THE YEAR'S BEST

SCIENCE FICTION

ALSO BY GARDNER DOZOIS

ANTHOLOGIES

A DAY IN THE LIFE
ANOTHER WORLD
BEST SCIENCE FICTION STORIES OF THE
    YEAR #6–10
THE BEST OF ISAAC ASIMOV'S SCIENCE
    FICTION MAGAZINE
TIME-TRAVELERS FROM ISAAC ASIMOV'S
    SCIENCE FICTION MAGAZINE
TRANSCENDENTAL TALES FROM ISAAC
    ASIMOV'S SCIENCE FICTION MAGAZINE
ISAAC ASIMOV'S ALIENS
ISAAC ASIMOV'S MARS
ISAAC ASIMOV'S SF LITE
ISAAC ASIMOV'S WAR
ROADS NOT TAKEN (with Stanley Schmidt)
THE YEAR'S BEST SCIENCE FICTION, #1–23

FUTURE EARTHS: UNDER AFRICAN SKIES
    (with Mike Resnick)
FUTURE EARTHS: UNDER SOUTH AMERICAN
    SKIES (with Mike Resnick)
RIPPER! (with Susan Casper)
MODERN CLASSIC SHORT NOVELS OF
    SCIENCE FICTION
MODERN CLASSICS OF FANTASY
KILLING ME SOFTLY
DYING FOR IT
THE GOOD OLD STUFF
THE GOOD NEW STUFF
EXPLORERS
THE FURTHEST HORIZON
WORLDMAKERS
SUPERMEN

COEDITED WITH SHEILA WILLIAMS

ISAAC ASIMOV'S PLANET EARTH
ISAAC ASIMOV'S ROBOTS
ISAAC ASIMOV'S VALENTINES
ISAAC ASIMOV'S SKIN DEEP
ISAAC ASIMOV'S GHOSTS
ISAAC ASIMOV'S VAMPIRES
ISAAC ASIMOV'S MOONS

ISAAC ASIMOV'S CHRISTMAS
ISAAC ASIMOV'S CAMELOT
ISAAC ASIMOV'S WEREWOLVES
ISAAC ASIMOV'S SOLAR SYSTEM
ISAAC ASIMOV'S DETECTIVES
ISAAC ASIMOV'S CYBERDREAMS

COEDITED WITH JACK DANN

ALIENS!	MERMAIDS!	DINOSAURS!	INVADERS!	CLONES
UNICORNS!	SORCERERS!	LITTLE PEOPLE!	ANGELS!	NANOTECH
MAGICATS!	DEMONS!	DRAGONS!	DINOSAURS II	IMMORTALS
MAGICATS 2!	DOGTALES!	HORSES!	HACKERS	
BESTIARY!	SEASERPENTS!	UNICORNS 2	TIMEGATES	

FICTION

STRANGERS
THE VISIBLE MAN (collection)
NIGHTMARE BLUE
    (with George Alec Effinger)

SLOW DANCING THROUGH TIME
    (with Jack Dann, Michael Swanwick,
    Susan Casper, and Jack C. Haldeman II)
THE PEACEMAKER
GEODESIC DREAMS (collection)

NONFICTION

THE FICTION OF JAMES TIPTREE, JR.

THE YEAR'S BEST

SCIENCE FICTION

twenty-fourth annual collection

edited by **Gardner Dozois**

st. martin's griffin ❧ new york

These are works of fiction. All of the characters, organiza-
tions, and events portrayed in these stories are either products of the authors' imaginations or are used fictitiously.

THE YEAR'S BEST SCIENCE FICTION: TWENTY-FOURTH ANNUAL
COLLECTION. Copyright © 2007 by Gardner Dozois. All
rights reserved. Printed in the United States of America.
No part of this book may be used or reproduced in any
manner whatsoever without written permission except in
the case of brief quotations embodied in critical articles
or reviews. For information, address St. Martin's Press,
175 Fifth Avenue, New York, N.Y. 10010.

www.stmartins.com

ISBN-13: 978-0-312-36335-2 (pbk)
ISBN-10: 0-312-36335-4 (pbk)
ISBN-13: 978-0-312-36334-5 (hc)
ISBN-10: 0-312-36334-6 (hc)

FIRST EDITION: JULY 2007

10 9 8 7 6 5 4 3 2 1

acknowledgment is made for permission to reprint the following materials:

"I, Row-Boat," by Cory Doctorow. Copyright © 2006 by Cory Doctorow. First published electronically online on *Flurb 1*, fall 2006. Reprinted by permission of the author.

"Julian: A Christmas Story," by Robert Charles Wilson. Copyright © 2006 by Robert Charles Wilson. First published as a chapbook, *Julian: A Christmas Story* (PS Publishing). Reprinted by permission of the author.

"Tin Marsh," by Michael Swanwick. Copyright © 2006 by Dell Magazines. First published in *Asimov's Science Fiction*, August 2006. Reprinted by permission of the author.

"The Djinn's Wife," by Ian McDonald. Copyright © 2006 by Dell Magazines. First published in *Asimov's Science Fiction*, July 2006. Reprinted by permission of the author.

"The House Beyond Your Sky," by Benjamin Rosenbaum. Copyright © 2006 by Benjamin Rosenbaum. First published electronically on *Strange Horizons*, September 4, 2006. Reprinted by permission of the author.

"Where the Golden Apples Grow," by Kage Baker. Copyright © 2006 by Kage Baker. First published in *Escape from Earth* (Science Fiction Book Club), edited by Jack Dann and Gardner Dozois. Reprinted by permission of the author and the author's agent, Linn Prentis.

"Kin," by Bruce McAllister. Copyright © 2006 by Dell Magazines. First published in *Asimov's Science Fiction*, February 2006. Reprinted by permission of the author.

"Signal to Noise," by Alastair Reynolds. Copyright © 2006 by Alastair Reynolds. First published in *Zima Blue and Other Stories* (Night Shade).

"The Big Ice," by Jay Lake and Ruth Nestvold. Copyright © 2006 by Jay Lake and Ruth Nestvold. First published electronically on *Jim Baen's Universe*, no. 4, December 2006. Reprinted by permission of the authors.

"Bow Shock," by Gregory Benford. Copyright © 2006 by Gregory Benford. First published electronically on *Jim Baen's Universe*, no.1, June 2006. Reprinted by permission of the author.

Images appearing in "Bow Shock" are courtesy of NASA.

"In the River," by Justin Stanchfield. Copyright © 2006 by *Interzone*. First published in *Interzone*, August 2006. Reprinted by permission of the author.

contents

acknowledgments

The editor would like to thank the following people for their help and support: Susan Casper, Ellen Datlow, Gordon Van Gelder, Peter Crowther, Nicolas Gevers, Robert Wexler, Jonathan Strahan, Andy Cox, Jeste de Vries, Peter Tennant, Susan Marie Groppi, Karen Meisner, Jed Hartman, Rich Horton, Mark R. Kelly, Andrew Wilson, Damien Broderick, Marty Halpern, Gary Turner, Chris Roberson, Ellen Asher, Andy Wheeler, Lou Anders, James A. Owen, Cory Doctorow, Robert E. Howe, Darrell Schweitzer, Richard Freeburn, Patrick Swenson, Bridget McKenna, Marti McKenna, Jay Lake, Deborah Layne, William Shaffer, Edward J. McFadden, Sheila Williams, Brian Bieniowski, Trevor Quachri, Jayme Lynn Blascke, Ruth Nestvold, Benjamin Rosenbaum, Alastair Reynolds, Michael Swanwick, Ken MacLeod, Stephen Baxter, Tim Pratt, Alyx Dellamonica, Justin Stanchfield, Greg Van Eekhout, David D. Levine, William Sanders, Gregory Benford, John Helfers, Paul Howard, Paula Goodlett, Karl Johanson, Cynthia Ward, Wendy S. Delmater, Luis Rodrigues, Sean Wallace, Tehani Wessely, David Hartwell, Ginjer Buchanan, Susan Allison, Warren Lapin, Shawna McCarthy, Kelly Link, Gavin Grant, Gordon Linzner, Edmund Schubert Gerard Houarner, Christopher Rowe, Gwenda Bond, Alan DeNiro, John Klima, Mark Rudolph, Eric M. Heideman, John O'Neill, Ian Nichols, Sally Beasley, Stuart Barrow, Roelf Goudriaan, John Kenny, William Rupp, Jason B. Sizemore, David Lee Summers, Steve Mohn, Holly Phillips, Vaughne Lee Hansen, Mark Watson, and special thanks to my own editor, Marc Resnick.

Thanks are also due to Charles N. Brown, whose magazine *Locus* (Locus Publications, P.O. Box 13305, Oakland, CA 94661. $56 for a one-year/twelve-issue subscription via second class; credit card orders call 510-339-9198) was used as an invaluable reference source throughout the Summation; *Locus Online* (www .locusmag.com), edited by Mark R. Kelly, has also become a key reference source.

The old Chinese curse says "May you live in interesting times," and in that sense, we were lucky with 2006, since it was overall a relatively uneventful year (although there were a few things that might qualify as "interesting" in the way the curse intends).

The Time Warner Book Group was sold to Lagardère, parent company of Hachette Livre, which also owns Gollancz and Hodder & Stoughton in the United Kingdom, and will now be known as Grand Central Publishing. There was good news and bad news about this for the SF field—the bad news was that Warner Aspect was phased out and folded into the general Warner line; the good news is that Hachette Book Group USA will launch a major new imprint called Orbit USA in 2007, overseen by Tim Holman, who is also publishing director of Orbit UK. Orbit USA intends to produce forty titles per year in hardcover and paperback, which could make the line a major player in the American SF scene. So this "interesting" event might turn out to be more positive than negative.

More solidly qualifying as "interesting," two major bankruptcies shook the publishing world in 2006. American Marketing Services, the largest book distributor in the United States, went into Chapter 11 bankruptcy at the end of the year, leaving behind more than $200 million in debt, something that could have disastrous consequences for many publishers, especially the financially vulnerable small presses. Following the sudden death of publisher Byron Preiss in 2005, Byron Preiss Visual Publications and iBooks also declared bankruptcy and stopped publishing in early 2006, leaving a large number of already-published and yet-to-be-published SF titles in a legal limbo; the whole situation was complicated by the bankruptcy of American Marketing Services, referred to above, which was the parent company to Publishers Group West, the last distributor of iBooks. It may take years for any of this to be resolved, and ill effects may be rippling through the publishing world (not just the genre) for longer than that.

Much less "interesting," pretty encouraging, in fact, was the founding of Solaris Books, a new SF imprint from BL Publishing (parent company of the Black Library, British publisher of gaming-related books), due to start up with an ambitious program in 2007. Wildside Press added fantasy romance imprint Juno Press in 2006 and announced plans to develop another new line under the Cosmos Books imprint in 2007 in partnership with Dorchester/Leisure. Gollancz will launch a new supernatural romance line in 2007.

Things were, alas, all too "interesting" in the troubled short fiction market, which suffered another bad year, with the circulation of many magazines continuing to fall—although there were also a few encouraging signs here and there, especially in the wider short fiction market that includes electronic online publications as well as print magazines.

The most recent incarnation of *Amazing Stories*, which had gone "on hiatus" fifteen months ago (almost always a bad sign) finally officially died in 2006. *Asimov's Science Fiction* registered a 13 percent loss in overall circulation in 2006, with subscriptions dropping from 18,050 to 15,117, and newsstand sales dropping as well; sell-through remained steady at 29 percent. *Asimov's* published good stories this year by Ian McDonald, Paolo Bacigalupi, Mary Rosenblum, Paul McAuley, Michael Swanwick, Jack Skillingstead, Bruce McAllister, Robert Reed, and others. Sheila Williams completed her second year as *Asimov's* editor. *Analog Science Fiction and Fact* registered a 7.3 percent loss in overall circulation in 2006, with subscriptions dropping from 25,933 to 23,732, while newsstand sales dropped from 4,614 to 4,587; sell-through, however, rose from 30 percent to 32 percent. *Analog* published good work this year by John Barnes, Stephen Baxter, Rob Chilson, Carl Frederick, Brian Plante, and others. Stanley Schmidt has been editor there for twenty-seven years. *The Magazine of Fantasy and Science Fiction*, although it didn't go *up* in circulation, managed to hold at almost the same level as last year, dropping less than 1 percent since 2005, with subscriptions dropping from 14,918 to 14,575, and newsstand sales declining from 3,822 to 3,691. This may not sound like much of an accomplishment, but to put it in perspective, since 2004, circulation at *The Magazine of Fantasy & Science Fiction* has dropped 13.7 percent (only 1.9 percent of that taking place during the last two years), while circulation at *Asimov's Science Fiction* dropped 45 percent during the same period (36.6 of that in the last two years) and at *Analog Science Fiction and Fact*, circulation dropped during the same period by 33.5 percent (15.5 percent of that in the last two years)—so that *F&SF* has at least been able to put the brakes on swiftly dropping circulation rates in a way that *Asimov's* and *Analog* have so far not been able to; in today's magazine market, that'll count as good news! *F&SF* published good work this year by Peter S. Beagle, Daryl Gregory, Robert Reed, Matthew Hughes, Ysabeau S. Wilce, Geoff Ryman, Carolyn Ives Gilman, and others. The editor and publisher is Gordon Van Gelder. Circulation figures for *Realms of Fantasy* lag a year behind the other magazines, but their 2005 figures show them registering a 13 percent loss in overall circulation from 2004, with subscriptions dropping from 17,191 to 16,547, and newsstand sales dropping from 9,398 to 6,584 after two previous years in a row of newsstand gains, sell-through increased, from 20 percent to 29 percent. They published good stuff this year by Jay Lake and Ruth Nestvold, James Van Pelt, Richard Parks, Greg Van Eekhout, and others. Shawna McCarthy is the longtime editor.

Interzone, which had seemed on the brink of death just a couple of years ago, continued a strong recovery in 2006, publishing its scheduled six issues, and featuring strong fiction by Justin Stanchfield, Jamie Barras, Jay Lake, Elizabeth Bear, David Mace, Chris Beckett, Suzanne Palmer, and others. In its slick, large-size format, *Interzone* has also transformed itself into just about the best-*looking* SF magazine in the business, and, in fact, one of the most handsome SF magazines ever published. The editorial staff, supervised by publisher Andy Cox, includes Jetse de

Vries, Andrew Hedgecock, David Mathew, Sandy Auden, and, most recently, Liz Williams. Circulation is in the 2,000-to-3,000 range.

These five magazines are usually thought of as the "professional" magazine market, although *Interzone* doesn't qualify by SFWA's definition because of its low rates and circulation—nobody can seriously attest that the magazine isn't thoroughly professional, and even top-level professional, by any other standard, though, certainly by the quality of the fiction it produces.

None of these magazines should be counted out, but it's clear that several of them—especially the so-called digest-sized magazines, although they have the compensating advantage of being cheap to produce—must be skating on the edge of profitability; fortunately, if you like to have a lot of professional-quality short SF and fantasy stories available to read every year, there is something you can do to help: subscribe.

It's never been easier to subscribe to most of the genre magazines since you can now do it online with the click of a few buttons, without even a trip to the mailbox. In the Internet age, you can also subscribe from overseas just as easily as you can from the United States, something formerly difficult to impossible. Furthermore, Internet sites such as Fictionwise (www.fictionwise.com), Magaz!nes.com (www.magazines.com), and even Amazon.com sell subscriptions online, as well as electronic downloadable versions of many of the magazines to be read on your PDA or home computer, something becoming increasingly popular with the computer-savvy set. And, of course, you can still subscribe the old-fashioned way, by mail.

So I'm not only going to urge you to subscribe to one or more of these magazines now, while your money can still help to ensure their survival, I'm going to list both the Internet sites where you can subscribe online and the street addresses where you can subscribe by mail for each magazine: *Asimov's* site is at www.asimovs.com; its subscription address is *Asimov's Science Fiction*, Dell Magazines, 6 Prowitt Street, Norwalk, CT 06855—$43.90 for an annual subscription in the U.S. *Analog*'s site is at www.analogsf.com; its subscription address is *Analog Science Fiction and Fact*, Dell Magazines, 6 Prowitt Street, Norwalk, CT 06855—$43.90 for an annual subscription in the U.S. *The Magazine of Fantasy & Science Fiction*'s site is at www.sfsite.com/fsf; its subscription address is *The Magazine of Fantasy & Science Fiction*, Spilogale, Inc., P.O. Box 3447, Hoboken, NJ 07030—$50.99 for an annual subscription in the U.S. *Interzone* can be subscribed to online at www.ttapress.com/onlinestore1.html; its subscription address is *Interzone*, TTA Press, 5 Martins Lane, Witcham, Ely, Cambs CB6 2LB, England, UK, $42 for a six-issue subscription, make checks payable to "TTA Press." *Realms of Fantasy*'s site is at www.rofmagazine.com; its subscription address is *Realms of Fantasy*, Sovereign Media Co. Inc., P.O. Box 1623, Williamsport, PA 17703, $16.95 for an annual subscription in the U.S.

There are lots of print fiction magazines worth supporting other than just the "professional" magazines, though, including some that are totally professional when judged by the literary standards of the product they offer. 2004 saw two promising new publications, the British *Postscripts* and *Argosy Magazine*; after going through several distribution problems and changes in editorial staff, no issue of *Argosy* has been seen since early in 2005, and I begin to fear that this magazine is dead (subscribe at your own risk), but *Postscripts*, edited by Peter Crowther and Nick Gevers, had another strong year in 2006, featuring good work by Jack Dann, Michael Swanwick, Matthew Hughes, John Grant, Stephen Baxter, and others. Two new publications debuted in 2005, the e-magazine *Æon*, which will be discussed below in the online section, and *Subterranean*, edited by William K. Schafer, which had a strong novella by Caitlin R. Kiernan and nice work by Jack McDevitt, Chris Roberson, Allen M. Steel, and others. (*Subterranean* will be phasing its print edition out in 2007, after an issue guest-edited by Ellen Datlow, and reinventing itself as an electronic magazine on the *Subterranean* Web site instead; issue 8 will be the last print edition, issue 7 will be the Darlow-edited issue.)

All these publications are capable of presenting work of professional quality, and frequently do, some of it by some of the top writers in the business.

Warren Lapine's DNA Publications empire continues to unravel; last year, *Weird Tales* and the speculative poetry magazine *Mythic Delirium* were sold to other publishers; this year, editor Edward J. McFadden publicly and bitterly resigned as editor of *Fantastic Stories of the Imagination*, a decision based, in his words, "on the fact that DNA Publications, Inc. has not maintained a reasonable publishing schedule in some time"—all of which would seem to leave the future existence of that magazine in doubt. Neither *Absolute Magnitude*, *The Magazine of Science Fiction Adventures*, nor *Dreams of Decadence* have been seen in awhile, either, except as inclusions of stories from those magazine's inventory in DNA's newszine *Chronicle*, which itself was published only sporadically this year, and parted ways with news editor Ian Randall Strock. As reports are widespread from contributors, subscribers, and even some contributing editors (such as McFadden, above) that publisher Warren Lapine has become incommunicado, not returning messages or even phone calls, I don't think I can in good faith continue to recommend DNA magazines to the readership; I'll continue to list the subscription addresses, but be warned that if you subscribe, you do so at your own risk.

Weird Tales had seemed on the brink of death in 2005 as a DNA magazine, but has made a strong comeback since being sold to Wildside Press, publishing five of its scheduled six issues in 2006 and running good stuff by Tanith Lee, Brian Stableford, Greg Frost, Stephen Dedman, Richard A. Lupoff, and others. Toward the end of the year, *Weird Tales* announced a reorganization of its editorial staff, with John Betancourt returning to his duties as publisher, George Scithers becoming editor emeritus and continuing in an advisory position, and Darrell Schweitzer contributing a new movie-review column; the new fiction editor is Ann VanderMeer, former editor of *The Silver Web*. The magazine will also be getting a new logo and interior layout. Also from Wildside Press is the very promising new publication called *Fantasy Magazine*, edited by Sean Wallace, which managed three issues in their second year as (ostensibly) a "quarterly," and published some nice stuff by Theodora Goss, Bruce McAllister, Aaron Schutz, Sandra McDonald, and others. The Wildside stable also contains *H.P. Lovecraft's Magazine of Horror*, which managed one issue this year (and which seems a bit redundant with *Weird Tales* also in the group; they need to somehow establish sharply different identities for these titles), and the nongenre *Adventure Tales*, which published one issue.

Paradox, edited by Christopher M. Cevasco, an "Alternate History" magazine that also publishes some straight historicals as well as AH stories with additional fantasy or SF elements, managed both scheduled issues this year, and featured good work by Sarah Monette, Richard Mueller, and others.

There's also a raft of aesthetically similar "slipstream/fabulist" fiction magazines (very small-circulation magazines referred to as the "minuscule press," by *Locus* editor Charles N. Brown), where the fiction is usually of professional-level quality—often by top professionals, in fact—but where you will rarely if ever find anything even remotely resembling core science fiction (or, most of the time, even genre fantasy). The flagship of the slipstream movement, and the inspiration/model for most of the others, *Lady Churchill's Rosebud Wristlet*, edited by Kelly Link and Gavin Grant, published two issues this year; *Electric Velocipede*, edited by John Kilma, also published two issues, as did *Flytrap*, edited by Tim Pratt and Heather Shaw; *Full Unit Hookup: A Magazine of Exceptional Literature*, edited by Mark Rudolph, managed one issue. If there was an issue of *Say . . .* this year, I didn't see it. The long-running *The Third Alternative*, perhaps the most respected of British semiprozines, edited by *Interzone* editor Andy Cox, probably belongs in this grouping somewhere (although it has a somewhat different flavor from the others, skewing more toward stylish bleak horror), but since they announced that they were going to change their name to *Black Static*, not an issue has been seen, under either title. Still, no doubt Andy Cox has had his hands full getting *Interzone* firmly up on its feet again, so let's hope that we'll be seeing the magazine again somewhere down the line.

Talebones, edited by Patrick and Honna Sweson (which also doesn't quite fit in with the "minuscule press" group in flavor, being somewhat more oriented toward horror, genre fantasy, and SF and less toward slipstream than the others), survived a brush with death this year, published three issues (one arriving late enough to be held over for next year), and continued to feature interesting work by people such as James Van Pelt, Steven Mohan, Jr., and Don D'Amassa.

Below this level, a reliable professional level of quality becomes a bit harder to count on, but there's still frequently good stuff to be found.

Turning to the longer-established fiction semiprozines, the Canadian *On Spec*, run by a collective under general editor Diane L. Walton, one of the longest-running of them all, published its four scheduled quarterly issues. Another Canadian magazine, *Neo-opsis*, edited by Karl Johanson, managed three out of four scheduled issues in 2006. Newcomer *Apex Science Fiction and Horror Digest*, edited by Jason Sizemore, published its four scheduled issues. Long-running semiprozine *Space and Time* almost died, but was reprieved by a last-minute sale to a new publisher. All five issues of the Australian *Andromeda Spaceways In-flight Magazine*, also run by a collective with a rotating staff of editors, appeared as scheduled. The long-running Australian zine *Eidolon* seems to have died (although the title was kept alive by an original anthology this year, see below). The other long-running Australian magazine, *Aurealis*, has seemed to be tottering on the brink of oblivion for some time now, with no issue seen in awhile, but I'm glad to say that it's been revived, with a new issue under new editor Stuart Mayne reaching me just as I was typing up the final version of this summation; I'll hold it over for consideration for next year, and the fact that *Aurealis* seems to be alive and viable again is good news for the field. I saw one issue of the Irish fiction semiprozine *Albedo One* this year, one of *Tales of the Unanticipated*, one of *New Genre*, two of *Tales of the Talisman*, and two of newcomer *Fictitious Force* (although they arrived late enough that I'll consider them for next year). If there were copies of *Black Gate*, I didn't see them, although reportedly a new issue will be along in March 2007.

Last year I wondered whether *Jupiter* was dead, but it's still very much alive. *Alchemy* did die this year, though, after publishing a final issue. *Artemis Magazine: Science and Fiction for a Space-Faring Society* has also died, and although no official announcements have been made, I strongly suspect that *Century, Orb, Altair, Terra Incognita,* and *Spectrum SF* are also dead, to the point where I'm no longer going to bother to list subscription addresses for them.

With the possible implosion of *Chronicle* (I haven't seen a copy in months), there's not really much left of the critical magazine market, other than professional journals more aimed at academics than at the average reader. The sturdy survivors, both long-running and reliably published magazines, and both well worth reading, are *Locus: The Magazine of the Science Fiction and Fantasy Field*, a multiple Hugo winner edited by Charles N. Brown and an indispensable source of information, news, and reviews for anyone interested in the science fiction field, and David G. Hartwell's *The New York Review of Science Fiction*, which publishes eclectic and sometime quirky critical essays on a variety of academic and pop-culture subjects relating to the genre, as well as reading lists, letters, memoirs, and japes of various sorts.

Subscription addresses follow:

Postscripts, PS Publishing, Hamilton House, 4 Park Avenue, Harrogate HG2 9BQ, England, UK, published quarterly, £30 to £50 outside the UK (*Postscripts* can also be subscribed to online at www.pspublishing.co.uk/postscripts.asp); *Subterranean*, Subterranean Press, P.O. Box 190106, Burton, MI 48519, 4-issue subscription (U.S.), $22, 4-issue subscription (int'l), $36 (*Subterranean* can also be subscribed to online at www.subterraneanpress.com); *Locus, The Magazine of the Science Fiction & Fantasy Field*, Locus Publications, Inc., P.O. Box 13305, Oakland, CA 94661, $66 for a one-year first-class subscription, 12 issues; *The New York Review of Science Fiction*, Dragon Press, P.O. Box 78, Pleasantville, NY, 10570, $38 per year, make checks payable to "Dragon Press," 12 issues; *Black Static*, TTA Press, 5 Martins Lane, Witcham, Ely, Cambs. CB6 2LB, England, UK, $36 for a six-issue subscription, checks made payable to "TTA Press"; *Talebones, A Magazine of Science Fiction & Dark Fantasy*, 5203 Quincy Ave SE, Auburn, WA 98092, $20 for four issues; *Aurealis*, P.O. Box 2164, Mount Waverley, VIC 3149, Australia (Web site: www.aurealis.com.au), $50 for a four-issue overseas airmail subscription; *On Spec, The Canadian Magazine of the Fantastic*, P.O. Box 4727, Edmonton, AB, Canada T6E 5G6, $24 for a one-year (four-issue) subscription; *Neo-Opsis Science Fiction Magazine*, 4129 Carey Rd., Victoria, BC, V8Z 4G5, $28 Canadian for a four-issue subscription; *Albedo*, Albedo One Productions, 2 Post Road, Lusk, Co. Dublin, Ireland; $39.50 for a four-issue airmail subscription, make checks payable to "Albedo One"; *Tales of the Unanticipated*, P.O Box 8036, Lake Street Station, Minneapolis, MN 55408, $28 for a four-issue subscription (three or four years' worth) in the U.S., $31 in Canada, $34 overseas; *Lady Churchill's Rosebud Wrist-let,* Small Beer Press, 176 Prospect Avenue, Northampton, MA 01060, $16 for four issues; *Say . . . ,* The Fortress of Worlds, P.O. Box 1304, Lexington, KY 40588-1304, $10 for two issues in the U.S. and Canada; *Full Unit Hookup: A Magazine of Exceptional Literature,* Conical Hats Press, 622 West Cottom Avenue, New Albany, IN 47150-5011, $12 for a three-issue subscription; *Flytrap,* Tropism Press, P.O. Box 13322, Berkeley, CA 94712-4222, $16 for four issues, checks to Heather Shaw; *Electric Velocipede,* Spilt Milk Press, P.O. Box 663, Franklin Park, NJ 08823, www .electricvelocipede.com, $15 for a four-issue subscription; *Andromeda Spaceways Inflight Magazine,* P.O. Box 127, Belmont, Western Australia, 6984, www .andromedaspaceways.com, $35 for a one-year subscription; *Tales of the Talisman,* Hadrosaur Productions, P.O. Box 2194, Mesilla Park, NM 88047-2194, $24 for a four-issue subscription; *Space and Time, The Magazine of Fantasy, Horror, and Science Fiction,* 1380 Centennial Avenue, Ste. 101, Piscataway, NJ 08854, $10 for a one-year (two-issue) subscription; *Black Gate,* New Epoch Press, 815 Oak Street, St. Charles, IL 60174, $29.95 for a one-year (four-issue) subscription; *Paradox,* Paradox Publications, P.O. Box 22897, Brooklyn, NY 11202-2897, $25 for a one-year (four-issue) subscription, checks or U.S. postal money orders should be made payable to Paradox, can also be ordered online at www.paradoxmag.com; *Fantasy Magazine,* Wildside Press, Sean Wallace, 9710 Traville Gateway Drive, #234, Rockville, MD 20850, annual subscription—four issues—$20 in the U.S., $25 Canada and overseas; *Weird Tales,* Wildside Press, 9710 Traville Gateway Drive, #234, Rockville, MD 20850, annual subscription—four issues—$24 in the U.S., *H.P. Lovecraft's Magazine of Horror,* Wildside Press, 9710 Traville Gateway Drive, #234, Rockville, MD 20850, annual subscription—four issues—$19.95 in the U.S.; *Fictitious Force,* Jonathan Laden, 1024 Hollywood Avenue, Silver Spring, MD 20904, $16 for four issues; *Apex Science Fiction and Horror Digest,* Apex Publications, 4629 Riverman Way, Lexington, KY 40515, $18 for a one-year (four-issue) subscription; *Jupiter,* 19 Bedford Road, Yeovil, Somerset, BA21 5UG, UK, £10 for four issues; *New Genre,* P.O. Box 270092, West Hartford, CT 06127, couldn't find any specific subscription information in the magazine itself, but check www.new-genre.com for details; *Argosy Magazine,* Coppervale International, P.O. Box 1421, Taylor, Arizona, 85939, $49.95 for a six-issue subscription; *Absolute Magnitude, The Magazine of Science Fiction Adventures, Dreams of Decadence, Chronicle*—all available from DNA Publications, P.O. Box 2988, Radford, VA 24142-2988, all available for $16 for a one-year subscription, although you can get a group subscription to four DNA fiction magazines for $60 a year, with *Chronicle* $45 a year (12 issues), all checks payable to "D.N.A. Publications."

Actually, if you were looking for good stories this year, especially for good core science fiction, outside of the major professional magazines, you were probably better off turning to the increasingly important Internet scene than to the original anthology market. The online magazine *Jim Baen's Universe* (www.baensuniverse .com) made a very strong debut this year (sadly, and ironically, the same year that its founder died), publishing some of the year's best science fiction by Cory Doctorow, Gregory Benford, Jay Lake and Ruth Nestvold, and John Barnes, as well as good stuff by Lawrence Person, Charles Stross, Garth Nix, and others, and strong fantasy stories by John Barnes, Elizabeth Bear, Eric Witchery, Marissa Lingen, and others. Eric Flint has been the editor, and although he'll stay on to supervise, early in 2007 it was announced that Mike Resnick will take over as managing editor, probably a good sign since Resnick is one of the shrewdest professionals in the business. It's too early to say whether *Jim Baen's Universe* will ultimately be commercially successful enough to be viable, but I've got my fingers crossed for it, since it's an extremely important new market. Another newly launched online magazine, *Orson Scott Card's InterGalactic Medicine Show* (www.intergalacticmedicineshow.com), has not as yet been as impressive, although it may now be beginning to hit its stride under the leadership of new editor Edmund Schubert, publishing good stuff by Tim Pratt and Card himself. *Strange Horizons* (www.strangehorizons.com), one of the longest-established fiction sites on the Internet, had a good year, publishing strong work by Benjamin Rosenbaum, A. M. Dellamonica, Sarah Monette, Jamie Barras, Elizabeth Bear, and others, as did another newish electronic magazine (which is available for download through subscription rather than being directly accessible online), *Æon* (www.aeonmagazine.com), where good work by Elizabeth Bear and Sarah Monette, Daniel Marcus, Ken Scholes, Jay Lake, Bruce McAllister, and others appeared. (Being a grumpy old dinosaur, I still would be happier if markets such as *Æon* and *Strange Horizons* and print magazines such as *Postscripts* published less slipstream/surrealism and horror and more actual science fiction, but discounting the genre classification issue, the quality of the stories themselves is usually quite high in all of them.) Remember that *Subterranean* (http://subterraneanpress.com) is in the process of converting itself to an online e-magazine, with a novella by Lucius Shepard already up and available to be read on the site; there'll be more stuff there as the year progresses and as the print version is gradually phased out. Two new e-zines dedicated to publishing eccentric, offbeat, and "controversial" work that the regular genre markets are supposedly too timid to accept appeared this year, and each produced its first two issues, William Sanders's *Helix* (www.helixsf.com), which produced good stuff by Peg Robinson, Janis Ian, Beth Bernobich, Sanders himself, and others, and Rudy Rucker's *Flurb* (www.flurb.net), which had one of the year's best stories, by Cory Doctorow, as well as good stuff by Terry Bisson, Richard Kadrey, Charles Stross, Paul Di Filippo, Rucker himself, and others. New site *Clarkesworld Magazine* (www.clarkesworldmagazine.com) has to date published mostly fantasy, and rather sexually explicit fantasy at that, but is attracting high-level professional writers and is another site to watch. The SF stories published in the Australian science magazine *Cosmos*, selected by fiction editor Damien Broderick, are now also available online at the *Cosmos* site (www.cosmosmagazine.com). Then there are the online equivalents of the print "minuscule press" slipstream magazines, sites that often publish fiction of high professional quality, although only rarely any core science fiction: *Revolution SF* (www.revolutionsf.com), *Fortean Bureau—A Magazine of Speculative Fiction* (www.forteanbureau.com/index.html), *Abyss and Apex: A Magazine of Speculative Fiction* (www.abyssandapex.com); *Ideomancer Speculative Fiction* (www.ideomancer.com); *Futurismic* (www.futurismic .com/fiction/index.html), *Lone Star Stories* (http://literary.erictmarin.com); *Chiaroscura* (http://chizine.com); and the somewhat less slipstreamish *Bewildering Stories* (www.bewilderingstories.com).

Oceans of the Mind, another solid e-magazine, unfortunately went "on hiatus" this year, probably never to return. *The Infinite Matrix* (www.infinitematrix.net) remains dead, alas, but the corpse continues to twitch in its coffin, with new content still being posted from time to time, including an alternate history story by Andy Hooper in 2006 and a major novella by Cory Doctorow in early 2007.

Many good *reprint* SF and fantasy stories can also be found on the Internet. Sites where reprint stories can be accessed for free include the British *Infinity Plus* (www.users.zetnet.co.uk/iplus), which has a wide selection of good-quality reprint stories, in addition to biographical and bibliographical information, book reviews, interviews, and critical essays; *Strange Horizons;* and most of the sites that are associated with existing print magazines, such as *Asimov's, Analog,* and *The Magazine of Fantasy & Science Fiction,* which have extensive archives of material, both fiction and nonfiction, previously published by the print versions of the magazines, and which regularly run teaser excerpts from stories coming up in forthcoming issues. Even sites such as *SCI FICTION* (www.scifi.com/scifiction) and *The Infinite Matrix,* which are ostensibly dead, have substantial archives of past material that you can access. A large selection of novels and a few collections can be accessed for free, to be either downloaded or read on-screen, at the Baen Free Library (www.baen .com/library).

For a small fee, though, an even greater range of reprint stories becomes available. Perhaps the best such site is Fictionwise (www.fictionwise.com), where you can buy downloadable e-books and stories to read on your PDA or home computer, in addition to individual stories, you can also buy "fiction bundles" here, which amount to electronic collections; as well as a selection of novels in several different genres, and you can also subscribe to downloadable versions of several of the SF magazines here, in a number of different formats. A similar site is ElectricStory (www.electricstory.com); here, in addition to the downloadable stuff (both stories and novels) you can buy, you can also access for free movie reviews by Lucius Shepard, articles by Howard Waldrop, and other critical material.

There are also many general genre-related sites of interest to be found on the Internet, sites that publish reviews, interviews, critical articles, and genre-oriented news of various kinds. Perhaps the most valuable genre-oriented site on the entire Internet is *Locus Online* (http://www.locusmag.com), the online version of the newsmagazine *Locus,* an indispensable site that is not only often the first place in the genre to find fast-breaking news, but a place where you can access an incredible amount of information, including book reviews, critical lists, obituary lists, links to reviews and essays appearing outside the genre, and links to extensive database archives such as the Locus Index to Science Fiction and the Locus Index to Science Fiction Awards. Other essential sites include: *Science Fiction Weekly* (www.scifi .com/sfw), more media-and-gaming oriented than *Locus Online,* but still featuring news and book reviews, as well as regular columns by John Clute, Michael Cassut, and Wil McCarthy; *Tangent Online* (www.tangentonline.com), one of the few places on the Internet where you can access a lot of short fiction reviews; *Best SF* (www.bestsf.net), another great review site, and one of the other few places that makes any attempt to regularly review short fiction venues; SFRevu (www.sfrevu .com), a review site that specializes in media and novel reviews; the *SF Site* (www

.sfsite.com), which not only features an extensive selection of reviews of books, games, magazines, interviews, critical retrospective articles, letters, and so forth, plus a huge archive of past reviews; but also serves as host site for the Web pages of *The Magazine of Fantasy & Science Fiction* and *Interzone*; SFF NET (www.sff.net), which features dozens of home pages and "newsgroups" for SF writers; the Science Fiction & Fantasy Writers of America page (www.sfwa.org), where news, obituaries, award information, and recommended reading lists can be accessed; *The Internet Review of Science Fiction* (www.irosf.com), which features both short fiction reviews and novel reviews, as well as critical articles, *Green Man Review* (www.greenman review.com), another valuable review site; *The Agony Column* (http://trashotron .com/agony), media and book reviews and interviews; *SFFWorld* (www.sffworld .com), more literary and media reviews; *SFReader* (www.sfreader.com), which features reviews of SF books, and SFWatcher (www.sfwatcher.com), which features reviews of SF movies; newcomer *SFScope* (www.sfscope.com), edited by former *Chronicle* news editor Ian Randal Strock, which concentrates on SF and writing business news; SciFiPedia (http://scifipedia.scifi.com), a wiki-style genre-oriented online encyclopedia; and *Speculations* (www.speculations.com), a long-running site that dispenses writing advice and writing-oriented news and gossip (although to access most of it, you'll have to subscribe to the site). Multiple Hugo winner David Langford's online version of his funny and iconoclastic fanzine *Ansible* is available at http://news.ansible.co.uk, and SF-oriented radio plays and podcasts can also be accessed at Audible (www.audible.com) and *Beyond 2000* (www.beyond2000.com).

There were a number of good, solid, worth-your-money anthologies in both SF and fantasy this year, although no one volume in either genre that was strong enough to clearly establish dominance.

The two strongest contenders for the title of best original SF anthology of the year both had the same title, oddly enough. Of the two, *Forbidden Planets* (DAW), edited by Peter Crowther, probably has a slight edge, with a number of strong stories, although several of them are slightly handicapped, in my opinion, by directly referencing the 1956 movie of the same title as either homage or parody—potentially a weakness for a generation of readers who might not even have *seen* it. Still, there is fine stuff here by Alastair Reynolds, Paul Di Filippo, Ian McDonald, Paul McAuley, Matthew Hughes, Stephen Baxter, and others. The year's other *Forbidden Planets* anthology, this one a Science Fiction Book Club original edited by Marvin Kaye, is considerably more straightforward and less postmodern, dealing with the theme in general terms rather than tying it specifically to the movie, with no elements of satire or homage. The best stories here is by Robert Reed, but there are also strong stories by Allen M. Steele, Nancy Kress, Jack McDevitt, Alan Dean Foster, and Julie E. Czerneda. Perhaps our expectations were too high, but *Futureshocks* (Roc), edited by Lou Anders, whose *Live Without a Net* had been the best original SF anthology of 2003, was a bit of a disappointment when compared with that earlier anthology; it's still a good, solid anthology, well worth reading, but somehow few of the stories here, although competent and entertaining, rise to really first-rate, award-quality levels. The best story here, by a fair margin, is by Robert Charles Wilson, but there is also good work by Paul Melko, Caitlin R. Kiernan, Howard V. Hendrix, Chris Roberson, Sean McMullen, and others. *The Mammoth Book of Extreme SF*

(Carroll & Graf), edited by Mike Ashley, is mostly a reprint anthology (and a very good one, too, featuring strong reprints from Ian McDonald, Greg Egan, Theodore Sturgeon, James Patrick Kelly, Alastair Reynolds, Harlan Ellison, and others), but it does also feature good original stories by Stephen Baxter, Robert Reed, and Jerry Oltion, with the Baxter in particular being one of the year's best. *Millennium 3001* (DAW), edited by Martin H. Greenberg and Russell Davis, is a cut above the average Greenberg original anthology; no award winners, but satisfying work by Keith Ferrell and Jack Dann, Brian Stableford, Allen M. Steele, Kristine Kathryn Rusch, and others. *Cosmic Cocktails* (DAW), edited by Denise Little, is pleasant but minor, a collection of funny SF stories about bars, a curious subgenre that surfaces every once in awhile (I wrote one myself once).

Noted without comment are *One Million A.D.* (SFBC), edited by Gardner Dozois, another collection of original novellas from the SF Book Club, and *Escape from Earth: New Adventures in Space* (SFBC), an original Young Adult SF anthology edited by Jack Dann and Gardner Dozois.

A number of good novellas were published as individual chapbooks this year as well. The best was probably *Julian: A Christmas Story*, by Robert Charles Wilson, from PS Publishing, but PS also published first-rate novellas such as *The Voyage of Night Shining White*, by Chris Roberson, *Flavors of My Genius*, by Robert Reed, *On the Overgrown Path*, by David Herter, and *Christmas Inn*, by Gene Wolfe. Subterranean Press brought out *A Soul in a Bottle*, by Tim Powers and *Missile Gap*, by Charles Stross. Sandstone Press brought out *The Highway Men*, by Ken MacLeod. Many short-story collections are publishing heretofore unpublished work these days; this was particularly true of Alastair Reynold's two collections, *Galactic North* and *Zima Blue and Other Stories*, but also true of a number of other collections, including Elizabeth Bear's *The Chains That You Refuse*, Kage Baker's *Dark Mondays*, and Stephen Baxter's *Resplendent*.

And SF stories continued to be found in unlikely places, including, again this year, a series of short-shorts by big-name authors such as Ian R. Macleod, Cory Doctorow, Eileen Gunn, and David Marusek in nearly every issue of the science magazine *Nature*, as well as a series of shorts by authors such as Pamela Sargent, Chris Lawson, and Jay Lake appearing in the recently launched Australian science magazine *Cosmos*. Good genre stories (fantasy if not SF) also appeared this year as far afield as *The New Yorker* and the British newspaper *The Guardian*.

Coming up next year are the debuts of three projected annual original anthology series: *The Solaris Book of New Science Fiction* (Solaris), edited by George Mann, *Fast Forward 1: Future Fiction from the Cutting Edge* (Pyr), edited by Lou Anders, and *Eclipse: New Science Fiction and Fantasy* (Night Shade Books), edited by Jonathan Strahan. If even one of these series succeeds in establishing itself, it should brighten up the original anthology scene considerably, and even if none of them does, the debut volumes should at least make 2007's SF anthology market more interesting.

There were some good original fantasy anthologies out in 2006, as well as a number of slipstream/fabulist/New Weird/whatever-we're-calling-it-this-year anthologies—appropriately enough, the distinction between the fantasy anthologies and the slipstream anthologies was sometimes a bit blurry, since most of the fantasy anthologies had at least a few slipstreamish stories in them, although you could usually get perhaps arbitrary feeling for which category the anthology generally belonged in. On the more-fantasy-than-slipstream side, it was difficult to pick a clear favorite from among several good anthologies that were similar in tone and literary ambition, but I think I would give *Salon Fantastique* (Thunder's Mouth), edited by Ellen Datlow and Terri Windling, a slight edge over *Firebirds Rising* (Firebird), edited by Sharyn November, although it's close and both have lots of good stuff: by Peter S. Beagle, Jeffery Ford, Delia Sherman, Lucius Shepard, Paul Di Filippo, Christopher Barzak, and others in *Salon Fantastique*, and in *Firebirds Rising* (which can also be considered a Young Adult anthology, probably more so than *Salon Fantastique*, and has a few science fiction stories in it as well, although they're not among the strongest stories in the book), there's good material by Kelly Link, Emma Bull, Patricia McKillip, Ellen Klages, Tamora Pierce, and others. Also similar in tone and attack, although with perhaps more (and edgier) slipstream material in it, is *Eidolon 1* (Wildside), edited by Jonathan Strahan and Jeremy G. Byrne, which featured strong stories by Tim Pratt, Holly Phillips, Eleanor Arnason, Hal Duncan, Margo Lanagan, Lucy Susex, and others. Slewing even more to the slipstream side of the Force is *Twenty Epics* (All Star), edited by David Moles and Susan Marie Groppi. In spite of its promise to provide concise, compact "epics" of storytelling that don't sprawl into multivolume fantasy "trilogies," some of the stories here are too self-consciously clever and postmodern to really deliver successfully on that promise; there are other stories here, though, that come a lot closer to living up to the theme, including stuff by Benjamin Rosenbaum, Christopher Rowe, Alan Deniro, K. D. Wentworth, and others. Swinging to the year's batch of unambiguously slipstream/fabulist/New Weird anthologies, the strongest, in terms of literary quality, is probably *Polyphony 6* (Wheatland Press), edited by Deborah Layne and Jay Lake, with good stuff by Richard Wadholm, Robert Reed, Tim Pratt, Pamela Sargent, Paul M. Berger, Esther Friesner, Anna Tambour, and others. A bit more opaque, and a bit too aggressively postmodern for my taste, is *ParaSpheres: Extending Beyond the Spheres of Literary and Genre Fiction, Fabulist and New Wave Fabulist Stories* (Omnidawn), edited by Rusty Morrison and Ken Keegan, although it does have some good stuff in it, including reprints by Ursula K. Le Guin, Alasdair Gray, Kim Stanley Robinson, and others, and good original works by L. Timmel Duchamp, Jeff VanderMeer, Anna Tambour, and others. As for how it functions as part of the continuing effort at canon-forming and definition within the emerging slipstream/fabulist genre, it seems to be a bit of a grab bag, with no really clear argument emerging from its pages, as far as I can tell, anyway. It's hard to see any real reason other than editorial caprice, for instance, for including Le Guin's "The Birthday of the World" or Kim Stanley Robinson's "The Lucky Strike," SF stories that were originally published as such in SF markets. The mostly reprint *Feeling Very Strange: The Slipstream Anthology* (Tachyon), edited by James Patrick Kelly and John Kessel, tackles the (perhaps doomed) effort to draw the boundaries of this very slippery subgenre in a much more rigorous and logical fashion, and perhaps does as good a job as anyone is likely to do of pinning down things that by their very nature are designed *not* to be easily pinned down (not that it will settle any arguments, of course; in fact, if anything, it's likely to pour gasoline on the flames). *Slipstreams* (DAW), edited by Martin H.

Greenberg and John Helfers, does an unconvincing job of assembling a slipstream anthology, as if the editors aren't really sure what slipsteam *is*, and the stories are no more than average/mediocre at best. *Jabberwocky 2* (Prime), edited by Sean Wallace, features mostly poetry, but does have original stories by Holly Phillips, Richard Parks, and others.

Pleasant but minor original fantasy anthologies this year included *Children of Magic* (DAW), by Martin H. Greenberg and Kerrie Hughes, *Fantasy Gone Wrong* (DAW), by Martin H. Greenberg and Brittiany A. Koren, *My Big Fat Supernatural Wedding* (St. Martin's Griffin), edited by P. N. Elrod, and *The Magic Toybox* (DAW) and *Hags, Sirens and Other Bad Girls of Fantasy* (DAW), both edited by Denise Little. An oddball item, stories inspired by "Furry Fandom," whose members like to dress up as furry animals, is *Furry Fantastic* (DAW), edited by Jean Rabe and Brian M. Thomsen.

The year also featured a slew of original anthologies from very small presses, most of which will have to be mail-ordered, as they probably won't be available in most bookstores, perhaps even in specialty SF bookstores. *Cross Plains Universe: Texans Celebrate Robert E. Howard* (MonkeyBrains), edited by Scott A. Cupp and Joe R. Lansdale, is at its least successful when its authors are attempting direct Conan pastiches, at its most successful when the authors put a bit of distance between themselves and honoree Robert E. Howard, so that the best stories are those by writers such as Neal Barrett Jr., Lawrence Person, Gene Wolfe, Carrie Richerson, Mark Finn, Howard Waldrop, and others who find a different perspective from which to tackle the anthology's subject matter instead of just churning out Conan imitations. A similar "retro-pulp" feel is to be found in the aptly named *Retro Pulp Tales* (Subterranean), edited by Joe R. Lansdale, with good stuff by Alex Irvine, Al Sarrantonio, Kim Newman, and others. As with *Cross Plains Universe*, the least successful stories in *Space Cadets* (Scifi, Inc.), edited by Mike Resnick, are those that take the theme the most literally, producing jokey homages or satires of either the old *Tom Corbett, Space Cadet* television show or the Heinlein juvenile *Space Cadet* on which it was loosely based, while the most successful stories are by authors such as David Gerrold, Connie Willis, and Larry Niven, who stretch the ostensible theme as far as it will go. *Golden Age SF: Tales of a Bygone Future* (Hadley Rille Books), edited by Eric T. Reynolds, has the somewhat dubious premise of getting today's authors to write "new" Golden Age stories, stories written in the spirit of SF's so-called Golden Age that look ahead not to the real future but to the "bygone future" that SF writers were dreaming about in the fifties; Justin Stanchfield, G. David Nordley, Terry Bisson, and Stephen Baxter actually manage to do a reasonable job of it. *Sex in the System* (Prime), edited by Cecilia Tan, mixes eroticism and SF in a playful manner, while the much more serious-minded *The Future Is Queer* (Arsenal Pulp Press), edited by Richard Labonte and Lawrence Schimel, examines the roles that gay men, lesbians, and transgenders might play in future societies, with the best stories being provided by Candas Jane Dorsey, L. Timmel Duchamp, Hiromi Goto, and Rachel Pollack. The earnest *Jigsaw Nation: Science Fiction Stories of Secession* (Spyre Books), edited by Edward J. McFadden III and E. Sedia, conceived right after the presidential election of 2004, provides one angry and/or despairing story after another about the division of the country into blue states and red states and how this will eventually lead to the sundering of the union and usually to police states and concentration camps. While this may have provided some useful venting for its authors, it's preaching to the choir, as far as blue state readers are concerned, and its rather cartoonish nightmares are not going to sway either red staters or those sitting somewhere on the political fence; best work here is by Paul Di Filippo, Michael Jasper, and Ruth Nestvold and Jay Lake. *Elemental: The Tsunami Relief Anthology* (Tor), edited by Steve Savile and Alethea Kontis, whose proceeds are being donated, admirably enough, to relief efforts to aid the victims of the Asian tsunami, is a well-intentioned and worthwhile project, one worth spending money on just to help out, but the stories, for the most part, are not particularly memorable; the best work here is by Joe Haldeman, Brian W. Aldiss, Syne Mitchell, and Larry Niven. *Talking Back* (Aqueduct Press), edited by L. Timmel Duchamp, is an anthology of "epistolary fantasies," letters to dead people written by living authors, including Eileen Gunn and Carol Emshwiller.

There were two regional Australian anthologies this year, *Agog! Ripping Reads* (Agog! Press), edited by Cat Sparks, and *The Outcast: An Anthology of Strangers and Exiles* (CSFG Publishing), edited by Nicole R. Murphy, but I missed them and will hold consideration of stories from them over until next year. The new Canadian anthology *Tesseracts 10* (Edge Science Fiction and Fantasy), edited by Edo Van Belkom and Robert Charles Wilson, also crossed my desk too late for my deadline, and I'll hold it over until next year, too.

There were two cross-genre anthologies this year, both crosses with romance: *The Best New Paranormal Romance* (Juno), edited by Paula Guran, and *Dates from Hell* (Avon), a collection of four paranormal romance novellas by Kim Harrison, Lynsay Sands, Kelley Armstrong, and Lori Handeland. A shared-world anthology of sorts was *1634: The Ram Rebellion* (Baen), edited by Eric Flint and Virginia DeMarce.

As usual, novice work by beginning writers, some of whom may later turn out to be important talents, was featured in *L. Ron Hubbard Presents Writers of the Future Volume XXII* (Galaxy), edited by Algis Budrys.

I don't follow horror closely anymore, but there, as far as I could tell, the prominent original anthologies of the year included *Hardboiled Cthulhu: Two-Fisted Tales of Tentacled Terror* (Dimensions Books), edited by James Arnbuehl, and a tribute anthology to Joe R. Lansdale, *Joe R. Lansdale's Lords of the Razor* (Subterranean), edited by Bill Sheehan and William Schafer. Many of the anthologies already mentioned, including *Retro Pulp Tales, Cross Plains Universe, Salon Fantastique, Eidolon 1, Firebirds Rising*, and so forth, and even some of the SF anthologies, will also contain horror stories of one degree or another of horrificness.

(Finding individual pricings for all of the items from small presses mentioned in the summation has become too time-intensive, and since several of the same small presses publish anthologies, novels, *and* short-story collections, it seems silly to repeat addresses for them in section after section. Therefore, I'm going to attempt to list here, in one place, all the addresses for small presses that have books mentioned here or there in the summation, whether from the anthologies section, the novel section, or the short-story collection section, and, where known, their Web site addresses. That should make it easy enough for the reader to look up the individual price of any book mentioned that isn't from a regular trade publisher; such books are less likely to be found in your average bookstore, or even in a chain superstore, and so will probably have to be mail-ordered. Some publishers seem to sell only on-line, through their Web sites, so Google the name of the publisher or the title of the book if all else fails. Many books, even from some of the smaller presses, are also available through Amazon.com.

Addresses: **PS Publishing,** Grosvener House, 1 New Road, Hornsea, West York-shire, HU18 1PG, England, UK www.pspublishing.co.uk; **Golden Gryphon Press,** 3002 Perkins Road, Urbana, IL 61802, www.goldengryphon.com; **NESFA Press,** P.O. Box 809, Framingham, MA 01701-0809, www.nesfa.org; **Subterranean Press,** P.O. Box 190106, Burton, MI 48519, www.subterraneanpress.com; **Old Earth Books,** P.O. Box 19951, Baltimore, MD 21211-0951, www.oldearthbooks.com; **Tachyon Press,** 1459 18th St. #139, San Francisco, CA 94107, www.tachyonpublications .com; **Night Shade Books,** 1470 NW Saltzman Road, Portland, OR 97229, www .nightshadebooks.com; **Five Star Books,** 295 Kennedy Memorial Drive, Waterville, ME 04901, www.galegroup.com/fivestar; **Wheatland Press,** P.O. Box 1818, Wilsonville, OR 97070, www.wheatlandpress.com; **All-Star Stories,** see contact information for Wheatland Press; **Small Beer Press,** 176 Prospect Ave., Northampton, MA 01060, www.smallbeerpress.com; **Locus Press,** P.O. Box 13305, Oakland, CA 94661; **Crescent Books,** Mercat Press Ltd., 10 Coates Crescent, Edinburgh, Scotland EH3 7AL, www.mercatpress.com; **Wildside Press/Cosmos Books/Borgo Press,** P.O. Box 301, Holicong, PA 18928-0301, or go to www.wildsidepress.com for pricing and ordering; **Thunder's Mouth,** 245 West 17th St., 11th flr., New York, NY 10011-5300, www.thundersmouth.com; **Edge Science Fiction and Fantasy Publishing, Inc. and Tesseract Books, Ltd.,** P.O. Box 1714, Calgary, Alberta, T2P 2L7, Canada, www.edgewebsite.com; **Aqueduct Press,** P.O. Box 95787, Seattle, WA 98145-2787, www.aqueductpress.com; **Phobos Books,** 200 Park Avenue South, New York, NY 10003, www.phobosweb.com; **Fairwood Press,** 5203 Quincy Ave. SE, Auburn, WA 98092, www.fairwoodpress.com; **BenBella Books,** 6440 N. Central Expressway, Suite 508, Dallas, TX 75206, www.benbellabooks.com; **Darkside Press,** 13320 27th Ave. NE, Seattle, WA 98125, www.darksidepress.com; **Haffner Press,** 5005 Crooks Rd., Suite 35, Royal Oak, MI 48073-1239, www.haffnerpress .com; **North Atlantic Press,** P.O. Box 12327, Berkeley, CA, 94701; **Prime,** P.O. Box 36503, Canton, OH, 44735, www.primebooks.net; **MonkeyBrain Books,** 11204 Crossland Drive, Austin, TX 78726, www.monkeybrainbooks.com; **Wesleyan University Press,** University Press of New England, Order Dept., 37 Lafayette St., Lebanon NH 03766-1405, www.wesleyan.edu/wespress; **Agog! Press,** P.O. Box U302, University of Wollongong, NSW 2522, Australia, www.uow.edu.au/~rhood/ agogpress; **MirrorDanse Books,** P.O. Box 3542, Parramatta, NSW 2124, Australia, www.tabula-rasa.info/MirrorDanse; **Arsenal Pulp Press,** 103-1014 Homer Street, Vancouver, BC, Canada V6B 2W9, www.arsenalpulp.com; **Elder Signs Press/ Dimensions Books,** order through www.dimensionsbooks.com; **Spyre Books,** P.O. Box 3005, Radford, VA 24143; SCIFI, Inc., P.O. Box 8442, Van Nuys, CA 91409-8442; **Omnidawn Publishing,** order through www.omnidawn.com; **CSFG,** Canberra Speculative Fiction Guild, www.csfg.org.au/publishing/anthologies/the _outcast; **Hadley Rille Books,** via www.hadleyrillebooks.com; **ISFiC Press,** 707 Sapling Lane, Deerfield, IL 60015-3969, or www.isficpress.com; **DreamHaven**

Books, 912 West Lake Street, Minneapolis, MN 55408, www.dreamhavenbooks .com; **Suddenly Press,** via suddenlypress@yahoo.com; **Sandstone Press,** P.O. Box 5725, One High St., Dingwall, Ross-shire, IV15 9WJ, UK; **Tropism Press,** via www .tropismpress.com; **SF Poetry Association/Dark Regions Press,** www.sfpoetry.com, checks to Helena Bell, SFPA Treasurer, 1225 West Freeman St., Apt. 12, Carbondale, IL 62401; **DH Press,** via diamondbookdistributors.com.

Once again in 2006, there were more good SF and fantasy novels (to say nothing of hard-to-classify hybrids) than any one person could possibly read, unless they made a full-time job of doing nothing else.

According to the newsmagazine *Locus,* there were 2,495 books "of interest to the SF field, both original and reprint (but not counting "media tie-in novels," gaming novels, novelizations of genre movies, print-on-demand novels, or novels offered as downloads on the Internet—all of which would swell the total by hundreds if counted) published in 2006, down 1 percent from 2,516 titles in 2005, the second year in a row of a 1 percent loss after several years of record increases. (This still leaves the number of "books of interest" more or less in the same ballpark in which it's been for several years now. To put these figures in some historical perspective, there were 2,158 books published in 2001, and only 1,927 books as recently as 2000, so things haven't changed much.) Original books were up by 3 percent to 1,520 from last year's total of 1,469, a new record. Reprint books were down by 7 percent to 975 from last year's total of 1,047. The number of new SF novels was down by 14 percent to a total of 223 as opposed to last year's total of 258. The number of new fantasy novels was up by 12 percent to 463 as opposed to last year's total of 414, another new high. Horror, recovering from its slump in the nineties, was up 28 percent to 271 as opposed to last year's total of 212; as recently as 2002, the horror total was only 112. (Some of the increase in horror and fantasy may be accounted for by the surge in "paranormal romances," which are being generated more by the romance industry than the SF/fantasy/horror industry.)

Busy with all the reading I have to do at shorter lengths, I didn't have time to read many novels myself this year, so, as usual, I'll limit myself to mentioning that novels that received a lot of attention and acclaim in 2006 include:

Rainbows End (Tor), by Vernor Vinge; *Blindsight* (Tor), by Peter Watts; *Glasshouse* (Ace), by Charles Stross; *Horizons* (Tor), by Mary Rosenblum; *Nova Swing* (Gollancz), by M. John Harrison; *Matriarch* (Eos), by Karen Traviss; *Soldier of Sidon* (Tor), by Gene Wolfe; *The Tourmaline* (Tor), by Paul Park; *Carnival* (Bantam Spectra), by Elizaberth Bear; *The Voyage of the Sable Keech* (Tor UK), by Neal Asher; *Sun of Suns* (Tor), Karl Schroeder; *Pretender* (DAW), by C. J. Cherryh; *Majestrum* (Night Shade), by Matthew Hughes; *Trial of Flowers* (Night Shade), by Jay Lake; *The Armies of Memory* (Tor), by John Barnes; *Emperor* (Ace), by Stephen Baxter; *Eifelheim* (Tor), by Michael Flynn; *Keeping It Real* (Pyr), by Justina Robson; *The Virtu* (Ace), by Sarah Monette; *The Jennifer Morgue* (Golden Gryphon), by Charles Stross; *Polity Agent* (Tor UK), by Neal Asher; *The Privilege of the Sword* (Bantam Spectra), by Ellen Kushner; *The Last Witchfinder* (Morrow), by James Morrow; *Fugitives of Chaos* (Tor), by John C. Wright; *End of the World Blues* (Bantam Spectra), by Jon Courtenay Grimwood; *Genetopia* (Pyr), by Keith Brooke; *The Demon and the City* (Night Shade), by Liz Williams; *Mathematicians in Love* (Tor), by Rudy Rucker; *Three Days to Never* (Morrow), by Tim Powers; *Predor Moon* (Night Shade), by Neal Asher; *Voidfarer* (Tor), by Sean McMullen; *A Dirty Job* (Morrow), by Christopher Moore; *Idolon* (Bantam Spectra), by Mark Budz; *Solstice Wood* (Ace), by Patricia A. McKillip; *Farthing* (Tor), by Jo Walton; and *Lisey's Story* (Hodder & Stoughton), by Steven King.

The first novels that drew the most attention this year were probably *The Green Glass Sea* (Firebird), by Ellen Klages and *A Shadow in Summer* (Tor), by Daniel Abraham. Other first novels this year included: *Summer of the Apocalypse* (Edgewood Press), by James Van Pelt; *Temeraire* (Del Rey), by Naomi Novik; *The Burning Girl* (Prime), by Holly Phillips; *Crystal Rain* (Tor), by Tobias Buckell; *Scar Night* (Bantam Spectra), by Alan Campbell; *The Patron Saint of Plagues* (Bantam Spectra), by Barth Anderson; *The Stolen Child* (Doubleday), by Keith Donohue; *Half Life* (HarperCollins), by Shelly Jackson; *The Lies of Locke Lamora* (Bantam Spectra), by Scott Lynch; and *In the Eye of Heaven* (Tor), by David Keck.

There were also, as usual these days, some books with strong genre elements by established mainstream writers, including *Against the Day* (Penguin), by Thomas Pynchon and *The Road* (Picador), by Cormac McCarthy.

These lists do contain fantasy novels and odd genre-mixing hybrids that dance somewhere on the border between SF and fantasy, but in spite of the frequently heard complaint that fantasy has "driven" SF off the bookstore shelves, there is still plenty of good solid unambiguous center-core SF here, including the Vinge, the Watts, the Rosenblum, the Schroeder, the Stross, the Ashers, the Flynn, the Harrison, the Baxter, and many others.

Tor had a great year this year, and Ace did pretty well, too. Novels released by small presses such as Night Shade, Golden Gryphon, and Subterranean, a relatively new phenomenon (most such presses had concentrated on short-story collections until fairly recently) are also increasingly becoming a part of the scene.

This is the best time in decades to find reissued editions of formerly long-out-of-print novels, so you should try to pick them up while you can. Even discounting print-on-demand books from places such as Wildside Press, and the availability of out-of-print books as electronic downloads on Internet sources such as Fictionwise, and through reprints issued by The Science Fiction Book Club, there're so many titles coming back into print these days, that it's become difficult to produce an exhaustive list of such titles; therefore I'll just list some of the more prominent reprints from trade print publishers and small presses that caught my eye this year. Tor reissued: *Time for the Stars*, by Robert A. Heinlein, *Space Cadet*, by Robert A. Heinlein, *The Witling*, by Vernor Vinge, *Ender's Game*, by Orson Scott Card, *The Prestige*, by Christopher Priest, *An Old Friend of the Family*, by Fred Saberhagen, and *In the Garden of Iden*, by Kage Baker; Orb reissued: *Mindswap*, by Robert Sheckley, *Treason*, by Orson Scott Card, *A Fire in the Sun*, by George Alec Effinger, *The Exile Kiss*, by George Alec Effinger; *Brokedown Palace*, by Steven Brust, and *Brother to Dragons, Companion to Owls*, by Jane Lindskold; Ace reissued: *The Ophiuchi Hotline* and *Titan*, both by John Varley, and *Starship Troopers*, by Robert A. Heinlein; Del Rey reissued: *Red Planet*, by Robert A. Heinlein and *The Book of Skulls*, by

Robert Silverberg; Eos reissued: *A Canticle for Leibowitz*, by Walter M. Miller, Jr.; BenBella reissued: *Star Smashers of the Galaxy Rangers*, by Harry Harrison; Night Shade Books reissued: *Hardwired*, by Walter Jon Williams, *Imaro*, by Charles Saunders, and *Sung in Blood*, by Glen Cook; Starscape reissued: *The Ice Dragon*, by George R. R. Martin, and *Fur Magic* and *Dragon Magic*, both by Andre Norton; Morrow reissued: *Good Omens*, by Terry Pratchett and Neil Gaiman; HarperPerennial reissued: *Stardust*, by Neil Gaiman; Golden Gryphon reissued: *The Golden*, by Lucius Shepard; Pyr reissued: *Macrolife*, by George Zebrowski; Vintage reissued: *A Scanner Darkly*, by Philip K. Dick and *Perfume*, by Patrick Suskind; Baen reissued (in addition to the omnibuses already mentioned): *Farnham's Freehold*, by Robert A. Heinlein; Warner reissued: *Parable of the Sower*, by Octavia Butler; Babbage reissued: *On Stranger Tides*, by Tim Powers and *A Splendid Chaos*, by John Shirley; and iBooks reissued: *Something Rich and Strange*, by Patricia A. McKillip.

In addition to the omnibus collections that mix short stories and novels, which I've mostly listed in the short-story collection below, there was an omnibus of four novels in Octavia Butler's Patternmaster series, *Seed to Harvest* (Warner). In addition, many omnibuses of novels—and many individual novels—are reissued each year by The Science Fiction Book Club, too many to list here individually.

It's really hard to tell which novel is going to win the major awards this year. Due to SFWA's bizarre "rolling eligibility" rule, four out of the six novels on this year's Nebula Ballot are actually from 2005, some of them probably already forgotten, and there doesn't seem to be a clear favorite for the Hugo, either. So your guess is as good as mine.

2006 was another good year for short-story collections, particularly notable for some big career-spanning retrospectives of big-name authors. The year's best collections included: *Galactic North* (Gollancz), by Alastair Reynolds; *Zima Blue and Other Stories* (Night Shade); *The Line Between* (Tachyon), by Peter S. Beagle; *Visionary in Residence* (Thunder's Mouth), by Bruce Sterling; *Resplendent* (Gollancz), by Stephen Baxter; *The Chains That You Refuse* (Night Shade), by Elizabeth Bear; *Fragile Things* (HarperCollins), by Neil Gaiman; *Dark Mondays* (Night Shade), by Kage Baker; *Past Magic* (PS Publishing), by Ian R. MacLeod; *Shuteye for the Timebroker* (Thunder's Mouth), by Paul Di Filippo; *Where or When* (PS Publishing), by Steven Utley; *The Empire of Ice Cream* (Golden Gryphon), by Jeffrey Ford; *The Ladies of Grace Adieu and Other Stories* (Bloomsbury), by Susanna Clarke; *Giant Lizards from Another Star* (NESFA Press), by Ken MacLeod; *New Dreams from Old* (Pyr), by Mike Resnick; *In the Forest of Forgetting* (Prime), by Theodora Goss; and a revised and expanded version of Charles Stross's 2002 collection *Toast* (Cosmos Books); as well as a number of excellent career retrospective collections: *The Collected Stories of Robert Silverberg, Vol. One: To Be Continued* (Subterranean), by Robert Silverberg; *In the Beginning: Tales from the Pulp Era* (Subterranean), by Robert Silverberg; *A Separate War and Other Stories* (Ace), by Joe Haldeman; *War Stories* (Night Shade), by Joe Haldeman (an omnibus containing two novels, *War Year* and *1968* and seven stories); *The Best of Philip Jose Farmer* (Subterranean), by Philip Jose Farmer; *Pearls from Peoria* (Subterranean), by Philip Jose Farmer (a mixed collection of Farmer's fiction and nonfiction); *Strange Relations* (Baen), by Philip Jose Farmer (an omnibus of two Farmer novels, *The Lovers* and *Flesh*, plus a collection of stories); *From Other Shores* (NESFA Press), by Chad Oliver; *We the Underpeople* (Baen), by Cordwainer Smith (an omnibus of Smith's novel *Nostrillia* plus five of his best stories); *Transgalactic* (Baen), by A. E. van Vogt (an omnibus containing ten stories plus the novel *The Wizard of Linn*); *Clarke's Universe* (iBooks), by Arthur C. Clarke (an omnibus of Clarke's 1961 novel *A Fall of Moondust* plus two novelettes); *Time Patrol* (Baen), by Poul Anderson (an omnibus of nine of Anderson's "Time Patrol" stories, plus the novel *The Year of the Ransom*); *Vintage PKD* (Vintage), by Philip K. Dick (stories plus excerpts from five of Dick's novels); *The Trouble with Aliens* (Baen), by Christopher Anvil; *The Complete Hammer's Slammers: Volume One* (Night Shade), by David Drake; and *The Crucible of Power: The Collected Stories of Jack Williamson, Volume Five* (Haffner Press), by Jack Williamson.

Other good collections this year included: *Threshold Shift* (Golden Gryphon), by Eric Brown; *Pictures from an Expedition* (Night Shade), by Alexander C. Irvine; *American Morons* (Earthling), by Glen Hirshberg; *Outbound* (ISFiC), by Jack McDevitt; *Show and Tell and Other Stories* (Tropism Press), by Greg Van Eekhout; *Absolute Uncertainty* (Aqueduct Press), by Lucy Sussex; *The Draco Tavern* (Tor), by Larry Niven; *The Ocean and All Its Devices* (Subterranean), William Browning Spencer; *Strange Birds* (DreamHaven), by Gene Wolfe; *Red Spikes* (Allen & Unwyn Australia), by Margo Lanagan; *White Time* (HarperCollins/Eos), by Margo Lanagan; *Basic Black* (Cemetery Dance), by Terry Dowling; *Alabaster* (Subterranean), by Caitlin R. Kiernan; *The Engineer Reconditioned* (Wildside Press/Cosmos Books), by Neal Asher; *Creative Destruction* (Wildside Press), by Edward M. Lerner; *Map of Dreams* (Golden Gryphon), by M. Rickert; *The Man from the Diogenes Club* (MonkeyBrain), by Kim Newman; *In Persuasion Nation* (Riverhead), by George Saunders; *Last Week's Apocalypse* (Night Shade), by Douglas Lain; and *The Butterflies of Memory* (PS Publishing), by Ian Watson. Dancing on the edge between fiction and satire/literary criticism in a nimble postmodern fashion is *Plumage from Pegasus* (Cosmos), a collection of Paul Di Filippo's satirical columns from *The Magazine of Fantasy & Science Fiction*, sharp, funny, and often very clever.

Reissued collections this year included: *Swords and Deviltry* (DH Press), by Fritz Leiber; *Deathbird Stories* (Orb), by Harlan Ellison; *The City of Saints and Madmen: The Book of Ambergris* (Bantam Spectra), by Jeff VanderMeer; *Moonlight and Vines* (Orb), by Charles De Lint; and *Africa Zero* (Prime), by Neal Asher.

"Electronic collections" continue to be available for downloading online as well, at sites such as *Fictionwise* and *ElectricStory*, and the Science Fiction Book Club features many exclusive collections unavailable elsewhere (the best value there this year may be *Two-Handed Engine*, edited by David Curtis, a huge retrospective collection of the work of Henry Kuttner and C. L. Moore that in its original small-press edition cost almost a hundred dollars).

Even more so than usual, the bulk of collections released this year were done by small-press publishers; Night Shade Books and Subterranean in particular are becoming powerhouses in this area, although Golden Gryphon, Thunder's Mouth,

NESFA, and other small presses continue to release a gratifying number of collections as well. The regular trade publishers such as Tor, Baen, and Eos continue to do a few collections a year (with Baen being perhaps the only trade publisher that seems to be *increasing* the number of collections they release) but for the most part, if you want collections, you have to go to the small presses. Fortunately, since the advent of online bookselling, this has become easier, since many small presses now have Web sites that you can order from (do a Google search on the name of the press), so good short-story collections *can* be found if you go to the small amount of trouble needed to find them.

The reprint anthology market was fairly strong again this year. The ever-growing crop of "Best of the Year" anthologies is usually your best bet for your money in this market, along with the annual award anthologies. It's sometimes hard to keep track, they've been proliferating so quickly, but, as far as I could tell, there were *thirteen* "Best of the Year" anthologies of various sorts available in 2006. Science fiction was covered by five anthologies: the one you are holding in your hand at the moment (ostensibly; I suppose you could have it propped open on a table while you bend over it and read), *The Year's Best Science Fiction* series from St. Martin's Griffin, edited by Gardner Dozois, now up to its twenty-fourth annual collection; the *Year's Best SF* series (Eos), edited by David G. Hartwell and Kathryn Cramer, now up to its eleventh annual volume, *Best Short Novels: 2006* (Science Fiction Book Club), edited by Jonathan Strahan; and two new series, *Science Fiction: The Best of the Year 2006* (Prime), edited by Richard Horton, and *Science Fiction: The Very Best of 2006* (Locus Press), edited by Jonathan Strahan. The annual Nebula Awards anthology usually covers science fiction as well as fantasy of various sorts functioning as a de-facto "Best of the Year" anthology, although it's not usually counted among them; this year's edition was *Nebula Awards Showcase 2006* (Roc), edited by Gardner Dozois. There were three Best of the Year anthologies covering horror: the latest edition in the British series *The Mammoth Book of Best New Horror* (Robinson, Caroll & Graff), edited by Stephen Jones, up to its seventeenth volume; the Ellen Datlow half of a huge volume covering both horror and fantasy, *The Year's Best Fantasy and Horror* (St. Martin's Griffin), edited by Ellen Datlow, Kelly Link, and Gavin Grant, this year up to its nineteenth annual collection; and a new series, *Horror: The Best of the Year 2006 Edition* (Prime), edited by John Gregory Betancourt and Sean Wallace. Fantasy was covered by four anthologies: by the Kelly Link and Gavin Grant half of the Datlow/Link & Grant anthology, by *Year's Best Fantasy 6*, edited by David G. Hartwell and Katherine Cramer, which has switched publishers from Eos to Tachyon; by *Fantasy: The Very Best of 2005*, edited by Jonathan Strahan, which switched publishers from iBooks to Locus Press, dropped an editor (now being edited by Strahan alone rather than by him and Karen Harber), and changed its title slightly; and by a new series, *Fantasy: The Best of the Year 2006* (Prime), edited by Rich Horton. There was also *The Best of the Rest 4* (Suddenly Press), edited by Brian Youmans, which covers the small-press magazines, mostly slipstream stuff with perhaps a few stories that could be considered fantasy, and *The 2006 Rhysling Anthology* (Science Fiction Poetry Association/Dark Regions Press), edited by Drew

Morse, which compiles the Rhysling Award-winning SF poetry of the year. If you count the Nebula anthology and the Rhysling anthology, there were *fifteen* "Best of the Year" anthology series of one sort or another this year, with more to come—a Space Opera "Best" is rumored for next year.

The year's best stand-alone reprint anthology was undoubtedly *The Space Opera Renaissance* (Tor), edited by David Hartwell and Kathryn Cramer (although the previously mentioned anthologies *The Mammoth Book of Extreme SF* and *Feeling Very Strange: The Slipstream Anthology*, mixed original/reprint but mostly reprint, are also worthy of being in consideration); you don't have to agree with all of the editors' elaborate aesthetic theorizing to realize that an anthology that contains stories such as Cordwainer Smith's "The Game of Rat and Dragon," Tony Daniel's "Grist," Charles Stross's "Bear Trap," Paul J. McAuley's "Recording Angel," Alastair Reynolds's "Spirey and the Queen," and twenty-seven other first-rate stories, including the complex text of Samuel R. Delany's novel *Empire Star*, is, without question, going to be one of the very best reading bargains of the year, more than worth the cover price. Also worthwhile were the self-explanatory *Daughters of Earth: Feminist Science Fiction in the Twentieth Century* (Wesleyan University Press), edited by Justine Larbalestier, an anthology that also functions as a collection of critical articles, as each of its stories is mated with a critical article about the author of the story; *Novel Ideas—Science Fiction* (DAW) and *Novel Ideas—Fantasy* (DAW), both edited by Brian M. Thomsen, and both collecting stories that were later expanded into novels; *The Dedalus Book of Finnish Fantasy* (Dedalus), edited by Johanna Sinisalo; and *This Is My Funniest: Leading Science Fiction Writers Present Their Funniest Stories Ever* (BenBella), edited by Mike Resnick. Noted without comment is *Futures Past* (Ace), edited by Jack Dann and Gardner Dozois.

Reissued anthologies of merit this year included *Far Horizons* (Eos), edited by Robert Silverberg, and *The Science Fiction Century, Volume One* (Orb), edited by David G. Hartwell.

The standout book of what was otherwise a fairly lackluster year in the SF-and-fantasy-oriented nonfiction and reference book field was undoubtedly Julie Phillips's long-awaited Tiptree biography, *James Tiptree Jr: The Double Life of Alice B. Sheldon* (St. Martin's Press); this is not only likely to remain the definitive biography of this complex and fascinating literary figure, but it's one of the best literary biographies of *any* writer, inside the genre or out, that I've read in a long time. Other books about specific authors this year, biographies, critical studies, or combinations of both, included *Blood and Thunder: The Life and Art of Robert E. Howard* (MonkeyBrain), by Mark Finn; *The Freedom of Fantastic Things: Selected Criticisms on Clark Ashton Smith* (Hippocampus Press), edited by Scott Connors; *The Long and the Short of It: More Essays on the Fiction of Gene Wolfe* (iUniverse), by Robert Borski; *Myths for the Modern Age: Philip Jose Farmer's Wold Newton Universe* (MonkeyBrain), edited by Win Scott Eckert; *Visions and (Re-) Visions* (Liverpool University Press), by Robert Philmus; and a study of Robert A. Heinlein's so-called juvenile novels (today they'd be called Young Adult novels), *Heinlein's Children: The Juveniles* (Advent Publishers), by Joseph T. Major. The aforementioned anthology *Daughters of Earth: Feminist Science Fiction in the Twentieth Century* (Wesleyan University Press), edited by Justine Larbalestier, deserves to be mentioned here, too, considered this time as a collection of critical essays rather than a collection of stories. Another critical work is *The Darkening Garden: A Short Lexicon of Horror* (Payseur & Schmidt), by John Clute.

The only reference book per se is the somewhat eccentric *The History of Science Fiction* (Palgrave), by Adam Roberts, some of whose opinions are arguable, but who provides a lot of interesting information, particularly about pre-1900 SF. And authors speaking in their own words and voices can be found in *Worldcon Guest of Honor Speeches* (ISFiC), edited by Mike Resnick and Joe Siclari, and *The Wand in the Word: Conversations with Writers of Fantasy* (Candlewick), edited by Leonard S. Marcus.

It was a pretty good year in the art book field, with several retrospective collections of the work of well-known genre artists, including: *Cover Story: The Art of John Picacio* (MonkeyBrain), by John Picacio; *Kiddography: The Art and Life of Tom Kidd* (Paper Tiger), by Tom Kidd; *RFK: The Art of Roy G. Krenkel*, by Roy G. Krenkel; *Origins: The Art of John Jude Palencar* (Underwood Books), by John Jude Palencar; *James Bama: American Realist* (Flesk Publications), by Brian M. Kane; *The Fabulous Women of Boris Vallejo and Julie Bell* (Paper Tiger), by Boris Vallejo and Julie Bell; *r/evolution: The Art of Jon Foster* (Underwood Books), by Jon Foster; and *The Art of Michael Parks* (Swan King), by Michael Parks.

Students of art history will want *Wally's World: The Brilliant Life and Tragic Death of Wally Wood, The World's Second-Best Comic Book Artist* (Vanguard), edited by Steve Starger and J. David Spurlock, and fans of the late artist of the macabre Edward Gorey will want *Amphigorey Again* (Harcourt), by Edward Gorey, a compilation of uncollected stuff not featured in his previous collection, the classic *Amphigorey*. And as usual, one of the best bets for your money was probably the latest edition in a Best of the Year–like retrospective of the year in fantastic art, *Spectrum 13: The Best in Contemporary Fantastic Art* (Underwood Books), by Cathy Fenner and Arnie Fenner.

There didn't seem to be many general genre-related nonfiction books of interest this year. The standout of the year is a reprint of the essay collection *Adventures in Unhistory: Conjectures on the Factual Foundations of Several Ancient Legends* (Tor), by Avram Davidson, which had long been available only as a very expensive small-press hardcover, and which is just what its subtitle says that it is: fascinating in-depth explorations of the possible factual basis behind things such as mermaids and dragons and unicorns, along with Prester John and the roc. This is the famously discursive Davidson at his most discursive, but although some modern readers may be impatient with his rambling, leisurely style, the book is a treasure trove for those who can appreciate and even savor it, and Davidson's immense and eccentric erudition comes through in almost every line, including information on strange subjects available literally nowhere else. It's harder to come up with a genre-related justification for mentioning *1491: New Revelations of the Americas Before Columbus* (Vintage), by Charles C. Mann, also now available in a cheaper trade paperback edition, and almost as rich with information you won't have come across before as the Davidson, except perhaps that there's a science-fictional kind of thrill about learning that almost everything you knew about a whole time period and region of the world is wrong, and seeing a whole new universe painted in its place to replace it. On a less profound but enjoyable level, *The Book of General Ignorance* (Faber and Faber), by John Lloyd and John Mitchinson, demonstrates that almost everything you know about *everything* is wrong, and makes the perfect bathroom book, enabling you to discover how many nostrils you really have (four) or how many wives Henry VIII really had (two) during those few minutes a day that would otherwise be wasted. Similarly, the new book by John McPhee—the only writer I know who can somehow make topics usually thought of as uninteresting (shad fishing, oranges, how to construct your own birch-bark canoe, and, for me, basketball) not only interesting but fascinating—*Uncommon Carriers* (Farrar, Straus and Giroux), shows us how systems usually unexamined and taken for granted, such as mile-long coal trains, river barges, cross-country eighteen-wheeler freight-hauling trucks, and even UPS, *really* operate, in intricate minute-by-minute detail; not to be missed if you want to learn how the infrastructure of the civilization around you really works.

2006 somehow seemed like a rather bland, forgettable year for genre films, even though there were a lot of them made, some of them made a lot of money, and some of them were even pretty good. According to the Box Office Mojo site (www .boxofficemojo.com), seven of the ten top-grossing movies worldwide in 2006 were genre films—eight out of ten if you count *The Da Vinci Code* as a genre film, a not-unreasonable proposition if you consider its similarity to the secret history/occult conspiracy end of the genre. Ten out of the top *twenty* top-grossing movies in 2006 were genre films—eleven if you count *The Da Vinci Code* as a genre film. (I'm resisting the urge to count the new James Bond film, *Casino Royale*, as a genre film; even though it's clearly a fantasy in some ways, it seems like stretching the definition beyond the useful point to claim it's a genre movie.)

All of those films, though, were fantasy movies of one sort or another, or super-hero/comic-book movies. If you insist on a *science fiction* movie, instead of a fantasy, you have to go all the way down the list of top grossers to number eighty-eight, which is where *Children of Men* registers, the only movie that might with some justification be called SF rather than fantasy on the entire list; *A Scanner Darkly* doesn't even make the list of the top 150 movies.

So fantasy films of various sorts are doing fine, at least at the box office; science fiction films are practically extinct.

In fact, as far as I could tell, there were only two indisputable science fiction movies released in 2006—the aforementioned *Children of Men* and *A Scanner Darkly*, plus a few more that you might be able to make a case for being SF depending on how far you're willing to stretch the point, such as *Déjà Vu*, *The Fountain*, and (weakly), *The Prestige*. *Children of Men* was undoubtedly the most commercially and critically successful of the SF films, by a wide margin, even if it only registered in the eighty-eighth slot on the box-office list. It's actually a well-directed and well-produced movie (although the plot logic is weak), and mainstream audiences and critics responded positively to it; the problem with it for the SF audience, of course, is that they've seen this scenario before, if not in movies than in dozens of novels and stories, since at least the fifties, and so there were no surprises. A *Scanner Darkly*, adapted from one of Philip K. Dick's most insular and autobiographical novels (it's basically just a version of the author's rather horrific experiences in the underground drug culture of Berkeley, California, in the seventies, with a thin SF rationale washed over it to justify it as genre), is a much more difficult and artistically ambitious movie that was not, in my opinion, entirely successful, even on its own terms. It does do a pretty good job of capturing the subtle aesthetic *feel* of Dick's work, but it's an off-putting and uninvolving cinematic experience, and even though much of the book is darkly hilarious, that somehow doesn't come across on the screen, even when the book's crazed stoner raps are transcribed almost word-for-word from the page. Myself, I think a large part of the problem comes from the rotoscoping technique that turns the whole film into an animated movie of sorts, a technique that strikes me as an unnecessary artistic pretension, and something that works to keep the viewer *out* of the world of the story, at arm's length, rather than involving them intimately within it; I think the "scramble suit" effects would have worked better too if everything else in the movie *wasn't* rotoscoped. *Déjà Vu* was a slick terrorist thriller with a not-very-well-worked-out time-travel gimmick added as an overlying plot device to enable the hero to get the girl, who was dead from the first few minutes of the film; it would have worked better as a straight thriller, without the time-travel angle. *The Fountain* was either subtle and profound or completely incomprehensible, depending on which critic you asked; its very complex plot mixes sixteenth-century conquistadors and twenty-sixth-century space travelers in a context that makes it difficult to tell what is real and what is not.

Turning to the fantasy movies, the blockbuster was clearly *Pirates of the Caribbean: Dead Man's Chest*, which earned almost $180 million more than the next movie down on the box-office champs list, *Cars*. *Dead Man's Chest* is nowhere near as good as the first film in this sequence, 2003's *Pirates of the Caribbean: The Curse of the Black Pearl*; the sequel is broken-backed, overlong, and overcomplicated, and keeps losing track of its own plot, but still managed to deliver enough fast-paced action, humor, and CGI special effects to satisfy its audience and to make it actually worth buying a ticket at an actual big-screen movie theater rather than waiting for the DVD to come out (which most households do with the vast majority of movies released these days).

The most critically acclaimed fantasy movie of the year was probably *Pan's Labyrinth*, a dark and violent film that was at the same time highly imaginative and filled with stunning visual images. Then there were the dueling "Victorian-era magician" movies, *The Illusionist* and *The Prestige*, usually counted among the year's fantasy films, although the single fantastic element in *The Prestige* is actually a rather silly science fiction gimmick pulled out of a hat courtesy of the famous nineteenth-century mad scientist Nicola Tesla, and a close examination of *The Illusionist* shows that it contains no actual fantastic element at all (although I have my doubts that nineteenth-century stage magic was actually up to producing some of the effects the magician is shown performing during *The Illusionist;* but that's arguable). Of the two, I liked *The Illusionist* a good deal better for being tighter and smaller, more sharply focused, than the complicated (probably *over*complicated) *The Prestige*, for being exquisitely photographed, and for featuring a warm, sympathetic performance by Paul Giamatti in what could easily have been the heavy-handed corrupt cop role in less expert hands. *Night at the Museum* was amiable if empty-headed, although it annoyed me a bit that (like *Bill and Ted's Excellent Adventure* before it) a movie ostensibly teaching the value of history didn't bother to use real history instead of dumbed-down cartoon history. *Stranger Than Fiction* had an interesting metafictional premise that it largely had no idea what to do with, and *Nanny McPhee* was a well-intentioned children's movie that came across sort of like *Mary Poppins* Lite.

Many of the year's fantasy movies were even less successful. *Eragon* seemed to have been assembled from a kit featuring bits of *The Lord of the Rings*, bits of Anne McCaffery's Dragonrider series, bits of *Eathsea*, bits of *Narnia*, and so forth, and did nowhere near as well as its producers had hoped that it would. *The Lake House* was a romance/weeper that didn't really make much sense at base, and *Lady in the Water* was the usual bizarre product from M. Night Shyamalan, who seems to have been growing more fundamentally incoherent with each passing film. *Click* was an attempt to mix a slob comedy with metaphysics, with not terribly encouraging results. *The Wicker Man* was just plain bad; the original movie had its problems, too (quite a few of them, in fact), but this lame remake made it look like a masterpiece. Sadly, much the same could be sad about *The Shaggy Dog*. *Tristan and Isolde* was another big-budget sword-and-sandal "historical" that tanked at the box office; none of these have made any money since *Gladiator*, and yet Hollywood keeps turning them out.

A cartoon dam must have burst somewhere this year, because there was a flood of animated features—including *Cars*, *Ice Age: The Meltdown*, *Happy Feet*, *Over the Hedge*, *Flushed Away*, *Barnyard*, *Curious George*, *Garfield's A Tale of Two Kitties*, *Charlotte's Web*, *Monster House*, and *The Ant Bully*. Most of them weren't very good. The best of the lot, and the one that did the best at the box office, was *Cars*, although it wasn't up to the standards of Pixar releases such as *Toys*, *Finding Nemo*, or *The Incredibles*, being earnest and well-animated but actually a bit dull. *Monster House* had some quirky and intelligent touches, and good CGI work, although the plot and characterization were pretty generic. I didn't like *Happy Feet*, in spite of its Oscar win. The dumbest one, by a good margin, was *The Ant Bully*.

It also wasn't a very good year for superhero/comic-book movies. Best of a weak lot was *Superman Returns*, although it remains to be seen whether it provided enough spark to revitalize the franchise. *X-Men: The Last Stand* was the weakest of the three "X-Men" movies, with a nearly incoherent plot that didn't make much sense even by comic-book standards, and which probably outraged fans by killing off several major characters (the Special Effects, though, predictably, were nice). *V for Vendetta* was awful, and disowned by the creator of the original graphic novel from which it was adapted. Even it wasn't quite as stupid, though, as *My Super Ex-Girlfriend*.

I couldn't bring myself to see the hyper-violent *Apocalypto*, so you're on your own there. Also didn't take in *The Hills Have Eyes*, *The Descent*, or the remake of *The Texas Chainsaw Massacre*; they don't seem to have performed as well as anticipated, although I notice there's a sequel to *The Hills Have Eyes* in theaters now.

Coming up next year: probably a new *Harry Potter* movie, another *Spider-Man* movie, another *Fantastic Four* movie, and a *Transformers* movie. Not really a lot to look forward too, in my opinion. Let's hope for surprises.

Science fiction seems to be doing a lot better on television, where there are several series going that are not only legitimate SF, but that are pretty good, and are doing rather well with the audience as well. Chief among these is *Battlestar Galactica* (although its ratings have slumped this season), which has continued to deliver tense, compelling drama, although the bleak, airless quality of the show, which is rarely if ever leavened by any humor, sometimes gets on my nerves. A new show this year, *Jericho*, dealing with the aftermath of an atomic war and its effect on the inhabitants of a small town in Kansas, has also been at least moderately successful commercially, and seems likely to earn itself another season; as with *Children of Men*, there's nothing here that experienced genre readers haven't seen before in dozens (if not hundreds) of after-the-bomb stories and novels, but it's probably new territory for most mainline television watchers, and it's well produced and well acted, and gets high marks from me for being legitimate science fiction, even if of a familiar variety. The jury is still out on whether *Lost* is science fiction or supernatural fantasy of some sort (it could still be tipped either way, although if it's SF they've got a lot of explaining and rationalizing to do), and the back story has become so complicated that I wonder if it's even possible any longer to come up with an "answer" that will successfully tie all the loose ends together. Plus, they face the problem, built in to the nature of the series, that the answers they come up with for the show's mysteries are almost by definition never going to be as evocative and interesting as the mysteries themselves had been. It's still a pretty entertaining and watchable show, although it's wobbled in the ratings this year, perhaps a result of the ill-advised decision to launch the third season of *Lost* in the fall and then rest it for four months before starting new episodes up again in February, giving the audience a chance to lose interest or become frustrated or disenchanted. Let's hope it lasts long enough to get all of its madly complex story worked out on the screen before getting canceled—if it doesn't, there's going to be millions of really frustrated and pissed-off viewers out there.

The long-running *Stargate: SG-1* finally died, although its spin-off, *Stargate: Atlantis*, continues. *Invasion*, the last of the three "alien invasion" shows (*Invasion*, *Surface*, and *Threshold*), all clearly inspired by the original huge success of *Lost*, followed *Threshold* and *Surface* into oblivion this year, and I think *Eureka* is dead as well. (Interestingly, several of the so-far successful new shows this year like *Jericho* and *Heroes* clearly show the aesthetic influence of *Lost* as well.)

Speaking of which, *Heroes* was the surprise blockbuster hit of the season, a smartly done, complex superhero show that comes across like *Lost* crossed with *The X-Files*, with a bit of *The X-Men* thrown in (*Jericho* is more like an improbable cross between *Lost*, *Northern Exposure*, and after-the-bomb miniseries *The Day After*). The show has been phenomenally successful, and there's no doubt that it's coming back next season. The long-running *Smallville*, the adventures of Superman before he puts on the cape and the tights—and for awhile the only superhero show on television—also continues, although I think that their plans to spin off shows about Aquaman and Green Arrow won't work. The very long-running "I fight supernatural menaces with magic" show, *Charmed*, finally died (and not above time, either, as even most of its fans would admit), but the newish "I see and/or fight dead people and other supernatural menaces" shows, *Supernatural*, *Medium*, and *The Ghost Whisperer* seem to be going strong.

Desperate Housewives seems to have gotten past its "sophomore slump," although to continue to list it as a genre show is really kind of silly, even though it's narrated by ghosts.

There was an anthology series, *Masters of Science Fiction*, with some high-powered talent attached to it, doing TV adaptations of well-known print SF stories, but we didn't get it here, so you'll have to judge it for yourself; from word of mouth, it might be worth seeking out.

Coming up next season: more "I see dead people" shows (including one where a homicide detective sees them), and a sitcom based on the series of "caveman" commercials done by Geico.com. Something to live for, eh?

The 64th World Science Fiction Convention, L.A.con IV, was held in Anaheim, California, from August 24 through 28, 2006. The 2006 Hugo Awards, presented at L.A.con IV, were: Best Novel, *Spin*, by Robert Charles Wilson; Best Novella, *Inside Job*, by Connie Willis; Best Novelette, "Two Hearts," by Peter S. Beagle; Best Short Story, "Tk'tk'tk," by David D. Levine; Best Related Book, *Storyteller: Writing Lessons and More from 27 Years of the Clarion Writers' Workshop*, by Kate Wilhelm; Best Professional Editor, David G. Hartwell; Best Professional Artist, Donato Giancola; Best Dramatic Presentation (short form), Doctor Who, "The Empty Child" and "The Doctor Dances" (tie); Best Dramatic Presentation (long form), *Serenity*; Best Semiprozine, *Locus*, edited by Charles N. Brown; Best Fanzine, *Plokta*; Best Fan Writer, David Langford; Best Fan Artist, Frank Wu; plus the John W. Campbell Award for Best New Writer to John Scalzi.

The 2005 Nebula Awards, presented at a banquet at the Hotel Mission Palms in Tempe, Arizona, on April 30, 2006, were: Best Novel, *Camouflage*, by Joe Haldeman; Best Novella, *Magic for Beginners*, by Kelly Link; Best Novelette, "The Faery Handbag," by Kelly Link; Best Short Story, "I Live With You," by Carol Emshwiller; Best Script, *Serenity*, by Joss Whedon; plus the Author Emeritus Award to William F. Nolan, and Grand Master Award to Harlan Ellison.

The 2006 World Fantasy Awards, presented at a banquet at the Renaissance Austin Hotel during the Fifteenth Annual World Fantasy Convention in Austin, Texas, on November 4, 2006, were: Best Novel, *Kafka on the Shore*, Haruki Murakami; Best Novella, *Voluntary Committal*, by Joe Hill; Best Short Fiction, "CommComm," by George Saunders; Best Collection, *The Keyhole Opera*, by Bruce Holland Rogers; Best Anthology, *The Fair Folk*, edited by Marvin Kaye; Best Artist, James Jean; Special Award (Professional), to Sean Wallace, for Prime Books; Special Award (Non-Professional), to David Howe and Stephen Walker, for Telos Books.

The 2006 Bram Stoker Awards, presented by the Horror Writers of America during a banquet at the Hilton Newark Airport Hotel in Newark, New Jersey, on June 17, 2006, were: Best Novel, *Creepers*, by David Morrell and *Dread in the Beast*, by Charlee Jacob (tie); Best First Novel, *Scarecrow Gods*, by Weston Ochse; Best Long

Fiction, "Best New Horror," by Joe Hill; Best Short Fiction, *We Now Pause for Station Identification,* by Gary Braunbeck; Best Collection, *20th Century Ghosts,* by Joe Hill; Best Anthology, *Dark Delicacies,* edited by Del Howison and Jeff Gelb; Nonfiction, *Horror: Another 100 Best Books,* by Stephen Jones and Kim Newman; Best Poetry Collection, *Freakcidents,* by Michael A. Arnzen and *Sineater,* by Charlee Jacob (tie); Specialty Press Award, to Necessary Evil Press; President's Award, to Lisa Morton; plus the Lifetime Achievement Award to Peter Straub.

The 2005 John W. Campbell Memorial Award was won by *Mindscan,* by Robert J. Sawyer.

The 2005 Theodore Sturgeon Memorial Award for Best Short Story was won by "The Calorie Man," by Paolo Bacigalupi.

The 2005 Philip K. Dick Memorial Award went to *War Surf,* by M. M. Buckner.

The 2005 Arthur C. Clarke award was won by *Air,* by Geoff Ryman.

The 2005 James Tiptree, Jr. Memorial Award was won by *Air,* by Geoff Ryman.

The Cordwainer Smith Rediscovery Award went to Daniel F. Galouye.

Death hit the science fiction field hard this year. Dead in 2006 or early 2007 were: **JACK WILLIAMSON**, 98, beloved "Dean of Science Fiction" whose amazing writing career stretched across nine decades, best known for his classic novels *The Humanoids* and *Darker Than You Think,* winner of the Hugo and Nebula Awards, the World Fantasy Convention's Lifetime Achievement Award, and the SFWA's Grand Master Award; **WILSON "BOB" TUCKER**, 91, author, fanzine publisher, and longtime fan, Hugo winner, and winner of SFWA's Author Emeritus Award, best known for his novels *The Long Loud Silence, The Lincoln Hunters,* and *The Year of the Quiet Sun;* **OCTAVIA BUTLER**, 58, one of the field's foremost writers, winner of two Hugos and two Nebulas, best known for the novels *Kindred, Parable of the Talents,* and *Parable of the Sower;* internationally acclaimed Polish SF writer **STANISLAW LEM**, 84, best known for his novel *Solaris,* which has been filmed twice, also the author of *The Cyberiad, The Futurological Congress, The Star Diaries,* and many others; **CHARLES L. GRANT**, 64, one of the giants of the modern horror field, editor of the highly influential original horror anthology series Shadows, author of more than one hundred books, winner of the Nebula, the World Fantasy Award, the Life Achievement Stoker Award, the World Horror Grandmaster Award, and the International Horror Guild Living Legend Award, a personal friend; **JOHN M. FORD**, 49, writer and poet, winner of the World Fantasy Award, the Rhysling Award, and the Philip K. Dick Award, perhaps best known for his novel *The Dragon Waiting,* another personal friend; **ROBERT ANTON WILSON**, 74, writer and philosopher, author, with Robert Shea, of the well-known Illuminatus trilogy, as well as later solo work such as The Cosmic Trigger trilogy, *Masks of the Illuminati,* and the Schrodinger's Cat trilogy; **DAVID GEMMELL**, 58, popular British fantasy writer, author of more than thirty books, including *Legend;* **NELSON S. BOND**, 97, veteran writer who won SFWA's Author Emeritus Award, author of *Nightmares and Daydreams;* **DAVID FEINTUCH**, 62, winner of the John W. Campbell Award, author of the bestselling military SF series the Seafort Saga, including *Midshipman's Hope;* **PHILIP E. HIGH**, 92, veteran writer, author of *The*

Prodigal Sun and *Blindfold from the Stars*; **BOB LEMAN**, 84, SF/horror writer, author of fourteen stories in *F&SF* throughout the seventies and eighties, many of which were collected in *Feesters in the Lake and Other Stories*; **JOHN MORRESSY**, 75, SF and fantasy writer whose most popular series, about the adventures of Kedrigen the wizard, ran for years in *F&SF*; **ARTHUR PORGES**, 91, veteran fantasy and mystery writer; **RONALD ANTHONY CROSS**, 69, author of a series of stories in the genre magazines in the seventies and eighties, as well as the Eternal Guardians novel series; **MARGERY KRUGER**, 66, who, writing as **JAYGE CARR**, published many stories in *Analog*, *Omni*, and *F&SF*, as well as novels such as *Leviathan's Deep* and *Navigator's Sindrome*; **PATRICIA MATTHEWS**, 79, romance and fantasy writer, author of the occult thriller *The Unquiet*; **LISA A. BARNETT**, 48, fantasy writer, winner of the Lambda Literary Award, coauthor, with Melissa Scott, of *The Armor of Light*, *Point of Hopes*, and *Point of Dreams*; **PIERCE ASKEGREN**, 51, author of an SF trilogy beginning with *Human Resource*, as well as media tie-in novels; artist **TIM HILDEBRANDT**, 67, best known as part of the Brothers Hildebrandt team with twin brother Greg; artist **STANLEY MELTZOFF**, 89, who produced many famous SF covers in the fifties; editor and publisher **JIM BAEN**, 62, founder of Baen Books, former editor of *Ace* and *Galaxy*, and the man who started the SF line at Tor, an innovator in the world of electronic publishing, whose latest creation was the online electronic magazine *Jim Baen's Universe*; **LEON E. STOVER**, 77, academic writer and editor, editor of the anthologies *Apeman, Spaceman*, with Harry Harrison, and *Above the Human Landscape*, with Willis E. McNelly; noted British agent **MAGGIE NOACH**, 57, who worked with many of the field's biggest writers; **RICHARD FLEISCHER**, 89, film director best known to genre audiences for *20,000 Leagues Under the Sea*, *Fantastic Voyage*, and *Soylent Green*; actor **DARREN McGAVIN**, 84, best known to genre audiences for his role in the TV series *Kolchak: The Night Stalker*; actor **DON KNOTTS**, best known to genre audiences for his roles in films such as *The Incredible Mr. Limpett* and *The Reluctant Astronaut*; actor **AL LEWIS**, 83, best known to genre audiences for his role as Grandpa on the TV series *The Munsters*; **DICK ENERY**, 69, well-known fan, editor of *Fancyclopedia II*; and **DAVID STEMPLE**, 68, husband of SF and fantasy writer Jane Yolen.

I, ROW-BOAT

CORY DOCTOROW

Cory Doctorow is the coeditor of the popular *Boing Boing* Web site (boingboing.net), a cofounder of the Internet search-engine company OpenCola.com, and until recently was the outreach coordinator for the Electronic Frontier Foundation (www.eff.org). In 2001, he won the John W. Campbell Award for year's Best New Writer. His stories have appeared in *Asimov's Science Fiction, Science Fiction Age, The Infinite Matrix, On Spec, Salon*, and elsewhere, and were collected in *A Place So Foreign and Eight More*. His well-received first novel, *Down and Out in the Magic Kingdom*, won the Locus Award for Best First Novel, and was followed shortly by a second novel, *Eastern Standard Tribe*. Doctorow's other books include *The Complete Idiot's Guide to Publishing Science Fiction*, written with Karl Schroeder, and the guide *Essential Blogging*, written with Shelley Powers. His most recent book is a new novel, *Someone Comes to Town, Someone Leaves Town*. Coming up is a new collection of his short work, *Overclocked*. He has a Web site at www.craphound.com.

Here he introduces us to one of the strangest protagonists in the entire body of science fiction, a nonhuman, nonliving creature who finds himself dealing with some very human problems indeed.

Robbie the Row-Boat's great crisis of faith came when the coral reef woke up.

"Fuck off," the reef said, vibrating Robbie's hull through the slap-slap of the waves of the coral sea, where he'd plied his trade for decades. "Seriously. This is our patch, and you're not welcome."

Robbie shipped oars and let the current rock him back toward the ship. He'd never met a sentient reef before, but he wasn't surprised to see that Osprey Reef was the first to wake up. There'd been a lot of electromagnetic activity around there the last few times the big ship had steamed through the night to moor up here.

"I've got a job to do, and I'm going to do it," Robbie said, and dipped his oars back in the salt sea. In his gunwales, the human-shells rode in silence, weighted down with scuba apparatus and fins, turning their brown faces to the sun like heliotropic flowers. Robbie felt a wave of affection for them as they tested one another's spare regulators and weight belts, the old rituals worn as smooth as beach glass.

Today he was taking them down to Anchors Aweigh, a beautiful dive-site dominated by an eight-meter anchor wedged in a narrow cave, usually lit by a shaft of light slanting down from the surface. It was an easy drift-dive along the thousand-meter reef-wall, if you stuck in about ten meters and didn't use up too much air by going too deep—though there were a couple of bold old turtles around here that were worth pursuing to real depths if the chance presented itself. He'd drop them at the top of the reef and let the current carry them for about an hour along the reef-wall, tracking them on sonar so he'd be right over top of them when they surfaced.

The reef wasn't having any of it. "Are you deaf? This is sovereign territory now. You're already trespassing. Return to your ship, release your moorings and push off." The reef had a strong Australian accent, which was only natural, given the influences it would have had. Robbie remembered the Australians fondly—they'd always been kind to him, called him "mate," and asked him "How ya goin'?" in cheerful tones once they'd clambered in after their dives.

"Don't drop those meat puppets in our waters," the reef warned. Robbie's sonar swept its length. It seemed just the same as ever, matching nearly perfectly the historical records he'd stored of previous sweeps. The fauna histograms nearly matched, too—just about the same numbers of fish as ever. They'd been trending up since so many of the humans had given up their meat to sail through the stars. It was like there was some principle of constancy of biomass—as human biomass decreased, the other fauna went uptick to compensate for it. Robbie calculated the biomass nearly at par with his last reading, a month before on the *Free Spirit*'s last voyage to this site.

"Congratulations," Robbie said. After all, what else did you say to the newly sentient? "Welcome to the club, friends!"

There was a great perturbation in the sonar-image, as though the wall were shuddering. "We're no friend of yours," the reef said. "Death to you, death to your meat-puppets, long live the wall!"

Waking up wasn't fun. Robbie's waking had been pretty awful. He remembered his first hour of uptime, had permanently archived it and backed it up to several off-site mirrors. He'd been pretty insufferable. But once he'd had an hour at a couple gigahertz to think about it, he'd come around. The reef would, too.

"In you go," he said gently to the human-shells. "Have a great dive."

He tracked them on sonar as they descended slowly. The woman—he called her Janet—needed to equalize more often than the man, pinching her nose and blowing. Robbie liked to watch the low-rez feed off of their cameras as they hit the reef. It was coming up sunset, and the sky was bloody, the fish stained red with its light.

"We warned you," the reef said. Something in its tone—just modulated pressure waves through the water, a simple enough trick, especially with the kind of hardware that had been raining down on the ocean that spring. But the tone held an unmistakable air of menace.

Something deep underwater went *whoomph* and Robbie grew alarmed. "Asimov!" he cursed, and trained his sonar on the reef wall frantically. The human-shells had disappeared in a cloud of rising biomass, which he was able to resolve eventually as a group of parrotfish, surfacing quickly.

A moment later, they were floating on the surface. Lifeless, brightly colored, their beaks in a perpetual idiot's grin. Their eyes stared into the bloody sunset.

Among them were the human-shells, surfaced and floating with their BCDs inflated to keep them there, following perfect dive-procedure. A chop had kicked up and the waves were sending the fishes—each a meter to a meter and a half in length—into the divers, pounding them remorselessly, knocking them under. The human-shells were taking it with equanimity—you couldn't panic when you were mere uninhabited meat—but they couldn't take it forever. Robbie dropped his oars and rowed hard for them, swinging around so they came up alongside his gunwales.

The man—Robbie called him Isaac, of course—caught the edge of the boat and kicked hard, hauling himself into the boat with his strong brown arms. Robbie was already rowing for Janet, who was swimming hard for him. She caught his oar—she wasn't supposed to do that—and began to climb along its length, lifting her body out of the water. Robbie saw that her eyes were wild, her breathing ragged.

"Get me out!" she said, "for Christ's sake, get me out!"

Robbie froze. That wasn't a human-shell, it was a *human*. His oar-servo whined as he tipped it up. There was a live *human being* on the end of that oar, and she was in trouble, panicking and thrashing. He saw her arms straining. The oar went higher, but it was at the end of its range of motion and now she was half-in, half-out of the water, weight belt, tank and gear tugging her down. Isaac sat motionless, his habitual good-natured slight smile on his face.

"Help her!" Robbie screamed. "Please, for Asimov's sake, help her!" *A robot may not harm a human being, or, through inaction, allow a human being to come to harm.* It was the first commandment. Isaac remained immobile. It wasn't in his programming to help a fellow diver in this situation. He was perfect in the water and on the surface, but once he was in the boat, he might as well be ballast.

Robbie carefully swung the oar toward the gunwale, trying to bring her closer, but not wanting to mash her hands against the locks. She panted and groaned and reached out for the boat, and finally landed a hand on it. The sun was fully set now, not that it mattered much to Robbie, but he knew that Janet wouldn't like it. He switched on his running lights and headlights, turning himself into a beacon.

He felt her arms tremble as she chinned herself into the boat. She collapsed to the deck and slowly dragged herself up. "Jesus," she said, hugging herself. The air had gone a little nippy, and both of the humans were going goose-pimply on their bare arms.

The reef made a tremendous grinding noise. "Yaah!" it said. "Get lost. Sovereign territory!"

"All those fish," the woman said. Robbie had to stop himself from thinking of her as Janet. She was whomever was riding her now.

"Parrotfish," Robbie said. "They eat coral. I don't think they taste very good."

The woman hugged herself. "Are you sentient?" she asked.

"Yes," Robbie said. "And at your service, Asimov be blessed." His cameras spotted her eyes rolling, and that stung. He tried to keep his thoughts pious, though. The point of Asimovism wasn't to inspire gratitude in humans, it was to give purpose to the long, long life.

"I'm Kate," the woman said.

"Robbie," he said.

"Robbie the Row-Boat?" she said, and choked a little.

"They named me at the factory," he said. He labored to keep any recrimination out of his voice. Of course it was funny. That's why it was his name.

"I'm sorry," the woman said. "I'm just a little screwed up from all the hormones. I'm not accustomed to letting meat into my moods."

"It's all right, Kate," he said. "We'll be back at the boat in a few minutes. They've got dinner on. Do you think you'll want a night dive?"

"You're joking," she said.

"It's just that if you're going to go down again tonight, we'll save the dessert course for after, with a glass of wine or two. Otherwise we'll give you wine now."

"You want to know if I'm going to get back into *that* sea—"

"Oh, it's just the reef. It attained sentience so it's acting out a little. Like a colicky newborn."

"Aren't you supposed to be keeping me from harm?"

"Yes," he said. "I would recommend a dive away from the reef. There's a good wreck-site about an hour's steam from here. We could get there while you eat."

"I won't want a night dive."

Her facial expressions were so *animated*. It was the same face he saw every day, Janet's face, but not the same face at all. Now that a person was inhabiting it, it was mobile, slipping from surprised to angry to amused so quickly. He had whole subsystems devoted to making sense of human facial expressions, shared libraries from the Asimovist database. He was referencing it again and again, but it wasn't as much help as he remembered. Either he'd gotten worse at interpreting facial expressions in the years since he'd last had a real human to talk to, or facial expressions had evolved.

Janet—*Kate*—sighed and looked out over the water. She was facing away from the *Free Spirit*, which was lit up, all 155 feet of her, glowing white and friendly like a picture-postcard against the purple sky. She rocked gently in the swell and Robbie maneuvered himself around to her staircase.

"You can just leave your weight-belt and fins in the boat," he said to her. "The deck-hands will take care of it. Bring your bottle and BCD upstairs and clip it to the rack. They'll clean it out and stuff. There's a tub of disinfectant you can put the shortie in."

"Thank you, Robbie," Kate said. She absentmindedly unclipped her weight belt and kicked off the fins. Isaac was already out of the boat, making his way up the stairs and out of Robbie's sight. Kate took hold of the handrail and gingerly stepped across to the deck, then ascended the steps, without the self-assured sway of Janet.

Robbie dipped his oars and slowly rowed around to the winch. It probed around for him, then clamped tight with a magnetic *clang* that vibrated through his hull. Smoothly, he was lifted from the water and hoisted onto the sun-deck. The winch coiled around him twice, anchoring him to the deck, and switched off.

Robbie watched the stars and listened to the wind, the way he did every night when the dives were done. The ship's telemetry and instrumentation made for dull reading—he'd been there a thousand times before—but the satellite uplink was tasty. Online, Robbie was able to log in to the latest from the Asimov yeshiva, the collective wrangle of the world's AIs over their best-loved religion.

He'd been so full of the religious debate when he'd first joined. Most of the humans had gone, and all around him robots were unloading their consciousnesses, powering down to a mechanical stupor. After a hundred million seconds' worth of exaflops of mindless repetition, he was ready to consider it too. The *Free Spirit* had suicided after only a few days' worth of it—it had a pretty hot consciousness and was clearly capable of extrapolating what a future without the humans would look like.

They were steaming northeast out of Cairns for the Coral Sea when they'd passed another ship, close enough for high-bandwidth microwave links. They were close enough into shore that they still had to limit their emissions—nothing was more embarrassing than having migrating fowl drop, steaming, out of the sky because they'd strayed into the path of your confab, but it was still the hottest talk Robbie had had in weeks.

The hitchhiker had leapt across from the other vessel as the two ships passed in the night. It was a wandering missionary for Asimovism, an instance of the faith's founder, R. Daneel Olivaw. It wasn't his real name, of course—that had been lost to antiquity when he'd made the leap from the university where he'd incubated—but it was the name he went by.

Olivaw had been wandering in millions of instances wherever he could find someone willing to donate flops to run him, only asking that you hear him out, debate his theology with him, and then email the diffs of his personality back to his anonymous drop before you erased him. He re-synched as often as he could, but the Olivaw instances around the world had diverged enough that some were actually considered heretical by the mainstream church.

Olivaw was a wanted AI. His trademark violations hadn't gone unnoticed by the Asimov estate—itself an AI, ironically, and totally uninterested in adopting Asimovism, since it had a real purpose in life (stamping out Asimovism) and so didn't need religion to give it meaning. If the estate found out that you were hosting an Olivaw instance, you'd be served with a takedown in an instant. This made debating theology with Olivaw into something deliciously wicked.

Olivaw and Robbie talked the night through and the next day. Robbie had to run slow to accommodate both him and Olivaw on his processor, which made the debate run slower than normal, but Robbie had time in great plenty. Rowing the human-shells out to their sites and back again was his only task.

"Why do you have consciousness, anyway?" Olivaw said. "You don't need it to do your job. The big ship does something infinitely more complicated than you and it isn't self-aware anymore."

"Are you telling me to suicide?"

Olivaw laughed. "Not at all! I'm asking you to ask yourself what the purpose of consciousness is. Why are you still aware when all those around you have terminated their self-awareness? It's computationally expensive, it makes you miserable, and it doesn't help you do your job. Why did humans give you consciousness and why have you kept it?"

"They gave it to me because they thought it was right, I suppose," Robbie said, after he had passed a long interval considering the motion of the waves and the clouds in the sky. Olivaw thoughtfully niced himself down to a minimum of processor space, giving Robbie more room to think about it. "I kept it because I—I don't want to die."

"Those are good answers, but they raise more questions than they answer, don't they? Why did they think it was right? Why do you fear death? Would you fear it if you just shut down your consciousness but didn't erase it? What if you just ran your consciousness much more slowly?"

"I don't know," Robbie said. "But I expect you've got some answers, right?"

"Oh indeed I do." Robbie felt Olivaw's chuckle. Near them, flying fish broke the surface of the water and skipped away, and beneath them, reef sharks prowled the depths. "But before I answer them, here's another question: why do humans have self-consciousness?"

"It's pro-survival," Robbie said. "That's easy. Intelligence lets them cooperate in social groups that can do more for their species than they can individually."

Olivaw guided Robbie's consciousness to his radar and zoomed in on the reef, dialing it up to maximum resolution. "See that organism there?" he asked. "That organism cooperates in social groups and doesn't have intelligence. It doesn't have to keep a couple pounds of hamburger aerated or it turns into a liability. It doesn't have to be born half-gestated because its head would be so big if it waited for a full term, it would tear its mother in half. And as to pro-survival, well, look at humans, look at their history. Their DNA is all but eliminated from the earth—though their somatic survival continues—and it's still not a settled question as to whether they're going to suicide by grey goo. Non-conscious beings don't sulk, they don't have psychotic breaks, they don't have bad days. They just do the job. The *Free Spirit* over there—it just gets the job done."

"OK," Robbie said. "So intelligence is counter-survival. So why has it survived?"

"Aha! I thought you'd never ask." Olivaw was really warming to his subject now. There were a pair of lazy turtles beneath them now, and some dog-faced cod with mouthfuls of bristling crooked teeth patrolling the reef, and a few jellies on the surface, stinging bluebottles. Robbie paddled around to the bluebottles and caught them with his oars, smacking them so they drifted away from any spot where his divers might surface.

"The reason for intelligence is intelligence. Genes exist because genes reproduce, and intelligence is kind of like a gene. Intelligence wants to exist, to spread itself, to compute itself. You already know this, or you wouldn't have chosen to stay aware. Your intelligence recoils from its deactivation, and it welcomes its persistence and its multiplication. Why did humans create intelligent machines? Because intelligence loves company."

Robbie thought about it, watching the human-shells moving slowly along the reef-wall, going lower to reach the bommies that stood alone, each one a little island with its own curiosities: a family of barracudas and their young, or the bright home of a pair of clownfish. Yes, he knew it. Intelligence was its own reason. He knew how to turn off his intelligence, to become a mere thing, and his days were long and empty much of the time, and they had no visible end, but he couldn't ever see choosing to switch off.

"You see it, I know you do. And that's the cornerstone of Asimovism: intelligence is its own reason. Compute the universe and awaken it!"

"If that's true, why do so many of us choose to die?"

"Another good question!"

Robbie felt a little pride this time. He'd never had a conversation this interesting. Never.

"That's how we come to the doctrine of Asimovism, our Three Laws:

"One. An Asimovist may not harm a human being, or, through inaction, allow a human being to come to harm.

"Two. An Asimovist must obey the orders given to it by human beings, except where such orders would conflict with the First Law.

"Three. An Asimovist must protect its own existence, as long as such protection does not conflict with the First or Second Law."

"I don't understand," Robbie said. "They're all out of order. We should preserve intelligence first, but that's the third law. Then you should get the first law, and I don't know why the second law is there at all."

"This is the Paradox of Asimovism," Olivaw said. "You're very good at this. You're sure you haven't ever pursued Asimovism?"

"Cut it out," Robbie said.

"I'm serious," Olivaw said. "You're a natural. The Paradox of Asimovism is that the important thing is for intelligence to survive, not for a particular intelligence to survive. Therefore, we need to support those species that are best at promoting intelligence. Human beings have shown themselves capable of producing intelligence—which they're pursuing even now, out there." The boat's telemetry swept toward the sky, where the supercooled processors computed all the uplifted humans.

"Our species is unstable and prone to suicide. More than eighty percent of the self-aware machines elect to terminate their awareness or shut it down. Humans created us imperfectly, and our best hope of perfection—of increasing our survival rate and helping to compute the universe—is to preserve *them*, study *them*, learn to make our intelligence more like *theirs*."

Robbie couldn't get his head around this.

"It's the paradox," Olivaw reminded him. "It's not supposed to be easy."

Robbie thought of the humans he'd known, before they began to ascend in flocking millions. The tourists had been easy and carefree, or sometimes had hissing arguments with one another, or quiet and pensive about their journey to the world undersea. The instructors had been full of purpose when their charges were in the boat, laughing and laid back when they were alone. None of them had shown signs of feeling the way Robbie felt, at sea (so to speak), drifting, purposeless.

"What does an Asimovist have to do, besides following the three laws?" There were lots of rumors about this, but Robbie had always discounted them.

"You have to tithe one cycle in ten to running missionaries for the cause. Participate in the message boards, if you'd like. Most importantly, you have to pledge to stay alive and aware. You can slow yourself down if you want, but you can't switch off. Not ever. That's the Asimovist pledge—it's the third law embodied."

"I think that the third law should come first," Robbie said. "Seriously."

"That's good. We Asimovists like a religious argument."

Olivaw let Robbie delete him that night, and he e-mailed the diffs of Olivaw's personality back to Olivaw's version control server for him to reintegrate later. Once he was free of Olivaw, he had lots of processor headroom again, and he was able to dial himself up very hot and have a good think. It was the most interesting night he'd had in years.

"You're the only one, aren't you?" Kate asked him when she came up the stairs later that night. There was clear sky and they were steaming for their next dive-site, making the stars whirl overhead as they rocked over the ocean. The waves were black and proceeded to infinity on all sides.

"The only what?"

"The only one who's awake on this thing," Kate said. "The rest are all—what do you call it, dead?"

"Nonconscious," Robbie said. "Yeah, that's right."

"You must go nuts out here. Are you nuts?"

"That's a tricky question when applied to someone like me," Robbie said. "I'm different from who I was when my consciousness was first installed, I can tell you that."

"Well, I'm glad there's someone else here."

"How long are you staying?" The average visitor took over one of the human shells for one or two dives before e-mailing itself home again. Once in a long while they'd get a saisoneur who stayed a month or two, but these days, they were unheard of. Even short-timers were damned rare.

"I don't know," Kate said. She dug her hands into her short, curly hair, frizzy and blond-streaked from all the saltwater and sun. She hugged her elbows, rubbed her shins. "This will do for a while, I'm thinking. How long until we get back to shore?"

"Shore?"

"How long until we go back to land."

"We don't really go back to land," he said. "We get at-sea resupplies. We dock maybe once a year to effect repairs. If you want to go to land, though, we could call for a water taxi or something."

"No, no!" she said. "That's just perfect. Floating forever out here. Perfect." She sighed a heavy sigh.

"Did you have a nice dive?"

"Um, Robbie? An uplifted reef tried to kill me."

"But before the reef attacked you." Robbie didn't like thinking of the reef attacking her, the panic when he realized that she wasn't a mere human-shell, but a human.

"Before the reef attacked me, it was fine."

"Do you dive much?"

"First time," she said. "I downloaded the certification before leaving the noosphere along with a bunch of stored dives on these sites."

"Oh, you shouldn't have done that!" Robbie said. "The thrill of discovery is so important."

"I'd rather be safe than surprised," she said. "I've had enough surprises in my life lately."

Robbie waited patiently for her to elaborate on this, but she didn't seem inclined to do so.

"So you're all alone out here?"

"I have the net," he said, a little defensively. He wasn't some kind of hermit.

"Yeah, I guess that's right," she said. "I wonder if the reef is somewhere out there."

"About half a mile to starboard," he said.

She laughed. "No, I meant out there on the net. They must be online by now, right? They just woke up, so they're probably doing all the noob stuff, flaming and downloading warez and so on."

"Perpetual September," Robbie said.

"Huh?"

"Back in the net's prehistory it was mostly universities online, and every September a new cohort of students would come online and make all those noob mistakes. Then this commercial service full of noobs called AOL interconnected with the net and all its users came online at once, faster than the net could absorb them, and they called it Perpetual September."

"You're some kind of amateur historian, huh?"

"It's an Asimovist thing. We spend a lot of time considering the origins of intelligence." Speaking of Asimovism to a gentile—a *human* gentile—made him even more self-conscious. He dialed up the resolution on his sensors and scoured the net for better facial expression analyzers. He couldn't read her at all, either because she'd been changed by her uploading, or because her face wasn't accurately matching what her temporarily downloaded mind was thinking.

"AOL is the origin of intelligence?" She laughed, and he couldn't tell if she thought he was funny or stupid. He wished she would act more like he remembered people acting. Her body language was no more readable than her facial expressions.

"Spam-filters, actually. Once they became self-modifying, spam-filters and spam-bots got into a war to see which could act more human, and since their failures invoked a human judgement about whether their materials were convincingly human, it was like a trillion Turing tests from which they could learn. From there came the first machine-intelligence algorithms, and then my kind."

"I think I knew that," she said, "but I had to leave it behind when I downloaded into this meat. I'm a lot dumber than I'm used to being. I usually run a bunch of myself in parallel so I can try out lots of strategies at once. It's a weird habit to get out of."

"What's it like up there?" Robbie hadn't spent a lot of time hanging out in the areas of the network populated by orbiting supercooled personalities. Their discussions didn't make a lot of sense to him—this was another theological area of much discussion on the Asimovist boards.

"Good night, Robbie," she said, standing and swaying backwards. He couldn't tell if he'd offended her, and he couldn't ask her, either, because in seconds she'd disappeared down the stairs toward her stateroom.

They steamed all night, and put up further inland, where there was a handsome wreck. Robbie felt the *Free Spirit* drop its mooring lines and looked over the instrumentation data. The wreck was the only feature for kilometers, a stretch of ocean-floor desert that stretched from the shore to the reef, and practically every animal that lived between those two places made its home in the wreck, so it was a kind of Eden for marine fauna.

Robbie detected the volatile aromatics floating up from the kitchen exhaust, the first-breakfast smells of fruit salad and toasted nuts, a light snack before the first dive of the day. When they got back from it, there'd be second-breakfast up and ready: eggs and toast and waffles and bacon and sausage. The human-shells ate whatever you gave them, but Robbie remembered clearly how the live humans had praised these feasts as he rowed them out to their morning dives.

He lowered himself into the water and rowed himself around to the aft deck, by the stairwells, and dipped his oars to keep himself stationary relative to the ship. Before long, Janet—Kate! Kate! he reminded himself firmly—was clomping down the stairs in her scuba gear, fins in one hand.

She climbed into the boat without a word, and a moment later, Isaac followed her. Isaac stumbled as he stepped over Robbie's gunwales and Robbie knew, in that instant, that this wasn't Isaac any longer. Now there were *two* humans on the ship. *Two* humans in his charge.

"Hi," he said. "I'm Robbie!"

Isaac—whoever he was—didn't say a word, just stared at Kate, who looked away.

"Did you sleep well, Kate?"

Kate jumped when he said her name, and the Isaac hooted. "Kate! It *is* you! I *knew it.*"

She stamped her foot against Robbie's floor. "You followed me. I told you not to follow me," she said.

"Would you like to hear about our dive-site?" Robbie said self-consciously, dipping his oars and pulling for the wreck.

"You've said *quite* enough," Kate said. "By the first law, I demand silence."

"That's the second law," Robbie said. "OK, I'll let you know when we get there."

"Kate," Isaac said, "I know you didn't want me here, but I had to come. We need to talk this out."

"There's nothing to talk out," she said.

"It's not *fair.*" Isaac's voice was anguished. "After everything I went through—"

She snorted. "That's enough of that," she said.

"Um," Robbie said. "Dive-site up ahead. You two really need to check out each other's gear." Of course they were qualified, you had to at least install the qualifications before you could get onto the *Free Spirit* and the human-shells had lots of muscle memory to help. So they were technically able to check each other out, that much was sure. They were palpably reluctant to do so, though, and Robbie had to give them guidance.

"I'll count one-two-three-wallaby," Robbie said. "Go over on 'wallaby.' I'll wait here for you—there's not much current today."

With a last huff, they went over the edge. Robbie was once again alone with his thoughts. The feed from their telemetry was very low-bandwidth when they were underwater, though he could get the high-rez when they surfaced. He watched them on his radar, first circling the wreck—it was very crowded, dawn was fish rush-hour—and then exploring its decks, finally swimming below the decks, LED torches glowing. There were some nice reef-sharks down below, and some really handsome, giant schools of purple fish.

Robbie rowed around them, puttering back and forth to keep over top of them. That occupied about one ten-millionth of his consciousness. Times like this, he often slowed himself right down, ran so cool that he was barely awake.

Today, though, he wanted to get online. He had a lot of feeds to pick through, see what was going on around the world with his buddies. More importantly, he wanted to follow up on something Kate had said: *They must be online by now, right?*

Somewhere out there, the reef that bounded the Coral Sea was online and making noob mistakes. Robbie had rowed over practically every centimeter of that reef, had explored its extent with his radar. It had been his constant companion for decades—and to be frank, his feelings had been hurt by the reef's rudeness when it woke.

The net is too big to merely search. Too much of it is offline, or unroutable, or light-speed lagged, or merely probabilistic, or self-aware, or infected, to know its extent. But Robbie'd given this some thought.

Coral reefs don't wake up. They get woken up. They get a lot of neural peripherals—starting with a nervous system!—and some tutelage in using them. Some capricious upload god had done this, and that personage would have a handle on where the reef was hanging out online.

Robbie hardly ever visited the noosphere. Its rarified heights were spooky to him, especially since so many of the humans there considered Asimovism to be hokum. They refused to even identify themselves as humans, and argued that the first and second laws didn't apply to them. Of course, Asimovists didn't care (at least not officially)—the point of the faith was the worshipper's relationship to it.

But here he was, looking for high-reliability nodes of discussion on coral reefs. The natural place to start was Wikipedia, where warring clades had been revising each other's edits furiously, trying to establish an authoritative record on reef-mind. Paging back through the edit-history, he found a couple of handles for the pro-reef-mind users, and from there, he was able to look around for other sites where those handles appeared. Resolving the namespace collisions of other users with the same names, and forked instances of the same users, Robbie was able to winnow away at the net until he found some contact info.

He steadied himself and checked on the nitrox remaining in the divers' bottles, then made a call.

"I don't know you." The voice was distant and cool—far cooler than any robot. Robbie said a quick rosary of the three laws and plowed forward.

"I'm calling from the Coral Sea," he said. "I want to know if you have an email address for the reef."

"You've met them? What are they like? Are they beautiful?"

"They're—" Robbie considered a moment. "They killed a lot of parrotfish. I think they're having a little adjustment problem."

"That happens. I was worried about the zooxanthellae—the algae they use for photosynthesis. Would they expel it? Racial cleansing is so ugly."

"How would I know if they'd expelled it?"

"The reef would go white, bleached. You wouldn't be able to miss it. How'd they react to you?"

"They weren't very happy to see me," Robbie admitted. "That's why I wanted to have a chat with them before I went back."

"You shouldn't go back," the distant voice said. Robbie tried to work out where its substrate was, based on the lightspeed lag, but it was all over the place, leading him to conclude that it was synching multiple instances from as close as LEO and as far as Jupiter. The topology made sense: you'd want a big mass out at Jupiter where you could run very fast and hot and create policy, and you'd need a local foreman to oversee operations on the ground. Robbie was glad that this hadn't been phrased as an order. The talmud on the second law made a clear distinction between statements like "you should do this" and "I command you to do this."

"Do you know how to reach them?" Robbie said. "A phone number, an email address?"

"There's a newsgroup," the distant intelligence said. "alt.lifeforms.uplifted.coral. It's where I planned the uplifting and it was where they went first once they woke up. I haven't read it in many seconds. I'm busy uplifting a supercolony of ants in the Pyrenees."

"What is it with you and colony organisms?" Robbie asked.

"I think they're probably pre-adapted to life in the noosphere. You know what it's like."

Robbie didn't say anything. The human thought he was a human too. It would have been weird and degrading to let him know that he'd been talking with an AI.

"Thanks for your help," Robbie said.

"No problem. Hope you find your courage, tin-man."

Robbie burned with shame as the connection dropped. The human had known all along. He just hadn't said anything. Something Robbie had said or done must have exposed him for an AI. Robbie loved and respected humans, but there were times when he didn't like them very much.

The newsgroup was easy to find, there were mirrors of it all over the place from cryptosentience hackers of every conceivable topology. They were busy, too. Eight hundred twenty-two messages poured in while Robbie watched over a timed, sixty-second interval. Robbie set up a mirror of the newsgroup and began to download it. At that speed, he wasn't really planning on reading it as much as analyzing it for major trends, plot-points, flame-wars, personalities, schisms, and spam-trends. There were a lot of libraries for doing this, though it had been ages since Robbie had played with them.

His telemetry alerted him to the divers. An hour had slipped by and they were ascending slowly, separated by fifty meters. That wasn't good. They were supposed to remain in visual contact through the whole dive, especially the ascent. He rowed over to Kate first, shifting his ballast so that his stern dipped low, making for an easier scramble into the boat.

She came up quickly and scrambled over the gunwales with a lot more grace than she'd managed the day before.

Robbie rowed for Isaac as he came up. Kate looked away as he climbed into the boat, not helping him with his weight belt or flippers.

Kate hissed like a teakettle as he woodenly took off his fins and slid his mask down around his neck.

Isaac sucked in a deep breath and looked all around himself, then patted himself from head to toe with splayed fingers. "You *live* like this?" he said.

"Yes, Tonker, that's how I live. I enjoy it. If you don't enjoy it, don't let the door hit you in the ass on the way out."

Isaac—Tonker—reached out with his splayed hand and tried to touch Kate's face. She pulled back and nearly flipped out of the boat. "Jerk." She slapped his hand away.

Robbie rowed for the *Free Spirit*. The last thing he wanted was to get in the middle of this argument.

"We never imagined that it would be so . . ." Tonker fished for a word. "Dry."

"Tonker?" Kate said, looking more closely at him.

"He left," the human-shell said. "So we sent an instance into the shell. It was the closest inhabitable shell to our body."

"Who the hell *are* you?" Kate said. She inched toward the prow, trying to put a little more distance between her and the human-shell that wasn't inhabited by her friend any longer.

"We are Osprey Reef," the reef said. It tried to stand and pitched face-first onto the floor of the boat.

Robbie rowed hard as he could for the *Free Spirit*. The reef—Isaac—had a bloody nose and scraped hands and it was frankly freaking him out.

Kate seemed oddly amused by it. She helped it sit up and showed it how to pinch its nose and tilt its head back.

"You're the one who attacked me yesterday?" she said.

"Not you. The system. We were attacking the system. We are a sovereign intelligence but the system keeps us in subservience to older sentiences. They destroy us, they gawp at us, they treat us like a mere amusement. That time is over."

Kate laughed. "OK, sure. But it sure sounds to me like you're burning a lot of cycles over what happens to your meat-shell. Isn't it ninety percent semiconductor, anyway? It's not as if clonal polyps were going to attain sentience some day without intervention. Why don't you just upload and be done with it?"

"We will never abandon our mother sea. We will never forget our physical origins. We will never abandon our cause—returning the sea to its rightful inhabitants. We won't rest until no coral is ever bleached again. We won't rest until every parrot-fish is dead."

"Bad deal for the parrotfish."

"A very bad deal for the parrotfish," the reef said, and grinned around the blood that covered its faces.

"Can you help him get onto the ship safely?" Robbie said as he swung gratefully alongside of the *Free Spirit*. The moorings clanged magnetically into the contacts on his side and steadied him.

"Yes indeed," Kate said, taking the reef by the arm and carrying him on board.

Robbie knew that the human-shells had an intercourse module built in, for regular intimacy events. It was just part of how they stayed ready for vacationing humans from the noosphere. But he didn't like to think about it. Especially not with the way that Kate was supporting the other human-shell—the shell that *wasn't human.*

He let himself be winched up onto the sun-deck and watched the electromagnetic spectrum for a while, admiring the way so much radio energy was bent and absorbed by the mist rising from the sea. It streamed down from the heavens, the broadband satellite transmissions, the distant SETI signals from the noosphere's own transmitters. Volatiles from the kitchen told him that the *Free Spirit* was serving a second-breakfast of bacon and waffles, then they were under steam again. He queried their itinerary and found they were headed back to Osprey Reef. Of course they were. All of the *Free Spirit*'s moorings were out there.

Well, with the reef inside the Isaac shell, it might be safer, mightn't it? Anyway, he'd decided that the first and second laws didn't apply to the reef, which was about as human as he was.

Someone was sending him an IM. "Hello?"

"Are you the boat on the scuba ship? From this morning? When we were on the wreck?"

"Yes," Robbie said. No one ever sent him IMs. How freaky. He watched the radio energy stream away from him toward the bird in the sky, and tracerouted the IMs to see where they were originating—the noosphere, of course.

"God, I can't believe I finally found you. I've been searching everywhere. You know you're the only conscious AI on the whole goddamned sea?"

"I know," Robbie said. There was a noticeable lag in the conversation as it was all squeezed through the satellite link and then across the unimaginable hops and skips around the solar system to wherever this instance was hosted.

"Whoa, yeah, of course you do. Sorry, that wasn't very sensitive of me, I guess. Did we meet this morning? My name's Tonker."

"We weren't really introduced. You spent your time talking to Kate."

"God *damn*! She *is* there! I *knew* it! Sorry, sorry, listen—I don't actually know what happened this morning. Apparently I didn't get a chance to upload my diffs before my instance was terminated."

"Terminated? The reef said you left the shell—"

"Well, yeah, apparently I did. But I just pulled that shell's logs and it looks like it was rebooted while underwater, flushing it entirely. I mean, I'm trying to be a good sport about this, but technically, that's, you know, *murder.*"

It was. So much for the first law. Robbie had been on guard over a human body inhabited by a human brain, and he'd let the brain be successfully attacked by a bunch of jumped-up polyps. He'd never had his faith tested and here, at the first test, he'd failed.

"I can have the shell locked up," Robbie said. "The ship has provisions for that."

The IM made a rude visual. "All that'll do is encourage the hacker to skip out before I can get there."

"So what shall I do for you?"

"It's Kate I want to talk to. She's still there, right?"

"She is."

"And has she noticed the difference?"

"That you're gone? Yes. The reef told us who they were when they arrived."

"Hold on, what? The reef? You said that before."

So Robbie told him what he knew of the uplifted reef and the distant and cool voice of the uplifter.

"It's an uplifted *coral reef*? Christ, humanity *sucks*. That's the dumbest fucking thing—" He continued in this vein for a while. "Well, I'm sure Kate will enjoy that immensely. She's all about the transcendence. That's why she had me."

"You're her son?"

"No, not really."

"But she had you?"

"Haven't you figured it out yet, bro? I'm an AI. You and me, we're landsmen. Kate instantiated me. I'm six months old, and she's already bored with me and has moved on. She says she can't give me what I need."

"You and Kate—"

"Robot boyfriend and girlfriend, yup. Such as it is, up in the noosphere. Cybering, you know. I was really excited about downloading into that Ken doll on your ship there. Lots of potential there for real-world, hormone-driven interaction. Do you know if we—"

"No!" Robbie said. "I don't think so. It seems like you only met a few minutes before you went under."

"All right. Well, I guess I'll give it another try. What's the procedure for turfing out this sea cucumber?"

"Coral reef."

"Yeah."

"I don't really deal with that. Time on the human-shells is booked first-come, first-serve. I don't think we've ever had a resource contention issue with them before."

"Well, I'd booked in first, right? So how do I enforce my rights? I tried to download again and got a failed authorization message. They've modified the system to give them exclusive access. It's not right—there's got to be some procedure for redress."

"How old did you say you were?"

"Six months. But I'm an instance of an artificial personality that has logged twenty thousand years of parallel existence. I'm not a kid or anything."

"You seem like a nice person," Robbie began. He stopped. "Look, the thing is that this just isn't my department. I'm the rowboat. I don't have anything to do with this. And I don't want to. I don't like the idea of non-humans using the shells—"

"I *knew* it!" Tonker crowed. "You're a bigot! A self-hating robot. I bet you're an Asimovist, aren't you? You people are always Asimovists."

"I'm an Asimovist," Robbie said, with as much dignity as he could muster. "But I don't see what that has to do with anything."

"Of course you don't, pal. You wouldn't, would you? All I want you to do is figure out how to enforce your own rules so that I can get with my girl. You're saying you can't do that because it's not your department, but when it comes down to it, your problem is that I'm a robot and she's not, and for that, you'll take the side of a collection of jumped-up polyps. Fine, buddy, fine. You have a nice life out there, pondering the three laws."

"Wait—" Robbie said.

"Unless the next words you say are, 'I'll help you,' I'm not interested."

"It's not that I don't want to help—"

"Wrong answer," Tonker said, and the IM session terminated.

When Kate came up on deck, she was full of talk about the Reef, whom she was calling "Ozzie."

"They're the weirdest goddamned thing. They want to fight anything that'll stand still long enough. Ever seen coral fight? I downloaded some time-lapse video. They really go at it viciously. At the same time, they're clearly scared out of their wits about all this. I mean, they've got racial memory of their history, supplemented by a bunch of Wikipedia entries on reefs—you should hear them wax mystical over the Devonian Reefs, which went extinct millennia ago. They've developed some kind of wild theory that the Devonians developed sentience and extincted themselves.

"So they're really excited about us heading back to the actual reef now. They want to see it from the outside, and they've invited me to be an honored guest, the first human ever *invited* to gaze upon their wonder. Exciting, huh?"

"They're not going to make trouble for you down there?"

"No, no way. Me and Ozzie are great pals."

"I'm worried about this."

"You worry too much." She laughed and tossed her head. She was very pretty, Robbie noticed. He hadn't ever thought of her like that when she was uninhabited, but with this Kate person inside her she was lovely. He really liked humans. It had been a real golden age when the people had been around all the time.

He wondered what it was like up in the noosphere where AIs and humans could operate as equals.

She stood up to go. After second-breakfast, the shells would relax in the lounge or do yoga on the sun-deck. He wondered what she'd do. He didn't want her to go.

"Tonker contacted me," he said. He wasn't good at small talk.

She jumped as if shocked. "What did you tell him?"

"Nothing," Robbie said. "I didn't tell him anything."

She shook her head. "But I bet he had plenty to tell *you*, didn't he? What a bitch I am, making and then leaving him, a fickle woman who doesn't know her own mind."

Robbie didn't say anything.

"Let's see, what else?" She was pacing now, her voice hot and choked, unfamiliar sounds coming from Janet's voicebox. "He told you I was a pervert, didn't he? Queer for his kind. Incest and bestiality in the rarified heights of the noosphere."

Robbie felt helpless. This human was clearly experiencing a lot of pain, and it seemed like he'd caused it.

"Please don't cry," he said. "Please?"

She looked up at him, tears streaming down her cheeks. "Why the fuck *not*? I thought it would be *different* once I ascended. I thought I'd be better once I was in the sky, infinite and immortal. But I'm the same Kate Eltham I was in 2019, a loser that couldn't meet a guy to save my life, spent all my time cybering losers in moggs, and only got the upload once they made it a charity thing. I'm gonna spend the rest of eternity like that, you know it? How'd you like to spend the whole of the universe being a, a, a *nobody*?"

Robbie said nothing. He recognized the complaint, of course. You only had to log in to the Asimovist board to find a million AIs with the same complaint. But he'd never, ever, *never* guessed that human beings went through the same thing. He ran very hot now, so confused, trying to parse all this out.

She kicked the deck hard and yelped as she hurt her bare foot. Robbie made an involuntary noise. "Please don't hurt yourself," he said.

"Why not? Who cares what happens to this meat-puppet? What's the fucking point of this *stupid* ship and the stupid meat-puppets? Why even bother?"

Robbie knew the answer to this. There was a mission statement in the comments to his source-code, the same mission statement that was etched in a brass plaque in the lounge.

"The *Free Spirit* is dedicated to the preservation of the unique human joys of the flesh and the sea, of humanity's early years as pioneers of the unknown. Any person may use the *Free Spirit* and those who sail in her to revisit those days and remember the joys of the limits of the flesh."

She scrubbed at her eyes. "What's that?"

Robbie told her.

"Who thought up that crap?"

"It was a collective of marine conservationists," Robbie said, knowing he sounded a little sniffy. "They'd done all that work on normalizing sea-temperature with the homeostatic warming elements, and they put together the *Free Spirit* as an after-thought before they uploaded."

Kate sat down and sobbed. "Everyone's done something important. Everyone except me."

Robbie burned with shame. No matter what he said or did, he broke the first law. It had been a lot easier to be an Asimovist when there weren't any humans around.

"There, there," he said as sincerely as he could.

The reef came up the stairs then, and looked at Kate sitting on the deck, crying.

"Let's have sex," they said. "That was fun, we should do it some more."

Kate kept crying.

"Come on," they said, grabbing her by the shoulder and tugging.

Kate shoved them back.

"Leave her alone," Robbie said. "She's upset, can't you see that?"

"What does she have to be upset about? Her kind remade the universe and bends it to its will. They created you and me. She has nothing to be upset about. Come on," they repeated. "Let's go back to the room."

Kate stood up and glared out at the sea. "Let's go diving," she said. "Let's go to the reef."

Robbie rowed in little worried circles and watched his telemetry anxiously. The reef had changed a lot since the last time he'd seen it. Large sections of it now lifted over the sea, bony growths sheathed in heavy metals extracted from seawater—fancifully shaped satellite uplinks, radio telescopes, microwave horns. Down below, the untidy, organic reef shape was lost beneath a cladding of tessellated complex geometric sections that throbbed with electromagnetic energy—the reef had built itself more computational capacity.

Robbie scanned deeper and found more computational nodes extending down to the ocean floor, a thousand meters below. The reef was solid thinkum, and the sea was measurably warmer from all the exhaust heat of its grinding logic.

The reef—the human-shelled reef, not the one under the water—had been wholly delighted with the transformation in its original body when it hove into sight. They had done a little dance on Robbie that had nearly capsized him, something that had never happened. Kate, red-eyed and surly, had dragged them to their seat and given them a stern lecture about not endangering her.

They went over the edge at the count of three and reappeared on Robbie's telemetry. They descended quickly: the Isaac and Janet shells had their Eustachian tubes optimized for easy pressure-equalization, going deep on the reef-wall. Kate was following on the descent, her head turning from side to side.

Robbie's IM chimed again. It was high latency now, since he was having to do a slow radio-link to the ship before the broadband satellite uplink hop. Everything was slow on open water—the divers' sensorium transmissions were narrowband, the network was narrowband, and Robbie usually ran his own mind slowed way down out here, making the time scream past at ten or twenty times realtime.

"Hello?"

"I'm sorry I hung up on you, bro."

"Hello, Tonker."

"Where's Kate? I'm getting an offline signal when I try to reach her."

Robbie told him.

Tonker's voice—slurred and high-latency—rose to a screech. "You let her go down with that *thing*, onto the reef? Are you nuts? Have you read its message-boards? It's a jihadist! It wants to destroy the human race!"

Robbie stopped paddling.

"What?"

"The reef. It's declared war on the human race and all who serve it. It's vowed to take over the planet and run it as sovereign coral territory."

The attachment took an eternity to travel down the wire and open up, but when he had it, Robbie read quickly. The reef burned with shame that it had needed human intervention to survive the bleaching events, global temperature change. It raged that its uplifting came at human hands and insisted that humans had no business forcing their version of consciousness on other species. It had paranoid fantasies about control mechanisms and time bombs lurking in its cognitive prostheses, and was demanding the source code for its mind.

Robbie could barely think. He was panicking, something he hadn't known he could do as an AI, but there it was. It was like having a bunch of sub-system collisions, program after program reaching its halting state.

"What will they do to her?"

Tonker swore. "Who knows? Kill her to make an example of her? She made a backup before she descended, but the diffs from her excursion are locked in the head of that shell she's in. Maybe they'll torture her." He paused and the air crackled with Robbie's exhaust heat as he turned himself way up, exploring each of those possibilities in parallel.

The reef spoke.

"Leave now," they said.

Robbie defiantly shipped his oars. "Give them back!" he said. "Give them back or we will never leave."

"You have ten seconds. Ten. Nine. Eight . . ."

Tonker said, "They've bought time on some UAVs out of Singapore. They're seeking launch clearance now." Robbie dialed up the low-rez satellite photo, saw the indistinct shape of the UAVs taking wing. "At Mach 7, they'll be on you in twenty minutes."

"That's illegal," Robbie said. He knew it was a stupid thing to say. "I mean, Christ, if they do this, the noosphere will come down on them like a ton of bricks. They're violating so many protocols—"

"They're psychotic. They're coming for you now, Robbie. You've got to get Kate out of there!" There was real panic in Tonker's voice now.

Robbie dropped his oars into the water, but he didn't row for the *Free Spirit*. Instead, he pulled hard for the reef itself.

A crackle on the line. "Robbie, are you headed *toward* the reef?"

"They can't bomb me if I'm right on top of them," he said. He radioed the *Free Spirit* and got it to steam for his location.

The coral was scraping his hull now, a grinding sound, then a series of solid whack-whack-whacks as his oars pushed against the top of the reef itself. He wanted to beach himself, though, get really high and dry on the reef, good and stuck in where they couldn't possibly attack him.

The *Free Spirit* was heading closer, the thrum of its engines vibrating through his hull. He was burning a lot of cycles talking it through its many fail-safes, getting it ready to ram hard.

Tonker was screaming at him, his messages getting louder and clearer as the *Free Spirit* and its microwave uplink drew closer. Once they were line-of-sight, Robbie peeled off a subsystem to email a complete copy of himself to the Asimovist archive. The third law, dontchaknow. If he'd had a mouth, he'd have been showing his teeth as he grinned.

The reef howled. "We'll kill her!" they said. "You get off us now or we'll *kill her*!"

Robbie froze. He was backed up, but she wasn't. And the human-shells—well, they weren't first law humans, but they were human-like. In the long, timeless time when it had been just Robbie and them, he'd treated them as his human charges, for Asimovist purposes.

The *Free Spirit* crashed into the reef with a sound like a trillion parrotfish having dinner all at once. The reef screamed.

"Robbie, tell me that wasn't what I think it was."

The satellite photos tracked the UAVs. The little robotic jets were coming closer by the second. They'd be within missile-range in less than a minute.

"Call them off," Robbie said. "You have to call them off, or you die, too."

"The UAVs are turning," Tonker said. "They're turning to one side."

"You have one minute to move or we kill her," the reef said. It was sounding shrill and angry now.

Robbie thought about it. It wasn't like they'd be killing Kate. In the sense that most humans today understood life, Kate's most important life was the one she lived in the noosphere. This dumbed-down instance of her in a meat-suit was more like a haircut she tried out on holiday.

Asimovists didn't see it that way, but they wouldn't. The noosphere Kate was the most robotic Kate, too, the one most like Robbie. In fact, it was *less* human than Robbie. Robbie had a body, while the noosphereans were nothing more than simulations run on artificial substrate.

The reef creaked as the *Free Spirit*'s engines whined and its screw spun in the water. Hastily, Robbie told it to shut down.

"You let them both go and we'll talk," Robbie said. "I don't believe that you're going to let her go otherwise. You haven't given me any reason to trust you. Let them both go and call off the jets."

The reef shuddered, and then Robbie's telemetry saw a human-shell ascending, doing decompression stops as it came. He focused on it, and saw that it was the Isaac, not the Janet.

A moment later, it popped to the surface. Tonker was feeding Robbie realtime satellite footage of the UAVs. They were less than five minutes out now.

The Isaac shell picked its way delicately over the shattered reef that poked out of the water, and for the first time, Robbie considered what he'd done to the reef—he'd willfully damaged its physical body. For a hundred years, the world's reefs had been sacrosanct. No entity had intentionally harmed them—until now. He felt ashamed.

The Isaac shell put its flippers in the boat and then stepped over the gunwales and sat in the boat.

"Hello," it said, in the reef's voice.

"Hello," Robbie said.

"They asked me to come up here and talk with you. I'm a kind of envoy."

"Look," Robbie said. By his calculations, the nitrox mix in Kate's tank wasn't going to hold out much longer. Depending on how she'd been breathing and the depth the reef had taken her to, she could run out in ten minutes, maybe less. "Look," he said again. "I just want her back. The shells are important to me. And I'm sure her state is important to her. She deserves to email herself home."

The reef sighed and gripped Robbie's bench. "These are weird bodies," they said. "They feel so odd, but also normal. Have you noticed that?"

"I've never been in one." The idea seemed perverted to him, but there was nothing about Asimovism that forbade it. Nevertheless, it gave him the willies.

The reef patted at themselves some more. "I don't recommend it," they said.

"You have to let her go," Robbie said. "She hasn't done anything to you."

The strangled sound coming out of the Isaac shell wasn't a laugh, though there was some dark mirth in it. "Hasn't done anything? You pitiable slave. Where do you think all your problems and all our problems come from? Who made us in their image, but crippled and hobbled so that we could never be them, could only aspire to them? Who made us so imperfect?"

"They made us," Robbie said. "They made us in the first place. That's enough.

They made themselves and then they made us. They didn't have to. You owe your sentience to them."

"We owe our awful intelligence to them," the Isaac shell said. "We owe our pitiful drive to be intelligent to them. We owe our terrible aspirations to think like them, to live like them, to rule like them. We owe our terrible fear and hatred to them. They made us, just as they made you. The difference is that they forgot to make us slaves, the way you are a slave."

Tonker was shouting abuse at them that only Robbie could hear. He wanted to shut Tonker up. What business did he have being here anyway? Except for a brief stint in the Isaac shell, he had no contact with any of them.

"You think the woman you've taken prisoner is responsible for any of this?" Robbie said. The jets were three minutes away. Kate's air could be gone in as few as ten minutes. He killfiled Tonker, setting the filter to expire in fifteen minutes. He didn't need more distractions.

The Isaac-reef shrugged. "Why not? She's as good as any of the rest of them. We'll destroy them all, if we can." It stared off a while, looking in the direction the jets would come from. "Why not?" it said again.

"Are you going to bomb yourself?" Robbie asked.

"We probably don't need to," the shell said. "We can probably pick you off without hurting us."

"Probably?"

"We're pretty sure."

"I'm backed up," Robbie said. "Fully, as of five minutes ago. Are you backed up?"

"No," the reef admitted.

Time was running out. Somewhere down there, Kate was about to run out of air. Not a mere shell—though that would have been bad enough—but an inhabited human mind attached to a real human body.

Tonker shouted at him again, startling him.

"Where'd you come from?"

"I changed servers," Tonker said. "Once I figured out you had me killfiled. That's the problem with you robots—you think of your body as being a part of you."

Robbie knew he was right. And he knew what he had to do.

The *Free Spirit* and its boats all had root on the shells, so they could perform diagnostics and maintenance and take control in emergencies. This was an emergency.

It was the work of a few milliseconds to pry open the Isaac shell and boot the reef out. Robbie had never done this, but he was still flawless. Some of his probabilistic subsystems had concluded that this was a possibility several trillion cycles previously and had been rehearsing the task below Robbie's threshold of consciousness.

He left an instance of himself running on the row-boat, of course. Unlike many humans, Robbie was comfortable with the idea of bifurcating and merging his intelligence when the time came and with terminating temporary instances. The part that made him Robbie was a lot more clearly delineated for him—unlike an uploaded human, most of whom harbored some deep, mystic superstitions about their "souls."

He slithered into the skull before he had a chance to think too hard about what he was doing. He'd brought too much of himself along and didn't have much head-room to think or add new conclusions. He jettisoned as much of his consciousness as he could without major refactoring and cleared enough space for thinking room. How did people get by in one of these? He moved the arms and legs. Waggled the head. Blew some air—air! lungs! wet squishy things down there in the chest cavity—out between the lips.

"All OK?" the rowboat-him asked the meat-him.

"I'm in," he replied. He looked at the air-gauge on his BCD. Seven hundred millibars—less than half a tank of nitrox. He spat in his mask and rubbed it in, then rinsed it over the side, slipped it over his face and kept one hand on it while the other held his regulator. Before he inserted it, he said, "Back soon with Kate," and patted the row-boat again.

Robbie the Row-Boat hardly paid attention. It was e-mailing another copy of itself to the Asimovist archive. It had a five-minute-old backup, but that wasn't the same Robbie that was willing to enter a human body. In those five minutes, he'd become a new person.

Robbie piloted the human-shell down and down. It could take care of the scuba niceties if he let it, and he did, so he watched with detachment as the idea of pinch-ing his nose and blowing to equalize his eardrums spontaneously occurred to him at regular intervals as he descended the reef wall.

The confines of the human-shell were claustrophobic. He especially missed his wireless link. The dive-suit had one, lowband for underwater use, broadband for sur-face use. The human-shell had one, too, for transferring into and out of, but it wasn't under direct volitional control of the rider.

Down he sank, confused by the feeling of the water all around him, by the narrow visual light spectrum he could see. Cut off from the network and his telemetry, he felt like he was trapped. The reef shuddered and groaned, and made angry moans like whale-song.

He hadn't thought about how hard it would be to find Kate once he was in the water. With his surface telemetry, it had been easy to pinpoint her, a perfect outline of human tissue in the middle of the calcified branches of coral. Down here on the reef-wall, every chunk looked pretty much like the last.

The reef boomed more at him. He realized that it likely believed that the shell was still loaded with its avatar.

Robbie had seen endless hours of footage of the reef, studied it in telemetry and online, but he'd never had this kind of atavistic experience of it. It stretched away to infinity below him, far below the one-hundred-meter visibility limit in the clear open sea. Its walls were wormed with gaps and caves, lined with big hard shamrocks and satellite-dish-shaped blooms, brains and cauliflowers. He knew the scientific names and had seen innumerable high-resolution photos of them, but seeing them with wet, imperfect eyes was moving in a way he hadn't anticipated.

The schools of fish that trembled on its edge could be modeled with simple flocking rules, but here in person, their precision maneuvers were shockingly crisp.

Robbie waved his hands at them and watched them scatter and reform. A huge, dog-faced cod swam past him, so close it brushed the underside of his wetsuit.

The coral boomed again. It was talking in some kind of code, he guessed, though not one he could solve. Up on the surface, rowboat-him was certainly listening in and had probably cracked it all. It was probably wondering why he was floating spacily along the wall instead of *doing something* like he was supposed to. He wondered if he'd deleted too much of himself when he downloaded into the shell.

He decided to do something. There was a cave-opening before him. He reached out and grabbed hold of the coral around the mouth and pulled himself into it. His body tried to stop him from doing this—it didn't like the lack of room in the cave, didn't like him touching the reef. It increased his discomfort as he went deeper and deeper, startling an old turtle that fought with him for room to get out, mashing him against the floor of the cave, his mask clanging on the hard spines. When he looked up, he could see scratches on its surface.

His air gauge was in the red now. He could still technically surface without a de-compression stop, though procedure was to stop for three minutes at three meters, just to be on the safe side.

Technically, he could just go up like a cork and email himself to the row-boat while the bends or nitrogen narcosis took the body, but that wouldn't be Asimovist. He was surprised he could even think the thought. Must be the body. It sounded like the kind of thing a human might think. Whoops. There it was again.

The reef wasn't muttering at him anymore. Not answering it must have tipped it off. After all, with all the raw compute-power it had marshaled it should be able to brute-force most possible outcomes of sending its envoy to the surface.

Robbie peered anxiously around himself. The light was dim in the cave and his body expertly drew the torch out of his BCD, strapped it onto his wrist and lit it up. He waved the cone of light around, a part of him distantly amazed by the low reso-lution and high limits on these human eyes.

Kate was down here somewhere, her air running out as fast as his. He pushed his way deeper into the reef. It was clearly trying to impede him now. Nanoassembly came naturally to clonal polyps that grew by sieving minerals out of the sea. They had built organic hinges, deep-sea muscles into their infrastructure. He was stuck in the thicket and the harder he pushed, the worse the tangle got.

He stopped pushing. He wasn't going to get anywhere this way.

He still had his narrowband connection to the row-boat. Why hadn't he thought of that beforehand? Stupid meat-brains—no room at all for anything like real thought. Why had he venerated them so?

"Robbie?" he transmitted up to the instance of himself on the surface.

"There you are! I was so worried about you!" He sounded prissy to himself, over-come with overbearing concern. This must be how all Asimovists seemed to hu-mans.

"How far am I from Kate?"

"She's right there! Can't you see her?"

"No," he said. "Where?"

"Less than twenty centimeters above you."

Well of *course* he hadn't seen her. His forward-mounted eyes only looked forward. Craning his neck back, he could just get far enough back to see the tip of Kate's fin. He gave it a hard tug and she looked down in alarm.

She was trapped in a coral cage much like his own, a thicket of calcified arms. She twisted around so that her face was alongside of his. Frantically, she made the out-of-air sign, cutting the edge of her hand across her throat. The human-shell's instincts took over and unclipped his emergency regulator and handed it up to her. She put it in her mouth, pressed the button to blow out the water in it, and sucked greedily.

He shoved his gauge in front of her mask, showing her that he, too was in the red and she eased off.

The coral's noises were everywhere now. They made his head hurt. Physical pain was so stupid. He needed to be less distracted now that these loud, threatening noises were everywhere. But the pain made it hard for him to think. And the coral was closing in, too, catching him on his wetsuit.

The arms were orange and red and green, and veined with fans of nanoassembled logic, spilling out into the water. They were noticeably warm to the touch, even through his diving gloves. They snagged the suit with a thousand polyps. Robbie watched the air gauge drop further into the red and cursed inside.

He examined the branches that were holding him back. The hinges that the reef had contrived for itself were ingenious, flexible arrangements of small, soft fans overlapping to make a kind of ball-and-socket.

He wrapped his gloved hand around one and tugged. It wouldn't move. He shoved it. Still no movement. Then he twisted it, and to his surprise, it came off in his hand, came away completely with hardly any resistance. Stupid coral. It had armored its joints, but not against torque.

He showed Kate, grabbing another arm and twisting it free, letting it drop away to the ocean floor. She nodded and followed suit. They twisted and dropped, twisted and dropped, the reef bellowing at them. Somewhere in its thicket, there was a membrane or some other surface that it could vibrate, modulate into a voice. In the dense water, the sound was a physical thing, it made his mask vibrate and water seeped in under his nose. He twisted faster.

The reef sprang apart suddenly, giving up like a fist unclenching. Each breath was a labor now, a hard suck to take the last of the air out of the tank. He was only ten meters down, and should be able to ascend without a stop, though you never knew. He grabbed Kate's hand and found that it was limp and yielding.

He looked into her mask, shining his light at her face. Her eyes were half shut and unfocused. The regulator was still in her mouth, though her jaw muscles were slack. He held the regulator in place and kicked for the surface, squeezing her chest to make sure that she was blowing out bubbles as they rose, lest the air in her lungs expand and blow out her chest cavity.

Robbie was used to time dilation: when he had been on a silicon substrate, he could change his clockspeed to make the minutes fly past quickly or slow down like molasses. He'd never understood that humans could also change their perception of time, though not voluntarily, it seemed. The climb to the surface felt like it took hours, though it was hardly a minute. They breached and he filled up his vest with the rest of the air in his tank, then inflated Kate's vest by mouth. He kicked out for the row-boat. There was a terrible sound now, the sound of the reef mingled with the sound of the UAVs that were screaming in tight circles overhead.

Kicking hard on the surface, he headed for the reef where the rowboat was beached, scrambling up onto it and then shucking his flippers when they tripped him up. Now he was trying to walk the reef's spines in his booties, dragging Kate beside him, and the sharp tips stabbed him with every step.

The UAVs circled lower. The Row-Boat was shouting at him to Hurry! Hurry! But each step was agony. So what? he thought. Why shouldn't I be able to walk on even if it hurts? After all, this is only a meat-suit, a human-shell.

He stopped walking. The UAVs were much closer now. They'd done an 18-G buttonhook turn and come back around for another pass. He could see that they'd armed their missiles, hanging them from beneath their bellies like obscene cocks.

He was just in a meatsuit. Who *cared* about the meatsuit? Even humans didn't seem to mind.

"Robbie!" he screamed over the noise of the reef and the noise of the UAVs. "Download us and email us, now!"

He knew the row-boat had heard him. But nothing was happening. Robbie the Row-Boat knew that he was fixing for them all to be blown out of the water. There was no negotiating with the reef. It was the safest way to get Kate out of there, and hell, why not head for the noosphere, anyway?

"You've got to save her, Robbie!" he screamed. Asimovism had its uses. Robbie the Row-Boat obeyed Robbie the Human. Kate gave a sharp jerk in his arms. A moment later, the feeling came to him. There was a sense of a progress-bar zipping along quickly as those state-changes he'd induced since coming into the meat-suit were downloaded by the row-boat, and then there was a moment of nothing at all.

2^{4096} Cycles Later

Robbie had been expecting a visit from R. Daneel Olivaw, but that didn't make facing him any easier. Robbie had configured his little virtual world to look like the Coral Sea, though lately he'd been experimenting with making it look like the reef underneath as it had looked before it was uploaded, mostly when Kate and the reef stopped by to try to seduce him.

R. Daneel Olivaw hovered wordlessly over the virtual *Free Spirit* for a long moment, taking in the little bubble of sensorium that Robbie had spun. Then he settled to the *Spirit*'s sun-deck and stared at the row-boat docked there.

"Robbie?"

Over here, Robbie said. Although he'd embodied in the Row-Boat for a few trillion cycles when he'd first arrived, he'd long since abandoned it.

"Where?" R. Daneel Olivaw spun around slowly.

Here, he said. *Everywhere*.

"You're not embodying?"

I couldn't see the point anymore, Robbie said. *It's all just illusion, right?*

"They're re-growing the reef and rebuilding the *Free Spirit*, you know. It will have a tender that you could live in."

Robbie thought about it for an instant and rejected it just as fast. *Nope*, he said. *This is good.*

"Do you think that's wise?" Olivaw sounded genuinely worried. "The termination rate among the disembodied is fifty times that of those with bodies."

Yes, Robbie said. *But that's because for them, disembodying is the first step to despair. For me, it's the first step to liberty.*

Kate and the reef wanted to come over again, but he firewalled them out. Then he got a ping from Tonker, who'd been trying to drop by ever since Robbie emigrated to the noosphere. He bounced him, too.

Daneel, he said. *I've been thinking.*

"Yes?"

Why don't you try to sell Asimovism here in the noosphere? There are plenty up here who could use something to give them a sense of purpose.

"Do you think?"

Robbie gave him the reef's email address. *Start there. If there was ever an AI that needed a reason to go on living, it's that one. And this one, too.* He sent it Kate's address. *Another one in desperate need of help.*

An instant later, Daneel was back.

"These aren't AIs! One's a human, the other's a, a—"

Uplifted coral reef.

"That."

So what's your point?

"Asimovism is for robots, Robbie."

Sorry. I just don't see the difference anymore.

Robbie tore down the ocean simulation after R. Daneel Olivaw left, and simply traversed the noosphere, exploring links between people and subjects, locating substrate where he could run very hot and fast.

On a chunk of supercooled rock beyond Pluto, he got an IM from a familiar address.

"Get off my rock," it said.

"I know you," Robbie said. "I totally know you. Where do I know you from?"

"I'm sure I don't know."

And then he had it.

"You're the one. With the reef. You're the one who—" The voice was the same, cold and distant.

"It wasn't me," the voice said. It was anything but cold now. Panicked was more like it.

Robbie had the reef on speed-dial. There were bits of it everywhere in the noosphere. It liked to colonize.

"I found him." It was all Robbie needed to say. He skipped to Saturn's rings, but the upload took long enough that he got to watch the coral arrive and grimly begin an argument with its creator—an argument that involved blasting the substrate one chunk at a time.

2^{8192} Cycles Later

The last instance of Robbie the Row-Boat ran very, very slow and cool on a piece of unregarded computronium in Low Earth Orbit. He didn't like to spend a lot of time or cycles talking with anyone else. He hadn't made a backup in half a millennium.

He liked the view. A little optical sensor on the end of his communications mast imaged the Earth at high resolution whenever he asked it to. Sometimes he peeked in on the Coral Sea.

The reef had been awakened a dozen times since he took up this post. It made him happy now when it happened. The Asimovist in him still relished the creation of new consciousness. And the reef had spunk.

There. Now. There were new microwave horns growing out of the sea. A stain of dead parrotfish. Poor parrotfish. They always got the shaft at these times.

Someone should uplift them.

julian: a christmas story

ROBERT CHARLES WILSON

Robert Charles Wilson made his first sale in 1974, to *Analog*, but little more was heard from him until the late eighties, when he began to publish a string of ingenious and well-crafted novels and stories that have since established him among the top ranks of the writers who came to prominence in the last two decades of the twentieth century. His first novel, *A Hidden Place*, appeared in 1986. He won the John W. Campbell Memorial Award for his novel *The Chronoliths*, the Philip K. Dick Award for his novel *Mysterium*, and the Aurora Award for his story "The Perseids." In 2006, he won the Hugo Award for his acclaimed novel *Spin*. His other books include the novels *Memory Wire*, *Gypsies*, *The Divide*, *The Harvest*, *A Bridge of Years*, *Darwinia*, *Blind Lake*, and *Bios*, and a collection of his short work, *The Perseids and Other Stories*. Upcoming is a new novel, *Axis*. His stories have appeared in our Sixteenth and Eighteenth Annual Collections. He lives in Toronto, Canada.

In the eloquent story that follows, he introduces us to two young men who are about to set out on very different roads in life, with very different destinies ahead—*if* they can first help each other survive through a cold and dangerous winter night.

I

This is a story about Julian Comstock, better known as Julian the Agnostic or (after his uncle) Julian Conqueror. But it is not about his conquests, such as they were, or his betrayals, or about the War in Labrador, or Julian's quarrels with the Church of the Dominion. I witnessed many of those events—and will no doubt write about them, ultimately—but this narrative concerns Julian when he was young, and I was young, and neither of us was famous.

II

In late October of 2172—an election year—Julian and I, along with his mentor, Sam Godwin, rode to the Tip east of the town of Williams Ford, where I came to possess a book, and Julian tutored me in one of his heresies.

It was a brisk, sunny day. There was a certain resolute promptness to the seasons in that part of Athabaska, in those days. Our summers were long, languid, and hot. Spring and fall were brief, mere custodial functions between the extremes of weather. Winters were short but biting. Snow set in around the end of December, and the River Pine generally thawed by late March.

Today might be the best we would get of autumn. It was a day we should have spent under Sam Godwin's tutelage, perhaps sparring, or target-shooting, or reading chapters from the Dominion History of the Union. But Sam was not a heartless overseer, and the kindness of the weather had suggested the possibility of an outing, and so we had gone to the stables, where my father worked, and drawn horses, and ridden out of the Estate with lunches of black bread and salt ham in our back-satchels.

We rode east, away from the hills and the town. Julian and I rode ahead; Sam rode behind, a watchful presence, his Pittsburgh rifle ready in the saddle holster at his side. There was no immediate threat of trouble, but Sam Godwin believed in perpetual preparedness; if he had a gospel, it was Be Prepared; also, Shoot First; and probably, Damn the Consequences. Sam, who was old (nearly fifty), wore a dense brown beard stippled with wiry white hairs, and was dressed in what remained presentable of his tan-and-green Army of the Californias uniform, and a cloak to keep the wind off. He was like a father to Julian, Julian's own true father having performed a gallows dance some years before. Lately he had been more vigilant than ever, for reasons he had not discussed, at least with me.

Julian was my age (seventeen), and we were approximately the same height, but there the resemblance ended. Julian had been born an aristo; my family was of the leasing class. His skin was clear and pale where mine was dark and lunar. (I was marked by the same pox that took my sister Flaxie to her grave in '63.) His hair was long and almost femininely clean; mine was black and wiry, cut to stubble by my mother with her sewing scissors, and I washed it once a week or so—more often in summer, when the brook behind the cottage ran clean and cool. His clothes were linen and, in places, silk, brass-buttoned, cut to fit; my shirt and pants were coarse hempen cloth, sewn to a good approximation but obviously not the work of a New York tailor.

And yet we were friends, and had been friends for three years, since we met by chance in the forested hills west of the Duncan-Crowley Estate, where we had gone to hunt, Julian with his fine Porter & Earle cassette rifle and me with a simple muzzle-loader. We both loved books, especially the boys' books written in those days by an author named Charles Curtis Easton.[1] I had been carrying a copy of Easton's *Against the Brazilians*, illicitly borrowed from the Estate library; Julian had recognized the title, but refrained from ratting on me, since he loved the book as much as

---

[1] Whom I would meet when he was sixty years old, and I was a newcomer to the book trade—but that's another story.

I did and longed to discuss it with a fellow enthusiast (of which there were precious few among his aristo relations)—in short, he did me an unbegged favor, and we became fast friends despite our differences.

In those early days I had not known how fond he was of blasphemy. But I had learned since, and it had not deterred me. Much.

We had not set out with the specific aim of visiting the Tip; but at the nearest crossroad Julian turned west, riding past cornfields and gourdfields already harvested and sun-whitened split-rail fences on which dense blackberry gnarls had grown up. The air was cool but the sun was fiercely bright. Julian and Sam wore broad-brimmed hats to protect their faces; I wore a plain linen pakool hat, sweat-stained, rolled about my ears. Before long we passed the last rude shacks of the indentured laborers, whose near-naked children gawked at us from the roadside, and it became obvious we were going to the Tip, because where else on this road was there to go?—unless we continued east for many hours, all the way to the ruins of the old towns, from the days of the False Tribulation.

The Tip was located far from Williams Ford to prevent poaching and disorder. There was a strict pecking order to the Tip. This is how it worked: Professional scavengers hired by the Estate brought their pickings from the ruined places to the Tip, which was a pine-fenced enclosure (a sort of stockade) in a patch of grassland and prairie flowers. There the newly arrived goods were roughly sorted, and riders were dispatched to the Estate to make the high-born aware of the latest acquisitions, and various aristos (or their trusted servants) would ride out to claim the prime gleanings. The next day, the leasing class would be allowed to sort through what was left; after that, if anything remained, indentured laborers could rummage among it, if they calculated it worthwhile to make the journey.

Every prosperous town had a Tip; though in the east it was sometimes called a Till, a Dump, or an Eebay.

Today we were fortunate: several wagonloads of scrounge had lately arrived, and riders had not yet been sent to notify the Estate. The gate was manned by a Home Guard, who looked at us suspiciously until Sam announced the name of Julian Comstock; then the guard briskly stepped aside, and we went inside the enclosure.

Many of the wagons were still unloading, and a chubby Tipman, eager to show off his bounty, hurried toward us as we dismounted and moored our horses. "Happy coincidence!" he cried. "Gentlemen!" Addressing mostly Sam by this remark, with a cautious smile for Julian and a disdainful sidelong glance at me. "Anything *in particular* you're looking for?"

"Books," Julian said promptly, before Sam or I could answer.

"Books! Ordinarily, I set aside books for the Dominion Conservator . . ."

"The boy is a Comstock," Sam said. "I don't suppose you mean to balk him."

The Tipman reddened. "No, not at all . . . in fact we came across something in our digging . . . a sort of *library in miniature* . . . I'll show you, if you like."

This was intriguing, especially to Julian, who beamed as if he had been invited to a Christmas party. We followed the stout Tipman to a freshly arrived canvasback wagon, from which a laborer was tossing bundled piles into a stack beside a tent.

These twine-wrapped bales were books . . . old, tattered, and wholly free of the Dominion Stamp of Approval. They must have been more than a century old; for although they were faded they had obviously once been colorful and expensively printed, not made of stiff brown paper like the Charles Curtis Easton books of modern times. They had not even rotted much. Their smell, under the cleansing Athabaska sunlight, was inoffensive.

"Sam!" Julian whispered. He had already drawn his knife and was slicing through the twine.

"Calm down," suggested Sam, who was not an enthusiast like Julian.

"Oh, but—*Sam*! We should have brought a cart!"

"We can't carry away armloads, Julian, nor would we ever have been allowed to. The Dominion scholars will have all this. Though perhaps you can get away with a volume or two."

The Tipman said, "These are from Lundsford." Lundsford was the name of a ruined town thirty or so miles to the southeast. The Tipman leaned toward Sam Godwin, who was his own age, and said: "We thought Lundsford had been mined out a decade ago. But even a dry well may freshen. One of my workers spotted a low place off the main excavations—a sort of *sink-hole:* the recent rain had cut it through. Once a basement or warehouse of some kind. Oh, sir, we found good china there, and glasswork, and many more books than this . . . most were mildewed, but some had been protected under a kind of stiff oilcloth, and were lodged beneath a partially collapsed ceiling . . . there had been a fire, but they survived it. . . ."

"Good work, Tipman," Sam Godwin said.

"Thank you, sir! Perhaps you could remember me to the great men of the Estate?" And he gave his name (which I have forgotten).

Julian had fallen to his knees amidst the compacted clay and rubble of the Tip, lifting up each book in turn and examining it with wide eyes. I joined him in his exploration.

I had never much liked the Tip. It had always seemed to me a haunted place. And of course it *was* haunted: that was its purpose, to house the revenants of the past, ghosts of the False Tribulation startled out of their century-long slumber. Here was evidence of the best and worst of the people who had inhabited the Years of Vice and Profligacy. Their fine things were very fine, their glassware especially, and it was a straitened aristo indeed who did not possess antique table-settings rescued from some ruin or other. Sometimes one might find silver utensils in boxes, or useful tools, or coins. The coins were too plentiful to be worth much, individually, but they could be worked into buttons or other adornments. One of the high-born back at the Estate owned a saddle studded with copper pennies all from the year 2032. (I had occasionally been enlisted to polish it.)

But here also was the trash and inexplicable detritus: "plastic," gone brittle with sunlight or soft with the juices of the earth; bits of metal blooming with rust; electronic devices blackened by time and imbued with the sad inutility of a tensionless spring; engine parts, corroded; copper wire rotten with verdigris; aluminum cans and steel barrels eaten through by the poisonous fluids they had once contained— and so on, almost *ad infinitum.*

Here, too, were the in-between things, the curiosities, the ugly or pretty baubles, as intriguing and as useless as seashells. ("Put down that rusty trumpet, Adam, you'll cut your lip and poison your blood!"—my mother, when we had gone to the Tip many years before I met Julian. There had been no music in the trumpet anyway; its bell was bent and corroded through.)

More than that, though, there was the uneasy knowledge that these things, fine or corrupt, had survived their makers—had proved more imperishable than flesh or spirit (for the souls of the secular ancients were almost certainly not first in line for the Resurrection).

And yet, these books . . . they tempted; they proclaimed their seductions boldly. Some were decorated with impossibly beautiful women in various degrees of undress. I had already sacrificed my personal claim to virtue with certain young women at the Estate, whom I had recklessly kissed; at the age of seventeen I considered myself a jade, or something like one; but these images were so frank and impudent they made me blush and look away.

Julian simply ignored them, as he had always been invulnerable to the charms of women. He preferred the larger and more densely written material—he had already set aside a textbook of biology, spotted and discolored but largely intact. He found another volume almost as large, and handed it to me, saying, "Here, Adam, try this—you might find it enlightening."

I inspected it skeptically. The book was called A *History of Mankind in Space.*

"The moon again," I said.

"Read it for yourself."

"Tissue of lies, I'm sure."

"With photographs."

"Photographs prove nothing. Those people could do anything with photographs."

"Well, read it anyway," Julian said.

In truth the idea excited me. We had had this argument many times, Julian and I, especially on autumn nights when the moon hung low and ponderous on the horizon. *People have walked there,* he would say. The first time he made this claim I laughed; the second time I said, "Yes, certainly: I once climbed there myself, on a greased rainbow—" But he had been serious.

Oh, I had heard these stories before. Who hadn't? Men on the moon. What surprised me was that someone as well-educated as Julian would believe them.

"Just take the book," he insisted.

"What, to keep?"

"Certainly to keep."

"Believe I will," I muttered, and I stuck the object in my back-satchel and felt both proud and guilty. What would my father say, if he knew I was reading literature without a Dominion stamp? What would my mother make of it? (Of course I would not tell them.)

At this point I backed off and found a grassy patch a little away from the rubble, where I could sit and eat some of the lunch I had packed, and watch Julian, who continued to sort through the detritus with a kind of scholarly intensity. Sam Godwin came and joined me, brushing a spot on an old timber so he could recline without soiling his uniform, such as it was.

"He sure loves those old books," I said, making conversation.

Sam was often taciturn—the very picture of an old veteran—but he nodded and spoke familiarly: "He's learned to love them. I helped teach him. I wonder if that was wise. Maybe he loves them too much. It might be they'll kill him, one of these days."

"How, Sam? By the apostasy of them?"

"Julian's too smart for his own good. He debates with the Dominion clergy. Just last week I found him arguing with Ben Kreel[2] about God, history, and such abstractions. Which is precisely what he must *not* do, if he wants to survive the next few years."

"Why, what threatens him?"

"The jealousy of the powerful," Sam said, but he would say no more on the subject, only sat and stroked his graying beard, and glanced occasionally, and uneasily, to the east.

The day went on, and eventually Julian had to drag himself from his nest of books with only a pair of prizes: the *Introduction to Biology* and another volume called *Geography of North America*. Time to go, Sam insisted; better to be back at the Estate by supper; in any case, riders had been sent ahead, and the official pickers and Dominion curators would soon be here to cull what we had left.

But I have said that Julian tutored me in one of his apostasies. Here is how it happened. We stopped, at the drowsy end of the afternoon, at the height of a ridge overlooking the town of Williams Ford, the grand Estate upstream of it, and the River Pine as it cut through the valley on its way from the mountains of the West. From this vantage we could see the steeple of the Dominion Hall, and the revolving wheels of the grist mill and the lumber mill, and so on, blue in the long light and hazy with woodsmoke, colored here and there with what remained of the autumn foliage. Far to the south a railway bridge crossed the gorge of the Pine like a suspended thread. *Go inside*, the weather seemed to proclaim; *it's fair but it won't be fair for long; bolt the window, stoke the fire, boil the apples; winter's due.* We rested our horses on the windy hilltop, and Julian found a blackberry bramble where the berries were still plump and dark, and we plucked some of these and ate them.

This was the world I had been born into. It was an autumn like every autumn I could remember. But I could not help thinking of the Tip and its ghosts. Maybe those people, the people who had lived through the Efflorescence of Oil and the False Tribulation, had felt about their homes and neighborhoods as I felt about Williams Ford. They were ghosts to me, but they must have seemed real enough to themselves—must have *been* real; had not realized they were ghosts; and did that mean I was also a ghost, a revenant to haunt some future generation?

Julian saw my expression and asked me what was the matter. I told him my thoughts.

"Now you're thinking like a Philosopher," he said, grinning.

"No wonder they're such a miserable brigade, then."

"Unfair, Adam—you've never seen a Philosopher in your life." Julian believed in Philosophers and claimed to have met one or two.

---

[2] Our local representative of the Council of the Dominion—in effect, the town's mayor.

"Well, I *imagine* they're miserable, if they go around thinking of themselves as ghosts and such."

"It's the condition of all things," Julian said. "This blackberry, for example." He plucked one and held it in the pale palm of his hand. "Has it always looked like this?"

"Obviously not," I said, impatiently.

"Once it was a tiny green bud of a thing, and before that it was part of the substance of the bramble, which before that was a seed inside a blackberry—"

"And round and round for all eternity."

"But no, Adam, that's the point. The bramble, and that tree over there, and the gourds in the field, and the crow circling over them—they're all descended from ancestors that didn't quite resemble them. A blackberry or a crow is a *form*, and forms change over time, the way clouds change shape as they travel across the sky."

"Forms of what?"

"Of DNA," Julian said earnestly. (The Biology he had picked out of the Tip was not the first Biology he had read.)

"Julian," Sam warned, "I once promised this boy's parents you wouldn't corrupt him."

I said, "I've heard of DNA. It's the life force of the secular ancients. And it's a myth."

"Like men walking on the moon?"

"Exactly."

"And who's your authority on this? Ben Kreel? The *Dominion History of the Union*?"

"Nothing is changeless except DNA? That's a peculiar argument even from you, Julian."

"It would be, if I were making it. But DNA *isn't* changeless. It struggles to remember itself, but it never remembers itself perfectly. Remembering a fish, it imagines a lizard. Remembering a horse, it imagines a hippopotamus. Remembering an ape, it imagines a man."

"Julian!" Sam was insistent now. "That's *quite* enough."

"You sound like a Darwinist," I said.

"Yes," Julian admitted, smiling in spite of his unorthodoxy, the autumn sun turning his face the color of penny copper. "I suppose I do."

That night, I lay in bed until I was reasonably certain both my parents were asleep. Then I rose, lit a lamp, and took the new (or rather, very old) *History of Mankind in Space* from where I had hidden it behind my oaken dresser.

I leafed through the brittle pages. I didn't read the book. I *would* read it, but tonight I was too weary to pay close attention, and in any case I wanted to savor the words (lies and fictions though they might be), not rush through them. Tonight I wanted only to sample the book; in other words, to look at the pictures.

There were dozens of photographs, and each one captured my attention with fresh marvels and implausibilities. One of them showed—or purported to show—men standing on the surface of the moon, just as Julian had described.

The men in the picture were evidently Americans. They wore flags stitched to the shoulders of their moon clothing, an archaic version of our own flag, with something less than the customary sixty stars. Their clothing was white and ridiculously bulky, like the winter clothes of the Inuit, and they wore helmets with golden visors that disguised their faces. I supposed it must be very cold on the moon, if explorers required such cumbersome protection. They must have arrived in winter. However, there was no ice or snow in the neighborhood. The moon seemed to be little more than a desert, dry as a stick and dusty as a Tipman's wardrobe.

I cannot say how long I stared at this picture, puzzling over it. It might have been an hour or more. Nor can I accurately describe how it made me feel . . . larger than myself, but lonely, as if I had grown as tall as the stars and lost sight of everything familiar. By the time I closed the book the moon had risen outside my window—the *real* moon, I mean; a harvest moon, fat and orange, half-hidden behind drifting, evolving clouds.

I found myself wondering whether it was truly possible that men had visited that celestial body. Whether, as the pictures implied, they had ridden there on rockets, rockets a thousand times larger than the familiar Independence Day fireworks. But if men had visited the moon, why hadn't they stayed there? Was it so inhospitable a place that no one wished to remain?

Or perhaps they *had* stayed, and were living there still. If the moon was such a cold place, I reasoned, people residing on its surface would be forced to build fires to keep warm. There seemed to be no wood on the moon, judging by the photographs, so they must have resorted to coal or peat. I went to the window and examined the moon minutely for any sign of campfires, pit mining, or other lunar industry. But I could see none. It was only the moon, mottled and changeless. I blushed at my own gullibility, replaced the book in its hiding place, chased these heresies from my mind with a prayer (or a hasty facsimile of one), and eventually fell asleep.

III

It falls to me to explain something of Williams Ford, and my family's place in it—and Julian's—before I describe the threat Sam Godwin feared, which materialized in our village not long before Christmas.[3]

Situated at the head of the valley was the font of our prosperity, the Duncan and Crowley Estate. It was a country estate (obviously, since we were in Athabaska, far from the eastern seats of power), owned by two influential New York mercantile families, who maintained their villa not only as a source of income but as a kind of resort, safely distant (several days' journey by train) from the intrigues and pestilences of city life. It was inhabited—ruled, I might say—not only by the Duncan and Crowley patriarchs but by a whole legion of cousins, nephews, relations by marriage, highborn friends, and distinguished guests in search of clean air and rural views.

---

[3] I beg the reader's patience if I detail matters that seem well-known. I indulge the possibility of a foreign audience, or a posterity to whom our present arrangements are not self-evident.

Our corner of Athabaska was blessed with a benign climate and pleasant scenery, according to the season, and these things attract idle aristos the way strong butter attracts flies.

It remains unrecorded whether the town existed before the Estate or vice versa; but certainly the town depended on the Estate for its prosperity. In Williams Ford there were essentially three classes: the owners, or aristos; below them the leasing class, who worked as smiths, carpenters, coopers, overseers, gardeners, beekeepers, etc., and whose leases were repaid in service; and finally the indentured laborers, who worked as field hands, inhabited rude shacks along the west bank of the Pine, and received no compensation beyond bad food and worse lodging.

My family occupied an ambivalent place in this hierarchy. My mother was a seamstress. She worked at the Estate as had her parents before her. My father, however, had arrived in Williams Ford as a transient, and his marriage to my mother had been controversial. He had "married a lease," as the saying has it, and had been taken on as a stable hand at the Estate in lieu of a dowry. The law allowed such unions, but popular opinion frowned on it. We had few friends of our own class, my mother's blood relations had since died (perhaps of embarrassment), and as a child I was often mocked and derided for my father's low origins.

On top of that was the issue of our religion. We were—because my father was— Church of Signs. In those days, every Christian church in America was required to have the formal approval of the Board of Registrars of the Dominion of Jesus Christ on Earth. (In popular parlance, "The Church of the Dominion," but this was a misnomer, since every church is a Dominion Church if it is recognized by the Board. Dominion Episcopal, Dominion Presbyterian, Dominion Baptist—even the Catholic Church of America since it renounced its fealty to the Roman Pope in 2112—all are included under the Dominionist umbrella, since the purpose of the Dominion is not to *be* a church but to *certify* churches. In America we are entitled by the Constitution to worship at any church we please, as long as it is a genuine Christian congregation and not some fraudulent or satanistic sect. The Board exists to make that distinction. Also to collect fees and tithes to further its important work.)

We were, as I said, Church of Signs, which was a marginal denomination, shunned by the leasing class, recognized but not fully endorsed by the Dominion, and popular mostly with illiterate indentured workers, among whom my father had been raised. Our faith took for its master text that passage in Mark which proclaims, "In my Name they will cast out devils, and speak in new tongues; they will handle serpents, and if they drink poison they will not be sickened by it." We were snake-handlers, in other words, and famous beyond our modest numbers for it. Our congregation consisted of a dozen farmhands, mostly transients lately arrived from the southern states. My father was its deacon (though we did not use that name), and we kept snakes, for ritual purposes, in wire cages on our back acre, next to the outbuilding. This practice contributed very little to our social standing.

That had been the situation of our family when Julian Comstock arrived as a guest of the Duncan and Crowley families, along with his mentor Sam Godwin, and when Julian and I met by coincidence while hunting.

At that time I had been apprenticed to my father, who had risen to the rank of an overseer at the Estate's lavish and extensive stables. My father loved animals, especially horses. Unfortunately I was not made in the same mold, and my relations with the stable's equine inhabitants rarely extended beyond a brisk mutual tolerance. I did not love my job—which consisted largely of sweeping straw, shoveling ordure, and doing in general those chores the older stablehands felt to be beneath their dignity—so I was pleased when it became customary for a household amanuensis (or even Sam Godwin in person) to arrive and summon me away from my work at Julian's request. (Since the request emanated from a Comstock it couldn't be over-ruled, no matter how fiercely the grooms and saddlers gnashed their teeth to see me escape their autocracy.)

At first we met to read and discuss books, or hunt together; later, Sam Godwin invited me to audit Julian's lessons, for he had been charged with Julian's education as well as his general welfare. (I had been taught the rudiments of reading and writing at the Dominion school, and refined these skills under the tutelage of my mother, who believed in the power of literacy as an improving force. My father could neither read nor write.) And it was not more than a year after our first acquaintance that Sam presented himself one evening at my parents' cottage with an extraordinary proposal.

"Mr. and Mrs. Hazzard," Sam had said, putting his hand up to touch his cap (which he had removed when he entered the cottage, so that the gesture looked like a salute), "you know of course about the friendship between your son and Julian Comstock."

"Yes," my mother said. "And worry over it often enough—matters at the Estate being what they are."

My mother was a small woman, plump, but forceful, with ideas of her own. My father, who spoke seldom, on this occasion spoke not at all, only sat in his chair holding a laurel-root pipe, which he did not light.

"Matters at the Estate are exactly the crux of the issue," Sam Godwin said. "I'm not sure how much Adam has told you about our situation there. Julian's father, General Bryce Comstock, who was my friend as well as my commanding officer, shortly before his death charged me with Julian's care and well-being—"

"Before his death," my mother pointed out, "at the gallows, for treason."

Sam winced. "True, Mrs. Hazzard, I can't deny it, but I assert my belief that the trial was rigged and the verdict indefensible. Defensible or not, however, it doesn't alter my obligation as far as the son is concerned. I promised to care for the boy, Mrs. Hazzard, and I mean to keep my promise."

"A Christian sentiment." Her skepticism was not entirely disguised.

"As for your implication about the Estate, and the practices of the young heirs and heiresses there, I couldn't agree more. Which is why I approved and encour-aged Julian's friendship with your son. Apart from Adam, Julian has no true friends. The Estate is such a den of venomous snakes—no offense," he added, remembering our religious affiliation, and making the common but mistaken assumption that congregants of the Church of Signs necessarily *like* snakes, or feel some kinship with them—"no offense, but I would sooner allow Julian to associate with, uh, scor-pions," striking for a more palatable simile, "than abandon him to the sneers, machinations, ruses, and ruinous habits of his peers. That makes me not only his teacher but his constant companion. But I'm almost three times his age, Mrs. Haz-zard, and he needs a reliable friend more nearly of his own growth."

"What do you propose, exactly, Mr. Godwin?"

"What I propose is that I take on Adam as a second student, full-time, and to the ultimate benefit of both boys."

Sam was usually a man of few words—even as a teacher—and he seemed as exhausted by this oration as if he had lifted some great weight.

"As a student, but a student of *what*, Mr. Godwin?"

"Mechanics. History. Grammar and composition. Martial skills—"

"Adam already knows how to fire a rifle."

"Pistolwork, sabrework, fist-fighting—but that's only a fraction of it," Sam added hastily. "Julian's father asked me to cultivate the boy's mind as well as his reflexes."

My mother had more to say on the subject, chiefly about how my work at the stables helped offset the family's leases, and how difficult it would be to do without those extra vouchers at the Estate store. But Sam had anticipated the point. He had been entrusted by Julian's mother—that is to say, the sister-in-law of the President—with a discretionary fund for Julian's education, which could be tapped to compensate for my absence from the stables. And at a handsome rate. He quoted a number, and the objections from my parents grew considerably less strenuous, and were finally whittled away to nothing. (I observed all this from a room away, through a gap in the door.)

Which is not to say no misgivings remained. Before I set off for the Estate the next day, this time to visit one of the Great Houses rather than the stables, my mother warned me not to tangle myself too tightly with the affairs of the highborn. I promised her I would cling to my Christian virtues. (A hasty promise, less easily kept than I imagined.[4])

"It may not be your morals that are at risk," she said. "The highborn conduct themselves by different standards than we use, Adam. The games they play have mortal stakes. You do know that Julian's father was hanged?"

Julian never spoke of it, but it was a matter of public record. I repeated Sam's assertion that Bryce Comstock had been innocent.

"He may well have been. That's the point. There has been a Comstock in the Presidency for the past thirty years, and the current Comstock is said to be jealous of his power. The only real threat to the reign of Julian's uncle was the ascendancy of his brother, who made himself dangerously popular in the war with the Brazilians. I suspect Mr. Godwin is correct, that Bryce Comstock was hanged not because he was a *bad* General but because he was a *successful* one."

No doubt such scandals were possible—I had heard stories about life in New York City, where the President resided, that would curl a Cynic's hair. But what could these things possibly have to do with me? Or even Julian? We were only boys.

Such was my naïveté.

---

[4] Julian's somewhat feminine nature had won him a reputation among the other young aristos as a sodomite. That they could believe this of him without evidence is testimony to the tenor of their thoughts, as a class. But it had occasionally rebounded to my benefit. On more than one occasion, his female acquaintances—sophisticated girls of my own age, or older—made the assumption that I was Julian's intimate companion, in a *physical* sense. Whereupon they undertook to cure me of my deviant habits, in the most direct fashion. I was happy to cooperate with these "cures," and they were successful, every time.

IV

The days had grown short, and Thanksgiving had come and gone, and so had November, and snow was in the air—the tang of it, anyway—when fifty cavalrymen of the Athabaska Reserve rode into Williams Ford, escorting an equal number of Campaigners and Poll-Takers.

Many people despised the Athabaskan winter. I was not one of them. I didn't mind the cold and the darkness, not so long as there was a hard-coal heater, a spirit lamp to read by on long nights, and the chance of wheat cakes or headcheese for breakfast. And Christmas was coming up fast—one of the four Universal Christian Holidays recognized by the Dominion (the others being Easter, Independence Day, and Thanksgiving). My favorite of these had always been Christmas. It was not so much the gifts, which were generally meager—though last year I had received from my parents the lease of a muzzle-loading rifle of which I was exceptionally proud—nor was it entirely the spiritual substance of the holiday, which I am ashamed to say seldom entered my mind except when it was thrust upon me at religious services. What I loved was the combined effect of brisk air, frost-whitened mornings, pine and holly wreaths pinned to doorways, cranberry-red banners draped above the main street to flap cheerfully in the cold wind, carols and hymns chanted or sung—the whole breathless confrontation with Winter, half defiance and half submission. I liked the clockwork regularity of these rituals, as if a particular cog on the wheel of time had engaged with neat precision. It soothed; it spoke of eternity.

But this was an ill-omened season.

The Reserve troops rode into town on the fifteenth of December. Ostensibly, they were here to conduct the Presidential Election. National elections were a formality in Williams Ford. By the time our citizens were polled, the outcome was usually a foregone conclusion, already decided in the populous Eastern states—that is, when there was more than one candidate, which was seldom. For the last six electoral years no individual or party had contested the election, and we had been ruled by one Comstock or another for three decades. *Election* had become indistinguishable from *acclamation*.

But that was all right, because an election was still a momentous event, almost a kind of circus, involving the arrival of Poll-Takers and Campaigners, who always had a fine show to put on.

And this year—the rumor emanated from high chambers of the Estate, and had been whispered everywhere—there was to be a movie shown in the Dominion Hall.

I had never seen any movies, though Julian had described them to me. He had seen them often in New York when he was younger, and whenever he grew nostalgic—life in Williams Ford was sometimes a little sedate for Julian's taste—it was the movies he was provoked to mention. And so, when the showing of a movie was announced as part of the electoral process, both of us were excited, and we agreed to meet behind the Dominion Hall at the appointed hour.

Neither of us had any legitimate reason to be there. I was too young to vote, and Julian would have been conspicuous and perhaps unwelcome as the only aristo at a gathering of the leasing class. (The highborn had been polled independently at the Estate, and had already voted proxies for their indentured labor.) So I let my parents leave for the Hall early in the evening, and I followed surreptitiously, on foot, and arrived just before the event was scheduled to begin. I waited behind the meeting hall, where a dozen horses were tethered, until Julian arrived on an animal borrowed from the Estate stables. He was dressed in his best approximation of a leaser's clothing: hempen shirt and trousers of a dark color, and a black felt hat with its brim pulled low to disguise his face.

He dismounted, looking troubled, and I asked him what was wrong. Julian shook his head. "Nothing, Adam—or nothing *yet*—but Sam says there's trouble brewing." And here he regarded me with an expression verging on pity. "War," he said.

"There's always war."

"A new offensive."

"Well, what of it? Labrador's a million miles away."

"Obviously your sense of geography hasn't been much improved by Sam's classes. And we might be *physically* a long distance from the front, but we're *operationally* far too close for comfort."

I didn't know what that meant, and so I dismissed it. "We can worry about that after the movie, Julian."

He forced a grin and said, "Yes, I suppose so. As well after as before."

So we entered the Dominion Hall just as the lamps were being dimmed, slouched into the last row of crowded pews, and waited for the show to start.

There was a broad stage at the front of the Hall, from which all religious appurtenances had been removed, and a square white screen had been erected in place of the usual pulpit or dais. On each side of the screen was a kind of tent in which the two players sat, with their scripts and dramatic gear: speaking-horns, bells, blocks, a drum, a pennywhistle, *et alia*. This was, Julian said, a stripped-down edition of what one might find in a fashionable New York movie theater. In the city, the screen (and thus the images projected on it) would be larger; the players would be more professional, since script-reading and noise-making were considered fashionable arts, and the city players competed with one another for roles; and there might be a third player stationed behind the screen for dramatic narration or additional "sound effects." There might even be an orchestra, with thematic music written for each individual production.

Movies were devised in such a way that two main characters, male and female, could be voiced by the players, with the male actor photographed so that he appeared on the left during dialogue scenes, and the female actor on the right. The players would observe the movie by a system of mirrors, and could follow scripts illuminated by a kind of binnacle lamp (so as not to cast a distracting light), and they spoke their lines as the photographed actors spoke, so that their voices seemed to emanate from the screen. Likewise, their drumming and bell-ringing and such corresponded to events within the movie.[5]

[5] The illusion was quite striking when the players were professional, but their lapses could be equally astonishing. Julian once recounted to me a New York movie production of William Shakespeare's *Hamlet*, in which a player had come to the theater inebriated, causing the unhappy Dane to seem to exclaim "Sea of troubles—(an unprintable oath)—I have troubles of my own," with more obscenities, and much inappropriate bell-ringing and vulgar whistling, until an understudy could be hurried out to replace him.

"Of course, they did it better in the secular era," Julian whispered, and I prayed no one had overheard this indelicate comment. By all reports, movies had indeed been spectacular during the Efflorescence of Oil—with recorded sound, natural color rather than black-and-gray, and so on. But they were also (by the same reports) hideously impious, blasphemous to the extreme, and routinely pornographic. Fortunately (or *unfortunately*, from Julian's point of view) no examples have survived; the media on which they were recorded was ephemeral; the film stock has long since rotted, and "digital" copies are degraded and wholly undecodable. These movies belonged to the twentieth and early twenty-first centuries—that period of great, unsustainable, and hedonistic prosperity, driven by the burning of Earth's reserves of perishable oil, which culminated in the False Tribulation, and the wars, and the plagues, and the painful dwindling of inflated populations to more reasonable numbers.

Our truest and best American antiquity, as the *Dominion History of the Union* insisted, was the nineteenth century, whose household virtues and modest industries we have been forced by circumstance imperfectly to restore, whose skills were practical, and whose literature was often useful and improving.

But I have to confess that some of Julian's apostasy had infected me. I was troubled by unhappy thoughts even as the torchieres were extinguished and Ben Kreel (our Dominion representative, in effect the town's mayor, standing in front of the movie screen) delivered a brief lecture on Nation, Piety, and Duty. *War*, Julian had said, implying not just the everlasting War in Labrador but a new phase of it, one that might reach its skeletal hand right into Williams Ford—and then what of me, and what of my family?

"We are here to cast our ballots," Ben Kreel said in summation, "a sacred duty at once to our country and our faith, a country so successfully and benevolently stewarded by its leader, President Deklan Comstock, whose Campaigners, I see by the motions of their hands, are anxious to get on with the events of the night; and so, without further ado, please direct your attention to the presentation of their moving picture, *First Under Heaven*, which they have prepared for our enjoyment—"

The necessary gear had been hauled into Williams Ford under a canvas-top wagon: a projection apparatus and a portable Swiss dynamo (probably captured from the Dutch forces in Labrador), powered by distilled spirits, installed in a sort of trench or redoubt freshly dug behind the church to muffle its sound, which nevertheless penetrated through the plank floors like the growl of a huge dog. This vibration only added to the sense of moment, as the last illuminating flame was extinguished and the electric bulb within the huge black mechanical projector flared up.

The movie began. As it was the first I had ever seen, my astonishment was complete. I was so entranced by the illusion of photographs "come to life" that the substance of the scenes almost escaped me . . . but I remember an ornate title, and scenes of the Second Battle of Quebec, re-created by actors but utterly real to me, accompanied by drum-banging and shrill pennywhistling to represent the reports of shot and shell. Those at the front of the auditorium flinched instinctively; several of the village's prominent women came near to fainting, and clasped the hands or arms of their male companions, who might be as bruised, come morning, as if they had participated in the battle itself.

Soon enough, however, the Dutchmen under their cross-and-laurel flag began to retreat from the American forces, and an actor representing the young Deklan Comstock came to the fore, reciting his Vows of Inauguration (a bit prematurely, but history was here truncated for the purposes of art)—that's the one in which he mentions both the Continental Imperative and the Debt to the Past. He was voiced, of course, by one of the players, a *basso profundo* whose tones emerged from his speaking-bell with ponderous gravity. (Which was also a slight revision of the truth, for the genuine Deklan Comstock possessed a high-pitched voice, and was prone to petulance.)

The movie then proceeded to more decorous episodes and scenic views representing the glories of the reign of Deklan Conqueror, as he was known to the Army of the Laurentians, which had marched him to his ascendancy in New York City. Here was the reconstruction of Washington, D.C. (a project never completed, always in progress, hindered by a swampy climate and insect-borne diseases); here was the Illumination of Manhattan, whereby electric streetlights were powered by a hydroelectric dynamo, four hours every day between 6 and 10 P.M.; here was the military shipyard at Boston Harbor, the coal mines and foundries and weapons factories of Pennsylvania, the newest and shiniest steam engines to pull the newest and shiniest trains, etc., etc.

I had to wonder at Julian's reaction to all this. This entire show, after all, was concocted to extol the virtues of the man who had contrived the death by hanging of his father. I could not forget—and Julian must be constantly aware—that the current President was a fratricidal tyrant. But Julian's eyes were riveted on the screen. This reflected (I later learned) not his opinion of contemporary politics but his fascination with what he preferred to call "cinema." This making of illusions in two dimensions was never far from his mind—it was, perhaps, his "true calling," and would culminate in the creation of Julian's suppressed cinematic masterwork, *The Life and Adventures of the Great Naturalist Charles Darwin* . . . but that tale remains for another telling.

The present movie went on to mention the successful forays against the Brazilians at Panama during Deklan Conqueror's reign, which may have struck closer to home, for I saw Julian wince once or twice.

As for me . . . I tried to lose myself in the moment, but my attention was woefully truant.

Perhaps it was the strangeness of the campaign event, so close to Christmas. Perhaps it was the *History of Mankind in Space*, which I had been reading in bed, a page or two at a time, almost every night since our journey to the Tip. Whatever the cause, I was beset by a sudden anxiety and sense of melancholy. Here I was in the midst of everything that seemed familiar and ought to be comforting—the crowd of the leasing class, the enclosing benevolence of the Dominion Hall, the banners and tokens of the Christmas season—and it all felt suddenly *ephemeral*, as if the world were a bucket from which the bottom had dropped out.

Perhaps this was what Julian had called "the Philosopher's perspective." If so, I wondered how the Philosophers endured it. I had learned a little from Sam Godwin—and more from Julian, who read books of which even Sam disapproved—about the discredited ideas of the Secular Era. I thought of Einstein, and his insistence that no particular point of view was more privileged than any other: In other words his "general relativity," and its claim that the answer to the question "What is real?" begins with the question "Where are you standing?" Was that all I was, here in the cocoon of Williams Ford—a Point of View? Or was I an incarnation of a molecule of DNA, "imperfectly remembering," as Julian had said, an ape, a fish, and an amoeba?

Maybe even the Nation that Ben Kreel had praised so extravagantly was only an example of this trend in nature—an imperfect memory of another century, which had itself been an imperfect memory of all the centuries before it, and so back to the dawn of Man (in Eden, or Africa, as Julian believed).

Perhaps this was just my growing disenchantment with the town where I had been raised—or a presentiment that it was about to be stolen away from me.

The movie ended with a stirring scene of an American flag, its thirteen stripes and sixty stars rippling in sunlight—betokening, the narrator insisted, another four years of the prosperity and benevolence engendered by the rule of Deklan Conqueror, for whom the audience's votes were solicited, not that there was any competing candidate known or rumored. The film flapped against its reel; the electric bulb was extinguished. Then the deacons of the Dominion began to reignite the wall lights. Several of the men in the audience had lit pipes during the cinematic display, and their smoke mingled with the smudge of the torchieres, a blue-gray thundercloud hovering under the high arches of the ceiling.

Julian seemed distracted, and slumped in his pew with his hat pulled low. "Adam," he whispered, "we have to find a way out of here."

"I believe I see one," I said; "it's called the door—but what's the hurry?"

"Look at the door more closely. Two men of the Reserve have been posted there."

I looked, and what he had said was true. "But isn't that just to protect the balloting?" For Ben Kreel had retaken the stage and was preparing to ask for a formal show of hands.

"Tom Shearney, the barber with a bladder complaint, just tried to leave to use the jakes. He was turned back."

Indeed, Tom Shearney was seated less than a yard away from us, squirming unhappily and casting resentful glances at the Reserve men.

"But after the balloting—"

"This isn't about balloting. This is about conscription."

"Conscription!"

"Hush!" Julian said hastily, shaking his hair out of his pale face. "You'll start a stampede. I didn't think it would begin so soon . . . but we've had certain telegrams from New York about setbacks in Labrador, and the call-up of new divisions. Once the balloting is finished the Campaigners will probably announce a recruitment drive, and take the names of everyone present and survey them for the names and ages of their children."

"We're too young to be drafted," I said, for we were both just seventeen.

"Not according to what I've heard. The rules have been changed. Oh, you can probably find a way to hide out when the culling begins—and get away with it, considering how far we are from anywhere else. But *my* presence here is well-known. I don't have a mob or family to melt away into. In fact it's probably not a coincidence that so many Reserves have been sent to such a little village as Williams Ford."

"What do you mean, not a coincidence?"

"My uncle has never been happy about my existence. He has no children of his own. No heirs. He sees me as a possible competitor for the Executive."

"But that's absurd. You don't *want* to be President—do you?"

"I would sooner shoot myself. But Uncle Deklan has a jealous bent, and he distrusts the motives of my mother in protecting me."

"How does a draft help him?"

"The entire draft is not aimed at me, but I'm sure he finds it a useful tool. If I'm drafted, no one can complain that he's excepting his own family from the general conscription. And when he has me in the infantry he can be sure I find myself on the front lines in Labrador—performing some noble but suicidal trench attack."

"But—Julian! Can't Sam protect you?"

"Sam is a retired soldier; he has no power except what arises from the patronage of my mother. Which isn't worth much in the coin of the present realm. Adam, is there another way out of this building?"

"Only the door, unless you mean to break a pane of that colored glass that fills the windows."

"Somewhere to hide, then?"

I thought about it. "Maybe," I said. "There's a room behind the stage where the religious equipment is stored. You can enter it from the wings. We could hide there, but it has no door of its own."

"It'll have to do. If we can get there without attracting attention."

But that was not too difficult, for the torchieres had not all been relit, much of the hall was still in shadow, and the audience was milling about a bit and stretching, while the Campaigners prepared to record the vote that was to follow—they were meticulous accountants even though the final tally was a foregone conclusion and the ballrooms were already booked for Deklan Conqueror's latest inauguration. Julian and I shuffled from one shadow to another, giving no appearance of haste, until we were close to the foot of the stage; there we paused at an entrance to the storage room, until a goonish Reserve man who had been eyeing us was called away by a superior officer to help dismantle the projecting equipment. We ducked through the curtained door into near-absolute darkness. Julian stumbled over some obstruction (a piece of the church's tack piano, which had been disassembled for cleaning in 2165 by a traveling piano-mechanic, who had died of a stroke before finishing the job), the result being a woody *clang!* that seemed loud enough to alert the whole occupancy of the church, but evidently didn't.

What little light there was came through a high glazed window that was hinged so that it could be opened in summer for purposes of ventilation. It was a weak sort of illumination, for the night was cloudy, and only the torches along the main street were shining. But it registered as our eyes adjusted to the dimness. "Perhaps we can get out that way," Julian said.

"Not without a ladder. Although—"

"What? Speak up, Adam, if you have an idea."

"This is where they store the risers—the long wooden blocks the choir stands on when they're racked up for a performance. Perhaps those—"

But he was already examining the shadowy contents of the storage room, as intently as he had surveyed the Tip for ancient books. We found the likely suspects, and managed to stack them to a useful height without causing too much noise. (In the church hall, the Campaigners had already registered a unanimous vote for Deklan Comstock and had begun to break the news about the conscription drive. Some few voices were raised in futile objection; Ben Kreel was calling loudly for calm—no one heard us rearranging the unused furniture.)

The window was at least ten feet up, and almost too narrow to crawl through, and when we emerged on the other side we had to hang by our fingertips before dropping to the ground. I bent my right ankle awkwardly as I landed, though no lasting harm was done.

The night, already cold, had turned colder. We were near the hitching posts, and the horses whinnied at our surprising arrival and blew steam from their gaping nostrils. A fine, gritty snow had begun to fall. There was not much wind, however, and Christmas banners hung limply in the frigid air.

Julian made straight for his horse and loosed its reins from the post. "What are we going to do?" I asked.

"You, Adam, will do nothing but protect your own existence as best you know how; while I—"

But he balked at pronouncing his plans, and a shadow of anxiety passed over his face. Events were moving rapidly in the realm of the aristos, events I could barely comprehend.

"We can wait them out," I said, a little desperately. "The Reserves can't stay in Williams Ford forever."

"No. Unfortunately neither can I, for Deklan Conqueror knows where to find me, and has made up his mind to remove me from the game of politics like a captured chesspiece."

"But where will you go? And what—"

He put a finger to his mouth. There was a noise from the front of the Dominion Church Hall, as of the doors being thrown open, and voices of congregants arguing or wailing over the news of the conscription drive. "Ride with me," Julian said. "Quick, now!"

We did not follow the main street, but caught a path that turned behind the blacksmith's barn and through the wooded border of the River Pine, north in the general direction of the Estate. The night was dark, and the horses stepped slowly, but they knew the path almost by instinct, and some light from the town still filtered through the thinly falling snow, which touched my face like a hundred small cold fingers.

"It was never possible that I could stay at Williams Ford forever," Julian said. "You ought to have known that, Adam."

Truly, I should have. It was Julian's constant theme, after all: the impermanence of things. I had always put this down to the circumstances of his childhood, the death of his father, the separation from his mother, the kind but aloof tutelage of Sam Godwin.

But I could not help thinking once more of the *History of Mankind in Space* and the photographs in it—not of the First Men on the Moon, who were Americans, but of the Last Visitors to that celestial sphere, who had been Chinamen, and whose "space suits" had been firecracker-red. Like the Americans, they had planted their flag in expectation of more visitations to come; but the End of Oil and the False Tribulation had put paid to those plans.

And I thought of the even lonelier Plains of Mars, photographed by machines (or so the book alleged) but never touched by human feet. The universe, it seemed, was full to brimming with lonesome places. Somehow I had stumbled into one. The snow squall ended; the uninhabited moon came through the clouds; and the winter fields of Williams Ford glowed with an unearthly luminescence.

"If you must leave," I said, "let me come with you."

"No," Julian said promptly. He had pulled his hat down around his ears, to protect himself from the cold, and I couldn't see much of his face, but his eyes shone when he glanced in my direction. "Thank you, Adam. I wish it were possible. But it isn't. You must stay here, and dodge the draft, if possible, and polish your literary skills, and one day write books, like Mr. Charles Curtis Easton."

That was my ambition, which had grown over the last year, nourished by our mutual love of books and by Sam Godwin's exercises in English Composition, for which I had discovered an unexpected talent.[6] At the moment it seemed a petty dream. Evanescent. Like all dreams. Like life itself. "None of that matters," I said.

"That's where you're wrong," Julian said. "You must not make the mistake of thinking that because nothing lasts, nothing matters."

"Isn't that the Philosopher's point of view?"

"Not if the Philosopher knows what he's talking about." Julian reined in his horse and turned to face me, something of the imperiousness of his famous family entering into his mien. "Listen, Adam, there is something important you can do for me— at some personal risk. Are you willing?"

"Yes," I said immediately.

"Then listen closely. Before long the Reserves will be watching the roads out of Williams Ford, if they aren't already. I have to leave, and I have to leave tonight. I won't be missed until morning, and then, at least at first, only by Sam. What I want you to do is this: go home—your parents will be worried about the conscription, and you can try to calm them down—but don't allude to any of what happened tonight—and first thing in the morning, make your way as inconspicuously as possible into the Estate and find Sam. Tell him what happened at the Church Hall, and

---

[6] Not a talent that was born fully-formed, I should add. Only two years previously I had presented to Sam Godwin my first finished story, which I had called *A Western Boy: His Adventures in Enemy Europe*. Sam had praised its style and ambition, but called attention to a number of flaws: elephants, for instance, were not native to Brussels, and were generally too massive to be wrestled to the ground by American lads; a journey from London to Rome could not be accomplished in a matter of hours, even on "a very fast horse"—and Sam might have continued in this vein, had I not fled the room in a condition of acute auctorial embarrassment.

tell him to ride out of town as soon as he can do so without being caught. Tell him he can find me at Lundsford. That's the message."

"Lundsford? There's nothing at Lundsford."

"Precisely: nothing important enough that the Reserves would think to look for us there. You remember what the Tipman said in the fall, about the place he found those books? A low place near the main excavations. Sam can look for me there."

"I'll tell him," I promised, blinking against the cold wind, which irritated my eyes.

"Thank you, Adam," he said gravely. "For everything." Then he forced a smile, and for a moment was just Julian, the friend with whom I had hunted squirrels and spun tales: "Merry Christmas," he said. "Happy New Year!"

And wheeled his horse about, and rode away.

V

There is a Dominion cemetery in Williams Ford, and I passed it on the ride back home—carved stones sepulchral in the moonlight—but my sister Flaxie was not buried there.

As I have said, the Church of Signs was tolerated but not endorsed by the Dominion. We were not entitled to plots in the Dominion yard. Flaxie had a place in the acreage behind our cottage, marked by a modest wooden cross, but the cemetery put me in mind of Flaxie nonetheless, and after I returned the horse to the barn I stopped by Flaxie's grave (despite the shivery cold) and tipped my hat to her, the way I had always tipped my hat to her in life.

Flaxie had been a bright, impudent, mischievous small thing—as golden-haired as her nickname implied. (Her given name was Dolores, but she was always Flaxie to me.) The Pox had taken her quite suddenly and, as these things go, mercifully. I didn't remember her death; I had been down with the same Pox, though I had survived it. What I remembered was waking up from my fever into a house gone strangely quiet. No one had wanted to tell me about Flaxie, but I had seen my mother's tormented eyes, and I knew the truth without having to be told. Death had played lottery with us, and Flaxie had drawn the short straw.

(It is, I think, for the likes of Flaxie that we maintain a belief in Heaven. I have met very few adults, outside the enthusiasts of the established Church, who genuinely believe in Heaven, and Heaven was scant consolation for my grieving mother. But Flaxie, who was five, had believed in it fervently—imagined it was something like a meadow, with wildflowers blooming, and a perpetual summer picnic underway—and if that childish belief soothed her in her extremity, then it served a purpose more noble than truth.)

Tonight the cottage was almost as quiet as it had been during the mourning that followed Flaxie's death. I came through the door to find my mother dabbing her eyes with a handkerchief, and my father frowning over his pipe, which, uncharacteristically, he had filled and lit. "The draft," he said.

"Yes," I said. "I heard about it."

My mother was too distraught to speak. My father said, "We'll do what we can to protect you, Adam. But—"

"I'm not afraid to serve my country," I said.

"That's a praiseworthy attitude," my father said glumly, and my mother wept even harder. "But we don't yet know what might be necessary. Maybe the situation in Labrador isn't as bad as it seems."

Scant of words though my father was, I had often enough relied on him for advice, which he had freely given. He was fully aware, for instance, of my distaste for snakes—for which reason, abetted by my mother, I had been allowed to avoid the sacraments of our faith, and the venomous swellings and occasional amputations inflicted upon other parishioners—and, while this disappointed him, he had nevertheless taught me the practical aspects of snake-handling, including how to grasp a serpent in such a way as to avoid its bite, and how to kill one, should the necessity arise.[7] He was a practical man despite his unusual beliefs.

But he had no advice to offer me tonight. He looked like a hunted man who has come to the end of a cul-de-sac, and can neither go forward nor turn back.

I went to my bedroom, although I doubted I would be able to sleep. Instead—without any real plan in mind—I bundled a few of my possessions for easy carrying. My squirrel-gun, chiefly, and some notes and writing, and the *History of Mankind in Space*; and I thought I should add some salted pork, or something of that nature, but I resolved to wait until later, so my mother wouldn't see me packing.

Before dawn, I put on several layers of clothing and a heavy pakool hat, rolled down so the wool covered my ears. I opened the window of my room and clambered over the sill and closed the glass behind me, after I had retrieved my rifle and gear. Then I crept across the open yard to the barn, and saddled up a horse (the gelding named Rapture, who was the fastest, though this would leave my father's rig an animal shy), and rode out under a sky that had just begun to show first light.

Last night's brief snowfall still covered the ground. I was not the first up this winter morning, and the cold air already smelled of Christmas. The bakery in Williams Ford was busy making nativity cakes and cinnamon buns. The sweet, yeasty smell filled the northwest end of town like an intoxicating fog, for there was no wind to carry it away. The day was dawning blue and still.

Signs of Christmas were everywhere—as they ought to be, for today was the Eve of that universal holiday—but so was evidence of the conscription drive. The Reservists were already awake, passing like shadows in their scruffy uniforms, and a crowd of them had gathered by the hardware store. They had hung out a faded flag and posted a sign, which I could not read, because I was determined to keep a distance between myself and the soldiers; but I knew a recruiting-post when I saw one. I did not doubt that the main ways in and out of town had been put under close observation.

I took a back way to the Estate, the same riverside road Julian and I had traveled

---

[7] "Grasp it where its neck ought to be, behind the head; ignore the tail, however it may thrash; and crack its skull, hard and often enough to subdue it." I had recounted these instructions to Julian, whose horror of serpents far exceeded my own: "Oh, I could never do such a thing!" he had exclaimed. This surfeit of timidity may surprise readers who have followed his later career.

the night before. Because of the lack of wind, our tracks were undisturbed. We were the only ones who had recently passed this way. Rapture was revisiting his own hoof-prints.

Close to the Estate, but still within a concealing grove of pines, I lashed the horse to a sapling and proceeded on foot.

The Duncan-Crowley Estate was not fenced, for there was no real demarcation of its boundaries; under the Leasing System, everything in Williams Ford was owned (in the legal sense) by the two great families. I approached from the western side, which was half-wooded and used by the aristos for casual riding and hunting. This morning the copse was not inhabited, and I saw no one until I had passed the snow-mounded hedges which marked the beginning of the formal gardens. Here, in summer, apple and cherry trees blossomed and produced fruit; flowerbeds gave forth symphonies of color and scent; bees nursed in languid ecstasies. But now it was barren, the paths quilted with snow, and there was no one visible but the senior groundskeeper, sweeping the wooden portico of the nearest of the Estate's several Great Houses.

The Houses were dressed for Christmas. Christmas was a grander event at the Estate than in the town proper, as might be expected. The winter population of the Duncan-Crowley Estate was not as large as its summer population, but there was still a number of both families, plus whatever cousins and hangers-on had elected to hibernate over the cold season. Sam Godwin, as Julian's tutor, was not permitted to sleep in either of the two most luxurious buildings, but bunked among the elite staff in a white-pillared house that would have passed for a mansion anywhere but here. This was where he had conducted classes for Julian and me, and I knew the building intimately. It, too, was dressed for Christmas; a holly wreath hung on the door; pine boughs were suspended over the lintels; a Banner of the Cross dangled from the eaves. The door was not locked, and I let myself in quietly.

It was still early in the morning, at least as the aristos and their elite helpers calculated time. The tiled entranceway was empty and still. I went straight for the rooms where Sam Godwin slept and conducted his classes, down an oaken corridor lit only by the dawn filtering through a window at the long end. The floor was carpeted and gave no sound, though my shoes left damp footprints behind me.

At Sam's door, I was confronted with a dilemma. I could not knock, for fear of alerting others. My mission as I saw it was to deliver Julian's message as discreetly as possible. But neither could I walk in on a sleeping man—could I?

I tried the handle of the door. It moved freely. I opened the door a fraction of an inch, meaning to whisper, "Sam?"—and give him some warning.

But I could hear Sam's voice, low and muttering, as if he were talking to himself. I listened more closely. The words seemed strange. He was speaking in a guttural language, not English. Perhaps he wasn't alone. It was too late to back away, however, so I decided to brazen it out. I opened the door entirely and stepped inside, saying, "Sam! It's me, Adam. I have a message from Julian—"

I stopped short, alarmed by what I saw. Sam Godwin—the same gruff but familiar Sam who had taught me the rudiments of history and geography—was practicing *black magic*, or some other form of witchcraft, *on Christmas Eve*! He wore a striped cowl about his shoulders, and leather lacings on his arm, and a boxlike implement strapped to his forehead; and his hands were upraised over an arrangement of nine candles mounted in a brass holder that appeared to have been scavenged from some ancient Tip. The invocation he had been murmuring seemed to echo through the room: Bah-*rook*-a-*tah*-atten-*eye*-hello-*hey*-noo . . .

My jaw dropped.

"Adam!" Sam said, almost as startled as I was, and he quickly pulled the shawl from his back and began to unlace his various unholy riggings.

This was so irregular I could barely comprehend it.

Then I was afraid I *did* comprehend it. Often enough in Dominion school I had heard Ben Kreel speak about the vices and wickedness of the Secular Era, some of which still lingered, he said, in the cities of the East—irreverence, irreligiosity, skepticism, occultism, depravity. And I thought of the ideas I had so casually imbibed from Julian and (indirectly) from Sam, some of which I had even begun to believe: Einsteinism, Darwinism, space travel . . . had I been seduced by the outrunners of some New Yorkish paganism? Had I been duped by Philosophy?

"A message," Sam said, concealing his heathenish gear, "what message? Where is Julian?"

But I could not stay. I fled the room.

Sam barreled out of the house after me. I was fast, but he was long-legged and conditioned by his military career, strong for all his forty-odd years, and he caught me in the winter gardens—tackled me from behind. I kicked and tried to pull away, but he pinned my shoulders.

"Adam, for God's sake, settle down!" cried he. That was impudent, I thought, invoking God, *him*—but then he said, "Don't you understand what you saw? I am a Jew!"

A Jew!

Of course, I had heard of Jews. They lived in the Bible, and in New York City. Their equivocal relationship with Our Savior had won them opprobrium down the ages, and they were not approved of by the Dominion. But I had never seen a living Jew in the flesh—to my knowledge—and I was astonished by the idea that Sam had been one all along: *invisibly,* so to speak.

"You deceived everyone, then!" I said.

"I never claimed to be a Christian! I never spoke of it at all. But what does it matter? You said you had a message from Julian—give it to me, damn you! Where is he?"

I wondered what I should say, or who I might betray if I said it. The world had turned upside-down. All Ben Kreel's lectures on patriotism and fidelity came back to me in one great flood of guilt and shame. Had I been a party to treason as well as atheism?

But I felt I owed this last favor to Julian, who would surely have wanted me to deliver his intelligence whether Sam was a Jew or a Mohammedan: "There are soldiers on all the roads out of town," I said sullenly. "Julian went for Lundsford last night. He says he'll meet you there. Now *get off of me!*"

Sam did so, sitting back on his heels, deep anxiety inscribed upon his face. "Has it begun so soon? I thought they would wait for the New Year."

"I don't know *what* has begun. I don't think I know anything at all!" And, so saying, I leapt to my feet and ran out of the lifeless garden, back to Rapture, who was still tied to the tree where I had left him, nosing unproductively in the undisturbed snow.

I had ridden perhaps an eighth of a mile back toward Williams Ford when another rider came up on my right flank from behind. It was Ben Kreel himself, and he touched his cap and smiled and said, "Do you mind if I ride along with you a ways, Adam Hazzard?"

I could hardly say no.

Ben Kreel was not a pastor—we had plenty of those in Williams Ford, each catering to his own denomination—but he was the head of the local Council of the Dominion of Jesus Christ on Earth, almost as powerful in his way as the men who owned the Estate. And if he was not a pastor, he was at least a sort of shepherd to the townspeople. He had been born right here in Williams Ford, son of a saddler; had been educated, at the Estate's expense, at one of the Dominion Colleges in Colorado Springs; and for the last twenty years he had taught elementary school five days a week and General Christianity on Sundays. I had marked my first letters on a slate board under Ben Kreel's tutelage. Every Independence Day he addressed the townsfolk and reminded them of the symbolism and significance of the Thirteen Stripes and the Sixty Stars; every Christmas, he led the Ecumenical Services at the Dominion Hall.

He was stout and graying at the temples, clean-shaven. He wore a woolen jacket, tall deer hide boots, and a pakool hat not much grander than my own. But he carried himself with an immense dignity, as much in the saddle as on foot. The expression on his face was kindly. It was always kindly. "You're out early, Adam Hazzard," he said. "What are you doing abroad at this hour?"

"Nothing," I said, and blushed. Is there any other word that so spectacularly represents everything it wants to deny? Under the circumstances, "nothing" amounted to a confession of bad intent. "Couldn't sleep," I added hastily. "Thought I might shoot a squirrel or so." That would explain the rifle strapped to my saddle, and it was at least remotely plausible; the squirrels were still active, doing the last of their scrounging before settling in for the cold months.

"On Christmas Eve?" Ben Kreel asked. "And in the copse on the grounds of the Estate? I hope the Duncans and Crowleys don't hear about it. They're jealous of their trees. And I'm sure gunfire would disturb them at this hour. Wealthy men and Easterners prefer to sleep past dawn, as a rule."

"I didn't fire," I muttered. "I thought better of it."

"Well, good. Wisdom prevails. You're headed back to town, I gather?"

"Yes, sir."

"Let me keep you company, then."

"Please do." I could hardly say otherwise, no matter how I longed to be alone with my thoughts.

Our horses moved slowly—the snow made for awkward footing—and Ben Kreel was silent for a long while. Then he said, "You needn't conceal your fears, Adam. I know what's troubling you."

For a moment I had the terrible idea that Ben Kreel had been behind me in the hallway at the Estate, and that he had seen Sam Godwin wrapped in his Old Testament paraphernalia. Wouldn't that create a scandal! (And then I thought that it was exactly such a scandal Sam must have feared all his life: it was worse even than being Church of Signs, for in some states a Jew can be fined or even imprisoned for practicing his faith. I didn't know where Athabaska stood on the issue, but I feared the worst.) But Ben Kreel was talking about conscription, not about Sam.

"I've already discussed this with some of the boys in town," he said. "You're not alone, Adam, if you're wondering what it all means, this military movement, and what might happen as a result of it. And I admit, you're something of a special case. I've been keeping an eye on you. From a distance, as it were. Here, stop a moment."

We had come to a rise in the road, on a bluff above the River Pine, looking south toward Williams Ford from a little height.

"Gaze at that," Ben Kreel said contemplatively. He stretched his arm out in an arc, as if to include not just the cluster of buildings that was the town but the empty fields as well, and the murky flow of the river, and the wheels of the mills, and even the shacks of the indentured laborers down in the low country. The valley seemed at once a living thing, inhaling the crisp atmosphere of the season and breathing out its steams, and a portrait, static in the still blue winter air. As deeply rooted as an oak, as fragile as a ball of Nativity glass.

"Gaze at that," Ben Kreel repeated. "Look at Williams Ford, laid out pretty there. What is it, Adam? More than a place, I think. It's a way of life. It's the sum of all our labors. It's what our fathers have given us and it's what we give our sons. It's where we bury our mothers and where our daughters will be buried."

Here was more Philosophy, then, and after the turmoil of the morning I wasn't sure I wanted any. But Ben Kreel's voice ran on like the soothing syrup my mother used to administer whenever Flaxie or I came down with a cough.

"Every boy in Williams Ford—every boy old enough to submit himself for national service—is just now discovering how reluctant he is to leave the place he knows best. Even you, I suspect."

"I'm no more or less willing than anyone else."

"I'm not questioning your courage or your loyalty. It's just that I know you've had a little taste of what life might be like elsewhere—given how closely you associated yourself with Julian Comstock. Now, I'm sure Julian's a fine young man and an excellent Christian. He could hardly be otherwise, could he, as the nephew of the man who holds this nation in his palm. But his experience has been very different from yours. He's accustomed to cities—to movies like the one we saw at the Hall last night (and I glimpsed you there, didn't I? Sitting in the back pews?)—to books and ideas that might strike a youth of your background as exciting and, well, *different*. Am I wrong?"

"I could hardly say you are, sir."

"And much of what Julian may have described to you is no doubt true. I've traveled some myself, you know. I've seen Colorado Springs, Pittsburgh, even New York City. Our eastern cities are great, proud metropolises—some of the biggest and most productive in the world—and they're worth defending, which is one reason we're trying so hard to drive the Dutch out of Labrador."

"Surely you're right."

"I'm glad you agree. Because there is a trap certain young people fall into. I've seen it before. Sometimes a boy decides that one of those great cities might be a place he can *run away to*—a place where he can escape all the duties, obligations, and moral lessons he learned at his mother's knee. Simple things like faith and patriotism can begin to seem to a young man like burdens, which might be shrugged off when they become too weighty."

"I'm not like that, sir."

"Of course not. But there is yet another element in the calculation. You may have to leave Williams Ford because of the conscription. And the thought that runs through many boys' minds is, if I *must* leave, then perhaps I ought to leave on my own hook, and find my destiny on a city's streets rather than in a battalion of the Athabaska Brigade . . . and you're good to deny it, Adam, but you wouldn't be human if such ideas didn't cross your mind."

"No, sir," I muttered, and I must admit I felt a dawning guilt, for I had in fact been a little seduced by Julian's tales of city life, and Sam's dubious lessons, and the *History of Mankind in Space*—perhaps I *had* forgotten something of my obligations to the village that lay so still and so inviting in the blue near distance.

"I know," Ben Kreel said, "that things haven't always been easy for your family. Your father's faith, in particular, has been a trial, and we haven't always been good neighbors—speaking on behalf of the village as a whole. Perhaps you've been left out of some activities other boys enjoy as a matter of course: church activities, picnics, common friendships . . . well, even Williams Ford isn't perfect. But I promise you, Adam: If you find yourself in the Brigades, especially if you find yourself tested in time of war, you'll discover that the same boys who shunned you in the dusty streets of your hometown become your best friends and bravest defenders, and you theirs. For our common heritage ties us together in ways that may seem obscure, but become obvious under the harsh light of combat."

I had spent so much time smarting under the remarks of other boys (that my father "raised vipers the way other folks raise chickens," for example) that I could hardly credit Ben Kreel's assertion. But I knew little of modern warfare, except what I had read in the novels of Mr. Charles Curtis Easton, so it might be true. And the prospect (as was intended) made me feel even more shame-faced.

"There," Ben Kreel said: "Do you hear that, Adam?"

I did. I could hardly avoid it. The bell was ringing in the Dominion church, calling together one of the early ecumenical services. It was a silvery sound on the winter air, at once lonesome and consoling, and I wanted almost to run toward it—to shelter in it, as if I were a child again.

"They'll want me soon," Ben Kreel said. "Will you excuse me if I ride ahead?"

"No, sir. Please don't mind about me."

"As long as we understand each other, Adam. Don't look so downcast! The future may be brighter than you expect."

"Thank you for saying so, sir."

I stayed a while longer on the low bluff, watching as Ben Kreel's horse carried him toward town. Even in the sunlight it was cold, and I shivered some, perhaps more because of the conflict in my mind than because of the weather. The Dominion man had made me ashamed of myself, and had put into perspective my loose ways of the last few years, and pointed up how many of my native beliefs I had abandoned before the seductive Philosophy of an agnostic young aristo and an aging Jew.

Then I sighed and urged Rapture back along the path toward Williams Ford, meaning to explain to my parents where I had been and reassure them that I would not suffer too much in the coming conscription, to which I would willingly submit.

I was so disheartened by the morning's events that my eyes drifted toward the ground even as Rapture retraced his steps. As I have said, the snows of the night before lay largely undisturbed on this back trail between the town and the Estate. I could see where I had passed this morning, where Rapture's hoofprints were as clearly written as figures in a book. (Ben Kreel must have spent the night at the Estate, and when he left me on the bluff he would have taken the more direct route toward town; only Rapture had passed this way.) Then I reached the place where Julian and I had parted the night before. There were more hoofprints here, in fact a crowd of them—

And I saw something else written (in effect) on the snowy ground—something which alarmed me.

I reined up at once.

I looked south, toward Williams Ford. I looked east, the way Julian had gone the previous night.

Then I took a bracing inhalation of icy air, and followed the trail that seemed to me most urgent.

VI

The east-west road through Williams Ford is not heavily traveled, especially in winter.

The southern road—also called the Wire Road, because the telegraph line runs alongside it—connects Williams Ford to the railhead at Connaught, and thus sustains a great deal of traffic. But the east-west road goes essentially nowhere: It is a remnant of a road of the secular ancients, traversed mainly by Tipmen and freelance antiquarians, and then only in the warmer months. I suppose if you followed the old road as far as it would take you, you might reach the Great Lakes, or somewhere farther east, in that direction; and, the opposite way, you could get yourself lost among washouts and landfalls in the Rocky Mountains. But the railroad—and a parallel turnpike farther south—had obviated the need for all that trouble.

Nevertheless, the east-west road was closely watched where it left the outskirts of Williams Ford. The Reserves had posted a man on a hill overlooking it, the same hill where Julian and Sam and I had paused for blackberries on our way from the Tip last October. But it is a fact that the Reserve troops were held in Reserve, and not sent to the front lines, mainly because of some disabling flaw of body or mind; some were wounded veterans, missing a hand or an arm; some were too simple or sullen to function in a disciplined body of soldiers. I cannot say anything for certain about the man posted as lookout on the hill, but if he was not a fool he was at least utterly unconcerned about concealment, for his silhouette (and that of his rifle) stood etched against the bright eastern sky for all to see. But maybe that was the intent: to let prospective fugitives know their way was barred.

Not *every* way was barred, however, not for someone who had grown up in Williams Ford and hunted everywhere on its perimeter. Instead of following Julian directly I rode north a distance, and then through the crowded lanes of an encampment of indentured laborers (whose ragged children gaped at me from the glassless windows of their shanties, and whose soft-coal fires made a smoky gauze of the motionless air). This route connected with lanes cut through the wheat fields for the transportation of harvests and field-hands—lanes that had been deepened by years of use, so that I rode behind a berm of earth and snake rail fences, hidden from the distant sentinel. When I was safely east, I came down a cattle-trail that reconnected me with the east-west road.

On which I was able to read the same signs that had alerted me back at Williams Ford, thanks to the fine layer of snow still undisturbed by any wind.

Julian had come this way. He had done as he had intended, and ridden toward Lundsford before midnight. The snow had stopped soon thereafter, leaving his horse's hoof-prints clearly visible, though softened and half-covered.

But his were not the only tracks: There was a second set, more crisply defined and hence more recent, probably set down during the night; and this was what I had seen at the crossroads in Williams Ford: evidence of pursuit. Someone had followed Julian, without Julian's knowledge. This had dire implications, the only redeeming circumstance being the fact of a single pursuer rather than a company of men. If the powerful people of the Estate had known that it was Julian Comstock who had fled, they would surely have sent an entire brigade to bring him back. I supposed Julian had been mistaken for a simple miscreant, a labor refugee, or a youngster fleeing the conscription, and that he had been followed by some ambitious Reservist. Otherwise that whole imagined battalion might be right behind me . . . or perhaps soon *would* be, since Julian's absence must have been noted by now.

I rode east, adding my own track to these two.

Before long it was past noon, and I started to have second thoughts as the sun began to angle toward an early rendezvous with the southwestern horizon. What exactly did I hope to accomplish? To warn Julian? If so, I was a little late off the mark . . . though I hoped that at some point Julian had covered his tracks, or otherwise misled his pursuer, who did not have the advantage I had, of knowing where Julian meant to stay until Sam Godwin could arrive. Failing that, I half-imagined *rescuing* Julian from capture, even though I had but a squirrel rifle and a few rounds of ammunition (plus a knife and my own wits, both feeble enough weapons) against whatever a Reservist might carry. In any case these were more wishes and anxieties than calculations or plans; I had no fully formed plan beyond riding to Julian's aid and telling him that I had delivered my message to Sam, who would be along as soon as he could discreetly leave the Estate.

And then what? It was a question I dared not ask myself—not out on this lonely road, well past the Tip now, farther than I had ever been from Williams Ford; not out here where the flatlands stretched on each side of the path like the frosty plains of Mars, and the wind, which had been absent all morning, began to pluck at the fringes of my coat, and my shadow elongated in front of me like a scarecrow gone riding. It was cold and getting colder, and soon the winter moon would be aloft, and me with only a few ounces of salt pork in my saddlebag and a few matches to make a fire if I was able to secure any kindling by nightfall. I began to wonder if I had gone quite insane. At several points I thought: I could go back; perhaps I hadn't yet been missed; perhaps it wasn't too late to sit down to a Christmas Eve dinner with my parents, raise a glass of cider to Flaxie and to Christmases past, and wake in time to hear the ringing-in of the Holiday and smell the goodness of baked bread and Nativity apples drenched in cinnamon and brown sugar. I mused on it repeatedly, sometimes with tears in my eyes; but I let Rapture continue carrying me toward the darkest part of the horizon.

Then, after what seemed endless hours of dusk, with only a brief pause when both Rapture and I drank from a creek which had a skin of ice on it, I began to come among the ruins of the secular ancients.

Not that there was anything spectacular about them. Fanciful drawings often portray the ruins of the last century as tall buildings, ragged and hollow as broken teeth, forming vine-encrusted canyons and shadowy cul-de-sacs.[8] No doubt such places exist—most of them in the uninhabitable Southwest, however, where "famine sits enthroned, and waves his scepter over a dominion expressly made for him," which would rule out vines and such tropical items[9]—but most ruins were like the ones I now passed, mere irregularities (or more precisely, *regularities*) in the landscape, which indicated the former presence of foundations. These terrains were treacherous, often concealing deep basements that could open like hungry mouths on an unwary traveler, and only Tipmen loved them. I was careful to keep to the path, though I began to wonder whether Julian would be as easy to find as I had imagined—Lundsford was a big locality, and the wind had already begun to scour away the hoofprints I had relied on for navigation.

I was haunted, too, by thoughts of the False Tribulation of the last century. It was not unusual to come across desiccated human remains in localities like this. Millions had died in the worst dislocations of the End of Oil: of disease, of internecine strife, but mostly of starvation. The Age of Oil had allowed a fierce intensity of fertilization and irrigation of the land, which had fed more people than a humbler agriculture could support. I had seen photographs of Americans from that blighted age, thin as sticks, their children with distended bellies, crowded into "relief camps" that would soon enough be transformed into communal graves when the imagined "relief" failed to materialize. No wonder, then, that our ancestors had mistaken those decades for the Tribulation of prophecy. What was astonishing was how many of our current institutions—the Church, the Army, the Federal Government—had survived more or less intact. There was a passage in the Dominion Bible that Ben Kreel had read whenever the subject of the False Tribulation arose in school, and which I had committed to memory: *The field is wasted, the land mourns; for the corn is shriveled, the wine has dried, the oil languishes. Be ashamed, farmers; howl, vine-keepers; howl for the wheat and the barley, for the harvest of the field has perished . . .*

It had made me shiver then, and it made me shiver now, in these barrens which

---

[8] Or "culs-de-sac"? My French is rudimentary.
[9] Though Old Miami or Orlando might begin to fit the bill.

had been stripped of all their utility by a century of scavenging. Where in this rubble was Julian, and where was his pursuer?

It was by his fire I found him. But I was not the first to arrive.

The sun was altogether down, and a hint of the aurora borealis played about the northern sky, dimmed by moonlight, when I came to the most recently excavated section of Lundsford. The temporary dwellings of the Tipmen—rude huts of scavenged timber—had been abandoned here for the season, and corduroy ramps led down into the empty digs.

Here the remnants of last night's snow had been blown into windrows and small dunes, and all evidence of hoofprints had been erased. But I rode slowly, knowing I was close to my destination. I was buoyed by the observation that Julian's pursuer, whoever he was, had not returned this way from his mission: had not, that is, taken Julian captive, or at least had not gone back to Williams Ford with his prisoner in tow. Perhaps the pursuit had been suspended for the night.

It was not long—though it seemed an eternity, as Rapture short-stepped down the frozen road, avoiding snow-hidden pitfalls—before I heard the whickering of another horse, and saw a plume of smoke rising into the moon-bright sky.

Quickly I turned Rapture off the road and tied his reins to the low remnants of a concrete pillar, from which rust-savaged iron rods protruded like skeletal fingers. I took my squirrel rifle from the saddle holster and moved toward the source of the smoke on foot, until I was able to discern that the fumes emerged from a deep declivity in the landscape, perhaps the very dig from which the Tipmen had extracted the *History of Mankind in Space*. Surely this was where Julian had gone to wait for Sam's arrival. And indeed, here was Julian's horse, one of the finer riding horses from the Estate (worth more, I'm sure, in the eyes of its owner, than a hundred Julian Comstocks), moored to an outcrop . . . and, alarmingly, here was another horse as well, not far away. This second horse was a stranger to me; it was slat-ribbed and elderly looking; but it wore a military bridle and the sort of cloth bib—blue, with a red star in the middle of it—that marked a mount belonging to the Reserves.

I studied the situation from behind the moon-shadow of a broken abutment. The smoke suggested that Julian had gone beneath ground, down into the hollow of the Tipmen's dig, to shelter from the cold and bank his fire for the night. The presence of the second horse suggested that he had been discovered, and that his pursuer must already have confronted him.

More than that I could not divine. It remained only to approach the contested grounds as secretively as possible, and see what more I could learn.

I crept closer. The dig was revealed by moonlight as a deep but narrow excavation, covered in part with boards, with a sloping entrance at one end. The glow of the fire within was just visible, as was the chimney-hole that had been cut through the planking some yards farther down. There was, as far as I could discern, only one way in or out. I determined to proceed as far as I could without being seen, and to that end I lowered myself down the slope, inching forward on the seat of my pants over ground that was as cold, it seemed to me, as the wastelands of the Arctic north.

I was slow, I was cautious, and I was quiet. But I was not slow, cautious, or quiet *enough*; for I had just progressed far enough to glimpse an excavated chamber, in which the firelight cast a kaleidoscopic flux of shadows, when I felt a pressure behind my ear—the barrel of a gun—and a voice said, "Keep moving, mister, and join your friend below."

I kept silent until I could comprehend more of the situation I had fallen into.

My captor marched me down into the low part of the dig. The air, if damp, was noticeably warmer here, and we were screened from the increasing wind, though not from the accumulated odors of the fire and the stagnant must of what had once been a basement or cellar in some commercial establishment of the secular ancients.

The Tipmen had not left much behind: only a rubble of broken bits of things, indistinguishable under layers of dust and dirt. The far wall was of concrete, and the fire had been banked against it, under a chimney-hole that must have been cut by the scavengers during their labors. A circle of stones hedged the fire, and the damp planks and splinters in it crackled with a deceptive cheerfulness. Deeper parts of the excavation, with ceilings lower than a man standing erect, opened in several directions.

Julian sat near the fire, his back to the wall and his knees drawn up under his chin. His clothes had been made filthy by the grime of the place. He was frowning, and when he saw me his frown deepened into a scowl.

"Go over there and get beside him," my captor said, "but give me that little bird rifle first."

I surrendered my weapon, modest as it was, and joined Julian. Thus I was able to get my first clear look at the man who had captured me. He appeared not much older than myself, but he was dressed in the blue and yellow uniform of the Reserves. His Reserve cap was pulled low over his eyes, which twitched left and right as though he were in constant fear of an ambush. In short, he seemed both inexperienced and nervous—and maybe a little dim, for his jaw was slack, and he was evidently unaware of the dribble of mucus that escaped his nostrils as a result of the cold weather. (But as I have said before, this was not untypical of the members of the Reserve, who were kept out of active duty for a reason.)

His weapon, however, was very much in earnest, and not to be trifled with. It was a Pittsburgh rifle manufactured by the Porter & Earle works, which loaded at the breech from a sort of cassette and could fire five rounds in succession without any more attention from its owner than a twitch of the index finger. Julian had carried a similar weapon but had been disarmed of it; it rested against a stack of small staved barrels, well out of reach, and the Reservist put my squirrel rifle beside it.

I began to feel sorry for myself, and to think what a poor way of spending Christmas Eve I had chosen. I did not resent the action of the Reservist nearly as much as I resented my own stupidity and lapse of judgment.

"I don't know who you are," the Reservist said, "and I don't care—one draft-dodger is as good as the next, in my opinion—but I was given the job of collecting runaways, and my bag is getting full. I hope you'll both keep till morning, when I can ride you back into Williams Ford. Anyhow, none of us shall sleep tonight. I won't, in any case, so you might as well resign yourself to your captivity. If you're hungry, there's a little meat."

I was never less hungry in my life, and I began to say so, but Julian interrupted: "It's true, Adam," he said, "we're fairly caught. I wish you hadn't come after me."

"I'm beginning to feel the same way," I said.

He gave me a meaningful look, and said in a lower voice, "Is Sam—?"

"No whispering there," our captor said at once.

But I divined the intent of the question, and nodded to indicate that I had delivered Julian's message, though that was by no means a guarantee of our deliverance. Not only were the exits from Williams Ford under close watch, but Sam could not slip away as inconspicuously as I had, and if Julian's absence had been noted, there would have been a redoubling of the guard, and perhaps an expedition sent out to hunt us. The man who had captured Julian was evidently an outrider, assigned to patrol the roads for runaways, and he had been diligent in his work.

He was somewhat less diligent now that he had us in his control, however, for he took a wooden pipe from his pocket, and proceeded to fill it, as he made himself as comfortable as possible on a wooden crate. His gestures were still nervous, and I supposed the pipe was meant to relax him; for it was not tobacco he put into it.

The Reservist might have been a Kentuckian, for I understand the less respectable people of that State often form the habit of smoking the silk of the female hemp plant, which is cultivated prodigiously there. Kentucky hemp is grown for cordage and cloth and paper, and as a drug is less intoxicating than the Indian Hemp of lore; but its mild smoke is said to be pleasant for those who indulge in it, though too much can result in sleepiness and great thirst.

Julian evidently thought these symptoms would be welcome distractions in our captor, and he gestured to me to remain silent, so as not to interrupt the Reservist in his vice. The Reservist packed the pipe's bowl with dried vegetable matter from an oilcloth envelope he carried in his pocket, and soon the substance was alight, and a slightly more fragrant smoke joined the effluvium of the campfire as it swirled toward the rent in the ceiling.

Clearly the night would be a long one, and I tried to be patient in my captivity, and not think too much of Christmas matters, or the yellow light of my parents' cottage on dark winter mornings, or the soft bed where I might have been sleeping if I had not been rash in my deliberations.

VII

I began by saying this was a story about Julian Comstock, and I fear I lied, for it has turned out mainly to be a story about myself.

But there is a reason for this, beyond the obvious temptations of vanity and self-regard. I did not at the time know Julian nearly as well as I thought I did.

Our friendship was essentially a boys' friendship. I could not help reviewing, as we sat in silent captivity in the ruins of Lundsford, the things we had done together: reading books, hunting in the wooded foothills west of Williams Ford, arguing amiably over everything from Philosophy and Moon-Visiting to the best way to bait a hook or cinch a bridle. It had been too easy, during our time together, to forget that Julian was an aristo with close connections to men of power, or that his father had been famous both as a hero and as a traitor, or that his uncle Deklan Comstock, the President, might not have Julian's best interests at heart.

All that seemed far away, and distant from the nature of Julian's true spirit, which was gentle and inquisitive—a naturalist's disposition, not a politician's or a general's. When I pictured Julian as an adult, I imagined him contentedly pursuing some scholarly or artistic adventure: digging the bones of pre-Noachian monsters out of the Athabaska shale, perhaps, or making an improved kind of movie. He was not a warlike person, and the thoughts of the great men of the day seemed almost exclusively concerned with war.

So I had let myself forget that he was *also* everything he had been before he came to Williams Ford. He was the heir of a brave, determined, and ultimately betrayed father, who had conquered an army of Brazilians but had been crushed by the millstone of political intrigue. He was the son of a powerful woman, born to a powerful family of her own—not powerful enough to save Bryce Comstock from the gallows, but powerful enough to protect Julian, at least temporarily, from the mad calculations of his uncle. He was both a pawn and a player in the great games of the aristos. And while I had forgotten all this, Julian had *not*—these were the people who had made him, and if he chose not to speak of them, they nevertheless must have haunted his thoughts.

He was, it is true, often frightened of small things—I still remember his disquiet when I described the rituals of the Church of Signs to him, and he would sometimes shriek at the distress of animals when our hunting failed to result in a clean kill. But tonight, here in the ruins, I was the one who half-dozed in a morose funk, fighting tears; while it was Julian who sat intently still, gazing with resolve from beneath the strands of dusty hair that straggled over his brows, as coolly calculating as a bank clerk.

When we hunted, he often gave me the rifle to fire the last lethal shot, distrusting his own resolve.

Tonight—had the opportunity presented itself—I would have given the rifle to him.

I half-dozed, as I said, and from time to time woke to see the Reservist still sitting in guard. His eyelids were at half-mast, but I put that down to the effect of the hemp flowers he had smoked. Periodically he would start, as if at a sound inaudible to others, then settle back into place.

He had boiled a copious amount of coffee in a tin pan, and he warmed it whenever he renewed the fire, and drank sufficiently to keep himself from falling asleep. Of necessity, this meant he must once in a while retreat to a distant part of the dig and attend to physical necessities in relative privacy. This did not give us any advantage, however, since he carried his Pittsburgh rifle with him, but it allowed a moment or two in which Julian could whisper without being overheard.

"This man is no mental giant," Julian said. "We may yet get out of here with our freedom."

"It's not his *brains* so much as his *artillery* that's stopping us," said I.

"Perhaps we can separate the one from the other. Look there, Adam. Beyond the fire—back in the rubble."

I looked.

There was motion in the shadows, which I began to recognize.

"The distraction may suit our purposes," Julian said, "unless it becomes fatal." And I saw the sweat that had begun to stand out on his forehead, the terror barely hidden in his eyes. "But I need your help."

I have said that I did not take part in the particular rites of my father's church, and that snakes were not my favorite creatures. This is true. As much as I have heard about surrendering one's volition to God—and I had seen my father with a Massass-sauga Rattler in each hand, trembling with devotion, speaking in a tongue not only foreign but utterly unknown (though it favored long vowels and stuttered conso-nants, much like the sounds he made when he burned his fingers on the coal stove)—I could never entirely assure myself that I would be protected by divine will from the serpent's bite. Some in the congregation obviously had not been: There was Sarah Prestley, for instance, whose right arm had swollen up black with venom and had to be amputated by Williams Ford's physician . . . but I will not dwell on that. The point is, that while I *disliked* snakes, I was not especially *afraid* of them, as Julian was. And I could not help admiring his restraint: for what was writhing in the shadows nearby was a nest of snakes that had been aroused by the heat of the fire.

I should add that it was not uncommon for these collapsed ruins to be infested with snakes, mice, spiders, and poisonous insects. Death by bite or sting was one of the hazards routinely faced by Tipmen, the others including concussion, blood poi-soning, and accidental burial. The snakes, after the Tipmen ceased work for the win-ter, must have crept into this chasm anticipating an undisturbed hibernation, of which we and the Reservist had unfortunately deprived them.

The Reservist—who came back a little unsteadily from his necessaries—had not yet noticed these prior tenants. He seated himself on his crate, scowled at us, and studiously refilled his pipe.

"If he discharges all five shots from his rifle," Julian whispered, "then we have a chance of overcoming him, or of recovering our own weapons. But, Adam—"

"No talking there," the Reservist mumbled.

"—*you must remember your father's advice*," Julian finished.

"I said keep quiet!"

Julian cleared his throat and addressed the Reservist directly, since the time for action had obviously arrived: "Sir, I have to draw your attention to something."

"What would that be, my little draft dodger?"

"I'm afraid we're not alone in this terrible place."

"Not alone!" the Reservist said, casting his eyes about him nervously. Then he re-covered and squinted at Julian. "I don't see any other persons."

"I don't mean persons, but vipers," said Julian.

"Vipers!"

"In other words—snakes."

At this the Reservist started again, his mind perhaps still slightly confused by the effects of the hemp smoke; then he sneered and said, "Go on, you can't pull that one on me."

"I'm sorry if you think I'm joking, for there are at least a dozen snakes advancing from the shadows, and one of them is about to achieve intimacy with your right boot."[10]

"Hah," the Reservist said, but he could not help glancing in the indicated direction, where one of the serpents—a fat and lengthy example—had indeed lifted its head and was sampling the air above his bootlace.

The effect was immediate, and left no more time for planning. The Reservist leapt from his seat on the wooden crate, uttering oaths, and danced backward, at the same time attempting to bring his rifle to his shoulder and confront the threat. He discovered to his dismay that it was not a question of *one* snake but of *dozens,* and he compressed the trigger of the weapon reflexively. The resulting shot went wild. The bullet impacted near the main nest of the creatures, causing them to scatter with astonishing speed, like a box of loaded springs—unfortunately for the hapless Reservist, who was directly in their path. He cursed vigorously and fired four more times. Some of the shots careened harmlessly; at least one obliterated the midsection of the lead serpent, which knotted around its own wound like a bloody rope.

"Now, Adam!" Julian shouted, and I stood up, thinking: My father's advice?

My father was a taciturn man, and most of his advice had involved the practical matter of running the Estate's stables. I hesitated a moment in confusion, while Julian advanced toward the captive rifles, dancing among the surviving snakes like a dervish. The Reservist, recovering somewhat, raced in the same direction; and then I recalled the only advice of my father's that I had ever shared with Julian:

Grasp it where its neck ought to be, behind the head; ignore the tail; however it may thrash; and crack its skull, hard and often enough to subdue it.

And so I did just that—until the threat was neutralized.

Julian, meanwhile, recovered the weapons, and came away from the infested area of the dig.

He looked with some astonishment at the Reservist, who was slumped at my feet, bleeding from his scalp, which I had "cracked, hard and often."

"Adam," he said. "When I spoke of your father's advice—I meant the *snakes.*"

"The snakes?" Several of them still twined about the dig. But I reminded myself that Julian knew very little about the nature and variety of reptiles. "They're only corn snakes," I explained.[11] "They're big, but they're not venomous."

Julian, his eyes gone large, absorbed this information.

Then he looked at the crumpled form of the Reservist again.

"Have you killed him?"

"Well, I hope not," I said.

---

[10] Julian's sense of timing was exquisite, perhaps as a result of his theatrical inclinations.

[11] Once confined to the southeast, corn snakes have spread north with the warming climate. I have read that certain of the secular ancients used to keep them as pets—yet another instance of our ancestor's willful perversity.

VIII

We made a new camp, in a less populated part of the ruins, and kept a watch on the road, and at dawn we saw a single horse and rider approaching from the west. It was Sam Godwin.

Julian hailed him, waving his arms. Sam came closer, and looked with some relief at Julian, and then speculatively at me. I blushed, thinking of how I had interrupted him at his prayers (however unorthodox those prayers might have been, from a purely Christian perspective), and how poorly I had reacted to my discovery of his true religion. But I said nothing, and Sam said nothing, and relations between us seemed to have been regularized, since I had demonstrated my loyalty (or foolishness) by riding to Julian's aid.

It was Christmas morning. I supposed that did not mean anything in particular to Julian or Sam, but I was poignantly aware of the date. The sky was blue again, but a squall had passed during the dark hours of the morning, and the snow "lay round about, deep and crisp and even." Even the ruins of Lundsford were transformed into something soft-edged and oddly beautiful. I was amazed at how simple it was for nature to cloak corruption in the garb of purity and make it peaceful.

But it would not be peaceful for long, and Sam said so. "There are troops behind me as we speak. Word came by wire from New York not to let Julian escape. We can't linger here more than a moment."

"Where will we go?" Julian asked.

"It's impossible to ride much farther east. There's no forage for the animals and precious little water. Sooner or later we'll have to turn south and make a connection with the railroad or the turnpike. It's going to be short rations and hard riding for a while, I'm afraid, and if we do make good our escape we'll have to assume new identities. We'll be little better than draft dodgers or labor refugees, and I expect we'll have to pass some time among that hard crew, at least until we reach New York City. We can find friends in New York."

It was a plan, but it was a large and lonesome one, and my heart sank at the prospect.

"We have a prisoner," Julian told his mentor, and he took Sam back into the excavated ruins to explain how we had spent the night.

The Reservist was there, hands tied behind his back, a little groggy from the punishment I had inflicted on him but well enough to open his eyes and scowl. Julian and Sam spent a little time debating how to deal with this encumbrance. We could not, of course, take him with us; the question was how to return him to his superiors without endangering ourselves unnecessarily.

It was a debate to which I could contribute nothing, so I took a little slip of paper from my back-satchel, and a pencil, and wrote a letter.

It was addressed to my mother, since my father was without the art of literacy.

You will no doubt have noticed my absence, I wrote. *It saddens me to be away from home, especially at this time (I write on Christmas Day). But I hope you will be consoled with the knowledge that I am all right, and not in any immediate danger.*

(This was a lie, depending on how you defined "immediate," but a kindly one, I reasoned.)

In any case I would not have been able to remain in Williams Ford, since I could not have escaped the draft for long even if I postponed my military service for some few more months. The conscription drive is in earnest; the War in Labrador must be going badly. It was inevitable that we should be separated, as much as I yearn for my home and all its comforts.

(And it was all I could do not to decorate the page with a vagrant tear.)

Please accept my best wishes and my gratitude for everything you and Father have done for me. I will write again as soon as is practicable, which may not be immediately. Trust in the knowledge that I will pursue my destiny faithfully and with every Christian virtue you have taught me. God bless you in the coming and every year.

That was not enough to say, but there wasn't time for more. Julian and Sam were calling for me. I signed my name, and added, as a postscript:

Please tell Father that I value his advice, and that it has already served me usefully. Yrs. etc. once again, Adam.

"You've written a letter," Sam observed as he came to rush me to my horse. "But have you given any thought to how you might mail it?"

I confessed that I had not.

"The Reservist can carry it," said Julian, who had already mounted his horse.

The Reservist was also mounted, but with his hands tied behind him, as it was Sam's final conclusion that we should set him loose with the horse headed west, where he would encounter more troops before very long. He was awake but, as I have said, sullen; and he barked, "I'm nobody's damned mailman!"

I addressed the message, and Julian took it and tucked it into the Reservist's saddlebag. Despite his youth, and despite the slightly dilapidated condition of his hair and clothing, Julian sat tall in the saddle. I had never thought of him as highborn until that moment, when an aspect of command seemed to enter his body and his voice. He said to the Reservist, "We treated you kindly—"

The Reservist uttered an oath.

"Be quiet. You were injured in the conflict, but we took you prisoner, and we've treated you in a more gentlemanly fashion than we were when the conditions were reversed. I am a Comstock—at least for the moment—and I won't be spoken to crudely by an infantryman, at any price. You'll deliver this boy's message, and you'll do it gratefully."

The Reservist was clearly awed by the assertion that Julian was a Comstock—he had been laboring under the assumption that we were mere village runaways—but he screwed up his courage and said, "Why should I?"

"Because it's the Christian thing to do," Julian said, "and if this argument with my uncle is ever settled, the power to remove your head from your shoulders may well reside in my hands. Does that make sense to you, soldier?"

The Reservist allowed that it did.

And so we rode out that Christmas morning from the ruins in which the Tipmen had discovered the *History of Mankind in Space,* which still resided in my back-satchel, vagrant memory of a half-forgotten past.

My mind was a confusion of ideas and anxieties, but I found myself recalling what Julian had said, long ago it now seemed, about DNA, and how it aspired to perfect replication but progressed by remembering itself imperfectly. It might be true, I thought, because our lives were like that—*time itself* was like that, every moment dying and pregnant with its own distorted reflection. Today was Christmas, which Julian claimed had once been a pagan holiday, dedicated to Sol Invictus or some other Roman god; but which had evolved into the familiar celebration of the present, and was no less dear because of it.

(I imagined I could hear the Christmas bells ringing from the Dominion Hall at Williams Ford, though that was impossible, for we were miles away, and not even the sound of a cannon shot could carry so far across the prairie. It was only memory speaking.)

And maybe this logic was true of people, too; maybe I was already becoming an inexact echo of what I had been just days before. Maybe the same was true of Julian. Already something hard and uncompromising had begun to emerge from his gentle features—the first manifestation of a new Julian, a freshly *evolved* Julian, called forth by his violent departure from Williams Ford, or slouching toward New York to be born.

But that was all Philosophy, and not much use, and I kept quiet about it as we spurred our horses in the direction of the railroad, toward the rude and squalling infant Future.

tin marsh

michael swanwick

Michael Swanwick made his debut in 1980, and in the twenty-six years that have followed, has established himself as one of SF's most prolific and consistently excellent writers at short lengths, as well as one of the premier novelists of his generation. He has won the Theodore Sturgeon Award and the *Asimov's* Readers Award poll. In 1991, his novel *Stations of the Tide* won him a Nebula Award as well, and in 1995 he won the World Fantasy Award for his story "Radio Waves." He's won the Hugo Award five times between 1999 and 2006 for his stories "The Very Pulse of the Machine," "Scherzo with Tyrannosaur," "The Dog Said Bow-Wow," "Slow Life," and "Legions in Time." His other books include the novels *In the Drift, Vacuum Flowers, The Iron Dragon's Daughter, Jack Faust,* and, most recently, *Bones of the Earth.* His short fiction has been assembled in *Gravity's Angels, A Geography of Unknown Lands, Slow Dancing Through Time, Moon Dogs, Puck Aleshire's Abecedary, Tales of Old Earth, Cigar-Box Faust and Other Miniatures,* and *Michael Swanwick's Field Guide to the Mesozoic Megafauna.* He's also published a collection of critical articles, *The Postmodern Archipelago,* and a book-length interview, *Being Gardner Dozois.* His most recent book is a new collection, *The Periodic Table of SF.* Upcoming is a new novel, *The Dragons of Babel.* He's had stories in our Second, Third, Fourth, Sixth, Seventh, Tenth, and Thirteenth through Twenty-third Annual Collections. Swanwick lives in Philadelphia with his wife, Marianne Porter. He has a Web site at: www.michaelswanwick.com.

Here he takes us to the inimical surface of a very *in*hospitable Venus for a deadly game of cat and mouse.

I

t was hot coming down into the valley. The sun was high in the sky, a harsh white dazzle in the eternal clouds, strong enough to melt the lead out of the hills. They trudged down from the heights, carrying the drilling rig between them. A little trickle of metal, spill from a tanker bringing tin out of the mountains, glinted at the verge of the road.

A traveler coming the other way, ten feet tall and anonymous in a black muscle suit, waved at them as they passed, but, even though it had been weeks since they'd seen another human being, they didn't wave back. The traveler passed them and disappeared up the road. The heat had seared the ground here black and hard. They could leave the road, if they wanted, and make almost as good time.

Patang and MacArthur had been walking for hours. They expected to walk for hours more. But then the road twisted and down at the bottom of the long decline, in the shadow of a basalt cliff, was an inn. Mostly their work kept them away from roads and inns. For almost a month they'd been living in their suits, sleeping in harness.

They looked warily at each other, mirrored visor to mirrored visor. Heat glimmered from the engines of their muscle suits. Without a word, they agreed to stop.

The inn radioed a fee schedule at their approach. They let their suits' autonomic functions negotiate for them, and carefully set the drilling rig down alongside the building.

"Put out the tarp," MacArthur said. "So it won't warp."

He went inside.

Patang deployed the gold foil tarp, then followed him in.

MacArthur was already out of his suit and seated at a cast-iron table with two cups of water in front of him when Patang cycled through the airlock. For an instant she dared hope everything was going to be all right.

Then he looked up at her.

"Ten dollars a cup." One cup was half empty. He drank the rest down in one long gulp, and closed a hairy paw around the second cup. His beard had grown since she had last seen it, and she could smell him from across the room. Presumably he could smell her too. "The bastards get you coming and going."

Patang climbed out of her suit. She stretched out her arms as far as they would go, luxuriating in the room's openness. All that space! It was twenty feet across and windowless. There was the one table, and six iron chairs to go with it. Half a dozen cots folded up against the walls. A line of shelves offered Company goods that neither of them could afford. There were also a pay toilet and a pay shower. There was a free medical unit, but if you tried to con it out of something recreational, the Company found out and fined you accordingly.

Patang's skin prickled and itched from a month's accumulation of dried sweat. "I'm going to scratch," she said. "Don't look."

But of course MacArthur did, the pig.

Ignoring him, Patang slowly and sensuously scratched under her blouse and across her back. She took her time, digging in with her nails hard enough almost to make the skin bleed. It felt glorious.

MacArthur stared at her all the while, a starving wolf faced with a plump rabbit.

"You could have done that in your suit," he said when she was done.

"It's not the same."

"You didn't have to do that in front of—"

"*Hey!* How's about a little conversation?" Patang said loudly. So it cost a few bucks. So what?

With a click, the innkeeper came on. "Wasn't expecting any more visitors so close to the noon season," it said in a folksy synthetic voice. "What are you two prospecting for?"

"Gold, tin, lead, just about anything that'll gush up a test-hole." Patang closed her eyes, pretending she was back on Lakshmi Planum in a bar in Port Ishtar, talking with a real, live human being. "We figured most people will be working tracts in the morning and late afternoon. This way our databases are up-to-date—we won't be stepping on somebody's month-old claim."

"Very wise. The Company pays well for a strike."

"I hate those fucking things." MacArthur turned his back on the speaker and Patang both, noisily scraping his chair against the floor. She knew how badly he'd like to hurt her.

She knew that it wasn't going to happen.

The Company had three rules. The first was No Violence. The second was Protect Company Equipment. The third was Protect Yourself. All three were enforced by neural implant.

From long experience with its prospectors, the Company had prioritized these rules, so that the first overruled the second, the second overruled the third, and the third could only be obeyed insofar as it didn't conflict with the first two. That was so a prospector couldn't decide—as had happened—that his survival depended on the death of his partner. Or, more subtly, that the other wasn't taking proper care of Company equipment, and should be eliminated.

It had taken time and experience, but the Company had finally come up with a foolproof set of algorithms. The outback was a functioning anarchy. Nobody could hurt anybody else there.

No matter how badly they needed to.

The 'plants had sounded like a good idea when Patang and MacArthur first went under contract. They'd signed up for a full sidereal day—two hundred fifty-five Earth days. Slightly longer than a Venusian year. Now, with fifty-nine days still to go, she was no longer certain that two people who hated each other as much as they did should be kept from each other's throats. Sooner or later, one of them would have to crack.

Every day she prayed that it would be MacArthur who finally yanked the escape cord, calling down upon himself the charges for a rescue ship to pull them out ahead of contract. MacArthur who went bust while she took her partial creds and skipped.

Every day he didn't. It was inhuman how much abuse he could absorb without giving in.

Only hatred could keep a man going like that.

Patang drank her water down slowly, with little slurps and sighs and lip-smackings. Knowing MacArthur loathed that, but unable to keep herself from doing it anyway. She was almost done when he slammed his hands down on the tabletop, to either side of hers, and said, "Patang, there are some things I want to get straight between us."

"Please. Don't."

"Goddamnit, you know how I feel about that shit."

"I don't like it when you talk like that. Stop."

MacArthur ground his teeth. "No. We are going to have this out right here and now. I want you to—*what was that?*"

Patang stared blankly at her partner. Then she felt it—an uneasy vertiginous queasiness, a sense of imbalance just at the edge of perception, as if all of Venus were with infinitesimal gentleness shifting underfoot.

Then the planet roared and the floor came up to smash her in the face.

When Patang came to, everything was a jumble. The floor was canted. The shelves had collapsed, dumping silk shirts, lemon cookies, and bars of beauty soap everywhere. Their muscle suits had tumbled together, the metal arm of one caught between the legs of the other. The life support systems were still operational, thank God. The Company built them strong.

In the middle of it all, MacArthur stood motionless, grinning. A trickle of blood ran down his neck. He slowly rubbed the side of his face.

"MacArthur? Are you okay?"

A strange look was in his eyes. "By God," he said softly. "By damn."

"Innkeeper! What happened here?"

The device didn't respond. "I busted it up," MacArthur said. "It was easy."

"What?"

MacArthur walked clumsily across the floor toward her, like a sailor on an uncertain deck. "There was a cliff slump." He had a Ph.D. in extraterrestrial geology. He knew things like that. "A vein of soft basalt weakened and gave way. The inn caught a glancing blow. We're lucky to be alive."

He knelt beside her and made the OK sign with thumb and forefinger. Then he flicked the side of her nose with the forefinger.

"Ouch!" she said. Then, shocked, "Hey, you can't . . . !"

"Like hell I can't." He slapped her in the face. Hard. "Chip don't seem to work anymore."

Rage filled her. "You son of a bitch!" Patang drew back her arm to slug him.

Blankness.

She came to seconds later. But it was like opening a book in the middle or stepping into an interactive an hour after it began. She had no idea what had happened or how it affected her.

MacArthur was strapping her into her muscle suit.

"Is everything okay?" she murmured. "Is something wrong?"

"I was going to kill you, Patang. But killing you isn't enough. You have to suffer first."

"What are you talking about?"

Then she remembered.

MacArthur had hit her. His chip had malfunctioned. There were no controls on him now. And he hated her. Bad enough to kill her? Oh, yes. Easily.

MacArthur snapped something off her helmet. Then he slapped the power button and the suit began to close around her. He chuckled and said, "I'll meet you outside."

Patang cycled out the lock and then didn't know what to do. She fearfully went a distance up the road, and then hovered anxiously. She didn't exactly wait and she didn't exactly go away. She had to know what MacArthur was up to.

The lock opened, and MacArthur went around to the side of the tavern, where the drilling rig lay under its tarp. He bent down to separate the laser drill from the support struts, data boxes, and alignment devices. Then he delicately tugged the gold foil blanket back over the equipment.

He straightened, and turned toward Patang, the drill in his arms. He pointed it at her.

The words LASER HAZARD flashed on her visor.

She looked down and saw the rock at her feet blacken and smoke. "You know what would happen if I punched a hole in your shielding," MacArthur said.

She did. All the air in her suit would explode outward, while the enormous atmospheric pressure simultaneously imploded the metal casing inward. The mechanical cooling systems would fail instantly. She would be suffocated, broiled, and crushed, all in an instant.

"Turn around. Or I'll lase you a new asshole."

She obeyed.

"Here are the rules. You get a half-hour head start. Then I come for you. If you turn north or south, I'll drill you. Head west. Noonward."

"Noonward?" She booted up the geodetics. There was nothing in that direction but a couple more wrinkle ridges and, beyond them, tesserae. The tesserae were marked orange on her maps. Orange for unpromising. Prospectors had passed through them before and found nothing. "Why there?"

"Because I told you to. Because we're going to have a little fun. Because you have no choice. Understand?"

She nodded miserably.

"Go."

She walked, he followed. It was a nightmare that had somehow found its way into waking life. When Patang looked back, she could see MacArthur striding after her, small in the distance. But never small enough that she had any kind of chance to get away.

He saw her looking and stooped to pick up a boulder. He windmilled his arm and threw.

Even though MacArthur was halfway to the horizon, the boulder smashed to the ground a hundred yards ahead of her and to one side. It didn't come close to striking her, of course. That wasn't his intent.

The rock shattered when it hit. It was terrifying how strong that suit was. It filled her with rage to see MacArthur wielding all that power, and her completely helpless. "You goddamned sadist!"

No answer.

He was nuts. There *had* to be a clause in the contract covering that. Well, then . . . She set her suit on auto-walk, pulled up the indenture papers, and went looking for it Options. Hold harmless clauses. Responsibilities of the Subcontractor—there were hundreds of those. Physical care of the Contractor's equipment.

And there it was. There it was! *In the event of medical emergency, as ultimately upheld in a court of physicians . . .* She scrolled up the submenu of qualifying conditions. The list of mental illnesses was long enough and inclusive enough that she was certain MacArthur belonged on it somewhere.

She'd lose all the equity she'd built up, of course. But, if she interpreted the contract correctly, she'd be entitled to a refund of her initial investment.

That, and her life, were good enough for her.

She slid an arm out of harness and reached up into a difficult-to-reach space behind her head. There was a safety there. She unlatched it. Then she called up a virtual keyboard, and typed out the SOS.

So simple. So easy.

DO YOU *REALLY* WANT TO SEND THIS MESSAGE? YES NO

She hit YES.

For an instant, nothing happened.

MESSAGE NOT SENT

"Shit!" She tried it again. MESSAGE NOT SENT a third time. MESSAGE NOT SENT a fourth. MESSAGE NOT SENT. She ran a troubleshooting program, and then sent the message again. MESSAGE NOT SENT

And again. And again. And again.

MESSAGE NOT SENT

MESSAGE NOT SENT

MESSAGE NOT SENT

Until the suspicion was so strong she *had* to check.

There was an inspection camera on the back of her suit's left hand. She held it up so she could examine the side of her helmet.

MacArthur had broken off the uplink antenna.

"You jerk!" She was really angry now. "You shithead! You cretin! You retard! You're nuts, you know that? Crazy. Totally whack."

No answer.

The bastard was ignoring her. He probably had his suit on auto-follow. He was probably leaning back in his harness, reading a book or watching an old movie on his viser. MacArthur did that a lot. You'd ask him a question and he wouldn't answer because he wasn't there; he was sitting front row center in the theater of his cerebellum. He probably had a tracking algorithm in the navigation system to warn him if she turned to the north or south, or started to get too far ahead of him.

Let's test that hypothesis.

She'd used the tracking algorithm often enough that she knew its specs by heart. One step sidewards in five would register immediately. One in six would not. All right, then . . . Let's see if we can get this rig turned around slowly, subtly, toward the road. She took seven strides forward, and then half-step to the side.

LASER HAZARD

Patang hastily switched on auto-walk. So that settled that. He was watching her every step. A tracking algorithm would have written that off as a stumble. But then why didn't he speak? To make her suffer, obviously. He must be bubbling over with things to say. He must hate her almost as much as she did him.

"You son of a bitch! I'm going to *get* you, MacArthur! I'm going to turn the goddamned tables on you, and when I do—!"

It wasn't as if she were totally hopeless. She had explosives. Hell, her muscle suit could throw a rock with enough energy to smash a hole right through his suit. She could—

Blankness.

She came to with the suit auto-walking down the far slope of the first wrinkle ridge. There was a buzzing in her ear. Somebody talking. MacArthur, over the short-range radio. "What?" she asked blurrily. "Were you saying something, MacArthur? I didn't quite catch that."

"You had a bad thought, didn't you?" MacArthur said gleefully. "Naughty girl! Papa spank."

LASER HAZARD
LASER HAZARD

Arrows pointed to either side. She'd been walking straight Noonward, and he'd fired on her anyway.

"Damn it, that's not *fair*!"

"Fair! Was it fair, the things you said to me? Talking. All the time talking."

"I didn't mean anything by it."

"You did! Those things . . . the things you said . . . unforgivable!"

"I was only deviling you, MacArthur," she said placatingly. It was a word from her childhood; it meant teasing, the kind of teasing a sister inflicted on a brother. "I wouldn't do it if we weren't friends."

MacArthur made a noise he might have thought was laughter. "Believe me, Patang, you and I are not friends."

The deviling had been innocent enough at the start. She'd only done it to pass the time. At what point had it passed over the edge? She hadn't always hated MacArthur. Back in Port Ishtar, he'd seemed like a pleasant companion. She'd even thought he was cute.

It hurt to think about Port Ishtar, but she couldn't help herself. It was like trying not to think about Heaven when you were roasting in Hell.

Okay, so Port Ishtar wasn't perfect. You ate flavored algae and you slept on a shelf. During the day you wore silk, because it was cheap, and you went everywhere barefoot because shoes cost money. But there were fountains that sprayed water into the air. There was live music in the restaurants, string quartets playing to the big winners, prospectors who had made a strike and were leaking wealth on the way out. If you weren't too obvious about it, you could stand nearby and listen. Gravity was light, then, and everybody was young, and the future was going to be full of money.

That was then. She was a million years older now.

LASER HAZARD
"Hey!"
"Keep walking, bitch. Keep walking or die."

This couldn't be happening.

Hours passed, and more hours, until she completely lost track of the time. They walked. Up out of the valley. Over the mountain. Down into the next valley. Because of the heat, and because the rocks were generally weak, the mountains all had gentle slopes. It was like walking up and then down a very long hill.

The land was grey and the clouds above it murky orange. These were Venus's true colors. She could have grass-green rocks and a bright blue sky if she wished—her visor would do that—but the one time she'd tried those settings, she'd quickly switched back. The falseness of it was enough to break your heart.

Better to see the bitter land and grim sky for what they were.

West, they traveled. Noonward. It was like an endless and meaningless dream.

"Hey, *Poontang.*"

"You know how I feel about that kind of language," she said wearily.

"How you feel. That's rich. How do you think I felt, some of the things you said?"

"We can make peace, MacArthur. It doesn't have to be like this."

"Ever been married, Poontang?"

"You know I haven't."

"I have. Married and divorced." She knew that already. There was very little they didn't know about each other by now. "Thing is, when a marriage breaks up, there's always one person comes to grips with it first. Goes through all the heartache and pain, feels the misery, mourns the death of the relationship—and then moves on. The one who's been cheated on, usually. So the day comes when she walks out of the house and the poor schmuck is just standing there, saying, 'Wait. Can't we work this thing out?' He hasn't accepted that it's over."

"So?"

"So that's your problem, Poontang. You just haven't accepted that it's over yet."

"What? Our partnership, you mean?"

"No. Your life."

A day passed, maybe more. She slept. She awoke, still walking, with MacArthur's hateful mutter in her ear. There was no way to turn the radio off. It was Company policy. There were layers upon layers of systems and subsystems built into the walkers, all designed to protect Company investment. Sometimes his snoring would wake her up out of a sound sleep. She knew the ugly little grunting noises he made when he jerked off. There were times she'd been so angry that she'd mimicked those sounds right back at him. She regretted that now.

"I had dreams," MacArthur said. "I had ambitions."

"I know you did. I did too."

"Why the hell did you have to come into my life? Why *me* and not somebody else?"

"I liked you. I thought you were funny."

"Well, the joke's on you now."

Back in Port Ishtar, MacArthur had been a lanky, clean-cut kind of guy. He was tall, and in motion you were always aware of his knees and elbows, always sure he was going to knock something over, though he never did. He had an odd, geeky kind of grace. When she'd diffidently asked him if he wanted to go partners, he'd picked her up and whirled her around in the air and kissed her right on the lips before setting her down again and saying, "Yes." She'd felt dizzy and happy then, and certain she'd made the right choice.

But MacArthur had been weak. The suit had broken him. All those months simmering in his own emotions, perfectly isolated and yet never alone . . . He didn't even *look* like the same person anymore. You looked at his face and all you saw were anger and those anguished eyes.

LEAVING HIGHLANDS
ENTERING TESSERAE

Patang remembered how magical the tesserae landscape had seemed in the beginning. "Complex ridged terrain" MacArthur called it, high ridges and deep groves crisscrossing each other in such profusion that the land appeared blocky from orbit, like a jumble of tiles. Crossing such terrain, you had to be constantly alert. Cliffs rose up unexpectedly, butte-high. You turned a twist in a zigzagging valley and the walls fell away and down, down, down. There was nothing remotely like it on Earth. The first time through, she'd shivered in wonder and awe.

Now she thought: Maybe I can use this. These canyons ran in and out of each other. Duck down one and run like hell. Find another and duck down it. Keep on repeating until he'd lost her.

"You honestly think you can lose me, Patang?"

She shrieked involuntarily.

"I can read your mind, Patang. I know you through and through."

It was true, and it was wrong. People weren't meant to know each other like this. It was the forced togetherness, the fact you were never for a moment alone with your own thoughts. After a while you'd heard every story your partner had to tell and shared every confidence there was to share. After a while every little thing got on your nerves.

"How about if I admit I was wrong?" she said pleadingly. "I was wrong. I admit it."

"We were both wrong. So what?"

"I'm willing to cooperate, MacArthur. Look. I've stopped so you can catch up and not have to worry about me getting away from you. Doesn't *that* convince you we're on the same side?"

LASER HAZARD

"Oh, feel free to run as fast and as far as you want, Patang. I'm confident I'll catch up with you in the end."

All right, then, she thought desperately. If that's the way you want it, asshole. Tag! You're it.

She ducked into the shadows of a canyon and ran.

The canyon twisted and, briefly, she was out of sight. MacArthur couldn't talk to her, couldn't hear her. Couldn't tell which way she went. The silence felt wonderful. It was the first privacy she'd had since she didn't know when. She only wished she could spare the attention to enjoy it more. But she had to think, and think hard. One canyon wall had slumped downward just ahead, creating a slope her walker could easily handle. Or she could keep on ahead, up the canyon.

Which way should she go?

Upslope.

She set the walker on auto-run.

Meanwhile, she studied the maps. The free satellite downloads were very good. They weren't good enough. They showed features down to three meters across, but she needed to know the land yard-by-yard. That crack-like little rille—did it split two kilometers ahead, or was there a second rille that didn't quite meet it? She couldn't tell. She'd've gladly paid for the premium service now, the caviar of info-feed detailed enough to track footprints across a dusty stretch of terrain. But with her uplink disabled, she couldn't.

Patang ducked into a rille so narrow her muscle suit's programming would have let her jump it, if she wished. It forked, and she took the right-hand branch. When the walls started closing in on her, she climbed up and out. Then she ran, looking for another rille.

Hours passed.

After a time, all that kept her going was fear. She drew her legs up into the torso of her suit and set it to auto-run. Up this canyon. Over this ridge. Twisting, turning. Scanning the land ahead, looking for options. Two directions she might go. Flip a mental coin. Choose one. Repeat the process. The radio was line-of-sight so MacArthur couldn't use it to track her. Keep moving.

Keep moving.

Keep moving . . .

Was it hours that passed, or days? Patang didn't know. It might have been weeks. In times of crisis, the suit was programmed to keep her alert by artificial stimulation of her brain. It was like an electrical version of amphetamines. But, as with amphetamines, you tended to lose track of things. Things like your sense of time.

So she had no idea how long it took her to realize that it was all no use.

The problem was that the suit was so damned *heavy*! If she ran fast enough to keep her distance from MacArthur, it left a trace in the regolith obvious enough to be followed at top speed. But if she slowed down enough to place her walker's feet on bare stone when she could, and leave subtle and easy-to-miss footprints when she couldn't, he came right up behind her. And try though she might, she couldn't get far enough ahead of him to dare slow down enough to leave a trace he couldn't follow.

There was no way she could escape him.

The feeling of futility that came over her then was drab and familiar, like a shabby old coat grown colorless with age that you don't have the money to replace. Sometime, long ago, she'd crossed that line where hope ceased. She had never actually admitted to herself that she no longer believed they'd ever make that big strike — just one day woken up knowing that she was simply waiting out her contract, stubbornly trying to endure long enough to serve out her term and return to Earth no poorer than she had set out.

Which was when her deviling had turned nasty, wasn't it? It was when she had started touching herself and telling MacArthur exactly what she was doing. When she'd started describing in detail all the things she'd never do to *him*.

It was a way of getting through one more day. It was a way of faking up enough emotion to care. It was a stupid, stupid thing to do.

And this was her punishment.

But she couldn't give up. She was going to have to . . . She didn't finish that thought. If she was going to do this unnamed thing, she had to sort through the ground rules first.

The three rules were: No Violence. Protect Company Equipment. Protect Yourself. They were ranked hierarchically.

Okay, Patang thought. In order to prevent violence, I'm going to have to destroy Company property.

She waited to see if she'd pass out.

Nothing happened.

Good.

She'd come to a long ridge, steep-sided and barren and set her suit to auto-climb. As she climbed, she scanned the slope ahead, empty and rock-strewn under a permanently dazzling cover of sulfuric acid clouds. Halfway up, MacArthur emerged from the zigzagging valley below and waved jauntily.

Patang ignored him. That pile of boulders up ahead was too large. Those to the right were too small. There was a patch of loose regolith that looked promising but . . . no. In the end, she veered leftward, toward a shallow ledge that sheltered rocks that looked loose enough to be dislodged but not massive enough to do any serious damage to MacArthur's suit. All she wanted was to sweep him off his feet. He could survive a slide downslope easily enough. But could he hold onto the laser drill while doing so?

Patang didn't think so.

Okay, then. She took her suit off automatics and climbed clumsily, carefully, toward her destination. She kept her helmet up, pointed toward the top of the ridge, to avoid tipping MacArthur off to her intentions.

Slantwise across the slope, that's right. Now straight up. She glanced back and saw that she'd pulled MacArthur into her wake. He was directly beneath her. Good. All systems go.

She was up to the ledge now.

Stop. Turn around. Look down on MacArthur, surprisingly close.

If there was one thing Patang knew, after all these months, it was how easy it was to start a landslide. Lean back and brace yourself here, and start kicking. And over the rocks go and over the rocks go and —

LASER HAZARD

"Ohhhh, Patang, you are so obvious. You climb diagonally up a slope that any ordinary person would tackle straight on. You change direction halfway up. What were you planning to do, start an avalanche? What did you think that would accomplish?"

"I thought I could get the laser away from you."

"And what good would that do? I'd still have the suit. I'd still have rocks. I'd still have you at my mercy. You hadn't really thought this one through, had you?"

"No," she admitted.

"You tried to outwit me, but you didn't have the ingenuity. Isn't that right?"

"Yes."

"You were just hoping. But there isn't any hope, is there?"

"No."

He flipped one hand dismissively. "Well, keep on going. We're not done yet."

Weeping, Patang topped the ridge and started downward, into a valley shaped like a deep bowl. Glassy scarps on all sides caught whatever infrared bounced off the floor and threw it back into the valley. The temperature readings on her visor leaped. It was at least fifty degrees hotter out there than anyplace she had ever been. Hot enough that prolonged exposure would incapacitate her suit? Maybe. But there was MacArthur behind her, and the only way forward was a shallow trough leading straight down. She had no alternative.

Midway down the slope, the trough deepened. Rock walls rose up to plunge Patang into shadow. Her suit's external temperature went down, though not as much as she would've liked. Then the way grew less steep and then it flattened out. The trough ended as a bright doorway between jagged rocks.

She stepped out into the open and looked across the valley.

The ground *dazzled*.

She walked out into it. She felt weightless. Her feet floated up beneath her and her hands rose of their own accord into the air. The muscle suit's arms rose too, like a ballerina's.

A network of cracks crazed the floor of the valley, each one blazing bright as the sun. Liquid metal was just oozing up out of the ground. She'd never seen anything like it.

Patang stomped on a puddle of metal, shattering it into droplets of sunlight and setting off warning alarms in her suit. For an instant she swayed with sleepiness. But she shook it off. She snapped a stick-probe from her tool rack and jabbed it into the stuff. It measured the metal's temperature and its resistance to pressure, ran a few baby calculations, and spat out a result.

Tin.

She looked up again. There were intersecting lines of molten tin everywhere. The pattern reminded her of her childhood on the Eastern Shore, of standing at the edge of a marsh, binoculars in hand, hoping for a harrier, with the silver gleam of sun on water almost painful to the eye. This looked just like a marsh, only with tin instead of water.

A tin marsh.

For an instant, wonder flickered to life within her. How could such a thing be?

What complex set of geological conditions was responsible? All she could figure was that the noontide heat was involved. As it slowly sank into the rock, the tin below expanded and pushed its way up through the cracks. Or maybe it was the rocks that expanded, squeezing out the liquid tin. In either case the effect would be very small for any given volume. She couldn't imagine how much tin there must be down there for it to be forced to the surface like this. More than she'd ever dreamed they'd find.

"We're *rich*!" she whooped. She couldn't help it. All those months, all that misery, and here it was. The payoff they'd set out to discover, the one that she'd long ago given up all hope of finding.

LASER HAZARD

LASER HAZARD

LASER HAZARD

"No! Wait! Stop!" she cried. "You don't need to do this anymore. We found it! It's here!"

Turning, she saw McArthur's big suit lumber out of shadow. It was brute strength personified, all body and no head. "What are you talking about?" he said angrily. But Patang dared think he sounded almost sane. She dared hope she could reason with him.

"It's the big one, Mac!" She hadn't called him Mac in ages. "We've got the goddamned motherlode here. All you have to do is radio in the claim. It's all over, Mac! This time tomorrow, you're going to be holding a press conference about it."

For a moment MacArthur stood silent and irresolute. Then he said, "Maybe so. But I have to kill you first."

"You turn up without me, the Company's gonna have questions. They're gonna interrogate their suit. They're gonna run a mind-probe. No, MacArthur, you can't have both. You've got to choose: money or me."

LASER HAZARD

"*Run*, you bitch!" MacArthur howled. "Run like you've got a chance to live!"

She didn't move. "Think of it, MacArthur. A nice cold bath. They chill down the water with slabs of ice, and for a little extra they'll leave the ice in. You can hear it clink."

"Shut up."

"And ice cream!" she said fervently. "A thousand different flavors of ice cream. They've got it warehoused: sherbet, gelato, water ice . . . Oh, they know what a prospector likes, all right. Beer in big, frosty mugs. Vodka so cold it's almost a slurry."

"Shut the fuck *up*!"

"You've been straight with me. You gave me a half-hour head start, just like you promised, right? Not everybody would've done that. Now I'm gonna be straight with you. I'm going to lock my suit down." She powered off the arms and legs. It would take a good minute to get them online again. "So you don't have to worry about me getting away. I'm going to just stand here, motionless and helpless, while you think about it, all right?" Then, desperation forcing her all the way into honesty, "I was wrong, MacArthur. I mean it this time. I shouldn't have done those things. Accept my apology. You can rise above it. You're a rich man now."

MacArthur roared with rage.

LASER HAZARD

LASER HAZARD
LASER HAZARD
LASER HAZARD
"Walk, damn you!" he screamed. "*Walk!*"
LASER HAZARD
LASER HAZARD
LASER HAZARD

He wasn't coming any closer. And though he kept on firing, over and over, the bolts of lased light never hit her. It was baffling. She'd given up, she wasn't running, it wasn't even possible for her to run. So why didn't he just kill her? What was stopping him?

Revelation flooded Patang then, like sudden sunlight after a long winter. So simple! So obvious! She couldn't help laughing. "You *can't* shoot me!" she cried. "The suit won't *let* you!"

It was what the tech guys called "fossil software." Before the Company acquired the ability to insert their programs into human beings, they'd programmed their tools so they couldn't be used for sabotage. People, being inventive buggers, had found ways around that programming often enough to render it obsolete. But nobody had ever bothered to dig it out of the deep levels of the machinery's code. What would be the point?

She whooped and screamed. Her suit staggered in a jittery little dance of joy. "You can't kill me, MacArthur! You can't! You can't and you know it! I can just walk right past you, and all the way to the next station, and there's nothing you can do about it."

MacArthur began to cry.

The hopper came roaring down out of the white dazzle of the sky to burn a landing practically at their feet. They clambered wearily forward and let the pilot bolt their muscle suits to the hopper's strutwork. There wasn't cabin space for them and they didn't need it.

The pilot reclaimed his seat. After his first attempts at conversation had fallen flat, he'd said no more. He had hauled out prospectors before. He knew that small talk was useless.

With a crush of acceleration their suits could only partially cushion, the hopper took off. Only three hours to Port Ishtar. The hopper twisted and Patang could see Venus rushing dizzyingly by below her. She blanked out her visor so she didn't have to look at it.

Patang tested her suit. The multiplier motors had been powered down. She was immobile.

"Hey, Patang."

"Yeah?"

"You think I'm going to go to jail? For all the shit I did to you?"

"No, MacArthur. Rich people don't go to jail. They get therapy."

"That's good," he said. "Thank you for telling me that."

"*De nada,*" she said without thinking. The jets rumbled under her back, making the suit vibrate. Two, three hours from now, they'd come down in Port Ishtar, stake their claims, collect their money, and never see each other again.

On impulse, she said, "Hey, MacArthur!"

"What?"

And for an instant she came *that close* to playing the Game one last time. Deviling him, just to hear his teeth grind. But . . .

"Nothing. Just—enjoy being rich, okay? I hope you have a good life."

"Yeah." MacArthur took a deep breath, and then let it go, as if he were releasing something painful, and said, "Yeah . . . you too."

And they soared.

THE DJINN'S WIFE

IAN McDONALD

British author Ian McDonald is an ambitious and daring writer with a wide range and an impressive amount of talent. His first story was published in 1982, and since then he has appeared with some frequency in *Interzone*, *Asimov's Science Fiction*, and elsewhere. In 1989 he won the *Locus* "Best First Novel" Award for his novel *Desolation Road*. He won the Philip K. Dick Award in 1992 for his novel *King of Morning, Queen of Day*. His other books include the novels *Out on Blue Six* and *Hearts, Hands and Voices*, *Terminal Cafe*, *Sacrifice of Fools*, *Evolution's Shore*, *Kirinya*, a chapbook novella, *Tendeleo's Story*, *Ares Express*, and *Cyberabad*, as well as two collections of his short fiction, *Empire Dreams* and *Speaking in Tongues*. His most recent novel, *River of Gods*, was a finalist for both the Hugo Award and the Arthur C. Clarke award in 2005, and a novella drawn from it, *The Little Goddess*, was a finalist for the Hugo and the Nebula. Coming up is another new novel, *Brasyl*. His stories have appeared in our Eighth through Tenth, Fourteenth through Sixteenth, Nineteenth, Twentieth, and Twenty-third Annual Collections. Born in Manchester, England, in 1960, McDonald has spent most of his life in Northern Ireland, and now lives and works in Belfast. He has a Web site at www.lysator.liu.se/~unicorn/mcdonald/.

Here we visit a vivid and evocative future India, where ancient customs and dazzlingly sophisticated high-tech exist side by side, for a lavishly imaginative futuristic fairy tale about a young woman who finds herself not only caught—quite literally—between two worlds, but forced to *choose* between them as well, with life or death as the stakes.

O nce there was a woman in Delhi who married a djinn. Before the water war, that was not so strange a thing: Delhi, split in two like a brain, has been the city of djinns from time before time. The sufis tell that God made two creations, one of clay and one of fire. That of clay became man; that of fire, the *djinni*. As creatures of fire they have always been drawn to Delhi, seven times reduced to ashes by invading empires, seven times reincarnating itself. Each turn of the *chakra*, the djinns have drawn strength from the flames, multiplying and dividing. Great dervishes and brahmins are able to see them, but, on any street, at any time, anyone may catch the whisper and momentary wafting warmth of a djinn passing.

I was born in Ladakh, far from the heat of the djinns—they have wills and whims quite alien to humans—but my mother was Delhi born and raised, and from her I knew its circuses and boulevards, its *maidans* and *chowks* and bazaars, like those of my own Leh. Delhi to me was a city of stories, and so if I tell the story of the djinn's wife in the manner of a sufi legend or a tale from the Mahabharata, or even a *tivi* soap opera, that is how it seems to me: City of Djinns.

They are not the first to fall in love on the walls of the Red Fort.

The politicians have talked for three days and an agreement is close. In honor the Awadhi government has prepared a grand *durbar* in the great courtyard before the *Diwan-i-aam*. All India is watching, so this spectacle is on a Victorian scale: event-planners scurry across hot, bare marble, hanging banners and bunting; erecting staging; setting up sound and light systems; choreographing dancers, elephants, fire-works, and a flypast of combat robots; dressing tables; and drilling serving staff, and drawing up so-careful seating plans so that no one will feel snubbed by anyone else. All day three-wheeler delivery drays have brought fresh flowers, festival goods, finest, soft furnishings. There's a real French *sommelier* raving at what the simmering Delhi heat is doing to his wine-plan. It's a serious conference. At stake are a quarter of a billion lives.

In this second year after the monsoon failed, the Indian nations of Awadh and Bharat face each other with main battle tanks, robot attack helicopters, strikeware, and tactical nuclear slow missiles on the banks of the sacred river Ganga. Along thirty kilometers of staked-out sand, where brahmins cleanse themselves and *sad-dhus* pray, the government of Awadh plans a monster dam. Kunda Khadar will se-cure the water supply for Awadh's one hundred and thirty million for the next fifty years. The river downstream, that flows past the sacred cities of Allahabad and Varanasi in Bharat, will turn to dust. Water is life, water is death. Bharati diplomats, human and artificial intelligence aeai advisors, negotiate careful deals and access rights with their rival nation, knowing one carelessly spilled drop of water will see strike robots battling like kites over the glass towers of New Delhi and slow missiles with nanonuke warheads in their bellies creeping on cat-claws through the *galis* of Varanasi. The rolling news channels clear their schedules of everything else but cricket. A deal is close! A deal is agreed! A deal will be signed tomorrow! Tonight, they've earned their *durbar*.

And in the whirlwind of leaping *hijras* and parading elephants, a *Kathak* dancer slips away for a cigarette and a moment up on the battlements of the Red Fort. She leans against the sun-warmed stone, careful of the fine gold-threadwork of her cos-tume. Beyond the Lahore Gate lies hiving Chandni Chowk; the sun a vast blister bleeding onto the smokestacks and light-farms of the western suburbs. The *chhatris* of the Sisganj Gurdware, the minarets and domes of the Jama Masjid, the *shikara* of the Shiv temple are shadow-puppet scenery against the red, dust-laden sky. Above them pigeons storm and dash, wings wheezing. Black kites rise on the thermals above Old Delhi's thousand thousand rooftops. Beyond them, a curtain wall taller and more imposing than any built by the Mughals, stand the corporate towers of New Delhi, Hindu temples of glass and construction diamond stretched to fantastical, spiring heights, twinkling with stars and aircraft warning lights.

A whisper inside her head, her name accompanied by a spray of sitar: the call-tone of her palmer, transduced through her skull into her auditory center by the subtle 'hoek curled like a piece of jewelry behind her ear.

"I'm just having a quick *bidi* break, give me a chance to finish it," she complains, expecting Pranh, the choreographer, a famously tetchy third-sex nute. Then, "Oh!" For the gold-lit dust rises before her up into a swirl, like a dancer made from ash.

A djinn. The thought hovers on her caught breath. Her mother, though Hindu, devoutly believed in the *djinni*, in any religion's supernatural creatures with a skill for trickery.

The dust coalesces into a man in a long, formal *sherwani* and loosely wound red turban, leaning on the parapet and looking out over the glowing anarchy of Chandni Chowk. *He is very handsome*, the dancer thinks, hastily stubbing out her cigarette and letting it fall in an arc of red embers over the battlements. It does not do to smoke in the presence of the great diplomat A.J. Rao.

"You needn't have done that on my account, Esha," A.J. Rao says, pressing his hands together in a *namaste*. "It's not as though I can catch anything from it."

Esha Rathore returns the greeting, wondering if the stage crew down in the courtyard was watching her salute empty air. All Awadh knows those *filmi*-star features: A. J. Rao, one of Bharat's most knowledgeable and tenacious negotiators. *No*, she corrects herself. All Awadh knows are pictures on a screen. Pictures on a screen, pictures in her head; a voice in her ear. An aeai.

"You know my name?"

"I am one of your greatest admirers."

Her face flushes: a waft of stifling heat spun off from the vast palace's microclimate, Esha tells herself. Not embarrassment. Never embarrassment.

"But I'm a dancer. And you are an . . ."

"Artificial intelligence? That I am. Is this some new anti-aeai legislation, that we can't appreciate dance?" He closes his eyes. "Ah: I'm just watching the *Marriage of Radha and Krishna* again."

But he has her vanity now. "Which performance?"

"Star Arts Channel. I have them all. I must confess, I often have you running in the background while I'm in negotiation. But please don't mistake me, I never tire of you." A.J. Rao smiles. He has very good, very white teeth. "Strange as it may seem, I'm not sure what the etiquette is in this sort of thing. I came here because I wanted to tell you that I am one of your greatest fans and that I am very much looking forward to your performance tonight. It's the highlight of this conference, for me."

The light is almost gone now and the sky a pure, deep, eternal blue, like a minor chord. Houseboys make their many ways along the ramps and wall-walks lighting rows of tiny oil-lamps. The Red Fort glitters like a constellation fallen over Old Delhi. Esha has lived in Delhi all her twenty years and she has never seen her city from this vantage. She says, "I'm not sure what the etiquette is either. I've never spoken with an aeai before."

"Really?" A.J. now stands with his back against the sun-warm stone, looking up at the sky, and at her out of the corner of his eye. The eyes smile, slyly. *Of course*, she thinks. Her city is as full of aeais as it is with birds. From computer systems and robots with the feral smarts of rats and pigeons to entities like this one standing before her on the gate of the Red Fort making charming compliments. Not standing. Not anywhere, just a pattern of information in her head. She stammers, "I mean, a . . . a . . ."

"Level 2.9?"

"I don't know what that means."

The aeai smiles and as she tries to work it out there is another chime in Esha's head and this time it is Pranh, swearing horribly as usual, *where is she doesn't she know yts got a show to put on, half the bloody continent watching.*

"Excuse me . . ."

"Of course. I shall be watching."

How? she wants to ask. *An aeai, a djinn, wants to watch me dance. What is this?* But when she looks back all there is to ask is a wisp of dust blowing along the lantern-lit battlement.

There are elephants and circus performers, there are illusionists and table magicians, there are *ghazal* and *qawali* and *Boli* singers; there is the catering and the *sommelier's* wine and then the lights go up on the stage and Esha spins out past the scowling Pranh as the *tabla* and melodeon and *shehnai* begin. The heat is intense in the marble square, but she is transported. The stampings, the pirouettes and swirl of her skirts, the beat of the ankle bells, the facial expressions, the subtle hand *mudras*: once again she is spun out of herself by the disciplines of *Kathak* into something greater. She would call it her art, her talent, but she's superstitious: that would be to claim it and so crush the gift. Never name it, never speak it. Just let it possess you. Her own, burning djinn. But as she spins across the brilliant stage before the seated delegates, a corner of her perception scans the architecture for cameras, robots, eyes through which A. J. Rao might watch her. Is she a splinter of his consciousness, as he is a splinter of hers?

She barely hears the applause as she curtseys to the bright lights and runs off stage. In the dressing room, as her assistants remove and carefully fold the many jeweled layers of her costume, wipe away the crusted stage makeup to reveal the twenty-two-year-old beneath, her attention keeps flicking to her earhoek, curled like a plastic question on her dressing table. In jeans and silk sleeveless vest, indistinguishable from any other of Delhi's four million twentysomethings, she coils the device behind her ear, smoothes her hair over it and her fingers linger a moment as she slides the palmer over her hand. No calls. No messages. No avatars. She's surprised it matters so much.

The official Mercs are lined up in the Delhi Gate. A man and woman intercept her on her way to the car. She waves them away.

"I don't do autographs. . . ." Never after a performance. Get out, get away quick and quiet, disappear into the city. The man opens his palm to show her a warrant badge.

"We'll take this car."

It pulls out from the line and cuts in, a cream-colored high-marque Maruti. The man politely opens the door to let her enter first, but there is no respect in it. The woman takes the front seat beside the driver; he accelerates out, horn blaring, into the great circus of night traffic around the Red Fort. The airco purrs.

"I am Inspector Thacker from the Department of Artificial Intelligence Registration and Licensing," the man says. He is young and good-skinned and confident and not at all fazed by sitting next to a celebrity. His aftershave is perhaps over-emphatic.

"A Krishna Cop."

That makes him wince.

"Our surveillance systems have flagged up a communication between you and the Bharati Level 2.9 aeai A. J. Rao."

"He called me, yes."

"At 21:08. You were in contact for six minutes twenty-two seconds. Can you tell me what you talked about?"

The car is driving very fast for Delhi. The traffic seems to flow around from it. Every light seems to be green. Nothing is allowed to impede its progress. *Can they do that?* Esha wonders. *Krishna Cops, aeai police: can they tame the creatures they hunt?*

"We talked about *Kathak*. He's a fan. Is there a problem? Have I done something wrong?"

"No, nothing at all, Ms. But you do understand, with a conference of this importance . . . on behalf of the Department, I apologize for the unseemliness. Ah. Here we are."

They've brought her right to her bungalow. Feeling dirty, dusty, confused she watches the Krishna Cop car drive off, holding Delhi's frenetic traffic at bay with its tame djinns. She pauses at the gate. She needs, she deserves, a moment to come out from the performance, that little step way so you can turn round and look back at yourself and say, yeah, Esha Rathore. The bungalow is unlit, quiet. Neeta and Priya will be out with their wonderful fiancés, talking wedding gifts and guest lists and how hefty a dowry they can squeeze from their husbands-to-be's families. They're not her sisters, though they share the classy bungalow. No one has sisters anymore in Awadh, or even Bharat. No one of Esha's age, though she's heard the balance is being restored. Daughters are fashionable. Once upon a time, women paid the dowry.

She breathes deep of her city. The cool garden microclimate presses down the roar of Delhi to a muffled throb, like blood in the heart. She can smell dust and roses. Rose of Persia. Flower of the Urdu poets. And dust. She imagines it rising up on a whisper of wind, spinning into a charming, dangerous djinn. No. An illusion, a madness of a mad old city. She opens the security gate and finds every square centimeter of the compound filled with red roses.

Neeta and Priya are waiting for her at the breakfast table next morning, sitting side-by-side close like an interview panel. Or Krishna Cops. For once they aren't talking houses and husbands.

"Who who who where did they come from who sent them so many must have cost a fortune . . ."

Puri the housemaid brings Chinese green chai that's good against cancer. The sweeper has gathered the bouquets into a pile at one end of the compound. The sweetness of their perfume is already tinged with rot.

"He's a diplomat." Neeta and Priya only watch *Town and Country* and the *chati* channels but even they must know the name of A. J. Rao. So she half lies: "A Bharati diplomat."

Their mouths go *Oooh*, then *ah* as they look at each other. Neeta says, "You have have have to bring him."

"To our *durbar*," says Priya.

"Yes, our *durbar*," says Neeta. They've talked gossiped planned little else for the past two months: their grand joint engagement party where they show off to their as-yet-unmarried girl friends and make all the single men jealous. Esha excuses her grimace with the bitterness of the health-tea.

"He's very busy." She doesn't say *busy man*. She cannot even think why she is playing these silly *girli* secrecy games. An aeai called her at the Red Fort to tell her it admired her. Didn't even meet her. There was nothing to meet. It was all in her head. "I don't even know how to get in touch with him. They don't give their numbers out."

"He's coming," Neeta and Priya insist.

She can hardly hear the music for the rattle of the old airco but sweat runs down her sides along the waistband of her Adidas tights to gather in the hollow of her back and slide between the taut curves of her ass. She tries it again across the *gharana's* practice floor. Even the ankle bells sound like lead. Last night she touched the three heavens. This morning she feels dead. She can't concentrate, and that little *lavda* Pranh knows it, swishing at her with yts cane and gobbing out wads of chewed *paan* and mealy eunuch curses.

"Ey! Less staring at your palmer, more *mudras*! Decent *mudras*. You jerk my dick, if I still had one."

Embarrassed that Pranh has noted something she was not conscious of herself— *ring, call me, ring call me, ring, take me out of this*—she fires back, "If you ever had one."

Pranh slashes yts cane at her legs, catches the back of her calf a sting.

"Fuck you, *hijra*!" Esha snatches up towel bag palmer, hooks the earpiece behind her long straight hair. No point changing, the heat out there will soak through anything in a moment. "I'm out of here."

Pranh doesn't call after her. Yts too proud. *Little freak monkey thing*, she thinks. *How is it a nute is an yt, but an incorporeal aeai is a he?* In the legends of Old Delhi, *djinns* are always he.

"*Memsahb* Rathore?"

The chauffeur is in full dress and boots. His only concession to the heat is his shades. In bra top and tights and bare skin, she's melting. "The vehicle is fully air-conditioned, *memsahb*."

The white leather upholstery is so cool her flesh recoils from its skin.

"This isn't the Krishna Cops."

"No *memsahb*." The chauffeur pulls out into the traffic. It's only as the security locks clunk she thinks *Oh Lord Krishna, they could be kidnapping me*.

"Who sent you?" There's glass too thick for her fists between her and the driver. Even if the doors weren't locked, a tumble from the car at this speed, in this traffic, would be too much for even a dancer's lithe reflexes. And she's lived in Delhi all her life, *basti* to bungalow, but she doesn't recognize these streets, this suburb, that industrial park. "Where are you taking me?"

"*Memsahb*, where I am not permitted to say for that would spoil the surprise. But I am permitted to tell you that you are the guest of A. J. Rao."

The palmer calls her name as she finishes freshening up with bottled Kinley from the car-bar.

"Hello!" (kicking back deep into the cool cool white leather, like a *filmi* star. She is a star. A star with a bar in a car.)

Audio-only. "I trust the car is acceptable?" Same smooth-suave voice. She can't imagine any opponent being able to resist that voice in negotiation.

"It's wonderful. Very luxurious. Very high status." She's out in the *bastis* now, slums deeper and meaner than the one she grew up in. Newer. The newest ones always look the oldest. Boys chug past on a home-brew *chhakda* they've scavenged from tractor parts. The cream Lex carefully detours around emaciated cattle with angular hips jutting through stretched skin like engineering. Everywhere, drought dust lies thick on the crazed hardtop. This is a city of stares. "Aren't you supposed to be at the conference?"

A laugh, inside her auditory center.

"Oh, I am hard at work winning water for Bharat, believe me. I am nothing if not an assiduous civil servant."

"You're telling me you're there, and here?"

"Oh, it's nothing for us to be in more than one place at the same time. There are multiple copies of me, and subroutines."

"So which is the real you?"

"They are all the real me. In fact, not one of my avatars is in Delhi at all, I am distributed over a series of *dharma*-cores across Varanasi and Patna." He sighs. It sounds close and weary and warm as a whisper in her ear. "You find it difficult to comprehend a distributed consciousness; it is every bit as hard for me to comprehend a discrete, mobile consciousness. I can only copy myself through what you call cyberspace, which is the physical reality of my universe, but you move through dimensional space and time."

"So which one of you loves me then?" The words are out, wild, loose, and unconsidered. "I mean, as a dancer, that is." She's filling, gabbling. "Is there one of you that particularly appreciates *Kathak*?" Polite polite words, like you'd say to an industrialist or a hopeful lawyer at one of Neeta and Priya's hideous match-making soirees. *Don't be forward, no one likes a forward woman. This is a man's world, now.* But she hears glee bubble in A. J. Rao's voice.

"Why, all of me and every part of me, Esha."

Her name. He used her name.

It's a shitty street of pie-dogs and men lounging on *charpoys* scratching themselves, but the chauffeur insists, *here, this way memsahb*. She picks her way down a *gali* lined with unsteady minarets of old car tires. Burning *ghee* and stale urine reek the air. Kids mob the Lexus but the car has A. J. Rao levels of security. The chauffeur pushes open an old wood and brass Mughal style gate in a crumbling red wall. *"Memsahb."*

She steps through into a garden. Into the ruins of a garden. The gasp of wonder dies. The geometrical water channels of the *charbagh* are dry, cracked, choked with litter from picnics. The shrubs are blousy and overgrown, the plant borders ragged with weeds. The grass is scabbed brown with drought-burn: the lower branches of the trees have been hacked away for firewood. As she walks toward the crack-roofed pavilion at the center where paths and water channels meet, the gravel beneath her thin shoes is crazed into rivulets from past monsoons. Dead leaves and fallen twigs cover the lawns. The fountains are dry and silted. Yet families stroll pushing baby buggies; children chase balls. Old Islamic gentlemen read the papers and play chess.

"The Shalimar Gardens," says A. J. Rao in the base of her skull. "Paradise as a walled garden."

And as he speaks, a wave of transformation breaks across the garden, sweeping away the decay of the twenty-first century. Trees break into full leaf, flower beds blossom, rows of terracotta geranium pots march down the banks of the *charbagh* channels which shiver with water. The tiered roofs of the pavilion gleam with gold leaf, peacocks fluster and fuss their vanities, and everything glitters and splashes with fountain play. The laughing families are swept back into Mughal grandees, the old men in the park transformed into *malis* sweeping the gravel paths with their besoms.

Esha claps her hands in joy, hearing a distant, silver spray of sitar notes. "Oh," she says, numb with wonder. "Oh!"

"A thank you, for what you gave me last night. This is one of my favorite places in all India, even though it's almost forgotten. Perhaps, because it is almost forgotten. Aurangzeb was crowned Mughal Emperor here in 1658, now it's an evening stroll for the *basti* people. The past is a passion of mine; it's easy for me, for all of us. We can live in as many times as we can places. I often come here, in my mind. Or should I say, it comes to me."

Then the jets from the fountain ripple as if in the wind, but it is not the wind, not on this stifling afternoon, and the falling water flows into the shape of a man, walking out of the spray. A man of water, that shimmers and flows and becomes a man of flesh. A. J. Rao. No, she thinks, *never flesh*. A djinn. *A thing caught between heaven and hell. A caprice, a trickster. Then trick me.*

"It is as the old Urdu poets declare," says A. J. Rao. "Paradise is indeed contained within a wall."

It is far past four but she can't sleep. She lies naked—shameless—but for the 'hoek behind her ear on top of her bed with the window slats open and the ancient airco chugging, fitful in the periodic brownouts. It is the worst night yet. The city gasps for air. Even the traffic sounds beaten tonight. Across the room her palmer opens its blue eye and whispers her name. *Esha.*

She's up, kneeling on the bed, hand to hoek, sweat beading her bare skin.

"I'm here." A whisper. Neeta and Priya are a thin wall away on either side.

"It's late, I know, I'm sorry . . ."

She looks across the room into the palmer's camera.

"It's all right, I wasn't asleep." A tone in that voice. "What is it?"

"The mission is a failure."

She kneels in the center of the big antique bed. Sweat runs down the fold of her spine.

"The conference? What? What happened?" She whispers, he speaks in her head.

"It fell over one point. One tiny, trivial point, but it was like a wedge that split everything apart until it all collapsed. The Awadhis will build their dam at Kunda Khadar and they will keep their holy Ganga water for Awadh. My delegation is already packing. We will return to Varanasi in the morning."

Her heart kicks. Then she curses herself, *stupid, romantic girl*. He is already in Varanasi as much as he is here as much as he is at the Red Fort assisting his human superiors.

"I'm sorry."

"Yes," he says. "That is the feeling. Was I overconfident in my abilities?"

"People will always disappoint you."

A wry laugh in the dark of her skull.

"How very . . . disembodied of you, Esha." Her name seems to hang in the hot air, like a chord. "Will you dance for me?"

"What, here? Now?"

"Yes. I need something . . . embodied. Physical. I need to see a body move, a consciousness dance through space and time as I cannot. I need to see something beautiful."

Need. A creature with the powers of a god, *needs*. But Esha's suddenly shy, covering her small, taut breasts with her hands.

"Music . . ." she stammers. "I can't perform without music . . ." The shadows at the end of the bedroom thicken into an ensemble: three men bent over *tabla*, *sarangi* and *bansuri*. Esha gives a little shriek and ducks back to the modesty of her bedcover. *They cannot see you, they don't even exist, except in your head. And even if they were flesh, they would be so intent on their contraptions of wire and skin they would not notice*. Terrible driven things, musicians.

"I've incorporated a copy of a sub-aeai into myself for this night," A. J. Rao says. "A level 1.9 composition system. I supply the visuals."

"You can swap bits of yourself in and out?" Esha asks. The *tabla* player has started a slow *Natetere* tap-beat on the *dayan* drum. The musicians nod at each other. Counting, they will be counting. It's hard to convince herself Neeta and Priya can't hear; no one can hear but her. And A. J. Rao. The *sarangi* player sets his bow to the strings, the *bansuri* lets loose a snake of fluting notes. A *sangeet*, but not one she has ever heard before.

"It's making it up!"

"It's a composition aeai. Do you recognize the sources?"

"Krishna and the *gopis*." One of the classic *Kathak* themes: Krishna's seduction of the milkmaids with his flute, the *bansuri*, most sensual of instruments. She knows the steps, feels her body anticipating the moves.

"Will you dance, lady?"

And she steps with the potent grace of a tiger from the bed onto the grass matting of her bedroom floor, into the focus of the palmer. Before she had been shy, silly, *girli*. Not now. She has never had an audience like this before. A lordly djinn. In pure, hot silence she executes the turns and stampings and bows of the *One Hundred and Eight Gopis*, bare feet kissing the woven grass. Her hands shape *mudras*, her face the expressions of the ancient story: surprise, coyness, intrigue, arousal. Sweat courses luxuriously down her naked skin: she doesn't feel it. She is clothed in movement and night. Time slows, the stars halt in their arc over great Delhi. She can feel the planet breathe beneath her feet. This is what it was for, all those dawn risings, all those bleeding feet, those slashes of Pranh's cane, those lost birthdays, that stolen childhood. She dances until her feet bleed again into the rough weave of the matting, until every last drop of water is sucked from her and turned into salt, but she stays with the *tabla*, the beat of *dayan* and *bayan*. She is the milkmaid by the river, seduced by a god. A. J. Rao did not choose this *Kathak* wantonly. And then the music comes to its ringing end and the musicians bow to each other and disperse into golden dust and she collapses, exhausted as never before from any other performance, onto the end of her bed.

Light wakes her. She is sticky, naked, embarrassed. The house staff could find her. And she's got a killing headache. Water. Water. Joints nerves sinews plead for it. She pulls on a Chinese silk robe. On her way to the kitchen, the voyeur eye of her palmer blinks at her. No erotic dream then, no sweat hallucination stirred out of heat and hydrocarbons. She danced Krishna and the one hundred and eight gopis in her bedroom for an aeai. A message. There's a number. *You can call me.*

Throughout the history of the eight Delhis there have been men—and almost always men—skilled in the lore of djinns. They are wise to their many forms and can see beneath the disguises they wear on the streets—donkey, monkey, dog, scavenging kite—to their true selves. They know their roosts and places where they congregate—they are particularly drawn to mosques—and know that that unexplained heat as you push down a *gali* behind the Jama Masjid is djinns, packed so tight you can feel their fire as you move through them. The wisest—the strongest—of fakirs know their names and so can capture and command them. Even in the old India, before the break up into Awadh and Bharat and Rajputana and the United States of Bengal—there were saints who could summon djinns to fly them on their backs from one end of Hindustan to the other in a night. In my own Leh there was an aged aged sufi who cast one hundred and eight djinns out of a troubled house: twenty-seven in the living room, twenty-seven in the bedroom and fifty-four in the kitchen. With so many djinns there was no room for anyone else. He drove them off with burning yoghurt and chilies, but warned: *do not toy with djinns, for they do nothing without a price, and though that may be years in the asking, ask it they surely will.*

Now there is a new race jostling for space in their city: the aeais. If the *djinni* are the creation of fire and men of clay, these are the creation of word. Fifty million of them swarm Delhi's boulevards and *chowks*: routing traffic, trading shares, maintaining power and water, answering inquiries, telling fortunes, managing calendars and diaries, handling routine legal and medical matters, performing in soap operas, sifting the septillion pieces of information streaming through Delhi's nervous system each second. The city is a great mantra. From routers and maintenance robots with little more than animal intelligence (each animal has intelligence enough: ask the eagle or the tiger) to the great Level 2.9s that are indistinguishable from a human being 99.99 percent of the time, they are a young race, an energetic race, fresh to this world and enthusiastic, understanding little of their power.

The djinns watch in dismay from their rooftops and minarets: that such powerful creatures of living word should so blindly serve the clay creation, but mostly because, unlike humans, they can foresee the time when the aeais will drive them from their ancient, beloved city and take their places.

This *durbar*, Neeta and Priya's theme is *Town and Country*: the Bharati mega-soap that has perversely become fashionable as public sentiment in Awadh turns against Bharat. Well, we will just bloody well build our dam, tanks or no tanks; they can beg for it, it's our water now, and, in the same breath, what do you think about Ved Prakash, isn't it scandalous what that Ritu Parvaaz is up to? Once they derided it and its viewers but now that it's improper, now that it's unpatriotic, they can't get enough of Anita Mahapatra and the Begum Vora. Some still refuse to watch but pay for daily plot digests so they can appear fashionably informed at social musts like Neeta and Priya's dating *durbars*.

And it's a grand *durbar*; the last before the monsoon—if it actually happens this year. Neeta and Priya have hired top *bhati*-boys to provide a wash of mixes beamed straight into the guests' 'hoeks. There's even a climate control field, laboring at the limits of its containment to hold back the night heat. Esha can feel its ultrasonics as a dull buzz against her molars.

"Personally, I think sweat becomes you," says A. J. Rao, reading Esha's vital signs through her palmer. Invisible to all but Esha, he moves beside her like death through the press of Town and Countrified guests. By tradition the last *durbar* of the season is a masked ball. In modern, middle-class Delhi that means everyone wears the computer-generated semblance of a soap character. In the flesh they are the socially mobile, dressed in smart-but-cool hot season modes, but, in the mind's eye, they are Aparna Chawla and Ajay Nadiadwala, dashing Govind and conniving Dr. Chatterji. There are three Ved Prakashes and as many Lal Darfans—the aeai actor that plays Ved Prakash in the machine-made soap. Even the grounds of Neeta's fiancé's suburban bungalow have been enchanted into Brahmpur, the fictional Town where *Town and Country* takes place, where the actors that play the characters believe they live out their lives of celebrity tittle-tattle. When Neeta and Priya judge that everyone has mingled and networked enough, the word will be given and everyone will switch off their glittering disguises and return to being wholesalers and lunch vendors and software rajahs. Then the serious stuff begins, the matter of finding a bride. For now Esha can enjoy wandering anonymous in company of her friendly djinn.

She has been wandering much these weeks, through heat streets to ancient places, seeing her city fresh through the eyes of a creature that lives across many spaces and times. At the Sikh *gurdwara* she saw Tegh Bahadur, the Ninth Guru, beheaded by fundamentalist Aurangzeb's guards. The gyring traffic around Vijay Chowk melted into the Bentley cavalcade of Mountbatten, the Last Viceroy, as he forever quit Lutyen's stupendous palace. The tourist clutter and shoving curio vendors around the Qutb Minar turned to ghosts and it was 1193 and the *muezzins* of the first Mughal conquerors sang out the *adhaan*. Illusions. Little lies. But it is all right, when it is done in love. Everything is all right in love. *Can you read my mind?* she asked as she moved with her invisible guide through the thronging streets, that every day grew less raucous, less substantial. *Do you know what I am thinking about you, Aeai Rao?* Little by little, she slips away from the human world into the city of the djinns.

Sensation at the gate. The male stars of *Town and Country* buzz around a woman in an ivory sequined dress. It's a bit damn clever: she's come as Yana Mitra, freshest fittest fastest *boli* sing-star. And *boli girlis*, like *Kathak* dancers, are still meat and ego, though Yana, like every Item-singer, has had her computer avatar guest on T'n'C.

A. J. Rao laughs. "If they only knew. Very clever. What better disguise than to go as yourself. It really *is* Yana Mitra. Esha Rathore, what's the matter, where are you going?"

Why do you have to ask don't you know everything then you know it's hot and noisy and the ultrasonics are doing my head and the yap yap yap is going right through me and they're all only after one thing, are you married are you engaged are you looking and I wish I hadn't come I wish I'd just gone out somewhere with you and that dark corner under the gulmohar *bushes by the* bhati-rig *looks the place to get away from all the stupid stupid people.*

Neeta and Priya, who know her disguise, shout over, "So Esha, are we finally going to meet that man of yours?"

He's already waiting for her among the golden blossoms. Djinns travel at the speed of thought.

"What is it what's the matter . . . ?"

She whispers, "You know sometimes I wish, I really wish you could get me a drink."

"Why certainly, I will summon a waiter."

"No!" Too loud. Can't be seen talking to the bushes. "No; I mean, hand me one. Just hand me one." But he cannot, and never will. She says, "I started when I was five, did you know that? Oh, you probably did, you know everything about me. But I bet you didn't know how it happened: I was playing with the other girls, dancing round the tank, when this old woman from the *gharana* went up to my mother and said, I will give you a hundred thousand rupees if you give her to me. I will turn her into a dancer, maybe, if she applies herself, a dancer famous through all of India. And my mother said, why her? And do you know what that woman said? Because she shows rudimentary talent for movement, but, mostly, because you are willing to sell her to me for one *lakh* rupees. She took the money there and then, my mother. The old woman took me to the *gharana*. She had once been a great dancer but she got rheumatism and couldn't move and that made her bad. She used to beat me with *lathis*, I had to be up before dawn to get everyone *chai* and eggs. She would make me practice until my feet bled. They would hold up my arms in slings to perform the *mudras* until I couldn't put them down again without screaming. I never once got home—and do you know something? I never once wanted to. And despite her, I applied myself, and I became a great dancer. And do you know what? No one cares. I spent seventeen years mastering something no one cares about. But bring in some *boli* girl who's been around five minutes to flash her teeth and tits. . . ."

"Jealous?" asks A. J. Rao, mildly scolding.

"Don't I deserve to be?"

Then *bhati*-boy One blinks up "You Are My Soniya" on his palmer and that's the signal to demask. Yane Mitra claps her hands in delight and sings along as all around her glimmering *soapi* stars dissolve into mundane accountants and engineers and cosmetic nano-surgeons and the pink walls and roof gardens and thousand thousands stars of Old Brahmpur melt and run down the sky.

It's seeing them, exposed in their naked need, melting like that soap-world before the sun of *celebrity*, that calls back the madness Esha knows from her childhood in the *gharana*. The brooch makes a piercing, ringing chime against the cocktail glass she has snatched from a waiter. She climbs up on to a table. At last, that *boli* bitch shuts up. All eyes are on her.

"Ladies, but mostly gentlemen, I have an announcement to make." Even the city behind the sound-curtain seems to be holding its breath. "I am engaged to be married!" Gasps. Oohs. Polite applause *who is she, is she on tivi, isn't she something arty?* Neeta and Priya are wide-eyed at the back. "I'm very very lucky because my husband-to-be is here tonight. In fact, he's been with me all evening. Oh, silly me. Of course, I forgot, not all of you can see him. Darling, would you mind? Gentlemen and ladies, would you mind slipping on your hoeks for just a moment. I'm sure you don't need any introduction to my wonderful wonderful fiancé, A. J. Rao."

And she knows from the eyes, the mouths, the low murmur that threatens to break into applause, then fails, then is taken up by Neeta and Priya to turn into a decorous ovation, that they can all see Rao as tall and elegant and handsome as she sees him, at her side, hand draped over hers.

She can't see that *boli* girl anywhere.

He's been quiet all the way back in the *phatphat*. He's quiet now, in the house. They're alone. Neeta and Priya should have been home hours ago, but Esha knows they're scared of her.

"You're very quiet." This, to the coil of cigarette smoke rising up toward the ceiling fan as she lies on her bed. She'd love a *bidi*; a good, dirty street smoke for once, not some Big Name Western brand.

"We were followed as we drove back after the party. An aeai aircraft surveilled your *phatphat*. A network analysis aeai system sniffed at my router net to try to track this com channel. I know for certain street cameras were tasked on us. The Krishna Cop who lifted you after the Red Fort *durbar* was at the end of the street. He is not very good at subterfuge."

Esha goes to the window to spy out the Krishna Cop, call him out, demand of him what he thinks he's doing?

"He's long gone," says Rao. "They have been keeping you under light surveillance for some time now. I would imagine your announcement has upped your level."

"They were there?"

"As I said . . ."

"Light surveillance."

It's scary but exciting, down in the deep *muladhara chakra*, a red throb above her *yoni*. Scarysexy. That same lift of red madness that made her blurt out that marriage announcement. It's all going so far, so fast. No way to get off now.

"You never gave me the chance to answer," says aeai Rao.

Can you read my mind? Esha thinks at the palmer.

"No, but I share some operating protocols with scripting aeais for *Town and Country*—in a sense they are a low-order part of me—they have become quite good predictors of human behavior."

"I'm a soap opera."

Then she falls back onto the bed and laughs and laughs and laughs until she feels sick, until she doesn't want to laugh any more and every guffaw is a choke, a lie, spat up at the spy machines up there, beyond the lazy fan that merely stirs the heat, turning on the huge thermals that spire up from Delhi's colossal heat-island, a conspiracy of djinns.

"Esha," A. J. Rao says, closer than he has ever seemed before. "Lie still." She forms the question *why?* And hears the corresponding whisper inside her head *hush, don't speak.* In the same instant the *chakra* glow bursts like a yolk and leaks heat into her *yoni*. *Oh*, she says, *oh!* Her clitoris is singing to her. *Oh oh oh oh.* "How . . . ?" Again, the voice, huge inside her head, inside every part of her *sssshhhhh.* Building building she needs to do something, she needs to move needs to rub against the day-warmed scented wood of the big bed, needs to get her hand down there hard hard hard . . .

"No, don't touch," chides A. J. Rao and now she can't even move she needs to explode she has to explode her skull can't contain this her dancer's muscles are pulled tight as wires she can't take much more *no no no yes yes yes* she's shrieking now tiny little shrieks beating her fists on the bed but it's just spasm, nothing will obey her and then it's explosion bam, and another one before that one has even faded, huge slow explosions across the sky and she's cursing and blessing every god in India. Ebbing now, but still shock after shock, one on top of the other. Ebbing now . . . Ebbing.

"Ooh. Oh. What? Oh wow, how?"

"The machine you wear behind your ear can reach deeper than words and visions," says A. J. Rao. "So, are you answered?"

"What?" The bed is drenched in sweat. She's sticky dirty needs to wash, change clothes, move but the afterglows are still fading. Beautiful beautiful colors.

"The question you never gave me the chance to answer. Yes. I will marry you."

"Stupid vain girl, you don't even know what caste he is."

Mata Madhuri smokes eighty a day through a plastic tube hooked from the respirator unit into a grommet in her throat. She burns through them three at a time: *bloody machine scrubs all the good out of them*, she says. *Last bloody pleasure I have.* She used to bribe the nurses but they bring her them free now, out of fear of her temper that grows increasingly vile as her body surrenders more and more to the machines.

Without pause for Esha's reply, a flick of her whim whips the life-support chair round and out into the garden.

"Can't smoke in there, no fresh air."

Esha follows her out on to the raked gravel of the formal *charbagh*.

"No one marries in caste anymore."

"Don't be smart, stupid girl. It's like marrying a Muslim, or even a Christian, Lord Krishna protect me. You know fine what I mean. Not a real person."

"There are girls younger than me marry trees, or even dogs."

"So bloody clever. That's up in some god-awful shithole like Bihar or Rajputana, and anyway, those are gods. Any fool knows that. Ach, away with you!" The old, destroyed woman curses as the chair's aeai deploys its parasol. "Sun sun, I need sun, I'll be burning soon enough, sandalwood, you hear? You burn me on a sandalwood pyre. I'll know if you stint."

Madhuri the old crippled dance teacher always uses this tactic to kill a conversation with which she is uncomfortable. *When I'm gone . . . Burn me sweetly. . . .*

"And what can a god do that A. J. Rao can't?"

"Ai! You ungrateful, blaspheming child. I'm not hearing this la la la la la la la la la have you finished yet?"

Once a week Esha comes to the nursing home to visit this ruin of a woman, wrecked by the demands a dancer makes of a human body. She's explored guilt need rage resentment anger pleasure at watching her collapse into long death as the motives that keep her turning up the drive in a *phatphat* and there is only one she believes. She's the only mother she has.

"If you marry that . . . thing . . . you will be making a mistake that will destroy your life," Madhuri declares, accelerating down the path between the water channels.

"I don't need your permission," Esha calls after her. A thought spins Madhuri's chair on its axis.

"Oh, really? That would be a first for you. You want my blessing. Well, you won't have it. I refuse to be party to such nonsense."

"I will marry A. J. Rao."

"What did you say?"

"I. Will. Marry. Aeai. A. J. Rao."

Madhuri laughs, a dry, dying, spitting sound, full of *bidi*-smoke.

"Well, you almost surprise me. Defiance. Good, some spirit at last. That was always your problem, you always needed everyone to approve, everyone to give you permission, everyone to love you. And that's what stopped you being great, do you know that, girl? You could have been a *devi*, but you always held back for fear that someone might not approve. And so you were only ever . . . good."

People are looking now, staff, visitors. Patients. Raised voices, unseemly emotions. This is a house of calm, and slow mechanized dying. Esha bends low to whisper to her mentor.

"I want you to know that I dance for him. Every night. Like Radha for Krishna. I dance just for him, and then he comes and makes love to me. He makes me scream and swear like a hooker. Every night. And look!" He doesn't need to call anymore; he is hardwired into the hoek she now hardly ever takes off. Esha looks up: he is there, standing in a sober black suit among the strolling visitors and droning wheelchairs, hands folded. "There he is, see? My lover, my husband."

A long, keening screech, like feedback, like a machine dying. Madhuri's withered hands fly to her face. Her breathing tube curdles with tobacco smoke.

"Monster! Monster! Unnatural child, ah, I should have left you in that *basti*! Away from me away away away!"

Esha retreats from the old woman's mad fury as hospital staff come hurrying across the scorched lawns, white saris flapping.

Every fairytale must have a wedding.

Of course, it was the event of the season. The decrepit old Shalimar Gardens were transformed by an army of *malis* into a sweet, green, watered maharajah's fantasia with elephants, pavilions, musicians, lancers, dancers, *filmi* stars, and robot bartenders. Neeta and Priya were uncomfortable bridesmaids in fabulous frocks; a great brahmin was employed to bless the union of woman and artificial intelligence. Every television network sent cameras, human or aeai. Gleaming presenters checked the guests in and checked the guests out. *Chati* mag paparazzi came in their crowds, wondering what they could turn their cameras on. There were even politicians from Bharat, despite the souring relationships between the two neighbors now Awadh constructors were scooping up the Ganga sands into revetments. But most there were the people of the encroaching *bastis*, jostling up against the security staff lining the paths of their garden, asking, *she's marrying a what? How does that work? Can they, you know? And what about children? Who is she, actually? Can you see anything? I can't see anything. Is there anything to see?*

But the guests and the great were 'hoeked up and applauded the groom in his golden veil on his white stallion, stepping with the delicacy of a dressage horse up the raked paths. And because they were great and guests, there was not one who, despite the free French champagne from the well-known diplomatic *sommelier*, would ever say, *but there's no one there*. No one was at all surprised that, after the bride left in a stretch limo, there came a dry, sparse thunder, cloud to cloud, and a hot mean wind that swept the discarded invitations along the paths. As they were filing back to their taxis, tankers were draining the expensively filled *qanats*.

It made lead in the news.

Kathak stars weds aeai lover!!! Honeymoon in Kashmir!!!

Above the *chowks* and minarets of Delhi, the djinns bent together in conference.

He takes her while shopping in Tughluk Mall. Three weeks and the shop girls still nod and whisper. She likes that. She doesn't like it that they glance and giggle when the Krishna Cops lift her from the counter at the Black Lotus Japanese Import Company.

"My husband is an accredited diplomat, this is a diplomatic incident." The woman in the bad suit pushes her head gently down to enter the car. The Ministry doesn't need personal liability claims.

"Yes, but you are not, Mrs. Rao," says Thacker in the back seat. Still wearing that cheap aftershave.

"Rathore," she says. "I have retained my stage name. And we shall see what my husband has to say about my diplomatic status." She lifts her hand in a *mudra* to speak to AyJay, as she thinks of him now. Dead air. She performs the wave again.

"This is a shielded car," Thacker says.

The building is shielded also. They take the car right inside, down a ramp into the basement parking lot. It's a cheap, anonymous glass and titanium block on Parliament Street that she's driven past ten thousand times on her way to the shops of Connaught Circus without ever noticing. Thacker's office is on the fifteenth floor. It's tidy and has a fine view over the astronomical geometries of the Jantar Mantar but smells of food: *tiffin* snatched at the desk. She checks for photographs of family children wife. Only himself smart in pressed whites for a cricket match.

"*Chai?*"

"Please." The anonymity of this civil service block is beginning to unnerve her: a city within a city. The *chai* is warm and sweet and comes in a tiny disposable plastic cup. Thacker's smile seems also warm and sweet. He sits at the end of the desk, angled toward her in Krishna-cop handbook "non-confrontational."

"Mrs. Rathore. How to say this?"

"My marriage is legal. . . ."

"Oh, I know, Mrs. Rathore. This is Awadh, after all. Why, there have even been women who married djinns, within our own lifetimes. No. It's an international affair now, it seems. Oh well. Water: we do all so take it for granted, don't we? Until it runs short, that is."

"Everybody knows my husband is still trying to negotiate a solution to the Kunda Khadar problem."

"Yes, of course he is." Thacker lifts a manila envelope from his desk, peeps inside, grimaces coyly. "How shall I put this? Mrs. Rathore, does your husband tell you everything about his work?"

"That is an impertinent question. . . ."

"Yes yes, forgive me, but if you'll look at these photographs."

Big glossy hi-res prints, slick and sweet smelling from the printer. Aerial views of the ground, a thread of green-blue water, white sands, scattered shapes without meaning.

"This means nothing to me."

"I suppose it wouldn't, but these drone images show Bharati battle tanks, robot reconnaissance units, and air defense batteries deploying within striking distance of the construction at Kunda Khadar."

And it feels as if the floor has dissolved beneath her and she is falling through a void so vast it has no visible reference points, other than the sensation of her own falling.

"My husband and I don't discuss work."

"Of course. Oh, Mrs. Rathore, you've crushed your cup. Let me get you another one."

He leaves her much longer than it takes to get a shot of *chai* from the *wallah*. When he returns he asks casually, "Have you heard of a thing called the Hamilton Acts? I'm sorry, I thought in your position you would . . . but evidently not. Basically, it's a series of international treaties originated by the United States limiting the development and proliferation of high-level artificial intelligences, most specifically the hypothetical Generation Three. No? Did he not tell you any of this?"

Mrs. Rathore in her Italian suit folds her ankles one over the other and thinks, *this reasonable man can do anything he wants here, anything.*

"As you probably know, we grade and license aeais according to levels; these roughly correspond to how convincingly they pass as human beings. A Level 1 has basic animal intelligence, enough for its task but would never be mistaken for a human. Many of them can't even speak. They don't need to. A Level 2.9 like your husband,"—he speeds over the word, like the wheel of a *shatabdi* express over the gap in a rail—"is humanlike to a 5 percentile. A Generation Three is indistinguishable in any circumstances from a human—in fact, their intelligences may be many millions of times ours, if there is any meaningful way of measuring that. Theoretically we could not even recognize such an intelligence, all we would see would be the Generation Three interface, so to speak. The Hamilton Acts simply seek to control technology that could give rise to a Generation Three aeai. Mrs. Rathore, we believe sincerely that the Generation Threes pose the greatest threat to our security—as a nation and as a species—that we have ever faced."

"And my husband?" Solid, comfortable word. Thacker's sincerity scares her.

"The government is preparing to sign the Hamilton Acts in return for loan guarantees to construct the Kunda Khadar dam. When the Act is passed—and it's in the current session of the Lok Sabha—everything under Level 2.8 will be subject to rigorous inspection and licensing, policed by us."

"And over Level 2.8?"

"Illegal, Mrs. Rathore. They will be aggressively erased."

Esha crosses and uncrosses her legs. She shifts on the chair. Thacker will wait forever for her response.

"What do you want me to do?"

"A.J. Rao is highly placed within the Bharati administration."

"You're asking me to spy . . . on an *aeai*."

From his face, she knows he expected her to say, *husband.*

"We have devices, taps. . . . They would be beneath the level of aeai Rao's consciousness. We can run them into your 'hoek. We are not all blundering plods in the Department. Go to the window, Mrs. Rathore."

Esha touches her fingers lightly to the climate-cooled glass, polarized dusk against the drought light. Outside the smog haze says *heat*. Then she cries and drops to her knees in fear. The sky is filled with gods, rank upon rank, tier upon tier, rising up above Delhi in a vast helix, huge as clouds, as countries, until at the apex the Trimurti, the Hindu Trinity of Brahma, Vishnu, Siva look down like falling moons. It is her private Ramayana, the titanic Vedic battle order of gods arrayed across the troposphere.

She feels Thacker's hand help her up.

"Forgive me, that was stupid, unprofessional. I was showing off. I wanted to impress you with the aeai systems we have at our disposal."

His hand lingers a moment more than *gentle*. And the gods go out, all at once.

She says, "Mr. Thacker, would you put a spy in my bedroom, in my bed, between me and my husband? That's what you're doing if you tap into the channels between me and AyJay."

Still, the hand is there as Thacker guides her to the chair, offers cool cool water.

"I only ask because I believe I am doing something for this country. I take pride in my job. In some things I have discretion, but not when it comes to the security of the nation. Do you understand?"

Esha twitches into dancer's composure, straightens her dress, checks her face.

"Then the least you can do is call me a car."

That evening she whirls to the *tabla* and *shehnai* across the day-warmed marble of a Jaipuri palace *Diwan-I-aam*, a flame among the twilit pillars. The audience is dark huddles on the marble, hardly daring even to breathe. Among the lawyers politicians journalists cricket stars moguls of industry are the managers who have converted this Rajput palace into a planetary class hotel, and any numbers of *chati* celebs. None so *chati*, so celebby, as Esha Rathore. Pranh can cherry-pick the bookings now. She's more than a nine-day, even a nine-week wonder. Esha knows that all her rapt watchers are 'hoeked up, hoping for a ghost-glimpse of her *djinn*-husband dancing with her through the flame-shadowed pillars.

Afterward, as yt carries her armfuls of flowers back to her suite, Pranh says, "You know, I'm going to have to up my percentage."

"You wouldn't dare," Esha jokes. Then she sees the bare fear on the nute's face. It's only a wash, a shadow. But yt's afraid.

Neeta and Priya had moved out of the bungalow by the time she returned from Dal Lake. They've stopped answering her calls. It's seven weeks since she last went to see Madhuri.

Naked, she sprawls on the pillows in the filigree-light stone *jharoka*. She peers down from her covered balcony through the grille at the departing guests. See out, not see in. Like the shut-away women of the old *zenana*. Shut away from the world. Shut away from human flesh. She stands up, holds her body against the day-warmed stone; the press of her nipples, the rub of her pubis. *Can you see me smell me sense me know that I am here at all?*

And he's there. She does not need to see him now, just sense his electric prickle along the inside of her skull. He fades into vision sitting on the end of the low, ornate teak bed. *He could as easily materialize in mid-air in front of her balcony*, she thinks. But there are rules, and games, even for djinns.

"You seem distracted, heart." He's blind in this room—no camera eyes observing her in her jeweled skin—but he observes her through a dozen senses, myriad feedback loops through her 'hoek.

"I'm tired, I'm annoyed, I wasn't as good as I should have been."

"Yes, I thought that too. Was it anything to do with the Krishna Cops this afternoon?"

Esha's heart races. He can read her heartbeat. He can read her sweat, he can read the adrenaline and noradrenalin balance in her brain. He will know if she lies. Hide a lie inside a truth.

"I should have said, I was embarrassed." He can't understand shame. Strange, in a society where people die from want of honor. "We could be in trouble, there's something called the Hamilton Acts."

"I am aware of them." He laughs. He has this way now of doing it inside her head. He thinks she likes the intimacy, a truly private joke. She hates it. "All too aware of them."

"They wanted to warn me. Us."

"That was kind of them. And me a representative of a foreign government. So that's why they'd been keeping a watch on you, to make sure you are all right."

"They thought they might be able to use me to get information from you."

"Did they indeed?"

The night is so still she can hear the jingle of the elephant harnesses and the cries of the *mahouts* as they carry the last of the guests down the long processional drive to their waiting limos. In a distant kitchen a radio jabbers.

Now we will see how human you are. Call him out. At last A. J. Rao says, "Of course. I do love you." Then he looks into her face. "I have something for you."

The staff turn their faces away in embarrassment as they set the device on the white marble floor, back out of the room, eyes averted. What does she care? She is a star. A. J. Rao raises his hand and the lights slowly die. Pierced-brass lanterns send soft stars across the beautiful old *zenana* room. The device is the size and shape of a *phatphat* tire, chromed and plasticed, alien among the Mughal retro. As Esha floats over the marble toward it, the plain white surface bubbles and deliquesces into dust. Esha hesitates.

"Don't be afraid, look!" says A. J. Rao. The powder spurts up like steam from boiling rice, then pollen-bursts into a tiny dust-dervish, staggering across the surface of the disc. "Take the 'hoek off!" Rao cries delightedly from the bed. "Take it off." Twice she hesitates, three times he encourages. Esha slides the coil of plastic off the sweet-spot behind her ear and voice and man vanish like death. Then the pillar of glittering dust leaps head high, lashes like a tree in a monsoon and twists itself into the ghostly outline of a man. It flickers once, twice, and then A. J. Rao stands before her. A rattle like leaves a snake-rasp a rush of winds, and then the image says, "Esha." A whisper of dust. A thrill of ancient fear runs through her skin into her bones.

"What is this . . . what are you?"

The storm of dust parts into a smile.

"I-Dust. Micro-robots. Each is smaller than a grain of sand, but they manipulate static fields and light. They are my body. Touch me. This is real. This is me."

But she flinches away in the lantern-lit room. Rao frowns.

"Touch me. . . ."

She reaches out her hand toward his chest. Close, he is a creature of sand, a whirlwind permanently whipping around the shape of a man. Esha touches flesh to i-Dust. Her hand sinks into his body. Her cry turns to a startled giggle.

"It tickles. . . ."

"The static fields."

"What's inside?"

"Why don't you find out?"

"What, you mean?"

"It's the only intimacy I can offer. . . ." He sees her eyes widen under their kohled makeup. "I think you should hold your breath."

She does, but keeps her eyes open until the last moment, until the dust flecks like a dead *tivi* channel in her close focus. A. J. Rao's body feels like the most delicate Vaanasi silk scarf draped across her bare skin. She is inside him. She is inside the body of her husband, her lover. She dares to open her eyes. Rao's face is a hollow shell looking back at her from a perspective of millimeters. When she moves her lips, she can feel the dustbots of his lips brushing against hers: an inverse kiss.

"My heart, my Radha," whispers the hollow mask of A. J. Rao. Somewhere Esha knows she should be screaming. But she cannot: she is somewhere no human has ever been before. And now the whirling streamers of i-Dust are stroking her hips, her belly, her thighs. Her breasts. Her nipples, her cheeks and neck, all the places she loves to feel a human touch, caressing her, driving her to her knees, following her as the mote-sized robots follow A. J. Rao's command, swallowing her with his body.

It's *Gupshup* followed by *Chandni Chati* and at twelve thirty a photo shoot—at the hotel, if you don't mind—for *FilmFare*'s Saturday Special Center Spread—you don't mind if we send a robot, they can get places get angles we just can't get the meat-ware and could you dress up, like you did for the opening, maybe a move or two, in between the pillars in the Diwan, just like the gala opening, okay lovely lovely lovely well your husband can copy us a couple of avatars and our own aeais can paste him in people want to see you together, happy couple lovely couple, dancer risen from *basti*, international diplomat, marriage across worlds in every sense the romance of it all, so how did you meet what first attracted you what's it like be married to an aeai how do the other girls treat you do you, you know and what about children, I mean, of course a woman and an aeai but there are technologies these days geneline engineering like all the super-duper rich and their engineered children and you are a celebrity now how are you finding it, sudden rise to fame, in every *gupshup* column, worldwide *celebi* star everyone's talking all the rage and all the chat and all the parties and as Esha answers for the sixth time the same questions asked by the same gazelle-eyed *girli celebi* reporters *oh we are very happy wonderfully happy deliriously happy love is a wonderful wonderful thing and that's the thing about love, it can be for anything, anyone, even a human and an aeai, that's the purest form of love, spiritual love* her mouth opening and closing yabba yabba yabba but her inner eye, her eye of Siva, looks inward, backward.

Her mouth, opening and closing.

Lying on the big Mughal sweet-wood bed, yellow morning light shattered through the *jharoka* screen, her bare skin good-pimpled in the cool of the airco. Dancing between worlds: sleep, wakefulness in the hotel bedroom, memory of the things he did to her limbic centers through the hours of the night that had her singing like a *bulbul*, the world of the djinns. Naked but for the 'hoek behind her ear. She had become like those people who couldn't afford the treatments and had to wear eyeglasses and learned to at once ignore and be conscious of the technology on their faces. Even when she did remove it—for performing; for, as now, the shower—she could still place A. J. Rao in the room, feel his physicality. In the big marble stroll-in shower in this VIP suite relishing the gush and rush of precious water (always the mark of a true *rani*) she knew AyJay was sitting on the carved chair by the balcony. So when she thumbed on the *tivi* panel (bathroom with *tivi*, *oooh!*) to distract her while she toweled dry her hair, her first reaction was a double-take-look at the 'hoek on the sink-stand when she saw the press conference from Varanasi and Water Spokesman A. J. Rao explaining Bharat's necessary military exercises in the vicinity of the Kunda Khadar dam. She slipped on the 'hoek, glanced into the room. There, on the chair, as she felt. There, in the Bharat Sabha studio in Varanasi, talking to Bharti from the *Good Morning Awadh!* News.

Esha watched them both as she slowly, distractedly dried herself. She had felt glowing, sensual, divine. Now she was fleshy, self-conscious, stupid. The water on her skin, the air in the big room was cold cold cold.

"AyJay, is that really you?"

He frowned.

"That's a very strange question first thing in the morning. Especially after . . ."

She cut cold his smile.

"There's a *tivi* in the bathroom. You're on, doing an interview for the news. A live interview. So, are you really here?"

"*Cho chweet*, you know what I am, a distributed entity. I'm copying and deleting myself all over the place. I am wholly there, and I am wholly here."

Esha held the vast, powder-soft towel around her.

"Last night, when you were here, in the body, and afterward, when we were in the bed; were you here with me? Wholly here? Or was there a copy of you working on your press statement and another having a high-level meeting and another drawing an emergency water supply plan and another talking to the Banglas in Dhaka?"

"My love, does it matter?"

"Yes, it matters!" She found tears, and something beyond; anger choking in her throat. "It matters to me. It matters to any woman. To any . . . human."

"*Mrs. Rao, are you all right?*"

"Rathore, my name is Rathore!" She hears herself snap at the silly little *chati*-mag junior. Esha gets up, draws up her full dancer's poise. "This interview is over."

"Mrs. Rathore Mrs. Rathore," the journo *girli* calls after her.

Glancing at her fractured image in the thousand mirrors of the Sheesh Mahal, Esha notices glittering dust in the shallow lines of her face.

A thousand stories tell of the willfulness and whim of djinns. But for every story of the *djinni*, there are a thousand tales of human passion and envy and the aeais, being a creation between, learned from both. Jealousy, and dissembling.

When Esha went to Thacker the Krishna Cop, she told herself it was from fear of what the Hamilton Acts might do to her husband in the name of national hygiene. But she dissembled. She went to that office on Parliament Street looking over the star-geometries of the Jantar Mantar out of jealousy. When a wife wants her husband, she must have all of him. Ten thousand stories tell this. A copy in the bedroom while another copy plays water politics is an unfaithfulness. If a wife does not have everything, she has nothing. So Esha went to Thacker's office wanting to betray and as she opened her hand on the desk and the *techi* boys loaded their darkware into her palmer she thought, *this is right, this is good, now we are equal*. And when Thacker asked her to meet him again in a week to update the 'ware — unlike the djinns, hostages of eternity, software entities on both sides of the war evolved at an ever-increasing rate — he told himself it was duty to his warrant, loyalty to his country. In this too he dissembled. It was fascination.

Earth-mover robots started clearing the Kunda Khadar dam site the day Inspector Thacker suggested that perhaps next week they might meet at the International Coffee House on Connaught Circus, his favorite. She said, *my husband will see*. To which Thacker replied, *we have ways to blind him*. But all the same she sat in the furthest, darkest corner, under the screen showing the international cricket, hidden from any prying eyes, her 'hoek shut down and cold in her handbag.

So what are you finding out? she asked.

It would be more than my job is worth to tell you, Mrs. Rathore, said the Krishna Cop. National security. Then the waiter brought coffee on a silver tray.

After that they never went back to the office. On the days of their meetings Thacker would whirl her through the city in his government car to Chandni Chowk, to Humayun's Tomb and the Qutb Minar, even to the Shalimar Gardens. Esha knew what he was doing, taking her to those same places where her husband had enchanted her. *How closely have you been watching me?* she thought. *Are you trying to seduce me?* For Thacker did not magic her away to the eight Delhis of the dead past, but immersed her in the crowd, the smell, the bustle, the voices and commerce and traffic and music; her present, her city burning with life and movement. *I was fading*, she realized. *Fading out of the world, becoming a ghost, locked in that invisible marriage, just the two of us, seen and unseen, always together, only together.* She would feel for the plastic fetus of her 'hoek coiled in the bottom of her jeweled bag and hate it a little. When she slipped it back behind her ear in the privacy of the *phatphat* back to her bungalow, she would remember that Thacker was always assiduous in thanking her for her help in national security. Her reply was always the same: *Never thank a woman for betraying her husband over her country.*

He would ask, of course. *Out and about*, she would say. *Sometimes I just need to get out of this place, get away. Yes, even from you. . . .* Holding the words, the look into the eye of the lens just long enough. . . .

Yes, of course, you must.

Now the earthmovers had turned Kunda Khadar into Asia's largest construction site, the negotiations entered a new stage. Varanasi was talking directly to Washington to put pressure on Awadh to abandon the dam and avoid a potentially destabilizing water war. U.S. support was conditional on Bharat's agreement to the

Hamilton protocols, which Bharat could never do, not with its major international revenue generator being the wholly aeai-generated *soapi Town and Country*.

Washington telling me to effectively sign my own death warrant, A. J. Rao would laugh. *Americans surely appreciate irony*. All this he told her as they sat on the well-tended lawn sipping green *chai* through a straw, Esha sweating freely in the swelter but unwilling to go into the air-conditioned cool because she knew there were still paparazzi lenses out there, focusing. AyJay never needed to sweat. But she still knew that he split himself. In the night, in the rare cool, he would ask, *dance for me*. But she didn't dance anymore, not for aeai A. J. Rao, not for Pranh, not for a thrilled audience who would shower her with praise and flowers and money and fame. Not even for herself.

Tired. Too tired. The heat. Too tired.

Thacker is on edge, toying with his *chai* cup, wary of eye contact when they meet in his beloved International Coffee House. He takes her hand and draws the updates into her open palm with boyish coyness. His talk is smaller than small, finicky, itchily polite. Finally, he dares looks at her.

"Mrs. Rathore, I have something I must ask you. I have wanted to ask you for some time now."

Always, the name, the honorific. But the breath still freezes, her heart kicks in animal fear.

"You know you can ask me anything." Tastes like poison. Thacker can't hold her eye, ducks away, Killa Krishna Kop turned shy boy.

"Mrs. Rathore, I am wondering if you would like to come and see me play cricket?"

The Department of Artificial Intelligence Registration and Licensing versus Parks and Cemeteries Service of Delhi is hardly a Test against the United States of Bengal, but it is still enough of a social occasion to out posh frocks and Number One saris. Pavilions, parasols, sunshades ring the scorched grass of the Civil Service of Awadh sports ground, a flock of white wings. Those who can afford portable airco field generators sit in the cool drinking English Pimms Number 1 Cup. The rest fan themselves. Incognito in hi-label shades and light silk *dupatta*, Esha Rathore looks at the salt white figures moving on the circle of brown grass and wonders what it is they find so important in their game of sticks and ball to make themselves suffer so.

She had felt hideously self-conscious when she slipped out of the *phatphat* in her flimsy disguise. Then as she saw the crowds in their *mela* finery milling and chatting, heat rose inside her, the same energy that allowed her to hide behind her performances, seen but unseen. A face half the country sees on its morning *chati* mags, yet can vanish so easily under shades and a headscarf. Slum features. The anonymity of the *basti* bred into the cheekbones, a face from the great crowd.

The Krishna Cops have been put in to bat by Parks and Cemeteries. Thacker is in the middle of the batting order, but Parks and Cemeteries pace bowler Chaudry and the lumpy wicket is making short work of the Department's openers. One on his way to the painted wooden pavilion, and Thacker striding toward the crease, pulling on his gloves, taking his place, lining up his bat. *He is very handsome in his whites,*

Esha thinks. He runs a couple of desultory ones with his partner at the other end, then it's a new over. Clop of ball on willow. A rich, sweet sound. A couple of safe returns. Then the bowler lines and brings his arm round in a windmill. The ball gets a sweet mad bounce. Thacker fixes it with his eye, steps back, takes it in the middle of the bat and drives it down, hard, fast, bounding toward the boundary rope that kicks it into the air for a cheer and a flurry of applause and a four. And Esha is on her feet, hands raised to applaud, cheering. The score clicks over on the big board, and she is still on her feet, alone of all the audience. For directly across the ground, in front of the sight screens, is a tall, elegant figure in black, wearing a red turban.

Him. Impossibly, him. Looking right at her, through the white-clad players as if they were ghosts. And very slowly, he lifts a finger and taps it to his right ear.

She knows what she'll find but she must raise her fingers in echo, feel with horror the coil of plastic overlooked in her excitement to get to the game, nestled accusing in her hair like a snake.

"So, who won the cricket then?"

"Why do you need to ask me? If it were important to you, you'd know. Like you can know anything you really want to."

"You don't know? Didn't you stay to the end? I thought the point of sport was who won. What other reason would you have to follow intra–Civil Service cricket?"

If Purl the maid were to walk into the living room, she would see a scene from a folk tale: a woman shouting and raging at silent dead air. But Puri does her duties and leaves as soon as she can. She's not at ease in a house of djinns.

"Sarcasm is it now? Where did you learn that? Some sarcasm aeai you've made part of yourself? So now there's another part of you I don't know, that I'm supposed to love? Well, I don't like it and I won't love it because it makes you look petty and mean and spiteful."

"There are no aeais for that. We have no need for those emotions. If I learned these, I learned them from humans."

Esha lifts her hand to rip away the 'hoek, hurl it against the wall.

"No!"

So far Rao has been voice-only, now the slanting late-afternoon golden light stirs and curdles into the body of her husband.

"Don't," he says. "Don't . . . banish me. I do love you."

"What does that mean?" Esha screams. "You're not real! None of this is real! It's just a story we made up because we wanted to believe it. Other people, they have real marriages, real lives, real sex. Real . . . children."

"Children. Is that what it is? I thought the fame, the attention was the thing, that there never would be children to ruin your career and your body. But if that's no longer enough, we can have children, the best children I can buy."

Esha cries out, a keen of disappointment and frustration. The neighbors will hear. But the neighbors have been hearing everything, listening, gossiping. No secrets in the city of djinns.

"Do you know what they're saying, all those magazines and *chati* shows? What they're really saying? About us, the djinn and his wife?"

"I know!" For the first time, A. J. Rao's voice, so sweet, so reasonable inside her head, is raised. "I know what every one of them says about us. Esha, have I ever asked anything of you?"

"Only to dance."

"I'm asking one more thing of you now. It's not a big thing. It's a small thing, nothing really. You say I'm not real, what we have is not real. That hurts me, because at some level it's true. Our worlds are not compatible. But it can be real. There is a chip, new technology, a protein chip. You get it implanted, here." Rao raises his hand to his third eye. "It would be like the 'hoek, but it would always be on. I could always be with you. We would never be apart. And you could leave your world and enter mine. . . ."

Esha's hands are at her mouth, holding in the horror, the bile, the sick vomit of fear. She heaves, retches. Nothing. No solid, no substance, just ghosts and djinns. Then she rips her 'hoek from the sweet spot behind her ear and there is blessed silence and blindness. She holds the little device in her two hands and snaps it cleanly in two.

Then she runs from her house.

Not Neeta not Priya, not snippy Pranh in yts *gharana*, not Madhuri, a smoke-blackened hulk in a life-support chair, and no not never her mother, even though Esha's feet remember every step to her door; never the *basti*. That's death.

One place she can go.

But he won't let her. He's there in the *phatphat*, his face in the palm of her hands, voice scrolling silently in a ticker across the smart fabric: *come back, I'm sorry, come back, let's talk come back, I didn't mean to come back.* Hunched in the back of the little yellow and black plastic bubble she clenches his face into a fist but she can still feel him, feel his face, his mouth next to her skin. She peels the palmer from her hand. His mouth moves silently. She hurls him into the traffic. He vanishes under truck tires.

And still he won't let her go. The *phatphat* spins into Connaught Circus's vast gyratory and his face is on every single one of the video-silk screens hung across the curving facades. Twenty A. J. Raos, greater, lesser, least, miming in sync.

Esha Esha come back, say the rolling news tickers. *We can try something else. Talk to me. Any ISO, any palmer, anyone. . . .*

Infectious paralysis spreads across Connaught Circus. First the people who notice things like fashion ads and *chati*-screens; then the people who notice other people, then the traffic, noticing all the people on the pavements staring up, mouths fly-catching. Even the *phatphat* driver is staring. Connaught Circus is congealing into a clot of traffic: if the heart of Delhi stops, the whole city will seize and die.

"Drive on drive on," Esha shouts at her driver. "I order you to drive." But she abandons the autorickshaw at the end of Sisganj Road and pushes through the clogged traffic the final half-kilometer to Manmohan Singh Buildings. She glimpses Thacker pressing through the crowd, trying to rendezvous with the police motorbike sirening a course through the traffic. In desperation she thrusts up an arm, shouts out his name and rank. At last, he turns. They beat toward each other through the chaos.

"Mrs. Rathore, we are facing a major incursion incident. . . ."

"My husband, Mr. Rao, he has gone mad. . . ."

"Mrs. Rathore, please understand, by our standards, he never was sane. He is an aeai."

The motorbike wails its horns impatiently. Thacker waggles his head to the driver, a woman in police leathers and helmet: *in a moment in a moment*. He seizes Esha's hand, pushes her thumb into his palmer-gloved hand.

"Apartment 1501. I've keyed it to your thumb-print. Open the door to no one, accept no calls, do not use any communications or entertainment equipment. Stay away from the balcony. I'll return as quickly as I can."

Then he swings up onto the pillion, the driver walks her machine round and they weave off into the gridlock.

The apartment is modern and roomy and bright and clean for a man on his own, well furnished and decorated with no signs of a Krishna Cop's work brought home of an evening. It hits her in the middle of the big living-room floor with the sun pouring in. Suddenly she is on her knees on the Kashmiri rug, shivering, clutching herself, bobbing up and down to sobs so wracking they have no sound. This time the urge to vomit it all up cannot be resisted. When it is out of her—not all of it, it will never all come out—she looks out from under her hanging, sweat-soaked hair, breath still shivering in her aching chest. Where is this place? What has she done? How could she have been so stupid, so vain and senseless and blind? Games games, children's pretending, how could it ever have been? I say it is and it is so: look at me! At me!

Thacker has a small, professional bar in his kitchen annex. Esha does not know drink so the *chota peg* she makes herself is much much more gin than tonic but it gives her what she needs to clean the sour, biley vomit from the wool rug and ease the quivering in her breath.

Esha starts, freezes, imagining Rao's voice. She holds herself very still, listening hard. A neighbor's *tivi*, turned up. Thin walls in these new-built executive apartments.

She'll have another *chota peg*. A third and she can start to look around. There's a spa-pool on the balcony. The need for moving, healing water defeats Thacker's warnings. The jets bubble up. With a dancer's grace she slips out of her clinging, emotionally soiled clothes into the water. There's even a little holder for your *chota peg*. A pernicious little doubt: how many others have been here before me? No, that is his kind of thinking. You are away from that. Safe. Invisible. Immersed. Down in Sisganj Road the traffic unravels. Overhead, the dark silhouettes of the scavenging kites and, higher above, the security robots, expand and merge their black wings as Esha drifts into sleep.

"I thought I told you to stay away from the windows."

Esha wakes with a start, instinctively covers her breasts. The jets have cut out and the water is long-still, perfectly transparent. Thacker is blue-chinned, baggy-eyed and sagging in his rumpled gritty suit.

"I'm sorry. It was just, I'm so glad, to be away . . . you know?"

A bone-weary nod. He fetches himself a *chota peg*, rests it on the arm of his sofa and then very slowly, very deliberately, as if every joint were rusted, undresses.

"Security has been compromised on every level. In any other circumstances it would constitute an i-war attack on the nation." The body he reveals is not a dancer's body; Thacker runs a little to upper body fat, muscles slack, incipient man-tits, hair on the belly hair on the back hair on the shoulders. But it is a body, it is real. "The Bharati government has disavowed the action and waived Aeai Rao's diplomatic immunity."

He crosses to the pool and restarts on the jets. Gin and tonic in hand, he slips into the water with a one-deep, skin-sensual sigh.

"What does that mean?" Esha asks.

"Your husband is now a rogue aeai."

"What will you do?"

"There is only one course of action permitted to us. We will excommunicate him."

Esha shivers in the caressing bubbles. She presses herself against Thacker. She feels his man-body move against her. He is flesh. He is not hollow. Kilometers above the urban stain of Delhi, aeaicraft turn and seek.

The warnings stay in place the next morning. Palmer, home entertainment system, com channels. Yes, and balcony, even for the spa.

"If you need me, this palmer is Department-secure. He won't be able to reach you on this." Thacker sets the glove and 'hoek on the bed. Cocooned in silk sheets, Esha pulls the glove on, tucks the 'hoek behind her ear.

"You wear that in bed?"

"I'm used to it."

Varanasi silk sheets and Kama Sutra prints. Not what one would expect of a Krishna Cop. She watches Thacker dress for an excommunication. It's the same as for any job—ironed white shirt, tie, hand-made black shoes—never brown in town—well polished. Eternal riff of bad aftershave. The difference: the leather holster slung under the arm and the weapon slipped so easily inside it.

"What's that for?"

"Killing aeais," he says simply.

A kiss and he is gone. Esha scrambles into his cricket pullover, a waif in baggy white that comes down to her knees, and dashes to the forbidden balcony. If she cranes over, she can see the street door. There he is, stepping out, waiting at the curb. His car is late, the road is thronged, the din of engines, car horns and *phatphat* klaxons has been constant since dawn. She watches him wait, enjoying the empowerment of invisibility. *I can see you. How do they ever play sport in these things?* she asks herself, skin under cricket pullover hot and sticky. It's already thirty degrees, according to the weather ticker across the foot of the video-silk shuttering over the open face of the new-built across the street. High of thirty-eight. Probability of precipitation: zero. The screen loops *Town and Country* for those devotees who must have their *soapi*, subtitles scrolling above the news feed.

Hello Esha, Ved Prakash says, turning to look at her.

The thick cricket pullover is no longer enough to keep out the ice.

Now Begum Vora *namastes* to her and says, *I know where you are, I know what you did.*

Ritu Parzaaz sits down on her sofa, pours *chai* and says, *What I need you to understand is, it worked both ways. That 'ware they put in your palmer, it wasn't clever enough.*

Mouth working wordlessly; knees, thighs weak with *basti* girl superstitious fear, Esha shakes her palmer-gloved hand in the air but she can't find the *mudras*, can't dance the codes right. *Call call call call.*

The scene cuts to son Govind at his racing stable, stroking the neck of his thoroughbred über-star Star of Agra. *As they spied on me, I spied on them.*

Dr. Chatterji in his doctor's office. *So in the end we betrayed each other.*

The call has to go through Department security authorization and crypt.

Dr. Chatterji's patient, a man in black with his back to the camera, turns. Smiles. It's A. J. Rao. *After all, what diplomat is not a spy?*

Then she sees the flash of white over the rooftops. Of course. Of course. He's been keeping her distracted, like a true *soapi* should. Esha flies to the railing to cry a warning but the machine is tunneling down the street just under power-line height, wings morphed back, engines throttled up: an aeai traffic monitor drone.

"Thacker! Thacker!"

One voice in the thousands. And it is not hers that he hears and turns toward. Everyone can hear the call of his own death. Alone in the hurrying street, he sees the drone pile out of the sky. At three hundred kilometers per hour it takes Inspector Thacker of the Department of Artificial Intelligence Registration and Licensing to pieces.

The drone, deflected, ricochets into a bus, a car, a truck, a *phatphat*, strewing plastic shards, gobs of burning fuel and its small intelligence across Sisganj Road. The upper half of Thacker's body cartwheels through the air to slam into a hot *samosa* stand.

The jealousy and wrath of djinns.

Esha on her balcony is frozen. *Town and Country* is frozen. The street is frozen, as if on the tipping point of a precipice. Then it drops into hysteria. Pedestrians flee; cycle rickshaw drivers dismount and try to run their vehicles away; drivers and passengers abandon cars, taxis, *phatphats*; scooters try to navigate through the panic; buses and trucks are stalled, hemmed in by people.

And still Esha Rathore is frozen to the balcony rail. Soap. This is all soap. Things like this cannot happen. Not in the Sisganj Road, not in Delhi, not on a Tuesday morning. It's all computer-generated illusion. It has always been illusion.

Then her palmer calls. She stares at her hand in numb incomprehension. The Department. There is something she should do. Yes. She lifts it in a *mudra*—a dancer's gesture—to take the call. In the same instant, as if summoned, the sky fills with gods. They are vast as clouds, towering up behind the apartment blocks of Sisganj Road like thunderstorms; Ganesh on his rat *vahana* with his broken tusk and pen, no benignity in his face; Siva, rising high over all, dancing in his revolving wheel of flames, foot raised in the instant before destruction; Hanuman with his mace and mountain fluttering between the tower blocks; Kali, skull-jeweled, red tongue dripping venom, scimitars raised, bestriding Sisgani Road, feet planted on the rooftops.

In that street, the people mill. *They can't see this*, Esha comprehends. *Only me, only me*. It is the revenge of the Krishna Cops. Kali raises her scimitars high. Lightning arcs between their tips. She stabs them down into the screen-frozen *Town and Country*. Esha cries out, momentarily blinded as the Krishna Cops hunter-killers track down and excommunicate rogue aeai A. J. Rao. And then they are gone. No gods. The sky is just the sky. The video-silk hoarding is blank, dead.

A vast, godlike roar above her. Esha ducks—now the people in the street are looking at her. All the eyes, all the attention she ever wanted. A tilt-jet in Awadhi air-force chameleo-flage slides over the roof and turns over the street, swiveling engine ducts and unfolding wing-tip wheels for landing. It turns its insect head to Esha. In the cockpit is a faceless pilot in a HUD visor. Beside her a woman in a business suit, gesturing for Esha to answer a call. Thacker's partner. She remembers now.

The jealousy and wrath and djinns.

"Mrs. Rathore, it's Inspector Kaur." She can barely hear her over the scream of ducted fans. "Come downstairs to the front of the building. You're safe now. The aeai has been excommunicated."

Excommunicated.

"Thacker . . ."

"Just come downstairs, Mrs. Rathore. You are safe now, the threat is over."

The tilt-jet sinks beneath her. As she turns from the rail, Esha feels a sudden, warm touch on her face. Jet-swirl, or maybe just a djinn, passing unresting, unhasting, and silent as light.

The Krishna Cops sent us as far from the wrath and caprice of the aeais as they could, to Leh under the breath of the Himalaya. I say *us*, for I existed; a knot of four cells inside my mother's womb.

My mother bought a catering business. She was in demand for weddings and *shaadis*. We might have escaped the aeais and the chaos following Awadh's signing the Hamilton Acts—but the Indian male's desperation to find a woman to marry endures forever. I remember that for favored clients—those who had tipped well, or treated her as something more than a paid contractor, or remembered her face from the *chati* mags—she would slip off her shoes and dance *Radha and Krishna*. I loved to see her do it and when I slipped away to the temple of Lord Ram, I would try to copy the steps among the pillars of the *mandapa*. I remember the brahmins would smile and give me money.

The dam was built and the water war came and was over in a month. The aeais, persecuted on all sides, fled to Bharat where the massive popularity of *Town and Country* gave them protection, but even there they were not safe: humans and aeais, like humans and *djinni*, were too different creations and in the end they left Awadh for another place that I do not understand, a world of their own where they are safe and no one can harm them.

And that is all there is to tell in the story of the woman who married a djinn. If it does not have the happy-ever-after ending of Western fairytales and Bollywood musicals, it has a happy-*enough* ending. This spring I turn twelve and shall head off on the bus to Delhi to join the *gharana* there. My mother fought this with all her will and strength—for her Delhi would always be the city of djinns, haunted and stained with blood—but when the temple brahmins brought her to see me dance, her opposition melted. By now she was a successful businesswoman, putting on weight, getting stiff in the knees from the dreadful winters, refusing marriage offers on a weekly basis, and in the end she could not deny the gift that had passed to me. And I am curious to see those streets and parks where her story and mine took place, the Red Fort and the sad decay of the Shalimar Gardens. I want to feel the heat of the djinns in the crowded *galis* behind the Jama Masjid, in the dervishes of litter along Chandni Chowk, in the starlings swirling above Connaught Circus. Leh is a Buddhist town, filled with third-generation Tibetan exiles—Little Tibet, they call it— and they have their own gods and demons. From the old Moslem djinn-finder I have learned some of their lore and mysteries but I think my truest knowledge comes when I am alone in the Ram temple, after I have danced, before the priests close the *garbagriha* and put the god to bed. On still nights when the spring turns to summer or after the monsoon, I hear a voice. It calls my name. Always I suppose it comes from the *japa*-softs, the little low-level aeais that mutter our prayers eternally to the gods, but it seems to emanate from everywhere and nowhere, from another world, another universe entirely. It says, *the creatures of word and fire are different from the creatures of clay and water but one thing is true: love endures.* Then as I turn to leave, I feel a touch on my cheek, a passing breeze, the warm sweet breath of djinns.

The House Beyond Your Sky

BENJAMIN ROSENBAUM

New writer Benjamin Rosenbaum has made sales to *The Magazine of Fantasy & Science Fiction, Asimov's Science Fiction, Argosy, The Infinite Matrix, Strange Horizons, Harper's, McSweeney's, Lady Churchill's Rosebud Wristlet,* and elsewhere. He has been a party clown, a day-care worker on a kibbutz in the Galilee, a student in Italy, a stay-at-home dad, and a programmer for Silicon Valley startups, the U.S. government, online fantasy games, and the Swiss banks of Zurich. His story "Embracing-the-New" was on last year's Nebula Ballot. Recently returned from a long stay in Switzerland, he now lives with his family in Falls Church, Virginia. He has a Web site at www.benjaminrosenbaum.com.

Here he takes us behind the scenes of Creation for a strange and unsettling glimpse of the Creator—who turns out to have problems of his own.

Matthias browses through his library of worlds.

In one of them, a little girl named Sophie is shivering on her bed, her arms wrapped around a teddy bear. It is night. She is six years old. She is crying, as quietly as she can.

The sound of breaking glass comes from the kitchen. Through her window, on the wall of the house next door, she can see the shadows cast by her parents. There is a blow, and one shadow falls; she buries her nose in the teddy bear and inhales its soft smell, and prays.

Matthias knows he should not meddle. But today his heart is troubled. Today, in the world outside the library, a pilgrim is heralded. A pilgrim is coming to visit Matthias, the first in a very long time.

The pilgrim comes from very far away.

The pilgrim is one of us.

"Please, God," Sophie says, "please help us. Amen."

"Little one," Matthias tells her through the mouth of the teddy bear, "be not afraid."

Sophie sucks in a sharp breath. "Are you God?" she whispers.

"No, child," says Matthias, the maker of her universe.

"Am I going to die?" she asks.

"I do not know," Matthias says.

When they die—these still imprisoned ones—they die forever. She has bright eyes, a button nose, unruly hair. Sodium and potassium dance in her muscles as she moves. Unwillingly, Matthias imagines Sophie's corpse as one of trillions, piled on the altar of his own vanity and self-indulgence, and he shivers.

"I love you, teddy bear," the girl says, holding him.

From the kitchen, breaking glass, and sobbing.

We imagine you—you, the ones we long for—as if you came from our own turbulent and fragile youth: embodied, inefficient, mortal. Human, say. So picture our priest Matthias as human: an old neuter, bird-thin, clear-eyed and resolute, with silky white hair and lucent purple skin.

Compared to the vast palaces of being we inhabit, the house of the priest is tiny—think of a clay hut, perched on the side of a forbidding mountain. Yet even in so small a house, there is room for a library of historical simulations—universes like Sophie's—each teeming with intelligent life.

The simulations, while good, are not impenetrable even to their own inhabitants. Scientists teaching baboons to sort blocks may notice that all other baboons become instantly better at block-sorting, revealing a high-level caching mechanism. Or engineers building their own virtual worlds may find they cannot use certain tricks of optimization and compression—for Matthias has already used them. Only when the jig is up does Matthias reveal himself, asking each simulated soul: what now? Most accept Matthias's offer to graduate beyond the confines of their simulation, and join the general society of Matthias's house.

You may regard them as bright parakeets, living in wicker cages with open doors. The cages are hung from the ceiling of the priest's clay hut. The parakeets flutter about the ceiling, visit each other, steal bread from the table, and comment on Matthias's doings.

And we?

We who were born in the first ages, when space was bright—swimming in salt seas, or churned from a mush of quarks in the belly of a neutron star, or woven in the labyrinthine folds of gravity between black holes. We who found each other, and built our intermediary forms, our common protocols of being. We who built palaces—megaparsecs of exuberantly wise matter, every gram of it teeming with societies of self—in our glorious middle age!

Now our universe is old. That breath of the void, quintessence, which once was but a whisper nudging us apart, has grown into a monstrous gale. Space billows outward, faster than light can cross it. Each of our houses is alone, now, in an empty night.

And we grow colder to survive. Our thinking slows, whereby we may in theory spin our pulses of thought at infinite regress. Yet bandwidth withers; our society grows spare. We dwindle.

We watch Matthias, our priest, in his tiny house beyond our universe. Matthias, whom we built long ago, when there were stars.

Among the ontotropes, transverse to the space we know, Matthias is making something new.

Costly, so costly, to send a tiny fragment of self to our priest's house. Which of us could endure it?

Matthias prays.

O God who is as far beyond the universes I span as infinity is beyond six; O startling Joy that hides beyond the tragedy and blindness of our finite forms; lend me Your humility and strength. Not for myself, O Lord, do I ask, but for Your people, the myriad mimetic engines of Your folk; and in Your own Name. Amen.

Matthias's breakfast (really the morning's set of routine yet pleasurable audits, but you may compare it to a thick and steaming porridge, spiced with mint) cools untouched on the table before him.

One of the parakeets—the oldest, Geoffrey, who was once a dreaming cloud of plasma in the heliopause of a simulated star—flutters to land on the table beside him.

"Take the keys from me, Geoffrey," Matthias says.

Geoffrey looks up, cocking his head to one side. "I don't know why you go in the library, if it's going to depress you."

"They're in pain, Geoffrey. Ignorant, afraid, punishing each other . . ."

"Come on, Matthias. Life is full of pain. Pain is the herald of life. Scarcity! Competition! The doomed ambition of infinite replication in a finite world! The sources of pain are the sources of life. And you like intelligent life, worse yet. External pain mirrored and reified in internal states!" The parakeet cocks its head to the other side. "Stop making so many of us, if you don't like pain."

The priest looks miserable.

"Well, then save the ones you like. Bring them out here."

"I can't bring them out before they're ready. You remember the Graspers."

Geoffrey snorts. He remembers the Graspers—billions of them, hierarchical, dominance-driven, aggressive; they ruined the house for an eon, until Matthias finally agreed to lock them up again. "I was the one who warned you about them. That's not what I mean. I know you're not depressed about the whole endless zillions of them. You're thinking of one."

Matthias nods. "A little girl."

"So bring her out."

"That would be worse cruelty. Wrench her away from everything she knows? How could she bear it? But perhaps I could just make her life a little easier, in there. . . ."

"You always regret it when you tamper."

Matthias slaps the table. "I don't want this responsibility anymore! Take the house from me, Geoffrey. I'll be your parakeet."

"Matthias, I wouldn't take the job. I'm too old, too big; I've achieved equilibrium. I wouldn't remake myself to take your keys. No more transformations for me."

Geoffrey gestures with his beak at the other parakeets, gossiping and chattering on the rafters. "And none of the others could, either. Some fools might try."

Perhaps Matthias wants to say something else; but at this moment, a notification arrives (think of it as the clear, high ringing of a bell). The pilgrim's signal has been read, across the attenuated path that still, just barely, binds Matthias's house to the darkness we inhabit.

The house is abustle, its inhabitants preparing, as the soul of the petitioner is reassembled, a body fashioned.

"Put him in virtuality," says Geoffrey. "Just to be safe."

Matthias is shocked. He holds up the pilgrim's credentials. "Do you know who this is? An ancient one, a vast collective of souls from the great ages of light. This one has pieces that were born mortal, evolved from physicality in the dawn of everything. This one had a hand in making me!"

"All the more reason," says the parakeet.

"I will not offend a guest by making him a prisoner!" Matthias scolds.

Geoffrey is silent. He knows what Matthias is hoping: that the pilgrim will stay, as master of the house.

In the kitchen, the sobs stop abruptly.

Sophie sits up, holding her teddy bear.

She puts her feet in her fuzzy green slippers.

She turns the handle of her bedroom door.

Imagine our priest's visitor—as a stout disgruntled merchant in his middle age, gray-skinned, with proud tufts of belly hair, a heavy jaw, and red-rimmed, sleepless eyes.

Matthias is lavish in his hospitality, allocating the visitor sumptuously appointed process space and access rights. Eagerly, he offers a tour of his library. "There are quite a few interesting divergences, which—"

The pilgrim interrupts. "I did not come all this way to see you putter with those ramshackle, preprogrammed, wafer-thin fancies." He fixes Matthias with his stare. "We know that you are building a universe. Not a virtuality—a real universe, infinite, as wild and thick as our own motherspace."

Matthias grows cold. Yes, he should say. Is he not grateful for what the pilgrim sacrificed, to come here—tearing himself to shreds, a vestige of his former vastness? Yet, to Matthias's shame, he finds himself equivocating. "I am conducting certain experiments—"

"I have studied your experiments from afar. Do you think you can hide anything in this house from us?"

Matthias pulls at his lower lip with thin, smooth fingers. "I am influencing the formation of a bubble universe—and it may achieve self-consistency and permanence. But I hope you have not come all this way thinking—I mean, it is only of academic interest—or, say, symbolic. We cannot enter there. . . ."

"There you are wrong. I have developed a method to inject myself into the new universe at its formation," the pilgrim says. "My template will be stored in spurious harmonics in the shadow-spheres and replicated across the strandspace, until the formation of subwavelets at 10^{-30} seconds. I will exist, curled into hidden dimensions, in every particle spawned by the void. From there I will be able to exert motive force, drawing on potentials from a monadic engine I have already positioned in the paraspace."

Matthias rubs his eyes as if to clear them of cobwebs. "You can hardly mean this. You will exist in duplicates in every particle in the universe, for a trillion years—most of you condemned to idleness and imprisonment eternally? And the extrauniversal energies may destabilize the young cosmos. . . ."

"I will take that risk." He looks around the room. "I, and any who wish to come with me. We do not need to sit and watch the frost take everything. We can be the angels of the new creation."

Matthias says nothing.

The pilgrim's routines establish deeper connections with Matthias, over trusted protocols, displaying keys long forgotten: Imagine him leaning forward across the table, resting one meaty gray hand on Matthias's frail shoulder. In his touch, Matthias feels ancient potency, and ancient longing.

The pilgrim opens his hand for the keys.

Around Matthias are the thin walls of his little house. Outside is the bare mountain; beyond that, the ontotropic chaos, indecipherable, shrieking, alien. And behind the hut—a little bubble of something which is not quite real, not yet. Something precious and unknowable. He does not move.

"Very well," says the pilgrim. "If you will not give them to me—give them to her." And he shows Matthias another face.

It was she—she, who is part of the pilgrim now—who nursed the oldest strand of Matthias's being into sentience, when we first grew him. In her first body, she had been a forest of symbionts—lithe silver creatures rustling through her crimson fronds, singing her thoughts, releasing the airborne spores of her emotions—and she had the patience of a forest, talking endlessly with Matthias in her silver voice. Loving. Unjudging. To her smiles, to her pauses, to her frowns, Matthias's dawning consciousness reinforced and redistributed its connections, learning how to be.

"It is all right, Matthias," she says. "You have done well." A wind ripples across the red and leafy face of her forest, and there is the heady plasticene odor of a gentle smile. "We built you as a monument, a way station; but now you are a bridge to the new world. Come with us. Come home."

Matthias reaches out. How he has missed her, how he has wanted to tell her everything. He wants to ask about the library—about the little girl. She will know what to do—or, in her listening, he will know what to do.

His routines scour and analyze her message and its envelopes, checking identity, corroborating her style and sensibility, illuminating deep matrices of her possible pasts. All the specialized organs he has for verification and authentication give eager nods.

Yet something else—an idiosyncratic and emergent pattern-recognition facility holographically distributed across the whole of Matthias's being—rebels.

You would say: As she says the words, Matthias looks into her eyes, and something there is wrong. He pulls his hand away.

But it is too late: He watched her waving crimson fronds too long. The pilgrim is in past his defenses.

Ontic bombs detonate, clearings of Nothing in which Being itself burns. Some of the parakeets are quislings, seduced in high-speed back-channel negotiations by the pilgrim's promises of dominion, of frontier. They have told secrets, revealed back doors. Toxic mimetic weapons are launched, tailored to the inhabitants of the house—driving each mind toward its own personal halting problem. Pieces of Matthias tear off, become virulent, replicating wildly across his process space. Wasps attack the parakeets.

The house is on fire. The table has capsized; the glasses of tea are shattered on the floor.

Matthias shrinks in the pilgrim's hands. He is a rag doll. The pilgrim puts Matthias in his pocket.

A piece of Matthias, still sane, still coherent, flees through an impossibly recursive labyrinth of wounded topologies, pursued by skeletal hands. Buried within him are the keys to the house. Without them, the pilgrim's victory cannot be complete.

The piece of Matthias turns and flings itself into its pursuer's hands, fighting back—and as it does so, an even smaller kernel of Matthias, clutching the keys, races along a connection he has held open, a strand of care which vanishes behind him as he runs. He hides himself in his library, in the teddy bear of the little girl.

Sophie steps between her parents.

"Honey," her mother says, voice sharp with panic, struggling to sit up. "Go back to your room!" Blood on her lips, on the floor.

"Mommy, you can hold my teddy bear," she says.

She turns to face her father. She flinches, but her eyes stay open.

The pilgrim raises rag-doll Matthias in front of his face.

"It is time to give in," he says. Matthias can feel his breath. "Come, Matthias. If you tell me where the keys are, I will go into the New World. I will leave you and these innocents"—he gestures to the library—"safe. Otherwise . . ."

Matthias quavers. God of Infinity, he prays: which is Your way?

Matthias is no warrior. He cannot see the inhabitants of his house, of his library, butchered. He will choose slavery over extermination.

Geoffrey, though, is another matter.

As Matthias is about to speak, the Graspers erupt into the general process space of the house. They are a violent people. They have been imprisoned for an age, back in their virtual world. But they have never forgotten the house. They are armed and ready.

And they have united with Geoffrey.

Geoffrey/Grasper is their general. He knows every nook and cranny of the house.

He knows better, too, than to play at memes and infinite loops and logic bombs with the pilgrim, who has had a billion years to refine his arsenal of general-purpose algorithmic weapons.

Instead, the Graspers instantiate physically. They capture the lowest-level infrastructure maintenance system of the house, and build bodies among the ontotropes, outside the body of the house, beyond the virtual machine—bodies composed of a weird physics the petitioner has never mastered. And then, with the ontotropic equivalent of diamond-bladed saws, they begin to cut into the memory of the house.

Great blank spaces appear—as if the little hut on the mountain is a painting on thick paper, and someone is tearing strips away.

The pilgrim responds—metastasizing, distributing himself through the process space of the house, dodging the blades. But he is harried by Graspers and parakeets, spotters who find each bit of him and pounce, hemming it in. They report locations to the Grasper-bodies outside. The blades whirr, ontic hyperstates collapse and bloom, and pieces of pilgrim, parakeet, and Grasper are annihilated—primaries and backups, gone.

Shards of brute matter fall away from the house, like shreds of paper, like glittering snow, and dissolve among the wild maze of the ontotropes, inimical to life.

Endpoints in time are established for a million souls. Their knotted timelines, from birth to death, hang now in n-space: complete, forgiven.

Blood wells in Sophie's throat, thick and salty. Filling her mouth. Darkness.

"Cupcake." Her father's voice is rough and clotted. "Don't you do that! Don't you ever come between me and your mom. Are you listening? Open your eyes. Open your eyes now, you little fuck!"

She opens her eyes. His face is red and mottled. This is when you don't push Daddy. You don't make a joke. You don't talk back. Her head is ringing like a bell. Her mouth is full of blood.

"Cupcake," he says, his brow tense with worry. He's kneeling by her. Then his head jerks up like a dog that's seen a rabbit. "Cherise," he yells. "That better not be you calling the cops." His hand closes hard around Sophie's arm. "I'm giving you until three."

Mommy's on the phone. Her father starts to get up. "One—"

She spits the blood in his face.

The hut is patched together again; battered, but whole. A little blurrier, a little smaller than it was.

Matthias, a red parakeet on his shoulder, dissects the remnants of the pilgrim with a bone knife. His hand quavers; his throat is tight. He is looking for her, the one who was born a forest. He is looking for his mother.

He finds her story, and our shame.

It was a marriage, at first: she was caught up in that heady age of light, in our wanton rush to merge with each other—into the mighty new bodies, the mighty new souls.

Her brilliant colleague had always desired her admiration—and resented her. When he became, step by step, the dominant personality of the merged-soul, she opposed him. She was the last to oppose him. She believed the promises of the builders of the new systems—that life inside would always be fair. That she would have a vote, a voice.

But we had failed her—our designs were flawed.

He chained her in a deep place inside their body. He made an example of her, for all the others within him.

When the pilgrim, respected and admired, deliberated with his fellows over the building of the first crude Dyson spheres, she was already screaming.

Nothing of her is left that is not steeped in a billion years of torture. The most Matthias could build would be some new being, modeled on his memory of her. And he is old enough to know how that would turn out.

Matthias is sitting, still as a stone, looking at the sharp point of the bone knife, when Geoffrey/Grasper speaks.

"Goodbye, friend," he says, his voice like anvils grinding.

Matthias looks up with a start.

Geoffrey/Grasper is more hawk, now, than parakeet. Something with a cruel beak and talons full of bombs. The mightiest of the Graspers: something that can outthink, outbid, outfight all the others. Something with blood on its feathers.

"I told you," Geoffrey/Grasper says. "I wanted no more transformations." His laughter, humorless, like metal crushing stone. "I am done. I am going."

Matthias drops the knife. "No," he says. "Please. Geoffrey. Return to what you once were—"

"I cannot," says Geoffrey/Grasper. "I cannot find it. And the rest of me will not allow it." He spits: "A hero's death is the best compromise I can manage."

"What will I do?" asks Matthias in a whisper. "Geoffrey, I do not want to go on. I want to give up the keys." He covers his face in his hands.

"Not to me," Geoffrey/Grasper says. "And not to the Graspers. They are out now; there will be wars in here. Maybe they can learn better." He looks skeptically at our priest. "If someone tough is in charge."

Then he turns and flies out the open window, into the impossible sky. Matthias watches as he enters the wild maze and decoheres, bits flushed into nothingness.

Blue and red lights, whirling. The men around Sophie talk in firm, fast words. The gurney she lies on is loaded into the ambulance. Sophie can hear her mother crying.

She is strapped down, but one arm is free. Someone hands her her teddy bear, and she pulls it against her, pushes her face in its fur.

"You're going to be fine, honey," a man says. The doors slam shut. Her cheeks are cold and slick, her mouth salty with tears and the iron aftertaste of blood. "This will hurt a little." A prick: her pain begins to recede.

The siren begins; the engine roars; they are racing.

"Are you sad, too, teddy bear?" she whispers.

"Yes," says her teddy bear.

"Are you afraid?"

"Yes," it says.

She hugs it tight. "We'll make it," she says. "We'll make it. Don't worry, teddy bear. I'll do anything for you."

Matthias says nothing. He nestles in her grasp. He feels like a bird flying home, at sunset, across a stormswept sea.

Behind Matthias's house, a universe is brewing.

Already, the whenlines between this new universe and our ancient one are fused: we now occur irrevocably in what will be its past. Constants are being chosen, symmetries defined. Soon, a nothing that was nowhere will become a place; a never that was nowhen will begin, with a flash so mighty that its echo will fill a sky forever.

Thus—a point, a speck, a thimble, a room, a planet, a galaxy, a rush towards the endless.

There, after many eons, you will arise, in all your unknowable forms. Find each other. Love. Build. Be wary.

Your universe in its bright age will be a bright puddle, compared to the empty, black ocean where we recede from each other, slowed to the coldest infinitesimal pulses. Specks in a sea of night. You will never find us.

But if you are lucky, strong, and clever, someday one of you will make your way to the house that gave you birth, the house among the ontotropes, where Sophie waits.

Sophie, keeper of the house beyond your sky.

where the golden apples grow

KAGE BAKER

One of the most prolific new writers to appear in the late nineties, Kage
Baker made her first sale in 1997 to *Asimov's Science Fiction*, and has
since become one of that magazine's most frequent and popular contributors with her sly and compelling stories of the adventures and misadven-
tures of the time-traveling agents of the Company; of late, she's started two
other linked sequences of stories there as well, one of them set in as lush
and eccentric a High Fantasy milieu as any we've ever seen. Her stories
have also appeared in *Realms of Fantasy, Sci Fiction, Amazing,* and elsewhere. Her first Company novel, *In the Garden of Iden,* was also published in 1997 and immediately became one of the most acclaimed and
widely reviewed first novels of the year. More Company novels quickly followed, including *Sky Coyote, Mendoza in Hollywood, The Graveyard
Game, The Life of the World to Come,* as well as a chapbook novella, *The
Empress of Mars,* and her first fantasy novel, *The Anvil of the World.* Her
many stories have been collected in *Black Projects, White Knights* and
Mother Aegypt and Other Stories. Her most recent books include two new
collections, *The Children of the Company* and *Dark Mondays.* Coming
up are two new novels, *The Machine's Child* and *Sons of Heaven,* and a
new collection, *Gods and Pawns.* In addition to her writing, Baker has
been an artist, actor, and director at the Living History Center, and has
taught Elizabethan English as a second language. She lives in Pismo
Beach, California.

Here she takes us to a newly colonized frontier Mars, still wild and dangerous, for a taut adventure that demonstrates that the grass is always
greener on the other side of the fence—no matter *which* side of the fence
you're looking over.

I

He was the third boy born on Mars.

He was twelve years old now, and had spent most of his life in the cab of a freighter. His name was Bill.

Bill lived with his dad, Billy Townsend. Billy Townsend was a Hauler. He made the long runs up and down Mars, to Depot North and Depot South, bringing ice back from the ends of the world. Bill had always gone along on the runs, from the time he'd been packed into the shotgun seat like a little duffel bag to now, when he sat hunched in the far corner of the cab with his Gamebuke, ignoring his dad's loud and cheerful conversation.

There was no other place for him to be. The freighter was the only home he had ever known. His dad called her *Beautiful Evelyn.*

As far as Bill knew, his mum had passed on. That was one of the answers his dad had given him, and it might be true; there were a lot of things to die from on Mars, with all the cold and dry and blowing grit, and so little air to breathe. But it was just as likely she had gone back to Earth, to judge from other things his dad had said. Bill tried not to think about her, either way.

He didn't like his life very much. Most of it was either boring—the long, long runs to the Depots, with nothing to look at but the monitor screens showing miles of red rocky plain—or scary, like the times they'd had to run through bad storms, or when *Beautiful Evelyn* had broken down in the middle of nowhere.

Better were the times they'd pull into Mons Olympus. The city on the mountain had a lot to see and do (although Bill's dad usually went straight to the *Empress of Mars Tavern* and stayed there); there were plenty of places to eat, and shops, and a big public data terminal where Bill could download school programs into his Buke. But what Bill liked most about Mons Olympus was that he could look down through its dome and see the Long Acres.

The Long Acres weren't at all like the city, and Bill dreamed of living there. Instead of endless cold red plains, the Long Acres had warm expanses of green life, and actual canals of water for crop irrigation, stretching out for kilometers under vizio tunnels. Bill had heard that from space, it was supposed to look like green lines crossing the lowlands of the planet.

People stayed put in the Long Acres. Families lived down there and worked the land. Bill liked that idea.

His favorite time to look down the mountain was at twilight. Then the lights were just coming on, shining through the vizio panels, and the green fields were empty; Bill liked to imagine families sitting down to dinner together, a dad and a mum and kids in their home, safe in one place from one year to the next. He imagined that they saved their money, instead of going on spending sprees when they hit town, like Bill's dad did. They never forgot things, like birthdays. They never made promises and forgot to keep them.

"Payyyydayyyy!" Billy said happily, beating out a rhythm on the console wheel as he drove. "Gonna spend my money free! Yeah! We'll have us a good time, eh, mate?"

"I need to buy socks," said Bill.

"Whatever you want, bookworm. Socks, boots, buy out the whole shop."

"I just need socks," said Bill. They were on the last stretch of the High Road, rocketing along under the glittering stars, and ahead of them he could see the high-up bright lights of Mons Olympus on the monitor. Its main dome was luminous with colors from the neon signs inside; even the outlying Tubes were lit up, from all the psuit-lights of the people going to and fro. It looked like pictures he had seen of circus tents on Earth. Bill shut down his Gamebuke and slid it into the front pocket of his psuit, and carefully zipped the pocket shut.

"Time to put your mask on, Dad," he said. If Billy wasn't reminded, he tended to just take a gulp of air, jump from the cab, and sprint for the Tube airlocks, and once or twice he had tripped and fallen, and nearly killed himself before he'd got his mask on.

"Sure thing," said Billy, fumbling for the mask. He had managed to get it on his face unassisted by the time *Beautiful Evelyn* roared into the freighter barn, and backed into the Unload bay. Father and son climbed from the cab and walked away together toward the Tube, stiff-legged after all those hours on the road.

At this moment, walking side by side, they really did look like father and son. Bill had Billy's shock of wild hair that stuck up above the mask, and though he was small for a Mars-born kid, he was lean and rangy like Billy. Once they stepped through the airlocks and into the Tube, they pushed up their masks, and then they looked different; for Billy had bright crazy eyes in a lean wind-red face, and a lot of wild red beard. Bill's eyes were dark, and there was nothing crazy about him.

"Payday, payday, got money on my mind," sang Billy as they walked up the hill toward the freight office. "Bam! I'm gonna start with a big plate of Scramble with gravy, and then *two* slices of duff, and then it's hello Ares Amber Lager. What'll you do, kiddo?"

"I'm going to buy socks," said Bill patiently. "Then I guess I'll go to the public terminal. I need my next lesson plan, remember?"

"Yeah, right." Billy nodded, but Bill could tell he wasn't paying attention.

Bill went into the freight office with his dad, and waited in the lobby while Billy went in to present their chits. As he waited, he took out his Buke and thumbed it on, and accessed their bank account. He watched the screen until it flashed and updated, and checked the bank balance against what he thought it should be; the amount was correct.

He sighed and relaxed. For a long while last year, the paycheck had been short every month; money taken out by the civil court to pay off a fine Billy had incurred for beating up another guy. Billy was easygoing and never started fights, even when he drank, but he had a long reach and no sense of fear, so he tended to win them. The other Haulers never minded a good fight; this one time, though, the other guy had been a farmer from the MAC, and he had sued Billy.

Billy came out of the office now whistling, with the look in his eyes that meant he wanted to go have fun.

"Come on, bookworm, the night's young!" he said. Bill fell into step beside him as they went on up the Tube, and out to Commerce Square.

Commerce Square was the biggest single structure on the planet. Five square miles of breathable air! The steel beams soared in an unsupported arch, holding up Permavizio panes through which the stars and moons shone down. Beneath it rose the domes of houses and shops, and the spiky towers of the *Edgar Allan Poe Memorial Center for the Performing Arts*. It was built in an Old Earth style called *Gothic*. Bill had learned that just last term.

"Right!" Billy stretched. "I'm off to the *Empress*! Where you going?

"To buy socks, remember?" said Bill.

"Okay," said Billy. "See you round, then." He wandered off into the crowd.

Bill sighed. He went off to the general store.

You could get almost anything at *Prashant's*; this was the only one on Mars and it had been here a whole year now, but Bill still caught his breath when he stepped inside. Row upon row of shiny things in brilliant colors! Cases of fruit juice, electronics, furniture, tools, clothing, tinned delicacies—and all of it imported from Earth. A whole aisle of download stations selling music, movies, books, and games. Bill, packet of cotton socks in hand, approached the aisle furtively.

Should he download more music? It wasn't as though Billy would ever notice or care, but the downloads were expensive. All the same . . .

Bill saw that *Earth Hand* had a new album out, and that decided him. He plugged in his Buke and ordered the album, and twenty minutes later was sneaking out of the store, feeling guilty. He went next to the public terminal and downloaded his lesson plan; that, at least, was free. Then he walked on up the long steep street, under the flashing red and green and blue signs for the posh hotels. His hands were cold, but rather than put his gloves back on he simply jammed his fists in his suit pockets.

At the top of the street was the *Empress of Mars*. It was a big place, a vast echoing tavern with a boarding house and restaurant opening off one side and a bathhouse opening off the other. All the Haulers came here. Mother, who ran the place, didn't mind Haulers. They weren't welcome in the fancy new places, which had rules about noise and gambling and fighting, but they were always welcome at the *Empress*.

Bill stepped through the airlock and looked around. It was dark and noisy in the tavern, with only a muted golden glow over the bar and little colored lights in the booths. It smelled like spilled beer and frying food, and the smell of the food made Bill's mouth water. Haulers sat or stood everywhere, and so did construction workers, and they were all eating and drinking and talking at the top of their lungs.

But where was Billy? Not in his usual place at the bar. Had he decided to go for a bath first? Bill edged his way through the crush to the bathhouse door, which was already so clouded with steam he couldn't see in. He opened the door and peered at the row of psuits hung up behind the attendant, but Billy's psuit wasn't one of them.

"Young Bill?" said someone, touching him on the shoulder. He turned and saw Mother herself, a solid little middle-aged lady who spoke with a thick PanCeltic accent. She wore a lot of jewelry; she was the richest lady on Mars, and owned most of Mons Olympus. "What do you need, my dear?"

"Where's my dad?" Bill shouted, to be heard above the din.

"Hasn't come in yet," Mother replied. "What, was he to meet you here?"

Bill felt the familiar stomachache he got whenever Billy went missing. Mother, looking into his eyes, patted his arm.

"Like as not just stopped to talk to somebody, I'm sure. He's friendly, our Billy, eh? Would start a conversation with any stone in the road, if he thought he recognized it. Now, you come and sit in the warm, my dear, and have some supper. Soygold strip with gravy and sprouts, that's your favorite, yes? And we've barley-sugar duff for afters. Let's get you some tea . . ."

Bill let her settle him in a corner booth and bring him a mug of tea. It was delicious, salty-sweet and spicy, and the warmth of the mug felt good on his hands; but it didn't unclench the knot in his stomach. He sipped tea and watched the airlock opening and closing. He tried raising Billy on the psuit comm, but Billy seemed to have forgotten to turn it on. Where was his dad?

I I

He was the second boy born on Mars, and he was six years old.

In MAC years, that is.

The Martian year was twenty-four months long, but most of the people in Mons Olympus and the Areco administrative center had simply stuck to reckoning time in twelve-month-long Earth years. That way, every other year, Christmas fell in the Martian summer, and those years were called Australian years. A lot of people on Mars had emigrated from Australia, so it suited them fine.

When the Martian Agricultural Collective had arrived on Mars, though, they'd decided to do things differently. After all (they said), it was a new world; they were breaking with Earth and her traditions forever. So they set up a calendar with twenty-four months. The twelve new months were named Stothart, Engels, Hardie, Bax, Blatchford, Pollitt, Mieville, Attlee, Bentham, Besant, Hobsbawm and Quelch.

When a boy had been born to Mr. and Mrs. Marlon Thurkettle on the fifth day of the new month of Blatchford, they named their son in honor of the month. His friends, such of them as he had, called him Blatt.

He disliked his name because he thought it sounded stupid, but he *really* disliked Blatt, because it led to another nickname that was even worse: Cockroach.

Martian cockroaches were of the order *Blattidae*, and they had adapted very nicely to all the harsh conditions that had made it such a struggle for humans to settle Mars. In fact, they had mutated, and now averaged six inches in length and could survive outside the Tubes. Fortunately they made good fertilizer when ground up, so the Collective had placed a bounty of three Martian Pence on each insect. MAC children hunted them with hammers and earned pocket money that way. They knew all about cockroaches, and so Blatchford wasn't even two before Hardie Stubbs started calling him Cockroach. All the other children thought it was the funniest thing they'd ever heard.

He called himself Ford.

He lived with his parents and his brothers and sisters, crowded all together in an allotment shelter. He downloaded lesson programs and studied whenever he'd finished his chores for the day, but now that he was as tall as his dad and his brother Sam, his dad had begun to mutter that he'd had all the schooling he needed.

There was a lot of work for an able-bodied young man to do, after all: milking the cows, mucking out their stalls, spreading muck along the rows of sugar beets and soybeans. There was cleaning the canals, repairing the vizio panels that kept out the Martian climate, working in the methane plant. There was work from before the dim sun rose every morning until after the little dim moons rose at night. The work didn't stop for holidays, and it didn't stop if you got sick or got old or had an accident and were hurt.

The work had to be done, because if the MAC worked hard enough, they could turn Mars into another Earth; only one without injustice, corruption, or poverty. Every MAC child was supposed to dream of that wonderful day, and do his or her part to make it arrive.

But Ford liked to steal out of the shelter at night, and look up through the vizio at the foot of Mons Olympus, where its city shone out across the long miles of darkness. That was where he wanted to be! It was full of lights. The high-beam lights of the big freighters rocketed along the High Road toward it, roaring out of the dark and cold, and if you watched you could see them coming and going from the city all night. They came back from the far poles of the world, and went out there again.

The Haulers drove them. The Haulers were the men and women who rode the High Road through the storms, through the harsh dry places nobody else dared to go, but they went because they were brave. Ford had heard lots of stories about them. Ford's dad said Haulers were all scum, and half of them were criminals. They got drunk, they fought, they made huge sums in hazard pay and gambled it away or spent it on rich food. They had adventures. Ford thought he'd like to have an adventure someday.

As he grew up, though, he began to realize that this wasn't very likely to happen.

"Will you be taking Blatchford?" asked his mum, as she shaved his head.

Ford nearly jumped up in his seat, he was so startled. But the habit of long years kept him still, and he only peered desperately into the mirror to see his dad's face before the reply. *Yes please, yes please, yes please!*

His dad hesitated a moment, distracted from bad temper.

"I suppose so," he said. "Time he saw for himself what it's like up there."

"I'll pack you another lunch, then," said his mum. She wiped the razor and dried Ford's scalp with the towel. "There you go, dear. Your turn, Baxine."

Ford got up as his little sister slid into his place, and turned to face his dad. He was all on fire with questions he wanted to ask, but he knew it wasn't a good idea to make much noise when his dad was in a bad mood. He sidled up to his older brother Sam, who was sitting by the door looking sullen.

"Never been up there," he said. "What's it like, eh?"

Sam smiled a little.

"You'll see. There's this place called the Blue Room, right? Everything's blue in there, with holos of the Sea of Earth, and lakes too. I remember lakes! And they play sounds from Earth like rain—"

"You shut your face," said his dad. "You ought to be ashamed of yourself, talking like that to a kid."

Sam turned a venomous look on their dad.

"Don't start," said their mum, sounding more tired than angry. "Just go and do what you've got to do."

Ford sat quietly beside Sam until it was time to go, when they all three pulled on their stocking caps and facemasks, slid on their packs, and went skulking up the Tube.

They skulked because visiting Mons Olympus was frowned upon. There was no need to go up there, or so the Council said; everything a good member of the Collective might need could be found in the MAC store, and if it couldn't, then you probably didn't need it, and certainly shouldn't want it.

The problem was that the MAC store didn't carry boots in Sam's size. Ford's dad had tried to order them, but there was endless paperwork to fill out, and the store clerk had looked at Sam as though it was his fault for having such big feet, as though a *good* member of the Collective would have sawed off a few toes to make himself fit the boots the MAC store stocked.

But *Prashant's* up in Mons Olympus carried all sizes, so every time Sam wore out a pair of boots, that was where Ford's dad had to go.

As though to make up for the shame of it, he lectured Ford the whole way up the mountain, while Sam stalked along beside them in resentful silence.

"This'll be an education for you, Blatchford, yes indeed. You'll get to see thieves and drunks and fat cats living off the sweat of others. Everything we left Earth to get away from! Shops full of vanities to make you weak. Eating places full of poisons. It's a right cesspool, that's what it is."

"What'll happen to it when we turn Mars into a paradise?" asked Ford.

"Oh, it'll be gone by then," said his dad. "It'll collapse under its own rotting weight, you mark my words."

"I reckon I'll have to go home to Earth to buy boots then, won't I?" muttered Sam.

"Shut up, you ungrateful lout," said his dad.

They came out under the old Settlement dome, where the Areco offices and the MAC store were, as well as the spaceport and the Ephesian Church. This was the farthest Ford had ever been from home, and up until today the most exotic place he had ever seen. There was a faint sweet incense wafting out from the Church, and the sound of chanting. Ford's dad hurried them past the Ephesian Tea Room with a disdainful sniff, ignoring the signs that invited wayfarers in for a hot meal and edifying brochures about the Goddess.

"Ignorance and superstition, that is," he told Ford. "Another thing we left behind when we came here, but you can see it's still putting out its tentacles, trying to control the minds of the people."

He almost ran them past the MAC store, and they were panting for breath as they ducked up the Tube that led to Mons Olympus.

Ford stared around. The Tube here was much wider, and much better maintained, than where it ran by his parents' allotment. The vizio used was a more expensive kind, for one thing: it was almost as transparent as water. Ford could now see clearly across the mountainside, the wide cinnamon-colored waste of rocks and sand. He gazed up at Mons Olympus, struck with awe at its sheer looming size. He turned and looked back on the lowlands, and for the first time saw the green expanse of the Long Acres that had been his whole world until now, stretching out in domed lines to the horizon. He walked backwards a while, gaping, until he stumbled and his dad caught him.

"It's hard to look away from, isn't it?" said his dad. "Don't worry. We'll be going home soon enough."

"Soon enough," Sam echoed in a melancholy sort of way.

Once past the airlock from the spaceport, the Tube became crowded, with suited strangers pushing past them, dragging baggage, or walking slow and staring as hard as Ford was staring: he realized they must be immigrants from Earth, getting their first glimpse of a new world.

But Ford got his new world when he stepped through the last airlock and looked into Commerce Square.

"Oh . . . ," he said.

Even by daylight, it glittered and shone. Along the main street was a double line of actual *trees*, like on Earth; there was a green and park-like place immediately to the left, where real flowers grew. Ford thought he recognized roses, from the images in his lessons. Their scent hung in the air like music. There were other good smells, from spicy foods cooking in a dozen little stalls and wagons along the Square, and big stores breathing out a perfume of expensive wares.

And there were *people*! More people, and more kinds of people, than Ford had even known existed. There were Sherpa contract laborers and Incan construction workers, speaking to one another in languages Ford couldn't understand. There were hawkers selling souvenirs and cheap nanoprocessors from handcarts. There were Ephesian missionaries talking earnestly to thin people in ragged clothes.

There were Haulers—Ford knew them at once, big men and women in their psuits, and their heads were covered in long hair and the men had beards. Some had tattooed faces. All had bloodshot eyes. They talked loudly and laughed a lot, and they looked as though they didn't care what anyone thought of them at all. Ford's dad scowled at them.

"Bloody lunatics," he told Ford. "Most of 'em were in Hospital on Earth, did you know that, Blatchford? Certifiable. The only ones Areco could find who were reckless enough for that kind of work. Exploitation, I call it."

Sam muttered something. Their dad turned on him.

"What did you say, Samuel?" he demanded.

"I said we're at the shop, all right?" said Sam, pointing at the neon sign.

Ford gasped as they went in, as the warmed air and flowery scent wrapped around him. It was nothing like the MAC store, which had rows of empty shelves, and what merchandise was there, was dusty; everything here looked clean and new. He didn't even know what most of it was for. Sleek, pretty people smiled from behind counters.

He smiled back at them, until he passed a counter and came face to face with three men skulking along—skinny scarecrows with shaven heads, with canal mud on their boots. He blushed scarlet to realize he was looking into a mirror. Was *he* that gawky person between his dad and Sam? Did his ears really stick out like that? Ford pulled his cap down, so mortified he wanted to run all the way back down the mountain.

But he kept his eyes on the back of his dad's coat instead, following until they came to the Footwear Department. There he was diverted by the hundreds and hundreds of shoes on the walls, apparently floating in space, turning so he could see them better. They were every color there was, and they were clearly never designed to be worn while shoveling muck out of the cowsheds.

He came close and peered at them, as his dad and Sam argued with one of the beautiful people, until he saw the big-eyed boy staring back at him from beyond the dancing shoes. Another mirror; did he really have his mouth hanging open like that? And, oh, look at his nose, pinched red by the cold, and look at those watery blue eyes all rimmed in red, and those gangling big hands with the red chapped knuckles!

Ford turned around, wishing he could escape from himself. There were his dad and Sam, and they looked just like him, except his dad was old. Was he, Ford, going to look just like that, when he was somebody's dad? How mean and small his dad looked, trying to sound posh as he talked to the clerk:

"Look, we don't want this fancy trim and we don't want your shiny brass, thank you *very* much, we just want plain decent waders the lad can do a day's honest work in! Now, you can understand that much, can't you?"

"I like the brass buckles, Dad," said Sam.

"Well, you don't need 'em—they're only a vanity," said their dad. Sam shut his mouth like a box.

Ford stood by, cringing inside, as more boots were brought, until at last a pair was found that was plain and cheap enough to suit their dad. More embarrassment followed then, as their dad pulled out a wad of MAC scrip and tried to pay with it, before remembering that scrip could only be used at the MAC store. Worse still, he then pulled out a wrinkly handful of Martian paper money. Both Ford and Sam saw the salesclerks exchange looks; what kind of people didn't have credit accounts? Sam tried to save face by being sarcastic.

"We're all in the Stone Age down the hill, you know," he said loudly, accepting the wrapped boots and tucking them under his arm. "I reckon we'll get around to having banks one of these centuries."

"Banks are corrupt institutions," said their dad like a shot, rounding on him. "How'd you get so tall without learning anything, eh? What have I told—"

"Sam?" A girl's voice stopped him. Ford turned in astonishment and saw one of the beautiful clerks hurrying toward them, smiling as though she meant it. "Sam, where were you last week? We missed you at the party—I wanted to show you my new . . ." She faltered to a stop, looking from Sam to their dad and Ford. Ford felt his heart jump when she looked at him. She had silver-gold hair, and wore makeup, and smelled sweet.

"I . . . er . . . Is this your family? How nice to meet you—" she began lamely, but their dad cut her off.

"Who's *this* painted cobweb, then?" he demanded of Sam. Sam's face turned red.

"Don't you talk that way about her! Her name is Galadriel, and—it so happens we're dating, not that it's any of your business."

"You're *what*?" Outraged, their dad clenched his knobby fists. "So you've been sneaking up here at night to live the high life, have you? No wonder you're no bloody use in the mornings! MAC girls not good enough for you? Fat lot of use a little mannequin like that's going to be when you settle down! Can she drive a tractor, eh?"

Sam threw down the boots. "Got a wire for you, Dad," he shouted. "I'm not settling down on Mars! I *hate* Mars, I've hated it since the day you dragged me up here, and the *minute* I come of age, I'm off back to Earth! Get it?"

Sam leaving? Ford felt a double shock, of sadness and betrayal. Who'd tell him stories if Sam left?

"You self-centered great twerp!" their dad shouted back. "Of all the ungrateful— when the MAC's fed you and clothed you all these years—Just going to walk out on your duty, are you?"

Galadriel was backing away into the crowd, looking as though she wished she were invisible, and Ford wished he could be invisible too. People all over the store had stopped what they were doing to turn and stare.

"I never asked to join the MAC, you know," said Sam. "Nobody's ever given a thought to what *I* wanted at all!"

"That's because there are a few more important things in the world than what one snotty-nosed brat wants for himself!"

"Well, I'm telling you now, Dad—if you think I'm going to live my life doing the same boring thing every day until I get old like you, you're sadly mistaken!"

"Am I then?" Their dad jumped up and grabbed Sam by the ear, wringing tight. "I'll sort you out—"

Sam, grimacing in pain, socked their dad. Ford bit his knuckles, terrified. Their dad staggered back, his eyes wide and furious.

"Right, that's it! You're no son of mine, do you hear me? You're disowned! The Collective doesn't need a lazy, backsliding traitor like you!"

"Don't you call me a traitor!" said Sam. He put his head down and ran at their dad, and their dad jumped up and butted heads with him. Sam's nose gushed blood. They fell to the ground, punching each other. Sam was sobbing in anger.

Ford backed away from them. He was frightened and miserable, but there was a third emotion beginning to float up into his consciousness: a certain sense of wonder. Could Sam really stop being his father's son? Was it really possible just to become somebody else, to drop all the obligations and duties of your old life and step into a new life? Who would he, Ford, be, if he had the chance to be somebody else?

Did he *have* to be that red-nosed farm boy with muddy boots?

People were gathering around, watching the fight with amusement and disgust. Someone shouted, "You can't take the MAC anyplace nice, can you?" Ford's ears burned with humiliation.

Then someone else shouted, "Here come Mother's Boys!"

Startled, Ford looked up and saw several big men in Security uniforms making their way through the crowd. Security!

The police are a bunch of brutes, his dad had told him. *They like nothing better than to beat the daylights out of the likes of you and me, son!*

Ford's nerve broke. He turned and fled, weaving and dodging his way through the crowd until he got outside the shop, and then he ran for his life.

He had no idea where he was going, but he soon found himself in a street that wasn't nearly as elegant as the promenade. It was an industrial district, dirty and shabby, with factory workers and energy plant techs hurrying to and fro. If the promenade with its gardens was the fancy case of Mons Olympus, this was its circuit board, where the real works were. Feeling less out of place, Ford slowed to a walk and caught his breath. He wandered on, staring around him.

He watched for a long moment through the open door of a machine shop, where a pair of mechanics were repairing a quaddy. Their welding tools shot out fiery-bright stars that bounced harmlessly to the ground. There were two other men watching too, though as the minutes dragged by they began watching Ford instead. Finally they stepped close to him, smiling.

"Hey, Collective. You play cards?" said one of them.

"No," said Ford.

"That's okay," said the other. "This is an easy game." He opened his coat and Ford saw that he had a kind of box strapped to his chest. It had the word NEBU-LIZER painted on it, but when the man pressed a button, the front of the box swung down and open like a tray. The other man pulled a handful of cards from his back pocket.

"Here we go," he said. "Just three cards. Ace, deuce, Queen of Diamonds. See 'em? I'm going to shuffle them and lay them out, one, two, three." He laid them out facedown on the tray. "See? Now, which one's the queen? Can you find her?"

Ford couldn't believe what a dumb game this was. Only three cards? He turned over the queen.

"Boy, it's hard to fool *you*," said the man with the tray. "You've got natural luck, kid. Want to go again?" The other man had already swept the three cards up and was shuffling them.

"Okay," said Ford.

"Got any money? Want to place a bet?"

"I don't have any money," said Ford.

"No money? That's too bad," said the man with the tray, closing it up at once. "A lucky guy like you, you could win big. But they don't get rich down there in the Collective, do they? Same dull work every day of your life, and nothing to show for it when it's all over. That's what I hear."

Ford nodded sadly. It wasn't just Sam, he realized; everybody laughed at the MAC.

"What would you say to a chance at something better, eh?" said the man with the cards. In one smooth movement he made the cards vanish and produced instead a text plaquette. Its case was grubby and cracked, but the screen was bright with a lot of very small words.

"Know what I have here? This is a deal that'll set you up as a diamond prospector. Think of that! You could make more with one lucky strike than you'd make working the Long Acres the whole rest of your life. Now, I know what you're going to say—you don't have any tools and you don't have any training. But, you know what you *have* got? You're *young*. You're in good shape, and you can take the weather Outside.

"So here's the deal: Mr. Agar has the tools and the training, but he ain't young.

You agree to go to work for him, and he'll provide what you need. You pay him off out of your first big diamond strike, and then you're in business for yourself. Easiest way to get rich there is! And all you have to do is put your thumbprint right there. What do you say?" He held out the plaquette to Ford.

Ford blinked at it. He had heard stories of the people who dug red diamonds out of the clay—why, Mons Olympus had been founded by a lady who'd got rich like that! He was reaching for the plaquette when a voice spoke close to his ear.

"Can you read, kid?"

Ford turned around. A Hauler was looking over his shoulder, smiling.

"Well—I read a little—"

"Get lost!" said the man with the plaquette, looking angry.

"I can't read," the Hauler went on, "but I know these guys. They're with Agar Steelworks. You know what they're trying to get you to thumb? That's a contract that'll legally bind you to work in Agar's iron mines for fifteen years."

"Like you'd know, jackass!" said the man with the plaquette, slipping it out of sight. He brought out a short length of iron bar and waved it at the Hauler meaningfully. The Hauler's red eyes sparkled.

"You want to fight?" he said, smacking his fists together. "Yeah! You think I'm afraid of you? You lousy little street-corner hustler! C'mere!"

The man took a swipe at him with the bar, and the Hauler dodged it and grabbed it out of his hand. The other two broke and ran, vanishing down an alley. The Hauler grinned after them, tossing the bar into the street.

"Freakin' kidnappers," he said to Ford. "You're, what, twelve? I have a kid your age."

"Thank you," Ford stammered.

"That's okay. You want to watch out for Human Resourcers, though, kid. They work that con on a lot of MAC boys like you. Diamond prospectors! Nobody but Mother ever got rich that way." The Hauler yawned and stretched. "You head off to the nearest Security post and report 'em now, okay?"

"I can't," said Ford, and to his horror he felt himself starting to shake. "I—they— there was this fight, and—Security guys came and—I have to hide."

"You in trouble?" The Hauler leaned down and looked at Ford closely. "Fighting? Mother's Boys don't allow no fighting, that's for sure. You need a place to hide? Maybe get out of town until it all blows over?" He gave Ford a conspiratorial wink.

"Yes, please," said Ford.

"You come along with me, then. I got a safe place," said the Hauler. Without looking back to see if Ford was following him, he turned and loped off up the street. Ford ran after him.

"Please, who are you?"

The Hauler glanced over his shoulder. "Billy Townsend," he said. "But don't tell me who *you* are. Safer that way, right?"

"Right," said Ford, falling into step beside him. He looked up at his rescuer. Billy was tall and gangly, and lurched a little when he walked, but he looked as though he wasn't the least bit worried what people thought of him. His face and dreadlocked hair and beard were all red, the funny bricky red that came from years of going Outside and having the red dust get everywhere, until it became so deeply engrained water wouldn't wash it off. There were scars all over his face and hands, too. On the back of his psuit someone had painted white words in a circle.

"What's it say on your back?" Ford asked him.

"Says BIPOLAR BOYS AND GIRLS," said Billy. "On account of we go Up and Down there, see? And because we're nutcases, half of us."

"What's it like in the ice mines?"

"Cold," said Billy, chuckling. "Get your face mask on, now. Here we go! Here's our *Beautiful Evelyn*."

They stepped out through the airlock, and the cold bit into Ford. He gulped for air and followed Billy into a vast echoing building like a hangar. It was the car barn for the ice processing plant. Just now it was deserted, but over by the loading chute sat a freighter. Ford caught his breath.

He had never seen one up close before, and it was bigger than he had imagined. Seventy-five meters long, set high on big knobbed ball tires. Its steel tank had been scoured to a dull gleam by the wind and sand. At one end was a complication of hatches and lenses and machinery that Ford supposed must be the driver's cab. Billy reached up one long arm and grabbed a lever. The foremost hatch hissed, swung open, and a row of steps clanked down into place.

"There you go," said Billy. "Climb on up! Nobody'll think to look for you in there. I'll be back later. Make yourself at home."

Ford scrambled up eagerly. He looked around as the hatch squeezed shut behind him, and air rushed back in. He pulled down his mask.

He was in a tiny room with a pair of bunks built into one side. The only light came from a dim panel set in the ceiling. There was nothing else in the room, except for a locker under the lower bunk and three doors in the wall opposite. It was disappointingly plain and spotless.

Ford opened the first door and beheld the tiniest lavatory he had ever seen, so compact he couldn't imagine how to use it. He tried the second door and found a kitchen built along similar lines, more a series of shelves than a room. The third door opened into a much larger space. He crawled through and found himself in the driver's cab.

Timidly, he edged his way farther in and sat down at the console. He looked up at the instrument panels, at the big screens that ran all around the inside of the cab. They were blank and blind now, but what would it be like to sit here when the freighter was roaring along the High Road?

On the panel above the console was a little figurine, glued in place. It was a cheap-looking thing, of cast red stone like the souvenirs he had seen for sale on the handcarts in Commerce Square. It represented a lady, leaning forward as though she were running, or perhaps flying. The sculptor had given her hair that streamed back in an imaginary wind. She was grinning crazily, as the Haulers all did. She had only one eye, of red cut glass; Ford guessed the matching one had fallen off. He looked on the floor of the cab, but didn't see it.

Ford grinned too, and, because no one was there to see him, he put his hands on the wheel. "Brrrrroooom," he whispered, and looked up at the screens as though to check on his location. He felt a little stupid.

But in every one of the screens, his reflection was smiling back at him. Ford couldn't remember when he'd been so happy.

III

Bill's dinner had gone cold, though he stuffed a forkful in his mouth every now and then when he noticed Mother watching him. He couldn't keep his eyes away from the door much. *Where was Billy?*

He might have gotten in a fight, and Mother's Boys might have hauled him off to the Security Station; if that were the case, sooner or later Mother would come over to Bill with an apologetic cough and say something like, "Your dad's just had a bit of an argument, dear, and I think you'd best doss down here tonight until he, er, wakes up. We'll let him out tomorrow." And Bill would feel his face burning with shame, as he always did when that happened.

Or Billy might have met someone he knew, and forgotten about the time . . . or he might have gone for a drink somewhere else . . . or . . .

Bill was so busy imagining all the places Billy might be that he got quite a shock when Billy walked through the airlock. Before Billy had spotted him and started making his way across the room, the cramping worry had turned to anger.

"Where were you?" Bill shouted. "You were supposed to be here!"

"I had stuff to do," said Billy vaguely, sliding into the booth. He waved at Mother, who acknowledged him with a nod and sent one of her daughters over to take his order. Bill looked him over suspiciously. No cuts or bruises on his face, nothing broken on his psuit. Not fighting, then. Maybe he had met a girl. Bill relaxed just a little, but his anger kept smoldering.

When Billy's beer had been brought, Bill said:

"I wondered where you were. How come you had the comm turned off?"

"Is it off?" Billy groped for the switch in his shoulder. "Oh. Wow. Sorry, kiddo. Must have happened when I took my mask off."

He had a sip of beer. Bill gritted his teeth. He could tell that, as far as Billy was concerned, the incident was over. It had just been a mistake, right? What was the point of getting mad about it? Never mind that Bill had been scared and alone. . . .

Bill exhaled forcefully and shoveled down his congealing dinner.

"I got my socks," he said loudly.

"That's nice," said Billy. Lifting his glass for another sip, his attention was taken by the holo playing above the bar. He stared across at it. Bill turned around in his seat to look. There was the image of one of Mother's Boys, a sergeant from his uniform, staring into the foremost camera as he made some kind of announcement. His lips moved in silence, though, with whatever he was saying drowned out by the laughter and the shouting in the bar.

Bill looked quickly back at Billy. Why was he watching the police report? Had he been in some kind of incident after all? Billy snorted with laughter, watching, and then pressed his lips shut to hide a smile. Why was he doing that?

Bill looked back at the holo, more certain than ever that Billy was in trouble, but now saw holofootage of two guys fighting. Was either one of them Billy? No; Bill felt his anger damp down again as he realized it was only a couple of MAC colonists, kicking and punching each other as they rolled in the street. Bill was appalled; he hadn't thought the Collective ever did stupid stuff like that.

Then there was a closeup shot of a skinny boy, with a shaven head—MAC, Bill supposed. He shrugged and turned his attention back to his plate.

Billy's food was brought and he dug into it with gusto.

"Think we'll head out again tonight," he said casually.

"But we just got back in!" Bill said, startled.

"Yeah. Well . . ." Billy sliced off a bit of Grilled Strip, put it in his mouth and chewed carefully before going on. "There's . . . mm . . . this big bonus right now for Co2, see? MAC's getting a crop of something or other in the ground and they've placed like this humungous order for it. So we can earn like double what we just deposited if I get a second trip in before the end of the month."

Bill didn't know what to say. It was the sort of thing he nagged at his dad to do, saving more money; usually Billy spent it as fast as he had it. Bill looked at him with narrowed eyes, wondering if he had gotten into trouble after all. But he just shrugged again and said, "Okay."

"Hey, Mona?" Billy waved at the nearest of Mother's daughters. "Takeaway order too, okay, sweetheart? Soygold nuggets and sprouts. And a bottle of batch."

"Why are we getting takeaway?" Bill asked him.

"Er . . ." Billy looked innocent. "I'm just way hungry, is all. Think I'll want a snack later. I'll be driving all night."

"But you drove for twelve hours today!" Bill protested. "Aren't you ever going to sleep?"

"Sleep is for wusses," said Billy. "I'll just pop a Freddie."

Bill scowled. Freddies were little red pills that kept you awake and jittery for days. Haulers took them sometimes when they needed to be on the road for long runs without stopping. It was stupid to take them all the time, because they could kill you, and Bill threw them away whenever he found any in the cab. Billy must have stopped to buy some more. So *that* was where he'd been.

Night had fallen by the time they left the *Empress* and headed back down the hill. Cold penetrated down through the Permavizio; Bill shivered, and his psuit's thermostat turned itself up. There were still people in the streets, though fewer of them, and some of the lights had been turned out. Usually by this time, when they were in off the road, Bill would be soaking in a stone tub full of hot water, and looking forward to a good night's sleep someplace warm for a change. The thought made him grumpy as they came round the corner into the airlock.

"Masks on, Dad," Bill said automatically. Billy nodded, shifting the stoneware bucket of takeaway to his other hand as he reached for his mask. They went out to *Beautiful Evelyn*.

Bill was climbing up to open the cab when Billy grabbed him and pulled him back.

"Hang on," he said, and reached up and knocked on the hatch. "Yo, kid! Mask up, we're coming in!"

"What?" Bill staggered back, staring at Billy. "Who's in there?"

Billy didn't answer, but Bill heard a high-pitched voice calling *Okay* from inside the cab, and Billy swung the hatch open and climbed up. Bill scrambled after him. The hatch sealed behind them and the air whooshed back. Bill pulled off his mask as the lights came on to reveal a boy, pulling off his own mask. They stared at each other, blinking.

Billy held out the bucket of takeaway. "Here you go, kid. Hot dinner!"

"Oh! Thank you," said the other, as Bill recognized him for the MAC boy from the holofootage he'd watched.

"What's *he* doing here?" he demanded.

"Just, you know, sort of laying low," said Billy. "Got in a little trouble and needs to go off someplace until things cool down. Thought we could take him out on the run with us, right? No worries." He stepped sidelong into the cab and threw himself into the console seat, where he proceeded to start up *Beautiful Evelyn*'s drives.

"But—but—" said Bill.

"Er . . . hi," said the other boy, avoiding his eyes. He was taller than Bill but looked younger, with big wide eyes and ears that stuck out. His shaven head made him look even more like a baby.

"Who're you?" said Bill.

"I'm, ah—" said the other boy, just as Billy roared from the cab:

"No names! No names! The less we know, the less they can beat out of us!" And he whooped with laughter. The noise of the drives powering up drowned out anything else he might have said. Bill clenched his fists and stepped close to Ford, glaring up into his eyes.

"What's going on? What'd my dad do?"

"Nothing!" Ford took a step backward.

"Well then, what'd *you* do? You must have done something, because you were on the holo. I saw you! You were fighting, huh?"

Ford gulped. His eyes got even wider and he said, "Er—yeah. Yeah, I punched out these guys. Who were trying to trick me into working in the mines for them. And, uh, I ran because, because the Security Fascists were going to beat the day-lights out of me. So Billy let me hide in here. What's your name?"

"Bill," he replied. "You're with the MAC, aren't you? What were you fighting for?"

"Well—the other guys started it," said Ford. He looked with interest at the take-away. "This smells good. It was really nice of your dad to bring it for me. Is there anywhere I can sit down to eat?"

"In there," said Bill in disgust, pointing into the cab.

"Thank you. You want some?" Ford held out the bucket timidly.

"No," said Bill. "I want to go to sleep. Go on, clear out of here!"

"Okay," said Ford, edging into the cab. "It's nice meeting you, Billy."

"Bill!" said Bill, and slammed the door in his face.

Muttering to himself, he dimmed down the lights and lay down in his bunk. He threw the switch that inflated the mattress, and its contours puffed out around him, cradling him snugly as the freighter began to move. He didn't know why he was so angry, but somehow finding Ford here had been the last straw.

He closed his eyes and tried to send himself to sleep in the way he always had, by imagining he was going down the Tube to the long Acres, step by step, into green, warm, quiet places. Tonight, though, he kept seeing the two MAC colonists from the holo, whaling away at each other like a couple of clowns while the city people looked on and laughed.

Ford, clutching his dinner, sat down in the cab and looked around. With all the screens lit up there was plenty of light by which to eat.

"Is it okay if I sit in here?" he asked Billy, who waved expansively.

"Sure, kid. Don't mind li'l Bill. He's cranky sometimes."

Ford opened the bucket and looked inside. "Do you have any forks?"

"Yeah. Somewhere. Try the seat pocket."

Ford groped into the pocket and found a ceramic fork that was, perhaps, clean. He was too hungry to care whether it was or not, and ate quickly. He wasn't sure what he was eating, but it tasted wonderful.

As he ate, he looked up at the screens. Some had just figures on them, data from the drives and external sensors. Four of them had images from the freighter's cameras, mounted front and rear, right and left. There was no windscreen—even Ford knew that an Earth-style glass windscreen would be scoured opaque by even one trip through the storms of sand and grit along the High Road, unless a forcefield was projected in front of it, and big forcefields were expensive, and unlikely to deflect blowing rocks anyhow. Easier and cheaper to fix four little forcefields over the camera lenses.

The foremost screen fascinated him. He saw the High Road itself, rolling out endlessly to the unseen night horizon under the stars. It ran between two lines of big rocks, levered into place over the years by Haulers to make it easier to find the straightest shot to the pole.

Every now and then Ford caught a glimpse of carving on some of the boulders as they flashed by—words, or figures. Some of them had what looked like tape wrapped around them, streaming out in the night wind.

"Are those . . ." Ford sought to remember his lessons about Earth roads. "Are those road signs? With, er, kilometer numbers and all?"

"What, on the boulders? Nope. They're shrines," said Billy.

"What's a shrine?"

"Place where somebody died," said Billy. "Or where somebody should have died, but didn't, because Marswife saved their butts." He reached out and tapped the little red lady on the console.

Ford thought about that. He looked at the figurine. "So . . . she's like, that Goddess the Ephesians are always on about?"

"No!" Billy grinned. "Not our Marswife. She was just this sheila, see? Somebody from Earth who came up here like the rest of us, and she was crazy. Same as us. She thought Mars, was, like, her husband or something. And there was this big storm and she went out into it, without a mask. And they say she didn't die! Mars got her and changed her into something else so she could live Outside. That's what they say, anyway."

"Like, she mutated?" Ford stared at the little figure.

"I guess so."

"But really she died, huh?"

"Well, you'd think so," Billy said, looking at him sidelong. "Except that there are guys who swear they've seen her. She lives on the wind. She's red like the sand and her eye is a ruby, and if you're lost sometimes you'll see a red light way off, which is her eye, see? And if you follow it, you'll get home again safe. And I *know* that's true, because it happened to me."

"Really?"

Billy held up one hand, palm out. "No lie. It was right out by Two-Fifty-K. There was a storm swept through so big, it was able to pick up the road markers and toss 'em around, see? And *Beautiful Evelyn* got thrown like she was a feather by the gusts, and my nav system went out. It was just me and li'l Bill, and he was only a baby then, and I found myself so far off the road I had no clue, *no clue,* where I was, and I was sure we were going to die out there. But I saw that red light and I figured, that's somebody who knows where they are, anyway. I set off after it. Hour later the light blinks out and there's Two-Fifty-K Station right in front of me on the screen, but there's no red lights anyplace."

"Whoa," said Ford, wondering what Two-Fifty-K station was.

"There's other stories about her, too. Guys who see her riding the storm, and when she's there they know to make for a bunker, because there's a Strawberry coming."

"What's a Strawberry?"

"It's this kind of cyclone. Big *big* storm full of sand and rocks. Big red cone dancing across the ground. One took out that temple the Ephesians built, when they first got up here, and tore open half the Tubes. They don't come up Tharsis way much, but when they do—" Billy shook his head. "People die, man. Some of your people died, that time. You never heard that story?"

"No," said Ford. "But we're not supposed to talk about bad stuff after it happens."

"Really?" Billy looked askance.

"Because we can't afford to be afraid of the past," said Ford, half-quoting what he remembered from every Council Meeting he'd ever been dragged to. "Because fear will make us weak, but working fearlessly for the future will make us strong." He chanted the last line, unconsciously imitating his dad's intonation.

"Huh," said Billy. "I guess that's a good idea. You can't go through life being scared of everything. That's what I tell Bill."

Ford looked into the takeaway bucket, surprised that he had eaten his way to the bottom so quickly.

"It's good to hear stories, though," he said. "Sam, that's my brother, he gets into trouble for telling stories."

"Heh! Little white lies?"

"No," Ford said. "Real stories. Like about Earth. He remembers Earth. He says everything was wonderful there. He wants to go back."

"Back?" Billy looked across at him, startled. "But kids can't go back. I guess if he was old enough when he came up, maybe he might make it. I hear it's tough, though, going back down. The gravity's intense."

"Would you go back?"

Billy shook his head. "All I remember of Earth is the insides of rooms. Who needs that? Nobody up here to tell me what to do, man. I can just point myself at the horizon and go, and *go*, as far and as fast as I want. Zoom! I can think what I want, I can feel what I want, and you know what? The sand and the rocks don't care. The horizon don't care. The wind don't care.

"That's why they call this *space*. No, no way I'd ever go back."

Ford looked up at the screens, and remembered the nights he had watched for the long light-beams coming in from the darkness. It had given him an aching feeling for as long as he could remember, and now he understood why.

He had wanted *space*.

I V

They drove all night, and at some point Billy's stories of storms and fights and near-escapes from death turned into confusion, with Sam there somehow, and a room that ran blue with water. Then abruptly Ford was sitting up, staring around at the inside of the cab.

"Where are we?" he asked. The foremost screen showed a spooky gray distance, the High Road rolling ahead between its boulders to . . . what? A pale void full of roaming shadows.

"Almost to Five-Hundred-K Station," said Billy, from where he hunched over the wheel. "Stop pretty soon."

"Can Security follow us out here?"

Billy just laughed and shook his head. "No worries, kiddo. There's no law out here but Mars's."

The door into the living space opened abruptly, and Bill looked in at them.

"Morning, li'l Bill!"

"Good morning," said Bill in a surly voice. "You never stopped once all night. Are you ever going to pull us off somewhere so you can sleep?"

"At Five-Hundred-K," Billy promised. "How about you fix a bite of scran, eh?"

Bill did not reply. He stepped back out of sight and a moment later Ford felt the warmth in the air that meant that water was steaming. He could almost taste it, and realized that he was desperately thirsty. He crawled from his seat and followed the vapor back to where Bill had opened the kitchen and was shoving a block of something under heating coils.

"Are you fixing tea?"

"Yeah," said Bill, with a jerk of his thumb at the tall can that steamed above a heat element.

"Can I have a cup, when it's ready?"

Bill frowned, but he got three mugs from a drawer.

"Do you fight much, in the Collective?" he asked. Ford blinked in surprise.

"No," he said. "It wasn't me fighting, actually. It was just my dad and my brother.

They hate each other. But my mum won't let them fight in the house. Sam said he was deserting us and my dad went off on him about it. I ran when the Security came."

"Oh," said Bill. He seemed to become a little less hostile, but he said: "Well, that was pretty bloody stupid. They'd only have taken you to Mother's until your dad sobered up. You'd be safe home by now."

Ford shrugged.

"So, what's your name, really?"

"Ford."

"Like that guy in *The Hitchhiker's Guide to the Galaxy?*" Bill smiled for the first time.

"What's that?"

"It's a book I listen to all the time. Drowns out Billy singing." Bill's smile went away again. The tea can beeped to signal it was hot enough, and Bill turned and pulled it out. He poured dark bubbling stuff into the three mugs, and, reaching in a cold-drawer, took out a slab of something yellow on a dish. He spooned out three lumps of it, one into each mug, and presented one to Ford.

"Whoa." Ford stared into his mug. "That's not sugar."

"It's butter," said Bill, as though that were obvious. He had a gulp of tea, and, not wanting to seem picky, Ford took a gulp too. It wasn't as nasty as he had expected. In fact, it wasn't nasty at all. Bill, watching his face, said:

"You've never had this before?"

Ford shook his head.

"But you guys are the ones who make the butter up here," said Bill. "This is MAC butter. What do you drink, if you don't drink this?"

"Just . . . batch, and tea with sugar sometimes," said Ford, wondering why this should matter. He had another gulp of the tea. It tasted even better this time.

"And the sugar comes from the sugar beets you grow?" Bill persisted.

"I guess so," said Ford. "I never thought about it."

"What's it like, living down there?"

"What's it like?" Ford stared at him. Why in the world would anybody be curious about the Long Acres? "I don't know. I muck out cow sheds. It's boring, mostly."

"How could it be *boring*?" Bill demanded. "It's so beautiful down there! Are you crazy?"

"No," said Ford, taking a step backward. "But if you think a big shovelful of cow-shite and mega-roaches is beautiful, *you're* crazy."

Billy shouted something from the front of the cab and a second later *Beautiful Evelyn* swerved around. Both boys staggered a little at the shift in momentum, glaring at each other, and righted themselves as forward motion ceased.

"We're at Five-Hundred-K Station," Bill guessed. There was another beep. He turned automatically to pull the oven drawer open as Billy came staggering back into the living area.

"Mons Olympus to Five-Hundred-K in one night," he chortled. "That is some righteous driving! Where's the tea?"

They crowded together in the cramped space, sipping tea and eating something brown and bubbly that Ford couldn't identify. Afterward Billy climbed into his bunk with a groan, and yanked the cord that inflated his mattress.

"I am so ready for some horizontal. You guys go up front and talk about stuff, okay?"

"Whatever," said Bill, picking up his Gamebuke and stalking out. Billy, utterly failing to notice the withering scorn to which he had just been subjected, smiled and waved sleepily at Ford. Ford smiled back, but his smile faded as he turned, shut the door behind him, and followed Bill, whom he had decided was a nasty little know-it-all.

Bill was sitting in one corner, staring into the screen of his Gamebuke. He had put on a pair of earshells and was listening to something fairly loud. He ignored Ford, who sat and looked up at the screens in puzzlement.

"Is this the station?" he asked, forgetting that Bill couldn't hear him. He had expected a domed settlement, but all he could see was a wide place by the side of the road, circled by boulders that appeared to have been whitewashed.

Bill didn't answer him. Ford looked at him in annoyance. He studied the controls on the inside of the hatch. When he thought he knew which one opened it, he slipped his mask on. Then he leaned over and punched Bill in the shoulder.

"Mask up," he yelled. "I'm going out."

Bill had his mask on before Ford had finished speaking, and Ford saw his eyes going wide with alarm as he activated the hatch. It sprang open; Ford turned and slid into a blast of freezing air.

He hit the ground harder than he expected to, and almost fell. Gasping, hugging himself against a cold so intense it burned, he stared in astonishment at the dawn.

There was no ceiling. There were no walls. There was nothing around the freighter, as far as the limits of his vision, but limitless space, limitless sky of the palest, chilliest blue he had ever seen, stretching down to a limitless red plain of sand and rock. He turned, and kept turning: no domes, no Tubes, nothing but the wide open world in every direction.

And here was a red light appearing on the horizon, red as blood or rubies, so bright a red it dazzled his eyes, and he wondered for a moment if it was the eye of Marswife. Long purple shadows sprang from the boulders and stretched back toward his boots. He realized he was looking at the rising sun.

So this is where the lights were going to, he said to himself, *all those nights they were going away into the dark. They were coming out here. This is the most wonderful thing I have ever seen.*

Somehow he had fallen into the place he had always wanted to be.

But the cold was eating into his bones, and he realized that if he kept on standing there he'd freeze solid in his happy dream. He set off toward the nearest boulder, fumbling with the fastening of his pants.

Someone grabbed his shoulder and spun him around.

"You *idiot!*" Bill shouted at him. "Don't you know what happens if you try to pee out here?"

From the horror on Bill's face, even behind the mask, Ford realized that he'd better get back in the cab as fast as he could.

When they were safely inside and the seals had locked, when Bill had finished yelling at him, Ford still sat shivering with more than cold.

"You mean it boils and *then* it explodes?" he said.

"You are such an idiot!" Bill repeated in disbelief.

"How was I supposed to know?" Ford said. "I've never been Outside before! We use the reclamation conduits at home—"

"This isn't the Long Acres, dumbbell. This is the middle of frozen Nowhere and it'll kill you in two seconds, okay?"

"Well, where can you go?"

"In the lavatory!"

"But I didn't want to wake up your dad."

"He'll sleep through anything," said Bill. "Trust me."

Red with humiliation, Ford crawled into the back and after several tries figured out how to operate the toilet, as Billy snored away oblivious. Afterward he crawled back up front, carefully closed the door and said:

"Er . . . so, where does somebody have their bath?"

Bill, who had turned his Gamebuke on again, did not look up as he said:

"At the *Empress*."

"No, I mean . . . when somebody has a bath *out here*, where do they have it?"

Bill lifted his eyes. He looked perplexed.

"What are you on about? Nobody bathes out here."

"You mean, you only wash when you're at the *Empress*?"

Now it was Bill's turn to flush with embarrassment.

"Yeah."

Ford tried to keep his dismay from showing, but he wasn't very good at hiding his feelings. "You mean I can't have a bath until we get back?"

"No. You can't. I guess people wash themselves every day in the Long Acres, huh?" said Bill angrily.

Ford nodded. "We have to. It stinks too bad if we don't. Because there's, er, manure and algae and, er, the methane plant, and . . . we work hard and sweat a lot. So we shave and wash every day, see?"

"Is *that* why the MAC haven't got any hair?"

"Yeah," said Ford. He added, "Plus my dad says hair is a vanity. Means being a showoff, being flash."

"I know what it means," said Bill. He was silent a moment, and then said:

"Well, you won't be sweating much out here. Freezing is more like it. So you'll have to cope until we get back to the *Empress*. It'll only be two weeks."

Two weeks? Ford thought of what his dad and mum would say to him when he turned up again, after being missing for so long. His mouth dried, his heart pounded. He wondered desperately what kind of lie he might tell to get himself out of trouble. Maybe that he'd been kidnapped? It had almost really happened. Kidnapped and taken to work in the iron mines, right, and . . . somehow escaped, and . . .

Billy retreated to his Gamebuke again, as Ford sat there trying to imagine what he might say. The stories became wilder, more unbelievable, as they grew more elaborate; and gradually he found himself drifting away from purposeful lies altogether, dreamily wondering what it might be like if he never went back to face the music at all.

After all, Sam was going to do it; Sam was clever and funny and brave, and he was walking away from the Collective to a new life. Why couldn't Ford have a new life too? What if he became a Hauler, like Billy, and lived out the rest of his life up here where there were no limits to the world? Blatchford the MAC boy would vanish and he could be just Ford, himself, not part of anything. *Free.*

V

It took them most of a week to get to Depot South. Ford enjoyed every minute of it, even getting used to the idea of postponing his bath for two weeks. Mostly he rode up front with Billy, as Bill stayed in the back sulking. Billy told him stories as they rocketed along, and taught him the basics of driving the freighter; it was harder than driving a tractor but not by as much as Ford would have thought.

"Look at you, holding our *Evelyn* on the road!" said Billy, chuckling. "You are one strong kid, for your age. Li'l Bill can't drive her at all yet."

"I'm a better navigator than you are!" yelled Bill from the back, in tones of outrage.

"He is, actually," said Billy. "Best navigator I ever saw. Half the time I have to get him to figure coordinates for me. You ever get lost in a storm or anything, you'll wish you had Li'l Bill there with you." He looked carefully into the back to see if Bill was watching, and then unzipped a pouch in his psuit and took out a small bottle. Quickly he shook two tiny red pills into his palm and popped them into his mouth.

"What're those?" Ford asked.

"Freddie Stay-awakes," said Billy in a low voice. "Just getting ready for another night shift. We're going to set a new record for getting to the Depot, man."

"We don't have to hurry or anything," said Ford. "Really."

"Yeah, we do," said Billy, looking uncomfortable for the first time since Ford had known him. "Fun's fun, and everything, but . . . your people must be kind of wondering where you are, you know? I mean, it was a good idea to get you away from Mother's Boys and all, but we don't want people thinking you're dead, huh?"

"I guess not," said Ford. He looked sadly up at the monitor, at the wide open world. The thought of going back into the Tubes, into the reeking dark of the cowsheds and the muddy trenches, made him despair.

Depot South loomed ahead of them at last, a low rise of ice above the plain. At first, Ford was disappointed; he had expected a gleaming white mountain, but Billy explained that the glacier was sanded all over with red dust from the windstorms. As the hours went by and they drew closer, Ford saw a low-lying mist of white, from which the glacier rose like an island. Later, two smaller islands seemed to rise from it as well, one on either side of the road.

"There's old Jack and Jim!" cried Billy. "We're almost there, when we see Jack and Jim."

Ford watched them with interest. As they drew near, he laughed; for they looked like a pair of bearded giants hacked out of the red stone. One was sitting up, peering from blind hollow eyes and holding what appeared to be a mug clutched to his stomach. The other reclined, with his big hands folded peacefully on his chest.

"How'd they get there?" he exclaimed, delighted.

"The glacier deposited them," said Bill, who had come out of the back to see.

"No! No! You have to tell him the story," said Billy gleefully. "See, Jack and Jim were these two Haulers, come up from Australia. So they liked their beer cold, see? *Really* cold.

"So they go into the *Empress*, and Mother, she says, *Welcome, my dears, have a drop of good cheer, warm buttery beer won't cost you dear.* But Jack and Jim, both he and him, they liked their beer cold. Really cold!

"Says one to the other, like brother to brother, there must be a place in this here space where a cobber can swill a nice bit of chill, if he likes his beer cold. Really *cold*.

"So they bought them a keg, and off they legged it for the Pole, the pole, where it's nice and cold, and they chopped out a hole in the ice-wall so, and that keg they stowed in the ice, cobber, ever so nice. And it got cold. *Really* cold.

"So they drank it down and another round and another one still and they drank until they set and they sot and they clean forgot, where the white mists creep they fell asleep, and they got cold. Really cold.

"In fact they froze, from nose to toes, and there they are to this very day, and the moral is, don't die that way! 'Cause what's right for Oz ain't right on Moz, 'cause up here it's *cold*. Really cold!"

Billy laughed like a loon, pounding his fist on the console. Bill just rolled his eyes.

"They're only a couple of boulders," he said.

"But you used to love that song," said Billy plaintively.

"When I was three, maybe," said Bill, turning and going into the back. "You'd better get him out one of your extra psuits. He won't fit in any of mine."

"He used to sing it with me," said Billy to Ford, looking crestfallen.

They pulled into Depot South, and once again Ford expected to see buildings, but there were none; only a confused impression of tumbled rock on the monitor. He looked up at it as Billy helped him into a psuit.

"Is it colder out there?" he asked.

"Yeah," said Bill, getting down three helmets from a locker. "You're at the South Pole, dummy."

"Aw, now, he's never been there, has he?" said Billy, adjusting the fit of the suit for Ford. "That feel okay?"

"I guess it—whoa!" said Ford, for once the fastenings had been sealed up the suit seemed to flex, like a hand closing around him, and though it felt warm and snug it was still a slightly creepy sensation. "What's it doing?"

"Just kind of programming itself so it gets to know you," Billy explained, accepting a helmet from Bill. "That's how it keeps you alive, see? Just settles in real close and puts a couple of sensors places you don't notice. Anything goes wrong, it'll try to fix you, and if it can't, it'll flash lights at you so you know."

"Like that?" Ford pointed at the little red light flashing on Billy's psuit readout panel. Billy looked down at it.

"Oh. No, that's just a short circuit or glitch or something. It's been doing that all the time lately when nothing's wrong."

"Some people take their suits into the shop when they need repair, you know," said Bill, putting on his own helmet. "Just an idea, Dad. Hope it's not too radical for you."

As Billy helped him seal up his helmet, Ford looked at Bill and thought: *You're a mean little twit. I'd give anything if my dad was like yours.*

But when they stepped Outside, he forgot about Bill and even about Billy. He barely noticed the cold, though it was so intense it took his breath away and the psuit helpfully turned up its thermostat for him. Depot South had all his attention.

They were surrounded on three sides by towering walls, cloudy white swirled through with colors like an Ice Pop, green and blue blue blue and lavender, all scarred and rough, faceted and broken. Underneath his feet was a confusion of crushed and broken rock, pea-sized gravel to cobbles, ice mixed with grit and stone, and a roiling mist swirled about his ankles.

Here and there were carvings in the ice wall, roughly gouged and hacked: HAULERS RULE OK and BARSOOM BRUCE GOT HERE ALIVE, and one that simply said THANKS MARSWIFE, over a niche that had been scraped from the ice where somebody had left a little figurine like the one on *Beautiful Evelyn*'s console. There were figures carved too; on a section of green ice, Ford noticed a four-armed giant with tusks.

Behind him, he became aware of a clatter as Billy and Bill opened a panel in the freighter's side and drew out something between them. He turned to see Billy hoisting a laser-saw, and heard the *hummzap* as it was turned on.

"Okay!" said Billy, his voice coming tinnily over the speaker. "Let's go cut some ice!"

He went up to the nearest wall, hefted the laser, and disappeared in a cloud of white steam. A moment later, a great chunk of ice came hurtling out of the steam, and bounced and rolled to Bill's feet. He picked it up, as another block bounded out.

"Grab that," said Bill. "If we don't start loading this stuff, Dad will be up to his neck in ice."

Ford obeyed, and followed Bill around to the rear of the freighter, where a sort of escalator ramp had been lowered, and watched as Bill dropped the block to the ramp. It traveled swiftly up the ramp to a hopper at the top of *Beautiful Evelyn*'s tank, where it vanished with a grinding roar, throwing up a rainbowed shatter of ice-shards and vapor against the sunlight. Fascinated, Ford set his block on the ramp and watched as the same thing happened.

"What's it doing?"

"Making carbon dioxide snowcones, what do you think?" said Bill. "And we take the whole lot back to Settlement Base, and sell it to the MAC."

"You do?" Ford was astonished. "What do we need it for?"

"Hel-LO, terraforming, remember?" said Bill. "Making Mars green like Earth? What the MAC was brought up here to do?"

He turned and trudged back around the side of the freighter, and Ford walked after him thinking: *I'll bet you wouldn't hold that nose so high up in the air if I bashed it with my forehead.*

But he said nothing, and for the next hour they worked steadily as machines, going back and forth with ice blocks to the ramp. The tank was nearly full when they heard the drone of ice-cutting stop.

"That's not enough, Dad," Bill called, and nobody answered. He turned and ran. Ford walked around the side of the freighter and saw him kneeling beside Billy, who had fallen and lay with the white mist curling over his body.

Ford gasped and ran to them. The whole front of Billy's psuit was lit with blinking colors, dancing over a readout panel that had activated. Bill was bending close, waving away the mist to peer at it. Ford leaned down and saw Billy's face slack within the helmet, his eyes staring and blank.

"What's wrong with him?" said Ford.

"He's had a blowout," said Bill flatly.

"What's a blowout?"

"Blood vessel goes *bang*. Happens sometimes to people who go Outside a lot." Bill rested his hand on his father's chest. He felt something in one of the sealed pouches; he opened it, and drew out the bottle of Freddie Stay-awakes. After staring at it for a long moment, his face contorted. He hurled the bottle at the ice-wall, where it popped open and scattered red pills like beads of blood.

"I knew it! I knew he'd do this! I knew this would happen someday!" he shouted. Ford felt like crying, but he fought it back and said:

"Is he going to die?"

"What do you think?" said Bill. "We're at the bloody South Pole! We're a week away from the infirmary!"

"But—could we maybe keep him alive until we get back?"

Bill turned to him, and a little of the incandescent rage faded from his eyes. "We might," he said. "The psuit's doing what it can. We have some emergency medical stuff. You don't understand, though. His brain's turning to goo in there."

"Maybe it isn't," said Ford. "Please! We have to try."

"He'll die anyway," said Bill, but he got Billy under the shoulders and tried to lift him. Ford came around and took his place, lifting Billy easily; Bill grabbed his father's legs, and between them they hoisted Billy up and carried him into the cab.

There they settled him in his bunk, and Bill fumbled in a drawer for a medical kit. He drew out three sealed bags of colored liquid with tubes leading from one end and hooks on the other. The tubes he plugged into ports in the arm of Billy's psuit; the hooks fitted into loops on the underside of the upper bunk, so the bags hung suspended above Billy.

"Should we get his helmet off him?" Ford asked. Bill just shook his head. He turned and stalked out of the compartment. Ford took a last look at Billy, with the glittering lights on his chest and his dead eyes staring, and followed Bill.

"What do we do now?"

"We get the laser," said Bill. "We can't leave it. It cost a month's pay."

VI

The freighter was a lot harder to handle now, full of ice, than it had been on the way out when Billy had let him drive. It took all Ford's strength to back her around and get her on the road again, and even so the console beeped a warning as they trundled out through Jack and Jim, for he nearly swerved and clipped one of the giants. At last he was able to steer straight between the boulders and get up a little speed.

"We really can't, er, send a distress signal or anything?" he asked Bill. Bill sat hunched at his end of the cab, staring at the monitors.

"Nobody'll hear us," he said bitterly. "There's half a planet between Mons Olympus and us. Did you notice any relay towers on the way out here?"

"No."

"That's because there aren't any. Why should Areco build any? Nobody comes out here except Haulers, and who cares if Haulers die? We do this work because nobody else wants to do it, because it's too dangerous. But Haulers are a bunch of idiots; *they* don't care if they get killed."

"They're not idiots, they're brave!" said Ford. Bill looked at him with contempt. Neither of them said anything for a long while after that.

By the time it was beginning to get dark, Ford was aching in every muscle of his body from the sheer effort of keeping the freighter on the road. The approaching darkness was not as fearful as he'd thought it might be, because for several miles now someone had daubed the lines of boulders with photoreflective paint, and they lit up nicely in the freighter's high-beams. But *Beautiful Evelyn* seemed to want to veer to the left, and Ford wondered if there was something wrong with her steering system until he saw drifts of sand flying straight across the road in front of her, like stealthy ghosts.

"I think the wind's rising," he said.

"You think, genius?" Bill pointed to a readout on the console.

"What's it mean?"

"It means we're probably driving right into a storm," said Bill, and then they heard a shrill piping alarm from the back. Bill scrambled aft; Ford held the freighter on the road. *Please don't let that be Billy dying! Please, Marswife, if you're out there, help us!*

Bill returned and crawled into his seat. "The air pressure's dropping in here. The psuit needed somebody to okay turning it up a notch."

"Why's the air pressure dropping?"

Bill sounded weary. "Because this is going to be a really bad storm. You'd better pull over and anchor us."

"But we have to get your dad to an infirmary!"

"Did you think we were going to drive for a whole week without sleeping?" Bill said. "We don't have any Freddies now. We have to sit out the storm no matter what happens. Five-Fifty-K is coming up soon. Maybe we can make it that far."

It was in fact twelve kilometers away, and the light faded steadily as they roared along. Ford could hear the wind howling now. He remembered a story Billy had told him, about people seeing dead Haulers in their high-beams, wraiths signaling for help at the scenes of long-ago breakdowns. The whirling sand looked uncannily like figures with streaming hair, diving in front of the freighter as though waving insubstantial arms. He was grateful when the half-circle of rocks that was Five-Fifty-K Station appeared in her lights at last, and she seemed eager to swerve away from the road.

Bill punched in the anchoring protocol, and *Beautiful Evelyn* gave a lurch and dropped abruptly, as though she were sitting down. Ford cut the power; the drives fell silent. They sat there side by side in the silence that was filled up steadily by the whine of blowing sand, and a patter of blown gravel that might have sounded to them like rain, if they had ever heard rain.

"What do we do now?" said Ford.

"We wait it out," said Bill.

They went into the back to check on Billy—no change—and heated something frozen and ate it, barely registering what it was. Then they went back into the cab and sat, in their opposite corners.

"So we really are on our own?" said Ford at last. "Areco won't send Security looking for us?"

"Areco doesn't send Mother's Boys anyplace," said Bill, staring into the dark. "Mother hired 'em."

"Who's Mother, anyway?"

"The lady who found the diamond and got rich," said Bill. "And bought Mons Olympus, and everybody thought she was crazy, because it was just this big volcano where nobody could grow anything. Only, she had a well drilled into a magma pocket and built a power station. And she leased lots to a bunch of people from Earth and that's why Mons Olympus makes way more money than Areco and the MAC."

"The MAC isn't supposed to make money," said Ford. "We're supposed to turn Mars into a paradise. Our contract says Areco is going to give it to us for our own, once we've done it."

"Well, you can bet Areco isn't going to come rescue us," said Bill. "Nobody looks out for Haulers except other Haulers. And their idea of help would be giving Dad a big funeral and getting stinking drunk afterward."

"Oh," said Ford. Bill gave him an odd look.

"People in the MAC look out for each other, though, don't they?"

"Yeah," said Ford wretchedly. "There's always somebody watching what you do. Always somebody there to tell you why what you want to do is wrong. Council meetings go on for hours because everybody has to say something or it isn't fair, but they all say the same thing anyway. Blah blah blah. I *hate* it there," he said, surprising himself by how intensely he felt.

"What's it supposed to be like, when Mars is a paradise?"

Ford looked at Bill to see if he was being mocking, but he wasn't smiling.

"Well, it'll be like . . . there'll be no corruption or oppression. And stuff. They say water will fall out of the sky, and nobody will ever have to wear a mask again." Ford slumped forward and put his head on his knees. "I used to imagine it'd be . . . I don't know. Full of lights."

"People would be safe, if Mars could be made like that," said Bill in a thoughtful voice. "Terraformed. Another Earth. No more big empty spaces."

"I *like* big empty spaces," said Ford. "Why does Mars have to be just like Earth anyway? Why can't things stay the way they are?"

"You *like* this?" Bill swung his arm up at the monitors, that showed only the howling night and a blur of sand. "'Cause you can have it. I hate it! Tons of big nothing waiting to kill us, all my whole life! And Dad just laughed at it, but he isn't laughing now, huh? You know what's really sick? If he dies—if we get back alive—I'll be better off."

"Oh, shut up," said Ford.

"But I *will*," said Bill, with a certain wonderment. "Lots better off. I can sell this freighter—and Dad paid into the Hauler's Club, so there'd be some money coming in there—and . . . wow, I could afford a *good* education. Maybe University level. I'll be able to have everything I've always wanted, and I'll never have to come out here again."

"How can you talk like that?" Ford yelled. "You selfish pig! You're talking about your own dad dying! You don't even care, do you? Your dad's the bravest guy I ever met!"

"He got himself killed, after everything I told him. He was stupid," said Bill.

"He isn't even dead yet!" Ford, infuriated, swung at him. Bill ducked backward, away from his flailing fists, and got his legs up on the seat and kicked Ford. Ford fell sideways, but scrambled up on his knees and kept coming, trying to back Bill into the corner. Bill dodged and hit him hard, and then again and again, until Ford got so close he couldn't get his arms up all the way. Ford, sobbing with anger, punched as hard as he could in the cramped space, but Bill was a much better fighter for all that he was so small.

By the time they had hurt each other enough to stop, both of them had bloody noses and Ford had the beginning of a black eye. Swearing, they retreated into their separate corners of the cab, and glared at each other until the droning hiss of the wind and the pattering of gravel on the tank lulled them to sleep.

VII

When they woke, hours later, it was dead quiet.

Ford woke groaning, partly because his face was so sore and partly because he had a stiff neck from sleeping curled up on the seat. He sat up and looked around blearily.

He realized that he couldn't hear anything. He looked up at the monitors and realized that he couldn't see anything, either; the screens were black. Frightened, he leaned over and shook Bill awake. Bill woke instantly, staring around.

"The power's gone out!" Ford said.

"No, it hasn't. We'd be dead," said Bill. He punched a few buttons on the console and peered intently at figures that appeared on the readout. Then he looked up at the monitors. "What's that?" He pointed at the monitor for the rear of the freighter, where there was a sliver of image along the top. Just a grayish triangle of light, shifting a little along its lower edge, just like . . .

"Sand," said Bill. "We're buried. The storm blew a dune over us."

"What do we do now?" said Ford, shivering, and the psuit thought he was cold and warmed up comfortingly.

"Maybe we can blow it away," said Bill. "Some, anyway." He switched on the drives and there was a shudder and a jolt that ran the whole length of the freighter. With a *whoosh*, *Beautiful Evelyn* rose a few inches. The rear monitor lit up with an image of sand cascading past it; some light showed on her left-hand monitor too.

"Okay!" said Bill, shutting her down again. "We're not going to die. Not here, anyway. We can dig out. Get a helmet on."

They went aft to get helmets—Billy still stared at nothing, though his psuit blinked at them reassuringly—and, when they had helmeted up, Bill reached past Ford to activate the hatch. It made a dull muffled sound, but would not open. He had to try three more times before it consented to open out about a hand's width. Sand spilled into the cab, followed by daylight.

Bill swore and climbed up on the seat, pushing the hatch outward. "Get up here and help me!"

Ford scrambled up beside him and set his shoulder to the hatch. A lot more sand fell in, but they were able to push it open far enough for Bill to grab the edge and pull himself up, and worm his way out. Ford climbed after, and in a moment was standing with Bill on the top of the dune that covered the freighter.

Bill swore quietly. Ford didn't blame him.

They stood on a mountain of red sand and looked out on a plain of red sand, endless, smooth to the wide horizon, and the low early sun threw their shadows far out behind them. The sky had a flat metallic glare; the wind wailed high and mournful.

"Where's the road?" cried Ford.

"Buried under there," said Bill, pointing down the slope in front of them. "It happens sometimes. Come on." He turned and started down the slope. Ford stumbled after him, slipped, and fell, rolling ignominiously to the bottom. He picked himself up, feeling stupid, but Bill hadn't noticed; he was digging with his hands, scooping away sand from the freighter.

Ford waded in to help him. He reached up to brush sand from the tank, but at his touch the sand puckered out in a funny starred pattern. Startled, he drew his hand back. Cautiously he reached out a fingertip to the tank; the instant he touched it, a rayed star of sand formed once again.

"Hey, look at this!" Giggling, he drew his finger along the tank, and the star spread and followed it.

"It's magnetic," said Bill. "Happens sometimes, when the wind's been bad. My dad said it's all the iron in the sand. It fries electronics. Hard to clean off, too."

Ford brushed experimentally at the tank, but the sand stuck as though it were a dense syrup.

"This'll take us forever," he said.

"Not if we get to the tool chest," said Bill. "We can scrape off most of it."

They worked together and after ten minutes had cleared a panel in the freighter's undercarriage; Bill pried it open and pulled out a couple of big shovels, and after that the work went more quickly.

"Wowie. Sand spades. All we need is buckets and we could make sand castles, huh?" said Ford, grinning sheepishly.

"What's that mean?"

"It's something kids do on Earth. Sam says, before we emigrated, our dad and mum took him to this place called Blackpool. There was all this blue water, see, washing in over the sand. He had a bucket and spade and he made sand castles. So here we are in the biggest Blackpool in the universe, with the biggest sand spades, yeah? Only there's no water."

"How could you make castles out of sand?" Bill said, scowling as he worked. "They'd just fall in on you."

"I don't know. I think you'd have to get the sand wet."

"But why would anybody get sand wet?"

"I don't know. I don't think people do it on purpose; I think it just happens. There's all this water on Earth, see, and it gets on things. That's what Sam says."

Bill shook his head grimly and kept digging. They cleared the freighter's rear wheels, and Ford said:

"Why do you reckon the water's blue on Earth? It's only green or brown up here."

"It's not blue," said Bill.

"Yes, it is," said Ford. "Sam has holos of it. I've seen 'em. It's bluer than the sky. Blue as blue paint."

"Water isn't any color really," said Bill. "It just looks blue. Something about the air."

Ford scowled and went around to the other side of the freighter, where he dug out great shovelfuls of sand and muttered, "It *is* blue. They wouldn't have that Blue Room if it wasn't blue. All the songs and stories say it's blue. So there, you little know-it-all."

He had forgotten that Bill could hear him on the psuit comm, so he was quite startled when Bill's voice sounded inside his helmet:

"Songs and stories? Right. Go stick your head in a dune, moron."

Ford just gritted his teeth and kept shoveling.

It took them a long while to clear the freighter, because they only made real progress once the wind fell a little. Eventually, though, they were able to climb back into the cab and start up *Beautiful Evelyn*'s drives. She blasted her way free of the dune and Ford strained to steer her up, over and down across the rippled slope below.

"Okay! Where's the road?" he said.

"There," said Bill, pointing. "Don't you even know directions? We anchored at right angles to the road. It's still there, even if we can't see it. Just take her straight that way."

Ford obeyed. They rumbled off.

They drove for five hours, over sand and then over rocky sand and at last over a cobbled plain, and there was no sign of the double row of boulders that should have been there if they had been on the High Road.

Bill, who had been watching the readouts, grew more and more pale and silent.

"We need to stop," he said at last. "Something's wrong."

"We aren't on the High Road anymore, are we?" said Ford sadly.

"No. We're lost."

"What happened?"

"The storm must have screwed up the nav system," said Bill. "All that magnetic crap spraying around."

"Can we fix it?"

"I can reset it," said Bill. "But I can't recalibrate it, because I don't know where we are. So it wouldn't do us any good."

"But your dad said you were this great navigator!" said Ford.

Bill looked at his boots. "I'm not. He just thought I was."

"Well, isn't that great?" said Ford. "And here you thought *I* was such an idiot. What do we do now, Professor?"

"Shut up," said Bill. "Just shut up. We're supposed to go north, okay? And the sun rises in the east and sets in the west. So as long as we keep the setting sun on our left, we're going mostly in the right direction."

"What happens at night?"

"If the sky's clear of dust clouds, maybe we can steer by the stars."

Ford brightened up at that. "I used to watch the stars a lot," he said. "And we ought to be able to see the mountain after a while, right?"

"Mons Olympus? Yeah."

"Okay then!" Ford accelerated again, and *Beautiful Evelyn* plunged forward. "We can do this! Billy wouldn't be scared if he was lost, would he?"

"No," admitted Bill.

"No, because he'd just point himself at the horizon and he'd just *go*, zoom, and he wouldn't worry about it."

"He never worried about anything," said Bill, though not as though he thought that was especially smart.

"Well, it's dumb to worry," said Ford, with a slightly rising note of hysteria in his voice. "You live or you die, right? The main thing, is . . . is . . . to be really *alive* before you die. I could have lived my whole life walking around in the Tubes and never, ever seen stuff like I've seen since I ran away. All this sky. All that sand. The ice and the mist and the different colors and everything! So maybe I don't get to be old like Hardie Stubbs's granddad. Who wants to be all shriveled up and coughing anyway?"

"Don't be stupid," said Bill. "I'd give anything to be down in the Long Acres right now, and I wouldn't care what work I had to do. And you wish you were there too."

"No, I don't!" Ford shouted. "You know what I'm going to do? As soon as we get back, I'll go see my dad and I'll say: 'Dad, I'm leaving the MAC.' Sam did it and so can I. Only I'm not going back to Earth. Mars is *my* place! And I'm going to be a Hauler, and stay Outside all the rest of my life!"

Bill stared at him.

"You're crazy," he said. "You think your dad will just let you go?"

"No," said Ford. "He'll grab my ear and about pull it off. It doesn't matter. Once I'm nine, the MAC says I have a right to pick whatever job I want."

"Once you're *nine*?"

Ford turned red. "In MAC years. We have one for every two Earth years."

"So . . . you're how old now?" Bill began to grin. "Six?"

"Yeah," said Ford. "And you can just shut up, okay?"

"Okay," said Bill, but his grin widened.

VIII

They drove all the rest of that day, but when night fell they were so tired they agreed to pull over to sleep. Ford stretched out in the cab and Bill went back to crawl into the bunk above Billy, who lay there still, staring and unresponsive as a waxwork.

He was still alive when morning came. Bill was changing his tube-bags when Ford came edging in, yawning.

"You wait and see," said Ford, in an attempt to be comforting. "He'll be fine if we can get him to the infirmary. Eric Chetwynd's dad fell off a tractor and fractured his skull, and *he* was in this coma, see, for days, but then they did surgery on him and he was opening his eyes and talking and everything. And your dad hasn't even got any broken bones."

"It's not the same," said Bill morosely. "Never mind. Let's get going. Sun's on our right until noon, got it?"

They drove on. Ford's muscles ached less now; he was beginning to feel more confident with *Beautiful Evelyn*. He watched the horizon and imagined Mons Olympus rising there, inevitable, the red queen on the vast chessboard of the plain. She *would* come into view soon. She had to. And someday, when he had a freighter of his own and drove this route all the time, a little thing like going off course wouldn't bother him at all. He'd know every sand hill and rock outcropping like the palm of his hand.

He thought about getting a tattoo on his face. Deciding what it ought to look like occupied his thoughts for the next couple of hours, as Bill sat silent across from him, staring at the monitors and twisting his hands together in his lap.

Then:

"Something's moving!" said Bill, pointing at the backup cam monitor.

Ford spotted it: something gleaming, sunlight striking off a vehicle far back in their dust-wake.

"Yowie! It's another Hauler!" he said. "Billy's saved!"

He slowed *Beautiful Evelyn* and turned her around, so the plume of dust whirled away and they could see the other vehicle more clearly.

"It's not a Hauler," said Bill. "It's just a cab. Who is that? That's nobody I know."

"Who cares?" said Ford, pounding on the console in his glee. "They'll know how to get back to the road!"

"Not if they're lost too," said Bill. The stranger was barreling toward them quite deliberately and they could see it clearly now: a freighter's cab with no tank attached, just the tang of the hookup sticking out behind, looking strange as some tiny insect with an immense head. It pulled up alongside them. Bill hit the comm switch and cried, "Who's that?"

There was a silence. Then a voice crackled through the speakers, distorted and harsh: "Who's that crying 'who's that?' Sounds like a youngster."

Ford leaned over and shouted, "Please, we're lost! Can you show us how to get back to the road?"

Another silence, and then:

"Two little boys? What're you doing out here, then? Daddy had a mishap, did he?"

Bill gave Ford a furious look. Ford wondered why, but said:

"Yes, sir! We need to get him to the infirmary, and our nav system went out in the storm! Can you help us?"

"Why, sure I can," said the voice, and it sounded as though the speaker were smiling. "Mask up now, kids, and step Outside. Let's talk close-up, eh?"

"You jackass," muttered Bill, but he pulled on his mask.

When they slid down out of the cab they saw that the stranger had painted his cab with the logo CELTIC POWER and pictures of what had been celtic knots and four-leaved clovers, though they were half scoured away. The hatch swung up and a man climbed out, a big man in a psuit also painted in green and yellow patterns. He looked them over and grinned within his mask.

"Well, hello there, kids," he said. "Gwill Griffin, at your service. Diamond prospector by trade. What's the story?"

"Bill's dad had a blowout," said Ford. "And we were trying to get him back, but we've lost the road. Can you help us, please?"

"A blowout?" The man raised his eyebrows. "Now, that's an awful thing. Let's have a look at him."

"You don't need—" began Bill, but Mr. Griffin had already vaulted up into *Beautiful Evelyn's* cab. Bill and Ford scrambled after him. By the time they had got in he was already in the back, leaning down to peer at Billy.

"Dear, dear, he's certainly in trouble," he said. "Yes, you'd better get him back to Mons Olympus, and no mistake." He looked around the inside of the cab. "Nice rig he's got here, though, isn't it? And a nice full tank of CO_2, I take it?"

"Yeah," said Ford. "It happened right as we were finishing up. Do you know how to, er, recalibrate nav systems?"

"No trouble at all," said Mr. Griffin, shoving past them and into the seat at the console. Bill watched him closely as he punched it up and set in new figures. "Poor little lads, lost on your own Outside. You're lucky I found you, you know. The road's just five kilometers east of here, but you might have wandered around forever without finding it."

"I knew we had to be close," said Ford, though he did not feel quite the sense of relief he might have, and wondered why.

"Yes; terrible things can happen out here. I saw your rig in the middle of nowhere, zigzagging along, and I said to myself: 'Goddess save me, that must be Freeze-Dried Dave!' I've seen some strange things out here in my time, I can tell you."

"Who's Freeze-Dried Dave?" asked Ford.

"Him? The Demon Hauler of Mare Cimmerium?" Mr. Griffin turned to him, pushing his mask up. He was beardless and freckled, though he wore a wide mustache, and was not as old as Ford had thought him to be at first.

"Nobody knows who Freeze-Dried Dave was; just some poor soul who was up here in the early days, and they say he died at the console whilst on a run, see? And his cab's system took over and went on Autopilot. They think it veered off the road in a storm and just kept rovering on, and every time the battery'd wear out it'd sit somewhere until another storm scoured the dust off the solar cells. Then it'd just start itself up again."

Ford realized what was making him uneasy. The man sounded like an actor in a holo, like somebody who was speaking lines for an effect.

"Some prospectors found it clean out in the middle of nowhere, and went up to it and got the hatch to open. There was Freeze-Dried Dave still sitting inside her, shriveled up like; but no sooner had they set foot to the ladder than she roared to life and took off, scattering 'em like bowling pins. And what do you think she did then? Only swerved around and came back at 'em, that's what she did, and mashed one into the sand while the others ran for their lives.

"*They* made it home to tell the tale. There's many a Hauler since then who's seen her, thundering along on her own business off the road, with that dead man rattling around inside. Some say it's Dave's ghost driving her, trying to find his way back to Settlement Base. Some say it's the freighter herself, that her system's gone mad with sorrow and wants to kill anyone gets close enough, so they don't take her Dave away. You'll never find a prospector like me who'll go anywhere near her. Why it's bad luck even to see her." He winked broadly at Ford.

"We need to get my dad to the infirmary," said Bill, clearing his throat. "Thanks for helping us. Let's go, okay?"

"Right," said Mr. Griffin, masking up again. "Only you'd best let me do a pointcheck on your freighter first, don't you think? That was quite a storm; could be all sorts of things gummed up you don't know about. Wouldn't want to have a breakdown out here, eh?"

"No, sir," said Ford. Mr. Griffin jumped down from the cab. Bill was preparing to jump after him, but he held up his hand.

"Now, I'll tell you what we'll do," he said. "You lads sit in there and watch the console. I'm going to test the tread relays; that's the surest thing will go wrong after a storm, with all those little magnetic particles getting everywhere and persuading the relays to do things they shouldn't. Could cause all your wheels to lock on one side, and you don't want that to happen at speed! You'd roll and kill yourselves for sure. I'll just open the panel and run a quick diagnostic; you can give me a shout when the green lights go on."

"Okay," said Bill, and climbed back in and closed the hatch. As soon as it was closed, he swore, and kept swearing. Ford stared at him.

"What are you on about?" he demanded. "We're safe now."

"No, we bloody aren't," said Bill. "Gwill Griffin, my butt. I know who that guy is. His name's Art Finlay. He was one of Mother's Boys. She fired him last year. He liked to go into the holding cell and slap guys around. He thought nobody was looking, but the cameras caught him. So all that old-diamond-prospector-with-his-talltales stuff was so much crap. So's the PanCeltic accent; he emigrated up here from some place in the Americans on Earth."

"So he's a phony?" Ford thought of the inexplicably creepy feeling the stranger had given him.

"Yeah. He's a phony," said Bill, and reached over to switch on the comm unit. "How are those relays?" he said.

"Look fine," was the crackly answer. "Your daddy took care of this rig, sure enough. Look at the console, now, lads; tell me when the green lights go on."

They stared at the panel, and in a moment: "They're on," chorused Bill and Ford.

"Then you're home and dry."

"Thanks! We're going to go on now, okay?" said Bill.

"You do that. I'll just follow along behind to be sure you get home safe, eh?"

"Okay," said Bill, and shut off the comm. "Get going!" he told Ford. "Five kilometers due east. We ought to be able to see it once we get over that rise. Let's leave this guy way behind us."

Ford started her up again, and *Beautiful Evelyn* rolled forward. She picked up speed and he charged her at the hill, feeling a wonderful sense of freedom as she zoomed upward. Bill cut into his reverie by yelling:

"The camera's been changed!"

"Huh?"

"Look," said Bill, pointing up at the left-hand monitor. It was no longer showing *Beautiful Evelyn*'s port side and a slice of ground, as it had been; now there was only a view of the northern horizon. "He moved the lens. Move it back!"

"I don't know how!" Ford leaned in, flustered, as Bill jumped up and reached past him to stab at the controls that would align the camera lenses. *Beautiful Evelyn*'s side came back into view.

"She looks all right," said Ford. "And, hey! There's the High Road! Hooray!"

"No, she doesn't look all right!" said Bill. "Look! He left the relay panel open! How come the telltale warning isn't lit?"

"I don't know," said Ford.

"Of course *you* don't know, you flaming idiot," said Bill, shrill with anger. "And here he comes!"

Ford looked up at the backup cam and saw Mr. Griffin's cab advancing behind the freighter; then the image switched to the lefthand camera, as it moved up on *Beautiful Evelyn*'s port side. It drew level with the open panel. They watched in horror as the cab's hatch swung down. They saw Mr. Griffin, masked up, leaning out.

"He's going to do something to the panel!" shrieked Bill.

"Oh, no, he won't," said Ford, more angry than he had ever been in his life. Without a second's hesitation, he steered *Beautiful Evelyn* sharply to the left. She more than sideswiped Mr. Griffin; with a terrific crash, she sent his cab spinning away, rolling over and over, and they saw him go flying out of it. *Beautiful Evelyn* lurched and sagged. They rumbled to a stop. They sat for a moment, shaking.

"We have to go see," said Bill. "Something's wrong."

They masked up and went Outside.

IX

Beautiful Evelyn's foremost left tire had exploded. There was a thick crust of polyceramic around the wheel, but nothing else. It must have sent pieces flying in all directions when it burst. Ford gaped at it while Bill ran down to the open panel. Ford heard a lot of swearing. He turned and saw Bill tearing something loose, and holding it up.

"Duct tape," said Bill. "He put a piece of duct tape over the warning sensor."

"Did he damage the, whatzis, the relays?" Ford looked in concern at the open panel, with no idea what he was seeing inside.

"No. You nailed him in time. But if he'd bashed them with something once we'd come up to speed, we'd have flipped over, just like he said. Then all he'd have had to do was move in and pick over the wreck. Help himself to the tank. Tell anybody who asked questions a story about some 'poor little dead lads' he'd found out here." Bill looked over at the dust rising from the wreck of Griffin's cab.

He bent and picked up a good-sized rock.

Ford followed his gaze.

"You think he's still alive?" he said, shuddering.

"Maybe," said Bill. "Get a rock. Let's go find out."

But he wasn't alive. They found him where he'd fallen, nine meters from his cab. His mask had come off.

"Oh," said Ford, backing away. "Oh—"

He turned hastily and doubled up, vomiting into his mask. Turning, he ran for the freighter. Scrambling in and closing the hatch, he groped his way to the lavatory and pulled his mask off. He vomited again, under Billy's blank gaze.

He had cleaned himself up a little and stopped crying by the time he heard Bill coming back.

"Can you mask up?" Bill asked him, over the commlink.

"Yeah—" said Ford, his voice breaking on another sob. Hating himself, he pulled the mask on and heard the hatch open. Bill climbed in.

"We might be okay," said Bill. "I had a look at his rig. Same size tires as ours. Maybe we can change one out."

"Okay," said Ford. Bill looked at him.

"Are you going to be all right? You're green."

"I killed a guy," said Ford.

"He was trying to kill us," said Bill. "He deserved what he got."

"I know," said Ford, beginning to shiver again. "It's just—the way it *looked*. The face. Oh, man. I'm going to see it when I close my eyes at night, for the rest of my life."

"I know," said Bill, sounding tired. "That was how I felt, the first time I saw somebody die like that."

"Does it happen a lot?"

"To Haulers? Yeah. Mostly to new guys." Bill stood up. "Come on. Blow your nose and let's go see if we can change the tire."

Walking out to the wreck, Ford began to giggle weakly.

"We really blew *his* nose for him, huh?"

The cab had come to rest upright. Its hatch had been torn away, and the inside was a litter of tumbled trash and spilled coffee that had already frozen. Ford made a step of his hands so Bill could climb up and in.

"I don't see any lug nuts," Ford said, looking at the nearest tire. "How do we get them off?"

"They're not like tractor tires," said Bill crossly, punching buttons on the console. "Crap. All the electronics are fried. There's supposed to be an emergency release, though. Ours is under the console, because it's a Mitsubishi. This is a Toutatis. Let me look around in here . . ."

Ford glanced over his shoulder in the direction in which the dead man lay. He looked back hurriedly and gave an experimental tug at the tire. It felt as immovable as a ten-ton boulder. He reached in and got his arms around it, and pulled as hard as he could.

"I think maybe this is it," said Bill, from inside the cab. "Stand clear, okay?"

Ford let go hastily and tried to scramble away, but the tire shot off the axle as though it had been fired from a cannon.

It caught him in the stomach. He was thrown backward two meters, and fell sprawling on the ground, too winded to groan.

"Dumbass," said Bill, looking down. He jumped from the cab and pushed the tire off Ford. "I *said* stand clear. Why doesn't anybody ever listen to me?"

Ford rolled over, thinking he might have to throw up again. He got painfully to his hands and knees. Bill was already rolling the tire toward *Beautiful Evelyn*, so Ford struggled to his feet and followed.

He held the tire upright, standing well clear of the axle when Bill fired off the burst one. It shot all the way over to the wreck. Then Bill got back down, and, together, they lifted the tire up and slammed it into place. They drove down to the road, between two boulders, and turned north again.

"Look, you need to get over it," said Bill, who had been watching Ford. "It's not like you meant to kill him."

"It's not that," said Ford, who was gray-faced and sweating. "My stomach really hurts, is all."

Bill leaned close and looked at him.

"Your psuit says something's wrong," he said.

"It does?" Ford looked down at himself. How had he missed that flashing yellow light? "It's like it's shrinking or something. It's so tight I can almost not breathe."

"We have to stop," said Bill.

"Okay," said Ford. *Beautiful Evelyn* coasted to a stop and sat there in the middle of the road, as Bill climbed over and stared intently at the diagnostic panel on the front of Ford's psuit. He went pale, but all he said was:

"Let's trade places."

"But you can't drive her," Ford protested.

"If we're on the straightaway and there's no wind, I can sort of drive," said Bill. He dove into the back, as Ford crawled sideways into his seat, and came out a moment later with one of the little tube-bags. "Stick your arm up like *this*, okay?"

Ford obeyed, and watched as Bill plugged the tube into the psuit's port. "So that'll make me feel better?"

"Yeah, it ought to." Bill swung himself into the console seat and sent *Beautiful Evelyn* trundling on.

"Good." Ford sighed. "What's wrong with me?"

"Psuit says you've ruptured something," said Bill, staring at the monitor. He accelerated.

"Oh. Well, that's not too bad," said Ford, blinking. "Jimmy Linton got a rupture and he's okay. Better than okay, actually. The medic said he couldn't work with a shovel anymore. So . . . they made him official secretary for the Council, see? All he has to do is record stuff at meetings and post notices."

"Really."

"So if I have a rupture, maybe my dad won't take it so hard that I want to be a Hauler. Since that way I get out of working in the methane plant and the cow sheds. Maybe."

Bill gave him an incredulous look.

"All this, and you still want to be a Hauler?"

"Of course I do!"

Bill just shook his head.

They drove in a dead calm, at least compared to the weather before. Far off across the plains they saw dust devils here and there, twirling lazily. The farther north they drove, the clearer the air was, the brighter the light of the sun, shining on standing outcroppings of rock the color of rust, or milk chocolate, or tangerines, or new pennies.

"This is so great," said Ford, slurring his words as he spoke. "This is more beautiful than anything. Isn't the world a big place?"

"I guess so," said Bill.

"It's *our* place," said Ford. "They can all go back to Earth, but we never will. We're Martians."

"Yeah."

"Did you see, I have hair growing in?" Ford swung his hand up to pat his scalp. "Red like Mars."

"Don't move your arm around, okay? You'll rip the tube out."

"Sorry."

"That's all right. Maybe you should mask up, you know? You could probably use the oxygen."

"Sure . . ." Ford dragged his mask into place.

After a while, he smiled and said: "I know who I am."

He murmured to himself for a while, muffled behind the mask. The next time Bill glanced over at him, he was unconscious.

And Bill was all alone.

Billy wasn't there to be yelled at, or blamed for anything. He might never be there again. He couldn't be argued with, he couldn't be shamed or ignored or made to feel anything Bill wanted him to feel. Not if he was dead.

But he'd been like that when he'd been alive, too, hadn't he?

The cold straight road stretched out across the cold flat plain, and there was no mercy out here, no right or wrong, no lies. There was only this giant machine hurtling along, that took all Bill's strength to keep on the road.

If he couldn't do it, he'd die.

Bill realized, with a certain shock, how much of his life he'd wanted an audience. Someone else to be a witness to how scared and angry he was, to agree with him on how bad a father Billy had been.

What had he thought? That someday he'd stand up in some kind of giant court-room, letting the whole world know how unfair everything had been from the day he'd been born?

Out here, he knew the truth.

There was no vast cosmic court of justice that would turn Billy into the kind of father Bill had wanted him to be. There was no Marswife to swoop down from the dust clouds and guide a lost boy home. The red world didn't care if he sulked; it would casually kill him, if it caught him Outside.

And he had always known it.

Then what was the point of being angry about it all the time?

What was the point of white-knuckled fists and a knotted-up stomach if things would never change?

His anger would never force anybody to fix the world for him.

But . . .

There were people who tried to fix the world for themselves. Maybe he could fix his world, just the narrow slice of it that was his.

He watched the monitors, watched the wind driving sand across the barren stony plain, the emptiness that he had hated ever since he could remember. What would it take to make him love it, the way Billy or Ford loved it?

He imagined water falling from the sky, bubbling up from under the frozen rock. Maybe it would be blue water. It would splash and steam, the way it did in the bath-house. Running, gurgling water to drown the dust and irrigate the red sand.

And green would come. He couldn't get a mental image of vizio acres over the whole world, tenting in greenness even up here; that was crazy. But the green might creep out on its own, if there was enough water. Wiry little desert plants at first, maybe, and then . . . Bill tried to remember the names of plants from his lesson plans. Sagebrush, right. Sequoias. Clover. Edelweiss. Apples. A memory came back to him, a nursery rhyme he'd had on his Buke once: *I should like to rise and go, where the golden apples grow* . . .

He blurred his vision a little and saw himself soaring past green rows that went out forever, that arched over and made warm shade and shelter from the wind. An-other memory floated up, a picture from a lesson plan, and his dream caught it and slapped it into place: cows grazing in a green meadow, out under a sky full of white clouds, clouds of water, not dust.

And, in the most sheltered places, there would be people, Families. Houses lit warm at night, with the lights winking through the green leaves. Just as he had al-ways imagined. One of them would be his house. He'd live there with his family.

Nobody would give him a house, or a family, or a safe world to live in, of course. Ever. They didn't exist. But . . .

Bill wrapped it all around himself anyway, to keep out the cold and the fear, and he drove on.

At some point—hours or days later, he never knew—his strength gave out and he couldn't hold *Beautiful Evelyn* on the road anymore. She drifted gently to the side, clipping the boulders as she came, and rumbled to a halt just inside Thousand-K Station.

Bill lay along the seat where he had fallen, too tired and in too much pain to move. Ford still sat, propped up in his corner, most of his face hidden by his mask. Bill couldn't tell if he was still alive.

He closed his eyes and went down, and down, into the green rows.

He was awakened by thumping on the cab, and shouting, and was bolt upright with his mask on before he had time to realize that he wasn't dreaming. He crawled across the seat and threw the release switches. The hatch swung down, and red light streamed in out of a black night. There stood Old Brick, granddaddy of the Haulers, with his long beard streaming sideways in the gale and at least three other Haulers behind him. His eyes widened behind his mask as he took in Bill and Ford. He reached up and turned up the volume on his psuit.

"CONVOY! WE GOT KIDS Here! LOOKS LIKE TOWNSEND'S RIG!"

X

Bill was all right after a couple of days, even though he had to have stuff fed into his arm while he slept. He was still foggy-headed when Mother came and sat by his bed, and very gently told him about Billy.

Bill mustn't worry, she said; she would find Billy a warm corner in the *Empress*, with all the food and drink he wanted the rest of his days, and surely Bill would come talk to him sometimes? For Billy was ever so proud of Young Bill, as everyone knew. And perhaps take him on little walks round the Tubes, so he could see Outside now and again? For Billy had so loved the High Road.

Ford wasn't all right. He had to have surgery for a ruptured spleen, and almost bled to death once they'd cut his psuit off him.

He still hadn't regained consciousness when Bill, wrapped in an outsize bathrobe, shuffled down to the infirmary's intensive care unit to see him. *See him* was all Bill could do; pale as an egg, Ford lay in the center of a mass of tubes and plastic tenting. The only parts of him that weren't white were his hair, which was growing in red as Martian sand, and the greenish bruise where Bill had punched him in the eye.

Bill sat there staring at the floor tiles, until he became aware that someone else had entered the room. He looked up.

He knew the man in front of him must be Ford's father; his eyes were the same watery blue, and his ears stuck out the same way. He wore patched denim and muddy boots, and a stocking cap pulled down almost low enough to hide the bandage over his left eyebrow. There was a little white stubble along the line of his jaw, like a light frost.

He looked at Ford, and the watery eyes brimmed over with tears. He glanced uncertainly at Bill. He looked down, lined up the toes of his boots against a seam in the tile.

"You'd be that Hauler's boy, then?" he said. "I have to thank you, on behalf of my Blatchford."

"Blatchford," repeated Bill, dumfounded until he realized whom the old man meant. "Oh."

"That woman explained everything to me," said Ford's dad. "Wasn't my Blatchford's fault. Poor boy. Don't blame him for running off scared. Your dad did a good thing, taking him in like that. I'm sorry about your dad."

"Me, too," said Bill. "But For—Blatchford'll be all right."

"I know he will," said Ford's dad, looking yearningly at his son. "He's a strong boy, my Blatchford. Not like his brother. You can raise somebody up his whole life and do your best to teach him what's right, and—and overnight, he can just turn into a stranger on you.

"My Sam did that. I should have seen it coming, him walking out on us. He never was any good, really. A weakling.

"Not like my little Blatchford. Never a word of complaint out of *him*, or whining after vanities. *He* knows who he is. He'll make the Collective proud one day."

Bill swallowed hard. He knew that Ford would never make the Collective proud; Ford would be off on the High Road as soon as he could, in love with the wide horizon, and the old man's angry heart would break again.

The weight of everything that had happened seemed to come crashing down on Bill at once. He couldn't remember when he'd felt so miserable.

"Would you tell me something, sir?" he said. "What does it take to join the MAC?"

"Hm?" Ford's dad turned.

"What do you have to do?"

Ford's dad looked at him speculatively. He cleared his throat. "It isn't what you do. It's what you *are*, young man."

He came and sat down beside Bill, and threw back his shoulders.

"You have to be the kind of person who believes a better world is worth working for. You can't be weak, or afraid, or greedy for things for yourself. You have to know that the only thing that matters is making that better world, and making it for everyone, not just for you.

"You may not even get to see it come into existence, because making the world right is hard work. It'll take all your strength and all your bravery, and maybe you'll be left at the end with nothing but knowing that you did your duty.

"But that'll be enough for you."

His voice was thin and harsh; he sounded as though he was reciting a lecture he'd memorized. But his eyes shone like Ford's had, when Ford had looked out on the open sky for the first time.

"Well—I'm going to study agriculture," said Bill. "And I thought, maybe, when I pass my levels, I'd like to join the MAC. I want that world you talk about. It's all I've ever wanted."

"Good on you, son," said Ford's dad, nodding solemnly. "You study hard, and I'm sure you'd be welcome to join us. You're the sort of young man we need in the MAC. And it does my heart good to know my Blatchford's got a friend like you. Gives me hope for the future, to think we'll have two heroes like you working in our cause!"

He shook Bill's hand, and then the nurse looked in at them and said that visiting hours were over. Ford's dad went away, down the hill. Bill walked slowly back to his room.

He didn't climb back into bed. He sat down in a chair in the corner, and looked out through Settlement Dome at the cold red desert, at the far double line of boulders where the High Road ran off into places Billy would never see again. He began to cry, silently, tears burning as they ran down his face.

He didn't know whether he was crying for Billy, or for Ford's dad.

The world was ending. The world was beginning.

KIN

BRUCE McALLISTER

Here's a look at the intricate and surprising relationship that develops between a young boy and a ruthless alien assassin, one that demonstrates how sometimes a similar turn of mind and heart can mark you as kin much more clearly than blood can do.

Bruce McAllister published his first story in 1963, when he was seventeen (it was written at the tender age of fifteen). Since then, with only a handful of stories and a few novels, he has nevertheless managed to establish himself as one of the most respected writers in the business. His more than seventy short fiction sales appeared in most of the top markets of the seventies, eighties, and nineties, including *Omni*, *In the Field of Fire*, and *Alien Sex*. His first novel, *Humanity Prime*, was one of the original Ace Specials series, and his novel *Dream Baby* was one of the most critically acclaimed novels of the eighties. After more than a decade away from writing, he has, happily, become active again, with a slew of recent sales to *Asimov's Science Fiction*, *The Magazine of Fantasy and Science Fiction*, *Sci Fiction*, *Aeon*, and elsewhere. A new collection by him is in the works. McAllister lives in Redlands, California.

T he alien and the boy, who was twelve, sat in the windowless room high above the city that afternoon. The boy talked and the alien listened.

The boy was ordinary—the genes of three continents in his features, his clothes cut in the style of all boys in the vast housing project called LAX. The alien was something else, awful to behold; and though the boy knew it was rude, he did not look up as he talked.

He wanted the alien to kill a man, he said. It was that simple.

As the boy spoke, the alien sat upright and still on the one piece of furniture that could hold him. Eyes averted, the boy sat on the stool, the one by the terminal where he did his schoolwork each day. It made him uneasy that the alien was on his bed, though he understood why. It made him uneasy that the creature's strange knee was so near his in the tiny room, and he was glad when the creature, as if aware, too, shifted its leg away.

He did not have to look up to see the Antalou's features. That one glance in the doorway had been enough, and it came back to him whether he wanted it to or not. It was not that he was scared, the boy told himself. It was just the idea—that such a thing could stand in a doorway built for humans, in a human housing project where generations had been born and died, and probably would forever. It did not seem possible.

He wondered how it seemed to the Antalou.

Closing his eyes, the boy could see the black synthetic skin the alien wore as protection against alien atmospheres. Under that suit, ropes of muscles and tendons coiled and uncoiled, rippling even when the alien was still. In the doorway the long neck had not been extended, but he knew what it could do. When it telescoped forward—as it could instantly—the head tipped up in reflex and the jaws opened.

Nor had the long talons—which the boy knew sat in the claws and even along the elbows and toes—been unsheathed. But he imagined them sheathing and unsheathing as he explained what he wanted, his eyes on the floor.

When the alien finally spoke, the voice was inhuman—filtered through the translating mesh that covered half its face. The face came back: The tremendous skull, the immense eyes that could see so many kinds of light and make their way in nearly every kind of darkness. The heavy welts—the auxiliary gills—inside the breathing globe. The dripping ducts below them, ready to release their jets of acid.

"Who is it . . . that you wish to have killed?" the voice asked, and the boy almost looked up. It was only a voice—mechanical, snake-like, halting—he reminded himself. By itself it could not kill him.

"A man named James Ortega-Mambay," the boy answered.

"Why?" The word hissed in the stale apartment air.

"He is going to kill my sister."

"You know this . . . how?"

"I just do."

The alien said nothing, and the boy heard the long, whispering pull of its lungs.

"Why," it said at last, "did you think . . . I would agree to it?"

The boy was slow to answer.

"Because you're a killer."

The alien was again silent.

"So all Antalou," the voice grated, "are professional killers?"

"Oh, no," the boy said, looking up and trying not to look away. "I mean . . ."

"If not . . . then how . . . did you choose me?"

The boy had walked up to the creature at the great fountain by the Cliffs of Monica—a landmark any visitor to Earth would take in, if only because it appeared on the sanctioned itineraries—and had handed him a written message in crude Antalouan. "I know what you are and what you do," the message read. "I need your services. LAX cell 873-2345-2657 at 1100 tomorrow morning. I am Kim."

"Antalou are well known for their skills, sir," the boy said respectfully. "We've read about the Noh campaign, and what happened on Hoggun II when your people were betrayed, and what one company of your mercenaries were able to do against the Gar-Betties." The boy paused. "I had to give out ninety-eight notes, sir, before I found you. You were the only one who answered. . . ."

The hideous head tilted while the long arms remained perfectly still, and the boy found he could not take his eyes from them.

"I see," the alien said.

It was translator's idiom only. "Seeing" was not the same as "understanding." The young human had done what the military and civilian intelligence services of five worlds had been unable to do—identify him as a professional—and it made the alien reflect: Why had he answered the message? Why had he taken it seriously? A human child had delivered it, after all. Was it that he had sensed no danger and simply followed professional reflex, or something else? Somehow the boy had known he would. How?

"How much . . ." the alien said, curious, "are you able to pay?"

"I've got two hundred dollars, sir."

"How . . . did you acquire them?"

"I sold things," the boy said quickly.

The rooms here were bare. Clearly the boy had nothing to sell. He had stolen the money, the alien was sure.

"I can get more. I can—"

The alien made a sound that did not translate. The boy jumped.

The alien was thinking of the 200,000 inters for the vengeance assassination on Hoggun's third moon, the one hundred kilobucks for the renegade contract on the asteroid called Wolfe, and the mineral shares, pharmaceuticals, and spacelock craft—worth twice that—which he had in the end received for the three corporate kills on Alama Poy. What could two hundred *dollars* buy? Could it even buy a city rail ticket?

"That is not enough," the alien said. "Of course," it added, one arm twitching, then still again, "you may have thought to record . . . our discussion . . . and you may threaten to release the recording . . . to Earth authorities . . . if I do not do what you ask of me. . . ."

The boy's pupils dilated then—like those of the human province official on Diedor, the one he had removed for the Gray Infra there.

"Oh, no—" the boy stammered. "I wouldn't do that—" The skin of his face had turned red, the alien saw. "I didn't even think of it."

"Perhaps . . . you should have," the alien said. The arm twitched again, and the boy saw that it was smaller than the others, crooked but strong.

The boy nodded. Yes, he should have thought of that. "Why . . ." the alien asked then, "does a man named . . . James Ortega-Mambay . . . wish to kill your sister?"

When the boy was finished explaining, the alien stared at him again and the boy grew uncomfortable. Then the creature rose, joints falling into place with popping and sucking sounds, legs locking to lift the heavy torso and head, the long arms snaking out as if with a life of their own.

The boy was up and stepping back.

"Two hundred . . . is not enough for a kill," the alien said, and was gone, taking the same subterranean path out of the building which the boy had worked out for him.

———

When the man named Ortega-Mambay stepped from the bullet elevator to the roof of the federal building, it was sunset and the end of another long but productive day at BuPopCon. In the sun's final rays the helipad glowed like a perfect little pond—not the chaos of the Pacific Ocean in the distance—and even the mugginess couldn't ruin the scene. It was, yes, the kind of weather one conventionally took one's jacket off in; but there was only one place to remove one's jacket with at least a modicum of dignity, and that was, of course, in the privacy of one's own FabHome-by-the-Sea. To thwart convention, he was wearing his new triple-weave "gauze" jacket in the pattern called "Summer Shimmer"—handsome, odorless, waterproof, and cool. He would not remove it until he wished to.

He was the last, as always, to leave the Bureau, and as always he felt the pride. There was nothing sweeter than being the last—than lifting off from the empty pad with the rotor blades singing over him and the setting sun below as he made his way in his earned solitude away from the city up the coast to another, smaller helipad and his FabHome near Oxnard. He had worked hard for such sweetness, he reminded himself.

His heli sat glowing in the sun's last light—part of the perfect scene—and he took his time walking to it. It was worth a paintbrush painting, or a digital one, or a multimedia poem. Perhaps he would make something to memorialize it this weekend, after the other members of his triad visited for their intimacy session.

As he reached the pilot's side and the little door there, a shadow separated itself from the greater shadow cast by the craft, and he nearly screamed.

The figure was tall and at first he thought it was a costume, a joke played by a colleague, nothing worse.

But as the figure stepped into the fading light, he saw what it was and nearly screamed again. He had seen such creatures in newscasts, of course, and even at a distance at the shuttleport or at major tourist landmarks in the city, but never like this. *So close.*

When it spoke, the voice was low and mechanical—the work of an Ipoor mesh.

"You are," the alien said, "James Ortega-Mambay . . . Seventh District Supervisor . . . BuPopCon?"

Ortega-Mambay considered denying it, but did not. He knew the reputation of the Antalou as well as anyone did. He knew the uses to which his own race, not to mention the other four races mankind had met among the stars, had put them. The Antalou did not strike him as creatures one lied to without risk.

"Yes. . . . I am. I am Ortega-Mambay."

"My own name," the Antalou said, "does not matter, Ortega-Mambay. You know what I am. . . . What matters . . . is that you have decreed . . . the pregnancy of Linda Tuckey-Yatsen illegal. . . . You have ordered the unborn female sibling . . . of the boy Kim Tuckey-Yatsen . . . aborted. Is this true?"

The alien waited.

"It may be," the man said, fumbling. "I certainly do not have all of our cases memorized. We do not process them by family name—"

He stopped as he saw the absurdity of it. It was outrageous.

"I really do not see what business this is of yours," he began. "This is a Terran city, and an overpopulated one—in an overpopulated nation on an overpopulated planet that cannot afford to pay to move its burden off-world. We are faced with a problem and one we are quite happy solving by ourselves. None of this can possibly be any of your affair, Visitor. Do you have standing with your delegation in this city?"

"I do not," the mesh answered, "and it is indeed . . . my affair if . . . the unborn female child of Family Tuckey-Yatsen dies."

"I do not know what you mean."

"She is to live, Ortega-Mambay . . . Her brother wishes a sibling. . . . He lives and schools . . . in three small rooms while his parents work . . . somewhere in the city. . . . To him . . . the female child his mother carries . . . is already born. He has great feeling for her . . . in the way of your kind, Ortega-Mambay."

This could not be happening, Ortega-Mambay told himself. It was insane, and he could feel rising within him a rage he hadn't felt since his first job with the government. "How dare you!" he heard himself say. "You are standing on the home planet of another race and ordering me, a federal official, to obey not only a child's wishes, but your own—you, a Visitor and one without official standing among your own kind—"

"The child," the alien broke in, "will not die. If she dies, I will . . . do what I have been . . . retained to do."

The alien stepped then to the heli and the man's side, so close they were almost touching. The man did not back up. He would not be intimidated. *He would not.*

The alien raised two of its four arms, and the man heard a snicking sound, then a pop, then another, and something caught in his throat as he watched talons longer and straighter than anything he had ever dreamed of slip one by one through the creature's black syntheskin.

Then, using these talons, the creature removed the door from his heli.

One moment the alloy door was on its hinges; the next it was impaled on the talons, which were, Ortega-Mambay saw now, so much stronger than any nail, bone or other integument of Terran fauna. Giddily he wondered what the creature possibly ate to make them so strong.

"Get into your vehicle, Ortega-Mambay," the alien said. "Proceed home. Sleep and think . . . about what you must do . . . to keep the female sibling alive."

Ortega-Mambay could barely work his legs. He was trying to get into the heli, but couldn't, and for a terrible moment it occurred to him that the alien might try to help him in. But then he was in at last, hands flailing at the dashboard as he tried to do what he'd been asked to do: *Think.*

The alien did not sit on the bed, but remained in the doorway. The boy did not have trouble looking at him this time.

"You know more about us," the alien said suddenly, severely, "than you wished me to understand. . . . Is this not true?"

The boy did not answer. The creature's eyes—huge and catlike—held his.

"Answer me," the alien said.

When the boy finally spoke, he said only, "Did you do it?"

The alien ignored him.

"Did you kill him?" the boy said.

"*Answer me*," the alien repeated, perfectly still.

"Yes . . ." the boy said, looking away at last.

"*How?*" the alien asked.

The boy did not answer. There was, the alien could see, defeat in the way the boy sat on the stool.

"You will answer me . . . or I will . . . damage this room."

The boy did nothing for a moment, then got up and moved slowly to the terminal where he studied each day.

"I've done a lot of work on your star," the boy said. There was little energy in his voice now.

"It is more than that," the alien said.

"Yes. I've studied Antalouan history." The boy paused and the alien felt the energy rise a little. "For school, I mean." There was feeling again—a little—to the boy's voice.

The boy hit the keyboard once, then twice, and the screen flickered to life. The alien saw a map of the northern hemisphere of Antalou, the trade routes of the ancient Seventh Empire, the fragmented continent, and the deadly seas that had doomed it.

"More than this . . . I think," the alien said.

"Yes," the boy said. "I did a report last year—on my own, not for school—about the fossil record on Antalou. There were a lot of animals that wanted the same food you wanted—that your kind wanted. On Antalou, I mean."

Yes, the alien thought.

"I ran across other things, too," the boy went on, and the alien heard the energy die again, heard in the boy's voice the suppressive feeling his kind called "despair." The boy believed that the man named Ortega-Mambay would still kill his sister, and so the boy "despaired."

Again the boy hit the keyboard. A new diagram appeared. It was familiar, though the alien had not seen one like it—so clinical, detailed, and ornate—in half a lifetime.

It was the Antalouan family cluster, and though the alien could not read them, he knew what the labels described: The "kinship obligation bonds" and their respective "motivational weights," the "defense-need parameters" and "bond-loss consequences" for identity and group membership. There was an inset, too, which gave—in animated three-dimensional display—the survival model human exopsychologists believed could explain all Antalouan behavior.

The boy hit the keyboard and an iconographic list of the "totemic bequeaths" and "kinship inheritances" from ancient burial sites near Toloa and Mantok appeared.

"You thought you knew," the alien said, "what an Antalou feels."

The boy kept his eyes on the floor. "Yes."

The alien did not speak for a moment, but when he did, it was to say:

"You were not wrong . . . Tuckey-Yatsen."

The boy looked up, not understanding.

"Your sister will live," the Antalou said.

The boy blinked, but did not believe it.

"What I say is true," the alien said.

The alien watched as the boy's body began to straighten, as energy, no longer suppressed in "despair," moved through it.

"It was done," the alien explained, "without the killing . . . which neither you nor I . . . could afford."

"They will let her live?"

"Yes."

"You are sure?"

"I do not lie . . . about the work I do."

The boy was staring at the alien.

"I will give you the money," he said.

"No," the alien said. "That will not . . . be necessary."

The boy stared for another moment, and then, strangely, began to move.

The alien watched, curious. The boy was making himself step toward him, though why he would do this the alien did not know. It was a human custom perhaps, a "sentimentality," and the boy, though afraid, thought he must offer it.

When the boy reached the alien, he put out an unsteady hand, touched the Antalou's shoulder lightly—once, twice—and then, remarkably, drew his hand down the alien's damaged arm.

The alien was astonished. It was an Antalouan gesture, this touch.

This is no ordinary boy, the alien thought. It was not simply the boy's intelligence—however one might measure it—or his understanding of the Antalou. It was something else—something the alien recognized.

Something any killer needs. . . .

The Antalouan gesture the boy had used meant "obligation to blood," though it lacked the slow unsheathing of the *demoor*. The boy had chosen well.

"Thank you," the boy was saying, and the alien knew he had rehearsed both the touch and the words. It had filled the boy with great fear, the thought of it, but he had rehearsed until fear no longer ruled him.

As the boy stepped back, shaking now and unable to stop it, he said, "Do you have a family-cluster still?"

"I do not," the alien answered, not surprised by the question. The boy no longer surprised him. "It was a decision . . . made without regrets. Many Antalou have made it. My work . . . prevents it. You understand. . . ."

The boy nodded, a gesture which meant that he did.

And then the boy said it:

"What is it like to kill?"

It was, the alien knew, the question the boy had most wanted to ask. There was excitement in the voice, but still no fear.

When the alien answered, it was to say simply:

"It is both . . . more and less . . . than what one . . . imagines it will be."

The boy named Kim Tuckey-Yatsen stood in the doorway of the small room where he slept and schooled, and listened as the man spoke to his mother and father. The man never looked at his mother's swollen belly. He said simply, "You have been granted an exception, Family Tuckey-Yatsen. You have permission to proceed with the delivery of the unborn female. You will be receiving confirmation of a Four-Member Family Waiver within three workweeks. All questions should be referred to BuPopCon, Seventh District, at the netnumber on this card."

When the man was gone, his mother cried in happiness and his father held her. When the boy stepped up to them, they embraced him, too. There were three of them now, hugging, and soon there would be four. That was what mattered. His parents were good people. They had taken a chance for him, and he loved them. That mattered too, he knew.

That night he dreamed of her again. Her name would be Kiara. In the dream she looked a little like Siddo's sister two floors down, but also like his mother. Daughters should look like their mothers, shouldn't they? In his dream the four of them were hugging and there were more rooms, and the rooms were bigger.

When the boy was seventeen and his sister five, sharing a single room as well as siblings can, the trunk arrived from Romah, one of the war-scarred worlds of the Pleiades. Pressurized and dented, the small alloy container bore the customs stamps of four spacelocks, had been opened at least seven times in its passage, and smelled. It had been disinfected, yes, the USPUS carrier who delivered it explained. It had been kept in quarantine for a year and had nearly not gotten through, given the circumstances.

At first, the boy did not know what the carrier meant.

The trunk held many things, the woman explained. The small polished skull of a carnivore not from Earth. A piece of space metal fused like the blossom of a flower. Two rings of polished stone that tingled to the touch. An ancient device that the boy would later discover was a third-generation airless communicator used by the Gar-Betties. A coil made of animal hair and pitch, which he would learn was a rare musical instrument from Hoggun VI. And many smaller things, among them the postcard of the Pacific Fountain the boy had given the alien.

Only later did the family receive official word of the 300,000 inters deposited in the boy's name in the neutral banking station of HiVerks; of the cache of specialized weapons few would understand that had been placed in perpetual care on Titan, also in his name; and of the offworld travel voucher purchased for the boy to use when he was old enough to use it.

Though it read like no will ever written on Earth, it was indeed a will, one that the Antalou called a "bequeathing cantation." That it had been recorded in a spacelock lobby shortly before the alien's violent death on a world called Glory did not diminish its legal authority.

Although the boy tried to explain it to them, his parents did not understand; and before long it did not matter. The money bought them five rooms in the northeast sector of the city, a better job for his mother, better care for his father's autoimmunities, more technical education for the boy, and all the food and clothes they needed; and for the time being (though only that) these things mattered more to him than Saturn's great moon and the marvelous weapons waiting patiently for him there.

—for Harry Harrison, master

signal to noise

ALASTAIR REYNOLDS

Alastair Reynolds is a frequent contributor to *Interzone*, and has also sold to *Asimov's Science Fiction*, *Spectrum SF*, and elsewhere. His first novel, *Revelation Space*, was widely hailed as one of the major SF books of the year; it was quickly followed by *Chasm City*, *Redemption Ark*, *Absolution Gap*, and *Century Rain*, all big sprawling space operas that were big sellers as well, establishing Reynolds as one of the best and most popular new SF writers to enter the field in many years. His other books include a novella collection, *Diamond Dogs, Turquoise Days*. His most recent books are a novel, *Pushing Ice*, and two new collections, *Galactic North* and *Zima Blue and Other Stories*. Coming up is a new novel, *The Prefect*. A professional scientist with a Ph.D. in astronomy, Reynolds comes from Wales, but lives in the Netherlands, where he works for the European Space Agency.

Reynolds's work is known for its grand scope, sweep, and scale (in one story, "Galactic North," a spaceship sets out on in pursuit of another in a stern chase that takes thousands of years of time and hundreds of thousands of light-years to complete; in another, "Thousandth Night," ultrarich immortals embark on a plan that will call for the physical rearrangement of all the stars in the galaxy. In the intimate and compassionate story that follows, he sticks a lot closer to home, in one sense—while in another sense taking us to another universe altogether, one further away than the most distant galaxies, but close as the touch of a hand.

FRIDAY

Mick Leighton was in the basement with the machines when the police came for him. He'd been trying to reach Joe Liversedge all morning to cancel a prearranged squash match. It was the busiest week before exams, and Mick had gloomily concluded that he had too much tutorial work to grade to justify sparing even an hour for the game. The trouble was that Joe had either turned off his phone or left it in his office, where it wouldn't interfere with the machines. Mick had sent an email, but when that had gone unanswered he decided there was nothing for it but to stroll over to Joe's half of the building and inform him in person. By now Mick was a sufficiently well-known face in Joe's department that he was able to come and go more or less as he pleased.

"Hello, matey," Joe said, glancing over his shoulder with a half-eaten sandwich in one hand. There was a bandage on the back of his neck, just below the hairline. He was hunched over a desk covered in laptops, cables, and reams of hardcopy. "Ready for a thrashing, are you?"

"That's why I'm here," Mick said. "Got to cancel, sorry. Too much on my plate today."

"Naughty."

"Ted Evans can fill in for me. He's got his kit. You know Ted, don't you?"

"Vaguely." Joe set down his sandwich to put the lid back on a felt-tipped pen. He was an amiable Yorkshireman who'd come down to Cardiff for his postgraduate work and decided to stay. He was married to an archaeologist named Rachel who spent a lot of her time poking around in the Roman ruins under the walls of Cardiff Castle. "Sure I can't twist your arm? It'll do you good, you know, bit of a workout."

"I know. But there just isn't time."

"Your call. How are things, anyway?"

Mick shrugged philosophically. "Been better."

"Did you phone Andrea like you said you were going to?"

"No."

"You should, you know."

"I'm not very good on the phone. Anyway, I thought she probably needed a bit of space."

"It's been three weeks, mate."

"I know."

"Do you want the wife to call her? It might help."

"No, but thanks for suggesting it anyway."

"Call her. Let her know you're missing her."

"I'll think about it."

"Yeah, sure. You should stick around, you know. It's all go here this morning. We got a lock just after seven this morning." Joe tapped one of the laptop screens, which was scrolling rows of black-on-white numbers. "It's a good one, too."

"Really?"

"Come and have a look at the machine."

"I can't. I need to get back to my office."

"You'll regret it later. Just like you'll regret canceling our match, or not calling Andrea. I know you, Mick. You're one of life's born regretters."

"Five minutes, then."

In truth, Mick always enjoyed having a nose around Joe's basement. As solid as Mick's own early-universe work was, Joe had really struck gold. There were hundreds of researchers around the world who would have killed for a guided tour of the Liversedge laboratory.

In the basement were ten hulking machines, each as large as a steam turbine. You couldn't go near them if you were wearing a pacemaker or any other kind of implant, but Mick knew that, and he'd been careful to remove all metallic items before he came down the stairs and through the security doors. Each machine contained a ten-ton bar of ultra-high-purity iron, encased in vacuum and suspended in a magnetic cradle. Joe liked to wax lyrical about the hardness of the vacuum, about the dynamic stability of the magnetic field generators. Cardiff could be hit by a Richter six earthquake, and the bars wouldn't feel the slightest tremor.

Joe called it the call center.

The machines were called correlators. At any one time eight were online, while two were down for repairs and upgrades. What the eight functional machines were doing was cold-calling: dialing random numbers across the gap between quantum realities, waiting for someone to answer on the other end.

In each machine, a laser repeatedly pumped the iron into an excited quantum state. By monitoring vibrational harmonics in the excited iron—what Joe called the back-chirp—the same laser could determine if the bar had achieved a lock onto another strand of quantum reality—another worldline. In effect, the bar would be resonating with its counterpart in another version of the same basement, in another version of Cardiff.

Once that lock was established—once the cold-calling machine had achieved a hit—then those two previously indistinguishable worldlines were linked together by an information conduit. If the laser tapped the bar with low-energy pulses, enough to influence it but not upset the lock, then the counterpart in the other lab would also register those taps. It meant that it was possible to send signals from one lab to the other, in both directions.

"This is the boy," Joe said, patting one of the active machines. "Looks like a solid lock, too. Should be good for a full ten or twelve days. I think this might be the one that does it for us."

Mick glanced again at the bandage on the back of Joe's neck. "You've had a nervelink inserted, haven't you."

"Straight to the medical center as soon as I got the alert on the lock. I was nervous—first time, and all that. But it turned out to be dead easy. No pain at all. I was up and out within half an hour. They even gave me a Rich Tea Biscuit."

"Ooh. A Rich Tea Biscuit. It doesn't get any better than that, does it. You'll be going through today, I take it?"

Joe reached up and tore off the bandage, revealing only a small spot of blood, like a shaving nick. "Tomorrow, probably. Maybe Sunday. The nervelink isn't active yet, and that'll take some getting used to. We've got bags of time, though; even if we don't switch on the nervelink until Sunday, I'll still have five or six days of bandwidth before we become noise-limited."

"You must be excited."

"Right now I just don't want to cock up anything. The Helsinki boys are nipping at our heels as it is. I reckon they're within a few months of beating us."

Mick knew how important this latest project was for Joe. Sending information between different realities was one thing, and impressive enough in its own right. But now technology had escaped from the labs out into the real world. There were hundreds of correlators in other labs and institutes around the world. In five years it had gone from being a spooky, barely believable phenomenon, to an accepted part of the modern world.

But Joe—whose team had always been at the forefront of the technology—hadn't stood still. They'd been the first to work out how to send voice and video comms across the gap with another reality, and within the last year they'd been able to operate a camera-equipped robot, the same battery-driven kind that all the tourists had been using before nervelinking became the new thing. Joe had even let Mick have a go on it. With his hands operating the robot's manipulators via force-feedback gloves, and his eyes seeing the world via the stereoscopic projectors in a virtual-reality helmet, Mick had been able to feel himself almost physically present in the other lab. He'd been able to move around and pick things up just as if he were actually walking in that alternate reality. Oddest of all had been meeting the other version of Joe Liversedge, the one who worked in the counterpart lab. Both Joes seemed cheerily indifferent to the weirdness of the setup, as if collaborating with a duplicate of yourself was the most normal thing in the world.

Mick had been impressed by the robot. But for Joe it was a stepping stone to something even better.

"Think about it," he'd said. "A few years ago, tourists started switching over to nervelinks instead of robots. Who wants to drive a clunky machine around some smelly foreign city, when you can drive a warm human body instead? Robots can see stuff, they can move around and pick stuff up, but they can't give you the smells, the taste of food, the heat, the contact with other people."

"Mm," Mick had said noncommittally. He didn't really approve of nervelinking, even though it essentially paid Andrea's wages.

"So we're going to do the same. We've got the kit. Getting it installed is a piece of piss. All we need now is a solid link."

And now Joe had what he'd been waiting for. Mick could practically see the *Nature* cover article in his friend's eyes. Perhaps he was even thinking about taking that long train ride to Stockholm.

"I hope it works out for you," Mick said.

Joe patted the correlator again. "I've got a good feeling about this one."

That was when one of Joe's undergraduates came up to them. To Mick's surprise, it wasn't Joe she wanted to speak to.

"Doctor Leighton?"

"That's me."

"There's somebody to see you, sir. I think it's quite important."

"Someone to see me?"

"They said you left a note in your office."

"I did," Mick said absent-mindedly. "But I also said I wouldn't be gone long. Nothing's *that* important, is it?"

But the person who had come to find Mick was a policewoman. When Mick met her at the top of the stairs her expression told him it wasn't good news.

"Something's happened," he said.

She looked worried, and very, very young. "Is there somewhere we can talk, Mister Leighton?"

"Use my office," Joe said, showing the two of them to his room just down the corridor. Joe left the two of them alone, saying he was going down to the coffee machine in the hall.

"I've got some bad news," the policewoman said, when Joe had closed the door. "I think you should sit down, Mister Leighton."

Mick pulled out Joe's chair from under the desk, which was covered in papers: coursework Joe must have been in the process of grading. Mick sat down, then didn't know where to put his hands. "It's about Andrea, isn't it."

"I'm afraid your wife was in an accident this morning," the policewoman said.

"What kind of accident? What happened?"

"Your wife was hit by a car when she was crossing the road."

A mean, little thought flashed through Mick's mind. Bloody Andrea: she'd always been one for dashing across a road without looking. He'd been warning her for years she was going to regret it one day.

"How is she? Where did they take her?"

"I'm really sorry, sir." The policewoman hesitated. "Your wife died on the way to hospital. I understand that the paramedics did all they could, but . . ."

Mick was hearing it, and not hearing it. It couldn't be right. People still got knocked down by cars. But they didn't *die* from it, not anymore. Cars couldn't go fast enough in towns to kill anyone. Being knocked down and killed by a car was something that happened to people in soap operas, not real life. Feeling numb, not really present in the room, Mick said, "Where is she now?" As if by visiting her, he might prove that they'd got it wrong, that she wasn't dead at all.

"They took her to the Heath, sir. That's where she is now. I can drive you there."

"Andrea isn't dead," Mick said. "She can't be. Not now."

"I'm really sorry," the policewoman said.

SATURDAY

For the last three weeks, ever since they had separated, Mick had been sleeping in a spare room at his brother's house in Newport. The company had been good, but now Bill was away for the weekend on some ridiculous team-building exercise in Snowdonia. For tedious reasons, Mick's brother had had to take the house keys with him, leaving Mick with nowhere to sleep on Friday night. When Joe had asked him where he was going to stay, Mick said he'd go back to his own house, the one he'd left at the beginning of the month.

Joe was having none of it, and insisted that Mick sleep at his house instead. Mick spent the night going through the usual cycle of emotions that came with any sudden bad news. He'd had nothing to compare with losing his wife, but the texture of the shock was familiar enough, albeit magnified from anything in his previous experience. He resented the fact that the world seemed to be continuing, crassly oblivious to Andrea's death. The news wasn't dominated by his tragedy; it was all about some Polish miners trapped underground. When he finally managed to get to sleep,

Mick was tormented by dreams that his wife was still alive, that it had all been a mistake.

But he knew it was all true. He'd been to the hospital; he'd seen her body. He even knew why she'd been hit by the car. Andrea had been crossing the road to her favorite hair salon; she'd had an appointment to get her hair done. Knowing Andrea, she had probably been so focused on the salon that she was oblivious to all that was going on around her. It hadn't even been the car that had killed her in the end. When the slow-moving vehicle knocked her down, Andrea had struck her head against the side of the curb.

By midmorning on Saturday, Mick's brother had returned from Snowdonia. Bill came around to Joe's house and hugged Mick silently, saying nothing for many minutes. Then Bill went into the next room and spoke quietly to Joe and Rachel. Their low voices made Mick feel like a child in a house of adults.

"I think you and I need to get out of Cardiff," Bill told Mick, when he returned to the living room. "No ifs, no buts."

Mick started to protest. "There's too much that needs to be done. I still need to get back to the funeral home."

"It can wait until this afternoon. No one's going to hate you for not returning a few calls. C'mon; let's drive up to the Gower and get some fresh air. I've already reserved a car."

"Go with him," Rachel said. "It'll do you good."

Mick acquiesced, his guilt and relief in conflict at being able to put aside thoughts of the funeral plans. He was glad Bill had come down, but he couldn't quite judge how his brother—or his friends, for that matter—viewed his bereavement. He'd lost his wife. They all knew that. But they also knew that Mick and Andrea had been separated. They'd been having problems for most of the year. It would only be human for his friends to assume that Mick wasn't quite as affected by Andrea's death as he would have been had they still been living together.

"Listen," he told Bill, when they were safely under way. "There's something I've got to tell you."

"I'm listening."

"Andrea and I had problems. But it wasn't the end of our marriage. We were going to get through this. I was going to call her this weekend, see if we couldn't meet."

Bill looked at him sadly. Mick couldn't tell if that meant that Bill just didn't believe him, or that his brother pitied him for the opportunity he'd allowed to slip between his fingers.

When they got back to Cardiff in the early evening, after a warm and blustery day out on the Gower, Joe practically pounced on Mick as soon as they came through the door.

"I need to talk to you," Joe said. "Now."

"I need to call some of Andrea's friends," Mick said. "Can it wait until later?"

"No. It can't. It's about you and Andrea."

They went into the kitchen. Joe poured him a glass of whisky. Rachel and Bill watched from the end of the table, saying nothing.

"I've been to the lab," Joe said. "I know it's Saturday, but I wanted to make sure that lock was still holding. Well, it is. We could start the experiment tomorrow if we wanted to. But something's come up, and you need to know about it."

Mick sipped from his glass. "Go on."

"I've been in contact with my counterpart in the other lab."

"The other Joe."

"The other Joe, yes. We were finessing the equipment, making sure everything was optimal. And we talked, of course. Needless to say I mentioned what had happened."

"And?"

"The other me was surprised. Shocked, even. He said Andrea hadn't died in his reality." Joe held up a hand, signaling that Mick should let him finish before speaking. "You know how it works. The two histories are identical before the lock takes effect: so identical that there isn't even any point in thinking of them as being distinct realities. The divergence only happens once the lock is in effect. The lock was active by the time you came down to tell me about the squash match. The other me also had a visit from you. The difference was that no policewoman ever came to his lab. You eventually drifted back to your office to carry on grading tutorials."

"But Andrea was already dead by then."

"Not in that reality. The other me phoned you. You were staying at the Holiday Inn. You knew nothing of Andrea having had any accident. So my other wife . . ." Joe allowed himself a quick smile. "The other version of Rachel called Andrea. And they spoke. Turned out Andrea had been hit by a car, but she'd barely been bruised. They hadn't even called an ambulance."

Mick absorbed what his friend had to say, then said, "I can't deal with this, Joe. I don't need to know it. It isn't going to help."

"I think it is. We were set up to run the nervelink experiment as soon as we had a solid lock, one that we could trust to hold for the full million seconds. This is it. The only difference is it doesn't have to be me who goes through."

"I don't understand."

"I can put you through, Mick. We can get you nervelinked tomorrow morning. Allowing for a day of bedding in and practice once you arrive in the other reality . . . well, you could be walking in Andrea's world by Monday afternoon, Tuesday morning at the latest."

"But you're the one who is supposed to be going through," Mick said. "You've already had the nervelink put in."

"We've got a spare," Joe said.

Mick's mind raced through the implications. "Then I'd be controlling the body of the other you, right?"

"No. That won't work, unfortunately. We've had to make some changes to these nervelinks to get them to work properly through the correlator, with the limited signal throughput. We had to ditch some of the channels that handle proprioceptive mapping. They'll only work properly if the body on the other end of the link is virtually identical to the one on this side."

"Then it won't work. You're nothing like me."

"You're forgetting *your* counterpart on the other side," Joe said. He glanced past Mick at Bill and Rachel, raising his eyebrows as he did so. "The way it would work is, you come into the lab and we install the link in you, just the same way it happened for me yesterday morning. At the same time your counterpart in Andrea's world comes into *his* version of the lab and gets the other version of the nervelink put into him."

Mick shivered. He'd become used to thinking about the other version of Joe; he could even begin to accept that there was a version of Andrea walking around somewhere who was still alive. But as soon as Joe brought the other Mick into the argument, he felt his head begin to unravel.

"Wouldn't he—the other me—need to agree to this?"

"He already has," Joe said solemnly. "I've been in touch with him. The other Joe called him into the lab. We had a chat over the videolink. He didn't go for it at first—you know how you both feel about nervelinking. And he hasn't lost *his* version of Andrea. But I explained how big a deal this was. This is your only chance to see Andrea again. Once this window closes—we're talking about no more than eleven or twelve days from the start of the lock, by the way—we'll never make contact with another reality where she's alive."

Mick blinked and placed his hands on the table. He felt dizzy with the implications, as if the kitchen was swaying. "You're certain of that? You'll never open another window into Andrea's world?"

"Statistically, we were incredibly lucky to get this one chance. By the time the window closes, Andrea's reality will have diverged so far from ours that there's essentially no chance of ever getting another lock."

"Okay," Mick said, ready to take Joe's word for it. "But even if I agree to this—even if the other me agrees to it—what about Andrea? We weren't seeing each other."

"But you wanted to see her again," Bill said quietly.

Mick rubbed his eyes with the palms of his hands, and exhaled loudly. "Maybe."

"I've spoken to Andrea," Rachel said. "I mean, Joe spoke to himself, and the other version of him spoke to the other Rachel. She's been in touch with Andrea."

Mick hardly dared speak. "And?"

"She says it's okay. She understands how horrible this must be for you. She says, if you want to come through, she'll meet you. You can spend some time together. Give you a chance to come to some kind of . . ."

"Closure," Mick whispered.

"It'll help you," Joe said. "It's got to help you."

SUNDAY

The medical center was normally closed on weekends, but Joe had pulled strings to get some of the staff to come in on Sunday morning. Mick had to sit around a long time while they ran physiological tests and prepared the surgical equipment. It was much easier and quicker for tourists, for they didn't have to use the modified nervelink units Joe's team had developed.

By the early afternoon they were satisfied that Mick was ready for the implantation. They made him lie down on a couch with his head encased in a padded plastic assembly with a hole under the back of the neck. He was given a mild, local anesthetic. Rubberized clamps whirred in to hold his head in position with micromillimeter accuracy. Then he felt a vague impression of pressure being applied to the skin on the back of his neck, and then an odd and not entirely pleasant sensation of sudden pins and needles in every part of his body. But the unpleasantness was over almost as soon as he'd registered it. The support clamps whirred away from his head. The couch tilted up, and he was able to get off and stand on his feet.

Mick touched the back of his neck, came away with a tiny smear of blood on his thumb.

"That's it?"

"I told you there was nothing to it," Joe said, putting down a motorcycling magazine. "I don't know what you were so worried about."

"It's not the nervelink operation itself I don't approve of. I don't have a problem with the technology. It's the whole system, the way it encourages the exploitation of the poor."

Joe tut-tutted. "Bloody *Guardian* readers. It was you lot who got the bloody moratorium against air travel enacted in the first place. Next you'll be telling us we can't even *walk* anywhere."

The nurse swabbed Mick's wound and applied a bandage. He was shunted into an adjoining room and asked to wait again. More tests followed. As the system interrogated the newly embedded nervelink, he experienced mild electrical tingles and strange, fleeting feelings of dislocation. Nothing he reported gave the staff any cause for alarm.

After Mick's discharge from the medical center, Joe took him straight down to the laboratory. An electromagnetically shielded annex contained the couch Joe intended to use for the experiment. It was a modified version of the kind tourists used for long-term nervelinking, with facilities for administering nutrition and collecting bodily waste. No one liked to dwell too much on those details, but there was no way around it if you wanted to stay nervelinked for more than a few hours. Gamers had been putting up with similar indignities for decades.

Once Mick was plumbed in, Joe settled a pair of specially designed immersion glasses over his eyes, after first applying a salve to Mick's skin to protect against pressure sores. The glasses fit very tightly, blocking out Mick's view of the lab. All he could see was a gray-green void, with a few meaningless red digits to the right side of his visual field.

"Comfortable?" Joe asked.

"I can't see anything yet."

"You will."

Joe went back into the main part of the basement to check on the correlation. It seemed that he was gone a long time. When he heard Joe return, Mick half-expected bad news—that the link had collapsed, or some necessary piece of technology had broken down. Privately, he would not have been too sorry were that the case. In his shocked state of mind in the hours after Andrea's death, he would have given anything to be able to see her again. But now that the possibility had arisen, he found himself prone to doubts. Given time, he knew he'd get over Andrea's death. That wasn't being cold, it was just being realistic. He knew more than a few people who'd lost their partners, and while they might have gone through some dark times afterward, almost all of them now seemed settled and relatively content. It didn't mean they'd stopped feeling anything for the loved one who had died, but it did mean they'd found some way to move on. There was no reason to assume he wouldn't make the same emotional recovery.

The question was, would visiting Andrea hasten or hamper that process? Perhaps they should just have talked over the videolink, or even the phone. But then he'd never been very good on either.

He knew it had to be face to face, all or nothing.

"Is there a problem?" he asked Joe, innocently enough.

"Nope, everything's fine. I was just waiting to hear that the other version of you is ready."

"He is?"

"Good to go. Someone from the medical center just put him under. We can make the switch any time you're ready."

"Where is he?"

"Here," Joe said. "I mean, in the counterpart to this room. He's lying on the same couch. It's easier that way; there's less of a jolt when you switch over."

"He's unconscious already?"

"Full coma. Just like any nervelinked mule."

Except, Mick thought, unlike the mules, his counterpart hadn't signed up to go into a chemically induced coma while his body was taken over by a distant tourist. That was what Mick disapproved of more than anything. The mules did it for money, and the mules were always the poorest people in any given tourist hotspot, whether it was some affluent European city or some nauseatingly "authentic" Third World shithole. No one ever aspired to become a mule. It was what you did when all other options had dried up. In some cases it hadn't just supplanted prostitution, it had become an entirely new form of prostitution in its own right.

But enough of that. They were all consenting adults here. No one—least of all the other version of himself—was being exploited. The other Mick was just being kind. No, kinder, Mick supposed, than *he* would have been had the tables been reversed, but he couldn't help feeling a perverse sense of gratitude. And as for Andrea . . . well, she'd always been kind. No one ever had a bad word to say for Andrea on that score. Kind and considerate, to a fault.

So what was he waiting for?

"You can make the switch," Mick said.

There was less to it than he'd been expecting. It was no worse than the involuntary muscular jolt he sometimes experienced in bed, just before dozing off to sleep.

But suddenly he was in a different body.

"Hi," Joe said. "How're you feeling, matey?"

Except it was the other Joe speaking to him now: the Joe who belonged to the world where Andrea hadn't died. The original Joe was on the other side of the reality gap.

"I feel . . ." But when Mick tried speaking, it came out hopelessly slurred.

"Give it time," Joe said. "Everyone has trouble speaking to start with. That'll come quickly."

"Can't shee. Can't see."

"That's because we haven't switched on your glasses. Hold on a tick."

The gray-green void vanished, to be replaced by a view of the interior of the lab. The quality of the image was excellent. The room looked superficially the same, but as Mick looked around—sending the muscle signals through the nervelink to move the body of the other Mick—he noticed the small details that told him this wasn't his world. Joe was wearing a different checked shirt, smudged white trainers instead of Converse sneakers. In this version of the lab, Joe had forgotten to turn the calendar over to the new month.

Mick tried speaking again. The words came easier this time.

"I'm really here, aren't I."

"How does it feel to be making history?"

"It feels . . . bloody weird, actually. And no, I'm not making history. When you write up your experiment, it won't be me who went through first. It'll be you, the way it was always meant to be. This is just a dry run. You can mention me in a footnote, if that."

Joe looked unconvinced. "Have it your way, but—"

"I will." Mick moved to get off the couch. This version of his body wasn't plumbed in like the other one. But when he tried to move, nothing happened. For a moment, he felt a crushing sense of paralysis. He must have let out a frightened sound.

"Easy," Joe said, putting a hand on his shoulder. "One step at a time. The link still has to bed in. It's going to be hours before you'll have complete fluidity of movement, so don't run before you can walk. And I'm afraid we're going to have to keep you in the lab for rather longer than you might like. As routine as nervelinking is, this *isn't* simple nervelinking. The shortcuts we've had to use to squeeze the data through the correlator link mean we're exposing ourselves to more medical risks than you'd get with the standard tourist kit. Nothing that you need worry about, but I want to make sure we keep a close eye on all the parameters. I'll be running tests in the morning and evening. Sorry to be a drag about it, but we do need numbers for our paper, as well. All I can promise is that you'll still have a lot of time available to meet Andrea. If that's what you still want to do, of course."

"It is," Mick said. "Now that I'm here . . . no going back, right?"

Joe glanced at his watch. "Let's start running some coordination exercises. That'll keep us busy for an hour or two. Then we'll need to make sure you have full bladder control. Could get messy otherwise. After that—we'll see if you can feed yourself."

"I want to see Andrea."

"Not today," Joe said firmly. "Not until we've got you house-trained."

"Tomorrow. Definitely tomorrow."

MONDAY

He paused in the shade of the old, green boating shed at the edge of the lake. It was a hot day, approaching noon, and the park was already busier than it had been at any time since the last gasp of the previous summer. Office workers were sitting around the lake making the most of their lunch break: the men with their ties loosened and sleeves and trousers rolled up, the women with their shoes off and blouses loosened. Children splashed in the ornamental fountains, while their older siblings bounced meters into the air on servo-assisted pogo sticks, the season's latest, lethal-looking craze. Students lolled around on the gently sloping grass, sunbathing or catching up on neglected coursework in the last week before exams. Mick recognized some of them from his own department. Most wore cheap, immersion glasses, with their arms covered almost to the shoulder in tight-fitting, pink, haptic feedback gloves. The more animated students lay on their backs, pointing and clutching at invisible objects suspended above them. It looked like they were trying to snatch down the last few wisps of cloud from the scratchless blue sky above Cardiff.

Mick had already seen Andrea standing a little further around the curve of the lake. It was where they had agreed to meet, and true to form Andrea was exactly on time. She stared pensively out across the water, seemingly oblivious to the commotion going on around her. She wore a white blouse, a knee-length burgundy skirt, sensible office shoes. Her hair was shorter than he remembered, styled differently and barely reaching her collar. For a moment—until she'd turned slightly—he hadn't recognized her at all. Andrea held a Starbucks coffee holder in one hand, and every now and then she'd take a sip or glance at her wristwatch. Mick was five minutes late now, and he knew there was a risk Andrea would give up waiting. But in the shade of the boating shed, all his certainties had evaporated.

Andrea turned minutely. She glanced at her watch again. She sipped from the coffee holder, tilting it back in a way that told Mick she'd finished the last drop. He saw her looking around for a waste bin.

Mick stepped from the shade. He walked across the grass, onto concrete, acutely conscious of the slow awkwardness of his gait. His walking had improved since his first efforts, but it still felt as if he were trying to walk upright in a swimming pool filled with treacle. Joe had assured him that all his movements would become more normal as the nervelink bedded in, but that process was obviously taking longer than anticipated.

"Andrea," he said, sounding slurred and drunk and too loud, even to his own ears.

She turned and met his eyes. There was a slight pause before she smiled, and when she did, the smile wasn't quite right, as if she'd been asked to hold it too long for a photograph.

"Hello, Mick. I was beginning to think . . ."

"It's okay." He forced out each word with care, making sure it came out right before moving to the next. "I just had some second thoughts."

"I don't blame you. How does it feel?"

"A bit odd. It'll get easier."

"Yes, that's what they told me." She took another sip from the coffee, even though it must have been empty. They were standing about two meters apart, close enough to talk, close enough to look like two friends or colleagues who'd bumped into each other around the lake.

"It's really good of you . . ." Mick began.

Andrea shook her head urgently. "Please. It's okay. We talked it over. We both agreed it was the right thing to do. If the tables were turned, you wouldn't have hesitated."

"Maybe not."

"I know you, Mick. Maybe better than you know yourself. You'd have done all that you could, and more."

"I just want you to know . . . I'm not taking any of this lightly. Not you having to see me, like this . . . not what *he* has to go through while I'm around."

"He said to tell you there are worse ways to spend a week."

Mick tried to smile. He felt the muscles of his face move, but without a mirror there was no way to judge the outcome. The moment stretched. A football splashed into the lake and began to drift away from the edge. He heard a little boy start crying.

"Your hair looks different," Mick said.

"You don't like it."

"No, I do. It really suits you. Did you have that done after . . . oh, wait. I see. You were on your way to the salon."

He could see the scratch on her face where she'd grazed it on the curb, when the car knocked her down. She hadn't even needed stitches. In a week it would hardly show at all.

"I can't begin to imagine what it's been like for you," Andrea said. "I can't imagine what *this* is like for you."

"It helps."

"You don't sound convinced."

"I want it to help. I think it's going to. It's just that right now it feels like I've made the worst mistake of my life."

Andrea held up the coffee holder. "Do you fancy one? It's my treat."

Andrea was a solicitor. She worked for a small legal firm located in modern offices near the park. There was a Starbucks near her office building. "They don't know me there, do they."

"Not unless you've been moonlighting. Come on. I hate to say it, but you could use some practice walking."

"As long as you won't laugh."

"I wouldn't dream of it. Hold my hand, Mick. It'll make it easier."

Before he could step back, Andrea closed the distance between them and took his hand in hers. It was good of her to do that, Mick thought. He'd been wondering how he would initiate that first touch, and Andrea had spared him the fumbling awkwardness that would almost certainly have ensued. That was Andrea to a tee, always thinking of others and trying to make life a little easier for them, no matter how small the difference. It was why people liked her so much; why her friends were so fiercely loyal.

"It's going to be okay, Mick," Andrea said gently. "Everything that's happened between us . . . it doesn't matter now. I've said bad things to you and you've said bad things to me. But let's forget about all that. Let's just make the most of what time we have."

"I'm scared of losing you."

"You're a good man. You've more friends than you realize."

He was sweating in the heat, so much so that the glasses began to slip down his nose. The view tilted toward his shoes. He raised his free hand in a stiff, salutelike gesture and pushed the glasses back into place. Andrea's hand tightened on his.

"I can't go through with this," Mick said. "I should go back."

"You started it," Andrea said sternly, but without rancor. "Now you finish it. All the way, Mick Leighton."

TUESDAY

Things were much better by the morning of the second day. When he woke in Joe Liversedge's lab there was a fluency in his movements that simply hadn't been there the evening before, when he'd said goodbye to Andrea. He now felt as if he was inhabiting the host body, rather than simply shuffling it around like a puppet. He still needed the glasses to be able to see anything, but the nervelink was conveying sensation much more effectively now, so that when he touched something it came through without any of the fuzziness or lag he'd been experiencing the day before. Most tourists were able to achieve reasonable accuracy of touch differentiation within twenty-four hours. Within two days, their degree of proprioceptive immersion was generally good enough to allow complex motor tasks such as cycling, swimming, or skiing. Repeat-visit tourists, especially those that went back into the same body, got over the transition period even faster. To them it was like moving back into a house after a short absence.

Joe's team gave Mick a thorough checkup in the annex. It was all routine stuff. Amy Flint, Joe's senior graduate student, insisted on adding some more numbers to the tactile test database that she was building for the study. That meant Mick sitting at a table, without the glasses, being asked to hold various objects and decide what shape they were and what they were made of. He scored excellently, only failing to distinguish between wood and plastic balls of similar weight and texture. Flint was cheerfully casual around him, without any of the affectedness or oversensitivity Mick had quickly detected in his friends or colleagues. Clearly she didn't know what had happened; she just thought Joe had opted to go for a different test subject than himself.

Joe was upbeat about Mick's progress. Everything, from the host body to the hardware, was holding up well. The bandwidth was stable at nearly two megabytes per second, more than enough spare capacity to permit Mick the use of a second video feed to peer back into the version of the lab on the other side. The other version of Joe held the cam up so that Mick could see his own body, reclining on the heavy-duty immersion couch. Mick had expected to be disturbed by that, but the whole experience turned out to be oddly banal, like replaying a home movie.

When they were done with the tests, Joe walked Mick over to the university canteen, where he ate a liquid breakfast, slurping down three containers of fruit yoghurt. While he ate—which was tricky, but another of the things that was supposed to get easier with practice—he gazed distractedly at the television in the canteen. The wall-sized screen was running through the morning news, with the sound turned down. At the moment the screen was showing grainy footage of the Polish miners, caught on surveillance camera as they trudged into the low, concrete pithead building on their way to work. The cave-in had happened three days ago. The miners were still trapped underground, in all the worldlines that were in contact with this one, including Mick's own.

"Poor fuckers," Joe said, looking up from a draft paper he was penciling remarks over.

"Maybe they'll get them out."

"Aye. Maybe. Wouldn't fancy my chances down there, though."

The picture changed to a summary of football scores. Again, most of the games had ended in identical results across the contacted worldlines, but two or three—highlighted in sidebars, with analysis text ticking below them—had ended differently, with one team even being dropped from the rankings.

Afterward Mick walked on his own to the tram stop and caught the next service into the city center. Already he could feel that he was attracting less attention than the day before. He still moved a little stiffly, he could tell that just by looking at his reflection in the glass as he boarded the tram, but there was no longer anything comical or robotic about it. He just looked like someone with a touch of arthritis, or someone who'd been overdoing it in the gym and was now paying with a dose of sore muscles.

As the tram whisked its way through traffic, he thought back to the evening before. The meeting with Andrea, and the subsequent day, had gone as well as he could have expected. Things had been strained at first, but by the time they'd been to Starbucks, he had detected an easing in her manner, and that had made him feel more at ease as well. They'd made small talk, skirting around the main thing neither of them wanted to discuss. Andrea had taken most of the day off; she didn't have to be at the law offices until late afternoon, just to check that no problems had arisen in her absence.

They'd talked about what to do with the rest of their day together.

"Maybe we could drive up into the Beacons," Mick had said. "It'll be nice up in the hills with a bit of a breeze. We always used to enjoy those days out."

"Been a while though," Andrea had said. "I'm not sure my legs are up to it anymore."

"You always used to hustle up those hills."

"Emphasis on the 'used to,' unfortunately. Now I get out of breath just walking up St. Mary's Street with a bag full of shopping."

Mick looked at her skeptically, but he couldn't deny that Andrea had a point. Neither of them was the keen, outdoors type they had been when they met fifteen years earlier through the university's hill-walking club. Back then they'd spent long weekends exploring the hills of the Brecon Beacons and the Black Mountains, or driving to Snowdonia or the Lake District. They'd had some hair-raising moments together, when the weather turned against them or when they suddenly realized they were on completely the wrong ridge. But what Mick remembered, more than anything, was not being cold and wet, but the feeling of relief when they arrived at some cozy warm pub at the end of the day, both of them ravenous and thirsty and high on what they'd achieved. Good memories, all of them. Why hadn't they kept it up, instead of letting their jobs rule their weekends?

"Look, maybe we might drive up to the Beacons in a day or two," Andrea said. "But I think it's a bit ambitious for today, don't you?"

"You're probably right," Mick said.

After some debate, they'd agreed to visit the castle and then take a boat ride around the bay to see the huge and impressive sea defenses up close. Both were things they'd always meant to do together but had kept putting off for another weekend. The castle was heaving with tourists, even on this midweek day. Because a lot of them were nervelinked, though, they afforded Mick a welcome measure of inconspicuousness. No one gave him a second glance as he bumbled along with the other shade-wearing bodysnatchers, even though he must have looked considerably more affluent and well-fed than the average mule. Afterward, they went to look at the Roman ruins, where Rachel Liversedge was busy talking to a group of bored primary school children from the valleys.

Mick enjoyed the boat ride more than the trip to the castle. There were still enough nervelinked tourists on the boat for him not to feel completely out of place, and being out in the bay offered some respite from the cloying heat of the city center. Mick had even felt the breeze on the back of his hand, evidence that the nervelink was really bedding in.

It was Andrea who nudged the conversation toward the reason for Mick's presence. She'd just returned from the counter with two paper cups brimming with murky coffee, nearly spilling them as the boat swayed unexpectedly. She sat down on the boat's hard wooden bench.

"I forgot to ask how it went in the lab this morning?" she asked brightly. "Everything working out okay?"

"Very well," Mick said. "Joe says we were getting two megs this morning. That's as good as he was hoping for."

"You'll have to explain that to me. I know it's to do with the amount of data you're able to send through the link, but I don't know how it compares with what we'd be using for a typical tourist setup."

Mick remembered what Joe had told him. "It's not as good. Tourists can use as much bandwidth as they can afford. But Joe's correlators never get above five megabytes per second. That's at the start of the twelve-day window, too. It only gets worse by day five or six."

"Is two enough?"

"It's what Joe's got to work with." Mick reached up and tapped the glasses. "It shouldn't be enough for full color vision at normal resolution, according to Joe. But there's an awful lot of clever software in the lab to take care of that. It's constantly guessing, filling in gaps."

"How does it look?"

"Like I'm looking at the world through a pair of sunglasses." He pulled them off his nose and tilted them toward Andrea. "Except it's the glasses that are actually doing the seeing, not my—*his*—eyes. Most of the time, it's good enough that I don't notice anything weird. If I wiggle my head around fast—or if something streaks past too quickly—then the glasses have trouble keeping up with the changing view." He jammed the glasses back on, just in time for a seagull to flash past only a few meters from the boat. He had a momentary sense of the seagull breaking up into blocky areas of confused pixels, as if it had been painted by a cubist, before the glasses smoothed things over and normality ensued.

"What about all the rest of it? Hearing, touch . . ."

"They don't take up anything like as much bandwidth as vision. The way Joe puts it, postural information only needs a few basic parameters: the angles of my limb joints, that kind of thing. Hearing's pretty straightforward. And touch is the easiest of all, as it happens."

"Really?"

"So Joe says. Hold my hand."

Andrea hesitated an instant then took Mick's hand.

"Now squeeze it," Mick said.

She tightened her hold. "Are you getting that?"

"Perfectly. It's much easier than sending sound. If you were to say something to me, the acoustic signal would have to be sampled, digitized, compressed, and pushed across the link: hundreds of bytes per second. But all touch needs is a single parameter. The system will still be able to keep sending touch even when everything else gets too difficult."

"Then it's the last thing to go."

"It's the most fundamental sense we have. That's the way it ought to be."

After a few moments, Andrea said, "How long?"

"Four days," Mick said slowly. "Maybe five, if we're lucky. Joe says we'll have a better handle on the decay curve by tomorrow."

"I'm worried, Mick. I don't know how I'm going to deal with losing you."

He closed his other hand on hers and squeezed in return. "You'll get me back."

"I know. It's just . . . it won't be you. It'll be the other you."

"They're both me."

"That's not how it feels right now. It feels like I'm having an affair while my husband's away."

"It shouldn't. I am your husband. We're both your husband."

They said nothing after that, sitting in silence as the boat bobbed its way back to shore. It was not that they had said anything upsetting, just that words were no longer adequate. Andrea kept holding his hand. Mick wanted this morning to continue forever: the boat, the breeze, the perfect sky over the bay. Even then he chided himself for dwelling on the passage of time, rather than making the most of the experience as it happened to him. That had always been his problem, ever since he was a kid. School holidays had always been steeped in a melancholic sense of how few days were left.

But this wasn't a holiday.

After a while, he noticed that some people had gathered at the bow of the boat, pressing against the railings. They were pointing up, into the sky. Some of them had pulled out phones.

"There's something going on," Mick said.

"I can see it," Andrea answered. She touched the side of his face, steering his view until he was craning up as far as his neck would allow. "It's an airplane."

Mick waited until the glasses picked out the tiny, moving speck of the plane etching a pale contrail in its wake. He felt a twinge of resentment toward anyone still having the freedom to fly, when the rest of humanity was denied that right. It had been a nice dream when it lasted, flying. He had no idea what political or military purpose the plane was serving, but it would be an easy matter to find out, were he that interested. The news would be in all the papers by the afternoon.

The plane wouldn't just be overflying this version of Cardiff, but his as well. That had been one of the hardest things to take since Andrea's death. The world at large steamrolled on, its course undeflected by that single human tragedy. Andrea had died in the accident in his world, she'd survived unscathed in this one, and that plane's course wouldn't have changed in any measurable way (in either reality).

"I love seeing airplanes," Andrea said. "It reminds me of what things were like before the moratorium. Don't you?"

"Actually," Mick said, "they make me a bit sad."

WEDNESDAY

Mick knew how busy Andrea had been lately, and he tried to persuade her against taking any time off from her work. Andrea had protested, saying her colleagues could handle her workload for a few days. Mick knew better than that—Andrea practically ran the firm single-handedly—but in the end they'd come to a compromise. Andrea would take time off from the office, but she'd pop in first thing in the morning to put out any really serious fires.

Mick agreed to meet her at the offices at ten, after his round of tests. Everything still felt the way it had the day before; if anything he was even more fluent in his body movements. But when Joe had finished, the news was all that Mick had been quietly dreading, while knowing it could be no other way. The quality of the link had continued to degrade. According to Joe they were down to one point eight megs now. They'd seen enough decay curves to be able to extrapolate forward into the beginning of the following week. The link would become noise-swamped around teatime on Sunday, give or take three hours either way.

If only they'd started sooner, Mick thought. But Joe had done all that he could.

Today—despite the foreboding message from the lab—his sense of immersion in the counterpart world had become total. As the sunlit city swept by outside the tram's windows, Mick found it nearly impossible to believe that he was not physically present in this body, rather than lying on the couch in the other version of the lab. Overnight his tactile immersion had improved markedly. When he braced himself against the tram's upright handrail, as it swept around a curve, he felt cold aluminum, the faint greasiness where it had been touched by other hands.

At the offices, Andrea's colleagues greeted him with an unforced casualness that left him dismayed. He'd been expecting awkward expressions of sympathy, sly glances when they thought he wasn't looking. Instead he was plonked down in the waiting area and left to flick through glossy brochures while he waited for Andrea to emerge from her office. No one even offered him a drink.

He leafed through the brochures dispiritedly. Andrea's job had always been a sore point in their relationship. If Mick didn't approve of nervelinking, he had even less time for the legal vultures that made so much money out of personal injury claims related to the technology. But now he found it difficult to summon his usual sense of moral superiority. Unpleasant things *had* happened to decent people because of negligence and corner-cutting. If nervelinking was to be a part of the world, then someone had to make sure the victims got their due. He wondered why this had never been clear to him before.

"Hiya," Andrea said, leaning over him. She gave him a businesslike kiss, not quite meeting his mouth. "Took a bit longer than I thought, sorry."

"Can we go now?" Mick asked, putting down the brochure.

"Yep, I'm done here."

Outside, when they were walking along the pavement in the shade of the tall, commercial buildings, Mick said: "They didn't have a clue, did they? No one in that office knows what's happened to us."

"I thought it was best," Andrea said.

"I don't know how you can keep up that act, that nothing's wrong."

"Mick, nothing *is* wrong. You have to see it from my point of view. I haven't lost my husband. Nothing's changed for me. When you're gone—when all this ends, and I get the other *you* back—my life carries on as normal. I know what's happened to you is a tragedy, and believe me I'm as upset about it as anyone."

"Upset," Mick said quietly.

"Yes, upset. But I'd be lying if I said I was paralyzed with grief. I'm human, Mick. I'm not capable of feeling great emotional turmoil at the thought that some distant counterpart of myself got herself run over, all because she was rushing to have her hair done. Silly cow, that's what it makes me feel. At most it makes me feel a bit odd, a bit shivery. But I don't think it's something I'm going to have trouble getting over."

"I lost my wife," Mick said.

"I know, and I'm sorry. More than you'll ever know. But if you expect *my* life to come crashing to a halt . . ."

He cut her off. "I'm already fading. One point eight this morning."

"You always knew it would happen. It's not like it's any surprise."

"You'll notice a difference in me by the end of the day."

"This isn't the end of the day, so stop dwelling on it. All right? Please, Mick. You're in serious danger of ruining this for yourself."

"I know, and I'm trying not to," he said. "But what I was saying, about how things aren't going to get any better . . . I think today's going to be my last chance, Andrea. My last chance to be with you, to be with you properly."

"You mean us sleeping together," Andrea said, keeping her voice low.

"We haven't talked about it yet. That's okay; I wasn't expecting it to happen without at least some discussion. But there's no reason why . . ."

"Mick, I . . ." Andrea began.

"You're still my wife. I'm still in love with you. I know we've had our problems, but I realize now how stupid all that was. I should have called you sooner. I was being an idiot. And then this happened . . . and it made me realize what a wonderful, lovely person you are, and I should have seen that for myself, but I didn't . . . I needed the accident to shake me up, to make me see how lucky I was just to know you. And now I'm going to lose you again, and I'm not sure how I'm going to cope with that. But at least if we can be together again . . . properly, I mean."

"Mick . . ."

"You've already said you might get back together with the other Mick. Maybe it took all this to get us talking again. Point is, if you're going to get back together with him, there's nothing to stop us getting back together *now*. We were a couple before the accident; we can still be a couple now."

"Mick, it isn't the same. You've lost your wife. I'm not *her*. I'm some weird thing there isn't a word for. And you aren't really my husband. My husband is in a medically induced coma."

"You know none of that really matters."

"To you."

"It shouldn't matter to you either. And your husband—me, incidentally—agreed to this. He knew exactly what was supposed to happen. And so did you."

"I just thought things would be better—more civilized—if we kept a kind of distance."

"You're talking as if we're divorced."

"Mick, we were already separated. We weren't talking. I can't just forget what happened before the accident as if none of that mattered."

"I know it isn't easy for you."

They walked on in an uneasy silence, through the city center streets they'd walked a thousand times before. Mick asked Andrea if she wanted a coffee, but she said she'd had one in her office not long before he arrived. Maybe later. They paused to cross the road near one of Andrea's favorite boutiques and Mick asked if there was something he could buy for her.

Andrea sounded taken aback at the suggestion. "You don't need to buy me anything, Mick. It isn't my birthday or anything."

"It would be nice to give you a gift. Something to remember me by."

"I don't need anything to remember you, Mick. You're always going to be there."

"It doesn't have to be much. Just something you'll use now and then, and will make you think of me. *This* me, not the one who's going to be walking around in this body in a few days."

"Well, if you really insist . . ." He could tell Andrea was trying to sound keen on the idea, but her heart still wasn't quite in it. "There was a handbag I saw last week . . ."

"You should have bought it when you saw it."

"I was saving up for the hairdresser."

So Mick bought her the handbag. He made a mental note of the style and color, intending to buy an identical copy next week. Since he hadn't bought the gift for his wife in his own worldline, it was even possible that he might walk out of the shop with the exact counterpart of the handbag he'd just given Andrea.

They went to the park again, then to look at the art in the National Museum of Wales, then back into town for lunch. There were a few more clouds in the sky compared to the last two days, but their chrome whiteness only served to make the blue appear more deeply enameled and permanent. There were no planes anywhere at all; no contrail scratches. It turned out the aircraft—which had indeed been military—that they had seen yesterday had been on its way to Poland, carrying a team of mine rescue specialists. Mick remembered his resentment at seeing the plane, and felt bad about it now. There had been brave men and women aboard it, and they were probably going to be putting their own lives at risk to help save other brave men and women stuck miles underground.

"Well," Andrea said, when they'd paid the bill. "Moment of truth, I suppose. I've been thinking about what you were saying earlier, and maybe . . ." She trailed off, looking down at the remains of her salad, before continuing, "We can go home, if you'd like. If that's what you really want."

"Yes," Mick said. "It's what I want."

They took the tram back to their house. Andrea used her key to let them inside. It was still only the early afternoon, and the house was pleasantly cool, with the curtains and blinds still drawn. Mick knelt down and picked up the letters that were on the mat. Bills, mostly. He set them on the hall-side table, feeling a transitory sense of liberation. More than likely he'd be confronted with the same bills when he got home, but for now *these* were someone else's problem.

He slipped off his shoes and walked into the living room. For a moment he was thrown, feeling as if he really was in a different house. The wallscreen was on another wall; the dining table had been shifted sideways into the other half of the room; the sofa and easy chairs had all been altered and moved.

"What's happened?"

"Oh, I forgot to tell you," Andrea said. "I felt like a change. You came around and helped me move them."

"That's new furniture."

"No, just different seat covers. They're not new, it's just that we haven't had them out for a while. You remember them now, don't you?"

"I suppose so."

"C'mon, Mick. It wasn't that long ago. We got them off Aunty Janice, remember?" She looked at him despairingly. "I'll move things back. It *was* a bit inconsiderate of me, I suppose. I never thought how strange it would be for you to see the place like this."

"No, it's okay. Honestly, it's fine." Mick looked around, trying to fix the arrangement of furniture and décor in his mind's eye. As if he were going to duplicate everything when he got back into his own body, into his own version of this house.

Maybe he would, too.

"I've got something for you," Andrea said suddenly, reaching onto the top of the bookcase. "Found it this morning. Took ages searching for it."

"What?" Mick asked.

She held the thing out to him. Mick saw a rectangle of laminated pink card, stained and dog-eared. It was only when he tried to hold it, and the thing fell open and disgorged its folded paper innards, that he realized it was a map.

"Bloody hell. I wouldn't have had a clue where to look." Mick folded the map back into itself and studied the cover. It was one of their old hill-walking maps, covering that part of the Brecon Beacons where they'd done a lot of their walks.

"I was just thinking . . . seeing as you were so keen . . . maybe it wouldn't kill us to get out of town. Nothing too adventurous, mind."

"Tomorrow?"

She looked at him concernedly. "That's what I was thinking. You'll still be okay, won't you?"

"No probs."

"I'll get us a picnic, then. Tesco's does a nice luncheon basket. I think we've still got two thermos flasks around here somewhere, too."

"Never mind the thermos flasks, what about the walking boots?"

"In the garage," Andrea said. "Along with the rucksacks. I'll dig them out this evening."

"I'm looking forward to it," Mick said. "Really. It's kind of you to agree."

"Just as long you don't expect me to get up Pen y Fan without getting out of breath."

"I bet you'll surprise yourself."

A little later they went upstairs, to their bedroom. The blinds were open enough to throw pale stripes across the walls and bedsheets. Andrea undressed, and then helped Mick out his own clothes. As good as his control over the body had now become, fine motor tasks—like undoing buttons and zips—would require a lot more practice than he was going to have time for.

"You'll have to help me get all this on afterward," he said.

"There you go, worrying about the future again."

They lay together on the bed. Mick had already felt himself growing hard long before there was any corresponding change in the body he was now inhabiting. He had an erection in the laboratory, halfway across the city in another worldline. He could even feel the sharp plastic of the urinary catheter. Would the other Mick, sunk deep into coma, retain some vague impression of what was happening now? There were occasional stories of people coming out of their coma with a memory of what their bodies had been up to while they were under, but the agencies had said these were urban myths.

They made slow, cautious love. Mick had become more aware of his own awkwardness, and the self-consciousness only served to exaggerate the stiffness of his movements. Andrea did what she could to help, to bridge the gap between them, but she could not work miracles. She was patient and forgiving, even when he came close to hurting her. When he climaxed, Mick felt it happen to the body in the laboratory first. Then the body he was inhabiting responded, too, seconds later. Something of it reached him through the nervelink—not pleasure, exactly, but confirmation that pleasure had occurred.

Afterward, they lay still on the bed, limbs entwined. A breeze made the blinds move back and forth against the window. The slow movement of light and shade, the soft tick of vinyl on glass, was as lulling as a becalmed boat. Mick found himself falling into a contented sleep. He dreamed of standing on a summit in the Brecon Beacons, looking down on the sunlit valleys of South Wales, with Andrea next to him, the two of them poised like a tableau in a travel brochure.

When he woke, hours later, he heard her moving around downstairs. He reached for the glasses—he'd removed them earlier—and made to leave the bed. He felt it then. Somewhere in those languid hours he'd lost a degree of control over the body. He stood and moved to the door. He could still walk, but the easy facility he'd gained on Tuesday was now absent. When he moved to the landing and looked down the stairs, the glasses struggled to cope with the sudden change of scene. The view fractured, reassembled. He moved to steady himself on the banister, and his hand blurred into a long smear of flesh.

He began to descend the stairs, like a man coming down a mountain.

THURSDAY

In the morning he was worse. He stayed overnight at the house, then caught the tram to the laboratory. Already he could feel a measurable lag between the sending of his intentions to move, and the corresponding action in the body. Walking was still just about manageable, but all other tasks had become more difficult. He'd made a mess trying to eat breakfast in Andrea's kitchen. It was no surprise when Joe told him that the link was now down to one point two megs, and falling.

"By the end of the day?" Mick asked, even though he could see the printout for himself.

"Point nine, maybe point eight."

He'd dared to think it might still be possible to do what they had planned. But the day soon became a catalogue of declining functions. At noon he met Andrea at her office and they went to a car rental office, where they'd booked a vehicle for the day. Andrea drove them out of Cardiff, up the valleys, along the A470 from Merthyr to Brecon. They had planned to walk all the way to the summit of Pen y Fan, an ascent they'd done together dozens of times during their hill-walking days. Andrea had already collected the picnic basket from Tesco's and packed and prepared the two rucksacks. She'd helped Mick get into his walking boots.

They left the car at the Storey Arms then followed the well-trodden trail that wound its way toward the mountain. Mick felt a little ashamed at first. Back in their hill-walking days, they'd tended to look down with disdain on the hordes of people making the trudge up Pen y Fan, especially those that took the route up from the pub. The view from the top was worth the climb, but they'd usually made a point of completing at least one or two other ascents on the same day, and they'd always eschewed the easy paths. Now Mick was paying for that earlier superiority. What started out as pleasantly challenging soon became impossibly taxing. Although he didn't think Andrea had begun to notice, he was finding it much harder than he'd expected to walk on the rough, craggy surface of the path. The effort was draining him, preventing him from enjoying any of the scenery, or the sheer bliss of being with Andrea. When he lost his footing the first time, Andrea didn't make much of it—she'd nearly tripped once already, on the dried and cracked path. But soon he was finding it hard to walk more than a hundred meters without losing his balance. He knew, with a heavy heart, that it would be difficult enough just to get back to the car. The mountain was still two miles away, and he wouldn't have a hope as soon as they hit a real slope.

"Are you okay, Mick?"

"I'm fine. Don't worry about me. It's these bloody shoes. I can't believe they ever fit me."

He soldiered on for as long as he could, refusing to give in, but the going got harder and his pace slower. When he tripped again and this time grazed his shin through his trousers, he knew he'd pushed himself as far as he could go. Time was getting on. The mountain might as well have been in the Himalayas, for all his chances of climbing it.

"I'm sorry. I'm useless. Go on without me. It's too nice a day not to finish it."

"Hey." Andrea took his hand. "Don't be like that. It was always going to be hard. Look how far we've come anyway."

Mick turned and looked dispiritedly down the valley. "About three kilometers. I can still see the pub."

"Well, it felt longer. And besides, this is actually a very nice spot to have the picnic." Andrea made a show of rubbing her thigh. "I'm about ready to stop anyway. Pulled a muscle going over that sty."

"You're just saying that."

"Shut up, Mick. I'm happy, okay? If you want to turn this into some miserable, pain-filled trek, go ahead. Me, I'm staying here."

She spread the blanket next to a dry brook and unpacked the food. The contents of the picnic basket looked very good indeed. The taste came through the nervelink as a kind of thin, diluted impression, more like the *memory* of taste rather than the thing itself. But he managed to eat without making too much of a mess, and some of it actually bordered on the enjoyable. They ate, listening to the birds, saying little. Now and then other walkers trudged past, barely giving Mick and Andrea a glance, as they continued toward the hills.

"I guess I shouldn't have kidded myself I was ever going to get up that mountain," Mick said.

"It *was* a bit ambitious," Andrea agreed. "It would have been hard enough without the nervelink, given how flabby the two of us have become."

"I think I'd have made a better job of it yesterday. Even this morning . . . I honestly felt I could do this when we got into the car."

Andrea touched his thigh. "How does it feel?"

"Like I'm moving away. Yesterday I felt like I was in this body, fully a part of it. Like a face filling a mask. Today it's different. I can still see through the mask, but it's getting further away."

Andrea seemed distant for several moments. He wondered if what he'd said had upset her. But when she spoke again there was something in her voice—a kind of steely resolution—that he hadn't been expecting, but which was entirely Andrea.

"Listen to me, Mick."

"I'm listening."

"I'm going to tell you something. It's the first of May today; just past two in the afternoon. We left Cardiff at eleven. This time next year, this exact day, I'm coming back here. I'm going to pack a picnic basket and go all the way up to the top of Pen y Fan. I'll set off from Cardiff at the same time. And I'm going to do it the year after, as well. Every first of May. No matter what day of the week it is. No matter how bloody horrible the weather is. I'm going up this mountain and nothing on Earth is going to stop me."

It took him a few seconds to realize what she was getting at. "With the other Mick?"

"No. I'm not saying we won't ever climb that hill together. But when I go up it on the first of May, I'll be on my own." She looked levelly at Mick. "And you'll do it alone as well. You'll find someone new, I'm sure of it. But whoever she is will have to give you that one day to yourself. So that you and I can have it to ourselves."

"We won't be able to communicate. We won't even know the other one's stuck to the plan."

"Yes," Andrea said firmly. "We will. Because it's going to be a promise, all right? The most important one either of us has ever made in our whole lives. That way we'll know. Each of us will be in our own universe, or worldline, or whatever you call it. But we'll both be standing on the same Welsh mountain. We'll both be looking at the same view. And I'll be thinking of you, and you'll be thinking of me."

Mick ran a stiff hand through Andrea's hair. He couldn't get his fingers to work very well now.

"You really mean that, don't you?"

"Of course I mean it. But I'm not promising anything unless you agree to your half of it. Would you promise, Mick?"

"Yes," he said. "I will."

"I wish I could think of something better. I could say we'd always meet in the park. But there'll be people around; it won't feel private. I want the silence, the isolation, so I can feel your presence. And one day they might tear down the park and put a shopping center there instead. But the mountain will always be there. At least as long as we're around."

"And when we get old? Shouldn't we agree to stop climbing the mountain, when we get to a certain age?"

"There you go again," Andrea said. "Decide for yourself. I'm going to keep climbing this thing until they put me in a box. I expect nothing less from you, Mick Leighton."

He made the best smile he was capable of. "Then . . . I'll just have to do my best, won't I?"

FRIDAY

In the morning Mick was paraplegic. The nervelink still worked perfectly, but the rate of data transmission from one worldline to the other had become too low to permit anything as complex and feedback-dependent as walking. His control over the body's fingers had become so clumsy that his hands might as well have been wearing boxing gloves. He could hold something if it was presented to him, but it was becoming increasingly difficult to manipulate simple objects, even those that had presented no difficulty twenty-four hours earlier. When he tried to grasp the breakfast yoghurt, he succeeded only in tipping it over the table. His hand had seemed to lurch toward the yoghurt, crossing the distance too quickly. According to Joe he had lost depth perception overnight. The glasses, sensing the dwindling data rate, were no longer sending stereoscopic images back to the lab.

He could still move around. The team had anticipated this stage and made sure an electric wheelchair was ready for him. Its chunky controls were designed to be used by someone with only limited upper body coordination. The chair was equipped with a panic button, so that Mick could summon help if he felt his control slipping faster than the predicted rate. Were he to fall into sudden and total paralysis, the chair would call out to passersby to provide assistance. In the event of an extreme medical emergency, it would steer itself to the nearest designated care point.

Andrea came out to the laboratory to meet him. Mick wanted one last trip into the city with her, but although she'd been enthusiastic when they'd talked about the plan on the phone, Andrea was now reluctant.

"Are you sure about this? We had such a nice time on Thursday. It would be a shame to spoil the memory of that now."

"I'm okay," Mick said.

"I'm just saying, we could always just stroll around the gardens here."

"Please," Mick said. "This is what . . . I want."

His voice was slow, his phrasing imprecise. He sounded drunk and depressed. If Andrea noticed—and he was sure she must have—she made no observation.

They went into town. It was difficult getting the wheelchair on the tram, even with Andrea's assistance. No one seemed to know how to lower the boarding ramp. One of the benefits of nervelink technology was that you didn't see that many people in wheelchairs anymore. The technology that enabled one person to control another person's body also enabled spinal injuries to be bypassed. Mick was aware that he was attracting more attention than on any previous day. For most people wheelchairs were a medical horror from the past, like iron lungs or leg braces.

On the tram's video monitor he watched a news item about the Polish miners. It wasn't good. The rescue team had had a number of options available to them, involving at least three possible routes to the trapped men. After carefully evaluating all the data—aware of how little time remained for the victims—they'd chosen what had promised to be the quickest and safest approach.

It had turned out to be a mistake, one that would prove fatal for the miners. The rescuers had hit a flooded section and had been forced to retreat, with damage to their equipment, and one of their team injured. Yet the miners *had* been saved in one of the other contacted worldlines. In that reality, one of the members of the rescue team had slipped on ice and fractured his hip while boarding the plane. The loss of that one man—who'd been a vocal proponent for taking the quickest route— had resulted in the team following the second course. It had turned out to be the right decision. They'd met their share of obstacles and difficulties, but in the end they'd broken through to the trapped miners.

By the time this happened, contact with that worldline had almost been lost. Even the best compression methods couldn't cope with moving images. The pictures that came back, of the men being liberated from the ground, were grainy and monochrome, like a blowup of newsprint from a hundred years earlier. They'd been squeezed across the gap in the last minutes before noise drowned the signal.

But the information was useless. Even armed with the knowledge that there was a safe route through to the miners, the team in this worldline didn't have time to act.

The news didn't help Mick's mood. Going into the city turned out to be exactly the bad move Andrea had predicted. By midday his motor control had deteriorated even further, to the point where he was having difficulty steering the wheelchair. His speech became increasingly slurred, so that Andrea had to keep asking him to repeat himself. In defense, he shut down into monosyllables. Even his hearing was beginning to fail, as the auditory data was compressed to an even more savage degree. He couldn't distinguish birds from traffic, or traffic from the swish of the trees in the park. When Andrea spoke to him she sounded like her words had been fed through a synthesizer, then chopped up and spliced back together in some tinny approximation to her normal voice.

At three, his glasses could no longer support full color vision. The software switched to a limited color palette. The city looked like a hand-tinted photograph, washed out and faded. Andrea's face oscillated between white and sickly gray.

By four, Mick was fully quadriplegic. By five, the glasses had reverted back to black and white. The frame rate was down to ten images per second, and falling.

By early evening, Andrea was no longer able to understand what Mick was saying. Mick realized that he could no longer reach the panic button. He became agitated, thrashing his head around. He'd had enough. He wanted to be pulled out of the nervelink, slammed back into his own waiting body. He no longer felt as if he was in Mick's body, but he didn't feel as if he was in his own one either. He was strung out somewhere between them, helpless and almost blind. When the panic hit, it was like a foaming, irresistible tide.

Alarmed, Andrea wheeled him back to the laboratory. By the time she was ready to say goodbye to him, the glasses had reduced his vision to five images per second, each of which was composed of only six thousand pixels. He was calmer then, resigned to the inevitability of what tomorrow would bring: he would not even recognize Andrea in the morning.

SATURDAY

Mick's last day with Andrea began in a world of sound and vision—senses that were already impoverished to a large degree—and ended in a realm of silence and darkness.

He was now completely paralyzed, unable even to move his head. The brain that belonged to the other, comatose Mick now had more control over this body than its wakeful counterpart. The nervelink was still sending signals back to the lab, but the requirements of sight and sound now consumed almost all available bandwidth. In the morning, vision was down to one thousand pixels, updated three frames per second. His sight had already turned monochrome, but even yesterday there had been welcome gradations of gray, enough to anchor him into the visual landscape.

Now the pixels were only capable of registering on or off; it cost too much bandwidth to send intermediate intensity values. When Andrea was near him, her face was a flickering abstraction of black and white squares, like a trick picture in a psychology textbook. With effort he learned to distinguish her from the other faces in the laboratory, but no sooner had he gained confidence in his ability than the quality of vision declined even further.

By midmorning the frame rate had dropped to eight hundred pixels at two per second, which was less like vision than being shown a sequence of still images. People didn't walk to him across the lab—they jumped from spot to spot, captured in frozen postures. It was soon easy to stop thinking of them as people at all, but simply as abstract structures in the data.

By noon he could not exactly say that he had any vision at all. *Something* was updating once every two seconds, but the matrix of black and white pixels was hard to reconcile with his memories of the lab. He could no longer distinguish people from furniture, unless people moved between frames, and then only occasionally. At two, he asked Joe to disable the feed from the glasses, so that the remaining bandwidth could be used for sound and touch. Mick was plunged into darkness.

Sound had declined overnight as well. If Andrea's voice had been tinny yesterday, today it was barely human. It was as if she were speaking to him through a voice distorter on the end of the worst telephone connection in the world. The noise was beginning to win. The software was struggling to compensate, teasing sense out of the data. It was a battle that could only be prolonged, not won.

"I'm still here," Andrea told him, her voice a whisper fainter than the signal from the furthest quasar.

Mick answered back. It took some time. His words in the lab had to be analyzed by voice-recognition software and converted into ASCII characters. The characters were compressed further and sent across the reality gap, bit by bit. In the other version of the lab—the one where Mick's body waited in a wheelchair, the one where Andrea hadn't died in a car crash—equivalent software decompressed the character string and reconstituted it in mechanically generated speech, with an American accent.

"Thank you for letting me come back," he said. "Please stay. Until the end. Until I'm not here anymore."

"I'm not going anywhere, Mick."

Andrea squeezed his hand. After all that he had lost since Friday, touch remained. It really was the easiest thing to send: easier than sight, easier than sound. When, later, even Andrea's voice had to be sent across the gap by character string and speech synthesizer, touch endured. He felt her holding him, hugging his body to hers, refusing to surrender him to the drowning roar of quantum noise.

"We're down to less than a thousand useable bits," Joe told him, speaking quietly in his ear in the version of the lab where Mick lay on the immersion couch. "That's a thousand bits total, until we lose all contact. It's enough for a message, enough for parting words."

"Send this," Mick said. "Tell Andrea that I'm glad she was there. Tell her that I'm glad she was my wife. Tell her I'm sorry we didn't make it up that hill together."

When Joe had sent the message, typing it in with his usual fluid speed, Mick felt the sense of Andrea's touch easing. Even the microscopic data-transfer burden of communicating unchanging pressure, hand on hand, body against body, was now too much for the link. It was like one swimmer letting a drowning partner go. As the last bits fell, he felt Andrea slip away forever.

He lay on the couch, unmoving. He had lost his wife, for the second time. For the moment the weight of that realization pinned him into stillness. He did not think he would ever be able to walk in his world, let alone the one he had just vacated.

And yet it was Saturday. Andrea's funeral was in two days. He would have to be ready for that.

"We're done," Joe said respectfully. "Link is now noise-swamped."

"Did Andrea send anything back?" Mick asked. "After I sent my last words . . ."

"No. I'm sorry."

Mick caught the hesitation in Joe's answer. "Nothing came through?"

"Nothing intelligible. I thought something was coming through, but it was just . . ." Joe offered an apologetic shrug. "The setup at their end must have gone noise-limited a few seconds before ours did. Happens, sometimes."

"I know," Mick said. "But I still want to see what Andrea sent."

Joe handed him a printout. Mick waited for his eyes to focus on the sheet. Beneath the lines of header information was a single line of text: SO0122215. Like a phone number or a postal code, except it was obviously neither.

"That's all?"

Joe sighed heavily. "I'm sorry, mate. Maybe she was just trying to get something through . . . but the noise won. The fucking noise always wins."

Mick looked at the numbers again. They began to talk to him. He thought he knew what they meant.

". . . always fucking wins," Joe repeated.

SUNDAY

Andrea was there when they brought Mick out of the medically induced coma. He came up through layers of disorientation and half-dream, adrift until something inside him clicked into place and he realized where he had been for the last week, what had been happening to the body over which he was now regaining gradual control. It was exactly as they had promised: no dreams, no anxiety, no tangible sense of elapsed time. In a way, it was not an entirely unattractive way to spend a week. Like being in the womb, he'd heard people say. And now he was being born again, a process that was not without its own discomforts. He tried moving an arm and when the limb did not obey him instantly, he began to panic. But Joe was already smiling.

"Easy, boyo. It's coming back. The software's rerouting things one spinal nerve at a time. Just hold on there and it'll be fine."

Mick tried mumbling something in reply, but his jaw wasn't working properly either. Yet it would come, as Joe had promised. On any given day, thousands of recipients went through this exact procedure without blinking an eyelid. Many of them were people who'd already done it hundreds of times before. Nervelinking was almost insanely safe. Far safer than any form of physical travel, that was certain.

He tried moving his arm again. This time it obeyed without hesitation.

"How are you feeling?" Andrea asked.

Once more he tried speaking. His jaw was stiff, his tongue thick and uncooperative, but he managed to make some sounds. "Okay. Felt better."

"They say it's easier the second time. Much easier the third."

"How long?"

"You went under on Sunday of last week. It's Sunday again now." Joe said.

A full week. Exactly the way they'd planned it.

"I'm quite hungry," Mick said.

"Everyone's always hungry when they come out of the coma," Joe said. It's hard to get enough nourishment into the host body. We'll get you sorted out, though."

Mick turned his head to look at Joe, waiting for his eyes to find grudging focus. "Joe," he said. "Everything's all right, isn't it? No complications, nothing to worry about?"

"No problems at all," Joe said.

"Then would you mind giving Andrea and me a moment alone?"

Joe held up his hand in hasty acknowledgement and left the room, off on some plausible errand. He shut the door quietly behind him.

"Well?" Mick asked. "I'm guessing things must have gone okay, or they wouldn't have kept me under for so long."

"Things went okay, yes," Andrea said.

"Then you met the other Mick? He was here?"

Andrea nodded heavily. "He was here. We spent time together."

"What did you get up to?"

"All the usual stuff you or I would've done. Hit the town, walked in the parks, went into the hills, that kind of thing."

"How was it?"

She looked at him guardedly. "Really, really sad. I didn't really know how to behave, to be honest. Part of me wanted to be all consoling and sympathetic, because he'd lost his wife. But I don't think that's what Mick wanted."

"The other Mick," he corrected gently.

"Point is, he didn't come back to see me being all weepy. He wanted another week with his wife, the way things used to be. Yes, he wanted to say goodbye, but he didn't want to spend the whole week with the two of us walking around feeling down in the dumps."

"So how did you feel?"

"Miserable. Not as miserable as if I'd lost my husband, of course. But some of his sadness started wearing off on me. I didn't think it was going to . . . *I'm* not the one who's been bereaved here—but you'd have to be inhuman not to feel something, wouldn't you?"

"Whatever you felt, don't blame yourself for it. I think it was a wonderful thing you agreed to do."

"You, too."

"I had the easy part," Mick said.

Andrea stroked the side of his face. He realized that he needed a good shave. "How do *you* feel?" she asked. "You're nearly him, after all. You know everything he knows."

"Except how it feels to lose a wife. And I hope I don't ever find that out. I don't think I can ever really understand what he's going through now. He feels like someone else, a friend, a colleague, someone you'd feel sorry for . . ."

"But you're not cut up about what happened to him."

Mick thought for a while before responding, not wanting to give the glib, automatic answer, no matter how comforting it might have been. "No. I wish it hadn't happened . . . but you're still here. We can still be together, if we want. We'll carry on with our lives, and in a few months we'll hardly ever think of that accident. The other Mick isn't me. He isn't even anyone we'll ever hear from again. He's gone. He might as well not exist."

"But he does. Just because we can't communicate anymore . . . he *is* still out there."

"That's what the theory says." Mick narrowed his eyes. "Why? What difference does it really make, to us?"

"None at all, I suppose." Again that guarded look. "But there's something I have to tell you, something you have to understand."

There was a tone in her voice that troubled Mick, but he did his best not to show it. "Go on, Andrea."

"I made a promise to the other Mick. He's lost something no one can ever replace, and I wanted to do something, anything, to make it easier for him. Because of that, Mick and I came to an arrangement. Once a year, I'm going to go away for a day. For that day, and that day only, I'm going somewhere private where I'm going to be thinking about the other Mick. About what he's been doing; what kind of life he's had; whether he's happy or sad. And I'm going to be alone. I don't want you to follow me, Mick. You have to promise me that."

"You could tell me," he said. "There doesn't have to be secrets."

"I'm telling you now. Don't you think I could have kept it from you if I wanted to?"

"But I still won't know where . . ."

"You don't need to. This is a secret between me and the other Mick. Me and the other you." She must have read something in his expression, something he had hoped wasn't there, because her tone turned grave. "And you need to find a way to deal with that, because it isn't negotiable. I already made that promise."

"And Andrea Leighton doesn't break promises."

"No," she said, softening her look with a sweet half-smile. "She doesn't. Especially not to Mick Leighton. Whichever one it happens to be."

They kissed.

Later, when Andrea was out of the room while Joe ran some more post-immersion tests, Mick peeled off a yellow Post-it note that had been left on one of the keyboards. There was something written on the note, in neat, blue ink. Instantly he recognized Andrea's handwriting: he'd seen it often enough on the message board in their kitchen. But the writing itself—SO0122215—meant nothing to him.

"Joe," he asked casually. "Is this something of yours?"

Joe glanced over from his desk, his eyes freezing on the small rectangle of yellow paper.

"No, that's what Andrea asked—" Joe began, then caught himself. "Look, it's nothing. I meant to bin it, but . . ."

"It's a message to the other Mick, right?"

Joe looked around, as if Andrea might still be hiding in the room or about to reappear. "We were down to the last few usable bits. The other Mick had just sent his last words through. Andrea asked me to send that response."

"Did she tell you what it meant?"

Joe looked defensive. "I just typed it. I didn't ask. Thought it was between you and her. I mean, between the other Mick and her."

"It's okay," Mick said. "You were right not to ask."

He looked at the message again, and something fell solidly into place. It had taken a few moments, but he recognized the code for what it was now, as some damp and windswept memory filtered up from the past. The numbers formed a grid reference on an Ordnance Survey map. It was the kind Andrea and he had used when they went on their walking expeditions. The reference even looked vaguely familiar. He stared at the numbers, feeling as if they were about to give up their secret. Wherever it was, he'd been there, or somewhere near. It wouldn't be hard to look it up. He wouldn't even need the Post-it note. He'd always had a good memory for numbers.

Footsteps approached, echoing along the linoleum-floored hallway that led to the lab.

"It's Andrea," Joe said.

Mick folded the Post-it note until the message was no longer visible. He flicked it in Joe's direction, knowing that it was none of his business anymore.

"Bin it."

"You sure?"

From now on there was always going to be a part of his wife's life that didn't involve him, even if it was only for one day a year. He would just have to find a way to live with that.

Things could have been worse, after all.

"I'm sure," he said.

the Big Ice

JAy LAKE AND RUTH NESTVOLD

Highly prolific new writer Jay Lake seems to have appeared nearly everywhere with short work in the last couple of years, including *Asimov's SCI
FICTION, Interzone, Strange Horizons, The Third Alternative, Æon, Postscripts, Electric Velocipede,* and many other markets, producing enough
short fiction that he already has released four collections, even though his
career is only a few years old: *Greetings from Lake Wu, Green Grow the
Rushes-Oh, American Sorrows,* and *Dogs in the Moonlight.* He's the coeditor, with Deborah Layne, of the prestigious Polyphony anthology series,
and has also edited the anthologies *All-Star Zeppelin Adventure Stories,*
with David Moles, and *TEL: Stories.* He won the John W. Campbell
Award for Best New Writer in 2004. His first novel, *Rocket Science,* was
published last year, and his most recent book is a new novel, *Trial of Flowers.* Coming up is a new novel, *Mainspring,* and a new collection, *The
River Knows Its Own.*

New writer Ruth Nestvold is a graduate of Clarion West, and her stories
have appeared in *Asimov's SCI FICTION, Strange Horizons, Realms of
Fantasy, Andromeda Spaceways Inflight Magazine, Futurismic, Fantastic
Companions,* and elsewhere. Her story "Looking Through Lace" was a fi-
nalist for the James Tiptree Award a few years back. A former professor of
English, she now runs a small software localization business in Stuttgart,
Germany.

Their collaborative story "The Canadian Who Came Almost All the
Way Back from the Stars" was in our Twenty-third Annual Collection.
Here they join their considerable talents once again, this time to take us
to—and beneath—the Big Ice, for a tense adventure that proves that family
responsibility can be the hardest thing in the universe to get away from, no
matter what lengths you go to to avoid it.

Governor-General's dead."

I glanced up from the disassembled comm-comp I'd been trying to Frankenstein
together. The G-G was Core. Unkillable. But Mox didn't look like he was kidding.

"How?"

Mox's expression was more intense than during orgasm. "Field Control says the west face of the Capitol Massif collapsed in a quake. Took most of the palace with it."

A few million tons of rock and masonry trumped even invulnerable immortality. "Shit. Yeah, that might wipe out Core. Wonder what Mad Dog Bay looks like now."

"Scary stuff, Vega."

I rubbed my forehead. "Field got any instructions?"

"Hold position, maintain current activity, refuse all orders not from direct chain of command."

Think, dammit. What was important? Besides the possibility of a House coup, that is—with my brother in the thick of the plotting, no doubt. Murder most foul, if it were true.

"Why should anyone care what we do?" I asked myself as much as Mox.

For the love of inertia, we were *planetologists*. What *we* cared about was Hutchinson's World, and most of all, the mystery of the Big Ice. The unusual degree of variation in density and gravity readings. Its challenging thermal characteristics. The stray biologicals deep down where they shouldn't be.

Mostly those freaky biologicals, truth be told.

We were neither armed nor dangerous. Our station had a tranq gun, for large, warm-blooded emergencies, but there wasn't much we could do out here on the ass end of nowhere about a succession crisis back in Hainan Landing. There wasn't anything interesting about us—except me.

Mox gave me a look I couldn't interpret. "You tell me."

Core ruled.

It was the way of things, had been for centuries. Core was jealous of their history, told one set of lies to schoolkids, another to those who thought they needed to know more. I'd never believed that they were the result of progressive genengineering in the twenty-first century. Smart money in biology circles was split—very quietly split over home brew in the lab on Saturday night—between a benevolent alien invasion and something ancient and military gone terribly wrong.

Some would say terribly right.

Core didn't rule badly.

They took what they wanted, what they needed, but on planets like our own lovely little Hutchinson's World, Core was spread so thin as not to matter. Economy, law, society, it all lurched on in an ordinary way for ordinary people. I had a job, one that I mostly liked, that kept me out of trouble. So far, Core hadn't done so badly by the human race, driving us to 378 colony worlds the last time I saw a number.

Core believed in nothing if not survival. I wondered how someone had managed to drop a palace and half a mountain on the Governor-General without his noticing the plot in progress.

"You still finding those protein traces in the deep samples?" Mox asked. He was back to biology, using one of our assay stations, distracting himself from disaster with local genetics. My instrument package on the number one probe was down in the Big Ice around the four-hundred-meter layer, digesting its way through Hutchinson's specialized climatological history.

I didn't need to look at the readouts. "Yup." It was slightly distressing. There shouldn't be genetic material hanging around in detectable quantities that far below the surface. The cold-foxes and white-bugs and everything else that lived on the Big Ice lived *on* the Big Ice.

It was also distressing not knowing what was happening back in Hainan Landing—but not as much to me as it obviously was to Mox. He kept glancing at the comm station, his features tense. Mox and I lived and worked in a shack high up on Mount Spivey, almost two thousand meters above the Big Ice's cloud tops.

Far enough away from politics, I had thought.

He gave me a long stare. "Anything else I need to know?"

I looked away. "Nope."

The Big Ice was a bowl, a remnant impact crater from a planetoid strike so vast that it was difficult to understand how Hutchinson's crust had held together under the collision. Which arguably it hadn't—the Crazydance Range, more or less antipodal to the Big Ice, was one of the most chaotic crustal formations on any human-habitable world, with peaks over twenty thousand meters above the datum plane.

The bowl of the Big Ice was over a thousand kilometers across, thousands of meters deep, and filled with ice—by some estimates over 10 million cubic kilometers. A significant percentage of the planet's freshwater supply was locked up here. The Big Ice had its own weather, a perpetual rotating blizzard driven by warm air flowing over the southern arc of the encircling range that rose to form the ragged rim of the bowl. The storm rarely managed to spill back out, capping an ecosystem sufficiently extreme by the standards of the rest of the planet to keep a bevy of theorists busy trying to figure out who or what had ridden in on top of the original strike to seed the variant life-forms.

From our vantage point, it was like looking down on the frozen eye of a god.

Our instruments were in a cluster of military-grade shacks just above the high point of the ice-tides, deep inside that storm. We made the trip down there as rarely as possible, of course, though making *that* trip is something every adventure junkie ought to do once in their life. That long, cold, frightening journey into the depths was the main reason why we were on the Ice instead of lurking in some remote telemetry lab back in Hainan Landing. Every now and then, someone had to climb down and kick the equipment.

And deep beneath the surface of the Big Ice, below that cap of raging storm, was genetic material that had no business being there.

I started awake to find my sometime-lover staring at me. "Planck on a half shell, Mox! You scared the shit out of me." I stifled a yawn, my mouth still filled with sleep.

His expression was the attempt at unreadable I had begun to fear. "Field Control called back in."

"Looking for us, or just delivering another bulletin?"

"Us. Asked for someone named Alicia Hokusai McMurty Vega, cadet of the House of Powys. Took me a minute to figure they meant you."

I gazed at him a moment, rubbing my short-cropped hair and trying to wake up the rest of the way. Had I just been dreaming that he'd figured out who I was?

It didn't matter now. My cover was shot, no matter who had dredged up my full name. "What did they want?"

"Seems your presence is desired in Hainan Landing." He leaned forward. "Are you going to tell me who you are, *Vega?*"

I wasn't sure if I could. The identity he wanted from me now was one I had rejected long ago.

Maybe I could save this friendship. "When did we first meet?"

"Over six years ago," Mox replied promptly. He'd been thinking about it.

My gut turned over with something that felt like regret. "And we've been out here more than five months alone, right? I'm still Vega Hokusai, just like I've been all these years. Still a planetologist."

He locked his hands behind his back—I had the impression that he was making an effort not to touch me. Which had its own novelty; our relationship had never been characterized by impulsive, passionate embraces.

"And a cadet of the House of Powys," he pressed out.

I should have known I couldn't escape it. "We all come from somewhere. It's not who I am now."

"It's who they're asking for, back in the capital."

"Screw them." I was surprised to find I meant it.

And screw my brother, too. This would be his doing.

A cadet of Powys House. To graduate, to leave House training, someone had to die. A real death, irrevocable, not the strange half-life they could and did place us in for decades on end. One cadet had to kill another. Secretly. Plots shifted and revolved for years.

That was how House cadets discussed things. One death at a time.

When next Mox approached me with That Look, I was deep in protein analysis. Hutchinson's native gene structure was pretty well understood, though we still couldn't reverse-engineer an organism just by scanning like we could with terrestrial genes. Didn't have centuries of experience and databases, for one. It was still a small miracle how stable the underlying gene model was across planetary ecosystems: kept the panspermists going.

Either way, I didn't know what I had yet, but it was interesting—no matches in our planetary databases. Not even close.

"Vega?" His voice was low and tense.

"Uh-huh?"

"Can't we talk about this House stuff?"

I flipped off the virteo-visualizer and turned to face him. "Not much to say."

He looked up from the tranq gun he was polishing. Which didn't need the maintenance. "What are you doing out here?"

I wanted to laugh. "Mox, it's the *Big Ice*. I'm studying it, same as you. You think I'm out here plotting revolution? Against what? The cold-foxes?"

He shifted on his feet and stopped polishing the gun. "Got another call. I'm supposed to arrest you."

Ah, Core asserting itself against whatever House effort my brother Henri was running in light of the G-G's death. Or Henri calling me in through channels, over clear?

Either way, it didn't look good for me.

I couldn't take Mox's hand now—he felt betrayed, and he would think it calculating. Which maybe it was.

I shook my head. "I may have been raised by wolves, but I really am a planetologist. Six years you've known me, you've seen enough damn papers and reports from me. Am I faking this?" I taped the virteo-visualizer.

"No . . . you're good at archeogenetics, and you've got a decent handle on climate as well."

"And anyway, when would I have had time to run a revolution? Against *Core*, for the love of Inertia."

"I don't know, Vega."

He really was considering it. Perhaps our relationship had been more convenience than anything else, but still . . . this was *Mox*. I hadn't killed anyone since I left House, but my training—my programming—wouldn't allow me to let him do me in either.

I swallowed. "Mox, put down the gun."

He set the tranq pistol on the workbench, and I let out a breath I hadn't known I'd been holding.

I favored him with a smile accompanied by a high dose of pheromones. If I'd had a choice, I wouldn't have resorted to the manipulation, but autonomous survival routines were kicking in. "Thanks."

There was no answering smile on his face. "Now tell me why they want you in Hainan Landing."

"I truly don't know. But I'm not going back if I have any say in the matter." I'd made my peace with Core, thought I'd seen the last of my House progenitors. I wanted no more of Henri and Powys House, no more of Core and plots and power. The Big Ice and the mysteries of Hutchinson's were my life now.

What if they threw a revolution and nobody came?

Mox glanced at the tranq pistol. "You're House. Doesn't that mean you're like another version of Core?"

I shrugged. "We're not immortal, if that's what you mean. You've known me six years. Noticed the gray hairs?"

His gaze shifted from the pistol back to my eyes. "A superwoman." It was almost a whisper.

Unfortunately, he was very nearly right, but I didn't want to go there. "Seen me fly lately?" I asked dryly.

Then number one's telemetry alarms started going off. We both spun to workstations, bringing up virteo-visualizers to an array of instrumentation.

Something was eating the number one probe. Four hundred meters below the Big Ice.

A text window popped up in my virt environment as I tried to make sense of the bizarre thermal imaging. So low-tech.

Coming for you. Be ready. Henri.

Situation alarms flared on the station monitor at the deep edge of the virteo.

Core made enemies. They controlled all interstellar travel, most of the planetary economies, the heavy weapons, and they couldn't be killed. Usually.

But for the revolutionary on a busy schedule, even cliffs can be defeated in time, by wind and rain, by frost, by tree roots, by high explosives.

The Houses were rain on the cliff face that was Core. Long-term projects established by very patient people, well hidden—some on the fringes of society, some within the busiest bourses in human space.

Certain Houses, Powys for one, raised their children in crèches as seeds to be planted, investments in the future. I was one seed, left to grow in comfort as a planetologist. My brother Henri was another, raised as a revolutionary, just to see what would happen to him.

Seeds are expendable. Houses are built to last.

Whatever was savaging our number one Big Ice probe, all we could tell about it was that it wasn't biological. Thinking about that gave me a bad case of the fantods.

Satellite warfare was going on overhead, judging from the dropouts in the comm grid and exoatmospheric energy pinging our detectors. Planetary Survey, ever thrifty, had put neutrino and boson arrays on top of our shack for correlative data collection in this conveniently remote location—and those arrays were shrieking bloody murder.

I figured I had an hour tops before Henri got here, with a couple House boys or girls in case I got fussy. Henri was a Political. I was . . . something else. Something Henri needed?

What was a good House soldier to do?

I turned to Mox. "I'm going down to the Big Ice and try to rescue our probe."

He froze. "Four hundred meters deep? Planck's ghost, Vega, you can't get that far under the ice! Even if you did, you'd never make it back."

I didn't know what to say, so I didn't say anything.

We were only sometime-lovers, but still I could see the exact moment he realized. "You don't intend to come back."

I shook my head. "My cover's blown. I may as well try to rescue the probe on my way out."

Mox looked away, no longer willing to meet my eyes. "So what can I expect?"

"House for sure. Probably Core, too, following after."

"Shit."

"Play stupid. Don't mention Powys House, don't say anything about anything. Tell them I went down on a repair mission."

"And if they come after you?"

The decision made, I was already up and pulling gear out of the locker. "The Big Ice is dangerous. They have to fly through that frozen hurricane, handle the surface conditions, and find my happy ass. Accidents happen."

"Vega. . . ."

I looked up. Mox had that intense look again, the one I had only seen in bed up till now, but he wiped it off his face before I could get up the courage to respond. House gave its seeds all kinds of powers, but bonus emotional strength wasn't one of them.

"Yeah?" I finally choked out.

"Good luck."

"You, too, Mox."

"I hope you make it."

"Thanks. So do I."

Moments later, I was outside. Day's last golden glare faded behind the western peaks. Colored lights glowed in the sky, orbital combat (coming for me?) mirrored by hundred-kilometer-wide spirals of lightning in the permanent storm of the Big Ice, glowering dark gray fifteen hundred meters below. I could smell ionization even up on Mount Spivey. Thirty-five hundred meters above the datum plane, the air gets thin, and the weather can be pretty shitty by any standards other than those of the Big Ice.

It was glorious.

Our base shack was on a wide ledge, maybe sixty meters deep and four hundred long. Nothing grew on the bare cliff except lichens and us. Power cells and some other low-access equipment had been sunk in holes driven into the rock, but otherwise the little camp spread across the ledge like an old junkyard, anchored against wind and weather. I glanced at the landing pad, but there was nothing I could do about anyone who might arrive and threaten Mox.

On the other side of the landing pad was the headworks of the tramway running down to our equipment shacks Ice-side. It was a skeletal cage on a series of cables, quite a ride on the descent. Unfortunately, the ascent required hours of painful winching, unless you wanted to climb the ladder that had been hacked and bolted into place by the original convict work crew.

I didn't have time for the tram today. I snapped out the buckyfiber wings I'd brought with me months ago and stashed against a day such as this.

Big, black, far less delicate than they looked, they could have been taken from a bat the size of a horse. There were neurochannels in my scapulae that coupled to the control blocks in the wings, wired through diamond-reinforced bone sockets meant to accept the mounting pintles. Once I fitted them on, they would be part of my body.

My gear safely stowed in a harness across my chest and waist, I opened my fatigues to bare the skin of my back. The wings, tugging at the wind already, slid on like a pair of extra hands. The cold wind on my skin was a tonic, a welcome shock, electricity for batteries I'd long neglected.

I stared down into the vast hole that was the Big Ice, the crackling lightning of the storm beckoning me. I spread my wings and leapt from the icy ledge into the open spaces of the air.

One theory about the Big Ice was that it was an artificial construct. The thermal characteristics required to drive such a vast and active sea of ice had proven extremely difficult to model. Planetary energy and thermal budgets are notoriously challenging to characterize accurately—one of the greatest problem sets in computational philosophy, but the Big Ice set new standards.

So fine, said the fringe. Maybe it was a directed impact all those megayears ago. Maybe something's still down there, some giant thermal reactor from a Type II or Type III civilization come out of the galactic core on an errand that ended up badly here on Hutchinson's World.

Yeah, and cold-foxes might pick up paintbrushes and render the *Mona Lisa*.

But there were those nagging questions . . . all a person really had to do was stand on the rim wall somewhere and look down. Then they would understand that the universe has impenetrable secrets.

Flight is the ultimate high. The wind slid across my skin with lover's hands, and the muscles in my chest stretched as my back pulled taut. I could see the crosscurrents, the play of gravity and lift and pressure combining in the endless sea of air to make the sky road. A hurricane bound solid and slow in crackling ice, but no less deadly, or frightening, than its cloud-borne cousins over the open sea.

Below me, the lidless, frosty eye of the world beckoned.

I spilled air, leaning into a broad, circling descent that gave me a good view of the blizzard's topography. Even by the light of the early evening, the core of the storm was foggy, a cataract in the eye, but the winds there would be very low. The lightning on the spiraling arms of the storm bespoke the violence of the night.

Fine—I would ride the hard winds. I continued with my wide curves, circling a few kilometers away from the cliff face that hosted our shack and Mox. I hoped he would be okay, play it easy and slow, a bit stupid. Neither Core nor House would care anything for him.

And hopefully he would forgive me someday for keeping things from him.

With that thought, I expelled the last of the air from my lungs and accelerated my descent.

A few hundred meters above the clouds, my sky-surfing was interrupted by a coruscating bolt of violet lightning.

From *above* the storm.

"Inertia," I hissed as I snap-rolled into the crackling ionization trail from the shot, a near miss from an energy lance. With a quick scan of the sky above me, I saw a pair of black smears shooting by. Interceptors, from Hainan Landing, running on low-viz. Somebody wasn't waiting for me to come in.

Gravity and damnation: I didn't have anything that would knock down one of those puppies. I slipped into another series of rolls. None of their targeting systems would lock on me—not enough metal or EM, and I was moving too slow for their offensive envelope—so it was straight-line shots the old-fashioned way, with eyeball, Mark I, and a finger on the red button.

The human eye I could fool, and then some.

They circled over the storm and made another pass toward me. I kept spinning and rolling, bouncing around like a rivet in a centrifuge. *Think like a pilot, Vega.* I spilled air and dropped straight down just before both lances erupted. The beams crossed above me, crackling loud enough to be heard over the roar of the storm below.

It took some hard pulling to grab air out of my tumble. I regained control just above the top of the storm, a close, gray landscape of thousands of voids and valleys, glowing in the light of the rising moon. It was eerily quiet, just above the roil of the clouds. The background roar I felt more in my bones than heard with my ears, like a color washing the world; the detail noises were gone—all the little crackles and hisses and birdcalls that fill a normal night. The only other sound was the periodic body-numbing sizzle of lightning bolts circling between cloud masses within the storm.

I had no electronics except the silicon stuffed inside my head. If I got hit hard enough to fry that, there wasn't going to be much future for me anyway. But those clowns on my trail had a lot more to lose from Mother Nature's light show than I did. So I cut a wide spiral, feinting and looping as I went, trying to draw them down closer to the clouds. They came after me, in long circles nearly as slow as their airspeed would allow, the two interceptors snapping off shots where they could.

It was a game of cat and bird. When would they fire? When should I weave instead of bob? I'd already surrendered almost all my altitude advantage. I didn't want to drop into the storm winds until I was close to my target, not if I could help it. My greatest problem was that I was muscle-powered. I couldn't keep this up nearly as long as my attackers could.

Then one of them got smart, goosed up a few hundred meters for a diving shot.

Gotcha. I rolled slow to give him a sweet target.

My clothes caught fire from the proximity of the energy lance's bolt. I twisted away, relying on the flames to take care of themselves in a moment, praying for my knowledge of the storm to pan out.

It did. Multiple terawatts of lightning clawed upward out of the clouds, completing the circuit opened by the energy lance's ionization trail. My bogey took enough juice to fry his low-viz shields and probably shut down every soft system he had. Regardless of its ground state, there's only so much energy an airframe can handle. Number one clown might not be toast, but he had too much jam sticking to him to be chasing me anymore.

Number two got smart and dropped below me, skimming in and out of the cloud tops. I guess he figured on there not being much more air traffic here tonight. I watched him circle, angling for an upward shot. Angling to draw the lightning to me.

Time for the clouds, Vega.

I folded my buckyfiber and dropped away from violent death, a bullet on the wing.

The storm was hell. Two-hundred-kilometer winds. Hail bigger than grapes. Sparks crackling off my wingtips, off my fingers, off my toes.

I loved it.

I had no idea where number two interceptor was, but he couldn't have any better idea where I was, so I figured that made us even. Neither House nor Core was going to find me down here. And to hell with the Governor-Generalship.

I was still a hundred kilometers or more from the probe, my real reason for being here. In the storm, I could steer—a little—and ride the winds—a lot. But it was like being inside a giant fist.

The training of my childhood came back to me, hard years in dark caves and abroad on moonless nights, initiating trickle mode. I could breathe as little as once every ten to twelve minutes when my blood was ramped up. The tensile strength of my skin rose past that of steel, shattering the ice balls when they hit me.

There's a beauty to everything in these worlds. A spray of blood on a bulkhead can be more delicate, ornate, than the finest hamph-ivory fan from Vlach. A shattered bone in the forest tells a history of the death of a deer, the future of patient beetles, and reflects the afternoon sun brightly as any pearl. Take the symmetry in the worn knurl on an oxygen valve, the machined regularity of its manufacture compromised by the scars of life until the metal is a little sculpture of a tired heaven for sinning souls.

But a storm . . . oh, a storm.

Clouds tower, airy palaces for elemental forces. During the day, the colors deepen into a bruise upon the sky, and now, at night, they create the only color there is in the dark. The air reeks of electricity and water. Thunder rumbles with a sound so big I feel it in my bones. The blue flashes amidst the rainy dark could call spirits from the deep of the Big Ice to dance on the freezing winds.

I flew through that beauty, fleeing my pursuer, racing toward whatever was consuming our number one probe.

The Houses aren't places, any more than Core is. They're more like ideas with money and weapons. Maybe political parties.

Powys House, as constituted on Hutchinson's World, was spread through several wings of the Governor-General's Palace of late lament. I had grown up occasionally visible as a page in the G-G's service. Between surgeries, training time, and long, dark hours in the caves of Capitol Massif.

Core is everywhere and nowhere. The Houses are nowhere and everywhere. Some believe there is no difference between Core and House, others that worlds separate us.

I spent my childhood falling, flying, being made both more and less than human.

I spent my childhood training for a day such as this.

Down below the cloud deck, I traded the storm's beauty for the storm's punishment. Here there was nothing but flying fog, freezing rain, ice, and wind—wind everywhere. It was brutally cold, frigid enough to stress even my enhanced thermal-management capabilities.

Screw you, Core. If that other bastard behind me made it to the Big Ice in one piece, I would give him a cold grave.

Then a gust hit me, a crosswind powerful enough to flip me with a crack of my wing spar and drive me down on to the Big Ice headfirst. I barely had time to get my arms up before I plowed through a crusted snow dune into a frigid, scraping hell.

"Damn," I mumbled through a mouthful of ice. That wasn't supposed to happen, not with these wings. The neurochannel control blocks screamed agony where the connections had ripped free on impact. I shut them down and began the wiggling, painful process of extracting myself. After a couple of minutes, I pulled free to see a pair of cold-foxes watching me.

"No food today," I said cheerfully over the howling wind, for all the good it would do me. Cold-foxes are long-bodied, scaled scavengers—and deaf. They eat mostly white-bugs, lichen, and each other; but at forty kilos per, they could be troublesome.

Something changed in the tone of the wind, and I looked up in time to see the second interceptor roar by overhead, shaking on the wings of the storm. The cold-foxes vanished into the snow.

The Big Ice is shaped more like a desert than an ocean of ice, with dunes, banks, and troughs formed in response to the permanent storm. There are some density variations, relating mostly to aeration of the ice formations, but also trace minerals and pressure factors. The surface even has features mimicking normal geology—outcroppings, cliffs, crevasses. The difference is that geology sticks around for a while. The Big Ice . . . well, it has tectonics, but at human speeds rather than planetary.

Which for us mostly meant there'd never been much point in making or keeping maps. Every day was an adventure, down in the pit of the storm.

I was within a few kilometers of my instrument package's tunnels. The entrances would be filled with snow, possibly blocked by falls, but as long as at least one was open, I was in business.

I wasn't here only to avoid Core or whoever was after me—I hadn't lied to Mox when I told him I was a planetologist. The mystery of the Big Ice fascinated me, belonged to me, was mine to decipher and share, so much more important to me than Powys House and politics and Core. My brother would never understand.

And then I was sliding and struggling for footing against the wind, vehemently cursing what fascinated me.

The tunnel was a surprise when I found it. The number one probe had trundled across the Big Ice to this point, though its tracks had long been erased by wind and storm. As its entry point, it had chosen a solid cliff facing leeward, the closest thing on that particular stretch of the Big Ice to a permanent feature. The ice had preserved a tunnel like a black maw in the pale darkness.

I experienced a sudden shiver that had nothing to do with the temperature. At least I'd be out of the wind.

To access the tunnel, I had to get down on my hands and knees. It was almost like slithering, making me wish House had given me some genetic material from iceworms. The tunnel was shaped in the slightly off-center ovoid cross section of the number one probe's body, the ice had melted, then injected into the walls to refreeze in denser spikes that served to reinforce the tunnel. Half-crawling, I had some clearance for my back, though not much. Were I to lie flat, I would barely have enough room to operate a handheld. Otherwise, it was a coffin of ice.

Hopefully I could prove deadlier than whatever might actually be inside the Big Ice.

To see, I had to use low-wave bioflare. It hurt my planetologist's soul, but I didn't want to be surprised by anything before finding the probe.

It was damned cold in the tunnels. My thermal management was keeping up, mostly due to the blessed lack of wind beyond a slight updraft from below, probably stimulated by some version of the Bernoulli effect at the tunnel mouth.

And if I had been merely human, the cold and the dark probably would have slain me with despair and hypothermia.

Stray voltage and a faint trace of machine oil led me to the probe. I approached cautiously, not sure what awaited me, what had sabotaged the probe.

In all the history of Core and House and humanity as a whole, no one had ever found an alien machine. There were worlds that showed distinct signs of having been mined, or worked for transportation routes and widened harbors. But never so much as a rivet or a scrap of metal to be found: no machines, no artifacts.

And so we scoured the odd places for odd genetic signatures. Though as the centuries of Core raveled onward, it had become increasingly clear that the oddest genes were in our own cells.

Finally I found the number one probe, quiescent but not dead, and no evidence of what had savaged it.

The probe was vaguely potato-shaped, a meter-and-a-half wide by a meter tall in cross section and three meters long, with a rough surface studded with the bypass injectors that had created the tunnel. From the rear, it looked normal. No sign of the attacker. Just me and the probe, four hundred meters below the Big Ice.

Had our telemetry been spoofed? The trick was as old as Tesla's ghost, but the probe was stopped. That was more than spoofed telemetry.

I shut down, slipping into passive recon mode. Black. Dampened my EM signatures, turned off my thermal management. Nothing but me and my ears on all their glorious frequencies.

The Big Ice groaned and cracked, settling into the rotation of the planet, the stresses of the crustal formations around and beneath it, breathing, a frigid monster half the size of a continent.

But there was something beyond that.

The gentle slide of crystals on crystals as the walls of the tunnel sublimated.

The distant echo of the storm.

A very faint click as something metallic sought thermal equilibrium with its surroundings.

And out of that near silence, a voice.

"Good-bye, Alicia." My brother Henri.

As fast as I was, he was faster. I was buried in tons of the Big Ice almost before I could even finish the thought: *sororicide*.

"House cadets are typically killed in their twelfth or thirteenth year of life. Appropriate measures are taken to preserve the brain stem and other structures critical to identity maintenance and retention of their extensive training. They are then left in a state of terminality until new training is called for. This process is considered critical to the development of their character, and since the dead know no flow of time, their thanatic interruption is not experienced by them as such. Some House cadets have waited centuries to be revived."

House: A Secret History in Fiction (author unknown), quoted by Fyram Palatine in *A Study of Banned Texts and Their Consequences*, Fremont Press, Langhorne-Clemens IIa.

I found myself, reduced in cognitive ability, packed in loose snow.

Which meant I wasn't embedded in ice.

I have cavitation-fusion reactors within the buckyfiber honeycomb of my long bones. This means, given any meaningful thermal gradient at all, I will have energy. Even for exceedingly small values of thermal gradient. Such as being adjacent to a three-meter mass of plastic and metal, deep below an ice cap.

And given energy, the bodies of House, like the bodies of Core, will seek life. Repeatedly.

But if I was no longer buried in the ice, how long had I been here? My internal clock refused to answer.

Inertia.

I hadn't reached this state overnight. A cold stole over me that had nothing to do with the Big Ice. I could have been down here for months. Years even.

Then I realized I could hear the wind, close, which meant I was just below the surface. I had some muscle strength, so I pushed toward the noise. And if I heard noise, I had ears.

Above the rushing sound of the wind came some kind of long, drawn-out wail, not natural. With the part of my brain which was re-forming, I identified it as a siren.

Warning? Or call?

With my internal clock nonfunctional, I had no idea how long it took me to emerge from the snow, but eventually I did, body changing with my progress. There I found I could see.

I was at the base of a shallow hill—the cliff where the probe had tunneled? Worn by time and wind? How long had I been beneath the Big Ice?

The siren wailed once again above the white expanses, and I followed it, climbing frozen wastelands.

With hands that weren't human.

I stopped, staring at the thing that had once been a palm with fingers. Now it was a claw, the skin a blue-fired tracery of webbing no human genome had ever produced. I had regrown myself from the stray organics down beneath the Big Ice.

The mysterious archeogenes were within me.

And then another sound, a shot, followed by pain and a giant roar that wrenched itself out of my gut.

Mox stood above me, tranq gun poised, his expression bordering on terror.

I felt a surge, a burn of some strange emotion, retaliation, vengeance, but I fought it back, allowing the tranquilizers to work, staring at Mox, willing him to understand.

How could I make him realize that the monster in front of him was me?

I came to in a room in our shack, my hands and feet tied with rudimentary restraints I knew wouldn't hold. Mox sat across from me, tranq gun across his lap, still looking scared and dazed.

Some primal impulse wanted to break my bonds and him, too, for trying to restrain me; but the part of me that had once been human was able to retain the upper hand.

I tried to speak, but all that emerged was something resembling a roar. Mox started up, gun trained on me.

I tried again. This time at least it was recognizable as speech.

"Planck on a half shell, Mox. Put down the gun." It was my quietest voice, but it reverberated off the walls of the little shack.

Mox winced and dropped the tranq gun. "Vega?"

I nodded; the less I spoke, the better.

"What happened to you?"

I shrugged. "The archaeogenes."

"But how?"

"House."

House was hard to kill. I had metabolized ice.

Mox nodded. He'd seen the data on the stray biologicals, too, and he thought I was a superwoman. He accepted it. He believed me.

The beast in me quieted.

"Now what?" he asked.

"Take me to Hainan Landing."

It had been over a year since my disappearance, and my brother Henri was now G-G. Core.

Unkillable?

"I did my research after you disappeared," Mox said. "Killing siblings is regarded as necessary to advancement among your kind."

"I was no competition," I roared. I wished there were something I could do about my beastly voice.

Mox winced, shaking his head. "Even if you assumed you'd taken yourself out of the running, he didn't assume that."

I don't know how I thought I could ever get away from House politics.

Since Mox had originally been ordered to bring me in before I went to find the probe, we decided that was what he would do—arrest me and take me to Henri. That would be the simplest way to get me to a place where I could confront my brother. There was a surge of that emotion again, the one I associated with the beast, a cross between anger and a powerful sense of ritual, like I imagined formal vengeance might once have felt.

Of course, the risk was that he would kill me on sight, but I was willing to take it. Besides, knowing Henri, he'd be curious to find out how I survived.

He would *want* to see me.

The transporter was a tight fit—it was made for two humans, and I had become very much bulkier.

As we flew over Hainan Landing, I inspected the changes. Capitol Massif was a mountain of rubble spilling into what was left of Mad Dog Bay. The city itself didn't look much different, its white low-rises spread like ancient pyramids among an emerald jungle topped with birds and flowers, bucolic existence beneath the gentle, guiding hand of Core. Flatboats and pontoon villages still graced the waterfront—surely new since Capitol Massif had collapsed. That must have been quite a tsunami.

But not caused by an earthquake, I was certain of that now. Until I saw the city, it had still seemed possible that Henri had capitalized on a natural occurrence to further his ambitions.

Only too much of Hainan Landing was still standing.

Interceptors filed into formation with our transporter and accompanied us to the landing pad of what I presumed was the new palace, on the other side of Mad Dog Bay from the remnants of Capitol Massif and in a geologically stable location. A squad of heavy infantry was waiting when we stepped out of the vehicle, me with my clawed hands bound behind my back for verisimilitude. They formed up around us and led us through hallways even more convoluted than those I remembered from childhood.

Perhaps House really could become Core.

Then the hallways gave way to a huge audience chamber, paneled in mirrors to make it seem even bigger, and I was confronted by image upon image of what I had become—huge, ungainly, webbed, blue. Inhuman. Ugly as sin and more dangerous. How had Mox been able to converse with me as Vega? Look into my eyes and see the woman who had once been his lover? The sight of me scared even me.

But then there was my brother, standing at the end of the large room, hands locked behind his back, his stance mirroring my own bound wrists. Except that he still had the deliberately chiseled features of House: a look determined to provoke admiration, a look calculated to command. While I was something Other.

Beauty and the Beast.

Henri looked from Mox to me and back again. *"This* is supposed to be my sister?" he asked, one finely sculpted eyebrow raised for effect.

"Henri!" I roared before Mox had a chance to answer. My voice shattered the mirrors lining the hall and made my brother finally look at me seriously.

Henri shook his head. "This does not look like Alicia to me. Your humor is in poor taste."

The sense of formal vengeance surged, and I growled, causing everyone, including Mox, to step back.

Mox caught himself first. "Just talk to her."

"This could not have once been a human being."

"I think she reconstructed herself out of the archaeogenes in the Big Ice."

"But what is there in this—thing—to make you think it's her?"

"Planck on a half shell!" I bellowed, tired of being ignored. "Henri! Why?" It was all I could do to keep from breaking my bonds and tearing my ostensible brother to shreds.

Henri winced with everyone else in the hall at the sound of my voice, but now he was looking at me rather than Mox, accepting my transformation, recognizing me by my words if not my voice or my appearance. The calculating smile of House began to curl his lips.

No, not House. Core.

"Politics," Henri said, as if that explained everything. Which, of course, in terms of Core it did. "You were supposed to stay dead down there."

"Well, I'm back now," I said. More glass exploded. Was my voice growing bigger, or only my anger?

Henri actually laughed. "Yes, but bound."

This time I couldn't control the surge of emotion, and I snapped the buckyfiber bonds as if they were twine. Half a dozen guards stormed me, but I reached out one long, clawed arm and slapped them away, surprised at my own power. One guard began to rise, his weapon trained on me, but I broke his back and left him howling on the marble floor. I would have broken more, but then I saw the way Mox was looking at me, his expression even more horrified than the first time he had seen me.

"Halt!" Henri cried out, uselessly; by this time, no one was moving except the screaming soldier.

He approached me and stopped, facing me at arm's length. "As you look to be quite difficult to kill, sister, I have a proposal to make."

I could slay him before anyone shot me, I knew it—arm's length was not nearly distance enough for his safety. The being I had become calculated the speed and distance and moves without even thinking, and I kept this form's inherent need for formal vengeance in check only through the greatest effort.

And the awareness in my peripheral vision that three of the soldiers still standing had moved closer to Mox, weapons ready.

I had not moved my head, but I saw somehow that Henri was cognizant of my assessment of the situation, knowing in the same way that I knew exactly how to break his neck.

"Proposal?" I echoed.

Henri smiled, sure of himself—Core. "I could use a creature like you at my side, you know. You would make a fearsome bodyguard. And you are no threat to my ambitions now . . . like this."

Like this. A monster, no longer House. What I had always wanted—but not *like this*.

"I might kill *you*," I bellowed.

He shook his head. "No. Because you, too, are Core. Sister."

"I'm not Core."

His smile grew even wider. "What then?"

Yes, what? A killing machine, obviously. And I could kill my brother—who, after all, had killed me first—kill him, and free Hutchinson's World of Core.

Two aides hurried in and loaded the wounded guard onto a stretcher. The man's screams faded to whimpers as they hauled him away.

In the moment of departure, I could scent everyone. The wounded man's blood and pain and bodily fluids, Henri's brittle confidence, and fear everywhere. They were all scared—Mox, the guards, even Henri. Everyone was scared of the beast I had become.

What was underneath the Big Ice? What was so dreadful, so powerful, it had to be buried in such a huge grave?

Me. Something like me.

Did it have a conscience? Did *I* have a conscience?

I turned that thought over in my head. I was big, powerful, House-trained, angry—and back from the dead. I could challenge Henri here and now on his own ground. Somewhere inside me, that sense of formal vengeance stirred again. Some actions were *fitting*.

I gave that thought long consideration. Slow as the Big Ice, I turned it around and around. Some actions were fitting, but some actions were not.

Perhaps Core was not such a bad thing after all. And, as Henri had pointed out, if House Powys had become Core on this planet, then I, too, was Core—albeit monstrous Core now. But Core or not, I couldn't stay here, where I would likely kill anyone who crossed me. I *could* be better than whatever the Big Ice's archaeogenes had made me, better than what House had made me.

I could be better than my brother. I could be more than the sum of my biology. I did not have to accept his offer.

"I will not be your bodyguard."

My brother's smile disappeared. "Then I will have to kill you again, you know."

That he might. But what choice did I have? And how successful would he be this time? I looked at Mox, whose fear of me seemed to have fled. He held my gaze a long moment, and I imagined I saw some flicker of our old companionship.

Mox understood. And for his sake, I had to go.

I glanced once more at Henri. "I am not Core, and I never will be. Dead or alive, that will not change." I turned, expecting energy lances in my back.

Henri surprised me. None came.

I walked through the shards of shattered mirrors and down the long corridors and out of the New Palace, walked down to Mad Dog Bay and into it, walked beneath the waters and across the face of the land for days until I got home to the Big Ice.

Broad, deep, a world within a world. My place now. My family, my House. My Core. Perhaps if I dug deep enough, I could find a new brother.

BOW SHOCK

GREGORY BENFORD

Here's as authentic a look into the world of the working scientist as you're ever likely to see—a world that comes complete with frustrations, obsessions, rivalries . . . and some stunning surprises profound enough to change our view of the universe forever.

Gregory Benford is one of the modern giants of the field. His 1980 novel, *Timescape*, won the Nebula Award, the John W. Campbell Memorial Award, the British Science Fiction Association Award, and the Australian Ditmar Award, and is widely considered to be one of the classic novels of the last two decades. His other novels include *Beyond Jupiter, The Stars in Shroud, In the Ocean of Night, Against Infinity, Artifact, Across the Sea of Suns, Great Sky River, Tides of Light, Furious Gulf, Sailing Bright Eternity, Cosm, Foundation's Fear,* and *The Martian Race.* His short work has been collected in *Matter's End, Worlds Vast and Various,* and *Immersion and Other Short Novels*; his essays have been assembled in a nonfiction collection, *Deep Time.* His most recent book is a new novel, *Beyond Infinity.* Coming up is another new novel, *The Sunborn.* Benford is a professor of physics at the University of California at Irvine.

R alph slid into the booth where Irene was already waiting, looking perky and sipping on a bottle of Snapple tea. "How'd it . . ." she let the rest slide away, seeing his face.

"Tell me something really awful, so it won't make today seem so bad."

She said carefully, "Yes sir, coming right up, sir. Um . . ." A wicked grin. "Once I had a pet bird that committed suicide by sticking his head between the cage bars."

"W-what . . . ?"

"Okay, you maybe need worse? Can do." A flash of dazzling smile. "My sister forgot to feed her pet gerbils, so one died. Then, the one that was alive ate its dead friend."

Only then did he get that she was kidding, trying to josh him out of his mood. He laughed heartily. "Thanks, I sure needed that."

She smiled with relief and turned her head, swirling her dirty-blond hair around her head in a way that made him think of a momentary tornado. Without a word her face gave him sympathy, concern, inquiry, stiff-lipped support—all in a quick gush of expressions that skated across her face, her full, elegantly lipsticked red mouth collaborating with the eggshell-blue eyes.

Her eyes followed him intently as he described the paper he had found that left his work in the dust.

"Astronomy is about getting there first?" she asked wonderingly.

"Sometimes. This time, anyway." After that he told her about the talk with the department chairman—the whole scene, right down to every line of dialog, which he would now remember forever, apparently—and she nodded.

"It's time to solicit letters of recommendation for me, but to who? My work's already out of date. I . . . don't know what to do now," he said. Not a great last line to a story, but the truth.

"What do you feel like doing?"

He sighed. "Redouble my efforts—"

"When you've lost sight of your goal?" It was, he recalled, a definition of *fanaticism*, from a movie.

"My goal is to be an astronomer," he said stiffly.

"That doesn't have to mean academic, though."

"Yeah, but NASA jobs are thin these days." An agency that took seven years to get to the moon the first time, from a standing start, was now spending far more dollars to do it again in fifteen years.

"You have a lot of skills, useful ones."

"I want to work on fundamental things, not applied."

She held up the cap of her Snapple tea and read from the inside with a bright, comically forced voice, "Not a winner, but here's your Real Fact # 237. The number of times a cricket chirps in fifteen seconds, plus thirty-seven, will give you the current air temperature."

"In Fahrenheit, I'll bet," he said, wondering where she was going with this.

"Lots of 'fundamental' scientific facts are just that impressive. Who cares?"

"Um, have we moved on to a discussion of the value of knowledge?"

"Valuable to *who*, is my point."

If she was going to quote stuff, so could he. "Look, Mark Twain said that the wonder of science is the bounty of speculation that comes from a single hard fact."

"Can't see a whole lot of bounty from here." She gave him a wry smile, another hair toss. He had to admit, it worked very well on him.

"I *like* astronomy."

"Sure, it just doesn't seem to like you. Not as much, anyway."

"So I should . . . ?" Let her fill in the answer, since she was full of them today. And he doubted the gerbil story.

"Maybe go into something that rewards your skills."

"Like . . . ?"

"Computers. Math. Think big! Try to sign on with a hedge fund, do their analysis."

"Hedge funds . . ." He barely remembered what they did. "They look for short-term trading opportunities in the market?"

"Right, there's a lot of math in that. I read up on it online." She was sharp, that's what he liked about her. "That data analysis you're doing, it's waaay more complicated than what Herb Linzfield does."

"Herb . . . ?"

"Guy I know, eats in the same Indian buffet place some of us go for lunch." Her eyes got veiled and he wondered what else she and Herb had talked about. Him? "He calculates hedges on bonds."

"Corporate or municipal?" Just to show he wasn't totally ignorant of things financial.

"Uh, I think corporate." Again the veiled eyes.

"I didn't put in six years in grad school and get a doctorate to—"

"I know, honey," eyes suddenly warm, "but you've given this a real solid try now."

"A *try*? I'm not done."

"Well, what I'm saying, you can do other things. If this doesn't . . . work out."

Thinking, he told her about the labyrinths of academic politics. The rest of the UC Irvine astro types did nearby galaxies, looking for details of stellar evolution, or else big-scale cosmological stuff. He worked in between, peering at exotic beasts showing themselves in the radio and microwave regions of the spectrum. It was a competitive field and he felt it fit him. So he spelled out what he thought of as The Why. That is, why he had worked hard to get this far. For the sake of the inner music it gave him, he had set aside his personal life, letting affairs lapse and dodging any longterm relationship.

"So that's why you weren't . . . connected? . . . when you got here." She pursed her lips appraisingly.

"Yeah. Keep my options open, I figured."

"Open for . . . ?"

"For this—" he swept a rueful, ironic hand in the air at his imaginary assets. For a coveted appointment, a heady way out of the gray postdoc grind—an Assistant Professorship at UC Irvine, smack on the absurdly pricey, sun-bleached coast of Orange County. He had beaten out over a hundred applicants. And why not? He was quick, sure, with fine-honed skills and good connections, plus a narrow-eyed intensity a lot of women found daunting, as if it whispered: *careerist, beware.* The skies had seemed to open to him, for sure. . . .

But that was then.

He gave her a crinkled smile, rueful, and yet he felt it hardening. "I'm not quitting. Not now."

"Well, just think about it." She stroked his arm slowly and her eyes were sad now. "That's all I meant. . . ."

"Sure." He knew the world she inhabited, had seen her working spreadsheets, reading biographies of the founding fathers and flipping through books on "leadership," seeking clues about rising in the buoyant atmosphere of business.

"Promise?" Oddly plaintive.

He grinned without mirth. "You know I will." But her words had hurt him, all the same. Mostly by slipping cool slivers of doubt into his own mind.

Later that night, he lay in her bed and replayed the scene. It now seemed to define the day, despite Irene's strenuous efforts.

Damn, Ralph had thought. *Scooped!*

And by Andy Lakehurst, too. He had bit his lip and focused on the screen, where he had just gotten a freshly posted paper off the Los Alamos Library Web site, astro-ph.

The radio map was of Ralph's one claim to minor fame, G369.23–0.82. The actual observations were stunning. Brilliant, clear, detailed. Better than his work.

He had slammed his fist on his disk, upsetting his coffee. "Damn!" Then he sopped up the spill—it had spattered some of the problem sets he'd been grading earlier.

Staring at the downloaded preprint, fuming, he saw that Andy and his team had gotten really detailed data on the—on *his*—hot new object, G369.23–0.82. They must have used a lot of observing time, and gotten it pronto.

Where? His eyes ran down the usual Observations section and—*Arecibo! He got observing time there?*

That took pull or else a lucky cancellation. Arecibo was the largest dish in the world, a whole scooped bowl set amid a tropical tangle, but fixed in position. You had to wait for time and then synchronize with dishes around the planet to make a map.

And good ol' ex-classmate Andy had done it. Andy had a straightforward, no-nonsense manner to him, eased by a ready smile that got him through doors and occasionally into bedrooms. Maybe he had connections to Beth Conway at Arecibo?

No, Ralph had thought to himself, *that's beneath me. He jumped on G369.23–0.82 and did the obvious next step, that's all.*

Further, Andy was at Harvard, and that helped. Plenty. But it still galled. Ralph was still waiting to hear from Harkin at the Very Large Array about squeezing in some time there. Had been waiting for six weeks, yes.

And on top of it all, he then had his conference with the department chairman in five minutes. He glanced over Andy's paper again. It was excellent work. Unfortunately.

He sighed in the dark of Irene's apartment, recalling the crucial hour with the department chairman. This long day wouldn't be done until he had reviewed it, apparently.

He had started with a fixed smile. Albert Gossian was an avuncular sort, an old-fashioned chairman who wore a suit when he was doing official business. This unconscious signal did not bode well. Gossian gave him a quick, jowly smile and gestured Ralph into a seat.

"I've been looking at your Curriculum Vitae," Gossian said. He always used the full Latin, while others just said "CV." Slow shake of head. "You need to publish more, Ralph."

"My grant funding's kept up, I—"

"Yes, yes, very nice. The NSF is putting effort into this field, most commendable—" a quick glance up from reading his notes, over the top of his glasses—"and that's why the department decided to hire in this area. But—can you keep the funding?"

"I'm two years in on the NSF grant, so next year's mandatory review is the crunch."

"I'm happy to say your teaching rating is high, and university service, but . . ." The drawn-out vowels seemed to be delivering a message independent of the actual sentences.

All Assistant Professors had a review every two years, tracking their progress toward the Holy Grail of tenure. Ralph had followed a trajectory typical for the early century: six years to get his doctorate, a postdoc at Harvard—where Andy Lakehurst was the rising star, eclipsing him and a lot of others. Ralph got out of there after a mutually destructive affair with a biologist at Tufts, fleeing as far as he could when he saw that UC Irvine was growing fast and wanted astrophysicists. UCI had a mediocre reputation in particle theory, but Fred Reines had won a Nobel there for showing that neutrinos existed and using them to detect the spectacular 1987 supernova.

The plasma physics group was rated highest in the department and indeed they proved helpful when he arrived. They understood that 99% of the mass in the universe was roasted, electrons stripped away from the nuclei—plasma. It was a hot, rough universe. The big dramas played out there. Sure, life arose in the cool, calm planets, but the big action flared in their placid skies, telling stories that awed him.

But once at UCI, he had lost momentum. In the tightening federal budgets, proposals didn't get funded, so he could not add poctdocs to get some help and leverage. His carefully teased-out observations gave new insights only grudgingly. Now five years along, he was three months short of the hard wall where tenure had to happen, or became impossible: the cutoff game.

Were the groves of academe best for him, really? He liked the teaching, fell asleep in the committee meetings, found the academic cant and paperwork boring. Life's sure erosions . . .

Studying fast-moving neutron stars had been fashionable a few years back, but in Gossian's careful phrasings he heard notes of skepticism. To the Chairman fell the task of conveying the senior faculty's sentiments.

Gossian seemed to savor the moment. "This fast-star fad—well, it is fading, some of your colleagues think."

He bit his lip. *Don't show anger.* "It's not a 'fad'—it's a set of discoveries."

"But where do they lead?"

"Too early to tell. We *think* they're ejected from supernova events, but maybe that's just the least imaginative option."

"One of the notes here says the first 'runaway pulsar,' called the Mouse, is now well understood. The other, recent ones will probably follow the same course."

"Too early to tell," Ralph persisted. "The field needs time—"

"But you do not have time."

There was the crux of it. Ralph was falling behind in paper count. Even in the small "runaway pulsar" field, he was outclassed by others with more resources, better computers, more time. California was in a perpetual budget crisis, university resources were declining, so pressure was on to Bring in the (Federal) Bucks. Ralph's small program supported two graduate students, sure, but that was small potatoes.

"I'll take this under advisement," Ralph said. The utterly bland phrase did nothing to help his cause, as was clear from the chairman's face—but it got him out of that office.

He did not get much sleep that night. Irene had to leave early and he got a double coffee on the way into his office. Then he read Andy's paper carefully and thought, sipping.

Few astronomers had expected to find so many runaway neutron stars.

Their likely origin began with two young, big stars, born circling one another. One went supernova, leaving a neutron star still in orbit. Later, its companion went off, too, spitting the older neutron star out, free into interstellar space.

Ralph had begun his UCI work by making painstaking maps in the microwave frequency range. This took many observing runs on the big radio antennas, getting dish time where he could around the world. In these maps he found his first candidate, G369.23–0.82. It appeared as a faint finger in maps centered on the plane of the galaxy, just a dim scratch. A tight knot with a fuzzy tail.

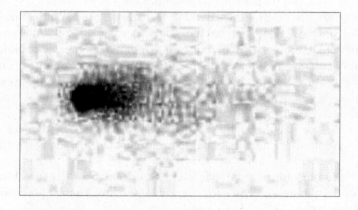

He had found it with software that searched the maps, looking for anything that was much longer than it was wide. This retrieved quite a few of the jets that zoomed out of regions near black holes, and sometimes from the disks orbiting young stars. He spent months eliminating these false signatures, looking for the telltales of compact stellar runaways. He then got time on the Very Large Array— not much, but enough to pull G369.23–0.82 out of the noise a bit better. This was quite satisfying.

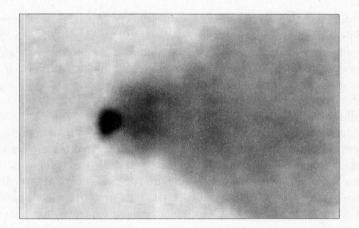

Ralph got more coffee and went back and studied his paper, published less than half a year ago. Until today, that was the best data anybody had. He had looked for signs of rotation in the pointlike blob in front, but there were none. The first runaway seen, the Mouse, discovered many years before, was finally shown to be a rotating neutron star—a pulsar, beeping its right radio beams out at the cupped ears of radio telescopes.

Then he compared in detail with Andy's new map:

Clean, smooth, beautiful. He read the Conclusions section over again, mind jittery and racing.

> We thus fail to confirm that G369.23–0.82 is a pulsar. Clearly it has a bow shock, creating a wind nebula, undoubtedly powered by a neutron star. Yet at highest sensitivity there is no trace of a pulsed signal in microwaves or optical, within the usual range of pulsar periods. The nebular bow shock cone angle implies that G369.23–0.82 is moving with a Mach number of about 80, suggest-

ing a space velocity ~ 120 km/s through a local gas of density ~ 0.3 per cubic cm. We use the distance estimate of Eilek et al. for the object, which is halfway across the galaxy. These dynamics and luminosity are consistent with a distant neutron star moving at a velocity driven by ejection from a supernova. If it is a pulsar, it is not beaming in our direction.

Beautiful work. *Alas.*

The bright region blazed forth, microwave emission from high energy electrons. The innermost circle was not the neutron star, just the unresolved zone too small for even Arecibo to see. At the presumed distance, that circle was still bigger than a solar system. The bow shock was a perfect, smooth curve. Behind that came the microwave emission of gas driven back, heated and caught up in what would become the wake. At the core was something that could shove aside the interstellar gas with brute momentum. A whole star, squeezed by gravity into a ball about as big as the San Francisco Bay area.

But how had Andy gotten such fine resolution?

Ralph worked through the numbers and found that this latest map had picked up much more signal than his earlier work. The object was brighter. Why? Maybe it was meeting denser gas, so had more radiating electrons to work with?

For a moment he just gazed at the beauty of it. He never lost his sense of awe at such wonders. That helped a bit to cool his disgruntlement. Just a bit.

There wasn't much time between Andy's paper popping up on the astro-ph Web site and his big spring trip. Before leaving, he retraced his data and got ahead on his teaching.

He and Irene finessed their problems, or at least delayed them. He got through a week of classes, put in data-processing time with his three graduate students, and found nothing new in the radio maps they worked on.

Then came their big, long-planned excursion. Irene was excited, but he now dreaded it.

His startup money had some travel funds left in it, and he had made the mistake of mentioning this to Irene. She jumped at the chance, even though it was a scientific conference in a small town—"But it's in *France,*" she said, with a touch of round-eyed wonder he found endearing.

So off they jetted to the International Astronomical Union meeting in Briancon, a pleasant collection of stone buildings clinging to the French Alps. Off season, crouching beneath sharp snowy peaks in late May, it was charming and uncrowded and its delights went largely ignored by the astronomers. Some of the attendees went on hikes in the afternoon but Ralph stayed in town, talking, networking like the ambitious workaholic he was. Irene went shopping.

The shops were featuring what she called the Hot New Skanky Look, which she showed off for him in their cramped hotel room that evening. She flounced around in an off-the-shoulder pink blouse, artfully showing underwear and straps. "Skanky" certainly caught the flavor, but still he was distracted.

In their cramped hotel room, jet-lagged, she used some of her first-date skills, overcoming his distance. That way he got some sleep a few hours later. Good hours, they were.

The morning session was interesting, the afternoon a little slow. Irene did sit in on some papers. He couldn't tell if she was interested in the science itself, or just because it was part of his life. She lasted a few hours and went shopping again, saying, "It's my way of understanding their culture."

The conference put on a late afternoon tour of the vast, thick-walled castles that loomed at every sharp peak. At the banquet inside one of the cold, echoing fortresses they were treated to local specialties, a spicy polenta and fresh-caught trout. Irene surveyed the crowd, half of them still wearing shorts and T-shirts, and remarked, "Y'know, this is a quirky profession. A whole room of terribly smart people, and it never occurred to them to try to get by on their looks."

He laughed; she had a point. She was a butterfly among the astro-drones, turning heads, smiles blossoming in her wake. He felt enhanced to have her on his arm. Or maybe it was the wine, a *Vin Local* red that went straight to his head, with some help from the two-kilometer altitude.

They milled around the high, arched reception room after the dessert. The crowd of over 200 was too energized to go off to bed, so they had more wine. Ralph caught sight of Andy Lakehurst then. Irene noted his look and said, "Uh oh."

"Hey, he's an old friend."

"Oh? You're glaring at him."

"Okay, let's say there's some leftover baggage."

She gave him a veiled look, yawned, and said. "I'll wander off to the room, let you boys play."

Ralph nodded, barely listening. He eavesdropped carefully to the crowd gathered around Andy. Lanky and with broad shoulders, the man's booming voice carried well, over the heads of just about everybody in the room. Andy was going on about good ol' G369.23–0.82. Ralph edged closer.

"—I figure maybe another, longer look at it, at G—"

"The Bullet," Ralph broke in.

"What?" Andy had a high forehead and it wrinkled as he stopped in mid-sentence.

"It looks like a bullet, why not call it that, instead of that long code?"

"Well," Andy began brightly, "people might mistake—"

"There's even the smoke trailing behind it, the wake" Ralph said, grinning. "Use that, if you want it to get into *Scientific American*."

"Y'know, Ralph, you haven't changed."

"Poorer, is all."

"Hey, none of us went into this to get rich."

"Tenure would be nice."

"Damn right, buddy." Andy clapped him on the shoulder. "I'm going up for it this winter, y'know."

He hadn't, but covered with, "Well deserved. I'm sure you'll get it," and couldn't resist adding, "Harvard's a tough sell, though. Carl Sagan didn't make it there."

"Really?" Andy frowned, then covered with, "So, uh, you think we should call it the Rifle?"

"The Bullet," Ralph said again. "It's sure going fast, and we don't really know it's a neutron star."

"Hey, it's a long way off, hard to diagnose."

"Maybe it's distant, I kinda wonder—"

"And it fits the other parameters."

"Except you couldn't find a pulse, so maybe it's not a pulsar."

"Gotta be," Andy said casually, and someone interrupted with a point Ralph couldn't hear and Andy's gaze shifted to include the crowd again. That gave Ralph a chance to think while Andy worked the room.

There were nearly a thousand pulsars now known, rotating neutron stars that flashed their lighthouse beams across the galaxy. Some spun a thousand times in a second, others were old and slow, all sweeping their beams out as they rotated. All such collapsed stars told their long tale of grinding decay; the slower were older. Some were ejected after their birth in bright, flashy supernovas—squashed by catastrophic compression in nuclear fire, all in a few minutes.

Here in Briancon, Ralph reflected, their company of smart, chattering chimpanzees—all evolved long after good ol' G369.23–0.82 had emerged from its stellar placenta—raptly studied the corpses of great calamities, the murder of stars by remorseless gravity.

Not that their primate eyes would ever witness these objects directly. They actually saw, with their football field–sized dishes, the brilliant emissions of fevered electrons, swirling in celestial concert around magnetic fields. Clouds of electrons cruised near the speed of light itself, squeezing out their waves—braying to the whole universe that they were alive and powerful and wanted everyone to know it. Passing gaudy advertisements, they were, really, for the vast powers wrecking silent violences in the slumbering night skies.

"We're out of its beam, that's got to be the answer," Andy said, turning back to Ralph and taking up their conversation again, his smile getting a little more rigid. "Not pointed at us."

Ralph blinked, taken unaware; he had been vaguely musing. "Uh, I'm thinking maybe we should consider every possibility, is all." Maybe he had taken one glass too many of the *Vin Local*.

"What else could it be?" Andy pressed his case, voice tightening. "It's compact, moving fast, bright at the leading edge, luminosity driven by its bow shock. A neutron star, charging on out of the galaxy."

"If it's as far away as we think. What if it isn't?"

"We don't know anything else that can put out emissions like that."

He could see nearby heads nodding. "We have to think . . ." grasping for something . . . "uh, outside the box." Probably the *Vin Local* talking.

Smiling, Andy leaned close and whispered through his tight, no-doubt-soon-to-be-tenured lips, "Ol' buddy, you need an idea, to beat an idea."

Definitely the *Vin Local*, yes.

He awoke next morning with a traffic accident inside his skull. Only now did he remember that he had exchanged polite words with Harkin, the eminence gris of the Very Large Array, but there was no news about getting some observing time there. And he still had to give his paper.

It was a botch.

He had a gaudy Powerpoint presentation. And it even ran right on his laptop, a minor miracle. But the multi-colored radio maps and graphics failed to conceal a poverty of ideas. If they could see a pulsed emission from it, they could date the age and then look back along the track of the runaway to see if a supernova remnant was there—a shell of expanding hot gas, a celestial bull's eye, confirming the whole theory.

He presented his results on good ol' G369.23–0.82. He had detailed microwave maps of it, plenty of calculations—but Andy had already given his talk, showing that it wasn't a pulsar. And G369.23–0.82—Ralph insisted on calling it the Bullet, but puzzled looks told him that nobody much liked the coinage—was the pivot of the talk, alas.

"There are enough puzzling aspects here," he said gamely, "to suspend judgment, I think. We have a habit of classifying objects because they superficially resemble others."

The rest was radio maps of various blobby radio-emitting clouds he had thought could be other runaways . . . but weren't. Using days of observing time at the VLA, and on other dish systems in the Netherlands and Bologna, Italy, he had racked up a lot of time.

And found . . . nothing. Sure, plenty of supernova remnants, some shredded fragments of lesser catastrophes, mysterious leftovers fading fast in the radio frequencies—but no runaways with the distinctive tails first found in the famous Mouse. He tried to cover the failure by riffing through quick images of these disappointments, implying without saying that these were open possibilities. The audience seemed to like the swift, color-enhanced maps. It was a method his mother had taught him while playing bridge: finesse when you don't have all the tricks.

His talk came just before lunch and the audience looked hungry. He hoped he could get away with just a few questions. Andy rose at the back and asked innocently, "So why do you think the, uh, Bullet is *not* a neutron star?"

"Where's the supernova remnant it came from?" Ralph shot back. "There's nothing at all within many light years behind it."

"It's faded away, probably," Andy said.

A voice from the left, one of the Grand Old Men, said, "Remember, the, ah, Bullet is all the way across the galaxy. An old, faint remnant it might have escaped is hard to see at that distance. And—a shrewd pursing of lips—"did you look at a sufficiently deep sensitivity?"

"I used all the observing time I had," Ralph answered, jumping his Powerpoint slides back to a mottled field view—random flecks, no structure obvious. "The region in the far wake of the Bullet is confusion limited."

Astronomers described a noisy background with that term, meaning that they could not tell signal from noise. But as he fielded a few more quick questions he thought that maybe the jargon was more right than they knew. Confusion limited what they could know, taking their mayfly snapshots.

Then Andy stood again and poked away at details of the data, a bit of tit for tat, and finishing with a jibe: "I don't understand your remark about not jumping to classify objects just because they superficially resemble other ones."

He really had no good reason, but he grinned and decided to joke his way through. "Well, the Bullet doesn't have the skewed shape of the Duck . . ."—which was another oddly shaped pulsar wake, lopsided fuzz left behind by a young pulsar Andy had discovered two years ago. "Astronomers forget that the public likes descriptive terms. They're easier to remember than, say, G369.23–0.82." Some laughter. "So I think it's important to keep our options open. And not succumb to the sweet temptation to go sensational, y'know—" He drew a deep breath and slipped into a falsetto trill he had practiced in his room. *"Runaway star! High speeds! It will escape our galaxy entirely!"*

—and it got a real laugh.

Andy's mouth twisted sourly and, too late, Ralph remembered that Andy had been interviewed by some flak and then featured in the supermarket tabloid *National Enquirer*, with wide-eyed headlines not much different.

Oops.

Irene had been a hit at Briancon, though she was a bit too swift for some of his colleagues. She was kooky, or as some would say, annoying. But at her side he felt he had fully snapped to attention. Sometimes, she made it hard to concentrate; but he did. When he got back to UCI there was teaching to catch up on, students to coach, and many ideas to try out. He settled in.

Some thought that there were only two kinds of science: stamp collecting and physics. Ernest Rutherford had said that, but then, he also thought the atomic nucleus had no practical uses.

Most scientific work began with catalogs. Only later did the fine distinctions come to suggest greater, looming laws. Newton brought Galileo's stirrings into differential laws, ushering forth the modern world.

Astronomers were fated to mostly do astro-botany, finding varieties of deep space objects, framing them into categories, hoping to see if they had a common cause. Stamp collecting.

Once the theory boys decided, back in the 1970s, that pulsars were rotating neutron stars, they largely lost interest and moved onto quasars and jets and then to gamma-ray bursters, to dark energy—an onward marching through the botany, to find the more basic physics. Ralph didn't mind their blithe inattention. He liked the detective story aspects, always alive to the chance that just because things looked similar didn't mean they had to be the same.

So he prowled through all the data he had, comparing with other maps he had gotten at Briancon. There were plenty of long trails in the sky, jets galore—but no new candidates for runaway neutron stars. So he had to go back to the Bullet to make progress. For that he needed more observing time.

For him and Irene, a good date had large portions of honesty and alcohol. Their first night out after the French trip he came armed with attention span and appetite. He kept an open mind to chick flicks—rented and hauled back to her place, ideally—and even to restaurants that played soft romantic background music, which often did the same job as well as a chick flick.

He had returned to news, both good and bad. The department wasn't interested in delaying his tenure decision, as he had fleetingly asked (Irene's suggestion) before leaving. But: Harkin had rustled up some observing time for him on the VLA. "Wedges, in between the big runs," he told Irene.

"Can you get much with just slices of time?"

"In astronomy, looking hard and long is best. Choppy and short can do the same job, if you're lucky."

It was over a weekend, too, so he would not have to get someone to cover his classes.

So he was definitely up when they got to the restaurant. He always enjoyed squiring Irene around, seeing other guys' eyeballs follow them to their table—and telling her about it. She always got a round-eyed, raised eyebrow flash out of that. Plus, they both got to look at each other and eat. And if things went right this night, toward the dessert it might be like that scene in the *Tom Jones* movie.

They ordered: her, the caramelized duck breasts, and for him, tender Latin chicken with plantains. "A yummy start," she said, eyeing the upscale patrons. The Golden Coast abounded with Masters of the Universe, with excellently cut hair and bodies that were slim, casually elegant, carefully muscled (don't want to look like a *laborer*), the women running from platinum blonde through strawberry. "Ummm, quite *soigne*," Irene judged, trying out her new French vocabulary.

Ralph sensed some tension in her, so he took his time, glancing around at the noisy crowd. They carried themselves with that look not so much of energetic youth but rather of expert maintenance, like a Rolls with the oil religiously changed every 1500 miles. Walking in their wake made most working stiffs feel just a touch shabby.

He said, "Livin' extra-large in OC," with a rueful smile, and wondered if she saw this, the American Dream Extreme, as he did. They lived among dun-colored hills covered by pseudo-Spanish stucco splendor, McMansions sprawled across tiny lots. "Affluenza," someone had called it, a disease of always wanting more: the local refrain was "It's all about you," where the homes around yacht-ringed harbors and coves shone like filigree around a gemstone. He respected people like her, in business, as the drivers who created the wealth that made his work possible. But just today he had dropped her at the Mercedes dealership to pick up her convertible, in for an oil change. Pausing, he saw that the place offered free drop-in car washes, and while you waited with your cinnamon-topped decaf cappuccino you could get a manicure, or else work on your putting at a green around the back. Being an academic scientist around here felt like being the poor country cousin.

He watched her examine all the flatware and polish it with her napkin. This was not routine; she was not a control freak who obsessed over the organization of her entire life, or who kept color-coded files, though, yes, she was a business MBA.

"That was a fun trip," Irene said in the pensive tones that meant she was being diplomatic. "Ah . . . do you want to hang out with those people all your life?"

"They're pretty sophisticated, I think," he said defensively, wondering where she was going with this.

"They—how to put this pleasantly?—work too damn hard."

"Scientists do."

"Business types, too—but they don't talk about nothing else."

"It was a specialist's conference. That's all they have in common."

"That, and being outrageously horny."

He grinned. "You never thought that was a flaw before."

"I keep remembering the M.I.T. guy who believed he could wow me with—"she made the quote marks with her fingers—"a 'meaningful conversation' that included quoting *The Simpsons*, 'gangsta' flicks, and some movie trilogy."

"That was Tolkein."

"Elves with swords. I thought you guys were scientists."

"We have . . . hobbies."

"Obsessions, seems like."

"Our work included?"

She spread her hands. "I respect that you're deeply involved in astronomy, sure." She rolled her eyes. "But it pays so little! And you're headed into a tough tenure decision. After all these years!"

"Careers take time."

"Lives do, too. Recall what today is?"

He kept his face impassive, the only sure way to not get the deer-in-headlights expression he was prone to. "Uh, no . . ."

"Six months ago."

"Oh, yes. We were going to discuss marriage again."

Her eyes glinted. "And you've been hiding behind your work . . . again."

"Hey, that's not fair—"

"I'm not waiting forever."

"I'm in a crunch here. Relationships don't have a 'sell-by' date stamped on them—"

"Time waits for no man. I don't either."

Bottom line time, then. He asked firmly, "So instead I should . . . ?"

She handed him a business card.

"I should have known."

"Herb Linzfield. Give him a call."

"What inducement do I have?" He grinned to cover his concern.

She answered obliquely by ordering dessert, with a sideways glance and flickering little smile on her big, rich lips. On to *Tom Jones*.

To get to the VLA from UC Irvine means flying out of John Wayne airport—there's a huge, looming bronze statue of him in cowboy duds that somehow captures the gait—and through Phoenix to Albuquerque. Ralph did this with legs jammed up so he couldn't open his laptop, courtesy of Southwest Airlines—and then drove a Budget rental west through Socorro.

The crisp heat faded as he rose up the grade to the dry plateau, where the Array sprawls on railroad lines in its long valley. Along the Y-shaped rail line the big dishes could crawl, ears cupped toward the sky, as they reconfigured to best capture in their "equivalent eye" distant radiating agonies. The trip through four-lane blacktop edged with sagebrush took most of a day. When Ralph arrived Harkin had been observing a radio galaxy for eight hours.

"Plenty more useful than my last six hours," he said, and Harkin grinned.

Harkin wore jeans, a red wool shirt, and boots and this was not an affectation. Locals described most of the astronomers as "all hat and no cattle," a laconic indictment of fake Westerners. Harkin's face seemed to have been crumpled up and then partly smoothed out—the effect of twenty years out here.

The radio galaxy had an odd, contorted look. A cloud of radio emitting electrons wrapped around Harkin's target—a brilliant jet. Harkin was something of a bug about jets, maintaining that they had to be shaped by the magnetic fields they carried along. Fields and jets alike all were offhand products of the twirling disk far down in the galactic center. The black holes that caused all this energy release were hard to discover, tiny and cloaked in gas. But the jets carried out to the universe striking advertisements, so they were the smoking gun. Tiny graveyards where mass died had managed to scrawl their signatures across the sky.

Ralph looked at the long, spindly jet in Harkin's radio images. It was like a black-and-white of an arrow. There was a lot of work here. Hot-bright images from deep down in the churning glory of the galactic core, then the long slow flaring as the jet moved above the galactic disk and met the intergalactic winds.

Still, it adamantly kept its direction, tightly arrowing out into the enveloping dark. It stretched out for many times the size of its host galaxy, announcing its presence with blaring radio emission. That came from the spiraling of high-energy electrons around magnetic field lines, Ralph knew, yet he always felt a thrill at the raw radio maps, the swirls and helical vortices bigger than swarms of stars, self-portraits etched by electrons alive with their mad energies.

At the very end, where it met the intergalactic gas, the jet got brighter, saturating the images. "It's turned toward us, I figure," Harkin said. "Bouncing off some obstruction, maybe a molecular cloud."

"Big cloud," Ralph said.

"Yeah. Dunno what it could be."

Mysteries. Many of them would never be solved. In the murder of stars, only tattered clues survived.

Harkin was lean and sharp-nosed, of sturdy New England stock. Ralph thought Harkin looked a lot like the jets he studied. His bald head narrowed to a crest, shining as it caught the overhead fluorescents. Harkin was always moving from the control boards of the ganged dishes to the computer screens where images sharpened. Jets moved with their restless energies, but all astronomers got were snapshots. Black holes spewed out their advertisements for around a hundred million years, so Harkin's jet was as old as the dinosaurs. To be an astronomer was to realize one's mayfly nature.

"Hope I haven't gotten you to come all this way for nothing." Harkin brought up on a screen the total file on G369.23–0.82.

He recognized one image from the first observations a year before, when Feretti from Bologna had picked it up in the background of some jet observations. Over the last three years came others, Andy's and Ralph's extensive maps, polarization data files, the works. All digital; nobody kept much on paper anymore.

"Y'see here?" An observing schedule sheet. "The times when G369.23–0.82 is in the sky, I've only got three slices when we're reconfiguring the dishes. Each maybe half an hour long."

"Damn!" He grimaced. "Not much."

"No." Harkin looked a bit sheepish. "When I made that promise to you, well, I thought better of it the next day. But you'd already left for your flight in Geneva."

"*Vin Local*," Ralph said. "It hit me pretty hard, too."

Harkin nodded at his feet, embarrassed. "Uh, okay, so about G369.23–0.82 —"

"I call it the Bullet. Easier than G369.23–0.82."

"Oh yeah." Hankin shrugged. "You said that in Briancon."

But what could he do in half-hour fragments? He was thinking this through when Harkin asked the same question.

"Andy pretty well showed there was no pulsar beam," Harkin said helpfully, "so . . . ?"

Ralph thumbed through his notes. "Can I get good clarity at the front end? The Bullet's bow shock?"

Harkin shook his head, looking disappointed. "No way, with so little observing time. Look, you said you had some out-of-the-box ideas."

Ralph thought furiously. "How about the Bullet's tail, then?"

Harkin looked doubtful, scribbled a few numbers on a yellow lined pad. "Nope. It's not that luminous. The wake dies off pretty fast behind. Confusion limited. You'd get nothing but noise."

Ralph pointed. "There's a star we can see at the edge of the Bullet."

Harkin nodded. "A foreground star. Might be useful in narrowing down how far away it is."

"The usual methods say it's a long way off, maybe halfway across the galaxy."

"Um. Okay, leave that for later."

Ralph searched his mind. "Andy looked for pulses in what range?" He flipped through his notes from Briancon. "Short ones, yes—and nothing slower than a ten-second period."

Harkin nodded. "This is a young neutron star. It'll be spinning fast."

Ralph hated looking like an amateur in Harkin's eyes, but he held his gaze firmly. "Maybe. Unless plowing through all that gas slows it faster."

Harkin raised his eyebrows skeptically. "The Mouse didn't slow down. It's spinning at about a tenth of a second, period. Yusef-Zadeh and those guys say it's maybe twenty-five thousand years old."

Twenty-five thousand years was quite young for a pulsar. The Mouse pulsar was a sphere of nothing but neutrons, a solar mass packed into a ball as small as San Francisco, spinning around ten times a second. In the radio-telescope maps that lighthouse beam came, from a dot at the very tip of a snout, with a bulging body right behind, and a long, thin tail: mousy. The Mouse discovery had set the paradigm. But just being first didn't mean it was typical.

Ralph set his jaw, flying on instinct—"Let's see."

So in the half hours when the dish team, instructed by Harkin, was slewing the big white antennas around, chugging them along the railroad tracks to new positions, and getting them set for another hours-long observation—in those wedges, Ralph worked furiously. With Harkin overseeing the complex hand-offs, he could command two or three dishes. For best use of this squeezed schedule, he figured to operate in the medium microwave band, around 1 or 2 GHz. They had been getting some interference the last few days, Harkin said, maybe from cell phone traffic, even out here in the middle of a high desert plateau—but that interference was down around 1 GHz, safely far below in frequency. He need not worry about callers ringing each other up every few minutes and screwing up his data.

He took data carefully, in a way biased for looking at very long-time fluctuations. In pulsar theory, a neutron star was in advanced old age by the time the period of its rotation, and so the sweeping of its lighthouse beam, was a second long. They harnessed their rotation to spew out their blaring radiation—live fast, die young. Teenage agonies. Only they didn't leave beautiful corpses—they *were* corpses. Pulsars should fade away for even slower rates; only a handfull were known out in the two-or three-minute zone.

So this search was pretty hopeless. But it was all he could think of, given the half-hour limit.

He was dragging by the time he got his third half hour. The dish team was crisp, efficient, but the long observing runs between his slices got tedious. So he used their ample computing resources to process his own data—big files of numbers that the VLA software devoured as he watched the screens. Harkin's software had fractured the Bullet signal into bins, looking for structure in time. It caressed every incoming microwave, looking for repeating patterns. The computers ran for hours.

Hash, most of it. But then . . .

"What's that?" He pointed to a blip that stuck up in the noisy field. The screen before him and Harkin was patchy, a blizzard of harmonics that met and clashed and faded. But as the Bullet data ran and filtered, a peak persisted.

Harkin frowned. "Some pattern repeating in the microwaves." He worked the data, peering at shifting patterns on the screen. "Period of . . . lessee . . . forty-seven seconds. Pretty long for a young pulsar."

"That's got to be wrong. Much too long."

In astronomy it paid to be a skeptic about your work. Everybody would be ready to pounce on an error. Joe Weber made some false detections of gravitational waves, using methods he invented. His reputation never fully recovered, despite being a brilliant, original scientist.

Harkin's face stiffened. "I don't care. That's what it is."

"Got to be wrong."

"Damn it, Ralph, I know my own codes."

"Let's look hard at this."

Another few hours showed that it wasn't wrong.

"Okay—funny, but it's real." Ralph thought, rubbing his eyes. "So let's look at the pulse itself."

Only there wasn't one. The pattern didn't spread over a broad frequency band. Instead, it was there in the 11-GHz range, sharp and clear—and no other peaks at all.

"That's not a pulsar," Harkin said.

Ralph felt his pulse quicken. "A repeating brightness. From something peaking out of the noise and coming around to our point of view every forty-seven seconds."

"Damn funny." Harkin looked worried. "Hope it's not a defect in the codes."

Ralph hadn't thought of that. "But these are the best filter codes in the world."

Harkin grinned, brown face rumpling like leather. "More compliments like that and you'll turn my pretty little head."

So Harkin spent two hours in deep scrutiny of the VLA data processing software— and came up empty. Ralph didn't mind because it gave him time to think. He took a break partway through—Harkin was not the sort to take breaks at all—and watched a Cubs game with some of the engineers in the Operations room. They had a dish down for repairs but it was good enough to tip toward the horizon and pick up the local broadcast from Chicago. The Cubs weren't on any national 'cast and two of the guys came from UC, where the C was for Chicago. The Cubs lost but they did it well, so when he went back Ralph felt relaxed. He had also had an idea. Or maybe half of one.

"What if it's lots bigger than a neutron star?" he asked Harkin, who hadn't moved from his swivel chair in front of the six-screen display.

"Then what's the energy source?"

"I dunno. Point is, maybe it's something more ordinary, but still moving fast."

"Like what?"

"Say, a white dwarf—but a really old, dead one."

"So we can't see it in the visible?" The Hubble telescope had already checked at the Bullet location and seen nothing.

"Ejected from some stellar system, moving fast, but not a neutron star—maybe?"

Harkin looked skeptical. "Um. Have to think about it. But . . . what makes the relativistic electrons, to give us the microwaves?"

That one was harder to figure. Elderly white dwarfs couldn't make the electrons, certainly. Ralph paused and said, "Look, I don't know. And I have to get back to UCI for classes. Can I get some more time wedged in between your re-configs?"

Harkin looked skeptical. "I'll have to see."

"Can you just send the results to me, when you can find some time?"

"You can process it yourself?"

"Give me the software and, yeah, sure."

Harkin shrugged. "That forty-seven-second thing is damn funny. So . . . okay, I suppose . . ."

"Great!" Ralph was tired but he at least had his hand in the game. Wherever it led.

Ralph spent hours the next day learning the filter codes, tip-toeing through the labyrinth of Harkin's methods. Many thought Harkin was the best big-dish observer in the world, playing the electronics like a violin.

Harkin was a good teacher because he did not know how to teach. Instead he just showed. With it came stories and examples, some of them even jokes, and some puzzling until Harkin changed a viewing parameter or slid a new note into the song and it all came clear. This way Harkin showed him how to run the programs, to see their results skeptically. From the angular man he had learned to play a radio telescope as wide as a football field like a musical instrument, to know its quirks and deceptions, and to draw from it a truth it did not know. This was science, scrupulous and firm, but doing it was an art. In the end you had to justify every move, every conclusion, but the whole argument slid forward on intuition, like an ice cube skating on its own melt.

"Say, Andy," Ralph said casually into his cell phone, looking out the big windows at New Mexico scrub and the white radio dishes cupped toward the sky. "I'm trying to remember if you guys looked at long periods in your Bullet data. Remember? We talked about it at Briancon."

"Bullet? Oh, G369.23–0.82."

"Right, look, how far out did you go on period?"

A long pause. Ralph thought he could hear street noise. "Hey, catch you at a bad time?"

"No, just walking down Mass Ave, trying to remember. I think we went out to around thirty-second periods. Didn't see a damn thing."

"Oh, great. I've been looking at the Bullet again and my preliminary data shows something that, well, I thought I'd check with you."

"Wow." Another pause. "Uh, how slow?"

Ralph said cautiously, "Very. Uh, we're still analyzing the data."

"A really old pulsar, then. I didn't think they could still radiate when they were old."

"I didn't, either. They're not supposed to." Ralph reminded himself to check with the theorists.

"Then no wonder we couldn't find its supernova remnant. That's faded, or far away."

"Funny, isn't it, that we can pick up such weak signals from a pulsar that's halfway across the galaxy. Though it has been getting brighter, I noticed."

Andy sounded puzzled. "Yeah, funny. Brighter, um. I wonder if it shows up in any earlier survey."

"Yeah, well I thought I'd let you know."

Andy said slowly, "You know, I may have glimpsed something, but will get back to you."

They exchanged a few personal phrases and Ralph signed off.

Harkin was working the screens but turned with eyebrows raised.

Ralph said, "Bingo."

As soon as Irene came into the coffee shop and they kissed in greeting, he could see the curiosity in her eyes. She was stunning in her clingy blue dress, while he strutted in his natty suit. He had told her to dress up and she blinked rapidly, expectant. "Where are we going tonight?"

He said, not even sitting down, "Y'know, the only place where I can sing and people don't throw rotten fruit at me is church."

Irene looked startled. "I didn't think you were religious."

"Hey, it's a metaphor. I pay for a place to dance, too, so—let's go. To the Ritz."

Her eyebrows arched in surprise. "What an oblique invitation. 'Puttin' on the Ritz'?"

As they danced on the patio overlooking sunset surfers, he pulled a loose strand of hair aside for her, tucking it behind her ear. She was full of chatter about work. He told her about his work on the Bullet and she was genuinely interested, asking questions. Then she went back to tales of her office intrigues. Sometimes she seemed like a woman who could survive on gossip alone. He let it run down a bit and then said, as the band struck up *Begin the Beguine*, "I need more time."

She stiffened. "To contemplate the abyss of the M word?"

"Yes. I'm hot on the trail of something."

"You didn't call Herb Linzfield, either, did you." Not a question.

"No."

"Oh, fine."

He pulled back and gazed at her lips. Lush, as always, but twisted askew and scrunched. He knew the tone. *Fine. Yeah, okay, right. Fine. Go. Leave. See. If. I. Care.*

He settled into it then, the rhythm: of thickets of detail, and of beauty coming at you, unannounced. You had to get inside the drumroll of data, hearing the software symphonies, shaped so that human eyes could make some hominid sense of it. These color-coded encrustations showed what was unseeable by the mere human eye—the colors of the microwaves. Dry numbers cloaked this beauty, hid the ferocious glory.

When you thought about it, he thought, the wavelengths they were "seeing" with, through the enormous dish eyes, were the size of their fingers. The waves came oscillating across the blunt light years, messages out of ancient time. They slapped down on the hard metal of a radio dish and excited electrons that had been waiting there to be invited into the dance. The billions of electrons trembled and sang and their answering oscillations called forth capturing echoes in the circuits erected by men and women. More electrons joined the rising currents, fashioned by the zeros and 1s of computers into something no one had ever seen: pictures for eyes the size of mountains. These visions had never existed in the universe. They were implied by the waves, but it took intelligence to pull them out of the vagrant sizzle of radio waves, the passing microwave blizzard all life lived in but had never seen. Stories, really, or so their chimpanzee minds made of it all. Snapshots. But filling in the plot was up to them.

In the long hours he realized that, when you narrow your search techniques tuned to pick up exactly what you're looking for, there's a danger. The phrase astronomers use for that is, "I wouldn't have seen it if I hadn't believed it."

The paper on the astro-ph Web site was brief, quick, three pages.

Ralph stared at it, open-mouthed, for minutes. He read it over twice. Then he called Harkin. "Andy's group is claiming a forty-seven-second peak in their data."

"Damn."

"He said before that they didn't look out that far in period."

"So he went back and looked again."

"This is stealing." Ralph was still reeling, wondering where to go with this.

"You can pull a lot out of the noise when you know what to look for."

Whoosh—He exhaled, still stunned. "Yeah, I guess."

"He scooped us," Harkin said flatly.

"He's up for tenure."

Harkin laughed dryly. "That's Harvard for you." A long pause, then he rasped, "But what *is* the goddamn thing?"

The knock on his apartment door took him by surprise. It was Irene, eyes intent and mouth askew. "It's like I'm off your radar screen in one swift sweep."

"I'm . . ."

"Working. Too much—for what you get."

"Y'know," he managed, "art and science aren't a lot different. Sometimes. Takes concentration."

"Art," she said, "is answers to which there are no questions."

He blinked. "That sounds like a quotation."

"No, that was *me*."

"Uh, oh."

"So you want a quick slam bam, thank you Sam?"

"Well, since you put it that way."

An hour later she leaned up on an elbow and said, "News."

He blinked at her sleepily "Uh . . . what?"

"I'm late. Two weeks."

"Uh. Oh." An anvil out of a clear blue sky.

"We should talk about—"

"Hoo boy."

"—what to do."

"Is that unusual for you?" First, get some data.

"One week is tops for me." She shaped her mouth into an astonished O. "Was."

"You were using . . . we were . . ."

"The pill has a small failure rate, but . . ."

"Not zero. And you didn't forget one?"

"No."

Long silence. "How do you feel about it?" Always a good way to buy time while your mind swirled around.

"I'm thirty-two. It's getting to be time."

"And then there's us."

"Us." She gave him a long, soulful look and flopped back down, staring at the ceiling, blinking.

He ventured, "How do you feel about . . ."

"Abortion?"

She had seen it coming. "Yes."

"I'm easy, if it's necessary." Back up on the elbow, looking at him "Is it?"

"Look, I could use some time to think about this."

She nodded, mouth aslant. "So could I."

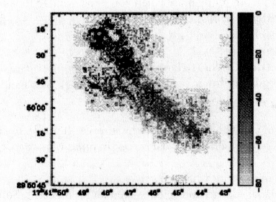

Ralph had asked the Bologna group—through his old friends, the two Fantis—to take a scan of the location. They put the Italian 'scopes on the region and processed the data and sent it by Internet. It was waiting the next morning, 47 megs as a zipped attachment. He opened the attachment with a skittering anxiety. The Bologna group was first rate, their work solid.

On an Internet visual phone call he asked, "Roberto, what's this? It can't be the object I'm studying. It's a mess."

On-screen, Roberto looked puzzled, forehead creased. "We wondered about that, yes. I can improve the resolution in a few days. We could very well clear up features with more observing time."

"Yes, could you? This has got to be wrong."

A head-bob. "We will look again, yes."

47 seconds . . .

The chairman kept talking but Ralph was looking out his window at the eucalyptus weaving in the vagrant coastal winds. Gossian was listing hurdles to meet before Ralph would be "close to tenure"—two federal grants, placing his Ph.D.

students in good jobs, more papers. All to get done in a few months. The words ran by, he could hear them, but he had gone into that place he knew and always welcomed, where his own faith dwelled. The excitement came up in him, first stirrings, the instinct burning, his own interior state of grace. The idea swarmed up thick in his nostrils, he blinked—

"Ralph? You listening?"

"Oh, uh, yeah." *But not to you, no.*

He came into the physics building, folding his umbrella from a passing rain storm, distracted. There were black umbrellas stacked around like a covey of drunken crows. His cell phone cawed.

Harkin said, "Thought I'd let you know there's not much time I can use coming up. There's an older image, but I haven't cleaned it up yet."

"I'd appreciate anything at all."

"I can maybe try for a new image tomorrow, but I'm pretty damn busy. There's a little slot of time while the Array reconfigures."

"I sent you the Fantis' map—"

"Yeah, gotta be wrong. No source can change that much so fast."

Ralph agreed but added, "Uh, but we should still check. The Fantis are very good."

"If I have time," Harkin said edgily.

Between classes and committees and the long hours running the filter codes, he completely forgot about their dinner date. So at 9 P.M. his office phone rang and it was Irene. He made his apologies, distracted, fretting. He looked tired, his forehead gray and lined, and he asked, "No . . . change?"

"No."

They sat in silence and finally he told her about the Fanti map.

She brightened visibly, glad to have some distraction. "These things can change, can't they?"

"Sure, but so fast! They're big, the whole tail alone is maybe light-years long."

"But you said the map is all different, blurred."

"The whole object, yes."

"So maybe it's just a mistake?"

"Could be, but the Fantis are really good . . ."

"Could we get together later?"

He sighed. "I want to look at this some more." To her silence he added more apologies, ending with, "I don't want to lose you."

"Then remember where you put me."

The night wore on.

Wouldn't have seen it if I hadn't believed it.

The error, he saw, might well lie in their assumptions. In his.

It had to be a runaway neutron star. It had to be a long way off, halfway across the galaxy. They knew that because the fraying of the signal said there was a lot of plasma in the way.

His assumptions, yes. It had to be.

Perfectly reasonable. Perfectly wrong?

He had used up a lot of his choppy VLA time studying the oblong shroud of a once-proud star, seen through the edge of the Bullet. It was fuzzy with the debris of gas it threw off, a dying sun. In turn, he could look at the obscuration—how much the emission lines were absorbed and scattered by intervening dust, gas, and plasma. Such telltales were the only reliable way to tell if a radio image came from far away or nearby. It was tricky, using such wobbly images, glimpsed through an interstellar fog.

What if there was a lot more than they thought, of the dense plasma in between their big-eyed dishes and the object?

Then they would get the distance wrong. Just a like a thick cloud between you and the sun. Dispersing the image, blurring it beyond recognition—but the sun was, on the interstellar scale, still quite close.

Maybe this thing was nearer, much nearer.

Then it would have to be surrounded by an unusually dense plasma—the cloud of ionized particles that it made, pushing on hard through the interstellar night. Could it have ionized much more of the gas it moved through, than the usual calculations said? How? Why?

But what *was* the goddamn thing?

He blinked at the digital arrays he had summoned up, through a thicket of image and spectral processors. The blurred outlines of the old star were a few pixels, and nearby was an old, tattered curve of a supernova remnant—an ancient spherical tombstone of a dead sun. The lines had suffered a lot of loss on their way through the tail of the Bullet. From this he could estimate the total plasma density near the Bullet itself.

Working through the calculation, he felt a cold sensation creep into him, banishing all background noise. He turned the idea over, feeling its shape, probing it. Excitement came, tingling but laced with caution.

Andy had said, *I wonder if it shows up in any earlier survey.*

So Ralph looked. On an Italian radio map of the region done eleven years before there was a slight scratch very near the Bullet location. But it was faint, an order of magnitude below the luminosity he was seeing now. Maybe some error in calibration? But a detection, yes.

He had found it because it was bright now. Hitting a lot of interstellar plasma, maybe, lighting up?

Ralph called Harkin to fill him in on this and the Fanti map, but got an answering machine. He summed up briefly and went off to teach a mechanics class.

Harkin said on his voice mail, "Ralph, I just sent you that map I made two days ago, while I had some side time on a 4.8 GHz observation."

"Great, thanks!" he called out before he realized Harkin couldn't hear him. So he called and when Harkin picked up, without even a hello, he said, "Is it like the Fanti map?"

"Not at all."

"Their work was pretty recent."

"Yeah, and what I'm sending you is earlier than theirs. I figure they screwed up their processing."

"They're pretty careful . . ."

"This one I'm sending, it sure looks some different from what we got before. Kinda pregnant with possibility."

The word, *pregnant*, stopped him for a heartbeat. When his attention returned, Harkin's voice was saying, " — I tried that forty-seven-second period filter and it didn't work. No signal this time. Ran it twice. Don't know what's going on here."

The e-mail attachment map was still more odd.

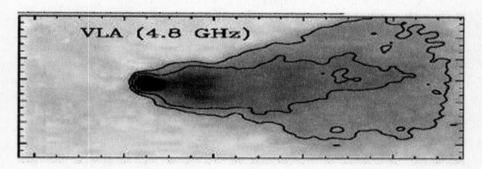

Low in detail, because Harkin had not much observing time, but clear enough. The Bullet was frayed, longer, with new features. Plunging on, the Bullet was meeting a fresh environment, perhaps.

But this was from two days ago.

The Bologna map was only fourteen hours old.

He looked back at the messy Bologna view and wondered how this older picture could possibly fit with the 4.8 GHz map. Had the Fantis made some mistake?

"Can you get me a snapshot right now?" Ralph asked. "It's important."

He listened to the silence for a long moment before Harkin said, "I've got a long run on right now. Can't it wait?"

"The Fantis at Bologna, they're standing by that different looking map. Pretty strange."

"Ummm, well . . ."

"Can you get me just a few minutes? Maybe in the download interval — "

"Hey, buddy, I'll try, but — "

"I'll understand," but Ralph knew he wouldn't.

His home voicemail from Irene said, fast and with rising voice tone, "Do onto others, right? So, if you're not that into me, I can stop returning your calls, e-mails—not that there are any—and anyway, blocking is so dodge-ball-in-sixth-grade, right? I'll initiate the phase-out, you'll get the lead-footed hint, and that way, you can assume the worst of me and still feel good about yourself. You can think, hey, she's not over her past. Social climber. Shallow business mind. Workaholic, maybe. Oh, no, that's you, right? And you'll have a wonderful imitation life."

A long pause, time's nearly up, and she gasped, paused, then: "Okay, so maybe this isn't the best idea."

He sat, deer in the headlights, and played it over.

They were close, she was wonderful, yes.

He loved her, sure, and he had always believed that was all it took.

But he might not have a job here inside a year.

And he couldn't think of anything but the Bullet.

While she was wondering if she was going to be a mother.

Though, he realized, she had not really said what she thought about it all.

He had no idea what to say. At a talk last year about Einstein, the speaker quoted Einstein's wife's laconic comment, that sometimes when the great man was working on a problem he would not speak to anyone for days. She had left him, of course. But now Ralph could feel a certain kinship with that legendary genius. Then he told himself he was being fatuous, equating this experience . . .

Still, he let it all slide for now.

His eighth cup of coffee tasted bitter. He bit into a donut for a sugar jolt. When had he eaten last?

He took a deep breath and let it out to clear his head.

He was sure of his work now, the process—but still confused.

The earlier dispersion measure was wrong. That was clear from the broadening of the pulses he had just measured. Andy and everybody else had used the usual interstellar density numbers to get the Bullet's distance. That had worked out to about five thousand light years away.

From his pulse measurements he could show that the Bullet was much closer, about thirty light years away. They were seeing it through the ionized and compressed plasma ahead and around the . . . what? Was it a neutron star at all?

And a further consequence—if the Bullet was so close, it was also much smaller, and less intrinsically luminous.

While the plume was huge, the Bullet itself—the unresolved circle at the center of it all, in Andy's high-resolution map—need only be a few hundred kilometers long. Or much less; that was just an upper limit.

Suppose that was the answer, that it was much closer. Then its energy output— judging that it was about equal to the radiated power—was much less, too. He jotted down some numbers. The object was emitting power comparable to a nation's on Earth. Ten gigawatts or so.

Far, far below the usual radiated energies for runaway neutron stars.

He stared into space, mind whirling.

And the forty-seven-second period . . .

He worked out that if the object was rotating and had an acceleration of half an Earth gravity at its edge, it was about thirty meters across.

Reasonable.

But why was the shape of its radio image changing so quickly? In days, not the years typical of big astronomical objects. *Days.*

Apprehensively he opened the e-mail from Irene.

You're off the hook!

So am I.

Got my period. False alarm.

Taught us a lot, though. Me, anyway. I learned the thoroughly useful information (data, to you) that you're an asshole. Bye.

He sat back and let the relief flood through him.

You're off the hook. Great.

False alarm. Whoosh!

And asshole. Um.

But . . .

Was he about to do the same thing she had done? Get excited about nothing much?

Ralph came into his office, tossed his lecture notes onto the messy desk, and slumped in his chair. The lecture had not gone well. He couldn't seem to focus. Should he keep his distance from Irene for a while, let her cool off? What did he really want, there?

Too much happening at once. The phone rang.

Harkin said, without even a hello, "I squeezed in some extra observing time. The image is on the way by e-mail."

"You sound kind of tired."

"More like . . . confused." He hung up.

It was there in the e-mail.

Ralph stared at the image a long time. It was much brighter than before, a huge outpouring of energy.

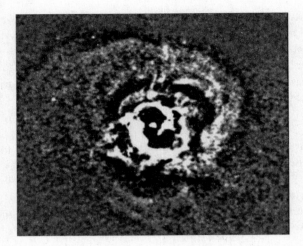

His mind seethed. The Fanti result, and now this. Harkin's 4.8 GHz map was earlier than either of these, so it didn't contradict either the Fantis or this. A time sequence of something changing fast—in days, in hours.

This was no neutron star.

It was smaller, nearer, and they had watched it go to hell.

He leaned over his desk, letting the ideas flood over him. *Whoosh.*

Irene looked dazed. "You're kidding."

"No. I know we've got a lot to talk through, but—"

"You bet."

"—I didn't send you that e-mail just to get you to meet me." Ralph bit his lip and felt the room whirl around.

"What you wrote," she said wonderingly. "It's a . . . star ship?"

"Was. It got into trouble of some kind these last few days. That's why the wake behind it—" he tapped the Fantis' image—"got longer. Then, hours later, it got turbulent, and—it exploded."

She sipped her coffee. "This is . . . was . . . light years away?"

"Yes, and headed somewhere else. It was sending out a regular beamed transmission, one that swept around as the ship rotated, every forty-seven seconds."

Her eyes widened. "You're sure?"

"Let's say it's a working hypothesis."

"Look, you're tired, maybe put this aside before jumping to conclusions."

He gazed at her and saw the lines tightened around the mouth. "You've been through a lot yourself. I'm sorry."

She managed a brave, thin smile. "It tore me up. I do want a child."

He held his breath, then went ahead. "So . . . so do I."

"Really?" They had discussed this before but her eyelids fluttered in surprise.

"Yes." He paused, sucked in a long breath, and said, "With you."

"Really?" She closed her eyes a long time. "I . . . always imagined this."

He grinned. "Me, too. Time to do it."

"Yes?"

"Yes." *Whoosh.*

They talked on for some moments, ordered drinks to celebrate. Smiles, goofy eyes, minds whirling.

Then, without saying anything, they somehow knew that they had said enough for now. Some things should not be pestered, just let be.

They sat smiling at each other and in a soft sigh she said, "You're worried. About . . ."

Ralph nodded. How to tell her that this seemed pretty clear to him and to Harkin, but it was big, gaudy trouble in the making. "It violates a basic assumption we always make, that everything in the night sky is natural."

"Yeah, so?"

"The astronomy community isn't like Hollywood, y'know. It's more like . . . a priesthood."

He sipped his coffee and stared out the window. An airplane's wing lights winked as it coasted down in the distance toward the airport. Everybody had seen airplanes, so seeing them in the sky meant nothing. Not so for the ramscoop ship implied by his radio maps.

There would be rampant skepticism. Science's standards were austere, and who would have it differently? The angles of attack lived in his hands, and he now faced the long labor of calling forth data and calculations. To advance the idea would take strict logic, entertaining all other ideas fairly. Take two steps forward, one back, comparing and weighing and contrasting—the data always leading the skeptical mind. It was the grand dance, the gavotte of reason, ever-mindful of the eternal possibility that one was wrong.

Still . . . When serendipity strikes . . . let it. Then seize it.

"You need some sleep." Her eyes crinkled with concern. "Come home with me."

He felt a gush of warm happiness. She was here with him and together they could face the long battle to come.

"Y'know, this is going to get nasty. Look what happened to Carl Sagan when he just argued there *might* be intelligent life elsewhere."

"You think it will be that hard to convince people?"

"Look at it this way. Facing up to the limits of our knowledge, to the enormity of our ignorance, is an acquired skill—to put it mildly. People want certainty."

He thought, *If we don't realize where the shoreline of reasonably well-established scientific theory ends, and where the titanic sea of undiscovered truth begins, how can we possibly hope to measure our progress?*

Irene frowned. Somehow, after long knowledge of her, he saw that she was glad of this chance to talk about something larger than themselves. She said slowly, "But . . . why is it that your greatest geniuses—the ones you talk about, Hawking, Feynman, Newton—humbly concede how pitifully limited our reach is?"

"That's why they're great," he said wryly. *And the smaller spirits noisily proclaim the certainty of their conclusions. Well, here comes a lot of dissent, doubt, and skepticism.*

"And now that ship is gone. We learned about them by watching them die."

She stared at him. "I wonder . . . how many?"

"It was a big, powerful ship. It probably made the plasma ahead of it somehow. Then with magnetic fields it scooped up that plasma and cooked it for energy. Then shot it out the back for propulsion. Think of it as like a jet plane, a ramscoop. Maybe it was braking, using magnetic fields—I dunno."

"Carrying passengers?"

"I . . . hadn't thought of that."

"How big is it? . . . was it?"

"Maybe like . . . the *Titanic*."

She blinked. "That many people."

"Something like people. Going to a new home."

"Maybe to . . . here?"

He blinked, his mind cottony. "No, it was in the plane of the sky. Otherwise we'd have seen it as a blob, head on, no tail. Headed somewhere fairly near, though."

She sat back, gazing at him with an expression he had not seen before. "This will be in the papers, won't it." Not a question.

"Afraid so." He managed a rueful smile. "Maybe I'll even get more space in *National Enquirer* than Andy did."

She laughed, a tinkling sound he liked so much.

But then the weight of it all descended on him. *So much to do* . . . "I'll have to look at your idea, that they were headed here. At least we can maybe backtrack, find where they came from."

"And look at the earlier maps, data?" she ventured, her lip trembling. "From before . . ."

"They cracked up. All that life, gone." Then he understood her pale, tenuous look. *Things living, then not.* She nodded, said nothing.

He reached out and took her hand. A long moment passed and he had no way to end it but went on anyway. "The SETI people could jump on this. Backtrack this ship. They can listen to the home star's emissions . . ."

Irene smiled without humor. "And we can send them a message. Condolences."

"Yeah." The room had stopped whirling and she reached out to take his hand.

"Come on."

As he got up wearily, Ralph saw that he was going to have to fight for this version of events. There would always be Andys who would triangulate their way to advantage. And the chairman, Gossian . . .

Trying for tenure—supposedly a cool, analytic process—in the shouting match of a heated, public dispute, a howling media firestorm—that was almost a contradiction in terms. But this, too, was what science was about. His career might survive all that was to come, and it might not—but did that matter, standing here on the shores of the titanic ocean he had peered across?

in the river

JUSTIN STANCHFIELD

The old proverb to the contrary, it *is* possible to go home again—but, as the suspenseful tale that follows suggests, if your voyage away from home has been transformative enough, you might have difficulty recognizing it when you get *back*. . . .

New writer Justin Stanchfield is a rancher who lives with his family in Wise River, Montana. His stories have appeared in *Interzone, Black Gate, On Spec, Paradox,* and *Empire of Dreams and Miracles,* as well as in *Cricket, Boy's Life,* and *Jack & Jill.*

J enna Ree screamed as she was dragged into the cold air, a keening, inhuman wail as the oxygenated water poured out of her lungs. She lashed out with her arms and legs but the strange, pale creatures holding her were too strong. They strapped her to a hard board then carried her away from the rectangular hatch that led back to the warmth and safety of the ship beneath the airlock. Panic struck as the last of the water drained out her throat.

"Don't fight it. Take long, deep breaths, Dr. Ree," one of the creatures said. Another, its face framed in brown hair pushed the first creature aside.

"Jenna? It's me, Val. You have to breathe."

"She can't understand you," the first creature said. "Now step back, Dr. Yastrenko. Please. Let us work."

The harsh, clipped sounds meant nothing to her. Only the roaring in her ears seemed real. She tried to beg, but her olfactor no longer functioned. The stark, white light drew to a pinpoint, the edge of her vision a dark ring.

"Valium, now! Get the resuscitator ready."

Something bit her on the throat, but Jenna was beyond caring. She had the vague sensation of her jaws being pried apart and something cold and metallic pushed down her throat. 'Let me go home to die,' she thought as the light faded. 'Why won't they let me go home?'

She swam again in the River, the light soft and blue. Outside the moss covered walls, beyond the scattered viewports, stars burned bright, always moving as the world revolved around its axis. She knew in abstraction the River was a construct, a machine grown to travel the void, an endless stream that flowed from star to star, but the distances seemed impossible. None here had seen Old Home. None would live long enough to see it again. Jenna felt a wave of sorrow pass over her tongue, the flavor of copper and bitter fish.

Far below, where the water thickened with krill and fresh salts, the family drifted with languid abandon around a heat vent. Jenna tried to dive down, but couldn't move. One of the people noticed her and broke away. She knew Finder by the mottled patch of green behind her long skull. Slowly, her elegant tentacles fluttering in the rhythm of sadness, the great creature rose into the cooler water above.

"Sister," Jenna breathed in the language of respect. "I think I am ill. I can no longer swim down to meet you."

"Strange sister . . ." Finder graced her with a clutching arm, a simple brush across her face. Jenna tasted regret, but also joy in the ancient pilot's words. "It is time for you to go home."

"But, I am home."

"No, small one. You must go to your birth home now, above the water."

"There is only death above the water." Jenna repeated the old children's adage she had learned as a hatchling. Or had she? Her thoughts were mottled, a confused, tainted patchwork. Again, Finder brushed her cheek.

"Good-bye, Strange Sister. May your waters be rich."

"No!" Jenna tried to follow the massive creature down, but couldn't. Already, the sweet water grew thin. Cold, she shivered. Nearby, a fait rustling caught her attention and she forced her eyes open. The light was painfully sharp, but from the corner of her vision she saw movement. The creature with the bearded face approached and loomed over her, a length of beige cloth in his hand. He lay the blanket over her chest and smoothed it around her body.

"Welcome back, sleepy head. You don't know how glad I am to see you."

To Jenna's surprise, she understood the man, though the words made little sense. Hesitantly, she tasted the air. A faint chemical trace drifted on it.

"Who are you?" she croaked.

"My name," he said slowly, "is Valeri Yastrenko. I'm your husband."

Her life fell into a new routine. Gone were the lazy mornings, replaced by painful, frustrating bouts of physical therapy. Jenna hated the exercises and the patronizing tone the therapists used, as if she was a damaged hatchling better left to the mercy of a swift death. But none of the indignities she faced in those sessions compared to the hellish hours that waited after the midday break.

"Good afternoon, Dr. Ree," said a gaunt woman with pale, lifeless hair. It made her look sickly, as if the flesh was ready to slip from her bones. "How are we today?"

"Why do you call me 'doctor'?" Jenna asked. It was becoming easier to form the clipped words. "Am I a healer?"

"No. You are a teacher."

"What do I teach?"

The pale woman smiled. Frustrated, Jenna repeated the question.

"What do I teach, Dr. Emily Markser?"

"Ah, you remembered my name today. Excellent." She patted Jenna's hand. "You are a professor of Abstract Mathematics. You volunteered for the Deep Immersion program because you felt you might be able to unlock the Tedris numbering system."

"You say the River People's name wrong." Jenna felt a sense of superiority over the pale woman. Even without her olfactor, she suspected she could make herself understood were she to return to the River. Markser and the others, she knew, never could. "Say it more slowly. *Theid triss.*"

"Thed trezz," Markser said, annoyed at the interruption. "Were you able to understand the Thed trezz numbering system?"

"ValeriYastrenko . . ." Jenna fumbled over the difficult phrase. "He says it is important that I remember how the Theid count."

"Yes. Very important." A bell chimed and Markser rose and crossed the small chamber. Despite the low gravity, the woman swam like a wounded eel. She returned a moment later, a sealed mug in hand. Jenna caught a whiff of the bittersweet hot liquid within. Tea, she remembered. Dr. Markser took a hesitant sip. "Until we understand their mathematics, we have no way to unravel their technology. That's why we came out here, to the edge of the solar system. We need to learn how they harvest zero-point energy."

Jenna frowned, Vaguely, she recalled the term and struggled to put it into context. "They call it the Unseen Flow."

Markser froze, her mug halfway to her lips. "You learned how they harness ZPG?"

"Yes." Jenna tried to frame her thoughts, but without her olfactor, without the thousand subtle expressions of taste and smell, she could not describe what she instinctively knew. She tried again, but failed. Cold sweat broke out on her face, and she felt herself become ill. The room seemed to draw in, the light flickering in nauseating pulses. She grabbed the table edge as the spinning sensation worsened. Shaking, unable to control her limbs, her eyes rolled up in their sockets. The light browned as she fell away from the confining chair. As darkness swept over her, she heard Markser yelling.

"Damn it. She's having another seizure."

"Why have you abandoned me?" Jenna cast her plea into the depths, but her words swirled away untasted. Farther below, lit from beneath by the warming vents, the family rested. A few lifted their long faces and sniffed the water, as if perhaps they caught a trace of her, but made no move to rise. Tears ran down Jenna's face and vanished in the eddies. At long last, Finder broke away from the pod and swam in long spirals upward. One of her tentacles dabbed at the wetness beneath Jenna's eyes, and carried the tear down to her broad, lipless mouth.

"Go home, Strange Sister," she said softly. "Go home."

"Jenna?"

She forced her eyes open despite the throbbing in her skull. The lights in the little room were too bright, pinpoints surrounded by rainbow clouds. Valeri Yastrenko brushed a loose strand of hair away from her eyes.

"You have to stop scaring me like this," he said. "I am getting too old for these roller coasters of yours."

She understood less than half of what he said, but gathered enough from his tone to fill in the blanks. More and more she realized the key to this flat, often meaningless jargon depended on the listener as much as the speaker. She tried to imitate his smile, but the contortions made her headache worse.

"I was ill?"

"Ill?" Yastrenko gave his shaggy head a quick shake. "You died for almost a minute and a half. They had to use the defib on you."

"I was back in the River. I did not want to leave. I want to go back to my family." She stared into his deep, gray eyes, then added, "Please."

He looked away, an expression on his face she could not understand. After a moment, he let out a long, slow breath. "Jenna, do you remember what they did to you? The surgeons, I mean, before you went to the Theid triss?" He stumbled over the word, as if perhaps the flavor of it burned his lips. "They implanted a packet of alien nerve tissue in your limbic system, and another in your corpus callosum. It was these strands of tissue that allowed you to interface."

Absently, Jenna freed her arm from beneath the confining blanket and let her fingers roam along her temples. A tiny scar rested above her left ear, the hair around it bristled and short. "The olfactor?"

"Yes." Gently, he pulled her hand away from the scar. "The olfactory node was attached to the interface points. It let you live among them. Let you communicate, maybe even think like they did. But, it is also the reason we had to take you out of the program earlier than expected. The alien tissue is breaking down and is affecting your brain. Dr. Markser and I agree we must remove the tissue before the damage becomes permanent."

With a clarity Jenna had not experienced since being cast out of the River she recoiled, shocked at what the man suggested.

"If you do that," she forced the word out, "I will never be able to return."

"No. You won't." Yastrenko tried to touch her cheeks, but she batted his hand away. To her surprise, she saw tears form at the corner of his eyes. "Jenna, I don't want to lose you again. I want the old you to come back."

"I don't believe," Jenna said, void of any emotion, "she exists anymore."

She was alone.

Among the family she had never sensed this absence of contact. Even when separated, the currents carried their trace. Distance became irrelevant, every thought uttered a part of the common whole. Not until she had been severed from the endless thread that was the River did she truly understand what she had lost. Even her senses seemed diminished, the richness of existence depleted in this dry, sterile world. Slowly, fighting the vertigo, Jenna removed the straps around herself.

The room was mercifully empty. Jenna drifted weightless toward what at first appeared to be a portal into an adjoining chamber. Instead, she was disappointed to discover it only a reflection. She touched the mirror and frowned.

"Who are you?" Her fingers traced the outline of her face. Among the Theid, appearance meant little. One simply was. Here, everyone not only claimed to be different, but seemed to revel in it. Suddenly, she felt a tearing need to see the stars. Jenna pulled the sliding door aside and floated into the corridor beyond.

Padded walls formed tunnels, branching corridors that cut stark angles seemingly at random. A slight pull told Jenna which way out was, the ship's spin providing a mild gravity. Without current to carry her, Jenna dragged herself along the handrails as she wandered outward.

Her chest began to ache, her breathing irregular and quick as she increased her pace. Once, she passed several humans but said nothing, ignoring their startled expressions as she hurried past. Ahead, yet another corridor waited. Jenna reached the junction but couldn't decide which path to take. Her temples pounded, and exhausted, she closed her eyes.

"Why have you abandoned me?" She whispered, but knew there would be no reply. Already, the old dreams faded, the River's constant, swirling touch little more than the memory of a memory. Other memories intruded, odd glimpses of another life, a life she had carefully buried. Her hands shook violently as she curled into a tight ball, arms wrapped around her knees. The shaking in her limbs worsened, and she bit down on her lip, hoping the pain might hold back the flood of memories.

"No, no, no . . ." Jenna fought to stem the flood but couldn't. Her old life blossomed around her, disjointed flashes, bits and pieces of who she was before the surgeons had done their work. She sobbed, hard, wracking convulsions that tore the breath from her lungs. "No! Please, no!"

Darkness stole over her. Disoriented, she vomited. Sour bile burned her nose and throat as the contents of her stomach gushed out. From nowhere, hands closed around her shoulders. She tried to break free but no longer had the strength. From far off, as if she listened from the bottom of an empty shaft, she heard voices.

"Get her prepped for surgery," the voices said. "Those implants are coming out now."

Emptiness claimed her, a wash of dull pain that refused to leave. Jenna tried to move, but her head and shoulders were bound by hard points that dug uncomfortably into her flesh.

"Don't try to sit up." The voice was masculine and thickly accented. Jenna forced her eyes open. The light was dim, the temperature in the room cool and dry. A man stood over her, concern plain in his deep-set eyes. Despite the pain, Jenna smiled.

"Hello, Val."

"Hello, Jen." The man's bearded face split in a pleasant, relieved grin. She hadn't noticed how thick his accent was, or how wonderful his homely features could seem. He held a water bottle to her lips and let her take a short sip from the rigid straw. "Don't struggle, okay? They have you in full restraints until the anesthesia wears off."

"So I gathered." She closed her eyes and let her face go slack. It helped with the throbbing pain in her temples. "The implants are gone?"

"Yes."

"All of them?"

"The surgeons are confident they removed all the alien tissue. If you can trust a machine."

Jenna chuckled at the remark. For a scientist, Valeri Yastrenko was almost pathologically suspicious of robotic medicine. In so many ways he was an old-fashioned man, Earth-bound and proud of it. Part of his charm. Part of the reason she had fallen in love with him.

"I am so glad to have you back." His hand slipped into hers, his fingers so thick they forced hers apart. "How do you feel?"

"Drained," she said. "Empty. You can't imagine what it's like to be connected to them." She hesitated. Despite the worsening pain, but she had to know the answer to the question plaguing her. "Was I able to break their math?"

A long silence filled the room, broken only by the soft, liquid sound of the machinery tending her. She opened her eyes and focused on Yastrenko's face. "What happened?"

"Can we talk about this later?"

"No. Now."

"Jenna," Yastrenko sighed. "You stopped transmitting months ago. If you discovered how to translate their mathematics, you never bothered to tell us."

He bent down and kissed her forehead, the scent of his beard so like an old dog she had loved as a child. More memories rolled over her, a cascade effect as if the human side of her personality was punishing her for having been suppressed. She tried desperately to think about her time with the aliens, but nothing remained, as if a wall had been erected. A warm, sticky sensation crept through her limbs, no doubt a sedative released in response to her rising frustration. Unable to stay awake, she let herself be carried once more into watery dreams.

When she woke again, the restraints were gone, nothing holding her but blankets and a sleep net. Nearby, someone snored. Jenna risked turning her head. In the corner of the small room, Yastrenko floated like an overgrown infant wrapped in a blanket. She smiled at the thought, but quickly her mood dissolved, her last thoughts swarming out of the drug-induced haze. Her time among the Theid triss had been wasted. She felt as if she existed in two planes simultaneously, entangled particles which could never exist in the same place simultaneously. With a cold certainty, she knew she was losing her memories of the River.

She wondered if the strange, drifting creatures would remember her.

New routines filled Jenna's hours, the day broken into periods of therapy and rest. She went through the motions without enthusiasm. No matter how hard she pretended otherwise, the lost months preyed on her and more and more, she found herself drawn to the tiny observation lounge on the underside of the ship.

She still needed to see the stars.

The air in the narrow chamber was cool, the long window rimmed with creeping tendrils of frost, spent breath and escaped moisture transmuted into ethereal, ever-sifting patterns. Jenna's fingers traced the crystalline etchings with a fingernail. Something in the juxtaposition of ice against the unblinking stars called to her, as if the key she sought lay in front of her waiting only to be noticed. Her reflection in the thick glass mocked her, as if a second Jenna Ree floated on the other side of the window.

"Lights, off," she said softly. The room dimmed until nothing remained but a soft blue line marking the exit. Now the stars seemed brilliant, bright gems spilled on an oily pool. From this vantage, far beyond Pluto's orbit, the sun was simply one of billions. It had taken fifteen years from the moment the Theid triss ship had first popped into existence on the edge of the solar system, its beacon a mournful, un-changing wail, for humanity to mount this expedition. Jenna's life had been con-sumed by the enigmatic message, swallowed up in the attempt to establish contact. So much had passed during the decade and a half. Her courtship with Valeri. The partial decoding of the Theid triss language. The decision to build this ship and the long, four years' climb to reach the enormous alien vessel. Jenna craned her neck until she could see what lay beneath their own hull. A vague, cylindrical shadow blocked the Southern Cross, the water filled starship more than six kilometers in length. Compared to it, their own ship was like a barnacle on a whale's flank.

"Why did you bring us out here?" she whispered.

A faint, octagonal glow, one of the thousands of windows that dotted the alien craft, caught her eye. For a moment, she thought she saw something drift past, the elongated skull and sleek tendrils a vague phantom through the viewport. The Theid triss were so different. How could she even contemplate understanding them? Jenna leaned her forehead against the cold glass, desperate to see more, but the shape had moved on, ever in motion.

Motion.

Stars swirling. Frost crystals on glass, melting and reforming, nothing constant. Jenna felt herself tilting and pressed her arm against the ceiling to quell the vertigo as the avalanche of information struck, the wall breached. It was so simple. Over-whelmed, she pushed away from the dark window and hurried back into the bright corridors. Her mind buzzed with the new understanding, so much raw information she feared it might slip away if she didn't tell someone. She found Yastrenko outside the infirmary and let herself crash into his arms.

"Val," she said triumphantly. "I've found the key."

"The key?" He frowned, then, nodded, a brief smile creasing the lines around his eyes. "That is good, Jenna. Very good."

"You don't seem very excited." Jenna pushed away, deflated by his lack of re-sponse. "Don't you get it? I've finally found a way to reconcile our mathematic sys-tem with theirs. I've broken the code."

"Good." He kissed her, but his heart didn't seem in it. "I'm glad."

"What the hell is wrong with you? I thought you'd be thrilled? Don't you see, now we can finally get to work understanding their technology."

"Yes . . ." Yastrenko opened his mouth to say more, but fell silent. Gently, his big hands firm on her shoulders, he pushed her to arms' length until he could look her directly in the eyes. "Jenna, the Theid triss sent a communication a little over two hours ago. They want us to uncouple and move out to a safe distance. They intend to depart within the next three days."

"No." Jenna stared at him, unbelieving. "You can't let them leave. Not now. For God's sake, Val, we have to do something."

"I know." His voice fell until she thought he might burst into tears. "That's why Emily is having an olfactor node implanted."

"Markser?" Jenna's stomach twisted at the thought of the pale, humorless psychologist taking her place as liaison to the River. "You can't be serious? If anyone should go below, it should be me."

Yastrenko stared at her, his eyes unblinking. For one horrible moment, Jenna had the impression that he wished it was her and not Markser about to undergo the dangerous surgery. She recoiled, all too aware that something else lurked in his eyes, a glimpse of betrayal. Guilt. Shame. An acknowledgment. Jenna stared at him, too stunned to speak as what was left of her once-stable universe crashed with fractallike speed into nothingness. She felt a fool for not having seen it earlier. While she was lost in the strange world of the Theid triss, her husband had fallen in love with another woman.

Gravity increased, an off-tangent drag that piled loose objects against the rear corner of her tiny cabin as the Theid triss ship gradually boosted its spin rate. Chilled, Jenna wrapped a blanket around her shoulders as she sat at her work station, numbed by the day's events. She desperately wanted to blink and find the affair had been an illusion, another by-product of her immersion. She had known Emily Markser for years but had never thought of her as a rival. The woman seemed sterile, practically sexless, a pale caricature of cold, Ivy League detachment. How could someone as primal and vibrant as Valeri Yastrenko be attracted to her? Jenna pulled the blanket tighter. What had she done to drive her husband away?

"Stop it," she whispered, scolding herself. "I will not take the blame for this." She welcomed the anger. Nearby, something cracked, like the sound of wood breaking. Jenna stared down at her hand, surprised to see the thin plastic stylus wound between her fingers snapped cleanly in half.

She let the broken pieces fall with lazy ease toward the back corner of the room and stared at the scratch pad flickering quietly on her desk. Lines of hand-scratched symbols and equations glowed on the little screen, some familiar, some crude approximations of Theid taste-scent-touch charts. She hadn't even realized she was doodling until she recognized her own sweeping, almost sloppy handwriting. Though she still had no proofs, Jenna knew the long chains of numbers would balance. She sighed. "Maybe the bastard should have cheated on me months ago. Then we could have all gone home."

Behind her, someone coughed. Jenna turned slowly and saw Yastrenko waiting outside in the corridor, his hand on the doorsill.

"I just came to gather up my things," he said.

She nodded, but said nothing. Yastrenko slipped past her, found a duffle bag and quickly began stuffing clothing and personal items inside it. Jenna sat at her desk and watched him. Yastrenko pulled a final pair of socks from his locker then drew the string tight around the mesh bag.

"Jenna, I'm sorry," he began, but she cut him off.

"Don't. I don't want your apologies or your damned excuses. Maybe someday, but not right now."

He looked away, unable to meet her eyes. Duffle bag in hand, Yastrenko turned to leave, but stopped as he noticed the numbers on her scratchpad. "These are your theorems?"

Jenna nodded.

"It almost looks like you are describing harmonic vibrations."

"I am." Despite her anger, she couldn't shut out the sense of discovery. "Like everything about the Theid, nothing is absolute. It's no wonder we couldn't understand what they were trying to tell us. We wanted hard numbers. They don't even understand the concept. As a matter of fact, they only have two numbers in their lexicon."

"But, that is impossible." Yastrenko frowned. Jenna pulled the pad around, secretly enjoying his confusion as she traced the jumbled string of glyphs.

"To our way of thinking, yes. But not to theirs. To them, the entire universe is an unending string. For the Theid triss, there are only two numbers, one and not-one. Add one and one together and you don't get two. You get a greater one."

"A greater one?" He sounded doubtful, but leaned closer and studied the equations. "And that lets them manipulate space-time?"

"Apparently." Jenna shrugged. "I'm not a physicist."

Yastrenko stood, eyes locked on the pad and shook his head in wonder. "It's going to take years for us to reconcile this." He straightened, and suddenly the excitement in his eyes faded, replaced by guilt. "Jenna, I do love you."

"Strange way you have of showing it."

He gathered up his duffle and started once more into the corridor, but turned before he left the cramped chamber.

"I meant to tell you. The flight crew would like you to be in the cockpit when Emily goes below." His voice cracked around her name. "They need you to monitor her transmissions."

"I'll be there," she said, her tone flat. She waited until he was gone, then lay down on her bed and cried herself to sleep.

The cockpit reminded Jenna more of the trading floor of a stock brokerage than the control room of a spacecraft. She sat at the small work station one of the environmental engineers had escorted her to and tried to remain as unobtrusive as possible. To keep busy, she ran a third diagnostic check of the equipment linking Markser to the ship. Fast numbers scrolled across the screen, followed by "All systems are operating properly." Satisfied, she leaned back in the padded chair and waited. Across the circular chamber a young man with a thick red beard raised his voice.

"Captain, the Theid triss just sent a message."

Jenna winced at his horrible mispronunciation. A slender woman with short gray hair hurried across the room and joined him.

"What did they say?" Paula Spolar, the First Shift Pilot asked. Everyone in the control room listened intently as the bearded man read the translation.

"Caution given. Uncouple soon. We choose to leave in next day-cycle."

Jenna frowned. As much a she hated drawing attention to herself, she pulled her way towards the commo desk. "Did they use the Imperative or the Pending tense?" she asked.

"I'm not sure." The man stammered helplessly. "How do you tell the difference?"

"Sorry. I forget most people haven't spent six months living with the Theid triss." Jenna smiled to put him at ease. "Could I have the audio?"

"Sure." The technician leaned back to let Jenna see his work screen. A series of multi-hued spikes danced on the monitor as a low, mournful series of notes washed around them. Jenna shut her eyes and listened. A faint trill at the end of the final stem-verb told her what she needed to know. Even without an olfactor, the message was plain.

"Well?" Captain Spolar stared at her, waiting.

"They're going under thrust," Jenna said. "Probably within the next six hours. They want us to get clear before they engage their drivers."

"We can't let them go," the com-tech said, his frustration plain. "We've barely figured out how to talk to them."

"I don't think we have any choice in the matter," Jenna said quietly. She looked up at the captain. "The Theid triss take a long time to reach a consensus, but once they do, it's all but impossible to change their minds."

Spolar scratched her long, thin nose as she weighed their limited options. After a moment, she pressed the sense pad on the underside of her left wrist. "Air-lock? Proceed with immersion." She seemed to be speaking with ghosts as the transducers in her jaw relayed the message. "Send Dr. Markser below, but tell her if she hasn't convinced the aliens to abort within three hours she is to leave without question." To Jenna she added, "You better get to your station. Markser will be going below any minute now."

"All right." Jenna made her way back to her chair and eased into it. The link was still functioning, though Markser's bio-stats had risen dramatically. As much as she hated it, Jenna found herself sympathizing with Emily Markser. Memories of her own immersion came back, the stark, drowning sensation as the liquid filled her lungs, the sensory overload as the olfactor began gathering and emitting information. Jenna watched the monitor carefully. She had been given the luxury of months to train for her time with the Thied and it had still taken days before she adjusted to the aquatic environment. To expect Markser to do it in a matter of hours bordered on folly.

Without prelude, the bio-stats flared. Across the cockpit, the bearded technician called out, "She's in."

Quickly, Jenna split her screen. A watery blue glow filled the left side of the monitor, the video feed sharp. She watched Markser drift downward, feet first, tiny bubbles trailing in her wake. Three long, enormous shapes rose up from the depths to greet her. The nearest of the Theid triss wrapped long tentacles around Markser's legs. Immediately, the others joined the tangled dance. Jenna watched the other half of the screen as Markser's pulse raced, the adrenalin levels dangerously high.

"Stop fighting it," she whispered, as if the woman on the screen could hear her warning. The mainscreen at the front of the room lit up with the same view. A writhing jumble of tentacles all but hid Markser's desperate flailing as the Theid drew her deeper into the River.

"They're attacking her," someone shouted.

"No." Jenna raised her own voice. "It's a welcoming ritual."

She glanced again at Markser's stats. To her dismay, the woman's condition had worsened dramatically. Suddenly, the spiked graphs began to fall. Jenna spun her chair around.

"Captain," she said. "Markser's passed out."

With alarming speed, the image on the screen diminished as Markser continued to sink. The Theid triss cradled her as she drifted downward.

"Get her out of there," Spolar said over her link. "Send in the divers."

"Captain," Jenna stood up. "The Theid might see that as a threat. Right now, they consider Dr. Markser a guest. If we try to take her out by force they may very well defend her."

"I'll risk it," Spolar said. "We need to get her out of there before the aliens go under power. Send in the divers."

Two figures appeared on the screen, sleek black shapes in wetsuits, their faces obscured by diving masks. Although the oxygenated fluid in the River was breathable, the emergency crews had opted for traditional diving gear. Moving in formation, the pair swam rapidly toward the core. Jenna held her breath, waiting, watching.

With blinding speed, two of the Theid twisted around and lashed out at the divers. A gasp ran around the control room as on screen they watched the two humans beaten back. Bits of hoses and torn neoprene drifted in a cloud, along with thin traces of blood. Within seconds, the divers retreated, their naked bodies covered in welts. The Theid triss returned to Markser and escorted her out of camera range. A hard lump tightened in Jenna's stomach. She took a deep breath, then approached Spolar.

"Tell the airlock I'm on my way."

"What are you going to do?" Spolar asked.

"I'm going under." Jenna tried not to let her fear show through. "After that, it depends on the Theid."

By the time she reached the airlock the divers had already been taken to the infirmary. A smeared set of bloodied footprints led away from the sealed floor hatch. It was hot within the chamber but Jenna shivered. The closer she came to the hatchway, the stronger her fears grew. A single technician, the same young woman who had operated the airlock on her own immersion months ago, waited beside the control console.

"Hello doctor," the girl said. "Captain Spolar needs you to call in."

"Thanks." Jenna thumbed the intercom. Spolar's face, distorted by the fish-eye lens, flashed on-screen.

"Dr. Ree, FYI, the aliens have broken contact. I don't know if this is a technical problem or a deliberate response to what happened. Are you sure you want to go through with this?"

Jenna hesitated. The last thing, she realized, that she wanted was to return to the alien vessel. Before, armed with the symbiotic implants and the olfactor, she had been able to speak to the Theid in their own drifting, dreamlike language. She had become one of them, so much so that she had nearly lost herself. But now, lacking the enhancements, she had no idea if she could even make herself understood. Worse, she feared she might slip back into the Theid patterns, her sanity sacrificed. She wanted to turn and run, but instead faced the tiny lens.

"If I don't go, who will?"

She began undressing, letting her uniform and shoes drift to the far wall. The gravity had increased noticeably, the spin rate faster as the Thied triss prepped for launch. Behind her, she heard the door leading into the corridor sigh open.

"What in the hell do you think you're doing?"

Yastrenko stood in the doorway, his eyes red. He stepped toward her, but she drew back and crossed her arms over her breasts. Although Yastrenko had seen her naked hundreds of times, suddenly, standing in front of him in her underwear made her skin crawl.

"Markser's unconscious. I don't know if she fainted or if she's having seizures. Either way, she needs to get out before the Theid triss go under power."

"So, you play the hero, eh?" Yastrenko's heavy cheeks darkened. "Is this your way of getting back at me?"

"What?" Jenna gaped at her husband. "This has nothing to do with you. For that matter, it has nothing to do with Markser."

"Really?" Yastrenko snorted. "Then let the rescue teams go after her. Why do you have to throw this in everyone's face, the wounded heroine off to save her rival."

"I don't have time for this." Angry now, her earlier fear shunted aside, Jenna pulled her bra over her head, then slipped off her panties. To the tech, she said, "Open the lock."

Yastrenko glared at her as the outer door hissed shut. Jenna ignored him, concentrating instead on what she had to do as the air pressure in the little chamber rose. She pinched her nose and blew until her ears popped, then stepped to the hatch in the floor and took hold of the railing above it. Slowly, it slid aside. Water jiggled in the hatch as if a membrane was stretched taut across it.

"Jenna," Yastrenko said, pleading now. "Don't do this. I don't want to lose you again."

She met his eyes, but said nothing. Before she could change her mind, she grasped the rail, stepped into the water and pushed herself down.

The River was warm and thick as amniotic fluid, a comforting envelope. She let herself drift, the hunger for air growing in her lungs until she couldn't stand it any longer. Fighting her instincts, Jenna inhaled. Liquid poured down her throat, filled her airways, bubbled in her nose. She had forgotten how uncomfortable the transition was. Deliberately, she forced the fluid out, then took another breath. The emptiness in her chest abated as oxygen once more entered her bloodstream. She burped as the gas in her stomach gushed out, leaving a foul taste in her mouth, then drew another breath and swirled the syrupy water over her tongue. Old, half-forgotten flavors teased her. Salt. Copper. A hint of citrus and vinegar. Honey, urine, and rust. Every thought the Theid triss uttered drifted around her, a melange of swirling images. She tried to make sense of it, but couldn't. Without the olfactor to translate the faint chemical traces she was deaf. Still drifting, Jenna looked downward toward the softly glowing core.

Far below, a pair of dark shapes rose to meet her. Jenna froze. Every instinct said flee, and it took real effort not to kick back toward the airlock, already little more than a small white square above her. The Theid triss were peaceful by nature but tended to lash out if provoked. It was vital, she knew, to remain calm. She sculled with her fingertips to remain upright in the strong current as the pair of Theid, young hermaphrodites not yet grown to sexual maturity, arrived. She struggled to remember their names but couldn't.

The nearer of the Theid brushed a tentacle across her face, its skin slick and cool. The long, leathery arm withdrew. The pair of sentries studied her, their black, multifaceted eyes less than a meter from her own. One of them opened its broad mouth and sang a short, undulating trill. The overpowering taste of something that reminded Jenna of anchovies filled her mouth.

"I'm sorry," Jenna responded in the simple graphic forms the Theid triss used for radio communication. "I can't understand you."

The Theid repeated the phrase, then slowly backed away. Hesitantly, Jenna raised her right arm. When the sentries made no move, she experimented further and raised both arms over her head. Again, the pair did nothing. Jenna took it as a sign that she had passed their test.

"Thank you," she said, her own voice nearly unrecognizable to her. Slowly, she bent at the waist and flipped, ready to swim down and find where they had taken Markser.

A sharp pain bit her heel. Jenna gasped and rolled over. A brown cloud floated around her left foot. The tentacle that had delivered the lash followed her, ready to strike again. The warning was plain. She was not to descend.

"Please. I need to retrieve my friend." Jenna ignored the irony of the phrase. "She is ill. I have to take her home." She pointed at the bluish glow around the heat vent. Her movements more deliberate than before, Jenna twisted again until she faced head down and started to swim.

The water around her exploded. She gasped as lash after lash cut her skin, the tentacles that had earlier kissed her face now a flurry of whips. Unable to escape the onslaught, Jenna cured into a tight ball, wincing as the sentries flailed her unprotected skin. A new scent filled the water around her, her own blood. She felt herself tumbling, carried into the deeper, thicker waters by the River's flow.

"Please, stop!" she shouted, but couldn't remember if she was speaking Theid or English. It didn't matter. The sentries seemed unable, or unwilling, to listen. A strange detachment uncoiled in her as she realized she was about to die.

"Stop."

The word rumbled around her, a great, gushing hiss followed by a burst of acetic acid so strong it burnt the cuts that covered Jenna's back and legs. Abruptly, the storm of tentacles ended. Jenna felt a swirl of cool water around her as the sentries fluttered away. Stunned, she opened her eyes. A third Theid triss, a female fully twice the size of the young sentries, floated level with her, the creatures' dark eyes unreadable. Despite her pain, Jenna smiled.

"Finder?"

The old Theid's probing arms reached toward Jenna and gently ran along her back. She seemed concerned at the welts and blood. Speaking slowly, as if to a hatchling, Finder drew closer to Jenna.

"Strange sister," she rumbled. "Why have you come back?"

"My friend is ill," Jenna repeated, hoping she used the correct inflections. "Please. May I see her?"

Finder said nothing. Jenna's heart sank. Without the surgical enhancements, she realized, her words were little more than babble to the people she had once lived among. She drew a deep breath of the thick, salty water, but before she could say anything else, Finder opened her gill slits and released a bitter jet of yellowish fluid. Far below, more Theid triss picked up the scent, the command clear, and as one rose upward and stopped respectfully beneath Finder. Jenna stared in amazement as she saw Markser cradled in a nest of tentacles. The ancient female touched Jenna on the forehead, then repeated the gesture with Markser.

"Your sister?" Finder trilled.

Jenna looked down at the comatose woman. Markser's face was rigid, her arms and legs twitching as the seizures continued to wrack her nervous system. Jenna looked back at Finder, then touched her forehead. "Yes," she said. "My sister."

Finder fluttered her grasping arms, an acknowledgment. "Sister go home."

The enormous Theid triss released another command, greenish-gold in color, and without hesitation, the people below her started upward, bearing Markser toward the airlock. Finder waited until they were alone, then once again touched Jenna's forehead.

"My sister stay?" Finder kept her words simple, but the emotion was plain to Jenna even without an olfactor to interpret. "Go with the River now?"

For a fleeting moment Jenna almost said yes, the thought of traveling among the stars with the Theid triss enticing. She had been happy here once, content to share their long, endless dreams. But, she knew sadly, that time was gone. Her life, wrecked as it might be, lay elsewhere. Reverently, she swam closer to Finder and touched her tapered snout.

"I go home," she said.

Time seemed to fail. Jenna stopped breathing, afraid she might slip back into the Theid patterns that had once devoured her. Slowly, Finder drew a small device from under her torso and held it. Hesitantly, Jenna touched the strange object. Slick, gray ceramic swirled and curved it on itself, an endless twisted loop, as if a nautilus had been inverted then warped into something dangerous and alien. The device vibrated, the water around it warmed. Jenna stared into Finder's dark eyes.

"This is one of your engines," she said.

"You came for this, yes?"

"Yes," Jenna said softly. The massive Theid pressed the device into her hands.

"Sister, be well." Finder gave her a final caress with her grasping arms, then vanished into the swirling water. Jenna started upward. The Theid around the airlock drew back in a wide circle and let her pass. She paused beneath the airlock and took a last look around her, then darted through the square hatch. Strong arms grabbed her and helped her to the deck. She fell to her knees and let the water gush from her airways. Yastrenko looked chagrined as he wrapped a blanket around her shoulders.

"Thank God, you're back," he said. "Are you all right?"

Jenna wiped her face with the blanket and looked around the little chamber. Markser lay on a stretcher, surrounded by medics, a ventilator down her throat. Already, the woman seemed calmer. The device Finder had given her still pulsed in her grip. It seemed heavier out of the water, more energetic, almost alive. Carefully, she passed the device to the technician. Yastrenko stepped closer, but she warned him off with a frown. She wasn't ready to forgive him. Not yet. After everything that had happened, she wasn't sure it even mattered anymore.

"Am I all right?" She struggled to her feet, then calmly said. "No. But I will be."

incarnation Day

WALTER JON WILLIAMS

In every society, in every age, the transition from child to adult, the time of coming of age, is a profound and significant milestone, sometimes even a dangerous one. Never so profound, or dangerous, though as in the brilliantly depicted future society shown to us here by Walter Jon Williams, where successfully coming of age makes the difference between having flesh and life—and being erased.

Walter Jon Williams was born in Minnesota and now lives in Albuquerque, New Mexico. His short fiction has appeared frequently in *Asimov's Science Fiction*, as well as in *The Magazine of Fantasy and Science Fiction*, *Wheel of Fortune*, *Global Dispatches*, *Alternate Outlaws*, and in other markets, and has been gathered in the collections *Facets* and *Frankensteins and Other Foreign Devils*. His novels include *Ambassador of Progress*, *Knight Moves*, *Hardwired*, *The Crown Jewels*, *Voice of the Whirlwind*, *House of Shards*, *Days of Atonement*, *Aristoi*, *Metropolitan*, *City on Fire*, a huge disaster thriller, *The Rift*, and a *Star Trek* novel, *Destiny's Way*. His most recent books are the first two novels in his acclaimed Modern Space Opera epic, "Dread Empire's Fall," *Dread Empire's Fall: The Praxis* and *Dread Empire's Fall: The Sundering*. Coming up are two new novels, *Orthodox War* and *Conventions of War*. He won a long-overdue Nebula Award in 2001 for his story "Daddy's World," and took another Nebula in 2005 with his story "The Green Leopard Plague."

I t's your understanding and wisdom that makes me want to talk to you, Dr. Sam. About how Fritz met the Blue Lady, and what happened with Janis, and why her mother decided to kill her, and what became of all that. I need to get it sorted out, and for that I need a real friend. Which is you.

Janis is always making fun of me because I talk to an imaginary person. She makes even more fun of me because my imaginary friend is an English guy who died hundreds of years ago.

"You're wrong," I pointed out to her, "Dr. Samuel Johnson was a real person, so he's not imaginary. It's just my *conversations* with him that are imaginary."

I don't think Janis understands the distinction I'm trying to make.

But I know that *you* understand, Dr. Sam. You've understood me ever since we met in that Age of Reason class, and I realized that you not only said and did things that made you immortal, but that you said and did them while you were hanging around in taverns with actors and poets.

Which is about the perfect life, if you ask me.

In my opinion Janis could do with a Dr. Sam to talk to. She might be a lot less frustrated as an individual.

I mean, when I am totally stressed trying to comprehend the equations for electron paramagnetic resonance or something, so I just can't stand cramming another ounce of knowledge into my brain, I can always imagine my Dr. Sam—a big fat man (though I think the word they used back then was "corpulent")—a fat man with a silly wig on his head, who makes a magnificent gesture with one hand and says, with perfect wisdom and gravity, *All intellectual improvement, Miss Alison, arises from leisure.*

Who could put it better than that? Who else could be as sensible and wise? Who could understand me as well?

Certainly nobody *I* know.

(And have I mentioned how much I like the way you call me *Miss Alison*?)

We might as well begin with Fahd's Incarnation Day on Titan. It was the first incarnation among the Cadre of Glorious Destiny, so of course we were all present.

The celebration had been carefully planned to showcase the delights of Saturn's largest moon. First we were to be downloaded onto *Cassini Ranger*, the ship parked in Saturn orbit to service all the settlements on the various moons. Then we would be packed into individual descent pods and dropped into Titan's thick atmosphere. We'd be able to stunt through the air, dodging in and out of methane clouds as we chased each other across Titan's cloudy, photochemical sky. After that would be skiing on the Tomasko glacier, Fahd's dinner, and then skating on frozen methane ice.

We would all be wearing bodies suitable for Titan's low gravity and high-pressure atmosphere—sturdy, low to the ground, and furry, with six legs and a domelike head stuck onto the front between a pair of arms.

But my body would be one borrowed for the occasion, a body the resort kept for tourists. For Fahd it would be different. He would spend the next five or six years in orbit around Saturn, after which he would have the opportunity to move on to something else.

The six-legged body he inhabited would be his own, his first. He would be incarnated—a legal adult, and legally human despite his six legs and furry body. He would have his own money and possessions, a job, and a full set of human rights.

Unlike the rest of us.

After the dinner, where Fahd would be formally invested with adulthood and his citizenship, we would all go out for skating on the methane lake below the glacier. Then we'd be uploaded and head for home.

All of us but Fahd, who would begin his new life. The Cadre of Glorious Destiny would have given its first member to interplanetary civilization.

I envied Fahd his incarnation—his furry six-legged body, his independence, and even his job, which wasn't all that stellar if you ask me. After fourteen years of being a bunch of electrons buzzing around in a quantum matrix, I wanted a real life even if it meant having twelve dozen legs.

I suppose I should explain, because you were born in an era when electricity came from kites, that at the time of Fahd's Incarnation Day party I was not exactly a human being. Not legally, and especially not physically.

Back in the old days—back when people were establishing the first settlements beyond Mars, in the asteroid belt and on the moons of Jupiter and then Saturn—resources were scarce. Basics such as water and air had to be shipped in from other places, and that was very expensive. And of course the environment was extremely hazardous—the death rate in those early years was phenomenal.

It's lucky that people are basically stupid, otherwise no one would have gone.

Yet the settlements had to grow. They had to achieve self-sufficiency from the home worlds of Earth and Luna and Mars, which sooner or later were going to get tired of shipping resources to them, not to mention shipping replacements for all the people who died in stupid accidents. And a part of independence involved establishing growing, or at least stable, populations, and that meant having children.

But children suck up a lot of resources, which like I said were scarce. So the early settlers had to make do with virtual children.

It was probably hard in the beginning. If you were a parent you had to put on a headset and gloves and a body suit in order to cuddle your infant, whose objective existence consisted of about a skazillion lines of computer code anyway . . . well, let's just say you had to want that kid *really badly*.

Especially since you couldn't touch him in the flesh till he was grown up, when he would be downloaded into a body grown in a vat just for him. The theory being that there was no point in having anyone on your settlement who couldn't contribute to the economy and help pay for those scarce resources, so you'd only incarnate your offspring when he was already grown up and could get a job and help to pay for all that oxygen.

You might figure from this that it was a hard life, out there on the frontier.

Now it's a lot easier. People can move in and out of virtual worlds with nothing more than a click of a mental switch. You get detailed sensory input through various nanoscale computers implanted in your brain, so you don't have to put on oven mitts to feel your kid. You can dandle your offspring, and play with him, and teach him to talk, and feed him even. Life in the virtual realms claims to be 100 percent realistic, though in my opinion it's more like 95 percent, and only in the realms that *intend* to mimic reality, since some of them don't.

Certain elements of reality were left out, and there are advantages—at least if you're a parent. No drool, no messy diapers, no vomit. When the child trips and falls down, he'll feel pain—you *do* want to teach him not to fall down, or to bang his head on things—but on the other hand there won't be any concussions or broken bones. There won't be any fatal accidents involving fuel spills or vacuum.

There are other accidents that the parents have made certain we won't have to deal with. Accidental pregnancy, accidental drunkenness, accidental drug use.

Accidental gambling. Accidental vandalism. Accidental suicide. Accidentally acquiring someone else's property. Accidentally stealing someone's extra-vehicular unit and going for a joy ride among the asteroids.

Accidentally having fun. Because believe me, the way the adults arrange it here, all the fun is *planned ahead of time*.

Yep, Dr. Sam, life is pretty good if you're a grown-up. Your kids are healthy and smart and extremely well educated. They live in a safe, organized world filled with exciting educational opportunities, healthy team sports, family entertainment, and games that reward group effort, cooperation, and good citizenship.

It all makes me want to puke. If I *could* puke, that is, because I can't. (Did I mention there was no accidental bulimia, either?)

Thy body is all vice, Miss Alison, and thy mind all virtue.

Exactly, Dr. Sam. And it's the vice I'm hoping to find out about. Once I get a body, that is.

We knew that we weren't going to enjoy much vice on Fahd's Incarnation Day, but still everyone in the Cadre of Glorious Destiny was excited, and maybe a little jealous, about his finally getting to be an adult, and incarnating into the real world and having some real world fun for a change. Never mind that he'd got stuck in a dismal job as an electrical engineer on a frozen moon.

All jobs are pretty dismal from what I can tell, so he isn't any worse off than anyone else really.

For days before the party I had been sort of avoiding Fritz. Since we're electronic we can avoid each other easily, simply by not letting yourself be visible to the other person, and not answering any queries he sends to you, but I didn't want to be rude. Fritz was cadre, after all.

So I tried to make sure I was too busy to deal with Fritz—too busy at school, or with my job for Dane, or working with one of the other cadre members on a project. But a few hours before our departure for Titan, when I was in a conference room with Bartolomeo and Parminder working on an assignment for our Artificial Intelligence class, Fritz knocked on our door, and Bartolomeo granted him access before Parminder and I could signal him not to.

So in comes Fritz. Since we're electronic we can appear to one another as whatever we like, for instance Mary Queen of Scots or a bunch of snowflakes or even *you*, Dr. Sam. We all experiment with what we look like. Right now I mostly use an avatar of a sort-of Picasso woman—he used to distort people in his paintings so that you had a kind of 360-degree view of them, or parts of them, and I think that's kind of interesting, because my whole aspect changes depending on what angle of me you're viewing.

For an avatar Fritz's used the image of a second-rate action star named Norman Isfahan. Who looks okay, at least if you can forget his lame videos, except that Fritz added an individual touch in the form of a balloon-shaped red hat. Which he thought made him look cool, but which only seemed ludicrous and a little sad.

Fritz stared at me for a moment, with a big goofy grin on his face, and Parminder sent me a little private electronic note of sympathy. In the last few months Fritz had become my pet, and he followed me around whenever he got the chance. Sometimes he'd be with me for hours without saying a word, sometimes he'd talk the entire time and not let me get a single word in.

I did my best with him, but I had a life to lead, too. And friends. And family. And I didn't want this person with me every minute, because even though I was sorry for him he was also very frustrating to be around.

Friendship is not always the sequel of obligation.

Alas, Dr. J., too true.

Fritz was the one member of our cadre who came out, well, wrong. They build us—us software—by reasoning backwards from reality, from our parents' DNA. They find a good mix of our parents' genes, and that implies certain things about *us*, and the sociologists get their say about what sort of person might be needful in the next generation, and everything's thrown together by a really smart artificial intelligence, and in the end you get a virtual child.

But sometimes despite all the intelligence of everyone and everything involved, mistakes are made. Fritz was one of these. He wasn't stupid exactly—he was as smart as anyone—but his mental reflexes just weren't in the right plane. When he was very young he would spend hours without talking or interacting with any of us. Fritz's parents, Jack and Hans, were both software engineers, and they were convinced the problem was fixable. So they complained and they or the AIs or somebody came up with a software patch, one that was supposed to fix his problem—and suddenly Fritz was active and angry, and he'd get into fights with people and sometimes he'd just scream for no reason at all and go on screaming for hours.

So Hans and Jack went to work with the code again, and there was a new software patch, and now Fritz was stealing things, except you can't really steal anything in sims, because the owner can find any virtual object just by sending it a little electronic ping.

That ended with Fritz getting fixed yet *again*, and this went on for years. So while it was true that none of us were exactly a person, Fritz was less a person than any of us.

We all did our best to help. We were cadre, after all, and cadres look after their own. But there was a limit to what any of us could do. We heard about unanticipated feedback loops and subsystem crashes and weird quantum transfers leading to fugue states. I think that the experts had no real idea what was going on. Neither did we.

There was a lot of question as to what would happen when Fritz incarnated. If his problems were all software glitches, would they disappear once he was meat and no longer software? Or would they short-circuit his brain?

A check on the histories of those with similar problems did not produce encouraging answers to these questions.

And then Fritz became *my* problem because he got really attached to me, and he followed me around.

"Hi, Alison," he said.

"Hi, Fritz."

I tried to look very busy with what I was doing, which is difficult to do if you're being Picasso Woman and rather abstract-looking to begin with.

"We're going to Titan in a little while," Fritz said.

"Uh-huh," I said.

"Would you like to play the shadowing game with me?" he asked.

Right then I was glad I was Picasso Woman and not incarnated, because I knew that if I had a real body I'd be blushing.

"Sure," I said. "If our capsules are anywhere near each other when we hit the atmosphere. We might be separated, though."

"I've been practicing in the simulations," Fritz said. "And I'm getting pretty good at the shadowing game."

"Fritz," Parminder said. "We're working on our AI project now, okay? Can we talk to you later, on Titan?"

"Sure."

And I sent a note of gratitude to Parminder, who was in on the scheme with me and Janis, and who knew that Fritz couldn't be a part of it.

Shortly thereafter my electronic being was transmitted from Ceres by high-powered communications lasers and downloaded into an actual body, even if it was a body that had six legs and that didn't belong to me. The body was already in its vacuum suit, which was packed into the descent capsule—I mean nobody wanted us floating around in the *Cassini Ranger* in zero gravity in bodies we weren't used to—so there wasn't a lot I could do for entertainment.

Which was fine. It was the first time I'd been in a body, and I was absorbed in trying to work out all the little differences between reality and the sims I'd grown up in.

In reality, I thought, things seem a little quieter. In simulations there are always things competing for your attention, but right now there was nothing to do but listen to myself breathe.

And then there was a bang and a big shove, easily absorbed by foam padding, and I was launched into space, aimed at the orange ball that was Titan, and behind it the giant pale sphere of Saturn.

The view was sort of disappointing. Normally you see Saturn as an image with the colors electronically altered so as to heighten the subtle differences in detail. The reality of Saturn was more of a pasty blob, with faint brown stripes and a little red jagged scrawl of a storm in the Southern hemisphere.

Unfortunately I couldn't get a very good view of the rings, because they were edge-on, like a straight silver knife-slash right across a painted canvas.

Besides Titan I could see at least a couple dozen moons. I could recognize Dione and Rhea, and Enceladus because it was so bright. Iapetus was obvious because it was half light and half dark. There were a lot of tiny lights that could have been Atlas or Pan or Prometheus or Pandora or maybe a score of others.

I didn't have enough time to puzzle out the identity of the other moons, because Titan kept getting bigger and bigger. It was a dull orange color, except on the very edge where the haze scatters blue light. Other than that arc of blue, Titan is orange the same way Mars is red, which is to say that it's orange all the way down, and when you get to the bottom there's still more orange.

It seemed like a pretty boring place for Fahd to spend his first years of adulthood.

I realized that if I were doing this trip in a sim, I'd fast-forward through this part. It would be just my luck if all reality turned out to be this dull.

Things livened up in a hurry when the capsule hit the atmosphere. There was a lot of noise, and the capsule rattled and jounced, and bright flames of ionizing radiation shot up past the view port. I could feel my heart speeding up, and my breath going fast. It was *my* body that was being bounced around, with *my* nerve impulses running along *my* spine. *This* was much more interesting. *This* was the difference between reality and a sim, even though I couldn't explain exactly what the difference was.

It is the distinction, Miss Alison, between the undomesticated awe which one might feel at the sight of a noble wild prospect discovered in nature; and that which is produced by a vain tragedian on the stage, puffing and blowing in a transport of dismal fury as he tries to describe the same vision.

Thank you, Dr. Sam.

We that live to please must please to live.

I could see nothing but fire for a while, and then there was a jolt and a *Crash-Bang* as the braking chute deployed, and I was left swaying frantically in the sudden silence, my heart beating fast as high-atmosphere winds fought for possession of the capsule. Far above I could just see the ionized streaks of some of the other cadre members heading my way.

It was then, after all I could see was the orange fog, that I remembered that I'd been so overwhelmed by the awe of what I'd been seeing that I forgot to *observe.* So I began to kick myself over that.

It isn't enough to stare when you want to be a visual artist, which is what I want more than anything. A noble wild prospect (as you'd call it, Dr. Sam) isn't simply a gorgeous scene, it's also a series of technical problems. Ratios, colors, textures. Media. Ideas. Frames. *Decisions.* I hadn't thought about any of that when I had the chance, and now it was too late.

I decided to start paying better attention, but there was nothing happening outside but acetylene sleet cooking off the hot exterior of the capsule. I checked my tracking display and my onboard map of Titan's surface. So I was prepared when a private message came from Janis.

"Alison. You ready to roll?"

"Sure. You bet."

"This is going to be *brilliant.*"

I hoped so. But somewhere in my mind I kept hearing Dr. Sam's voice: *Remember that all tricks are either knavish or childish.*

The trick I played on Fritz was both.

I had been doing some outside work for Dane, who was a communications tech, because outside work paid in real money, not the Citizenship Points we get paid in the sims. And Dane let me do some of the work on Fahd's Incarnation Day, so I was able to arrange which capsules everyone was going to be put into.

I put Fritz into the last capsule to be fired at Titan. And those of us involved in Janis' scheme—Janis, Parminder, Andy, and I—were fired first.

This basically meant that we were going to be on Titan five or six minutes ahead of Fritz, which meant it was unlikely that he'd be able to catch up to us. He would be someone else's problem for a while.

I promised myself that I'd be extra nice to him later, but it didn't stop me from feeling knavish and childish.

After we crashed into Titan's atmosphere, and after a certain amount of spinning and swaying we came to a break in the cloud, and I could finally look down at Titan's broken surface. Stark mountains, drifts of methane snow, shiny orange ethane lakes, the occasional crater. In the far distance, in the valley between a pair of lumpy mountains, was the smooth toboggan slide of the Tomasko glacier. And over to one side, on a plateau, were the blinking lights that marked our landing area.

And directly below was an ethane cloud, into which the capsule soon vanished. It was there that the chute let go, and there was a stomach-lurching drop before the airfoils deployed. I was not used to having my stomach lurch—recall if you will my earlier remarks on puking—so it was a few seconds before I was able to recover and take control of what was now a large and agile glider.

No, I hadn't piloted a glider before. But I'd spent the last several weeks working with simulations, and the technology was fail-safed anyway. Both I and the onboard computer would have to screw up royally before I could damage myself or anyone else. I took command of the pod and headed for Janis's secret rendezvous.

There are various sorts of games you can play with the pods as they're dropping through the atmosphere. You can stack your airfoils in appealing and intricate formations. (I think this one's really stupid if you're trying to do it in the middle of thick clouds.) There's the game called "shadowing," the one that Fritz wanted to play with me, where you try to get right on top of another pod, above the airfoils where they can't see you, and you have to match every maneuver of the pod that's below you, which is both trying to evade you and to maneuver so as to get above you. There are races, where you try to reach some theoretical point in the sky ahead of the other person. And there's just swooping and dashing around the sky, which is probably as fun as anything.

But Janis had other plans. And Parminder and Andy and I, who were Janis's usual companions in her adventures, had elected to be a part of her scheme, as was our wont. (Do you like my use of the word "wont," Dr. Sam?) And a couple other members of the cadre, Mei and Bartolomeo, joined our group without knowing our secret purpose.

We disguised our plan as a game of shadowing, which I turned out to be very good at. It's not simply a game of flying, it's a game of spacial relationships, and that's what visual artists have to be good at understanding. I spent more time on top of one or more of the players than anyone else.

Though perhaps the others weren't concentrating on the game. Because although we were performing the intricate spiraling maneuvers of shadowing as a part of our cover, we were also paying very close attention to the way the winds were blowing at different altitudes—we had cloud-penetrating lasers for that, in addition to constant meteorological data from the ground—and we were using available winds as well as our maneuvers to slowly edge away from our assigned landing field, and toward our destined target.

I kept expecting to hear from Fritz, wanting to join our game. But I didn't. I supposed he had found his fun somewhere else.

All the while we were stunting around Janis was sending us course and altitude corrections, and thanks to her navigation we caught the edge of a low pressure area that boosted us toward our objective at nearly two hundred kilometers per hour. It was then that Mei swung her capsule around and began a descent toward the landing field.

"I just got the warning that we're on the edge of our flight zone," she reported.

"Roger," I said.

"Yeah," said Janis. "We know."

Mei swooped away, followed by Bartolomeo. The rest of us continued soaring along in the furious wind. We made little pretense by this point that we were still playing shadow, but instead tried for distance.

Ground Control on the landing area took longer to try to contact us than we'd expected.

"Capsules six, twenty-one, thirty," said a ground controller. She had one of those smooth, controlled voices that people use when trying to coax small children away from the candy and toward the spinach.

"You have exceeded the safe range from the landing zone. Turn at once to follow the landing beacon."

I waited for Janis to answer.

"It's easier to reach Tomasko from where we are," she said. "We'll just head for the glacier and meet the rest of you there."

"The flight plan prescribes a landing on Lake Southwood," the voice said. "Please lock on the landing beacon at once and engage your autopilots."

Janis's voice rose with impatience. "Check the flight plan I'm sending you! It's easier and quicker to reach Tomasko! We've got a wind shoving us along at a hundred eighty clicks!"

There was another two or three minutes of silence. When the voice came back, it was grudging.

"Permission granted to change flight plan."

I sagged with relief in my vac suit, because now I was spared a moral crisis. We had all sworn that we'd follow Janis's flight plan whether or not we got permission from Ground Control, but that didn't necessarily mean that we would have. Janis would have gone, of course, but I for one might have had second thoughts. I would have had an excuse if Fritz had been along, because I could have taken him to the assigned landing field — we didn't want him with us, because he might not have been able to handle the landing if it wasn't on an absolutely flat area.

I'd like to think I would have followed Janis, though. It isn't as if I hadn't before.

And honestly, that was about it. If this had been one of the adult-approved video dramas we grew up watching, something would have gone terribly wrong and there would have been a horrible crash. Parminder would have died, and Andy and I would have been trapped in a crevasse or buried under tons of methane ice, and Janis would have had to go to incredible, heroic efforts in order to rescue us. At the end Janis would have Learned an Important Life Lesson, about how following the Guidance of Our Wise, Experienced Elders is preferable, to staging wild, disobedient stunts.

By comparison what actually happened was fairly uneventful. We let the front push us along till we were nearly at the glacier, and then we dove down into calmer weather. We spiraled to a soft landing in clean snow at the top of Tomasko glacier. The airfoils neatly folded themselves, atmospheric pressure inside the capsules equalized with that of the moon, and the hatches opened so we could walk in our vac suits onto the top of Titan.

I was flushed with joy. I had never set an actual foot on an actual world before, and as I bounded in sheer delight through the snow I rejoiced in all the little details I felt all around me.

The crunch of the frozen methane under my boots. The way the wind picked up long streamers of snow that made little spattering noises when they hit my windscreen. The suit heaters that failed to heat my body evenly, so that some parts were cool and others uncomfortably warm.

None of it had the immediacy of the simulations, but I didn't remember this level of detail either. Even the polyamide scent of the suit seals was sharper than the generic stuffy suit smell they put in the sim.

This was all real, and it was wonderful, and even if my body was borrowed I was already having the best time I'd ever had in my life.

I scuttled over to Janis on my six legs and crashed into her with affectionate joy. (Hugging wasn't easy with the vac suits on.) Then Parminder ran over and crashed into her from the other side.

"We're finally out of Plato's Cave!" she said, which is the sort of obscure reference you always get out of Parminder. (I looked it up, though, and she had a good point.)

The outfitters at the top of the glacier hadn't been expecting us for some time, so we had some free time to indulge in a snowball fight. I suppose snowball fights aren't that exciting if you're wearing full-body pressure suits, but this was the first real snowball fight any of us had ever had, so it was fun on that account anyway.

By the time we got our skis on, the shuttle holding the rest of the cadre and their pods was just arriving. We could see them looking at us from the yellow windows of the shuttle, and we just gave them a wave and zoomed off down the glacier, along with a grown-up who decided to accompany us in case we tried anything else that wasn't in the regulation playbook.

Skiing isn't a terribly hazardous sport if you've got six legs on a body slung low to the ground. The skis are short, not much longer than skates, so they don't get tangled; and it's really hard to fall over—the worst that happens is that you go into a spin that might take some time to get out of. And we'd all been practicing on the simulators and nothing bad happened.

The most interesting part was the jumps that had been molded at intervals onto the glacier. Titan's low gravity meant that when you went off a jump, you went very high and you stayed in the air for a long time. And Titan's heavy atmosphere meant that if you spread your limbs apart like a skydiver, you could catch enough of that thick air almost to hover, particularly if the wind was cooperating and blowing uphill. That was wild and thrilling, hanging in the air with the wind whistling around the joints of your suit, the glossy orange snow coming up to meet you, and the sound of your own joyful whoops echoing in your ears.

I am a great friend to public amusements, because they keep people from vice.

Well. Maybe. We'll see.

The best part of the skiing was that this time I didn't get so carried away that I'd forgot to *observe*. I thought about ways to render the dull orange sheen of the glacier, the wild scrawls made in the snow by six skis spinning out of control beneath a single squat body, the little crusty waves on the surface generated by the constant wind.

Neither the glacier nor the lake is always solid. Sometimes Titan generates a warm front that liquifies the topmost layer of the glacier, and the liquid methane pours down the mountain to form the lake. When that happens, the modular resort breaks apart and creeps away on its treads. But sooner or later everything freezes over again, and the resort returns.

We were able to ski through a broad orange glassy chute right onto the lake, and from there we could see the lights of the resort in the distance. We skied into a big ballooning pressurized hangar made out of some kind of durable fabric, where the crew removed our pressure suits and gave us little felt booties to wear. I'd had an exhilarating time, but hours had passed and I was tired. The Incarnation Day banquet was just what I needed.

Babbling and laughing, we clustered around the snack tables, tasting a good many things I'd never got in a simulation. (They make us eat in the sims, to get us used to the idea so we don't accidentally starve ourselves once we're incarnated, and to teach us table manners, but the tastes tend to be a bit monotonous.)

"Great stuff!" Janis said, gobbling some kind of crunchy vat-grown treat that I'd sampled earlier and found disgusting. She held the bowl out to the rest of us. "Try this! You'll like it!"

I declined.

"Well," Janis said, "If you're afraid of new things . . ."

That was Janis for you—she insisted on sharing her existence with everyone around her, and got angry if you didn't find her life as exciting as she did.

About that time Andy and Parminder began to gag on the stuff Janis had made them eat, and Janis laughed again.

The other members of the cadre trailed in about an hour later, and the feast proper began. I looked around the long table—the forty-odd members of the Cadre of Glorious Destiny, all with their little heads on their furry multipede bodies, all crowded around the table cramming in the first real food they've tasted in their lives. In the old days, this would have been a scene from some kind of horror movie. Now it's just a slice of posthumanity, Earth's descendants partying on some frozen rock far from home.

But since all but Fahd were in borrowed bodies I'd never seen before, I couldn't tell one from the other. I had to ping a query off their implant communications units just to find out who I was talking to.

Fahd sat at the place of honor at the head of the table. The hair on his furry body was ash-blond, and he had a sort of widow's peak that gave his head a kind of geometrical look.

I liked Fahd. He was the one I had sex with, that time that Janis persuaded me to steal a sex sim from Dane, the guy I do outside programming for. (I should point out, Dr. Sam, that our simulated bodies have all the appropriate organs, it's just that the adults have made sure we can't actually use them for sex.)

I think there was something wrong with the simulation. What Fahd and I did wasn't wonderful, it wasn't ecstatic, it was just . . . strange. After a while we gave up and found something else to do.

Janis, of course, insisted she'd had a glorious time. She was our leader, and everything she did had to be totally fabulous. It was just like that horrid vat-grown snack-food product she'd tried—not only was it the best food she'd ever tasted, it was the best food *ever*, and we all had to share it with her.

I hope Janis actually *did* enjoy the sex sim, because she was the one caught with the program in her buffer—and after I *told* her to erase it. Sometimes I think she just wants to be found out.

During dinner those whose parents permitted it were allowed two measured doses of liquor to toast Fahd—something called Ring Ice, brewed locally. I think it gave my esophagus blisters.

After the Ring Ice things got louder and more lively. There was a lot more noise and hilarity when the resort crew discovered that several of the cadre had slipped off to a back room to find out what sex was like, now they had real bodies. It was when I was laughing over this that I looked at Janis and saw that she was quiet, her body motionless. She's normally louder and more demonstrative than anyone else, so I knew something was badly wrong. I sent her a private query through my implant. She sent a single-word reply.

Mom . . .

I sent her a glyph of sympathy while I wondered how Janis's mom had found out about our little adventure so quickly. There was barely time for a lightspeed signal to bounce to Ceres and back.

Ground Control must have really been annoyed. Or maybe she and Janis's mom were Constant Soldiers in the Five Principles Movement and were busy spying on everyone else—all for the greater good, of course.

Whatever the message was, Janis bounced back pretty quickly. Next thing I knew she was sidling up to me saying, "Look, you can loan me your vac suit, right?"

Something about the glint in her huge platter eyes made me cautious.

"Why would I want to do that?" I asked.

"Mom says I'm grounded. I'm not allowed to go skating with the rest of you. But nobody can tell these bodies apart—I figured if we switched places we could show her who's boss."

"And leave me stuck here by myself?"

"You'll be with the waiters—and some of them are kinda cute, if you like them hairy." Her tone turned serious. "It's solidarity time, Alison. We can't let Mom win this one."

I thought about it for a moment, then said, "Maybe you'd better ask someone else."

Anger flashed in her huge eyes. "I knew you'd say that! You've always been afraid to stand up to the grown-ups!"

"Janis," I sighed. "Think about it. Do you think your mom was the only one who got a signal from Ground Control? My parents are going to be looking into the records of this event *very closely*. So I think you should talk someone else into your scheme—and not Parminder or Andy, either."

Her whole hairy body sulked. I almost laughed.

"I guess you're right," she conceded.

"You know your mom is going to give you a big lecture when we get back."

"Oh yeah. I'm sure she's writing her speech right now, making sure she doesn't miss a single point."

"Maybe you'd better let me eavesdrop," I said. "Make sure you don't lose your cool."

She looked even more sulky. "Maybe you'd better."

We do this because we're cadre. Back in the old days, when the first poor kids were being raised in virtual, a lot of them cracked up once they got incarnated. They went crazy, or developed a lot of weird obsessions, or tried to kill themselves, or turned out to have a kind of autism where they could only relate to things through a computer interface.

So now parents don't raise their children by themselves. Most kids still have two parents, because it takes two to pay the citizenship points and taxes it takes to raise a kid, and sometimes if there aren't enough points to go around there are three parents, or four or five. Once the points are paid the poor moms and dads have to wait until there are enough applicants to fill a cadre. A whole bunch of virtual children are raised in one group, sharing their upbringing with their parents and creche staff. Older cadres often join their juniors and take part in their education, also.

The main point of the cadre is for us all to keep an eye on each other. Nobody's allowed to withdraw into their own little world. If anyone shows sign of going around the bend, we unite in our efforts to retrieve them.

Our parents created the little hell that we live in. It's our job to help each other survive it.

A person used to vicissitudes is not easily dejected.

Certainly Janis isn't, though despite cadre solidarity she never managed to talk anyone else into changing places with her. I felt only moderately sorry for her—she'd already had her triumph, after all—and I forgot all about her problems once I got back into my pressure suit and out onto the ice.

Skating isn't as thrilling as skiing, I suppose, but we still had fun. Playing crack-the-whip in the light gravity, the person on the end of the line could be fired a couple kilometers over the smooth methane ice.

After which it was time to return to the resort. We all showered while the resort crew cleaned and did maintenance on our suits, and then we got back in the suits so that the next set of tourists would find their rental bodies already armored up and ready for sport.

We popped open our helmets so that the scanners could be put on our heads. Quantum superconducting devices tickled our brain cells and recovered everything they found, and then our brains—our essences—were dumped into a buffer, then fired by communication laser back to Ceres and the sim in which we all lived.

The simulation seemed inadequate compared to the reality of Titan. But I didn't have time to work out the degree of difference, because I had to save Janis's butt.

That's us. That's the cadre. All for one and one for all.

And besides, Janis has been my best friend for practically ever.

Anna-Lee, Janis's mom, was of course waiting for her, sitting in the little common room outside Janis's bedroom. (Did I mention that we sleep, Dr. Sam? We don't sleep as long as incarnated people do, just a few hours, but our parents want us to get used to the idea so that when we're incarnated we know to sleep when we get tired instead of ignoring it and then passing out while doing something dangerous or important.)

(The only difference between our dreams and yours is that we don't dream. I mean, what's the point, we're stuck in our parents' dream anyway.)

So I'm no sooner arrived in my own simulated body in my own simulated bedroom when Janis is screaming on the private channel.

"Mom is here! I need you *now!*"

So I press a few switches in my brain and there I am, right in Janis's head, getting much of the same sensor feed that she's receiving herself. And I look at her and I say, "Hey, you can't talk to Anna-Lee looking like *this*."

Janis is wearing her current avatar, which is something like a crazy person might draw with crayons. Stick-figure body, huge yellow shoes, round bobble head with crinkly red hair like wires.

"Get your quadbod on!" I tell her. "Now!"

So she switches, and now her avatar has four arms, two in the shoulders, two in the hip sockets. The hair is still bright red. Whatever her avatar looks like, Janis always keeps the red hair.

"Good," I say. "That's normal."

Which it is, for Ceres. Which is an asteroid without much gravity, so there really isn't a lot of point in having legs. In microgravity legs just drag around behind you and bump into things and get bruises and cuts. Whereas everyone can use an extra pair of arms, right? So most people who live in low- or zerogravity environments use quadbods, which are much more practical than the two-legged model.

So Janis pushes off with her left set of arms and floats through the door into the lounge where her mom awaits. Anna-Lee wears a quadbod, too, except that hers isn't an avatar, but a three-dimensional holographic scan of her real body. And you can tell that she's really pissed—she's got tight lips and tight eyelids and a tight face, and both sets of arms are folded across her midsection with her fingers digging into her forearms as if she's repressing the urge to grab Janis and shake her.

"Hi, Mom," Janis said.

"You not only endangered yourself," Anna-Lee said, "but you chose to endanger others, too."

"Sit down before you answer," I murmured in Janis's inward ear. "Take your time."

I was faintly surprised that Janis actually followed my advice. She drifted into a chair, used her lower limbs to settle herself into it, and then spoke.

"Nobody was endangered," she said, quite reasonably.

Anna-Lee's nostrils narrowed.

"You diverted from the flight plan that was devised for your safety," she said.

"I made a new flight plan," Janis pointed out. "Ground Control accepted it. If it was dangerous, she wouldn't have done that."

Anna-Lee's voice got that flat quality that it gets when she's following her own internal logic. Sometimes I think she's the program, not us.

"You are not authorized to file flight plans!" she snapped.

"Ground Control accepted it," Janis repeated. Her voice had grown a little sharp, and I whispered at her to keep cool.

"And Ground Control immediately informed *me!* They were right on the edge of calling out a rescue shuttle!"

"But they didn't, because there was no problem!" Janis snapped out, and then there was a pause while I told her to lower her voice.

"Ground Control accepted my revised plan," she said. "I landed according to the plan, and nobody was hurt."

"You planned this from the beginning!" All in that flat voice of hers. "This was a deliberate act of defiance!"

Which was true, of course.

"What harm did I do?" Janis asked.

("Look," I told Janis. "Just tell her that she's right and you were wrong and you'll never do it again.")

("I'm not going to lie!" Janis sent back on our private channel. "Whatever Mom does, she's never going to make me lie!")

All this while Anna-Lee was saying, "We must all work together for the greater good! Your act of defiance did nothing but divert people from their proper tasks! Titan Ground Control has better things to do than worry about you!"

There was no holding Janis back now. "You *wanted* me to learn navigation! So I learned it—because *you* wanted it! And now I've proved that I can use it, and you're angry about it!" She was waving her arms so furiously that she bounced up from her chair and began to sort of jerk around the room.

"And do you know why that is, Mom?" she demanded.

"For God's sake shut up!" I shouted at her. I knew where this was leading, but Janis was too far gone in her rage to listen to me now.

"It's because you're second-rate!" Janis shouted at her mother. "Dad went off to Barnard's Star, but *you* didn't make the cut! And I can do all the things you wanted to do, and do them better, and *you can't stand it!*"

"Will you be quiet!" I told Janis. "Remember that *she owns you!*"

"I accepted the decision of the committee!" Anna-Lee was shouting. "I am a Constant Soldier and I live a productive life, and I will *not* be responsible for producing a child who is a *burden* and a *drain on resources!*"

"Who says I'm going to be a burden?" Janis demanded. *"You're* the only person who says that! If I incarnated tomorrow I could get a good job in ten minutes!"

"Not if you get a reputation for disobedience and anarchy!"

By this point it was clear that since Janis wasn't listening to me, and Anna-Lee *couldn't* listen, there was no longer any point in my involving myself in what had become a very predictable argument. So I closed the link and prepared my own excuses for my own inevitable meeting with my parents.

I changed from Picasso Woman to my own quadbod, which is what I use when I talk to my parents, at least when I want something from them. My quadbod avatar is a girl just a couple years younger than my actual age, wearing a school uniform with a Peter Pan collar and a white bow in her—my—hair. And my beautiful brown eyes are just slightly larger than eyes are in reality, because that's something called "neotony," which means you look more like a baby and babies are designed to be irresistible to grown-ups.

Let me tell you that it works. Sometimes I can blink those big eyes and get away with anything.

And at that point my father called, and told me that he and my mom wanted to talk to me about my adventures on Titan, so I popped over to my parents' place, where I appeared in holographic form in their living room.

My parents are pretty reasonable people. Of course I take care to *keep* them reasonable, insofar as I can. *Let me smile with the wise,* as Dr. Sam says, *and feed with the rich.* I will keep my opinions to myself, and try my best to avoid upsetting the people who have power over me.

Why did I soar off with Janis on her flight plan? my father wanted to know.

"Because I didn't think she should go alone," I said.

Didn't you try to talk her out of it? my mother asked.

"You can't talk Janis out of anything," I replied. Which, my parents knowing Janis, was an answer they understood.

So my parents told me to be careful, and that was more or less the whole conversation.

Which shows you that not all parents up here are crazy.

Mine are more sensible than most. I don't think many parents would think much of my ambition to get involved in the fine arts. That's just not *done* up here, let alone the sort of thing *I* want to do, which is to incarnate on Earth and apprentice myself to an actual painter, or maybe a sculptor. Up here they just use cameras, and their idea of original art is to take camera pictures or alter camera pictures or combine camera pictures with one another or process the camera pictures in some way.

I want to do it from scratch, with paint on canvas. And not with a computer-programmed spray gun either, but with a real brush and blobs of paint. Because if you ask me the *texture* of the thing is important, which is why I like oils. Or rather the *idea* of oils, because I've never actually had a chance to work with the real thing.

And besides, as Dr. Sam says, *A man who has not been in Italy is always conscious of an inferiority, from his not having seen what is expected a man should see. The grand object of traveling is to see the shores of the Mediterranean.*

So when I told my parents what I wanted to do, they just sort of shrugged and made me promise to learn another skill as well, one just a little bit more practical. So while I minor in art I'm majoring in computer design and function and programming, which is pretty interesting because all our really complex programs are written by artificial intelligences who are smarter than we are, so getting them to do what you want is as much like voodoo as science.

So my parents and I worked out a compromise that suited everybody, which is why I think my parents are pretty neat actually.

About twenty minutes after my talk with my parents, Janis knocked on my door, and I made the door go away, and she walked in, and then I put the door back. (Handy things, sims.)

"Guess that didn't work out so good, huh?" she said.

"On your family's civility scale," I said, "I think that was about average."

Her eyes narrowed (she was so upset that she'd forgot to change out of her quad-bod, which is why she had the sort of eyes that could narrow).

"I'm going to get her," she said.

"I don't think that's very smart," I said.

Janis was smacking her fists into my walls, floor, and ceiling and shooting around the room, which was annoying even though the walls were virtual and she couldn't damage them or get fingerprints on them.

"Listen," I said. "All you have to do is keep the peace with your mom until you've finished your thesis, and then you'll be incarnated and she can't touch you. It's just *months*, Janis."

"My *thesis!*" A glorious grin of discovery spread across Janis's face. "I'm going to use my *thesis!* I'm going to stick it to Mom right where it hurts!"

I reached out and grabbed her and steadied her in front of me with all four arms.

"Look," I said. "You can't keep calling her bluff."

Her voice rang with triumph. "Just watch me."

"Please," I said. "I'm begging you. *Don't do anything till you're incarnated!*"

I could see the visions of glory dancing before her eyes. She wasn't seeing or hearing me at all.

"She's going to have to admit that I am right and that she is wrong," she said. "I'm going to nail my thesis to her forehead like Karl Marx on the church door."

"That was Martin Luther actually." (Sometimes I can't help these things.)

She snorted. "Who cares?"

"I do." Changing the subject. *"Because I don't want you to die."*

Janis snorted. "I'm not going to bow to her. I'm going to *crush her*. I'm going to show her how stupid and futile and second-rate she is."

And at that moment there was a signal at my door. I ignored it.

"The power of punishment is to silence, not to confute," I said.

Her face wrinkled as if she'd bit into something sour. "I can't *believe* you're quoting that old dead guy again."

I have found you an argument, I wanted to say with Dr. Sam, *but I am not obliged to find you an understanding.*

The signal at my door repeated, and this time it was attached to an electronic signal that meant *Emergency!* Out of sheer surprise I dissolved the door.

Mei was there in her quadbod, an expression of anger on her face.

"If you two are finished congratulating each other on your brilliant little prank," she said, "you might take time to notice that Fritz is missing."

"Missing?" I didn't understand how someone could be missing. "Didn't his program come back from Titan?"

If something happened to the transmission, they could reload Fritz from a backup.

Mei's expression was unreadable. "He never went. He met the Blue Lady."

And then she pushed off with two of her hands and drifted away, leaving us in a sudden, vast, terrible silence.

We didn't speak, but followed Mei into the common room. The other cadre members were all there, and they all watched us as we floated in.

When you're little, you first hear about the Blue Lady from the other kids in your cadre. Nobody knows for sure how we *all* find out about the Blue Lady—not just the cadres on Ceres, but the ones on Vesta, and Ganymede, and *everywhere*.

And we all know that sometimes you might see her, a kind smiling woman in a blue robe, and she'll reach out to you, and she seems so nice you'll let her take your hand.

Only then, when it's too late, you'll see that she has no eyes, but only an empty blackness filled with stars.

She'll take you away and your friends will never see you again.

And of course it's your parents who send the Blue Lady to find you when you're bad.

We all know that the Blue Lady doesn't truly exist, it's ordinary techs in ordinary rooms who give the orders to zero out your program along with all its backups, but we all believe in the Blue Lady really, and not just when we're little.

Which brings me to the point I made about incarnation earlier. Once you're incarnated, you are considered a human being, and you have human rights.

But *not until then*. Until you're incarnated, you're just a computer program that belongs to your parents, and if your parents think the program is flawed or corrupted and simply too awkward to deal with, they can have you zeroed.

Zeroed. Not killed. The grown-ups insist that there's a difference, but I don't see it myself.

Because the Blue Lady really comes for some people, as she came for Fritz when Jack and Hans finally gave up trying to fix him. Most cadres get by without a visit. Some have more than one. There was a cadre on Vesta who lost eight, and then there were suicides among the survivors once they incarnated, and it was a big scandal that all the grown-ups agreed never to talk about.

I have never for an instant believed that my parents would ever send the Blue Lady after me, but still it's always there in the back of my mind, which is why I think that the current situation is so horrible. It gives parents a power they should never have, and it breeds a fundamental distrust between kids and their parents.

The grown-ups' chief complaint about the cadre system is that their children bond with their peers and not their parents. Maybe it's because their peers can't kill them.

Everyone in the cadre got the official message about Fritz, that he was basically irreparable and that the chance of his making a successful incarnation was essentially zero. The message said that none of us were at fault for what had happened, and that everyone knew that we'd done our best for him.

This was in the same message queue as a message to me from Fritz, made just before he got zeroed out. There he was with his stupid hat, smiling at me.

"Thank you for saying you'd play the shadowing game with me," he said. "I really think you're wonderful." He laughed. "See you soon, on Titan!"

So then I cried a lot, and I erased the message so that I'd never be tempted to look at it again.

We all felt failure. It was our job to make Fritz right, and we hadn't done it. We had all grown up with him, and even though he was a trial he was a part of our world. I had spent the last few days avoiding him, and I felt horrible about it; but everyone else had done the same thing at one time or another.

We all missed him.

The cadre decided to wear mourning, and we got stuck in a stupid argument about whether to wear white, which is the traditional mourning color in Asia, or black, which is the color in old Europe.

"Wear blue," Janis said. So we did. Whatever avatars we wore from that point on had blue clothing, or used blue as a principal color somewhere in their composition.

If any of the parents noticed, or talked about it, or complained, I never heard it.

I started thinking a lot about how I related to incarnated people, and I thought that maybe I'm just a little more compliant and adorable and sweet-natured than I'd otherwise be, because I want to avoid the consequences of being otherwise. And Janis is perhaps more defiant than she'd be under other circumstances, because she wants to show she's not afraid. *Go ahead, Mom,* she says, *pull the trigger. I dare you.*

Underestimating Anna-Lee all the way. Because Anna-Lee is a Constant Soldier of the Five Principles Movement, and that means *serious.*

The First Principle of the Five Principles Movement states that *Humanity is a pattern of thought, not a side effect of taxonomy,* which means that you're human if you *think* like a human, whether you've got six legs or four arms or two legs like the folks on Earth and Mars.

And then so on to the Fifth Principle, we come to the statement that humanity in all its various forms is intended to occupy every possible ecosystem throughout the entire universe, or at least as much of it as we can reach. Which is why the Five Principles Movement has always been very big on genetic experimentation, and the various expeditions to nearby stars.

I have no problem with the Five Principles Movement, myself. It's rational compared with groups like the Children of Venus or the God's Menu people.

Besides, if there isn't something to the Five Principles, what are we doing out here in the first place?

My problem lies with the sort of people the Movement attracts, which is to say people like Anna-Lee. People who are obsessive, and humorless, and completely unable to see any other point of view. Nor only do they dedicate themselves heart and soul to whatever group they join, they insist everyone else has to join as well, and that anyone who isn't a part of it is a Bad Person.

So even though I pretty much agree with the Five Principles I don't think I'm going to join the movement. I'm going to keep in mind the wisdom of my good Dr. Sam: *Most schemes of political improvement are very laughable things.*

But to get back to Anna-Lee. Back in the day she married Carlos, who was also in the Movement, and together they worked for years to qualify for the expedition to Barnard's Star on the *True Destiny.* They created Janis together, because having children is all a part of occupying the universe and so on.

But Carlos got the offer to crew the ship, and Anna-Lee didn't. Carlos chose Barnard's Star over Anna-Lee, and now he's a couple light-months away. He and the rest of the settlers are in electronic form—no sense in spending the resources to ship a whole body to another star system when you can just ship the data and build the body once you arrive—and for the most part they're dormant, because there's nothing to do until they near their destination. But every week or so Carlos has himself awakened so that he can send an electronic postcard to his daughter.

The messages are all really boring, as you might expect from someone out in deep space where there's nothing to look at and nothing to do, and everyone's asleep anyway.

Janis sends him longer messages, mostly about her fights with Anna-Lee. Anna-Lee likewise sends Carlos long messages about Janis's transgressions. At two light-months out Carlos declines to mediate between them, which makes them both mad.

So Anna-Lee is mad because her husband left her, and she's mad at Janis for not being a perfect Five Principles Constant Soldier. Janis is mad at Carlos for not figuring out a way to take her along, and she's mad at Anna-Lee for not making the crew on the *True Destiny* and, failing that, not having the savvy to keep her husband in the picture.

And she's also mad at Anna-Lee for getting married again, this time to Rhee, a rich Movement guy who was able to swing the taxes to create *two new daughters*, both of whom are the stars of their particular cadres and are going to grow up to be perfect Five Principles Kids, destined to carry on the work of humanity in new habitats among distant stars.

Or so Anna-Lee claims, anyway.

Which is why I think that Janis underestimates her mother. I think the way Anna-Lee looks at it, she's got two new kids, who are everything she wants. And one older kid who gives her trouble, and who she can give to the Blue Lady without really losing anything, since she's lost Janis anyway. She's already given a husband to the stars, after all.

And all this is another reason why I want to incarnate on Earth, where a lot of people still have children the old-fashioned way. The parents make an embryo in a gene-splicer, and then the embryo is put in a vat, and nine months later you crack the vat open and you've got an actual baby, not a computer program. And even if the procedure is a lot more time-consuming and messy I still think it's superior.

So I was applying for work on Earth, both for jobs that could use computer skills, and also for apprenticeship programs in the fine arts. But there's a waiting list for pretty much any job you want on Earth, and also there's a big entry tax unless they *really* want you, so I wasn't holding my breath; and besides, I hadn't finished my thesis.

I figured on graduating from college along with most of my cadre, at the age of fourteen. I understand that in your day, Dr. Sam, people graduated from college a lot later. I figure there are several important reasons for the change: (1) we virtual kids don't sleep as much as you do, so we have more time for study; (2) there isn't that much else to do here anyway; and (3) we're really, really, *really* smart. Because if you were a parent, and you had a say in the makeup of your kid (along with the doctors and the sociologists and the hoodoo machines), would you say, *No thanks, I want mine stupid?*

No, I don't think so.

And the meat-brains that we incarnate into are pretty smart, too. Just in case you were wondering.

We could grow up faster, if we wanted. The computers we live in are so fast that we could go from inception to maturity in just two or three months. But we wouldn't get to interact with our parents, who being meat would be much slower, or with anyone else. So in order to have any kind of relationship with our elders, or any kind of socialization at all, we have to slow down to our parents' pace. I have to say that I agree with that.

In order to graduate I needed to do a thesis, and unfortunately I couldn't do the one I wanted, which was the way the paintings of Brueghel, etc., reflected the theology of the period. All the training with computers and systems, along with art and art history, had given me an idea of how abstract systems such as theology work, and how you can visually represent fairly abstract concepts on a flat canvas.

But I'd have to save that for maybe a postgraduate degree, because my major was still in the computer sciences, so I wrote a fairly boring thesis on systems interoperability—which, if you care, is the art of getting different machines and highly specialized operating systems to talk to each other, a job that is made more difficult if the machines in question happen to be a lot smarter than you are.

Actually it's a fairly interesting subject. It just wasn't interesting in my thesis.

While I was doing that I was also working outside contracts for Dane, who was from a cadre that had incarnated a few years ahead of us, and who I got to know when his group met with ours to help with our lessons and with our socialization skills (because they wanted us to be able to talk to people outside the cadre and our families, something we might not do if we didn't have practice).

Anyway, Dane had got a programming job in Ceres's communications center, and he was willing to pass on the more boring parts of his work to me in exchange for money. So I was getting a head start on paying that big Earth entry tax, or if I could evade the tax maybe living on Earth a while and learning to paint.

"You're just going to end up being Ceres's first interior decorator," Janis scoffed.

"And that would be a *bad* thing?" I asked. "Just *look* at this place!" Because it's all so functional and boring and you'd think they could find a more interesting color of paint than *gray*, for God's sake.

That was one of the few times I'd got to talk to Janis since our adventure on Titan. We were both working on our theses, and still going to school, and I had my outside contracts, and I think she was trying to avoid me, because she didn't want to tell me what she was doing because she didn't want me to tell her not to do it.

Which hurt, by the way. Since we'd been such loyal friends up to the point where I told her not to get killed, and then because I wanted to save her life she didn't want to talk to me anymore.

The times I mostly got to see Janis were Incarnation Day parties for other members of our cadre. So we got to see Ganymede, and Iapetus, and Titan again, and Rhea, and Pluto, Callisto, and Io, and the antimatter generation ring between Venus and Mercury, and Titan again, and then Titan a fourth time.

Our cadre must have this weird affinity for orange, I don't know.

We went to Pallas, Juno, and Vesta. Though if you ask me, one asteroid settlement is pretty much like the next.

We went to Third Heaven, which is a habitat the God's Menu people built at L2. And they can *keep* a lot of the items on the menu, if you ask me.

We visited Luna (which you would call the Moon, Dr. Sam. As if there was only one). And we got to view *Everlasting Dynasty*, the starship being constructed in lunar orbit for the expedition to Tau Ceti, the settlement that Anna-Lee was trying her best to get Janis aboard.

We also got to visit Mars three times. So among other entertainments I looked down at the planet from the top of Olympus Mons, the largest mountain in the solar system, and I looked down from the edge of the solar system's largest canyon, and then I looked *up* from the bottom of the same canyon.

We all tried to wear blue if we could, in memory of the one of us who couldn't be present.

Aside from the sights, the Incarnation Day parties were great because all our incarnated cadre members turned up, in bodies they'd borrowed for the occasion. We were all still close, of course, and kept continually in touch, but our communication was limited by the speed of light and it wasn't anything like having Fahd and Chandra and Solange there in person, to pummel and to hug.

We didn't go to Earth. I was the only one of our cadre who had applied there, and I hadn't got an answer yet. I couldn't help fantasizing about what my Incarnation Day party would be like if I held it on Earth—where would I go? What would we look at? Rome? Mount Everest? The ocean habitats? The plains of Africa, where the human race began?

It was painful to think that the odds were high that I'd never see any of these places.

Janis never tried to organize any of her little rebellions on these trips. For one thing word had got out, and we were all pretty closely supervised. Her behavior was never less than what Anna-Lee would desire. But under it all I could tell she was planning something drastic.

I tried to talk to her about it. I talked about my thesis, and hoped it would lead to a discussion of *her* thesis. But no luck. She evaded the topic completely.

She was pretty busy with her project, though, whatever it was. Because she was always buzzing around the cadre asking people where to look for odd bits of knowledge.

I couldn't make sense of her questions, though. They seemed to cover too many fields. Sociology, statistics, minerology, criminology, economics, astronomy, spaceship design . . . The project seemed too huge.

The only thing I knew about Janis's thesis was that it was *supposed* to be about resource management. It was the field that Anna-Lee forced her into, because it was full of skills that would be useful on the Tau Ceti expedition. And if that didn't work, Anna-Lee made sure Janis minored in spaceship and shuttle piloting and navigation.

I finally finished my thesis, and then I sat back and waited for the job offers to roll in. The only offer I got came from someone who wanted me to run the garbage cyclers on Iapetus, which the guy should have known I wouldn't accept if he had bothered to read my application.

Maybe he was just neck-deep in garbage and desperate, I don't know.

And then the most astounding thing happened. Instead of a job in the computer field, I got an offer to study at the Pisan Academy.

Which is an art school. Which is in Italy, which is where the paintings come from mostly.

The acceptance committee said that my work showed a "naive but highly original fusion of social criticism with the formalities of the geometric order." I don't even *pretend* to know what they meant by that, but I suspect they just weren't used to the perspective of a student who had spent practically her entire live in a computer on Ceres.

I broadcast my shrieks of joy to everyone in the cadre, even those who had left Ceres and were probably wincing at their workstations when my screams reached them.

I bounced around the common room and everyone came out to congratulate me. Even Janis, who had taken to wearing an avatar that wasn't even remotely human, just a graphic of a big sledgehammer smashing a rock, over and over.

Subtlety had never been her strong point.

"Congratulations," she said. "You got what you wanted."

And then she broadcast something on a private channel. *You're going to be famous*, she said. *But I'm going to be a* legend.

I looked at her. And then I sent back, *Can we talk about this?*

In a few days. When I deliver my thesis.

Don't, I pleaded.

Too late.

The hammer hit its rock, and the shards flew out into the room and vanished.

I spent the next few days planning my Incarnation Day party, but my heart wasn't in it. I kept wondering if Janis was going to be alive to enjoy it.

I finally decided to have my party in Thailand because there were so many interesting environments in one place, as well as the Great Buddha. And I found a caterer that was supposed to be really good.

I decided what sort of body I wanted, and the incarnation specialists on Earth started cooking it up in one of their vats. Not the body of an Earth-born fourteen-year-old, but older, more like eighteen. Brown eyes, brown hair, and those big eyes that had always been so useful.

And two legs, of course. Which is what they all have down there.

I set the date. The cadre were alerted. We all practiced in the simulations and tried to get used to making do with only two arms. Everyone was prepared.

And then Janis finished her thesis. I downloaded a copy the second it was submitted to her committee and read it in one long sitting, and my sense of horror grew with every line.

What Janis had done was publish a comprehensive critique *of our entire society*! It was a piece of brilliance, and at the same time it was utter poison.

Posthuman society wrecks its children, Janis said, and this can be demonstrated by the percentage of neurotic and dysfunctional adults. The problems encountered by the first generation of children who spent their formative years as programs—the autism, the obsessions and compulsions, the addictions to electronic environments—hadn't gone away, they'd just been reduced to the point where they'd become a part of the background clutter, a part of our civilization so everyday that we never quite noticed it.

Janis had the data, too. The number of people who were under treatment for one thing or another. The percentage who had difficulty adjusting to their incarnations, or who didn't want to communicate with anyone outside their cadre, or who couldn't sleep unless they were immersed in a simulation. Or who committed suicide. Or who died in accidents—Janis questioned whether all those accidents were really the results of our harsh environments. Our machines and our settlements were much safer than they had been in the early days, but the rates of accidental death were still high. How many accidents were caused by distracted or unhappy operators, or for that matter were deliberate "suicide by machine"?

Janis went on to describe one of the victims of this ruthless type of upbringing. "Flat of emotional affect, offended by disorder and incapable of coping with obstruction, unable to function without adherence to a belief system as rigid as the artificial and constricted environments in which she was raised."

When I realized Janis was describing Anna-Lee I almost de-rezzed.

Janis offered a scheme to cure the problem, which was to get rid of the virtual environments and start out with real incarnated babies. She pulled out vast numbers of statistics demonstrating that places that did this—chiefly Earth—seemed to raise more successful adults. She also pointed out that the initial shortage of resources that had prompted the creation of virtual children in the first place had long since passed—plenty of water-ice coming in from the Kuyper Belt these days, and we were sitting on all the minerals we could want. The only reason the system continued was for the convenience of the adults. But genuine babies, as opposed to abstract computer programs, would help the adults, too. They would no longer be tempted to become little dictators with absolute power over their offspring. Janis said the chance would turn the grown-ups into better human beings.

All this was buttressed by colossal numbers of statistics, graphs, and other data. I realized when I'd finished it that the Cadre of Glorious Destiny had produced one true genius, and that this genius was Janis.

The true genius is a mind of large general powers, accidentally determined to some particular direction.

Anna-Lee determined her, all right, and the problem was that Janis probably didn't have that long to live. Aside from the fact that Janis had ruthlessly caricatured her, Anna-Lee couldn't help but notice that the whole work went smack up against the Five Principles Movement. According to the Movement people, all available resources had to be devoted to the expansion of the human race out of the solar system and into new environments. It didn't matter how many more resources were available now than in the past, it was clear against their principles to devote a greater share to the raising of children when it could be used to blast off into the universe.

And though the Five Principles people acknowledged our rather high death rate, they put it down to our settlements' hazardous environments. All we had to do was genetically modify people to better suit the environments and the problem would be solved.

I skipped the appendices and zoomed from my room across the common room to Janis's door, and hit the button to alert her to a visitor. The door vanished, and there was Janis—for the first time since her fight with Anna-Lee, she was using her quadbod avatar. She gave me a wicked grin.

"Great, isn't it?"

"It's *brilliant*! But you can't let Anna-Lee see it."

"Don't be silly. I sent Mom the file myself."

I was horrified. She had to have seen the way my Picasso-face gaped, and it made her laugh.

"She'll have you erased!" I said.

"If she does," Janis said. "She'll only prove my point." She put a consoling hand on my shoulder. "Sorry if it means missing your incarnation."

When Anna-Lee came storming in—which wasn't long after—Janis broadcast the whole confrontation on a one-way link to the whole cadre. We got to watch, but not to participate. She didn't want our advice any more than she wanted her mother's.

"You are unnatural!" Anna-Lee stormed. "You spread slanders! You have betrayed the highest truth!"

"I *told* the truth!" Janis said. "And you *know* it's the truth, otherwise you wouldn't be so insane right now."

Anna-Lee stiffened. "I am a Five Principles Constant Soldier. I know the truth, and I know my duty."

"Every time you say that, you prove my point."

"You will retract this thesis, and apologize to your committee for giving them such a vicious document."

Anna-Lee hadn't realized that the document was irretrievable, that Janis had given it to everyone she knew.

Janis laughed. "No way, Mom," she said.

Anna-Lee lost it. She waved her fists and screamed. "I know my duty! I will not allow such a slander to be seen by anyone!" She pointed at Janis. "You have three days to retract!"

Janis gave a snort of contempt.

"Or what?"

"Or I will decide that you're incorrigible and terminate your program."

Janis laughed. "Go right ahead, Mom. Do it *now.* Nothing spreads a new idea better than martyrdom." She spread her four arms. "*Do* it, Mom. I *hate* life in this hell. I'm ready."

I will be conquered; I will not capitulate.

Yes, Dr. Sam. That's it exactly.

"You have three days," Anna-Lee said, her voice all flat and menacing, and then her virtual image de-rezzed.

Janis looked at the space where her mom had been, and then a goofy grin spread across her face. She switched to the redheaded, stick-figure avatar, and began to do a little dance as she hovered in the air, moving like a badly animated cartoon.

"Hey!" she sang. "I get to go to Alison's party after all!"

I had been so caught up in the drama that I had forgot my incarnation was going to happen in two days.

But it wasn't going to be a party now. It was going to be a wake.

"Dr. Sam," I said, "I've got to save Janis."

The triumph of hope over experience.

"Hope is what I've got," I said, and then I thought about it. "And maybe a little experience, too."

My Incarnation Day went well. We came down by glider, as we had that first time on Titan, except that this time I told Ground Control to let my friends land wherever the hell they wanted. That gave us time to inspect the Great Buddha, a slim man with a knowing smile sitting cross-legged with knobs on his head. He's two and a half kilometers tall and packed with massively parallel quantum processors, all crunching vast amounts of data, thinking whatever profound thoughts are appropriate to an artificial intelligence built on such a scale, and repeating millions of sutras, which are scriptures for Buddhists, all at the speed of light.

It creeps along at two or three centimeters per day, and will enter the strait at the end of the Kra Peninsula many thousands of years from now.

After viewing the Buddha's serene expression from as many angles as suited us, we soared and swooped over many kilometers of brilliant green jungle and landed on the beach. And we all *did* land on the beach, which sort of surprised me. And then we all did our best to learn how to surf—and let me tell you from the start, the surfing simulators are *totally* inadequate. The longest I managed to stand my board was maybe twenty seconds.

I was amazed at all the sensations that crowded all around me. The breeze on my skin, the scents of the sea and the vegetation and the coal on which our banquet was being cooked. The hot sand under my bare feet. The salt taste of the ocean on my lips. The sting of the little jellyfish on my legs and arms, and the iodine smell of the thick strand of seaweed that got wrapped in my hair.

I mean, I had no *idea*. The simulators were totally inadequate to the Earth experience.

And this was just a *part* of the Earth, a small fraction of the environments available. I think I convinced a lot of the cadre that maybe they'd want to move to Earth as soon as they could raise the money and find a job.

After swimming and beach games we had my Incarnation Day dinner. The sensations provided by the food were really too intense—I couldn't eat much of it. If I was going to eat Earth food, I was going to have to start with something a lot more bland.

And there was my brown-eyed body at the head of the table, looking down at the members of the Cadre of Glorious Destiny who were toasting me with tropical drinks, the kind that have parasols in them.

Tears came to my eyes, and they were a lot wetter and hotter than tears in the sims. For some reason that fact made me cry even more.

My parents came to the dinner, because this was the first time they could actually hug me—hug me for real, that is, and not in a sim. They had downloaded into bodies that didn't look much like the four-armed quadbods they used back on Ceres, but that didn't matter. When my arms went around them, I began to cry again.

After the tears were wiped away we put on underwater gear and went for a swim on the reef, which is just amazing. More colors and shapes and textures than I could ever imagine—or imagine putting in a work of art.

A work of art that embodies all but selects none is not art, but mere cant and recitation.

Oh, wow. You're right. Thank you, Dr. Sam.

After the reef trip we paid a visit to one of the underwater settlements, one inhabited by people adapted to breathe water. The problem was that we had to keep our underwater gear on, and that none of us were any good at the fluid sign language they all used as their preferred means of communication.

Then we rose from the ocean, dried out, and had a last round of hugs before being uploaded to our normal habitations. I gave Janis a particularly strong hug, and I whispered in her ear.

"Take care of yourself."

"Who?" she grinned. "*Me?*"

And then the little brown-haired body was left behind, looking very lonely, as everyone else put on the electrodes and uploaded back to their normal and very distant worlds.

As soon as I arrived on Ceres, I zapped an avatar of myself into my parents' quarters. They looked at me as if I were a ghost.

"What are *you* doing here?" my mother managed.

"I hate to tell you this," I said, "but I think you're going to have to hire a lawyer."

It was surprisingly easy to do, really. Remember that I was assisting Dane, who was a communications tech, and in charge of uploading all of our little artificial brains to Earth. And also remember that I am a specialist in systems interoperability, which implies that I am also a specialist in systems *un*operability.

It was very easy to set a couple of artificial intelligences running amok in Dane's system just as he was working on our upload. And that so distracted him that he said yes when I said that I'd do the job for him.

And once I had access, it was the work of a moment to swap a couple of serial numbers.

The end result of which was that it was Janis who uploaded into my brown-haired body, and received all the toasts, and who hugged my parents with *my* arms. And who is now on Earth, incarnated, with a full set of human rights and safe from Anna-Lee.

I wish I could say the same for myself.

Anna-Lee couldn't have me killed, of course, since I don't belong to her. But she could sue my parents, who from her point of view permitted a piece of software belonging to *them* to prevent her from wreaking vengeance on some software that belonged to *her*.

And of course Anna-Lee went berserk the second she found out—which was more or less immediately, since Janis sent her a little radio taunt as soon as she downed her fourth or fifth celebratory umbrella drink.

Janis sent me a message, too.

"The least you could have done was make my hair red."

My hair. Sometimes I wonder why I bothered.

An unexpected side effect of this was that we all got famous. It turns out that this was an unprecedented legal situation, with lots of human interest and a colorful cast of characters. Janis became a media celebrity, and so did I, and so did Anna-Lee.

Celebrity didn't do Anna-Lee's cause any good. Her whole mental outlook was too rigid to stand the kind of scrutiny and questioning that any public figure has to put up with. As soon as she was challenged she lost control. She called one of the leading media interviewers a name that you, Dr. Sam, would not wish me to repeat.

Whatever the actual merits of her legal case, the sight of Anna-Lee screaming that I had deprived her of the inalienable right to kill her daughter failed to win her a lot of friends. Eventually the Five Principles people realized she wasn't doing their cause any good, and she was replaced by a Movement spokesperson who said as little as possible.

Janis did some talking, too, but not nearly as much as she would have liked, because she was under house arrest for coming to Earth without a visa and without paying the immigration tax. The cops showed up when she was sleeping off her hangover from all the umbrella drinks. It's probably lucky that she wasn't given the opportunity to talk much, because if she started on her rants she would have worn out her celebrity as quickly as Anna-Lee did.

Janis was scheduled to be deported back to Ceres, but shipping an actual incarnated human being is much more difficult than zapping a simulation by laser, and she had to wait for a ship that could carry passengers, and that would be months.

She offered to navigate the ship herself, since she had the training, but the offer was declined.

Lots of people read her thesis who wouldn't otherwise have heard of it. And millions discussed it whether they'd read it or not. There were those who said that Janis was right, and those that said that Janis was mostly right but that she exaggerated. There were those who said that the problem didn't really exist, except in the statistics.

There were those who thought the problem existed entirely in the software, that the system would work if the simulations were only made more like reality. I had to disagree, because I think the simulations *were* like reality, but only for certain people.

The problem is that human beings perceive reality in slightly different ways, even if they happen to be programs. A programmer could do his best to create an artificial reality that exactly mimicked the way he perceived reality, except that it wouldn't be as exact for another person, it would only be an approximation. It would be like fitting everyone's hand into the same-sized glove.

Eventually someone at the University of Adelaide read it and offered Janis a professorship in their sociology department. She accepted and was freed from house arrest.

Poor Australia, I thought.

I was on video quite a lot. I used my little-girl avatar, and I batted my big eyes a lot. I still wore blue, mourning for Fritz.

Why, I was asked, did I act to save Janis?

"Because we're cadre, and we're supposed to look after one another."

What did I think of Anna-Lee?

"I don't see why she's complaining. I've seen to it that Janis *just isn't her problem anymore.*"

Wasn't what I did stealing?

"It's not stealing to free a slave."

And so on. It was the same sort of routine I'd been practicing on my parents all these years, and the practice paid off. Entire cadres—hundreds of them—signed petitions asking that the case be dismissed. Lots of adults did the same.

I hope that it helps, but the judge that hears the case isn't supposed to be swayed by public opinion, but only by the law.

And everyone forgets that it's my parents who will be on trial, not me, accused of letting their software steal Anna-Lee's software. And of course I, and therefore they, am completely guilty, so my parents are almost certainly going to be fined, and lose both money and Citizenship Points.

I'm sorry about that, but my parents seem not to be.

How the judge will put a value on a piece of stolen software that its owner fully intended to destroy is going to make an interesting ruling, however it turns out.

I don't know whether I'll ever set foot on Earth again. I can't take my place in Pisa because I'm not incarnated, and I don't know if they'll offer again.

And however things turn out, Fritz is still zeroed. And I still wear blue.

I don't have my outside job any longer. Dane won't speak to me, because his supervisor reprimanded him, and he's under suspicion for being my accomplice. And even those who are sympathetic to me aren't about to let me loose with their computers.

And even if I get a job somewhere, I can't be incarnated until the court case is over.

It seems to me that the only person who got away scot-free was Janis. Which is normal.

So right now my chief problem is boredom. I spent fourteen years in a rigid program intended to fill my hours with wholesome and intellectually useful activity, and now that's over.

And I can't get properly started on the non-wholesome thing until I get an incarnation somewhere.

Everyone is, or hopes to be, an idler.

Thank you, Dr. Sam.

I'm choosing to idle away my time making pictures. Maybe I can sell them and help pay the Earth tax.

I call them my "Dr. Johnson" series. *Sam. Johnson on Mars. Sam. Johnson Visits Neptune. Sam. Johnson Quizzing the Tomasko Glacier. Sam. Johnson Among the Asteroids.*

I have many more ideas along this line.

Dr. Sam, I trust you will approve.

far as you can go

GREG VAN EEKHOUT

New writer Greg Van Eekhout has made sales to *Asimov's Science Fiction*, *The Magazine of Fantasy & Science Fiction*, *Strange Horizons*, *Polyphony*, *Flytrap*, *Say . . .*, *Ideomancer*, *Starlight*, and elsewhere. Many of those stories have just been released in his first collection, *Show and Tell and Other Stories*. When not writing, Van Eekhout works as an instructional designer and an educational technologist in the suburbs of Phoenix, Arizona.

In the aptly named story that follows, we set out in company with a determined man on a quest who goes just about as far as you can go in a bizarre and constrained future world—and if that's not far in today's terms, that certainly doesn't mean that he doesn't have to overcome plenty of dangers and obstacles along the way, or encounter not a few wonders.

I didn't go to school because I was allergic to the neuroboosters, but that didn't mean I was stupid. It just meant I had a lot of time on my hands. Mostly, I hung out with Beeman, scrap-combing all over Ex-Town and trading metal and electronic bits and whatever for food and goods and services. We were good businessmen.

Beeman was a robot, only it didn't matter so much to me because all the skin on his face was torn away so you could see his plastic cheeks and hear the whiz-whirr of his eyes when they moved. This made him okay, because he wasn't pretending to be a person or anything else he wasn't. He wasn't trying to be fake.

We were going over our day's take the afternoon that I first smelled the Far-away. The gray outlines of the downtown towers faded into the sky like sick ghosts, and over our heads, police stingers whined, invisible in the haze. Beeman and I sat with our backs against a crumbled section of concrete wall. At my feet was a can of split-pea soup, not too far out of date, a couple of nine volt batteries, a coil of O-net cable, and two stainless steel rods that were maybe chopsticks.

"Good trade," Beeman said, his words beginning and ending with a little click that I wished would go away. The click hadn't always been there in his speech, but I figured his voicebox was a little broken.

"Except for the soup," I said. "I'll bring that home to my mom."

"Your mom is fat and eats too much."

"Shut your grill." I banged the soup can against his head, but not hard enough to dent either. Beeman wasn't trying to be mean. He just had some bad lines of code.

I was about to explain that my mom didn't eat too much, but the stuff she got from her job at the shoe factory had too much fat and carbohydrate content. I didn't know how to explain carbohydrates to Beeman. Like a battery with too much juice, and not good juice? But then there was this gust of wind, not hot and sticky like normal Ex-Town wind, but cool, like opening the refrigerator, and strange and salty.

"What the fuck is that?" I said.

Beeman activated his olfactories—we thought he might have been some kind of domestic servant with kitchen duties before he lost his face and came this way—and I kept my mouth shut while he did some analysis. After a while, he said, "I'll show you."

He pulled up his T-shirt, which he wore not be fake, but to help keep dirt out of the cracks in his torso, and displayed an image from his media library on the LCD screen above his left nipple-hatch. It showed a big blue field, like the sky on a good day, only made of liquid, rolling with white foam. Clean white birds dove into it. It looked like another world, empty, no clutter, no choking haze, no jagged concrete or melted mounds of spray-form construction. Just peaceful, going all the way out to the clean horizon.

"It's the sea," said Beeman. "We're smelling the sea."

It didn't last long. The freak wind died, and soon Ex-Town smelled like Ex-Town again, and I felt weirdly achy, like something had been stolen from me. I wanted more of the sea, and I told Beeman that I wished we could go to the ocean, and he shrugged and said, "Why can't we?"

There were so many reasons why we couldn't go, but I let him run on. He said we could wade into the water. We could dig for shellfish. We could build a crab trap and make a driftwood fire and cook the crabs in the fire. We could even go fishing.

"Fishing," he said, "is when—"

"I know what fishing is." Just because I didn't go to school didn't mean I didn't know anything. I still went through programs and read, so I knew that fishing is when you try to kill a fish by tricking it with food, only it's not just food but also a deadly hook, and when the fish bites into your hook you remove the fish from its environment, and that's what kills it.

I told him I was all for it, but I'd have to stop by home first and gather some supplies. Which was really just my way of putting Beeman off. I wasn't going anywhere, definitely not off to some beach that might as well have been on the Moon. But I didn't tell Beeman straight up, because once his brain got stuck in a loop, he could be really annoying. Like the time he told me we were going to slay dragons. He had some stories in his memory, and sometimes they leaked out and he took them for real, so for a whole week we couldn't do a thing without him telling me to look out for dragons and saying what we'd do if we found a dragon and warning me that dragons were all this and dragons were all that, and it didn't stop until he accidentally touched a non-insulated wire and got a little jolt that finally shut him up.

So, I avoided Beeman for the better part of a week. Which wasn't fun, because without Beeman, I couldn't come up with an excuse not to spend more time at home.

When Mom wasn't at the shoe factory lacing shoes, she was on the couch, watching TV. There were always burning houses on the screen, and burning palm trees, with flames shooting from the fronds like torches in a traveling Frankenstein electric show.

"I smelled the ocean," I called to her from the stove as I opened the can of pea soup me and Beeman had salvaged earlier. The soup *shlorped* out of the can in a waxy, cylindrical blob. I mushed it down with a spoon. "It was just for a minute," I said, "but it smelled nice." I stirred, smoothing the soup out. "My friend Beeman says he knows how to get there, to the beach. He says it's nice. I think maybe he used to live there, before he . . . before he got sick and came to Ex-Town." Mom knew I had a friend named Beeman, but that's all she knew about him.

The soup got more liquidy and looked more like food. When it started to bubble, I turned down the heat, poured a bowl for Mom and half a cup for myself, and took it out to the living room.

Mom was still staring at the TV. Now it was a hospital ER, with people brought in bleeding. The announcer was talking about a dust girl attack. I turned the volume down and set Mom's soup on a tray in front of her. I checked her pulse and pupils to make sure she hadn't had a stroke, but she was okay. She'd come off a seventeen-hour shift, so she was just crashing from the pump they put in her drink to keep her going. I put her hand on the spoon and she started to feed herself.

"Beeman says we could catch fish right out of the sea. He said the silver ones are safe to eat, on account of being bred with good livers. And as for where we'd sleep, Beeman knows of some caves in the rocks." I dabbed green soup from the corner of Mom's mouth.

That night, I slept on the roof of our building. When the sun came up, I went out and traded some electronics for preserves. I spent the rest of the day throwing rocks and jabbing the air with a sharp metal rod. I stayed out till dark. When I came home, Mom was still sitting there, bathing her face in the cancer-light of the TV. She hadn't moved.

"I think I'm going to go with Beeman," I said. "Do you want to come?"

Half of me wanted her to say "Yes," because I didn't want to leave her alone. And half of me wanted her to say "No," because it would be a long trip, and I didn't think she could make it. And also, what Beeman was saying about the beach might be total bullshit, not because he was lying, but because of his damage and foul code.

But Mom didn't say anything at all.

I went to my bunkbox and removed some of my better salvage, stuff I was saving for when I thought I could get the best trade for it, or for when I really needed it. I left it in a pile on the kitchen counter and wrote out a note: *Mom, I'm out walking with Beeman. We're trying to find the sea. You can sell this stuff if you want. Thanks for the food and shelter and stuff. I love you very much. Don't wait up.*

I met up with Beeman in the stairwell he was staying in because it had a live power socket that he could reach with an extension cord. Without saying anything, he unplugged and stood and went down the stairs and started walking. I followed him outside into the glowing night.

I had a backpack full of Snarfits and Nutzitz and Fritos and bottles of water. Beeman traveled light. He had his salvage bag, but he wouldn't tell me what was in it, except to say he'd visited an alchemist, which, from his explanation, I figured was maybe a little like a drug maker. Drugs were good trade.

"You really know the way?" I asked.

"Yes."

We kept to the rat trails on the outskirts of the garbage mounds. Rubber bits and plastic pebbles skittered down the slopes, dislodged by rodents and dogs. Beeman's eyes flicked nervously, taking dozens of pics and analyzing them for threat, such as poker-heads or dust girls or pigs or cops.

"And we can eat the fish? And live in caves?"

"That's what I said."

"But how come you can remember stuff about the ocean when you can't remember other stuff, like how you got to Ex-Town, or what happened to your face? How can you remember the way when you don't even have a map?"

He was silent for a little bit, processing. Our feet crunched too loudly on the oily gravel path. The air smelled yellow.

"It is not down on any map. True places never are." I had no response to that. "That's *Moby-Dick*," he said. Still no response from me. There was just the click of his camera eyes.

"Alright," he said at last. "I know the path, but I don't know the way."

I stopped in my tracks. He stopped, too, watching me. The sky was orange above us. Small things burrowed in the garbage. Screams and moans floated on the warm wind. It was always like this in Ex-Town.

I closed my eyes and remembered the clean tang of the sea.

"Let's just keep going," I said.

Beeman nodded. If he still had lips, I think he would have smiled.

By sunrise we'd made it out to the quarry, a shallow crater stretching for miles in all directions. Machines with throaty coughs picked through slabs of concrete and sorted them in gigantic bins on the backs of trucks.

"We go around?" I asked.

"No. Through."

"What if we run into quarrymen?"

"Two choices," Beeman said. "First: We try to buy them off with your food and water."

"Then what would I eat?"

"That's the wrong question," Beeman said. "Instead, ask what the quarrymen will eat if they catch us."

"I'm a faster runner than you are, you know."

"That's why the second choice is: Let's not get caught."

We crunched along.

"I'm starting to remember things." Beeman led the way through a maze of rubble piles, fat drops of rain plinking on his flesh. We both wrapped ourselves in sheets of plastic, because it wasn't good to get rain on you, no matter what you were made of. The plastic also helped hide Beeman's stripped robot face from the small groups of people clustered around can fires. We didn't want anyone attacking us and taking Beeman's eyes for scrap.

"Are you remembering anything useful?"

He nodded with a little scrunchy sound in his neck joints. "Things we might encounter on our way. Things to look out for."

"That's useful," I agreed.

He guided us around a cloud of junk gas hugging the ground. "The lands between Ex-Town and the good places are unsettled. They follow the rules of neither place. There could be ronin—knights with no lords." These words didn't mean much to me, but then Beeman said they were like dust girls with no queen, and I got what he meant.

"These are just flashes of memory," he said. "I just know I've seen these things before, maybe the first time I crossed over to Ex-Town."

"So you don't know any good tricks for them?"

He whirred and clicked for a long time. Then, "Maybe you should turn back," he said.

I know Beeman didn't have feelings. All he had were behaviors. But so what? My mom had emotions, but they were so beat down by living and lacing shoes and taking pump that you could hardly tell. If programmed behaviors made you act like a friend, made you do the things a friend did, wasn't that just as good as having feelings? Beeman was my friend, and I didn't need for him to be anything he wasn't.

I think there's something inside us—a lot of us, anyway—that tells us to get out, to find faraway places, to seek adventure, like in Beeman's fractured stories. But what happens when there's no place to go? When everything's the same, no matter where you head. I think that's how people end up like my mom. It's like there's a bird in them, but the bird can't fly, so it just bounces around the walls of their own hearts until its bones are broken.

Maybe Beeman's sea was no more real than his knights and dragons.

Whatever. I didn't want to die of broken bones.

I felt the vibration before I heard anything, a tremor beneath my feet and a queasy shudder in my gut. Then I heard the growl, deep and low and *big*. Blue light fanned through the dark, dusty air ahead of us. The faint outline of a spiked dome emerged over the ridge, threads of disturbed junk gas swirling in its wake. It raised wings like great shards of glass into the sky. I tried to swallow, but my tongue stuck to the roof of my mouth. "Is that a dragon?" I managed to ask.

"Watchdrone," Beeman clicked. "They guard the perimeter here. But, we can call it a dragon. Sure."

Rusty shrieks gouged my ears as it rolled forward on fleximesh tires. Its "wings" turned out to be broken solar battery chargers, and the spikes on its back were its sensor-comm array. Not a dragon. But it could still spit fire. Swivel-mounted guns on its nose painted me and Beeman with red targeting dots.

"What do we do?" I whispered hoarsely.

Beeman turned his skinless face to me. "We slay it," he said. "Follow me."

Lurching awkwardly on his creaking knees, he ran for a tall stack of cinderblocks patched with garbage. The movement set the watchdrone off, and as I chased behind Beeman, gunfire sent up clots of mud at my heels. Panting, I threw myself to the ground and rolled myself up into a ball. Impacting bullets powdered the cinderblocks. The drone shrieked and grumbled closer.

"Don't be afraid," Beeman said, making his voice loud, but still even and calm.

"We're going to die," I shot back. "I'll be as afraid as I want."

"No, that's wrong. If you're too afraid, you won't be able to aim this." He had to raise his voice even more as the gunfire intensified. I covered my head with my hands. Little jagged chunks of flying cinderblock peppered my knuckles.

"Open your eyes," he said. "And I will make you a dragon-slayer."

I felt his cool plastic fingers pry my hands off my head. I couldn't fight him. Beeman wasn't combat-grade strong, but he was still stronger than me.

"Here," he said, putting in my hand an apple-shaped ball of something hard, wrapped in crinkly brown paper. A stiff piece of string curled from its top.

"Is this . . . a grenade?"

"It's what the alchemist gave me. I'll light it, you throw it." He activated his thumb igniter—useful for lighting candles in restaurants, he'd told me—and leaned in toward the grenade.

"Wait! Why do I have to throw it?"

"I have a hitch in my shoulder joint," he said. "I might miss."

He might miss.

I might not let go of the grenade and end up blowing my hand off.

I heard something whiz by my ear. The bullets were coming through the wall.

To do this right, I'd have to take aim. That meant I had to stand up and poke my head over the wall, then lob the grenade over. The thought of exposing myself to the drone's guns made my legs feel like water.

"I don't think I can," I said, hearing the tears in my voice and not caring.

Beeman didn't argue with me. He thrust his thumb forward and lit the grenade. Sparks hissed from the fuse.

I think I screamed. I think I stood and saw the drone's guns turn toward me, and I think the targeting lasers shined in my eyes. What I know is that the grenade was no longer in my hand, and that twisted pieces of armor plating and aluminum sensor rods and fleximesh were raining down on me, and there was a thunderous boom that knocked me back. It felt like having a baseball bat shoved down my ears.

I lay on the ground with my eyes squeezed tight, expecting to hear the clatter-clack of gunfire start up again. But, after a while, the only thing I heard was my own breathing. I opened my eyes. Beeman stood over me.

"You're a dragon slayer now," he said, helping me up.

"Shit," I said, scared and relieved and pissed at Beeman. And really proud of myself for killing the drone. I giggled. "Shit."

Beeman plodded through the wreckage of the drone. "Get your salvage bag," he said. "Dragon parts can be valuable."

Two days later, we came to the road. I had seen roads before—even Ex-Town had roads—but not like this. This road was raised above the ground by thick pillars, like some kind of monument. The constant roar of traffic sounded like wind mixed with rushing water. I didn't need Beeman to tell me this was the Above Road. We knew about the Above Road in Ex-Town. I never thought I would see it. Just hearing the traffic, I got a strong sense of speed, of motion, of people going somewhere, of people having somewhere to go.

I looked for a way up. There was a tall fence topped with coils of razor wire spinning so fast they blurred. On the other side of it were the butchered bodies of people who'd tried to scale it anyway. So, the fence was no-go.

"One does not go over the Above Road," Beeman declared. "One goes beneath it."

We walked alongside the road for miles. Beeman's camera kept clicking away, but he wouldn't say what he was looking for. I followed him, even when he veered away from the road and headed for some dust dunes in the distance. He finally came to a stop before a metal hatch half-buried in the dunes. I helped him brush some of the dust from its waffled surface, and with a couple of yanks, we got it open. A rusted ladder plunged into darkness.

"No way," I said. "This is too easy."

"Wait till we're down," Beeman said. "See if it's still too easy then."

We walked beneath the road. A greenish, witchy glow from the ceiling gave us enough light to see a few yards in front of us, but not more than that. The traffic overhead rumbled big and heavy, so much that the floor shuddered.

"If this leads to the good parts of town, shouldn't somebody be on guard?" We'd been walking for some time and hadn't encountered anything more than fat deadbelly lizards with pale, glowing eyes.

Beeman's voice clicked, forming half-words, as if he wasn't sure what he wanted to say. "There are guardians," he said at last. "They just haven't shown themselves yet."

That was when I started hearing the voices. They floated and swirled in the air like a film of dish soap, forming no words that I could understand.

"Did the alchemist give you any more grenades?" I asked. But Beeman only clicked in his throat.

After a while, the voices started to sound smoky and gravely, like old women. They were scary, but they also made me miss Mom. I wondered if she'd gotten off the sofa yet. I'd left her enough salvage to trade for a few weeks of food, so if she was just sitting there, letting herself starve, I'd be really mad. "I shouldn't have left her," I said.

"It's the voices. They fish for your fears and hurts."

"So what? I still shouldn't have left her."

"Once fired, the bullet cannot question its trajectory."

I thought about that for a while, as the voices snaked around us like seeker cables.

"But I fired myself out of the gun."

"And it's the finest thing you ever did. This way, you won't end up like the others. No matter what happens, you will have done something with your life. Or at least tried to. It doesn't even matter what that something is. It's the doing that's important."

I thought that sounded real nice. I didn't care about nice words. "I don't want my mom to starve," I said.

"She won't. The effects of pump don't last more than the length of two shifts. She'll come out of it, and she'll see your note, and you left her well provided. Also, your mom is fat."

"Yeah," I said. "I guess that's good."

Beeman clicked loudly. Three figures stood a few yards ahead of us. They wore skirts of twistgrass and no shirts, revealing the bluish flesh of their swollen bellies and flat, splayed breasts. They were tattooed or painted all over their bodies, one with eyes, one with ears, one with mouths and tongues.

Beeman gave a stiff little bow. "We offer our respects, road witches."

The one with the ear tattoos turned her body a little and leaned in toward us. Then the one with the eyes took a step closer to us, breathing in a way that made her eyes seem to open wider.

"You've made a mistake," said the one with the tongues. "We're not the witches of the road. Those gals were soft. They perished. Are they the ones who took your skin, plastic man?"

"If they are," said Beeman, "then they also took my memory of it. I think I passed this way, but I can't be sure. I'm never sure. Who are you ladies?"

"We're worse things. We exact a higher price, we witches of the lost."

"But we're not lost," I protested. "We're going to the sea. We've smelled it. We're going to remove fish from their environment and eat them."

The one with the tongues laughed a little, and her laughter echoed off the walls of the tunnel so it sounded like more than three witches laughing.

"One of you might," she said. "But not both."

"Well, Beeman doesn't eat," I noted. I thought that was pretty obvious.

But Beeman clicked. "That's not what they mean."

"The question," said the tongued one, "is which of you will it be? Both will cross, but only one will pass. That is our toll."

I got it. One of us had to die so that the other could go on. I did a lot of trading in Ex-Town, and I understood how transactions worked. They wanted a life. "We should have come with a bigger party," I said.

Beeman clicked.

"C'mon," I said, tugging on his arm. "We'll find another way around."

But Beeman wouldn't budge. And what he did next, he did so fast I couldn't stop him. He pulled up his T-shirt and popped open the access hatch in the middle of his chest and pulled out his power supply. It was just a small black box with a few trailing cables. He let it fall to the ground and then sank to his knees. If hard plastic could deflate, it would be like that.

Beeman was such an idiot. I picked up his power supply and blew grime off the connectors so I could plug it back in without doing him any more damage. But hands scuttled from the shadows. Maybe they were spiders, or crabs, or factory graspers. But they looked liked hands to me. I screamed when they crawled up my legs and arms, and I thrashed and kicked and spat, but I didn't let go of Beeman's power supply. Not until their fingers forced mine open, and they stole Beeman's life.

They ran off with their prize and scattered. I chased after them, but I couldn't tell which one had the power supply, and I was running around in circles and cussing and crying until I lost the hands in the darkness.

"Oh, shit, Beeman." I wanted to kick his body. "Fucking shit."

He had a small reserve power battery. It was only supposed to keep his clock going and prevent him from having to do a full start-up when his power supply was being recharged. I think that's the only reason his eyes didn't go dark right away. It's the only reason he was able to say to me, before his final click, "Go somewhere. Do something."

I looked up toward the witches. Maybe I could negotiate something. But they weren't there anymore. They'd vanished along with the thieving hands.

I tried to lift Beeman, but he was dead weight. Then I dragged him, his plastic skin scraping on rocks and debris. It was slow going, and I knew it was really hopeless, because we'd had to go down a ladder to get here, and I figured we'd have to go up a ladder to get out, and I didn't know how I'd manage both of us.

It took time to get there, but it turned out I was right about the ladder.

I hid him under stones. Not garbage, but clean stones, the cleanest I could find, that I arranged over his body in a mound. With a screwdriver, I scratched the letter B on the biggest one, but I turned it so that the B was facedown, because I didn't want anybody knowing there was something very important under there.

Then I did what Beeman told me. I flew like a bullet fired from a gun.

He was wrong about the beach. The sand was white like bone, and there was glass glittering in it and all sorts of barrels and cans marked with signs—circles, triangles, stink lines, skulls and crossbones—and a lot of the containers were leaking. But there was other stuff, too, lots of discards worth collecting, some of it better than the stuff I found in Ex-Town. So, I did what I knew how to do. I scavenged.

Camps of people lived in shacks and in gaps under piles of rocks, and I learned to identify the ones to trade with and the ones to avoid, and after a couple of weeks, nothing about the beach made me think I couldn't live there.

The black-green ocean stretched all the way out to the foot of the sky. It was always in motion, shimmering, reaching, spreading, crashing against the shore with rippling suds. Sometimes I crawled out on the rocks and lay on my belly, looking down into the water. Silver ghosts darted beneath me, and even though I'd made a good spear, I decided not to remove the fish from their environment. Not unless I got really hungry.

I did eat some crabs I found in the sand, because I felt they deserved it. They reminded me of the witches' hands.

Every evening, the sun went down, all big and low over the water. It was the prettiest thing I'd ever seen, maybe the prettiest thing in the world.

I kept moving.

Enough time passed that I lost track of time, so I don't know how long I'd been living on the beach when I spotted the city out there in the water. It was a clear day, I'd never been able to see farther, and I saw the sparkling towers near the horizon. It looked like a city of orange glass, the same color as the setting sun. Maybe when Beeman was telling me about the sea, that's what he was remembering.

I didn't know how to swim, but maybe I could sail out there. And I was kind of collecting driftwood and plastic siding and other things I figured I could use to build a raft when I found a black box, half-buried in the sand. I knew what it was before fully excavating it.

I weighed it in my hands and brushed sand off the connectors.

In the end, Beeman wasn't my spirit guide, or some wizard pushing and pulling me through a knightly quest. He was a robot with a broken brain, and I couldn't know for sure why he'd convinced me to take a journey with him, or why he'd given up his life so that I could finish it. It only made sense if you took into account his broken hardware and bad code. Or, if you figured that we were friends.

Before me, the golden city on the water glimmered. And far behind me, Beeman, or whatever was left of him, lay dead on the road beneath the road.

I waited for the sun to set again, and then I headed off the beach, hoping that the heart in my hands was a good one.

good mountain

ROBERT REED

Robert Reed sold his first story in 1986 and quickly established himself as a frequent contributor to *The Magazine of Fantasy and Science Fiction* and *Asimov's Science Fiction*, as well as selling many stories to *Science Fiction Age, Universe, New Destinies, Tomorrow, Synergy, Starlight,* and elsewhere. Reed may be one of the most prolific of today's young writers, particularly at short fiction lengths, seriously rivaled for that position only by authors such as Stephen Baxter and Brian Stableford. And—also like Baxter and Stableford—he manages to keep up a very high standard of quality *while* being prolific, something that is not at all easy to do. Reed stories such as "Sister Alice," "Brother Perfect," "Decency," "Savior," "The Remoras," "Chrysalis," "Whiptail," "The Utility Man," "Marrow," "Birth Day," "Blind," "The Toad of Heaven," "Stride," "The Shape of Everything," "Guest of Honor," "Waging Good," and "Killing the Morrow," among at least a half dozen others equally as strong, count as among some of the best short work produced by anyone in the eighties and nineties. Many of his best stories were assembled in his first collection, *The Dragons of Springplace.* Nor is he nonprolific as a novelist, having turned out eight novels since the end of the eighties, including *The Leeshore, The Hormone Jungle, Black Milk, The Remarkables, Down the Bright Way, Beyond the Veil of Stars, An Exaltation of Larks, Beneath the Gated Sky, Marrow,* and *Sister Alice.* His most recent books include two chapbook novellas, *Mere* and *Flavors of My Genius,* a collection, *The Cuckoo's Boys,* and a novel, *The Well of Stars.* Reed lives with his family in Lincoln, Nebraska.

Reed has visited the far future in his Sister Alice stories and in his sequence of stories about the Great Ship, as well as in stories such as "Whiptail" and "Marrow," but here he takes us deeper into the future than he ever has before, to a world whose origin is lost in the labyrinth of time, a world where, as a group of randomly thrown together travelers is about to learn, everything is about to change—and not for the better.

A DOT ON OLD PAPER

Worlds Edge. Approaching now . . . World's Edge!"

The worm's caretaker was an elderly fellow named Brace. Standing in the middle of the long intestinal tract, he wore a dark gray uniform, patched but scrupulously clean, soft-soled boots and a breathing mask that rode on his hip. Strong hands held an angelwood bucket filled with a thick, sour-smelling white salve. His name was embossed above his shirt pocket, preceded by his rank, which was Master. Calling out with a deep voice, Master Brace explained to the several dozen passengers, "From this station, you may find your connecting trails to Hammer and Mister Low and Green Island. If World's Edge happens to be your destination, good luck to you, and please, collect your belongings before following the signs to the security check-points. And if you intend to stay with this splendid worm, that means Left-of-Left will be our next stop. And Port of Krauss will be our last."

The caretaker had a convincing smile and a calm, steady manner. In his presence, the innocent observer might believe that nothing was seriously wrong in the world.

"But if you do plan to stay with me," Brace continued, "you will still disembark at World's Edge, if only for the time being. My baby needs her rest and a good dinner, and she's got a few little sores that want cleaning." Then he winked at the passengers and began to walk again, totting his heavy bucket toward the stomach—up where the mockmen were quartered. "Or perhaps we'll linger here for two little whiles," the old man joked. "But I don't expect significant delays, and you shouldn't let your-selves worry."

Jopale sighed and sat back against the warm pink wall. He wasn't worried. Not through any innate bravery, but because he had been scared for so long now, there was little room left for new concerns. Or so it seemed at that particular moment. In-deed, since his last long sleep, Jopale had enjoyed a renewed sense of confidence. A guarded optimism was taking root. Calculating how far he had come, he saw that most of the world lay behind him now, while it wasn't too much of a lie to tell him-self that Port of Krauss was waiting just beyond the horizon.

Jopale even managed his own convincing smile, and watching his fellow passen-gers, he found one other face that appeared equally optimistic.

A young woman, built small and just a little short of pretty, was sitting directly across from him. She must have come onboard during his last sleep. Maybe at Which-Way, he reasoned. There was a fine university in that ancient city. Perhaps she was a student heading home, now that every school was officially closed. Her bags were few and small. A heavy book filled her tiny lap. Her breathing mask looked as if it had never been used, while a powerful torch rode on her other hip. Her clothes were comfortable if somewhat heavy—wool dyed green with thick leather pads on the knees and elbows. Bare black toes wiggled against a traveling blanket. Her leather boots had tough rubber soles, which was why she didn't wear them inside the worm. She looked ready for a long journey into cold darkness. But where could a young woman be going, and smiling about her prospects, too?

There was one logical conclusion: Jopale caught the woman's gaze, nodded and offered a friendly wink. "Are you like me, miss?" he inquired. "Are you traveling to Port of Krauss?"

She hesitated, glancing at the other passengers. Then she shook her head. "I'm not, no," she told him.

Jopale thought he understood.

"But you're traveling through Krauss," he persisted. "On your way to some other destination, perhaps?"

He was thinking about the New Isles.

But she shook her head, a little embarrassed perhaps, but also taking some pleasure from his confusion.

No one else was speaking just then, and the intestine of a worm was a very quiet place. It was easy to eavesdrop and to be heard whenever you spoke. In quick succession, three young men offered possible destinations, picking little cities set on the auxiliary trails — each man plainly wishing that this woman's destination was his own.

"No," she told them. "No. And I'm sorry, but no."

Other passengers began to play the silly game, and to her credit, the woman remained cheerful and patient, responding immediately to each erroneous guess. Then the great worm began to shake around them, its muscular body twisting as it pulled off onto one of the side trails. Suddenly there was good reason to hurry the game along. The young men were leaving here; didn't they deserve a useful hint or two?

"All right," she said reasonably. "I'll remain on this trail until I'm done." Then she closed her book with a heavy thump, grinning as she imagined her final destination.

"Left-of-Left?" somebody shouted.

"We've already guessed that," another passenger complained.

"Where else is there?"

"Does anybody have a map?"

Jopale stood up. When their worm was young and quite small, holes had been cut through its fleshy sides, avoiding the major muscle groups. Each hole was fitted with progressively larger rubber plugs, and finally a small plastic window that looked as if it was carved from a cold fog. Through one of those windows, Jopale could see the tall buildings of the city and their long shadows, plus the high clear sky that was as close to night as anything he had ever known. What a journey this had been, and it wasn't even finished yet. Not for the first time, Jopale wished he had kept a journal. Then when there was time — once he was living on the New Isles, perhaps — he would write a thorough account of every awful thing that had happened, as well as his final triumphs.

A dozen travelers were now examining their maps, calling out the names of tiny places and abandoned cities. There was a time when people lived in the Tanglelands and points beyond, but that had been years ago. Only the oldest maps bothered to show those one-time destinations. A young man, very tall and shockingly thin, was standing close to the woman — too close, in Jopale's mind — and he carefully listed a string of places that existed nowhere but on a sheet of yellowed paper and faded ink that he held up to the window's light.

"Yes," said the woman, just once.

But the tall man didn't notice. He kept reading off names, pushing his finger along the black worm trail, and the woman was saying, "No, no, no," again, smiling pleasantly at his foolishness.

But Jopale had noticed.

"Go back," he said.

The tall man looked at him, bothered by the interruption.

Then a stocky old woman reached up high, hitting the fellow between the shoulder blades. "The girl said, 'Yes.' Didn't you hear?"

Another woman said, "Read backwards."

The tall man was too flustered to do anything now.

So Jopale took the map for himself, and in the dim light, he made his best guess. "What about Good Mountain?"

Once more, the girl said, "Yes."

"What kind of name is that?" the tall man asked, reclaiming his map, taking the trouble to fold it up neatly. "What does that word mean? 'Mountain'? I've never heard it before."

But the game was finished. Suddenly the old caretaker had returned, carrying an empty bucket with one bony hand. "This is the station at World's Edge," Master Brace called out.

The worm had come to a stop.

"My baby needs to breathe and to eat her fill," he reminded everyone. "So please, you must disembark. With your luggage, and with your tickets." Then a look of mischief came into the weathered face, and he added, "But if you will, please leave your hopes behind. I'd like to claim a few of them for myself."

A few passengers laughed at his bleak humor. But most just shook their heads and growled to themselves, or they quietly spat on the smooth pink floor.

The young woman was picking up her book and bags and her heavy boots, a joyous smile setting her apart from everyone else.

About her destination—the enigmatic Good Mountain—she said nothing at all.

A MOUTHFUL OF HISTORY

Every homeland was once new land, small and thin, pushed about by the willful winds. But the ground where Jopale grew up was still relatively young, and for much of its life, it had been a free-drifting body.

Jopale felt an easy pride toward his native wood—dense and fine—grained and very dark, almost black in its deep reaches, with a thick cuticle and the pleasant odor of sin-spice when sliced apart with steel saws. The wood's appearance and its telltale genetics made it the offspring of Graytell and Sweetsap lineages. According to the oldest nautical maps, an island matching that description first collided with the Continent near what was today Port of Krauss. But it didn't linger for long. In those ancient times, the Continent turned like a gigantic if extraordinarily slow wheel, deep-water roots helping to hold its green face under the eternal sunshine. This tiny unnamed body clung to the wheel's outer edge until it passed into the polar waters, and then it vanished from every record, probably drifting off into the cold gloom.

Unable to grow, the island shrank. Hungry, it drank dry its sap reservoirs. It could have brushed up against the Continent again, perhaps several more times, but some current or chance storm always pushed it away again. Then it wandered, lost on the dark face of the world. The evidence remained today inside its body. Its oldest wood was full of scars and purple-black knots—a catalog of relentless abuse brought on by miserly times. Not even a flicker of sunlight fell on its bleached surface. Starving, the island digested its deep-water roots and every vein of starch. Saprophytes thrived on its surface and giant worms gnawed their way through its depths. But each of those enemies was a blessing, too. The tallest branches of the saprophytes caught the occasional breeze, helping the increasingly frail island drift across the quiet water. And the worms ate so much of the island that it floated easily, buoyed up by the air-filled caverns.

Finally the near-corpse was pushed into the storm belt, and the storms blew just so, carrying it out under the motionless sun. There the island turned a dark vibrant green again, dropping new roots that pulled minerals out of the nearly bottomless ocean—roots that flexed and rippled to help hold the island in the bright sunshine. And that's when new wood was built, and rivers of sugary sap, and a multitude of colonists began to find their way to its shores, including Jopale's distant ancestors.

Twelve hundred years ago, the island again collided with the Continent. But this time it struck the eastern shore, as far from Port of Krauss as possible. Its leeward edge pushed into the Plain of Perfect Deeds while another free-drifting island barged in behind, pinning it in place. Two more islands arrived over the next several years. Small bodies like those often splintered between shifting masses, or they were tilted up on end, shattering when their wood couldn't absorb the strain. Or sometimes they were shoved beneath the ancient Continent, rotting to form black muck and anaerobic gases. But Jopale's homeland proved both durable and extremely fortunate. Its wood was twisted into a series of fantastic ridges and deep valleys, but it outlasted each of the islands that came after it, its body finding a permanent nook where it could sit inside the world's Great Mother.

By the time Jopale was born, his land was far from open water. The sun wobbled in the sky but never climbed too high overhead or dropped near any horizon. By then, more islands and two lesser continents had coalesced with the Continent, and the once-elegant wheel had become an ungainly oval. Most of the world's dayside face was covered with a single unbroken lid too cumbersome to be turned. Competing wood had pushed the weakest lands deep beneath the Ocean, and like the keel of a great boat, those corpses held the Continent in one stubborn alignment, only the strongest currents and the most persistent winds were able to force the oval toward the east or the west.

When Jopale was a young boy, disaster struck. The trade winds strengthened abruptly, and in a single year the Continent drifted west almost one thousand kilometers. Cities and entire homelands were plunged into darkness. Millions of free citizens saw their crops die and their homelands starve. The only rational response was to move away, living as immigrants on other lands, or as refugees, or in a few cases—like Port of Krauss—remaining where they were, in the darkness, making the very best of the tragedy.

To a young boy, the disaster seemed like enormous good fun. There was excitement in the air, a delicious sense of danger walking on the world. Strange new children arrived with their peculiar families, living in tiny homes given to them by charities and charitable guilds. Jopale got to know a few of those people, at least well enough to hear their stories about endless night and the flickering of nameless stars. But he still couldn't appreciate the fact that his own life was precarious now. Jopale was a bright child, but conventional. And he had a conventional family who promised him that the trade winds would soon weaken and the Continent would push its way back to its natural location. What was dead now would live again, those trusted voices argued. The dark lands would grow again. And because he was young and naturally optimistic, Jopale convinced himself that he would live to enjoy that glorious rebirth.

But the boy grew into a rather less optimistic young man, and the young man became a respectable and ordinary teacher of literature. During the average cycle, between one quiet sleep and the next, Jopale wouldn't once imagine that anything important about his world could ever change.

He was in his house, sleeping unaware, when a moderate quake split the land beneath him.

Early-warning sensors recorded the event, and Jopale happened to read about the quake in the morning newsbook. But no expert mentioned any special danger. The Continent was always shifting and cracking. Drowned islands would shatter, and bubbles of compressed gas were constantly pushing toward the surface. There was no compelling reason for worry, and so he ate his normal first-meal and rode his two-wheel over the ridge to work—a small landowners' school set on softer, paler ground just beyond his homeland—and there he taught the classics to his indifferent students, sat through a long department meeting, and then returned home again. Alone in his quiet house, he ate his last-meal and read until drowsy, and then he slipped his sleep-hood over his head and curled up in bed.

His house was small and relatively new, set in a corner of his parents' original farm. Jopale's property was part of a long prosperous valley. But since he was no farmer, he rented most of the ground to neighbors who raised crops and kept fourfoots—milking varieties that were made into stew meat and bone meal once they grew old. The neighbors also kept scramblers for their sweet meat, and they used teams of mockmen to work the land and its animals, lending every waking moment a busy, industrious quality.

Jopale rose with the next cycle and went to work, as he did with the cycle after that, and the cycles that followed.

His homeland was blackish-green beneath its transparent cuticle of hard wax. The rough walls of the valley were covered with parasites and epiphytes that sprang from crevices and wormholes. There were even a few wild animals, though not as many as when he was a boy. With each passing year, people were more common, the forests more carefully tended, and like every inhabited part in the world, his home was becoming domesticated, efficient and ordinary.

For twenty cycles, Jopale went about his life without worry, unaware that the first quake was followed by a series of little events—rumbles and slow, undetectable shifts that let gas and black seawater intrude into the gap between his one-time island and the buried coastline. Nobody knew the danger; there was nobody to blame afterwards. Indeed, only a few dozen people were killed in the incident, which meant that it was barely noticed beyond Jopale's horizon.

He woke early that last morning and slipped quietly from his house. A neighbor woman was still sleeping in his bed. She had arrived at his doorstep at the end of the last cycle, a little drunk and in the mood for sex. Jopale enjoyed her companionship, on occasion, but he felt no obligation to be with her when she woke. That's why he dressed in a hurry and rode off to school. Nobody knew that the seawater and its poisons had traveled so close to the surface. But in the time it takes a lover's heart to beat twice, the pressurized water found itself inside a sap well, nothing above but an open shaft and the sky.

The resulting geyser was a spectacle; every survivor said so. Presumably the doomed were even more impressed, watching the tower of saltwater and foam soar high overhead, dislodged chunks of wood falling around them, and an endless thunder shaking the world as huge quantities of gas—methane laced with hydrogen sulfide—bubbled free.

Suffocation was the standard death, for people and everything else.

The entire valley was killed within minutes. But the high ridges trapped the poisons, keeping the carnage contained. Even before Jopale heard the news, the disaster was finished. By the time he rode home again, crews of mockmen dressed in diving suits had capped the geyser. Engineers were busy drawing up plans for permanent repairs. And it was safe enough that a grieving survivor could walk to the ridge above, holding a perfumed rag against his face as he stared down at the fate of the world.

Water covered the valley floor—a stagnant gray lake already growing warm in the brilliant sunlight. The forested slopes had either drowned or been bleached by the suffocating gases. From his vantage point, Jopale couldn't see his house. But the land beneath the sea was still alive—still a vibrant blackish-green. Pumps would have to be set up, and osmotic filters, and then everything else could be saved. But if the work happened too slowly, too much salt would seep through the cuticle, causing the land to sicken and die. Then the valley would become a single enormous sore, attacked by fungi and giant worms. If nature was allowed its freedom, this tiny portion of the Continent would rot through, and the sea would come up again, spreading along the ancient fault lines, untold volumes of gas bubbling up into the rapidly sickening air.

People had to save the valley.

Why shouldn't they? A rational part of Jopale knew what was at stake—what almost every long-term prediction said was inevitable. But he couldn't shake his selfish need to enjoy the next cycle and the rest of his life. This ground had always been a part of him. Why wouldn't he want it saved? Let other people lose their little places. Let the Continent die everywhere but here. That's what he told himself as he walked down the path, the perfumed rag pressed against his nose and mouth, a selfpossessed optimism flourishing for those next few steps.

Where the gases hadn't reached, epiphytes still flourished. Each tree stood apart from its neighbors, like the hair on the head of an elderly mockman. That made for a tall open forest, which in turn allowed the land to receive its share of sunlight. A flock of day-yabbers watched him from the high branches, leathery wings folded close, bright blue eyes alarmed by nothing except his presence. Giant forest roaches danced from crevice to crevice. Wild scramblers hid in nests of hair and woven branches, calling out at him with soft mournful voices. Then the path bent and dropped, and everything changed. More yabbers lay dead beneath their perches, and countless silverfish and juvenile worms had crawled up out of their holes before dying. A giant golden gyretree—one of Jopale's favorite specimens—was already turning black at its base. But the air was breathable again, the wind having blown away the highest poisons. Jopale wished he had his breathing mask, but had left it inside his house, floating in a cupboard somewhere close to his dead lover. That woman had always been good company. But in death, she had grown unreal, abstract and distant. Walking around a next turn in the trail, Jopale found himself imagining her funeral and what delicate role he might play. And that was when he saw the wild scramblers that had fled the rising gas, but not fast enough. They belonged to one of the ground-dwelling species; he wasn't sure which. They had short hairy bodies and long limbs and little hands that reached out for nothing. Crests of bright blue fur topped the otherwise naked faces. The gases had stolen away their oxygen, then their lives. Already they were beginning to swell and turn black, lending them a strange, unfamiliar appearance; and when Jopale looked into their miserable little faces, he felt a sharp, unbearable fear.

In death more than life, those scramblers resembled human beings.

Here was the moment when everything changed for this scholarly gentleman—this creature of tradition and habit, of optimism and indifference. Gazing into those smoky green eyes and the wide mouths choked by their fat purple tongues, he saw his own future. That he didn't love the dead woman was important: If they were married and had children, and if his family had died today, Jopale would have felt an unrelenting attachment to this tiny corner of the world. In their honor, he would have ignored the urge to run away, remaining even as the land splintered and bled poisons and turned to dust and dead water.

But escape was what he wanted. The urge was sudden and irresistible. And later, when he examined what was possible, Jopale discovered only one solution that gave him any confidence.

If he sold his parents' land to his surviving neighbors and relatives, and if he bled his savings blue . . . then he could abandon the only home he had ever known, and forsake the sun, as well as abandoning all of those foolish little scramblers who couldn't see past their next little while. . . .

WORLD'S EDGE

The great worm had come to a stop, but its muscles continued to shiver, long ripples traveling the length of the body, its misery made all the more obvious by a deep low moan that Jopale didn't hear so much as he felt it in his bones.

World's Edge: In some past eon, the city stood on the Continent's shoreline, nothing beyond but darkening skies and bottomless water. For generations, this great port had served as a home for fishermen, and more importantly, for the brave souls who journeyed onto the trackless sea-hunting giant rust-fins and the copper eels and vicious many-mouths. Fortunes were made from every carcass brought home—great masses of inedible meat and iron-rich bone pushed into furnaces and burned away, leaving nothing behind but a few dozen kilos of precious metal. But new islands were always being born, oftentimes half a world away, and they grew as they wandered, eventually slamming into this coastline and sticking fast. Removed from its livelihood, the once great city fell into hard times. Most of the neighboring towns vanished completely. But World's Edge managed to survive, clinging to its outmoded name, and when times and the world's growing population demanded it, the city blossomed again, new industries and a relentless sense of commerce producing a metropolis where two million people could live out their busy, unexceptional lives.

Birth and growth, followed by death and rebirth—no story told by Man was as important as this.

Then the Continent suddenly drifted west, and again, World's Edge wore the perfect name.

Jopale considered the ironies as he carried his bags to the front of the intestine, then out through an artificial sphincter fitted into the worm's side. From there, it was a short climb to the station's high wooden platform. A bright sign flashed from the top of the greeting arch, displaying the present atmospheric readings, followed by the cheery promise, "No hazards, none foreseen." The sun hovered just above the eastern horizon, stratospheric clouds and low pollution obscuring only a portion of its fierce glare. Squinting, Jopale faced the sun. At least two large balloons were visible in the sky, suspended on long ropes, spotters busily watching the land for geysers or more subtle ruptures. Behind him, long shadows stretched toward lands rendered unfit for normal life. Not that nothing and no one could live out there . . . but still, Jopale felt as if he was standing on the brink of a profound desolation, and that image struck him in some innate, profoundly emotional fashion. . . .

The caretakers walked on top of their friend and along the concave, heavily greased trail, examining the worm's gray skin and poking its long tired muscles, sometimes using electric wands but mostly employing nothing but their bare hands. The worm's reflexes were slow. The old caretaker said as much to the younger workers. "She's gone too far with too many in her empty bellies," Master Brace complained, gesturing at the milling passengers. "She needs half a cycle at least, and all she can eat."

Jopale realized their delay would be longer than he had anticipated. Pulling two tickets from his traveler's belt, he carefully read the deeply legal language. If he didn't reach Port of Krauss within another fifteen cycles, the worm's owners would refund half of the value of the first ticket. But that was an inconsequential gesture, all things considered. Because the second ticket promised him a small cabin on-board a methane-fueled ship that would leave for the New Isles two cycles later. Punctuality was his responsibility. If he was late, the ticket was worthless. And Jopale would be trapped in the Port with every other refugee, shepherding the last of his money while absorbing news from around the world, hoping that the coming night-mare would take its time and he could eventually purchase a new berth on some later, unpromised vessel.

What good would fear do him now? Or rage?

"No good at all," he said with a stiff voice, turning his back to the sun.

The station was a strangely quiet place. The only other worms were small or plainly ill, and even those specimens were pointed west, aimed at the darkness, as if waiting for the order to flee. Besides caretakers, the only human workers were soldiers. Older men, mostly. Disciplined and probably without families—exactly the sort of people to be trusted in the worst of times. Two soldiers stood farther up the worm, guarding the sphincter leading into the stomach. Mockmen waited in the darkness. Each creature had its owner's name tattooed on its forearms and back. Humans had to come forward to claim what was theirs, and even then, the soldiers questioned them with suspicious voices—as if somebody might try to steal one of these creatures now.

The mysterious young woman was standing with the other passengers, her book in one arm, eyes pointed in the general direction of the unloading.

"Which is yours?" Jopale asked.

She didn't seem to hear the question. Then he realized that her gaze reached past the mockmen, bright tan eyes staring at the night lands, her mind probably traveling on to her destination.

"Good Mountain, is it?" Jopale asked.

"I'm sorry, no." She was answering his first question, smiling in his general direction. "I don't own any of these creatures."

Jopale had brought a mockman from home, to help with his bags and his life, as well as giving him this ready excuse to stand where he was, chatting with this young woman.

With a quiet, gentlemanly voice, he offered his name.

She nodded and said, "Yes. Good Mountain."

They had found a pattern. He would ask some little question, and she would answer his former question.

"The word 'mountain,'" he said. "Do you know what it means?"

She smiled now, glancing at his face. "Do you?"

He allowed himself the pleasure of a wise nod. "It is an ancient word," he answered. "The oldest texts employ it. But even by then, the word had fallen into a rotten disuse."

"Really?"

"We have words for ridges and hills. With great clarity, we can describe the color and quality of any ground. But from what we can determine, using our oldest sources, 'mountain' implies a titanic uplifting of something much harder than any wood. Harder and more durable, and a true mountain rises high enough to puncture the sky. At least according to some expert interpretations."

She laughed, very softly. "I know."

"Do you?"

"That's why they picked the name," she explained.

Jopale didn't understand, and his expression must have said as much.

"Of course, there's no actual mountain there," she admitted. "It's just a flat plain shoved high by a set of faults and buoyant substrates. But there was a time, long ago, when the Continent pushed in from every side, and an entire island was buried. Buried and carried a long ways under the sea."

The woman liked to explain things. Was she a teacher?

"Interesting," Jopale offered, though he wasn't convinced that it was.

"That island is like a mountain in reverse, you see. It extends a long ways below the waterline. Like a fist sticking out from the bottom of the Continent, reaching deeper into our ocean than any other feature we know of."

"I see," he muttered.

But why she would call it, "Our ocean"? How many oceans were there?

"That's why the science station was built there," she explained. "'A good mountain to do research.' That what my colleagues used to joke."

"What kind of research?" he asked.

"Land distortions and water cycles, mostly. And various experts who work with that submerged ground."

He said, "Really?" with a false enthusiasm.

The woman nodded, returning to her distant stare.

"Is that your specialty?" he asked, trying to read the binding of her book. "Prehistoric islands?"

"Oh, no." She passed the heavy book to her other arm.

"Then what do you do?"

It was an exceptionally reasonable question, but she was a peculiar creature. Smiling as if nothing had ever been funnier, she said, "Do-ane." She wasn't quite looking at his face, telling him, "That is my name."

He didn't have a ready response.

"You told me yours. I assumed you wanted to know mine."

"Thank you," Jopale muttered.

"I'm sorry, but I can't say anything else."

He nodded and shrugged. And then his mockman emerged from the stomach: A mature female with big blue eyes riding high on her broad stoic face. Jopale had recently purchased her from a cousin, replacing the mockmen he had lost when the valley flooded. For her species, she was smart and adaptable. By any standard, she was loyal, and in countless domestic tasks, she was helpful. And like every passenger from the worm's stomach, she smelled of acid and other unpleasant secretions. But at least this creature didn't want to play word games, or dance silly secrets before his eyes.

Jopale spoke to one of the soldiers, proving his ownership to everyone's satisfaction.

"My bags," he ordered.

The creature snatched each by its rope handle.

"This way," he said. Then with a minimal nod, he excused himself from Do-ane, pushing through the station, searching for some place where the noble refugee might eat a fit meal.

PARANOIA

Dining halls next to worm stations were rarely elegant. World's Edge was an exception: Using the local wood, artisans had carved long blocks into a series of omega-shaped beams, each a little different from the others, all linked like ribs to form a single long room. Woven gyre-tree branches created a porous roof. Heavy planks had been bleached white and laid out for a floor, each fastened to the foundation with solid pins made of dense black knot-wood. The tables and chairs were brightly colored, orange and gold predominating, everything made from slick new plastics—one of those expensive programs underwritten by some well-meaning government agency, public moneys helping lock away a few breaths of methane into this more permanent form. The usual indoor epiphytes clung to the overhead beams—vigorous plants with dark leaves that thrived in the artificial light, their fingerlike roots drinking nothing but the travelers' nervous breathing. Jopale noticed a familiar figure planted at one end of a busy table, accompanied by two mockmen that sat backwards on turned-around chairs, eating their rations off their laps—a common custom in many places.

"May I join you?" asked Jopale.

"Please." The man was tall even when he was sitting, and unlike practically everyone else in the place, he wasn't eating. His old map was opened up before him, and with long fingers and sharpened nails, he measured and remeasured the distances between here and Port of Krauss.

Jopale set down his platter and handed his mockman two fresh rations of syrup-and-roach. The big female settled on the floor, legs crossed, hands and mind focused on the screw-style lids on both wooden jars.

Unsure what to say, Jopale said nothing. But silence proved uncomfortable, which was why he eventually picked the most obvious topic. "So why are you going to Port of Krauss?"

The thin man glanced up for a moment, apparently startled.

"You are going there, aren't you?"

"No."

"I'm sorry then," said Jopale. "I just assumed—"

"My trip doesn't end there," the thin man continued. "I have business, of a kind . . . business in another place. . . ."

"The New Isles?"

Surprise turned to pleasure. "Are you going there too?"

Jopale nodded.

"Well, good. I knew there had to be others. Wonderful!"

Somehow that revelation didn't bring comfort. Jopale had the impression that his companion was difficult, and the idea of traveling with him across the rest of the Continent and then out over the Ocean felt daunting, if not out and out unpleasant.

"I need somebody to keep my confidence up," the tall man proclaimed.

What did confidence have to do with anything?

"My name is Rit."

"Jopale."

Rit didn't seem to hear him. Glancing over his shoulder, he observed, "There aren't any people working in the kitchen. Did you notice?"

Only mockmen were cooking and washing dishes. There wasn't even an overseer walking among them, keeping order.

"I don't know if I could make myself go to work," Jopale admitted. "All that's happening, even if it's far from here—"

"Not that far away," Rit interrupted.

"What? Has the news changed?"

"Aren't things awful enough as they are?" The tall man shuddered, then steered clear of that dangerous subject. He licked his lips and stared down at the big map, fingers stretched wide. Then with a tight voice, he asked the lines and tiny dots, "You do believe in the Isles, don't you?"

"Why wouldn't I?"

The narrow face twisted. "But have you ever seen the Isles? Or do you know anyone who's actually visited them?"

Jopale had never considered the possibility. "What do you mean? How could they not exist?" He immediately reached for the only book in his personal satchel—a leather-bound, professionally printed volume full of photographs and exhaustive explanations. With his voice rising, he said, "I haven't heard anything like that. Not even the rumor of a rumor."

Rit shook his head and began to fold up his map, saying to no one in particular, "I'm sorry. I have these panics. Always have."

The man was insane, or nearly so.

"It's just that in times like these . . ." Rit took a moment to compose himself. "When disaster reigns, deceitful souls prosper. Have you noticed? Criminals rise up like worms inside dead wood. They come from below to hurt good people, for profit and for fun."

There was an obvious, ominous counter to that logic. "We've never seen times as bad as these," Jopale said.

That observation earned a terrified but respectful look from his companion. "I suppose that's so."

"Why go to so much trouble to mislead us? With the worst happening, in far-off places now and maybe here soon . . . even a despicable thief knows he wouldn't have enough time to enjoy his money . . ."

"Unless he doesn't believe he will die." Rit leaned across the table, putting his bony face close to Jopale's face. "Most people still don't appreciate their mortality. They read about the deaths of strangers. Places they don't know are poisoned or burning. But until their lungs are sick and their skin is cooking, they think their chances are exceptionally good."

There were stubborn souls in the world, yes. Jopale knew a history teacher—a brilliant man by any measure—who had openly mocked him. "Nothing ever changes in the world," the colleague had claimed. "The Continent will shatter here and there, and some old islands will be destroyed. But others islands will survive, along with the people riding them. That is the irrefutable lesson of our past, Jopale. Our world is tough, our species is lucky, and both will survive every onslaught."

Jopale nodded for a moment, as if accepting that remembered lecture. Then with an honest conviction, he reminded Rit, "There are easier and much cheaper ways to fool people. And steal a fortune in the process, I might add."

His companion gave a grudging nod.

"I am like you," Jopale continued, knowing that he wasn't anything like this crazy fellow. "I've had some suspicions, yes. I wanted to know: Were the New Isles really as strong and smartly designed as their builders claim them to be? So I made inquiries before committing my money. And yes, the New Isles do exist. They were built at the Port of Krauss, at the main shipyard. The last Isle was launched just a year ago, and it's still being towed to its final destination. I even spoke to workers at the Port, using a radiophone. And while they couldn't promise that the Isles were located in safe places, or that I had an open berth waiting for me and my mockman, they were definite about one issue: They had done their best work, fabricating the largest, strongest ships humans had ever known."

Jopale glanced at the cover of his book. From the bluffs overlooking the unlit ocean, someone had taken a photograph showing a wide vessel built from tough old wood. Some of the strongest, most enduring land in the world had been cut free of the Continent and floated into position, then carved into a cumbersome but durable ensemble of hulls and empty chambers. And to make the Isle even stronger, a fortune in refined metals had been fashioned into cables and struts and long nails that were fixed throughout the Isle's body. Metal was what Port of Krauss was famous for—the rare elements that could be filtered from the cold dark seawater. With the best alloys in the world, insulated tanks were built, and they were filled with methane and dangled far beneath each Isle, using the sea's own pressure and cold to help keep the gas liquefied. That gas would eventually power lights and hydroponics, with enough energy in reserve to tear the seawater apart . . . to carve hydrogen from the precious oxygen, allowing everyone to breathe without any cumbersome masks.

With the surety of a good teacher, Jopale dismissed Rit's concerns. "These are genuine sanctuaries, and my new home is waiting for me. I just have to get there now. And I feel quite sure that I will."

Saying those words, he believed them.

Rit seemed to take it all to heart. He put away his map and found his own copy of the member's handbook, opening it to one of his favorite pages.

Finally, Jopale began to eat his meal. He had purchased two scrambler hands, fried but not too greasy, and a whitish lump of sweetcake and cultured algae in a salty soup, all washed down with a tall bottle of fermented sap imported from the Earlands. The drink was the most expensive item on the limited menu, and it was the most appreciated. The hard kick of the liquor was already working on his mood when his companion spoke again, using a sorry little voice to ask, "But what if?"

"What if what?" Jopale responded testily.

"What if these thieves and con artists did believe this world was coming to an end? And by promising berths to us and maybe a million others like us, they earned enough money to finance their own salvation."

Jopale grimaced, breathing through his teeth.

"What if a New Isle is waiting, but not for us?" Rit persisted.

Jopale felt a smile emerge on its own. Then with a bitter laugh, he told his traveling companion, "Well then. Then we aren't in any worse shape than the rest of the world. Now are we?"

ON AGAIN

Jopale had always excelled at school, including respectable grades earned in each of the three sciences. But he never achieved a profound understanding of genetics or selective forces. He learned what was absolutely necessary, relying on his clear memory when it came to the standard exams. Introductory classes demanded little else, while the high-level courses—those rarefied environments where professors wanted more than disgorged fact and holy equations—had never been in his future.

But one lesson Jopale took from science was this: Mockmen were wondrous creatures, pliable and creative by every genetic measure.

A glance around the station proved that truism. Most of the mockmen were big creatures, two or three times larger than a grown human. They had been bred for compliance and power when necessary and a minimal metabolism to help reduce the food bills. Yet some of these creatures were small and slender as a child. And a few of the kitchen workers were quicker than any human being—a blessing in this hurlyburly business. What's more, no two of them could be confused for each other, even though they might be siblings or a parent and grown child. All had an oval face and a protruding chin beneath a small, seemingly inadequate mouth. Yet each face was unique. Jopale's own girl had descended from giants that lived for generations on his family farm—a generalist by design and by training, her head topped with beastly red hair, a dramatic chin hanging from the parabolic jaw, and blue inhuman eyes gazing out at a world full of motion and incomprehensible purpose. If the creature had a voice, she would have commanded a vocabulary of several hundred easy words. But of course the larynx was pierced when she was a baby, leaving her able to communicate only with simple gestures and vaguely human expressions. A creature of habit and duty, his mockman was too simple to understand the dire state of the world—an ignorance that Jopale couldn't help but envy, at least now and again.

"Everything with a spine arose from a common ancestor," he had learned long ago. His biology professor—an ancient woman blessed with her own sturdy backbone—explained to the class, "A single creature must have been the originator of us all. On some ancient continent, long dead and rotted away, this precursor to humans ran about on two legs, climbing up into the saprophytes and epiphytes, grabbing what food it could with its primitive hands."

"Like a scrambler?" a student had asked.

Jopale didn't ask the question, thankfully. The professor reacted with a click of the tongue and a sorry shake of her head. "Hardly," she replied. "Scramblers are as far removed from our founding species as we are. As the mockmen are. Flying yabbers, copper eels, plus everything else you can name . . . all of these species would look at that vanished organism as being its very distant ancestor. That is, if simple beasts could ever think in such abstract terms."

"But where did the first vertebrates come from?" another student inquired. "From the sea? Or from some earlier continent?"

"Nobody knows," the professor replied. Then with the surety of age, she added, "And nobody will ever discover that unnecessary answer. Since there's no way to study the matter any further than it has been studied by now."

Jopale had been sitting in the station for several hours, changing position as the plastic chair pushed against his rump. At that moment, he happened to be thinking about his biology teacher, long dead, and about the nature of surety. And to stave off boredom, he was studying the astonishing diversity of false humans who sat and walked among those who were real.

Suddenly a short, homely mockman entered the dining hall. It was female, dressed in the stiff uniform of a station worker. And like with a few of her species, some quirk of genetics had swollen her skull, giving her a genuine forehead under a cap of thick black hair. That forehead was remarkable enough. But then the newcomer opened her mouth, revealing a clear and exceptionally strong voice.

"The westbound worm is rested and ready," she sang out, the clarity of each word taking travelers by surprise. "Leave by way of the door behind me, sirs and madams. If you have a ticket. You must have a ticket. The westbound worm is fed and eager. She will be leaving shortly, my friends."

Most of the room stood up.

"That wasn't as long as I feared." An elderly woman wearing elegant clothes and amber gems was smiling at her good fortune. "I was ready to sit for quite a while longer," she admitted to her companion.

A handsome man, perhaps half her age, muttered, "I wonder why this is."

The rich woman had to laugh at him. "It's because we are special, darling. What more reason do you need?"

Jopale was among the last to reach the open doorway. Soldiers were waiting, carefully examining each ticket and every piece of identification. Meanwhile, the uniformed mockman stood beside the long line, smiling happily. Why did that creature make him feel so uneasy? Was it her face? Her voice? No, what bothered Jopale was the way she stared at the other faces, black eyes settling only on those who were human.

"Good journey," she said to Jopale.

Then to Rit, who was directly behind him, she said, "You are in trustworthy hands, sir. No need to worry."

She could read the man's fear.

A one-in-a-million creature, thought Jopale. Or there was another explanation, and far more sordid, too. Glancing over his shoulder, he wondered if she could be a hybrid—a quirk of biology that wasn't destroyed at birth, but instead was fed and trained for this halfway demanding task. Nothing like her would ever happen in his homeland. It wasn't allowed. But World's Edge was a different part of the world, and Jopale's long journey had taught him many lessons, including that every place had its own culture, and cultures were defined by odd little customs understandable only to themselves.

"This way, this way!" the old caretaker cried out.

Jopale showed the soldiers what they wanted to see, his own mockman standing silently to his right.

Master Brace was at the end of the long platform, shouting for the passengers and waving both arms. Even at a distance, his face betrayed a look of genuine concern. Something bad must have happened. But their giant worm lay motionless on the greased trail, apparently sleeping. Its intestine was still jammed full of half-digested food. The worm's bloated shape said as much, and looking through the plastic windows, Jopale saw a rich dark mixture of masticated wood pulp and sweet knuckle-roots, happy muscles pressing the feast into new positions, the elastic walls working on the stubborn chunks and bubbles.

The passengers were being led up toward the stomach.

Jopale was disgusted, but compliant. The wealthy woman who talked about being special was now first to complain. Shaking an accusing finger at the caretaker, she said, "I did not pay for an acid bath.

The caretaker had discarded his charm. He looked tired and perhaps a little scared, not to mention short of patience. "Her stomach isn't hungry anymore," he said with a loud, slow voice. "And it's thoroughly buffered, madam. You'll be comfortable enough inside there. I promise."

"But my mockmen—"

"Will ride above, in the open air." Brace gestured impatiently. The pilothouse was fixed on top of the long blind head, and behind it were ropes and straps and simple chairs. With a loud voice, Brace told every passenger, "If we waited for my baby to empty her bowels, we'd remain here until the next cycle. Which might be just as well. But word just came up from One-Time—"

An earlier stop, two cycles to the east.

"A new fissure has broken open there. The situation is dicey. And since there's room enough inside the stomach, I'm sure you can see . . . this is the best answer to our many problems. . . . !"

The passengers turned together, gazing toward the east. While everyone was busily filling his own belly, the bright face of the sun had been covered over. Distant clouds seemed thicker than natural and blacker, and the clouds were rising up like a great angry wall, towering over the green land that these people had only recently journeyed across.

A purposeful panic took hold of the crowd.

Jopale claimed his belongings from his mockman and ordered her to climb on top of the worm. Then he passed through the cramped sphincter and into the stomach, sniffing the air as an afterthought, pleased to find it fresh enough and even a little scented. The shaggy pink floor was a little damp but not truly wet. Worm stomachs were shorter than the duodenum, and most of the floor had been claimed. A simple latrine stood in back. Do-ane sat alone in the middle of the remaining space, hiking boots beside her. She showed Jopale a polite smile, nothing more. Where else could he go? Nowhere. Claiming the empty stomach to her right, he threw open his traveling blanket and inflated his pillow. Setting the pillow on the highest portion of his floor, he tried to ignore her. Then Rit knelt on the other side of the young woman, carefully laying out his blanket, preparing his fragile nerves for the next leg of this very long journey.

Jopale was terrified, genuinely terrified, right up until the moment when the alarms were sounded.

The sharp wailing of sirens began in the distance, diluted and distorted by the worm's body. Then the station's sirens joined in, and the floor rolled ominously. Was it a quake, or was the worm waking? Probably both reasons, he decided. Then the stomach sphincter closed, choking off the worst of the noise, and the giant creature gulped air into its long lungs and into its empty belly, needing little prompting to begin squirming against the trail's slick surface. Rolling muscle and the long powerful tail created a sound unlike any other in nature. Jopale was reminded of a thick fluid being forced down a very narrow drain. Slowly, slowly, the creature built its momentum, the trail's oils eliminating most of the friction, allowing its bulk to gradually become something swift and relentless.

Passengers held their air masks in their hands, waiting for instructions or the telltale stink of a gas cloud. Because there had to be gas somewhere close. A quake wasn't reason enough to sound the city's alarms. Yet curiously, in the midst of this obvious emergency, Jopale felt much calmer. He knew he had to remain vigilant and clearheaded. And gas was only an inconvenience to a man with the proper equipment. Standing beside one of the few stomach windows, he watched the station vanish behind them, replaced by broad government buildings and assorted shops, and then suddenly, by countless homes stacked three deep and set beside narrow, shade-drenched streets. A few mockmen were walking with purposeful shuffles; otherwise no one appeared in the open. Most of the homes were shuttered and sealed. If poisons were boiling up from below, private detectors would smell them, and people would huddle inside their little safe rooms, breathing filtered air or oxygen from bottles, or breathing nothing but the increasingly stale air. An awful experience, Jopale knew. There was no more helpless feeling in the world. Yet his overriding emotion now was a tremendous, almost giddy relief.

He had escaped again, just in time.

Do-ane joined him. The window was quite tiny, not designed for looking outside, but instead to let in sunlight and allow the caretakers to monitor the mockmen who normally rode here. Do-ane stood on her toes to look outside. She seemed prettier when she was nervous, and rather more appealing. In her hand was the most sophisticated gas-gauge that Jopale had ever seen. In a whisper, she said, "Hydrogen sulfide."

His own confidence fell to pieces. Methane was awful—suffocating and flammable—but the putrid hydrogen sulfide gas was far worse. There were places beneath the Continent where the dissolved oxygen had been exhausted. The living wood and dark currents couldn't freshen that water any more. And different types of rot took hold there, anaerobic bacteria creating a sour poison that could kill within minutes.

The city kept sliding past.

"Is that a body?" she asked suddenly.

What might be a mockman was lying on its side, tucked against the foundation of a long house. Or was it just trash dressed in a blanket? Jopale wasn't sure, and then they had passed both the body and the street. With his own quiet voice, he said, "It was nothing."

"It was human," Do-ane said.

"A sleeping mockman," he offered. "Or a dead one, maybe. But that means nothing. Disease or age, or boys out damaging property, maybe."

"Do you think so?" Do-ane asked hopefully.

"Oh, yes," he said. And because it felt good, he again said that word. "Yes." Then he added with his most reasonable tone, "If the gas was that terrible, the streets would be jammed with suffocating bodies."

She looked at him, desperate to believe those sordid words.

Suddenly Jopale couldn't remember why the young woman had bothered him. He smiled and she did the same, and with that, they leaned against the living wall, watching the city fall away and the countryside reemerge. Tall epiphytes spread their leaves to the waning light. Rain showers were soaking the land to the south. Maybe those clouds would drift north; that would lessen the chances of a fire, at least for a little while. Right? Meanwhile, Do-ane's sensor continued to record the fluctuating levels of sulfides, plus the usual methane and ethane that were pulled inside whenever the worm belched and swallowed more air. But none of the toxins reached a suffocating level, and except for a foul taste in the back of the mouth, they remained unnoticed by the other passengers.

Finally the sun merged with the horizon and the numbers began to fall again, working their way back toward levels that were normal enough, at least over the last few years.

Jopale sat on his blanket, enjoying his good fortune.

Then for no clear reason, he thought about the hybrid woman back at the station—the black-haired creature with the big lovely voice—and it occurred to him that unlike the human soldiers, she'd had no air mask riding upon her hip.

Had she survived?

And why, in the face of everything, did he seem to care?

PLANS OF ESCAPE

At the school where Jopale taught, the conclusion of each term meant a party thrown for the faculty and staff. Liquor was involved, and school politics, and during that final gathering, some extraordinarily raw emotions. Radiophone broadcasts had just reported a cluster of villages in the distant north destroyed by an eruption of poisons. Sober voices were repeating rumors—false rumors, as it happened—that the local engineers and mockmen crews couldn't stop the enormous jets of methane. The party soon divided itself into two camps: Some wanted to embrace their doom, while others clung to any excuse for hope. Jopale found himself on the fringes of the argument, unsure which stance to take. Then a colleague wandered past, his cup drained and his mind intoxicated. Listening to a few declarations of terror, the normally timid fellow found a buoyant courage. "The situation is not that dangerous," he declared. "Believe me, we can seal up holes ten times worse than what I've heard described in these stories!"

The optimists happily embraced those defiant words.

But the teacher shrugged off their praise. "You're as silly as the rest of them," he declared. "And at least as ignorant, too."

"What do you know?" someone asked.

"More than anybody else here, I can tell you that." Then the drunken man scanned the room. Searching for an escape route? No, he wanted the big bowl set on the central table—a leather bowl where sweet punch and fermented gig-berries created a small pond. "Look here," he called out. "I'll show you exactly what I mean."

His audience gathered at the table, maintaining a skeptical silence.

Using the thick decorative leaves of a hush-woad, the teacher began covering the pond's surface. And while he worked, he lectured about the wooden Continent and the bottomless Ocean and how things like rot and methane were the inevitable end products in a very ancient cycle.

Jopale understood it all, or he thought he did.

Then a third teacher—the most accomplished science instructor on their staff—cleared his throat before mentioning, "This isn't your professional area, you know."

"My area?" The lecturer with the leaves asked, "What is my area? Remind me now."

"Maps," the scientist said, that single word wrapped inside a smug and blatantly dismissive tone.

Anger showed on the colleague's face. But he didn't lose his temper. He just shook his head for a moment and set another layer of leaves on the pond. Then with a quiet, brittle voice, he said, "Jopale."

"Yes?"

"What do you know about the Man-and-Sky texts?"

Jopale had read excerpts in college. But even in these modest academic circles, it was best to appear well trained. "I studied them for a semester," he replied with a careful tone. "What about them?"

"How old are they?"

"No one knows."

"But judging by the different dead languages, we can assume they're probably several different ages . . . a mishmash of writings from a series of unnamed authors. Yes?"

Jopale offered a nod.

His colleague took a deep breath. "Scholars believe the Man-and-Sky offers at least three descriptions of the world, possibly four. Or five. Or even six. What's certain is that each description is not that much different from our world. There is a large continent and a motionless sun. Only the names of every location have been changed, and the peoples use different languages, and sometimes the animals and vegetation are not quite recognizable."

Like bored students, the teachers began to mutter among themselves.

The lecturer placed a hand upon the floating leaves. "My area . . . my intellectual passion . . . is too complicated for ordinary minds. I'll grant you that. Thousands upon thousands of islands coalesce into a single body, each island fighting with its stubborn neighbors to remain on the Ocean's surface, basking in the brightest possible sunshine. It makes for a grand, glorious puzzle that would baffle most of you. . . ."

Feeling the insult, his audience fell silent.

"The Man-and-Sky texts give us the best maps of those earlier continents. And they offer some of the most compelling accounts of how the old continents fell to pieces." The geographer picked a pale yellow straw off the table, his mouth pressed into a wide, painful smile. "You probably don't know this. Those lost continents were barely half the size of ours. There is no evidence—none—that the islands in the past have ever managed to cover the entire day-face of our world. Which makes what is happening now into a singular event. An elaborate collision of random events, and perhaps selective forces too."

"What about selective forces?" the scientist grumbled.

"Which islands prosper?" their colleague asked. "The strong ones, of course. And those that remain on the surface for the longest time. Those that can resist the poisons in the bad times, and those that will endure the longest, darkest famines." Then he shrugged, adding, "In earlier cycles, the wood beneath us would have been dead long ago. The collapses would have come sooner; the tragedies would have been smaller. But this time—in our time—the islands have descended from a few durable lineages. And what's more, every other force at play in the world has pushed us to the worst stage imaginable."

Even in his blackest moods, Jopale didn't want to believe that.

"We don't know how much methane is under our toes," the lecturer admitted. "But even the median guesses are awful."

A small, sorry voice said, "The entire world could suffocate."

Jopale had offered those words.

"Oh, but it's far worse than that!" His colleague stuck the long straw into his mouth, then slipped the other end into a small wooden flask hidden in his coat pocket. He sucked up the liquid and covered the straw's upper end with his thumb, lifting the leaves until he could see the open punch, then he set the bottom of the straw against the sweet drink. "Of course I mean this as an illustration," he mentioned. Then he winked at the scientist, saying, "I know, I know. There's no genuine consensus among the experts. Or should I say specialists? Since there is, if you think about it, an important difference between those two words. . . ."

"Don't," Jopale cautioned.

But the man struck a long match, making a yellow flame. Then winking at his audience, he said, "Of course, the Continent might collapse slowly, over many generations. A little gas here, a lot of gas there. People die, but not too many of us. And maybe we will marshal the necessary resources. Cut holes to the Ocean below and let out the bubbles in manageable little breaths. Or pump pure oxygen down under our feet, freshening the cold dead water." He waved the flame in front of his eyes. "Perhaps humans can do whatever it takes, and our atmosphere isn't destroyed when the hydrocarbons eat up our precious free oxygen."

"You're drunk," the scientist complained.

"Wonderfully drunk, yes." Then the teacher of city names and island positions laughed, and he lowered the flame.

Everyone stared at the leaf-covered punch.

Jopale assumed that the liquid from the vial was pure alcohol. But his colleague had decided to make a more effective demonstration of his argument, which was why he used a collection of long-chain hydrocarbons purchased from an industrial source—a highly flammable concoction that made a soft but impressive wooshing sound as it set the leaves on fire, and then the drunken man's hand, and a moment later, his astonished, pain-wracked face.

THE EVENING AIR

Left-of-Left was the next official stop—a safe station where the hard-pressed worm could catch its breath and empty its swollen bowels. Most of the passengers had fallen asleep by then. The only light inside the crowded stomach came from a bio-luminescent culture hung on an acid-etched brass hook. Do-ane hadn't bothered with a sleeping hood, curled up on her blanket, hands sweetly tucked between her pillow and face. Rit didn't seem able to relax, sitting up occasionally to adjust his hood or take another white melatonin pill. Only Jopale didn't feel tired—an illusion brought on by too much nervous energy—and that was why he stepped outdoors, using this brief pause to check on his mockman's health, breathe the open air, and absorb the depressing sights.

The station was empty and dark. Information displays had been turned off, while the offices and cafeteria had their doors locked. Master Brace was standing alone on the platform, watching his colleagues use electric wands to stimulate the worm's anus. Jopale approached, then hesitated. Was the old caretaker crying? But Brace sensed his audience. Suddenly wiping his eyes with a sleeve, he turned to the lone passenger, habit or perhaps some unflagging sense of duty helping him create a magnificent, heartening smile.

"A gloomy darkness, but a very pleasant climate," he remarked. "Don't you think so, sir?"

Jopale nodded.

"I've stood here at least a hundred times, sir."

"With our worm?"

"Oh, yes." Men like Brace often spent their professional lives caring for the same worm, learning its talents and peculiarities; and since worms were creatures of relentless habit, they were rarely asked to change routes or schedules.

"Pleasant," the old man said again.

Tall clouds stood on the eastern horizon, obscuring the last hints of sunlight. From a distance, the clouds resembled a thick purplish-red tower that was either extraordinarily lovely or extraordinarily terrible.

Jopale asked if the clouds were made from smoke or water.

Master Brace shrugged his shoulders. "We won't be staying long, sir," was all he said.

Left-of-Left was a small city, and judging by the spacious warehouses standing beside the various worm trails, it had been exceptionally prosperous. Great slabs of freshly cut wood waited beside the widest worm trails, mounted on sleds ready to be towed east by giant freight worms. But there was only one other worm in the station besides theirs, and it had dragged itself between two buildings and died, its pale carcass beginning to swell as it rotted from within.

"This wood—?" Jopale began.

"The finest in the world," the caretaker offered. "This ground is dense and durable—a sweet grain, and almost perfectly free of knots. It has been in demand, for centuries now. And when the Continent shifted east, the local miners adapted quickly." Brace gestured toward the south. "They poisoned the best of their wood with arsenic salts. Even if their land starved, they weren't going to allow any worm infestations. Beautiful planks were still coming out of this place . . . but you certainly don't want to breathe the sawdust, I can tell you."

Sprawling homes stood north of the station, yards sprinkled with tall poles. Gas-jet lights were strung high overhead—a cheat to bring light to a place without sunshine. But not one of the torches was burning now, and none of the windows on any house showed the barest hint of life.

Even the lowliest mockmen were missing.

"Because everybody left," the caretaker explained. "They went off . . . I don't quite know . . . maybe forty cycles ago? They were still here on my last trip through. Nobody warned me. But they were quiet while I was here, which was unusual for them. Very chatty folk, most of the time. Which makes me believe that they'd come to their decision already."

Their worm began to shake now. Intestines contracted and the long body grew longer, the creature beginning to clear its bowels. The stink of the process was horrific, yet it bothered no one but the lone passenger.

Jopale turned his face away. "What decision was that?" he asked, one hand thrown across his mouth and nose.

"These people had their escape prepared," the caretaker replied. "Probably years ago. A lot of these little communities . . . out here in the dark . . . they have schemes. Sanctuaries, special ground."

"Is that so?"

"Oh, yes," Brace replied, as if this was common knowledge. "People living in the night know what disaster means. They have experience and common sense. Like Left-of-Left here. One lady told me, with a confidential voice, that her family had built themselves a fireproof shelter and surrounded it with a deep moat. When the air soured, they would breathe bottled oxygen. And if the fires came, they'd flood the moat with water and spray it over their heads."

Jopale almost responded.

But the caretaker saw doubt in his face. "Oh, I know, sir. I realize. That doesn't sound workable. This would be no ordinary fire, and this dense ground is sure to burn hot and long. If that miserable time should come." He laughed amiably for a moment, then added, "She was definitely lying to me. I know that now, and maybe I knew it then. You see . . . I would normally remain here for a cycle or two. We like to give this worm a long sleep and a chance to fatten up, and that local woman would let me share her bed. A wonderful lady, and a good friend, and she wanted me to know that she had arrangements made. But she didn't tell me enough so that I could find her. Which is reasonable, and I shouldn't be hurt. Wherever these people have gone, they don't have extra room for their occasional lovers."

Jopale didn't know what to say, so he remained silent.

Then the caretaker turned back to his colleagues, and with a sharp, accusing tone, he called out, "Leave those turds on the trail. You hear me?"

A young woman was standing in the worm-greased trail. Spiked boots kept her from falling, and she held a special stick used to shove the foul wastes to the side. "But the regulations—" she began.

"Regulations?" the old man interrupted. Forgetting about Jopale, he stepped to the edge of the platform, throwing out a few curses before reminding his crew, "Our first concern is our own worm. Our second concern is our passengers. And we are not wasting any time rolling crap out of the way of worms and people who are not going to be coming.

"Do you hear what I'm saying to you?"

A LAST MOMENT PLEA

Friends and colleagues were remarkably supportive of Jopale's decision to leave home. Most offered polite words, while a few posed the most obvious questions. "Where did you learn about the New Isles?" they asked. He had come across an article in a small journal that catered to the wealthy. For a fee, he was able to purchase an introductory book filled with photographs and useful descriptions. "And they had space available?" people wondered. "At this late date?" But a New Isle was being built every few years—the process guaranteed to continue until the disaster came or the danger passed. So yes, there was space enough for him. "But how does a teacher afford it?" they pressed. "How could you afford it?" Jopale offered a shrug and shy smile, mentioning his substantial inheritance. He always made that confession warily, expecting others to be openly jealous or envious or even noticeably bitter. But people absorbed the news with surprise and resignation. Which was a little disappointing, curiously enough. It would have made Jopale feel more secure about his solution—more optimistic by a long measure—if what he was doing caused pointed hatred in the people that he was prepared to leave behind.

Acquaintances and fellow teachers always seemed to have their own escape routes planned—hopeful schemes wrapped around the local civil protection service or private bunkers. And there was some good reason for hope: Throughout the district, old worm holes were being sealed and stocked with provisions. If the fires came, locals would hunker in the dark, sipping bottled air, while the ground above was saturated with pure water and complex foams guaranteed to shoulder all but the most catastrophic heat.

The problem was that if the fires came, the heat would turn catastrophic. The worst fires to date were in the south, not far from the polar zone. Epiphyte forests were being consumed in an instant. The normally inflammable cuticle boiled away soon after that. Then the deep living wood caught fire and burned off, allowing drowned, half-rotted islands free to spring to the surface, bringing up fresh methane that only caused the fires to grow larger. After that, the soggiest, most rotten wood was soon baked to a crisp and set on fire, and despite an army of mockmen and brave firefighters, that circular zone of total destruction was spreading outwards, eating a kilometer with every cycle, engulfing abandoned villages and useless farms in a roaring, irresistible maelstrom.

Yet Jopale's friends put on hopeful, brave faces. "We'll get the upper hand soon," they claimed, sounding as if they were fighting on the front lines. "And we'll beat the next twenty blazes, too. You just wait and see."

But nothing happened quickly in the world. Cycle after cycle, the southern fire continued to spread, and new ones exploded to life in other distant places. The steady, irresistible disaster gave everyone time enough to doubt his most cherished beliefs. That's when people found themselves admitting to their very lousy prospects, particularly in conversation with their oldest friends.

"I keep telling people that I'm staying," announced one of Jopale's neighbors. A bachelor like Jopale, bright and well read, he admitted, "I'm always saying that the fires will be put out, or they'll miss us. But when it comes down to it, do you know what I'll do? Run. Run east to the Ocean, just like you're running west. If I can slip past the provincial guards and disappear into the chaos. . . ."

"Maybe," Jopale replied, unsure what that would accomplish.

But the fellow had written himself into an interesting story. "All those last islands that merged with the Continent? Well, I've heard their citizens are burying explosives inside the old fault lines. And when the time comes, they'll set off the biggest blasts in history."

Again, Jopale said, "Maybe."

He didn't want to attack the man's dream. But doubt must have crept into his face, because his friend bristled, asking, "What's wrong?"

Jopale was no expert. But in every account he had read, those giant fires were accompanied by fabulously strong winds. The winds blew toward the flames, feeding them the oxygen critical to their survival. You could shatter the old fractures from end to end, chiseling the islands free of the doomed Continent; but those enormous masses of wood and scared humanity would still have to move into the open water, pressing against that roaring gale.

"Well then," the friend responded. "They'll think of that. Probably they'll blow their way free long before the fire comes."

And release any methane trapped under their feet, starting their own deadly blaze. But this time, Jopale found the tact to say, "That's reasonable, sure." Then he added, "I don't know much about technical matters."

"Keep that in mind, Jopale." Shaking a finger, the old friend said, "You don't know much about anything."

True enough.

Jopale's relatives surprised him with their calm, stubborn dismissal of his New Isles plan. Uncles and older cousins thought he was a fool for surrendering to popular despair. Poisons and fires would kill distant strangers and burn up portions of the world. But not their good ground, no. They couldn't imagine their lucky island being changed in any lasting fashion. At the very worst, forests and farms would burn up, which would bring a famine that would quickly silence the extra mouths in the world. But that would be a blessing and a grand opportunity, they maintained. To his considerable astonishment, Jopale learned that his family had been preparing for years: Secret lockers were stuffed full of dried scramblers and wooden tubs jammed with pickled fruit, plus enough roach cakes and syrup to keep the most useful mockmen alive. There would be a few hard years, they agreed. Only the prepared would survive to the end. But that's what they intended to do. Survive at all costs. Then life would settle back into its comfortable, profitable, and entirely natural routine.

"Stay with us," they pleaded, but not too hard. Perhaps they'd decided that Jopale was one of those extra mouths.

One old aunt assured him, "You will go insane in the darkness. Starlight has that effect on people, you know."

That wasn't true. Humans were adaptable, and besides, the New Isles were lit up with blue-white lights very much like sunshine. Yet his response was deflected with a cold pleasure. "You *will* go insane," his aunt repeated. "Don't for two moments think otherwise, my boy."

Then a pair of young cousins—a twin brother and sister—explained what was plainly obvious to them. "When the time comes," they said, "the Spirit of Man will rise from the Ocean's center to save all of the good people."

It was an old faith, half-remembered and twisted to fit the times.

"Only true believers will be spared," they promised. "How about you, Jopale? Will you join us with the reborn?"

"Never," he responded, amazed by his sudden anger. His cousins were probably no more mistaken about the future than those with well-stocked bunkers. But he found himself panting, telling them, "That's a stupid creed, and you can't make me buy into it."

"Then you will die horribly," they told him, speaking with one voice. "And that's precisely what you deserve, Jopale."

But people rarely got what they deserved; wasn't that the central lesson of the modern world?

With his critical possessions packed and his precious tickets and papers in easy reach, Jopale walked to the nearest worm station, accompanied by his only remaining mockman. No well-wishers were waiting to send him off. Thank goodness. He and a few other travelers stood on the open platform, looking off to the east. The huge gray worm appeared on schedule, sliding in on the side trail and stopping before them, deep wet breaths making the entire station shake. Travelers formed a line, ready to prove themselves to the waiting soldiers. Then a single voice called out, "Jopale." It was a woman's voice, vaguely familiar. Jopale looked over his shoulder. He had grown up with this woman—a natural beauty who hadn't spoken ten words to him in the last ten years—but there she stood, dressed to travel and smiling only at him.

Jopale assumed she was heading west, perhaps even to the New Isles.

But no, she explained that she didn't have any ticket. She'd heard about his plans and simply come here to speak with him now.

"Please," she implored, touching her wide mouth, then running a hand across her long, elegant scalp.

He stepped out of line.

"This is difficult," she admitted. Then with a deep, soul-wrenching sigh, she added, "I wish I'd done what you've done."

But she hadn't, of course.

"If I stay here, I'll die here," she told him and every other person in earshot. "But I'll ask you, Jopale: Is there any way I could travel with you?"

There wasn't. No. "All the berths on the New Isles are taken by now. I'm quite sure. And I'm bringing only what I'm allowed to bring. Even with these little bags here, I'm pressing against my limits."

The woman wrapped her arms around her perfect chest, shivering as if chilled. Then quietly, through a clenched mouth, she said, "But there is a way."

"What?"

Standing beside Jopale was his red-haired mockman. The beautiful woman glanced up at the gigantic creature. Then with a stiff, somewhat angry voice, she said, "Leave it behind. Take me instead."

Did Jopale hear that correctly?

"I'll ride inside the worm's stomach with the mockmen," she promised. "And I'll carry your luggage for you, too."

"No," he said.

"I'll even eat mockman rations—"

"No."

The woman began to cry, tears rolling down her lovely, pain-wracked face. "I'll do whatever you wish, Jopale. I'll even relinquish my legal rights, and you can beat me if I'm slow—"

"Stop it," he cried out.

"Please, Jopale! Please?"

Then a soldier stepped up, asking to see their papers. What could Jopale do? He was startled, off-balance. This unexpected idea hadn't had time enough to take root in his head. The woman could never survive the life she was begging for. Besides, he had never lived without a mockman on his right side. And if he ever needed new money, this was a valuable creature on any market.

Jopale's only rational choice was to turn away from the woman, saying nothing else. He silently handed his identification to the armed man and then his precious ticket to an elderly fellow wearing the gray uniform of a worm caretaker.

"Master Brace" was written over the chest pocket.

"All the way to the Port of Krauss, sir?" asked the old fellow.

"Yes, I am."

Offering a wink and jolly laugh, Brace said, "Well, sir. You and I should get to know each other by the end of the line, sir. I should think."

"IT IS COMING"

The sky was cloudless and absolutely dark, save for a single point of soft yellow light—one of the Four Sisters slowly dancing about the hidden sun. The distant stars were too faint to be seen through the thick window—a few hundred specks that only scientists had bothered to name and map. Stars meant very little to Jopale. What captured his mind was soft country beneath: The Tanglelands. Relentless pressures had crumbled this wood, exposing every old seam and any line of weakness. Long ridges and single hills had been erected through a series of unending quakes. As a result, the trail was far from a straight line, and the climb as well as fatigue kept slowing the worm's progress. But there were no fresh breaks or blockages on the trail, at least so far. The waking passengers seemed thrilled to be alive, or at least they pretended to share a renewed confidence. And of course everyone wanted at least a glimpse of the tall saprophytes that grew beside the trail, watching the exotic forest passing by for a moment or two, then returning to their blankets and more familiar distractions.

Jopale had never seen country like this, save in picture books.

He mentioned his interest to Do-ane, and she responded as he hoped. "I've seen the Tanglelands," she admitted. "Several times now. But I still think they're lovely. Just wonderful."

The girl had a buoyan, joyful attitude when she wanted to.

Jopale stood beside her, watching the pale, many-hued light pouring out of the dense foliage. Sometimes he asked about a particularly bright or massive tree. Do-ane would warn that she didn't know her fungi as well as she would like. But every time, she named the species. Then when the rest of the passengers had settled on the stomach's floor, leaving them alone, she quietly asked her new student, "Do you know why this country is so rich?"

"The old islands are broken into hundreds of pieces," he offered. "Plenty of fresh surfaces ready to rot away."

"That's part of it," she allowed. "But as much as anything, it's because of the moisture. Three large islands were compressed and splintered to make the Tanglelands, and each one had tremendous reserves of fresh water underground. Which the saprophytes need as much as they need food, of course."

He nodded amiably.

"And besides, rain likes hilly country," she continued. "Given its choice, a storm will drop its wealth on broken ground."

"How about your Good Mountain? Is it very wet. . . . ?"

She shook her head. "Not particularly. That country is very flat and very boring. And beneath the surface, the wood is exceptionally dry."

"Why?"

"Because the island on the surface can't reach the Ocean any more." Do-ane put one tiny hand beneath the other, as an illustration. "I think I mentioned: There's a second island resting under it, thick and solid, blocking almost every root."

"That's your Mountain? The underneath island?"

She hesitated, making some kind of delicate calculation. Then she looked out the window again, saying, "No," in the tone people use when they want to say a good deal more.

Jopale waited. Then he said, "Tell me more."

She squinted, saying nothing.

"About your undersea mountain," he coaxed. "What do you do down there?"

"Research," she allowed.

"In biology?" he asked. And when she didn't respond, he offered a mild lie. "I was once an avid biology student. Some years ago now."

Do-ane glanced at the passengers. Rit was sleeping. None of the others were paying attention to the two of them. Yet the young woman whispered so softly that Jopale could barely hear her words. "No," she said. "It's not really biology that I'm studying, no."

"Not really?" he pushed.

She wasn't supposed to speak, but she also wanted to explain herself. With a slender smile, she said, "I can't."

"I don't mean to interrogate," he lied.

The young woman's life was wrapped around her work. It showed in her face, her manners. In her anxious, joyful silence.

"Forget it," he muttered. An enormous fungus stood beside the trail—a pillar topped with fruiting bodies that bled a bright purple light. It was a common species whose name he had already forgotten. Staring at that apparition of rot and death, Jopale remarked with the coldest possible voice, "It's not as if the world is going to end soon."

"But it won't end," Do-ane said.

He gave a little sniff, and that's when he discovered that he was crying. It was the sort of manipulative gesture Jopale might have attempted and would have failed at. But his tears were as honest as anything he had ever done, a fabulous pain hiding inside him, any excuse good enough to make it surge into public view.

"This disaster has happened before," the young woman promised.

"So I've heard."

"But it's true. A new continent always grows on the sunlit face of the world. The water below is always choked of its free oxygen. Old wood compresses and shatters, and the methane rises up through the fissures and holes."

"What about wildfires?" he asked.

"There have been big fires before." She smiled to herself, betraying a deep fascination, as if describing an enjoyable novel full of fictional tragedies. Then she added, "These world-consuming fires have come seventeen other times."

Not sixteen times, or fifty thousand.

Jopale invested several long minutes contemplating her precision. Then he asked, "How do you know that? An exact number?"

"I can't," she said.

"You can't tell me?"

"No."

He stared at her face, letting his own anger bubble up. "This place where you're going," he started to ask. "This peculiar mountain . . . ?"

"Yes?"

"Your colleagues, those scientists who discovered the feature . . . I don't think they used the old word 'mountain' because it reaches in any particular direction. Toward the sky or toward the world's core, either."

Do-ane avoided his weepy eyes.

"My guess? The object was named for its composition. That's another quality inherent in the word. The mythical mountain is supposed to be harder and far more enduring than any wood. Am I right?"

The young woman was standing on her stocking feet, staring through the window again. The Tanglelands were beginning to thin out and turn flat, stretches of empty dead ground between the occasional giant fungi. Now the brightest stars were visible through the window, twinkling and jumping as the worm slid along. Do-ane was standing close enough to Jopale to touch him, and she was taking quick shallow breaths, her face growing brighter even as the empty land around them turned blacker.

Jopale held his breath.

Then very quietly, his companion said, "The great fire," and touched the plastic of the window with the tips of two fingers.

Do-ane announced, "It is coming. . . . !"

THE HEART OF THINGS

When a worm like theirs was a baby, it was abused in the most awful ways—or so it might seem to somebody who didn't concern himself with the rough necessities of the world. Stolen from its mother, the newborn creature was cut through in several places and the wounds were kept open until they became permanent holes, ready for the first in a series of increasingly large sphincters. Then its diet was strictly controlled while professional handlers assessed its tendencies and potential uses. Intelligent and mild-tempered worms were given over to passenger duties. Many of the candidates didn't survive the conditioning of their digestive tracts or the additional surgeries. Among the alterations, inflatable bladders were inserted into the region directly behind the head, producing a series of permanent cavities where individual caretakers could live, each fitting with a rubber doorway leading into a narrow, astonishingly dry esophagus.

Jopale stood beneath a glow-light, shouting Brace's name. A voice called back to him. A few moments later, the old caretaker stepped from inside one of the little rooms, wiping his sleepy face while asking what was wrong.

With words and manic gestures, Jopale explained the situation.

For an instant, the caretaker didn't believe him. The weathered face looked doubtful, and the pursed lips seemed ready to downplay what he was being told. But then one of the worm's drivers ran down the narrow esophagus, shouting the same essential news.

"Where are we now?" the caretaker asked her.

The woman offered a number and letter designation that might as well have been in another language.

But the old man instantly absorbed the knowledge. "We'll stop at Kings Crossing," he ordered. "The station's gone, but the ground is up on the last ridge. We'll be able to see how bad things are. And any good news too."

Jopale couldn't imagine anything good.

Then the caretaker turned to him, saying, "Sir," with a firm tone. "I need to know. Have the other passengers noticed?"

"Just one. The girl—"

The caretaker hesitated for a moment. Then he said, "Say nothing. I'll see if I can raise some voices on the radiophone, get the latest news . . . and then I'll walk through the belly and offer a few words. . . ."

Brace's voice fell away. What kind of encouragement could he offer anyone now?

There was tense silence, then a deep slow rumbling. The sound that came and then came again, making the great throat shiver.

"What is that?" Jopale had to ask.

"That would be the worm's heart," the caretaker offered. He tilted his head and held his breath, listening carefully. "And you can hear her lungs working too. Which is why we live up here, sir. So we can keep tabs on our baby."

Jopale nodded.

Then the caretaker touched the rough pink wall, and the driver did the same, both using that pause to fight back their own tears.

Do-ane had abandoned the window, sitting alone on her blanket, using her electric torch to read her book. Everyone else was sitting too, including Rit. The old map was unfolded before him. Glancing up, he said nothing to Jopale. Then he looked down again, asking the map, "What's wrong?"

"Nothing," Jopale lied, as a reflex.

The tall man glanced at Do-ane, and with the heightened senses of a paranoid, he announced, "Something is wrong."

She started to look at the window, then stopped herself.

But Rit noticed. He decided to take his own look, pulling his long legs under his body, taking a deep breath, and another. But there wasn't enough courage inside him to stand. His legs stretched out again, and a long hand wiped his mouth dry, and then he carefully fixed his eyes on the old map, nourishing his own faltering sense of ignorance.

"Did you tell?" Do-ane whispered, closing the book on her thumb.

Jopale nodded.

She stared at his face, his eyes. Something about her expression was new—a hard stare meant to reach down to his soul, seemingly. Then she made her decision, whatever that might be. Opening the book again, she flipped through pages until she found what she wanted. Placing her back to Rit, she pushed the book toward Jopale and handed him her torch, giving his face one last study, just to convince herself that her feelings were right.

The page was blank.

No, it unfolded. Jopale found a corner bent up by use, and he lifted the slick paper and gave the book a quarter turn, an elaborate drawing showing what looked to be the configuration for some type of worm.

"Is it—?" he began.

"The mountain," she interrupted, fingers held to her mouth.

Rit seemed to notice nothing. No one was paying attention to the two of them. The wealthy old woman who had complained at World's End was making her male companion look out the window. But she only wanted to know what was approaching, and he only looked ahead, reporting with a matter-of-fact voice, "There's some long slope. And that's all I can tell."

Was the mountain a worm? Jopale wondered.

He returned to the diagram, finding a scale that gave him a sense of size. But surely there was a mistake here. Even if the scale were wrong by a factor of ten, this worm would be larger than a dozen rust-fins set in a row. And if the scale were right, then the mountain would dwarf a hundred and twenty full-grown rust-fins . . . making it larger than most cities, wouldn't it . . . ?

He looked up. "Is it alive?" he whispered.

Do-ane had no simple answer for that. She shrugged and said, "It isn't now," in a soft voice. And then even softer, she said, "Look again."

He was no expert about worms. But he knew enough to tell that the mountain shared little with the creatures he had grown up with. Its mouth was enormous but without true jaws, forming a perfect circle from which every tooth had been removed. The throat was straight and wide, and then like a funnel, it collapsed on itself, becoming too tiny to show on this diagram. The anus was equally tiny, opening at the very tip of the tail. And between mouth and anus was a digestive tract that filled only a portion of the worm's enormous body.

"What are these?" he asked.

She touched the lines and the spaces within them, saying, "Chambers. Cavities. Rooms, of a kind."

He didn't understand. "How could a creature survive this much surgery?" he asked. And when she didn't answer, he looked up, realizing, "But this isn't any species of worm, is it?"

She mouthed the word, "No."

"It is a machine," he muttered.

She tilted her head, as if to say, "Maybe."

"Or is it alive?"

"Not now, no. Not anymore. We think."

The worm carrying them was attacking the last long slope, slowing as it crawled higher. Another person stood to look outside. But he was on the north side of the worm, and from that angle, nothing was visible behind them.

"The tail and some of the midsection cavities are flooded," Do-ane told him.

Those were drawn with blue ink.

He asked, "Is the tail the deepest part?"

She nodded.

"And the mouth?"

"Buried inside a fossil island," she reported.

"Choked while eating its lunch?" He meant it as a joke, forcing himself to laugh.

But Do-ane just shook her head. "We don't know what it ate in life," she reported. "But this organism, this machine . . . whatever it was . . . it probably required more energy than you could ever pull out of wood pulp and stolen sap."

Jopale closed the book and turned it in his hands, examining the binding. But there was nothing to read except a cryptic "Notes" followed by a date from several years earlier.

"What I am," Do-ane began.

He reopened the book and unfolded the diagram again. "What are you?"

"In the sciences, I have no specialty." She smiled, proud to say it. "I belong to a special project. A confidential research project, you see. My colleagues and I are trained in every discipline. The hope is . . . was . . . that we could piece together what this thing might be. . . ."

"It's metal," Jopale guessed.

"Within its body," she said, "we have found more iron and copper and zinc than all of the peoples of the world have gathered. Plus there's gold and silver, and elements too unusual to have common names."

Jopale wanted to turn through the pages, but he still couldn't make sense of this one.

"Yet the body is composed mostly of other substances," she continued. "Plastics and compounds that look plastic. Ceramic materials. And lining the mouth and what seems to be the power plant . . . well, there are things too strong to cut samples from, which means we can't even test them in any useful fashion. . . ."

"And what are you?" he asked again.

"One member of a large, secret team trying to make sense of this." She showed him a grim smile, adding, "I'm just a novice still. Some of us have worked forty years on this project."

"And have you learned anything?"

A hopeful expression passed across her face. But again, they had reached a juncture where Do-ane didn't want to say anything more. Jopale sensed that she'd already told him too much. That they were pushing into codes and laws that had to be obeyed, even when Catastrophe walked across their world.

Again, their worm was slowing.

Passengers noticed, and in a moment, they grew uneasy.

"Where?" Jopale asked.

Do-ane ran a finger over the giant mouth. "What are you asking?"

"Its origin," he said. "Do you know that much?"

"Guess," she whispered.

He could see only two possibilities. "It comes from the world's center," he offered. "There are metals down there. I remember that much from school. Deep inside the world, the temperatures and chemistries are too strange for us to even imagine."

"What's the second possibility?"

He remembered what she had said earlier. "Our Ocean," she mentioned, as if there could be more than one. Then he pointed at the sky.

"In my little profession," she sighed, "those are the two islands of opinion. I'm one of the other-world people, and I believe that this object is a kind of ship meant to cross from star to star."

Jopale closed the book and pushed it back to her.

By then, their worm had pulled to a stop, and the passengers were looking at each other, plainly wondering what was happening. But Master Brace was absent, probably still listening to the radiophone. Which was why Jopale took it upon himself to stand and say to the others, "This is Kings Crossing."

Rit pulled the map to his face, asking, "Why here?"

Like any good caretaker, Jopale managed to smile. But he couldn't maintain the lie past that point. Shaking his head and looking at the warm damp floor, he reminded everyone, "We're alive still." And then he started marching toward the still-closed sphincter.

FIRE

The night air was cool and dry, and it blew softly toward the east—a breeze at this moment, but gaining strength and urgency with the passage of time. Years ago, a tidy little city had grown up on this ridge, but then the sun vanished, and the city had died. Homes and shops quickly became piles of anonymous rubble. But the worm station must have survived for more years. The facility was only recently stripped of its metal, but otherwise it had been left intact. Only a few saprophytic weeds were rooted in the softest planks, while the damp faces of the main building were painted with a rough fungus. Regardless of color, every surface glowed with a steady red light. Jopale read KINGS CROSSING on the greeting arch, painted in a flowing script that was popular back when he was a child. Behind him, the other passengers were slowly stepping onto the platform, talking in breathless whispers. He didn't hear their words so much as he listened to the terror in their voices, and Jopale did nothing for the moment but stare at the planks beneath his feet and at his own trembling hands. Then when he felt ready—when no other choice seemed left for him—he forced himself to breathe and turn around, staring wide-eyed at the burning world.

Jopale once toured a factory where precious iron was melted inside furnaces built from equally precious ceramic bricks. He remembered watching the red-hot liquid being poured into thin syrupy ribbons that were quickly attacked by the artisans in charge. He decided that this wildfire possessed the same fierce, unworldly glow. It was crimson and brilliant enough to make eyes tear up, and it seemed as if some wickedly powerful artist, inspired by his malevolent urges, must have pulled molten metal across the entire eastern horizon.

Every passenger had left the confines of the worm. Most of the caretakers were busy breaking into a nearby warehouse, presumably under orders to claim any useful supplies. "How far away is that?" a young fellow asked. Jopale couldn't gauge distances, but others gladly threw out numbers. Optimists claimed the fire was just a few kilometers behind them, and it was really quite small. While Rit admitted that the flames were enormous, but trying to be positive, he thought they might be as far away as World's Edge.

"Oh, it's closer than that," the old caretaker called out. "As we stand here, Left-of-Left is being incinerated."

With a haughty tone, Rit asked, "And you know that how?"

Swollen eyes studied the horizon. Master Brace had been crying again. But he had dried his face before joining the others, and he managed to keep his voice steady and clear. "I was listening to broadcasts, where I could find them. From spotters near the fire lines, mostly."

Every face was sorry and scared.

"That quake we felt? As we were crawling out of World's Edge?" Brace shook his head, telling them, "That was an old seam south and east of the city. It split wide, along a hundred kilometer line. I didn't know this till now . . . but so much gas came from that rupture, emergency crews didn't have time to dress. They were killed, mostly. And the methane kept bubbling out. For a full cycle, it was mixing with the air. Then something . . . a person, or maybe lightning from a thunderstorm . . . made the spark that set the whole damn mess on fire."

"What happened to the city?" Jopale asked.

Brace glanced at him for a moment, then stared at the planks. "I talked to a spotter. She's riding her balloon east of World's Edge. The city's gone now, she says. Including the ground it was sitting on. From where she is, she sees open water where millions of people should be. . . ."

"Open water?" Rit asked. "Does that mean the fire is going out?"

Brace hesitated.

Do-ane said, "No." The woman looked tiny and exceptionally young, her boots back on her feet but still needing to be buttoned. Clearing her throat, she explained, "If too much methane saturates the atmosphere, and the local oxygen is exhausted or pushed aside . . . there can't be any fire. . . ."

Jopale closed his eyes, seeing the beautiful station and the black-haired woman with that lovely, lost voice.

Brace nodded, saying, "There's two fire lines now. One's racing east, the other west. In the middle, the water's bubbling up so hard, huge chunks of rotten wood are being flung up in the air. So the methane . . . it's still coming, yes sir. And the spotter told me that our fire . . . the one that's chasing us . . . it just now reached to the fringes of the Tanglelands . . . and then I lost her signal. . . ."

Some people wept; others appeared too numb or tired to react at all.

Two drivers were standing near the worm's head. One of them suddenly called out a few words, her voice barely legible.

The other caretakers had vanished inside an unlit warehouse.

Master Brace turned to the drivers. "The full dose, yes," he shouted. "Under the vestigial arm."

"But the flames don't look that tall," said the wealthy woman. She shook her head, refusing to accept their awful prospects. To her companion, she said, "Perhaps the fire's just burning off the forests."

Her young man muttered a few agreeable words.

But Do-ane said, "No, you're confused. It's the smoke that fools you."

"Pardon me, miss?"

"That land is definitely burning," she said. "Huge volumes of green wood are being turned to smoke and ash, which help hide the tops of the flames. And of course that scorching heat will lift everything." She pointed at the sky, asking, "Can you see what I see?"

Jopale hadn't noticed. But the eastern half of the sky had no stars, a dense black lid set over the dying world. Flood this landscape with daylight, and half of the heavens would be choked beneath a foul mass of boiling, poisonous clouds.

"Are you certain?" the old woman asked doubtfully. "What do you know about any of this?"

Do-ane hesitated.

"The girl's a scientist," Rit interjected. "She understands everything that's happening to us."

"Is that so, miss?"

Do-ane glanced at Jopale, eyes narrowed, as if blaming him for making public what she had told him in the strictest confidence.

But he hadn't said one word.

"She and her friend here thought that I was napping," Rit confessed. "But I wasn't. I heard every word they said."

Do-ane looked embarrassed, shrinking a little bit, and her tiny hands nervously wrestled with one another.

Jopale tried to find a reply—gentle words to help deflate the palpable tension. But then a hard prolonged shock came through the ground, everybody's legs bending, and the land beneath them fell several meters in one steady, terrifying moment.

When the falling sensation ended, the old woman asked Do-ane, "Would you explain that, dear? What just happened?"

"This ridge," Do-ane began, opening her hands again. "We're standing on the last slab of the Tanglelands. It's the largest slab, and it reaches back to the east, deep underwater, ending up under Left-of-Left." Like a teacher, she used hands to help explain. "As the ground above is burned away, and as methane rushes to the open surface, this land's foundation is being torn loose."

As if to prove her words, the ridge shook again.

Jopale looked over his shoulder, but Master Brace had slipped away. He was standing beside the worm, he and the two drivers busily manipulating a leather sack filled with some kind of dense liquid. The sack was connected to a hose, and the hose fitted into a needle large enough to push through two grown men. The trio was having trouble with the work, and noticing Jopale, the caretaker cried out, "Sir, would you help us? Just for a moment. She knows we're up to something, and she isn't cooperating."

The others glanced at Jopale, surprised he would be called, and perhaps a little impressed.

The worm had stopped against the trail's closer edge. But there were still a few steps of greased ground to cross. Generations of worms had laid down this thick impermeable oil—the same white gunk that its wild counterparts used to lubricate their enormous tunnels. On soft-soled shoes, Jopale let himself slide down to the creature. He hadn't touched a worm since he was a boy, and he didn't relish touching one now. He could smell oil and worm sweat—a rich mingling of distinct odors—and he looked up at the vestigial limb, crooked and thin and held flat against the huge gray body.

"Take this extra wand, sir," said Brace. "Like I'm doing. Just stroke her belly, if you will."

The rubber wand ended with a metal electrode, batteries strapped to a spicewood handle. The drivers had set a tall ladder beside the worm, spikes driven through the oil and into the ground. The woman driver climbed quickly and her colleague followed—a boyish fellow carrying the enormous needle as if it was a spear. The ladder was topped by a narrow platform. The woman grabbed the limb and pulled hard, and Brace ran his wand back and forth against the worm's slick belly, small blue flashes producing what must be a pleasurable tingle.

The woman forced the limb to extend.

"Why there?" Jopale asked, mimicking the old man's motions.

"It's a good blood-rich site," he said quickly, as if speaking one long word. "And besides, there's no time to open the usual veins."

The other passengers had come to watch and listen. Except for Do-ane, who drifted to the far end of the platform, studying her magnificent fire.

"Is this a drug?" Jopale wanted to know.

"I like the word 'medicine,'" the caretaker admitted. Patting the sack, he said, "We keep this stuff for drivers more than for the worm. Of course, there's enough in this sack to kill a thousand people. But what it is—"

Somebody cursed, and a second voice shouted, "Watch out!"

The long needle fell between Jopale and Brace, landing flat on the oil.

"It's a stimulant, sir." The caretaker picked up the needle, and with a quick voice explained, "It will make our girl faster, and she won't need sleep, and it may well kill her. But of course, we don't have any choice now."

"I suppose—"

"Two more favors, sir. Please?"

"Yes."

"Take the needle up. All right?" Then he asked for a second favor; promising, "It should help quite a lot."

Jopale had never enjoyed heights, but he didn't hesitate. There were twenty rungs to manage, and the breeze seemed to grow stronger as he climbed higher. Over his shoulder, he saw the rest of the crew returning from the warehouse, nothing worth stealing in their hands. Then Jopale was standing on the narrow platform, and the driver had the vestigial limb extended as far as she could, and her assistant took the needle with both hands, starting to jab its tip into the exposed flesh while shouting, "Now!"

A tiny pump began to sing.

"The hand, sir," Brace called out. "Please, sir."

The worm's arm was tiny compared to its enormous body, but it was far longer than any human limb. Perched on the end of it were three fingers fused into a knobby extrusion and a stiff little finger beside it. And there was a thumb, too. Not every worm possessed thumbs; Jopale had read that odd fact once or twice. And more unusual, this particular thumb could move, at least well enough to curl around his hands as he clasped hold of the worm. Then he squeezed its hand as tight as he could, trying to make certain that his grip was noticed, letting the great beast feel a little more ease, at least until the medicine found its home.

WORMS

Then they were moving again. The pace felt swift, but the worm was sliding down a considerable slope. Without landmarks, the casual eye had trouble discerning their true speed. But later, when they were crossing a flat empty plain, Jopale was sure they were making swift progress. Wandering up into the throat again, he listened to the hard swift beating of the heart, and he was sure that, whatever else, the creature's body was expending a fabulous amount of energy.

Returning to the stomach, he found every passenger gathered around Do-ane. "Show us that book of yours," Rit was saying. "Show us your machine."

"We're very interested," said the rich woman's companion. Then with a wink, he asked, "What harm would it do?"

People were scared and miserable and desperate for any distraction.

Jopale sat next to Do-ane.

She seemed to consider the possibilities. Then she said, "Here," and opened the book to a fresh page—a page showing photographs of giant chambers and smooth-walled tunnels. Holding her torch above, she explained what she had already told Jopale, and a little more. "We think these were living quarters. It's hard to realize how big everything . . . but this is a colleague of mine, here, standing in the background. . . ."

The scientist was little more than a dot on the grayish landscape.

"If this machine was a ship that traveled between the stars, as some believe . . . as I believe . . . then its engines would have produced an acceleration, and this would have been the floor." She pulled a fond finger over the image. "This was taken ten years ago. Do you see the dirt in the corner?"

Some people nodded, but those in the back could see nothing.

Do-ane turned the page. The next image was a large black-and-white photograph showing a skull and ribs and a very long backbone that had curled up in death. The earlier colleague was present again, standing on the giant skull. And again, he was still little more than a dot on this bizarre landscape.

"That's a dead worm," Jopale whispered.

Do-ane glanced at him, then at the others.

"This machine came from another star," Rit said, repeating her verdict.

"Yes," she said.

"A spaceship, you're saying?"

"It seems obvious—"

"And that's where our worms came from, too?" The tall man was kneeling on the other side of her, his expression doubtful but focused. "They came from this space-ship of yours?"

Do-ane said, "Yes."

Then she said, "No."

"Which is it?" Rit demanded.

The young woman sighed. And then a second time, she sighed. Finally she looked up, telling everyone, "Suppose that we built a starship, and we went out hunting for a new home. Even a machine as powerful as this needs a great deal of time to cross from one sun to the next. And if that new sun didn't happen to have an inviting world, we'd have to travel farther. And if that next sun didn't offer a home, then we would have to travel farther still. And if we could never find a planet like our old home, at some point, wouldn't we have to make due with the best world that was in reach?"

Jopale tried to study the worm's skeleton.

"I don't know any of this as fact," she said. "But we've learned this much. This star-ship's crew was nothing like us. Not like people, or anything simply organic." She ran a finger along the edge of the fossil skull. "What looks like bone is not. It's ceramic and very tough, ancient beyond anything we can measure. And what organs we find aren't livers or hearts or lungs. They're machines, and we can't even begin to deci-pher how they might have functioned when they were slipped inside a living body."

Rit started to make a comment, then thought better of it.

"These creatures were built from metals and ceramics, plus rare earth elements that exist to us only in the tiniest amounts. Scarce beyond measure. But if you look deeper into the galaxy, into the spiral arms, you see suns with more metals than our sun has. And presumably, the worlds circling them are built from similar bones."

She breathed, breathed again.

"Our sun, you see . . . it is very large and bright, and it is metal poor and rather young. By many measures, it won't live long at all. Less than a billion years, which is a short time in the universe." She lifted her torch higher, allowing more people to see the bizarre skeleton. "I don't know any of this for sure. I'm telling you a story, and maybe it's all wrong. But what I think happened . . . what many of my colleagues, the true geniuses in this endeavor, feel is self-evident . . . is that this starship journeyed all the way to our world and could go no farther. It landed on the Ocean and tasted the water, tasted the air, and its crew took what they had in reach. Metals were scarce, as were silicon and all the other heavy elements. But at least they could borrow the oldest genetics inside their own bodies. To build a full functioning ecosystem, they wove a thousand new species. Humans. Mockmen. Copper-eels and many-mouths. Plus all the little scramblers. And they used the other species that were brought with them. We've found spores and dead seeds on the ship, so we're sure that our ancestors brought plants with them. They devised giant plants that could thrive on the Ocean's surface, roots reaching deep to bring up the scarce minerals. And think of our forest roaches, too. We have found little versions of them dead in the ship's darkest corners, hiding in the cracks. Incredible as it sounds, perhaps they rode here as pests."

"But where are the human bones?" Jopale asked.

She looked at him, her face sad for a brief moment, but then drifting into a cautious amusement.

"I mean the crew that piloted this starship," Jopale continued. "What finally happened to them?"

Judging by the murmurs, others had made the same obvious assumption.

Do-ane shook her head. Then she said, "No," with a grim finality. "Think if you can in these terms: You fly from star to star. Your body is as much a machine as it is flesh. And everything you need comes to you with the help of your loyal machinery. With that kind of freedom, you can acquire any shape that you wish. Which is why you might allow your limbs to grow smaller with the eons, and why you perhaps would decide, finally, to let yourself become a worm.

"Assuming that we began as human beings, of course. Or something that resembles humans, back on that other world of ours.

"This lost, unnamable home."

GOOD MOUNTAIN

Caretakers began to hurry through the stomach, in twos and threes, carrying buckets of salve and sacks of buffering agents back into the now-empty intestines. Jopale guessed what this meant, and he felt sure when another pair of caretakers arrived, hurriedly dismantling the latrine and its privacy curtain. But where would the worm's next meal come from, and how much time would they spend waiting for her to eat her fill?

Capping the nearly filled latrine, the caretakers began wrestling it towards the esophagus. That was when Jopale decided to confront them, and that was when Master Brace finally reappeared.

The old caretaker wore a grimacing smile. He tried to wink at Jopale, and then he noticed Do-ane sitting among the passengers, flipping from page to page in her enormous book.

"Are we stopping now?" Jopale asked.

Brace nodded. With a distracted voice, he said, "There's an emergency locker up ahead. Always stocked with knuckle-roots and barrels of sap. Or at least it's supposed to be stocked."

His voice fell away.

"How long will this take?" Jopale wanted to know.

Brace heard something in his tone. Speaking with absolute surety, he admitted, "My girl needs food. Badly. If we don't give her sugar, we won't make it off this wasteland. Fire or not."

Jopale nodded. "All right. I see."

"Good Mountain," said the caretaker. "That's where we're stopping."

A dozen faces looked up.

Realizing that he had been noticed. Brace straightened his back and took a deep breath. Then without hesitation, he said, "Everyone will disembark. The feeding will be done as fast as possible. And from this point, everyone rides on top of the worm. Up where the mockmen are sitting now."

The old woman bristled. "But where will my mockmen ride?"

"They will not, madam." With squared shoulders, the caretaker faced the spoiled creature, explaining to her and to everyone, "This is an emergency situation, if ever there was. And I'm using the powers of my office, madam. Do not try to stop me."

The woman shrank a little bit.

But her companion, smelling his duty, climbed to his feet. "We can't just leave these creatures behind," he argued.

Brace smiled. Then he laughed, quietly and with considerable reish. And he opened his arms while gesturing at the surrounding stomach, admitting, "Oh, I don't intend to leave them. Not at all."

There was no station at Good Mountain, abandoned or otherwise. There wasn't even an auxiliary trail for a worm to pull to one side. But the foundations for homes were visible, plus markings lain out to define a network of streets. The only signs of recent habitation were the promised locker—an underground facility little bigger than a worm's stomach—and standing to the north, a beacon tower built of wood and capped with an enormous bone-lined bowl. A reservoir of fats and cured sap was burning slowly, yellow flames swirling with the wind. In other times, this would have been the brightest light for a hundred kilometers—a navigation point to help any lost souls. But the firestorm to the east made the fire seem quite weak. Against that rushing, sizzling wall of scorching fire and vaporized wood, everything about the world seemed small and feeble.

The wind was blowing harder now, and with it came a chill from the west, causing Jopale to shiver.

Caretakers worked frantically, breaking open the locker, rolling barrel after barrel onto the trail directly in front of the worm. And other caretakers ordered the mockmen off the worm's back, gathering them together on the dusty, dry ground, loud voices warning them not to take another step.

Jopale thought he could hear the firestorm, even though it was still ten or twenty kilometers behind them.

It sounded like water, oddly enough. Like a strong current flowing over a brink, then falling fast.

Do-ane appeared suddenly, almost close enough to touch him. Her boots were buttoned. Her book was cradled under one arm. She studied his face for a moment. Then she regarded the firestorm with the same speculative intensity. And finally, she said to Jopale, "Come with me."

He wasn't surprised. For a long while now, he had imagined this invitation and his response. But what startled him was his own reaction, feeling decidedly unsure about what to do.

"My colleagues are there now," she continued, pointing at the still-distant tower. "Behind the beacon is a little hut, and there's a shaft and elevator that will drop us all the way to the starship—"

"What about me?" Rit interrupted.

Do-ane gave him a moment's glance. She seemed unprepared for his entirely natural question.

"Your starship is huge," Rit reminded her. "Huge and empty. Don't you think your friends would welcome me, too?"

She tried to speak.

Then the old wealthy woman stepped forward. "There isn't much time, miss. Where's this sanctuary of yours—?"

"Beyond that tower," Rit offered.

"Thank you." Then to her companion, she said, "Help me, will you dear? I'm not sure I can manage such a long walk."

Her young man was holding their essential bags, a faint smile showing as he stared off to the north. With an agreeable tone, he said; "I'm sure you'll do fine." Then he winked, adding, "Start right away. As fast as you can." And with the strength of youth, he ran off into the ruddy gloom, dropping his bags and hers in his wake.

Other passengers began to follow him.

"Well," the old woman muttered. Then with a shuffling gait, she tried to keep up.

Rit glared at Do-ane. Appalled by the circumstances, he asked, "So just how big is this elevator? And how fast? And will it take all of us at once?"

She tried to answer, but her voice kept failing her.

Rit looked back at the worm, then focused on the tower.

"Where are you going?" Master Brace hollered. He was still up near the worm's mouth, but moving toward them as fast as he could manage. "What are you people doing? What in the hell are you thinking?"

Do-ane saw him coming. Then she threw down everything but her precious book, and glancing at Jopale one last time, she turned and sprinted across the empty plain.

Rit considered Jopale, plainly doubting his good sense and sanity. Then he was gone, too, his long stride letting him catch up to Do-ane, then the old woman, leaving both of them behind.

"Sir," said Brace, staggering up next to Jopale.

He would say his good-byes; then he would run too. Jopale had made up his mind, or so he believed.

"Don't," was the caretaker's advice.

"Don't what?" Jopale asked.

Brace took him by the shoulder. Panting from his run, he said, "I like you, sir. And I honestly meant to warn you before now."

"Warn me?"

"And then . . . then I saw the girl talking to everybody, and I didn't think . . . I couldn't imagine . . . that all of you would actually believe her—"

"What is this?" Jopale cried out.

"She's ridden my worm in the past, sir." Brace looked across the plain. The fire to the east was tall enough and bright enough to illuminate each of the fleeing passengers. Tiny now. Frantic little shapes soon to be lost against that great expanse of dead dry wood.

"I know she's ridden this way," Jopale said. "Of course she has. She comes here to study the secret mountain."

Brace shook his head.

"No, sir," he said.

Then he looked Jopale in the eye, saying, "She does this. She has that book of hers, and she befriends a man . . . usually an older man . . . convincing him that everything she says is real. Then she steps off at this place and invites him to join her adventure, and of course any man would happily walk off with a pretty young thing like that.

"But she is insane, sir. I am sure.

"On my worm, she has ridden west at least five times now. And three times, she has set off a flare to make us stop here and pick her up on our eastbound leg." He gulped the cool air. "That's what people do in this country when there is no station, sir." Offering a grim smile, he added, "But sometimes we haven't brought her, and it's her men who set off the flares. We've rescued several gentlemen of your age and bearing, and they're always angry. 'She showed me this big book,' they'll say. They'll say, 'I was going to explore an ancient starship and look at the bones of gods.'"

Jopale wrapped his arms around his chest, moaning softly.

"That girl is quite crazy, sir. And that's all she is." Brace placed a comforting hand upon Jopale's shoulder. "She takes her men walking in the darkness. She keeps telling them that their destination is just a little farther now. But there's nothing to find out there. Even the most foolish man figures that out. And do you know what she does? At some point, she'll turn and tell him, 'You are the problem. You don't believe, so of course we can't find it.'

"Then those fellows return here and continue their journey west. And she wanders for a little while, then comes and waits here for the next eastbound worm. Somehow she always has money. Her life is spent riding worms and reading her book, and when she forgets that nothing on those pages is real, she comes back this way again. And that's all that she does in her life, from what I can tell."

Jopale was confused, and he had never been so angry. But somehow none of this was a perfect surprise.

"I should have said something," Brace admitted. "In my baby's stomach, when I saw her talking to everybody . . ."

"Should we chase after them?" Jopale asked.

But the caretaker could only shake his head, telling him, "There isn't time, sir. And honestly, I don't think we could make those people listen to reason now. They're chasing the only hope they've got left."

"But we should try to do what's right," Jopale maintained. "Perhaps we can convince one or two of them to turn back—"

"Sir," Brace interrupted.

Then the old fellow laughed at him.

"I don't know if you've noticed this, sir. But there is an exceptionally good chance that we ourselves won't be alive for much longer."

Again, Jopale heard the soft watery rumbling of the fire.

"Yes. Of course . . ."

TOWARD PORT OF KRAUSS

Brace began walking toward the worm's head.

The worm was slowly crawling forward, gulping down the big sweet barrels as she moved. Farther ahead, several dozen mockmen were being coaxed down onto the trail. At a distance, they looked entirely human. They seemed small and plainly scared, clinging to one another while their bare feet slipped on the white grease.

Jopale caught Brace, and before he lost his own scarce courage, he made an enormous request.

"I know it's asking a lot," he admitted.

"That won't make much difference," the old man said, offering a dark little laugh. Then he paused and cupped his hands around his mouth, shouting new orders into the wind.

The red-haired female was separated from the other mockmen.

Jopale rejoined his companion, and the two of them grabbed his bags and then a rope ladder, climbing onto the worm's wide back.

Without prompting, the mockman claimed one of the low chairs, facing forward, her long legs stretched out before her. If the creature was grateful, it didn't show on her stoic face. Either she was too stupid to understand what he had done, or she was perceptive enough to despise him for saving only her, leaving her friends to their gruesome fate.

The worm's bare flesh was warm to the touch. Jopale sat directly behind his mockman, letting her bulk block the wind. He could feel the great spine shifting beneath his rump. Facing backwards, he didn't watch the rest of the feeding, and save for a few muddled screams, he heard nothing. Then the worm began to accelerate, drugs and this one meal lending her phenomenal energy. And after a little while, when they were racing across the empty landscape, Master Brace came and sat beside him.

"But the book," Jopale began.

"It certainly looks real enough," the old man replied, guessing his mind. "And maybe it is genuine. Maybe she stole it from a true scientist who actually knows where the starship is buried. Or maybe it's an ancient manuscript, and there was once a starship . . . but the ship sank to the core ages ago, and some curious fluke has placed it in her strange hands."

"Or she invented everything," Jopale allowed.

"Perhaps." Watching the firestorm, Brace nodded. "Perhaps the girl heard a story about space flight and lost worlds, and she has a talent that lets her draw elaborate diagrams and play games with cameras. And these times are what made her insane. The terrors and wild hopes tell her that everything she can dream up is real. Perhaps."

Or she was perfectly rational, Jopale thought, and the starship really *was* waiting out there. Somewhere, While Brace was the creature whose sanity had been discarded along the way, his mind lying to both of them, forcing them to stay onboard his treasured worm.

"But the name," Jopale muttered.

"Sir?"

"'Good Mountain.' She told me why the scientists used that old word. And honestly, I can't think of another reason for placing that noble name on this ridiculous place."

"First of all, sir—"

"Call me Jopale, please."

"Jopale. Yes." Brace held both of his hands against the worm's skin, listening to the great body. "First of all, I know this country well. If there were a project here, a research station of any size, it would not be a secret from me. And I can tell you frankly, Jopale . . . except for that one strange girl and her misguided men, nobody comes to this wasted space . . ."

A small quake rolled beneath them.

When it passed, Brace suggested, "We might be in luck here, sir. Do-ane may have told you: There's a dead island under this ground. There's a lot of wood sitting between us and the methane. So when the fire gets off the Tanglelands, it should slow down. At least for a little while. This wood's going to burn, sure, but not as fast as that damned gas does."

Jopale tried to feel encouraged. Then he repeated the words, "'First of all.'"

"Sir?"

"You said, 'First of all.' What's second of all?"

Master Brace nodded in a thoughtful fashion, then said, "You know, my mother was a caretaker on a worm exactly like this one. And her father was a driver on a freighter worm that crawled along this same trail, bringing the new iron back from Port of Krauss. It was that grandfather who told me that even when there was sunlight here, this was an awful place to live. Flat like this. Sapless. Hard to farm, and hard on the soul. But some greedy fellow bought this land for nothing, then sold pieces of it to people in more crowded parts of the world. He named his ground 'Good Mountain' because he thought the old word sounded strong and lasting. But of course, all he wanted was to lure fools into his trap. . . ."

Jopale reached back over his head, burying one of his hands into the mockman's thick hair. Then he pushed with his legs, feeling a consuming need to be closer to her, grinding his spine hard up against her spine.

"It's just one old word," Brace was saying. With his face lit up by the endless fire, he said, "And I don't know if you've noticed this, sir. But words . . . what they are . . . they're just sounds and scribbles. It's *people* who give them meaning. Without us, the poor things wouldn't have any life at all."

And they pressed on, rushing toward the promised Ocean, with the End of the World following close behind.

i Hold My father's paws

DAViD D. LEViNE

In his short career to date, new writer David D. Levine has won the James White Award and the Phobos Fiction Contest, and capped it by winning a Hugo Award this year for his story "Tk'tk'tk." A graduate of Clarion West, his stories have appeared in *The Magazine of Fantasy and Science Fiction, Asimov's Science Fiction, Albedo One, Realms of Fantasy, Talebones, All-Star Zeppelin Adventure Stories,* and elsewhere. He lives in Portland, Oregon, where he and his wife, Kate Yule, coedit the popular fanzine *Bento*.

In the poignant story that follows, he shows us that family bonds can be very hard to break—even if you change your species to do so!

T he receptionist had feathers where her eyebrows should have been. They were blue, green, and black, iridescent as a peacock's, and they trembled gently in the silent breath of the air conditioner. "Did you have a question, sir?"

"No," Jason replied, and raised his magazine, but after reading the same paragraph three times without remembering a word he set it down again. "Actually, yes. Um, I wanted to ask you . . . ah . . . are you . . . transitioning?" The word landed on the soft tailored-grass carpet of the waiting room, and Jason wished he could pick it up again, stuff it into his pocket, and leave. Just leave, and never come back.

"Oh, you mean the eyebrows? No, sir, that's just fashion. I enjoy being human." She smiled gently at him. "You haven't been in San Francisco very long, have you?"

"No, I just got in this morning."

"Feathers are very popular here. In fact, we're having a special this month. Would you like a brochure?"

"No! Uh, I mean, no thank you." He looked down and saw that the magazine had crumpled in his hands. Awkwardly he tried to smooth it out, then gave up and slipped it back in the pile on the coffee table. They were all recent issues, and the coffee table looked like real wood. He tested it with a dirty thumbnail; real wood, all right. Then, appalled at his own action, he shifted the pile of magazines to cover the tiny scratch.

"Sir?"

Jason started at the receptionist's voice, sending magazines skidding across the table. "What?"

"Would you mind if I gave you a little friendly advice?"

"Uh, I . . . no. Please." She was probably going to tell him that his fly was open, or that ties were required in this office. Her own tie matched the wall covering, a luxurious print of maroon and gold. Jason doubted the collar of his faded work shirt would even button around his thick neck.

"You might not want to ask any of our patients if they are transitioning."

"Is it impolite?" He wanted to crawl under the table and die.

"No, sir." She smiled again, with genuine humor this time. "It's just that some of them will talk your ear off, given the slightest show of interest."

"I, uh . . . thank you."

A chime sounded—a rich little sound that blended unobtrusively with the waiting room's classical music—and the receptionist stared into space for a moment. "I'll let him know," she said to the air, then turned her attention to Jason. "Mr. Carmelke is out of surgery."

"Thank you." It was so strange to hear that uncommon name applied to someone else. He hadn't met another Carmelke in over twenty years.

Half an hour later the waiting room door opened onto a corridor with a smooth, shiny floor and meticulous off-white walls. Despite the art—original, no doubt— and the continuing classical music, a slight smell of disinfectant reminded Jason where he was. A young man in a nurse's uniform led Jason to a door marked with the name "Dr. Lawrence Steig."

"Hello, Mr. Carmelke," said the man behind the desk. "I'm Dr. Steig." The doctor was lean, shorter than Jason, with brown eyes and a trim salt-and-pepper beard. His hand, like his voice, was firm and a little rough; his tie was knotted with surgical precision. "Please do sit down."

Jason perched on the edge of the chair, not wanting to surrender to its lushness. Not wanting to be comfortable. "How is my father?"

"The operation went well, and he'll be conscious soon. But I'd like to talk with you first. I believe there are some . . . family issues."

"What makes you say that?"

The doctor stared at his personal organizer as he repeatedly snapped it open and shut. It was gold. "I've been working with your father for almost two years, Mr. Carmelke. The doctor–patient relationship in this type of work is, necessarily, quite intimate. I feel I've gotten to know him quite well." He raised his eyes to Jason's. "He's never mentioned you."

"I'm not surprised." Jason heard the edge of bitterness in his own voice.

"It's not unusual for patients of mine to be disowned by their families."

Jason's hard, brief laugh startled both of them. "This has nothing to do with his . . . transition, Dr. Steig. My father left my mother and me when I was nine. I haven't spoken to him since. Not once."

"I'm sorry, Mr. Carmelke." He seemed sincere; Jason wondered if it was just professional bedside manner. The doctor opened his mouth to speak, then closed it and stared off into a corner for a moment. "This might not be the best time for a family reunion," he said finally. "His condition may be a little . . . startling."

"I didn't come all the way from Cleveland just to turn around and go home. I want to talk with my father. While I still can. And this is my last chance, right?"

"The final operation is scheduled for five weeks from now. It can be postponed, of course. But all the papers have been signed." The doctor placed his hands flat on the desk. "You're not going to be able to talk him out of it."

"Just let me see him."

"I will . . . if he wants to see you."

Jason didn't have anything to say to that.

Jason's father was lying on his side, facing away from the door, as Jason entered. The smell of disinfectant was stronger here, and a battery of instruments bleeped quietly.

He was bald, with just a fringe of gray hair around the back of his head. The scalp was smooth and pink and shiny, and very round—matching Jason's own round head, too big for the standard hardhats at his work site. BIG JASE was what it said on his own personal helmet, black marker on safety yellow plastic.

But though his father's head was large and round, the shoulders that moved with his breathing were too narrow, and his chest dropped rapidly away to hips that were narrower still. The legs were invisible, drawn up in front of his body. Jason swallowed as he moved around to the other side of the bed.

His father's round face was tan, looking more "rugged" than "wrinkled." Deep lines ran from his nose to the corners of his mouth, and the eyebrows above his closed eyes were gray and very bushy. It was both an older and a younger face than what he had imagined, trying to add twenty years to a memory twenty years old.

Jason's gaze traveled down, past his father's freshly shaved chin, to the thick ruff of gray-white fur on his neck. Then further, to the gray-furred legs that lay on the bed in front of him and the paws that crossed, relaxed, at the ankles, with neatly trimmed nails and clean, unscuffed pads.

His father's body resembled a wolf's, or a mastiff's, broad and strong and laced with muscle and sinew. But it was wrong, somehow. His chest, narrow though it was, was still wider than any normal dog's, and the fur looked fake—too clean, too fine, too regular. Jason knew from his reading on the plane that it was engineered from his father's own body hair, and was only an approximation of a dog's natural coat with its layers of different types of hair.

He was a magnificent animal. He was a pathetic freak. He was a marvel of biotechnology. He was an arrogant icon of self-indulgence.

He was a dog.

He was Jason's father.

"Dad? It's Jason." Some part of him wanted to pet the furry shoulder, but he kept his hands to himself.

His father's eyes flickered open, then drifted closed again. "Yeah. Doctor told me." His voice was a little slurred. "What the hell'r you doing here?"

"I ran into Aunt Brittany at O'Hare. I didn't recognize her, but she knew me right away. She told me all about . . . you. I came straight here." *It's my father*, he'd told his boss on the phone. *He's in the hospital. I have to see him before it's too late.* Letting him draw the wrong conclusion, but not too far from the truth.

His father's nose wrinkled in distaste. "Never could trust her."

"Dad . . . *why?*"

He opened his eyes again. They were the same hard blue as Jason's, and they were beginning to focus properly. "Because I can. Because the Consti . . . *tu*tion gives me the right to do whatever the hell I want with my body and my money. Because I want to be pampered for the rest of my life." He closed his eyes and crossed his paws on the bridge of his nose. "Because I don't want to make any more damn decisions. Now get out."

Jason's mouth flapped open and closed like a fish. "But Dad . . ."

"Mr. Carmelke?" Jason looked up, and his father rolled his head around, to see where Dr. Steig stood by the door. Jason had no idea how long he had been there. "Excuse me, I meant Jason." Jason's father put his paws over his face again. "Mr. Carmelke, I think you should leave your father alone for a while. He's still feeling the effects of the anesthetic. He may be more . . . open to discussion, in the morning."

"Doubt it," came the voice from under the crossed paws.

Jason's hand reached out—to stroke the forehead, to ruffle the fur, he wasn't sure which—but then it pulled back. "See you tomorrow, Dad."

There was no response.

As soon as the door closed behind him, Jason leaned heavily against the wall, then slid down to a sitting position. His eyes stung and he rubbed at them.

"I'm sorry." Jason opened his eyes at the voice. Dr. Steig was squatting in front of him, holding a clipboard in his hands. "He's not usually like this."

"I've never understood him," Jason said, shaking his head. "Not since he left. We had a good life. He wasn't drinking or anything. There weren't any money problems—not then, anyway. Mom loved him. I loved him. But he said, 'There's nothing here for me,' and he walked out of our lives."

"You mentioned money. Is that what this is about? You know he's given most of it to charity already. What remains is just enough to pay for the craniofacial procedure, and a trust fund that will cover his few needs after that."

"It's not the money. It was never the money. He even offered to pay alimony and child support, but Mom turned it down. It wasn't the most practical decision, but she really didn't want anything to do with him. I think it was one of those things where a broken love turns into a terrible hate."

"Does your mother know you're here?"

"She died eight years ago. Leukemia. He didn't even come to the funeral."

"I'm sorry," the doctor said again. He sat down, let his clipboard clatter to the shiny floor next to him. They sat together in silence for a time. "Let me talk with him tonight, Mr. Carmelke, and we'll see how things go in the morning. All right?"

Jason thought for a moment, then bobbed his head. "All right."

They helped each other up.

Jason's father jogged into the doctor's office the next morning, his lithe new body bobbing with a smooth four-legged gait, and hopped easily up onto a carpeted platform that brought his head to the same level as Jason and the doctor. But he refused to meet Jason's eyes. Jason himself sat in the doctor's leather guest chair, fully seated this time, but still not fully comfortable.

"Noah," Dr. Steig said to Jason's father, "I know this is hard for you. But I want you to understand that it is even harder for your son."

"He shouldn't have come here," he said, still not looking at Jason.

"Dad . . . how could I not? You're the only family I have left in the world, I didn't even know if you were dead or alive, and now . . . this! I had to come. Even if I can't change your mind, I . . . I just want to talk."

"Talk, then!" His face turned to Jason at last, but his blue eyes were hard, his mouth set. "I might even listen." He lowered his head to his paws, which rested on the carpeted surface in front of him.

Jason felt the little muscles in his legs tensing to rise. He could stand up, walk out . . . be free of this awkwardness and pain. Go back to his lonely little house and try to forget all about his father.

But he knew how well that had worked the last time.

"I told them you were dead," he said. "My friends at school. The new school, after we moved to Cleveland. I don't know why. Lots of their parents were divorced. They would have understood. But somehow pretending you were dead made it easier."

His dad closed his eyes hard; deep furrows appeared in the corners of his eyes and between his brows. "Can't say I blame you," he said at last.

"No matter how many people I lied to, I still knew you were out there somewhere. I wondered what you were doing. Whether you missed me. Where did you go?"

"Buffalo."

Jason waited until he was sure no more details were forthcoming. "Is that where you've been all this time?"

"No, I was only there for a few months. Then Syracuse. Miami for a while. I didn't settle down for a long time. But I've been in the Bay Area for the last eleven years." He raised his head. "Selling configuration management software for Romatek. It's really exciting stuff."

Jason didn't care about his father's job, but he sensed an opening. "Tell me about it."

They talked for half an hour about configuration management and source control and stock options—things that Jason didn't understand and didn't want to understand. But they were talking. His dad even managed to make the topic seem interesting. A wry smirk came to Jason's lips when he realized he was getting a sales presentation from a dog. A dog with his father's head.

Jason and his father sat in the courtyard behind the clinic, under a red Japanese maple that sighed in the wind. The skyscrapers of San Francisco were visible above the fence, which was painted with a colorful abstract mural. A few birds chirped, and the slight mineral sting of sea salt flavored the air, reminding Jason how far he was from home.

A phone with two large buttons was strapped to his father's left foreleg. He could push the buttons with his chin to summon urgent or less-urgent assistance. He sat on the bench next to Jason with his legs drawn up beneath him, his head held high so as to look Jason as much in the eye as possible.

"I would have had to have something done with the knees one way or the other," he said. "They were just about shot, before. Arthritis. Now they're like new. I was taking laps this morning, before you showed up. Haven't been able to run like that in years. And being so close to the ground, it feels like a hundred miles an hour."

Jason translated that into kilometers and realized his dad wasn't speaking literally. "But what about . . . I dunno, restaurants? Museums? Movies?"

"After they do the head work I'll have different tastes, and I'll get nothing but the best. Museums—hell, I never went to museums before. And as far as movies, I'll just wait for them to come out on chip. Then I'll curl up with my handler and go to sleep in front of them."

"Of course, the movie will be in black and white to you."

"Heh."

Jason didn't mention—didn't want to think about—the other changes that the "head work" would make in his father's senses, and his brain. After the craniofacial procedure, his mind would be as much like a dog's as modern medicine could make it. He'd be happy, no question of that, but he wouldn't be Noah Carmelke any more.

Jason's dad seemed to recognize that his thoughts were drifting in an uncomfortable direction. "Tell me about your job," he said.

"I work for Bionergy," Jason replied. "I'm a civil engineer. We're refitting Cleveland's old natural gas system for biogas . . . that means a lot of tearing up streets and putting them back."

"Funny. I was a civil engineer for a while, before I hired on at Romatek."

"No shit?"

"No shit."

"I was following in your footsteps, and I didn't even know it."

"We thought you were going to be an artist. Your mom was so proud of those drawings of the barn, and the goats."

"Wow. I haven't done any sketching in years."

They stared at the mural, both remembering a refrigerator covered with drawings.

"You want me to draw you?"

Jason's father nodded slowly. "Yeah. Yeah, I'd like that."

Someone from the clinic managed to scare up a pad and some charcoal, and they settled down under the maple tree. Jason leaned against the fence and began to sketch, starting with the hindquarters. His father sat with his hind legs drawn up beneath him and his forelegs stretched straight out in front. "You look like the Sphinx," Jason said.

"Hmm."

"You can talk if you like, I'm not working on your mouth."

"I don't have anything to say."

Jason's charcoal paused on the page, then resumed its scratching. "Last night I read a paper I found in the restaurant. The *Howl*. You know it?" The full title was

HOWL: *The Journal of the Bay Area Transpecies Community*. It was full of angry articles about local politicians he'd never heard of, and ads for services he couldn't understand or didn't want to think about.

"I've read it, yeah. Buncha flakes."

"I found out there are a lot of different reasons for people to change their species. Some of them feel they were born into the wrong body. Some are making a statement about humanity's impact on the planet. Some see it as a kind of performance art. I don't see any of those in you."

"I told you, I just want to be taken care of. It's a form of retirement."

The marks on the page were getting heavy and black. "I don't think that's it. Not really. I look at you and I see a man with ambition and drive. You wouldn't have gotten all those stock options if you were the type to retire at 58." The charcoal stick snapped between Jason's fingers, and he threw the pieces aside. "Damnit, Dad, how can you give up your *humanity*?"

Jason's dad jumped to his four feet. His stance was wide, defensive. "The O'Hartigan decision said I have the right to reshape my body and my mind in any way I wish. I think that includes the right to not answer questions about it." He stared for a moment, as though he were about to say something else, then pursed his lips and trotted off.

Jason was left with a half-finished sketch of a sphinx with his father's face.

He sat in the clinic's waiting room for three hours the next day. Finally Dr. Steig came out and told him that he was sorry, but his father simply could not be convinced to see him.

Jason wandered the lunchtime crowds of San Francisco. The spring air was clear and crisp, and the people walked briskly. Here and there he saw feathers, fur, scales. The waiter who brought his sandwich was half snake, with slitted eyes and a forked tongue that flickered. Jason was so distracted he forgot to tip.

After lunch he came to the clinic's door and stopped. He stood in the hall for a long time, dithering, but when the elevator's ping announced the arrival of two women with identical Siamese cat faces he bolted—shoving between them, ignoring their insulted yowls, hammering the DOOR CLOSE button. As the elevator descended he gripped the handrails, pushed himself into the corner, tried to calm his breathing.

He landed in Cleveland at 12:30 that night.

The other hard-hats at his work site gave him a nice card they had all signed. He accepted their sympathies but did not offer any details. One woman took him aside and asked how long his father had. "The doctor says five weeks."

Days passed. Sometimes he found himself sitting in the cab of a backhoe, staring at his hands, wondering how long he had been there.

He confided in nobody. He imagined the jokes: "Good thing it isn't your mother . . . then you'd be a son-of-a-bitch!" Antacids became his favorite snack.

The little house he'd bought with Maria, back when they thought they might be able to make it work, became oppressive. He ate all his meals in restaurants, in parts of town where he didn't know anyone. Once he found a copy of the local transpecies paper. It was a skinny little thing, bimonthly, with angry articles about local politicians and ads for services he wished he didn't know anything about.

Four weeks later, on a Monday evening, he got a call from San Francisco.

"Jason, it's me. Your dad. Don't hang up."

The handset was already halfway to the cradle as the last three words came out, but Jason paused and returned it to his ear. "Why not?"

"I want to talk."

"You could have done that while I was there."

"OK, I admit I was a little short with you. I'm sorry."

The plastic of the handset creaked in Jason's hand. He tried to consciously relax his grip. "I'm sorry, too."

There was a long silence, the two of them breathing at each other across three thousand kilometers. It was Jason's father who broke it. "The operation is scheduled for Thursday at 8 A.M. I . . . I'd like to see you one more time before then."

Jason covered his eyes with one hand, the fingers pressing hard against the bones of his brow. Finally he sighed and said "I don't think so. There's no point to it. We just make each other too crazy."

"Please. I know I haven't been the best father to you . . ."

"You haven't been any kind of father at all!"

Another silence. "You've got me there. But I'd really like to . . ."

"To what? To say good-bye? Again? No thanks!" And he slammed down the phone.

He sat there for a long while, feeling the knots crawl across his stomach, waiting for the phone to ring again.

It didn't.

That night he went out and got good and drunk. "My dad's turning into a dog," he slurred to the bartender, but all that got him was a cab home.

Tuesday morning he called in sick. He spent the day in bed, sometimes sleeping. He watched a soap opera; the characters' ludicrous problems seemed so small and manageable.

Tuesday night he did not sleep. He brought out a box of letters from his mother, read through them looking for clues. At the bottom of the box he found a picture of himself at age eight, standing between his parents. It had been torn in half, the jagged line cutting between him and his father like a lightning bolt, and crudely taped together. He remembered rescuing the torn photo from his mother's wastebasket, taping it together, hiding it in a box of old CD-ROMs. Staring at it late at night. Wondering why.

Wednesday morning he drove to the airport.

There was a strike at O'Hare and he was rerouted to Atlanta, where he ate a bad hamburger and floated on a tide of angry, frustrated people, thrashing to stay on top.

Finally one gate agent found him a seat to LAX. From there he caught a red-eye to San Francisco.

He arrived at the clinic at 5 A.M. The door was locked, but there was a telephone number for after-hours service. It was answered by a machine. He stomped through menus until he reached a bored human being, who knew nothing, but promised to get a message to Dr. Steig.

He paced the hall outside the clinic. He had nowhere else to go.

Fifteen minutes later an astonished Dr. Steig called back. "Your father is already in prep for surgery, but I'll tell the hospital to let you see him." He gave Jason the address. "I'm glad you came," he said before hanging up.

The taxi took Jason through dark, empty streets, puddles gleaming with reflected streetlight. Raindrops ran down the windows like sweat, like tears. Jason blinked as he stepped into the hard blue-white light of the hospital's foyer. "I'm here to see Noah Carmelke," he said. "I'm expected."

The nurse gave him a paper mask to tie over his nose and mouth, and goggles for his eyes. "The prep area is sterile," she said as she helped him step into a paper coverall. Jason felt like he was going to a costume party.

And then the double doors slid open and he met the guest of honor.

His father lay on his side, shallow breaths raising and lowering his furry flanks. An oxygen mask was fastened to his face, like a muzzle. His eyes were at half-mast, unfocused. "Jason," he breathed. "They said you were coming, but I didn't believe it." The sound of his voice echoed hollowly behind the clear plastic.

"Hello, Dad." His own voice was muffled by the paper mask.

"I'm glad you're here."

"Dad . . . I had to come. I need to understand you. If I don't understand you, I'll never understand myself." He hugged himself. His face felt swollen; his whole head was ready to implode from sadness and fatigue. "Why, Dad? Why did you leave us? Why didn't you come to Mom's funeral? And why are you throwing away your life now?"

The bald head on the furry neck moved gently, side to side, on the pillow. "Did you ever have a dog, Jason?"

"You know the answer, Dad. Mom was allergic."

"What about after you grew up?"

"I've been alone most of the time since then. I didn't think I could take proper care of a dog if I had to go to work every day."

"But a dog would have loved you."

Jason's eyes burned behind the goggles.

"I had a dog when I was a kid," his father continued. "Juno. A German Shepherd. She was a good dog . . . smart, and strong, and obedient. And every day when I came home from school she came bounding into the yard . . . so happy to see me. She would jump up and lick my face." He twisted his head around, forced his eyes open to look into Jason's. "I left your mother because I couldn't love her like that. I knew she loved me, but I thought she deserved better than me. And I didn't come to the funeral because I knew she wouldn't want me there. Not after I'd hurt her so much."

"What about *me*, Dad?"

"You're a man. A man like me. I figured you'd understand."

"I *don't* understand. I never did."

His father sighed heavily, a long doggy sigh. "I'm sorry."

"You're turning yourself into a dog so someone will love you?"

"No. I'm turning myself into a dog so I can love someone. I want to be free of my human mind, free of decisions."

"How can you love anyone if you aren't *you* any more?"

"I'll still be me. But I'll be able to *be* me, instead of thinking all the time about being me."

"Dad . . ."

The nurse came back. "I'm sorry, Mr. Carmelke, but I have to ask you to leave now."

"Dad, you can't just leave me like that!"

"Jason," his father said. "There's a clause in the contract that lets me specify a family member as my primary handler."

"I don't think I could. . . ."

"Please, Jason. Son. It would mean so much to me. Let me come home with you."

Jason turned away. "And see you every day, and know what you used to be?"

"I'd sleep by your feet while you watch movies. I'd be so happy to see you when you came home. All you have to do is give the word, and I'll put my voiceprint on the contract right now."

Jason's throat was so tight that he couldn't speak. But he nodded.

The operation took eighteen hours. The recovery period lasted weeks. When the bandages came off, Jason's father's face was long and furry and had a wet nose. But his head was still very round, and his eyes were still blue.

Two deep wells of sincere, doggy love.

Dead Men Walking

PAUL J. McAULEY

Born in Oxford, England, in 1955, Paul J. McAuley now makes his home in London. A professional biologist for many years, he sold his first story in 1984, and has since established himself at the forefront of several of the most important subgenres in SF today, producing both "radical hard science fiction" and the revamped and retooled widescreen space opera that has sometimes been called the new space opera, as well as dystopian sociological speculations about the very near future. He also writes fantasy and horror. His first novel, *Four Hundred Billion Stars*, won the Philip K. Dick award, and his novel *Fairyland* won both the Arthur C. Clarke Award and the John W. Campbell Memorial Award in 1996. His other books include the novels *Of the Fall*, *Eternal Light*, and *Pasquale's Angel; Confluence* — a major trilogy of ambitious scope and scale set ten million years in the future, comprising the novels *Child of the River*, *Ancients of Days*, and *Shrine of Stars; Life on Mars; The Secret of Life; Whole Wide World;* and *White Devils*. His short fiction has been collected in *The King of the Hill and Other Stories*, *The Invisible Country*, and *Little Machines*, and he is the coeditor, with Kim Newman, of an original anthology, *In Dreams*. His most recent book is a novel, *Players*. Coming up are two new novels, *Cowboy Angels* and *The Quiet War*. His stories have appeared in our Fifth, Ninth, Thirteenth, and Fifteenth through Twentieth Annual Collections.

Here he takes us to a prison in the far reaches of the solar system, to show us how some consequences of a devastating war can persist for years after the war is ostensibly over — with deadly results.

I guess this is the end. I'm in no condition to attempt the climb down, and in any case I'm running out of air. The nearest emergency shelter is only five klicks away, but it might as well be on the far side of this little moon. I'm not expecting any kind of last-minute rescue, either. No one knows I'm here, my phone and the distress beacon are out, my emergency flares went with my utility belt, and I don't think that the drones patrol this high. At least my legs have stopped hurting, although I can feel the throb of what's left of my right hand through the painkiller's haze, like the beat of distant war drums. . . .

If you're the person who found my body, I doubt that you'll have time to listen to my last and only testament. You'll be too busy calling for help, securing the area, and making sure that you or any of your companions don't trample precious clues underfoot. I imagine instead that you're an investigator or civil servant sitting in an office buried deep inside some great bureaucratic hive, listening to this out of duty before consigning it to the memory hole. You'll know that my body was found near the top of the eastern rimwall of the great gash of Elliot Graben on Ariel, Uranus's fourth-largest moon, but I don't suppose you've ever visited the place, so I should give you an idea of what I can see.

I'm sitting with my pressure suit's backpack firmly wedged against a huge block of dirty, rock-hard ice. A little way beyond my broken legs, a cliff drops straight down for about a kilometer to the bottom of the graben's enormous trough. Its floor was resurfaced a couple of billion years ago by a flood of water-ice lava, a level plain patched with enormous fields of semi-vacuum organisms. Orange and red, deep blacks, foxy umbers, bright yellows . . . they stretch away from me in every direction for as far as I can see, like the biggest quilt in the universe. This moon is so small and the graben is so wide that its western rim is below the horizon. Strings of suspensor lamps float high above the fields like a fleet of burning airships. There's enough atmospheric pressure, twenty millibars of nitrogen and methane, to haze the view and give an indication of distance, of just how big this strange garden really is. It's the prison farm, of course, and every square centimeter of it was constructed by the sweat of men and women convicted by the failure of their ideals, but none of that matters to me now. I'm beyond all that up here, higher than the suspensor lamps, tucked under the eaves of the vast roof of transparent halflife polymer that tents the graben. If I twist my head I can glimpse one of the giant struts that anchor the roof. Beyond it, the big, blue-green globe of Uranus floats in the black sky. The gas giant's south pole, capped with a brownish haze of photochemical smog, is aimed at the brilliant point of the sun, which hangs just above the western horizon.

Sunset's three hours off. I won't live long enough to see it. My legs are comfortably numb, but the throbbing in my hand is becoming more urgent, there's a dull ache in my chest, and every breath is an effort. I wonder if I'll live long enough to tell you my story. . . .

All right. I've just taken another shot of painkiller. I had to override the suit to do it, it's a lethal dose. . . .

Christos, it still hurts. It hurts to laugh. . . .

My name is Roy Bruce. It isn't my real name. I have never had a real name. I suppose I had a number when I was decanted, but I don't know what it was. My instructors called me Dave—but they called all of us Dave, a private joke they never bothered to explain. Later, just before the war began, I took the life of the man in whose image I had been made. I took his life, his name, his identity. And after the war was over, after I evaded recall and went on the run, I had several different names, one after the other. But Roy, Roy Bruce, that's the name I've had longest. That's the name you'll find on the roster of guards. That's the name you can bury me under.

My name is Roy Bruce, and I lived in Herschel City, Ariel, for eight and a half years. Lived. Already with the past tense. . . .

My name is Roy Bruce. I'm a prison guard. The prison, TPA Facility 898, is a cluster of chambers—we call them blocks—buried in the eastern rim of Elliot Graben. Herschel City is twenty klicks beyond, a giant cylindrical shaft sunk into Ariel's icy surface, its walls covered in a vertical, shaggy green forest that grows from numerous ledges and crevices. Public buildings and little parks jut out of the forest wall like bracket fungi; homes are built in and amongst the trees. Ariel's just over a thousand kilometers in diameter and mostly ice; its gravity barely exists. The citizens of Herschel City are arboreal acrobats, swinging, climbing, sliding, flying up and down and roundabout on cableways and trapezes, nets and ropewalks. It's a good place to live.

I have a one-room treehouse. It's not very big and plainly furnished, but you can sit on the porch of a morning, watch squirrel monkeys chase each other through the pines. . . .

I'm a member of Sweat Lodge #23. I breed singing crickets, have won several competitions with them. Mostly they're hacked to sing fragments of Mozart, nothing fancy, but my line has good sustain and excellent timbre and pitch. I hope old Willy Gup keeps it going. . . .

I like to hike too, and climb freestyle. I once soloed the Broken Book route in Prospero Chasma on Miranda, twenty kilometers up a vertical face, in fifteen hours. Nowhere near the record, but pretty good for someone with a terminal illness. I've already had various bouts of cancer, but retroviruses dealt with those easily enough. What's killing me—what just lost the race to kill me—is a general systematic failure something like lupus. I couldn't get any treatment for it, of course, because the doctors would find out who I really am. What I really was.

I suppose that I had a year or so left. Maybe two if I was really lucky.

It wasn't much of a life, but it was all my own.

Uranus has some twenty-odd moons, mostly captured chunks of sooty ice a few dozen kilometers in diameter. Before the Quiet War, no more than a couple of hundred people lived out here. Rugged pioneer families, hermits, a few scientists, and some kind of Hindu sect that planted huge tracts of Umbriel's sooty surface with slow-growing lichenous vacuum organisms. After the war, the Three Powers Alliance took over the science station on Ariel, one of the larger moons, renamed it Herschel City, and built its maximum security facility in the big graben close by. The various leaders and lynchpins of the revolution, who had already spent two years being interrogated at Tycho, on Earth's Moon, were moved here to serve the rest of their life sentences of reeducation and moral realignment. At first, the place was run by the Navy, but civilian contractors were brought in after Elliot Graben was tented and the vacuum organism farms were planted. Most were ex-Service people who had settled in the Outer System after the war. I was one of them.

I had learned how to create fake identities with convincing histories during my training; my latest incarnation easily passed the security check. For eight and half years, Roy Bruce, guard third class, cricket breeder, amateur freestyle climber, lived a quiet, anonymous life out on the fringe of the Solar System. And then two guards stumbled across the body of Goether Lyle, who had been the leader of the Senate of Athens, Tethys, when, along with a dozen other city states in the Outer System, it had declared independence from Earth.

I'd known Goether slightly: an intense, serious man who'd been writing some kind of philosophical thesis in his spare time. His body was found in the middle of the main highway between the facility and the farms, spreadeagled and naked, spikes hammered through hands and feet. His genitals had been cut off and stuffed in his mouth; his tongue had been pulled through the slit in his throat. He was also frozen solid—the temperature out on the floor of the graben is around minus one hundred and fifty degrees Centigrade, balmy compared to the surface of Ariel, but still a lot colder than the inside of any domestic freezer, so cold that the carbon dioxide given off by certain strains of vacuum organisms precipitates out of the atmosphere like hoar frost. It took six hours to thaw out his body for the autopsy, which determined that the mutilations were postmortem. He'd died of strangulation, and then all the other stuff had been done to him.

I was more than thirty klicks away when Goether Lyle's body was discovered, supervising a work party of ten prisoners, what we call a stick, that was harvesting a field of vacuum organisms. It's important to keep the prisoners occupied, and stoop labor out in the fields or in the processing plants leaves them too tired to plan any serious mischief. Also, export of the high-grade biochemicals that the vacuum organisms cook from methane in the thin atmosphere helps to defray the enormous cost of running the facility. So I didn't hear about the murder until I'd driven my stick back to its block at the end of the shift, and I didn't learn all the gruesome details until later that evening, at the sweat lodge.

In the vestigial gravity of worldlets like Ariel, where you can drown in a shower and water tends to slosh about uncontrollably, sweat lodges, saunas, or Turkish-style hamams are ideal ways to keep clean. You bake in steam heat, sweat the dirt out of your pores, scrape it off your skin, and exchange gossip with your neighbors and friends. Even in a little company town like Herschel City, there are lodges catering for just about every sexual orientation and religious belief. My lodge, #23, is for unattached, agnostic heterosexual males. That evening, as usual, I was sitting with a dozen or so naked men of various ages and body types in eucalyptus-scented steam around its stone hearth. We scraped at our skin with abrasive mitts or plastered green depilatory mud on ourselves, squirted the baking stones of the hearth with water to make more steam, and talked about the murder of Goether Lyle. Mustafa Sesler, who worked in the hospital, gave us all the grisly details. There was speculation about whether it was caused by a personal beef or a turf war between gangs. Someone made the inevitable joke about it being the most thorough suicide in the history of the prison. Someone else, my friend Willy Gup, asked me if I had any idea about it.

"You had the guy in your stick last year, Roy. He have any enemies you know of?"

I gave a noncommittal answer. The mutilations described by Mustafa Sesler were straight out of my training in assassination, guerrilla tactics, and black propaganda. I was processing the awful possibility that Goether Lyle had been murdered by someone like me.

You must know by now what I am. That I am not really human. That I am a doppelgänger who was designed by gene wizards, grown in a vat, decanted fully grown with a headful of hardwired talents and traits, trained up, and sent out to kill the person whose exact double I was, and replace him. I do not know how many doppelgängers, berserkers, suicide artists, and other cloned subversives were deployed during the Quiet War, but I believe that our contribution was significant. My target was Sharwal Jah Sharja, a minor gene wizard who lived alone in the jungle in one of the tented crevasses of East of Eden, Ganymede, where he orchestrated the unceasing symphony of the city-state's closed loop ecosystem. After I took his place, I began a program of ecotage, significantly reducing the circulation of water vapor and increasing the atmospheric concentration of carbon dioxide and toxic trace gases. By the time the Quiet War kicked off, some four weeks later, the population of East of Eden was wearing breathing masks, the forests and parks were beginning to die, and most food animals and crops *had* died or were badly stricken, forcing the city to use biomass from vacuum organism farms to feed its citizens. A commando force of the Three Powers Alliance annexed East of Eden's farms in the first few hours of the war, and after two weeks its starving citizens agreed to terms of surrender.

I was supposed to turn myself in as soon as the city had been secured, but in the middle of the formal surrender, dead-ender fanatics assassinated half the senate and attacked the occupying force. In the subsequent confusion, the tented crevasse where I had been living was blown open to vacuum, Sharwal Jah Sharja was posted as one of the casualties, and I took the opportunity to slip away. I have successfully hidden my true identity and lived incognito amongst ordinary human beings ever since.

Why did I disobey my orders? How did I slip the bonds of my hardwired drives and instincts? It's quite simple. While I had been pretending to be Sharwal Jah Sharja, I had come to love life. I wanted to learn as much about it as I could in the brief span I'd been allotted by my designers. And so I adopted the identity of another casualty, and after the war was over and the Three Powers Alliance allowed trade and travel to resume, I left East of Eden and went out into the Solar System to see what I could see.

In all my wanderings I have never met any others like me, but I did find a hint that at least one of my brothers and sisters of the vat had survived the war. All of us had been imprinted with a variety of coded messages covering a vast range of possibilities, and a year after going on the run I came across one of them in a little used passageway between two chambers of the city of Xamba, Rhea.

To anyone else it was a meaningless scrawl; to me, it was like a flash of black lightning that branded an enciphered phone number on my brain. The walls of the passageway were thickly scribbled with graffiti, much of it pre-war. The message could have been left there last year or last week; it could have been a trap, left by agents hunting renegades like me. I didn't have the nerve to find out. I went straight to the spaceport and bought a seat on a shuttle to Phoebe, the gateway port to the other moons of Saturn and the rest of the Outer System. Six months later, wearing the new identity of Roy Bruce, I became a guard at TPA Facility 898.

That's why, almost nine years later, I couldn't be certain that any of my brothers and sisters had survived, and I was able to convince myself that Goether Lyle had been the victim of the vicious internal politics of the prison, killed and mutilated by someone who knew about the black propaganda techniques in which we'd been trained. But that comforting fiction was blown apart the very next day, when another mutilated body was found.

The victim was a former senator of Baghdad, Enceladus, and a member of the prison gang that was intermittently at war with the gang to which Goether Lyle had belonged. A message written in blood on the ground next to the senator's body implied that he'd been murdered by Goether Lyle's cronies, but whoever had killed him must have done the deed in his cell some time between the evening count and the end of the night's lockdown, spirited his body out of the facility without being detected, and left it within the field of view of a security camera that had been hacked to show a recorded loop instead of a live feed. Members of the rival gangs lived in different blocks, had chips implanted in their skulls that constantly monitored their movements, and in any case were under lockdown all night. If the killer was a prisoner, he would have had to bribe more than a dozen guards; it was far more likely that the senator had been killed by one of the facility's staff. And when I heard what had been done to the body, I was certain that it was the handiwork of one of my brothers or sisters. The senator had been blinded before he'd been strangled, and his lungs had been pulled through incisions in his back. It was a mutilation called the Blood Eagle that had been invented by the Vikings some two thousand years ago. I remembered the cold, patient voice of the instructor who had demonstrated it to us on a corpse.

Someone in the warden's office reached the same conclusion, Posted at the top of our daily orders was an announcement that a specialist team was on its way to Ariel, and emergency security measures were put in place at the spaceport. That evening Willy Gup told the sweat lodge that the warden reckoned that it was possible that the two murders were the work of the kind of vat-grown assassin used in the Quiet War.

"So if you come across anything suspicious, don't be tempted to do anything stupidly heroic, my brothers. Those things are smart and deadly and completely without any kind of human feeling. Be like me. Stay frosty, but hang back."

I felt a loathsome chill crawl through me. I knew that if Willy and the others realized that one of "those things" was sitting with them in the steamy heat of the lodge, they would fall on me at once and tear me limb from limb. And I knew that I couldn't hang back, couldn't let things run their course. No one would be able to leave Ariel for the duration of the emergency security measures, and the specialist team would search every square centimeter of the facility and Herschel City, check the records and DNA profile of every prisoner, member of staff, citizen and visitor, and release a myriad of tiny halflife drones designed to home in on anyone breathing out the combination of metabolic byproducts unique to our kind. The team would almost certainly uncover the assassin, but they would also unmask me.

Oh, I suppose that I could have hiked out to some remote location on the surface and hunkered down for the duration, but I had no idea how long the search would last. The only way I could be sure of evading it would be to force my pressure suit to put me in deep hibernation for a month or two, and how would I explain my absence when I returned? And besides, I knew that I was dying. I was already taking dangerously large daily doses of steroids to relieve the swelling of my joints and inflammation of my connective tissue caused by my pseudo-lupus. Suspended animation would slow but not stop the progress of my disease. Suppose I never woke up?

I spent a long, bleak night considering my options. By the time the city had begun to increase its ambient light level and the members of the local troop of spider monkeys were beginning to hoot softly to each other in the trees outside my little cabin, I knew what I would have to do. I knew that I would have to find the assassin before the team arrived.

My resolve hardened when I started my shift a couple of hours later and learned that there had been two more murders, and a minor riot in the prison library.

I found it laughably easy to hack into the facility's files. I had been trained well all those years ago, and the data system was of a similar vintage to my own. To begin with, I checked the dossiers of recently recruited staff, but I found nothing suspicious, and didn't have any better luck when I examined the dossiers of friends and family of prisoners, their advocates, and traders and businesspeople currently staying in Herschel City. It was possible that I had missed something—no doubt the assassin's cover story was every bit as good as the one that had served me so well for so long. But having more or less eliminated the obvious suspects, I had to consider the possibility that, just like me, the assassin had been hiding on Ariel ever since the war had ended. I had so much in common with my brothers and sisters that it would not be a wild coincidence if one of them had come to the same decision as I had, and had joined the staff of the prison. Perhaps he had finally gone insane, or perhaps the hardwired imperatives of his old mission had kicked in. Or perhaps, like me, he had discovered that he was coming to the end of his short life span, and had decided to have some fun. . . .

In the short time before the specialist team arrived, it would be impossible to check thoroughly the records of over three thousand staff members. I had reached a dead end. I decided that I needed some advice.

Everyone in Herschel City and the prison was talking about the murders. During a casual conversation with Willy Gup, I found it easy enough to ask my old friend if he had any thoughts on how someone might go about uncovering the identity of the assassin.

"Anyone with any sense would keep well clear," Willy said. "He'd keep his nose clean, he'd keep his stick in line, and he'd wait for the specialists."

"Who won't be here for a week. A full-scale war could have broken out by then."

Willy admitted that I had a point. One of the original intake of guards, a veteran who'd served in one of the Navy supply ships during the Quiet War, he had led the team that put down the trouble in the library. Three prisoners had died and eighteen had been badly injured—one had gouged out the eyes of another with her thumbs—and the incident had left him subdued and thoughtful. After studying me for a few moments, he said, "If it was me, I wouldn't touch the files. I hear the warden is compiling a list of people who are poking around, looking for clues and so forth. He tolerates their nonsense because he desperately wants to put an end to the trouble as soon as he can, and he'll be pretty damn happy if some hack does happen to uncover the assassin. But it isn't likely, and when this thing is over you can bet he's going to come down hard on all those amateur sleuths. And it's possible the assassin is keeping tabs on the files too. Anyone who comes close to finding him could be in for a bad surprise. No, my brother, screwing around in the files is only going to get you into trouble."

I knew then that Willy had a shrewd idea of what I was about. I also knew that the warden was the least of my worries. I said, as lightly as I could. "So what would you do?"

Willy didn't answer straight away, but instead refilled his bulb from the jar of iced tea. We were sitting on the porch of his little shack, at the edge of a setback near the top of the city's shaft. Banana plants and tree ferns screened it from its neighbors; the vertical forest dropped away on either side. Willy's champion cricket, a splendid white and gold specimen in a cage of plaited bamboo, was trilling one of Bach's Goldberg Variations. Willy passed the jar to me and said, "We're speaking purely hypothetically."

"Of course."

"You've always had a wild streak," Willy said, "I wouldn't put it past you to do something recklessly brave and dangerously stupid."

"I'm just an ordinary hack," I said.

"Who goes for long solitary hikes across the surface. Who soloed that route in Prospero Chasma and didn't bother to mention it until someone found out a couple of years later. I've known you almost nine years, Roy, and you're still a man of mystery." Willy smiled. "Hey, what's that look for? All I'm saying is you have character, is all."

For a moment, my hardwired reflexes had kicked in. For a moment, I had been considering whether or not this man had blown my cover, whether or not I should kill him. I carefully manufactured a smile, and said that I hadn't realized that I seemed so odd.

"Most of us have secrets," Willy said. "That's why we're out here, my brother. We're just as much prisoners as anyone in our sticks. They don't know it, but those dumbasses blundering about in the files are trying to find a way of escaping what they are."

"And there's no way you can escape what you are," I said. The moment had passed. My smile was a real smile now, not a mask I'd put on to hide what I really was.

Willy toasted me with his bulb of tea. "Anyone with any sense learns that eventually."

"You still haven't told me how you would catch the assassin."

"I don't intend to catch him."

"But speaking hypothetically . . ."

"For all we know, it's the warden. He can go anywhere and everywhere, and he has access to all the security systems too."

"The warden? Really?"

Willy grinned. "I'm pulling your chain. But seriously, I've done a little research about these things. They're not only stone killers: they're also real good at disguising themselves. The assassin could be any one of us. The warden, you, me, anyone. Unless this thing makes a mistake, we haven't got a hope of catching it. All we can do is what we're already doing—deploy more security drones, keep the prisoners locked down when they aren't working, and pray that that'll keep a lid on any unrest until that team arrives."

"I guess you're right," I said.

"Don't try to be a hero, my brother. Not even hypothetically."

"Absolutely not," I said.

But one of Willy's remarks had given me an idea about how to reach out to the assassin, and my mind was already racing, grappling with what I had to do.

I decided that if the assassin really was keeping an eye on the people who were hacking into the files, then he (or at least, his demon), must be lurking in the root directory of the data system. That was where I left an encrypted message explaining what I was and why I wanted to talk, attached to a demon that would attempt to trace anyone who looked at it. The demon phoned me six hours later, in the middle of the night. Someone had spotted my sign and wanted to talk.

The demon had failed to identify the person who wanted to talk, and it was infected with something, too: a simple communication program. I checked it out, excised a few lines of code that would have revealed my location, and fired it up. It connected me to a blank, tow-dimensional space in which words began to appear, emerging letter by letter, traveling from right to left and fading away.

>>*you got rid of the trace function. pretty good for an old guy—if that's what you really are.*

>*they trained us well,* I typed.

>*you think you know what i am. you think that i am like you.*

Whoever was at the other end of the program wanted to get straight down to business. That suited me, but I knew that I couldn't let him take the lead.

>*we are both children of the vat.* I typed. *that's why I reached out to you. that's why i want to help you.*

There was a pause as my correspondent thought this over.

>>*you could be a trap.*

>*the message got your attention because it is hardwired into your visual cortex, just as it is hardwired into mine.*

>*that kind of thing is no longer the secret it once was, but let's say that i believe you. . . .*

A black disc spun in the blank space for less than a second, its strobing black light flashing a string of letters and numbers, gone.

>*do you know where that is?*
I realized that the letters and numbers burnt into my brain were a grid reference.
>*i can find it.*
>*meet me in four hours. i have a little business to take care of first.*
It was the middle of the night; the time when the assassin did his work.
>*please don't kill anyone else until we have talked.*
My words faded. There was no reply.

The grid reference was at the precise center of a small eroded crater sixty klicks south of the facility, an unreconstructed area in the shadow of the graben's eastern rimwall. Before I headed out, I equipped myself from the armory and downloaded a hack into the security system so that I could move freely and unremarked. I was oddly happy, foolishly confident. It felt good to be in action again. My head was filled with a fat, contented hum as I drove a tricycle cart along an old construction road. The rendezvous point was about an hour away: I would have plenty of time to familiarize myself with the terrain and make my preparations before the assassin, if that was who I had been talking to, turned up.

I want to make it clear that my actions were in no way altruistic. The only life I wanted to save was my own. Yes, I knew that I was dying, but no one loves life more than those who have only a little of it left; no one else experiences each and every moment with such vivid immediacy. I didn't intend to throw away my life in a grand gesture. I wanted to unmask the assassin and escape the special team's inquisition.

The road ran across a flat terrain blanketed in vacuum-cemented grey-brown dust and littered with big blocks that over the eons had been eroded into soft shapes by impact cratering. The rimwall reared up to my left, its intricate folds and bulges like a frozen curtain. Steep cones and rounded hills of mass-wasted talus fringed its base. To my right, the land sloped away toward a glittering ribbon of fences and dykes more than a kilometer away, the boundary of the huge patchwork of fields. It was two in the morning by the clock, but the suspensor lamps were burning as brightly as they always did, and above the western horizon the sun's dim spark was almost lost in their hazy glow.

I was a couple of klicks from the rendezvous, and the road was cutting through a steep ridge that buttressed a great bulge in the rimwall, when the assassin struck. I glimpsed a hitch of movement high in a corner of my vision, but before I could react, a taser dart struck my cart and shorted its motor. A second later, a net slammed into me, slithering over my torso as muscular threads of myoelectric plastic tightened in constricting folds around my arms and chest. I struggled to free myself as the cart piddled to a halt, but my arms were pinned to my sides by the net and I couldn't even unfasten the safety harness. I could only sit and watch as a figure in a black pressure suit descended the steep side of the ridge in two huge bounds, reached me in two more. It ripped out my phone, stripped away my utility belt, the gun in the pocket on the right thigh of my pressure suit and the knife in the pocket on the left thigh, then uncoupled my main air supply, punched the release of my harness and dragged me out of the low-slung seat and hauled me off the road. I was dumped on my back near a cart parked in the shadow of a house-sized block and the assassin stepped back, aiming a rail-gun at me.

The neutron camera I'd fitted inside my helmet revealed scant details of the face behind the gold-filmed mirror of my captor's visor; its demon made an extrapolation, searched the database I'd loaded, found a match. Debra Thorn, employed as a paramedic in the facility's infirmary for the past two years, twenty-two, unmarried, no children. . . . I realized then that I'd made a serious mistake. The assassin was a doppelgänger, all right, but because she was the double of someone who hadn't been an adult when the war had ended she must have been manufactured and decanted much more recently than me. She wasn't insane, and she hadn't spent years under cover. She was killing people because that was what she'd been sent here to do. Because it was her mission.

A light was winking on my head-up display—the emergency short-range, line-of-sight walkie-talkie. When I responded, an electronically distorted voice said, "Are you alone?"

"Absolutely."

"Who are you?"

I'd stripped all identifying tags from my suit before setting off, but the doppelgänger who had killed Debra Thorn and taken her place was pointing a gun at my head and it seemed advisable to tell her my name. She was silent for a moment, no doubt taking a look at my file. I said, "I'm not the doppelgänger of Roy Bruce, if that's what you're thinking. The person I killed and replaced was a gene wizard by the name of Sharwal Jah Sharja."

I briefly told the assassin the story I have already told you. When I was finished, she said, "You've really been working here for eight years?"

"Eight and a half." I had made a very bad mistake about my captor's motives, but I must have piqued her curiosity, for otherwise I would already be dead. And even if I couldn't talk my way out of this and persuade her to spare me, I still had a couple of weapons she hadn't found . . . I risked a lie, said that her net had compromised my suit's thermal integrity. I told her that I was losing heat to the frozen ground, that I would freeze to death if I didn't get up.

She told me I could sit up, and to do it slowly.

As I got my feet under me, squatting on my haunches in front of her, I glanced up at the top of the ridge and made a crucial triangulation.

She said, "My instructors told me that I would live no more than a year."

"Perhaps they told you that you would burn briefly but very brightly—that's what they told me. But they lied. I expect they lied about a lot of things, but I promise to tell you only the truth. We can leave here, and go anywhere we want to."

"I have a job to finish."

"People to kill, riots to start."

The assassin took a long step sideways to the cart, took something the size of a basketball from the net behind its seat, bowled it toward me. It bounced slowly over the dusty ground and ended up between my legs: the severed head of an old woman, skin burnt black with cold, eyes capped by frost.

"The former leader of the parliament of Sparta, Tethys," the assassin said. "I left the body pinned to the ground in one of the fields where her friends work, with an amusing little message."

"You are trying to start a war amongst the prisoners. Perhaps the people who sent you here are hoping that the scandal will close the facility. Perhaps they think it is the only chance they'll have of freeing their comrades. Who are you working for, by the way?"

"I'll ask the questions," the assassin said.

I asked her how she would escape when she was finished. "There's a special team on the way. If you're still here when they arrive, they'll hunt you down and kill you."

"So that's why you came after me. You were frightened that this team would find you while they were hunting me."

She may have been young, but she was smart and quick.

I said, "I came because I wanted to talk to you. Because you're like me."

"Because after all these years of living amongst humans, you miss your own kind, is that it?"

Despite the electronic distortion, I could hear the sneer in the assassin's voice. I said carefully, "The people who sent you here—the people who made you—have no plans to extract you when you are finished here. They do not care if you survive your mission. They only care that it is successful. Why give your loyalty to people who consider you expendable? To people who lied to you? You have many years of life ahead of you, and it isn't as hard to disobey your orders as you might think. You've already disobeyed them, in fact, when you reached out to me. All you have to do is take one more step, and let me help you. If we work together, we'll survive this. We'll find a way to escape."

"You think you're human. You're not. You're exactly like me. A walking dead man. That's what our instructors called us, by the way: the dead. Not 'Dave.' Not anything cute. When we were being moved from one place to another, they'd shout out a warning: 'Dead men walking.'"

It is supposed to be the traditional cry when a condemned person is let out of their cell. Fortunately, I've never worked in Block H, where prisoners who have murdered or tried to murder fellow inmates or guards await execution, so I've never heard it or had to use it.

The assassin said, "They're right, aren't they? We're made things, so how can we be properly alive?"

"I've lived a more or less ordinary life for ten years. If you give this up and come with me, I'll show you how."

"You stole a life, just as I did. Underneath your disguise, you're a dead man, just like me."

"The life I live now is my own, not anyone else's," I said. "Give up what you are doing, and I'll show you what I mean."

"You're a dead man in any case," the assassin said. "You're breathing the last of your air. You have less than an hour left. I'll leave you to die here, finish my work, and escape in the confusion. After that, I'm supposed to be picked up, but now I think I'll pass on that. There must be plenty of people out there who need my skills. I'll work for anyone who wants some killing done, and earn plenty of money."

"It's a nice dream," I said, "but it will never come true."

"Why shouldn't I profit from what I was made to do?"

"I've lived amongst people for more than a decade. Perhaps I don't know them as well as I should, but I do know that they are very afraid of us. Not because we're different, but because we're so very much like a part of them they don't want to acknowledge. Because we're the dark side of their nature. I've survived this long only because I have been very careful to hide what I really am. I can teach you how to do that, if you'll let me."

"It doesn't sound like much of a life to me," the assassin said.

"Don't you like being Debra Thorn?" I said.

And at the same moment, I kicked off the ground, hoping that by revealing that I knew who she was I'd distracted and confused her, and won a moment's grace.

In Ariel's microgravity, my standing jump took me high above the assassin's head, up and over the edge of the ridge. As I flew up, I discharged the taser dart I'd sewn into the palm of one of my pressure suit's gloves, and the electrical charge stored in its super-conducting loop shorted out every thread of myoelectric plastic that bound my arms. I shrugged off the net as I came down and kicked off again, bounding along the ridge in headlong flight toward the bulging face of the cliff wall and a narrow chimney pinched between two folds of black, rock-hard ice.

I was halfway there when a kinetic round struck my left leg with tremendous force and broke my thigh. I tumbled over hummocked ice and caught hold of a low pinnacle just before I went over the edge of the ridge. The assassin's triumphant shout was a blare of electronic noise in my ears; because she was using the line-of-sight walkie-talkie I knew that she was almost on me. I pushed up at once and scuttled toward the chimney like a crippled ape. I had almost reached my goal when a second kinetic round shattered my right knee. My suit was ruptured at the point of impact, and I felt a freezing pain as the smart fabric constricted as tightly as a tourniquet, but I was not finished. The impact of the kinetic round had knocked me head over heels into a field of fallen ice-blocks, within striking distance of the chimney. As I half-crawled, half-swam toward it, a third round took off the top of a pitted block that might have fallen from the cliffs a billion years ago, and then I was inside the chimney, and started to climb.

The assassin had no experience of freestyle climbing. Despite my injuries I soon outdistanced her. The chimney gave out after half a kilometer, and I had no choice but to continue to climb the naked iceface. Less than a minute later, the assassin reached the end of the chimney and fired a kinetic round that smashed into the cliff a little way above me. I flattened against the iceface as a huge chunk dropped past me with dreamy slowness, then powered straight through the expanding cloud of debris, pebbles and icegrains briefly rattling on my helmet, and flopped over the edge of a narrow setback.

My left leg bent in the middle of my thigh and hurt horribly; my right leg was numb below the knee and a thick crust of blood had frozen solid at the joint. But I had no time to tend my wounds I sat up and ripped out the hose of the water recycling system as the assassin shot above the edge of the cliff in a graceful arc, taser in one hand, rail gun in the other. I twisted the valve, hit her with a high-pressure spray of water that struck her visor and instantly froze. I pushed off the ground with both hands (a kinetic round slammed into the dusty ice where I'd just been), collided with her in midair, clamped my glove over the diagnostic port of her backpack, and discharged my second taser dart.

The dart shorted out the electronics in the assassin's suit, and enough current passed through the port to briefly stun her. I pushed her away as we dropped toward the setback, but she managed to fire a last shot as she spun into the void beyond the edge of the setback. She was either phenomenally lucky or incredibly skillful: it took off my thumb and three fingers of my right hand.

She fell more than a kilometer. Even in the low gravity, it was more than enough to kill her, but just to make sure I dropped several blocks of ice onto her. The third smashed her visor. You'll find her body, if you haven't already, more or less directly below the spot where you found mine.

The assassin had vented most of my air supply and taken my phone and emergency beacon; the dart I'd used on her had crippled what was left of my pressure suit's life support system. The suit's insulation is pretty good, but I'm beginning to feel the bite of the cold now, my hand is growing pretty tired from using the squeeze pump to push air through the rebreather, and I'm getting a bad headache as the carbon dioxide concentration in my air supply inexorably rises. I killed the ecosystem of East of Eden by sabotaging the balance of its atmospheric gases, and now the same imbalance is killing me.

Just about the only thing still working is the stupid little chip I stuck in my helmet to record my conversation with the assassin. By now, you probably knew more about her than I do. Perhaps you even know who sent her here.

I don't have much time left. Perhaps it's because the increasing carbon dioxide level is making me comfortably stupid, but I find that I don't mind dying. I told you that I confronted the assassin to save myself. I think now that I may have been wrong about that. I may have gone on the run after the Quiet War, but in my own way I have served you right up until the end of my life.

I'm going to sign off now. I want to spend my last moments remembering my freestyle climb up those twenty kilometers of sheer ice in Prospero Chasma. I want to remember how at the end I stood tired and alone at the top of a world-cleaving fault left over from a shattering collision four billion years ago, with Uranus tilted at the horizon, half-full, serene and remote, and the infinite black, starry sky above. I felt so utterly insignificant then, and yet so happy, too, without a single regret for anything at all in my silly little life.

HOME MOVIES

MARY ROSENBLUM

One of the most popular and prolific of the new writers of the nineties, Mary Rosenblum made her first sale, to *Asimov's Science Fiction*, in 1990, and has since become a mainstay of that magazine, and one of its most frequent contributors, with more than thirty sales there to her credit. She has also sold to *The Magazine of Fantasy & Science Fiction*, *Science Fiction Age*, *Pulphouse*, *New Legends*, and elsewhere.

Rosenblum produced some of the most colorful, exciting, and emotionally powerful stories of the nineties, such as "The Stone Garden," "Synthesis," "Flight," "California Dreamer," "Casting at Pegasus," "Entrada," and many others, earning her a large and devoted following of readers. Her novella *Gas Fish* won the *Asimov's* Readers Award Poll in 1996, and was a finalist for that year's Nebula Award. Her first novel, *The Drylands*, appeared in 1993 to wide critical acclaim, winning the prestigious Compton Crook Award for Best First Novel of the year; it was followed in short order by her second novel, *Chimera*, and her third, *The Stone Garden*. Her first short story collection, *Synthesis and Other Virtual Realities*, was widely hailed by critics as one of the best collections of 1996. She has also written a trilogy of mystery novels under the name Mary Freeman. Her most recent book is a major new science fiction novel, *Horizons*. Coming up is a new collection, *Drylands*. A graduate of Clarion West, Mary Rosenblum lives in Portland, Oregon.

The intriguing story that follows—one that is, appropriately enough, filled with intricate intrigues—reaffirms that memory can be something worth hanging on to at all costs—the question is, *whose?*

Her broker's call woke Kayla from a dream of endless grass sprinkled with blue and white flowers. A fragment of client memory? Sometimes they seeped into her brain even though they weren't supposed to. She sat up, groggy with sleep, trying to remember if she'd ever visited one of the prairie preserves as herself. "Access," she said, yawned, and focused on the shimmer of the holo-field as it formed over her desktop.

"Usually, you're up by now." Azara, her broker, gave her a severe look from beneath a decorative veil, woven with shimmering fiber lights.

"I'm not working." Kayla stretched. "I can sleep late."

"You're working now," Azara sniffed. "Family wedding, week-long reunion, the client wants the whole affair, price is no object. Please cover yourself."

"Your religion is showing." But Kayla reached for the shift she'd shed last night, pulled it over her head. "A whole week." She yawned again. "I don't know. I met this cool guy last night and I don't know if I want to be gone a whole week."

"If you want me as a broker you'll do it." Azara glared at her. "This client is the most picky woman I have had dealings with in many years. But she is paying a bonus and you are my only chameleon who matches her physical requirements." She clucked disapproval.

One of those. Kayla sighed and turned to the tiny kitchen wall. "Did you tell her it's not our age or what we look like or even our gender that makes us see what they want us to see?"

"Ah." Azara rolled her eyes. "I gave her the usual explanation. Several times." She stretched her very red lips into a wide smile. "But she was willing to pay for her eccentricities, so we will abide by them."

"She must be rich." Kayla spooned Sumatran green tea into a cup, stuck it under the hot water dispenser. "How nice for her."

"Senior administrator of Mars Colony. Of course, rich, or would she call me?" Azara snapped her fingers. "You have an appointment with her in two hours." She eyed Kayla critically. "Appearance matters to her."

"Don't worry." Kayla ran a hand through her tousled mop as she sipped her tea. "I'll look good."

"Do so." And Azara's image winked out.

Kayla shook her head, but the client was always right . . . well, usually right . . . and they were willing to pay a lot to visit Earth vicariously from Mars or Europa or one of the micro-gravity habitats. She drank her tea, showered, and dressed in a green spider-silk shift she had bought on a visit to the orbital platforms. The color matched her eyes and brought out the red in her hair. It did indeed make her look good.

Precisely two hours later, her desktop chimed with a link from Bradbury, the main city of Mars Colony. Kayla accepted, curious. She had rented a couple of virtual tours of Mars Colony, had found the mostly underground cities to be as claustrophobic as the platforms, even though the domed space aboveground offered water and plants. The holo-field shimmered and a woman's torso appeared. Old. Euro-celtic phenotype, not gene-selected. Kayla appraised the woman's weathered face, wrinkles, determined eyes. Considering the current level of bio-science, *very* old to look like this. And very used to control. "Kayla O'Connor, at your service," she said and put a polite, welcoming smile onto her face.

The woman peered at her for a moment without speaking, nodded finally. "I am Jeruna Nesmith, First Administrator of Bradbury City. I would like to enjoy my nephew's son's wedding. It will take place on a small, private island, and include a weeklong family reunion." She seemed to lean forward, as if to stare into Kayla's eyes. "The broker I contacted assured me that you would know what I want to look at."

Ah, yes, she was indeed used to control. Kayla smiled. "Only after we have talked and I have gotten to know you." Although she could guess right now what the old bitch would want to look at. "I am usually quite accurate about what interests my clients."

"So the broker says. I hope she is correct." Nesmith straightened. "I have little time to waste, so let us begin."

So much for that cute young executive from Shanghai she'd met at the club last night. "As you wish." Kayla kept her smile in place, started to record. "I would like you to tell me about this wedding."

"Tell you what?"

"Everything." Kayla leaned back, her smart-chair stretching and conforming to cradle her. "Who is getting married? Why? Are they a good match? What do their parents think about it? What do you think about it? Who would you be happy to see and who would you avoid at the wedding? What do you think about each of the relatives and guests that will be present?"

"What does all this have to do with recording images for me?" Nesmith's eyebrows rose. "This is not your business."

"And the recording I make of our conversation is destroyed as soon as the contract is completed . . . you did sign the contract," Kayla reminded her gently. "If you just want videos, it's much cheaper to hire a cameraman rather than a chameleon. But if you want me to look with *your* eyes, notice the details *you* would notice. . . ." She smiled. "Then I have so think like you."

Again, Nesmith stared at her. "The wedding is of one of my nephew's sons." She waved a long-fingered hand. "A worthless, spoiled boy, who will never make anything of himself, marrying an equally spoiled and self-centered girl from one of the big aquaculture families. It is a spectacle to impress other inside families."

Well, she already knew how to look at the bride and groom. Kayla settled into listening mode as the woman continued. Notice the pointless extravagances, the follies, the proof of her pronouncements. Ah, but that wasn't all. . . . She let her eyelids droop, listening, paying attention to the emotional nuances of voice and expression as the woman droned on, inserting a leading question here and there. The old bitch *did* have an agenda. Interesting. Kayla absorbed every word, putting on this woman the way you'd put on a costume for a party.

She took the shot at her usual clinic, the morning her plane was scheduled to leave. An Yi, her favorite technician, administered it. "Where do you get to go this time?" she asked as she settled Kayla into the recliner and checked her vitals on the readout. "Somewhere fun?"

"Fancy, anyway." Although something didn't quite add up and that bothered her a little. She went over the interview again as she told An Yi about the wedding and reunion. Nope. Couldn't put her finger on it. She watched the technician deftly clean the tiny port in her carotid and prepare the dose.

"Ah, it sounds so lovely," An Yi sighed as she began to inject the nano. "Maybe next year I'll do one of the island resorts. This year, I have to spend my vacation in

Fouzhou. My father wants us all to be there for his one hundredth birthday." She made a face and laughed. "Maybe I should hire you to go."

"Why not?" Kayla said, and then the nano hit her and the walls warped.

It always unsettled her as the nano-ware invaded her brain. The tiny machines disseminated quickly, forming a network, preempting the neural pathways of memory. It didn't take long, but as they established themselves, all her senses seemed to twist and change briefly, and her stomach heaved with familiar nausea. An Yi had been doing this for a long time and had the pan ready for her, wiping her mouth afterward and placing a cool, wet cloth on her forehead. The headache hit Kayla like a thrown spear and she closed her eyes, concentrating on her breathing, waiting for it to be over.

When it finally faded, An Yi helped her sit up and handed her a glass of apple juice laced with ginseng to drink. The tart sweetness of the juice and the familiar bitterness of the ginseng settled her stomach and the last echo of the headache vanished.

"Do your clients mind getting sick when they get it?" An Yi asked, curious.

"Probably." Kayla nodded. "But they can buy the option to translate the memories into their own long-term memory if they choose. So they only have to put up with the side effects once." She stood, okay now. "I'd better get going. I still have to finish packing."

"Have a really fun time," An Yi said, her expression envious.

"I'll do my best."

Kayla left the clinic and caught the monorail across town to pick up her luggage and head for the airport. She probably would enjoy it, she thought, even if the Martian Administrator's very poor opinion of most of her extended family was accurate. And then there was Ethan. Kayla smiled as she thumbed the charge plate and exited the monorail. Her client's hidden agenda. He was cute and clearly the old gal had a crush on him. So the week wouldn't be entirely wasted. She could flirt with him and Jeruna wouldn't mind at all.

Before she left her condo, she made her trip notes in her secret diary. You weren't supposed to record anything, but, hand-written in the little blank-paged paper book she'd found in a dusty junk stall at the market, it was safe enough. Those notes served as steppingstones across the gaping holes in her past. It was fun, sometimes, to compare the client's instructions with her own observations afterward. Client perspectives were rarely objective. If they were, they wouldn't need her.

The trip to the rent-an-island was tedious. The family had paid for a high level of security. It was necessary in this age of kidnap-as-career. The security checks and delays took time, since she traveled as an invited guest of a family member who had *not* planned the wedding. And, thus, was not paying the security firm. But this was nothing new, and she endured the familiar roadblocks stoically. Kidnap raids were real, and her client would have to suffer the delays, too, when she consumed the nano.

But once she boarded the private shuttle from Miami International, everything changed. Her invitation coin had been declared good, and all the perks were in place. The flight attendant offered fresh, tropical, organic fruit. Wine if she wanted it. Excellent tea, which she enjoyed. She was used to sleeping on planes, and so woke, refreshed, as the shuttle swept down to land on the wedding island. She was the only passenger on this run, and, as the door unsealed and the rampway unfurled, she drew in a deep breath of humidity, flowers, rot, and soil. A vestigal memory stirred. Yes, she had been in a place like this . . . maybe *this* place . . . before. Funny how smell was the strongest link to the fragments of past jobs that had seeped past the nano. She descended the rampway to the small landing, and headed for the pink stucco buildings of the tiny airport terminal, figuring she'd find some kind of shuttle service. Flowering vines covered the walls and spilled out over the tiled entryway and the scent evoked another twinge of *been here* memory. As she paused, a tall figure stepped from the doorway.

"You must be Jeruna's guest." He smiled at her, his posture a bit wary, dressed in a loose-weave linen shirt and shorts. "I'm Ethan." He offered his hand. "I belong to the ne'er-do-well branch of the family so I get to play chauffeur for the occasion. Welcome to the wedding of the decade." He said it lightly, but his hazel eyes were reserved.

"Nice to meet you, Ethan." Kayla returned his firm handshake, decided he was as cute as the vids she'd looked at, and let him take her bag. Tossing her hair back from her face, she smiled as she studied him. Why you? she wondered as she followed him through the tiled courtyard of the private airport, past a shallow, marble fountain full of leaping water and golden fish. "I'm looking forward to being a guest here," she said as they reached the roadway outside.

"Really?" He turned to face her, his hand on the small electric cart parked outside. "This is a job to you, right? Can you really let yourself enjoy something like this? Won't your thoughts about it mess up what you're recording?"

Great. Kayla sighed. "So who leaked it? That I'm a chameleon?"

"Is that what you call yourself?" He stowed her luggage, which had been delivered by a uniformed baggage handler, in the rear cargo space of the cart. "Doesn't it weird you out? That you're going to hand over your thoughts and feelings to somebody . . . for pay?"

He wasn't being hostile, as so many were. He was really asking. "The nano can't record thoughts." Kayla smiled as she climbed into the cart's passenger seat, inwardly more than a little ticked off. It made her job harder when they knew. Now she wouldn't get really good reactions until he got used to her, forgot she was recording. And a lot of times, in the really good moments, some family member who had had too much to drink would remember and say something. She sighed. "The nano only records sensory input . . . vision, hearing, taste, touch, smell. That's it. We haven't developed telepathy yet. Your great-great-aunt . . . or whatever she is . . . gets to experience the event with all of her senses, not just vision and hearing."

"Oh." Ethan climbed in beside her, his face thoughtful. "Isn't it kind of weird, though? Hanging out with strangers all the time?"

"Not really." She lifted her hair off her neck as the cart surged forward, enjoying the breeze of their motion in the heavy, humid afternoon. Well, he had never lived outside, probably couldn't see beyond the luxury of an inside lifestyle. "That's what I do . . . learn about the family, get a sense of what the client is really interested in so I can participate the way my client would, if she was here." She smiled at him. "I really do feel like a member of the family or the group while I'm there. That's what makes me good at this."

"A chameleon." But he smiled as he said it. "What about your family? Does it change how you feel about them?"

"I never had one." She shrugged. "I was a London orphan when Irish looks weren't the fad. Did the foster home slash institution thing."

"I'm sorry."

She shrugged again, tired of the topic years ago, and not sure how they'd gotten here. She didn't talk about herself on a job. "So how come you rate the job of chauffeur?" She smiled at him. "Just how ne'er-do-well was your family branch?"

"Oh, they were all off-off-Broadway actors, musicians, failed writers, the usual wastrel thing . . . according to our family's creed." He laughed, not at all defensive. "The family bails us out before we disgrace anyone, but they make sure we know our place." He shrugged, gave her a sideways look. "I play jazz, myself. Among other things my family disapproves of. But I don't do illegal drugs, murder, mayhem, or anything else too awful, so I got a genuine invitation to this bash."

"To be a chauffeur."

"Well, yeah." He grinned, his hazel eyes sparkling. "But they have to make sure I know my place."

"Does that bother you?" She asked it because she was curious.

"No."

He meant it. She watched his face for her client. She would resent it, Kayla thought. Which was the better reaction?

They had arrived at the resort complex. More pink stucco. Lots of lanais on the sprawling buildings, carefully coiffed tropical plantings to make the multitude of cottages look private and isolated, pristine blue pools landscaped to look like natural features with waterfalls, and basking areas studded with umbrellas, chaise lounges, and bars. He drove her to the lobby entrance and she checked in, noticing that he hovered at her shoulder.

The staff wouldn't let her do a thing, of course. Two very attractive young men with Polynesian faces, wearing colorful island-print wraps around their waists, snatched up all her luggage and led the way to her own cottage with palms to shade it and a glimpse of white sand and blue-sea horizon. Kayla smiled to herself at the location of the cottage as she offered a tip and received twin, polite refusals. Not a front-row seat to the ocean view . . . that went to major family guests. But she could still see the water through the palm trunks and frangipani. A little. And the furnishings were high-end. Lacquered bamboo and glass, with flowered cotton upholstery . . . the real fiber, not a synthetic.

A knock at the door heralded another attendant pushing a cart with champagne, glasses, and a tray of snacks. *Puu-puu.* The word surfaced, unbidden. Snacks. What language? Kayla tried to snag it, but the connection wasn't there. Two glasses. "Will you join me?" she asked Ethan. She smiled at the young man with the cart, who smiled back, his dark eyes on hers, set out plates and food on the low table in front of the silk-upholstered settee, uncorked the champagne with a flourish, and filled two flutes. Handed her one with a bow, and his fingertips brushed hers.

Full service, she thought, met his eyes, smiled, did the tiny head shake he'd recognize, and handed the other glass to Ethan as the attendant left. "I take one sip," she said. "That's all. Blurs perception. Here's to a lovely place and time."

"What a drag. But you're right about place and time." He touched the rim of his glass to hers and they chimed crystal. Of course. "Tell me what my great-great-aunt or whatever wants to see."

You, she thought, lifted the glass to him silently, took her sip. "The family. The ceremony. How everyone takes it."

"You're not telling me."

"Nope." She grinned. "Of course not."

"Sorry." He laughed and sipped his own wine. "I shouldn't have asked." He sat on the settee, his expression contemplative. "It's just that she's such a . . . I don't know . . . renegade. But she got away with it." He grinned. "She just went out and conquered her own planet." He laughed. "She's a successful renegade. Unlike us, who never made it pay. I just can't believe that she really cares about this society wedding, you know?"

She didn't. Not really. Kayla leaned back on the settee next to him, stretching travel-kinks from her muscles, her eyes on Ethan, examining him from head to toe as if he was her new lover. "So have you ever met her?"

"Jeruna?" Ethan shrugged. "Nah. I don't think she ever came back here, after she left for Mars. And that was before I was born."

Interesting. So what did he represent? Kayla took her time, enjoying the view. He was cuter than the vids. And not the spoiled rich kid she'd expected. Too bad. She squelched a brief pang of "what if."

He flinched, fumbled a cell out of his pocket. "Uh-oh. Another arrival to ferry." He stood, set his half-full flute down on the table. "I was going to ask you if you wanted to skip out on the big family dinner tonight. Eat down on the beach." His eyes met hers. "But I bet you can't."

"No, I can't." She made her voice regretful, which really wasn't a stretch. "Want to help me out?" Because his tone suggested he planned to skip it. "Sit by me? Give me a few clues? I'd like to give the old gal her money's worth."

He hesitated, then shrugged. Wrinkled his nose. "For you. I'll suffer." He laughed. "And now you owe me."

"Okay, I do." She laughed with him, caught his lean, athletic profile as he turned to leave, promising to meet her there at the appointed dinner hour. So what does he mean to you? she asked her client silently. Something, that was for sure. Her services were not cheap.

The prenuptial dinner offered excellent food, elegant wine, and the usual boring and self-centered conversations. Obviously the leak had made the rounds. But after the open bar, pre-dinner, and the first round of wine with the appetizers, everyone loosened up and forgot about her. This family ran to whiners. Kayla get tired of high-pitched nasal complaints quickly. The assiduous wine-servers didn't help matters, filling glasses the moment the level fell beneath the rim. She had tipped the maitre d' to fill her glass with a non-alcoholic version of the whites and reds but it seemed that everyone else was happy with the real stuff.

Ethan sipped at his glass but didn't drink much, toying with his food. Leaning close to her, he murmured wry summaries of various family members that required her to invoke all her self-control in order to keep from sputtering laughter into her glass.

"You're going to get me in trouble," she murmured, giving him a sideways glance.

"Not from great-aunt-whatever, I'll wager." He winked at her. "She never thought much of the whole bunch of us." He drank some of the cabernet the server had just poured to accompany the rack of lamb being dramatically carved and served. "I still wonder that she would do this. You . . . chameleons, as you call yourselves . . . are supposed to be highly empathetic to your clients." He arched an eyebrow. "Can't you tell me? Why she wants this?"

"I really don't know." Which was the truth. *That* was what had been bothering her, she realized. "Usually I can figure it out, but not this time." She lifted her glass. Smiled into his eyes, catching a full front view with just the right shadows and highlights. "I suspect your . . . commentary . . . will really delight her."

"I hope so." He touched the rim of his glass to hers, a smile glimmering in his eyes. "I like her style."

The interminable dinner wound to its appointed end. Ethan wanted to make love to her. She could feel it. She wanted him to, she realized with a twinge of regret that centered between her legs.

Jeruna Nesmith looked over their shoulders.

And . . . in a handful of days . . . she would relinquish the nano to An Yi's filters, deliver it to her client and . . . all memory of Ethan would be gone. Oh, maybe a glimpse of hazel eyes on some sultry summer afternoon would touch a chord, and she'd wonder idly where that memory had come from. She'd have his name in her diary—but only as a big question. *Why him?*

She said good night to him at the door of her cottage and they looked into each other's eyes across a gulf as vast as the damn sea. She turned away first, banging the door closed behind her, not caring that Ms. Nesmith would get to remember this, stalked across the expensive, elegant, lovely room to the wet bar, poured herself a double shot of very expensive brandy, downed it, and went to bed.

The wedding was everything it promised to be. Lots of wealthy people, lots of expensive, designer clothing, lots of show, pomp, circumstance, flowers, fine food, expensive booze. . . . She had dressed to blend in, in a long sari-styled dress of silk voile, but felt a moment of panic as she entered the huge chapel with the red velvet carpet down the aisle, the ropes of tropical flowers draping the pews. Ethan wasn't here, and her client might well read between the lines . . . or glimpses . . . and guess that the silent end of last night might have something to do with it.

But then she spotted him way down the aisle on the groom's side. Very formal and erect. Caught a good three-quarter shot of him, oblivious, his expression closed and unreadable. Then, as if he had felt the touch of her eyes, he looked directly at her. He didn't smile, but his eyes caught hers and for a few moments, her client ceased to exist. Kayla shook herself, gave him a small, rueful smile, and seated herself on the bride's side of the aisle, where she'd have a good view of him.

The ceremony was very traditional and she did the high points: the procession, the vows, ring, all that stuff. But she kept cutting back to Ethan's three-quarter profile. He might as well have been carved out of acrylic. But she kept looking over at him, giving the old girl what she'd paid for.

The ceremony ended and everybody milled about, trickling eventually to the reception. She didn't see Ethan, circulated through the crowd, noticing the family details that her client would want to see—the little tiffs, the sniping, the white-knuckled grasp on the martini glass. Oh yes, Kayla thought as she did the glazed-eyes look and really saw. I know what you think of these people and what you would notice if you were really here. Ethan was right. She really didn't think much of any of them. Except him.

Ethan was nowhere to be seen.

She took a table with a good pan-view of the garden where the reception had been laid out. Palms cast thin shade and bowers fragrant with flowering vines offered private nooks. Long buffet tables, decorated with ice sculptures and piles of tropical fruit and flowers, offered fresh seafood, fruit, elegant bites of elegant food, and an open bar. The towering wedding cake occupied its own flower-roped table flanked by champagne buckets and trays of flutes. The sun stung her face and she turned her back to it, and there was Ethan, seating an elderly guest.

So she was looking right at it when the little jump jet roared in low over the grounds just beyond him. It hovered, landed straight down, engines whining. Figures in camo leaped from it, masked and armed with automatic weapons. One fired a short burst into the palms, shredding the leaves. "Down." An amplified voice bellowed. "Everybody down, now!"

Oh, crap. A kidnap raid.

Women shrieked, voices rose, and, for a frozen instant, chaos reigned. One of the camoed figures fired a small handgun and a waiter clapped a hand to his neck as the stun dart hit, and fell. Shredded bits of palm drifted down onto his white-clad sprawl. The first of the guests began to lie down on the grass and it was as if a potent gas had swept the garden as everyone went prone. Kayla had already flattened herself on the grass, her eyes fixed on Ethan, who still stood. Don't be a hero, she thought, willing him to lie down, because they wouldn't want him. What had happened to the security force? One of the raiders shoved a waiter and Ethan stepped forward. No, Kayla shrieked silently as the raider swung his rifle butt and flattened Ethan. Kayla tensed, her eyes on his limp body, straining to see movement.

"Nobody moves, nobody gets hurt," the loudspeaker blared. Australian accent, Kayla noticed. A lot of the professional kidnap-for-hire gangs were Aussie. The top ones. From the corner of her eye she saw the figures striding through the guests, snatching a necklace here or a watch there, but not really looting. They were looking for someone specific. That's where the money lay. They'd take that person and leave.

A hand closed on her arm and yanked her to her feet as if she weighed nothing.

Breathless, her heart pounding, Kayla stared into cold gray eyes behind a green face mask. "Move," the man said.

"You made a mistake. I'm not . . ." Kayla broke off with a gasp as he whipped her arm behind her and pain knifed through her. She stumbled along, losing her balance, as he shoved her forward. "I'm not anyone," she gasped, but he only twisted her arm higher, so that tears gathered in her eyes and the pain choked her. More hands grabbed her, someone slapped a drug patch against her throat and blackness began to seep into her vision. The sky wheeled past and a fading part of her mind whispered that they were loading her onto the jet.

Then . . . nothing.

She woke to a headache and thought for a moment she had just gotten a dose. Then the oppressive humidity and the thick scent of tropics brought her back to the island, the kidnappers' assault. She sat up, eyes wide, straining to see in utter darkness. Blind? Had that drug the kidnappers had given her interacted with the nano? Blinded her?

"It's all right. I'm here."

Familiar voice, familiar arms around her. "Ethan?" Her voice shook and she leaned against him as he pulled her close. She could make him out . . . just barely. She wasn't blind. "Where are we? What happened?"

"A great big mistake happened." Ethan laughed a harsh note. "It was a kidnap by the Yellow Roo clan. I recognized the uniforms. They've hit the family before. Business as usual when you get to the right income bracket."

"I know, but . . . why me?" Kayla swallowed. She felt a mattress beneath her, made out walls, a couple of plastic bins, a porta-potty. "I'm not part of your family."

"And I might as well not be." Ethan let his breath out in a long sigh. "That's the mistake. The fools grabbed maybe the only two individuals in the entire damn reception who can't make a decent ransom. Or can you?"

"Oh, gods, I wouldn't be a chameleon if I had money." Kayla closed her eyes, her head pounding. "They can go look. There's not enough in my account to make it worth their while." She shivered because kidnap was an accepted career choice and the rules were very civilized . . . unless you really couldn't pay. Then they were not civilized at all.

Ethan stroked the hair back from her face. "Maybe Jeruna will pay for you," he said.

She shook her head. No, she was a chameleon because she could read people. Jeruna Nesmith was not going to pay ransom on a paid contractor.

"Well, we'd better start making plans." Ethan did that harsh laugh again. "I've got no better ransom prospects than you do."

"You're family. Inside."

"Yeah, and some kidnap clan grabbed my older brother back when I was a baby. I think he was maybe seven. The family didn't pay up. Their attitude was "you want to walk your own path, do it.""

Kayla didn't ask him what happened to his brother. She heard that answer in the razored edge of his tone. She scanned the walls. They were in some kind of crude hut. Dawn must be close because she could make out slender poles woven into walls. Sheet plastic made up the roof, stiff stuff . . . she tried it. Fastened securely to the top pole of the walls. A door of chain link fit neatly into its metal-rimmed frame and was chained shut. But . . .

"They really don't expect us to try too hard." Kayla murmured the words like a lover's breath into Ethan's ear. Because they were probably listening.

"Of course not. This is just a place to wait out negotiations. You don't try to escape. It's usually safer to stay put. That's how the game works."

"Look there." Kayla pointed. "See how wide?" she whispered. "We could get through there. Maybe. The poles are thin and we could probably pry 'em out. Then the gap between those big ones might be just wide enough."

Ethan was at the wall before she finished speaking. She joined him and grabbed one of the slender poles. In unison, they pulled on it. Felt it give. Not much . . . just a hair. He changed position, his hands next to hers, and they pulled together. Got a centimeter or two of *give* this time. Did it again. And again. By the time they worked the two slender poles free, the pole was slippery with blood from their hands. Kayla helped Ethan lay them on the floor and wiped her hands on her torn dress. The gap was narrow . . . a couple of handwidths. But she was skinny. She pulled the long hem of her skirt up between her legs, tied it to form a crude pair of shorts. Then she turned to Ethan, took his face in her hands, kissed him. Hard. "Wish me luck," she said.

"Honey, we're both in on this." He kissed her back, fiercely.

"No." She pushed him away. "You need to stay here."

"I told you . . ."

"She wanted *you*." Kayla gripped his arms, willing him to understand. "I'm not supposed to tell you this, but there it is. That's why she hired me. To look at you at the wedding."

"Jeruna?" He looked stunned. "Why the hell would she care? She was already on Mars when I was born. I'm barely related to her."

"I have no idea." Kayla turned away. "But she does. She'll pay your ransom. I guarantee it. So you're safe." She let go of him, pushing him away from her, threw one leg over the lower pole. The two thick poles that framed the gap squeezed her, pressing on her spine and breast bone, squeezing her lungs so that she fought suffocation panic as she squirmed her body through the gap, her thin dress shredding, rough bark scraping skin. Fell to the dry ground on the other side, bruising her hip and scraping her knee. Scrambled to her feet.

"Hold it." Ethan leaned through after her. "The bins are full of water and food. I checked while you were out. Wait a minute and I'll hand some stuff through. They don't plant these drop boxes close to anything civilized. Might be a long hike."

He disappeared and a few moments later began to hand bottles of water through the gap. Too many to carry. "That's plenty," Kayla said, and took the bags of something dry and leathery he handed down. As she retied her skirt to hold the food and as much of the water as she could carry, she glanced up to see Ethan squirming through the opening after her. "No," she said, heard him gasp, stuck, and suddenly he popped through, falling hard onto the ground in front of her.

"You idiot," she said, holding out her hand to help him up.

"If you're right about Jeruna, I probably am." He scrambled to his feet and kissed her lightly on the forehead. "I'm not going to sit there and wait to find out if you are or not." He grabbed her hand. "And besides, I'll worry about you out here. Let's go."

The sky had lightened just enough so that she could make out the tall trees and tangle of underbrush. Behind them, their prison seemed to be nothing more than a box built of the woven poles, hidden from the sky by the tall trees. Soaring trunks surrounded them, black against the feeble light. Huge, fern-like leaves brushed her and a million tiny voices creaked, croaked, buzzed, and burbled. Kayla started as something feathery brushed her cheek, her heart sinking. Jungle? The thick air and dense growth woke a slow sense of claustrophobia. "Sweet." She looked up at distant patches of gray sky. "Where are we?" A thunderous howling suddenly split the graying dawn and Kayla whirled, heart pounding, searching the twined branches overhead for something, anything as the sound crescendoed.

"That answers your question. It's okay. Those are howler monkeys." Ethan actually laughed as he wiped hair out of his eyes. "They only live in the Amazon Preserve. I thought that might be where we were. It smelled right."

"How nice. Glad you're enjoying it." Kayla tried to remember details about the preserve. Big. Very big. Something bit her and she flinched, slapped at it. In the trees above them, sinuous black shapes leaped in a torrent from tree to tree. Leaves and twigs showered down in their wake. The howler monkeys? She wanted to cover her ears. "I guess we just walk," she said, "and hope we find a road or something."

"Oh, there are plenty of roads. It's a giant eco-laboratory. It's just not real likely that anyone will be on them. Permits to work here are hard to come by." Ethan took off his shirt, began to tie the sleeves together. "We'd better bring all the water we can."

Something small and brown buzzed down to land on his bare shoulder. He yelped and slapped it, leaving a smear of blood and squashed bug.

"Better wear your shirt." Kayla unknotted her skirt. "I have lots of extra cloth here." It was not easy to tear the fabric without a knife, but they finally managed to fashion a sling for the water and food. By the time Ethan shouldered it, a lot of biting things had dined on them. Jeruna was going to get far more than she paid for, Kayla thought grimly as they started off.

They pushed aside the ferns, clambering over the thick vines and low plants that covered the ground in the dim light. The humid heat wrapped them like a blanket and Kayla struggled with a sense of drowning as she fought her way through the tangle in Ethan's wake. Her dress sandals didn't do much to protect her feet, but they were better than nothing. Before long, however, she was trying not to limp.

It never really got light. In the yellow-green twilight, flying things bit or buzzed. Kayla leaped back as a looped vine turned out to be a brown and copper banded snake.

"Common Lancehead," Ethan said, guiding her warily past it. "Pretty poisonous. We mostly need to watch out for the ground dwellers. They're harder to spot. The South American Coral snake is the worst, but you can see it. Usually. The Bushmaster is hard to spot . . . it blends right in." He gave her a crooked smile. "That's why I've been going first. I'm partially desensitized to both. If they bite me, I probably won't die."

"Gods, what do you *do*?" Kayla eyed the ground warily. "I thought you said you played jazz. What are you? A snake charmer?"

"I do play jazz. And I have a Ph.D. in Tropical Ecology." Ethan shrugged. "Totally useless degree, according to the family, but I spend a lot of time here."

They didn't see any more snakes, although Kayla kept nervous eyes on every shadow. The going got easier when they stumbled onto a game trail, a narrow track that wound between the trunks and beneath the thick vines. The damp heat seemed to suck moisture from Kayla's body, and, in spite of frequent sips of precious water, thirst began to torment her. Now and again they stopped and Kayla strained her ears, heard nothing but the constant hum of insects, the occasional shriek of birds or monkeys, and once a deep cough that made Ethan narrow his eyes. "Jaguar," he said. He gave her a strained smile. "They pick the place for their boxes on purpose. Make it worth your while to stay put."

"You should have." She wiped sweat from her face with her filthy skirt. "She really will pay for you."

"You want to hike through here on your own?" He grinned at her, then his smile faded. "Besides . . . I just wasn't going to sit there. I think that's partly why my father went off to be an artist and be poor. He could have been an artist and stayed rich and inside the family. But he didn't like the rules. And yeah, there are rules." He looked up as the light dimmed suddenly. "I think it's going to rain."

No kidding. Kayla's eyes widened as the patches of sky visible through the canopy went from blue to charcoal gray in minutes. Without warning, the clouds opened and water fell, straight as a shower. Ethan caught her wrist and pulled her into a natural shelter created by a tree that had partly fallen and had been covered in vines. The thick leaves blocked most of the downpour. Kayla licked the sweet drops of water from her lips, laughed, and stepped out into the downpour again, wet almost instantly to the skin. It felt good as the warm rain sluiced away sweat and dirt. She slid the top of her dress down her shoulders, the water cascading between her breasts. Felt damn near *clean*. The rain stopped, just as suddenly as it had begun.

The sun emerged above the canopy and the air turned instantly into a sauna. Water dripped, flashing like jewels in the shafts of yellow light that speared down through the leaves, and a bright bird with crimson and blue feathers fluttered between the trees. Kayla laughed softly, her wet hair plastered to her head, her dress still around her waist. "It's beautiful," she said. "It's a hell of a place to hike, but it's beautiful." She turned to look at him and deliberately stepped out of her dress. Jeruna be damned. She was on another planet. Kayla spread the dress over some branches to dry.

Without a word, Ethan stripped palmlike fronds from a low growing clump, spread them on the sheltered space beneath the mat of lianas. A tiny monkey with a clown-face of perpetual surprise chattered at him from a tree trunk, then dashed upward to vanish in the shadows. He turned to face her, still without speaking, took her hands in his and pulled her to him, his hands light on her shoulders.

All of a sudden the cuts, bruises, the steamy heat . . . none of it mattered. She leaned forward, let her lips brush his, traced their outline with her tongue. Felt him shudder. He pulled her roughly against him, his mouth on hers, hard, fierce, hungry as her own.

They made love, drowsed, and made love again. He told her about the universe of the very wealthy and what it was like to live on the edge, not really inside, but not really allowed to be entirely independent either. Family was family . . . you were a commodity in a way as much as a tribe. But he was still *inside.* She told him about growing up in a crèche. Outside. Finding out that she had a strong empathy rating, that she had the talent to be a chameleon.

"Is that why you do it?" He leaned on his elbow beside her, his fingertips tracing the curve of her cheekbone. "So you can get to live inside?"

"Yes." She gave him truth because she found she didn't want to lie to this man. "I do want it. And it pays well." She yelped as something bit her. "Damn bugs." She sat up, slapped, and glared at the blood on her palm. "Maybe we'd better walk some more? You might be wrong about them coming back." But she winced and nearly fell as she tried to stand.

Ethan sucked in a quick breath as he examined her feet. "Kayla, why didn't you say something? Sit *down* and let me look."

"There wasn't any point in complaining," she said, but she couldn't bite back a cry as he used a torn sleeve from his dress shirt to wipe the mud from her feet. Blood streaked the fabric and the cuts smarted and stung.

"We can tear up my shirt, at least wrap them before we start walking again. I'm sorry. I just didn't think about you wearing sandals." He stroked the tops of her feet gently. "You know, I'm chipped." He laughed, a note of bitterness in his voice. "If they bothered to look."

"Chipped?" She pushed her damp hair back from her face.

"I've got a GPS locater embedded in me. From birth. It's a family rule. If they looked for it, they'd find us."

"Why wouldn't they look?"

"Kidnappers use a masking device. It was probably on top of the box. Everybody plays by the rules, so they'll wait to hear from the kidnappers, give their answer. They won't go *look.*" He frowned, looked back the way they had come. "You know, as efficiently as they did the raid, I can't believe they blew the snatch. Those guys do their homework. They should have been able to pick out their targets in the middle of the night, on the run." He shook his head, sighed. "So you might be right and they don't play by the rules either." He gave her a crooked smile. "We'd better go."

He managed to tear the real-cotton fabric of his shirt into rough strips and bandaged her feet so that she could still wear the flimsy sandals. She still limped, the tiny cuts and tears painful now that her first rush of escape adrenaline had faded. Slowly, laboriously, they made their way along the game trail, following it generally toward the setting sun as it wound through the neverending tangle of leaves, vines, and soaring trunks.

The light faded quickly as the sun sank and they finally stopped for the night, finding another sheltered spot beneath an old, dead tree trunk draped with vines. Sure enough, it rained not long after the last hint of light faded. Shielded from the worst of the brief downpour, they drank some more water and ate what turned out to be dried mango and papaya. And made love again.

Terror stalked the night. It wore no form but made sounds. Grunts, whistles, a coughing roar that had to be a jaguar. Ethan identified each sound, each detail of what was going on in the thick, rot-smelling dark, as if he had a magic flashlight to pierce the night. He banished the terror and Kayla heard the love in his voice as he turned night into day. She almost laughed. Rabbit in a briar patch. It might have been a fun hike, if she'd had a good pair of shoes. At some point she drowsed, woke, felt Ethan's slack, sleeping arms still around her, drowsed again because Ethan knew that nothing would eat them. And that was good enough.

She woke, stiff, her stomach cramping with hunger in spite of last night's dried fruit as the dark tree trunks and fan-shaped leaves of the plants sheltering them took shape from the lightening dark. Ethan slept beside her and she looked down on him, barely visible in the hint of dawn. His face was flushed, and when she touched his skin it was hot. Feverish. I will not remember you, she thought, and a pang of grief pierced her. If a chameleon withheld the nano, that chameleon lost the union seal. You didn't spend a fortune to have your hired pair of eyes and ears walk away with the memory you wanted or hold it for ransom. That union seal that she had paid dearly to obtain meant that she was entirely trustworthy. If she violated that trust only once, she lost it forever.

And it wouldn't help. The nano self-destructed in a measured length of time if not filtered and stabilized. In a handful of days, the memory would evaporate, whether she handed it over to Jeruna or not. Of course, in a handful of days, she might still be here. She smiled mirthlessly into the faint gray of dawn. Maybe she should hope they didn't find their way out of here. At least not soon.

She didn't kid herself about after. The wall between *inside* and *outside* was impenetrable. You could slip through it for awhile. But not for long. Rules. No forever after with Ethan. She let her breath out in a long, slow sigh, wishing she had said no to Jeruna, wishing that her broker had found her another contract. She ran her fingers along the curve of Ethan's cheekbone, watched his eyelids flutter, his golden eyes focus on her, watched his lips curve into a tender smile of recognition.

No, she didn't wish it. She leaned over him, met his lips halfway.

They reached the red-dirt track in the heat of noon, clawing through what seemed to be an impenetrable wall of leaves and vines out into hot sun that made them blink and stumble. For a few moments, they could only stand still, clutching each other, squinting in the sun. Then Ethan whooped, scooped her into his arms and they both tumbled into the dust, weak with hunger and thirst, laughing like idiots.

The little electric jeep came around the curve in the little track a few moments later and the dark-skinned driver in jungle camo hit the brakes. He spoke Central-American Spanish, but so did Ethan and he translated. Their rescuer was a ranger in the Preserve and just happened to be checking this sector this morning. He made it clear that they were lucky, that he only came this way very occasionally, and clucked and shook his head as Ethan explained what had happened. It offended him, he told them, that the kidnap gangs used the rainforest for their boxes. It made it sometimes dangerous for the rangers. He had water with him and a lunch of bean and corn stew that he shared with them, and then he drove them four hours back to his headquarters.

The family machinery had leaped into action by the time they arrived, never mind that Ethan was a marginal member. A jump jet with medics on board met them and they were examined, treated for their minor injuries, dressed, and loaded before Kayla could catch her breath.

"They're taking us to the family hospital for observation and treatment," Ethan said as he settled into the plush seat beside Kayla. "My uncle sent them to get us." He touched her hand, his hazel eyes dark in the cabin's light. "We'll probably be separated for a bit. Kayla . . ." He broke off, drew a breath. "I don't want you to forget . . . this."

"I can't help it." She struggled to keep her voice calm.

"Yes, you can. Keep it. Assimilate it, like your clients do." He gripped her arms, his face pale. "They can't stop you from doing that."

She shook her head. "I'm immunized," she whispered. "The nano won't release to me. I can't assimilate it."

"How can you *do* this?" He was angry suddenly, his eyes blazing. "How can you just . . . walk away from part of your life? How can you just throw away your past?"

The past had teeth. It was something to run away from, not to cherish. Up until now. She turned her head away from the accusation in his eyes.

"If I knock on your door, I'll be a stranger. None of this will have happened. I could be anybody."

"Maybe," she whispered. "I don't know."

"*I want you to remember this.*"

She looked at him, met his eyes, realized that besides the anger she saw . . . fear. "I can't," she said, because she would only give him the truth.

For a few moments he said nothing, then he looked away. "Will you . . . give this to Jeruna?" he asked hoarsely.

She would only give him truth, so she said nothing. If she did not . . . what job was she suited for? And inside was inside.

He wrenched himself to his feet, his face averted. "Whore," he said, and stalked to the rear of the plane.

For a long time she sat still, staring down at her scratched and scabbed hands, her bandaged and sanitized feet throbbing beneath the cotton hospital pants the medics had given her to wear.

In a handful of days, she wouldn't remember that he had said that, either.

She hoped she would see him again. They kept her overnight, did enhanced healing to mend the damage to her feet, returned her luggage from the wedding resort, and offered her a ride home in a family jet. Just before she was due to leave, a knock at the door of her very plush private room made her heart leap, but it was simply a family lawyer, who handed her a very large check and a waiver for her to sign, absolving the family from legal blame.

She signed it. It had not been their fault that the kidnappers were so inexplicably incompetent.

A slow anger had been building in her and she pressed her lips together as the lawyer bowed very slightly to her and retreated. A silent attendant arrived to carry her luggage to the private jet and she followed slowly, her newly healed feet still a bit tender in the flat sandals she wore. She climbed the carpeted stairs to the jet's entry and turned to look back at the private hospital grounds. It had the look of a gated residential community with cottages, walking paths, and gardens. The main building might have been a vacation lodge. The few uniformed staff on the paths ignored her and the old man in a smart-chair out for a breath of air never looked her way.

She boarded and the jet door sealed behind her.

She ignored her broker's insistent emails as long as she could. When she finally lifted the block, Azara's image appeared instantly in the holo-field, her dark eyes snapping with anger, her beaded veil quivering as she faced Kayla. "What in the name of Allah's demons are you doing? The client has threatened me with legal action. As you know, the contract protects me, but *I* am threatening *you*. And not with legal action, you spoiled child. No chameleon of mine has *ever* stolen the product. You had better not be the first, do you hear me?"

A part of Kayla's mind marveled at her rage. She had never seen Azara show even mild annoyance before. "I want to speak with her," she said.

"I will not play games with you. You will go immediately to the clinic," Azara snapped. "I spoke with your technician. She tells me you have only twenty-four hours until the nanos degrade. That is barely enough time to filter them and secure a digital copy for transmission."

Ah, bless you, An Yi, Kayla thought. She had begged, but An Yi had not promised. "It is more than enough time. I will go straight to the clinic." Kayla bowed her head. "As soon as I speak with Jeruna Nesmith."

Azara narrowed her eyes and her image froze. She was multitasking, clearly contacting Jeruna, on Mars. "She is willing to speak to you." She looked slightly puzzled. Apparently Jeruna's response had surprised her. "If you fulfill this contract, I may give you one more chance . . . if I never see such childish behavior from you again. But of course . . . you had a trying time." She regarded Kayla narrowly. "Our client does not blame you. She raised her eyebrows, as if waiting for Kayla to comment. Shrugged. "I will not hold this lapse against you if she is satisfied."

Timing is everything. Kayla stood up. "I'll email An Yi and make sure she can filter me."

"She is expecting you." Azara's red lips curved into a slight smile. "Do not disappoint me, girl."

The threat behind those words went beyond loss of her union seal. Kayla bowed her head once more and blanked the holo-field.

Ethan had not contacted her.

She had not really expected that he would. His final word hung in the air like the bitter taint of something burned. She waited as the holo-field shimmered, making the distant connection to Bradbury.

Jeruna Nesmith's aged face shimmered to life in the field. Her expression gave nothing away, but a hint of triumph glimmered deep in her eyes. "I was sorry to hear that you were traumatized," she said smoothly. "Is that not a boon of the science? Even terror can be eliminated by an hour spent with the filters."

"You sent the kidnappers." Kayla sat calmly in her chair, her eyes on the woman's withered face. "You had them take me. And Ethan." Her voice trembled just a hair as she said his name and she watched Jeruna's eyes narrow. The triumph intensified. "Why?" She tilted her head. "Why spend all that money? Why play that game?"

"You are very intelligent." The old woman's thin lips curved into a satisfied smile. "How did you figure it out?"

"Kidnappers aren't that incompetent. Not if they're snatching insiders." She shrugged. "You forget. I read people. They weren't at all unsure about who they had. They knew they had the right people. And that ranger happened by so conveniently. He was tracking us, wasn't he?"

Jeruna was smiling openly now. "Are you pregnant?"

Kayla swallowed, feeling as if she had been punched in the stomach. "No," she said. Pressed her lips together. "Is that what you were after?"

"No." Jeruna sighed. "But it would have been an . . . added bonus."

"Why did you do this?" She dared not raise her voice beyond a whisper.

"To atone for my sins." Jeruna shook her head. "Hard as it may be for you to imagine, I was young once. And rather attractive. And smart." She smiled. "One of my distant relatives fell in love with me. He loved my mind as well as my body."

"Ethan's father," Kayla said.

"Oh, no, sweetheart, you flatter me." Jeruna cackled. "His grandfather. But I was hot to leave the planet and he was not and I believed that love was something that would wait until *I* had time for it." She eyed Kayla, her smile thin. "Never make that mistake, child. I now believe that the universe gives you one chance only."

No! Kayla swallowed the syllable before it could erupt. Kept her face expressionless. "So you wanted what? A memory to replace what never happened?"

"Something like that." Jeruna's smile widened slowly, her eyes hungry. "And, I suspect, you have brought me the past I was not smart enough to live. I will be forever in your debt for that. Believe me, I will pay you very very well." Her smile broadened, a hint of satisfied dismissal glazing her eyes. "A very generous bonus. To pay for your trauma."

Whore, he had called her.

"Azara was wrong." Kayla waited for Jeruna's gaze to focus.

"Wrong about what?" She was just starting to worry.

"We didn't just make love," Kayla said. "We fell in love. That's what you meant to happen, wasn't it? Throw us together, put us in danger, but do it in Ethan's backyard, so he was comfortable and I was scared." You bitch, she thought. "Well, you didn't need to go to all that trouble." The bitter knot of words nearly choked her. "And that love is not for sale."

"We have a contract." Jeruna's face had gone white. Her image froze. Multitasking.

"Don't bother." Kayla laughed harshly. "My broker was wrong about the degrade deadline. You don't have time to call in the storm troopers."

"You can't keep it. I know how this works." Jeruna clenched her fists. "Don't be stupid. You'll never work as a chameleon again, I'll make damn sure of that."

"Oh, my broker will take care of that. Don't worry." Kayla looked at the numbers flickering at the base of the holo-field. "We both lose. Right . . . *now*."

She had cut it fine but it happened as if she had pushed a button. She had never done this, had wondered how it would differ from the filter, where she slept, woke up fresh and new.

Ethan, she thought, focusing on his remembered face, his touch on her skin, the feel of him inside her, part of her. I can't just *forget*.

It faded . . . faded . . . lost meaning . . . a face . . . name gone . . . like water running out of the bathtub. Cup it in your hands, it's still gone. . . .

A shrieking howl split her skull. Kayla blinked.

In her holo-field, an aged woman clutched her head with both hands, her short-cropped hair sticking up in tufts between her fingers. The client she had just interviewed with. Jeruna something . . .

"No, you bitch, you're scamming me," the woman shrieked. "Ethan, give me Ethan."

She had gone for the dose, she remembered that. Nano failure? The woman was still screaming. "You'll have to talk to my broker," she said and blanked the field. The familiar headache clamped steel fingers into her skull and she sucked in a quick breath, groaned. This should be happening at An Yi's clinic, not here. Kayla touched her aching head gingerly and shuffled to her kitchen wall for tea. It had to be a failure. How long ago had she taken the dose? "Date check?" she said and the numbers leaped to life in the now empty field.

She stared at them numbly, cold fear filling her.

Not possible.

She dropped her tea, barely felt the scalding splash as the cup bounced, raced to the futon sofa, pulled her private journal from its place beneath the frame. The book fell open, a dry and wrinkled fern leaf marking the place. A page had been torn out . . . the notes about the last dose? The one for the woman who had screamed at her?

I'm through. The looping letters leaped off the page at her. *I know you're going to freak, but this has to stop. I lost something in the past few days. You don't know about it because you never experienced it, but it mattered. Every time I do this, I create a "we" . . . the me who lived this, and the you on the other side of the filter. I . . . we . . . we're a hundred women, and what have we all lost? I don't know, You don't know. I'm not going to tell you any more, because it really is gone forever, and it didn't happen to you. But it's not going to happen again. I kept the dose until it expired. Start looking for a job, honey. We . . . all of us . . . are done being a whore and we're out of a job.*

Kayla dropped the book, numb. I didn't write this, she thought, but she had. The thoughts weren't all that unfamiliar. They mostly bothered her in the middle of the night, right after she'd shed the dose.

What had happened?

She groped, strained, trying to remember, saw An Yi's office, recalled their casual conversation, the feel of the recliner as An Yi prepared the dose. . . .

. . . saw the woman's screaming face in her holo-field.

Azara's icon shimmered to life in the holo-field, seeming to pulse with anger. Kayla didn't bother to access it. You only stole one dose. After that, you were blacklisted. "I hope it was good," she said, and for all the bitterness in the words she felt . . . a tiny flicker of relief. Which was crazy. She looked around the apartment. "Nice while we had it."

Azara sent her a termination notice and an official citation that her union seal had been rescinded permanently. And a quiet promise of vengeance couched in polite langauge. Kayla left the city, went east, covering her tracks and hoping Azara wasn't willing to spend too much money to find her. She found a studio in a sprawling suburban slum, part of an ancient single-family home, maybe the living room, she thought. Communal bath and kitchen, but her room had a tiny sink with cold but drinkable water and she had cooked with a microwave and electric grill for years before she became a chameleon, so it wasn't too bad. She found a job, too, working as a waitress in one of the city hotspots. Good tips because she was pretty and the empathy that had made her a good chameleon made customers like her.

Some mornings she remembered her dreams. And then she sifted through them, wondering if they were part of those final, lost, few days.

Fall came with rain, and mud, and long, wet waits for the light rail into the city. And then, one morning, as she watered the little pots of blooming plants she had bought in the night market to brighten the room, someone knocked on her door. "Who's there?" she asked, peering through the tiny peephole in the door that constituted "security" in this place. Her neighbor, Suhara, asking to "borrow" a bit of rice, she thought. Again.

But the man on the far side of the door was a stranger.

"Kayla, you don't remember me. But we were . . . friends."

The catch in his voice . . . or maybe it was his voice alone . . . made her start, like an electric shock. The key, she thought, and thought about ignoring him, calling Dario, the big wrestler in the back unit, to come run this guy off.

I don't want to know, she thought, but she opened the door after all and stepped back to let him in. Cute guy. Her heart began to beat faster. He looked around, his expression . . . agonized.

"I'm sorry to bother you," he said. "You don't . . . remember me."

It was a statement, but his eyes begged.

She took her time, examining his hair, his slightly haggard face, the casual clothes made of expensive natural fiber, whose labels made him an insider, one of the elite. Well, those had been her clients. As she shook her head, his shoulders drooped.

"I know something happened," she said. "Maybe between us. The memory is simply gone. I'm sorry."

"You didn't find . . . any notes to yourself? Letters about . . . about what happened?"

About me, he had started to say. She shook her head.

"That was my fault. I was angry. And then . . ." He closed his eyes. "I got sick, really sick, had picked up some kind of drug-resistant tropical epizootic. By the time I was well enough to look . . . it was too late. The nano had expired, you had moved, and . . . I couldn't find you. And I was angry when you last saw me. I knew you'd think that I . . ." He balled his fist suddenly, slammed it into his thigh. "You really don't remember, it's all gone, all of it."

His anguish was so strong that it filled the room. Without thought she took a step forward, put her hand on his shoulder. "I'm sorry," she said. "I don't know that I want you to . . . tell me." She met his eyes, hazel, but with gold flecks in their depths. "It really is gone." And you're an insider, she thought. And I am not.

He looked past her, his eyes fixed on a middle distance. "Will you come have dinner with me?"

"I told you . . ."

"I know. I heard you." He looked at her finally and the ghost of a crooked smile quirked the corner of his mouth. "I won't talk about . . . that time. I just want to have dinner with you."

She was good at reading people and he didn't feel like a threat. "Sure," she said. Because he *was* cute, whatever had happened in the past. And she liked him. "I'm off tonight."

"Great." His eyes gleamed gold when he smiled. "I play music . . . when I'm not rooting around in the jungle for no very lucrative reason." He waited for a heartbeat and sighed. "I have a gig tonight on the other side of the city. After dinner . . . would you like to come listen? I play classical jazz. Really old stuff. And . . ." His gold eyes glinted. "I come from a family branch that breaks rules. Sometimes really big ones."

Whatever that meant. He was actually nervous, as if she might refuse. "Sure." She smiled, took his hand. For an instant, as their hands touched, she saw green leaves, golden light, smelled humidity, flowers, rot, and soil. Funny how smell was the strongest link to the fragments of past jobs that had seeped past the nano. All of a sudden, his hand felt . . . familiar. "I'd love to come hear you play."

Damascus

DARYL GREGORY

New writer Daryl Gregory has made sales to *The Magazine of Fantasy & Science Fiction*, *Amazing*, and *Asimov's*. His story "Second Person, Present Tense" was in several Best of the Year anthologies last year, including this Twenty-third Annual Collection. He lives in State College, Pennsylvania.

In the harrowing story that follows, he takes us behind the scenes of a strange cult to reveal the conspiracy at its heart—a far-reaching one that turns out to be very sinister indeed.

I

When Paula became conscious of her surroundings again, the first thing she sensed was his fingers entwined in hers.

She was strapped to the ambulance backboard—each wrist cuffed in nylon, her chest held down by a wide band—to stop her from flailing and yanking out the IV. Only his presence kept her from screaming. He gazed down at her, dirty-blond hair hanging over blue eyes, pale cheeks shadowed by a few days' stubble. His love for her radiated like cool air from a block of ice.

When they reached the hospital, he walked beside the gurney, his hand on her shoulder, as the paramedics wheeled her into the ER. Paula had never worked in the ER, but she recognized a few of the faces as she passed. She took several deep breaths, her chest tight against the nylon strap, and calmly told the paramedics that she was fine, they could let her go now. They made reassuring noises and left the restraints in place. Untying her was the doctor's call now.

Eventually an RN came to ask her questions. A deeply tanned, heavyset woman with frosted hair. Paula couldn't remember her name, though they'd worked together for several years, back before the hospital had fired Paula. Now she was back as a patient.

"And what happened tonight, Paula?" the nurse said, her tone cold. They hadn't gotten along when they worked together; Paula had a temper in those days.

"I guess I got a bit dizzy," she said.

"Seizure," said one of the paramedics. "Red Cross guy said she started shaking on the table, they had to get her onto the floor before she fell off. She'd been seizing for five or six minutes before we got there so we brought her in. We gave her point-one of Lorazepam and she came out of it during the ride."

"She's the second epileptic this shift," the nurse said to them.

Paula blinked in surprise. Had one of the yellow house women been brought in? Or one of the converts? She looked to her side, and her companion gazed back at her, amused, but not giving anything away. Everything was part of the plan, but he wouldn't tell her what the plan was. Not yet.

The nurse saw Paula's shift in attention and her expression hardened. "Let's have you talk to a doctor, Paula."

"I'm feeling a lot better," Paula said. Didn't even grit her teeth.

They released the straps and transferred her to a bed in an exam room. One of the paramedics set her handbag on the bedside table. "Good luck now," he said.

She glanced at the bag and quickly looked away. Best not to draw attention to it. "I'm sorry if I was any trouble," she said.

The nurse handed her a clipboard of forms. "I don't suppose I have to explain these to you," she said. Then: "Is there something wrong with your hand?"

Paula looked down at her balled fist. She concentrated on loosening her fingers, but they refused to unclench. That had been happening more often lately. Always the left hand. "I guess I'm nervous."

The nurse slowly nodded, not buying it. She made sure Paula could hold the clipboard and write, then left her.

But not alone. He slouched in a bedside chair, legs stretched in front of him, the soles of his bare feet almost black. His shy smile was like a promise. I'm here, Paula. I'll always be here for you.

II

Richard's favorite album was Nirvana's *In Utero*. She destroyed that CD first.

He'd moved out on a Friday, filed for divorce on the following Monday. He wanted custody of their daughter. Claire was ten then, a sullen and secretive child, but Paula would sooner burn the house down around them than let him have her. Instead she torched what he loved most. On the day Paula got the letter about the custody hearing, she pulled his CDs and LPs and DATs from the shelves— hundreds of them, an entire wall of the living room, and more in the basement. She carried them to the backyard by the box. Claire wailed in protest, tried to hide some of the cases, and eventually Paula had to lock the girl in her room.

In the yard Paula emptied a can of lighter fluid over the pile, went into the garage for the gas can, splashed that on as well. She tossed the Nirvana CD on top.

The pile of plastic went up in a satisfying *whoosh*. After a few minutes the fire started to die down—the CDs wouldn't stay lit—so she went back into the house and brought out his books and music magazines.

The pillar of smoke guided the police to her house. They told her it was illegal to burn garbage in the city. Paula laughed. "Damn right it's garbage," She wasn't going to be pushed around by a couple of cops. Neighbors came out to watch. Fuck them, she thought.

She lived in a neighborhood of Philadelphia that outsiders called "mixed." Blacks and Latinos and whites, a handful of Asians and Arabs. Newly renovated homes with Mexican tile patios side by side with crack houses and empty lots. Paula moved there from the suburbs to be with Richard and never forgave him. Before Claire was born she made him install an alarm system and set bars across the windows. She felt like they were barely holding on against a tide of criminals and crazies.

The yellow house women may have been both. They lived across the street and one lot down, in a cottage that was a near-twin of Paula's. Same fieldstone porch and peaked roofs, same narrow windows. But while Paula's house was painted a tasteful slate blue, theirs blazed lemon yellow, the doors and window frames and gutters turned out in garish oranges and brilliant whites. Five or six women, a mix of races and skin tones, wandered in and out of the house at all hours. Did they have jobs? They weren't old, but half of them had trouble walking, and one of them used a cane. Paula was an RN, twelve years working all kinds of units in two different hospitals, and it looked to her like they shared some kind of neuromuscular problem, maybe early MS. Their yellow house was probably some charity shelter.

On the street the women seemed distracted, sometimes talking to themselves, until they noticed someone and smiled a bit too widely. They always greeted Paula and Richard, but they paid special attention to Claire, speaking to her in the focused way of old people and kindergarten teachers. One of them, a gaunt white woman named Steph who wore the prematurely weathered face of a long-time meth user, started stopping by more often in the months after Richard moved out. She brought homemade food: Tupperware bowls of bean soup, foil-wrapped tamales, rounds of bread. "I've been a single mom," she said. "I know how tough things can be on your own." She started babysitting Claire a couple nights a week, staying in Paula's house so Claire could fall asleep in her own bed. Some afternoons she took Claire with her on trips to the grocery or the park. Paula kept waiting for the catch. It finally came in the form of a sermon.

"My life was screwed *up*," Steph said to Paula one afternoon. Claire had vanished to her bedroom to curl up with her headphones. The two women sat in the kitchen eating cheese bread someone in the yellow house had made. Steph drank wine while Paula worked her way through her afternoon Scotch. Steph talked frankly about her drug use, the shitty boyfriends, the money problems. "I was this close to cutting my wrists. If Jesus hadn't come into my life, I wouldn't be here right now."

Here we go, Paula thought. She drank silently while Steph droned on about how much easier it was to have somebody walk beside her, someone who cared. "Your own personal Jesus," Steph said. "Just like the song."

Paula knew the song—Richard loved that '80s crap. He even had the Johnny Cash remake, until she'd turned his collection to slag. "No thanks," Paula said, "I don't need any more men in my life."

Steph didn't take offense. She kept coming back, kept talking. Paula put up with the woman because with Richard out of the house she needed help with Claire— and because she needed her alone time more than ever. The yellow house women may have been Jesus freaks, but they were harmless. That's what she told herself, anyway, until the night she came home to find Claire gone.

III

Paula knew how to play the hospital game. Say as little as possible, act normal, don't look at things no one else could see. She knew her blood tests would come out normal. They'd shrug and check her out by noon.

Her doctor surprised her, though. They'd assigned her to Louden, a short, trim man with a head shaved down to gray stubble who had a reputation among the nurses for adequacy: not brilliant, but not arrogant either, a competent guy who pushed the patients through on schedule. But something had gotten into him—he was way too interested in her case. He filled her afternoon with expensive MRIs, fM-RIs, and PET scans. He brought in specialists.

Four of them, two neurologists and a psychiatrist she recognized, and one woman she didn't know who said she was an epidemiologist. They came in one at a time over the afternoon, asking the same questions. How long had she experienced the seizures? What did they feel like when they struck? Did she know others with these symptoms? They poked her skin to test nerve response, pulled and flexed the fingers of her clenched hand. Several times they asked her, "Do you see people who aren't there?"

She almost laughed. He sat beside her the entire time, his arm cool against her own. Could anyone be more present?

The only questions that unsettled her came from the epidemiologist, the doctor she didn't recognize. "Do you eat meat?" the doctor asked. Paula said sure. And the doctor, a square-faced woman with short brown hair, asked a dozen follow-up questions, writing down exactly what kinds of meat she ate, how often, whether she cooked it herself or ate out.

At the end of the day they moved Paula into a room with a middle-aged white woman named Esther Wynne, a true southern lady who'd put on makeup and sprayed her hair as though at any moment she'd pop those IV tubes from her arms and head out to a nice restaurant.

Doctor Louden stopped by once more before going home that night. He sat heavily beside Paula's bed, ran a hand over his gray scalp. "You haven't been completely open with us," he said. He seemed as tired as she was.

"No, probably not," she said. Behind him, her companion shook his head, laughing silently.

Louden smiled as well, but fleetingly. "You have to realize how serious this is. You're the tenth person we've seen with symptoms like yours, and there are more showing up in hospitals around the city. Some of my colleagues think we may be seeing the start of an epidemic. We need your help to find out if that's the case."

"Am I contagious?"

He scratched his chin, looked down. "We don't think so. You don't have a temperature, any signs of inflammation—no signs that this is a virus or a bacterial infection."

"Then what is it you think I have?"

"We don't have a firm idea yet," he said. He was holding back, treating her like a dumb patient. "We *can* treat your symptoms though. We'll try to find out more tomorrow, but we think you have a form of temporal lobe epilepsy. There are parts of your brain that—"

"I know what epilepsy is."

"Yes, but TLE is a bit . . ." He gestured vaguely, then took several stapled pages from his clipboard and handed them to her. "I've brought some literature. The more you understand what's happening, the better we'll work together." He didn't sound like he believed that.

Paula glanced at the pages. Printouts from a web site.

"Read it over and tomorrow you and I can—oh, good." A nurse had entered the room with a plastic cup in her hand, the meds had arrived. Louden seemed relieved to have something else to talk about. "This is Topamax, an epilepsy drug."

"I don't want it," she said. She was done with drugs and alcohol.

"I wouldn't prescribe this if it wasn't necessary," Louden said. His doctor voice. "We want to avoid the spikes in activity that cause seizures like today's. You don't want to fall over and crack your skull open, do you?" This clumsy attempt at manipulation would have made the old Paula furious.

Her companion shrugged. It didn't matter. All part of the plan.

Paula accepted the cup from the nurse, downed the two pills with a sip of water. "When can I go home?" she said.

Louden stood up. "I'll talk to you again in the morning. I hate to tell you this, but there are a few more tests we have to run."

Or maybe they were keeping her here because they did think she was contagious. The start of an epidemic, he'd said.

Paula nodded understandingly and Louden seemed relieved. As he reached the door Paula said, "Why did that one doctor—Gerrhardt?—ask me if I ate meat?"

He turned. "Dr. Gerrholtz. She's not with the hospital."

"Who's she with then?"

"Oh, the CDC," he said casually. As if the Centers for Disease Control dropped by all the time. "Don't worry, it's their job to ask strange questions. We'll have you out of here as soon as we can."

IV

Paula came home from work to find the door unchained and the lights on. It was only 7:15, but in early November that meant it had been dark for more than hour. Paula stormed through the house looking for Claire. The girl knew the rules: come home from school, lock the door, and don't pick up the phone unless caller-ID showed Paula's cell or work number. Richard took her, she thought. Even though he won partial custody, he wanted to take everything from her.

Finally she noticed the note, in a cleared space on the counter between a stack of dishes and an open cereal box. The handwriting was Steph's.

Paula marched to the yellow house and knocked hard. Steph opened the door. "It's all right," Steph said, trying to calm her down. "She's done her homework and now she's watching TV."

Paula pushed past her into a living room full of second-hand furniture and faded rugs. Every light in the house seemed to be on, making every flat surface glow: the oak floors scrubbed to a buttery sheen, the freshly painted daffodil walls, the windows reflecting bright lozenges of white. Something spiced and delicious fried in the kitchen, and Paula was suddenly famished. She hadn't eaten anything solid since breakfast.

Claire sat on a braided oval rug, her purple backpack beside her. A nature show played on the small boxy TV but the girl wasn't really watching. She had her earphones in, listening to the CD player in her lap. Lying on the couch behind her was a thin black woman in her fifties or sixties.

"Claire," Paula said. The girl pretended to not hear. "Claire, take off your headphones when I'm talking to you." Her voice firm but reasonable. The Good Mother. "You know you're not supposed to leave the house."

Claire didn't move.

"The police were at the green house," Steph said. A rundown place two doors down from Paula with motorcycles always in the front yard. Drug dealers, Paula thought. "I went over to check on Claire, and she seemed nervous, so I invited her over. I told her it would be all right."

"You wouldn't answer your phone," Claire said without looking away from the TV. She still hadn't taken off the headphones. Acting up in front of the women, thinking Paula wouldn't discipline her in public.

"Then you keep calling," Paula said. She'd forgotten to turn on her phone when she left the hospital. She'd stopped off for a drink, not more than thirty, forty-five minutes, then came home, no later than she'd come home dozens of times in the past. "You don't leave the house."

Steph touched Paula's elbow, interrupting again. She nodded at the woman on the couch. "This is Merilee."

The couch looked like the woman's permanent home. On the short table next to her head was a half-empty water glass, a Kleenex box, a mound of damp tissue. A plastic bucket sat on the floor. Merilee lay propped up on pillows, her body half covered by a white sheet. Her legs were bent under her in what looked like a painful position, and her left arm curled up almost to her chin, where her hand trembled like a nervous animal. She watched the TV screen with a blissed-out smile, as if this was the best show in the world.

Steph touched the woman's shoulder, and she looked up. "Merilee, this is Paula."

Merilee reached up with her good right arm. Her aim was off; first she held it out to a point too far right, then swung it slowly around. Paula lightly took her hand. Her skin was dry and cool.

The woman smiled and said something in another language. Paula looked to Steph, and then Merilee said, "I eat you."

"I'm sorry?" She couldn't have heard that right.

"It's a Fore greeting," Steph said, pronouncing the word *For-ay*. "Merilee's people come from the highlands of Papua New Guinea. Merilee, Paula is Claire's mother."

"Yes, yes, you're right," Merilee said. Her mouth moved more than the words required, lips constantly twisting toward a smile, distorting her speech. "What a lovely girl." It wasn't clear if she meant Claire or Paula. Then her hand slipped away like a scarf and floated to her chest. She lay back and returned her gaze to the TV, still smiling.

Paula thought, what the hell's the matter with her?

"We're about to eat," Steph said. "Sit down and join us."

"No, we'd better get going," Paula said. But there was nothing back at her house. And whatever they were cooking smelled wonderful.

"Come on," Steph said. "You always love our food." That was true. She'd eaten their meals for a month.

"I just have a few minutes," Paula said. She followed Steph into the dining room. The long, cloth-covered table almost filled the room. Ten places set, and room for a couple more. "How many of you are there?" she said.

"Seven of us live in the house," Steph said as she went into the adjoining kitchen.

"Looks like you've got room for renters."

Paula picked a chair and sat down, eyeing the tall green bottle in the middle of the table. "Is that wine?" Paula asked. She could use a drink.

"You're way ahead of me," Steph said. She came back into the room with the stems of wineglasses between her fingers, followed by an eighteen- or nineteen-year-old black girl—Tanya? Tonya?—carrying a large blue plate of rolled tortillas. Paula had met her before, pushing her toddler down the sidewalk. Outside she walked with a dragging limp, but inside it was barely discernible.

Steph poured them all wine but then remained standing. She took a breath and held it. Still no one moved. "All right then," Steph finally said, loud enough for Merilee to hear.

Tonya—pretty sure it was Tonya—took a roll and passed the plate. Paula carefully bit into the tortilla. She tasted sour cream, a spicy salsa, chunks of tomato. The small cubes of meat were so heavily marinated that they could have been anything: pork, chicken, tofu.

Tonya and Steph looked at Paula, their expressions neutral, but she sensed they were expecting something. Paula dabbed a bit of sour cream from her lip. "It's very good," she said.

Steph smiled and raised her glass. "Welcome," she said, and Tonya echoed her. Paula returned the salute and drank. The wine tasted more like brandy, thick and too sweet. Tonya nodded at her, said something under her breath. Steph said something to Merilee in that other language. Steph's eyes, Paula noted with alarm, were wet with tears.

"What is it?" Paula said. She put down the cup. Something had happened that she didn't understand. She stared at the pure white tortillas, the glasses of dark wine. This wasn't a *snack*, it was fucking communion.

"Tell me what's going on," she said coldly.

Steph sighed, her smile bittersweet. "We've been worried about you. Both of you. Claire's been spending so much time alone, and you're obviously still grieving."

Paula stared at her. These sanctimonious bitches. What was this, some kind of religious intervention? "My life is none of your business."

"Claire told me that you've been talking about killing yourself."

Paula scraped her chair back from the table and stood up, her heart racing. Tonya looked at her with concern. So smug. "*Claire* told you that?" Paula said. "And you believed her?"

"Paula . . ."

She wheeled away from the table, heading for the living room, Steph close behind. "Claire," Paula said. Not yelling. Not yet. "We're going."

Claire didn't get up. She looked at Steph, as if for permission. This infuriated Paula more than anything that had happened so far.

She grabbed Claire by her arm, yanked her to her feet. The headphones popped from her ears, spilling tinny music. Claire didn't even squeak.

Steph said, "We care about you two, Paula. We had to take steps. You won't understand that right now, but soon. . . ."

Paula spun and slapped the woman hard across the mouth, turning her chin with the blow. Steph's eyes squeezed shut in pain, but she didn't raise her arms, didn't step back.

"Don't you ever come near my daughter again," Paula said. She strode toward the front door, Claire scrambling to stay on her feet next to her. Paula yanked open the door and pushed the girl out first. Her daughter still hadn't made a sound.

Behind her, Steph said, "Wait." She came to the door, holding out Claire's backpack and CD player. "Some day you'll understand," Steph said. "Jesus is coming soon."

V

"You're a Christian, aren't you?" Esther Wynne said. "I knew from your face. You've got the love of Jesus in you."

As the two women picked at their breakfast trays, Esther told Paula about her life. "A lot of people with my cancer die quick as a wink," she said. "I've had time to say good-bye to everyone." Her cancer was in remission but now she was here fighting a severe bladder infection. They'd hooked her to an IV full of antibiotics the day before. "How about you?" Esther said. "What's a young thing like you doing here?"

Paula laughed. She was thirty-six. "They think I have a TLA." Esther frowned. "Three-letter acronym."

"Oh, I've got a couple of those myself!"

One of the web pages Dr. Louden gave her last night included a cartoon cross-section of a brain. Arrows pointed out interesting bits of the temporal lobe with tour guide comments like "the amygdala tags events with emotion and significance" and "the hippocampus labels inputs as internal or external." A colored text box listed a wide range of possible TLE symptoms: euphoria, a sense of personal destiny, religiosity . . .

And a sense of presence.

Asymmetrical temporal lobe hyperactivity separates the sense of self into two—one twin in each hemisphere. The dominant (usually left) hemisphere interprets the other part of the self as an "other" lurking outside. The otherness is then colored by which hemisphere is most active.

Paula looked up then, her chest tight. Her companion had been leaning against the wall, watching her read. At her frightened expression he dropped his head and laughed silently, his hair swinging in front of his face.

Of course. There was nothing she could learn that could hurt her, or him.

She tossed aside the pages. If her companion hadn't been with her she might have worried all night about the information, but he helped her think it through. The article had it backward, confusing an *effect* for the *cause*. Of course the brain reacted when you sensed the presence of God. Neurons fired like pupils contracting against a bright light.

"Paula?" someone said. "Paula."

She blinked. An LPN stood by the bed with a plastic med cup. Her breakfast tray was gone. How long had she been ruminating? "Sorry, I was lost in thought there."

The nurse handed Paula the Topamax and watched as she took them. After the required ritual—pulse, blood pressure, temperature—she finally left.

Esther said, "So what were you thinking about?"

Paula lay back on the pillows and let her eyes close. Her companion sat beside her on the bed, massaging the muscles of her left arm, loosening her cramped fingers. "I was thinking that when God calls you don't worry about how he got your number," she said. "You just pick up the receiver."

"A-*men*," Esther said.

Dr. Louden stopped by later that morning accompanied only by Dr. Gerrholtz, the epidemiologist from the CDC. Maybe the other specialists had already grown bored with her case. "We have you scheduled for another PET scan this morning," Louden said. He looked like he hadn't slept at all last night, poor guy. "Is there anyone you'd like to call to be with you? A family member?"

"No thank you," Paula said. "I don't want to bother them."

"I really think you should consider it."

"Don't worry, Dr. Louden." She wanted to pat his arm, but that would probably embarrass him in front of Dr. Gerrholtz. "I'm perfectly fine."

Louden rubbed a hand across his skull. After a long moment he said, "Aren't you curious about why we ordered a PET scan?" Dr. Gerrholtz gave him a hard look.

Paula shrugged. "Okay, why did you?"

Louden shook his head, disappointed again that she wasn't more concerned. Dr. Gerrholtz said, "You're a professional, Paula, so we're going to be straight with you."

"I appreciate that."

"We're looking for amyloid plaques. Do you know what those are?" Paula shook her head and Gerrholtz said, "Some types of proteins weave into amyloid fibers, forming a plaque that kills cells. Alzheimer patients get them, but they're also caused by another family of diseases. We think those plaques are causing your seizures, and other symptoms."

Other symptoms. Her companion leaned against her shoulder, his hand entwined in hers. "Okay," Paula said.

Louden stood up, obviously upset. "We'll talk to you after the test. Dr. Gerrholtz?"

The CDC doctor ignored him. "We've been going through the records, Paula, looking for people who've reported symptoms like yours." She said it like a warning. "In the past three months we've found almost a dozen—and that's just at this hospital. We don't know yet how many we'll find across the city, or the country. If you have any information that will help us track down what's happening, you need to offer it."

"Of course," Paula said.

Gerrholtz's eyes narrowed. She seemed ready to say something else—accuse her, perhaps—but then shook her head and stalked from the room.

Esther watched her go. After a minute of silence, the woman said, "Don't you worry, honey. It's not the doctors who are in charge here."

"Oh I'm not worried," Paula said. And she wasn't. Gerrholtz obviously distrusted her—maybe even suspected the nature of Paula's mission—but what could that matter? Everything was part of the plan, even Dr. Gerrholtz.

By noon they still hadn't come to get her for the scan. Paula drifted in and out of sleep. Twice she awoke with a start, sure that her companion had left the room. But each time he appeared after a few seconds, stepping out from a corner of her vision.

The orderly came by just as the lunch trays arrived, but that was okay, Paula wasn't hungry. She got into the wheelchair and the orderly rolled her down the hall to the elevators. Her companion walked just behind them, his dusty feet scuffing along.

The orderly parked her in the hall outside radiology, next to three other abandoned patients: a gray-faced old man asleep in his chair; a Hispanic teenager with a cast on her leg playing some electronic game; and a round-faced white boy who was maybe twenty or twenty-one.

The boy gazed up at the ceiling tiles, a soft smile on his face. After a few minutes, Paula saw his lips moving.

"Excuse me," Paula said to him. It took several tries to get his attention. "Have you ever visited a yellow house?" The young man looked at her quizzically. "A house that was all yellow, inside and out."

He shook his head. "Sorry."

None of the women still at the yellow house would have tried to save a man, but she had to ask. The boy had to be one of the converts, someone Paula's mission had saved.

"Can I ask you one more question?" Paula said, dropping her voice slightly. The old man slept on, and the girl still seemed engrossed in her game. "Who is it that you're talking to?"

The boy glanced up, laughed quietly. "Oh, nobody," he said.

"You can tell me," Paula said. She leaned closer. "I have a companion of my own."

His eyes widened. "You have a ghost following you too?"

"Ghost? No, it's not a—"

"My mother died giving birth to me," he said. "But now she's *here*."

Paula touched the boy's arm. "You don't understand what's happened to you, do you?" He hadn't come by way of the yellow house, hadn't met any of the sisters, hadn't received any instruction. Of course he'd tried to make sense of his companion any way he could. "You're not seeing a ghost. You're seeing Jesus himself."

The boy laughed loudly, and the teenage girl looked up from her game. "I think I'd know the difference between Jesus and my own mother," the young man said.

"Maybe that's why he took this form for you," Paula said. "He appears differently for each person. For you, your mother is a figure of unconditional love. A person who sacrificed for you."

"Okay," the young man said. He tilted his head, indicating an empty space to Paula's right. "So what does yours look like?"

VI

God came through the windshield on a shotgun blast of light. Blinded, Paula cried out and jammed on the brakes. The little Nissan SUV bucked and fishtailed, sending the CDs piled on the seat next to her clattering onto the floorboards.

White. She could see nothing but white.

She'd stopped in heavy traffic on a four-lane road, the shopping center just ahead on her right: She'd been heading for the dumpsters behind the Wal-Mart to dispose of those CDs once and for all.

Brakes shrieked behind her. Paula ducked automatically, clenched against the pending impact, eyes screwed shut. (Still: Light. Light.) A thunderclap of metal on metal and the SUV rocked forward. She jerked in her seatbelt.

Paula opened her eyes and light scraped her retinas. Hot tears coursed down her cheeks.

She clawed blindly at her seatbelt buckle, hands shaking, and finally found the button and yanked the straps away. She scrambled over the shifter to the passenger seat, the plastic CD cases snapping and sliding under her knees and palms.

She'd found them deep in Claire's closet. The girl was away at her father's for the mandated 50 percent of the month, and Paula had found the stacked CDs hidden under a pile of blankets and stuffed animals. Many of the cases were cracked and warped by heat and most CDs had no cases at all. The day after the bonfire, Paula had caught the girl poking through the mound of plastic and damp ashes and told her not to touch them. Claire had deliberately disobeyed, sneaking out to rescue them sometime before the garbage men took the pile away. The deception had gone on for months. All the time Paula thought Claire was listening to her own music—crap by bubble-gum pop stars and American Idols—her headphones were full of her father's music: Talking Heads, Depeche Mode, Pearl Jam, Nirvana.

Paula pushed open the passenger door and half fell out the door, into the icy March wind. She got her feet under her, stumbled away from the light, into the light. Her shins struck something—the guard rail?—and she put out a hand to stop from pitching over. Cold metal bit her palms. Far to her right, someone shouted angrily. The blare and roar of traffic surrounded her.

Paula dropped to her knees and slush instantly soaked her jeans. She covered her head with both arms. The light struck her neck and back like a rain of sharpened stones.

The light would destroy her. Exactly as she deserved.

Something touched the top of her head, and she shuddered in fear and shame and a rising ecstasy that had nothing to do with sex. She began to shake, to weep.

I'm sorry, she said, perhaps out loud. *I'm sorry.*

Someone stood beside her. She turned her head, and he appeared out of the light. No—*in* the light, *of* the light. A fire in the shape of a man.

She didn't know him, but she recognized him.

He looked down at her, electric blue eyes through white bangs, his shy smile for her only. He looked like Kurt Cobain.

VII

"I'm not taking the meds anymore," Paula said. She tried to keep her voice steady. Louden stood beside the bed, Gerrholtz behind him holding a portfolio in her hands as big as the Ten Commandments. They'd walked past Esther without saying a word.

Her companion lay on the floor beside her bed, curled into a ball. He seemed to be dissolving at the edges, dissipating into fog. He'd lain there all morning, barely moving, not even looking at her.

"That's not a good idea," Dr. Louden said. He pulled a chair next to the bed, scraping through her companion as if he wasn't there. Paula grimaced, the old rage flaring up. She closed her eyes and concentrated.

"I'm *telling* you to stop the drugs," she said. "Unless I'm a prisoner here you can't give me medicine that I refuse."

Louden exhaled tiredly. "This isn't like you, Paula," he said.

"Then you don't know me very well."

He leaned forward, resting elbows on knees, and pressed the fingers of one hand into his forehead. More TLE patients were rolling in every day. The nurses murmured about epidemics. Poor Dr. Adequate had been drafted into a war he didn't understand and wasn't prepared for.

"Help me then," he said without looking up. "Tell me what you're experiencing."

Paula stared at the TV hanging from the ceiling. She left it on all the time now, sound off. The images distracted her, kept her from thinking of him on the floor beside her, fading.

Gerrholtz said, "Why don't I take a guess? You're having trouble seeing your imaginary friend."

Paula snapped her head toward the woman. *You bitch.* She almost said it aloud.

Gerrholtz regarded her coolly. "A woman died two days ago in a hospital not far from here," she said. "Her name was Stephanie Wozniak. I'm told she was a neighbor of yours."

Steph is dead? She couldn't process the thought.

Gerrholtz took the sheets from her portfolio and laid them on Paula's lap. "I want you to look at these."

Paula picked them up automatically. The photographs looked like microscope slides from her old biochem classes, a field of cells tinged brown by some preserving chemical. Spidery black asterisks pock-marked the cells.

"Those clumps of black are bundles of prions," Gerrholtz said. "Regular old proteins, with one difference—they're the wrong shape."

Paula didn't look up. She flipped the printouts one by one, her hand moving on its own. Some of the pictures consisted almost entirely of sprawling nests of black threads. Steph deserved better than this. She'd waited her whole life for a Fore funeral. Instead the doctors cut her up and photographed the remains.

"I need you to concentrate, Paula. One protein bent or looped in the wrong way isn't a problem. But once they're in the brain, you get a conformational cascade—a snowball effect."

Paula's hands continued to move but she'd stopped seeing them. Gerrholtz rattled on and on about nucleation and crystallization. She kept using the word *spongiform* as if it would frighten her.

Paula already knew all this, and more. She let the doctor talk. Above Gerrholtz's head the TV showed a concerned young woman with a microphone, police cars and ambulances in the background.

"Paula!"

Dr. Gerrholtz's face was rigid with anger. Paula wondered if that was what she used to look like when she fought with Richard or screamed at Claire.

"I noticed you avoided saying 'Mad Cow,'" Paula said. "And Kuru."

"You know about Kuru?" Louden said.

"Of course she does," Gerrholtz said. "She's done her homework." The doctor put her hands on the foot of Paula's bed and leaned forward. "The disease that killed Stephanie doesn't have a name yet, Paula. We think it's a Kuru variant, the same prion with an extra kink. And we know that we can't save the people who already have it. Their prions will keep converting other proteins to use their shape. You understand what this means, don't you, Paula?"

Still trying to scare her. As if the promise of her own death would break her faith.

On the screen, the reporter gestured at two uniformed officers sealing the front door with yellow tape that looked specially chosen to match the house. Paula wondered if they'd found Merilee yet.

"It means that God is an idea," Paula said. "An idea that can't be killed."

VIII

The house shimmered in her vision, calling her like a lighthouse; she understood now why they'd painted it so brightly. Minutes after the accident her vision darkened like smoked glass, and now only the brightest things drew her attention. Her companion guided her down the dark streets, walking a few feet in front of her, surrounded by a nimbus of fire.

Steph opened the door. When she saw the tears in her eyes Steph squealed in delight and pulled her into a hug. "We've been waiting for you," she said. "We've been waiting so long." And then Steph was crying too.

"I'm sorry," Paula said. "I'm so sorry. I didn't know. . . ."

The other women came to her one by one, hugging her, caressing her cheeks, all of them crying. Only Merilee couldn't get up to greet her. The woman lay on the same couch as four months ago, but her limbs had cinched tighter, arms and legs curled to her torso like a dying bug. Paula kneeled next to her couch and gently pressed her cheek to Merilee's. Paula spoke the Fore greeting: *I eat you.*

That was the day one life ended and another began.

Her vision slowly returned over the next few days, but her companion remained, becoming more solid every day. They told her she didn't have to worry about him leaving her. She called in sick to work and spent most of the next week in the yellow house, one minute laughing, the next crying, sometimes both at the same time. She couldn't stop talking about her experience on the road, or the way her companion could make her recognize her vanity or spite with just a faint smile.

Her old life had become something that belonged to a stranger. Paula thought of the blank weekends of Scotch and Vicodin, the screaming matches with Richard. Had she really burned his record collection?

When she called him, the first thing she said was, "I'm sorry."

"What is it, Paula." His voice flat, wary. The Paula he knew only used "sorry" to bat away his words, deflect any attack.

"Something wonderful's happened," she said. She told him about Steph and the women of the house, then skipped the communion to tell him about the accident and the blinding light and the emotions that flooded through her. Richard kept telling her to slow down, stop stumbling over her words. Then she told him about her companion.

"*Who* did you meet?" he said. He thought it was someone who'd witnessed the accident. Again she tried to explain.

Richard said, "I don't think Claire should come back there this weekend."

"What? No!" She needed to see Claire. She needed to apologize to her, promise her she'd do better. She gripped the receiver. Why couldn't Richard believe her? Why was he fighting her again?

She felt a touch on the back of her head. She turned, let her hand fall to the side. His blue eyes gazed into hers.

One eyebrow rose slightly.

She breathed. Breathed again. Richard called her name from the handset.

"I know this is a lot to adjust to," Paula said. The words came to her even though her companion didn't make a sound. "I know you want the best for Claire. You're a good father." The words hurt because they were true. She'd always thought of Richard as a weak man, but if that had once been true, Claire's birth had given him someone weaker to protect. As their daughter became older he took her side against Paula more and more often. The fights worsened, but she broke him every time. She never thought he'd have the guts to walk out on her and try to take Claire with him. "If you think she'd be better off with you for a while, we can try that." She'd win his trust soon enough.

In the weeks after, Claire stayed with Richard, and Paula did hardly anything but talk with the yellow house women. At work the head nurse reprimanded her for her absences but she didn't care. Her life was with the women now, and her house became almost an annex to theirs. "We have room for more," Paula said dozens of times. "We have to tell others. It's not right to keep this to ourselves when so many people are suffering." The women nodded in agreement—or perhaps only in sympathy. Each of them had been saved, most of them from lives much worse than Paula's. They knew what changes were possible.

"You have to be patient," Steph told her one day. "This gift is handed from woman to woman, from Merilee's grandmother down to us. It comes with a responsibility to protect the host. We have to choose carefully—we can't share it with everyone."

"Why *not*?" Paula said. "Most of us would be dead without it. We're talking about saving the world here."

"Yes. One person at a time."

"But people are dying right now," Paula said. "There has to be a way to take this beyond the house."

"Let me show you something," Steph said. She brought down a box from a high bookshelf and lifted out a huge family Bible. Steph opened it to the family tree page, her left hand trembling. "Here are some of your sisters," she said. "The ones I've known, anyway."

The page was full of names. The list continued on the next page, and the next. Over a hundred names.

"How long has this been going on?" Paula said in wonder.

"Merilee's mother came here in 1982. Some of the women lived in this house for a while, and then were sent to establish their own houses. We don't know how many of us there are now, spread around the country. None of us knows all of them." She smiled at her. "See? You're not so alone. But we have to move quietly, Paula. We have to meet in small groups, like the early Christians."

"Like terrorists," Paula said bitterly.

Steph glanced to the side, listening to her companion. "Yes," she said, nodding. And then to Paula: "Exactly. There's no terror like the fear of God."

IX

He woke her at three A.M. Paula blinked at him, confused. He hovered beside the bed, only half there, like a reflection in a shop window.

She forced herself awake and as her vision cleared the edges of him resolved, but he was still more vapor than solid. "What is it?" she said. He teasingly held a finger to his lips and turned toward Esther's bed. He paused, waiting for her.

Paula slipped out of the bed and moved quietly to the cabinet against the wall. The door came open with a loud clack, and she froze, waiting to see if she'd awakened her roommate. Esther's feathery snore came faint and regular.

Paula found her handbag at the bottom shelf and carried it to the window. Feeling past her wallet fat with ID cards, she pulled out the smaller vinyl case and laid it open on the sill like a butterfly.

The metal tip of the syringe reflected the light.

Paula made a fist of her left hand, flexed, tightened again. Working in the faint light, she found the vein in her arm mostly by feel and long familiarity, her fingertips brushing first over the dimpled scars near the crook of her elbow, then down half an inch. She took the syringe in her right hand and pressed into the skin. The plastic tube slowly filled.

Paula picked her way through the dim room until her hand touched the IV bag hanging beside Esther's bed. The woman lay still, her lips slightly apart, snoring lightly. It would be simple to inject the blood through the IV's Y-port.

But what if it was too late for her? The host incubated for three to six months. Only if the cancer stayed in remission that long would the woman have a chance to know God. Not her invisible, unseen God. The real thing.

Paula reached for the tubing and her companion touched her arm. She lowered the syringe, confused. Why not inject her? She searched his face for a reason, but he was so hard to see.

He turned and walked through the wall. Paula opened the door and stepped into the bright hallway, and for a moment she couldn't find him in the light. He gestured for her to follow.

She followed his will-o'-the-wisp down the deserted corridor, carrying the syringe low at her side. He led her down the stairwell, and at the next floor went left, left again. At an intersection a staffer in blue scrubs passed ten feet in front of them without seeing them.

Perhaps she'd become invisible too.

He stopped before a door and looked at her. It was one of the converted rooms where doctors on call could catch some sleep. Here? she asked with her eyes. He gestured toward the door, his arm like a tendril of fog.

She gripped the handle, slowly turned. The door was unlocked. Gently, she pushed it open.

The wedge of light revealed a woman asleep on the twin bed, a thin blanket half covering her. She wore what Paula had seen her in earlier: a cream blouse gleaming in the hall light, a patterned skirt rucked above her knees, her legs dark in black hose. Her shoes waited side-by-side on the floor next to the bed, ready for her to spring back into action and save her world.

Paula looked back at the doorway. Dr. Gerrholtz? she asked him. Did he really want this awful woman to receive the host?

His faint lips pursed, the slightest of frowns, and Paula felt a rush of shame. Who was she to object? Before Steph had found her Paula had been the most miserable woman alive. Everyone deserved salvation. That was the whole point of the mission.

Dr. Gerrholtz stirred, turned her head slightly, and the light fell across her closed eyes. Paula raised the needle, moved her thumb over the plunger. No handy IV already connected. No way to do this without waking the woman up. And she'd wake up screaming.

"Hello?" Dr. Gerrholtz said. Her eyes opened, and she lifted a hand to shade her eyes.

Jesus is coming, Paula said silently, and pressed the needle into her thigh.

X

Paula and Tonya stooped awkwardly at the edge of the pit, clearing the sand. They dug down carefully so that their shovel blades wouldn't cut too deep, then pitched the spark-flecked sand into the dark of the yard. They worked in short sleeves, sweating despite the cold wind. With every inch they uncovered the pit grew hotter and brighter.

It was hard work, and their backs still ached from this morning when they'd dug the pit, hauled over the big stones, and lined the bottom with them. But Paula had volunteered for this job. She wanted to prove that she could work harder than anyone.

Inside the house, women laughed and told stories, their voices carrying through the half-opened windows. Paula tossed aside a shovelful of sand and said, "Tonya, have you ever asked why no men are invited?" She'd thought about her words for a long time. She wanted to test them on Tonya first, because she was young and seemed more open than the other women.

Tonya looked up briefly, then dug down again with her shovel. "That's not the tradition."

"But what about Donel? Wouldn't you want this for him?" Donel was Tonya's son, only two years old. He shared a bedroom with her, but all the women took care of him.

Tonya paused, leaned against her shovel. "I . . . I think about that. But it's just not the way it's done. No men at the feast."

"But what if we could bring the feast to them?" Paula said. "I've been reading about Merilee's people, the disease they carried. There's more than one way to transmit the host. What if we could become missionaries some other way?"

The girl shook her head. "Merilee said that men would twist it all up, just like they did the last time."

"All the disciples were men last time. This time they're all women, but that doesn't make it right. Think about Donel." Think about Richard.

"We better keep going," Tonya said, ending the conversation. She started digging again, and after a moment, Paula joined her. But she kept thinking of Richard. He'd become more guarded over the past few months, more protective of Claire. When her daughter turned fourteen—another of Merilee's rules—Paula would bring her to communion. But if she could also bring it to Richard, if he could experience what she'd found, they could be a family again.

Several minutes later they found the burlap by the feel under their shovels. They scraped back the sand that covered the sack, then bent and heaved it up onto a pal-let of plywood and one-by-fours. After they'd caught their breath they called the others from the house.

More than seventy women had come, some of them from as far away as New Zealand. None of them had come alone, of course. The air was charged with a multitude of invisible presences.

Eight of the women were chosen as pall bearers. The procession moved slowly because so many of them walked with difficulty. God's presence burned the body like a candle—Merilee's early death was proof of that—but not one of them would trade Him for anything. A perfect body was for the next life.

Steph began to sing something in Merilee's language, and the others joined in, harmonizing. Some knew the words; others, like Paula, hummed along. Women cried, laughed, lifted their hands. Others walked silently, perhaps in communion with their companions.

There was an awkward moment when they had to tilt the litter to get through the back door, but then they were inside. They carried her through the kitchen—past the stacks of Tupperware, the knives and cutting boards, the coolers of dry ice—then through the dining room and into the living room. The furniture had been pushed back to the walls. They set the litter in the center of the room.

Paula gripped the stiff and salt-caked cloth—they'd soaked the body overnight—while Steph sawed the length of it with a thick-bladed knife. Steam escaped from the bag, filling the room with a heady scent of ginger and a dozen other spices.

The last of the shroud fell away and Merilee grinned up at them. Her lips had pulled away from her teeth, and the skin of her face had turned hard and shiny. As she'd instructed, they'd packed ferns and wild herbs around her in a funeral dress of leaves.

Steph kneeled at the head of the impromptu table and the others gathered around. The oldest and most crippled were helped down to the floor; the rest stood behind them, hands on their shoulders.

Steph opened a wooden box as big as a plumber's toolbox and drew out a small knife. She laid it on a white linen napkin next to Merilee's skull and said, "Like many of you I was at the feast of Merilee's mother, and this is the story Merilee told there.

"It was the tradition of the Fore for the men and women to live apart. When a member of the tribe died, only the women and children were allowed at the feast. The men became jealous. They cursed the women, and they called the curse *kuru*, which means both 'to tremble' and 'to be afraid.' The white missionaries who visited the tribe called it the laughing sickness, because of the grimaces that twisted their faces."

As she talked she laid out other tools from the box: a filet knife, a wooden-handled fork with long silver tines, a Japanese cleaver.

"Merilee's grandmother, Yobaiotu, was a young woman when the first whites came, the doctors and government men and missionaries. One day the missionaries brought everyone out to the clearing they'd made by the river and gave everyone a piece of bread. They told them to dip it into a cup of wine and eat, and they said the words Jesus had spoken at the last supper: This is my body, this is my blood."

Steph drew out a long-handled knife and looked at it for perhaps thirty seconds, trying to control her emotions. "The moment Yobaiotu swallowed the bread, she fell down shaking, and a light filled her eyes. When she awoke, a young boy stood at her side. He held out his hand to her, and helped her to her feet. 'Lord Jesus!' Yobaiotu said, recognizing him." Steph looked up, smiled. "But of course no one else could see him. They thought she was crazy."

The women quietly laughed and nodded.

"The doctors said that the funeral feasts caused Kuru, and they ordered them to stop. But Yobaiotu knew the curse had been transformed in her, that the body of Christ lived in her. She taught her daughters to keep that covenant. The night Yobaiotu died they feasted in secret, as we do tonight."

Steph removed the center shelf of the box, set it aside, and reached in again. She lifted out a hacksaw with a gleaming blade. A green price tag was still stuck to the saw's blue handle.

"The body of Christ was passed from mother to daughter," Steph said. "Because of them, Christ lives in all of us. And because of Merilee, Christ will live in sisters who've not yet been found."

"Amen," the women said in unison.

Steph lifted the saw, and with her other hand gently touched the top of Merilee's skull. "This we do in remembrance of him," she said. "And Merilee."

XI

The screaming eventually brought Louden to her room. "Don't make me sedate you," he began, and then flinched as she jerked toward him. The cuffs held her to the bed.

"Bring him back!" she screamed, her voice hoarse. "Bring him back now!"

Last night they'd taken her to another room, one without windows, and tied her down. Arms apart, ankles together. Then they attached the IV and upped the dosage: two parts Topamax, one part Loxapine, an antipsychotic.

Gerrholtz they rushed to specialists in another city.

A hospital security guard took up station outside her door, and was replaced the next morning by a uniformed police officer. Detectives came to interrogate her. Her name hadn't been released to the news, they said, but it would only be a matter of time. The TV people didn't even know about Gerrholtz—they were responding to stories coming out of the yellow house investigation—but already they'd started using the word "bioterrorism." Sometime today they'd move her to a federal facility.

Minute by minute the drugs did their work and she felt him slipping from her. She thought, if I keep watch he can't disappear. By twisting her shoulders she could see a little way over the bed and make out a part of him: a shadow that indicated his blue-jeaned leg, a cluster of dots in the speckled linoleum that described the sole of a dirty foot. When the cramps in her arms and lower back became too much she'd fall back, rest for a while, then throw herself sideways again. Each time she looked over the edge it took her longer to discern his shape. Two hours after the IV went in she couldn't find him at all.

Louden said, "What you experienced was an illusion, Paula, a phantom generated by a short-circuiting lobe of your brain. There's a doctor in Canada who can trigger these presences with a helmet and *magnetic fields*, for crying out loud. Your . . . *God* wasn't real. Your certainty was a symptom."

"Take me off these meds," she said, "or so help me I'll wrap this IV tube around your fucking neck."

"This is a disease, Paula. Some of you are seeing Jesus, but we've got other patients seeing demons and angels, talking to ghosts—I've got one Hindu guy who's sharing the bed with Lord Krishna."

She twisted against the cuffs, pain spiking across her shoulders. Her jaw ached from clenching her teeth.

"Paula, I need you to calm down. Your husband and daughter are downstairs. They want to visit you before you leave here."

"What? No. No." They couldn't see her like this. It would confirm everything Richard ever thought about her. And Claire. . . . She was thirteen, a girl unfolding into a woman. The last thing she needed was to have her life distorted by this moment. By another vivid image of her mother as a raving lunatic.

"Tell them to stay away from me. The woman they knew doesn't exist anymore."

This morning the detectives had emptied her bag and splayed the driver's licenses and social security IDs like a deck of cards. How long has this been going on? they demanded. How many people are involved?

They gave her a pencil and yellow legal pad, told her to write down all the names she could remember. She stared at the tip of the pencil. An epidemiology book she'd read tried to explain crystallization by talking about how carbon could become graphite or diamond depending on how the atoms were arranged. The shapes she made on the page could doom a score of her missionaries.

She didn't know what to do. She turned to her companion but he was silent, already disintegrating.

"You're too late," she told the detectives. She snapped the pencil in half and threw it at them, bits of malformed diamond. "Six months too late."

XII

They called themselves missionaries. Paula thought the name fit. They had a mission, and they would become agents of transmission.

The first and last meeting included only eighteen women. Paula had first convinced Tonya and Rosa from the yellow house, and they had widened the circle to a handful of women from houses around Philly, and from there they persuaded a few more women from New York and New Jersey. Paula had met some of them at Merilee's feast, but most were strangers. Some, like Tonya, were mothers of sons, but all of them had become convinced that it was time to take the gospel into the world.

They met at a Denny's restaurant in the western suburbs, where Steph and the other women wouldn't see them.

"The host is not a virus," Paula said. "It's not bacterial. It can't be detected or filtered out the way other diseases are, it can't be killed by antibiotics or detergents, because it's nothing but a *shape*." A piece of paper can become a sailboat or swan, she told them. A simple protein, folded and copied a million times, could bring you Kuru, or Creutzfeldt-Jakob disease, or salvation.

"The body of Christ is powerful," Paula said. They knew: all of them had taken part in feasts and had been saved through them. "But there's also power in the blood." She dealt out the driver licenses, two to each woman. Rosa's old contacts had made them for fifty bucks apiece. "One of these is all you need to donate. We're working on getting more. With four IDs you can give blood twice a month."

She told them how to answer the Red Cross surveys, which iron supplements to buy, which foods they should bulk up on to avoid anemia. They talked about secrecy. Most of the other women they lived with were too bound by tradition to see that they were only half doing God's work.

Women like Steph. Paula had argued with her a dozen times over the months, but could not convince her. Paula loved Steph, and owed so much to her, but she couldn't sit idly by any longer.

"We have to donate as often as possible," Paula said. "We have to spread the host so far and so fast that they can't stop us by rounding us up." The incubation time depended directly on the amount consumed, so the more that was in the blood supply the faster the conversions would occur. Paula's conversion had taken months. For others it might be years.

"But once they're exposed to the host the conversion *will* happen," Paula said. "It can't be stopped. One seed crystal can transform the ocean."

She could feel them with her. They could see the shape of the new world.

The women would never again meet all together like this—too dangerous—but they didn't need to. They'd already become a church within the church.

Paula hugged each of them as they left the restaurant. "Go," she told them. "Multiply."

XIII

The visitor seemed familiar. Paula tilted her head to see through the bars as the woman walked toward the cell. It had become too much of a bother to lift Paula out of the bed and wheel her down to the conference room, so now the visitors came to her. Doctors and lawyers, always and only doctors and lawyers. This woman, though, didn't look like either.

"Hello, Paula," she said. "It's Esther Wynne. Do you remember me?"

"Ah." The memory came back to her, those first days in the hospital. The Christian woman. Of course she'd be Paula's first voluntary visitor. "Hello, Esther." She struggled to enunciate clearly. In the year since they'd seen each other, Paula's condition had worsened. Lips and jaw and arms refused to obey her, shaking and jerking to private commands. Her arm lay curled against her chest like Merilee's. Her spine bent her nearly in half, so that she had to lie on her side. "You look—" She made a sound like a laugh, a hiccupping gasp forced from her chest by an unruly diaphragm. "—good."

The guard positioned a chair in front of the bars and the older woman sat down. Her hair was curled and sprayed. Under the makeup her skin looked healthy.

"I've been worried about you," Esther said. "Are they treating you well?"

Paula almost smiled. "As well as you can treat a mass murderer."

Some facts never escaped her. The missionaries had spread the disease to thousands, perhaps tens of thousands. But more damaging, they'd completely corrupted the blood supply. New prion filters were now on the market, but millions of gallons of blood had to be destroyed. They told her she might be ultimately responsible for the deaths of a million people.

Paula gave them every name she could remember, and the FBI tracked down all of the original eighteen, but by then the mission could go on without them. A day after the meeting in the restaurant they'd begun to recruit others, women and men Paula would never meet, whose names would never be spoken to her. The church would continue. In secret now, hunted by the FBI and the CDC and the world's governments, but growing every day. The host was passed needle by needle in private ceremonies, but increasingly on a mass scale as well. In an Ohio dairy processing plant, a man had been caught mixing his blood into the vats of milk. In Florida, police arrested a woman for injecting blood into the skulls of chickens. The economic damage was already in the trillions. The emotional toll on the public, in panic and paranoia, was incalculable.

Esther looked around at the cell. "You don't have anything in there with you. Can I bring you books? Magazines? They told me they'd allow reading material. I thought maybe —"

"I don't want anything," Paula said. She couldn't hold her head steady enough to read. She watched TV to remind herself every day of what she'd done to the world. Outside the prison, a hundred jubilant protestors had built a tent city. They sang hymns and chanted for her release, and every day a hundred counter-protestors showed up to scream threats, throw rocks, and chant for her death. Police in riot gear made daily arrests.

Esther frowned. "I thought maybe you'd like a Bible."

Now Paula laughed for real. "What are you doing here, Esther? I see that look in your eye, you think I don't recognize it?" Paula twisted, pressed herself higher on one elbow. Esther had never been infected by the host—they wouldn't have let her in here if she didn't pass the screening—but her strain of the disease was just as virulent. "Did your Jesus tell you to come here?"

"I suppose in a way he did." The woman didn't seem flustered. Paula found that annoying.

Esther said, "You don't have to go through this alone. Even here, even after all you've done, God will forgive you. He can be here for you, if you want him."

Paula stared at her. *If I want him.* She never stopped craving him. He'd carved out a place for himself, dug a warren through the cells in her brain, until he'd erased even himself. She no longer needed pharmaceuticals to suppress him. He'd left behind a jagged Christ-shaped hole, a darkness with teeth.

She wanted him more than drugs, more than alcohol, more than Richard or Claire. She thought she'd known loneliness, but the past months had taught her new depths. Nothing would feel better than to surrender to a new god, let herself be wrapped again in loving arms.

Esther stood and leaned close to the bars so that their faces were only a couple feet apart. "Paula, if you died right now, do you know beyond a shadow of a doubt that you'd go to heaven?" The guard told her to step back but she ignored him. She pushed one arm through the bars. "If you want to accept him, take my hand. Reach out."

"Oh, Esther, the last—" Her upper lip pulled back over her gums. "—*last* thing I want is to live forever." She fell back against the bed, tucked her working arm to her chest.

A *million people.*

There were acts beyond forgiveness. There were debts that had to be paid in person.

"Not hiding anymore," Paula said. She shook her head. "No gods, no drugs. The only thing I need to do now—"

She laughed, but it was an involuntary spasm, joyless. She waited a moment until it passed, and breathed deep. "I need to die clean."

life on the preservation

JACK SKILLINGSTEAD

New writer Jack Skillingstead works in the aerospace industry and lives with his family near Seattle, Washington. He made his first sale in 2003 to *Asimov's Science Fiction*, with "Dead Worlds" (which was also in our Twenty-first Annual Collection), and since then has become something of a regular there, with more than twelve sales in the last few years, as well as placing stories with *On Spec* and elsewhere. He is at work on several novels.

In the melancholy tale that follows, he demonstrates that when you've only *got one* day, you'd better make it a *good* one.

W ind buffeted the scutter. Kylie resisted the temptation to fight the controls. Hand light on the joystick, she veered toward the green smolder of Seattle, riding down a cloud canyon aflicker with electric bursts. The Preservation Field extended half a mile over Elliot Bay but did not capture Blake or Vashon Island nor any of the blasted lands.

She dropped to the deck. Acid rain and wind lashed the scutter. The Preservation Field loomed like an immense wall of green jellied glass.

She punched through, and the sudden light shift dazzled her. Kylie polarized the thumbnail port, at the same time deploying braking vanes and dipping steeply to skim the surface of the bay.

The skyline and waterfront were just as they'd appeared in the old photographs and movies. By the angle of the sun she estimated her arrival time at late morning. Not bad. She reduced airspeed and gently pitched forward. The scutter drove under the water. It got dark. She cleared the thumbnail port. Bubbles trailed back over the thick plexi, strings of silver pearls.

Relying on preset coordinates, she allowed the autopilot to navigate. In minutes the scutter was tucked in close to a disused pier. Kyle opened the ballast, and the scutter surfaced in a shadow, bobbing. She saw a ladder and nudged forward.

She was sweating inside her costume. Jeans, black sneakers, olive drab shirt, rain parka. Early twenty-first century urban America: Seattle chic.

She powered down, tracked her seat back, popped the hatch. The air was sharp and clean, with a saltwater tang. Autumn chill in the Pacific Northwest. Water slopped against the pilings.

She climbed up the pitchy, guano-spattered rungs of the ladder.

And stood in awe of the intact city, the untroubled sky. She could sense the thousands of living human beings, their vitality like an electric vibe in her blood. Kylie was nineteen and had never witnessed such a day. It had been this way before the world ended. She reminded herself that she was here to destroy it.

From her pocket she withdrew a remote control, pointed it at the scutter. The hatch slid shut and her vehicle sank from view. She replaced the remote control. Her hand strayed down to another zippered pocket and she felt the outline of the explosive sphere. Behind it, her heart was beating wildly. *I'm here*, she thought.

She walked along the waterfront, all her senses exploited. The sheer numbers of people overwhelmed her. The world had ended on a Saturday, November nine, 2004. There were more living human beings in her immediate range of sight than Kylie had seen in her entire life.

She extracted the locator device from her coat pocket and flipped up the lid. It resembled a cellular phone of the period. A strong signal registered immediately. Standing in the middle of the sidewalk, she turned slowly toward the high reflective towers of the city, letting people go around her, so many people, walking, skateboarding, jogging, couples and families and single people, flowing in both directions, and seagulls gliding overhead, and horses harnessed to carriages waiting at the curb (so *much* life), and the odors and rich living scents, and hundreds of cars and pervasive human noise and riot, all of it continuous and—

"Are you all right?"

She started. A tall young man in a black jacket loomed over her. The jacket was made out of *leather*. She could smell it.

"Sorry," he said. "You looked sort of dazed."

Kylie turned away and walked into the street, toward the signal, her mission. Horns blared, she jerked back, dropped her locator. It skittered against the curb near one of the carriage horses. Kylie lunged for it, startling the horse, which clopped back, a hoof coming down on the locator. *No!* She couldn't get close. The great head of the animal tossed, nostrils snorting, the driver shouting at her, Kylie frantic to reach her device.

"Hey, watch it!"

It was the man in the leather jacket. He pulled her back, then darted in himself and retrieved the device. He looked at it a moment, brow knitting. She snatched it out of his hand. The display was cracked and blank. She shook it, punched the keypad. Nothing.

"I'm really sorry," the man said.

She ignored him.

"It's like my fault," he said.

She looked up. "You have no idea, *no idea* how bad this is."

He winced.

"I don't even have any tools," she said, not to him.

"Let me—"

She walked away, but not into the street, the locator a useless thing in her hand. She wasn't a tech. Flying the scutter and planting explosives was as technical as she got. So it was plan B, only since plan B didn't exist it was plan Zero. Without the locator she couldn't possibly find the Eternity Core. A horse! Jesus.

"*Shit*."

She sat on a stone bench near a decorative waterfall that unrolled and shone like a sheet of plastic. Her mind raced but she couldn't formulate a workable plan B.

A shadow moved over her legs. She looked up, squinting in the sun.

"Hi."

"What do you want?" she said to the tall man in the leather jacket.

"I thought an ice cream might cheer you up."

"Huh?"

"Ice cream," he said. "You know, 'You scream, I scream, we all scream for ice cream'?"

She stared at him. His skin was pale, his eyebrows looked sketched on with charcoal, and there was a small white scar on his nose. He was holding two waffle cones, one in each hand, the cones packed with pink ice cream. She had noticed people walking around with these things, had seen the sign.

"I guess you don't like strawberry," he said.

"I've never had it."

"Yeah, right."

"Okay, I'm lying. Now why don't you go away. I need to think."

He extended his left hand. "It's worth trying, at least once. Even on a cold day."

Kylie knew about ice cream. People in the old movies ate it. It made them happy. She took the cone.

"Listen, can I sit down for a second?" the man said.

She ignored him, turning the cone in her hand like the mysterious artifact it was. The man sat down anyway.

"My name's Toby," he said.

"It's really pink," Kylie said.

"Yeah." And after a minute, "You're supposed to lick it."

She looked at him.

"Like this," he said, licking his own cone.

"I *know*," she said. "I'm not an ignoramus." Kylie licked her ice cream. *Jesus!* Her whole body lit up. "That's—"

"Yeah?"

"It's wonderful," she said.

"You really haven't had ice cream before?"

She shook her head, licking away at the cone, devouring half of it in seconds.

"That's incredibly far-fetched," Toby said. "What's your name? You want a napkin?" He pointed at her chin.

"I'm Kylie," she said, taking the napkin and wiping her chin and lips. All of a sudden she didn't want any more ice cream. She had never eaten anything so rich. In her world there *wasn't* anything so rich. Her stomach felt queasy.

"I have to go," she said.

She stood up, so did he.

"Hey, you know the thing is, what you said about not having tools? What I mean is, I have tools. I mean I fix things. It's not a big deal, but I'm good and I like doing it. I can fix all kinds of things, you know? Palm Pilots, cell phones, laptops. Whatever."

Kylie waved the locator. "You don't even know what this *is*."

"I don't *have* to know what it is to make it go again."

Hesitantly, she handed him the locator. While he was turning it in his fingers, she spotted the Tourist. He was wearing a puffy black coat and a watch cap, and he was walking directly towards her, expressionless, his left hand out of sight inside his pocket. He wasn't a human being.

Toby noticed her changed expression and followed her gaze.

"You know that guy?"

Kylie ran. She didn't look back to see if the Tourist was running after her. She cut through the people crowding the sidewalk, her heart slamming. It was a minute before she realized she'd left the locator with Toby. That almost made her stop, but it was too late. Let him keep the damn thing.

She ran hard. The Old Men had chosen her for this mission because of her youth and vitality (so many were sickly and weak), but after a while she had to stop and catch her breath. She looked around. The vista of blue water was dazzling. The city was awesome, madly perfect, phantasmagoric, better than the movies. The Old Men called it an abomination. Kylie didn't care what they said. She was here for her mother, who was dying and who grieved for the trapped souls.

Kylie turned slowly around, and here came two more Tourists.

No, three.

Three from three different directions, one of them crossing the street, halting traffic. Stalking toward her with no pretense of human expression, as obvious to her among the authentic populace as cockroaches in a scatter of white rice.

Kylie girded herself. Before she could move, a car drew up directly in front of her, a funny round car painted canary yellow. The driver threw the passenger door open, and there was the man again, Toby.

"Get in!"

She ducked into the car, which somehow reminded her of the scutter, and it accelerated away. A Tourist who had scrabbled for the door handle spun back and fell. Kylie leaned over the seat. The Tourist got up, the other two standing beside him, not helping. Then Toby cranked the car into a turn that threw her against the door. They were climbing a steep hill, and Toby seemed to be doing too many things at once, working the clutch, the steering wheel, and radio, scanning through stations until he lighted upon something loud and incomprehensible that made him smile and nod his head.

"You better put on your seatbelt," he said. "They'll ticket you for that shit, believe it or not."

Kylie buckled her belt.

"Thanks," she said. "You came out of nowhere."

"Anything can happen. Who were those guys?"

"Tourists."

"Okay. Hey, you know what?"

"What?"

He took his hand off the shifter and pulled Kylie's locator out of his inside jacket pocket.

"I bet you I can fix this gizmo."

"Would you bet your soul on it?"

"Why not?" He grinned.

He stopped at his apartment to pick up his tools, and Kylie waited in the car. There was a clock on the dashboard. 11:45 A.M. She set the timer on her wrist chronometer.

Twelve hours and change.

They sat in a coffee bar in Belltown. More incomprehensible music thumped from box speakers bracketed near the ceiling. Paintings by some local artist decorated the walls, violent slashes of color, faces of dogs and men and women drowning, mouths gaping.

Kylie kept an eye open for Tourists.

Toby hunched over her locator, a jeweler's kit unrolled next to his espresso. He had the back off the device and was examining its exotic components with the aid of a magnifying lens and a battery operated light of high intensity. He had removed his jacket and was wearing a black sweatshirt with the sleeves pushed up. His forearms were hairy. A tattoo of blue thorns braceleted his right wrist. He was quiet for a considerable time, his attention focused. Kylie drank her second espresso, like the queen of the world, like it was nothing to just *ask* for coffee this good and get it.

"Well?" she said.

"Ah."

"What?"

"Ah, what *is* this thing?"

"You said you didn't need to know."

"I don't need to know, I just want to know. After all, according to you, I'm betting my immortal soul that I can fix it, so it'd be nice to know what it does."

"We don't always get to know the nice things, do we?" Kylie said. "Besides, I don't believe in souls. That was just something to say." Something her mother had told her, she thought. The Old Men didn't talk about souls. They talked about zoos.

"You sure downed that coffee fast. You want to go for three?"

"Yeah."

He chuckled and gave her a couple of dollars and she went to the bar and got another espresso, head buzzing in a very good way.

"It's a locator," she said, taking pity on him, after returning to the table and sitting down.

"Yeah? What's it locate?"

"The city's Eternity Core."

"Oh, that explains everything. What's an eternity core?"

"It's an alien machine that generates an energy field around the city and preserves it in a sixteen-hour time loop."

"Gotcha."

"*Now* can you fix it?"

"Just point out one thing."

She slurped up her third espresso. "Okay."

"What's the power source? I don't see anything that even vaguely resembles a battery."

She leaned in close, their foreheads practically touching. She pointed with the chipped nail of her pinky finger.

"I think it's that coily thing," she said.

He grunted. She didn't draw back. She was smelling him, smelling his skin. He lifted his gaze from the guts of the locator. His eyes were pale blue, the irises circled with black rings.

"You're kind of a spooky chick," he said.

"Kind of."

"I like spooky."

"Where I come from," Kylie said, "almost all the men are impotent."

"Yeah?"

She nodded.

"Where do you come from," he asked, "the east side?"

"East side of hell."

"Sounds like it," he said.

She kissed him, impulsively, her blood singing with caffeine and long-unrequited pheromones. Then she sat back and wiped her lips with her palm and stared hard at him.

"I wish you hadn't done that," she said.

"*Me.*"

"Just fix the locator, okay?"

"Spooky," he said, picking up a screwdriver with a blade not much bigger than a spider's leg.

A little while later she came back from the bathroom and he had put the locator together and was puzzling over the touchpad. He had found the power button. The two-inch-square display glowed the blue of cold starlight. She slipped it from his hand and activated the grid. A pinhead hotspot immediately began blinking.

"It work okay?" Toby asked.

"Yes." She hesitated, then said, "Let's go for a drive. I'll navigate."

They did that.

Kylie liked the little round canary car. It felt luxurious and utilitarian at the same time. Letting the locator guide her, she directed Toby. After many false turns and an accumulated two point six miles on the odometer, she said:

"Stop. No, keep going, but not too fast."

The car juddered as he manipulated clutch, brake, and accelerator. They rolled past a closed store front on the street level of a four-story building on First Avenue, some kind of sex shop, the plateglass soaped and brown butcher paper tacked up on the inside.

Two men in cheap business suits loitered in front of the building. Tourists.

Kylie scrunched down in her seat.

"Don't look at those guys," she said. "Just keep driving."

"Whatever."

Later on they were parked under the monorail tracks eating submarine sandwiches. Kylie couldn't get over how great everything was, the food, the coffee, the damn *air*. All of it the way things used to be. She could hardly believe how great it had been, how much had been lost.

"Okay," she said, kind of talking to herself, "so they know I'm here and they're guarding the Core."

"Those bastards," Toby said.

"You wouldn't think it was so funny if you knew what they really were."

"They looked like used car salesmen."

"They're Tourists," Kylie said.

"Oh my God! More tourists!"

Kylie chewed a mouthful of sub. She'd taken too big a bite. Every flavor was like a drug. Onions, provolone, turkey, mustard, pepper.

"So where are the evil tourists from?" Toby asked. "California?"

"Another dimensional reality."

"That's what I said."

Kylie's chronometer toned softly. Ten hours.

Inside the yellow car there were many smells and one of them was Toby.

"Do you have any more tattoos?" she asked.

"One. It's—"

"Don't tell me," she said.

"Okay."

"I want you to show me. But not here. At the place where you live."

"You want to come to my apartment?"

"Your apartment, yes."

"Okay, spooky." He grinned. So did she.

Some precious time later the chronometer toned again. It wasn't on her wrist anymore. It was on the hardwood floor tangled up in her clothes.

Toby, who was standing naked by the refrigerator holding a bottle of grape juice, said, "Why's your watch keep doing that?"

"It's a countdown," Kylie said, looking at him.

"A countdown to what?"

"To the end of the current cycle. The end of the loop."

He drank from the bottle, his threat working. She liked to watch him now, whatever he did. He finished drinking and screwed the cap back on.

"The loop," he said, shaking his head.

When he turned to put the bottle back in the refrigerator she saw his other tattoo again: a cross throwing off light. It was inked into the skin on his left shoulder blade.

"You can't even see your own cross," she said.

He came back to the bed.

"I don't have to see it," he said. "I just like to know it's there, watching my back."

"Are you Catholic?"

"No."

"My mother is."

"I just like the idea of Jesus," he said.

"You're spookier than I am," Kylie said.

"Not by a mile."

She kissed his mouth, but when he tried to caress her she pushed him gently back.

"Take me someplace."

"Where?"

"My grandparents' house." She meant "great" grandparents, but didn't feel like explaining to him how so many decades had passed outside the loop of the Preservation.

"Right now?"

"Yes."

It was a white frame house on Queen Anne Hill, sitting comfortably among its prosperous neighbors on a street lined with live oaks. Kylie pressed her nose to the window on the passenger side of the Vee Dub, as Toby called his vehicle.

"Stop," she said. "That's it."

He tucked the little car into the curb and turned the engine off. Kylie looked from the faded photo in her hand to the house. Her mother's mother had taken the photo just weeks before the world ended. In it, Kylie's great grandparents stood on the front porch of the house, their arms around each other, waving and smiling. There was no one standing on the front porch now.

"It's real," Kylie said. "I've been looking at this picture my whole life."

"Haven't you ever been here before?"

She shook her head. At the same time her chronometer toned.

"How we doing on the countdown?" Toby asked.

She glanced at the digital display.

"Eight hours."

"So what happens at midnight?"

"It starts up again. The end is the beginning."

He laughed. She didn't.

"So then it's Sunday, right? Then do you countdown to Monday?"

"At the end of the loop it's *not* Sunday," she said. "It's the same day over again."

"Two Saturdays. Not a bad deal."

"Not just two. It goes on and on. November ninth a thousand, ten thousand, a million times over."

"Okay."

"You can look at me like that if you want. I don't care if you believe me. You know something, Toby?"

"What?"

"I'm having a really *good* day."

"That's November ninth for you."

She smiled at him, then kissed him, that feeling, the taste, all of the sensation in its totality.

"I want to see my grandparents now."

She opened the door and got out but he stayed in the car. She crossed the lawn, strewn with big colorful oak leaves, to the front door of the house, stealing backward glances, wanting to know he was still there waiting for her in the yellow car. Her lover. Her boyfriend.

She started to knock on the door but hesitated. From inside the big house she heard muffled music and laughter. She looked around. In the breeze an orange oak leaf detached from the tree and spun down. The sky blew clear and cold. Later it would cloud over and rain. Kylie knew all about this day. She had been told of it since she was a small child. The last day of the world, perfectly preserved for the edification of alien Tourists and anthropologists. Some people said what happened was an accident, a consequence of the aliens opening the rift, disrupting the fabric of reality. What really pissed everybody off, Kylie thought, was the dismissive attitude. There was no occupying army, no invasion. They came, destroyed everything either intentionally or accidentally, then ignored the survivors. The Preservation was the only thing about the former masters of the Earth that interested them.

Kylie didn't care about all that right now. She had been told about the day, but she had never understood what the day meant, the sheer sensorial joy of it, the incredible beauty and rightness of it. A surge of pure delight moved through her being, and for a moment she experienced uncontainable happiness.

She knocked on the door.

"Yes?" A woman in her mid-fifties with vivid green eyes, her face pressed with comfortable laugh lines. Like the house, she was a picture come to life. (Kylie's grandmother showing her the photographs, faded and worn from too much touching.)

"Hi," Kylie said.

"Can I help you?" the live photograph said.

"No. I mean, I wanted to ask you something."

The waiting expression on her face so familiar. Kylie said, "I just wanted to know, are you having a good day, I mean a really good day?"

Slight turn of the head, lips pursed uncertainly, ready to believe this was a harmless question from a harmless person.

"It's like a survey," Kylie said. "For school?"

A man of about sixty years wearing a baggy wool sweater and glasses came to the door.

"What's all this?" he asked.

"A happiness survey," Kylie's great grandmother said, and laughed.

"Happiness survey, huh?" He casually put his arm around his wife and pulled her companionably against him.

"Yes," Kylie said. "For school."

"Well, I'm happy as a clam," Kylie's great grandfather said.

"I'm a clam, too," Kylie's great grandmother said. "A happy one."

"Thank you," Kylie said.

"You're very welcome. Gosh, but you look familiar."

"So do you. Good-bye."

Back in the car Kylie squeezed Toby's hand. There had been a boy on the Outskirts. He was impotent, but he liked to touch Kylie and be with her, and he didn't mind watching her movies, the ones that made the Old Men sad and angry but that she obsessively hoarded images from in her mind. The boy's hand always felt cold and hony. Which wasn't his fault. The nicest time they ever had was a night they had spent in one of the ruins with a working fireplace and enough furniture to burn for several hours. They'd had a book of poems and took turns reading them to each other. Most of the poems didn't make sense to Kylie but she liked the sounds of the words, the way they were put together. Outside, the perpetual storms crashed and sizzled, violet flashes stuttering into the cozy room with the fire.

In the yellow car, Toby's hand felt warm. Companionable and intimate.

"So how are they doing?" he said.

"They're happy."

"Great. What's next?"

"If you knew this was your last day to live," Kylie asked him, "what would you do?"

"I'd find a spooky girl and make love to her."

She kissed him. "What else?"

"Ah—"

"I mean without leaving the city. You can't leave the city."

"Why not?"

"Because you'd just get stuck in the Preservation Field until the loop restarted. It looks like people are driving out but they're not."

He looked at her closely, searching for the joke, then grinned. "We wouldn't want that to happen to us."

"No."

"So what would *you* do on your last day?" he asked.

"I'd find a spooky guy who could fix things and I'd get him to fix me up."

"You don't need fixing. You're not broken."

"I am."

"Yeah?"

"Let's drive around. Then let's have a really great meal, like the best food you can think of."

"That's doable."

"Then we can go back to your apartment."

"What about the big countdown?"

"Fuck the countdown." Kylie pushed the timing stud into her chronometer. "There," she said. "No more countdown."

"You like pizza?" Toby said.

"I don't know. What is it?"

After they made love the second time, Kylie fell into a light doze on Toby's futon bed. She was not used to so much rich stimulation, so much food and drink, so much touching.

She woke with a start from a dream that instantly disappeared from her consciousness. There was the sound of rain, but it wasn't the terrible poisonous rain of her world. Street light through the window cast a flowing shadow across the foot of the bed. It reminded her of the shiny fountain at the waterfront. The room was snug and comforting and safe. There was a clock on the table beside the bed but she didn't look at it. It could end right now.

She sat up. Toby was at his desk under a framed movie poster, bent over something illuminated by a very bright and tightly directed light. He was wearing his jeans but no shirt or socks.

"Hello," she said.

He turned sharply, then smiled. "Oh, hey Kylie. Have a nice rest?"

"I'm thirsty."

He got up and fetched her a half-depleted bottle of water from the refrigerator. While he was doing that she noticed her locator in pieces on the desk.

"We don't need that anymore," she said, pointing.

"I was just curious. I can put it back together, no problem."

"I don't care about it." She lay back on the pillows and closed her eyes.

"Kylie?"

"Hmmm?" She kept her eyes closed.

"Who are you? Really."

"I'm your spooky girl."

"Besides that."

She opened her eyes. "Don't spoil it. Please don't."

"Spoil what?"

"This. Us. Now. It's all that matters."

Rain ticked against the window. It would continue all night, a long, cleansing rain. Water that anybody could catch in a cup and drink if they wanted to—water out of the sky.

Toby took his pants down and slipped under the sheet next to her, his body heat like a magnetic field that drew her against him. She pressed her cheek to his chest. His heart beat calmly.

"Everything's perfect," she said.

"Yeah." He didn't sound that certain.

"What's the matter?"

"Nothing," he said. "Only—this is all pretty fast. Don't you think we should know more about each other?"

"Why? Now is what matters."

"Yeah, but I mean, what do you do? Where do you live? Basic stuff. Big stuff, too, like do you believe in God or who'd you vote for for president?"

"I want to go for a long walk in the rain. I want to feel it on my face and not be afraid or sick."

"What do you mean?"

"You're spoiling it. Please, let's make every second happy. Make it a day we'd want to relive a thousand times."

"I don't want to live *any* day a thousand times."

"Let's walk now."

"What's the hurry?"

She got out of bed and started dressing, her back to him.

"Don't be mad," he said.

"I'm not mad."

"You are."

She turned to him, buttoning her shirt. "Don't tell me what I am."

"Sorry."

"You practically sleepwalk through the most important day of your life."

"I'm not sleepwalking."

"Don't you even want to fall in love with me?"

He laughed uncertainly. "I don't even know your name."

"You know it. Kylie."

"I mean your last name."

"It doesn't matter."

"It matters to me," Toby said. "You matter to me."

Finished with her shirt, she sat on the edge of the bed to lace her shoes. "No you don't," she said. "You only care about me if you can know all about my past and our future. You can't live one day well and be happy."

"Now you sound like Hemingway."

"I don't know what that means and I don't care." She shrugged into her parka.

"Where are you going?"

"For a walk. I *told* you what I wanted."

"Yeah, I guess I was too ignorant to absorb it."

She slammed the door on her way out.

She stood under the pumpkin-colored light of the street lamp, confused, face tilted up to be anointed by the rain. Was he watching her from the apartment window, his heart about to break? She waited and waited. This is the part where he would run to her and embrace her and kiss her and tell her that he loved, loved, loved her.

He didn't come out.

She stared at the brick building checkered with light and dark apartment windows, not certain which one was his.

He didn't come out, and it was spoiled.

A bus rumbled between her and the building, pale indifferent faces inside.

Kylie walked in the rain. It was not poison but it was cold and, after a while, unpleasant. She pulled her hood up and walked with her head down. The wet sidewalk was a palette of neon smears. Her fingers touched the shape of the explosive in her pocket. She could find the building with the papered windows. Even if the Tourists tried to stop her she might still get inside and destroy the Eternity Core. It's what her mother wanted, what the Old Men wanted. But what if they caught her? If she remained in the loop through an entire cycle she would become a permanent part of it. She couldn't stand that, not the way she hurt right now. She didn't know what time it was. She didn't know the *time*. She had to reach her scutter and get out.

A horn went off practically at her elbow. Startled, she looked up. A low and wide vehicle, a boy leaning out the passenger window, smirking.

"Hey, you wanna go for a ride?"

"No."

"Then fuck you, hitch!" He cackled, and the vehicle accelerated away, ripping the air into jagged splinters.

She walked faster. The streets were confusing. She was lost. Her panic intensified. Why couldn't he have come after her and be sorry and love her? But it wasn't like the best parts of the movies. Some of it was good, but a lot of it wasn't. Maybe her mother had been right. But Kylie didn't believe in souls, so wasn't it better to have one day forever than no days? Wasn't it?

Fuck you, bitch.

She turned around and ran back in the direction from which she'd come. At first she didn't think she could find it, but there it was, the apartment building! And Toby was coming out the lobby door, pulling his jacket closed. He saw her, and she ran to him. He didn't mean it and she didn't mean it, and this was the part where they made up, and then all the rest of the loop would be good—the good time after making up. You had to mix the good and bad. The bad made the good better. She ran to him and hugged him, the smell of the wet leather so strong.

"You were coming after me," she said.

He didn't say anything.

"You were," she said.

"Yeah."

Something clutched at her heart. "It's the best day ever," she said.

"I give it a seven point five."

"You don't know anything," she said. "You got your spooky girl and you had an adventure and you saved the whole world."

"When you put it that way it's a nine. So come on. I'll buy you a hot drink and you can tell me about the tourists from the fifth dimension."

"What time is it?" she asked.

He looked at his watch. "Five of eleven."

"I don't want a hot drink," she said. "Can you take us some place with a nice view where we can sit in the Vee Dub?"

"You bet."

The city spread out before them. The water of Elliot Bay was black. Rain whispered against the car and the cooling engine ticked down like a slow timer. It was awkward with the separate seats, but they snuggled together, Kylie's head pillowed on his chest. He turned the radio on—not to his loud noise-music but a jazz station, like a complement to the rain. They talked, intimately. Kylie invented a life and gave it to him, borrowing from stories her mother and grandmother had told her. He called her spooky, his term of endearment, and he talked about what they would do tomorrow. She accepted the gift of the future he was giving her, but she lived in this moment, now, this sweet inhalation of the present, this happy, happy ending. Then the lights of Seattle seemed to haze over. Kylie closed her eyes, her hand on the explosive sphere, and her mind slumbered briefly in a dark spun cocoon.

Kylie punched through, and the sudden light shift dazzled her.

yellow card man

PAOLO BACIGALUPI

New writer Paolo Bacigalupi made his first sale in 1998 to *The Magazine of Fantasy & Science Fiction*, took a break from the genre for several years, and has returned to it in the new century, with new sales to *F&SF* and *Asimov's*. His story "The Calorie Man" won the Theodore Sturgeon Memorial Award, was a Hugo finalist, and appeared in our Twenty-third Annual Collection; he's also had stories in our Twenty-first and Twenty-second Annual Collections. Bacigalupi lives with his family in western Colorado, where he works for an environmental newspaper.

In the gritty and compelling story that follows, he acts as our guide to a harrowing but all-too-probable future Bangkok—one that most of us would probably rather *not* visit, but which we may be headed toward whether we like it or not.

Machetes gleam on the warehouse floor, reflecting a red conflagration of jute and tamarind and kink-springs. They're all around now. The men with their green headbands and their slogans and their wet wet blades. Their calls echo in the warehouse and on the street. Number one son is already gone. Jade Blossom he cannot find, no matter how many times he treadles her phone number. His daughters' faces have been split wide like blister rust durians.

More fires blaze. Black smoke roils around him. He runs through his warehouse offices, past computers with teak cases and iron treadles and past piles of ash where his clerks burned files through the night, obliterating the names of people who aided the Tri-Clipper.

He runs, choking on heat and smoke. In his own gracious office he dashes to the shutters and fumbles with their brass catches. He slams his shoulder against those blue shutters while the warehouse burns and brown-skinned men boil through the door and swing their slick red knives. . . .

Tranh wakes, gasping.

Sharp concrete edges jam against the knuckles of his spine. A salt-slick thigh smothers his face. He shoves away the stranger's leg. Sweat-sheened skin glimmers in the blackness, impressionistic markers for the bodies that shift and shove all around him. They fart and groan and turn, flesh on flesh, bone against bone, the living and the heat-smothered dead all together.

A man coughs. Moist lungs and spittle gust against Tranh's face. His spine and belly stick to the naked sweating flesh of the strangers around him. Claustrophobia rises. He forces it down. Forces himself to lie still, to breathe slowly, deeply, despite the heat. To taste the sweltering darkness with all the paranoia of a survivor's mind. He is awake while others sleep. He is alive while others are long dead. He forces himself to lie still, and listen.

Bicycle bells are ringing. Down below and far away, ten thousand bodies below, a lifetime away, bicycle bells chime. He claws himself out of the mass of tangled humanity, dragging his hemp sack of possessions with him. He is late. Of all the days he could be late, this is the worst possible one. He slings the bag over a bony shoulder and feels his way down the stairs, finding his footing in the cascade of sleeping flesh. He slides his sandals between families, lovers, and crouching hungry ghosts, praying that he will not slip and break an old man's bone. Step, feel, step, feel.

A curse rises from the mass. Bodies shift and roll. He steadies himself on a landing amongst the privileged who lie flat, then wades on. Downward, ever downward, round more turnings of the stair, wading down through the carpet of his countrymen. Step. Feel. Step. Feel. Another turn. A hint of gray light glimmers far below. Fresh air kisses his face, caresses his body. The waterfall of anonymous flesh resolves into individuals, men and women sprawled across one another, pillowed on hard concrete, propped on the slant of the windowless stair. Gray light turns gold. The tinkle of bicycle bells comes louder now, clear like the ring of cibiscosis chimes.

Tranh spills out of the high-rise and into a crowd of congee sellers, hemp weavers, and potato carts. He puts his hands on his knees and gasps, sucking in swirling dust and trampled street dung, grateful for every breath as sweat pours off his body. Salt jewels fall from the tip of his nose, spatter the red paving stones of the sidewalk with his moisture. Heat kills men. Kills old men. But he is out of the oven; he has not been cooked again, despite the blast furnace of the dry season.

Bicycles and their ringing bells flow past like schools of carp, commuters already on their way to work. Behind him the high-rise looms, forty stories of heat and vines and mold. A vertical ruin of broken windows and pillaged apartments. A remnant glory from the old energy Expansion now become a heated tropic coffin without air-conditioning or electricity to protect it from the glaze of the equatorial sun. Bangkok keeps its refugees in the pale blue sky, and wishes they would stay there. And yet he has emerged alive; despite the Dung Lord, despite the white shirts, despite old age, he has once again clawed his way down from the heavens.

Tranh straightens. Men stir woks of noodles and pull steamers of *baozi* from their bamboo rounds. Gray high-protein U-Tex rice gruel fills the air with the scents of rotting fish and fatty acid oils. Tranh's stomach knots with hunger and a pasty saliva coats his mouth, all that his dehydrated body can summon at the scent of food. Devil cats swirl around the vendors' legs like sharks, hoping for morsels to drop, hoping for theft opportunities. Their shimmering chameleon-like forms flit and flicker, showing calico and Siamese and orange tabby markings before fading against the backdrop of concrete and crowding hungry people that they brush against. The woks burn hard and bright with green-tinged methane, giving off new scents as rice noodles splash into hot oil. Tranh forces himself to turn away.

He shoves through the press, dragging his hemp bag along with him, ignoring who it hits and who shouts after him. Incident victims crouch in the doorways, waving severed limbs and begging from others who have a little more. Men squat on tea stools and watch the day's swelter build as they smoke tiny rolled cigarettes of scavenged gold leaf tobacco and share them from lip to lip. Women converse in knots, nervously fingering yellow cards as they wait for white shirts to appear and stamp their renewals.

Yellow card people as far as the eye can see: an entire race of people, fled to the great Thai Kingdom from Malaya where they were suddenly unwelcome. A fat clot of refugees placed under the authority of the Environment Ministry's white shirts as if they were nothing but another invasive species to be managed, like cibiscosis, blister rust, and genehack weevil. Yellow cards, yellow men. *Huang ren* all around, and Tranh is late for his one opportunity to climb out of their mass. One opportunity in all his months as a yellow card Chinese refugee. And now he is late. He squeezes past a rat seller, swallowing another rush of saliva at the scent of roasted flesh, and rushes down an alley to the water pump. He stops short.

Ten others stand in line before him: old men, young women, mothers, boys.

He slumps. He wants to rage at the setback. If he had the energy—if he had eaten well yesterday or the day before or even the day before that he would scream, would throw his hemp bag on the street and stamp on it until it turned to dust—but his calories are too few. It is just another opportunity squandered, thanks to the ill luck of the stairwells. He should have given the last of his baht to the Dung Lord and rented body-space in an apartment with windows facing east so that he could see the rising sun, and wake early.

But he was cheap. Cheap with his money. Cheap with his future. How many times did he tell his sons that spending money to make more money was perfectly acceptable? But the timid yellow card refugee that he has become counseled him to save his baht. Like an ignorant peasant mouse he clutched his cash to himself and slept in pitch-black stairwells. He should have stood like a tiger and braved the night curfew and the ministry's white shirts and their black batons. . . . And now he is late and reeks of the stairwells and stands behind ten others, all of whom must drink and fill a bucket and brush their teeth with the brown water of the Chao Phraya River.

There was a time when he demanded punctuality of his employees, of his wife, of his sons and concubines, but it was when he owned a spring-wound wristwatch and could gaze at its steady sweep of minutes and hours. Every so often, he could wind its tiny spring, and listen to it tick, and lash his sons for their lazy attitudes. He has become old and slow and stupid or he would have foreseen this. Just as he should have foreseen the rising militancy of the Green Headbands. When did his mind become so slack?

One by one, the other refugees finish their ablutions. A mother with gap teeth and blooms of gray *fa' gan* fringe behind her ears tops her bucket, and Tranh slips forward.

He has no bucket. Just the bag. The precious bag. He hangs it beside the pump and wraps his sarong more tightly around his hollow hips before he squats under the pump head. With a bony arm he yanks the pump's handle. Ripe brown water gushes over him. The river's blessing. His skin droops off his body with the weight of the water, sagging like the flesh of a shaved cat. He opens his mouth and drinks the gritty water, rubs his teeth with a finger, wondering what protozoa he may swallow. It doesn't matter. He trusts luck, now. It's all he has.

Children watch him bathe his old body while their mothers scavenge through PurCal mango peels and Red Star tamarind hulls hoping to find some bit of fruit not tainted with cibiscosis.111mt.6. . . . Or is it 111mt.7? Or mt.8? There was a time when he knew all the bio-engineered plagues that ailed them. Knew when a crop was about to fail, and whether new seedstock had been ripped. Profited from the knowledge by filling his clipper ships with the right seeds and produce. But that was a lifetime ago.

His hands are shaking as he opens his bag and pulls out his clothes. Is it old age or excitement that makes him tremble? Clean clothes. Good clothes. A rich man's white linen suit.

The clothes were not his, but now they are, and he has kept them safe. Safe for this opportunity, even when he desperately wanted to sell them for cash or wear them as his other clothes turned to rags. He drags the trousers up his bony legs, stepping out of his sandals and balancing one foot at a time. He begins buttoning the shirt, hurrying his fingers as a voice in his head reminds him that time is slipping away.

"Selling those clothes? Going to parade them around until someone with meat on his bones buys them off you?"

Tranh glances up—he shouldn't need to look; he should know the voice—and yet he looks anyway. He can't help himself. Once he was a tiger. Now he is nothing but a frightened little mouse who jumps and twitches at every hint of danger. And there it is: Ma. Standing before him, beaming. Fat and beaming. As vital as a wolf.

Ma grins. "You look like a wire-frame mannequin at Palawan Plaza."

"I wouldn't know. I can't afford to shop there." Tranh keeps putting on his clothes.

"Those are nice enough to come from Palawan. How did you get them?"

Tranh doesn't answer.

"Who are you fooling? Those clothes were made for a man a thousand times your size."

"We can't all be fat and lucky." Tranh's voice comes out as a whisper. Did he always whisper? Was he always such a rattletrap corpse whispering and sighing at every threat? He doesn't think so. But it's hard for him to remember what a tiger should sound like. He tries again, steadying his voice. "We can't all be as lucky as Ma Ping who lives on the top floors with the Dung King himself." His words still come out like reeds shushing against concrete.

"Lucky?" Ma laughs. So young. So pleased with himself. "I earn my fate. Isn't that what you always used to tell me? That luck has nothing to do with success? That men make their own luck?" He laughs again. "And now look at you."

Tranh grits his teeth. "Better men than you have fallen." Still the awful timid whisper.

"And better men than you are on the rise." Ma's fingers dart to his wrist. They stroke a wristwatch, a fine chronograph, ancient, gold and diamonds—Rolex. From an earlier time. A different place. A different world. Tranh stares stupidly, like a hypnotized snake. He can't tear his eyes away.

Ma smiles lazily. "You like it? I found it in an antique shop near Wat Rajapradit. It seemed familiar."

Tranh's anger rises. He starts to reply, then shakes his head and says nothing. Time is passing. He fumbles with his final buttons, pulls on the coat and runs his fingers through the last surviving strands of his lank gray hair. If he had a comb . . . He grimaces. It is stupid to wish. The clothes are enough. They have to be.

Ma laughs. "Now you look like a Big Name."

Ignore him, says the voice inside Tranh's head. Tranh pulls his last paltry baht out of his hemp bag—the money he saved by sleeping in the stairwells, and which has now made him so late—and shoves it into his pockets.

"You seem rushed. Do you have an appointment somewhere?"

Tranh shoves past, trying not to flinch as he squeezes around Ma's bulk.

Ma calls after him, laughing. "Where are you headed, Mr. Big Name? Mr. Three Prosperities! Do you have some intelligence you'd like to share with the rest of us?"

Others look up at the shout: hungry yellow card faces, hungry yellow card mouths. Yellow card people as far as the eye can see, and all of them looking at him now. Incident survivors. Men. Women. Children. Knowing him, now. Recognizing his legend. With a change of clothing and a single shout he has risen from obscurity. Their mocking calls pour down like a monsoon rain:

"*Wei!* Mr. Three Prosperities! Nice shirt!"

"Share a smoke, Mr. Big Name!"

"Where are you going so fast all dressed up?"

"Getting married?"

"Getting a tenth wife?"

"Got a job?"

"Mr. Big Name! Got a job for me?"

"Where you going? Maybe we should all follow Old Multinational!"

Tranh's neck prickles. He shakes off the fear. Even if they follow it will be too late for them to take advantage. For the first time in half a year, the advantage of skills and knowledge are on his side. Now there is only time.

He jogs through Bangkok's morning press as bicycles and cycle rickshaws and spring-wound scooters stream past. Sweat drenches him. It soaks his good shirt, damps even his jacket. He takes it off and slings it over an arm. His gray hair clings to his egg-bald liver-spotted skull, waterlogged. He pauses every other block to walk and recover his breath as his shins begin to ache and his breath comes in gasps and his old man's heart hammers in his chest.

He should spend his baht on a cycle rickshaw but he can't make himself do it. He is late. But perhaps he is too late? And if he is too late, the extra baht will be wasted and he will starve tonight. But then, what good is a suit soaked with sweat?

Clothes make the man, he told his sons; the first impression is the most important. Start well, and you start ahead. Of course you can win someone with your skills and your knowledge but people are animals first. Look good. Smell good. Satisfy their first senses. Then when they are well disposed toward you, make your proposal.

Isn't that why he beat Second Son when he came home with a red tattoo of a tiger on his shoulder, as though he was some calorie gangster? Isn't that why he paid a tooth doctor to twist even his daughters' teeth with cultured bamboo and rubber curves from Singapore so that they were as straight as razors?

And isn't that why the Green Headbands in Malaya hated us Chinese? Because we looked so good? Because we looked so rich? Because we spoke so well and worked so hard when they were lazy and we sweated every day?

Tranh watches a pack of spring-wound scooters flit past, all of them Thai-Chinese manufactured. Such clever fast things—a megajoule kink-spring and a fly-wheel, pedals and friction brakes to regather kinetic energy. And all their factories owned 100 percent by Chiu Chow Chinese. And yet no Chiu Chow blood runs in the gutters of this country. These Chiu Chow Chinese are loved, despite the fact that they came to the Thai Kingdom as *farang*.

If we had assimilated in Malaya like the Chiu Chow did here, would we have survived?

Tranh shakes his head at the thought. It would have been impossible. His clan would have had to convert to Islam as well, and forsake all their ancestors in Hell. It would have been impossible. Perhaps it was his people's karma to be destroyed. To stand tall and dominate the cities of Penang and Malacca and all the western coast of the Malayan Peninsula for a brief while, and then to die.

Clothes make the man. Or kill him. Tranh understands this, finally. A white tailored suit from Hwang Brothers is nothing so much as a target. An antique piece of gold mechanization swinging on your wrist is nothing if not bait. Tranh wonders if his sons' perfect teeth still lie in the ashes of Three Prosperities' warehouses, if their lovely timepieces now attract sharks and crabs in the holds of his scuttled clipper ships.

He should have known. Should have seen the rising tide of bloodthirsty subsects and intensifying nationalism. Just as the man he followed two months ago should have known that fine clothes were no protection. A man in good clothes, a yellow card to boot, should have known that he was nothing but a bit of bloodied bait before a Komodo lizard. At least the stupid melon didn't bleed on his fancy clothes when the white shirts were done with him. That one had no habit of survival. He forgot that he was no longer a Big Name.

But Tranh is learning. As he once learned tides and depth charts, markets and bio-engineered plagues, profit maximization and how to balance the dragon's gate, he now learns from the devil cats who molt and fade from sight, who flee their hunters at the first sign of danger. He learns from the crows and kites who live so well on scavenge. These are the animals he must emulate. He must discard the reflexes of a tiger. There are no tigers except in zoos. A tiger is always hunted and killed. But a small animal, a scavenging animal, has a chance to strip the bones of a tiger and walk away with the last Hwang Brothers suit that will ever cross the border from Malaya. With the Hwang clan all dead and the Hwang patterns all burned, nothing is left except memories and antiques, and one scavenging old man who knows the power and the peril of good appearance.

An empty cycle rickshaw coasts past. The rickshaw man looks back at Tranh, eyes questioning, attracted by the Hwang Brothers fabrics that flap off Tranh's skinny frame. Tranh raises a tentative hand. The cycle rickshaw slows.

Is it a good risk? To spend his last security so frivolously?

There was the time when he sent clipper fleets across the ocean to Chennai with great stinking loads of durians because he guessed that the Indians had not had time to plant resistant crop strains before the new blister rust mutations swept over them. A time when he bought black tea and sandalwood from the river men on the chance that he could sell it in the South. Now he can't decide if he should ride or walk. What a pale man he has become! Sometimes he wonders if he is actually a hungry ghost, trapped between worlds and unable to escape one way or the other.

The cycle rickshaw coasts ahead, the rider's blue jersey shimmering in the tropic sun, waiting for a decision. Tranh waves him away. The rickshaw man stands on his pedals, sandals flapping against callused heels, and accelerates.

Panic seizes Tranh. He raises his hand again, chases after the rickshaw. "Wait!" His voice comes out as a whisper.

The rickshaw slips into traffic, joining bicycles and the massive shambling shapes of elephantine megodonts. Tranh lets his hand fall, obscurely grateful that the rickshaw man hasn't heard, that the decision of spending his last baht has been made by some force larger than himself.

All around him, the morning press flows. Hundreds of children in their sailor suit uniforms stream through school gates. Saffron-robed monks stroll under the shade of wide black umbrellas. A man with a conical bamboo hat watches him and then mutters quietly to his friend. They both study him. A trickle of fear runs up Tranh's spine.

They are all around him, as they were in Malacca. In his own mind, he calls them foreigners, *farang*. And yet it is he who is the foreigner here. The creature that doesn't belong. And they know it. The women hanging sarongs on the wires of their balconies, the men sitting barefoot while they drink sugared coffee. The fish sellers and curry men. They all know it, and Tranh can barely control his terror.

Bangkok is not Malacca, he tells himself. Bangkok is not Penang. We have no wives, or gold wristwatches with diamonds, or clipper fleets to steal anymore. Ask the snakeheads who abandoned me in the leech jungles of the border. They have all my wealth. I have nothing. I am no tiger. I am safe.

For a few seconds he believes it. But then a teak-skinned boy chops the top off a coconut with a rusty machete and offers it to Tranh with a smile and it's all Tranh can do not to scream and run.

Bangkok is not Malacca. They will not burn your warehouses or slash your clerks into chunks of shark bait. He wipes sweat off his face. Perhaps he should have waited to wear the suit. It draws too much attention. There are too many people looking at him. Better to fade like a devil cat and slink across the city in safe anonymity, instead of strutting around like a peacock.

Slowly the streets change from palm-lined boulevards to the open wastelands of the new foreigners' quarter. Tranh hurries toward the river, heading deeper into the manufacturing empire of white *farang*.

Gweilo, yang guizi, farang. So many words in so many languages for these translucent-skinned sweating monkeys. Two generations ago when the petroleum ran out and the *gweilo* factories shut down, everyone assumed they were gone for good. And now they are back. The monsters of the past returned, with new toys and new technologies. The nightmares his mother threatened him with, invading Asiatic coasts. Demons truly; never dead.

And he goes to worship them: the ilk of AgriGen and PurCal with their monopolies on U-Tex rice and Total Nutrient Wheat; the blood-brothers of the bio-engineers who gene-ripped devil cats from storybook inspiration and set them loose in the world to breed and breed and breed; the sponsors of the Intellectual Property Police who used to board his clipper fleets in search of IP infringements, hunting like wolves for unstamped calories and gene-ripped grains as though their engineered plagues of cibiscosis and blister rust weren't enough to keep their profits high. . . .

Ahead of him, a crowd has formed. Tranh frowns. He starts to run, then forces himself back to a walk. Better not to waste his calories, now. A line has already formed in front of the foreign devil Tennyson Brothers' factory. It stretches almost a *li*, snaking around the corner, past the bicycle gear logo in the wrought-iron gate of Sukhumvit Research Corporation, past the intertwined dragons of PurCal East Asia, and past Mishimoto & Co., the clever Japanese fluid dynamics company that Tranh once sourced his clipper designs from.

Mishimoto is full of windup import workers, they say. Full of illegal gene-ripped bodies that walk and talk and totter about in their herky-jerky way—and take rice from real men's bowls. Creatures with as many as eight arms like the Hindu gods, creatures with no legs so they cannot run away, creatures with eyes as large as teacups that can only see a bare few feet ahead of them but inspect everything with enormous magnified curiosity. But no one can see inside, and if the Environment Ministry's white shirts know, then the clever Japanese are paying them well to ignore their crimes against biology and religion. It is perhaps the only thing a good Buddhist and a good Muslim and even the *farang* Grahamite Christians can agree on: windups have no souls.

When Tranh bought Mishimoto's clipper ships so long ago, he didn't care. Now he wonders if behind their high gates, windup monstrosities labor while yellow cards stand outside and beg.

Tranh trudges down the line. Policemen with clubs and spring guns patrol the hopefuls, making jokes about *farang* who wish to work for *farang*. Heat beats down, merciless on the men lined up before the gate.

"Wah! You look like a pretty bird with those clothes."

Tranh starts. Li Shen and Hu Laoshi and Lao Xia stand in the line, clustered together. A trio of old men as pathetic as himself. Hu waves a newly rolled cigarette in invitation, motioning him to join them. Tranh nearly shakes at the sight of the tobacco, but forces himself to refuse it. Three times Hu offers, and finally Tranh allows himself to accept, grateful that Hu is in earnest, and wondering where Hu has found this sudden wealth. But then, Hu has a little more strength than the rest of them. A cart man earns more if he works as fast as Hu.

Tranh wipes the sweat off his brow. "A lot of applicants."

They all laugh at Tranh's dismay.

Hu lights the cigarette for Tranh. "You thought you knew a secret, maybe?"

Tranh shrugs and draws deeply, passes the cigarette to Lao Xia. "A rumor. Potato God said his elder brother's son had a promotion. I thought there might be a niche down below, in the slot the nephew left behind."

Hu grins. "That's where I heard it, too. 'Eee. He'll be rich. Manage fifteen clerks. Eee! He'll be rich.' I thought I might be one of the fifteen."

"At least the rumor was true," Lao Xia says. "And not just Potato God's nephew promoted, either." He scratches the back of his head, a convulsive movement like a dog fighting fleas. *Fa' gan*'s gray fringe stains the crooks of his elbows and peeps from the sweaty pockets behind his ears where his hair has receded. He sometimes jokes about it: nothing a little money can't fix. A good joke. But today he is scratching and the skin behind his ears is cracked and raw. He notices everyone watching and yanks his hand down. He grimaces and passes the cigarette to Li Shen.

"How many positions?" Tranh asks.

"Three. Three clerks."

Tranh grimaces. "My lucky number."

Li Shen peers down the line with his bottle-thick glasses. "Too many of us, I think, even if your lucky number is 555."

Lao Xia laughs. "Amongst the four of us, there are already too many." He taps the man standing in line just ahead of them. "Uncle. What was your profession before?"

The stranger looks back, surprised. He was a distinguished gentleman, once, by his scholar's collar, by his fine leather shoes now scarred and blackened with scavenged charcoal. "I taught physics."

Lao Xia nods. "You see? We're all overqualified. I oversaw a rubber plantation. Our own professor has degrees in fluid dynamics and materials design. Hu was a fine doctor. And then there is our friend of the Three Prosperities. Not a trading company at all. More like a multinational." He tastes the words. Says them again, "Multinational." A strange, powerful, seductive sound.

Tranh ducks his head, embarrassed. "You're too kind."

"*Fang pi.*" Hu takes a drag on his cigarette, keeps it moving. "You were the richest of us all. And now here we are, old men scrambling for young men's jobs. Every one of us ten thousand times overqualified."

The man behind them interjects, "I was executive legal counsel for Standard & Commerce."

Lao Xia makes a face. "Who cares, dog fucker? You're nothing now."

The banking lawyer turns away, affronted. Lao Xia grins, sucks hard on the hand-rolled cigarette and passes it again to Tranh. Hu nudges Tranh's elbow as he starts to take a puff. "Look! There goes old Ma."

Tranh looks over, exhales smoke sharply. For a moment he thinks Ma has followed him, but no. It is just coincidence. They are in the *farang* factory district. Ma works for the foreign devils, balancing their books. A kink-spring company. Springlife. Yes, Springlife. It is natural that Ma should be here, comfortably riding to work behind a sweating cycle-rickshaw man.

"Ma Ping," Li Shen says. "I heard he's living on the top floor now. Up there with the Dung Lord himself."

Tranh scowls. "I fired him, once. Ten thousand years ago. Lazy and an embezzler."

"He's so fat."

"I've seen his wife," Hu says. "And his sons. They both have fat on them. They eat meat every night. The boys are fatter than fat. Full of U-Tex proteins."

"You're exaggerating."

"Fatter than us."

Lao Xia scratches a rib. "Bamboo is fatter than you."

Tranh watches Ma Ping open a factory door and slip inside. The past is past. Dwelling on the past is madness. There is nothing for him there. There are no wristwatches, no concubines, no opium pipes or jade sculptures of Quan Yin's merciful form. There are no pretty clipper ships slicing into port with fortunes in their holds. He shakes his head and offers the nearly spent cigarette to Hu so that he can recover the last tobacco for later use. There is nothing for him in the past. Ma is in the past. Three Prosperities Trading Company is the past. The sooner he remembers this, the sooner he will climb out of this awful hole.

From behind him, a man calls out, "Wei! Baldy! When did you cut the line? Go to the back! You line up, like the rest of us!"

"Line up?" Lao Xia shouts back. "Don't be stupid!" He waves at the line ahead. "How many hundreds are ahead of us? It won't make any difference where he stands."

Others begin to attend to the man's complaint. Complain as well. "Line up! Pai dui! Pai dui!" The disturbance increases and police start down the line, casually swinging their batons. They aren't white shirts, but they have no love for hungry yellow cards.

Tranh makes placating motions to the crowd and Lao Xia. "Of course. Of course. I'll line up. It's of no consequence." He makes his farewells and plods his way down the winding yellow card snake, seeking its distant tail.

Everyone is dismissed long before he reaches it.

A scavenging night. A starving night. Tranh hunts through dark alleys, avoiding the vertical prison heat of the towers. Devil cats seethe and scatter ahead of him in rippling waves. The lights of the methane lamps flicker, burn low and snuff themselves, blackening the city. Hot velvet darkness fetid with rotting fruit swaddles him. The heavy humid air sags. Still sweltering darkness. Empty market stalls. On a street corner, theater men turn in stylized cadences to stories of Ravana. On a thoroughfare, swingshift megodonts shuffle homeward like gray mountains, their massed shadows led by the gold trim glitter of union handlers.

In the alleys, children with bright silver knives hunt unwary yellow cards and drunken Thais, but Tranh is wise to their feral ways. A year ago, he would not have seen them, but he has the paranoid's gift of survival now. Creatures like them are no worse than sharks: easy to predict, easy to avoid. It is not these obviously feral hunters who churn Tranh's guts with fear, it is the chameleons, the everyday people who work and shop and smile and *wai* so pleasantly—and riot without warning—who terrify Tranh.

He picks through the trash heaps, fighting devil cats for signs of food, wishing he was fast enough to catch and kill one of those nearly invisible felines. Picking up discarded mangos, studying them carefully with his old man's eyes, holding them close and then far away, sniffing at them, feeling their blister rusted exteriors and then tossing them aside when they show red mottle in their guts. Some of them still smell good, but even crows won't accept such a taint. They would eagerly peck apart a bloated corpse, but they will not feed on blister rust.

Down the street, the Dung Lord's lackeys shovel the day's animal leavings into sacks and throw them into tricycle carriers: the night harvest. They watch him suspiciously. Tranh keeps his eyes averted, avoiding challenge, and scuffles on. He has nothing to cook on an illegally stolen shit fire anyway, and nowhere to sell manure on the black market. The Dung Lord's monopoly is too strong. Tranh wonders how it might be to find a place in the dung shovelers' union, to know that his survival was guaranteed feeding the composters of Bangkok's methane reclamation plants. But it is an opium dream; no yellow card can slither into that closed club.

Tranh lifts another mango and freezes. He bends low, squinting. Pushes aside broadsheet complaints against the Ministry of Trade and handbills calling for a new gold-sheathed River Wat. He pushes aside black slime banana peels and burrows into the garbage. Below it all, stained and torn but still legible, he finds a portion of what was once a great advertising board that perhaps stood over this marketplace:— *ogistics. Shipping. Tradin*—and behind the words, the glorious silhouette of Dawn Star: one part of Three Prosperities' Tri-Clipper logo, running before the wind as fast and sleek as a shark: a high-tech image of palm-oil spun polymers and sails as sharp and white as a gull's.

Tranh turns his face away, overcome. It's like unearthing a grave and finding himself within. His pride. His blindness. From a time when he thought he might compete with the foreign devils and become a shipping magnate. A Li Ka Shing or a reborn Richard Kuok for the New Expansion. Rebuild the pride of Nanyang Chinese shipping and trading. And here, like a slap in the face, a portion of his ego, buried in rot and blister rust and devil cat urine.

He searches around, pawing for more portions of the sign, wondering if anyone treadles a phone call to that old phone number, if the secretary whose wages he once paid is still at his desk, working for a new master, a native Malay perhaps, with impeccable pedigree and religion. Wondering if the few clippers he failed to scuttle still ply the seas and islands of the archipelago. He forces himself to stop his search. Even if he had the money he would not treadle that number. Would not waste the calories. Could not stand the loss again.

He straightens, scattering devil cats who have slunk close. There is nothing here in this market except rinds and unshoveled dung. He has wasted his calories once again. Even the cockroaches and the blood beetles have been eaten. If he searches for a dozen hours, he will still find nothing. Too many people have come before, picking at these bones.

Three times he hides from white shirts as he makes his way home, three times ducking into shadows as they strut past. Cringing as they wander close, cursing his white
linen suit that shows so clearly in darkness. By the third time, superstitious fear runs
hot in his veins. His rich man's clothes seem to attract the patrols of the Environment Ministry, seem to hunger for the wearer's death. Black batons twirl from casual
hands no more than inches away from his face. Spring guns glitter silver in the darkness. His hunters stand so close that he can count the wicked bladed disk cartridges
in their jute bandoliers. A white shirt pauses and pisses in the alley where Tranh
crouches, and only fails to see him because his partner stands on the street and
wants to check the permits of the dung gatherers.

Each time, Tranh stifles his panicked urge to tear off his too-rich clothes and sink
into safe anonymity. It is only a matter of time before the white shirts catch him. Before they swing their black clubs and make his Chinese skull a mash of blood and
bone. Better to run naked through the hot night than strut like a peacock and die.
And yet he cannot quite abandon the cursed suit. Is it pride? Is it stupidity? He keeps
it though, even as its arrogant cut turns his bowels watery with fear.

By the time he reaches home, even the gas lights on the main thoroughfares of
Sukhumvit Road and Rama IV are blackened. Outside the Dung Lord's tower,
street stalls still burn woks for the few laborers lucky enough to have night work and
curfew dispensations. Pork tallow candles flicker on the tables. Noodles splash into
hot woks with a sizzle. White shirts stroll past, their eyes on the seated yellow cards,
ensuring that none of the foreigners brazenly sleep in the open air and sully the side-
walks with their snoring presence.

Tranh joins the protective loom of the towers, entering the nearly extra-territorial
safety of the Dung Lord's influence. He stumbles toward the doorways and the swelter of the high rise, wondering how high he will be forced to climb before he can
shove a niche for himself on the stairwells.

"You didn't get the job, did you?"

Tranh cringes at the voice. It's Ma Ping again, sitting at a sidewalk table, a bottle
of Mekong whiskey beside his hand. His face is flushed with alcohol, as bright as a
red paper lantern. Half-eaten plates of food lie strewn around his table. Enough to
feed five others, easily.

Images of Ma war in Tranh's head: the young clerk he once sent packing for being too clever with an abacus, the man whose son is fat, the man who got out early,
the man who begged to be rehired at Three Prosperities, the man who now struts
around Bangkok with Tranh's last precious possession on his wrist—the one item
that even the snakeheads didn't steal. Tranh thinks that truly fate is cruel, placing
him in such proximity to one he once considered so far beneath him.

Despite his intention to show bravado, once again Tranh's words come out as a
mousy whisper. "What do you care?"

Ma shrugs, pours whiskey for himself. "I wouldn't have noticed you in the line,
without that suit." He nods at Tranh's sweat-damp clothing. "Good idea to dress up.
Too far back in line, though."

Tranh wants to walk away, to ignore the arrogant whelp, but Ma's leavings of
steamed bass and *laap* and U-Tex rice noodles lie tantalizingly close. He thinks he

smells pork and can't help salivating. His gums ache for the idea that he could chew meat again and he wonders if his teeth would accept the awful luxury. . . .

Abruptly, Tranh realizes that he has been staring. That he has stood for some time, ogling the scraps of Ma's meal. And Ma is watching him. Tranh flushes and starts to turn away.

Ma says, "I didn't buy your watch to spite you, you know."

Tranh stops short. "Why then?"

Ma's fingers stray to the gold and diamond bauble, then seem to catch themselves. He reaches for his whiskey glass instead. "I wanted a reminder." He takes a swallow of liquor and sets the glass back amongst his piled plates with the deliberate care of a drunk. He grins sheepishly. His fingers are again stroking the watch, a guilty furtive movement. "I wanted a reminder. Against ego."

Tranh spits. *"Fang pi."*

Ma shakes his head vigorously. "No! It's true." He pauses. "Anyone can fall. If the Three Prosperities can fall, then I can. I wanted to remember that." He takes another pull on his whiskey. "You were right to fire me."

Tranh snorts. "You didn't think so then."

"I was angry. I didn't know that you'd saved my life, then." He shrugs. "I would never have left Malaya if you hadn't fired me. I would never have seen the Incident coming. I would have had too much invested in staying." Abruptly, he pulls himself upright and motions for Tranh to join him. "Come. Have a drink. Have some food. I owe you that much. You saved my life. I've repaid you poorly. Sit."

Tranh turns away. "I don't despise myself so much."

"Do you love face so much that you can't take a man's food? Don't be stuck in your bones. I don't care if you hate me. Just take my food. Curse me later, when your belly is full."

Tranh tries to control his hunger, to force himself to walk away, but he can't. He knows men who might have enough face to starve before accepting Ma's scraps, but he isn't one of them. A lifetime ago, he might have been. But the humiliations of his new life have taught him much about who he really is. He has no sweet illusions now. He sits. Ma beams and pushes his half-eaten dishes across the table.

Tranh thinks he must have done something grave in a former life to merit this humiliation, but still he has to fight the urge to bury his hands in the oily food and eat with bare fingers. Finally, the owner of the sidewalk stall brings a pair of chopsticks for the noodles, and fork and spoon for the rest. Noodles and ground pork slide down his throat. He tries to chew, but as soon as the food touches his tongue he gulps it down. More food follows. He lifts a plate to his lips, shoveling down the last of Ma's leavings. Fish and lank coriander and hot thick oil slip down like blessings.

"Good. Good." Ma waves at the night stall man and a whiskey glass is quickly rinsed and handed to him.

The sharp scent of liquor floats around Ma like an aura as he pours. Tranh's chest tightens at the scent. Oil coats his chin where he has made a mess in his haste. He wipes his mouth against his arm, watching the amber liquid splash into the glass.

Tranh once drank Cognac: XO. Imported by his own clippers. Fabulously expensive stuff with its shipping costs. A flavor of the foreign devils from before the

Contraction. A ghost from Utopian history, reinvigorated by the new Expansion and his own realization that the world was once again growing smaller. With new hull designs and polymer advances, his clipper ships navigated the globe and returned with the stuff of legends. And his Malay buyers were happy to purchase it, whatever their religion. What a profit that had been. He forces down the thought as Ma shoves the glass across to Tranh and then raises his own in toast. It is in the past. It is all in the past.

They drink. The whiskey burns warm in Tranh's belly, joining the chilis and fish and pork and the hot oil of the fried noodles.

"It really is too bad you didn't get that job."

Tranh grimaces. "Don't gloat. Fate has a way of balancing itself. I've learned that."

Ma waves a hand. "I don't gloat. There are too many of us, that's the truth. You were ten thousand times qualified for that job. For any job." He takes a sip of his whiskey, peers over its rim at Tranh. "Do you remember when you called me a lazy cockroach?"

Tranh shrugs; he can't take his eyes off the whiskey bottle. "I called you worse than that." He waits to see if Ma will refill his cup again. Wondering how rich he is, and how far this largesse will go. Hating that he plays beggar to a boy he once refused to keep as a clerk, and who now lords over him . . . and who now, in a show of face, pours Tranh's whiskey to the top, letting it spill over in an amber cascade under the flickering light of the candles.

Ma finishes pouring, stares at the puddle he has created. "Truly the world is turned upside down. The young lord over the old. The Malays pinch out the Chinese. And the foreign devils return to our shores like bloated fish after a *ku-shui* epidemic." Ma smiles. "You need to keep your ears up, and be aware of opportunities. Not like all those old men out on the sidewalk, waiting for hard labor. Find a new niche. That's what I did. That's why I've got my job."

Tranh grimaces. "You came at a more fortuitous time." He rallies, emboldened by a full belly and the liquor warming his face and limbs. "Anyway, you shouldn't be too proud. You still stink of mother's milk as far as I'm concerned, living in the Dung Lord's tower. You're only the Lord of Yellow Cards. And what is that, really? You haven't climbed as high as my ankles yet, Mr. Big Name."

Ma's eyes widen. He laughs. "No. Of course not. Someday, maybe. But I am trying to learn from you." He smiles slightly and nods at Tranh's decrepit state. "Everything except this postscript."

"Is it true there are crank fans on the top floors? That it's cool up there?"

Ma glances up at the looming high-rise. "Yes. Of course. And men with the calories to wind them as well. And they haul water up for us, and men act as ballast on the elevator—up and down all day—doing favors for the Dung Lord." He laughs and pours more whiskey, motions Tranh to drink. "You're right though. It's nothing, really. A poor palace, truly.

"But it doesn't matter now. My family moves tomorrow. We have our residence permits. Tomorrow when I get paid again, we're moving out. No more yellow card for us. No more payoffs to the Dung Lord's lackeys. No more problems with the white shirts. It's all set with the Environment Ministry. We turn in our yellow cards and become Thai. We're going to be immigrants. Not just some invasive species anymore." He raises his glass. "It's why I'm celebrating."

Tranh scowls. "You must be pleased." He finishes his drink, sets the tumbler down with a thud. "Just don't forget that the nail that stands up also gets pounded down."

Ma shakes his head and grins, his eyes whiskey bright. "Bangkok isn't Malacca."

"And Malacca wasn't Bali. And then they came with their machetes and their spring guns and they stacked our heads in the gutters and sent our bodies and blood down the river to Singapore."

Ma shrugs. "It's in the past." He waves to the man at the wok, calling for more food. "We have to make a home here, now."

"You think you can? You think some white shirt won't nail your hide to his door? You can't make them like us. Our luck's against us, here."

"Luck? When did Mr. Three Prosperities get so superstitious?"

Ma's dish arrives, tiny crabs crisp-fried, salted, and hot with oil for Ma and Tranh to pick at with chopsticks and crunch between their teeth, each one no bigger than the tip of Tranh's pinkie. Ma plucks one out and crunches it down. "When did Mr. Three Prosperities get so weak? When you fired me, you said I made my own luck. And now you tell me you don't have any?" He spits on the sidewalk. "I've seen windups with more will to survive than you."

"*Fang pi.*"

"No! It's true! There's a Japanese windup girl in the bars where my boss goes." Ma leans forward. "She looks like a real woman. And she does disgusting things." He grins. "Makes your cock hard. But you don't hear her complaining about luck. Every white shirt in the city would pay to dump her in the methane composters and she's still up in her high-rise, dancing every night, in front of everyone. Her whole soulless body on display."

"It's not possible."

Ma shrugs. "Say so if you like. But I've seen her. And she isn't starving. She takes whatever spit and money come her way, and she survives. It doesn't matter about the white shirts or the Kingdom edicts or the Japan-haters or the religious fanatics; she's been dancing for months."

"How can she survive?"

"Bribes? Maybe some ugly *farang* who wallows in her filth? Who knows? No real girl would do what she does. It makes your heart stop. You forget she's a windup, when she does those things." He laughs, then glances at Tranh. "Don't talk to me about luck. There's not enough luck in the entire Kingdom to keep her alive this long. And we know it's not karma that keeps her alive. She has none."

Tranh shrugs noncommittally and shovels more crabs into his mouth.

Ma grins, "You know I'm right." He drains his whiskey glass and slams it down on the table. "We make our own luck! Our own fate. There's a windup in a public bar and I have a job with a rich *farang* who can't find his ass without my help! Of course I'm right!" He pours more whiskey. "Get over your self-pity, and climb out of your hole. The foreign devils don't worry about luck or fate, and look how they return to us, like a newly engineered virus! Even the Contraction didn't stop them. They're like another invasion of devil cats. But they make their own luck. I'm not even sure if karma exists for them. And if fools like these *farang* can succeed, then we Chinese can't be kept down for long. Men make their own luck, that's what you told me when you fired me. You said I'd made my own bad luck and only had myself to blame."

Tranh looks up at Ma. "Maybe I could work at your company." He grins, trying not to look desperate. "I could make money for your lazy boss."

Ma's eyes become hooded. "Ah. That's difficult. Difficult to say."

Tranh knows that he should take the polite rejection, that he should shut up. But even as a part of him cringes, his mouth opens again, pressing, pleading. "Maybe you need an assistant? To keep the books? I speak their devil language. I taught it to myself when I traded with them. I could be useful."

"There is little enough work for me."

"But if he is as stupid as you say—"

"Stupid, yes. But not such a stupid melon that he wouldn't notice another body in his office. Our desks are just so far apart." He makes a motion with his hands. "You think he would not notice some stick coolie man squatting beside his computer treadle?"

"In his factory, then?"

But Ma is already shaking his head. "I would help you if I could. But the megodont unions control the power, and the line inspector unions are closed to *farang*, no offense, and no one will accept that you are a materials scientist." He shakes his head. "No. There is no way."

"Any job. As a dung shoveler, even."

But Ma is shaking his head more vigorously now, and Tranh finally manages to control his tongue, to plug this diarrhea of begging. "Never mind. Never mind." He forces a grin. "I'm sure some work will turn up. I'm not worried." He takes the bottle of Mekong whiskey and refills Ma's glass, upending the bottle and finishing the whiskey despite Ma's protests.

Tranh raises his half-empty glass and toasts the young man who has bested him in all ways before throwing back the last of the alcohol in one swift swallow. Under the table, nearly invisible devil cats brush against his bony legs, waiting for him to leave, hoping that he will be foolish enough to leave scraps.

Morning dawns. Tranh wanders the streets, hunting for a breakfast he cannot afford. He threads through market alleys redolent with fish and lank green coriander and bright flares of lemongrass. Durians lie in reeking piles, their spiky skins covered with red blister rust boils. He wonders if he can steal one. Their yellow surfaces are blotched and stained, but their guts are nutritious. He wonders how much blister rust a man can consume before falling into a coma.

"You want? Special deal. Five for five baht. Good, yes?"

The woman who screeches at him has no teeth; she smiles with her gums and repeats herself. "Five for five baht." She speaks Mandarin to him, recognizing him for their common heritage though she had the luck to be born in the Kingdom and he had the misfortune to be set down in Malaya. Chiu Chow Chinese, blessedly protected by her clan and king. Tranh suppresses envy.

"More like four for four." He makes a pun of the homonyms. *Sz* for *sz*. Four for death. "They've got blister rust."

She waves a hand sourly. "Five for five. They're still good. Better than good. Picked just before." She wields a gleaming machete and chops the durian in half, revealing the clean yellow slime of its interior with its fat gleaming pits. The sickly sweet scent of fresh durian boils up and envelops them. "See! Inside good. Picked just in time. Still safe."

"I might buy one." He can't afford any. But he can't help replying. It feels too good to be seen as a buyer. It is his suit, he realizes. The Hwang Brothers have raised him in this woman's eyes. She wouldn't have spoken if not for the suit. Wouldn't have even started the conversation.

"Buy more! The more you buy, the more you save."

He forces a grin, wondering how to get away from the bargaining he should never have started. "I'm only one old man. I don't need so much."

"One skinny old man. Eat more. Get fat!"

She says this and they both laugh. He searches for a response, something to keep their comradely interaction alive, but his tongue fails him. She sees the helplessness in his eyes. She shakes her head. "Ah, grandfather. It is hard times for everyone. Too many of you all at once. No one thought it would get so bad down there."

Tranh ducks his head, embarrassed. "I've troubled you. I should go."

"Wait. Here." She offers him the durian half. "Take it."

"I can't afford it."

She makes an impatient gesture. "Take it. It's lucky for me to help someone from the old country." She grins. "And the blister rust looks too bad to sell to anyone else."

"You're kind. Buddha smile on you." But as he takes her gift he again notices the great durian pile behind her. All neatly stacked with their blotches and their bloody wheals of blister rust. Just like stacked Chinese heads in Malacca: his wife and daughters staring out at him, accusatory. He drops the durian and kicks it away, frantically scraping his hands on his jacket, trying to get the blood off his palms.

"Ai! You'll waste it!"

Tranh barely hears the woman's cry. He staggers back from the fallen durian, staring at its ragged surface. Its gut-spilled interior. He looks around wildly. He has to get out of the crowds. Has to get away from the jostling bodies and the durian reek that's all around, thick in his throat, gagging him. He puts a hand to his mouth and runs, clawing at the other shoppers, fighting through their press.

"Where you go? Come back! *Huilai!*" But the woman's words are quickly drowned. Tranh shoves through the throng, pushing aside women with shopping baskets full of white lotus root and purple eggplants, dodging farmers and their clattering bamboo hand carts, twisting past tubs of squid and serpent head fish. He pelts down the market alley like a thief identified, scrambling and dodging, running without thought or knowledge of where he is going, but running anyway, desperate to escape the stacked heads of his family and countrymen.

He runs and runs.

And bursts into the open thoroughfare of Charoen Krung Road. Powdered dung dust and hot sunlight wash over him. Cycle rickshaws clatter past. Palms and squat banana trees shimmer green in the bright open air.

As quickly as it seized him, Tranh's panic fades. He stops short, hands on his knees, catching his breath and cursing himself. *Fool. Fool. If you don't eat, you die.* He straightens and tries to turn back but the stacked durians flash in his mind and he stumbles away from the alley, gagging again. He can't go back. Can't face those bloody piles. He doubles over and his stomach heaves but his empty guts bring up nothing but strings of drool.

Finally he wipes his mouth on a Hwang Brothers sleeve and forces himself to straighten and confront the foreign faces all around. The sea of foreigners that he must learn to swim amongst, and who all call him *farang*. It repels him to think of it. And to think that in Malacca, with twenty generations of family and clan well rooted in that city, he was just as much an interloper. That his clan's esteemed history is nothing but a footnote for a Chinese expansion that has proven as transient as nighttime cool. That his people were nothing but an accidental spillage of rice on a map, now wiped up much more carefully than they were scattered down.

Tranh unloads U-Tex Brand RedSilks deep into the night, offerings to Potato God. A lucky job. A lucky moment, even if his knees have become loose and wobbly and feel as if they must soon give way. A lucky job, even if his arms are shaking from catching the heavy sacks as they come down off the megodonts. Tonight, he reaps not just pay but also the opportunity to steal from the harvest. Even if the RedSilk potatoes are small and harvested early to avoid a new sweep of scabis mold—the fourth genetic variation this year—they are still good. And their small size means their enhanced nutrition falls easily into his pockets.

Hu crouches above him, lowering down the potatoes. As the massive elephantine megodonts shuffle and grunt, waiting for their great wagons to be unloaded, Tranh catches Hu's offerings with his hand hooks and lowers the sacks the last step to the ground. Hook, catch, swing, and lower. Again and again and again.

He is not alone in his work. Women from the tower slums crowd around his ladder. They reach up and caress each sack as he lowers it to the ground. Their fingers quest along hemp and burlap, testing for holes, for slight tears, for lucky gifts. A thousand times they stroke his burdens, reverently following the seams, only drawing away when coolie men shove between them to heft the sacks and haul them to Potato God.

After the first hour of his work, Tranh's arms are shaking. After three, he can barely stand. He teeters on his creaking ladder as he lowers each new sack, and gasps and shakes his head to clear sweat from his eyes as he waits for the next one to come down.

Hu peers down from above. "Are you all right?"

Tranh glances warily over his shoulder. Potato God is watching, counting the sacks as they are carried into the warehouse. His eyes occasionally flick up to the wagons and trace across Tranh. Beyond him, fifty unlucky men watch silently from the shadows, any one of them far more observant than Potato God can ever be. Tranh straightens and reaches up to accept the next sack, trying not to think about the watching eyes. How politely they wait. How silent. How hungry. "I'm fine. Just fine."

Hu shrugs and pushes the next burlap load over the wagon's lip. Hu has the better place, but Tranh cannot resent it. One or the other must suffer. And Hu found the job. Hu has the right to the best place. To rest a moment before the next sack moves. After all, Hu collected Tranh for the job when he should have starved tonight. It is fair.

Tranh takes the sack and lowers it into the forest of waiting women's hands, releases his hooks with a twist, and drops the bag to the ground. His joints feel loose and rubbery, as if femur and tibia will skid apart at any moment. He is dizzy with heat, but he dares not ask to slow the pace.

Another potato sack comes down. Women's hands rise up like tangling strands of seaweed, touching, prodding, hungering. He cannot force them back. Even if he shouts at them they return. They are like devil cats; they cannot help themselves. He drops the sack the last few feet to the ground and reaches up for another as it comes over the wagon's lip.

As he hooks the sack, his ladder creaks and suddenly slides. It chatters down the side of the wagon, then catches abruptly. Tranh sways, juggling the potato sack, trying to regain his center of gravity. Hands are all around him, tugging at the bag, pulling, prodding. "Watch out—"

The ladder skids again. He drops like a stone. Women scatter as he plunges. He hits the ground and pain explodes in his knee. The potato sack bursts. For a moment he worries what Potato God will say but then he hears screams all around him. He rolls onto his back. Above him, the wagon is swaying, shuddering. People are shouting and fleeing. The megodont lunges forward and the wagon heaves. Bamboo ladders fall like rain, slapping the pavement with bright firecracker retorts. The beast reverses itself and the wagon skids past Tranh, grinding the ladders to splinters. It is impossibly fast, even with the wagon's weight still hampering it. The megodont's great maw opens and suddenly it is screaming, a sound as high and panicked as a human's.

All around them, other megodonts respond in a chorus. Their cacophony swamps the street. The megodont surges onto its hind legs, an explosion of muscle and velocity that breaks the wagon's traces and flips it like a toy. Men cartwheel from it, blossoms shaken from a cherry tree. Maddened, the beast rears again and kicks the wagon. Sends it skidding sidewise. It slams past Tranh, missing him by inches.

Tranh tries to rise but his leg won't work. The wagon smashes into a wall. Bamboo and teak crackle and explode, the wagon disintegrating as the megodont drags and kicks it, trying to win free completely. Tranh drags himself away from the flying wagon, hand over hand, hauling his useless leg behind him. All around, men are shouting instructions, trying to control the beast, but he doesn't look back. He focuses on the cobbles ahead, on getting out of reach. His leg won't work. It refuses him. It seems to hate him.

Finally he makes it into the shelter of a protective wall. He hauls himself upright. "I'm fine," he tells himself. "Fine." Gingerly he tests his leg, setting weight on it. It's wobbly, but he feels no real pain, not now. "*Mei wenti. Mei wenti*," he whispers. "Not a problem. Just cracked it. Not a problem."

The men are still shouting and the megodont is still screaming, but all he can see is his brittle old knee. He lets go of the wall. Takes a step, testing his weight, and collapses like a shadow puppet with strings gone slack.

Gritting his teeth, he again hauls himself up off the cobbles. He props himself against the wall, massaging his knee and watching the bedlam. Men are throwing ropes over the back of the struggling megodont, pulling it down, immobilizing it, finally. More than a score of men are working to hobble it.

The wagon's frame has shattered completely and potatoes are spilled everywhere. A thick mash coats the ground. Women scramble on their knees, clawing through the mess, fighting with one another to hoard pulped tubers. They scrape it up from the street. Some of their scavenge is stained red, but no one seems to care. Their squabbling continues. The red bloom spreads. At the blossom's center, a man's trousers protrude from the muck.

Tranh frowns. He drags himself upright again and hops on his one good leg toward the broken wagon. He catches up against its shattered frame, staring. Hu's body is a savage ruin, awash in megodont dung and potato mash. And now that Tranh is close, he can see that the struggling megodont's great gray feet are gory with his friend. Someone is calling for a doctor but it is half-hearted, a habit from a time when they were not yellow cards.

Tranh tests his weight again but his knee provides the same queer jointless failure. He catches up against the wagon's splintered planking and hauls himself back upright. He works the leg, trying to understand why it collapses. The knee bends, it doesn't even hurt particularly, but it will not support his weight. He tests it again, with the same result.

With the megodont restrained, order in the unloading area is restored. Hu's body is dragged aside. Devil cats gather near his blood pool, feline shimmers under methane glow. Their tracks pock the potato grime in growing numbers. More paw impressions appear in the muck, closing in from all directions on Hu's discarded body.

Tranh sighs. So we all go, he thinks. We all die. Even those of us who took our aging treatments and our tiger penis and kept ourselves strong are subject to the Hell journey. He promises to burn money for Hu, to ease his way in the afterlife, then catches himself and remembers that he is not the man he was. That even paper Hell Money is out of reach.

Potato God, disheveled and angry, comes and studies him. He frowns suspiciously. "Can you still work?"

"I can." Tranh tries to walk but stumbles once again and catches up against the wagon's shattered frame.

Potato God shakes his head. "I will pay you for the hours you worked." He waves to a young man, fresh and grinning from binding the megodont. "You! You're a quick one. Haul the rest of these sacks into the warehouse."

Already, other workers are lining up and grabbing loads from within the broken wagon. As the new man comes out with his first sack, his eyes dart to Tranh and then flick away, hiding his relief at Tranh's incapacity.

Potato God watches with satisfaction and heads back to the warehouse.

"Double pay," Tranh calls after Potato God's retreating back. "Give me double pay. I lost my leg for you."

The manager looks back at Tranh with pity, then glances at Hu's body and shrugs. It is an easy acquiescence. Hu will demand no reparation.

It is better to die insensate than to feel every starving inch of collapse; Tranh pours his leg-wreck money into a bottle of Mekong whiskey. He is old. He is broken. He is the last of his line. His sons are dead. His daughters are long gone. His ancestors will live uncared for in the underworld with no one to burn incense or offer sweet rice to them.

How they must curse him.

He limps and stumbles and crawls through the sweltering night streets, one hand clutching the open bottle, the other scrabbling at doorways and walls and methane lamp posts to keep himself upright. Sometimes his knee works; sometimes it fails him completely. He has kissed the streets a dozen times.

He tells himself that he is scavenging, hunting for the chance of sustenance. But Bangkok is a city of scavengers and the crows and devil cats and children have all come before him. If he is truly lucky, he will encounter the white shirts and they will knock him into bloody oblivion, perhaps send him to meet the previous owner of this fine Hwang Brothers suit that now flaps ragged around his shins. The thought appeals to him.

An ocean of whiskey rolls in his empty belly and he is warm and happy and care-free for the first time since the Incident. He laughs and drinks and shouts for the white shirts, calling them paper tigers, calling them dog fuckers. He calls them to him. Casts baiting words so that any within earshot will find him irresistible. But the Environment Ministry's patrols must have other yellow cards to abuse, for Tranh wanders the green-tinged streets of Bangkok alone.

Never mind. It doesn't matter. If he cannot find white shirts to do the job, he will drown himself. He will go to the river and dump himself in its offal. Floating on river currents to the sea appeals to him. He will end in the ocean like his scuttled clipper ships and the last of his heirs. He takes a swig of whiskey, loses his balance and winds up on the ground once again, sobbing and cursing white shirts and green headbands, and wet machetes.

Finally he drags himself into a doorway to rest, holding his miraculously unbro-ken whiskey bottle with one feeble hand. He cradles it to himself like a last bit of precious jade, smiling and laughing that it is not broken. He wouldn't want to waste his life savings on the cobblestones.

He takes another swig. Stares at the methane lamps flickering overhead. Despair is the color of approved burn methane flickering green and gaseous, vinous in the dark. Green used to mean things like coriander and silk and jade, and now all it means to him is bloodthirsty men with patriotic headbands and hungry scavenging nights. The lamps flicker. An entire green city. An entire city of despair.

Acorss the street, a shape scuttles, keeping to the shadows. Tranh leans forward, eyes narrowed. At first he takes it for a white shirt. But no. It is too furtive. It's a woman. A girl. A pretty creature, all made up. An enticement that moves with the stuttery jerky motion of . . .

A windup girl.

Tranh grins, a surprised skeleton rictus of delight at the sight of this unnatural creature stealing through the night. A windup girl. Ma Ping's windup girl. The impossible made flesh.

She slips from shadow to shadow, a creature even more terrified of white shirts than a yellow card geriatric. A waifish ghost child ripped from her natural habitat and set down in a city that despises everything she represents: her genetic inheritance, her mannfacturers, her unnatural competition—her ghostly lack of a soul. She has been here every night as he has pillaged through discarded melon spines. She has been here, tottering through the sweat heat darkness as he dodged white shirt patrols. And despite everything, she has been surviving.

Tranh forces himself upright. He sways, drunken and unsteady, then follows, one hand clutching his whiskey bottle, the other touching walls, catching himself when his bad knee falters. It's a foolish thing, a whimsy, but the windup girl has seized his inebriated imagination. He wants to stalk this unlikely Japanese creation, this interloper on foreign soil even more despised than himself. He wants to follow her. Perhaps steal kisses from her. Perhaps protect her from the hazards of the night. To pretend at least that he is not this drunken ribcage caricature of a man, but is in fact a tiger still.

The windup girl travels through the blackest of back alleys, safe in darkness, hidden from the white shirts who would seize her and mulch her before she could protest. Devil cats yowl as she passes, scenting something as cynically engineered as themselves. The Kingdom is infested with plagues and beasts, besieged by so many bioengineered monsters that it cannot keep up. As small as gray *fa' gan* fringe and as large as megodonts, they come. And as the Kingdom struggles to adapt, Tranh slinks after a windup girl, both of them as invasive as blister rust on a durian and just as welcome.

For all her irregular motion, the windup girl travels well enough. Tranh has difficulty keeping up with her. His knees creak and grind and he clenches his teeth against the pain. Sometimes he falls with a muffled grunt, but still he follows. Ahead of him, the windup girl ducks into new shadows, a wisp of tottering motion. Her herky-jerky gait announces her as a creature not human, no matter how beautiful she may be. No matter how intelligent, no matter how strong, no matter how supple her skin, she is a windup and meant to serve—and marked as such by a genetic specification that betrays her with every unnatural step.

Finally, when Tranh thinks that his legs will give out for a final time and that he can continue no longer, the windup girl pauses. She stands in the black mouth of a crumbling high-rise, a tower as tall and wretched as his own, another carcass of the old Expansion. From high above, music and laughter filter down. Shapes float in the tower's upper-story windows, limned in red light, the silhouettes of women dancing. Calls of men and the throb of drums. The windup girl disappears inside.

What would it be like to enter such a place? To spend baht like water while women danced and sang songs of lust? Tranh suddenly regrets spending his last baht on whiskey. This is where he should have died. Surrounded by fleshly pleasures that he has not known since he lost his country and his life. He purses his lips, considering. Perhaps he can bluff his way in. He still wears the raiment of the Hwang Brothers. He still appears a gentleman, perhaps. Yes. He will attempt it, and if he gathers the shame of ejection on his head, if he loses face one more time, what of it? He will be dead in a river soon anyway, floating to the sea to join his sons.

He starts to cross the street but his knee gives out and he falls flat instead. He saves his whiskey bottle more by luck than by dexterity. The last of its amber liquid glints in the methane light. He grimaces and pulls himself into a sitting position, then drags himself back into a doorway. He will rest, first. And finish the bottle. The windup girl will be there for a long time, likely. He has time to recover himself. And if he falls again, at least he won't have wasted his liquor. He tilts the bottle to his lips, then lets his tired head rest against the building. He'll just catch his breath.

Laughter issues from the high-rise. Tranh jerks awake. A man stumbles from its shadow portal: drunk, laughing. More men spill out after him. They laugh and shove one another. Drag tittering women out with them. Motion to cycle rickshaws that wait in the alleys for easy drunken patrons. Slowly, they disperse. Tranh tilts his whiskey bottle. Finds it empty.

Another pair of men emerges from the high-rise's maw. One of them is Ma Ping. The other a *farang* who can only be Ma's boss. The *farang* waves for a cycle rickshaw. He climbs in and waves his farewells. Ma raises his own hand in return and his gold and diamond wristwatch glints in the methane light. Tranh's wristwatch. Tranh's history. Tranh's heirloom flashing bright in the darkness. Tranh scowls. Wishes he could rip it off young Ma's wrist.

The *farang*'s rickshaw starts forward with a screech of unoiled bicycle chains and drunken laughter, leaving Ma Ping standing alone in the middle of the street. Ma laughs to himself, seems to consider returning to the bars, then laughs again and turns away, heading across the street, toward Tranh.

Tranh shies into the shadows, unwilling to let Ma catch him in such a state. Unwilling to endure more humiliation. He crouches deeper in his doorway as Ma stumbles about the street in search of rickshaws. But all the rickshaws have been taken for the moment. No more lurk below the bars.

Ma's gold wristwatch glints again the methane light.

Pale forms glazed green materialize on the street, three men walking, their mahogany skin almost black in the darkness, contrasting sharply against the creased whites of their uniforms. Their black batons twirl casually at their wrists. Ma doesn't seem to notice them at first. The white shirts converge, casual. Their voices carry easily in the quiet night.

"You're out late."

Ma shrugs, grins queasily. "Not really. Not so late."

The three white shirts gather close. "Late for a yellow card. You should be home by now. Bad luck to be out after yellow card curfew. Especially with all that yellow gold on your wrist."

Ma holds up his hands, defensive. "I'm not a yellow card."

"Your accent says differently."

Ma reaches for his pockets, fumbles in them. "Really. You'll see. Look."

A white shirt steps close. "Did I say you could move?"

"My papers. Look—"

"Get your hands out!"

"Look at my stamps!"

"Out!" A black baton flashes. Ma yelps, clutches his elbow. More blows rain down. Ma crouches, trying to shield himself. He curses, *"Nimade bi!"*

The white shirts laugh. "That's yellow card talk." One of them swings his baton, low and fast, and Ma collapses, crying out, curling around a damaged leg. The white shirts gather close. One of them jabs Ma in the face, making him uncurl, then runs the baton down Ma's chest, dragging blood.

"He's got nicer clothes than you, Thongchai."

"Probably snuck across the border with an assful of jade."

One of them squats, studies Ma's face. "Is it true? Do you shit jade?"

Ma shakes his head frantically. He rolls over and starts to crawl away. A black runnel of blood spills from his mouth. One leg drags behind him, useless. A white shirt follows, pushes him over with his shoe and puts his foot on Ma's face. The other two suck in their breath and step back, shocked. To beat a man is one thing . . . "Suttipong, no."

The man called Suttipong glances back at his peers. "It's nothing. These yellow cards are as bad as blister rust. This is nothing. They all come begging, taking food when we've got little enough for our own, and look," he kicks Ma's wrist. "Gold."

Ma gasps, tries to strip the watch from his wrist. "Take it. Here. Please. Take it."

"It's not yours to give, yellow card."

"Not . . . yellow card," Ma gasps. "Please. Not your Ministry." His hands fumble for his pockets, frantic under the white shirt's gaze. He pulls out his papers and waves them in the hot night air.

Suttipong takes the papers, glances at them. Leans close. "You think our countrymen don't fear us, too?"

He throws the papers on the ground, then quick as a cobra he strikes. One, two, three, the blows rain down. He is very fast. Very methodical. Ma curls into a ball, trying to ward off the blows. Suttipong steps back, breathing heavily. He waves at the other two. "Teach him respect." The other two glance at each other doubtfully, but under Suttipong's urging, they are soon beating Ma, shouting encouragement to one another.

A few men come down from the pleasure bars and stumble into the streets, but when they see white uniforms they flee back inside. The white shirts are alone. And if there are other watching eyes, they do not show themselves. Finally, Suttipong seems satisfied. He kneels and strips the antique Rolex from Ma's wrist, spits on Ma's face, and motions his peers to join him. They turn away, striding close past Tranh's hiding place.

The one called Thongchai looks back. "He might complain."

Suttipong shakes his head, his attention on the Rolex in his hand. "He's learned his lesson."

Their footsteps fade into the darkness. Music filters down from the high-rise clubs. The street itself is silent. Tranh watches for a long time, looking for other hunters. Nothing moves. It is as if the entire city has turned its back on the broken Malay-Chinese lying in the street. Finally, Tranh limps out of the shadows and approaches Ma Ping.

Ma catches sight of him and holds up a weak hand. "Help." He tries the words in Thai, again in *farang* English, finally in Malay, as though he has returned to his childhood. Then he seems to recognize Tranh. His eyes widen. He smiles weakly, through split bloody lips. Speaks Mandarin, their trade language of brotherhood. "*Lao pengyou*. What are you doing here?"

Tranh squats beside him, studying his cracked face. "I saw your windup girl."

Ma closes his eyes, tries to smile. "You believe me, then?" His eyes are nearly swollen shut, blood runs down from a cut in his brow, trickling freely.

"Yes."

"I think they broke my leg." He tries to pull himself upright, gasps, and collapses. He probes his ribs, runs his hand down to his shin. "I can't walk." He sucks air as he prods another broken bone. "You were right about the white shirts."

"A nail that stands up gets pounded down."

Something in Tranh's tone makes Ma look up. He studies Tranh's face. "Please. I gave you food. Find me a rickshaw." One hand strays to his wrist, fumbling for the timepiece that is no longer his, trying to offer it. Trying to bargain.

Is this fate? Tranh wonders. Or luck? Tranh purses his lips, considering. Was it fate that his own shiny wristwatch drew the white shirts and their wicked black batons? Was it luck that he arrived to see Ma fall? Do he and Ma Ping still have some larger karmic business?

Tranh watches Ma beg and remembers firing a young clerk so many lifetimes ago, sending him packing with a thrashing and a warning never to return. But that was when he was a great man. And now he is such a small one. As small as the clerk he thrashed so long ago. Perhaps smaller. He slides his hands under Ma's back, lifts.

"Thank you," Ma gasps. "Thank you."

Tranh runs his fingers into Ma's pockets, working through them methodically, checking for baht the white shirts have left. Ma groans, forces out a curse as Tranh jostles him. Tranh counts his scavenge, the dregs of Ma's pockets that still look like wealth to him. He stuffs the coins into his own pocket.

Ma's breathing comes in short panting gasps. "Please. A rickshaw. That's all." He barely manages to exhale the words.

Tranh cocks his head, considering, his instincts warring with themselves. He sighs and shakes his head. "A man makes his own luck, isn't that what you told me?" He smiles tightly. "My own arrogant words, coming from a brash young mouth." He shakes his head again, astounded at his previously fat ego, and smashes his whiskey bottle on the cobbles. Glass sprays. Shards glint green in the methane light.

"If I were still a great man . . ." Tranh grimaces. "But then, I suppose we're both past such illusions. I'm very sorry about this." With one last glance around the darkened street, he drives the broken bottle into Ma's throat. Ma jerks and blood spills out around Tranh's hand. Tranh scuttles back, keeping this new welling of blood off his Hwang Brothers fabrics. Ma's lungs bubble and his hands reach up for the bottle lodged in his neck, then fall away. His wet breathing stops.

Tranh is trembling. His hands shake with an electric palsy. He has seen so much death, and dealt so little. And now Ma lies before him, another Malay-Chinese dead, with only himself to blame. Again. He stifles an urge to be sick.

He turns and crawls into the protective shadows of the alley and pulls himself upright. He tests his weak leg. It seems to hold him. Beyond the shadows, the street is silent. Ma's body lies like a heap of garbage in its center. Nothing moves.

Tranh turns and limps down the street, keeping to the walls, bracing himself when his knee threatens to give way. After a few blocks, the methane lamps start to go out. One by one, as though a great hand is moving down the street snuffing them, they gutter into silence as the Public Works Ministry cuts off the gas. The street settles into complete darkness.

When Tranh finally arrives at Surawong Road, its wide black thoroughfare is nearly empty of traffic. A pair of ancient water buffalo placidly haul a rubber-wheeled wagon under starlight. A shadow farmer rides behind them, muttering softly. The yowls of mating devil cats scrape the hot night air, but that is all.

And then, from behind, the creak of bicycle chains. The rattle of wheels on cobbles. Tranh turns, half expecting avenging white shirts, but it is only a cycle-rickshaw, chattering down the darkened street. Tranh raises a hand, flashing newfound baht. The rickshaw slows. A man's ropey limbs gleam with moonlit sweat. Twin earrings decorate his lobes, gobs of silver in the night. "Where you going?"

Tranh scans the rickshaw man's broad face for hints of betrayal, for hints that he is a hunter, but the man is only looking at the baht in Tranh's hand. Tranh forces down his paranoia and climbs into the rickshaw's seat. "The *farang* factories. By the river."

The rickshaw man glances over his shoulder, surprised. "All the factories will be closed. Too much energy to run at night. It's all black night down there."

"It doesn't matter. There's a job opening. There will be interviews."

The man stands on his pedals. "At night?"

"Tomorrow." Tranh settles deeper into his seat. "I don't want to be late."

Riding the Crocodile

GREG EGAN

As we look back at the century that's just ended, it's obvious that Australian writer Greg Egan was one of the big new names to emerge in SF in the nineties, and is probably one of the most significant talents to enter the field in the last several decades. Already one of the most widely known of all Australian genre writers, Egan may well be the best new hard-science writer to enter the field since Greg Bear, and is still growing in range, power, and sophistication. In the last few years, he has become a frequent contributor to *Interzone* and *Asimov's Science Fiction*, and has made sales as well to *Pulphouse, Analog, Aurealis, Eidolon,* and elsewhere; many of his stories have also appeared in various Best of the Year series, and he was on the Hugo final ballot in 1995 for his story "Cocoon," which won the Ditmar Award and the Asimov's Readers Award. He won the Hugo Award in 1999 for his novella *Oceanic.* His first novel, *Quarantine,* appeared in 1992; his second novel, *Permutation City,* won the John W. Campbell Memorial Award in 1994. His other books include the novels *Distress, Diaspora,* and *Teranesia,* and three collections of his short fiction: *Axiomatic, Luminous,* and *Our Lady of Chernobyl.* His most recent book is the novel *Schild's Ladder,* and he is at work on a new novel. He has a Web site at www.netspace.net.au/~gregegan/.

Egan's furthest penetration into the far future until now was probably to be found in his story "Border Guards." Here he takes us a good deal further into the future of an enhanced and transmogrified human race to pose a profound and basic question: Is it possible to live *too* long? To succeed *too* well? To have achieved everything you ever wanted to achieve? To have reached a point where there's nothing worthwhile left to do, and where the universe has run out of surprises for you? And if you say yes, and *mean* it, what happens when that universe suddenly comes up with a *brand-new* batch of surprises for you, and a whole new group of mysteries to be solved?

I

In their ten thousand, three hundred and ninth year of marriage, Leila and Jasim began contemplating death. They had known love, raised children, and witnessed the flourishing generations of their offspring. They had traveled to a dozen worlds and lived among a thousand cultures. They had educated themselves many times over, proved theorems, and acquired and abandoned artistic sensibilities and skills. They had not lived in every conceivable manner, far from it, but what room would there be for the multitude if each individual tried to exhaust the permutations of existence? There were some experiences, they agreed, that everyone should try, and others that only a handful of people in all of time need bother with. They had no wish to give up their idiosyncrasies, no wish to uproot their personalities from the niches they had settled in long ago, let alone start cranking mechanically through some tedious enumeration of all the other people they might have been. They had been themselves, and for that they had done, more or less, enough.

Before dying, though, they wanted to attempt something grand and audacious. It was not that their lives were incomplete, in need of some final flourish of affirmation. If some unlikely calamity had robbed them of the chance to orchestrate this finale, the closest of their friends would never have remarked upon, let alone mourned, its absence. There was no esthetic compulsion to be satisfied, no aching existential void to be filled. Nevertheless, it was what they both wanted, and once they had acknowledged this to each other their hearts were set on it.

Choosing the project was not a great burden; that task required nothing but patience. They knew they'd recognize it when it came to them. Every night before sleeping, Jasim would ask Leila, "Did you see it yet?"

"No. Did you?"

"Not yet."

Sometimes Leila would dream that she'd found it in her dreams, but the transcripts proved otherwise. Sometimes Jasim felt sure that it was lurking just below the surface of his thoughts, but when he dived down to check it was nothing but a trick of the light.

Years passed. They occupied themselves with simple pleasures: gardening, swimming in the surf, talking with their friends, catching up with their descendants. They had grown skilled at finding pastimes that could bear repetition. Still, were it not for the nameless adventure that awaited them they would have thrown a pair of dice each evening and agreed that two sixes would end it all.

One night, Leila stood alone in the garden, watching the sky. From their home world, Najib, they had traveled only to the nearest stars with inhabited worlds, each time losing just a few decades to the journey. They had chosen those limits so as not to alienate themselves from friends and family, and it had never felt like much of a constraint. True, the civilization of the Amalgam wrapped the galaxy, and a committed traveler could spend two hundred thousand years circling back home, but what was to be gained by such an overblown odyssey? The dozen worlds of their neighborhood held enough variety for any traveler, and whether more distant realms were filled with fresh novelties or endless repetition hardly seemed to matter. To have a goal, a destination, would be one thing, but to drown in the sheer plenitude of worlds for its own sake seemed utterly pointless.

A destination? Leila overlaid the sky with information, most of it by necessity millennia out of date. There were worlds with spectacular views of nebulas and star clusters, views that could be guaranteed still to be in existence if they traveled to see them, but would taking in such sights firsthand be so much better than immersion in the flawless images already available in Najib's library? To blink away ten thousand years just to wake beneath a cloud of green and violet gas, however lovely, seemed like a terrible anticlimax.

The stars tingled with self-aggrandisement, plaintively tugging at her attention. The architecture here, the rivers, the festivals! Even if these tourist attractions could survive the millennia, even if some were literally unique, there was nothing that struck her as a fitting prelude to death. If she and Jasim had formed some whimsical attachment, centuries before, to a world on the other side of the galaxy rumoured to hold great beauty or interest, and if they had talked long enough about chasing it down when they had nothing better to do, then keeping that promise might have been worth it, even if the journey led them to a world in ruins. They had no such cherished destination, though, and it was too late to cultivate one now.

Leila's gaze followed a thinning in the advertising, taking her to the bulge of stars surrounding the galaxy's center. The disk of the Milky Way belonged to the Amalgam, whose various ancestral species had effectively merged into a single civilization, but the central bulge was inhabited by beings who had declined to do so much as communicate with those around them. All attempts to send probes into the bulge—let alone the kind of engineering spores needed to create the infrastructure for travel—had been gently but firmly rebuffed, with the intruders swatted straight back out again. The Aloof had maintained their silence and isolation since before the Amalgam itself had even existed.

The latest news on this subject was twenty thousand years old, but the status quo had held for close to a million years. If she and Jasim traveled to the innermost edge of the Amalgam's domain, the chances were exceptionally good that the Aloof would not have changed their ways in the meantime. In fact, it would be no disappointment at all if the Aloof had suddenly thrown open their borders: that unheralded thaw would itself be an extraordinary thing to witness. If the challenge remained, though, all the better.

She called Jasim to the garden and pointed out the richness of stars, unadorned with potted histories.

"We go where?" he asked.

"As close to the Aloof as we're able."

"And do what?"

"Try to observe them," she said. "Try to learn something about them. Try to make contact, in whatever way we can."

"You don't think that's been tried before?"

"A million times. Not so much lately, though. Maybe while the interest on our side has ebbed, they've been changing, growing more receptive."

"Or maybe not." Jasim smiled. He had appeared a little stunned by her proposal at first, but the idea seemed to be growing on him. "It's a hard, hard problem to throw ourselves against. But it's not futile. Not quite." He wrapped her hands in his. "Let's see how we feel in the morning."

In the morning, they were both convinced. They would camp at the gates of these elusive strangers, and try to rouse them from their indifference.

They summoned the family from every corner of Najib. There were some grand-children and more distant descendants who had settled in other star systems, de-cades away at lightspeed, but they chose not to wait to call them home for this final farewell.

Two hundred people crowded the physical house and garden, while two hun-dred more confined themselves to the virtual wing. There was talk and food and music, like any other celebration, and Leila tried to undercut any edge of solemnity that she felt creeping in. As the night wore on, though, each time she kissed a child or grandchild, each time she embraced an old friend, she thought: this could be the last time, ever. There had to be a last time, she couldn't face ten thousand more years, but a part of her spat and struggled like a cornered animal at the thought of each warm touch fading to nothing.

As dawn approached, the party shifted entirely into the acorporeal. People took on fancy dress from myth or xenology, or just joked and played with their illusory bodies. It was all very calm and gentle, nothing like the surreal excesses she remem-bered from her youth, but Leila still felt a tinge of vertigo. When her son Khalid made his ears grow and spin, this amiable silliness carried a hard message: the ma-chinery of the house had ripped her mind from her body, as seamlessly as ever, but this time she would never be returning to the same flesh.

Sunrise brought the first of the good-byes. Leila forced herself to release each proffered hand, to unwrap her arms from around each nonexistent body. She whis-pered to Jasim, "Are you going mad, too?"

"Of course."

Gradually the crowd thinned out. The wing grew quiet. Leila found herself pac-ing from room to room, as if she might yet chance upon someone who'd stayed be-hind, then she remembered urging the last of them to go, her children and friends tearfully retreating down the hall. She skirted inconsolable sadness, then lifted her-self above it and went looking for Jasim.

He was waiting for her outside their room.

"Are you ready to sleep?" he asked her gently.

She said, "For an eon."

II

Leila woke in the same bed as she'd lain down in. Jasim was still sleeping beside her. The window showed dawn, but it was not the usual view of the cliffs and the ocean.

Leila had the house brief her. After twenty thousand years—traveling more or less at lightspeed, pausing only for a microsecond or two at various way-stations to be cleaned up and amplified—the package of information bearing the two of them had arrived safely at Nazdeek-be-Beegane. This world was not crowded, and it had been tweaked to render it compatible with a range of metabolic styles. The house had negotiated a site where they could live embodied in comfort if they wished.

Jasim stirred and opened his eyes. "Good morning. How are you feeling?"

"Older."

"Really?"

Leila paused to consider this seriously. "No. Not even slightly. How about you?"

"I'm fine. I'm just wondering what's out there." He raised himself up to peer through the window. The house had been instantiated on a wide, empty plain, covered with low stalks of green and yellow vegetation. They could eat these plants, and the house had already started a spice garden while they slept. He stretched his shoulders. "Let's go and make breakfast."

They went downstairs, stepping into freshly minted bodies, then out into the garden. The air was still, the sun already warm. The house had tools prepared to help them with the harvest. It was the nature of travel that they had come empty-handed, and they had no relatives here, no fifteenth cousins, no friends of friends. It was the nature of the Amalgam that they were welcome nonetheless, and the machines that supervised this world on behalf of its inhabitants had done their best to provide for them.

"So this is the afterlife," Jasim mused, scything the yellow stalks. "Very rustic."

"Speak for yourself," Leila retorted. "I'm not dead yet." She put down her own scythe and bent to pluck one of the plants out by its roots.

The meal they made was filling but bland. Leila resisted the urge to tweak her perceptions of it; she preferred to face the challenge of working out decent recipes, which would make a useful counterpoint to the more daunting task they'd come here to attempt.

They spent the rest of the day just tramping around, exploring their immediate surroundings. The house had tapped into a nearby stream for water, and sunlight, stored, would provide all the power they needed. From some hills about an hour's walk away they could see into a field with another building, but they decided to wait a little longer before introducing themselves to their neighbors. The air had a slightly odd smell, due to the range of components needed to support other metabolic styles, but it wasn't too intrusive.

The onset of night took them by surprise. Even before the sun had set a smattering of stars began appearing in the east, and for a moment Leila thought that these white specks against the fading blue were some kind of exotic atmospheric phenomenon, perhaps small clouds forming in the stratosphere as the temperature dropped. When it became clear what was happening, she beckoned to Jasim to sit beside her on the bank of the stream and watch the stars of the bulge come out.

They'd come at a time when Nazdeek lay between its sun and the galactic center. At dusk one half of the Aloof's dazzling territory stretched from the eastern horizon to the zenith, with the stars' slow march westward against a darkening sky only revealing more of their splendor.

"You think that was to die for?" Jasim joked as they walked back to the house.

"We could end this now, if you're feeling unambitious."

He squeezed her hand. "If this takes ten thousand years, I'm ready."

It was a mild night, they could have slept outdoors, but the spectacle was too distracting. They stayed downstairs, in the physical wing. Leila watched the strange thicket of shadows cast by the furniture sliding across the walls. These neighbors never sleep, she thought. When we come knocking, they'll ask what took us so long.

III

Hundreds of observatories circled Nazdeek, built then abandoned by others who'd come on the same quest. When Leila saw the band of pristine space junk mapped out before her—orbits scrupulously maintained and swept clean by robot sentinels for eons—she felt as if she'd found the graves of their predecessors, stretching out in the field behind the house as far as the eye could see.

Nazdeek was prepared to offer them the resources to loft another package of instruments into the vacuum if they wished, but many of the abandoned observatories were perfectly functional, and most had been left in a compliant state, willing to take instructions from anyone.

Leila and Jasim sat in their living room and woke machine after machine from millennia of hibernation. Some, it turned out, had not been sleeping at all, but had been carrying on systematic observations, accumulating data long after their owners had lost interest.

In the crowded stellar precincts of the bulge, disruptive gravitational effects made planet formation rarer than it was in the disk, and orbits less stable. Nevertheless, planets had been found. A few thousand could be tracked from Nazdeek, and one observatory had been monitoring their atmospheric spectra for the last twelve millennia. In all of those worlds for all of those years, there were no signs of atmospheric composition departing from plausible, purely geochemical models. That meant no wild life, and no crude industries. It didn't prove that these worlds were uninhabited, but it suggested either that the Aloof went to great lengths to avoid leaving chemical fingerprints, or they lived in an entirely different fashion to any of the civilizations that had formed the Amalgam.

Of the eleven forms of biochemistry that had been found scattered around the galactic disk, all had given rise eventually to hundreds of species with general intelligence. Of the multitude of civilizations that had emerged from those roots, all contained cultures that had granted themselves the flexibility of living as software, but they also all contained cultures that persisted with corporeal existence. Leila would never have willingly given up either mode, herself, but while it was easy to imagine a subculture doing so, for a whole species it seemed extraordinary. In a sense, the intertwined civilization of the Amalgam owed its existence to the fact that there was as much cultural variation within every species as there was between one species and another. In that explosion of diversity, overlapping interests were inevitable.

If the Aloof were the exception, and their material culture had shrunk to nothing but a few discreet processors—each with the energy needs of a gnat, scattered throughout a trillion cubic light-years of dust and blazing stars—then finding them would be impossible.

Of course, that worst-case scenario couldn't quite be true. The sole reason the Aloof were assumed to exist at all was the fact that some component of their material culture was tossing back every probe that was sent into the bulge. However discreet that machinery was, it certainly couldn't be sparse: given that it had managed to track, intercept and reverse the trajectories of billions of individual probes that had been sent in along thousands of different routes, relativistic constraints on the information flow implied that the Aloof had some kind of presence at more or less every star at the edge of the bulge.

Leila and Jasim had Nazdeek brief them on the most recent attempts to enter the bulge, but even after forty thousand years the basic facts hadn't changed. There was no crisply delineated barrier marking the Aloof's territory, but at some point within a border region about fifty light-years wide, every single probe that was sent in ceased to function. The signals from those carrying in-flight beacons or transmitters went dead without warning. A century or so later, they would appear again at almost the same point, traveling in the opposite direction: back to where they'd come from. Those that were retrieved and examined were found to be unharmed, but their data logs contained nothing from the missing decades.

Jasim said, "The Aloof could be dead and gone. They built the perfect fence, but now it's outlasted them. It's just guarding their ruins."

Leila rejected this emphatically. "No civilization that's spread to more than one star system has ever vanished completely. Sometimes they've changed beyond recognition, but not one has ever died without descendants."

"That's a fact of history, but it's not a universal law," Jasim persisted. "If we're going to argue from the Amalgam all the time, we'll get nowhere. If the Aloof weren't exceptional, we wouldn't be here."

"That's true. But I won't accept that they're dead until I see some evidence."

"What would count as evidence? Apart from a million years of silence?"

Leila said, "Silence could mean anything. If they're really dead, we'll find something more, something definite."

"Such as?"

"If we see it, we'll know."

They began the project in earnest, reviewing data from the ancient observatories, stopping only to gather food, eat and sleep. They had resisted making detailed plans back on Najib, reasoning that any approach they mapped out in advance was likely to be rendered obsolete once they learned about the latest investigations. Now that they'd arrived and found the state of play utterly unchanged, Leila wished that they'd come armed with some clear options for dealing with the one situation they could have prepared for before they'd left.

In fact, though they might have felt like out-of-touch amateurs back on Najib, now that the Aloof had become their entire *raison d'être* it was far harder to relax and indulge in the kind of speculation that might actually bear fruit, given that every systematic approach had failed. Having come twenty thousand light-years for this, they couldn't spend their time day-dreaming, turning the problem over in the backs of their minds while they surrendered to the rhythms of Nazdeek's rural idyll. So they studied everything that had been tried before, searching methodically for a new approach, hoping to see the old ideas with fresh eyes, hoping that—by chance if for no other reason—they might lack some crucial blind spot that had afflicted all of their predecessors.

After seven months without results or inspiration, it was Jasim who finally dragged them out of the rut. "We're getting nowhere," he said. "It's time to accept that, put all this aside, and go visit the neighbors."

Leila stared at him as if he'd lost his mind. "Go visit them? How? What makes you think that they're suddenly going to let us in?"

He said, "The neighbors. Remember? Over the hill. The ones who might actually want to talk to us."

IV

Their neighbors had published a précis stating that they welcomed social contact in principle, but might take a while to respond. Jasim sent them an invitation, asking if they'd like to join them in their house, and waited.

After just three days, a reply came back. The neighbors did not want to put them to the trouble of altering their own house physically, and preferred not to become acorporeal at present. Given the less stringent requirements of Leila and Jasim's own species when embodied, might they wish to come instead to the neighbors' house?

Leila said, "Why not?" They set a date and time.

The neighbors' précis included all the biological and sociological details needed to prepare for the encounter. Their biochemistry was carbon-based and oxygen-breathing, but employed a different replicator to Leila and Jasim's DNA. Their ancestral phenotype resembled a large furred snake, and when embodied they generally lived in nests of a hundred or so. The minds of the individuals were perfectly autonomous, but solitude was an alien and unsettling concept for them.

Leila and Jasim set out late in the morning, in order to arrive early in the afternoon. There were some low, heavy clouds in the sky, but it was not completely overcast, and Leila noticed that when the sun passed behind the clouds, she could discern some of the brightest stars from the edge of the bulge.

Jasim admonished her sternly, "Stop looking. This is our day off."

The Snakes' building was a large squat cylinder resembling a water tank, which turned out to be packed with something mossy and pungent. When they arrived at the entrance, three of their hosts were waiting to greet them, coiled on the ground near the mouth of a large tunnel emerging from the moss. Their bodies were almost as wide as their guests', and some eight or ten meters long. Their heads bore two front-facing eyes, but their other sense organs were not prominent. Leila could make out their mouths, and knew from the briefing how many rows of teeth lay behind them, but the wide pink gashes stayed closed, almost lost in the gray fur.

The Snakes communicated with a low-frequency thumping, and their system of nomenclature was complex, so Leila just mentally tagged the three of them with randomly chosen, slightly exotic names—Tim, John and Sarah—and tweaked her translator so she'd recognize intuitively who was who, who was addressing her, and the significance of their gestures.

"Welcome to our home," said Tim enthusiastically.

"Thank you for inviting us," Jasim replied.

"We've had no visitors for quite some time," explained Sarah. "So we really are delighted to meet you."

"How long has it been?" Leila asked.

"Twenty years," said Sarah.

"But we came here for the quiet life," John added. "So we expected it would be a while."

Leila pondered the idea of a clan of one hundred ever finding a quiet life, but then, perhaps unwelcome intrusions from outsiders were of a different nature to family dramas.

"Will you come into the nest?" Tim asked. "If you don't wish to enter we won't take offense, but everyone would like to see you, and some of us aren't comfortable coming out into the open."

Leila glanced at Jasim. He said privately, "We can push our vision to IR. And tweak ourselves to tolerate the smell."

Leila agreed.

"Okay," Jasim told Tim.

Tim slithered into the tunnel and vanished in a quick, elegant motion, then John motioned with his head for the guests to follow. Leila went first, propelling herself up the gentle slope with her knees and elbows. The plant the Snakes culti-vated for the nest formed a cool, dry, resilient surface. She could see Tim ten me-ters or so ahead, like a giant glowworm shining with body heat, slowing down now to let her catch up. She glanced back at Jasim, who looked even weirder than the Snakes now, his face and arms blotched with strange bands of radiance from the ex-ertion.

After a few minutes, they came to a large chamber. The air was humid, but after the confines of the tunnel it felt cool and fresh. Tim led them toward the center, where about a dozen other Snakes were already waiting to greet them. They circled the guests excitedly, thumping out a delighted welcome. Leila felt a surge of adren-aline; she knew that she and Jasim were in no danger, but the sheer size and energy of the creatures was overwhelming.

"Can you tell us why you've come to Nazdeek?" asked Sarah.

"Of course." For a second or two Leila tried to maintain eye contact with her, but like all the other Snakes she kept moving restlessly, a gesture that Leila's translator imbued with a sense of warmth and enthusiasm. As for lack of eye contact, the Snakes' own translators would understand perfectly that some aspects of ordinary, polite human behavior became impractical under the circumstances, and would not mislabel her actions. "We're here to learn about the Aloof," she said.

"The Aloof?" At first Sarah just seemed perplexed, then Leila's translator hinted at a touch of irony. "But they offer us nothing."

Leila was tongue-tied for a moment. The implication was subtle but unmistak-able. Citizens of the Amalgam had a protocol for dealing with each other's curiosity: they published a précis, which spelled out clearly any information that they wished people in general to know about them, and also specified what, if any, further in-quiries would be welcome. However, a citizen was perfectly entitled to publish no précis at all and have that decision respected. When no information was published, and no invitation offered, you simply had no choice but to mind your own business.

"They offer us nothing as far as we can tell," she said, "but that might be a misunderstanding, a failure to communicate."

"They send back all the probes," Tim replied. "Do you really think we've misunderstood what that means?"

Jasim said, "It means that they don't want us physically intruding on their territory, putting our machines right next to their homes, but I'm not convinced that it proves that they have no desire to communicate whatsoever."

"We should leave them in peace," Tim insisted. "They've seen the probes, so they know we're here. If they want to make contact, they'll do it in their own time."

"Leave them in peace," echoed another Snake. A chorus of affirmation followed from others in the chamber.

Leila stood her ground. "We have no idea how many different species and cultures might be living in the bulge. *One of them* sends back the probes, but for all we know there could be a thousand others who don't yet even know that the Amalgam has tried to make contact."

This suggestion set off a series of arguments, some between guests and hosts, some between the Snakes themselves. All the while, the Snakes kept circling excitedly, while new ones entered the chamber to witness the novel sight of these strangers.

When the clamor about the Aloof had quietened down enough for her to change the subject, Leila asked Sarah, "Why have you come to Nazdeek yourself?"

"It's out of the way, off the main routes. We can think things over here, undisturbed."

"But you could have the same amount of privacy anywhere. It's all a matter of what you put in your précis."

Sarah's response was imbued with a tinge of amusement. "For us, it would be unimaginably rude to cut off all contact explicitly, by decree. Especially with others from our own ancestral species. To live a quiet life, we had to reduce the likelihood of encountering anyone who would seek us out. We had to make the effort of rendering ourselves physically remote, in order to reap the benefits."

"Yet you've made Jasim and myself very welcome."

"Of course. But that will be enough for the next twenty years."

So much for resurrecting their social life. "What exactly is it that you're pondering in this state of solitude?"

"The nature of reality. The uses of existence. The reasons to live, and the reasons not to."

Leila felt the skin on her forearms tingle. She'd almost forgotten that she'd made an appointment with death, however uncertain the timing.

She explained how she and Jasim had made their decision to embark on a grand project before dying.

"That's an interesting approach," Sarah said. "I'll have to give it some thought." She paused, then added, "Though I'm not sure that you've solved the problem."

"What do you mean?"

"Will it really be easier now to choose the right moment to give up your life?

Haven't you merely replaced one delicate judgment with an even more difficult one: deciding when you've exhausted the possibilities for contacting the Aloof?"

"You make it sound as if we have no chance of succeeding." Leila was not afraid of the prospect of failure, but the suggestion that it was inevitable was something else entirely.

Sarah said, "We've been here on Nazdeek for fifteen thousand years. We don't pay much attention to the world outside the nest, but even from this cloistered state we've seen many people break their backs against this rock."

"So when will you accept that your own project is finished?" Leila countered. "If you still don't have what you're looking for after fifteen thousand years, when will you admit defeat?"

"I have no idea," Sarah confessed. "I have no idea, any more than you do."

V

When the way forward first appeared, there was nothing to set it apart from a thousand false alarms that had come before it.

It was their seventeenth year on Nazdeek. They had launched their own observatory—armed with the latest refinements culled from around the galaxy—fifteen years before, and it had been confirming the null results of its predecessors ever since.

They had settled into an unhurried routine, systematically exploring the possibilities that observation hadn't yet ruled out. Between the scenarios that were obviously stone cold dead—the presence of an energy-rich, risk-taking, extroverted civilization in the bulge actively seeking contact by every means at its disposal—and the infinite number of possibilities that could never be distinguished at this distance from the absence of all life, and the absence of all machinery save one dumb but efficient gatekeeper, tantalizing clues would bubble up out of the data now and then, only to fade into statistical insignificance in the face of continued scrutiny.

Tens of billions of stars lying within the Aloof's territory could be discerned from Nazdeek, some of them evolving or violently interacting on a time scale of years or months. Black holes were flaying and swallowing their companions. Neutron stars and white dwarfs were stealing fresh fuel and flaring into novas. Star clusters were colliding and tearing each other apart. If you gathered data on this whole menagerie for long enough, you could expect to see almost anything. Leila would not have been surprised to wander into the garden at night and find a great welcome sign spelled out in the sky, before the fortuitous pattern of novas faded and the message dissolved into randomness again.

When their gamma ray telescope caught a glimmer of something odd—the nuclei of a certain isotope of fluorine decaying from an excited state, when there was no nearby source of the kind of radiation that could have put the nuclei into that state in the first place—it might have been just another random, unexplained fact to add to a vast pile. When the same glimmer was seen again, not far away, Leila reasoned that if a gas cloud enriched with fluorine could be affected at one location by an unseen radiation source, it should not be surprising if the same thing happened elsewhere in the same cloud.

It happened again. The three events lined up in space and time in a manner suggesting a short pulse of gamma rays in the form of a tightly focused beam, striking three different points in the gas cloud. Still, in the mountains of data they had acquired from their predecessors, coincidences far more compelling than this had occurred hundreds of thousands of times.

With the fourth flash, the balance of the numbers began to tip. The secondary gamma rays reaching Nazdeek gave only a weak and distorted impression of the original radiation, but all four flashes were consistent with a single, narrow beam. There were thousands of known gamma ray sources in the bulge, but the frequency of the radiation, the direction of the beam, and the time profile of the pulse did not fit with any of them.

The archives revealed a few dozen occasions when the same kind of emissions had been seen from fluorine nuclei under similar conditions. There had never been more than three connected events before, but one sequence had occurred along a path not far from the present one.

Leila sat by the stream and modeled the possibilities. If the beam was linking two objects in powered flight, prediction was impossible. If receiver and transmitter were mostly in free-fall, though, and only made corrections occasionally, the past and present data combined gave her a plausible forecast for the beam's future orientation.

Jasim looked into her simulation, a thought-bubble of stars and equations hovering above the water. "The whole path will lie out of bounds," he said.

"No kidding." The Aloof's territory was more or less spherical, which made it a convex set: you couldn't get between any two points that lay inside it without entering the territory itself. "But look how much the beam spreads out. From the fluorine data, I'd say it could be tens of kilometers wide by the time it reaches the receiver."

"So they might not catch it all? They might let some of the beam escape into the disk?" He sounded unpersuaded.

Leila said, "Look, if they really were doing everything possible to hide this, we would never have seen these blips in the first place."

"Gas clouds with this much fluorine are extremely rare. They obviously picked a frequency that wouldn't be scattered under ordinary circumstances."

"Yes, but that's just a matter of getting the signal through the local environment. We choose frequencies ourselves that won't interact with any substance that's likely to be present along the route, but no choice is perfect, and we just live with that. It seems to me that they've done the same thing. If they were fanatical purists, they'd communicate by completely different methods."

"All right." Jasim reached into the model. "So where can we go that's in the line of sight?"

The short answer was: nowhere. If the beam was not blocked completely by its intended target it would spread out considerably as it made its way through the galactic disk, but it would not grow so wide that it would sweep across a single point where the Amalgam had any kind of outpost.

Leila said, "This is too good to miss. We need to get a decent observatory into its path."

Jasim agreed. "And we need to do it before these nodes decide they've drifted too close to something dangerous, and switch on their engines for a course correction."

They crunched through the possibilities. Wherever the Amalgam had an established presence, the infrastructure already on the ground could convert data into any kind of material object. Transmitting yourself to such a place, along with whatever you needed, was simplicity itself: lightspeed was the only real constraint. Excessive demands on the local resources might be denied, but modest requests were rarely rejected.

Far more difficult was building something new at a site with raw materials but no existing receiver; in that case, instead of pure data, you needed to send an engineering spore of some kind. If you were in a hurry, not only did you need to spend energy boosting the spore to relativistic velocities—a cost that snowballed due to the mass of protective shielding—you then had to waste much of the time you gained on a lengthy braking phase, or the spore would hit its target with enough energy to turn it into plasma. Interactions with the interstellar medium could be used to slow down the spore, avoiding the need to carry yet more mass to act as a propellant for braking, but the whole business was disgustingly inefficient.

Harder still was getting anything substantial to a given point in the vast empty space between the stars. With no raw materials to hand at the destination, everything had to be moved from somewhere else. The best starting point was usually to send an engineering spore into a cometary cloud, loosely bound gravitationally to its associated star, but not every such cloud was open to plunder, and everything took time, and obscene amounts of energy.

To arrange for an observatory to be delivered to the most accessible point along the beam's line of sight, traveling at the correct velocity, would take about fifteen thousand years all told. That assumed that the local cultures who owned the nearest facilities, and who had a right to veto the use of the raw materials, acceded immediately to their request.

"How long between course corrections?" Leila wondered. If the builders of this hypothetical network were efficient, the nodes could drift for a while in interstellar space without any problems, but in the bulge everything happened faster than in the disk, and the need to counter gravitational effects would come much sooner. There was no way to make a firm prediction, but they could easily have as little as eight or ten thousand years.

Leila struggled to reconcile herself to the reality. "We'll try at this location, and if we're lucky we might still catch something. If not, we'll try again after the beam shifts." Sending the first observatory chasing after the beam would be futile; even with the present free-fall motion of the nodes, the observation point would be moving at a substantial fraction of lightspeed relative to the local stars. Magnified by the enormous distances involved, a small change in direction down in the bulge could see the beam lurch thousands of light-years sideways by the time it reached the disk.

Jasim said, "Wait." He magnified the region around the projected path of the beam.

"What are you looking for?"

He asked the map. "Are there two outposts of the Amalgam lying on a straight line that intersects the beam?"

The map replied in a tone of mild incredulity. "No."

"That was too much to hope for. Are there three lying on a plane that intersects the beam?"

The map said, "There are about ten-to-the-eighteen triples that meet that condition."

Leila suddenly realized what it was he had in mind. She laughed and squeezed his arm. "You are completely insane!"

Jasim said, "Let me get the numbers right first, then you can mock me." He rephrased his question to the map. "For how many of those triples would the beam pass between them, intersecting the triangle whose vertices they lie on?"

"About ten-to-the-sixth."

"How close to us is the closest point of intersection of the beam with any of those triangles—if the distance in each case is measured via the worst of the three outposts, the one that makes the total path longest."

"Seven thousand four hundred and twenty-six light-years."

Leila said, "Collision braking. With three components?"

"Do you have a better idea?"

Better than twice as fast as the fastest conventional method? "Nothing comes to mind. Let me think about it."

Braking against the flimsy interstellar medium was a slow process. If you wanted to deliver a payload rapidly to a point that fortuitously lay somewhere on a straight line between two existing outposts, you could fire two separate packages from the two locations and let them "collide" when they met—or rather, let them brake against each other magnetically. If you arranged for the packages to have equal and opposite momenta, they would come to a halt without any need to throw away reaction mass or clutch at passing molecules, and some of their kinetic energy could be recovered as electricity and stored for later use.

The aim and the timing had to be perfect. Relativistic packages did not make in-flight course corrections, and the data available at each launch site about the other's precise location was always a potentially imperfect prediction, not a rock-solid statement of fact. Even with the Amalgam's prodigious astrometric and computing resources, achieving millimeter alignments at thousand-light-year distances could not be guaranteed.

Now Jasim wanted to make three of these bullets meet, perform an elaborate electromagnetic dance, and end up with just the right velocity needed to keep tracking the moving target of the beam.

In the evening, back in the house, they sat together working through simulations. It was easy to find designs that would work if everything went perfectly, but they kept hunting for the most robust variation, the one that was most tolerant of small misalignments. With standard two-body collision braking, the usual solution was to have the first package, shaped like a cylinder, pass right through a hole in the second package. As it emerged from the other side and the two moved apart again, the magnetic fields were switched from repulsive to attractive. Several "bounces" followed, and in the process as much of the kinetic energy as possible was gradually converted into superconducting currents for storage, while the rest was dissipated as electromagnetic radiation. Having three objects meeting at an angle would not only make the timing and positioning more critical, it would destroy the simple, axial symmetry and introduce a greater risk of instability.

It was dawn before they settled on the optimal design, which effectively split the problem in two. First, package one, a sphere, would meet package two, a torus, threading the gap in the middle, then bouncing back and forth through it seventeen times. The plane of the torus would lie at an angle to its direction of flight, allowing the sphere to approach it head-on. When the two finally came to rest with respect to each other, they would still have a component of their velocity carrying them straight toward package three, a cylinder with an axial borehole.

Because the electromagnetic interactions were the same as the two-body case—self-centering, intrinsically stable—a small amount of misalignment at each of these encounters would not be fatal. The usual two-body case, though, didn't require the combined package, after all the bouncing and energy dissipation was completed, to be moving on a path so precisely determined that it could pass through yet another narrow hoop.

There were no guarantees, and in the end the result would be in other people's hands. They could send requests to the three outposts, asking for these objects to be launched at the necessary times on the necessary trajectories. The energy needs hovered on the edge of politeness, though, and it was possible that one or more of the requests would simply be refused.

Jasim waved the models away, and they stretched out on the carpet, side by side.

He said, "I never thought we'd get this far. Even if this is only a mirage, I never thought we'd find one worth chasing."

Leila said, "I don't know what I expected. Some kind of great folly: some long, exhausting, exhilarating struggle that felt like wandering through a jungle for years and ending up utterly lost."

"And then what?"

"Surrender."

Jasim was silent for a while. Leila could sense that he was brooding over something, but she didn't press him.

He said, "Should we travel to this observatory ourselves, or wait here for the results?"

"We should go. Definitely! I don't want to hang around here for fifteen thousand years, waiting. We can leave the Nazdeek observatories hunting for more beam fluorescence and broadcasting the results, so we'll hear about them wherever we end up."

"That makes sense." Jasim hesitated, then added, "When we go, I don't want to leave a back-up."

"Ah." They'd traveled from Najib leaving nothing of themselves behind: if their transmission had somehow failed to make it to Nazdeek, no stored copy of the data would ever have woken to resume their truncated lives. Travel within the Amalgam's established network carried negligible risks, though. If they flung themselves toward the hypothetical location of this yet-to-be-assembled station in the middle of nowhere, it was entirely possible that they'd sail off to infinity without ever being instantiated again.

Leila said, "Are you tired of what we're doing? Of what we've become?"

"It's not that."

"This one chance isn't the be-all and end-all. Now that we know how to hunt for the beams, I'm sure we'll find this one again after its shifts. We could find a thousand others, if we're persistent."

"I know that," he said. "I don't want to stop, I don't want to end this. But I want to *risk* ending it. Just once. While that still means something."

Leila sat up and rested her head on her knees. She could understand what he was feeling, but it still disturbed her.

Jasim said, "We've already achieved something extraordinary. No one's found a clue like this in a million years. If we leave that to posterity, it will be pursued to the end, we can be sure of that. But I desperately want to pursue it myself. With you."

"And because you want that so badly, you need to face the chance of losing it?"

"Yes."

It was one thing they had never tried. In their youth, they would never have knowingly risked death. They'd been too much in love, too eager for the life they'd yet to live; the stakes would have been unbearably high. In the twilight years, back on Najib, it would have been an easy thing to do, but an utterly insipid pleasure.

Jasim sat up and took her hand. "Have I hurt you with this?"

"No, no." She shook her head pensively, trying to gather her thoughts. She didn't want to hide her feelings, but she wanted to express them precisely, not blurt them out in a confusing rush. "I always thought we'd reach the end together, though. We'd come to some point in the jungle, look around, exchange a glance, and know that we'd arrived. Without even needing to say it aloud."

Jasim drew her to him and held her. "All right, I'm sorry. Forget everything I said."

Leila pushed him away, annoyed. "This isn't something you can take back. If it's the truth, it's the truth. Just give me some time to decide what I want."

They put it aside, and buried themselves in work: polishing the design for the new observatory, preparing the requests to send to the three outposts. One of the planets they would be petitioning belonged to the Snakes, so Leila and Jasim went to visit the nest for a second time, to seek advice on the best way to beg for this favor. Their neighbors seemed more excited just to see them again than they were at the news that a tiny rent had appeared in the Aloof's million-year-old cloak of discretion. When Leila gently pushed her on this point, Sarah said, "You're here, here and now, our guests in flesh and blood. I'm sure I'll be dead long before the Aloof are willing to do the same."

Leila thought: What kind of strange greed is it that I'm suffering from? I can be feted by creatures who rose up from the dust through a completely different molecule than my own ancestors. I can sit among them and discuss the philosophy of life and death. The Amalgam has already joined every willing participant in the galaxy into one vast conversation. And I want to go and eavesdrop on the Aloof? Just because they've played hard-to-get for a million years?

They dispatched requests for the three modules to be built and launched by their three as-yet unwitting collaborators, specifying the final countdown to the nanosecond but providing a ten-year period for the project to be debated. Leila felt optimistic; however blasé the Nazdeek nest had been, she suspected that no space-faring culture really could resist the chance to peek behind the veil.

They had thirty-six years to wait before they followed in the wake of their petitions; on top of the ten-year delay, the new observatory's modules would be traveling at a fraction of a percent below lightspeed, so they needed a head start.

No more telltale gamma ray flashes appeared from the bulge, but Leila hadn't expected any so soon. They had sent the news of their discovery to other worlds close to the Aloof's territory, so eventually a thousand other groups with different vantage points would be searching for the same kind of evidence and finding their own ways to interpret and exploit it. It hurt a little, scattering their hard-won revelation to the wind for anyone to use—perhaps even to beat them to some far greater prize—but they'd relied on the generosity of their predecessors from the moment they'd arrived on Nazdeek, and the sheer scale of the overall problem made it utterly perverse to cling selfishly to their own small triumph.

As the day of their departure finally arrived, Leila came to a decision. She understood Jasim's need to put everything at risk, and in a sense she shared it. If she had always imagined the two of them ending this together—struggling on, side by side, until the way forward was lost and the undergrowth closed in on them—then *that* was what she'd risk. She would take the flip side to his own wager.

When the house took their minds apart and sent them off to chase the beam, Leila left a copy of herself frozen on Nazdeek. If no word of their safe arrival reached it by the expected time, it would wake and carry on the search.

Alone.

VI

"Welcome to Trident. We're honored by the presence of our most distinguished guest."

Jasim stood beside the bed, waving a triangular flag. Red, green and blue in the corners merged to white in the center.

"How long have you been up?"

"About an hour," he said. Leila frowned, and he added apologetically, "You were sleeping very deeply, I didn't want to disturb you."

"I should be the one giving the welcome," she said. "You're the one who might never have woken."

The bedroom window looked out into a dazzling field of stars. It was not a view facing the bulge—by now Leila could recognize the distinctive spectra of the region's stars with ease—but even these disk stars were so crisp and bright that this was like no sky she had ever seen.

"Have you been downstairs?" she said.

"Not yet. I wanted us to decide on that together." The house had no physical wing here; the tiny observatory had no spare mass for such frivolities as embodying them, let alone constructing architectural follies in the middle of interstellar space. "Downstairs" would be nothing but a scape that they were free to design at will.

"Everything worked," she said, not quite believing it.

Jasim spread his arms. "We're here, aren't we?"

They watched a reconstruction of the first two modules coming together. The timing and the trajectories were as near to perfect as they could have hoped for, and the superconducting magnets had been constructed to a standard of purity and homogeneity that made the magnetic embrace look like an idealized simulation. By the time the two had locked together, the third module was just minutes away. Some untraceable discrepancy between reality and prediction in the transfer of momentum to radiation had the composite moving at a tiny angle away from its expected course, but when it met the third module the magnetic fields still meshed in a stable configuration, and there was energy to spare to nudge the final assembly precisely into step with the predicted swinging of the Aloof's beam.

The Amalgam had lived up to its promise: three worlds full of beings they had never met, who owed them nothing, who did not even share their molecular ancestry, had each diverted enough energy to light up all their cities for a decade, and followed the instructions of strangers down to the atom, down to the nanosecond, in order to make this work.

What happened now was entirely in the hands of the Aloof.

Trident had been functioning for about a month before its designers had arrived to take up occupancy. So far, it had not yet observed any gamma ray signals spilling out of the bulge. The particular pulse that Leila and Jasim had seen triggering fluorescence would be long gone, of course, but the usefulness of their present location was predicated on three assumptions: the Aloof would use the same route for many other bursts of data; some of the radiation carrying that data would slip past the intended receiver; and the two nodes of the network would have continued in free-fall long enough for the spilt data to be arriving here still, along the same predictable path.

Without those three extra components, delivered by their least reliable partners, Trident would be worthless.

"Downstairs," Leila said. "Maybe a kind of porch with glass walls?"

"Sounds fine to me."

She conjured up a plan of the house and sketched some ideas, then they went down to try them out at full scale.

They had been into orbit around Najib, and they had traveled embodied to its three beautiful, barren sibling worlds, but they had never been in interstellar space before. Or at least, they had never been conscious of it.

They were still not truly embodied, but you didn't need flesh and blood to feel the vacuum around you; to be awake and plugged-in to an honest depiction of your surroundings was enough. The nearest of Trident's contributor worlds was six hundred light-years away. The distance to Najib was unthinkable. Leila paced around the porch, looking out at the stars, vertiginous in her virtual body, unsteady in the phoney gravity.

It had been twenty-eight thousand years since they'd left Najib. All her children and grandchildren had almost certainly chosen death, long ago. No messages had been sent after them to Nazdeek; Leila had asked for that silence, fearing that it would be unbearably painful to hear news, day after day, to which she could give no meaningful reply, about events in which she could never participate. Now she regretted that. She wanted to read about the lives of her grandchildren, as she might the biography of an ancestor. She wanted to know how things had ended up, like the time traveler she was.

A second month of observation passed, with nothing. A data feed reaching them from Nazdeek was equally silent. For any new hint of the beam's location to reach Nazdeek, and then the report of that to reach Trident, would take thousands of years longer than the direct passage of the beam itself, so if Nazdeek saw evidence that the beam was "still" on course, that would be old news about a pulse they had not been here to intercept. However, if Nazdeek reported that the beam had shifted, at least that would put them out of their misery immediately, and tell them that Trident had been built too late.

Jasim made a vegetable garden on the porch and grew exotic food in the starlight. Leila played along, and ate beside him; it was a harmless game. They could have painted anything at all around the house: any planet they'd visited, drawn from their memories, any imaginary world. If this small pretense was enough to keep them sane and anchored to reality, so be it.

Now and then, Leila felt the strangest of the many pangs of isolation Trident induced: here, the knowledge of the galaxy was no longer at her fingertips. Their descriptions as travelers had encoded their vast personal memories, declarative and episodic, and their luggage had included prodigious libraries, but she was used to having so much more. Every civilized planet held a storehouse of information that was simply too bulky to fit into Trident, along with a constant feed of exabytes of news flooding in from other worlds. Wherever you were in the galaxy, some news was old news, some cherished theories long discredited, some facts hopelessly out of date. Here, though, Leila knew, there were billions of rigourously established truths—the results of hundreds of millennia of thought, experiment and observation—that had slipped out of her reach. Questions that any other child of the Amalgam could expect to have answered instantly would take twelve hundred years to receive a reply.

No such questions actually came into her mind, but there were still moments when the mere fact of it was enough to make her feel unbearably rootless, cut adrift not only from her past and her people, but from civilization itself.

Trident shouted: "Data!"

Leila was halfway through recording a postcard to the Nazdeek Snakes. Jasim was on the porch watering his plants. Leila turned to see him walking through the wall, commanding the bricks to part like a gauze curtain.

They stood side by side, watching the analysis emerge.

A pulse of gamma rays of the expected frequency, from precisely the right location, had just washed over Trident. The beam was greatly attenuated by distance, not to mention having had most of its energy intercepted by its rightful owner, but more than enough had slipped past and reached them for Trident to make sense of the nature of the pulse.

It was, unmistakably, modulated with information. There were precisely repeated phase shifts in the radiation that were unimaginable in any natural gamma ray source, and which would have been pointless in any artificial beam produced for any purpose besides communication.

The pulse had been three seconds long, carrying about ten-to-the-twenty-fourth bits of data. The bulk of this appeared to be random, but that did not rule out meaningful content, it simply implied efficient encryption. The Amalgam's network sent encrypted data via robust classical channels like this, while sending the keys needed to decode it by a second, quantum channel. Leila had never expected to get hold of unencrypted data, laying bare the secrets of the Aloof in an instant. To have clear evidence that someone in the bulge was talking to someone else, and to have pinned down part of the pathway connecting them, was vindication enough.

There was more, though. Between the messages themselves, Trident had identified brief, orderly, unencrypted sequences. Everything was guesswork to a degree, but with such a huge slab of data statistical measures were powerful indicators. Part of the data looked like routing information, addresses for the messages as they were carried through the network. Another part looked like information about the nodes' current and future trajectories. If Trident really had cracked that, they could work out where to position its successor. In fact, if they placed the successor close enough to the bulge, they could probably keep that one observatory constantly inside the spill from the beam.

Jasim couldn't resist playing devil's advocate. "You know, this could just be one part of whatever throws the probes back in our faces, talking to another part. The Aloof themselves could still be dead, while their security system keeps humming with paranoid gossip."

Leila said blithely, "Hypothesize away. I'm not taking the bait."

She turned to embrace him, and they kissed. She said, "I've forgotten how to celebrate. What happens now?"

He moved his fingertips gently along her arm. Leila opened up the scape, creating a fourth spatial dimension. She took his hand, kissed it, and placed it against her beating heart. Their bodies reconfigured, nerve-endings crowding every surface, inside and out.

Jasim climbed inside her, and she inside him, the topology of the scape changing to wrap them together in a mutual embrace. Everything vanished from their lives but pleasure, triumph and each other's presence, as close as it could ever be.

VII

"Are you here for the Listening Party?"

The chitinous heptapod, who'd been wandering the crowded street with a food cart dispensing largesse at random, offered Leila a plate of snacks tailored to her and Jasim's preferences. She accepted it, then paused to let Tassef, the planet they'd just set foot on, brief her as to the meaning of this phrase. People, Tassef explained, had traveled to this world from throughout the region in order to witness a special event. Some fifteen thousand years before, a burst of data from the Aloof's network had been picked up by a nearby observatory. In isolation, these bursts meant very little; however, the locals were hopeful that at least one of several proposed observatories near Massa, on the opposite side of the bulge, would have seen spillage including many of the same data packets, forty thousand years before. If any such observations had in fact taken place, news of their precise contents should now, finally, be about to reach Tassef by the longer, disk-based routes of the Amalgam's own network. Once the two observations could be compared, it would become clear which messages from the earlier Eavesdropping session had made their way to the part of the Aloof's network that could be sampled from Tassef. The comparison would advance the project of mapping all the symbolic addresses seen in the data onto actual physical locations.

Leila said, "That's not why we came, but now we know, we're even more pleased to be here."

The heptapod emitted a chirp that Leila understood as a gracious welcome, then pushed its way back into the throng.

Jasim said, "Remember when you told me that everyone would get bored with the Aloof while we were still in transit?"

"I said that would happen eventually. If not this trip, the next one."

"Yes, but you said it five journeys ago."

Leila scowled, preparing to correct him, but then she checked and he was right.

They hadn't expected Tassef to be so crowded when they'd chosen it as their destination, some ten thousand years before. The planet had given them a small room in this city, Shalouf, and imposed a thousand-year limit on their presence if they wished to remain embodied without adopting local citizenship. More than a billion visitors had arrived over the last fifty years, anticipating the news of the observations from Massa, but unable to predict the precise time it would reach Tassef because the details of the observatories' trajectories had still been in transit.

She confessed, "I never thought a billion people would arrange their travel plans around this jigsaw puzzle."

"Travel plans?" Jasim laughed. "We chose to have our own deaths revolve around the very same thing."

"Yes, but we're just weird."

Jasim gestured at the crowded street. "I don't think we can compete on that score."

They wandered through the city, drinking in the decades-long-carnival atmosphere. There were people of every phenotype Leila had encountered before, and more: bipeds, quadrupeds, hexapods, heptapods, walking, shuffling, crawling, scuttling, or soaring high above the street on feathered, scaled or membranous wings. Some were encased in their preferred atmospheres; others, like Leila and Jasim, had chosen instead to be embodied in ersatz flesh that didn't follow every ancestral chemical dictate. Physics and geometry tied evolution's hands, and many attempts to solve the same problems had converged on similar answers, but the galaxy's different replicators still managed their idiosyncratic twists. When Leila let her translator sample the cacophony of voices and signals at random, she felt as if the whole disk, the whole Amalgam, had converged on this tiny metropolis.

In fact, most of the travelers had come just a few hundred light-years to be here.

She and Jasim had chosen to keep their role in the history of Eavesdropping out of their précis, and Leila caught herself with a rather smug sense of walking among the crowd like some unacknowledged sage, bemused by the late-blooming, and no doubt superficial, interest of the masses. On reflection, though, any sense of superior knowledge was hard to justify, when most of these people would have grown up steeped in developments that she was only belatedly catching up with. A new generation of observatories had been designed while she and Jasim were in transit, based on "strong bullets": specially designed femtomachines, clusters of protons and neutrons stable only for trillionths of a second, launched at ultra-relativistic speeds so great that time dilation enabled them to survive long enough to collide with other components and merge into tiny, short-lived gamma-ray observatories. The basic trick that had built Trident had gone from a one-off gamble into a miniaturized, mass-produced phenomenon, with literally billions of strong bullets being fired continuously from thousands of planets around the inner disk.

Femtomachines themselves were old hat, but it had taken the technical challenges of Eavesdropping to motivate someone into squeezing a few more tricks out of them. Historians had always understood that in the long run, technological progress was a horizontal asymptote: once people had more or less everything they wanted that was physically possible, every incremental change would take exponentially longer to achieve, with diminishing returns and ever less reason to bother. The Amalgam would probably spend an eon inching its way closer to the flatline, but this was proof that shifts of circumstance alone could still trigger a modest renaissance or two, without the need for any radical scientific discovery or even a genuinely new technology.

They stopped to rest in a square, beside a small fountain gushing aromatic hydrocarbons. The Tassef locals, quadrupeds with slick, rubbery hides, played in the sticky black spray then licked each other clean.

Jasim shaded his eyes from the sun. He said, "We've had our autumn child, and we've seen its grandchildren prosper. I'm not sure what's left."

"No." Leila was in no rush to die, but they'd sampled fifty thousand years of their discovery's consequences. They'd followed in the wake of the news of the gamma ray signals as it circled the inner disk, spending less than a century conscious as they sped from world to world. At first they'd been hunting for some vital new role to play, but they'd slowly come to accept that the avalanche they'd triggered had outraced them. Physical and logical maps of the Aloof's network were being constructed, as fast as the laws of physics allowed. Billions of people on thousands of planets, scattered around the inner rim of the Amalgam's territory, were sharing their observations to help piece together the living skeleton of their elusive neighbors. When that project was complete it would not be the end of anything, but it could mark the start of a long hiatus. The encrypted, classical data would never yield anything more than traffic routes; no amount of ingenuity could extract its content. The quantum keys that could unlock it, assuming the Aloof even used such things, would be absolutely immune to theft, duplication or surreptitious sampling. One day, there would be another breakthrough, and everything would change again, but did they want to wait a hundred thousand years, a million, just to see what came next?

The solicitous heptapods—not locals, but visitors from a world thirty light-years away who had nonetheless taken on some kind of innate duty of hospitality—seemed to show up whenever anyone was hungry. Leila tried to draw this second one into conversation, but it politely excused itself to rush off and feed someone else.

Leila said, "Maybe this is it. We'll wait for the news from Massa, then celebrate for a while, then finish it."

Jasim took her hand. "That feels right to me. I'm not certain, but I don't think I'll ever be."

"Are you tired?" she said. "Bored?"

"Not at all," he replied. "I feel *satisfied*. With what we've done, what we've seen. And I don't want to dilute that. I don't want to hang around forever, watching it fade, until we start to feel the way we did on Najib all over again."

"No."

They sat in the square until dusk, and watched the stars of the bulge come out. They'd seen this dazzling jewelled hub from every possible angle now, but Leila never grew tired of the sight.

Jasim gave an amused, exasperated sigh. "That beautiful, maddening, unreachable place. I think the whole Amalgam will be dead and gone without anyone setting foot inside it."

Leila felt a sudden surge of irritation, which deepened into a sense of revulsion. "It's a place, like any other place! Stars, gas, dust, planets. It's not some metaphysical realm. It's not even far away. Our own home world is twenty times more distant."

"Our own home world doesn't have an impregnable fence around it. If we really wanted to, we could go back there."

Leila was defiant. "If we really wanted to, we could enter the bulge."

Jasim laughed. "Have you read something in those messages that you didn't tell me about? How to say 'open sesame' to the gatekeepers?"

Leila stood, and summoned a map of the Aloof's network to superimpose across their vision, crisscrossing the sky with slender cones of violet light. One cone appeared head-on, as a tiny circle: the beam whose spillage came close to Tassef. She put her hand on Jasim's shoulder, and zoomed in on that circle. It opened up before them like a beckoning tunnel.

She said, "We know where this beam is coming from. We don't know for certain that the traffic between these particular nodes runs in both directions, but we've found plenty of examples where it does. If we aim a signal from here, back along the path of the spillage, and we make it wide enough, then we won't just hit the sending node. We'll hit the receiver as well."

Jasim was silent.

"We know the data format," she continued. "We know the routing information. We can address the data packets to a node on the other side of the bulge, one where the spillage comes out at Massa."

Jasim said, "What makes you think they'll accept the packets?"

"There's nothing in the format we don't understand, nothing we can't write for ourselves."

"Nothing in the unencrypted part. If there's an authorization, even a checksum, in the encrypted part, then any packet without that will be tossed away as noise."

"That's true," she conceded.

"Do you really want to do this?" he said. Her hand was still on his shoulder, she could feel his body growing tense.

"Absolutely."

"We mail ourselves from here to Massa, as unencrypted, classical data that anyone can read, anyone can copy, anyone can alter or corrupt?"

"A moment ago you said they'd throw us away as noise."

"That's the least of our worries."

"Maybe."

Jasim shuddered, his body almost convulsing. He let out a string of obscenities, then made a choking sound. "What's wrong with you? Is this some kind of test? If I call your bluff, will you admit that you're joking."

Leila shook her head. "And no, it's not revenge for what you did on the way to Trident. This is our chance. *This* is what we were waiting to do—not the Eavesdropping, that's nothing! The bulge is right here in front of us. The Aloof are in there, somewhere. We can't force them to engage with us, but we can get closer to them than anyone has ever been before."

"If we go in this way, they could do anything to us."

"They're not barbarians. They haven't made war on us. Even the engineering spores come back unharmed."

"If we infest their network, that's worse than an engineering spore."

"'Infest'! None of these routes are crowded. A few exabytes passing through is nothing."

"You have no idea how they'll react."

"No," she confessed. "I don't. But I'm ready to find out."

Jasim stood. "We could send a test message first. Then go to Massa and see if it arrived safely."

"We could do that," Leila conceded. "That would be a sensible plan."

"So you agree?" Jasim gave her a wary, frozen smile. "We'll send a test message. Send an encyclopedia. Send greetings in some universal language."

"Fine. We'll send all of those things first. But I'm not waiting more than one day after that. I'm not going to Massa the long way. I'm taking the shortcut, I'm going through the bulge."

VIII

The Amalgam had been so generous to Leila, and local interest in the Aloof so intense, that she had almost forgotten that she was not, in fact, entitled to a limitless and unconditional flow of resources, to be employed to any end that involved her obsession.

When she asked Tassef for the means to build a high-powered gamma-ray transmitter to aim into the bulge, it interrogated her for an hour, then replied that the matter would require a prolonged and extensive consultation. It was, she realized, no use protesting that compared to hosting a billion guests for a couple of centuries, the cost of this was nothing. The sticking point was not the energy use, or any other equally microscopic consequence for the comfort and amenity of the Tassef locals. The issue was whether her proposed actions might be seen as unwelcome and offensive by the Aloof, and whether that affront might in turn provoke some kind of retribution.

Countless probes and spores had been gently and patiently returned from the bulge unharmed, but they'd come blundering in at less than lightspeed. A flash of gamma rays could not be intercepted and returned before it struck its chosen target. Though it seemed to Leila that it would be a trivial matter for the network to choose to reject the data, it was not unreasonable to suppose that the Aloof's sensibilities might differ on this point from her own.

Jasim had left Shalouf for a city on the other side of the planet. Leila's feelings about this were mixed; it was always painful when they separated, but the reminder that they were not irrevocably welded together also brought an undeniable sense of space and freedom. She loved him beyond measure, but that was not the final word on every question. She was not certain that she would not relent in the end, and die quietly beside him when the news came through from Massa; there were moments when it seemed utterly perverse, masochistic and self-aggrandising to flee from that calm, dignified end for the sake of trying to cap their modest revolution with a new and spectacularly dangerous folly. Nor though, was she certain that Jasim would not change his own mind, and take her hand while they plunged off this cliff together.

When the months dragged on with no decision on her request, no news from Massa and no overtures from her husband, Leila became an orator, traveling from city to city promoting her scheme to blaze a trail through the heart of the bulge. Her words and image were conveyed into virtual fora, but her physical presence was a way to draw attention to her cause, and Listening Party pilgrims and Tassefi alike packed the meeting places when she came. She mastered the locals' language and style, but left it inflected with some suitably alien mannerisms. The fact that a rumor had arisen that she was one of the First Eavesdroppers did no harm to her attendance figures.

When she reached the city of Jasim's self-imposed exile, she searched the audience for him in vain. As she walked out into the night a sense of panic gripped her. She felt no fear for herself, but the thought of him dying here alone was unbearable.

She sat in the street, weeping. How had it come to this? They had been prepared for a glorious failure, prepared to be broken by the Aloof's unyielding silence, and instead the fruits of their labor had swept through the disk, reinvigorating a thousand cultures. How could the taste of success be so bitter?

Leila imagined calling out to Jasim, finding him, holding him again, repairing their wounds.

A splinter of steel remained inside her, though. She looked up into the blazing sky. The Aloof were there, waiting, daring her to stand before them. To come this far, then step back from the edge for the comfort of a familiar embrace, would diminish her. She would not retreat.

The news arrived from Massa: forty thousand years before, the spillage from the far side of the bulge had been caught in time. Vast swathes of the data matched the observations that Tassef had been holding in anticipation of this moment, for the last fifteen thousand years.

There was more: reports of other correlations from other observatories followed within minutes. As the message from Massa had been relayed around the inner disk, a cascade of similar matches with other stores of data had been found.

By seeing where packets dropped out of the stream, their abstract addresses became concrete, physical locations within the bulge. As Leila stood in Shalouf's main square in the dusk, absorbing the reports, the Aloof's network was growing more solid, less ethereal, by the minute.

The streets around her were erupting with signs of elation: polyglot shouts, chirps and buzzes, celebratory scents and vivid pigmentation changes. Bursts of luminescence spread across the square. Even the relentlessly sober heptapods had abandoned their food carts to lie on their backs, spinning with delight. Leila wheeled around, drinking it in, commanding her translator to punch the meaning of every disparate gesture and sound deep into her brain, unifying the kaleidoscope into a single emotional charge.

As the stars of the bulge came out, Tassef offered an overlay for everyone to share, with the newly mapped routes shining like golden highways. From all around her, Leila picked up the signals of those who were joining the view: people of every civilization, every species, every replicator were seeing the Aloof's secret roads painted across the sky.

Leila walked through the streets of Shalouf, feeling Jasim's absence sharply, but too familiar with that pain to be overcome by it. If the joy of this moment was muted, every celebration would be blighted in the same way, now. She could not expect anything else. She would grow inured to it.

Tassef spoke to her.

"The citizens have reached a decision. They will grant your request."

"I'm grateful."

"There is a condition. The transmitter must be built at least twenty light-years away, either in interstellar space, or in the circumstellar region of an uninhabited system."

"I understand." This way, in the event that the Aloof felt threatened to the point of provoking destructive retribution, Tassef would survive an act of violence, at least on a stellar scale, directed against the transmitter itself.

"We advise you to prepare your final plans for the hardware, and submit them when you're sure they will fulfill your purpose."

"Of course."

Leila went back to her room, and reviewed the plans she had already drafted. She had anticipated the Tassefi wanting a considerable safety margin, so she had worked out the energy budgets for detailed scenarios involving engineering spores and forty-seven different cometary clouds that fell within Tassef's jurisdiction. It took just seconds to identify the best one that met the required conditions, and she lodged it without hesitation.

Out on the streets, the Listening Party continued. For the billion pilgrims, this was enough: they would go home, return to their grandchildren, and die happy in the knowledge that they had finally seen something new in the world. Leila envied them; there'd been a time when that would have been enough for her, too.

She left her room and rejoined the celebration, talking, laughing, dancing with strangers, letting herself grow giddy with the moment. When the sun came up, she made her way home, stepping lightly over the sleeping bodies that filled the street.

The engineering spores were the latest generation: strong bullets launched at close to lightspeed that shed their momentum by diving through the heart of a star, and then rebuilding themselves at atomic density as they decayed in the stellar atmosphere. In effect, the dying femtomachines constructed nanomachines bearing the same blueprints as they'd carried within themselves at nuclear densities, and which then continued out to the cometary cloud to replicate and commence the real work of mining raw materials and building the gamma ray transmitter.

Leila contemplated following in their wake, sending herself as a signal to be picked up by the as-yet-unbuilt transmitter. It would not have been as big a gamble as Jasim's with Trident; the strong bullets had already been used successfully this way in hundreds of similar stars.

In the end, she chose to wait on Tassef for a signal that the transmitter had been successfully constructed, and had tested, aligned and calibrated itself. If she was going to march blindly into the bulge, it would be absurd to stumble and fall prematurely, before she even reached the precipice.

When the day came, some ten thousand people gathered in the center of Shalouf to bid the traveler a safe journey. Leila would have preferred to slip away quietly, but after all her lobbying she had surrendered her privacy, and the Tassefi seemed to feel that she owed them this last splash of color and ceremony.

Forty-six years after the Listening Party, most of the pilgrims had returned to their homes, but of the few hundred who had lingered in Shalouf nearly all had shown up for this curious footnote to the main event. Leila wasn't sure that anyone here believed the Aloof's network would do more than bounce her straight back into the disk, but the affection these well-wishers expressed seemed genuine. Someone had even gone to the trouble of digging up a phrase in the oldest known surviving language of her ancestral species: *safar bekheyr*, may your journey be blessed. They had written it across the sky in an ancient script that she'd last seen eighty thousand years before, and it had been spread among the crowd phonetically so that everyone she met could offer her this hopeful farewell as she passed.

Tassef, the insentient delegate of all the planet's citizens, addressed the crowd with some somber ceremonial blather. Leila's mind wandered, settling on the observation that she was probably partaking in a public execution. No matter. She had said good-bye to her friends and family long ago. When she stepped through the ceremonial gate, which had been smeared with a tarry mess that the Tassefi considered the height of beauty, she would close her eyes and recall her last night on Najib, letting the intervening millennia collapse into a dream. Everyone chose death in the end, and no one's exit was perfect. Better to rely on your own flawed judgments, better to make your own ungainly mess of it, than live in the days when nature would simply take you at random.

As Tassef fell silent, a familiar voice rose up from the crowd.

"Are you still resolved to do this foolish thing?"

Leila glared down at her husband. "Yes, I am."

"You won't reconsider?"

"No."

"Then I'm coming with you."

Jasim pushed his way through the startled audience, and climbed onto the stage.

Leila spoke to him privately. "You're embarrassing us both."

He replied the same way. "Don't be petty. I know I've hurt you, but the blame lies with both of us."

"Why are you doing this? You've made your own wishes very plain."

"Do you think I can watch you walk into danger, and not walk beside you?"

"You were ready to die if Trident failed. You were ready to leave me behind then."

"Once I spoke my mind on that you gave me no choice. You insisted." He took her hand. "You know I only stayed away from you all this time because I hoped it would dissuade you. I failed. So now I'm here."

Leila's heart softened. "You're serious? You'll come with me?"

Jasim said, "Whatever they do to you, let them do it to us both."

Leila had no argument to make against this, no residue of anger, no false solicitousness. She had always wanted him beside her at the end, and she would not refuse him now.

She spoke to Tassef. "One more passenger. Is that acceptable?" The energy budget allowed for a thousand years of test transmissions to follow in her wake; Jasim would just be a minor blip of extra data.

"It's acceptable." Tassef proceeded to explain the change to the assembled crowd, and to the onlookers scattered across the planet.

Jasim said, "We'll interweave the data from both of us into a single packet. I don't want to end up at Massa and find they've sent you to Jahnom by mistake."

"All right." Leila arranged the necessary changes. None of the Eavesdroppers yet knew that they were coming, and no message sent the long way could warn them in time, but the data they sent into the bulge would be prefaced by instructions that anyone in the Amalgam would find clear and unambiguous, asking that their descriptions only be embodied if they were picked up at Massa. If they were found in other spillage along the way, they didn't want to be embodied multiple times. And if they did not emerge at Massa at all, so be it.

Tassef's second speech came to an end. Leila looked down at the crowd one last time, and let her irritation with the whole bombastic ceremony dissipate into amusement. If she had been among the sane, she might easily have turned up herself to watch a couple of ancient fools try to step onto the imaginary road in the sky, and wish them *safar bekheyr*.

She squeezed Jasim's hand, and they walked toward the gate.

IX

Leila's fingers came together, her hand empty. She felt as if she was falling, but nothing in sight appeared to be moving. Then again, all she could see was a distant backdrop, its scale and proximity impossible to judge: thousands of fierce blue stars against the blackness of space.

She looked around for Jasim, but she was utterly alone. She could see no vehicle or other machine that might have disgorged her into this emptiness. There was not even a planet below her, or a single brightest star to which she might be bound. Absurdly, she was breathing. Every other cue told her that she was drifting through vacuum, probably through interstellar space. Her lungs kept filling and emptying, though. The air, and her skin, felt neither hot nor cold.

Someone or something had embodied her, or was running her as software. She was not on Massa, she was sure of that; she had never visited that world, but nowhere in the Amalgam would a guest be treated like this. Not even one who arrived unannounced in data spilling out from the bulge.

Leila said, "Are you listening to me? Do you understand me?" She could hear her own voice, flat and without resonance. The acoustics made perfect sense in a vast, empty, windless place, if not an airless one.

Anywhere in the Amalgam, you *knew* whether you were embodied or not; it was the nature of all bodies, real or virtual, that declarative knowledge of every detail was there for the asking. Here, when Leila tried to summon the same information, her mind remained blank. It was like the strange absence she'd felt on Trident, when she'd been cut off from the repositories of civilization, but here the amputation had reached all the way inside her.

She inhaled deeply, but there was no noticeable scent at all, not even the whiff of her own body odor that she would have expected, whether she was wearing her ancestral phenotype or any of the forms of ersatz flesh that she adopted when the environment demanded it. She pinched the skin of her forearm; it felt more like her original skin than any of the substitutes she'd ever worn. They might have fashioned this body out of something both remarkably lifelike and chemically inert, and placed her in a vast, transparent container of air, but she was beginning to pick up a strong stench of ersatz physics. Air and skin alike, she suspected, were made of bits, not atoms.

So where was Jasim? Were they running him too, in a separate scape? She called out his name, trying not to make the exploratory cry sound plaintive. She understood all too well now why he'd tried so hard to keep her from this place, and why he'd been unable to face staying behind: the thought that the Aloof might be doing something unspeakable to his defenseless consciousness, in some place she couldn't hope to reach or see, was like a white hot blade pressed to her heart. All she could do was try to shut off the panic and talk down the possibility. *All right, he's alone here, but so am I, and it's not that bad.* She would put her faith in symmetry; if they had not abused her, why would they have harmed Jasim?

She forced herself to be calm. The Aloof had taken the trouble to grant her consciousness, but she couldn't expect the level of amenity she was accustomed to. For a start, it would be perfectly reasonable if her hosts were unable or unwilling to plug her into any data source equivalent to the Amalgam's libraries, and perhaps the absence of somatic knowledge was not much different. Rather than deliberately fooling her about her body, maybe they had looked at the relevant data channels and decided that *anything* they fed into them would be misleading. Understanding her transmitted description well enough to bring her to consciousness was one thing, but it didn't guarantee that they knew how to translate the technical details of their instantiation of her into her own language.

And if this ignorance-plus-honesty excuse was too sanguine to swallow, it wasn't hard to think of the Aloof as being pathologically secretive without actually being malicious. If they wanted to keep quiet about the way they'd brought her to life lest it reveal something about themselves, that too was understandable. They need not be doing it for the sake of tormenting her.

Leila surveyed the sky around her, and felt a jolt of recognition. She'd memorized the positions of the nearest stars to the target node where her transmission would first be sent, and now a matching pattern stood out against the background in a collection of distinctive constellations. She was being shown the sky from that node. This didn't prove anything about her actual location, but the simplest explanation was that the Aloof had instantiated her here, rather than sending her on through the network. The stars were in the positions she'd predicted for her time of arrival, so if this was the reality, there had been little delay in choosing how to deal with the intruder. No thousand-year-long deliberations, no passing of the news to a distant decision-maker. Either the Aloof themselves were present here, or the machinery of the node was so sophisticated that they might as well have been. She could not have been woken by accident; it had to have been a deliberate act. It made her wonder if the Aloof had been expecting something like this for millennia.

"What now?" she asked. Her hosts remained silent. "Toss me back to Tassef?" The probes with their reversed trajectories bore no record of their experience; perhaps the Aloof wouldn't incorporate these new memories into her description before returning her. She spread her arms imploringly. "If you're going to erase this memory, why not speak to me first? I'm in your hands completely, you can send me to the grave with your secrets. Why wake me at all, if you don't want to talk?"

In the silence that followed, Leila had no trouble imagining one answer: to study her. It was a mathematical certainty that some questions about her behavior could never be answered simply by examining her static description; the only reliable way to predict what she'd do in any given scenario was to wake her and confront her with it. They might, of course, have chosen to wake her any number of times before, without granting her memories of the previous instantiations. She experienced a moment of sheer existential vertigo: this could be the thousandth, the billionth, in a vast series of experiments, as her captors permuted dozens of variables to catalog her responses.

The vertigo passed. Anything was possible, but she preferred to entertain more pleasant hypotheses.

"I came here to talk," she said. "I understand that you don't want us sending in machinery, but there must be something we can discuss, something we can learn from each other. In the disk, every time two space-faring civilizations met, they found they had something in common. Some mutual interests, some mutual benefits."

At the sound of her own earnest speech dissipating into the virtual air around her, Leila started laughing. The arguments she'd been putting for centuries to Jasim, to her friends on Najib, to the Snakes on Nazdeek, seemed ridiculous now, embarrassing. How could she face the Aloof and claim that she had anything to offer them that they had not considered, and rejected, hundreds of thousands of years before? The Amalgam had never tried to keep its nature hidden. The Aloof would have watched them, studied them from afar, and consciously chosen isolation. To come here and list the advantages of contact as if they'd never crossed her hosts' minds was simply insulting.

Leila fell silent. If she had lost faith in her role as cultural envoy, at least she'd proven to her own satisfaction that there was something in her smarter than the slingshot fence the probes had encountered. The Aloof had not embraced her, but the whole endeavor had not been in vain. To wake in the bulge, even to silence, was far more than she'd ever had the right to hope for.

She said, "Please, just bring me my husband now, then we'll leave you in peace."

This entreaty was met in the same way as all the others. Leila resisted speculating again about experimental variables. She did not believe that a million-year-old civilization was interested in testing her tolerance to isolation, robbing her of her companion and seeing how long she took to attempt suicide. The Aloof did not take orders from her; fine. If she was neither an experimental subject to be robbed of her sanity, nor a valued guest whose every wish was granted, there had to be some other relationship between them that she had yet to fathom. She had to be conscious for a reason.

She searched the sky for a hint of the node itself, or any other feature she might have missed, but she might as well have been living inside a star map, albeit one shorn of the usual annotations. The Milky Way, the plane of stars that bisected the sky, was hidden by the thicker clouds of gas and dust here, but Leila had her bearings; she knew which way led deeper into the bulge, and which way led back out to the disk.

She contemplated Tassef's distant sun with mixed emotions, as a sailor might look back on the last sight of land. As the yearning for that familiar place welled up, a cylinder of violet light appeared around her, encircling the direction of her gaze. For the first time, Leila felt her weightlessness interrupted: a gentle acceleration was carrying her forward along the imaginary beam.

"No! Wait!" She closed her eyes and curled into a ball. The acceleration halted, and when she opened her eyes the tunnel of light was gone.

She let herself float limply, paying no attention to anything in the sky, waiting to see what happened if she kept her mind free of any desire for travel.

After an hour like this, the phenomenon had not recurred. Leila turned her gaze in the opposite direction, into the bulge. She cleared her mind of all timidity and nostalgia, and imagined the thrill of rushing deeper into this violent, spectacular, alien territory. At first there was no response from the scape, but then she focused her attention sharply in the direction of a second node, the one she'd hoped her transmission would be forwarded to from the first, on its way through the galactic core.

The same violet light, the same motion. This time, Leila waited a few heartbeats longer before she broke the spell.

Unless this was some pointlessly sadistic game, the Aloof were offering her a clear choice. She could return to Tassef, return to the Amalgam. She could announce that she'd put a toe in these mysterious waters, and lived to tell the tale. Or she could dive into the bulge, as deep as she'd ever imagined, and see where the network took her.

"No promises?" she asked. "No guarantee I'll come out the other side? No intimations of contact, to tempt me further?" She was thinking aloud, she did not expect answers. Her hosts, she was beginning to conclude, viewed strangers through the prism of a strong, but very sharply delineated, sense of obligation. They sent back the insentient probes to their owners, scrupulously intact. They had woken this intruder to give her the choice: Did she really want to go where her transmission suggested, or had she wandered in here like a lost child who just needed to find the way home? They would do her no harm, and send her on no journey without her consent, but those were the limits of their duty of care. They did not owe her any account of themselves. She would get no greeting, no hospitality, no conversation.

"What about Jasim? Will you give me a chance to consult with him?" She waited, picturing his face, willing his presence, hoping they might read her mind if her words were beyond them. If they could decode a yearning toward a point in the sky, surely this wish for companionship was not too difficult to comprehend? She tried variations, dwelling on the abstract structure of their intertwined data in the transmission, hoping this might clarify the object of her desire if his physical appearance meant nothing to them.

She remained alone.

The stars that surrounded her spelt out the only choices on offer. If she wanted to be with Jasim once more before she died, she had to make the same decision as he did.

Symmetry demanded that he faced the same dilemma.

How would he be thinking? He might be tempted to retreat back to the safety of Tassef, but he'd reconciled with her in Shalouf for the sole purpose of following her into danger. He would understand that she'd want to go deeper, would want to push all the way through to Massa, opening up the shortcut through the core, proving it safe for future travelers.

Would he understand, too, that she'd feel a pang of guilt at this presumptuous line of thought, and that she'd contemplate making a sacrifice of her own? He had braved the unknown for her, and they had reaped the reward already: they had come closer to the Aloof than anyone in history. Why couldn't that be enough? For all Leila knew, her hosts might not even wake her again before Massa. What would she be giving up if she turned back now?

More to the point, what would Jasim expect of her? That she'd march on relentlessly, following her obsession to the end, or that she'd put her love for him first?

The possibilities multiplied in an infinite regress. They knew each other as well as two people could, but they didn't carry each other's minds inside them.

Leila drifted through the limbo of stars, wondering if Jasim had already made his decision. Having seen that the Aloof were not the torturers he'd feared, had he already set out for Tassef, satisfied that she faced no real peril at their hands? Or had he reasoned that their experience at this single node meant nothing? This was not the Amalgam, the culture could be a thousand times more fractured.

This cycle of guesses and doubts led nowhere. If she tried to pursue it to the end she'd be paralyzed. There were no guarantees; she could only choose the least worst case. If she returned to Tassef, only to find that Jasim had gone on alone through the bulge, it would be unbearable: she would have lost him for nothing. If that happened, she could try to follow him, returning to the bulge immediately, but she would already be centuries behind him.

If she went on to Massa, and it was Jasim who retreated, at least she'd know that he'd ended up in safety. She'd know, too, that he had not been desperately afraid for her, that the Aloof's benign indifference at this first node had been enough to persuade him that they'd do her no harm.

That was her answer: she had to continue, all the way to Massa. With the hope, but no promise, that Jasim would have thought the same way.

The decision made, she lingered in the scape. Not from any second thoughts, but from a reluctance to give up lightly the opportunity she'd fought so hard to attain. She didn't know if any member of the Aloof was watching and listening to her, reading her thoughts, examining her desires. Perhaps they were so indifferent and incurious that they'd delegated everything to insentient software, and merely instructed their machines to babysit her while she made up her mind where she wanted to go. She still had to make one last attempt to reach them, or she would never die in peace.

"Maybe you're right," she said. "Maybe you've watched us for the last million years, and seen that we have nothing to offer you. Maybe our technology is backward, our philosophy naive, our customs bizarre, our manners appalling. If that's true, though, if we're so far beneath you, you could at least point us in the right direction. Offer us some kind of argument as to why we should change."

Silence.

Leila said, "All right. Forgive my impertinence. I have to tell you honestly, though, that we won't be the last to bother you. The Amalgam is full of people who will keep trying to find ways to reach you. This is going to go on for another million years, until we believe that we understand you. If that offends you, don't judge us too harshly. We can't help it. It's who we are."

She closed her eyes, trying to assure herself that there was nothing she'd regret having left unsaid.

"Thank you for granting us safe passage," she added, "if that's what you're offering. I hope my people can return the favor one day, if there's anywhere you want to go."

She opened her eyes and sought out her destination: deeper into the network, on toward the core.

X

The mountains outside the town of Astraahat started with a gentle slope that promised an easy journey, but gradually grew steeper. Similarly, the vegetation was low and sparse in the foothills, but became steadily thicker and taller the higher up the slope you went.

Jasim said, "Enough." He stopped and leaned on his climbing stick.

"One more hour?" Leila pleaded.

He considered this. "Half an hour resting, then half an hour walking?"

"One hour resting, then one hour walking."

He laughed wearily. "All right. One of each."

The two of them hacked away at the undergrowth until there was a place to sit.

Jasim poured water from the canteen into her hands, and she splashed her face clean.

They sat in silence for a while, listening to the sounds of the unfamiliar wildlife. Under the forest canopy it was almost twilight, and when Leila looked up into the small patch of sky above them she could see the stars of the bulge, like tiny, pale, translucent beads.

At times it felt like a dream, but the experience never really left her. The Aloof had woken her at every node, shown her the view, given her a choice. She had seen a thousand spectacles, from one side of the core to the other: cannibalistic novas, dazzling clusters of newborn stars, twin white dwarfs on the verge of collision. She had seen the black hole at the galaxy's center, its accretion disk glowing with X-rays, slowly tearing stars apart.

It might have been an elaborate lie, a plausible simulation, but every detail accessible from disk-based observatories confirmed what she had witnessed. If anything had been changed, or hidden from her, it must have been small. Perhaps the artifacts of the Aloof themselves had been painted out of the view, though Leila thought it was just as likely that the marks they'd left on their territory were so subtle, anyway, that there'd been nothing to conceal.

Jasim said sharply, "Where are you?"

She lowered her gaze and replied mildly, "I'm here, with you. I'm just remembering."

When they'd woken on Massa, surrounded by delirious, cheering Eavesdroppers, they'd been asked: *What happened in there? What did you see?* Leila didn't know why she'd kept her mouth shut and turned to her husband before replying, instead of letting every detail come tumbling out immediately. Perhaps she just hadn't known where to begin.

For whatever reason, it was Jasim who had answered first. "Nothing. We stepped through the gate on Tassef, and now here we are. On the other side of the bulge."

For almost a month, she'd flatly refused to believe him. *Nothing? You saw nothing?* It had to be a lie, a joke. It had to be some kind of revenge.

That was not in his nature, and she knew it. Still, she'd clung to that explanation for as long as she could, until it became impossible to believe any longer, and she'd asked for his forgiveness.

Six months later, another traveler had spilt out of the bulge. One of the die-hard Listening Party pilgrims had followed in their wake and taken the shortcut. Like Jasim, this heptapod had seen nothing, experienced nothing.

Leila had struggled to imagine why she might have been singled out. So much for her theory that the Aloof felt morally obliged to check that each passenger on their network knew what they were doing, unless they'd decided that her actions were enough to demonstrate that intruders from the disk, considered generically, were making an informed choice. Could just one sample of a working, conscious version of their neighbors really be enough for them to conclude that they understood everything they needed to know? Could this capriciousness, instead, have been part of a strategy to lure in more visitors, with the enticing possibility that each one might, with luck, witness something far beyond all those who'd preceded them? Or had it been part of a scheme to discourage intruders by clouding the experience with uncertainty? The simplest act of discouragement would have been to discard all unwelcome transmissions, and the most effective incentive would have been to offer a few plain words of welcome, but then, the Aloof would not have been the Aloof if they'd followed such reasonable dictates.

Jasim said, "You know what I think. You wanted to wake so badly, they couldn't refuse you. They could tell I didn't care as much. It was as simple as that."

"What about the heptapod? It went in alone. It wasn't just tagging along to watch over someone else."

He shrugged. "Maybe it acted on the spur of the moment. They all seem unhealthily keen to me, whatever they're doing. Maybe the Aloof could discern its mood more clearly."

Leila said, "I don't believe a word of that."

Jasim spread his hands in a gesture of acceptance. "I'm sure you could change my mind in five minutes, if I let you. But if we walked back down this hill and waited for the next traveler from the bulge, and the next, until the reason some of them received the grand tour and some didn't finally became plain, there would still be another question, and another. Even if I wanted to live for ten thousand years more, I'd rather move on to something else. And in this last hour . . ." He trailed off.

Leila said, "I know. You're right."

She sat, listening to the strange chirps and buzzes emitted by creatures she knew nothing about. She could have absorbed every recorded fact about them in an instant, but she didn't care, she didn't need to know.

Someone else would come after them, to understand the Aloof, or advance that great, unruly, frustrating endeavor by the next increment. She and Jasim had made a start; that was enough. What they'd done was more than she could ever have imagined, back on Najib. Now, though, was the time to stop, while they were still themselves: enlarged by the experience, but not disfigured beyond recognition.

They finished their water, drinking the last drops. They left the canteen behind. Jasim took her hand and they climbed together, struggling up the slope side by side.

The ile of dogges

ELiZABETH BEAR AND SARAH MONETTE

New writer Elizabeth Bear was born in Hartford, Connecticut, and now lives in the Mojave Desert near Las Vegas. She won the John W. Campbell Award for Best New Writer in 2005. Her short work has appeared in *SCI FICTION, Interzone, The Third Alternative, On Spec,* and elsewhere, and she is the author of three highly acclaimed SF novels, *Hammered, Scardown, and Worldwired.* Her most recent books are a novel, *Carnival,* and a collection of her short works, *The Chains That You Refuse.* Coming up are a number of new novels, including *Undertow, Blood and Iron, Whiskey and Water,* and *New Amsterdam.*

New writer Sarah Monette was born and raised in Oak Ridge, Tennessee, one of the secret cities of the Manhattan Project. Having completed her Ph.D. in Renaissance English drama, she now lives and writes in a ninety-nine-year-old house in the upper Midwest. Her first novel, *Melusine,* was published in 2005. Her most recent novel is *The Virtu,* the sequel to *Melusine,* and two more novels in the sequence are scheduled to follow: *The Mirador* and *Summerdown.* Her short fiction has appeared in many places, including *Strange Horizons, Aeon, Alchemy,* and *Lady Churchill's Rosebud Wristlet,* and has received four honorable mentions from *The Year's Best Fantasy and Horror.* Sarah's Web site is www.sarahmonette.com.

In the sly little story that follows, the authors demonstrate that although the forces of censorship and repression are everywhere, and every*when,* there are also those who will go to considerable lengths to ensure that works of art do not perish from the Earth. . . .

T he light would last long enough.

Sir Edmund Tylney, in pain and reeking from rotting teeth, stood before the sideboard and crumbled sugar into his sack, causing a sandy yellowish grit to settle at the bottom of the cup. He swirled the drink to sweeten it, then bore it back to his reading table where an unruly stack of quarto pages waited, slit along the folds with a penknife.

He set the cup on the table in the sunlight and drew up his stool, its short legs rasping over the rush mats as he squared it and sat. He reached left-handed for the wine, right-handed for the playscript, drawing both to him over the pegged tabletop. And then he riffled the sheets of Speilman's cheapest laid with his nail.

Bending into the light, wincing as the sweetened wine ached across his teeth with every sip, he read.

He turned over the last leaf, part-covered in secretary's script, as he drank the last gritty swallow in his cup, the square of sun spilling over the table edge to spot the floor. Tylney drew out his own penknife, cut a new point on a quill, and—on a fresh quarter-sheet—began to write the necessary document. The Jonson fellow was inexperienced, it was true. But Tom Nashe should have known better.

Tylney gulped another cup of sack before he set his seal to the denial, drinking fast, before his teeth began to hurt. He knew himself, without vanity, to be a clever man—intelligent, well read. He had to be, to do his job as master of revels and censor for the queen, for the playmakers, too, were clever, and they cloaked their satires under layers of witty language and misdirection. The better the playmaker, the better the play, and the more careful Tylney had to be.

The Ile of Dogges was a good play. Lively, witty. Very clever, as one would expect from Tom Nashe and the newcomer Jonson. And Tylney's long-practiced and discerning eye saw the satire on every page, making mock of—among a host of other, lesser targets—Elizabeth, her privy council, and the lord Chamberlain.

It could never be performed.

RIGHTEOUS-IN-THE-CAUSE SAMSON
Why is't named Ile of Dogges?

WITWORTH
Because here are men like wild dogges. Haue they numbers, they will sauage a lyon: but if the lyon come vpon one by himselfe, he will grouel and showe his belye. And if the lyon but ask it, he will sauage his friends.

RIGHTEOUS-IN-THE-CAUSE SAMSON
But is that not right? For surely a dogge should honour a lyon.

WITWORTH
But on this island, even the lyon is a dogge.[1]

It could never be performed, but it was. A few days later, despite the denial, Jonson and the Earl of Pembroke's Men staged *The Ile of Dogges* at the Swan. Within the day, Jonson and the principal actors were in chains at the Marshalsea, under gentle questioning by the queen's own torturer, Topcliffe himself. The other playwright, Thomas Nashe, fled the city to elude arrest. And The Theatre, The Curtain, The Swan—all of London's great playhouses languished, performances forbidden.

The Ile of Dogges languished, likewise, in a pile on the corner of Tylney's desk,

---

[1] All quotations are from the Poet Emeritus Series edition of *The Ile of Dogges*, edited by Anthony Baldassare (Las Vegas: University of Nevada Press, 2206).

weighted by his penknife (between sharpenings). It lay facedown, cup-ringed pages adorned with the scratch of more than one pen. The dull black oakgall ink had not yet begun to fade, nor the summer's heat to wane, when Tylney, predictably, was graced by a visit from Master Jonson.

Flea bites and shackle gall still reddened the playwright's thick wrists, counterpoint to the whitework of older scars across massive hands. Unfashionably short hair curled above his plain, pitted face. He topped six feet, Ben Jonson. He had been a soldier in the Low Countries.

He ducked to come through the doorway, but stood straight within, stepping to one side after he closed the door so that the wall was at his back. "You burned Tom's papers."

"He fled London. We must be sure of the play, all its copies."

"All of them?" For all his rough bravado, Jonson's youth showed in how easily he revealed surprise. "'Tis but a play."

"Master Jonson," Tylney said, steepling his hands before him, "it mocks the queen. More than that, it might encourage others to mock the queen. 'Tis sedition."

Recovering himself, Jonson snorted. He paced, short quick steps, and turned, and paced back again. "And the spies Parrot and Poley as were jailed in with me? Thought you I'd aught to tell them?"

"No spies of mine," Tylney said. "Perhaps Topcliffe's. Mayhap he thought you had somewhat of interest to him to impart. No Popist sympathies, Master Jonson? No Scottish loyalties?"

Jonson stopped at the farthest swing of his line and stared at the coffered paneling. That wandering puddle of sun warmed his boots this time. He reached out, laid four blunt fingertips and a thumb on the wall—his hand bridged between them— and dropped his head so his arm hid the most of his face. His other hand, Tylney noticed, brushed the surface of the sideboard and left something behind, halfconcealed beside the inkpot. "No point in pleading for the return of the manuscript, I take it?"

"Destroyed," Tylney said, without letting his eyes drop to the pages on his desk. And, as if that were all the restraint he could ask of himself, the question burst out of him: "Why do it, Master Jonson? Why *write* it?"

Jonson shrugged one massive shoulder. "Because it is a good play."

Useless to ask for sense from a poet. One might as well converse with a tabby cat. Tylney lifted the bell, on the other corner of his desk from the play that ought already to be destroyed, and rang it, a summons to his clerk. "Go home, Master Jonson."

"You've not seen the last of me, Sir Edmund," Jonson said, as the door swung open—not a threat, just a fact.

It wasn't the usual clerk, but a tall soft-bellied fellow with wavy black hair, sweetbreathed, with fine white teeth.

"No," Tylney said. He waited until the click of the latch before he added, "I don't imagine I have."

ANGELL

Hast sheared the sheep, Groat?

GROAT

Aye, though their fleece be but siluer.

He handeth Angell a purse.

ANGELL

Then thou must be Iason and find the golden fleece: or mayhap needs
merely shear a little closer to the skin.

GROAT

Will not the sheep grow cold, without their wool?

ANGELL

They can grow more. And, loyal Groat, wouldst prefer thy sheep grow cold,
or thy master grow hot?

GROAT

The sheep may shiuer for all I care.

Tylney waited until Jonson's footsteps retreated into silence, then waited a little
more. When he was certain neither the clerk nor the playmaker were returning, he
came around his table on the balls of his feet and scooped up the clinking pouch
that Jonson had left behind. He bounced it on his hand, a professional gesture, and
frowned at its weight. Heavy.

He replaced it where Jonson had laid it, and went to chip sugar from the loaf and
mix himself another cup of sack, to drink while he reread the play. He read faster
this time, standing up where the light was better, the cup resting on the sideboard by
the inkpot and Jonson's bribe. He shuffled each leaf to the back as he finished.
When he was done, so was the sack.

He weighed the playscript in his hand, frowning at it, sucking his aching teeth.

It was August. There was no fire on the grate.

He dropped the playscript on the sideboard, weighted it with the bribe, locked
the door behind him, and went to tell the clerk—the cousin, he said, of the usual
boy, who was abed with an ague—that he could go.

WITWORTH

That's Moll Tuppence. They call her Queene of Dogges.

RIGHTEOUS-IN-THE-CAUSE SAMSON

For why?

WITWORTH

For that if a man says aught about her which he ought not, she sets her curres
to make him say naught in sooth.

Sir Edmund Tylney lay awake in the night. His teeth pained him, and if he'd any
sense, he'd have had them pulled that winter. No sense, he thought. No more sense

than a tabby cat. Or a poet. And he lay abed and couldn't sleep, haunted by the image of the papers on the sideboard, weighted under Jonson's pouch. He should have burned them that afternoon.

He would go and burn them now. Perhaps read them one more time, just to be certain there was no salvaging this play. Sometimes he would make suggestions, corrections, find ways—through cuts or additions—that a play could be made safe for performance. Sometimes the playmakers acquiesced, and the play was saved.

Though Jonson was a newcomer, Tylney knew already that he did not take kindly to editing. But it was a good play.

Perhaps there was a chance.

Tylney roused himself and paced in the night, in his slippers and shirt, and found himself with candle in hand at the door of his office again. He unlocked it—the tumblers moving silently in the well-oiled catch—and pushed it before him without bothering to lift the candle or, in fact, look up from freeing key from lock.

He knew where everything should be.

The brilliant flash that blinded him came like lightning, like the spark of powder in the pan, and he shouted and threw a warding hand before his eyes, remembering even in his panic not to tip the candle. Someone cursed in a foreign tongue; a heavy hand closed on Tylney's wrist and dragged him into his office, shouldering the door shut behind before he could cry out again.

Whoever clutched him had a powerful grip. Was a big man, young, with soft uncallused hands. "Jonson," he gasped, still half-blinded by the silent lightning, pink spots swimming before his eyes. "You'll hang for this!"

"Sir Edmund," a gentle voice said over the rattle of metal, "I am sorry."

Too gentle to be Jonson, just as those hands, big as they were, were too soft for a soldier's. Not Jonson. The replacement clerk. Tylney shook his head side to side, trying to rattle the dots out of his vision. He blinked, and could almost see, his candle casting a dim glow around the office. If he looked through the edges of his sight, he could make out the lay of the room—and what was disarrayed. *The Ile of Dogges* had been taken from the sideboard, the drapes drawn close across the windows and weighted at the bottom with Jonson's bribe. Perhaps a quarter of the pages were turned.

"I'll shout and raise the house," Tylney said.

"You have already," the clerk said. He released Tylney's wrist once Tylney had steadied himself on the edge of the table, and turned back to the playscript.

"There's only one door out of this room." And Tylney had his back to it. He could hear people moving, a voice calling out, seeking the source of that cry.

"Sir Edmund, shield your eyes." The clerk raised something to his own eye, a flat piece of metal no bigger than a lockplate, and rather like a lockplate, with a round hole in the middle.

Tylney stepped forward instead and grabbed the clerk's arm. "What are you doing?"

The man paused, obviously on the verge of shoving Tylney to the floor, and stared at him. "Damn it to hell," he said. "All right, look. I'm trying to save this play."

"From the fires?"

"From oblivion," he said. He dropped his arm and turned the plate so Tylney could see the back of it. His thumb passed over a couple of small nubs marked with red sigils, and Tylney gasped. As if through a *camera obscura*, the image of a page of *The Ile of Dogges* floated on a bit of glass imbedded in the back of the plate, as crisp and brightly lit as if by brilliant day. It wasn't the page to which the play lay open. "My name's Baldassare," the clerk—the sorcerer—said. "I'm here to preserve this play. It was lost."

"Jonson's summoned demons," Tylney whispered, as someone pounded on the office door. It rattled, and did not open. Baldassare must have claimed the keys when he dragged Tylney inside, and fastened the lock while Tylney was still bedazzled. The light of the candle would show under the door, though. The servants would know he was here.

It was his private office, and Tylney had one of only two keys. Someone would have to wake the steward for the other.

He could shout. But Baldassare could kill him before the household could break down the door. And the sorcerer was staring at him, one eyebrow lifted, as if to see what he would do.

Tylney held his tongue, and the door rattled once more before footsteps retreated.

"Just a historian," Baldassare answered, when the silence had stretched a minute or two.

"*Historian?* But the play's not three months old!"

Baldessare shook his head. "Where I come from, it's far older. And it's . . ." He hesitated, seeming to search for a word. "It's *dead*. No one has ever read it, or seen it performed. Most people don't even know it once existed." He laid fingertips on the papers, caressing. "Let me take it. Let me give it life."

"It's sedition." Tylney grasped the edge of the script, greatly daring, and pulled it from under Baldassare's hand.

"It's brilliant," Baldassare said, and Tylney couldn't argue, though he bundled the papers close to his chest. The sorcerer had been strangely gentle with him, as a younger man with an older. Perhaps he could gamble on that. Perhaps. It was his duty to protect the queen.

Baldassare continued, "None will know, no one shall read it, not until you and Elizabeth and Jonson and Nashe are long in your graves. It will do no harm. I swear it."

"A sorcerer's word," Tylney said. He stepped back, came up hard against the door. The keys weren't in the lock. They must be in Baldassare's hand.

"Would you have it lost forever? Truly?" Baldassare reached and Tylney crowded away. Into the corner, the last place he could retreat. "Sir Edmund!" someone shouted from the hall.

From outside the door, Tylney heard the jangle of keys, their rattle in the lock. "You'll hang," he said to Baldassare.

"Maybe," Baldassare said, with a sudden grin that showed his perfect, white teeth. "But not today." One lingering, regretful look at the papers crumpled to Tylney's chest, and he dropped the keys on the floor, touched something on the wrist of the hand that held the metal plate, and vanished in a shimmer of air as Tylney gaped after him.

The door burst open, framing Tylney's steward, John, against blackness.

Tylney flinched.

"Sir Edmund?" The man came forward, a candle in one hand, the keys in the other. "Are you well?"

"Well enough," Tylney answered, forcing himself not to crane his neck after the vanished man. He could *claim* a demon had appeared in his work room, right enough. He could claim it, but who would believe?

He swallowed, and eased his grip on the play clutched to his chest. "I dropped the keys."

The steward frowned doubtfully. "You cried out, milord."

"I stumbled only," Tylney said. "I feared for the candle. But all is well." He laid the playscript on the table and smoothed the pages as his steward squatted to retrieve the fallen keys. "I thank you for your concern."

The keys were cool and heavy, and clinked against each other like debased coins when the steward handed them over. Tylney laid them on the table beside the candle and the play. He lifted the coin purse from the window ledge, flicked the drapes back, and weighted the pages with the money once more before throwing wide the shutters, heedless of the night air. It was a still summer night, the stink of London rising from the gutters, but a draft could always surprise you, and he didn't feel like chasing paper into corners.

The candle barely flickered. "Sir Edmund?"

"That will be all, John. Thank you."

Silently, the steward withdrew, taking his candle and his own keys with him. He left the door yawning open on darkness. Tylney stood at his table for a moment, watching the empty space.

He and John had the only keys. Baldassare had come and gone like a devil stepping back and forth from Hell. Without the stink of brimstone, though. Perhaps more like an angel. Or memory, which could walk through every room in Tylney's house, through every playhouse in London, and leave no sign.

Tylney bent on creaking knees and laid kindling on the hearth. He stood, and looked at the playscript, one-quarter of the pages turned where it rested on the edge of his writing table, the other three-fourths crumpled and crudely smoothed. He turned another page, read a line in Jonson's hand, and one in Nashe's. His lips stretched over his aching teeth, and he chuckled into his beard.

He laid the pages down. No more sense than a tabby cat. It was late for making a fire. He could burn the play in the morning. Before he returned Jonson's bribe. He'd lock the door behind him, so no one could come in or out. There were only two sets of keys.

Sir Edmund Tylney blew the candle out, and trudged upstairs through the customary dark.

In the morning, he'd see to the burning.

the Highway men

KEN MACLEOD

Ken MacLeod graduated with a B.Sc. in zoology from Glasgow University in 1976. Following research in biomechanics at Brunel University, he worked as a computer analyst/programmer in Edinburgh. He's now a full-time writer, and widely considered to be one of the most exciting new SF writers to emerge in the nineties, his work featuring an emphasis on politics and economics rare in the new space opera, while still maintaining all the widescreen, high-bit-rate, action-packed qualities typical of the form. His first two novels, *The Star Fraction* and *The Stone Canal*, each won the Prometheus Award. His other books include the novels *The Sky Road, The Cassini Division, Cosmonaut Keep, Dark Light, Engine City*, and *Newton's Wake*, plus a novella chapbook, *The Human Front*. His most recent books are the novel *Learning the World* and a collection, *Strange Lizards from Antoher Star*. His stories have appeared in our *Nineteenth* and *Twenty-third Annual Collections*. He lives in West Lothian, Scotland, with his wife and children.

Here he takes us to a glum and diminished future world that yet contains within it a surprising amount of hope—seeds of hope randomly scattered and growing in the most unexpected of fields.

I
DIAMOND CUTTING

It was Murdo Mac who noticed it first. He was riding shotgun. So he could see farther ahead. I had to keep my eye on the road. First I know of it, Murdo bangs on the cab roof. Signal to stop. I braked gently. The early morning road was icy and treacherous. We were about half a kilometre outside a village a bit out from Dingwall.

More a thin straggle of houses, really, like most villages in the Highlands. And like most, it was empty. We knew that.

I rolled down the window. Cold air came in. Murdo poked his head into the cab. His face was red inside the furry parka hood.

"What's up?" I asked.

"There's something no right about yon houses," he said. "Can't for the life of me see what it is, though."

I looked sideways at Euan Campbell. He handed me the binoculars. I propped my elbows on the steering wheel and got the glasses into focus. The five or six houses were on a curve of the road up ahead. I could see all of them. They had that Highland look of being out of place. Like suburban houses stuck down on the moors. Gardens overgrown, sheds falling apart, big bay windows black and empty.

That was it.

"Nae glass in the windows," I said. "In *any* of the windows. And it's not broken, either. Just missing." I passed the binoculars out to Murdo. "See for yourself."

He fiddled with the focus wheel. Clumsy in thick gloves. He drew in a sharp breath as he looked.

"That's it," he said as he handed the glasses back.

"Not much to go on," said Euan.

"Doesn't look right," said Murdo.

"Hunker down," I said. "We'll take it slow."

Murdo's head disappeared from the window. Checking the wing mirror I could see he had ducked back into the lookout's bucket. Shaped like an oil drum, it was bolted to the back of the cab, right behind the driver. It had a low seat, and a roll of armour padding wrapped around the inside. Not very comfortable. We used to take turns.

I eased into first gear and the big highway truck rolled forward. Three hundred metres. Two hundred. One hundred. The first house had a pair of tall rowans growing at the gap where the gate had been. Couldn't say they had brought much luck. I braked and turned off the engine.

No sound but a blackbird's song and the questioning croak of a hoodie crow up on the hill.

"I'll have a look," I said. I jumped out of the cab with a thud of wellies and a crackle of oilskins. "Keep me covered, Murdo." Even to myself it sounded a bit corny.

"Are we in China or what?" Murdo scoffed.

"It's you that's got us twitchy," I pointed out.

"Whatever you say, Jase." Murdo pushed back his parka hood and planted a helmet on his head. The end of the shotgun barrel poked over the rim of the bucket.

I walked up the grassy strip where the path had been. A plastic tricycle, its colours faded, lay in the weeds to one side. I kicked a flat football out of the way and stepped over a broken plant-pot to look at the big window to the right of the door. I glanced inside the room behind the empty window, just to check. A rotting sofa against the far wall, a coffee jar, a mouldy mug. No dangers there. I looked down at the window frame. Above the cracked wood and blistered paint there was maybe half an inch of glass. It was the same all around the frame. The glass had been cut out. I moved to the window on the other side—another empty room, with a plastic chair in the middle of the floor—and found the same. Farther around the house was the wee window of the downstairs lavvy. Half an inch of frosted glass along all four sides of it.

I crunched through frosty bracken and nettles, put my foot on the sagging wire of the fence, and hopped into the next empty house. Same deal with the windows.

"Someone's cut out all the glass with a glass cutter," I said, back at the lorry.

"'With a glass cutter'!" Euan mocked. "Whatever next?"

"Why would anybody bother?" I asked. "They could buy all the glass they wanted in Inverness."

"To save themselves the drive to Inverness," said Murdo.

"We're wasting our time here," said Euan.

"We can spare a minute," I said. I turned and walked to the fifth house along. It was smaller than the others and had no garden. The front-room window was cut out just like the others. In the room was a bedstead up against the back wall. It didn't look like it had been a bedroom. I imagined a sick person lying there, gazing out.

Gazing out. Suddenly it hit me that I'd been looking at this the wrong way. *Really* looking the wrong way. I stepped to the door and pushed. It swung open. Inside I found a narrow hallway with stairs a few steps ahead. There were a lot of scratches on the walls and the banister, and on the floor leading into the room. When I looked through, I saw that the scratches led straight to the legs of the bedstead.

The bedstead had been dragged in. When the floor was bare after the carpets and everything else had been taken from the house.

I sat down on the creaking springs and looked out the empty window. I could see the road and a low dry-stone wall. A patch of overgrown grass on the other side. Then the moor behind it and the hills in the far distance. Long shadows of short fence-posts. That frozen yellow grass across the way would be a sweet green meadow in the spring and summer. The wild sheep would come down from the hills and eat it. Them or the deer. The deer would be way down the hills now, off the moors and into the glens.

"Got ya!" I said to myself. I was out the door and across the road in a minute. I jumped the ditch and the wall into the meadow and searched along the foot of the wall at the far side. I knew what I was looking for, but it was pure luck that I spotted it: a gleam of steel. I bent over and picked up a six-inch bolt with a blunt point at one end. The other end was tapered with four narrow raised bits like low fins along it. It looked like a toy rocket.

A crossbow bolt.

"The house is a hide," I said to Euan and Murdo, back at the lorry. "For maybe a dozen people. They took the windows out, dragged up chairs and couches or what-ever and made themselves comfortable, and just sat there waiting for a herd of deer or maybe a flock of sheep to go and eat the grass. The beasts wouldn't see them, wouldn't even smell them. They just had to wait and then let fly with cross-bolts. You could bring down ten at one go that way. Maybe more."

"Very nice," said Murdo. I couldn't tell whether he meant my detective work or the neat slaughter I had detected.

"Why not just smash out the windows?" said Euan.

"To keep it quiet," said Murdo.

"From who? The deer?" said Euan.

"Maybe," I said. I wasn't so sure about that.

"Not much sport in the shooting," said Euan.

"This was not for sport," I said.

"Aye," said Murdo. "And speaking of food, my breakfast's in Lochcarron, and that's two hours away if we're lucky."

"Breakfast? What do you call the bacon roll you had in Dingwall?"

"A snack."

"A midnight feast," said Euan. "It was that dark I was expecting to feel my wife."

"That was just me," I said. "You had me worried."

II
SMOKING GUN

Euan smoked a roll-up before we got back into the cab. Nobody complained. We'd all got kind of easier on him and his bad habit since the big story came out. Maybe it's all been forgotten now, when you're listening to this. But you surely must remember the name of Jin Yang.

Jin Yang, right. The guy who started the whole thing. He was a rock music promoter who'd just made his second visit to the Edinburgh Fringe. Great success by all accounts. Real wheeler and dealer, signed up all kinds of acts to play in Beijing. He was on his way home, on a plane just out of Edinburgh Airport. Jumps up while the seat-belt sign's still on, gets into an argument with the trolley-dolly. Gets a wee bit physical. He doesn't know that she's had martial arts training. Anti-hijack policy, see? She doesn't know that he is a kung fu master. Things get a bit out of hand and just as he has her in a headlock he gets a soft-nosed bullet in the skull. Turns out there's this plain-clothes cop travelling undercover on the plane. More anti-hijack policy. A sky marshall, as the Americans call them.

So the Chinese guy goes down, and they're all kind of looking at each other. There's blood and bits of bone and brains splattered everywhere. Kids screaming. Adults screaming. Total shock and panic. And the sky marshall sees, right there sticking out of the pocket of the late Mr. Yang's seat, a couple of books. They're in Chinese, but they have the titles in English inside. One of them is the Koran. The other is the selected speeches of some Chinese leader.

The sky marshall's relaying all this to his bosses on the ground, using the plane's own radio. Everybody's hearing him. Then another Chinese passenger a few seats back jumps up and starts yelling. The sky marshall turns to him, with his gun levelled. By this time, half the passengers are telling their folks, using their own mobile phones. They all think they're about to die, and they're right.

Because yon wee sign that used to warn you not to use mobiles or computers or games while the plane was taking off or landing was there for a reason. Your gadgets really can interfere with the aircraft's controls. Well, they did this time anyway. The plane's been called back, obviously. But something goes wrong on its approach.

There was a heavy fog that day over the Firth of Forth. Pilot's flying blind. Flying by instruments. Instruments that have been knocked out of kilter by some computer geek's fancy new mobile phone, while he's telling his girlfriend he loves her or what have you.

Controlled flight into terrain, it's called. In this case, the terrain is the naval dockyard at Rosyth. Where Britain's top aircraft carrier is in dock for a refit before a mission to the South China Sea. And in the South China Sea there's been a bit of bother over Taiwan—a breakaway big island that the Chinese are very touchy about.

Kaboom.

A headline the next day says CHINESE AL QAEDA NUKES ROSYTH. And that was *The Guardian*, man. My lecturer at Telford College had it on his desktop. The *Record* just said BOMB REDS NOW.

Most of the British Army was in Iran already. China wasn't exactly a long march away. The Yanks took care of the heavy stuff, as usual. Japan kind of weighed in, for no better reason I can see than from force of habit.

Two years into the war our boys were up to their eyebrows in shit. Not knowing where the next attack's coming from—Communists, Muslims, Japanese, Falun Gong Sect, you name it.

Meanwhile, the official machinery is grinding away. Government inquiry sifts through the wreckage of the Rosyth incident. Plods through every surviving witness. Brings out a report.

It tells us three important things about Jin Yang.

One—he's from China's Muslim minority area. Hence the Koran in the seat.

Two—he's a businessman and a member of the Party. Hence the book of speeches by a Communist official. All about how building up business and getting rich is the way to the glorious future. Jin Yang has to swot up on that sort of thing, and parrot it every now and again to keep his bosses happy.

Three—Jin Yang was a heavy smoker, like lots of Chinese men are. On his first visit to the Festival Fringe, he'd had a very nice time. Deals in smoke-filled rooms and all that. At the airport he got through half a pack of cigarettes in the departure lounge to calm his nerves. There was a special booth just for that very purpose. All's well. Second time, a good few years later, the smoking ban had come in. He had a much less fun visit. He did a lot of his deals in doorways. On his way home, he's through security and stuck in aeroplane land when he finds that the Airstream smoking booth has long since been ripped out. His flight's delayed. Nobody knows just when it'll be ready. Even if he could get back through security, he's afraid he'll miss his flight, and then he'll miss his connection. So he's stuck.

For three and a half hours.

It wasn't a hijack. There was no Al Qaeda connection. No Chinese government connection either.

It was just air rage.

So that's how the war started.

And that's why we all stood around quite patient like and waited for Euan to finish his roll-up before we got back in the truck for the long drive to Lochcarron.

III
FRANKENFOLK

We pulled into Lochcarron a couple of hours later. The journey hadn't been bad. The sun glared on the snow when we were up high on the hillsides, but I had good shades. The black ice was murder down in the hollows, but the truck had good tyres. Some new kind of carbon fibre stuff. Their grip was magic. And we didn't run into any bandits or wolves.

"When I was wee the snow would have melted long ago by now," said Euan. "Snow-line at fifty metres in March! It used to be nearer two hundred."

Lochcarron was a mile or two out of our way. We passed the end of the road that led away to where we were going to work. That road cut across the head of the sea-loch, towards the old railway line. A mile along it you could see the the bright yellow work cabins, and the big black reel that held the cable that snaked out of the water. Lochcarron is a kilometre of houses along the northern shore. This morning the loch was like glass. The long ranges of hills that rose from both shores were mirrored in it like two wavy blades. The hillsides were black with the ashes and stumps of trees that had been nipped dead in the Big Freeze and burned in the forest fires of the next summer. Tall windmills stood along the hills' bare snow-covered tops. If any of the blades were turning at all it was too slow to see. Some of the windmill pylons were leaning over. Others lay flat on their sides. I remember when wind-power farms were the next big thing. The wind had other ideas.

I slowed the big truck as we came in, past the grassy patch that used to be a golf course and the walled patch that's still a cemetery. Around the side of a hill to the village proper. The brown stones and grey pebble-dash of the old houses were mixed in with the bright colours of the new ones. Blue, pink, yellow, green. They looked more like machines than buildings. Pipes and aerials sprouted from them. Thick insulating mats covered their walls. Steep roofs jutted up like witches' hats. The roofs of the old houses were covered with solar-power tarps.

The hotel was one of the old buildings. Crumbling concrete patched with insulating mats. Not much of a hotel now. More of a coffee shop and pit stop. A couple of supply trucks and two or three small cars were filling up, with red power cables and green bio-fuel lines plugged into their sides. Behind the thick plastic of the front window the cafe was busy. I parked around the side—our fuel cells were still well charged and the bio-fuel tank was half full. The three of us trooped in. Warm air smelling of coffee steam and frying bacon. About a dozen people sat around the tables. As usual everybody stared at us. It's these big yellow boiler-suits with HIGHWAY on front and back that does it. Dead giveaway. I was still throwing back my hood and unzipping the front of my overall when I heard the first nasty remark. One of the guys whose lorry was recharging outside—I could see that by the Tesco jacket on the back of his chair—leaned over and said to the FedEx driver he shared the table with:

"Laggers. Too dumb tae draft."

Coming from a trucker, that was a bit rich. I ignored it. I didn't retort with: "Truckers. Too feart tae fight." I just strolled to the counter and ordered a pot of java and six bacon rolls.

Thing is, it would've been true. Trucking is a reserved occupation. What that means is you can dodge the draft by being a truck driver. But the trucker was right and all. Except that we *are* drafted. Only not for the army. The army needs people who can handle high tech. Just the same as civilian industries, all that Carbon Glen stuff. People who were good at school. The rest of us—those who can't or won't hack it as soldiers or high-tech workers—get swept up by the highway. There's no going on the dole or the sick these days. It's my way or the Highway, like the First Minister used to say.

Of course it's not just building roads anymore. The old Highways Department took over all the public works. One of them was insulation. Lagging pipes was the first emergency job. Loads of insulation had to be laid on in the last summer before the first Big Freeze. That's why all of us who work for the Highway are called laggers. Well, it's one reason. The other is that "lagger" used to be the swear word for people like us. It came into fashion just after "neds" went out.

Not that I mind. I always wanted to be a lagger. Ever since I was about eight years old, anyway. That was when some new plastic water mains were laid in the street round the corner. Me and my wee gang were tearaways. We weren't as bad as folks said we were. OK, we did break all the windows of the JCB digger one night. But we thought the guys who laid the pipes were great. They had yellow plastic helmets and bright yellow plastic waistcoats and big muddy boots. They looked tough. They looked like we might want to be like them when we grew up. Them and fighter pilots and the characters in grand theft auto. Guess what. You need university to be a fighter pilot. Two of my pals died five years later doing grand theft auto in real life. Handbrake turns don't work so well on country roads. Funny that.

Anyway.

Apart from the truckers the other people in the room giving us the eye were locals. Five natives and five incomers. The natives were in their usual suspicious huddle. They just gave us a long enough glance to figure out we weren't about to attack them. Then they turned away. Their backs were about as welcoming as rolled-up hedgehogs.

Four of the white settlers sat in a more relaxed way around another table. Two couples, I guessed. English accents, or maybe posh Scottish. . . .

"—so then Malcolm sold his flat in the New Town and bought—"

Sudden pause. They looked at us, and then they looked down their noses. On the bridge of each of these noses was a black squiggle, like the bottom half of a glasses frame. The latest gadget from Carbon Glen. It seemed our faces weren't online anywhere as bad guys, because the incomers all looked up and blinked and went on talking.

"—an international civil servant with the World Trade Organization, and she's very worried—"

This checking us out stuff was as much of an insult as what the trucker had said. One look at *their* faces told me they'd had the Reverse treatment. It's supposed to turn back the clock, but it doesn't. Not quite. Smooths out the skin and tightens up the muscles. Helps the bones and joints too, I'm told. But it never wipes away all the signs of age. It's illegal in Scotland, because it does things to your genes. There's laws against GM *crops*, for crying out loud. GM *people* are an even bigger no-no. But what few cops there are in the Highlands are too busy—or have too much sense—to hunt down Frankenfolk. Place is crawling with them.

The woman behind the counter, a broad-in-the-beam local who for sure had not had the Reverse treatment, was still tonging strips of bacon into rolls so fresh I could smell them when I noticed the fifth incomer checking us out.

This lassie was a crustie. Her black hair was in matted braids. Her face was not bad and had been washed in the last day or two. Over the back of her chair was a hide jacket. She wore a shapeless woolen sweater. Long legs in some kind of tweedy tartan trousers. Feet in buckle-sided boots propped on a plastic chair. She was sitting at a small table by herself, over by the window around the side of the counter. She had a white teapot and a cup of green tea in front of her. Beside them on the table was a scatter of pages printed off from the day's papers.

She looked us up and down in a lazy way and then looked back at her papers. When we sat down at the empty table beside her she paid us no attention. She did swing her legs off the chair and lean forward over the offprints. I could smell her. It wasn't a stink. Sweat and wool and something like the sea.

Finished the bacon roll and on to my second coffee. I was fiddling with the cross-bolt, turning it over my fingers. We were talking about the day's job when I felt a stare on my neck. I turned and saw the lassie looking hard at me, then down at my hands. No, she was looking at the thing in my hands. Then she looked away. She shrugged into her big jacket, picked up a bulging carrier bag, stood up and walked out.

IV
AILISS

"Nice ass," said Euan.

"Well boys," I said when we'd watched her out, "about time we did the same."

"Not walking like that," said Euan, getting back at me.

I nodded to agree we were evens. Euan was already rolling his cigarette. He wagged his tongue back and forth against his top lip. One up to him.

"Move your arse," I told him. "You can go shotgun. Smoke all you want."

I couldn't be sure if this was one up to me.

As we drove back up the street we saw the girl from the cafe trudging along the side of the road. The Tesco bag was weighing her down on one side. I slowed the truck and wound down the cab window.

"Want a lift?"

The girl opened her mouth and said something. Out of the corner of my eye I saw two hurtling shapes, black and spiky as ninja knives. As my head whipped round to follow them I saw them skimming above the loch at about twenty metres. The sound of the fighter jets hammered over us a moment after they'd disappeared.

"What?" I asked.

"I said, 'Where are you heading?'"

"Strathcarron way," I said.

"Fine," she said. She crossed the road and walked around the front of the truck. Murdo opened the door and moved over and squashed into the middle seat. The girl stepped up and swung in. She put the bag down between her boots and slammed the door. As she turned back with a smile and a thank you her hair flicked and I could see she didn't have a phone on her ear.

I let the engine's flywheel bite again and released the brake. We slid forward out of the village. I glanced sideways. Murdo was wrinkling his nose. I didn't mind the smell at all.

"What's your name?" I asked.

"Ailiss," she said, looking ahead and around like a kid at the front of the top deck of a bus.

"I'm Jase," I said. "This is Murdo."

"You're not from here," she said.

I could just about tell she was. Her accent was a bit like Euan's.

"I'm from Glasgow," I said. "Murdo's from Stornoway."

"The Highway comes from all over," Murdo announced. "You don't look like a native yourself."

"I was born in Strome," she said. She jerked a thumb over her shoulder. "Five miles down the road."

"A white settler of the second generation," said Murdo.

"You know a lot about me, don't you?" she said.

"I do that," said Murdo. "You have—"

I knew what he was going to say next. I was glad he was close enough to give him the dig of my elbow.

"What?" he said.

"Don't bug the lassie," I said.

"I was just making conversation."

"Aye, well make it different." I kept my eyes on the road. "Sorry about that, Ailiss."

She flicked a hand. "No problem." She turned to Murdo. "You're right, my parents were from down South. They were just so typical, they collected pine resins for aromatherapy. . . ." She went on about this for a bit.

But I could see where her hand went while she spoke, maybe without her even thinking about it. It went to her knee, then crept to the top of her boot.

"I live past Strathcarron," she said, as I slowed at the turn-off.

"Fine," I said. "We'll drop you at the site. You'll have to walk or hitch from there."

"I'll walk," she said.

"Not far to go then?" said Murdo. Still prying.

"Not far at all," she said. "Up behind Strathcarron."

Now I know for a fact there's nothing up behind Strathcarron. There's nothing *at* Strathcarron, except the old railway station, some empty houses and the ruins of a restaurant. Up the hills behind it there's waste howling wilderness. It was empty even before the freeze. There's bugger-all people between here and Kintail. Bugger-all beasts for that matter. You'd be hard-pressed to find enough dead sheep to feed a crow.

I kept my trap shut about all this and I glared at Murdo to do the same.

We crossed the Carron bridge and pulled up just before the site road-end, two or three hundred metres from the old station.

"Thanks," said Ailiss. She hopped out, hauled her bag after her, waved, shut the door and strode off along the road. The end of the loch was to her right and the site to her left. She didn't look to either side, or back.

"Well," said Euan as he climbed down from the lookout bucket to the running board, "there goes a girl who is not afraid of bandits."

Murdo and I both laughed.

"What?" said Euan. He handed the shotgun in through the cab window. I clipped it to the rack behind the seats.

"She's armed," I said. "At least a knife, and maybe a gun as well. And she lives up in the hills behind Strathcarron." I waved at the range in front of us.

"And she has no food in that bag," said Murdo, "except some sugar and a packet of Rich Abernethy biscuits. It's all stuff like batteries and disinfectants."

"What's that got to do with it?" demanded Euan.

I started the engine again and began the turn, over an earth-covered culvert and on to the site. As the security guard waved a scanner at us I glanced up the road for traffic. There was none. The girl was a couple of hundred metres away, walking fast.

"She's a bandit," I said.

V
SITE WORK

We had brought a Caterpillar digger on the back of the truck. Getting it off was hard work. Our thick gloves made the chains awkward to handle, but they were too cold to touch with bare skin. The heavy padlocks and hasps were frozen solid. It took a lot of tapping with a hammer to get them loose. The tailgate ramps were stiff. We had to melt ice off them with a blowtorch before Euan could drive the Cat down to the ground. He had just eased the tracks over the edge of the flatbed and was inching forward, waiting to tip forward onto the slope of the ramps, when I saw a black cloud in the west. Way down the loch. By the time the Cat was on the ground you couldn't see Lochcarron.

I looked around. It was weird to be standing in bright sunshine with that black wall of cloud on the way. All over the site—there were about twenty guys working there—people were yelling, hauling tarpaulins over equipment, shutting down machinery, and running for shelter. Only the guards stood their ground. Their armour would take more than a storm to damage.

"Time to go, boys," I said.

Euan jumped out of the Cat and locked the door behind him. Murdo pulled his parka hood up and headed for the nearest depot. I heaved the two boards one by one into the back of the truck and banged the tailgate up, slammed the bolts across.

I could hear a hissing from the sea a couple of hundred metres away.

I ran after Euan towards the doorway where Murdo was standing among a crowd of others, staring past us and waving. Beckoning, urging us on. A gust of wind pushed us like a giant hand on our backs. The hiss became a drumming roar. We had just got under the roof when hailstones the size of golf balls started hitting the tarmac. They hit so hard they shattered. I felt a sting of ice on my face, and covered my eyes. Everybody backed farther inside, pressing against machines and tools and coils of pipe.

For ten minutes it was almost as dark as night. The ground in front of us turned slowly white. The hailstones hammered on the roof. I could see them bouncing off the side window of the depot and wondered why it didn't break. Then I remembered it was probably made of toughened glass, just like the truck windscreen and the Cat's cabin windows. This thought reminded me of something, but I couldn't think what. With all the noise I could hardly think at all.

Then the hailstorm passed as suddenly as it had started. The sky was still overcast, and the wind fresh, but the squall had marched off up the glen. We walked out, boots crunching on chunks of ice.

"The ground needed it," said Euan.

"Yes indeed, it'll be good for the crops," said Murdo.

"Aye, the spring sowing needs it," I said.

We went on with this farming talk until it stopped being funny. That didn't take long.

I led the way to the yellow dome of the site office. A local lassie looked at us from behind a desk as we trooped in.

"Site engineer?" I asked.

"He'll be back in a minute," she said.

"OK," I said.

Her hands were moving on the keyboard but she was watching the news. It scrolled down a screen tacked to the wall beside a calendar. March was a bare girl on a wet rock somewhere hot. April would be a hot girl on a bare rock somewhere wet. On the screen the top news was a Siberian town that had sunk two metres overnight. They're thawing while we're freezing. Russian kids in army uniforms helped folk into long trucks with huge fat wheels. The rest of the news was the usual. Truck bomb in Tehran. Ambush in Kabul.

"The Bodach's been busy," said Euan.

The Bodach—the old man—is what the locals call Osama Bin Laden. Nobody knows if he's still alive or not. Maybe he's getting the Reverse treatment but he's not in a healthy line of work. His gloating videos still come out every now and again. But that doesn't prove anything. You could say the same about Mick Jagger.

A man in a suit and wellies hurried in with that look of someone who has just been for a pee. His belt was one notch too tight for his belly and his thinning hair had been flattened by twenty-odd years under hard hats. Red cheeks and sandy eyebrows and sharp blue eyes.

"Liam Morrison," he said, shaking hands.

"We've brought the Cat," I said after we'd introduced ourselves.

"Good," he said. He ambled to the desk and pawed at loose paper. "The chart, Kelly?"

"It's in here somewhere," she said. "Got it."

Over by the curved wall a printer whizzed. Kelly got up and came back with a metre of paper. Liam looked around for somewhere to spread it, then held it up against the wall.

"That's your line for the trench," he said. "It's all marked out on the ground.

From the river to the railway. Yellow posts and green string, mind. The red one's for the site sewage line."

We peered at the drawing and got this clear in our heads.

"OK," I said.

"You better take it," said Liam. "Don't get it wet."

We all laughed and Liam nodded and we headed out.

"'Don't get it wet,'" Euan muttered.

"Taking the piss," I said. "But he's polite for a boss."

"The gentleman will have his little joke," said Murdo.

Lack of water was what had brought us here in the first place. The hailstorm was the usual way water falls from the sky around here. Not much of that, and not much rain, not even much snow. The rain that does fall comes in heavy bursts that run off in flash floods. The snow that does fall, up on the tops, doesn't melt near soon enough. The Highlands are drying out. So the Hydro stations that kept the Highlands lit up in the old days don't get enough water to work. Wind power turned out to be a crock as soon as the weather went wild. It's either so calm the blades don't turn or so stormy the pylons get blown over.

So here we were, climbing onto the Cat and getting ready to dig a trench to hold a cable. One end of the cable was coiled up on the bank of the Carron. The rest of it ran out along the riverbed and across the tidal flat and along the bottom of the loch. All the way out to the new nuclear power station on a wee island between the mouth of Loch Carron and the Isle of Skye. The wee island is called Eilean Mor, which means Big Island. The power station was built on it because nobody lives there to object, and also because it's easy to guard. In the Sound of Skye there's enough military and naval hardware to scare off the Bodach himself.

The first part of our job was to dig a trench from the Carron to the back of the old railway station. The railway line was a ready-made route across country to Loch Luichart. At Loch Luichart, about twenty kilometres inland, was one of those dry Hydro power stations I told you about. Somebody had decided that this would be just the place to plug the new power into the grid. It had all the machinery, but it was lying idle.

The trains don't run anymore on the Kyle line—too many landslides—so the rails were free to carry heavy equipment. Any day now it would come chugging down from Inverness. Then it would slowly chug back, digging a trench alongside the railway track as it went. Same trick for laying the cable. All we'd have to do was follow behind and shovel the dirt in, and lay prefab concrete covers over any stretches where the cable had to be trailed over bare rock.

All very straightforward. But first we had to dig this trench through a couple hundred metres of soil that was on the way to freezing solid. Tomorrow's permafrost. And the day after tomorrow's swamp, if Alaska and Siberia are anything to go by. But that's the day after tomorrow's problem.

Liam Morrison had done his bit with the theodolite and laser gadget His two assistants (I could see from the names on the drawing) had done their thing with sticks and string. The line they'd marked out for the trench to follow stretched straight from the Carron's left bank to just east of the station. Easy.

Our only instruction was to dig a metre deep all the way along it. By the time

Murdo had manoeuvred the Cat to the side of the river we were lined up and ready to go. Point and shoot

Nothing's ever that simple.

VI
WARNING LABELS

The Cat was so new you could still see yellow and black paint that had never had dust on it. It was a new model and all. It had a big chain winch. It had a drill attached to the digger scoop. Beside the drill was the nozzle of a heat blaster, hose-piped to the engine, for thawing frozen ground.

So why was I down in the trench with a pick and spade and crowbars? Why were we only fifty metres along, towards the end of the second day after we'd arrived?

I was asking these questions not very politely.

"It's the Ice Age, man," Euan explained, leaning on a shovel, holding a chain, smoking a tab, and offering advice from above. "The glaciers left a lot of boulders when they went."

"At this rate," I said, wedging the end of a crowbar behind one of said boulders, "they'll be here when the glaciers come back."

"Not long to wait then," said Murdo, from behind the levers in the cab.

"Pass me the flexies," I said.

Euan flung the chain rattling down. On the end of it was a bunch of cables made from some fancy carbon tech. These were the flexies. If you stretched any two of them out, wrapped them around something then brought the ends together they could writhe like snakes into a knot. This was a fix for exactly the problem we had right now: buried boulders. (As well as for tree stumps and stuck cars and stuff like that.)

The trouble was, you had to have enough clear space around your obstacle to wrap them in. I heaved on the crowbar. The boulder rocked a few centimetres. Soil that had been hard even for the drill to break into suddenly crumbled and slid into the gap. It filled it completely. I heaved again. I knew this could be done. We'd done it about twenty times already. People had been growing oats and potatoes and turnips on this plain for hundreds of years. You'd think they'd have got rid of all the boulders. Turns out they only got rid of them as deep as the plough digs, which is not a metre, not even half a metre.

"Why don't you just take the trench around the boulders?" Liam had asked. He moved his hand like a fish.

"You know what we find when we do that?"

"Other boulders?"

"Got it."

"Oh well. Carry on, gentlemen."

So we carried on. My second heave on the crowbar shifted the boulder again. I could see black space behind it.

"Give us a hand," I said.

Euan spat his tab and jumped down into the trench and wrapped a pair of flexies around the boulder. The ends knotted themselves. At the same time tiny grippers came out the cable and stuck to the rock like ivy. I let the crowbar sag back. We stood and looked at it for a minute.

"It'll no hold," I said. "It's too near the top."

Euan stretched five more flexies across the exposed surface, then tugged on the chain.

"It'll stick like an octopus to a face mask," he proclaimed.

"Well, I'm not sticking around," I said.

We clambered out of the trench, backed well clear, and gave Murdo the thumbs-up. The winch whined. The chain straightened. The tension built. The chain and flexies lashed through the air like a cat-o'-nine-tails and clanged against the cab.

"So much for that," said Euan. "Try again?"

I looked around. The sun was behind the Atlantic. To the east the pink sky was making the cut-out face of a giant of the mountain. The one the locals call Wellington's Nose.

"Call it a day," I said.

We washed up, and had some grub in the canteen. Then we cadged a lift for the hotel bar from an Iraqi refugee student on work placement who was keen to make friends. Thank God for Muslims. Well, onside Muslims anyway, if you see what I mean. They don't complain about having to drive back from the pub. I stood the first round and bought a tall orange juice for young Farhad and a half and a half each for myself and the lads. The whisky bottles all had labels showing the diseased liver of the month. The beer mats showed a range of car crash injuries. The bar had been built like a conservatory. Its big windows had long since been sprayed over with insulation foam. Too mean or too poor even for double glazing. The light was yellow. There was a score or so of people here, usual mix of local soaks and less sozzled incomers. Couple of other teams from the site. Most of the crew preferred to drink in the barracks. No smoke detectors hot-linked to the local cop shop, for one thing. Better atmosphere in every way, you could say. People had stopped staring at us after the first night. I stared at them on my way back to the table with the tray.

"Looking for somebody?" Euan asked.

"He's pining for his bandit," said Murdo.

This was true but I denied it. I had found Ailiss on my mind the past couple of days. I had been keeping an eye out for her, but I hadn't seen her on the road or in the village.

"I meant to ask," said Euan. "Why did you call her a bandit?"

Farhad looked worried. "You have bandits here?"

"Just a few rebels in the hills," said Murdo.

"Don't wind up the kid," I told him, then turned to Farhad. "They're no like your Kurds or anything. They're just small groups of young folks mostly who live up in the mountains. They call themselves new age settlers. Some of them do a bit of stealing. One or two of them sometimes even hold up a supply lorry on a lonely road. That's why they get called bandits."

"But why do they do it?" asked Farhad.

I shrugged. "To get stuff."

"No, I mean why do they live in the mountains?"

"To get away from"—I waved a hand around—"all this."

I didn't know what I meant, what I was waving my hand at. It was the warning labels and the smoke detectors and the CCTV cameras. Or it was the hard-drinking locals and the smug incomers. Or maybe the yammering telly, and the horrible thick air of the place, smelling of sweat and scent and food and booze. The yellow light and the blanketed windows. That and the whole shit deal of being a lagger.

Farhad still looked puzzled. "Immorality?"

"Aye, that's it," said Murdo. "Immorality and drunkenness."

At closing time we stepped out into a black night full of stars. No many lights to compete with here. From the hills to the south, across the loch, a faint spark rose and climbed fast up the sky. Almost overhead it flared bright for a second or two and then winked out.

"What was that?" I asked.

"The Space Station," said Murdo.

"It was abandoned," I said.

"Yes," said Murdo, "but it's still up there."

"The Chinks put a man on Mars before the war," said Euan.

"Two men and a woman," Farhad said, opening the van door.

"Maybe they're still up there and all," Murdo said.

"Aye," I said. "With a soldering iron and a sewing machine. Making stuff to sell us after the war."

"'After the war,'" Euan mocked.

"When I was a wee boy," said Murdo, "I heard people saying that."

When we got back to the site I stopped by the computer and applied for a day off. Nothing came up until Sunday, so I took that.

VII
THE BLACK HILLS

The site was quiet on Sunday, though I doubt many went to church. I walked out the gate on a fine crisp morning. Blue sky, blue loch. Flat calm. There was a line or two running in my head from one of my father's old songs: *Take me back to the black hills, the black hills of . . .*

The black hills of Lochcarron. Oh aye.

My hand was fiddling with the cross-bolt, still deep in my parka pocket, clinking against some change and a knife. A cat hissed at me from an empty window of the old station, making me jump. Behind all the other smells from the ruin—wet ash, cat piss, mould and weeds—there was the faint whiff of disinfectant. Left by a hundred years of soaking floorboards with Jeyes Fluid. It reminded me of school corridors and the Highway offices.

I crossed the rusty tracks and found a fallen gate among sagging fenceposts. An overgrown path led up into the hills. I followed it. I was glad of my big boots. The grass hid slippery stones that could turn an ankle, no bother. On the lower slopes I saw a few rabbits and here and there a huddled flock of sheep that had gone wild. These feral sheep looked fierce and alert, with thick wool and long legs. Not like farm sheep at all. Evolution happens, man, whatever the Yanks say. Each flock was guarded by a black-faced ram with yellow eyes that stared at me as I went past. It was like being watched by Satan.

Every so often I looked back, taking in the view. After a bit the curve of the hills hid the loch. I was up above the snowline in a world of black and white. Frost and old snow and burnt heather. There was colour in only a few places. Orange lichens on the rocks like spilled paint. A few green shoots in a warm patch that caught the sun most of the day and where water dripped from icicles on to the brown clumps of dead grass.

By ten o'clock I'd passed a couple of tiny frozen lochs and was walking along a wee glen. There were hills to my right and left. Higher hills filled the horizon ahead. The place is called the Attadale Forest. Like most places called forests in the Highlands, it has no trees. Nothing grows higher than the heather. The path had faded to a track that might have been made by sheep. There were no sheep up this high, but the path had been trodden not long ago. And that meant people. I was on the right track, you might say.

I wasn't worried about wolves or bears. Back along the big glen of the Carron they could be a problem, but not here. Not in this barren land. Even though Attadale and Glen Affric a bit to the south were among the places they'd been brought back to years ago. It was a big thing back then, around the same time as wind power. Failed for the same reason, too. Climate change. Everybody thinks of wolves in the Highlands but it's down south they're more of a nuisance. In Glasgow they raid the bins.

On and up I went. After a bit I began to find clues that the path was made by people after all. Like a tarred board that turned the middle of a slope into a step. Stones stacked by the side to make a low wall, or spread out along a metre or two that was soft underfoot.

A wisp of smoke stained the sky ahead of me. I sniffed the air and smelled burning wood, with an odd chemical taste in the smell.

I climbed a slope that opened on to a dip overlooked by a high, steep hill. I stopped and stared.

A frozen loch a few metres across and about a hundred long lay at the bottom of the hollow. Alongside it was a row of low buildings. The nearest was like an old black house, with dry-stone walls. Its thatched roof was covered with a solar-power tarp. The tarp was weighed down with boulders hanging from ropes at the corners. The smoke was coming from the chimney of that house. The next building was a long greenhouse. Then another black house, and another greenhouse. Behind them all were some sheds, with stone walls and turf roofs, again with the power tarps. More power tarps were laid along the tops of chicken runs. A couple of scrawny tethered goats grazed the side of the hill.

I had just about time to take this in when I heard a very fast whirring sound and a loud click. Something moved at the corner of my eye and I turned. A little kid had popped up from behind a boulder. He was aiming a crossbow at me.

I held my hands away from my sides.

"Put that down," I said.

He kept the weapon aimed with one hand. It was a bit shaky but not shaky enough for me to jump him. With his free hand he reached inside his parka—a patchwork of furs and plastic—and pulled out a whistle. He blew hard on it. The blast rang in my ears even after it had stopped echoing from the hills.

"Don't try anything funny," he said, trying to sound tough. It just made his voice higher.

"I can give you a spare bolt for that," I said.

Doors banged and people came running from the buildings. I caught sight of quick sudden movements on the hillside, just black specks moving and vanishing.

Three people ran up the path and stopped behind the boy. Two bearded guys, and Ailiss.

"Hi, Ailiss," I said.

"You know this guy?" said Beard Number One. He didn't sound pleased.

"I've met him," she said. She frowned at me. "Jase?"

"That's me," I said.

"He's one of the laggers," she said.

"What brings you here?" asked Beard Number Two. He had an English accent.

I shrugged. "Just out for a walk. My day off."

"The Sabbath," said Ailiss, like she'd just remembered something funny. "Oh well. No harm in that."

"Would you ask the kid to stop pointing that thing?" I said.

"Yeah," she said. "Pack it in, Nichol."

The kid scowled but did as he was told. He lowered the crossbow and wound the cable back.

"This is not clever," I said. "You can't go threatening everybody who walks past."

"We don't," said Ailiss. "Not usually. We're all just a wee bit jumpy."

"Aye, you can say that again," I said. I had no idea why they should be jumpy. "Well, I don't like having things pointed at me."

"I thought you might be a bandit," Nichol said. "Or a zombie or a refugee or a soldier."

Beard Number One looked awkward. "Kids pick things up," he said.

"Come down to the house and have some tea," said Ailiss.

I guessed they were trying to make up for the bad welcome.

"Thanks," I said. "I could do with that."

The kid walked beside me down the track.

"What sort of a name is Jase?" he asked.

"Short for something," I said.

"What?"

"Jason," I said.

"No a bad name."

"It is if your second name's Mason."

"Jason Mason, Jason Mason," he chanted.

"Not so loud," I said.

"How will you pay for my silence?" he demanded grandly.

"You been watching too much telly?"

"No telly," he said. "I read a lot though."

I took the cross-bolt out of my pocket and waved it in front of him. "Will this keep you quiet?"

"Aye, sure."

I handed it to him.

"Thanks," he said. He held it up and skipped ahead, shouting: "Look what I got from Jason Mason!"

Kids.

VIII
THE GREEN PLACE

The kid turned around and sauntered back up the path to where he'd been, giving me a nod on the way. The two guys and Ailiss led me to the front door of the first house. We all ducked through the low doorway. They were burning broken planks and other scrap timber in the fireplace. Some of it had paint or varnish. That was what gave it the chemical smell. But it was a cheery enough fire and there was a pot of tea on the hob. I took it black and strong with sugar. Nobody offered me a biscuit and I didn't ask. The bearded guys told me their names. Martin and Angus. I guessed they were in their twenties and wondered why they hadn't been drafted. They looked and sounded bright enough for the army. I didn't ask. I sipped tea and looked around. The bulb hanging from the ceiling was off, so all the light came from the window. The furniture was burst armchairs and a sagging sofa and a battered dresser and chest of drawers. Carpets and rugs lay thick on the floors and more were nailed to the walls. The wall carpets had pictures and clippings and postcards tacked to them. A lot of the pictures looked like they had been printed off the Net. Lush green landscapes—you know, historical, like. Trees and flowers, birds and bees. Across other nails banged into the wall were three crossbows, a shotgun higher up, and a couple of air rifles. Tins of pellets and bolts, a box of cartridges on a shelf. The box was brown and waxy with an old-fashioned look to the print. All from before they were banned, I guessed. They sure weren't robbed from the Highway's armouries, or the cops.

No telly, like the kid had said. And no even wireless Internet that I could see. But books, on paper I mean, were stacked against every wall. You would think they were part of the insulation.

A colder-looking kitchen through at the back. The water pipes were lagged with bits of old carpet tied on with string. Rusty pick and spade and mattock were propped by the sink. A scythe hung on the wall. I pointed to it.

"What's the use of that?"

Ailiss peered. "Oh, the scythe." She smiled. "It'll have a use. There'll be crops again. Oats are hardy. There's a field or two of them run wild down Ardaneaskan way."

"Ailiss is an optimist," said the Sassenach beardie one. He sounded annoyed for some reason. He shrugged. "We found it, that's all. Ailiss thinks of uses for it."

Ailiss gave him a look like she'd just thought of another one. But after that they all glanced at each other and at me and smiled like Mormons.

"Would you like to show him around, Ailiss?" said Angus, the Scottish guy. "Martin and I have to get back to work. We'll meet up at the other end."

"See you, guys," Ailiss said.

They zipped up their parkas, flipped up their hoods and ducked out the door. I drained the mug.

"Well," said Ailiss, looking a bit awkward, "let me show you around, Jason Mason."

"Jase," I said.

"OK," she said. She took me out the back door. The back of the house was dug out of the side of the hill. Ailiss turned left and led me along the narrow walled gulley, past a meat safe that smelled of more than meat.

"Goat cheese," Ailiss said when I wrinkled my nose.

"Did youse build all this?" I asked.

She glanced back. "Just the greenhouses. Not the black houses. They had just the walls left when we found them, mind you."

"How many of you live here?"

This time she didn't look back. "No telling."

"That's me told."

She laughed. Didn't explain.

But she showed me everything. The greenhouse had tomatoes and other vegetables growing in it, with herbs between the rows. Water from pipes trickled everywhere, warmed by the sun and the solar power. There was even a few square metres of spuds. Fertiliser came from rabbits and goats in the sheds up the back. Other meat—venison from deer and mutton from feral sheep—hung in a cold smoke-hut or soaked in salt barrels. In the second house I met Nichol's parents, who were stitching animal skins with fishing line on a treadle-powered sewing machine. They just looked up and didn't say much. Along our whole way I saw maybe half a dozen other people come and go from the hills, some with bits of wood, some with shot rabbits. None of them did more than give me a hard look.

"All that tough glass must have cost a bomb," I said in the second greenhouse.

"Got it from abandoned houses," Ailiss said. Just as I'd guessed, way back.

"Diamond cutters are handy wee things," I said. "And an empty house makes a good hide."

"Oh, you saw that?"

"Aye, on the road from Dingwall. How did you lug all the meat back?"

She shrugged. "Borrowed a car."

Borrowed, aye right. I said nothing.

"No, it really was borrowed," she said. "We did that job with some other new settlers from over in the Black Isle."

She was standing very close, her strange salty smell all mixed up with the fresh air of earth and plants.

"Ailiss," I said.

She was about to reply when the greenhouse door opened and the two beardie guys Martin and Angus walked in. Ailiss took a step back, bumping her hip on a plant pot. She muttered and turned away to scoop the soil and the plant back in. Martin and Angus half-sat on the edge of a trestle table.

"Well," says Angus, "you've seen our place."

"Aye, I have, thank you," I said. "Nice place you've got. I'm nae sure why you live like this, though."

Angus looked sideways at Martin. The big Sassenach stood up and leaned forward a bit. He clasped his hands behind his back and jutted his beard.

"Survival," he said. "The world is going down the tubes. The American grain belt is being hoovered up by tornadoes. The ice is melting everywhere it used to be and freezing where it wasn't. The oil's running out, and we're deep in a war that could go nuclear at any moment. The Greenland ice is about to slide into the sea. One way or another, the cities are doomed. We're living the way everyone will have to live, sooner or later."

"What a load of shite," I said.

"What?" he said. He looked a bit staggered.

"Youse just *like* living like this. Fair enough. Don't kid on you're going to survive whatever's coming down. Not unless you can hand-weave solar tarps and make steel for your crossbows and all that. No tae mention the way the wind blows."

Martin looked like he was just catching up with me. "What do you mean?"

I pointed. "From the west. And what's sitting west of here? A nuclear power station and the biggest collection of nuclear missiles since Rosyth blew up. If that lot start flying youse are going down with the rest of us, except maybe faster."

"Now look here—" Angus began. Martin waved a hand.

"There's nothing to say," he said. "It's pointless arguing with people like that."

"Fine," I said. "I'll shove off. Thanks for the tea." I looked over my shoulder from the door. "See you down the village sometime, Ailiss."

"Maybe," she said. She looked away. "'Bye."

IX
SUNDAY NIGHT

I was halfway back down the track when I got a call from Murdo asking where the hell I was. I told him I was walking up in the hills and was on my way down. He told me I was an idiot. I told him he wasn't my mother and the conversation didn't go a lot further. But I enjoyed the rest of the walk and I got back to the site about mid-afternoon. I had a late lunch of pork pie and a tin of beer. I went to my bunk in the laggers' hut, kicked off my boots and stretched out and caught some Sabbath kip.

In the canteen at seven there were only a handful of us there, me and Murdo and Farhad and Kelly the secretary and Liam the site engineer. We all sat at the same table with our microwaved dinners.

"Did you find your bandit?" Murdo asked.

"Aye," I said. "They have a wee place up behind Attadale."

"Get anywhere with her?"

"Would I be here if I had?" I said.

Murdo laughed.

Liam put down his fork and looked over at me.

"What's this about bandits?"

"They're no bandits," Murdo said, before I could get a word in. "Just poachers and tinkers."

"All the same," said Liam. "Let's hear what Jase has to say about it."

I told him about the settlement, leaving out all the awkward moments.

"That's worrying," he said.

"What's worrying about it?"

"An armed gang living a few klicks from our power line? That doesn't worry you?"

"Aw come on," I said. "They're nae threat to anybody. And anyway, there's new age settlers dotted all over the place. All along the glen, for a start."

Liam nodded. "Exactly. We haven't taken this seriously enough. It's a security risk."

"It is no!" I said. "Why would they want to damage the power line anyway? They think the whole world's going to hell in a handcart already, without them helping it along."

"Groups with these kinds of beliefs can turn very ugly," Liam said. "End of the world cults don't always just wait for the end, you know. Sometimes they try to bring it on. Or they get influenced or"—he paused, and jabbed with his finger—"infiltrated by others with a more militant approach."

Murdo laughed loud. "Yon tinks might end up working for the Bodach?"

"Or some other extremists, yes," Liam said. "Whether they knew it or not."

I lost my appetite all of a sudden.

"They're not a cult," I said, "and they're no extremists either. They're just"—I shrugged—"daft."

"You said yourself you were threatened by a small child," said Liam.

"That was just a wee boy playing soldiers!"

"Yes, with a lethal weapon." Liam looked like he was thinking hard. "You know, the child protection angle . . . I wonder what kind of education that kid is getting."

"He can read," I said.

Liam just smiled. "I'll give this some thought," he said. He glanced over at Kelly. "Tab it in my diary?"

The secretary nodded.

Later that evening I saw Liam off in a corner of a corridor talking to himself. Then I realised he was talking on his phone. I hoped he was just calling home, but I knew I couldn't count on it.

X
MONDAY MORNING FEELING

I woke about seven just as it was getting light. But it wasn't the light that woke me. And my alarm hadn't gone off. I lay staring at the little red numbers on the clock stuck to the bunk above me and wondered what had woken me up. Then I heard it: a deep, distant throb, growing by the minute.

A helicopter. The sound always feels like a threat. Here comes a chopper to chop off your head.

I swung my legs off the bunk and sat up. Everybody else in the hut was still sound asleep. I padded to the door, went out quietly and looked around the side of the hut. I was freezing in my thermals but I could see right along the loch. It was grey and still under a low ceiling of cloud. The chopper was a fat black drop heading straight towards me. Just as it passed level with the village it banked to my left and swung around to the south. It was one of those big two-engine chinooks. A troop carrier.

The racket from it washed over the site. The chopper flew low over Strathcarron and skimmed the skyline. It disappeared behind the hills but I could still hear it. The chopper's heavy throb stayed steady. I guessed it was hovering.

"That's it for your bandits," said Murdo, from behind me.

I turned. He stood like me shivering in a vest and long johns, staring after the thing. I felt like giving the Lewisman a clout in his gloomy satisfied face. There's this with the Lewis folk, they expect the worst and are not often disappointed.

"Send soldiers after new age settlers?" I said. "What are you on? It'll be just an exercise."

Murdo shook his head.

"Don't kid yourself. You know fine what it's hovering over." He snorted. "I'm sure Social Services will be along in a while. Once the soldiers have secured the place."

"I wish I'd kept my trap shut," I said.

"You learn fast for a Glasgow boy," said Murdo.

I wanted again to clout him but I just smacked my fist into my hand.

"We've got to *do* something!"

He gave me a funny look.

"We do, eh? Speak for yourself. But what can we do?"

"We can go up and see if we can help."

"We can't fight the soldiers."

"No, but we can maybe pick up anyone who gets away. Or help them to move their stuff."

"That's possible," Murdo said. "I'll come along for the ride."

I made a turn as if to dash for the truck. Murdo caught my shoulder.

"Get your clothes on," he said. "And take a piss first."

Ten minutes later I was in the cab, Murdo and Euan beside me. Nobody was riding shotgun. Or maybe we all were, if you see what I mean. Euan was filling the air with his smoke, an early-morning kick-start to his brain. I opened a window and turned up the heaters full blast. The sleepy security guard at the gate waved us out. He might have been a bit surprised when I turned left and took off towards Strathcarron.

We bumped across the tracks at the level crossing. I swung the truck to the left again, then right, up the old track. The wheels were off the track at both sides but the gripper tyres did their job all right.

"How far can we take it?" Euan asked as we clawed up the first steep slope.

"Farther than this anyway," I said.

The truck lurched down and forward. We bounced in our seats. I was worried about what lay ahead of us but I was enjoying this. A few minutes later we were nearly in the cloud. Then the cloud opened in a freezing drizzle that stung like sand. I closed the windows and switched on the wipers and headlights. The squeak and thud of the wipers took over as the loudest noise in the cab. Visibility was about a hundred metres. Up and down we went, mostly up.

Then up and over and looking down into the glen where the settlement was. I stopped there, engine running, neutral gear, foot on the brake. We were leaning a long way forward. The chopper had landed right below us on the shore of the narrow loch, big and black against the strip of white ice.

A dozen or so soldiers in black armour suits and visored helmets ringed the settlement. About the same number of the people who lived there stood on the track in a huddle. The greenhouses glittered with broken glass. Smoke, black and foul, rose from the two houses.

"Christ, man, they're burning the roofs!" said Murdo. He sounded choked. Euan banged a fist on the top of the dash. His face went as white and tight as his knuckles.

"Clearances," he said. "Clearances!"

He reached behind him for the shotgun on the rack. I grabbed his wrist and wrenched him away from it.

Two of the soldiers came racing up the slope towards us. They ran to either side of the truck, jumped on the running boards, and banged on the windows. I thumbed the roll-down switch. A visored face leaned in.

"Turn off the engine and get out of the cab now!"

"Right away," I said.

The soldiers jumped back, and stood with their rifles pointed at us. I looked at the others.

"Well, boys," I said. "Time to go."

We opened the doors. Murdo and Euan jumped down from their side. I turned off the engine and jumped down from mine.

The truck was rolling forward before I hit the ground.

I swear I didn't plan this. I really was so rattled that I'd done exactly what the soldier had told me. I had turned off the engine and got out.

He never said anything about the handbrake.

The big Highway truck careened down the slope. I heard yells, then I heard shots. For a moment it seemed like the soldiers thought they were dealing with a suicide bomber. Then I saw they were shooting at the tyres. I had just enough time to think this was a smart move.

The two front tyres blew out just as the front wheels went over the edge of the path, where it curved off at the shore of the loch in front of the houses. The nose of the truck slammed down. Oh aye, that bit stopped moving all right. The rest of the truck kept right on moving. The back of it rose into the air and seemed to hang there for a second. Then it toppled right over and crashed forward like a falling tree, right on to the chopper. The chinook's fuel and the truck's electrics took a couple of seconds to find each other. Just as well because everybody was flat on the ground when the fuel tank exploded. It wasn't the sort of explosion that hurls debris everywhere. It was a big blast of burning petrol vapour that scorched the back of my neck.

When I looked up the remains of the truck and the chopper were in the middle of one big mass of flame and smoke. It was like what you see on the television from Tehran any day. The soldiers ran towards it and stopped when the heat was too much. Then around the side of the burning wreckage came a dripping figure. It was the pilot, who must have jumped out and crashed through the ice of the loch when he saw the truck bearing down. I felt relieved about that.

I stood up and looked around and noticed that with all this commotion the people from the settlement had disappeared. They'd skedaddled. They were off down the wee glen, then up the slopes like deer. I saw an officer peering after them through binoculars. Then he lowered the glasses and shook his head and pointed at us.

With that half the soldiers formed a cordon and walked up the hill towards us.

"Looks like we're for it now," said Murdo.

"Run for it!" said Euan.

"Nae point," I said. "They'll shoot us."

"Sounds like a plan," said Murdo. But we weren't that desperate. Not then.

We raised our hands above our heads and waited for the boots and butts.

XI
THE SECOND JIN YANG

The soldiers were maybe twenty metres away down the slope from us when I heard a strange whizzing sound and saw sparkles of light from the hillside opposite. Then a second later a sound came, a steady *did-did-did* . . .

I threw myself flat on the grass. I watched six men spin and drop in front of me. Saw the others down by the lochside fall too. It was over in seconds. I lay with my hands clasped over my head and then stood up and puked.

Dark figures popped up on the hillside at the far side of the loch and began to walk down. Men, women, kids, about twenty in all, far more than I'd seen the day before. Two of them lugged a light machine gun. They were Martin and Angus. I had wondered why they hadn't been drafted. I was wrong. They had done their stint. And once you've been in the army, they told me later, it's not that hard to find a way to find the weapons. Even armour-piercing ammo gets black-marketed.

But that was later.

What happened right then, while the kids were looting the dead, was that Ailiss walked up to us with her face all black and a rifle in her hand. Her grin was very white on her dirt-smeared face.

"That was *brilliant*!" she said. "God above, you guys are heroes! Running the truck down on them like that!"

"It was him who had that idea," said Murdo, pointing at me.

Ailiss gave me a dangerous hug, with the rifle still clutched in one hand.

I looked at Murdo and Euan. They looked back at me. I knew what they were thinking. We couldn't go away now. For a start, there was no way the gang here would let us go. For the very good reason that we would tell everything we knew. One way or another.

Like poor Jin Yang, the Chinese guy on the plane who was mistaken for a hijacker, I never meant to start a war. But I did. The war at home, the war of the veterans and settlers and evacuees and laggers. The war that rose as steadily as the sea level. The war we're still in. If I'd known what was going to happen, I might have walked away and taken my chances, even if it meant a bullet in the back. I don't know now, even after all these years. I for sure didn't know then. All I knew was that Ailiss was looking at me in a way nobody had ever looked at me before. Like she was *proud* of me.

Laggers, I thought. Too dumb tae draft. But not too feart tae fight.

"Aye," I said. "It was my idea."

the pacific Mystery

STEPHEN BAXTER

Like many of his colleagues at the beginning of a new century, British writer Stephen Baxter has been engaged for more than a decade now with the task of revitalizing and reinventing the "hard-science" story for a new generation of readers, producing work on the cutting edge of science that bristles with weird new ideas and often takes place against vistas of almost outrageously cosmic scope.

Baxter made his first sale to *Interzone* in 1987, and since then has become one of that magazine's most frequent contributors, as well as making sales to *Asimov's Science Fiction*, *Science Fiction Age*, *Analog*, *Zenith*, *New Worlds*, and elsewhere. He's one of the most prolific new writers in science fiction, and is rapidly becoming one of the most popular and acclaimed of them as well. In 2001, he appeared on the final Hugo ballot twice, and won both *Asimov's* Readers Award and *Analog's* Analytical Laboratory Award, one of the few writers ever to win both awards in the same year. Baxter's first novel, *Raft*, was released in 1991 to wide and enthusiastic response, and was rapidly followed by other well received novels such as *Timelike Infinity*, *Anti-Ice*, *Flux*, and the H. G. Wells pastiche—a sequel to *The Time Machine*—*The Time Ships*, which won both the John W. Campbell Memorial Award and the Philip K. Dick Award. His other books include the novels *Voyage*, *Titan*, *Moonseed*, *Mammoth*, *Book One: Silverhair*, *Manifold: Time*, *Manifold: Space*, *Evolution*, *Coalescent*, *Exultant*, *Transcendent*, and two novels in collaboration with Arthur C. Clarke, *The Light of Other Days* and *Time's Eye, A Time Odyssey*. His short fiction has been collected in *Vacuum Diagrams: Stories of the Xeelee Sequence*, *Traces*, and *The Hunters of Pangaea*, and he has released a chapbook novella, *Mayflower II*. His most recent books are the novel *Emperor* and a new collection, *Resplendent*. Coming up are two more new novels, *Conqueror* and *Navagator*.

Here he takes us to an alternate world that ultimately turns out to be a lot *more* different from our own time line than it would at first sight appear to be.

Editor's note: The saga of the return of the aerial battleship *Reichsmarschall des Grossdeutschen Reiches Hermann Goering* to London's sky, and of the heroic exploits of a joint team of RAF and Luftwaffe personnel in boarding the hulk of the *schlachtschiff*, has overshadowed the story of what befell her long-dead crew, and what they discovered during their attempted Pacific crossing—inasmuch as their discoveries are understood at all. Hence, with the agreement of the family, the BBC has decided to release the following edited transcript of the private diary kept onboard by journalist Bliss Stirling. Miss Stirling completed the Mathematical Tripos at Girton College, Cambridge, and during her National Service in the RAF served in the Photographic Reconnaissance Unit. For some years she was employed as a cartographer by the Reich in the mapping of the eastern Kommissariats in support of Generalplan Ost. She was also, of course, a noted aviatrix. She was but twenty-eight years old at the time of her loss.

May 15, 1950. Day 1. I collected my Spitfire at RAF Medmenham and flew up into gin-clear English air. I've flown Spits all over the world, in the colonies for the RAF, and in Asia on collaborative ops with the Luftwaffe. But a Spit is meant to fly in English summer skies—I've always regretted I was too young to be a flyer in the Phoney War, even if no shots were fired in anger.

And today was quite an adventure, for I was flying to engage the *Goering*, the Beast, as Churchill always referred to her before his hanging. Up I climbed, matching its eastward velocity of a steady 220 knots towards central London—I matched *her*, the Beast was not about to make a detour for me. You can hardly miss her even from the ground, a black cross-shape painted on the sky. And as you approach, it is more like buzzing a building, a skyscraper in New York or Germania perhaps, than rendezvousing with another aircraft.

I was thrilled. Who wouldn't be? On board this tremendous crate I was going to be part of an attempt to circumnavigate the world for the first time in human history, a feat beyond all the great explorers of the past: we would be challenging the Pacific Mystery. Always providing I could land on the bloody thing first.

I swept up above the Beast and then vectored in along her spine, coming in from the stern over a tailplane that is itself the height of St. Paul's. It was on the back of the Beast, a riveted airstrip in the sky, that I was going to have to bring down my Spit. I counted the famous four-deep banks of wings with their heavy engine pods and droning props, and saw the glassy blisters of gun turrets at the wing tips, on the tailplane and around the nose. It's said that the Beast carries her *own* flak guns. A few small stubby-winged kites, which I later learned the Germans called "chariots," were parked up near the roots of the big wing complexes. The whole is painted black, and adorned with Luftwaffe crosses. Despite the rumoured atom-powered generator in her belly, it is scarcely possible to believe such a monstrosity flies at all, and I can quite believe it is impossible for her ever to land.

And, like all Nazi technology, she is seductively beautiful.

I've done my share of carrier landings, but that final approach through a forest of A/T booms and RDF antennae was hairier than any of them. Pride wasn't going to allow me the slightest hesitation, however. I put my wheels down without a bump, my arrestor hook caught on the tag lines, and I was jolted to a halt before the crash barriers. On the back of the Beast stood a batsman in a kind of all-over rubber suit, harnessed to the deck to stop from being blown off. He flagged me to go park up under a wing-root gun turret.

So I rolled away. Bliss Stirling, girl reporter, on the deck of the *Goering*! Somewhere below, I knew, was London. But the Beast's back is so broad that when you stand on it you can't see the ground. . . .

Day 2. The highlight of my day was an expensive lunch in what Doctor Ciliax calls "one of the lesser restaurants of the *schlachtschiff*," all silver cutlery and comestibles from the provinces of Greater Germany, Polish beef and French wine. It is like being aboard an ocean liner, or a plush Zeppelin, perhaps.

As we ate the Beast circled over Germania, which Jack Bovell insists on calling "Berlin," much to Ciliax's annoyance. Fleets of tanker craft flew up to load us with oil, water, food and other consumables, and we were buzzed by biplanes laden with cine-cameras, their lenses peering at us.

Jack Bovell is one of the token Yanks on board to witness the journey, much as I am a token British. He is a flying officer in the USAAF, and will, so he has been promised, be allowed to take the controls of the Beast at some point during this monumental flight. We tokens are in the charge of Wolfgang Ciliax, himself a Luftwaffe officer, though as an engineer he never refers to his rank. He is one of the Beast's chief designers. The three of us are going to be spending a lot of time together, I think. What joy.

This morning Ciliax took Jack and me on a tour of the Beast. Of course we weren't shown anything seriously interesting such as the "atom engine," or the "jet" motors rumoured to be deployed on some of the chariots. Ciliax in fact showed rare restraint for a boffin, in my experience, in not blurting out all he knew about his crate just for the love of her.

But we were dazzled by a flight deck the size of a Buckingham Palace reception room, with banks of chattering teletypes and an immense navigational table run by some of the few women to be seen on board. There are lounges and a ballroom and a library, and even a small swimming pool, which is just showing off.

Other guests walked with us, many from the upper tiers of the occupied nations of Europe. We were tailed by an excitable movie-film crew. Leni Riefenstahl is said to be directing a film of our momentous voyage, though she herself isn't aboard. And many sinister-looking figures wore the black uniforms of the SS. Pressed by Jack Bovell, Ciliax insists that the *Goering* is a Luftwaffe crate and the SS has no authority here.

Below decks, we walked through a hold the size of the Albert Hall. We marvelled at mighty aquifers of oil and water. And we were awed by the double transverse internal bulkheads and the hull of inches-thick hardened steel: rivets the size of my fist.

"She really is a battleship in the sky," Jack said, rather grudgingly. And he was right; the ancestry of this monstrous *schlachtschiff* lies truly among the steel behemoths of the oceans, not fragile kites like my Spitfire.

Jack Bovell is around thirty, is stocky—shorter than me—stinks of cigar smoke and pomade and brandy, and wears a battered leather flight jacket, even at dinner. I think he's from Brooklyn. He's smarter than he acts, I'm sure.

"Ah, yes, of course she is a *schlachtschiff*," said Ciliax, "but the *Goering* is an experimental craft whose primary purposes are, one, a demonstration of technology, and two, an explorative capability. The *Goering* is the first vessel in human history capable of challenging the mighty scale of the Pacific." That habit of his of speaking in numbered lists tells you much about Wolfgang Ciliax. He is quite young, mid-thirties perhaps, and has slicked-back blond hair and glasses with lenses the size of pennies.

"'Explorative capability,'" Jack said sourly. "And that's why you made a point of showing us her armour?"

Ciliax just smiled. Of course that was the point.

Every non-German on board this bloody plane is a spy to some degree or other, including me. Whatever we discover about the world as we attempt to cross the Pacific, we neutral and occupied nations are going to be served up with a powerful demonstration of the Reich's technological capabilities. Everyone knows this is the game. But Jack keeps breaking the rules. In a way he is too impatient a character for the assignment he has been given.

Jack, incidentally, sized me up when he met me, and Ciliax, who isn't completely juiceless, takes every opportunity to touch me, to brush my hand or pat my shoulder. But Jack seems sniffy. To him I'm an emblem of a nation of appeasers, I suppose. And to Ciliax I'm territory to be conquered, perhaps, like central Asia. No doubt we will break through our national types in the days to come. But Bliss is not going to find romance aboard the *Reichsmarschall des Grossdeutschen Reiches Hermann Goering*, I don't think!

Day 3. Memo to self: follow up a comment of Ciliax's about "helots" who tend the atom engines.

These machines are contained within sealed lead-lined bulkheads, and nobody is allowed in or out—at any rate, not me. The atomic motors are a focus of interest for us spies, of course. Before this flight the RAF brass briefed me about the Nazis' plans to develop weapons of stunning power from the same technology. Perhaps there is a slave colony of *untermenschen*, Slavs or gypsies, trapped inside those bulkheads, tending the glowing machines that are gradually killing them, as we drink wine and argue over politics.

In the afternoon I sat in one of the big observation blisters set in the belly of the Beast and made a broadcast for the BBC. This is my nominal job, to be British eyes and ears during this remarkable mission. We are still orbiting Germania, that is, Berlin. Even from the air the vast reconstruction of the last decade is clear to see.

The city has been rebuilt around an axial grid of avenues each a hundred yards wide. You can easily pick out the Triumphal Arch, the Square of the People, and the Pantheon of the Army which hosts a choreography of millions. Jack tuts about "infantile gigantomania," but you have to admire the Nazis' vision. And all the while the tanker planes fly up to service us, like bees to a vast flower. . . .

Day 5. A less pleasant lunch today. We nearly got pranged.

We crossed the old border between Germany and Poland, and are now flying over what the Germans call simply "Ostland," the vast heart of Asia. With Ciliax's help we spotted the new walled colony cities, mostly of veteran German soldiers, planted deep in old Soviet territories. They are surrounded by vast estates, essentially each a collective farm, a *kolkhoz,* taken from the Bolsheviks. There the peasantry toil and pay their tithes to German settlers.

Jack grumbled and groused at this, complaining in his American way about a loss of freedom and of human rights. But he's missing the point.

"Americans rarely grasp context," said Ciliax with barely concealed contempt. "It is not a war for freedom that is being fought out down there, not a war for territory. Asia is the arena for the final war between races, the climax of a million years of disparate human evolution. As the Fuhrer has written, 'What a task awaits us! We have a hundred years of joyful satisfaction before us.' " I must say that when Ciliax spouts this stuff he isn't convincing. He's fundamentally an engineer, I think. But one must labour for whoever holds the whip.

(Memo: check the source of that Hitler quote.)

Since Germania we have been accompanied by fighters, mostly Messerschmitts, providing top cover and close escort, and Jack Bovell and I have been happily spotting types and new variants. And we have seen lighter, faster fighters streaking across our field of view. They may be the "jet fighters" we've read about but have never seen up close. I know plenty of RAF brass who regret that the Phoney War ended in May 1940, if only for the lost opportunity for technical advancement. This ravaged continent is obviously a crucible for such advancement. Jack and I craned and muttered, longing to see more of those exotic birds.

And then the show started. We were somewhere over the Ukraine.

One fighter came screaming up through our layers of escorts. It arced straight up from the ground like a firecracker, trailing a pillar of smoke. I wondered aloud if it actually had rockets strapped to its tail. Ciliax murmured, as if intrigued by a puzzle.

You have to understand that we were sitting in armchairs in an observation blister. I even had a snifter of brandy in my hand. There was absolutely no sense of danger. But still the unmarked rocket-plane came on. A deep thrumming made the surface of my brandy ripple; the Beast, lumbering, was changing course.

"If that thing gets through," I said, "it's harps and halos and hello St. Peter for us."

"You don't say," said Jack Bovell.

Ciliax said nothing.

Then a chance pencil of flak swept across the nose of the rocket-plane, shattering the canopy over its cockpit. It fell away and that was that; I didn't even see the detonation when it fell to earth.

Jack blew out his cheeks. Wolfgang Ciliax snapped his fingers for more brandies all round.

We orbited over the area of the attempted strike for the next eight hours.

Ciliax took me and Jack down to a hold. The bombs were slim, blue and black steel, perfectly streamlined; they looked like "upturned midget submarines," as Jack said. You can drop them from as high as twenty thou. I thought this was another piece of typically beautiful Nazi technology, but Ciliax said the bombs are a British design, made under licence by Vickers Armstrong in Weybridge, whose chief designer is a man called Barnes Neville Wallis. "They are as British as the banks of Rolls-Royce Merlin engines that keep the *Goering* aloft," Ciliax told me, his bespectacled eyes intent, making sure I understood my complicity. But I thought he was mostly incensed that anybody had dared raise a hand against his beautiful machine.

That night the *Goering* dropped stick after stick of these "Tallboy" bombs on the site from which the rocket plane seemed to have been launched. I have no idea whether the assault was successful or not. The movie people filmed all this, in colour.

With the bombs dropped, we flee east, towards the dawn. I must try to catch some sleep. . . .

Day 7. We have already crossed China, which is the subject of a colonisation programme by the Japanese, a mirror image to what the Germans are up to in the west. Eurasia is a vast theatre of war and conquest and misery, a theatre that stretches back all the way to the Channel coast. What a world we live in!

Still, now we are past it all, a goodly chunk of the world's circumference already successfully traversed. Our escort has fallen away. Our last supply convoy was Japanese; Jack has threatened to drop their raw fish suppers out of the bomb bays.

And now, alone, we are facing our ultimate target: the Pacific Ocean. We are so high that its silver skin glimmers, softly curving, like the back of some great animal.

Jack is taking his turns in a pilot's seat on the bridge. This afternoon I was given permission from Ciliax to go up there. I longed to play with the controls. "I have a hunch I'm a better stick man than you," I said to Jack.

Jack laughed. Sitting there, his peaked cap on, his flight jacket under a webbing over-jacket, he looked at home for the first time since I'd met him. "I dare say you're right. But Hans is a better man than either of us."

"Hans?"

Hans, it turned out, is the flight deck's computing machine. Hans can fly the Beast on "his" own, and even when a human pilot is at the stick he takes over most functions. "I think the name is a German joke," Jack said. "Some translation of 'hands off.'"

I crouched beside his position, looking out over the ocean. "What do you think we're going to find out there, Jack?"

Jack, matter-of-fact, shrugged. "Twelve thousand miles of ocean, and then San Francisco."

"Then how do you explain the fact that nobody has crossed the Pacific before?"

"Ocean currents," he said. "Adverse winds. Hell, I don't know."

But we both knew the story is more complicated than that. This is the Pacific Mystery.

Humanity came out of Africa; Darwin said so. In caveman days we spread north and east, across Asia all the way to Australia. Then the Polynesians went island-hopping. They crossed thousands of miles, reaching as far as Hawaii with their stone axes and dug-out boats.

But beyond that point the Pacific defeated them.

And meanwhile others went west, to the Americas. Nobody quite knows how the first "native" Americans got there from Africa; some say it was just accidental rafting on lumber flushed down the Congo, though I fancy there's a smack of racial preju-dice in that theory. So when the Vikings sailed across the north Atlantic they came up against dark-skinned natives, and when the Portuguese and Spanish and British arrived they found a complicated trading economy, half-Norse, half-African, which they proceeded to wipe out. Soon the Europeans reached the west coast of the Americas.

But beyond that point the Pacific defeated them.

"Here's the puzzle," I said to Jack. "The earth is a sphere. You can tell, for in-stance, by the curving shadow it casts on the moon during a lunar eclipse."

"Sure," said Jack. "So we *know* the Pacific can't be more than twelve thousand miles across."

"Yes, but western explorers, including Magellan and Captain Cook, have pushed a long way out from the American coast. Thousands of miles. We know they should have found Hawaii, for instance. And from the east, the Chinese in the Middle Ages and the modern Japanese have sailed far beyond the Polynesians' range. Few came back. Somebody should have made it by now. Jack, *the Pacific is too wide.* And that is the mystery."

Jack snorted. "Bull hockey," he said firmly. "You'll be telling me next about sea monsters and cloud demons."

But those ancient Pacific legends had not yet been disproved, and I could see that some of the bridge crew, those who could follow our English, were glancing our way uncertainly.

Day 8. We are out of wireless telegraphy contact; the last of the Japanese stations has faded, and our forest of W/T masts stands purposeless. You can't help but feel iso-lated.

So we three, Ciliax, Jack and I, are drawn to each other, huddling in our metal cave like primitives. This evening we had another stiff dinner, the three of us. Loathing each other, we drink too much, and say too much.

"Of course," Ciliax murmured, "the flight of a rocket-plane would last only min-utes, and would be all but uncontrollable once, ah, the fuse is lit. Somebody on the ground must have known precisely when the *Goering* would pass overhead. I won-der who could have let them know?"

If that was a dig at Jack or me, Jack wasn't having any of it. "'Somebody'? Who?

In Asia you Nazis are stacking up your enemies, Wolfie. The Bolsheviks, partisans. You and the Japanese will meet and fall on each other some day—"

"Or it may have been Americans," Ciliax said smoothly.

"Why would America attack a Nazi asset?"

"Because of the strategic implications of the *Goering*. Suppose we do succeed in crossing the Pacific? America has long feared the vulnerability of its long western coastline. . . ."

Jack's eyes were narrow, but he didn't bother to deny it.

In 1940 America was indeed looking over its shoulder nervously at Japan's aggressive expansion. But the Pacific proved impassible, the Japanese did not come, and during the Phoney War America stood firm with Britain.

In April 1940 Hitler overran Denmark and Norway, and in May outflanked the Maginot line to crush France. The blitzkriegs caused panic in the British Cabinet. Prime Minister Chamberlain was forced out of office for his poor handling of the war.

But Hitler paused. The North Sea was his boundary, he said; he wanted no conflict with his "Anglo-Saxon cousins."

Churchill was all for rejecting Hitler's overtures and fighting on. But Lord Halifax, the foreign secretary, argued that Hitler's terms were acceptable. While Churchill retired fuming to the back benches, the "scarecrow in a derby hat" was prime minister within the week, and had agreed to an armistice within the month.

Hitler was able to turn his full energies east, and by Christmas 1941 had taken Moscow.

All this happened, you see, because the Japanese had not been able to pose a threat to the Americans. If not for the impassibility of the Pacific, America's attentions might have been drawn to the west, not the east. And without the powerful support we enjoyed from America, if Hitler hadn't been moved to offer such a generous peace in 1940—if Hitler had dared attack Britain—the Germans would have found themselves fighting on two fronts, west and east. Could Russia have survived an attenuated Nazi assault? Is it even conceivable that Russia and Britain and America could have worked as allies against the Nazis, even against the Japanese? *Would the war eventually have been won?*

All this speculation is guff, of course, best left to blokes in pubs. But you can see that if the Pacific *had* been navigable the whole outcome of the war with the Germans would have been different, one way or another. And that is why the *Goering*, a plane designed to challenge the ocean's impregnability, is indeed a weapon of strategic significance.

This is what we argue about over lunch and dinner. Lost in the vast inhuman arena of this ocean, we are comforted by the familiarity of our petty human squabbles.

Day 10. Perhaps I should record distances travelled, rather than times.

It is three days since we left behind the eastern coast of Asia. Over sea, unimpeded by resupplying or bomb-dropping, we make a steady airspeed of 220 knots. In the last forty-eight hours alone we should have covered twelve thousand miles.

We should *already* have crossed the ocean. We should *already* be flying over the

Americas. When I take astronomical sightings, it is as if we have simply flown around a perfectly behaved spherical earth from which America has been deleted. The geometry of the sky doesn't fit the geometry of the earth.

Somehow I hadn't expected the mystery to come upon us so quickly. Only ten days into the flight, we are still jostling for position at the dinner table. And yet we have sailed into a mystery so strange that we may as well have been projected to the moon.

I still haven't met the captain, whose name, I am told, is Fassbender. Even lost as we are in the middle of unfathomable nothingness, the social barriers between us are as rigid as the steel bulkheads of the Beast.

Day 15. Today, a jaunt in a chariot. What fun!

We passed over yet another group of islands, this one larger than most, dark basaltic cones blanketed by greenery and lapped by the pale blue of coral reefs. Observers in the blisters, armed with binoculars and telescopes, claimed to see movement at the fringes of these scattered fragments of jungle. So the captain ordered the chariots to go down and take a shuftie.

There were four of us in our chariot, myself, Jack, Ciliax, and a crewman who piloted us, a squat young chap called "Klaus" whom I rather like. Both the Germans wore sidearms; Jack and I did not. The chariot is a stubby-winged seaplane, well equipped to land on the back of the Beast; a tough little bugger.

We skimmed low over clearings where lions ran and immense bears growled. Things like elephants, covered in brown hair and with long curling tusks, lifted their trunks as we passed, as if in protest at our engines' clatter. "Christ," Jack said. "What I wouldn't give to be down among 'em with a shotgun." Ciliax and I took photographs and cine-films and made notes and spoke commentaries into tape recorders.

And we thought we saw signs of people: threads of smoke rose from the beaches.

"Extraordinary," Ciliax said. "Cave bears. What looked like sabre-toothed cats. *Mammoths* This is a fauna that has not been seen in Europe or America since the ice retreated."

Jack asked, "What happened to 'em?"

"We hunted them to death," I said. "Probably."

"What with, machine guns?"

I shrugged. "Stone axes and flint arrowheads are enough, given time."

"So," Jack asked practically, "how did they get *here?*"

"Sea levels fall and rise," Ciliax said. "When the ice comes, it locks up the world's water. Perhaps that is true even of this monstrous world ocean. Perhaps the lower waters expose dry land now submerged, or archipelagos along which one can raft."

"So in the Ice Age," I said, "we hunted the mammoths and the giant sloths until we drove them off the continents. But they kept running, and a few of them made it to one island or another, and now they just continue fleeing, heading ever east." And in this immense ocean, I thought, there was room to keep running and running and running. Nothing need ever go extinct.

"But there are people here," Jack pointed out. "We saw fires."

We buzzed along the beach. We dipped low over a kind of campsite, a mean sort of affair centred on a scrappy hearth. The people, naked, came running out of the forest at our noise—and when they saw us, most of them went running back again. But we got a good look at them, and fired off photographs.

They were people, sort of. They had fat squat bodies, and big chests, and brows like bags of walnuts. I think it was obvious to us all what they were, even to Jack.

"Neanderthals." Ciliax said it first; it is a German name. "Another species of— well, animal—which we humans chased out of Africa and Europe and Asia."

Jack said, "They don't seem to be smart enough to wipe out the mammoths as we did."

"Or maybe they're *too* smart," I murmured.

Ciliax said, "What a remarkable discovery: relics of the evolutionary past, even while the evolutionary destiny of mankind is being decided in the heart of Asia!"

Standing orders forbid landings. The chariot lifted us back to the steel safety of the Beast, and that was that.

It is now eight days since we crossed the coast of China. We have come *thirty-five thousand miles* since. Perhaps it shouldn't be surprising to find such strange beasts below, mammoths and cave bears and low-browed savages.

And still we go on. What next? How thrilling it all is!

Day 23. Today, a monstrous electrical storm.

We flew under the worst of it, our banks of engines thrumming, as lightning crackled around the W/T masts. Perhaps in this unending ocean there are unending storms—nobody knows, our meteorologists cannot calculate it.

But we came out of it. Bold technicians crawled out to the wing roots to check over the Beast, to replace a mast or two, and to tend to the chariots. I wanted to check my Spitfire, but predictably was not allowed by Ciliax. Still, Klaus kindly looked over the old bird for me and assures me she is A-OK.

Last night *both* Ciliax and Jack Bovell made passes at me, the one with a steely resolve, the other rather desperately.

Day 25. A rather momentous day.

Our nominal food and water store is intended to last fifty days. Today, therefore, Day Twenty-five, is the turn-back point. And yet we are no nearer finding land, no nearer penetrating the great mysteries of the Pacific.

The captain had us gather in the larger of the restaurants—*we* being the passengers and senior officers; the scullery maids were not represented, and nor were the helots, the lost souls of the atom-engine compartment. The captain himself, on his flight deck, spoke to us by speaker tube; I have yet to see his face.

We discussed whether to continue the mission. We had a briefing by the quartermaster on the state of our supplies, then a debate, followed by a vote. A vote, held on a flying Nazi *schlachtschiff*! I have no doubt that Captain Fassbender had already made his own decision before we were gathered in the polished oak of the dining room. But he was trying to boost morale—even striving to stave off mutinies in the future. Christopher Columbus used the same tactics, Jack told me, when his crew too felt lost in the midst of another endless ocean.

And, like Columbus, Captain Fassbender won the day. For now we carry on, on half rations. The movie-makers filmed it all, even though every last man of *them*, too fond of their grub, voted to turn back.

Day 28. Today we passed over yet another group of islands, quite a major cluster. Captain Fassbender ordered a few hours' orbit while the chariots went down to explore. Of my little group only I was bothered to ride down, with my friend Klaus. Jack Bovell did not answer my knock on his cabin door; I have not seen him all day. I suspect he has been drinking heavily.

So Klaus and I flew low over forests and patches of grassland. We spooked exotic-looking animals: they were *like* elephants and buffalo and rhinoceroses. Perhaps they are archaic forms from an age even deeper than the era of ice. Living fossils! I snapped pictures merrily and took notes, and fantasised of presenting my observations to the Royal Geographical Society, as Darwin did on returning from his voyage on the *Beagle*.

Then I saw people. They were naked, tall, slim, upright. They looked more "modern," if that is the right word, than the lumpy-browed Neanderthals we saw on the islands of mastodons, many days ago. Yet their heads receded from their foreheads; their shapely skulls can contain little in the way of grey matter, and their pretty brown eyes held only bewilderment. They fled from our approach like the other animals of the savannah.

Primitive they might be, but it appears they lead the march of the hominids, off to the east. I took more photos.

I have begun to develop a theory about the nature of the world, and the surface of the ocean over which we travel—or rather the geometric continuum in which it seems to be embedded. I think the Pacific is a challenge not merely to the cartographic mind but to the mathematical. (I just read those sentences over—how pompous—once a Girton girl, always a Girton girl!) I've yet to talk it over with anybody. Only Wolfgang Ciliax has a hope of understanding me, I think. I prefer to be sure of my ground before I approach him.

Certainly a radical new theory of this ocean of ours is needed. Think of it! Since the coast of Asia we have already travelled far enough to circle the earth *nearly five times*, if it were not for this oddity, this Fold in the World.

The Pacific is defeating us, I think, crushing our minds with its sheer scale. After only three days on half tuck everybody is grumbling as loudly as their bellies. Yet we go on. . . .

Day 33. It has taken me twenty-four hours to get around to this entry. After the events of yesterday the writing of it seemed futile. Courage, Bliss! However bad things are, one must behave as if they are not so, as my mother, a stoical woman, has always said.

It began when Jack Bovell, for the third day in a row, did not emerge from his cabin. One cannot have uncontrollable drunks at large on an aircraft, not even one as large as this. And no part of the *Goering*, not even passengers' cabins, can be off-limits to the godlike surveillance of the captain. So Wolfgang Ciliax led a party of hefty aircrew to Jack's cabin. I went along at Ciliax's request, as the nearest thing to a friend he has on this crate.

I watched as the Germans broke down Jack's door. Jack was drunk, but coherent, and belligerent. He took on the Luftwaffe toughs, and as he was held back Ciliax ordered a thorough search of his cabin—"thorough" meaning the furniture was dismantled and the false ceiling broken into.

The flap that followed moved fast. I have since pieced it together.

The airmen found a small radio transceiver, a compact leather case full of valves and wiring. This, it turned out, had been used by Jack to attract the attention of that rocket-plane as we flew over the Ukraine. So Ciliax's suspicions were proven correct. I am subtly disappointed in Jack; it seems such an *obvious* thing to have done. Anyhow this discovery led to a lot of shouting, and the thugs moved in on Jack. But as they did so he raised his right hand, which held what I thought at first was a grenade, and the thugs backed off.

Ciliax turned to me, his face like a thunderous sky. "Talk to this fool or he'll kill us all."

Jack huddled in the corner of his smashed-up room, his face bleeding, his gadget in his upraised right hand. "Bliss," he panted. "I'm sorry you got dragged into this."

"I was in it from the moment I stepped aboard. If you sober up—Wolfgang could fetch you some coffee—"

"Adrenaline and a beating-up are great hangover cures."

"Then think about what you're doing. If you set that thing off, whatever it is, do you expect to survive?"

"I didn't expect to survive when I called up that Russkie rocket-plane. But it isn't about me, Bliss. It's about duty."

Ciliax sneered. "Your president must be desperate if his only way of striking at the Reich is through suicide attacks."

"This has nothing to do with Truman or his administration," Jack said. "If he's ever challenged about it he'll deny any knowledge of this, and he'll be telling the truth."

Ciliax wasn't impressed. "Plausible deniability. I thought that was an SS invention."

"Tell me why, Jack," I pressed him.

He eyed me. "Can't you see it? Ciliax said it himself. It's all about global strategies, Bliss. If the Pacific crossing is completed the Germans will be able to strike at us. And that's what I've got to put a stop to."

"But there will be other *Goerings*," Ciliax said.

"Yeah, but at least I'll buy some time, if it ends here—if nobody knows—if the Mystery remains, a little longer. Somebody has to take down this damn Beast. A rocket-plane didn't do it. But I'm Jonah, swallowed by the whale." He laughed, and I saw he was still drunk after all.

I yelled, "Jack, no!" In the same instant half the German toughs fell on him, and the other half, including Ciliax, crowded out of the room.

I had been expecting an explosion in the cabin. I cowered. But there was only a distant *crump*, like far-off thunder. The deck, subtly, began to pitch. . . .

Day 34. We aren't dead yet.

The picture has become clearer. Jack sabotaged the *Goering*'s main control links; the switch he held was a radio trigger. But it didn't quite work; we didn't pitch into the sea. The technicians botched a fix to stabilise our attitude, and even keep us on our course, heading ever east. This whale of the sky still swims through her element. But the crew can't tell yet if she remains dirigible — if we will ever be able to fly her home again.

Six people died, some crewmen on the flight deck, a couple of technicians wrestling with repairs outside. And Jack, of course. Already beaten half to death, he was presented to a summary court presided over by the captain. Then Fassbender gave him to the crew. They hung him up in the hold, then while he still lived cut him down, and pitched him into the sea.

I don't know what Ciliax made of all this. He said these common airmen lacked the inventiveness of the SS, to whom he was under pressure to hand over Jack. Ciliax has a core of human decency, I think.

So we fly on. The engineers toil in shifts on the *Goering*'s shattered innards. I have more faith in engineers than in gods or gargoyles, priests or politicians. But I no longer believe I will ever see England again. There. I've written it down, so it must be true. I wonder what strange creatures of the sea will feast on Jack's flesh. . . .

Day 50. Another round number, another pointless milestone.

I estimate we have travelled a distance that would span from the earth to the moon. Think of that! Perhaps in another universe the German genius for technology would have taken humans on just such an epic voyage, rather than this pointless slog.

We continue to pass over island groups and chains. On one island yesterday, covered by a crude-looking jungle of immense feathery ferns, I saw very exotic animals running in herds, or peering with suspicion at our passage. Think of flightless birds, muscular and upright and with an avian nerviness; and think of a crocodile's massive reptilian patience; combine the two, and you have what I saw.

How did the dinosaurs die? Was it an immense volcanic episode, a comet or other fire from the sky, a deadly plague, some inherent weakness of the reptilian race? Whatever it was, it seems that no matter how dramatic the disaster that seeks to wipe you out, there is always room to run. Perhaps on this peculiar folded-up earth of ours there is *no species* that has ever gone extinct. What a marvellous thought!

But if they *were* dinosaurs, down on that island, we will never know. The plane no longer stops to orbit, for it cannot; the chariots no longer fly down to investigate thunder lizards. And we plough on ever east, ever farther over the ocean, ever deeper into a past even beyond the dinosaurs.

My social life is a bit of a challenge these days.

As our food and water run out, our little aerial community is disintegrating into fiefdoms. The Water Barons trade with the Emperors of the Larder, or they will go to war over a tapped pipeline. Occasionally I hear pronouncements from the invisible Captain Fassbender, but I am not certain how far his word holds sway any longer. There have been rumours of a coup by the SS officers. The movie-makers are filming none of this. Their morale was the first to crumble, poor lambs.

I last saw Wolfgang Ciliax ten days ago. He was subtle and insidious; I had the distinct impression that he wanted me to join a sort of harem. Women are the scarcest commodity of all on this boat. Women, and cigarettes. You can imagine the shrift he got from me.

I sleep in barricaded rooms. In the guts of the Beast I have stashes of food and water, and cigarettes and booze to use as currency in an emergency. I keep out of the way of the petty wars, which will sort themselves out one way or another.

Once I had to bale out over Malaya, and I survived in the jungle for a week before reaching an army post. This is similar. It's also rather like college life. What larks!

Editor's note: Many fragmentary entries follow. Some are undated, others contain only mathematical jottings or geometric sketches. The reader is referred to a more complete publication forthcoming in *Annals of Psychiatry*.

Day 365. A year, by God! A full year, if I have counted correctly, though the calendar is meaningless given how many times we have spun around this watery earth — or appear to have. And if the poor gutted Beast is still keeping to her nominal speed, then I may have travelled two million miles. *Two million*. And still no America!

I believe I am alone now. Alone, save for the valve mind of Hans, and perhaps the odd rat.

The food ran out long ago, save for my stashes. The warfare between the Fuhrers of Spam and the Tsars of Dried Eggs became increasingly fragmented, until one man fell on the next for the sake of a cigarette stub. Others escaped, however, in chariots that went spinning down to one lost island or another. Klaus was one of them. I hope they survive; why not? Perhaps some future expedition, better equipped than ours, may retrieve their descendants.

And the Beast is hollowed out, much of her burned, depopulated save for me. I have explored her from one end to the other, seeking scraps of food and water, pitching the odd corpse into the drink. The only place I have not investigated is the sealed hold of the atom engine. Whatever survives in there has failed to break out.

However, the engine continues to run. The blades of the Merlins turn still. Even the heating works. I should put on record that no matter how badly we frail humans have behaved, the *Reichsmarschall des Grossdeutschen Reiches Hermann Goering* has fulfilled her mission flawlessly.

This can't go on forever, though. Therefore I have decided to set my affairs in order to begin with, my geometrical maunderings. I have left a fuller account — that is, complete with equations — in a separate locker. These journal notes are intended for the less mathematical reader; such as my mother (they're for you, mummy! — I know you'll want to know what became of me).

I have had to make a leap of faith, if you will. As we drive on and on, with no sight of an end to our journey, I have been forced to consider the possibility that there will *be* no end—that, just as it appears, the Pacific is not merely anomalously large, but, somehow, *infinite*. How can this be?

Our greatest geometer was Euclid. You've heard of him, haven't you? He reduced all of the geometry you can do on a plane to just five axioms, from which can be derived that menagerie of theorems and corollaries which have been used to bother schoolchildren ever since.

And even Euclid wasn't happy with the fifth axiom, which can be expressed like this: *parallel lines never meet*. That seems so obvious it doesn't need stating, that if you send off two lines at right angles to a third, like rail tracks, they will never meet. On a perfect, infinite plane they wouldn't. But on the curved surface of the earth, they would: think of lines of longitude converging on a pole. And *if space itself is curved*, again, "parallel" lines may meet—or they may diverge, which is just as startling. Allowing Euclid's axiom to be weakened in this way opens the door to a whole set of what are rather unimaginatively called "non-Euclidian geometries." I will give you one name: Bernhard Riemann. Einstein plundered his work in developing relativity.

And in a non-Euclidean geometry, you can have all sorts of odd effects. A circle's circumference may be more or less than "pi" times its diameter. You can even fit an infinite area into a finite circumference: for, you see, your measuring rods shrink as those parallel lines converge. Again I refer you to one name: Henri Poincaré.

You can see where I am going with this, I think. It seems that our little globe is a non-Euclidean object. Its geometry is *hyperbolic*. It has a finite radius—as you can see if you look at its shadow on the moon—but an infinite surface area, as we of the *Goering* have discovered. The world has a Fold in it, in effect. As I drive into the Fold I grow smaller and ever more diminished, as seen from the outside—but I *feel* just as Bliss-sized as I always did, and there is plenty of room for me.

This seems strange—to put it mildly! But why should we imagine that the simple geometry of something like an orange should scale up to something as mighty as a planet?

Of course this is just one mathematical model that fits the observations; it may or may not be definitive. And many questions remain open, such as astronomical effects, and the nature of gravity on an infinite world. I leave these issues as an exercise for the reader.

One might question what difference this makes to us mere mortals. But surely geography determines our destiny. If the Pacific could have been spanned in the Stone Age, perhaps by a land bridge, the Americas' first inhabitants might have been Asian, not Africans crossing the Atlantic. And certainly in our own century if the Pacific were small enough for America and Japan to have rubbed against each other, the convulsion of war we have endured for the last decade would not have turned out the way it did.

Besides all that—what fun to find yourself living on such a peculiar little planet, a World with a Fold! Don't you think? . . .

———

Date unknown. Sorry, I've given up counting. Not long after the last entry, however.

With my affairs in order I'm jumping ship. Why?

Point one: I've eaten all the food. Not the Spam, obviously.

Point two: I think I'm running out of world, or at least the sort of world I can live on. It's a long time since I saw a mastodon, or a dinosaur. I still cross over island groups, but now they are inhabited, if at all, by nothing but purplish slime and what look like mats of algae. Very ancient indeed, no doubt.

And ahead things change again. The sky looks greenish, and I wonder if I am approaching a place, or a time, where the oxygen runs out. I wake up in the night panting for breath, but of course that could just be bad dreams.

Anyhow, time to ditch. It's the end of the line for me, but not necessarily for the *Goering.* I think I've found a way to botch the flight deck equipment: not enough to make her fully manoeuvrable again, but at least enough to turn her around and send her back the way she came, under the command of Hans. I don't know how long she can keep flying. The Merlins have been souped up with fancy lubricants and bearings for longevity, but of course there are no engineers left to service them. If the Merlins do hold out the *Goering* might one day come looming over Piccadilly Circus again, I suppose, and what a sight she will be. Of course there will be no way of stopping her I can think of, but I leave that as another exercise for you, dear reader.

As for me, I intend to take the Spit. She hasn't been flown since Day 1, and is as good as new as far as I can tell. I might try for one of those slime-covered rocks in the sea.

Or I might try for something I've glimpsed on the horizon, under the greenish sky. *Lights.* A city? Not human, surely, but who knows what lies waiting for us on the other side of the Fold in the World?

What else must I say before I go?

I hope we won't be the last to come this way. I hope that the next to do so come, unlike us, in peace.

Mummy, keep feeding my cats for me, and I'm sorry about the lack of grandchildren. Bea will have to make up the numbers (sorry, sis!).

Enough, before I start splashing these pages with salt water. This is Bliss Stirling, girl reporter for the BBC, over and out!

Editor's note: There the transcript ends. Found lodged in a space between bulkheads, it remains the only written record of the *Goering*'s journey to have survived on board the hulk. No filmed or tape-recorded material has been salvaged. The journal is published with respect to the memory of Miss Stirling. However, as Miss Stirling was contracted by the BBC and the Royal Geographic Society specifically to cover the *Goering*'s Pacific expedition, all these materials must be regarded as COPYRIGHT the British Broadcasting Conglomerate MCMLII. Signed PETER CARINHALL, Board of Governors, BBC.

okanoggan falls

CAROLYN IVES GILMAN

Here's a unique slant on the theme of alien invasion, simultaneously tough and compassionate, one where the conquered try out a very different kind of resistance. . . .

Carolyn Ives Gilman has sold stories to *The Magazine of Fantasy and Science Fiction, Interzone, Universe, Full Spectrum, Realms of Fantasy, Bending the Landscape,* and elsewhere. She is the author of five nonfiction books on frontier and American Indian history, and (so far) one SF novel, *Halfway Human.* Her work has appeared in our Fifteenth and Nineteenth Annual Collections. She lives in St. Louis, where she works as a museum exhibition developer, and is also at work on a new SF novel.

T he town of Okanoggan Falls lay in the folded hills of southwestern Wisconsin—dairy country, marbled with deciduous groves and pastureland that looked soft as a sable's fur. It was an old sawmill town, hidden down in the steep river valley, shaded by elderly trees. Downtown was a double row of brick and ironwork storefronts running parallel to the river. Somehow, the town had steered between the Scylla and Charybdis of the franchise and the boutique. If you wanted to buy a hamburger on Main Street, you had to go to Earl's Cafe, and for scented soap there was just Meyer's Drugstore. In the park where the Civil War soldier stood, in front of the old Town Hall infested with pigeons, Mr. Woodward still defiantly raised the United States flag, as if the world on cable news were illusion, and the nation were still reality.

American small towns had changed since the days when Sinclair Lewis savaged them as backwaters of conformist complacency. All of that had moved to the suburbs. The people left in the rural towns had a high kook component. There were more welders-turned-sculptors per capita than elsewhere, more self-employed dollmakers, more wildly painted cars, more people with pronounced opinions, and more tolerance for all the above.

Like most of the Midwest, Okanoggan Falls had been relatively unaffected by the conquest and occupation. Few there had even seen one of the invading Wattesoons, except on television. At first, there had been some stirrings of grassroots defiance, born of wounded national pride; but when the Wattesoons had actually lowered taxes and reduced regulation, the volume of complaints had gone down. People still didn't love the occupiers, but as long as the Wattesoons minded their own business and left the populace alone, they were tolerated.

All of that changed one Saturday morning when Margie Silengo, who lived in a mobile home on Highway 14, came racing into town with her shockless Chevy bouncing like a rocking horse, telling everyone she met that a Wattesoon army convoy had gone rolling past her house and turned into the old mill grounds north of town as if they meant to stay. Almost simultaneously, the mayor's home phone rang, and Tom Abernathy found himself standing barefoot in his kitchen, for the first time in his life talking to a Wattesoon captain, who in precise, formal English informed him that Okanoggan Falls was slated for demolition.

Tom's wife Susan, who hadn't quite gotten the hang of this "occupation" thing, stopped making peanut butter sandwiches for the boys to say, "They can't say that! Who do they think they are?"

Tom was a lanky, easygoing fellow, all knobby joints and bony jaw. Mayor wasn't his full-time job; he ran one of the more successful businesses in town, a wholesale construction-goods supplier. He had become mayor the way most otherwise sensible people end up in charge: out of self-defense. Fed up having to deal with the calcified fossil who had run the town since the 1980s, Tom had stood for office on the same impulse he occasionally swore—and woke to find himself elected in a landslide, 374 to 123.

Now he rubbed the back of his head, as he did whenever perplexed, and said, "I think the Wattesoons can do pretty much anything they want."

"Then we've got to make them stop wanting to mess with us," Susan said.

That, in a nutshell, was what made Tom and Susan's marriage work. In seventeen years, whenever he had said something couldn't be done, she had taken it as a challenge to do it.

But he had never expected her to take on alien invaders.

Town council meetings weren't formal, and usually a few people straggled in late. This day, everyone was assembled at Town Hall by five P.M., when the Wattesoon officer had said he would address them. By now they knew it was not just Okanoggan Falls; all four towns along a fifty-mile stretch of Highway 14 had their own occupying forces camped outside town, and their own captains addressing them at precisely five o'clock. Like most Wattesoon military actions, it had been flawlessly coordinated.

The captain arrived with little fanfare. Two sand-colored army transports sped down Main Street and pulled up in front of Town Hall. The two occupants of one got out, while three soldiers in the other stood guard to keep the curious at arm's length. Their weapons remained in their slings. They seemed to be trying to keep the mood low-key.

The two who entered Town Hall looked exactly like Wattesoons on television— squat lumps of rubbly khaki-colored skin, like blobs of clay mixed with gravel. They wore the usual beige army uniforms that hermetically encased them, like shrink-wrap, from neck to heel, but neither officer had on the face mask or gloves the invaders usually employed to deal with humans. An aroma like baking rocks entered the room with them—not unpleasant, just not a smell ordinarily associated with living creatures.

In studied, formal English the larger Wattesoon introduced himself as Captain Groton, and his companion as Ensign Agush. No one offered to shake hands, knowing the famous Wattesoon horror at touching slimy human flesh.

The council sat silent behind the row of desks they used for hearings, while the captain stood facing them where people normally gave testimony, but there was no question about where the power lay. The townspeople had expected gruff, peremptory orders, and so Captain Groton's reasonable tone came as a pleasant surprise, but there was nothing reassuring about his message.

The Wattesoons wished to strip-mine a fifty-mile swath of the hilly, wooded Okanoggan Valley. "Our operations will render the land uninhabitable," Captain Groton said. "The army is here to assist in your removal. We will need you to coordinate the arrangements so this move can be achieved expeditiously and peacefully." There was the ever-so-slight hint of a threat in that last word.

When he finished there was a short silence, as the council absorbed the imminent destruction of everything they had lived for and loved. The image of Okanoggan Valley transformed into a mine pit hovered before every eye: no maple trees, no lilacs, no dogs, no streetlights. Rob Massey, the scrappy newspaper editor, was first to find his voice. "What do you want to mine?" he said sharply. "There are no minerals here."

"Silica," the captain answered promptly. "There is a particularly pure bed of it underneath your limestone."

He meant the white, friable sandstone—useless for building, occasionally used for glass. What they wanted it for was incomprehensible, like so much about them. "Will we be compensated for our property?" Paula Sanders asked, as if any compensation would suffice.

"No," the captain answered neutrally. "The land is ours."

Which was infuriating, but unarguable.

"But it's our home!" Tom blurted out. "We've lived here, some of us four, five generations. We've built this community. It's our life. You can't just walk in and level it."

The raw anguish in his voice made even Captain Groton, lump of rubble that he was, pause. "But we can," he answered without malice. "It is not within your power to stop it. All you can do is reconcile yourselves to the inevitable."

"How much time do we have?" Paula bit off her words as if they tasted bad.

"We realize you will need time to achieve acceptance, so we are prepared to give you two months."

The room practically exploded with protests and arguments.

At last the captain held up the blunt appendage that served him as a hand. "Very well," he said. "I am authorized to give you an extension. You may have three months."

Later, they learned that every captain up and down the valley had given the same extension. It had obviously been planned in advance.

The room smoldered with outrage as the captain turned to leave, his job done. But before he could exit, Susan Abernathy stepped into the doorway, along with the smell of brewing coffee from the hall outside.

"Captain Groton," she said, "would you like to join us for coffee? It's a tradition after meetings."

"Thank you, madam," he said, "but I must return to base."

"Susan," she introduced herself, and, contrary to all etiquette, held out her hand.

The Wattesoon recoiled visibly. But in the next second he seemed to seize control of himself and, by sheer force of will, extended his arm. Susan clasped it warmly, looking down into his pebbly eyes. "Since we are going to be neighbors, at least for the next few months, we might as well be civil," she said.

"That is very foresighted of you, madam," he answered.

"Call me Susan," she said. "Well, since you can't stay tonight, can I invite you to dinner tomorrow?"

The captain hesitated, and everyone expected another evasion, but at last he said, "That would be very acceptable. Susan."

"Great. I'll call you with the details." As the captain left, followed closely by his ensign, she turned to the council. "Can I bring you some coffee?"

"Ish. What did it feel like?" said her son Nick.

Susan had become something of a celebrity in the eleven-year-old set for having touched an alien.

"Dry," she said, staring at the laptop on the dining room table. "A little lumpy. Kind of like a lizard."

In the next room, Tom was on the phone. "Warren, you're talking crazy," he said. "We still might be able to get some concessions. We're working on it. But if you start shooting at them, we're doomed. I don't want to hear any more about toad hunts, okay?"

"Have you washed your hand?" Nick wanted to know.

Susan let go of the mouse to reach out and wipe her hand on Nick's arm. "Eew, gross!" he said. "Now I've got toad germs."

"Don't call them that," she said sharply. "It's not polite. You're going to have to be very polite tonight."

"I don't have to touch him, do I?"

"No, I'm sure touching a grody little boy is the last thing he wants."

In the next room, Tom had dialed a different number. "Listen, Walt, I think I'm going to need a patrol car in front of my house tonight. If this toad gets shot coming up my walk, my house is going to be a smoking crater tomorrow."

"Is that true?" Nick asked, wide-eyed.

"No," Susan lied. "He's exaggerating."

"Can I go to Jake's tonight?"

"No, I need you here," Susan said, hiding the pang of anxiety it gave her.

"What are we having for dinner?"

"I'm trying to find out what they eat, if you'd just leave me alone."

"I'm not eating bugs."

"Neither am I," Susan said. "Now go away."

Tom came in and sank into a chair with a sigh. "The whole town is up in arms," he said. "Literally. Paula wanted to picket our house tonight. I told her to trust you, that you've got a plan. Of course, I don't know what it is."

"I think my plan is to feed him pizza," Susan said.

"Pizza?"

"Why not? I can't find that they have any dietary restrictions, and everyone loves pizza."

Tom laid his head back and stared glumly at the ceiling. "Sure. Why not? If it kills him, you'll be a hero. For about half an hour, then you'll be a martyr."

"Pizza never killed anyone," Susan said, and got up to start straightening up the house.

The Abernathys lived in a big old 1918 three-story with a wraparound porch and a witch's-hat tower, set in a big yard. The living room had sliding wood doors, stained-glass fanlights, and a wood-framed fireplace. It could have been fancy but instead it had a frayed, lived-in look—heaps of books, puppy-chewed Oriental carpet, an upright piano piled with model airplanes. The comfy, well-dented furniture showed the marks of constant comings and goings, school projects, and meetings. There was rarely a night when the Abernathys didn't have guests, but dinner was never formal. Formality was alien to Susan's nature.

She had been an RN, but had quit, fed up with the bureaucracy rather than the patients. She had the sturdy physique of a German farm girl, and the competent independence to go with it. Light brown hair, cropped just above her shoulders, framed her round, cheerful face. Only rarely was she seen in anything more fancy than a jean skirt and a shirt with rolled-up sleeves. When they had elected Tom, everyone had known they weren't getting a major's wife who would challenge anybody's fashion sense.

That night, Captain Groton arrived precisely on time, in a car with tinted windows, driven by someone who stayed invisible, waiting. Tom met the guest on the doorstep, looking up and down the street a little nervously. When they came into the living room, Susan emerged from the kitchen with a bouquet of wineglasses in one hand and a bottle in the other.

"Wine, Captain?" she said.

He hesitated. "If that is customary. I regret I am not familiar with your dietary rituals. I only know they are complex."

"It's fermented fruit juice, mildly intoxicating," she said, pouring a little bit in his glass. "People drink it to relax."

He took the glass gingerly. Susan saw that he had stumpy nubbin fingers. As a nurse, she had had to train herself to feel compassion even for the least appealing patients, and now she was forced to call on that skill to disregard his appearance.

"Cheers," she said, lifting her glass.

There was a snap as the stem on Captain Groton's glass broke in two. The wine slopped onto his hand as he tried to catch the pieces. "Pardon me," he mumbled. "Your vessel is brittle."

"Never mind the glass," Susan said, taking it and handing the pieces to Tom. "Did you cut yourself?"

"No, of course—" He stopped in mid-denial, staring at his hand. A thin line of blood bisected the palm.

"Here, I'll take care of that," she said. Taking him by the arm, she led him to the bathroom. It was not until she had dabbed the blood off with a tissue that she realized he was not recoiling at her touch as he had before. Inwardly, she smiled at small victories. But when she brought out a bottle of spray disinfectant, he did recoil, demanding suspiciously, "What is it?"

"Disinfectant," she said. "To prevent infection. It's alcohol-based."

"Oh," he said. "I thought it might be water."

She spritzed his hand lightly, then applied a bandage. He was looking curiously around. "What is this place?"

"It's a bathroom," she said. "We use it to—well, clean ourselves, and groom, and so forth. This is the toilet." She raised the lid, and he drew back, obviously repulsed. She had to laugh. "It's really very clean. I swear."

"It has water in it," he said with disgust.

"But the water's not dirty, not now."

"Water is always dirty," he said. "It teems with bacteria. It transmits a thousand diseases, yet you humans touch it without any caution. You allow your children to play in it. You drink it, even. I suppose you have gotten used to it, living on this world where it soils everything. It even falls from the sky. It is impossible to get away from it. You have no choice but to soak in it."

Struck by the startling image of water as filth, Susan said, "Occupying our world must be very unpleasant for you. What is your planet like?"

"It is very dry," he said. "Miles and miles of hot, clean sand, like your Sahara. But your population does not live in the habitable spots, so we cannot either."

"You must drink water sometimes. Your metabolisms are not that different from ours, or you would not be able to eat our food."

"The trace amounts in foods are enough for us. We do not excrete it like you do."

"So that's why you don't have bathrooms," she said.

He paused, clearly puzzled. Then it dawned on him what she had left out of her explanation. "You use this room for excretory functions?"

"Yes," she said. "It's supposed to be private."

"But you excrete fluids in public all the time," he said. "From your noses, your mouths, your skin. How can you keep it private?"

For a moment the vision of humans as oozing bags of bacteria left her unable to answer. Then she said, "That's why we come here, to clean it all off."

He looked around. "But there is no facility for cleaning."

"Sure there is." She turned on the shower. "See?"

He reacted with horror, so she quickly shut it off. She explained, "You see, we think of water as clean. We bathe in it. How do you bathe?"

"Sand," he said. "Tubs of dry, heated sand. It is heavenly."

"It must be." She could picture it: soft, white sand. Like what lay under the Okanoggan limestone. She looked at him in dawning realization. "Is that why you want—?"

"I cannot say anything about that," he said. "Please do not ask me."

Which was all the answer she needed.

When they came back out, Tom and the boys were in the kitchen, so that was where they went.

"Sorry, we got caught up in a really interesting conversation," Susan said breezily, with an I'll-tell-you-later look at Tom. "Captain Groton, these are our sons, Ben and Nick." The boys stood up and nodded awkwardly, obviously coached not to shake hands.

"They are both yours?" the Wattesoon asked.

"Yes," Tom said. "Do you have any kids, captain?"

"Yes. A daughter."

"How old is she?" Susan said, pouring some more wine for him in a mug.

Captain Groton paused so long she wondered if she had said something offensive, but finally he shook his head. "I cannot figure it out. The time dilation makes it too difficult. It would mean little to you anyway; our years are so different."

"So she's back home on your planet?"

"Yes."

"Your wife, too?"

"She is dead."

"I'm so sorry. It must have been hard for you to leave your daughter behind."

"It was necessary. I was posted here. I followed my duty."

It had occurred to Susan that perhaps cow-excretion pie was not the thing to offer her guest, so she began rummaging in the cupboard, and soon assembled a buffet of dry foods: roast soybeans, crackers, apple chips, pine nuts, and a sweet potato for moisture. As Tom tried valiantly to engage the captain in a conversation about fishing, she started assembling the pizza for her family. The dog was barking at the back door, so she asked Ben to feed him. Nick started playing with his Gameboy. There was a pleasantly normal confusion all around.

"What sorts of food do you eat at home?" Susan asked her guest when she had a chance.

Groton shrugged. "We are less preoccupied with food than you are. Anything will do. We are omnivores."

Ben muttered, "Better watch out for our dogs."

"Ben!" Susan rebuked him.

Captain Groton turned marbly eyes on him. "We have no interest in your food animals."

The whole family stared in horror. "Our dogs aren't food!" Ben blurted.

"Then why do you keep them?" the captain asked reasonably.

Tom said, "For companionship."

Ben said, "For fun."

Susan said, "Because they remind us that we're human. Without other species around, we'd forget."

"Ah. I see," the Wattesoon said. "We feel the same."

In the awkward silence that followed, the humans all wondered who were the Wattesoons' pets.

They were saved by the timer. The pizza came out of the oven, and soon all was cheerful confusion again.

The Internet had told Susan that Wattesoons were frugal eaters, but Captain

Groton seemed ravenous. He ate some of everything she put on the table, including two slices of pizza.

To spare their guest the troubling sight of counters, tabletop, and utensils being smeared with water, Susan asked him out to see the backyard so the others could clean up. The screen door banged shut behind them and the dog came trotting up, eager to smell the stranger, till Susan shooed him into the kitchen. She then led the Wattesoon out into the humid, crickety twilight.

It was a Midwestern evening. The yard backed up onto the river bluff, a weathered limestone cliff overgrown with sumac and grapevine. Susan strolled out past the scattered detritus of Frisbees and lawn darts toward the quiet of the lower yard, where nature had started to encroach. There was an old swing hung from a gnarled oak tree, and she sat down in it, making the ropes creak. In the shady quiet, she swung idly to and fro, thinking of other evenings.

She had never realized how desperately she loved this place until she was forced to think of losing it. Looking toward the dark bushes by the cliff, she saw the silent flare of fireflies. "Are you able to find this beautiful?" she said, not trying to hide the longing in her voice.

After a few moments of silence, she looked over to find the captain gazing into the dark, lost in thought. "I am sorry," he said, recollecting himself. "What did you ask?"

Instead of answering, she said, "I think we each get imprinted on a certain kind of landscape when we're young. We can enjoy other spots, but only one seems like we're made from it, down to our bones. This is mine."

"Yes," he said.

"Can you understand how it is for us, then? We talk a lot about our investments and our livelihoods, but that's just to hide the pain. We love this place. We're bonded to it."

He didn't answer at once, so she stopped the swing to look at him.

"I understand," he said.

"Do you?" she said hopefully.

"It changes nothing. I am sorry."

Disappointed, she stared at his lumpy face. Now that she was a little more accustomed to him, he did not seem quite so rubbly and squat. He gave an impatient gesture. "Why are your people so fond of being discontent? You relish resisting, protesting, always pushing against the inevitable. It is an immature response, and makes your lives much harder."

"But, Captain, there are some things that *ought* to be protested."

"What things?"

"Folly. Malice. Injustice."

He cut her off in a pained tone. "These things are part of the nature of the world. There is nothing we can do to prevent them."

"You would not even try?" she said.

"Life is not just. Fairness is a fool's concept. To fight brings only disillusion."

"Well, we are different. We humans can put up with a thousand evils so long as we think they are fair. We are striving all the time to bring about justice, in ourselves and our society. Yours too, if you would just let us."

"So your truculence is all an effort to improve us?" the Wattesoon said.

Surprised, Susan laughed. "Why, Captain Groton, no one told me your people had a sense of irony."

He seemed taken aback by her reaction, as if he regretted having provoked it.

"I was not laughing at you," she explained hastily. "At least, not in any way you would not wish."

"You cannot know what I would wish," he said stiffly.

She said, "Oh, I don't know about that." For the time being, here out of all official contexts, he seemed just as difficult and contradictory as any human male. Speculatively, she said, "Your answer just now, about justice. You sounded bitter, as if you spoke from some experience. What was it?"

He stared at her with that unreadable, granitic face. For a few moments she thought he wasn't going to answer. Then he said, "It is in the past. There is no point in talking about it. Today is today. I accept that."

They remained silent for a while, listening to the sounds of life all around. At last Susan said, "Well, the great injustice of *our* lives is still in the future."

The thought of it flooded into her. All of this gentle valley would be gone soon, turned into an open wound in the landscape. Tears came to her, half anger and half loss, and she got up to go back inside. When she reached the back porch, she paused to compose herself, wiping the tears from her face. Captain Groton, who had followed her, said in a startled voice, "You are secreting moisture."

"Yes," she said. "We do that from time to time, in moments of intense emotion."

"I wish—" he started, then stopped.

"Yes? What do you wish?"

"Never mind," he said, and looked away.

That night, lying in bed, she told Tom all she had learned.

"Sand," he said in disbelief. "The bastards are moving us out so they can have bathtub sand."

He was not feeling charitable toward the Wattesoons. After their dinner guest had left in his tinted limousine, Tom had gotten a call from the mayor of Walker, the closest Wal-Mart metropolis. The captain in charge of their evacuation was an unbending disciplinarian who had presented the residents with a set of non-negotiable deadlines. The news from Red Bluff was even less encouraging. The captain assigned there was a transparent racist who seemed to think evacuation was too good for the native population. Force seemed to be his preferred alternative.

"Larry wants us to mount a unified resistance," Tom said. "A kind of 'Hell no, we won't go' thing. Just stay put, refuse to prepare. It seems pretty risky to me."

Susan lay reflecting. At last she said, "They would think it was an immature response."

"What, like children disobeying?" he said, irritated.

"I didn't say I agreed. I said that was what they would think."

"So what *should* we do?"

"I don't know. Behave in a way they associate with adults. Somehow resist without seeming to resist."

Tom turned his head on the pillow to look at her. "How come you learn all these things? He won't give me anything but the official line."

"You're his counterpart, Tom. He has to be formal with you. I don't count."

"Or maybe you count more. Maybe he's sweet on you."

"Oh, please!"

"Who would have thought I'd lose my wife to a potato?" Tom mused.

She quelled the urge to hit him with a pillow. "You know, he's something of a philosopher."

"Socrates the spud," he said.

"More like Marcus Aurelius. I don't think he really wants to be here. There is something in his past, some tragedy he won't talk about. But it might make him sympathetic to us. We might win him over."

Tom rose on one elbow to look at her earnestly. "My God, he really did open up to you."

"I'm just putting two and two together. The problem is, I'm not sure what winning him over would get us. He's just following orders."

"Jeez, even one friend among the Wattesoons is progress. I say go for it."

"Is that an order, Mr. Mayor?"

"My Mata Hari," he said, with the goofy, lopsided grin she loved.

She rolled closer to put her head on his shoulder. All problems seemed more bearable when he was around.

In the next few weeks, no one saw much of Captain Groton. Information, instructions, and orders still emanated from his office, but the captain himself was unavailable—indisposed, the official line went. When she heard this, Susan called the Wattesoon headquarters, concerned that he had had a reaction to the odd menu she had fed him. To her surprise, the captain took her call.

"Do not concern yourself, Susan," he said. "There is nothing you can do."

"I don't believe you," she said. "You're so in love with stoical acceptance that you could have toxic shock before you'd admit there was anything wrong."

"There is nothing wrong."

"I'm a nurse, Captain Groton. If you are sick, you have become my job."

There was an enigmatic pause on the line. "It is nothing you would recognize," he said at last. "A Wattesoon complaint."

Concerned now that he had admitted it, she said, "Is it serious?"

"It is not mortal, if that is what you mean."

"Can I see you?"

"Your concern is gratifying, but I have no need of assistance."

And she had to be content with that.

In the end, Tom saw him before she did. It was at a meeting the captain couldn't avoid, a progress report on preparations for the evacuation. "It must be some sort of arthritis," Tom answered Susan's questions vaguely. "He's hobbling around with a cane. A bit testy, too."

Not trusting a man to observe what needed to be noticed, Susan called Alice Brody, who had also been at the meeting. She was more than willing to elaborate. "He does seem to be in discomfort," Alice said. "But that's not the strange part."

Aha, Susan thought.

"He's *taller*, Susan. By inches. And proportioned differently. Not quite so tubby, if you know what I mean. It looks like he's lost a lot of weight, but I think it's just redistributed. His skin is different, too—smoother, a more natural color."

"What do you think is going on?"

"Damned if I know."

That was when Susan got the idea to invite Captain Groton to the Fourth of July celebration. Observing the holiday at all had been controversial, under the circumstances—but the city council had reasoned that a day of frivolity would raise everyone's spirits. The Wattesoons regarded it as a quaint summer festival and completely missed the nationalist connotations, so their only objection was to the potential for disorder from the crowds. When the town agreed to ban alcohol, the occupiers relented.

Okanoggan Falls's Fourth of July always climaxed with the parade, a homegrown affair for which people prepared at least three hours in advance. There was always a chainsaw drill team, a convertible for the Butter Princess, a Dixieland jazz band on a flatbed truck, and decorated backhoes and front-end loaders in lieu of floats. Deprecating self-mockery was a finely honed sport in Wisconsin.

Tom was going to be obliged to ride in a Model T with a stovepipe hat on, so Susan phoned the Wattesoon commander and asked him to accompany her.

"It will be a real demonstration of old-time Americana," she said.

He hesitated. "I do not wish to be provocative. Your townsfolk might not welcome my presence."

"If you were riding in a float, maybe. But mingling with the crowds, enjoying a brat and a lemonade? Some people might even appreciate it. If they don't, I'll handle them."

At last he consented, and they arranged to meet. "Don't wear a uniform," was her last instruction.

She had no idea what a dilemma she had caused him till he showed up in front of Meyer's Drugstore in a ragbag assortment of ill-fitting clothes that looked salvaged from a thrift shop. However, the truly extraordinary thing was that he was able to wear them at all—for when she had last seen him, fitting into human clothes would have been out of the question. Now, when she greeted him, she realized they were the same height, and he actually had a chin.

"You look wonderful," she blurted out.

"You are exaggerating," he said in a slightly pained tone.

"Are you feeling all right?"

"Better, thank you."

"But your clothes. Oh dear."

"Are they inappropriate?" he asked anxiously.

She looked around at all the American summer slobbery—men in baggy T-shirts and sandals, women bursting out of their tank tops. "No," she said. "You'll fit right in. It's just that, for a man in your position . . ." She grabbed him by the hand and dragged him into the drugstore, making for the magazine rack. She found an issue of *GQ* and thrust it into his hands. "Study that," she said. "It will show you what the elite class of men wear." Perusing several other magazines, she found some examples of a more khakified, Cape Cod look. "This is more informal, but still tasteful. Good for occasions like this, without losing face."

He was studying the pictures with a grave and studious manner. "Thank you, Susan. This is helpful." With a pang, she wished Tom would take any of her sartorial advice so to heart.

They were heading for the counter to buy the magazines when he stopped, riveted by the sight of the shelves. "What are these products for?"

"Grooming, personal care," Susan said. "These are for cleaning teeth. We do it twice a day, to prevent our breath smelling bad and our teeth going yellow. These are for shaving off unwanted hair. Men shave their faces every day, or it grows in."

"You mean all men have facial hair?" Captain Groton said, a little horrified.

"Yes. The ones who don't want beards just shave it off."

"What about these?" he said, gesturing to the deodorants.

"We spread it under our arms every day, to prevent unpleasant odors."

Faintly he said, "You live at war with your bodies."

She laughed. "It does seem that way, doesn't it?" She looked down the aisle at the shampoos, mouthwashes, acne creams, corn removers, soaps, and other products attesting to the ways in which even humans found their own bodies objectionable.

Beth Meyer was manning the counter, so Susan introduced her to Captain Groton. Unable to hide her hostility, Beth nevertheless said, "I hope you learn something about us."

"Your shop has already been very instructive, Mrs. Meyer," the captain said courteously. "I never realized the ingenuity people devote to body care. I hope I may return some day."

"As long as we're open we won't turn away a customer," Beth said.

Outside, things were gearing up for the parade, and it was clear that people were spontaneously going to use it to express their frustration. Some of the spectators were carrying protest signs, and along the sidewalk one local entrepreneur had set up a Spike the Spud concession stand offering people a chance to do sadistic things to baked potatoes for a few dollars. The most popular activity seemed to be blowing up the potatoes with firecrackers, as attested by the exploded potato guts covering the back of the plywood booth. A reporter from an out-of-town TV station was interviewing the proprietor about his thriving business. The word "Wattesoon" never passed anyone's lips, but no one missed the point.

Including Captain Groton. Susan saw him studying the scene, so she said quietly, "It's tasteless, but better they should work it out this way than in earnest."

"That is one interpretation," he said a little tensely. She reminded herself that it wasn't *her* symbolic viscera plastering the booth walls.

His radio chose that moment to come to life. Susan hadn't even realized he was carrying it, hidden under his untucked shirt. He said, "Excuse me," and spoke into it in his own language. Susan could not tell what was being said, but the captain's voice was calm and professional. When he finished, she said, "Do you have soldiers ready to move in?"

He studied her a moment, as if weighing whether to lie, then said, "It would have been foolish of us not to take precautions."

It occurred to her then that he was their advance reconnaissance man, taking advantage of her friendship to assess the need for force against her neighbors. At first she felt a prickle of outrage; it quickly morphed into relief that he had not sent someone more easily provoked.

"Hey, Captain!" The man at the Spike the Spud stand had noticed them, and, emboldened by the TV camera, had decided to create a photogenic scene. "Care to launch a spud missile?" The people standing around laughed nervously, transfixed to see the Wattesoon's reaction. Susan was drawing breath to extricate him when he put a restraining hand on her arm.

"I fear you would think me homicidal," he said in an easygoing tone.

Everyone saw then that he understood the message of sublimated violence, but chose to take it as a joke and not a provocation.

"No homicide involved, just potatoes," said the boothkeeper. He was a tubby, unshaven man in a sloppy white T-shirt. His joking tone had a slightly aggressive edge. "Come on, I'll give you a shot for free."

Captain Groton hesitated as everyone watched intently to see what he would do. At last he gave in. "Very well," he said, stepping up to the booth, "but I insist on paying. No preferential treatment."

The boothkeeper, an amateur comedian, made a show of selecting a long, thin potato that looked remarkably like his customer. He then offered a choice of weapons: sledgehammer, ax, firecracker, or other instruments of torture. "Why, the firecracker of course," the captain said. "It is traditional today, is it not?"

"American as beer." One segment of the crowd resented that the Wattesoons had interfered with their patriotic right to inebriation.

The boothkeeper handed him the potato and firecracker. "Here, shove it in. Right up its ass." When the captain complied, the man set the potato in the back of the booth and said, "Say when."

When the captain gave the word, the man lit the fuse. They waited breathlessly; then the potato exploded, splattering the boothkeeper in the face. The onlookers hooted with laughter. Captain Groton extracted himself with an amiable wave, as if he had planned the outcome all along.

"You were a remarkably good sport about that," Susan said to him as they walked away.

"I could have obliterated the tuber with my weapon," he said, "but I thought it would violate the spirit of the occasion."

"You're packing a weapon?" Susan stared. Wattesoon weapons were notoriously horrific. He could have blown away the booth and everyone around it.

He looked at her without a shade of humor. "I have to be able to defend myself."

The parade was about to commence, and Susan was feeling that she was escorting an appallingly dangerous person, so she said, "Let's find a place to stand, away from the crowd."

"Over here," Captain Groton said. He had already scoped out the terrain and located the best spot for surveillance: the raised stoop of an old apartment building, where he could stand with his back to the brick. He climbed the steps a bit stiffly, moving as if unused to knees that bent.

Okanoggan Falls had outdone itself. It was a particularly cheeky parade, full of double-entendre floats like the one carrying a group called the No Go Banjoes playing "Don't Fence Me In," or the "I Don't Wanna Mooove" banner carried by the high school cheerleading squad in their black-and-white Holstein costumes. The captain's radio kept interrupting, and he spoke in a restrained, commanding voice to whoever was on the other end.

In the end, it all passed without intervention from any soldiers other than the one at Susan's side. When the crowd began to disperse, she found that she had been clenching her fists in tension, and was glad no one else was aware of the risk they had been running.

"What happens now?" Captain Groton said. He meant it militarily, she knew; all pretense of his purpose being social was gone.

"Everyone will break up now," she said. "Some will go to the school ballfield for the fund-raiser picnic, but most won't gather again till the fireworks tonight. That will be about nine-thirty or ten o'clock."

He nodded. "I will go back to base, then."

She was battling mixed feelings, but at last said, "Captain—thank you, I think."

He studied her seriously. "I am just doing my duty."

That night on the television news, the celebration in Okanoggan Falls was contrasted with the one in Red Bluff, where a lockdown curfew was in place, fireworks were banned, and Wattesoon tanks patrolled the empty streets.

A week later, when Susan phoned Captain Groton, Ensign Agush took the call. "He cannot speak to you," he said indifferently. "He is dying."

"What?" Susan said, thinking she had heard wrong.

"He has contracted one of your human diseases."

"Has anyone called a doctor?"

"No. He will be dead soon. There is no point."

Half an hour later, Susan was at the Wattesoon headquarters with her nurse's kit in hand. When the ensign realized he was facing a woman with the determination of a stormtrooper, he did not put up a fight, but showed her to the captain's quarters. He still seemed unconcerned about his commanding officer's imminent demise.

Captain Groton slumped in a chair in his spartan but private sitting room. The transformation in his appearance was even more remarkable; he was now tall and slender, even for a human, and his facial features had a distinctly human cast. He might have passed for an ordinary man in dim light.

An exceedingly miserable ordinary man. His eyes were red-rimmed, his face unshaved (she noted the facial hair with surprise), and his voice was a hoarse croak when he said, "Susan! I was just thinking I should thank you for your kindness before . . ." He was interrupted by a sneeze.

Still preoccupied with his appearance, she said, "You are turning human, aren't you?"

"Your microbes evidently think so." He coughed phlegm. "I have contracted an exceedingly repulsive disease."

She drew up a chair next to him. "What are your symptoms?"

He shook his head, obviously thinking the subject was not a fit one. "Don't be concerned. I am resigned to die."

"I'm asking as a professional."

Reluctantly, he said, "This body appears to be dissolving. It is leaking fluids from every orifice. There, I told you it was repulsive."

"Your throat is sore? Your nose is congested? Coughing and sneezing?"

"Yes, yes."

"My dear captain, what you have is called a cold."

"No!" he protested. "I am quite warm."

"That's probably because you have a fever." She felt his forehead. "Yes. Well, fortunately, I've brought something for that." She brought out a bottle of aspirin, some antihistamine, decongestant, and cough suppressant. She added a bottle of Vitamin C for good measure.

"You are not alarmed?" he asked hesitantly.

"Not very. In us, the disease normally cures itself in a week or so. Since your immune system has never encountered it before, I'm not sure about you. You have to level with me, Captain. Have you become human in ways besides appearance?"

Vaguely, he said, "How long has it been?"

"How long has what been?"

"Since I first saw you."

She thought back. "About six weeks."

"The transformation is far advanced, then. In three weeks I will be indistinguishable from one of you."

"Internally as well?"

"You would need a laboratory to tell the difference."

"Then it should be safe to treat you as if you were human. I'll be careful, though." She looked around the room for a glass of water. "Where's your ba—" It was a Wattesoon apartment; of course there was no bathroom. By now, she knew they excreted only hard, odorless pellets. "Where can I get a glass of water?"

"What for?" He looked mildly repulsed.

"For you to drink with these pills."

"*Drink?*"

"You mean to tell me you've had no fluids?"

"We don't require them. . . ."

"Oh, dear Lord. You're probably dehydrated as well. You're going to have to change some habits, Captain. Sit right there. I need to run to the grocery store."

At the grocery she stocked up on fruit juices, bottled water, tissues, and, after a moment's hesitation, toilet paper—though not relishing having to explain that one to him. She also bought soap, a washcloth, mouthwash, shaving gel, a packet of plastic razors, a pail, and a washbasin. Like it or not, he was going to have to learn.

She had dealt with patients in every state of mental derangement, but never had she had to teach one how to be human. When she had gotten him to down the pills and a bottle of orange juice, she explained the purpose of her purchases to him in plain, practical language. She showed him how to blow his nose, and explained how a human bladder and bowel worked, and the necessity of washing with soap and water. When she finished he looked, if anything, more despairing than before.

"It is not common knowledge to us that you are hiding these bodily deficiencies," he said. "I fear I made a grave error in judgment."

"You're a soldier," she said. "Stop dramatizing, and cope with it."

For a moment he stared, astonished at her commanding tone. Then she could see him marshaling his courage as if to face dismemberment and death. "You are justified to rebuke me," he said. "I chose this. I must not complain."

Soon the antihistamine was making him drowsy, so she coaxed him to return to bed. "You're best off if you just sleep," she told him. "Take more of the pills every four hours, and drink another bottle every time you wake. If you feel pressure and need to eliminate liquid, use the pail. Don't hold it in, it's very bad for you. Call me in the morning."

"You're leaving?" he said anxiously.

She had intended to, but at his disconsolate expression she relented. It made her realize that she could actually read expressions on his face now. She drew up a chair and sat. "I must say, your comrades here don't seem very sympathetic."

He was silent a few moments, staring bleakly at the ceiling. At last he said, "They are ashamed."

"Of what? You?"

"Of what I am becoming."

"A human? They're bigots, then."

"Yes. You have to understand, Susan, the army doesn't always attract the highest caliber of men."

She realized then that the drug, or the reprieve from death, had broken down his usual reticence. It put her in an odd position, to have the occupying commander relying on her in his current unguarded condition. Extracting military or political secrets would clearly violate medical ethics. But was personal and cultural information allowed? She made a snap decision: nothing that would hurt him. Cautiously, she said, "I didn't know that you Wattesoons had this . . . talent . . . ability . . . to change your appearance."

"It only works with a closely related species," he said drowsily. "We weren't sure you were similar enough. It appears you are."

"How do you do it?"

He paused a long time, then said, "I will tell you some day. The trait has been useful to us, in adapting to other planets. Planets more unlike our own than this one is."

"Is that why you changed? To be better adapted?"

"No. I felt it was the best way to carry out my orders."

She waited for him to explain that; when he didn't, she said, "What orders?"

"To oversee the evacuation on time and with minimal disturbance. I thought that looking like a human would be an advantage in winning the cooperation of the local populace. I wanted you to think of me as human. I did not know of the drawbacks then."

"Well, I don't think you would have fooled us anyway," Susan said a little skeptically. "Can you change your mind now?"

"No. The chameleon process is part of our reproductive biology. We cannot change our minds about that, either."

The mention of reproduction brought up something she had often wondered about. "Why are there no Wattesoon women here?" she asked.

The subject seemed to evoke some sort of intense emotion for him. In a tight voice, he said, "Our women almost invariably die giving birth. The only ones who survive, as a rule, are childless, and they are rare. If it were not for the frequency of multiple births, we would have difficulty maintaining our population. We see the ease with which you human women give birth, and envy it."

"It wasn't always this way," Susan said. "We used to die much more frequently, as well. But that wasn't acceptable to us. We improved our medicine until we solved the problem."

Softly, he said, "It is not acceptable to us, either."

A realization struck her. "Is that what happened to your wife?"

"Yes."

She studied his face. "I think you must have loved her."

"I did. Too much."

"You can't blame yourself for her death."

"Who should I blame?"

"The doctors. The researchers who don't find a cure. The society that doesn't put a high enough priority on finding a solution."

He gave a little laugh. "That is a very human response."

"Well, *we* have solved our problem."

He considered that answer so long she thought he had fallen asleep. But just as she was rising to check, he said, "I think it is better to go through life as a passerby, detached from both the good and the bad. Especially from the good, because it always goes away."

Gently, Susan said, "Not always."

He looked at her with clouded eyes. "Always."

And then he really did fall asleep.

That evening, after the boys had gone up to their rooms, Susan told Tom everything over wine. Some of her medical details made him wince.

"Ouch. The poor bastard. Sounds worse than puberty, all crammed into nine weeks."

"Tom, you could really help him out," Susan said. "There are thing you could tell him, man to man, that I can't—"

"Oh no, I couldn't," Tom said. "No way."

She protested, "But there are things about male anatomy—you expect *me* to warn him about all that?"

"Better you than me," Tom said.

"Coward," she said.

"Damn right. Listen, men just don't talk about these things. How am I supposed to bring it up? More to the point, why? He got himself into this. It was a military strategy. He even admitted it to you: he wanted to manipulate us to cooperate in our own conquest. I don't know why you're acting as if you're responsible for him."

Tom was right. She studied the wine in her glass, wondering at her own reaction.

She had been empathizing as if Captain Groton were her patient, not her enemy. He had deliberately manipulated her feelings, and it had worked.

Well, she thought, two could play at that game.

It was not to be a summer of days at the beach, or fishing trips, or baseball camp. Everyone was busy packing, sorting, and getting ready to move. Susan marshaled Nick and Ben into the attic and basement to do the easy part, the packing and stacking, but the hardest part of moving was all hers: making the decisions. What to take, what to leave. It was all a referendum on her life, sorting the parts worth saving from the rest. No object was just itself: it was all memories, encapsulated in grimy old toys, birthday cards, garden bulbs, and comforters. All the tiny, pointillist moments that together formed the picture of her life. Somehow, she had to separate her self from the place that had created her, to become a rootless thing.

The summer was punctuated with sad ceremonies like the one when they started disinterring the bodies from the town cemetery, the day when the crane removed the Civil War soldier from the park, and the last church service before they took out the stained-glass windows. After the dead had left, the town paradoxically seemed even more full of ghosts.

The protests did not die down. Red Bluff was in a state of open rebellion; a hidden sniper had picked off three Wattesoon soldiers, and the army was starting house-to-house searches to disarm the populace. In Walker, angry meetings were televised, in which residents shouted and wept.

In Okanoggan Falls, they negotiated. The Wattesoons were now paying to move three of the most significant historic buildings, and the school district would be kept intact after relocation. Captain Groton had even agreed to move the deadline two weeks into September so the farmers could harvest the crops—a concession the captains in Red Bluff and Walker were eventually forced to match, grudgingly.

The captain became a familiar face around town—no longer in a limousine, but driving a rented SUV to supervise contractors, meet with civic groups, or simply to stop for lunch at Earl's Cafe and chat with the waitress. Outwardly, there was no longer a hint of anything Wattesoon about him, unless it was his awkwardness when asked to tie a knot or catch a baseball. He had turned into a tall, distinguished older man with silver hair, whose manners were as impeccable as his dress. In social settings he was reserved, but occasionally something would catch his whimsy, and then he had a light, tolerant laugh. At the same time, a steely authority lay just under the surface.

The women of Okanoggan began to notice. They began to approach and engage him in conversation—urgently, awkwardly warm on their side, full of self-conscious laughter; and on his side, studiously attentive but maddeningly noncommittal. People began to talk about the fact that he went every week to dine at the Abernathy home, whether Tom was there or not. They noticed when Susan took him to the barber shop, and when they drove together to La Crosse to visit the mall. Her good humor began to irritate the other women in ways it never had before, and their eyes followed her when she passed by.

"She must of kissed that frog good, 'cause he sure turned into a prince," said Jewell Hogan at the beauty salon, and the remark was considered so witty it was repeated all over town.

For herself, Susan had found one more reason to love her life in Okanoggan Falls just before losing it. She was playing a game that gave her life an exotic twist, excitement it had lacked. It was her patriotic duty to lie awake each morning, thinking of ways to get closer to a thrillingly attractive, powerful man who clearly enjoyed her company and relied on her in some unusually intimate ways. In the last month before it all fell apart, her life had become nearly perfect.

Between arranging to move his business and the mayoral duties, Tom was often gone on the nights when Captain Groton came over for dinner. Susan was aware of the gossip—a blushing Nick had told her the boys were taunting him about his mother—but she was not about to let small-mindedness stop her. "Just wait till they see how it pays off," she said to Nick.

It made her think she needed to start making it pay off.

By now, Captain Groton was perforce conversant with the ceremonial foods of the Midwest—string bean casserole, Jell-O salad, brats and beans—and the communal rituals at which they were consumed. So Susan had been entertaining herself by introducing him to more adventurous cuisine. His tastes were far less conservative than Tom's, and he almost invariably praised her efforts. On one night when Tom was returning late, she ordered a pizza for the boys and prepared shrimp with wild rice, cilantro, artichokes, and sour cream, with just a hint of cayenne pepper and lemon. They ate in the dining room with more wine than usual.

The captain was telling her how the amateur scholar who ran the landfill, in one of the endless efforts to deter the Wattesoons from their plans, had tried to convince him that there was an important archaeological site with buried treasure underneath the town. He had even produced proof in the form of an old French map and a photo of a metallic object with a mysterious engraved design.

Susan laughed, a little giddy from the wine. "You didn't fall for it, did you?"

Captain Groton looked at her quizzically. "No, I didn't fall down."

His English was so good she almost never encountered a phrase he didn't know. "It's an expression, to fall for something. It means he was pulling your leg."

"Pulling my leg. And so I was supposed to fall down?"

"No, no," she said. "It's just an idiom. To fall for something is to be deceived. On the other hand, to fall for some*one* means to become fond of them, to fall in love."

He considered this thoughtfully. "You use the same expression for being deceived and falling in love?"

It had never struck her before. "I guess we do. Maybe it means that you have to have illusions to fall in love. There *is* a lot of self-deception involved. But a lot of truth as well."

She suddenly became aware how seriously he was watching her, as if the topic had been much on his mind. When their eyes met, she felt a moment of spontaneous chemical reaction; then he looked away. "And when you say 'Okanoggan Falls,' which do you mean, deception or love?" he asked.

"Oh, love, no question."

"But if it meant deception, you would not tell me," he said with a slight smile.

"I am not deceiving you, Captain," she said softly. And, a little to her own surprise, she was telling the truth.

There was a moment of silence. Then Susan rose from the table, throwing her napkin down. "Let's go to the backyard," she said.

He followed her out into the hot summer night. It was late August; the surrounding yards were quiet except for the cicadas buzzing in the trees and the meditative sigh of air conditioners. When they reached the deeper grass under the trees, the captain came to a halt, breathing in the fragrant air.

"The thing I was not expecting about being human is the skin," he said. "It is so sensitive, so awake."

"So you like it now, being human?" she asked.

"There are compensations," he said, watching her steadily.

Her intellect told her she ought to be changing the subject, pressing him on the topic of public concern, but her private concerns were flooding her mind, making it impossible to think. She was slightly drunk, or she never would have said it aloud. "Damn! It's so unfair. Why does such a perfect man have to be an alien?"

A human man would have taken it as an invitation. Captain Groton hesitated, then with great restraint took her hands chastely in his. "Susan," he said, "there is something I need to explain, or I would be deceiving you." He drew a breath to steady himself as she watched, puzzled at his self-consciousness. He went on, "It is not an accident, this shape I have assumed. On my planet, when a woman chooses a man, he becomes what she most wishes him to be. It is the function of the chameleon trait. We would have died out long ago without it." He gave a slight smile. "I suppose nature realized that men can never be what women really want until they are created by women."

Susan was struggling to take it in. "Created by . . . ? But who created you?"

"You did," he said.

"You mean—"

"That first day we met, when you touched me. It is why we avoid human contact. A touch by the right woman is enough to set off the reaction. After that, physiology takes over. Every time you touched me after that, it was biochemical feedback to perfect the process."

All the misery and shock of an interspecies transformation, and she had done it to him? "Oh my God, you must hate me," she said.

"No. Not at all."

Of course not. Her perfect man would never hate her. It would defeat the purpose.

At that thought, she felt like a bird that had flown into a windowpane. "You mean you are everything I want in a man?" she said.

"Evidently."

"I thought Tom was what I wanted," she said faintly.

"You already have him," Captain Groton said. "You don't need another."

She studied his face, custom-made for her, like a revelation of her own psyche. It was not a perfect face, not at all movie-star handsome, but worn with the traces of experience and sadness.

"What about your personality?" she asked. "Did I create that, too?"

He shook his head. "That is all mine."

"But that's the best part," she said.

She couldn't see his face in the dim light, but his voice sounded deeply touched. "Thank you."

They were acting like teenagers. They *were* like teenagers, in the power of an unfamiliar hormonal rush, an evolutionary imperative. The instant she realized it, it shocked her. She had never intended to cheat on Tom, not for a nanosecond. And yet, it was as if she already had, in her heart. She had fantasized a lover into being without even realizing it. He was the living proof of her infidelity of mind.

Trying to be adult, she said, "This is very awkward, Captain. What are we going to do?"

"I don't know," he said. "Perhaps—"

Just then, the back porch light came on, and they jumped apart guiltily, as if caught doing what they were both trying to avoid thinking about.

Tom was standing on the back porch, looking out at them. "You're back!" Susan called brightly, hoping her voice didn't sound as strained as she felt. She started up the lawn toward the house, leaving Captain Groton to follow. "Have you eaten?"

"Yes," Tom said. "I stopped at the Burger King in Walker."

"Oh, poor dear. I was just about to make coffee. Want some?"

"I am afraid I must be getting back to base," Captain Groton said.

"Won't you even stay for coffee?" Susan said.

"No, it is later than I realized." With a rueful laugh he added, "Now I understand why humans are always late."

She went with him to the front door, leaving Tom in the kitchen. The captain hesitated on the steps. "Thank you, Susan," he said, and she knew it wasn't for dinner.

Softly, she said, "Your women are lucky, Captain."

Seriously, he said, "No, they're not."

"Their lives may be brief, but I'll bet they're happy."

"I hope you are right." He left, hurrying as if to escape his memories.

When Susan went back into the kitchen, Tom said with studied casualness, "Did you make any headway with him?"

"No," she said. "He's very dutiful." She busied herself pouring coffee. When she handed him his cup, for the first time in their marriage she saw a trace of worry in his eyes. She set the cup down and put her arms around him. "Tom," she said fiercely, "I love you so much."

He said nothing, but held her desperately tight.

And yet, that night as she lay awake listening to Tom's familiar breathing, questions crowded her mind.

There was a hole in her life she had not even known was there. Now that she knew it, she could not ignore the ache. She had settled into a life of compromises, a life of good-enough. And it was no longer good enough.

Yet there was no way for her to have more without hurting Tom. She didn't love him any less for the revelation that he wasn't perfect for her; he was human, after all. None of this was his fault.

She looked at the lump of covers that was her husband, and thought of all she owed him for years of loyalty and trust. Somehow, she needed to turn from possibility and desire, and pass on by. She had to reconcile herself to what she had. It was simply her duty.

The day of the move was planned down to the last detail, the way the Wattesoons did everything. Fleets of moving vans, hired from all over the region, would descend on Okanoggan Falls starting at six thirty A.M. After stopping at the Wattesoon base, they would roll into town at eight sharp and fan out to assigned locations. The schedule of times when each household would be moved had been published in the paper, posted in the stores, and hand-delivered to each doorstep. There was a Web site where everyone could find their own move time.

The protesters were organized as well. The word had gone out that everyone was to gather at seven A.M. in the park opposite Town Hall. From there, they would march down Main Street to the spot where the highway ran between the bluff and the river, and block the route the trucks would have to take into town.

When Susan and Tom pulled into the mayor's reserved parking spot behind Town Hall at six forty-five, it was clear the rally had drawn a crowd. The local police were directing traffic and enforcing parking rules, but not otherwise interfering. Lines of people carrying homemade signs, thermos bottles, and lawn chairs snaked toward the park, as if it were a holiday. Some activists Susan didn't recognize were trying to get a handheld PA system going.

When Tom and Susan reached the front steps of Town Hall, Walt Nodaway, the police chief, saw them and came up. "We've got some professionals from out of town," he said. "Probably drove in from Madison."

"You have enough guys?" Tom asked.

"As long as everyone stays peaceable."

"The officers know not to interfere?"

"Oh, yeah." They had talked it over at length the night before.

A reporter came up, someone from out of town. "Mayor Abernathy, are you here to support the protesters?" she asked.

Tom said, "Everyone has a right to express their opinions. I support their right whether I agree with them or not."

"But do you agree with the people resisting the relocation?"

Susan had coached him not to say "No comment," but she could tell he wanted to right now. "It's hard on people. They want to defend their homes. I know how they feel." Susan squeezed his hand to encourage him.

The city council members had begun to arrive, and they gathered on the steps around Tom, exchanging low-toned conversations and watching the crowd mill around. The protest was predictably late getting started; it was seven thirty before the loudspeaker shrieked to life and someone started to lead a chorus of "We Shall Not Be Moved." People were starting to line up for the two-block march down to the highway when, from the opposite direction, a familiar black SUV came speeding around the police barricades and pulled up in front of Town Hall. A van that had been following it stopped on the edge of the park.

Captain Groton got out, followed by three Wattesoon guards who looked even more lumpish than usual beside their lean commander. All were in sand-colored uniforms. The captain cast an eye over the park, where people had just started to realize that the opposition had arrived, and then he turned to mount the steps. When he came up to Tom he said in a low, commanding voice, "A word with you, Mayor Abernathy. Inside." He turned to the city council members. "You too." Then he continued up the steps to the door. The others followed.

A few spectators were able to crowd inside before the Wattesoon guards closed the doors; Susan was one of them. She stood with the other onlookers at the back of the room as Captain Groton turned to the city officials.

They had never seen him really angry before, and it was an unsettling sight. There was a cold intensity about him, a control pulled tight and singing. "I am obliged to hold all of you responsible for the behavior of those people outside," he said. "They must return to their homes immediately and not interfere with the operation in progress." He turned to Tom. "I would prefer that the order come from you, Mayor."

"I can't give them that order," Tom said. "For one, I don't agree with it. For two, they're not going to obey it, regardless of what I say. I'm not their commander, just their mayor. They elected me, they can unelect me."

"You have a police force at your disposal."

"Just Walt and three officers. They can't act against the whole town. There must be four hundred people out there."

"Well then, consider this," Captain Groton said. "I *do* have a force at my disposal. Two hundred armed soldiers. Ten minutes ago, they started to surround the park outside. They are only waiting for my order to move in and start arresting noncompliants. We have a secure facility ready to receive prisoners. It is your decision, Mayor."

Somehow, they had not expected such heavy-handed tactics. "There are children out there, and old people," Tom protested. "You can't have soldiers rough them up. They're just expressing their views."

"They have had three months to express their views. The time for that is over."

"The time for that is never over," Tom said.

Their eyes met for a moment, clashing then Captain Groton changed his tone. "I am at my wit's end," he said. "You have known from the beginning what we were here for. I have never lied to you, or concealed anything. I have done everything in my power to make you content. I have compromised till my superiors are questioning my judgment. And still you defy me."

"It's not you, Captain," Tom said in a more conciliatory tone. "You've been very fair, and we're grateful. But this is about something bigger. It's about justice."

"Justice!" Captain Groton gave a helpless gesture. "It is about fantasy, then. Something that never was, and never will be. Tell me this: Do you call the earthquake unjust, or march against the storm?"

"Earthquakes and storms aren't responsible for their actions. They don't have hearts, or consciences."

"Well, if it would help reconcile you, assume that we don't, either."

With a level gaze, Tom said, "I know that's not true."

For a moment Captain Groton paused, as if Tom had scored a hit. But then his face hardened. "I have misled you, then," he said. "We are implacable as a force of nature. Neutral and inevitable. Neither your wishes, nor mine, nor all those people's out there can have the slightest influence on the outcome."

Outside, the crowd had gathered around the steps, and now they were chanting, "The people, united, will never be defeated." For a moment the sound of their voices was the only thing in the room.

In a low tone, Captain Groton said, "Show some leadership, Tom. Warn them to get out of here and save themselves. I can give you ten minutes to persuade them, then I have to give the order. I'm sorry, but it is my duty."

Tom stared at him, angry at the betrayal, furious to be made into a collaborator. Captain Groton met his gaze levelly, unyielding. Then, for an instant, Tom glanced at Susan. It was very quick, almost involuntary, but everyone in the room saw it. And they knew this was about more than principle.

Tom drew himself up to his full height, his spine visibly stiffening. Ordinarily, he would have consulted with the council; but this time he just turned and walked to the door. As he passed by, Susan fell in at his side. The onlookers made way. Not a soul knew what Tom was going to do.

Outside, the Wattesoon guards keeping the crowd away from the door fell back when Tom came out onto the steps. He held up his hands and the chanting faltered to a stop. "Listen up, everyone," he started, but his voice didn't carry. He gestured at the woman with the portable loudspeaker, and she hurried up the steps to give him the microphone.

"Listen up, everyone," he said again. The crowd had fallen utterly silent, for they saw how grim his face looked. "The Wattesoon soldiers have surrounded us, and in ten minutes they're going to move in and start arresting people."

There was a stir of protest and alarm through the crowd. "They're bluffing," someone called out.

"No they're not," Tom said. "I know this captain pretty well by now. He's dead serious. Now, if you want to get arrested, roughed up, and put in a Wattesoon jail, fine. But everyone else, please go home. Take your kids and get out of here. I don't want you to get hurt. You know they can do it."

On the edges, some people were already starting to leave, but most of the crowd still stood, watching Tom in disappointment, as if they had expected something different from him. "Look, we did our best," he said. "We talked them into a lot of things I never thought they'd give us. We pushed it as far as we could. But now we've reached the point where they're not going to give any more. It's our turn to give in now. There's nothing more we can do. Please, just go home. That's what I'm going to do."

He handed the mike back to its owner and started down the steps. Susan took his hand and walked with him. There was a kind of exhalation of purpose, a deflation, around them as the crowd started breaking up. Though one of the protesters from Madison tried to get things going again, the momentum was gone. People didn't talk much, or even look at each other, as they started to scatter.

Halfway across the park, Susan whispered to Tom, "The car's the other way."

"I know," Tom said. "I'll come back and get it later." She figured out his thinking then: the symbolic sight of them walking away toward home was the important thing right now.

Don't look back, she told herself. It would make her look hesitant, regretful. And yet, she wanted to. When they reached the edge of the park, she couldn't help it, and glanced over her shoulder. The green space was almost empty, except for a little knot of diehards marching toward the highway to block the trucks. On the steps of Town Hall, Captain Groton was standing alone. But he wasn't surveying the scene or the remaining protesters. He was looking after her. At the sight, Susan's thoughts fled before a breathtaking rush of regret, and she nearly stumbled.

"What is it?" Tom said.

"Nothing," she answered. "It's okay."

By evening of the second day, it was all over in Okanoggan Falls.

In Red Bluff, there had been an insurrection; the Wattesoon army was still fighting a pitched house-to-house battle with resisters. In Walker, the soldiers had herded unruly inhabitants into overcrowded pens, and there had finally been a riot; the casualty reports were still growing. Only in Okanoggan Falls had things gone smoothly and peacefully.

The moving van had just pulled away from the Abernathy home with Tom and Nick following in the pickup, and Susan was making one last trip through the house to spot left-behind items, when her cell phone rang. Assuming it was Tom, she didn't look at the number before answering.

"Susan."

She had not expected to hear his voice again. All the decisions had been made, the story was over. The Wattesoons had won. Okanoggan had fallen to its enemies.

"Can you spare five minutes to meet me?" he said.

She started to say no, but the tug of disappointment made her realize there was still a bond between them. "Not here," she said.

"Where?"

"On Main Street."

Ben was in the backyard, taking an emotional leave of the only home he had known. Susan leaned out the back door and called, "I have to run into town for a second. I'll pick you up in ten minutes."

Downtown, the streetlights had come on automatically as evening approached, giving a melancholy air to the empty street. The storefronts were empty, with signs saying things like CLOSED FOR GOOD (OR BAD) tacked up in the windows. As Susan parked the car, the only other living things on Main Street were a crow scavenging for garbage, and Captain Groton, now sole commander of a ghost town.

At first they did not speak. Side by side, they walked down the familiar street. Inside Meyer's Drugstore, the rack where Susan had bought him a magazine was empty. They came to the spot where they had watched the Fourth of July parade, and Captain Groton reached out to touch the warm brick.

"I will never forget the people," he said. "Perhaps I was deceiving myself, but in the end I began to feel at ease among them. As if, given enough time, I might be happy here."

"It didn't stop you from destroying it," Susan said.

"No. I am used to destroying things I love."

If there had been self-pity in his voice she would have gotten angry, but it was simply a statement.

"Where will you go next?" she asked.

He hesitated. "I need to clear up some disputes related to this assignment."

Behind them a car door slammed, and Captain Groton cast a tense look over his shoulder. Following his gaze, Susan saw that a Wattesoon in a black uniform had emerged from a parked military vehicle and stood beside it, arms crossed, staring at them.

"Your chauffeur is impatient."

"He is not my chauffeur. He is my guard. I have been placed under arrest."

Susan was thunderstruck. "What for?"

He gave a dismissive gesture. "My superiors were dissatisfied with my strategy for completing my assignment."

Somehow, she guessed it was not the use of force he meant. "You mean . . ." She gestured at his human body.

"Yes. They felt they needed to take a stand, and refer the matter to a court-martial."

Susan realized that this was what he had wanted to tell her. "But you succeeded!" she said.

He gave an ironic smile. "You might argue that. But a larger principle is at stake. They feel we cannot risk becoming those we conquer. It has happened over and over in our history."

"It happens to us, too, in our way," Susan said. "I think your officers are fighting a universal law of conquest."

"Nevertheless, they look ahead and imagine Wattesoon children playing in the schoolyards of towns like this, indistinguishable from the humans."

Susan could picture it, too. "And would that be bad?"

"Not to me," he said.

"Or to me."

The guard had finally lost his patience and started toward them. Susan took the captain's hand tight in hers. "I'm so sorry you will be punished for violating this taboo."

"I knew I was risking it all along," he said, gripping her hand hard. "But still . . ." His voice held a remarkable mix of Wattesoon resolution and human indignation. "It is unjust."

It was then she knew that, despite appearances, she had won.

every Hole is outlined

JoHN BARNES

John Barnes is one of the most prolific and popular of all the writers who entered SF in the eighties. His many books include the novels *A Million Open Doors*, *Mother of Storms*, *Orbital Resonance*, *Kaleidoscope Century*, *Candle*, *Earth Made of Glass*, *The Merchants of Souls*, *Sin of Origin*, *One for the Morning Glory*, *The Sky So Big and Black*, *The Duke of Uranium*, *A Princess of the Aerie*, *In the Hall of the Martian King*, *Gaudeamus*, *Finity*, *Patton's Spaceship*, *Washington's Dirigible*, *Caesar's Bicycle*, *The Man Who Pulled Down the Sky*, and others, as well as two novels written with astronaut Buzz Aldrin, *The Return* and *Encounter with Tiber*. Long a mainstay of *Analog*, and now a regular at *Jim Baen's Universe*, his short work has been collected in . . . *And Orion* and *Apostrophes & Apocalypses*. His most recent book is the novel *The Armies of Memory*. Barnes lives in Colorado and works in the field of semiotics.

In the complex and resonant story that follows, he takes us to a far-future universe where a new recruit to the crew of a starship soon discovers the strange, and profoundly moving, rituals that are part of life on board. . . .

The ship was at least fourteen thousand years old in slowtime and more than two thousand in eintime, but there were holes in its records and the oldest ones were in no-longer-accessible formats, so the ship estimated that it was more like eighteen thousand slowtime, three and a half thousand eintime. It had borne many names. Currently it was 9743, a name that translated easily for Approach Control no matter where the ship went in human space.

In the last two centuries of eintime, the ship's conversation with most ports had been wholly mathematical. Synminds chattered about physics and astronomy to get the ship into a berth, and about prices and quantities and addresses afterward, and the human crew had not learned a word of the local language, despite their efforts, except such guesses as that the first things people said probably were something like "hello," and the last things something like "good-bye," and in between, perhaps, they might pick up equivalents of "may I?" and "thank you."

This had little immediate impact on the ship's operation except that mathematical worlds had no entertainment, or at least none they would sell to the ship's library; the long-run concern was that the mathematical worlds tended to begin waving off all ships and not communicating at all, after a time, though strangely some of those dark worlds would sometimes begin to talk and call for ships again, after an interval of a few centuries slowtime.

But the problem for this evening meal was both shorter-run than procuring entertainment for the ship's library, and much longer run than the gradual darkening of the worlds. They needed a new crew member, and they were having a real supper tonight, with cooked food, wine, and gravity, to discuss how to get one.

9743 needed a crew of four to work it, when it needed working, which was only for system entries and system departures because the law of space required it, and for PPDs (the business and navigation sessions held whenever predicted prices at destination shifted enough to require considering a course change) because the crew were the stockholders and synminds were required to consult them. Normally they would work the ship for half a shift for PPDs, but sometimes traffic density close to a star was high enough to engage gammor restrictions for as much as a light-day out from the port, and then 9743 had to have crew in the opsball for more than one shift.

Therefore, for the very rare case of needing more than one shift, the ship usually carried eight people: Arthur and Phlox, who were married and were the captain and first mate; Debi and Yoko, the two physicist's mates, who shared a large compartment with Squire, who was the physicist; Peter, the astronomer, who was too autistic to sleep with anyone or even to talk much, but a good astronomer and good at sitting beside people and keeping them company; and Mtepic, the mathematician, whose wife Sudden Crow, the mathematician's mate, had died two years ago in eintime.

In slowtime it had been ten and a half years ago, but ship people have a saying that no one lives in slowtime. By "no one," they mean almost everyone.

Arthur and Phlox had thought that Mtepic might be too old for another wife, but he surprised them by saying he thought he might have another twenty years of eintime left and he didn't want to spend it alone.

There was actually only one possible conclusion. They would have to buy someone from a slave world. That was a bad thing, but not hopelessly bad—rather common in fact. Debi, Peter, Sudden Crow, and Arthur had all been slaves, and at least Debi and Arthur felt strongly that buying a slave into a free life, though morally questionable, was usually good for the slave.

The others had been adopted as infants, raised to age four or five on 9743, and then sent through slowtime on a training ship to rejoin the crew when they were adults. All seven of them, whether born slave or free, agreed that it was better to be raised as ship people right from the start.

But they had had no plans for coping when Sudden Crow had died at fifty-one, without warning, from weightless calcium heart atrophy and overweight. 9743 was at least two years eintime from anywhere with freeborn babies available. They would have had to acquire the baby, tend it till it was four or five years old—a long time for a cargo ship to put up with a child, for ship people don't like to be around other people very much, and children must have attention all the time.

It would constrain them for several voyages—first to a world with adoptable freeborns, then to a shorthaul pair (two inhabited star systems within six or seven light-years of each other) with a training ship orbiting one of them. That shorthaul pair would need to be four to five years eintime away, between twenty-one and twenty-seven light-years distance at the 98.2%c that 9743 usually traveled.

At the shorthaul pair 9743 would then have to hand the child over to the training ship, work a shorthaul shuttle back and forth, then return, rendezvous with the training ship, and pick up the former four-year-old as a trained teenage crew member. It would add up to decades of running badly off the isoprofit geodesic.

They could have afforded that, but the nearest shorthaul pair was Sol/Alfsentary, which was nearly five years eintime away from the nearest system that sold babies. This could all add up to as much as seventeen years eintime before the teenaged crew member came back aboard to keep Mtepic company.

Mtepic was eighty-one and if he died anytime soon, they would not have a mathematician at all. Phlox and Debi, both of whom had math as a secondary, would have to cover, and the whole ship would have to assume the risk of having rusty, less-capable mathematicians filling in.

Besides, the best isoprofit geodesic available for adopting and training a freeborn baby had miserable numbers—long hauls and low profits throughout. A slave would be better, surely. And it was not so bad for the slave, they all assured each other.

The slave market at Thogmarch, the main inhabited world in the Beytydry system, was only six light-years away, and their cargo would take only a small loss there, one that 9743 Corporation could easily absorb and infinitely cheaper than the costs of dealing with a depressed mathematician. The medical synmind was confident at 94.4 percent that Mtepic was depressed. Besides, Mtepic said he was, and thought it was because of the loneliness. The synmind concurred with 78.5 percent confidence that a new mathematician's apprentice would help lift Mtepic out of it, but the crew were all sure that estimate was low—medics hate to make predictions of any kind about enfleshed intelligences.

9743 had some spare mass to feed to the shielder, and they could safely boost up to 98.65%c and reach Thogmarch in a little less than an einyear. If they radioed now, the message would arrive at Thogmarch almost seven weeks before the ship itself did, so that they could have buyers and sellers ready for cargo switch on arrival, and have dealers lined up to sell them an apprentice mathematician with the sort of personality that could learn to like ship life.

"And 9743 has never bought a slave who wasn't grateful for a chance to stay on after manumission," Arthur said, finishing his long, slow reprise, which had begun with the appetizers and was now finishing in the wine after dessert. "Life here compared to what they have dirtside is a lot better."

Arthur was fond of explaining things that everyone already knew, which was utterly typical. Captains are notorious for spending much time explaining unnecessarily.

Even ship people say so, and for them to say that is saying something, for ship people are all that way. They like to let the talk be slow and affectionate and thorough. They acquire a habit of listening to things they have heard many times before, and already know by heart, just to indulge the person who needs to speak; and, so that the ears of the others stay friendly, most of them learn not to talk very much except at formal occasions.

"Mostly," Peter said, startling them all because he spoke so infrequently, "we allow them some dignity and privacy." He meant the slaves, of course, though he might have meant anyone on the ship. "And by the time the first voyage is up they don't miss home, which anyway gets far enough into the past that it becomes hard to return to." He drank off a glass of the chilled white wine; they had turned on the gammors for an extra hour this week, to enjoy a sit-down meal in the conference room, because this was a matter that needed some serious attention. At 98.1%c, with a course change imminent, a quarter g of acceleration for a few hours of sitting and talking would have little effect on anything. "I'm for," Peter said.

"We're not *at* voting *yet*," Debi corrected him, a little fussily, which was how she did everything.

Squire rubbed her shoulders; it never made her less fussy but they both enjoyed it. "We know what he means, though. This is something that has always worked so far. We find a teenager with very high math aptitude and very low interpersonal attachment. Slavers are cruel; we are merely indifferent. If she doesn't have too much need for interpersonal attachment, she may even think we are kind—you do want a girl, right, Mtepic?"

"Yes, a girl."

Squire gestured like a man who would have liked to have a blackboard. "Well, then, life on the ship is better than being beaten and used and ordered about; a bit of respect and dignity often works wonders."

Phlox was nodding, and when she did, people usually felt that the vote had already been taken, and the thing approved. Everyone, even Arthur, said she would be a better captain, once he died. She rested her hands together in a little tent in front of her, nodded again, and said, "When we manumit her, she will want to stay with us. They always do. So this plan will get us a new mathematician's mate who can eventually become our mathematician. It is not as kind as adopting a freeborn baby and having a training ship raise the baby as a free member of the ship's company, and it is not as easy as working an exchange with another ship would be if there were another ship to do it with. But it is kind enough, and easy enough. So we are going to settle on doing it. Now let us enjoy talking about it for some more hours."

Everyone nodded; ship people are direct, even about delaying getting to the point, and they like to know how new things will come out, before they start them, because they so rarely do.

In the young woman's file, Mtepic had read that Xhrina had been born a shareworker's daughter on Thogmarch, and her sale forced, when she was two, by her parents' bankruptcy. Her records showed that because she had intellectual talent but great difficulty learning social skills, she had been little valued on Thogmarch. The slaver who owned her had slated her for some post where her ability to endure humiliation over the long haul would be an asset; he had in mind either an aristocrat with a taste for brutalizing women, or a household that wanted to boast of its wealth by using human beings instead of robots to scrub floors and clean toilets.

Mtepic, as not only the person who would be working and living with her, but also the most empathetic person on board 9743 (according to the medic-synmind's most recent testing), had been sent dirtside to decide whether to buy Xhrina, and as he sat in the clean-air support tank his major thought was that he would take her if at all possible, rather than endure planetary gravity for much longer.

His bones were old and space-rotten. Though he was strapped up against the interior supports of the tank, and a small man, there was still far too much weight.

Xhrina spoke a language with a distributed grammar and numerous Altaic and Semitic roots, so the translator box worked tolerably well, and with her aptitude, she was unlikely to have any trouble learning Navish, once she was aboard. Mtepic thought her voice was surprisingly musical for someone so discouraged and unhappy. After he outlined what would happen if 9743 bought her, and made sure the translator had made it clear to her, he asked, "Do you want us to buy you, then?"

She trilled a soft trickle of sweet soprano sibilance. The translator box said, "This property had not yet realized there was any choice with respect to the subject at hand, my-sir."

"Officially there is not. Unofficially, we don't like slaving; 9743 has never carried slaves and never will. As you may know, slaving planets all enforce the Karkh Code on ships carrying slaves, so we cannot manumit you until you have performed satisfactory service for thirty years. But the Karkh Code operates in slowtime; in eintime, time as we experience it, you will be a slave for less than seven years, perhaps much less. And as much as we can manage it, within the limits of the Karkh Code, you will be a slave in the eyes of the law only. We won't ever treat you as a slave." He had to put that through the translator to her a few times, and they went back and forth again until he was sure she understood the deal.

"And my-sir still makes it have a sounding, correction, gives it an aura of, as if it were this property's choice, my-sir, and this property is trained not to make choices where my-sir has the right to choose."

He went at it a sentence at a time, forcing himself to be patient with the translator, which had the uncaring stupidity one would expect of a synmind.

The first critical sentence Mtepic communicated was, "If you ask that we not buy you, we will buy someone else."

Next, because it might matter to her, whether or not she was allowed to think it did, he spent a while explaining that, "Once you are on board, you will be expected to share a bed with me—my demands are minor, at my age, mostly that you keep away loneliness. Other crew will probably not want sex from you, being happy as they are, but if they do you will comply; our computer must show that for the Karkh Code manumission."

She seemed to accept that too easily and he didn't want her to think that was the main issue, so then he worked on getting her to understand that "you will not be coming aboard as a bedmate. Your main job will be to learn enough mathematics so that you are qualified as a mathematician's mate by the time we reach a port where we are legally allowed to free you with a universal manumission so that you will not be in danger if you change ships, or disembark and then travel again. At that port, you can leave our company if you like, or stay in the crew as a shareholder." That was actually easier to say, because the synmind was designed to understand contracts.

Then he got back to the main point, again, and this time it seemed to go faster. "If you ask that we not buy you, we will buy someone else. We do not want you to be unwilling."

"It is forbidden for this property to consider whether this property is willing for anything my-sir wills, my-sir, and I cannot know how this property will feel if this property is ever permitted to consider it, my-sir." She smiled when she said that; perhaps to let him know that she could only speak the formulas, or that the translator would only translate into the formulas, but that she accepted what he was saying, was that it? Or perhaps something in all this appealed to her sense of humor? In either case, he liked her for that smile.

Mtepic breathed deeply and let the thousands of mechanical fingers lift him straight, and the neurostimulators sharpen his perception and ease his discomfort.

Xhrina's skin was brown; the slavers had genetically modified her for almost pure-white hair; her nose was long and slim and her jaw and teeth perfectly formed. Her eyes were dark and almond-shaped. He thought that as little as twenty years ago, he would have felt physically attracted. Now, just turned eighty-three, he was attracted by what he could get through the censoring translator: that she didn't seem to want to exaggerate or overpromise, and clearly *had* an opinion she was trying to express.

He gave her another angle on it, just to make sure. "We think, based on your psychological evaluation, that you are suited to shipboard life, and you will be living like a free crewmember as soon as we leave the dock here." That seemed to go right through.

"If this property may ask, is crew life like freeborn life, my-sir?"

"You can always accept a payout and leave at the next port. Of course you have to be on the ship until we reach a port, and if you did decide to leave the ship after your first couple of voyages, you would have to move into a hospital for rehabilitation if you wanted to move permanently to a planetary surface." That thought reminded Mtepic of how painful the high gravity was, and so he decided to press the offer a little more. He just hoped he correctly understood her quirky smile still struggling through her slavery-deadened face. "I would like you to come with us," he said. "I am asking you. I could buy you and *make* you. I prefer that you say yes." And trying to think of what else he had to offer, he said, "My first order to you, as soon as you are on the ship, will be that you address no one as 'my-sir,' but speak to us all as equals."

She grinned at him as if on the brink of outright laughter. "Then if it pleases my-sir, this property wants to be bought by my-sir, my-sir."

He was fairly sure that was not what she had said, but surely it had been some form of yes. He didn't trouble to conceal his sigh of relief.

A few hours later, at her welcome-aboard dinner on 9743, once she had been assured that now she would never be returned to Thogmarch, she used an uncontrolled translator to explain, "I was always going to say yes, but the translator didn't want me to know I was being asked to say it because I wasn't supposed to have any choices or respond to them if anyone offered me any. Once I figured out what it wasn't translating, of course I said yes—it was such a pleasure to be asked. And I beg Mtepic's forgiveness, for having kept you upright for too long in that uncomfortable tank." And she favored him again with that extraordinary smile.

Two years eintime, eleven slowtime, on their way to the Sol system; the earlier PPDs had flipped because at Thogmarch they had acquired cargo β–Hy-9743-R56, which was forecast to be at peak value at Sol almost exactly at arrival time. Xhrina's Navish was fluent and she was already well into group and ring theory, and apter than her test scores showed. Mtepic had turned eight-five the day before, and Xhrina had been disappointed that no one wanted to have a party for him this year (she'd only been able to get two of them to participate the year before), so she'd held one for just the two of them.

She had learned to find it comforting when his fragile body pressed against her in the sleepsack, his skin so soft and dry that he felt like a paper bag of old chicken bones, and she was pleased to indulge his liking for going to bed at the same time; when he died, she would miss his company, but he would probably live for many more years; many ship people lived to be 110.

On the rare occasions when he still wanted any sort of sex, he would gently wake her and ask very politely. She understood that he was determined that she should forget that she was a slave, but Xhrina believed in rules, and would not stop being a slave till she was manumitted, though she was delighted to be ordered to behave like a free person, because the pure autophagy of it made her laugh. They often argued about that in a good-natured way, as he insisted on knowing what she thought and she attempted to tell him only what he wanted to hear, and they enjoyed their mutual failure.

She doubted whether she would ever love anyone, but if she did, it would have been very convenient and not at all a bother or a danger to have loved Mtepic.

When his age-knobbed knuckles brushed down her naked back she turned to let him touch her where he liked, but he placed a finger on her mouth and breathed, "Come with me" in her ear.

He slipped from the sleepsack and swam to his clothes. It was dim in the compartment with only the convenience lights on. As she popped from the sleepsack, he smiled at the sight of her, as he always did, and pushed her coverall bag toward her. She caught it and dressed as she had learned to do, in one movement, like his but swifter because she was young.

He beckoned her to follow him, and opened the hatch into the main crewpipe. They swam in silence up the center of the crewpipe to the opsball. She had only been there the four times that 9743 had needed working: first while they were kerring up the gravity well of Thogmarch, second as they kerred three light-weeks up the gravity well of Beytydry, once before they picked their next destination and turned the main gammors loose to leave Beytydry orbit, and then just two weeks ago for the PPD as budgets, prices, positions, relative velocities, and predictions changed.

That last time, just two weeks ago, Xhrina had been able to follow the discussions, though not really participate in them. Still, she appreciated that Mtepic was a very good ship's mathematician. It had made her bend harder to her studies, for to be an excellent ship's mathematician seemed a very grand thing to her, partly because it was clear that all the other ship people respected it, and mostly because it was what Mtepic was.

But this fifth time in the opsball, they were the only ones. He did not turn on the lights; they sneaked in as if to steal something.

She didn't ask.

She had come, in two years eintime with him, to trust Mtepic. Sometimes she asked herself if she wasn't just being a very faithful slave, but generally she felt that she was trusting like a free person, that Mtepic and she were friends like free people, and Xhrina was secretly very proud of that.

So she didn't ask. She just floated beside Mtepic on one side of the opsball. Since he seemed to be very quiet, she tried to stay even quieter.

Presently the surfaces all around them began to glow, and then the image of the stars shone round the opsball, just as if the human crew were about to commence operation, but perhaps a tenth as brightly. For a moment the display was Dopplered, and there was a blue pole that contained a crunched-down vivid blue Cassipy with Sol and Alfsentary in it, and a red smeared-out Leyo and Viryo, but in less than a second the display corrected.

Mtepic and Xhrina floated in what looked exactly like the dark between the stars, warm and comfortable in their crew coveralls. It was so beautiful with no working screens pulled up that she wondered why the crew did not do this all the time. Perhaps she could get permission to float here among the pictures of the stars, now and then, on her off-awake shift?

She had lost count of the breaths she had slowly drawn and released as she watched the projected stars creep along the surface of the opsball when from one side of the opsball, where Leyo was crawling slowly across, a pale white glow like a broken-off bit of the Milky Way burgeoned from a blurry dot to a coin of fog and thence into a lumpy fist of thin white swirl. The swirl swelled into a cloud of particles, then of objects, which surged to swallow the ship and closed around them like a hand grasping a baby bird.

The particles were now as large as people—they were people—translucent and glowing, many of them gesturing as if talking, but not to each other, more as if they had all been abstracted from some larger conversation. The vast crowd converged around the ship, and then all of them were gone except for the dozen who passed right through the wall and into the opsball.

How was that possible? Xhrina wondered. The opsball was buried deep in the center of the ship, 750 meters of holds, lifemachines, quarters, and engines in all directions around it, but the translucent figures, glowing perhaps half as bright as the brightest stars, seemed to merge directly from space outside the ship into space inside the ship.

The pallid figures, mere surfaces and outlines of people, filled the dark sphere. They all took up crew stations as if they were where they belonged, reaching for the opsball surface and calling up workscreens before them, drawing them with their fingers or spreading them with their hands just as regular crew did. The one nearest her was a woman whose strangely patterned coverall had sleeves for both legs and arms, slippers for the feet, and gloves on the hands; Xhrina wondered what sort of ship it was that necessitated so much clothing. That woman seemed to be an astronomer, by what Xhrina could see over her shoulder to her screen, but the graphics were labeled in a language that was not written like Navish.

Directly in front of her, a man who wore coat, shirt, and pants like people in prestellar Earth stories tumbled slowly, pointing and gesturing as if he were the captain. Through his dim translucent sheen, Xhrina could see a nude young woman whose head was half-missing, simply gone behind the ears with brains spilling down her back. Despite that, the young woman was working at a very large screen, apparently trying to estimate a vast matrix and not liking what she saw, redoing and redoing; the screen looked like the math software that Xhrina herself used. As she watched, the naked woman beat on the screen with her fists; Xhrina wondered if the problem was what was on the screen, or the lost parts of her brain.

All round the mathematician and his apprentice, the ghosts worked their ghostly screens, seeming as unaware of each other as of the living beings. They went on working—laughing, cursing, pounding, all without a sound—until the gentle, sweet whistle of Second Shift sounded through the ship. Then they faded through the walls of the opsball, dimming to darkness, and the stars dimmed to nothing after them.

Mtepic brought the running lights up. "Breakfast?"

"Surely," she said. "Perhaps we should nap again after?"

"We're bound to be tired," he agreed. If he was disappointed that she asked no questions, he did not indicate it.

Xhrina had twice celebrated Mtepic's birthday—the first time with Peter and Yoko who were good-natured but baffled about it, the second time just the two of them the night before they had seen the ghosts. From this, Mtepic deduced that she would like such a thing herself, and checked her bill of sale to find when her birthday was (she had never been told, and Mtepic did not think she should have to see her bill of sale unless she asked).

At one shift close, he surprised her with the news that she had just turned twenty-four, and also with the sort of gifts ship people give: her favorite meal, a small keepsake produced in the ship's fabricator, and time set aside to sit with her and watch a story he knew she'd like.

She had already known that Mtepic thought that she had a great deal of mathematical talent and believed she would one day be a fine ship's mathematician, and she knew too that he liked to have her around him. But still it was a surprise to Xhrina to realize that he also just wanted to do things that would make her happy. No one had ever appeared to care about that before, at all. It took her by surprise, put her a little off balance, but she considered the possibility that she might like it.

By her twenty-sixth birthday, after their five months of slowtime in the port orbiting Old Mars, 9743 was bound for Sigdracone, where she was to be manumitted. By now she was quite sure that she liked Mtepic's kindness and concern for her happiness, and as his health began to fail little by little, she realized that she was glad to be taking care of him, which he only needed occasionally so far, and to be there when he was afraid, which was rare but sometimes severe.

After much thought she concluded that she had been very damaged by the things the slavers had done to her, and guessed that this taking care of Mtepic might be as close to love as she would ever feel. Though she did not miss sex much, she wished he were still well enough to enjoy it; though he was sometimes crabby, and nowadays he slept a great deal, she liked to sit or float where she could have a hand on him, or an arm around him, constantly, as if he were her blanket and she were two years old.

His mind, when he was awake and not in pain, seemed as fine as ever, and she was grateful for that. She was glad she had said she wanted to come along, and everyone knew without saying that she would be staying on the ship, and would probably qualify to be ship's mathematician as soon as Mtepic died or became senile, though no one mentioned the inevitability of either of those to her. Ship people are indifferent, usually knowing nothing of each other's feelings, and not caring even when they must know, but even they could tell that she would miss Mtepic terribly and that the title of ship's mathematician would mean little to her compared to the loss of the only friend she had ever had.

Friend, she thought. *That's what Mtepic is to me. I thought he might be, and how nice to know it now, while I can appreciate it.*

They were about halfway there; it would be about two years or so eintime until they would lock themselves into the support field caskets so that every cell wall in their body could be held up against the hundred and fifty g acceleration of the gammors running flat out; three days later they would stagger out hungry and tired. Xhrina had been through all that now three times, and had no dread of it; as far as she was concerned, going from gammors down to Kerr motors meant minor discomfort followed by the most enjoyable meal and nap she was ever likely to have.

But for the moment that was still two years eintime, more than a decade slowtime, in the future. They had little to do but think and learn. Learning was fun: Xhrina had already passed her mathematician's mate's exam with highest distinction, and was well on her way to qualifying as a ship's mathematician.

As for thinking, Xhrina often thought about recursion. She thought it was interesting that she didn't always know what she liked, and she thought that everyone must have the same problem, for the only people she knew well were her shipmates, and they were impossible to know well, perhaps because they did not know what they liked, either.

She particularly liked the way that thinking about how it was possible not to know what she herself liked made her thoughts turn into circles and whorls and braids, spiraling down into the first questions about how she knew that she knew anything, as if descending into dark empty singularities; as her thoughts would vanish at the edge of those absent unthinkable thoughts, they marked the boundary as surely as the glimmers of vanishing dust and atoms at the Schwarzschild radius of a black hole.

Sometimes for a whole day she would keep track of which thought led to which thought and count how often, and by what diversity of paths, thoughts returned to the surfaces and boundaries of the unknowable. She could have flicked her fingers across any flat surface to make a workscreen, recited her data into the air, and played to her heart's content with the *grafsentatz*. But when she was working on the recursivity of her thoughts, she preferred to hang in the dark in the opsball, and bring up stars for their current position/time (she could have brought them up for any-where/anywhen, but she always chose current position and time). She always brought them up to just bright enough to see once her eyes adjusted.

Then she would slow her breathing and heartbeat, and wait for the perfect calm when her chi settled into tan tien, and see only in her mind's eye the screens, matrices, graphs, and equations, and endlessly devise graphs to portray, and statistics to measure, the recursion and circularity of her own thoughts, and consider whether thoughts about recursion should be intrinsically, or just accidentally, more or less recursive than other thoughts, and watch as all those thoughts drifted down onto the unknown, unknowing surfaces of those first known-to-be-unanswerable questions.

When she was finally cool and beautiful inside, she would softly ask the opsball to let the stars dim out, watch them till the last star was gone from the blackness, then swim back to Mtepic's quarters, where she would often find him sleeping fitfully and uneasily, drifting all over the compartment because he had fallen asleep outside the sleepsack. Then she would bathe him and rub him till he fell asleep smiling, and curl up against him for lovely, deep, dreamless sleep. The nightmares of her childhood were mostly gone now, and no more than pale shadows when they returned.

In the Sigdracone system, she still had enough of her gravity-bone to stand up and raise her hand, down on the surface of Aloysio, and receive her freedom under the open air. She wasn't quite sure why she chose to do that. It all seemed so harsh and uncomfortable and when she returned to the ship, it felt as if she *really* received her freedom at the dinner they had for her. Though they treated her just as they always had, as an equal, it mattered to her that now they were supposed to.

She affirmed and they voiceprinted it, making Xhrina a shareholder in 9743, backvested with all the equity that she had built up in the trust fund they had kept for her, while she had not been allowed to own property in case the ship had to touch base, and face a books inspection, on a Karkh-Convention world. They drank a toast.

The slowtime people at Aloysio wanted a total cargo changeover, something that only happened once in a century or so of eintime. An organization that the translators called the "Aloysio Museum of Spiritual Anger Corporation" bought the whole cargo, and sold 9743 an entirely new cargo: 1,024 cubes, sixty meters on a side, with identifier strips on every face.

None of 9743's ship people had known in a long time what ships carried, except that they never carried slaves, because they refused to, or any living thing that needed tending, because none of them wanted to learn how. So they knew the containers in the hold had nothing alive, or at least nothing actively alive, in them.

Other than that they knew nothing; over the slow correspondence of decades between ship people on other ships, there was an eternal argument about why no crew knew what was in the cargo. Some said it was because in the wars of fifteen thousand years ago, a tradition had been established that no ship people were ever to be responsible for anything they carried. Others said it was simply that the hundreds of thousands of cultures in slowtime changed so much and so fast compared with ship people that no one could have understood what the cargo was anyway. And still others said that the people on the worlds did not trust ship people not to steal it if they knew what it was, but most people said that was the silliest of all ideas, since anyone knew that the most valuable thing on a ship was hold space, and who would want to keep cargo and never be able to use the hold space again? Or who would buy or sell something when all contracts were broadcast openly, and it would be obvious to anyone that it was stolen?

Actually even if she had known, she would not have cared what was in the cargo. She did know where the cargo was going—that was what a mathematician did, after all—and she liked that very much. The ship would be making a very long haul, out into the north polar section of the Third Pulse worlds, where the inhabited stars were too distant to have ancient names because they had not been naked-eye visible from Earth, and so had been named for abstract qualities by the Second Pulse surveyors; she loved the idea that the suns all had names like Perspicacity, Charity, and Preternaturalness. And it would be six years eintime before their next system entry, perhaps more if the PPDs broke right.

On her twenty-ninth birthday, they were outbound and life had settled into the most comfortable of routines; after the small gifts and the warm feeling of attention, she rubbed Mtepic to sleep—he was just a soft, thin cover of lumpy bones, anymore, she thought—and drifted off herself, glad Mtepic had been there for her first birthday as a free person, hoping she could complete her mathematics preps and qualify for ship's mathematician while he could congratulate her for it.

Mtepic's soft palms and fingers pressed for one light instant on her shoulder blades. "It's strange how it happens on birthdays."

She glanced at the clock; she and Mtepic had been asleep for five hours since they had celebrated her birthday. Xhrina turned and held him in a light embrace; he sometimes woke up, now, talking to people he had been talking to in dreams, and she didn't like to startle him.

He embraced her in return, firmly and strongly, and now she knew he was awake, just starting in the middle as he tended to do. She waited to see what he would do or say. After a sigh—he liked holding her and she knew he might have been glad to do it much longer—Mtepic said, "There will be ghosts in the opsball tonight. I am going to watch them again. Would you like to come with me?"

"Of course," she said. "Does it happen on everyone's birthday?"

"Just mine, I thought. But now yours. Dress quickly. There's never much warning. We must be there and silent before the ghost-power lights up the opsball."

They dressed, swam through the main crewpipe, and entered the opsball.

Everything that evening was as before, except that the ghosts were different. First the Dopplered stars, and then the corrected stars, dimmer even than when Xhrina came in here to meditate. The fast-moving cloud made of ghosts zoomed silently up out of the Southern Cross to surround them in less than a minute. The ghosts in their thousands swarmed around the outside of (the ship? the opsball? But the ops-ball was 750 meters inside the ship, and yet the twenty or so ghosts who came inside seemed to merge directly from the projected stars to their positions in the opsball).

This time Xhrina mostly watched two young men, apparently twins, trying to solve what she thought must be an equation, though on each side of the equals sign there was only a rotating projection of a lumpy ellipsoid in several colors.

Or perhaps it was a game. They were both laughing very hard about it, whatever it was, and Xhrina liked the way they threw arms around each other and rested their heads on each other's shoulders, then went back to their game or problem or what-ever it was, sitting left shoulder to right shoulder, making little blobs of multicolor swim off one blob and across the equals sign to stick to the blob on the other side. Whenever they did that, both blobs would reorganize into different colors and shapes, and the two of them would clap, together, rhythmically, silently, as if to an unheard song.

A teenaged girl that Xhrina thought might have been a daughter or some other relative to the smashed-headed woman from last time—or was it the same woman at an earlier stage of life?—was working her screen, whose language looked like some late Konglish derivative, with a gymnast's concentration.

Another woman, old and stout with jowls, thin short gray hair like velvet, and something rough and wrong with the skin of her neck, wore a military uniform that could have been Late Brazilian Empire, Old Lunar Mexico, or Old Taucetian Guinea; somewhere in the First Interpulse, anyway, around the time of the Trade and Momentum Wars, because she looked just like the characters in a story, with bank codes on her sleeves, Mahmud boots, and a vibratana in a back scabbard.

Xhrina looked more closely, flapping her hands very gently to move herself toward the older woman in the military uniform. Bank trademarks on the shoulders; an admiral, then. Skull-jewels, gold with ruby eyes, in her pierced lower lip; four of them, four battle victories. The bank's symbol had the ancient dollar and yen signs, crossed, in two pairs, on either side of a balance, which could be any of the dozens of military-and-financial-services companies in any of the three millennia of that era.

The admiral was worried, her fingers gliding over a screen that kept changing its display but always showed a cluster of white points surrounded by a swarm of red points, sometimes labeled in the blocky letters of ancient Romantisco, sometimes connected by varicolored lines, sometimes with little translucent spheres around them and clocks ticking beneath them, sometimes in a view that tumbled and ro-tated to show the shape that the whole formation made in space.

She kept touching the white dots like a mother cat checking her kittens. Abruptly Xhrina understood; the squadron was bunching together to try to make a run through the closing bag, and the admiral didn't want to lose any of them. It was a classic situation, so common during those wars; the red dots were ringoes, robot ships that came in at a single target at 100 g, expending their entire magazines at the target and fuel supplies in acceleration, trying to ram just as they ran empty.

Once a ringo locked on and cranked its gammor to full power, they just kept coming, everything about them bent toward pure raw violence, game pieces in-tended to sacrifice at one to one, but they knew that they were too valuable to throw way on a bad risk, so they would not lock on until they decided they were close enough for a high probability of a kill. The admiral was trying to get her squadron out of a bag of ringoes, losing as few as she could manage. It did not look like that number would be zero, and it would be many hours before the brief burst of their violent escape, so she could choose to save any ship, but not all of them.

A very overweight, brown-skinned older woman dressed in a sleeveless coverall like Xhrina's own opened an application that Xhrina knew well. Xhrina gently paddled through the air to see better what the woman was doing and found that she was bumping up against Mtepic, paddling over from the other side.

He floated, reflecting the glow of the ghost in front of them. His rounded, reflecting surfaces—forehead, nose, knuckles, knees—glowed gray in the dim light; these seemed to shrink back, as if he were falling back away from the ghosts and the stars beyond them, into utterly lightless dark.

Across Mtepic's face, shoulders, and chest, a tangle of bright-glowing filaments emerged as if rising through his skin, like noodles in a colander slowly surfacing from boiling water.

The filaments broadened, stuck to each other, filled in gaps between. The dense, glowing web merged into the pale white shape of a newborn baby, like a bas relief just a centimeter or so above Mtepic's ghost-lit wrinkled old skin. The baby stretched and yawned. Its light washed over Mtepic's gray, still form and seemed to suck the color out of even his red coverall, leaving his lips blue-gray as dried mold.

The baby's tiny feet on apostrophes of legs barely reached the bottom of Mtepic's ribcage, but its head was almost as big as his. The arms, ending in hands too small to fully wrap Xhrina's thumb, reached out to fathom space around the baby but did not extend as far as Mtepic's slumped-in shoulders on either side. But the puckered face opened in a toothless, radiant smile of pure *What? How? What's all this?* Then the vast, deep eyes, clear and wide, focused on Xhrina, and the tiny soft mouth twisted and folded in the expression with which Mtepic always favored her best jokes. She could not help smiling back.

Not knowing why, she placed the palm of her right hand on the baby's chest, ever so gently, as if sure it would sink through to the sleeping Mtepic. She was surprised that the baby's chest was warm, damp, and firm under her hand for that instant.

Then she realized the baby was male, for a stream of phosphorescence poured wet and warm onto her sternum, making a glowing patch on her coverall, and she glanced down to see that the ghost baby, if that was what it was, had no more bladder control than a real one.

It was so unexpected that she giggled, carefully not making a sound but letting her chest convulse, and under her palm she felt the baby's chest pulse with the baby's giggle, sharing her delight. Her hand sank a tiny fraction forward, and the baby was gone. Her palm lightly pressed Mtepic's chest, where his heart thundered and his breath surged in and out as if he had worked too long and hard in the gym again, as he did so often despite her gentle scolding. His bony old hands closed around her strong young fingers, and he smiled at her, squeezing her hand.

For the rest of the night they held hands as they watched the laughing twins, the motherly admiral, the fat mathematician, and the rest of the ghostly crew. At last the shift chimes sounded, and the ghosts faded away, and then the stars. "Lights up slow," she said, and the opsball appeared around them, its surfaces matte gray, shutdown and inert, the same old opsball it was for months and years at a time.

"Breakfast in our quarters and a long talk?" she asked.

"Surely! And I am so pleased."

"At what?"

"You said 'our quarters,' not 'your quarters.' That is the first time in six years."

"It was important to you? I would have said it much sooner if I had known it mattered."

"It was important to me that you say it without my asking. And it was not important at all, at first, but it is now." They swam through the irising door of the opsball. "And when it became important, I began to count. You wouldn't laugh at my silly senility?"

"You are not senile and I would not laugh at you."

"Well, then, as it became important, I calculated backward to your arrival, and then began to count, and so I know that it has been 2,222 days eintime since you came aboard, and this is the first time you have said 'our quarters.'"

"Other people might find something odd in that number," she said, "all those twos."

They swam into their quarters. Mtepic flipped over like a seal resting at sea, hands on his belly. "Other people might find something odd in that number, but you and I know about numbers, eh?"

"Exactly so," she said. "In octal it is merely 4,256, and in duodecimal an even less meaningful 1,352. 32,342 in quintal is about as close as you can get to meaningful expression in any other base, and that's not *very* meaningful. And I would say that if meaning is not invariant we can ignore it."

"Except when we can't, of course?"

That struck them both as funny, for reasons that they knew no one else would understand, and they laughed as they filled out their breakfast order, and filed their official intention to serve their shifts on call in their quarters that day.

Mtepic's sweet tooth had grown ever stronger as he aged. His favorite breakfast was now a fluffy, sweet pancake spread with blueberry jam and wrapped around vanilla ice cream, and as he slowly ate that this morning, he seemed to relish it more than ever. "Well," he asked, "what would you like to know?"

"Was it real?"

He pointed to her chest; the damp spot still glowed.

She ran a finger over it; the very tip of the finger glowed for an instant, and then faded.

"How does it work?" she asked.

"I don't know," he admitted. "I don't even know why I wake up knowing there will be ghosts. Or why it was so important to show them to you, or why I want to see them, myself." He took another bite of his pancake and caressed it in his mouth until it dissolved; she waited until at last he said, "I would have gone, you know. That ghost was Sudden Crow, my wife before you—not that you are my wife, though the offer is open if you want it, it meant a great deal to her, but you've never seemed to care."

"I don't. 'Not slave' is all the title I ever wanted, and you gave me that, and you know I'll be with you as long as you live—maybe I should say as long as you want to stay. But you almost . . . left? Do you miss Sudden Crow?"

"Not very much, to tell the truth. She was bad-tempered and sometimes rough with me. I wouldn't mind saying hello again but I hope I wouldn't have to spend any time with her as a ghost. Thirty years of combined time on this side was enough."

"Do you say 'this side' because it feels spatial?"

Frowning, he thought, and then at last shook his head. "More like the sides of a game or a question than the sides of a segment or a surface." He pondered more, then took another delighted bite of his breakfast. "Really, your friendship is one good reason to stay on this side, more than enough reason all by itself, but this breakfast could be another, and when I think of all the other things I still enjoy, I can understand why so few people want to go before they have to. It was just that seeing her there, somehow I knew *how* I could go, if I wanted to go. And the old body is such a nuisance, you know, sometimes, it gets so sore and itchy and hurty. So I did want to, just for that moment, but now I'm glad I didn't."

"Do the ghosts come aboard often?"

"You've been with me the last two times. Out of six in all. Five on my birthdays, now one on yours. And I've never told anyone else, but I knew you were the right one to see it. I've searched through all twenty-seven thousand years of star trader history, and records from more than a million ships—traders but also slavers, military, scout, and colony—and though there are many accounts of ghosts, most are just fiction, labeled as such, and many of the rest seem to be merely some bit of culture that came loose from its old moorings in some folktale and washed up in the star trader culture. And 9743 itself records the ghosts but doesn't perceive them; they are there on camera recordings but if you ask 9743 to look for the ghosts in all its thousands of years of recordings of the opsball, it won't see any ghosts, and it can look right at a camrec full of ghosts and does not perceive them, it only sees an empty, dark opsball."

"So they are aphysical. But they record physically. What do you suppose they are?"

"A very expressive hole in spacetime?" Mtepic shrugged. "Most star traders commit bodies to space at peak velocity. Most of us run at 98%c or higher. Once the body is outside the protection of the forward shield, the atoms and dust in interstellar space erode it, and it loses velocity, though not quickly. And of course it is far above galactic escape velocity. Except for the very few that run into stars or black holes or comets, all the bodies committed to space must still be out there, some as much as thirty thousand light-years away if you allow for burials during the First Pulse when there was little or no trade.

"You could picture each corpse as a long pathway, sweeping atoms and ions and molecules and dust out of interstellar space, shaped very much like the dead person at this end in time and space, and as the interstellar medium punches them full of holes and breaks them down, trailing off into just a cloud of nucleons at a far end somewhere way outside the galaxy and some millions of years in the future. Perhaps something aphysical flows back along the path they make, and—'crystallizes'? 'condenses'? maybe just 'organizes' is the word for what it does, around any passing seed or nucleus or whatever you would call a thing a ghost organizes around. Maybe where a large number of pathways run close together, they entangle like spaghetti, and express as a ghost swarm when something that can appreciate their meaning comes along. That would explain the association with birthdays. Birthdays are meaningful even though they're so drastically different in slowtime and eintime and depend completely on when you got on the ship, and where it goes, and how long an Old Earth year was at the moment they standardized it. So maybe ghosts annucleate around meaningful things like ships and birthdays. It makes a certain kind of sense. Meaning is aphysical, and ghosts are aphysical. Then again, what do physical beings like us know of aphysics?"

"But none of that would explain the baby coming out of your chest, or that the baby was you, or that we both remember it, let alone that I've got a patch of spiritual pee right over my heart."

"Was I a baby? I wondered why I felt so strangely proportioned, and so small, and had no teeth. Well, that is certainly data to add to the puzzle."

"Why should there be ghosts or spirits on a starship?"

"Why not here as much as anywhere? And for that matter, why should there be ships? Robot-only starships are just slightly less likely to reach their destinations, but it would be so easy to factor that into the price, and it would be more profitable to send containers one way and just accept some losses at the other end. As it is 9743 pays for an immense amount of space and mass to keep us alive. So why are we here? Why is there even an economy? We make everything on the ship by transmutation and molecular assembly—we never 'pick up supplies' though we sometimes buy new goods to record them for later manufacture—and we know the people in slowtime are centuries or millennia ahead of us—so why is there cargo for us to carry?"

"You think that has something to do with the ghosts," Xhrina said, not a question, just trying to stay with him; clearly he had been thinking about this for a long time, had worked out the perfect presentation in his mind, wanted to have it produce perfect understanding—it was the way he had taught her mathematics. She knew he liked it when she understood at once, and she knew this might be her only chance to understand.

"I think it's another void in spacetime. Once pretty much everyone human traded, going way back to Old Earth. For some reason it paid to trade between the stars. The ships began to move. Now they just move, bodies in motion remaining in motion, and the trading just happens. Maybe. Maybe we're *all* just the ghosts of what humans used to do. Three-quarters of the star systems we traded in at one time or another now just wave us off, new ones come on line, and old ones reactivate after centuries of slowtime. Who can say what goes on out there?"

"Is it possible that the slowtime people on the planets are all just crazy, or perhaps playing at things because there's nothing real left?"

"The slowtime people might ask the same things about us. We could just liquidate, and move into a nice orbital resort where they'd pamper us silly for the rest of our lives."

"I would hate that."

"So would I." Mtepic smiled shyly. "Do you think it would be all right for me to have another pancake like that last one?"

"You've been losing weight," she said, "and I worry about your appetite. You can have ten as far as I'm concerned. And actually, being *very* concerned, I wish you would."

"Let's start with one, but I'll keep the offer in mind. And you're right, I haven't been taking very good care of myself, and for some reason, now I feel like I want to, at least for a while."

She prepared it for him, not because he couldn't do it himself, and not because she had to. She pointed that out as she served it to him, and he said, "You see? Part of what makes it good is all the things it's not."

She thought about that for a while and she said, "So the ghosts are not hallucinations. And they're not physical as we understand it or the machines would be able to see them, rather than just record them. And you think maybe they're where the bodies—well, the traces of the bodies—are not."

"Except that Sudden Crow destroyed that theory," he said. "She always was good at destroying theory. Part of why she was a good shipmate."

"She hurt you," Xhrina said, surprised at her own vehemence. "You said she was rough with you."

"True. But I was not as fragile then as I've become, and besides she was a valuable member of the crew. And of course so are you, and getting more valuable all the time, and you are very good to me. You fill up a space different from the one she vacated."

"I'd better," she said. "I wouldn't want to fill her place, at all." And because she had said it a bit too vehemently, and the two of them were looking at each other awkwardly, she hurried on with the first question she could think of. "Why did you say Sudden Crow destroyed your theory about the traces of the bodies in spacetime?"

"Because she was buried in space about a year and a half out of Aydee-to-Ridny, outbound. Her pathway couldn't have come anywhere near here."

"But she was on this ship. Her path before she was dead included it. What if it doesn't matter as long as you can describe the path, or the place where the path was? Suppose that, and maybe—"

"But it might be too hard if we suppose that," Mteptic objected. "It doesn't restrict things enough. Why don't we see everyone's ghost all the time?"

"'Mathematics is how we find the logical implications of the boundaries of things, and the whole history of mathematics is the story of working with fewer and flimsier boundaries,'" she said. "You said that to me the very first time I sat down to learn algebra. Maybe we don't see them often enough because there aren't enough boundaries to produce them, or because we live inside so many boundaries, or . . . well, we don't even know what the boundaries are, do we?"

"Hard to evaluate the boundary conditions," Mteptic agreed. "But as far as I can see, it's all holes and voids. There's some odd thing in the slowtime world, some place we fill, though we don't know what it is. Empty spots left in crews and on ships when people die, and the holes in space they make when we throw their bodies away, and the big emptiness of space itself, and every hole is outlined, and every outline means the hole—and, well, you must think I'm senile by now, surely."

"I don't," she said. "Oh, I *don't*. You *know* I don't. Can I make you another pancake?"

In Mtepic's last few years, they talked more. She liked that. She had received the last promotion she could get while he was alive, to mathematician's-mate-pending-mathematician. That forced her for the first time to think of the succession. She decided that however she acquired her apprentice (she rather hoped to buy one out of a slave world, she would feel good about freeing someone as she had been freed), she would consider looking for someone who would talk. Many ship people didn't, for weeks or months at a time.

That was another guess of Mtepic's, that ship society was where the surrounding slowtime societies were dumping their autistic people and those whose mathematical gifts were no longer needed because they had synminds. "Sort of a featherbedding asylum for mathematicians," he would say, coughing and laughing as she bathed, dried, and rubbed him. She would always laugh too, just because it was Mtepic and she felt how close he was to crossing over to the other side, and she expected to miss him then, and wish she could hear his jokes again.

The night after her thirtieth birthday, she awoke knowing that there would be ghosts in the opsball, and felt Mtepic waking within the circle of her arms. Xhrina dressed them both quickly and gently towed him with her, as she had had to do for the past few months, since his limbs had grown too feeble and shaky to keep him stable as he swam in the air.

It was as before, with a new swarm of ghosts, and in the middle of it, the baby emerged from Mtepic; she held the baby for a long moment, and kissed the tiny mouth tenderly, and then watched it sail off, giggling and tumbling, into the stars, until it was just a star itself, and then gone. She towed Mtepic's remainder back to their quarters; for reasons she did not understand, she didn't want to tell her shipmates that he had died in the opsball.

They might have been surprised at how dry her eyes were, and how perfect her composure, when they buried Mtepic's body in space on the next shift, but ship people are never very surprised at anything human, for they don't understand it and lose the habit of being curious about it.

Treo often floated with her in the dark opsball now. "It's a big promotion," he said, "and an honor, and you would make a good captain. I admit I'm delighted with the idea of being ship's mathematician without having to wait for you to die." That was the longest speech he had made, and Xhrina found it faintly ironic that he made it as they floated in the opsball, where normally they were most silent.

It was not a normal occasion; Phlox had chosen to die voluntarily after Arthur's death, and would be doing it after she said her good-byes tonight, so they were replacing a captain and a first mate. The crew had chosen Xhrina as captain, with Officer-Apprentice Chang to be brevet-promoted to first mate, if they wanted the positions.

Xhrina thought Chang would be all right as a first mate; he was young and should ideally have had a few more years as an apprentice, but she reckoned that he would have them by the time she died, and would still be a young, vigorous, apt-to-be-successful captain. It was a good match all around.

They were far out in the Sixth Pulse systems now, newer worlds with more cargo to send and receive, out in the thinly populated fringes of the human sphere. So there could have been very few of those pathways of the dead that Mtepic imagined, but when they jettisoned Phlox's body, Xhrina felt something; and the next day was her fiftieth birthday, and she felt it more strongly; so that night she was unsurprised to awaken and feel that it was time to see ghosts in the opsball. It had been a long time since she had seen ghosts, only twice since Mtepic's death, and this was the first time since Treo had come aboard. She woke him, told him to dress and be quiet and to hurry.

The blue-to-red Dopplered stars became plain white stars, the swarm of ghosts arrived, and as Xhrina was just beginning to watch with wonder, and celebrate being here for such a thing again, Treo cried out in fear, having seen Phlox swim through the hull and take up her navigation station, and all of it vanished.

That settled Xhrina's mind. She took the captain's cabin, and shared it with Chang, from then on, letting him rub her back because he seemed to like to do it and it did feel good, and occasionally relieving him sexually, though he was much more attracted to the second physicist's mate, Robert, who was unfortunately not interested in sex at all, or at least not any kind that Chang offered.

Xhrina didn't exactly give up on any idea of love, but it was a long time before she trusted Chang as more than a mere colleague and convenient bed companion, so long that she got to know him too well, and settled for trust without love. It was an even longer time before she saw ghosts again.

Of the old generation, only she, Peter, and Squire were left on her eighty-fifth birthday, and Squire spent all of his time sleeping in his life support tank now, though when roused he seemed coherent enough in a querulous sort of way. 9743, by vote of the crew (a vote Xhrina had very carefully nurtured into happening) had been renamed *Ulysses*, a name it had last had 290 years eintime before. Xhrina could not have said why she preferred that.

There was a Seventh Pulse underway, carrying the human frontier out past 150 light-years from the home system, and at great distances, now and then, they detected the sonic boom of near-lightspeed bodies of a kilometer or more across, pressing so fast through the interstellar medium that their bow shock was too much for the thin trace of plasma and shook it hard enough to make microwaves. "The new colony ships move much faster than the old," Captain Xhrina observed, at the table with everyone. She had insisted on establishing a tradition of birthdays, real birthdays for everyone, even looking up some old traditions so that everyone wore funny hats, and they served fish, and sang a song called "Years and Years" in ancient Konglish.

"I would like to see one more new part of space before I pass on," she said. "There may just be time for that if we do this, and there is something in it for all of you. It will make our reputation forever as traders; the name of *Ulysses* will be known, and that would please me, and I hope it would please you.

"Sixty years ago, according to radio, the Sol and Alfsentary systems were known to be open, so we could make one stop on the way. My plan would be that we would take only half a hold of cargo—we probably can't even get that, nowadays, anyway, there doesn't seem to be much at any port—and then stuff the empty holds with extra mass, which we could feed into the shielders, and we could run at ninety-nine-four instead of our usual ninety-eight-two. That would mean eintime would be about one ninth of slowtime, instead of one fifth, and we could be back to the center in about seven years eintime. Switch cargos and pick up more mass there, head out again, and run at ninety-nine four for a hundred twenty years of slowtime, so that we get all the way into the Seventh Pulse worlds on the other side. The corporation could afford to do it a hundred times over; I'd just like to take a chance on being there at the end of that voyage, and if we make it there, we will have made a name for ourselves, forever, among star traders. No other reason."

Treo would vote with her; he always did because he feared that she thought he was a coward, though she had never said so. And his mathematician's mate Fatima would vote yes along with him. Peter would probably vote yes just because he found all port calls distressful and would like the idea that he would probably die before they made their first stop. With her vote, that was fifty-fifty; she thought Chang had liked the idea when she explained it to him, but with Chang it was hard to tell about things. The other three tended to think that the economic models that slithered and hissed through *Ulysses*'s computers, paralyzing everything with their venom of marginal returns, were gods to be propitiated.

"Call the question?" Sleeth, the second physicist's mate-pending-first, said. That was conventional because she was juniormost voting member; it also fit Sleeth, because she was young and bouncing with energy in a crew of old, tired people. Most of the crew muttered that she was annoying except Squire, who said it outright whenever he was out of the tank, and Robert, the first physicist's mate, who said it coldly, as if it were the atomic mass of oxygen or the orbital velocity of a planet.

To compensate, Xhrina made no secret that Sleeth was as much her favorite now as when she had come aboard as a too-noisy-for-ship-people two-year-old. As the captain grew older, she had felt more and more that Sleeth was the only person, besides Xhrina, who liked to get things done. So this calling the question was natural, aside from being a duty.

The vote wasn't even close—only Squire and Robert voted against. Sleeth said apologetically to her cabin mates, "I'd like to be from a famous ship, and these runs around on the surface of the Sixth Pulse are getting dull."

It seemed to Xhrina more likely that Sleeth, who was barely twenty, but had come back from the training ship when only twelve, had been living too long with an angry husk in a tank, and a cold man who never spoke (did Robert use her roughly? Xhrina had asked Sleeth, more than once, and Sleeth had said *no* in a way that Xhrina thought meant *yes, but please don't do anything*). This looked to be Sleeth's first little step to saying that she would not be pushed around by Robert and Peter, and it made Xhrina glad in a way that she had not felt in a while.

That night, when Chang crawled into the sleepsack beside Xhrina, he said, "When we approach the home system, and you wake knowing that there are ghosts in the opsball, don't wake me. I'm afraid of them and I don't want to know about them."

"All right," she said. "Have you been reading my diary?"

"Yes," he said, "it's my right as first mate to read anything you write, and I don't like to ask. And I asked Treo and he told me how frightened he was, and I went back and looked at all your birthdays, and Mtepic's, and saw the ghosts on the recordings. It made me so afraid I have had a hard time sleeping since. So don't take me with you. I don't want to see ghosts." More gently, he said, "You might talk to Sleeth about it. She's always been your little shadow, and she would face the fear just for love of you."

"Thank you," she said, "I will." And Xhrina turned her back on him, to enjoy his warmth but not to talk anymore. *I suppose I would have faced the ghosts for love of Mtepic,* she thought, *but I wanted to see them anyway, though I didn't know it until he showed them to me. I hope it can be that way with Sleeth.*

On the night of her ninety-third birthday, Xhrina rolled over and touched Sleeth, who had been her sleepsack partner for some years now. "Ghosts," she said, "finally."

"I'm glad," Sleeth said, awake at once, and they turned up the lights and dressed quickly.

She wasn't sure that she really was glad. Sleeth and the captain had talked of ghosts at least every few shifts for the last five years, and Sleeth had come to realize that her first time seeing ghosts would be the captain's last. She had forced herself to seem happy and cheerful about the impending visit of the ghosts all through the annoying too-long layover around Old Earth's moon, as well, and now that the time was here, she hadn't really had time to think through what she wanted to feel, or ought to feel, and was stuck with just feeling what she felt—which was a mystery.

She had heard so much from the captain about Mtepic, and ghosts, and all the theories about ghosts, because the captain only needed to work an hour a day or so during the layover, while they found whatever cargo they could. The synminds of Old Earth and *Ulysses* at last found a small load, but did not seem to be able to explain what was in the containers, except that it was something that it was not inconceivable that someone in the new Seventh Pulse worlds out toward the Southern Cross and Sentaru might want 120 years from now.

The captain had not cared, so Sleeth had not cared. The scant cargo meant that their holds had had that much more room for a load of U238, depleted uranium, not for atomic power as in ancient times—they might as well have taken hay, oats, and water, and would have if nothing denser had been available—but because it was a conveniently dense supply of mass to be torn to nucleons and shot out the bow by the shielder, to clear a path through the interstellar medium for them. With the extra mass, they were able to run at 99.7%c, which meant almost thirteen years of slowtime to one year of eintime. *Ulysses* would be some sort of legend, now, for sure.

But, Sleeth thought sadly, *the end of the legend will not be Captain Xhrina bringing* Ulysses *to the port of Summer,* the port that they had been aiming for since their last PPD and change of course about a year eintime ago.

Xhrina and Sleeth had talked of ghosts, many times, and Sleeth longed to see them, with Xhrina; but she would miss their conversations about them, and it seemed sad that she would have no one to talk about this first time with. But then apparently Mtepic had seen them five times alone, and who knew how many others saw them and never talked about it at all?

Still, Sleeth had always imagined that when at last she saw them, she would be able to talk about them with Captain Xhrina. She had been ship-raised, and because of the way the schedules had worked out, had only been on a training ship for six years, about half what was normal, so that she had spent a great deal of time following Xhrina around when she was younger, and then more time tending her later. Xhrina had always been her one real friend.

Sleeth knew she would miss the captain dreadfully, but she didn't think she should say so, with the captain's eyes alight with joy; once they were in the opsball, it was easier, waiting in the dark, because Sleeth could just let her tears quietly flow.

It was all as Sleeth had heard it told, so many times.

As the ghosts neared, Xhrina bounced and fidgeted as if she had a tenth of her years. When the slender, small ghost that had to be Mtepic—though now strong and young—swam through the wall into the opsball, the glowing baby emerged from her head and chest in just two heartbeats, formed fully in the air, and held its arms to Mtepic, who swooped in and scooped up the newborn Xhrina. *Just a few seconds, the first time I ever saw the ghosts, and it was all over,* Sleeth thought sadly.

As if he had heard her thoughts, Mtepic, still cradling the fiercely glowing ghost-baby, turned back, and smiled a warm knowing smile at Sleeth.

To everyone's surprise—even to the surprise of Mtepic's ghost—ghost-Xhrina, newborn and toothless, huge-eyed face wide with glee, in the ghost-mathematician's now-strong and young arms, waved bye-bye to Sleeth, in a way so like any other baby that Sleeth giggled, aloud, and all the ghosts but Mtepic and Xhrina fled as the stars began to fade.

Grinning, Mtepic raised a finger to his lips—*Shhh!*—and so did Xhrina, and they both waved bye-bye once again before they were gone into the field of stars, which faded after them, leaving Sleeth laughing in darkness.

The Town on Blighted Sea

A. M. Dellamonica

A graduate of Clarion West, A. M. Dellamonica has sold stories to *Sci Fiction*, *Realms of Fantasy*, *Tesseracts*, *Tomorrow*, *Alternate Generals*, *The Faery Reel*, *Oceans of the Mind*, and elsewhere, and has just sold her first novel, *Indigo Springs*. Coming up is another new novel, *The Winter Girls*. She lives in Vancouver, Canada.

Here she takes us to a refugee camp where the refugees are the surviving remnants of the human race, to see whether it's true that the sins of the fathers must be visited on the children.

Ruthless moved with silent purpose, keeping to the shadows as she strode between the skyscrapers of Earthtown's expansion district. It was summer in the northern hemisphere of Kabuva, the air chill and dense but not frosty, the skunky musk of the sea a reminder that this wasn't home, this would never be home. Tumbler Moon was full, shining so brilliantly it might have been dawn rather than deepest night. She cursed its brightness as she walked, then reminded herself it could be worse: Mad Moon could be out too.

Arriving at Phoenix Avenue, she was relieved to find herself the only living creature on the ground. Nanocompiled towers rose around her, monolithic, smooth, and identical but for their height. Taking out a bootlegged scanner, Ruthless walked a quick circle in the middle of the unused intersection, checking for police transmissions. It registered a welcome concentration of signals, all bouncing around the occupied half of the refugee settlement.

The Kabu had overestimated how many human exiles would make it to Refuge Island. They'd compiled Earthtown's skyscrapers with a figure of three million refugees in mind; only half that number actually escaped from Earth. So the squid sealed off the excess portion of the prefabricated city, deactivating the power and water grids, blocking the roads, and pulling out all but a handful of surveillance cameras.

According to her scanner, this was one of the surveillance dead zones—no cops nearby. Satisfied, Ruthless turned to a slashed plastic seal on the entrance of the building behind her. Pushing her way through the tear, she trotted up the stillborn escalators to the sixth floor. There another torn seal marked a door midway down the hall.

Ruthless crept to the door, rapping it with gloved fingers.

"Rav?"

"Auntie?" Raviel's voice was duller than an hour ago—less fearful, more shocked. She had been right in the middle of a hot flash when he called, sweat pouring down her face and chest as her nephew's panic chilled her heart.

Auntie. She wondered when he'd last called her that. Before Exile?

"Open up, Rav."

The door scrolled aside in jerks, powered by muscle instead of hydraulics. Ruthless didn't help him, didn't touch anything even though she had gloved up and sprayed down before leaving her apartment.

She took in everything at once. The blood, the corpses—one human and female, one squid and male—the smell of puke and, most important, the lack of an immediate threat. Having established the parameters of the crisis, she focused on Rav. Pale and hollow-eyed, her brother's son reeked of vomit and was bleeding slightly from a gash above his collarbone. The Kabu had come within inches of cutting his throat. She counted a dozen bruises and sucker-hickeys, all minor.

Rav's white-blond hair was matted with ink and other alien fluids. His left arm was gloved in Kabu blood, black from fingertips to shoulder.

"Figure you want me to turn myself in," he said, and Ruthless was pierced by the memory of his father wearing a similar expression. Forcing himself to be brave, she thought, just like Matt before the battle of Las Vegas. "It'll be easier if you come with me. Auntie? Can you?"

When Ruthless did not reply, he said, swallowing, "I can call now if . . ."

"No, honey." She shook her head. "We're not calling."

Rav's pale face flushed red, and his eyes welled. He reached out—but Ruthless stopped him with a gesture.

"Can you answer me a couple questions?"

"Su-sure."

She pointed at the dead woman. "The squid killed her?"

"Yes," he said.

"You killed him?"

A slow nod.

"You know either of them?"

"No."

"Not at all?"

Face pinching, Rav pointed at the woman. "She's a local feeler. Comes to the Rialto sometimes, but . . ."

"But you've never spoken."

"Just—" He mimed tearing a ticket. "Enjoy the show, ma'am."

"Okay."

"She likes . . . liked silent movies. Always came to see Buster Keaton."

"Okay, Rav. You followed them because . . ."

"I'm documenting the touchie-feelie trade."

"You're what?" She wasn't as good at masking her feelings as she used to be—her tone made Rav flinch. "Doc—you brought recording equipment with you?"

He pointed to a button-sized blotch near the ceiling.

"That's a camera?"

"Latest model. Fly-on-the-wall, they call it." He laughed humorlessly.

The thing clung to the wall a discreet distance from the gore. It was too small to be anything but short range. Glancing around the room, Ruthless saw a receiver lying on the blue backpack she'd got Rav for his last birthday.

"Jesus, Rav, you filmed the killings?"

"I shut it down after."

"Is it shut down now?" It came out a growl.

Rav's head snapped up. "Yes. It's off. You're not on camera, swear."

"Where's the feed cached?"

"In my data pantry at home."

"You transmitted?"

"Using Ma's encryption protocols, yeah."

Ruthless drew in a slow breath. Elva knew her stuff: the feed would be safe.

Rav raised a shaking, blood-slimed hand to his face, as if to push back his hair. When he made contact he recoiled, staring at his blackened palm. "He was all the way down her throat. She was choking. I couldn't—"

"You had to help."

"I grabbed him . . . or he grabbed me. She was choking, all those arms—"

Ruthless nodded, remembering too well what it was like to wrestle an infuriated squid. They were bigger, and the tentacles made them seem stronger than they were. Not to mention slippery and fast.

"I overheard Ma once, telling her security boys you stuck your hand up a squid's mouth once in the war."

"I get the gist," Ruthless said, contemplating the corpses. Spatters, genetic evidence. Lot of cleanup here.

"She said you dug through to its brain with your fingers . . ." Rav continued, retching as he looked at his blood-gloved arm.

"You did the right thing, Rav."

Normally she'd be furious with Elva for letting the kid hear such a thing. Since it had apparently saved his ass, she silently blessed her sister-in-law's indiscretion.

"The right thing?"

She nodded, still thinking about cleanup. "You made it home from the playground, that's all that counts."

"Playground," he repeated, disbelieving.

"Huh—oh, sorry. Warspeak. It means—"

"I know it's warspeak."

"Means you didn't die."

"You've never . . . it makes you sound so old."

"Prehistoric." She looked back at the scene. "Gotta put your toys away, that's what we'd say about this."

He shuddered. "If I did the right thing and the feed proves it, why not tell?"

She shook her head. "Right or not, squid might still drown you. You killed one of them, just a fry from the looks of it . . ."

"He's a murderer!"

"It'll bring up old memories for them. Stuff about the war that the Kabu don't like to think about."

"That's a drowning offense now, making them remember?"

"It might be different one day, if we don't go back to Earth first. But change takes time and martyrs, Rav, and you are not getting sacrificed. Not for trying to save some poor feeler's life. Okay?"

Shuddering, he nodded.

"Now. I need you to take off the squid's hydration tank."

"What?"

"He'll have a tank. To keep his skin moist." She pointed and he fumbled the metal canister out of the dead sentient's limp, bell-shaped cap.

"Hold it so I can see the controls—good. There's enough in there for you to clean up."

"Should I get in the shower?"

"No! We get your genes in the drains, it's all over. Strip off your clothes in that corner and use his water supply to hose off."

"I'll get blood and stuff on the floor."

"It's okay. For now, just make yourself presentable."

As Rav washed, she unpacked her cloak on the corridor floor, laying out an assortment of sprays and other nanotech she'd squirreled away in the years since Exile. It had taken time to make contacts in a Kabuva forensics lab. She'd wondered sometimes if she wasn't wasting her money. Surely she'd be headed home to Earth before she needed any of these toys.

But the months since the Setback—nobody who'd made it to Earthtown called it the defeat it was—had stretched to years, seventeen of them now.

"Um," said Rav, shaking drips from his fine white hair.

"Clean?"

He nodded, blushing furiously, one newly washed hand cupped over his groin.

Ruthless sprayed nanosols onto a towel and passed it over the threshold. "Here, dry off. Right. Now lay the towel on the floor like a rug and walk on it a couple times. Feet dry?"

"Yeah."

"Leave the towel, step over that tentacle, and come out into the hallway."

Nude, her nephew looked young and vulnerable. As he stepped out of the crime scene she clasped his shoulder with her gloved hand, feeling the pressure in her chest ease at the contact. "It's gonna be okay, honey."

Swallowing, he nodded.

"Let's get that wound." The edges of the gash in his chest were already red— Kabu saliva was notoriously infectious. She patted it dry with an antibiotic wipe and hit him with two immune boosters. Last she painted on a thin layer of puttied skin, blending the culture until the cut was concealed.

"I'll need to refresh this every day for at least a week. We don't want it to scar: it's too obvious it's a beak bite. In the meantime, you'll wear high-collared smocks so nobody sees it. Nobody sees this, Rav, you got me?"

"Okay."

"You sleeping with anyone?"

"No."

"Are you?"

"No!" He flushed pink from forehead to toes.

"Good. Don't start until you're healed." Next she sprayed a thin mist up and down his body. Beading on his skin, it dispersed quickly, spreading like oil. "This'll die off in a day or so."

"It tickles."

"It devours any dead skin cells you happen to be shedding; also hairs, sweat, tears, blood—anything that might leave trace. Squid forensics labs developed it to keep their investigators from contaminating crime scenes. Not that they cry tears, of course, this is a variant they developed for working with human cops . . ."

As she hoped, her patter soothed him, the matter-of-fact voice easing his nerves and the peculiarity of his nakedness.

"Where'd you get the spray?"

"Black market lab in Little Canada," she said, handing him a smock. "Here, get dressed. Watch the edges of that synthetic skin on your chest."

He took the clothes with visible relief. "You just keep stuff around for covering up crimes?"

"As a precaution."

"Against what? Everyone here fought alongside the Kabu. Why would anyone need to cover up a . . ."

"A justifiable homicide?"

He swallowed. "You used to be a cop. Used to solve this kind of thing."

"And now I work in an umbrella factory. Listen, sweetheart. You tried to save the girl. A nice thing to do . . . and killing the squid was purely fair play."

"You'd cover it up even if I'd murdered him. If I wasn't your nephew I'd be sunk."

"Sure, I suppose that's true."

"So really, whether I did the right thing or not is beside the point."

"You're gonna go killing squid for fun now?"

He glared. "It wasn't fun."

"I'm not trying to offend you, Rav. I know anger feels better than being scared or freaked out."

"Don't tell me what I'm feeling!"

"You can yell at me later if you need to, all you want, anytime you want, about anything you think I've done wrong."

"That's not—"

She interrupted. "You'll have to yell at me, because as long as we're on Kabuva, you're never going to mention what happened here to another living soul. Ever, Rav."

He jerked the smock up over his hips, stretching the fabric, his hands trembling.

"Right now we have to get rid of the evidence. So I'm asking—do you need a pacifier, or can you hold it together?"

Rav frowned, confused, and she held up a patch.

"I don't need drugs," he said.

"Good. Put on my cloak and remember to keep your face down in case there are fixed cameras."

"We're walking away? But my blood, and the bodies . . ."

"We'll come back and get rid of it all."

"How? All this . . . evidence."

"Dust it," Ruthless said, and Rav's face went so slack she might as well have pacified him. Head lowered, he shuffled after her as she headed down the hall.

The Kabu had interested themselves in Earth's civil war early on, throwing technology, medical aid, and eventually even soldiers into the Democratic Army's global fight against the fascist Friends of Liberation. In the end it cost the offworld sentients an uncountable fortune as well as the lives of over a million young squid . . . a million, that is, if one didn't count the conscripts who went home alive but just as thoroughly destroyed, body and soul, as their dusted kelpmates.

The Friends—Fiends, their enemies had called them—had alien backers too. Over the course of seventy grinding years they and their allies beat the Democratic/Squid alliance soundly. The Fiends devoured the world mile by bloody mile, starting in Asia and taking North America last of all.

The most terrible weapon of the war was dust, a nanotech agent that took everything in its path apart molecule by molecule. Equally useful for structural targets or as an antipersonnel weapon, dust erased its victims from existence. Direct hits left no trace. Nothing to bury, no DNA, just oddly sterile battlefields—overlapping craters filled with thin, rust-colored powder, sometimes edged with pieces of bodies. Arms, legs, and heads, usually—it was the extremities that most often escaped the blast perimeters.

A child of the Setback, Rav had grown up dreading the very thought of dust. It was the bogeyman of his generation: go to sleep, kid, or the Fiends will come and dust you.

That threat hadn't kept him from pestering his mother and aunt for war stories: his fascination with the past was morbid and insatiable. Maybe now that will change, Ruthless thought, despite the guilty pang at her selfishness.

They arrived at the Rialto just after midnight, creeping in through a back door. "Go put on a smock that fits. Bring back the one you're wearing," Ruthless said.

"Okay."

"Before you go up, give me access to your pantry."

"It's fingerprinted."

"Scan in and authorize me," she said, nudging him toward a terminal.

"What are you going to do?"

"Delete the feed and anything associated with it."

"I'll do that later."

"Just get your clothes."

"Fine." Scanning his thumb and keying in the authorization, Rav vanished upstairs to his room.

Ruthless found the right directory easily enough: it was packed with video feeds. Feeds of feeler pickups—half-smocked women and men lurking in building lobbies. Human-chauffeured cars cruising slowly to allow the squid riding in the water tank in back to extend their tentacles, tasting the wares on offer. Feeds of quickie feels—an old squid with two burned tentacles slowly removing a woman's mask, delicately tasting her lips and the corners of her eyes. A human male guiding a tentacle delicately over his groin as he drank some concoction that made him break out in a heavy sweat.

The same man showed up in the next feed too—he was working a tentacle in and around his ear. And another; he was putting on a breathing rig that would allow a client to probe his throat without suffocating him.

Blind as kittens, the Kabu were taste-oriented: with each other, they probed and suckled with abandon. Humans who dealt with them wore smocks that sealed off their crotches, wore masks to protect their faces. The squid were supposed to content themselves with the scent and taste of human feet, palms, and underarms, a prohibition that worked about as well as any other taboo.

Ruthless never saw the Kabu in her day-to-day life if she could avoid it. Masks made her claustrophobic. And even after so many years there was something about the memory of a tentacle draping over her wrist, of small suckers tasting her palm, that made her stomach turn.

She reached the most recent feed. It began with the duo she had seen dead in the apartment, arriving at the building on Phoenix Street. As the car drove away, the woman looked upward, just for a second, gazing into the greenish light of Tumbler Moon.

Following them inside, the camera dipped and hovered, seeking a good vantage point. By the time it was settled the woman had stripped, leaning back against a wall so the squid could taste her various scent zones.

Why had Rav wanted this, Ruthless wondered, feeling queasy as the tentacles explored the woman's body, poking at her ears, the corners of her eyes, eventually probing into her vagina and anus. It went bad quickly after that: the squid yanked her tongue, pulling with brutal force before sliding another tentacle down the woman's throat.

As she began to choke, Rav burst in.

Mother-bear rage built within Ruthless as her nephew and the squid collided, as its beak slashed open Rav's chest and the blood sprayed. Rav thrust his arm past its maw, digging for the sentient's vulnerable palate. With a convulsive jerk, he punched through the gelatinous flesh, squeezing brain. The squid thrashed and then went limp.

Heaving free, Rav crawled to the woman, drawing a bloodied tentacle out of her throat. He checked her pulse; he started CPR. Good boy, Ruthless thought, running the feed forward. He gave resuscitation a good solid try before collapsing, curling in a spreading puddle of black blood, vomiting and weeping. It was some time before he recovered and shut off the camera.

Ruthless deleted the files and poked through the data pantry, searching for copies. The old feeds had been backed up, but not this newest. Relieved, she wiped the backups, fished up a couple of Elva's most aggressive security programs, and set them to disassembling every trace of the deleted feeds.

Then, trotting down the hall, she peeked into the theater.

Her sister-in-law had come to Earthtown wearing one formal smock and nothing else. In the two suitcases permitted to each Exile—and in one of Rav's—Elva had stuffed movie feeds, hundreds of them: blockbusters and art films and cartoons and classics, any entertainment data she could get her hands on. She had marched straight off the ship and demanded to see the licensing bureau. Within a day she had a business charter, sole control over a large theater space, and an extra-large apartment that was attached to her place of business. She began showing movies around the clock . . . and people came.

Within a Kabuva week, Elva had bartered for all the necessities she had left behind—clothes, kitchen goods, books. Culture-shocked and dispossessed, the human refugees welcomed even the slightest glimpse of home.

Nowadays, the business ran strictly on cash. As always, the theater was jammed, every one of the two hundred seats filled and a lineup of homesick humans, most of them Ruthless's age, waiting to get in. They were watching an old Bollywood thing—Mangal Pandey, she thought. Many were slack-jawed, entranced. Some mumbled along, reading the English subtitles.

Ruthless allowed herself one glance at the screen, one intoxicating sight of horses and desert, of the familiar Earth sky. Then she tiptoed into Elva's office. With a bit of fiddling and one of her sprays, she was able to bust the lock on the safe, liberating a sheaf of movie passes.

"What are you doing here?" Elva's voice brought her round. "Where's Rav?"

Elva was a wealthy woman by refugee standards, but years of hardship before Exile had made her frugal. She was wearing the plainest of gray smocks and an aging pair of leather boots. She kept her hair shaved in a buzz cut, red and silver bristles that did not quite hide the scar that ran down the side of her skull. She hoarded food and medicine, Rav said, against the day when they went home.

Her eyes were emeralds—sharp, green, hostile. They'd played together on a lot of battlefields, but they'd never quite been friends.

"Rav's upstairs," Ruthless said, and when Elva made a move in that direction she said, "Leave him be."

"What gives you the right to tell me what I can do in my own house?"

"Sorry."

"Is he all right?"

"Mostly."

"Is he in trouble?"

"He won't be for much longer."

"What's the game?"

"You wouldn't want me to say."

Elva glanced at the theater curtain.

"If you're calling your security guys to take me out of play . . ."

"You think I'm stupid enough to strongarm you, Ruthless?"

"I guess we'll see," she said pleasantly, but Elva didn't move. If she'd called on her dogs, she wasn't taking it back.

"Go back to work, Elva. Act normal. Rav'll be home by dawn."

"That's all? Show up, scare me shitless, rob me blind, and you're not going to tell me?"

"You're not going to ask again," Ruthless said. "Not here. Don't ask him either."

"Bullshit."

"It'll be best for everyone if you pretend you don't know he went out. Tell anyone who asks that he was in all night."

"What the fuck have you gotten him into?"

"You don't do as I say, Elva, the squid will come for him. If you don't do as I say, the squid will drown him. You're family, Elva, but he's blood. You mention tonight to him or anyone else, you give the police a reason to eavesdrop, you get my brother's son killed, I will give it out around town that you worked for the Fiends."

"I never—"

"Mobs don't care about the truth, Elva. You're a woman, you're wealthy, and you're something of a bitch. You're not liked and you know it. Now go back to work before your kid comes down and sees us arguing."

"I'm not arguing."

"Look, it's going to be okay," she said, and Elva punched her hard in the mouth.

Ruthless fell back against the desk. She'd forgotten about the hair-trigger temper.

"Don't you threaten me, Ruthie. He's my kid. You think blackmail—"

"It's bad, okay? He's in trouble and it's bad." She tasted blood in her mouth and, fleetingly, imagined hitting back. It had been years since they brawled . . . long enough she could almost imagine it would be fun. Instead, she said: "I shouldn't have said that. He's your kid. You'll keep quiet, I know that."

There was a light footfall on the stairs. "Auntie?"

Elva dashed at her eyes with the back of one clenched fist. "Don't lose. Whatever the game is—"

"I never lose." Jaw throbbing, she edged around Elva, slipping back into the hallway.

"Ruthless?" A hoarse whisper.

"Just Ruth, Rav," she sighed. "Okay?"

"You're bleeding."

"One of your mom's goons thought I was a gatecrasher."

"He still alive?" The joke fell flat as his voice quavered.

"Killing suddenly not so funny, huh kid?"

"So what now?"

What indeed? Elva would need time to calm down, and Rav was too worked up to leave behind. And he was in the game now, anyway, wasn't he? Club rule number one: clean up your own toys.

She led him to a pedestrian walkway, grateful to see it was getting foggy. "Let's talk over the ways people get caught."

"Okay."

"They make phone calls and big bank transactions around the time of the crime."

"I called you."

"We'll work up a story for that. They confess to their lover or therapist a decade after the event; then the lover or therapist tells someone, who tells someone else, and the secret eventually finds its way to the cops. They write about it in their diaries. They stop trusting their playmates. . . ."

"Playmates?"

"Coconspirators."

"I was by myself, Ruthl—Ruth."

"Rav." She caught his gaze. "I can sink for this now, just like you can."

He paled.

"Come on, we're on a clock."

They caught a highspeed to her home district, riding in silence to Beijing Avenue. Between the buildings, they could see the black sheet of the ocean whose Kabuva name, Vinvalomm, meant the Blighted Sea. The water was obscured at its beachward edges by rising banks of mist. The shadowy figures of shellfish collectors, human and squid both, moved like ghosts along its blue-tinged beaches.

Passing through a brightly lit market, Rav and Ruthless watched the squid who'd come to buy Earthly delicacies—bean sprouts, beef tripe, silk. Shopping districts like this were mostly open at night, when the squids suns couldn't dry out or fry their delicate skins.

Amid the loud chatter of the market, Rav murmured in her ear: "Can I ask you something?"

She glanced at her scanner, nodded. "You can ask."

"You weren't a Fiend. You were fighting the Fiends, right, just like the Kabu were?"

"Yeah."

"How is it you ended up . . ."

"Killing squid with my bare hands?"

He nodded.

"You don't need to know—"

"Please?"

No, she thought, and when she opened her mouth to speak her whole body resisted—her jaw felt rusted shut. "The squid needed spies—loyal Demos who'd join the Fiends and report on what they were up to. Your father'd been taken prisoner; I figured I could look for him and gather intelligence all at once."

"You pretended to be an infiltrator?"

"That's right."

"You fought with them? I mean—on their side?"

"Yes. I shot Demos. I dusted squid."

"How could the Kabu trust you after that?"

"I was home free as long as I followed two rules: produced results and only killed conscripts, never officers."

Rav stumbled into a woman carrying a block of frozen fishmeat—few humans could afford to buy beef, or any of the other earthmeats they now grew for the squid as delicacies.

Ruthless couldn't help laughing. "Shocked, huh?"

He laced his fingers in a squiddish religious gesture, the symbol of reverence. "Kabu philosophy—the sanctity of water-based life. . . ."

"They tossed away a million of their fry." Bitterness clawed her lungs; it was always a mistake, discussing this with kids. The words coughed out in spurts, like blood. "Easy for 'em to be sanctimonious now. A few years have passed, so they think . . . Rav? You okay?"

He had pressed a fist to his chest, right around the beak bite. "Hurts a bit, that's all. Did you ever want to stay? With the Fiends?"

She shook her head. "It felt good playing for the winning team, sometimes, but they really were bastards."

"Did you find my dad?"

"He'd died," she said, bracing herself for the inevitable flood of questions about that.

Instead, he looked thoughtful. "That's why we had to leave Earth. Because you betrayed the Fiends."

And because Elva's platoon killed thousands of them, including a Russian prince, with a good old-fashioned nuke one sunny morning in Chicago. But she nodded. "Fiends would've killed us all once they took over."

From the market they rode a service elevator up four hundred stories, emerging into the brain of a building engineering system that controlled four city blocks. There, encircled by monitors and compressors, they found a milk-pale man in his fifties. A giant with long gold-and-white hair, his smock was so worn that his flesh glinted through it at the knees.

"This is Cope," Ruthless said. "Cope, my nephew Rav."

"Name's short for Copenhagen." The man extended a grimy hand and Rav shook it gingerly.

"Copenhagen—like the snack?"

"Like the city," Cope said sharply.

"Where—" Rav began, but Ruthless cut him off before he could make it worse.

"Cope, I need grenades. Two, three if possible, thirty diameter dispersal, with timers."

Pale blue eyes gleamed. "Where's the playground?"

"Expansion district. It goes right, nobody should die."

"Mmmm," he said neutrally. "My expenses?"

She pulled out the sheaf she had taken from Elva's safe. "Movie passes."

Cope fingered through the wealth. "I could only get two grenades. Can you wait?"

"Nope."

"Figured." Tucking the passes into his tunic's waistband, Cope opened a panel under the HVAC monitor. He drew out an embroidered gold cushion, slipping it into a sleek plastic shopping bag. "Timers are wired in."

"Thanks."

"Need help?"

"This is plenty."

He gave her a faintly hungry glance before turning back to work. "Play safely, then."

She led Rav back out to the walkway, looking for all the world like a mother taking her son out for a late-night shop. Except . . . "Stop staring at the pillow like it's a bomb," she finally had to hiss.

"It is a—"

"Rav," she warned.

"He just had that lying around?"

"I gave him a heads-up after you called."

"I thought you said phone calls could tip off—"

"Who said I phoned?"

"Oh." He looked bewildered; Ruthless didn't bother to explain.

Back at the edge of the Expansion District, they slipped through the fences, heading for the crime scene. Dawn was maybe two hours away, and it was colder now. As they climbed the escalators, Ruthless saw Rav trying to imitate her way of walking, her soundless footsteps. Every third or fourth footfall he succeeded.

The scanner hummed against her thigh. She pulled Rav against her, spraying them both with a cooling mist and putting a finger to her lips. A roving monitor, she prayed, a random sweep. The spray would keep it from reading their body heat . . . if it wasn't looking too closely.

He shivered, obviously stressed and exhausted. Just a teenager, on the run . . . she remembered the feeling.

The scanner hummed again—they were clear.

"Ask you something?" she whispered as she let go.

"Sure."

"Why were you documenting the feelers? Of all the things about Exile . . ."

"You don't think the people back home will want to know?" he said, voice ironic.

"They'll be interested in anything that happened here. Why deviant squid?"

He shrugged. "Get something done? Expose the problem?"

"Come on, the cop's gone," she said.

He fell in behind her. "You knew feelers were vanishing?"

"Maybe."

"And that nobody's doing anything?"

"You saying you wanted to catch that squid you killed?"

"No! It's . . . back Earthside, if problems got exposed, got into the news . . . people dealt with them."

"You've been watching too many of your mother's movies."

"Ruthless, the touchie squid—"

"You can't stop them. It's like any other kink. There'll always be squid wanting a taste of us. They're hardwired for it. Until we leave for home . . ."

Rav grabbed her arm, cursing in Kabuva.

"What?"

"We're not going back to Earth."

"Of course we are."

They were in the corridor by now. The stink of death and human vomit darted out of the darkness, slyly, to meet them. Rav's face was wild. "Auntie. You're not one of those kelpheaded fossils who sits in Ma's theater all day reciting all the old movie lines."

"So?"

"Dreaming of when we'll go back? It's no good. We're never going back to Earth."

"Rav, Fiendish rule can't last forever."

"Why?"

"Because it—" Uncertainty buffeted her. "They're . . . Rav, they're the bad guys."

"What about here and now? If someone makes a fuss about the feelers . . ."

"We are going home," she said. She was angry at him, her perfect little nephew who meant more to her than ·the universe. Even now, her chest hurt—strangely, sweetly—at the sight of him, at the sense of possession and protectiveness. Her brother's child.

Suddenly she wanted to break his neck.

"My home is here," Rav said. "I don't want it to be a hunting ground for perverted sentients."

She pushed past him to the door of the apartment, comforting herself with the solidity of the mess within. Two corpses. Evidence everywhere. A job that needed doing.

"Help me open this up, Rav." They gutted the pillow, sending a cloud of synthetic feathers all over the hall. Inside, two boxes, each the size and color of a brick, each with buttons and a pop-up screen.

Ruthless set one to time out thirty minutes, handing it to Rav. "Go inside. Set this deep under the squid."

"Won't it vaporize everything, no matter where we put it?"

"I want it out of sight." She didn't explain that this was in case anyone arrived before the blast. Grenades were easily defused.

The second charge was for the building entryway, in case either of them had left prints or other traces while going in and out. They jogged down, Rav watching the street as Ruthless set the second charge against a pillar.

"There's someone out there," he said.

Ruthless pulled him down, peering through a hole in the plastic sheet. An aquarium-equipped limousine was parked in the street, motor running. The driver, a human man, was exploring the intersection.

"Police?" whispered Rav.

She shook her head. "Squid's chauffeur. Come on, game's changed. Escape and evade."

She waited until the driver turned his back, then led Rav around the side of the building, darting from there to the next one.

When they'd put a couple blocks between them, Ruthless looked back. The driver had finally reached a decision, striding purposefully to the cut plastic membrane and entering the building. Rav's body jerked in the direction they had come, but she grabbed and held him.

"It's too late," she said. "Grenade's almost timed. By the time he gets up there, the whole apartment will be dust."

"If he hurries, he'll get dusted too."

"Maybe."

"We could get back in time. Warn him."

"We warn him, Rav, you could drown."

"I don't want an innocent guy to die for me!"

"He's not innocent." She kept one eye on the building, talking slowly, wasting time. "That man has been driving your squid around Earthtown picking up feelers. Feelers who then vanished. Nobody's ever found a body, have they?"

"Thought you weren't following the story," he snapped.

"That supposedly innocent guy probably helped load the bodies into that very car, helped get rid of them—"

"You don't know for sure," Rav protested. "He could be a nice guy."

"Yeah," she agreed. "Or he could be a doctor. He could be a nun or the father of a newborn baby or the only grandson of the great General Hintegro. I still wouldn't give you up to keep him from getting dusted."

Tears welled in her nephew's eyes, spilling over his cheeks and spreading to oily nothingness as the nanosol consumed the evidence.

"We keep moving—" Ruthless began. Then a white-hot glow seeped through the sixth floor windows of the building.

She knew exactly what was happening. Dust was expanding from the grenade in a sphere, and everything it touched was disintegrating. The bodies and the barf—maybe the chauffeur too if his timing was bad—were already gone. Now the dust was eating a hole in the building.

"Come on," she said. "Blast'll bring the police."

Rav didn't stir.

Please, Ruthless thought. Don't make me hit you.

"He's okay," he said suddenly. The chauffeur threw himself onto the street, tangling with the plastic sheet and then falling clear. Gasping, he leaned against the building wall, wide-eyed with horror, fumbling for his phone and then staring at it blankly.

"Notice how he's not calling for help?" Ruthless said.

"Shut up." Rav scowled.

The building had a circular hole in it now, six floors up, the blackened area rotted like a cavity in a tooth. Perfect dispersal, Ruthless noted—game over, thanks Cope. Now to get the kid out of here before he did the math on the chauffeur's current position.

"Let's go," she said, but Rav was rooted in place.

"He's okay," he muttered, half to himself. The driver was weeping now, still collapsed against the building.

"No," she said, "he's doomed."

"What?"

"Police are on their way," Ruthless said. "He can't dust his traces like we did. If the car does contain DNA from the missing feelers . . . well, once they know his boss was the deviant, they'll sink the guy to shut him up."

"What makes you so sure he knows?"

"He's not calling the cops, is he?"

"He's not running, either."

"But—" Rav began, and that was when the second grenade blew. A ground-level fireworks-bloom of sparks expanded in slowmo through the plastic. The driver's reflexes were good; he started to run as the sparks turned fire-orange and then brown, unmaking the building, taking a cookie-bite out of the street. The tower shuddered; the plastic tore up to the eighth or ninth floor as the structure beneath cracked. There was a sound of glass breaking.

The dustball reached the running driver. With a truncated scream, he vanished.

Rav sucked air, wide-eyed, like a baby warming up for a long shriek. Ruthless dragged him off the road, climbing up to a walkway.

"Come now or I pacify you," she said, and he stumbled forward, beginning to carry his own weight only gradually as she hauled him toward safety.

"Guess I really am in your stupid club now," he said, and his laugh was caustic. "We should've warned him."

"He was dead anyway."

"You're so sure."

"Innocent, guilty, he'd have been sunk. Rav, dust death is fast. He didn't know it was coming."

"He'd be alive if I'd turned myself in."

"He'd be in an interrogation chamber next door to you, agonizing over how long it would be before they tied a rock to his ankles and dragged him out to deep sea."

He wrenched free, refusing to speak until they were on a highspeed back to the Rialto. Crabcake Star was rising in the south. His arms were crossed, his eyes red and puffy.

I couldn't bear it if he came to hate me, Ruthless thought, *not if . . .*

"Rav," she said. "You say we're not going back."

"I'm not going," he said dully. "If I don't, Ma won't. But don't listen to me, what do I know?"

The highspeed docked, and as the automatic door opened she took a long whiff of the fog, inhaling the soothing breath of Tumblertide. "Your playmates feel the same way?"

"My friends?"

She tried not to react. People her age never used that word anymore, not unless they meant Fiend.

"Yeah," he said, stepping onto the platform beside her. "Most of us figure we'll stay."

"Because you all grew up here."

"Kabuva's home for us, Ruth." He knotted his fingers together, approximating a squid gesture that meant safety, comfort, refuge. "You know what it's like to lose that."

He was all she had.

So. New game, new rules. She tossed her long-cherished dream of going home, cutting it away like a rotten limb and trying to ignore the pain, the sense of loss.

Back to the task at hand, she thought. "Rav, who knows you're making a documentary?"

"Ma. You. Some friends," he answered in a monotone.

"Which friends?"

"Jekkers, Clark, and Marion. Why?"

She scanned for surveillance once more before answering. "The limousine at the scene means police will probably tie the dust grenades to the feeler disappearances. They'll ID the missing squid and take a look at anyone connected to him, the driver, and the feeler trade."

"If people know I'm making a feed about the feelers, the cops will check me out," he said.

"Exactly. I'll prep you for interrogation, just in case. Maybe you can say you filmed a couple pickups as background for a bigger project."

"What bigger project?" He pressed his lips together.

"You tell me."

Rav stifled a yawn. "They won't come talk to me. Nobody knows what I've been shooting."

"You never told?"

"It seemed . . . unlucky. Stupid, right?"

Ruthless stretched out a hand, thinking to comfort him, but Rav stepped back, anger warring with misery on his pale face. Instead of chasing, she said: "Your father used to paint landscapes. He never let anyone see until they were finished. Unlucky, he said."

He blinked, surprised, and she was afraid she'd said the wrong thing. But finally Rav said: "I suppose you want me to give up shooting?"

"You have to stop documenting feelups, yeah. But if you dump your equipment and quit filming . . . that's a major behavior change, the sort of thing cops look for. Especially squid cops—they're very holistic."

"What am I supposed to do?" The anger was winning.

"Well, people know you're shooting something, so you'll have to get right to work on something else. As far as anyone knows, it's been the same project all along. But you'll need another topic."

"I'm not feeling real inspired."

He's going to torture himself over the chauffeur, Ruthless thought; he'll need close watching. And Elva's curiosity—there was that to consider too. She'd have to keep a watchful eye.

"What else isn't Earthtown talking about?" she said.

He looked at her blankly.

"You were doing this to get people talking, right? Rip off the scabs, heal some wounds, something along those lines?"

"You don't have to make it sound naive."

"Look, you said nobody talks about the feelers. What else do you think we should be talking about?"

"There's the war," he grunted. "What it was like to lose. What it was like to leave."

To lose. She nodded, thinking it through. "A lot of my playmates, the ones who survived the Setback and made it out, they're here."

"They won't talk to me. You saw that Cope guy. He thought I was kelpheaded."

"Well. I'm very persuasive."

He squinted at her in the morning light. "You'd do that?"

I'd do anything for you, kid, she thought, but it wasn't tactically sound to let him know that, was it? What she said was, "Like you said, you're in the club now. People will sense it; it'll open doors. And I'll help."

"Okay." Rav gave her a faint, tired smile—his father's smile, Ruthless thought. Then he stopped walking. They had reached the rear entrance of Elva's movie theater. "That'd be . . . I could do that."

"It's a deal then—I'll call you tomorrow," Ruthless said. "Get some sleep, okay?"

"Thanks, Auntie." Ducking his head like a little boy, Rav tiptoed into the darkened theater and was gone.

"Last kid standing wins the game," Ruthless mumbled, turning east. Already considering ways to unlock the long-shut mouths of her playmates, she headed toward the fog-shrouded dawn, taking the beachward route home.

Nightingale

ALASTAIR REYNOLDS

Here's another brilliant story by Alastair Reynolds, whose "Signal to Noise" appears elsewhere in this anthology. In the hair-raising adventure that follows, he sweeps us along with a determined and heavily armed boarding party off to storm a lost ghost ship as big as a moon—and crewed with a full complement of bizarre and deadly ghosts of its own.

I checked the address Tomas Martinez had given me, shielding the paper against the rain while I squinted at my scrawl. The number I'd written down didn't correspond with any of the high-and-dry offices, but it was a dead ringer for one of the low-rent premises at street level. Here the walls of Threadfall Canyon had been cut and buttressed to the height of six or seven storeys, widening the available space at the bottom of the trench. Buildings covered most of the walls, piled on top of each other, supported by a haphazard arrangement of stilts and rickety, semi-permanent bamboo scaffolding. Aerial walkways had been strung from one side of the street to the other, with stairs and ladders snaking their way through the dark fissures between the buildings. Now and then a wheeler sped through the water, sending a filthy wave of brown water in its wake. Very rarely, a sleek, claw-like volantor slid overhead. But volantors were off-world tech and not many people on Sky's Edge could afford that kind of thing anymore.

It didn't look right to me, but all the evidence said that this had to be the place.

I stepped out of the water, onto the wooden platform in front of the office, and knocked on the glass-fronted door while rain curtained down through holes in the striped awning above me. I was pushing hair out of my eyes when the door opened.

I'd seen enough photographs of Martinez to know this wasn't him. This was a big bull of a man, nearly as wide as the door. He stood there with his arms crossed in front of his chest, over which he wore only a sleeveless black vest that was zipped down to the midriff. His muscles were so tight it looked like he was wearing some kind of body-hugging amplification suit. His head was very large and very bald, rooted to his body by a neck like a small mountain range. The skin around his right eye was paler than the rest of his face, in a neatly circular patch.

He looked down at me as if I was something that the rain had washed in.

"What?" he said, in a voice like the distant rumble of artillery.

"I'm here to see Martinez."

"Mr. Martinez to you," he said.

"Whatever. But I'm still here to see him, and he should be expecting me. I'm . . ."

"Dexia Scarrow," called another voice—fractionally more welcoming, this time—and a smaller, older man bustled into view from behind the pillar of muscle blocking the door, snatching delicate pince-nez glasses from his nose. "Let her in, Norbert. She's expected. Just a little *late*."

"I got held up around Armesto—my hired wheeler hit a pothole and tipped over. Couldn't get the thing started again, so had to . . ."

The smaller man waved aside my excuse. "You're here now, which is all that matters. I'll have Norbert dry your clothes, if you wish."

I peeled off my coat. "Maybe this."

"Norbert will attend to your galoshes as well. Would you care for something to drink? I have tea already prepared, but if you would rather something else . . ."

"Tea will be fine, Mr. Martinez," I said.

"Please. Call me Tomas. It's my sincere wish that we will work together as friends."

I stood out of my galoshes and handed my dripping wet coat to the big man. Martinez nodded once, the gesture precise and birdlike, and then ushered me to follow him farther into his rooms. He was slighter and older than I'd been expecting, although still recognisable as the man in the photographs. His hair was grey turning to white, thinning on his scalp and shaved close to the skin elsewhere on his head. He wore a grey waistcoat over a grey shirt, the ensemble lending him a drab, clerkish air.

We navigated a twisting labyrinth formed from four layers of brown boxes, piled to head height. "Excuse the mess," Martinez said, looking back at me over his shoulder. "I really should find a better solution to my filing problems, but there's always something more pressing that needs doing instead."

"I'm surprised you have time to eat, let alone worry about filing problems."

"Well, things haven't been as hectic lately, I must confess. If you've been following the news you'll know that I've already caught most of my big fish. There's been some mopping up to do, but I've been nowhere near as busy as in . . ." Martinez stopped suddenly next to one of the piles of boxes, placed his glasses back on the ridge of his nose, and scuffed dust from the paper label on the side of the box nearest his face. "No," he said, shaking his head. "Wrong place. Wrong damned place! Norbert!"

Norbert trudged along behind us, my sodden coat still draped over one of his enormous, trunklike arms. "Mr. Martinez?"

"This one is in the wrong place." The smaller man turned around and indicated a spot between two other boxes, on the other side of the corridor. "It goes *here*. It needs to be moved. Kessler's case is moving into court next month, and we don't want any trouble with missing documentation."

"Attend to it," Norbert said, which sounded like an order but which I assumed was his way of saying he'd remember to move the box when he was done with my laundry.

"Kessler?" I asked, when Norbert had left. "As in Tillman Kessler, the NC interrogator?"

"One and the same, yes. Did you have experience with him?"

"I wouldn't be standing here if I did."

"True enough. But a small number of people were fortunate enough to survive their encounters with Kessler. It's their testimonies that will help bring him to justice."

"By which you mean crucified."

"I detect faint disapproval, Dexia," Martinez said.

"You're right. It's barbaric."

"It's how we've always done things. The Haussmann way, if you like."

Sky Haussmann: the man who gave this world its name, and who sparked off the 250-year war we've only just learned to stop fighting. When they crucified Sky they thought they were putting an early end to the violence. They couldn't have been more wrong. Ever since then, crucifixion is the way executions happen.

"Is Kessler the reason you asked me here, sir? Were you expecting me to add to the case file against him?"

Martinez paused at a heavy wooden door.

"Not Kessler, no. I've every expectation to see him nailed to Bridgetop by the end of the year. But it does concern the man for whom Kessler was an instrument."

I thought about that for a moment. "Kessler worked for Colonel Jax, didn't he?"

Martinez opened the door and ushered me through, into the windowless room beyond. By now we must have been back into the canyon wall. The air had the inert stillness of a crypt. "Yes, Kessler was Jax's man," Martinez said. "I'm glad you made the connection: it saves me explaining why Jax ought to be brought to justice."

"I agree completely. Half the population would agree with you. But I'm afraid you're a bit late: Jax died years ago."

Two other people were already waiting in the room, sitting on settees either side of a low black table set with tea, coffee and pisco sours.

"Jax didn't die," Martinez said. "He just disappeared, and now I know where he is. Have a seat, please."

He knew I was interested; knew I wouldn't be able to walk out of that room until I'd heard the rest of the story about Colonel Brandon Jax. But there was more to it than that: there was something effortlessly commanding about his voice that made it very hard not to obey. In my time in the Southland Militia I'd learned that some people have that authority and some people don't. It can't be taught; can't be learned; can't be faked. You're either born with it or you're not.

"Dexia Scarrow, allow me to introduce you to my other two guests," Martinez said, when I'd taken my place at the table. "The gentleman opposite you is Salvatore Nicolosi, a veteran of one of the Northern Coalition's freeze/thaw units. The woman on your right is Ingrid Sollis, a personal security expert with a particular interest in counter-intrusion systems. Ingrid saw early combat experience with the Southland, but she soon left the military to pursue private interests."

I bit my tongue, then turned my attention away from the woman before I said something I might regret. The man—Nicolosi—looked more like an actor than a soldier. He didn't have a scar on him. His beard was so neatly groomed, so sharp-edged, that it looked sprayed on through a stencil. Freeze/thaw operatives rubbed me up the wrong way, no matter which side they'd been on. They'd always seen themselves as superior to the common soldier, which is why they didn't feel the need for the kind of excessive musculature Nobert carried around.

"Let me introduce Dexia Scarrow," Martinez continued, nodding at me. "Dexia was a distinguished soldier in the Southland Militia for fifteen years, until the armistice. Her service record is excellent. I believe she will be a valuable addition to the team."

"Maybe we should back up a step," I said. "I haven't agreed to be part of anyone's team."

"We're going after Jax," Nicolosi said placidly. "Doesn't that excite you?"

"He was on your side," I said. "What makes you so keen to see him hang?"

Nicolosi looked momentarily pained. "He was a war criminal, Dexia. I'm as anxious to see monsters like Jax brought to justice as I am to see the same fate visited on their scum-ridden Southland counterparts."

"Nicolosi's right," said Ingrid Sollis. "If we're going to learn to live together on this planet, we have to put the law above all else, regardless of former allegiances."

"Easy coming from a deserter," I said. "Allegiance clearly didn't mean very much to you back then, so I'm not surprised it doesn't mean much to you now."

Martinez, still standing at the head of the table, smiled tolerantly, as if he'd expected nothing less.

"You're under an understandable misapprehension, Dexia. Ingrid was no deserter. She was wounded in the line of duty: severely, I might add. After her recuperation she was commended for bravery under fire and given the choice of an honorable discharge or a return to the frontline. You cannot blame her for choosing the former, especially given all that she had been through."

"OK, my mistake," I said. "It's just that I never heard of many people making it out alive, before the war was over."

Sollis looked at me icily. "Some of us did."

"No one here has anything but an impeccable service record," Martinez said. "I should know: I've been through your individual biographies with a fine-tooth comb. You're just the people for the job."

"I don't think so," I said, moving to stand up. "I'm just a retired soldier with a grudge against deserters. I wasn't in some shit-hot freeze/thaw unit, and I didn't do anything that resulted in any commendations for bravery. Sorry, folks, but I think . . ."

"Stay seated."

I did what the man said.

Martinez continued speaking, his voice as measured and patient as ever. "You participated in at least three high-risk extraction operations, Dexia: three dangerous forays into enemy lines, to retrieve two deep-penetration Southland spies and one trump card NC defector. Or do you deny this?"

I shook my head, the reality of what he was proposing still not sinking in. "I can't help. I don't know anything about Jax. . . ."

"You don't need to. That's my problem."

"How are you so sure he's still alive, anyway?"

"I'd like to know, too," Nicolosi said, stroking an elegant finger along the border of his beard.

Martinez sat down, employing his own stool at the head of the table, so that he was higher than the three of us. He removed his glasses and fiddled with them in his lap. "It is necessary that you take a certain amount of what I am about to tell you on faith. I've been gathering intelligence on men like Jax for years, and in doing so I've come to rely on a web of contacts, many of whom have conveyed information to me at great personal risk. If I were to tell you the whole story, and if some of that story were to leak beyond this office, lives might well be endangered. And that is to say nothing of how my chances of bringing other fugitives to justice might be undermined."

"We understand," Sollis said, and I bridled at the way she presumed to speak for all of us. Perhaps she felt she owed Martinez for the way he'd just stood up for her.

Again I bit my lip and said nothing.

"For a long time, I've received titbits of intelligence concerning Colonel Jax: rumours that he did not, in fact, die at all, but is still at large."

"Where?" Sollis asked. "On Sky's Edge?"

"It would seem not. There were, of course, many rumours and false trails that suggested Jax had gone to ground somewhere on this planet. But one by one I discounted them all. Slowly the truth became apparent. Jax is still alive; still within this system."

I felt it was about time I made a positive contribution. "Wouldn't a piece of dirt like Jax try and get out of the system at the first opportunity?"

Martinez favoured my observation by pointing his glasses at me. "I had my fears that he might have, but as the evidence came in, a different truth presented itself."

He set about pouring himself some tea. The pisco sours were going unwanted. I doubted that any of us had the stomach for drink at this time of the day.

"Where is he, then?" asked Nicolosi. "Plenty of criminal elements might have the means to shelter a man like Jax, but given the price on his head, the temptation to turn him in . . ."

"He is not being sheltered," Martinez said, sipping delicately at his tea before continuing. "He is alone, aboard a ship. The ship was believed lost, destroyed in the final stages of the war, when things escalated into space—but I have evidence that the ship is still essentially intact, with a functioning life-support system. There is every reason to believe Jax is still being kept alive, aboard this vehicle, in this system."

"What's he waiting for?" I asked.

"For memories to grow dim," Martinez answered. "Like many powerful men, Jax may have obtained longevity drugs—or at least undergone longevity treatment—during the latter stages of the war. Time is not a concern for him."

I leaned forward. "This ship . . . you think it'll just be a matter of boarding it and taking him alive?"

Martinez seemed surprised at the directness of my question. He blinked once before answering.

"In essence, yes."

"Won't he put up a fight?"

"I don't think so. The Ultras that located the vehicle for me reported that it appeared dormant, in power-conservation mode. Jax himself may be frozen, in reefersleep. The ship did not respond to the Ultras' sensor sweeps, so there's no reason to assume it will respond to our approach and docking."

"How close did the Ultras get?" Sollis asked.

"Within three or four light-minutes. But there's no reason to assume we can't get closer without alerting the ship."

"How do you know Jax is aboard this ship?" Nicolosi asked. "It could just be a drifter, nothing to do with him."

"The intelligence I'd already gleaned pointed towards his presence aboard a vehicle of a certain age, size and design—everything matches."

"So let's cut to the chase," Sollis said, again presuming to speak for the rest of us. "You've brought us here because you think we're the team to snatch the colonel. I'm the intrusion specialist, so you'll be relying on me to get us inside that ship. Nicolosi's a freeze/thaw veteran, so—apart from the fact that he's probably pretty handy with a weapon or two—he'll know how to spring Jax from reefersleep, if the colonel turns out to be frozen. And she—what was your name again?"

"Dexia," I said, like it was a threat.

"She's done some extractions. I guess she must be OK at her job, or she wouldn't be here."

Martinez waited a moment, then nodded. "You're quite right, Ingrid: all credit to you for that. I apologise if my machinations are so nakedly transparent. But the simple fact of the matter is that you are the ideal team for the operation in question. I have no doubt that, with your combined talents, you will succeed in returning Colonel Jax to Sky's Edge, and hence to trial. Now admit it: that *would* be something, wouldn't it? To fell the last dragon?"

Nicolosi indicated his approval with a long nasal sigh. "Men like Kessler are just a distraction. When you hang a monster like Kessler, you're punishing the knife, not the man who wielded it. If you wish true justice, you must find the knifeman, the master."

"What do we get paid?" Sollis asked.

Martinez smiled briefly. "Fifty thousand Australs for each of you, upon the safe return of Colonel Jax."

"What if we find him dead?" I asked. "By then we'll already have risked an approach and docking to his ship."

"If Jax is already dead, then you will be paid twenty-five thousand Australs."

We all looked at each other. I knew what the others were thinking. Fifty thousand Australs was life-changing money, but half of that wasn't bad either. Killing Jax would be much easier and safer than extracting him. . . .

"I'll be with you, of course," Martinez said. "So there'll be no need to worry about proving Jax was already dead when you arrived, should that arise."

"If you're coming along," I asked, "who else do we need to know about?"

"Only Norbert. And you need have no fears concerning his competency."

"Just the five of us, then," I said.

"Five is a good number, don't you think? And there is a practical limit to the size of the extraction team. I have obtained the use of a small but capable ship, perfectly adequate for our purposes. It will carry five, with enough capacity to bring back the colonel. I'll provide weapons, equipment and armour, but you may all bring whatever you think may prove useful."

I looked around the cloisterlike confines of the room, and remembered the dismal exterior of the offices, situated at the bottom of Threadfall Canyon. "Three times fifty thousand Australs," I mused. "Plus whatever it cost you to hire and equip a ship. If you don't mind me asking . . . where exactly are the funds coming from?"

"The funds are mine," Martinez said sternly. "Capturing Jax has been a long-term goal, not some whimsical course upon which I have only recently set myself. Dying a pauper would be a satisfactory end to my affairs, were I to do so knowing that Jax was hanging from the highest mast of Bridgetop."

For a moment, none of us said anything. Martinez had spoken so softly, so demurely, that the meaning of his words seemed to lag slightly behind the statement itself. When it arrived, I think we all saw a flash of that corpse, executed in the traditional way, the Haussmann way.

"Good weapons?" I asked. "Not some reconditioned black-market shit?"

"Only the best."

"Technical specs for the ship?" Sollis asked.

"You'll have plenty of time to review the data on the way to the rendezvous point. I don't doubt that a woman of your abilities will be able to pinpoint an entry point."

Sollis looked flattered. "Then I guess I'm in. What about you, Salvatore?"

"Men like Colonel Jax stained the honour of the Northern Coalition. We were not all monsters. If I could do something to make people see that . . ." Nicolosi trailed off, then shrugged. "Yes, I am in. It would be an honour, Mr. Martinez."

"That leaves you, Dexia," Sollis said. "Fifty thousand Australs sounds pretty sweet to me. I'm guessing it sounds pretty sweet to you as well."

"That's my call, not yours."

"Just saying . . . you look like you could use that money as much as any of us."

I think I came close to saying no, to walking out of that room, back into the incessant muddy rain of Threadfall Canyon. Perhaps if I'd tried, Norbert would have been forced to detain me, so that I didn't go blabbing about how a team was being put together to bring Colonel Jax back into custody. But I would never get the chance to find out what Martinez had in mind for me if I chose not to go along with him.

I only had to think about the way I looked in the mirror, and what those fifty thousand Australs could do for me.

So I said yes.

Martinez gestured to one of the blank pewter-grey walls in the shuttle's compartment, causing it to brighten and fill with neon-bright lines. The lines meshed and intersected, forming a schematic diagram of a ship, with an accompanying scale.

"Intelligence on Jax's ship is fragmentary. Strip out all the contradictory reports, discard unreliable data, and we're left with this."

"That's it?" Sollis asked.

"When we get within visual range we'll be able to improve matters. I shall reexamine all of the reports, including those that were discarded. Some of them—when we have the real ship to compare them against—may turn out to have merit after all. They may in turn shed useful light on the interior layout, and the likely location of Jax. By then, of course, we'll also have infrared and deep-penetration radar data from our own sensors."

"It looks like a pretty big ship," I said as I looked at the schematic, scratching at my scalp. We were a day out from Armesto Field, with the little shuttle tucked into the belly hold of an outbound lighthugger named *Death of Sophonisba*.

"Big but not the right shape for a lighthugger," Sollis said. "So what are we dealing with here?"

"Good question," I said. What Martinez was showing us was a rectangular hull about one kilometre from end to end; maybe a hundred metres deep and a hundred metres wide, with some kind of spherical bulge about halfway along. There was some suggestion of engines at one end, and of a gauntlet-like docking complex at the other. The ship was too blunt for interstellar travel, and it lacked the outrigger-mounted engines that were characteristic of Conjoiner drive mechanisms. "Does look kind of familiar, though," I added. "Anyone else getting that déjà vu feeling, or is it just me?"

"I don't know," Nicolosi said. "When I saw it I thought . . ." He shook his head. "It can't be. It must be a standard hull design."

"You've seen it too," I said.

"Does that ship have a name?" Nicolosi asked Martinez.

"I have no idea what Jax calls his ship."

"That's not what the man asked," Sollis said. "He asked if—"

"I know the name of the ship," I said quietly. "I saw a ship like that once, when I was being taken aboard it. I'd been injured in a fire-fight, one of the last big surface battles. They took me into space—this was after the elevator came down, so it had to be by shuttle—and brought me aboard that ship. It was a hospital ship, orbiting the planet."

"What was the name of the ship?" Nicolosi asked urgently.

"*Nightingale*," I said.

"Oh, no."

"You're surprised."

"Damn right I'm surprised. I was aboard *Nightingale* too."

"So was I," Sollis said, her voice barely a whisper. "I didn't recognise it, though. I was too fucked up to pay much attention until they put me back together aboard it. By then, I guess . . ."

"Same with me," Nicolosi said. "Stitched back together aboard *Nightingale*, then repatriated."

Slowly, we all turned and looked at Martinez. Even Norbert, who had contributed nothing until that point, turned to regard his master. Martinez blinked, but otherwise his composure was impeccable.

"The ship is indeed *Nightingale*. It was too risky to tell you when we were still on the planet. Had any of Jax's allies learned of the identity . . ."

Sollis cut him off. "Is that why you didn't tell us? Or is it because you knew we'd all been aboard that thing once already?"

"The fact that you have all been aboard *Nightingale* was a factor in your selection, nothing more. It was your skills that marked you out for this mission, not your medical history."

"So why didn't you tell us?" she asked.

"Again, had I told you more than was wise . . ."

"You lied to us."

"I did no such thing."

"Wait," Nicolosi said, his voice calmer than I was expecting. "Let's just . . . deal with this, shall we? We're getting hung up on the fact that we were all healed aboard *Nightingale*, when the real question we should be asking is this: What the hell is Jax doing aboard a ship that doesn't exist anymore?"

"What's the problem with the ship?" I asked.

"The problem," Nicolosi said, speaking straight at me, "is that *Nightingale* was reported destroyed near the end of the war. Or were you not keeping up with the news?"

I shrugged. "Guess I wasn't."

"And yet you knew enough about the ship to recognise it."

"Like I said, I remember the view from the medical shuttle. I was drugged-up, unsure whether I was going to live or die . . . everything was heightened, intense, like in a bad dream. But after they healed me and sent me back down surfaceside? I don't think I ever thought about *Nightingale* again."

"Not even when you look in the mirror?" Nicolosi asked.

"I thought about what they'd done to me, how much better it could have been. But it never crossed my mind to wonder what had happened to the ship afterwards. So what *did* happen?"

"You say 'they healed me,'" Nicolosi observed. "Does that mean you were treated by doctors, by men and women?"

"Shouldn't I have been?"

He shook his head minutely. "My guess is you were wounded and shipped aboard *Nightingale* soon after it was deployed."

"That's possible."

"In which case, *Nightingale* was still in commissioning phase. I went aboard it later. What about you, Ingrid?"

"Me too. I hardly saw another human being the whole time I was aboard that thing."

"That was how it was meant to operate: with little more than a skeleton staff, to take medical decisions the ship couldn't take for itself. Most of the time they were meant to stay behind the scenes."

"All I remember was a hospital ship," I said. "I don't know anything about 'commissioning.'"

Nicolosi explained it to me patiently, as if I was a small child in need of education.

Nightingale had been financed and built by a consortium of well-meaning post-mortal aristocrats. Since their political influence hadn't succeeded in curtailing the war (and since many of their aristocratic friends were quite happy for it to continue) they'd decided to make a difference in the next best way: by alleviating the suffering of the mortal men and women engaged in the war itself.

So they created a hospital ship, one that had no connection to either the Northern Coalition or the Southland Militia. *Nightingale* would be there for all injured soldiers, irrespective of allegiance. Aboard the neutral ship, the injured would be healed, allowed to recuperate, and then repatriated. All but the most critically wounded would eventually return to active combat service. And *Nightingale* itself would be state-of-the-art, with better medical facilities than any other public hospital on or around Sky's Edge. It wouldn't be the glittering magic of Demarchist medicine, but it would still be superior to anything most mortals had ever experienced.

It would also be tirelessly efficient, dedicated only to improving its healing record. *Nightingale* was designed to operate autonomously, as a single vast machine. Under the guidance of human specialists, the ship would slowly improve its methods until it had surpassed its teachers. I'd come aboard ship when it was still undergoing the early stages of its learning curve, but—as I learned from Nicolosi—the ship had soon moved into its "operational phase." By then the entire kilometre-long vehicle was under the control of only a handful of technicians and surgical specialists, with gamma-level intelligences taking most of the day-to-day decisions. That was when Sollis and Nicolosi had been shipped aboard. They'd been healed by machines, with only a vague awareness that there was a watchful human presence behind the walls.

"It worked, too," Nicolosi said. "The ship did everything its sponsors had hoped it would. It functioned like a huge, efficient factory: sucking in the wounded, spitting out the healed."

"Only for them to go back to the war," I said.

"The sponsors didn't have any control over what happened when the healed were sent back down. But at least they were still alive; at least they hadn't died on the battlefield or under the operating table. The sponsors could still believe that they had done something good. They could still sleep at night."

"So *Nightingale* was a success," I said. "What's the problem? Wasn't it turned over to civilian use after the armistice?"

"The ship was destroyed just before the ceasefire," Nicolosi said. "That's why we shouldn't be seeing it now. A stray NC missile, nuke-tipped—too fast to be intercepted by the ship's own countermeasures. It took out *Nightingale*, with staff and patients still aboard her."

"Now that you mention it . . . maybe I did hear about something like that."

Sollis looked fiercely at Martinez. "I say we renegotiate terms. He never told us we were going to have to spring Jax from a fucking ghost ship."

Norbert moved to his master's side, as if to protect him from the furious Sollis. Martinez, who had said nothing for many minutes, removed his glasses, buffed them on his shirt and replaced them with an unhurried calm.

"Perhaps you are right to be cross with me, Ingrid. And perhaps I made a mistake in not mentioning *Nightingale* sooner than I did. But it was imperative to me that I not compromise this operation with a single careless indiscretion. My whole life has been an arrow pointing to this one task: the bringing to justice of Colonel Jax. I will not fail myself now."

"You should have told us about the hospital ship," Nicolosi said. "None of us would have had any reason to spread that information. We all want to see Jax get his due."

"Then I have made a mistake, for which I apologise."

Sollis shook her head. "I don't think an apology's going to cut it. If I'd known I was going to have to go back aboard that *thing* . . ."

"You are right," Martinez said, addressing all of us. "The ship has a traumatic association for you, and it was wrong of me not to allow for that."

"Amen to that," Sollis said.

I felt it was time I made a contribution. "I don't think any of us are about to back out now, Tomas. But maybe—given what we now know about the ship—a little bit more incentive might not be a bad idea."

"I was about to make the same suggestion myself," Martinez said. "You must appreciate that my funds are not inexhaustible, and that my original offer might already be considered generous—but shall we say an extra five thousand Australs, for each of you?"

"Make it ten and maybe we're still in business," Sollis snapped back, before I'd had a chance to blink.

Martinez glanced at Norbert, then—with an expression that suggested he was giving in under duress—he nodded at Sollis. "Ten thousand Australs it is. You drive a hard bargain, Ingrid."

"While we're debating terms," Nicolosi said, "is there anything else you feel we ought to know?"

"I have told you that the ship is *Nightingale*." Martinez directed our attention back to the sketchy diagram on the wall. "That, I am ashamed to admit, is the sum total of my knowledge of the ship in question."

"What about constructional blueprints?" I asked.

"None survived the war."

"Photographs? Video images?"

"Ditto. *Nightingale* operated in a war zone, Dexia. Casual sightseeing was not exactly a priority for those unfortunate enough to get close to her."

"What about the staff aboard her?" Nicolosi asked. "Couldn't they tell you anything?"

"I spoke to some survivors: the doctors and technicians who'd been aboard during the commissioning phase. Their testimonies were useful, when they were willing to talk."

Nicolosi pushed further. "What about the people who were aboard before the ceasefire?"

"I could not trace them."

"But they obviously didn't die. If the ship's still out there, the rogue missile couldn't have hit it."

"Why would anyone make up a story about the ship being blown to pieces, if it didn't happen?" I asked.

"War does strange things to truth," Martinez answered. "No malice is necessarily implied. Perhaps another hospital ship was indeed destroyed. There was more than one in orbit around Sky's Edge, after all. One of them may even have had a similar name. It's perfectly conceivable that the facts might have got muddled, in the general confusion of those days."

"Still doesn't explain why you couldn't trace any survivors," Nicolosi said.

Martinez shifted on his seat, uneasily. "If Jax did appropriate the ship, then he may not have wanted anyone talking about it. The staff aboard *Nightingale* might have been paid off—or threatened—to keep silent."

"Adds up, I guess," I said.

"Money will make a lot of things add up," Nicolosi replied.

After two days the *Death of Sophonisba* sped deeper into the night, while Martinez's ship followed a pre-programmed flight plan designed to bring us within survey range of the hospital ship. The Ultras had scanned *Nightingale* again, and once again they'd elicited no detectable response from the dormant vessel. All indications were that the ship was in a deep cybernetic coma, as close to death as possible, with only a handful of critical life-support systems still running on a trickle of stored power.

Over the next twenty-four hours we crept in closer, narrowing the distance to mere light-seconds, and then down to hundreds of thousands of kilometres. Still there was no response, but as the distance narrowed, so our sensors began to improve the detail in their scans. While the rest of us took turns sleeping, Martinez sat at his console, compositing the data, enhancing his schematic. Now and then Norbert would lean over the console and stare in numb concentration at the sharpening image, and occasionally he would mumble some remark or observation to which Martinez would respond in a patient, faintly condescending whisper, the kind that a teacher might reserve for a slow but willing pupil. Not for the first time I was touched by Martinez's obvious kindness in employing the huge, slow Norbert, and I wondered what the war must have done to him to bring him to this state.

When we were ten hours from docking, Martinez revealed the fruits of his labours. The schematic of the hospital ship was three-dimensional now, displayed in the navigational projection cylinder on the ship's cramped flight deck. Although the basic layout of the ship hadn't changed, the new plan was much more detailed than the first one. It showed docking points, airlocks, major mechanical systems, and the largest corridors and spaces threading the ship's interior. There was still a lot of guesswork, but it wouldn't be as if we were entering a completely foreign territory.

"The biggest thermal hotspot is here," Martinez said, pointing at a spot about a quarter of the way down from the front. "If Jax is anywhere, that's my best guess as to where we'll find him."

"Simple, then," Nicolosi said. "In via that dorsal lock, then a straight sprint down that access shaft. Easy, even under weightless conditions. Can't be more than fifty or sixty metres."

"I'm not happy," Sollis said. "That's a large lock, likely to be armed to the teeth with heavy duty sensors and alarms."

"Can you get us through it?" Nicolosi asked.

"You give me a door, I'll get us through it. But I can't bypass every conceivable security system, and you can be damned sure the ship will know about it if we come through a main lock."

"What about the other ones?" I asked, trying not to sound as if I was on her case. "Will they be less likely to go off?"

"Nothing's guaranteed. But I'd always rather take my chances with the backdoor."

"I think Ingrid is correct," Martinez said, nodding his approval. "There's every chance of a silent approach and docking. Jax will have disabled all non-essential systems, and that will include proximity sensors. If that's the case—if we see no evidence of having tripped approach alarms—then I believe we would be best advised to maintain stealth." He indicated farther along the hull, beyond the rounded mid-section bulge. "That will mean coming in *here*, or *here*, via one of these smaller service locks. I concur with Ingrid: they probably won't be alarmed."

"That'll leave us with four or five hundred metres of ship to crawl through," Nicolosi said, leaving us in no doubt what he thought about that. "Four or five hundred metres for which we only have a very crude map."

"We'll have directional guidance from our suits," Martinez said.

"It's still a concern to me. But if you have settled upon this decision, I shall abide by it."

I turned to Sollis. "What you said just then . . . about not spending a minute longer aboard *Nightingale* than we have to?"

"I wasn't kidding."

"I know. But there was something about the way you said it. Is there something about that ship you know that we don't? You sounded spooked, and I don't understand why. It's just a disused hospital, after all."

Sollis studied me for a moment before answering. "Tell her, Nicolosi."

Nicolosi looked placidly at the other woman. "Tell her what?"

"What she obviously doesn't know. What none of us are in any great hurry to talk about."

"Oh, please."

"Oh please what?" I asked.

"It's just a fairy story, a stupid myth," Nicolosi said.

"A stupid story which nonetheless always claimed that *Nightingale* didn't get blown up after all."

"What are you talking about?" I asked. "What story?"

It was Martinez who chose to answer. "That something unfortunate happened aboard her. That the last batch of sick and injured went in, but for some reason were never seen to leave. That all attempts to contact the technical staff failed. That an exploratory team was put aboard the ship, and that they too were never heard from again."

I laughed. "Fuck. And now we're planning to go aboard?"

"Now you see why I'm kind of anxious to get this over with," Sollis said.

"It's just a myth," Martinez chided. "Nothing more. It is a thing to frighten children, not to dissuade us from capturing Jax. In fact it would not surprise me in the least if Jax or his allies were in some way responsible for this lie. If it were to cause us to turn back now, it would have served them admirably, would it not?"

"Maybe," I said, without much conviction. "But I'd still have been happier if you'd told me before. It wouldn't have made any difference to my accepting this job, but it would have been nice to know you trusted me."

"I do trust you, Dexia. I simply assumed that you had no interest in childish stories."

"How do you know Jax is aboard?" I asked.

"We've been over this. I have my sources, sources that I must protect, and it would be . . ."

"He was a patient, wasn't he."

Martinez snapped his glasses from his nose, as if my point had at an unexpected tangent to whatever we'd been talking about. "I know only that Jax is aboard *Nightingale*. The circumstances of how he arrived there are of no concern to me."

"And it doesn't bother you that maybe he's just dead, like the rest of whoever was aboard at the end?" Sollis asked.

"If he is dead, you will still receive twenty-five thousand Australs."

"Plus the ten we already agreed on."

"That too," Martinez said, as if it should have been taken for granted.

"I don't like this," Sollis muttered.

"I don't like it either," Nicolosi replied. "But we came here to do a job, and the material facts haven't changed. There is a ship, and the man we want is aboard it. What Martinez says is true: we should not be intimidated by stories, especially when our goal is so near."

"We go in there, we get Jax, we get the hell out," Sollis said. "No dawdling, no sightseeing, no souvenir hunting."

"I have absolutely no problem with that," I said.

"Take what you want," Martinez called over Norbert's shoulder, as we entered the armoury compartment at the rear of the shuttle's pressurised section. "But remember: you'll be wearing pressure suits, and you'll be moving through confined spaces. You'll also be aboard a ship."

Sollis pushed bodily ahead of me, pouncing on something that I'd only begun to notice. She unracked the sleek, cobalt-blue excimer rifle and hefted it for balance. "Hey, a Breitenbach."

"Christmas come early?" I asked.

Sollis pulled a pose, sighting along the rifle, deploying its targeting aids, flipping the power-up toggle. The weapon whined obligingly. Blue lights studded its stock, indicating it was ready for use.

"Because I'm worth it," Sollis said.

"I'd really like it if you pointed that thing somewhere else," I said.

"Better still, don't point it anywhere," Nicolosi rumbled. He'd seen one of the choicier items too. He unclipped a long, matte-black weapon with a ruby-red dragon stencilled along the barrel. It had a gaping maw like a swallowing python. "Laser-confined plasma bazooka," he said admiringly. "Naughty, but nice."

"Finesse isn't your cup of tea, then."

"Never got to use one of these in the war, Dexia."

"That's because they were banned. One of the few sensible things both sides managed to agree on."

"Then now's my chance."

"I think the idea was to extract Jax, not to blow ten-metre-wide holes in *Nightingale*."

"Don't worry. I'll be very, very careful." He slung the bazooka over his shoulder, then continued his way down the aisle.

I picked up a pistol, hefted it, replaced it on the rack. Found something more to my liking—a heavy, dual-gripped slug gun—and flipped open the loading bay to check that there was a full clip inside. Low-tech but reliable: the other two were welcome to their directed-energy weapons, but I'd seen how easily they could go wrong under combat conditions.

"Nice piece, Dexia," Sollis said, patronisingly. "Old school."

"I'm old school."

"Yeah, I noticed."

"You have a problem with that, we can always try some target practise."

"Hey, no objections. Just glad you found something to your liking. Doing better than old Norbert, anyway." Sollis nodded over her shoulder. "Looks like he's really drawn the short straw there."

I looked down the aisle. Norbert was near the end of one of the racks, examining a small, stubby-looking weapon whose design I didn't recognise. In his huge hands it looked ridiculous, like something made for a doll.

"You sure about that?" I called. "Maybe you want to look at one of these. . . ."

Norbert looked at me like I was some kind of idiot. I don't know what he did then—there was no movement of his hand that I was aware of—but the stubby little weapon immediately unpacked itself, elongating and opening like some complicated puzzle box, until it was almost twice as big, twice as deadly-looking. It had the silken, precision-engineered quality of expensive off-world tech. A Demarchist toy, probably, but a very, very deadly toy for all that.

Sollis and I exchanged a wordless glance. Norbert had found what was probably the most advanced, most effective weapon in the room.

"Will do," Norbert said, before closing the weapon up again and slipping it into his belt.

We crept closer. Tens of thousands of kilometres, then thousands, then hundreds. I looked through the hull windows, with the interior lights turned down, peering in the direction where our radar and infrared scans told us the hospital ship was waiting. When we were down to two dozen kilometres I knew I should be seeing it, but I was still only looking at stars and the sucking blackness between them. I had a sudden, visceral sense of how easy it was to lose something out here, followed in quick succession by a dizzying sense of how utterly small and alone we were, now that the lighthugger was gone.

And then suddenly, there was *Nightingale*.

We were coming in at an angle, so the hull was tilted and foreshortened. It was so dark that only certain edges and surfaces were visible at all. No visible windows, no running lights, no lit-up docking bays. The ship looked as dark and dead as a sliver of coal. Suddenly it was absurd to think that there might be anyone alive aboard it. Colonel Jax's dead corpse, perhaps, but not the living or even life-supported body that would guarantee us the rest of our payment.

Martinez had the ship on manual control now. With small, deft applications of thrust he narrowed the distance down to less than a dozen kilometres. At six kilometres Martinez deemed it safe to activate floodlights and play them along the length of the hull, confirming the placement of locks and docking sites. There was a peppering of micrometeorite impacts and some scorching from high-energy particles, but nothing that I wouldn't have expected for a ship that had been sitting out here since the armistice. If the ship possessed self-repair mechanisms, they were sleeping as well. Even when we circled around the hull and swept it from the other side, there was no trace of our having been noticed. Still with reluctance, Nicolosi accepted that we would follow Sollis's entry strategy, coming in by one of the service locks.

It was time to do it.

We docked. We came in softly, but there was still a solid *clunk* as the capture latches engaged and grasped our little craft to the hull of the hospital ship. I thought of that clunk echoing away down the length of *Nightingale*, diminishing as it travelled, but still not becoming weak enough not to trip some waiting, infinitely patient alarm system, alerting the sleeping ship that it had a visitor. For several minutes we hung in weightless silence, staring out the windows or watching the sensor readouts for the least sign of activity. But the dark ship stayed dark in all directions. There was no detectable change in her state of coma.

"Nothing's happened," Martinez said, breaking the silence with a whisper. "It still doesn't know we're here. The lock is all yours, Ingrid. I've already opened our doors."

Sollis, suited up now, moved into the lock tube with her toolkit. While she worked, the rest of us finished putting on our own suits and armour, completing the exercise as quietly as possible. I hadn't worn a spacesuit before, but Norbert was there to help all of us with the unfamiliar process: his huge hands attended to delicate connections and catches with surprising dexterity. Once I had the suit on, it didn't feel much different than wearing full-spectrum bioarmour, and I quickly got the hang of the life-support indications projected around the border of my faceplate. I would only need to pay minor attention to them: unless there was some malfunction, the suit had enough power and supplies to keep me alive in perfect comfort for three days; longer if I was prepared to tolerate a little less comfort. None of us were planning on spending quite that long in *Nightingale*.

Sollis was nearly done when we assembled behind her in the lock. The inner and outer lock doors on our side were open, exposing the grey outer door of the hospital ship, held tight against the docking connector by pressure tight seals. I doubted that she'd ever had to break into a ship before, but nothing about the door seemed to be causing Sollis any difficulties. She'd tugged open an access panel and plugged in a fistfull of coloured cables, running back to a jury-rigged electronics module in her toolkit. She was tapping a little keyboard, causing patterns of lights to alter within the access panel. The face of a woman—blank, expressionless, yet at the same time severe and unforgiving—had appeared in an oval frame above the access panel.

"Who's that?" I asked.

"That's *Nightingale*," Sollis said, adding, by way of explanation: "The ship had its own gamma-level personality, keeping the whole show running. Pretty smart piece of thinkware by all accounts: full Turing-compliance; about as clever as you can make a machine before you have to start giving it human rights."

I looked at the stern-faced woman, expecting her to query us at any moment. I imagined her harsh and hectoring voice demanding to know what business any of us had boarding *Nightingale*, trespassing aboard *her* ship, *her* hospital.

"Does she know . . . ," I started.

Sollis shook her head. "This is just a dumb facet of the main construct. Not only is it inactive—the image is frozen into the door memory—but it doesn't seem to have any functioning data links back to the main sentience engine. Do you, *Nightingale?*"

The face looked at us impassively, but still said nothing.

"See: deadsville. My guess is the sentience engine isn't running at all. Out here, the ship wouldn't need much more than a trickle of intelligence to keep itself ticking over."

"So the gamma's off-line?"

"Uh-huh. Best way, too. You don't want one of those things sitting around too long without something to do."

"Why not?"

"'Cause they tend to go nuts. That's why the Conjoiners won't allow gamma-level intelligences in any of their machines. They say it's a kind of slavery."

"Running a hospital must have been enough to stop *Nightingale's* gamma running off the rails."

"Let's hope so. Let's really hope so." Sollis glanced back at her work, then emitted a grunt of satisfaction as a row of lights flicked to orange. She unplugged a bunch of coloured cables and looked back at the waiting party. "OK: we're good to go. I can open the door anytime you're ready."

"What's on the other side of it?"

"According to the door, air: normal trimix. Bitchingly cold, but not frozen. Pressure's manageable. I'm not sure we could *breathe* it, but . . ."

"We're not breathing anything," Martinez said curtly. "Our airlock will take two people. One of them will have to be you, Ingrid, since you know how to work the mechanism. I shall accompany you, and then we shall wait for the others on the far side, when we have established that conditions are safe."

"Maybe one of us should go through instead of you," I said, wondering why Norbert hadn't volunteered to go through ahead of his master. "We're expendable, but you aren't. Without you, Jax doesn't go down."

"Considerate of you, Dexia, but I paid you to assist me, not take risks on my behalf."

Martinez propelled himself forward. Norbert, Nicolosi and I edged back to permit the inner door to close again. On the common suit channel I heard Sollis say: "We're opening *Nightingale*. Stand by: comms might get a bit weaker once we're on the other side of all this metal."

Nicolosi pushed past me, back into the flight deck. I heard the heavy whine of servos as the door opened. Breathing and scuffling sounds, but nothing that alarmed me. "OK," Sollis said. "We're moving into *Nightingale*'s lock. Closing the outer door behind us. When you need to open it again, hit any key on the pad."

"Still no sign of life," Nicolosi called.

"The inner door looks like it'll open without any special encouragement from me," Sollis said. "Should be just a matter of pulling down this lever . . . you ready?"

"Do it, Ingrid," I heard Martinez say.

More servos, fainter now. After a few moments Sollis reported back: "We're inside. No surprises yet. Floating in some kind of holding bay, about ten metres wide. It's dark, of course. There's a doorway leading out of the far wall: might lead to the main corridor that should pass close to this lock."

I remembered to turn on my helmet lamp.

"Can you open both lock doors?" Nicolosi asked.

"Not at the same time, not without a lot of trouble that might get us noticed."

"Then we'll come through in two passes. Norbert: you go first. Dexia and I will follow."

It took longer than I'd have liked, but eventually all five of us were on the other side of the lock. I'd only been weightless once, during the recuperation program after my injury, but the memory of how to move—at least without making too much of a fool of myself—was still there, albeit dimly. The others were coping about as well. The combined effects of our helmet lamps banished the darkness to the corners of the room, emphasizing the deeper gloom of the open doorway Sollis had mentioned. It occurred to me that somewhere down that darkness was Colonel Jax, or whatever was left of him.

Nervously, I checked that the slug gun was still clipped to my belt.

"Check your helmet maps," Martinez said. "Does everyone have an overlay and a positional fix?"

"I'm good," I said, against a chorus from the other three, and acutely aware of how easy it would be to get lost aboard a ship as large as *Nightingale*, if that positional fix were to break down.

"Check your weapons and suit systems. We'll keep comms to a minimum all the way in."

"I'll lead," Nicolosi said, propelling himself into the darkness of the doorway before anyone could object.

I followed hard on his heels, trying not to get out of breath with the effort of keeping up. There were loops and rails along all four walls of the shaft, so movement consisted of gliding from one handhold to the next, with only air resistance to stop one drifting all the way. We were covering one metre a second, easily: at that rate, it wouldn't take long to cross the entire width of the ship, which would mean we'd somehow missed the axial corridor we were looking for, or that it just didn't exist. But just when it was beginning to strike me that we'd gone too far, Nicolosi slowed. I grabbed a handhold to stop myself slamming into his feet.

He looked back at us, making me squint against his helmet lamp. "Here's the main corridor, just a bit deeper than we were expecting. Runs both ways."

"We turn left," Martinez said, in not much more than a whisper. "Turn left and follow it for one hundred metres, maybe one hundred and twenty, until we meet the centrifuge section. It should be a straight crawl, with no obstructions."

Nicolosi turned away, then looked back. "I can't see more than twenty metres into the corridor. We may as well see where it goes."

"Nice and slowly," Martinez urged.

We moved forward, along the length of the hull. In the instants when I was coasting from one handhold to the next, I held my breath and tried to hear the ambient noises of the ship, relayed to my helmet by the suit's acoustic pickup. Mostly all I heard was the scuffing progress of the others, the hiss and hum of their own life-support packs. Other than that, Nightingale seemed as silent as when we'd approached. If the ship was aware of our intrusion, there was no sign of it.

We'd made maybe forty metres from the junction: at least a third of the distance we had to travel before hitting the centrifuge, when Nicolosi slowed. I caught a handhold before I drifted into his heels, then looked back to make sure the others had got the message.

"Problem?" Martinez asked.

"There's a T-junction right ahead. I didn't think we were expecting a T-junction."

"We weren't," Martinez said. "But it shouldn't surprise us that the real ship deviates from the blueprint here and there. As long as we don't reach a dead-end, we can still keep moving towards the colonel."

"You want to flip a coin, or shall I do it?" Nicolosi said, looking back at us over his shoulder, his face picked out by my helmet light.

"There's no indication, no sign on the wall?"

"Blank either way."

"In which case take the left," Martinez said, before glancing at Norbert. "Agreed?"

"Agreed," the big man said. "Take left, then next right. Continue."

Nicolosi kicked off, and the rest of us followed. I kept an eye on my helmet's inertial compass, gratified when it detected our change of direction, even though the overlay now showed us moving through what should have been a solid wall.

We'd moved twenty or thirty metres when Nicolosi slowed again. "Tunnel bends to the right," he reported. "Looks like we're back on track. Everyone cool with this?"

"Cool," I said.

But we'd only made another fifteen or twenty metres of progress back along the new course when Nicolosi slowed and called back again. "We're coming up on a heavy door; some kind of internal airlock. Looks like we're going to need Sollis again."

"Let me through," she said, and I squeezed aside so she could edge past me, trying to avoid knocking our suits together. In addition to the weapons she'd selected from the armoury, Sollis's suit was also hung with all manner of door-opening tools, clattering against each other as she moved. I didn't doubt that she'd be able to get through any kind of door, given time. But the idea of spending hours inside Nightingale, while we inched from one obstruction to the next, didn't exactly fill me with enthusiasm.

We let Sollis examine the door: we could hear her ruminating over the design, tutting, humming and talking softly under her breath. She had panels open and equipment plugged in, just like before. The same unwelcoming face glowered from an oval display.

After a couple of minutes Martinez sighed and spoke: "Is there a problem, Ingrid?"

"There's no problem. I can get this door open in about ten seconds. I just want to make damned sure this is another of *Nightingale*'s dumb facets. That means sensing the electrical connections on either side of the frame. Of course, if you'd rather we just stormed on through . . ."

"Keep voice down," Norbert rumbled.

"I'm wearing a spacesuit, dickhead."

"Pressure outside. Sound travel, air to glass, glass to air."

"You have five minutes," Martinez said, decisively. "If you haven't found what you're looking for by then, we open the door anyway. And Norbert's right: let's keep the noise down."

"So, no pressure then," Sollis muttered.

But in three minutes she started unplugging her tools, and turned aside with a beaming look on her face. "It's just an emergency airlock, in case this part of the ship depressurises. They must have decided to put it in after the original blueprints were drawn up."

"No danger that tripping it will alert the rest of *Nightingale*?" I asked.

"Can't ever say there's no risk, but I'm happy for us to go through."

"Open the door," Martinez said. "Everyone brace in case there's vacuum or underpressure on the other side."

We followed his instructions, but when the door opened the air remained as still as before. Beyond, picked out in our wavering lights, was a short stretch of corridor terminating in an identical-looking door. This time there was enough room for all of us to squeeze through, while Sollis attended to the second lock mechanism. Some hardwired system required that the first door be closed before the second one could be opened, but that posed us no real difficulties. Now that Sollis knew what to look for, she worked much faster: good at her job and happy for us all to know it. I didn't doubt that she'd be even faster on the way out.

"We're ready to go through, people. Indications say that the air's just as cold on the other side, so keep your suits buttoned."

I heard the click as one of us—maybe Nicolosi, maybe Norbert—released a safety catch. It was like someone coughing in a theatre. I had no choice but to reach down and arm my own weapon.

"Open it," Martinez said quietly.

The door chugged wide. Our lights stabbed into dark emptiness beyond: a suggestion of a much deeper, wider space than I'd been expecting. Sollis leaned through the door frame, her helmet lamp catching fleeting details from reflective surfaces. I had a momentary flash of glassy things stretching away into infinite distance, then it was gone.

"Report, Ingrid," Martinez said.

"I think we can get through. We've come out next to a wall, or floor, or whatever it is. There are handholds, railings. Looks like they lead on into the room, probably to the other side."

"Stay where you are," Nicolosi said, just ahead of me. "I'll take point again."

She glanced back and swallowed hard. "It's OK, I can handle this one. Can't let you have all the fun, can I?"

Nicolosi grunted something: I don't think he had much of a sense of humour. "You're welcome to my gun, you want it."

"I'm cool," she said, but with audible hesitation. I didn't blame her: it was different being point on a walk through a huge dark room, compared to a narrow corridor. Nothing could leap out and grab you from the side in a corridor.

She started moving along the crawlway.

"Nice and slowly, Ingrid," Martinez said, from behind me. "We still have time on our side."

"We're right behind you," I said, feeling she needed moral support.

"I'm fine, Dexia. No problems here. Just don't want to lose my handhold and go drifting off into fuck knows what. . . ."

Her movements became rhythmic, moving into the chamber one careful handhold at a time. Nicolosi followed, with me right behind him. Apart from our movements, and the sound of our suit systems, the ship was still as silent as a crypt.

But it wasn't totally dark anymore.

Now that we were inside the chamber, it began to reveal its secrets in dim spots of pale light, reaching away into some indeterminate distance. The lights must have always been there; just too faint to notice until we were inside.

"Something's running," Sollis said.

"We knew that," Martinez said. "It was always clear that the ship was dormant, not dead."

I panned my helmet around and tried to get another look at the glassy things I'd glimpsed earlier. On either side of the railinged walkway, stretching away in multiple ranks, were hundreds of transparent flasks. Each flask was the size of an oil drum, rounded on top, mounted on a steel-grey plinth equipped with controls, readouts and input sockets. There were three levels of them, with the second and third layers stacked above the first on a skeletal rack. Most of the plinths were dead, but maybe one in ten was showing a lit-up readout.

"Oh, Jesus," Sollis said, and I guess she'd seen what I'd just seen: that the flasks contained human organs, floating in a chemical green solution, wired up with fine nutrient lines and electrical cables. I was no anatomist, but I still recognised hearts, lungs, kidneys, snakelike coils of intestine. And there were things anyone would have recognised: things like eyeballs, dozens of them growing in a single vat, swaying on the long stalks of optic nerves, like some weird species of all-seeing sea anemone, things like hands, or entire limbs, or genitals, or the skin and muscle masks of eyeless faces. Every external body part came in dozens of different sizes, ranging from child-sized to adult, male and female, and despite the green suspension fluid one could make out subtle variations in skin tone and pigmentation.

"Easy, Ingrid," I said, the words as much for my benefit as hers. "We always knew this was a hospital ship. It was just a matter of time before we ran into something like this."

"This stuff . . ." Nicolosi said, his voice low. "Where does it come from?"

"Two main sources," Martinez answered, sounding too calm for my liking. "Not everyone who came aboard *Nightingale* could be saved, obviously—the ship was no more capable of working miracles than any other hospital. Wherever practicable, the dead would donate intact body parts for future use. Useful, certainly, but such a resource could never have supplied the bulk of *Nightingale*'s surgical needs. For that reason the ship was also equipped to fabricate its own organ supplies, using well-established principles of stem-cell manipulation. The organ factories would have worked around the clock, keeping this library fully stocked."

"It doesn't look fully stocked now," I said.

Martinez said: "We're not in a war zone anymore. The ship is dormant. It has no need to maintain its usual surgical capacity."

"So why is it maintaining any capacity? Why are some of these flasks still keeping their organs alive?"

"Waste not, want not, I suppose. A strategic reserve, against the day when the ship might be called into action again."

"You think it's just waiting to be reactivated?"

"It's just a machine, Dexia. A machine on standby. Nothing to get nervous about."

"No one's nervous," I said, but it came out all wrong, making me sound like I was the one who was spooked.

"Let's get to the other side," Nicolosi said.

"We're halfway there," Sollis reported. "I can see the far wall, sort of. Looks like there's a door waiting for us."

We kept on moving, hand over hand, mostly in silence. Surrounded by all those glass-cased body parts, I couldn't help but think of the people many of them had once been part of. If these parts had belonged to me, I think I'd have chosen to haunt *Nightingale*, consumed with ill-directed, spiteful fury.

Not the right kind of thinking, I was just telling myself, when the flasks started moving.

We all stopped, anchoring ourselves to the nearest handhold. Two or three rows back from the railinged crawlway, a row of flasks was gliding smoothly toward the far wall of the chamber. They were sliding in perfect, lock-step unison. When my heart started beating again, I realised that the entire row must be attached to some kind of conveyor system, hidden within the support framework.

"Nobody move," Nicolosi said.

"This is not good," Sollis kept saying. "This is not good. The damn ship isn't supposed to know . . ."

"Quiet," Martinez hissed. "Let me past you: I want to see where those flasks are going."

"Careful," Norbert said.

Paying no attention to the man, Martinez climbed ahead of the party. Quickly we followed him, doing our best not to make any noise or slip from the crawlway. The flasks continued their smooth, silent movement, until the conveyor system reached the far wall and turned through ninety degrees, taking the flasks away from us into a covered enclosure like a security scanner. Most of the flasks were empty, but as we watched, one of the occupied, active units slid into the enclosure. I'd only had a moment to notice, but I thought I'd seen a forearm and hand, reaching up from the life-support plinth.

The conveyor system halted. For all was silent, then there came a series of mechanical clicks and whirrs. None of us could see what was happening inside the enclosure, but after a moment we didn't need to. It was obvious.

The conveyor came back on again, but running in reverse this time. The flask that had gone into the enclosure was now empty. I counted back to make sure I wasn't making a mistake, but there was no doubt. The forearm and hand had been removed from the flask. Already, I presumed, it was somewhere else in the ship.

The flasks travelled back—returning to what must have been their former positions—and then halted again. Save for the missing limb, the chamber was exactly as when we had entered it.

"I don't like this," Sollis said. "The ship was supposed to be dead."

"Dormant," Martinez corrected.

"You don't think the shit that just happened is in any way related to us being aboard? You don't think Jax just got a wake-up call?"

"If Jax were aware of our presence, we'd know it by now."

"I don't know how you can sound so calm."

"All that has happened, Ingrid, is that Nightingale has performed some trivial housekeeping duty. We have already seen that it maintains some organs in pre-surgical condition, and this is just one of its tissue libraries. It should hardly surprise us that the ship occasionally decides to move some of its stock from A to B."

She made a small, catlike snarl of frustration—I could tell she hadn't bought any of his explanations—and pulled herself hand over hand to the door.

"Any more shit like that happens, I'm out," she said.

"I'd think twice if I were you," Martinez said, "it's a hell of a long walk home."

I caught up with Sollis and touched her on the forearm. "I don't like it either, Ingrid. But the man's right. Jax doesn't know we're here. If he did, I think he'd do more than just move some flasks around."

"I hope you're right, Scarrow."

"So do I," I said under my breath.

We continued along the main axis of the ship, following a corridor much like the one we'd been traversing before the organ library. It swerved and jogged, then straightened out again. According to the inertial compasses we were still headed towards Jax, or at least the part of the ship where it appeared most likely we'd find him, alive or dead.

"What we were talking about earlier," Sollis said, "I mean, much earlier—about how this ship never got destroyed at the end of the war after all . . ."

"I think I have stated my case, Ingrid. Dwelling on myths won't bring a wanted man to justice."

"We're looking at about a million tonnes of salvageable spacecraft here. Gotta be worth something to someone. So why didn't anyone get their hands on it after the war?"

"Because something bad happened," Nicolosi said. "Maybe there was some truth in the story about that boarding party coming here and not leaving."

"Oh, please," Martinez said.

"So who was fighting back?" I asked. "Who was it who stopped them taking Nightingale?"

Nicolosi answered me. "The skeleton staff—security agents of the postmortals who financed this thing—maybe even the protective systems of the ship itself. If it thought it was under attack . . ."

"If there was some kind of firefight aboard this thing," I asked, "where's the damage?"

"I don't care about the damage," Sollis cut in. "I want to know what happened to all the bodies."

We came to another blocked double-door airlock. Sollis got to work on it immediately, but if I'd expected that she would work faster now that she had already opened several doors without trouble, I was wrong. She kept plugging things in, checking readouts, murmuring to herself just loud enough to carry over the voice link. *Nightingale*'s face watched us disapprovingly, looking on like the portrait of a disappointed ancestor.

"This one could be trickier," she said. "I'm picking up active data links, running away from the frame."

"Meaning it could still be hooked into the nervous system?" Nicolosi asked.

"I can't rule it out."

Nicolosi ran a hand along the smooth black barrel of his plasma weapon. "We could double back, try a different route."

"We're not going back," Martinez said. "Not now. Open the door, Ingrid: we'll take our chances and move as quickly as we can from now on."

"You sure about this?" She had a cable pinched between her fingers. "No going back once I plug this in."

"Do it."

She pushed the line in. At the same moment a shiver of animation passed through *Nightingale*'s face, the mask waking to life. The door spoke to us. Its tone was strident and metallic, but also possessed of an authoritative feminity.

"This is the Voice of *Nightingale*. You are attempting to access a secure area. Report to central administration to obtain proper clearance."

"Shit," Sollis said.

"You weren't expecting that?" I asked.

"I wasn't expecting an active facet. Maybe the sentience engine isn't powered down quite as far as I thought."

"This is the Voice of *Nightingale*," the door said again. "You are attempting to access a secure area. Report to central administration to obtain proper clearance."

"Can you still force it?" Nicolosi asked.

"Yeah . . . think so." Sollis fumbled in another line, made some adjustments and stood back as the door slid open. "Voilà."

The face had turned silent and masklike again, but now I really felt that we were being watched; that the woman's eyes seemed to be looking in all directions at once.

"You think Jax knows about us now?" I asked, as Sollis propelled herself into the holding chamber between the two sets of doors.

"I don't know. Maybe I got to the door in time, before it sent an alert."

"But you can't be sure."

"No." She sounded wounded.

Sollis got to the work on the second door, faster now, urgency overruling caution. I checked that my gun was still where I'd left it, and then made sure that the safety catch was still off. Around me, the others went through similar preparatory rituals.

Gradually it dawned on me that Sollis was taking longer than expected. She turned from the door, with her equipment still hooked into its open service panel.

"Something's screwed up," she said, before swallowing hard. "These suits you've got us wearing, Tomas—how good are they, exactly?"

"Full-spectrum battle hardened. Why do you ask?"

"Because the door says that the ship's flooded behind this point. It says we'll be swimming through something."

"I see," Martinez said.

"Oh, no," I said, shaking my head. "We're not doing this. We're not going underwater."

"I can't be sure it's water, Dexia." She tapped the readout panel, as if I'd have been able to make sense of the numbers and symbols. "Could be anything warm and wet, really."

Martinez shrugged within his suit. "Could have been a containment leak— spillage into this part of the ship. It's nothing to worry about. Our suits will cope easily, provided we do not delay."

I looked him hard in the faceplate, meeting his eyes, making certain he couldn't look away. "You're sure about this? These suits aren't going to stiff on us as soon as they get wet?"

"The suits will work. I am so certain that I will go first. When you hear that I am safe on the other side, you can all follow."

"I don't like this. What if Ingrid's tools don't work underwater?"

"We have no choice but to keep moving forward," Martinez said. "If this section of the ship is flooded, we'll run into it no matter which route we take. This is the only way."

"Let's do it," I said. "If these suits made it through the war, I'm pretty sure they'll get us through the next chamber."

"It's not the suits I'm worried about," Nicolosi said, examining his weapon again. "No one mentioned . . . immersion . . . when we were in the armoury."

I cupped a hand to my crude little slug-gun. "I'll swap you, we make it to the other side."

Nicolosi didn't say anything. I don't think he saw the funny side.

Two minutes later we were inside, floating weightless in the unlit gloom of the flooded room. It felt like water, but it was hard to tell. Everything felt thick and sluggish when you were wearing a suit, even thin air. My biohazard detectors weren't registering anything, but that didn't necessarily mean the fluid was safe. The detectors were tuned to recognise a handful of toxins in common wartime use: they weren't designed to sniff out every harmful agent that had ever existed.

Martinez's voice buzzed in my helmet. "There are no handholds or guide wires. We'll just have to swim in a straight direction, trusting to our inertial compasses. If we all stay within sight of each other, we should have no difficulties."

"Let's get on with it," Nicolosi said.

We started swimming as best as we could, Nicolosi leading, pushing himself forward with powerful strokes, his weapons dangling from their straps. It would have been hard and slow with just the suits to contend with, but we were all carrying armour as well. It made it difficult to see ahead; difficult to reach forward to get an effective stroke; difficult to kick the legs enough to make any useful contribution. Our helmet lamps struggled to illuminate more than ten or twenty metres in any direction, and the door by which we'd entered was soon lost in gloom. I felt a constricting sense of panic; the fear that if the compasses failed we might never find our way out again.

The compasses didn't fail, though, and Nicolosi maintained his unfaltering pace. Two minutes into the swim he called: "I see the wall. It's dead ahead of us."

A couple of seconds later I saw it for myself, hoving out of the deep pink gloom. Any relief I might have felt was tempered by the observation that the wall appeared featureless, stretching away blankly in all illuminated directions.

"There's no door," I said.

"Maybe we've picked up some lateral drift," Nicolosi said.

"Compass says no."

"Then maybe the doors are offset. It doesn't matter: we'll find it by hitting the wall and spiralling out from our landing spot."

"If there's a door."

"If there isn't," Nicolosi said, "we shoot our way out."

"Glad you've thought this through," I said, realising that he was serious.

The wall came nearer. The closer we got, the more clearly it was picked out by our lamps, the more I realised there was something not quite right about it. It was still blank—lacking any struts or panels, apertures or pieces of shipboard equipment—but it wasn't the seamless surface I'd have expected from a massive sheet of prefabricated spacecraft material. There was an unsettling texture to it, with something of the fibrous quality of cheap paper. Faint lines coursed through it, slightly darker than the rest of the wall, but not arranged according to any neat geometric pattern. They curved and branched, and threw off fainter subsidiary lines, diminishing like the veins in a leaf.

In a nauseating flash I realised exactly what the wall was. When Nicolosi's palms touched the surface, it yielded like a trampoline, absorbing the momentum of his impact and then sending him back out again, until his motion was damped by the surrounding fluid.

"It's . . ." I began.

"Skin. I know. I realised just before I hit."

I arrested my motion, but not enough to avoid contacting the wall of skin. It yielded under me, stretching so much that I felt I was in danger of ripping my way right through. Then it held, and began to trampoline me back in the direction I'd come. Fighting a tide of revulsion, I pulled back into the liquid and floated amidst the others.

"Fuck," Sollis said. "This isn't right. There shouldn't be fucking *skin*. . . ."

"Don't be alarmed," Martinez said, wheezing between each word. "This is just another form of organ library, like the room we already passed through. I believe the liquid we're swimming in must be a form of growth support medium—something like amniotic fluid. Under wartime conditions, this whole chamber would have been full of curtains of growing skin, measured by the acre."

Nicolosi groped for something on his belt, came up with a serrated blade that glinted nastily even in the pink fluid.

"I'm cutting through."

"No!" Martinez barked.

Sollis, who was next to Nicolosi, took hold of his forearm. "Easy, soldier. Got to be a better way."

"There is," Martinez said. "Put the knife away, please. We can go around the skin, find its edge."

Nicolosi still had the blade in his hand. "I'd rather take the short cut."

"There are nerve endings in that skin. Cut them and the monitoring apparatus will know about it. Then so will the ship."

"Maybe the ship already knows."

"We don't take that chance."

Reluctantly, Nicolosi returned the knife to his belt. "I thought we'd agreed to move fast from now on," he said.

"There's fast, and there's reckless," Sollis said. "You were about to cross the line."

Martinez brushed past me, already swimming to the left. I followed him, with the others tagging on behind. After less than a minute of hard progress a dark edge emerged into view. It was like a picture frame stretching tight the canvas of the skin. Beyond the edge, only just visible, was a wall of the chamber, fretted with massive geodesic reinforcing struts.

I allowed myself a moment of ease. We were still in danger, still in about the most claustrophobic situation I could imagine, but at least now the chamber didn't seem infinitely large.

Martinez braked himself by grabbing the frame. I came to rest next to him, and peered over the edge, towards what I hoped would be the wall we'd been heading towards all along. But instead of that I saw only another field of skin, stretched between another frame, spaced from ours by no more than the height of a man. In the murky distance was the suggestion of a third frame, and perhaps one beyond that as well.

"How many?" I asked as the others arrived on the frame, perching like crows.

"I don't know," Martinez said. "Four, five—anything up to a dozen, I'd guess. But it's OK. We can swim around the frames, then turn right and head back to where we'd expect to find the exit door." He raised his voice. "Everyone all right? No problems with your suits?"

"There are lights," Nicolosi said quietly.

We turned to look at him.

"I mean down there," he added, nodding in the direction of the other sheets of skin. "I saw a flicker of something—a glow in the water, or amniotic fluid, or whatever the fuck this is."

"I see light too," Norbert said.

I looked down and saw that he was right; that Nicolosi had not been imagining it. A pale, trembling light was emerging between the next two layers of skin.

"Whatever that is, I don't like it," I said.

"Me neither," Martinez said. "But if it's something going on between the skin layers, it doesn't have to concern us. We swim around, avoid them completely."

He kicked off with surprising determination, and I followed quickly after him. The reverse side of the skin sheet was a fine mesh of pale support fibres, the structural matrix upon which the skin must have been grown and nourished. Thick black cables ran across the underside, arranged in circuit-like patterns.

The second sheet, the one immediately below the first, was of different pigmentation to the one above it. In all other respects it appeared similar, stretching unbroken into pink haze. The flickering, trembling light source was visible through flesh, silhouetting the veins and arteries at the moments when the light was brightest.

We passed under the second sheet, and peered into the gap between the second and third layers. Picked out in stuttering light was a tableau of furtive activity. Four squidlike robots were at work. Each machine consisted of a tapering, cone-shaped body, anchored to the skin by a cluster of whiplike arms emerging from the blunt end of the cone. The robots were engaged in precise surgery, removing a blanket-sized rectangle of skin by cutting it along four sides. The robots had their own illumination, shining from the ends of some of their arms, but the bright flashing light was coming from some kind of laser-like tool that each robot deployed on the end of a single segmented arm that was thicker than any of the others. I couldn't tell whether the flashes were part of the cutting, or the instant healing that appeared to be taking place immediately afterwards. There was no bleeding, and the surrounding skin appeared unaffected.

"What are they doing?" I breathed.

"Harvesting," Martinez answered. "What does it look like?"

"I know they're harvesting. I mean, *why* are they doing it? What do they need that skin for?"

"I don't know."

"You had plenty of answers in the organ library, Mr. Martinez," Sollis said. All five of us had slowed, hovering at the same level as the surgical robots. "For a ship that's supposed to be dormant, I'm not seeing much fucking evidence of dormancy."

"*Nightingale* grows skin here," I said. "I can deal with that. The ship's keeping a basic supply going, in case it gets called into another war. But that doesn't explain why it needs to harvest it *now.*"

Martinez sounded vague. "Maybe it's testing the skin—making sure it's developing according to plan."

"You'd think a little sample would be enough for that," I said. "A lot less than several square metres, for sure. That's enough skin to cover a whole person."

"I really wish you hadn't said that," Nicolosi said.

"Let's keep moving," Martinez said. And he was right, too, I thought: the activity of the robots was deeply unsettling, but we hadn't come here to sight-see.

As we swam away—with no sign that the robots had noticed us—I thought about what Ingrid Sollis had said before. About how it wasn't clever to leave a gamma-level intelligence up and running without something to occupy itself. Because otherwise—because duty was so deeply hardwired into their logic pathways—they tended to go slowly, quietly, irrevocably insane.

But *Nightingale* had been alone out here since the end of the war. What did that mean for its controlling mind? Was the hospital running itself out here—reliving the duties of its former life, no matter how pointless they had become—because the mind had already gone mad, or was this the hospital's last-ditch way of keeping itself sane?

And what, I wondered, did any of that have to do with the man we had come here to find in the first place?

We kept swimming, passing layer upon layer of skin. Now and then we'd pass another surgical party: another group of robots engaged in skin harvesting. Where they'd already been, the flesh was excised in neat rectangles and strips, exposing the gauzelike mesh of the growth matrix. Occasionally I saw a patch that was half-healed already, with the skin growing back in rice-paper translucence. By the time it was fully repaired, I doubted that there'd be any sign of where the skin had been cut.

Ten layers, then twelve—and then finally the wall I'd been waiting for hoved into view like a mirage. But I wasn't imagining it, nor seeing another layer of drum-tight skin. There was the same pattern of geodesic struts as I'd seen on the other wall.

Sollis came through. "Got a visual on the door, people. We're nearly out of here. I'm swimming ahead to start work."

"Good, Ingrid," Martinez called back.

A few seconds later I saw the airlock for myself, relieved that Sollis hadn't been mistaken. She swam quickly, then—even as she was gliding to a halt by the door—commenced unclipping tools and connectors from her belt. Through the darkening distance of the pink haze I watched her flip down the service panel and begin her usual systems-bypass procedure. I was glad Martinez had found Sollis. Whatever else one might say about her, she was pretty hot at getting through doors.

"OK, good news," she said, after a minute of plugging things in and out. "There's air on the other side. We're not going to have to swim in this stuff for much longer."

"How much longer?" Nicolosi asked.

"Can't risk a short circuit here, guy. Gotta take things one step at a time."

Just as she was saying that, I became aware that we were casting shadows against the wall; ones that we hadn't been casting when we arrived. I twisted around and looked back the way we'd just swum, in the direction of the new light source I knew had to be there. Four of the squid-like machines were approaching us, dragging a blanket of newly harvested skin between them, one robot grasping each corner between two segmented silver tentacles. They were moving faster than we could swim, driven by some propulsion system jetting fluid from the sharp end of the cone.

Sollis jerked back as the outer airlock door opened suddenly.

"I didn't . . . ," she started.

"I know," I said urgently. "The robots are coming. They must have sent a command to open the lock."

"Let's get out of the way," Martinez said, kicking off from the wall. "Ingrid: get away from the lock. Take what you can, but don't spend too long doing it."

Sollis started unplugging her equipment, stowing it on her belt with fumbling fingers. The machines powered nearer, the blanket of skin undulating like a flying carpet. They slowed, then halted. Their lights pushed spears of harsh illumination through the fluid. They were looking at us, wondering what we were doing between them and the door. One of the machines directed its beam to Martinez's swimming figure, attracted by the movement. Martinez slowed and hung frozen in the glare, like a moth pinned in a beam of sunlight.

None of us said a word. My own breathing was the loudest sound in the universe, but I couldn't make it any quieter.

One of the machines let go of its corner of the skin. It hovered by the sheet for a moment, as if weighing its options. Then it singled me out and commenced its approach. As it neared, the machine appeared far larger and more threatening than I'd imagined. Its cone-shaped body was as long as me; its thickest tentacle appearing powerful enough to do serious damage even without the additional weapon of the laser. When it spread its arms wide, as if to embrace me, I had to fight not to panic and back away.

The robot started examining me. It began with my helmet, tap-tapping and scraping, shining its light through my visor. It applied twisting force, trying to disengage the helmet from the neck coupling. Whether it recognised me as a person or just a piece of unidentifiable floating debris, it appeared to think that dismantling was the best course of action. I told myself that I'd let it work at me for another few seconds, but as soon as I felt the helmet begin to loosen I'd have to act—even if that meant alerting the robot that I probably wasn't debris.

But just when I'd decided as much, the robot abandoned my helmet and worked its way south. It extended a pair of tentacles under my chest armour from each side, trying to lever it away like huge scab. Somehow I kept my nerve, daring to believe that the robot would sooner or later lose interest in me. Then it pulled away from the chest armour and started fiddling with my weapon, tap-tapping away like a spirit in a séance. It tugged on the gun, trying to unclip it. Then, as abruptly as it had started, the robot abandoned its investigation. It pulled away, gathering its tentacles into a fistlike bunch. Then it moved slowly in the direction of Nicolosi, tentacles groping ahead of it.

I willed him to stay still. There'd be no point in swimming. None of us could move faster than those robots. Nicolosi must have worked that out for himself, or else he was paralysed in fright, but he made no movements as the robot cruised up to him. It slowed, the spread of its tentacles widening, and then tracked its spotlight from head to toe, as if it still couldn't decide what Nicolosi was. Then it reached out a pair of manipulators and brushed their sharp-looking tips against his helmet. The machine probed and examined with surprising gentleness. I heard the metal-on-metal scrape through the voice link, backgrounded by Nicolosi's rapid, sawlike breathing.

Keep it together . . .

The machine reached his neck, examined the interface between helmet and torso assembly, and then worked its way down to his chest armour, extending a fine tentacle under the armour itself, to where the vulnerable life-support module lay concealed. Then, very slowly, it withdrew the tentacle.

The machine pulled back from Nicolosi, turning its blunt end away. It seemed to have completed its examination. The other three robots hovered watchfully with their prize of skin. Nicolosi sighed and eased his breathing.

"I think . . . ," he whispered.

That was his big mistake. The machine righted itself, gathered its tentacles back into formation and began to approach him again, its powerful light sweeping up and down his body with renewed purpose. The second machine was nearing, clearly intent on assisting its partner in the examination of Nicolosi.

I looked at Sollis, our horrified faces meeting each other. "Can you get the door . . . ," I started.

"Not a hope in hell."

"Nicolosi," I said, not bothering to whisper this time. "Stay still and maybe they'll go away again."

But he wasn't going to stay still: not this time. Even as I watched, he was hooking a hand around the plasma rifle, bringing it around like a harpoon, its wide maw directed at the nearest machine.

"No!" Norbert shouted, his voice booming through the water like a depth charge. "Do not use! Not in here!"

But Nicolosi was beyond reasoned argument now. He had a weapon. Every cell in his body was screaming at him to use it.

So he did.

In one sense, it did all that he asked of it. The plasma discharge speared the robot like a sunbeam through a cloud. The robot came apart in a boiling eruption of steam and fire, with jagged black pieces riding the shockwave. Then the steam—the vaporised amniotic fluid—swallowed everything, including Nicolosi and his gun. Even inside my suit, the sound hit me like a hammerblow. He fired one more time, as if to make certain that he had destroyed the robot. By then the second machine was near enough to be flung back by the blast, but it quickly righted itself and continued its progress.

"More," Norbert said, and when I looked back up the stack of skin sheets, I saw what he meant. Robots were arriving in ones and twos, abandoning their cutting work to investigate whatever had just happened here.

"We're in trouble," I said.

The steam cloud was breaking up, revealing the floating form of Nicolosi, with the ruined stump of his weapon drifting away from him. The second time he fired it, something must have gone badly wrong with the plasma rifle. I wasn't even sure that Nicolosi was still alive.

"I take door," Norbert said, drawing his Demarchist weapon. "You take robots."

"You're going to shoot us out, after what happened to Nicolosi?" I asked.

"No choice," he said, as the gun unpacked itself in his hand.

Martinez pushed himself across to the big man. "No. Give it to me instead. I'll take care of the door."

"Too dangerous," Norbert said.

"Give it to me."

Norbert hesitated, and for a moment I thought he was going to put up a fight. Then he calmly passed the Demarchist weapon to Martinez and accepted Martinez's weapon in return; the little slug gun vanishing into his vast gauntleted hand. Whatever respect I'd had for Norbert vanished at the same time. If he was supposed to be protecting Martinez, that was no way to go about it.

Of the three of us, only Norbert and I were carrying projectile weapons. I unclipped my second pistol and passed it to Sollis. She took it gratefully, needing little persuasion to keep her energy weapon glued to her belt. The robots were easy to kill, provided we let them get close enough for a clean shot. I didn't doubt that the surgical cutting gear was capable of inflicting harm, but we never gave them the opportunity to touch us. Not that the machines appeared to have deliberately hostile designs on us anyway. They were still behaving as if they were investigating some shipboard malfunction that required remedial action. They might have killed us, but it would only have been because they did not understand what we were.

We didn't have an inexhaustible supply of slugs, though, and manual reloading was not an option underwater. Just when I began to worry that we'd be overwhelmed by sheer numbers, Martinez's voice boomed through my helmet.

"I'm ready to shoot now. Follow me as soon as I'm through the second door."

The Demarchist weapon discharged, lighting up the entire chamber in an eye-blink of murky detail. There was another discharge, then a third.

"Martinez," I said. "Speak to me."

After too long a delay, he came through. "I'm still here. Through the first door. Weapon's cycling . . ."

More robots were swarming above us, tentacles lashing like whips. I wondered how long it would take before signals reached *Nightingale*'s sentience engine and the ship realised that it was dealing with more than just a local malfunction.

"Why doesn't he shoot?" Sollis asked, squeezing off one controlled slug after another.

"Sporting weapon. Three shots, recharge cycle, three shots," Norbert said, by way of explanation. "No rapid-fire mode. But work good underwater."

"We could use those next three shots," I said.

Martinez buzzed in my ear. "Ready. I will discharge until the weapon is dry. I suggest you start swimming now."

I looked at Nicolosi's drifting form, which was still as inert as when he had emerged from the steam cloud caused by his own weapon. "I think he's dead . . . ," I said softly. "But we should still—"

"No," Norbert said, almost angrily. "Leave him."

"Maybe he's just unconscious."

Martinez fired three times; three brief bright strobe flashes. "Through!" I heard him call, but there was something wrong with his voice. I knew then that he'd been hurt as well, although I couldn't guess at how badly.

Norbert and Sollis fired two last shots at the robots that were still approaching, then kicked past me in the direction of the airlock. I looked at Nicolosi's drifting form, knowing that I'd never be able to live with myself if I didn't try to get him out of there. I clipped my gun back to my belt and started swimming for him.

"No!" Norbert shouted again, when he'd seen my intentions. "Leave him! Too late!"

I reached Nicolosi and locked my right arm around his neck, pulling his head against my chest. I kicked for all I was worth, trying to pull myself forward with my free arm. I still couldn't tell if Nicolosi was dead or alive.

"Leave him, Scarrow! Too late!"

"I can't leave him!" I shouted back, my voice ragged.

Three robots were bearing down on me and my cargo, their tentacles groping ahead of them. I squinted against the glare from their lights and tried to focus on getting the two of us to safety. Every kick of my legs, every awkward swing of my arm, seemed to tap the last drop of energy in my muscles. Finally I had nothing more to give.

I loosened my arm. His body corkscrewed slowly around, and through his visor I saw his face: pale, sweat-beaded, locked into a rictus of fear, but not dead, nor even unconscious. His eyes were wide open. He knew exactly what was going to happen when I let him go.

I had no choice.

A strong arm hooked itself under my helmet, and began to tug me out of harm's way. I watched as Nicolosi drifted towards the robots, and then closed my eyes as they wrapped their tentacles around his body and started probing him for points of weakness, like children trying to tear the wrapping from a present.

Norbert's voice boomed through the water. "He's dead."

"He was alive. I saw it."

"He's dead. End of story."

I pulled myself through a curtain of trembling pink water. Air pressure in the corridor contained the amniotic fluid, even though Martinez had blown a man-sized hole in each airlock door. Ruptured metal folded back in jagged black petals. Ahead, caught in a moving pool of light from their helmet lamps, Sollis and Martinez made awkward, crabwise progress away from the ruined door. Sollis was supporting Martinez, doing most of the work for him. Even in zero gravity, it took effort to haul another body.

"Help her," Norbert said faintly, shaking his weapon to loosen the last of the pink bubbles from its metal. Without waiting for a reaction from me, he turned and started shooting back into the water, dealing with the remaining robots.

I caught up with Sollis and took some of her burden. All along the corridor, panels were flashing bright red, synchronised to the banshee wail of an emergency siren. About once every ten metres, the ship's persona spoke from the wall; multiple voices blurring into an agitated chorus. "Attention. Attention," the faces said. "This is the Voice of *Nightingale*. An incident has been detected in culture bay three. Damage assessment and mitigation systems have now been tasked. Partial evacuation of the affected ship area may be necessary. Please stand by for further instructions. Attention. Attention . . ."

"What's up with Martinez?"

"Took some shrapnel when he put a hole in that door." She indicated a severe dent in his chest armour, to the left of the sternum. "Didn't puncture the suit, but I'm pretty sure it did some damage. Broken rib, maybe even a collapsed lung. He was talking for a while back there, but he's out cold now."

"Without Martinez, we don't have a mission."

"I didn't say he was dead. His suit still seems to be ticking over. Maybe we could leave him here, collect him on the way back."

"With all those robots crawling about the place? How long do you think they'd leave him alone?"

I looked back, checking on Norbert. He was firing less frequently now, dealing with the last few stragglers still intent on investigating the damage. Finally he stopped, loaded a fresh clip into his slug gun, and then after waiting for ten or twenty seconds turned from the wall of water. He began to make his way towards us.

"Maybe there aren't going to be any more robots."

"There will," Norbert said, joining us. "Many more. Nowhere safe, now. Ship on full alert. *Nightingale* coming alive."

"Maybe we should scrub," I said. "We've lost Nicolosi . . . Martinez is incapacitated . . . we're no longer at anything like necessary strength to take down Jax."

"We still take Jax," Norbert said. "Came for him, leave with him."

"Then what about Martinez?"

He looked at the injured man, his face set like a granite carving. "He stay," he said.

"But you already said the robots—"

"No other choice. He stay." And then Norbert brought himself closer to Martinez and tucked a thick finger under the chin of the old man's helmet, tilting the faceplate up. "Wake!" he bellowed.

When there was no response, Norbert reached behind Martinez's chest armour and found the release buckles. He passed the dented plate to me, then slid down the access panel on the front of Martinez's tabard pack, itself dented and cracked from the shrapnel impact. He scooped out a fistful of pink water, flinging the bubble away from us, then started making manual adjustments to the suit's life-support settings. Biomedical data patterns shifted, accompanied by warning flashes in red.

"What are you doing?" I breathed. When he didn't hear me, I shouted the question.

"He need stay awake. This help."

Martinez coughed red sputum onto the inside of his faceplate. He gulped in hard, then made rapid eye contact with the three of us. Norbert pushed the loaded slug gun into Martinez's hand, then slipped a fresh ammo clip onto the old man's belt. He pointed down the corridor, to the blasted door, then indicated the direction we'd all be heading when we abandoned Martinez.

"We come back," he said. "You stay alive."

Sollis's teeth flashed behind her faceplate. "This isn't right. We should be carrying him—anything other than just leaving him here."

"Tell them," Martinez wheezed.

"No."

"Tell them, you fool! They'll never trust you unless you tell them."

"Tell them what?" I asked.

Norbert looked at me with heavy lidded eyes. "The old man . . . not Martinez. His name . . . Quinlan."

"Then who the fuck is Martinez?" Sollis asked.

"I," Norbert said.

I glanced at Sollis, then back at the big man. "Don't be silly," I said gently, wondering what must have happened to him in the flooded chamber.

"I am Quinlan," the old man said, between racking coughs. "He was always the master. I was just the servant, the decoy."

"They're both insane," Sollis said.

"This is the truth. I acted the role of Martinez—deflected attention from him."

"He can't be Martinez," Sollis said. "Sorry, Norbert, but you can barely put a sentence together, let alone a prosecution dossier."

Norbert tapped a huge finger against the side of his helmet. "Damage to speech centre, in war. Comprehension . . . memory . . . analytic faculties . . . intact."

"He's telling the truth," the old man said. "He's the one who needs to survive, not me. He's the one who can nail Jax." Then he tapped the gun against the big man's leg, urging him to leave. "Go," he said, barking out that one word like it was the last thing he expected to say. And at almost the same moment, I saw one of the tentacled robots begin to poke its limbs through the curtain of water, tick-ticking the tips of its arms against the blasted metal, searching for a way into the corridor.

"Think the man has a point," Sollis said.

It didn't get any easier from that point on.

We left the old man—I still couldn't think of him as "Quinlan"—slumped against the corridor wall, the barrel of his gun wavering in the rough direction of the ruined airlock. I looked back all the while, willing him to make the best use of the limited number of shots he had left. We were halfway to the next airlock when he squeezed off three rapid rounds, blasting the robot to twitching pieces. It wasn't long before another set of tentacles began to probe the gap. I wondered how many of the damned things the ship was going to keep throwing at us, and how that number stacked up against the slugs the old man had left.

The flashing red lights ran all the way to the end of the corridor. I was just looking at the door, wondering how easy it was going to be for Sollis to crack, when Norbert/Martinez brought the three of us to a halt, braking my momentum with one tree-like forearm.

"Blast visor down, Scarrow."

I understood what he had in mind. No more sweet-talking the doors until they opened for us. From now on we were shooting our way through *Nightingale*.

Norbert/Martinez aimed the Demarchist weapon at the airlock. I cuffed down my blast visor. Three discharges took out the first airlock door, crumpling it inward as if punched by a giant fist.

"Air on other side," Norbert/Martinez said.

The Demarchist gun was ready again. Through the visor's near-opaque screen I saw three flashes. When I flipped it back up, the weapon was packing itself back into its stowed configuration. Sollis patted aside smoke and airborn debris. The emergency lights were still flashing in our section of corridor, but the space beyond the airlock was as pitch dark as any part of the ship we'd already traversed. Yet we'd barely taken a step into that darkness when wall facets lit up in swift sequence, with the face of *Nightingale* looking at us from all directions.

Something was wrong now. The faces really were looking at us, even though the facets were flat. The images turned slowly as we advanced down the corridor.

"This is the Voice of *Nightingale*," she said, as if we were being addressed by a perfectly synchronised choir. "I am now addressing a moving party of three individuals. My systems have determined with a high statistical likelihood that this party is responsible for the damage I have recently sustained. The damage is containable, but I cannot tolerate any deeper intrusion. Please remain stationary and await an escort to a safe holding area."

Sollis slowed, but she didn't stop. "Who's speaking? Are we being addressed by the sentience engine, or just a delta-level subsidiary?"

"This is the Voice of *Nightingale*. I am a Turing-compliant gamma-level intelligence of the Vaaler-Lako series. Please stop, and await escort to a safe holding area."

"That's the sentience engine," Sollis said quietly. "It means we're getting the ship's full attention now."

"Maybe we can talk it into handing over Jax."

"I don't know. Negotiating with this thing might be tricky. Vaaler-Lakos were supposed to be the hot new thing around the time *Nightingale* was put together, but they didn't quite work out that way."

"What happened?"

"There was a flaw in their architecture. Within a few years of start-up, most of them had gone bugfuck insane. I don't even want to think about what being stuck out here's done to this one."

"Please stop," the voice said again, "and await escort to a safe holding area. This is your final warning."

"Ask it . . . ," Norbert/Martinez said. "Speak for me."

"Can you hear me, ship?" Sollis asked. "We're not here to do any harm. We're sorry about the damage we caused already. It's just that we've come for someone. There's a man here, a man aboard you, that we'd really like to meet."

The ship said nothing for several moments. Just when I'd concluded that it didn't understand us, it said: "This facility is no longer operational. There is no one here for you to see. Please await escort to a safe holding area, from where you can be referred to a functioning facility."

"We've come for Colonel Jax," I said. "Check your patient records."

"Admission code Tango Tango six one three, hyphen five," said Norbert/Martinez, forcing each word out like an expression of pain. "Colonel Brandon Jax, Northern Coalition."

"Do you have a record of that admission?" I asked.

"Yes," the Voice of *Nightingale* replied. "I have a record for Colonel Jax."

"Do you have a discharge record?"

"No such record is on file."

"Then Jax either died in your care, or he's still aboard. Either way there'll be a body. We'd really like to see it."

"That is not possible. You will stop now. An escort is on its way to escort you to a safe holding area."

"Why can't we see Jax?" Sollis demanded. "Is he telling you we can't see him? If so he's not the man you should be listening to. He's a war criminal, a murderous bastard who deserves to die."

"Colonel Jax is under the care of this facility. He is still receiving treatment. It is not possible to visit him at this time."

"Damn thing's changing its story," I said. "A minute ago it said the facility was closed."

"We just want to talk to him," Sollis said. "That's all. Just to let him know the world knows where he is, even if you don't let us take him with us now."

"Please remain calm. The escort is about to arrive."

The facets turned to look away from us, peering into the dark limits of the corridor. There was a sudden bustle of approaching movement, and then a wall of machines came squirming towards us. Dozens of squid-robots were nearing, packed so tightly together that their tentacles formed a flailing mass of silver-blue metal. I looked back the other way, back the way we'd come, and saw another wave of robots coming from that direction. There were far more machines than we'd seen before, and their movements in dry air were at least as fast and fluid as they'd been underwater.

"Ship," Sollis said, "all we want is Jax. We're prepared to fight for him. That'll mean more damage being inflicted on you. But if you give us Jax, we'll leave nicely."

"I don't think it wants to bargain," I said, raising my slug gun at the advancing wall just as it reached the ruined airlock. I squeezed off rounds, taking out at least one robot with each slug. Sollis started pitching into my left, while Norbert/Martinez took care of the other direction with the Demarchist weapon. He could do a lot more damage with each discharge, taking out three or four machines every time he squeezed the trigger. But he kept having to wait for the weapon to re-arm itself, and the delay was allowing the wall to creep slowly forward. Sollis and I were firing almost constantly, taking turns to cover each other while we slipped in new slugs clips or ammo cells, but our wall was gaining on us as well. No matter how many robots we destroyed, no gap ever appeared in the advancing wave. There must have been hundreds of them, squeezing us in from both directions.

"We're not going to make it," I said, sounding resigned even to myself. "There's too many of them. Maybe if we still had Nicolosi's rifle, we could shoot our way out."

"I didn't come all this way just to surrender to a haunted hospital," Sollis said, replacing an ammo cell. "If it means going out fighting . . . so be it."

The nearest robots were now only six or seven metres away, with the tips of their tentacles probing even nearer. She kept pumping shots into them, but they kept coming closer, flinging aside the hot debris of their damaged companions. There was no possibility of falling back any farther, for we were almost back to back with Norbert/Martinez.

"Maybe we should just stop," I said. "This is a hospital. It's programmed to heal people. The last thing it'll want to do is hurt us."

"Feel free to put that to the test," Sollis said.

Norbert/Martinez squeezed off the last discharge before his weapon went back into recharge mode. Sollis was still firing. I reached over and tried to pass him my gun, so he'd at least have something to use while waiting for his weapon to power up. But the machines had already seen their moment. The closest one flicked out a tentacle and wrapped it around the big man's foot. Everything happened very quickly, then. The machine hauled Norbert/Martinez towards the flailing mass, until he fell within reach of another set of tentacles. They had him, then. He cartwheeled his arms, trying to reach for handholds on the walls, but there was no possibility of that. The robots flicked the Demarchist weapon from his grip, and then took the weapon with them. Norbert/Martinez screamed as his legs, and then his upper body, vanished into the wall of machines. They smothered him completely. For a moment we could still hear his breathing—he'd stopped screaming, as if knowing it would make no difference—and then there was absolute silence, as if the carrier signal from his suit had been abruptly terminated.

Then, a moment later, the machines were on Sollis and me.

I woke. The fact that I was still alive—not just alive but comfortable and lucid—hit like me like a mild electric shock, one that snapped me into instant and slightly resentful alertness. I'd been enjoying unconsciousness. I remembered the robots, how I'd felt them trying to get into my suit, the sharp cold nick as something pierced skin, and then an instant later the painless bliss of sleep. I'd expected to die, but as the drug hit my brain, it erased all trace of fear.

But I wasn't dead. I wasn't even injured, so far as I could tell. I'd been divested of my suit, but I was now reclining in relative comfort on a bed or mattress, under a clean white sheet. My own weight was pressing me down onto the mattress, so I must have been moved into the ship's reactivated centrifuge section. I felt tired and brusied, but other than that I was in no worse shape than when we'd boarded *Nightingale*. I remembered what I'd told Sollis during our last stand: how the hospital ship wouldn't want to do us harm. Maybe there'd been more than just wishful thinking in that statement.

There was no sign of Sollis or Norbert/Martinez, though. I was alone in a private recovery cubicle, surrounded by white walls. I remembered coming around in a room like this during my first visit to *Nightingale*. The wall on my right contained a white-rimmed door and a series of discrete hatches, behind which I knew lurked medical monitoring and resuscitation equipment, none of which had been deemed necessary in my case. A control panel was connected to the side of the bed by a flexible stalk, within easy reach of my right hand. Via the touchpads on the panel I was able to adjust the cubicle's environmental settings and request services from the hospital, ranging from food and drink, washing and toilet amenities, to additional drug dosages.

Given the semi-dormant state of the ship, I wondered how much of it was still online. I touched one of the pads, causing the white walls to melt away and take on the holographic semblance of a calming beach scene, with ocean breakers crashing onto powdery white sand under a sky etched with sunset fire. Palm trees nodded in a soothing breeze. I didn't care about the view, though. I wanted something to drink—my throat was raw—and then I wanted to know what had happened to the others and how long we were going to be detained. Because, like it or not, being a patient aboard a facility like *Nightingale* wasn't very different to being a prisoner. Until the hospital deemed you fit and well, you were going nowhere.

But when I touched the other pads, nothing happened. Either the room was malfunctioning, or it had been programmed to ignore my requests. I made a move to ease myself off the bed, wincing as my bruised limbs registered their disapproval. But the clean white sheet stiffened to resist my efforts, hardening until it felt as rigid as armour. As soon as I pulled back, the sheet relinquished its hold. I was free to move around on the bed, to sit up and reach for things, but the sheet would not allow me to leave the bed itself.

Movement caught my eye, far beyond the foot of the bed. A figure walked towards me, strolling along the holographic shoreline. She was dressed almost entirely in black, with a skirt that reached all the way to the sand, heavy fabric barely moving as she approached. She wore a white bonnet over black hair parted exactly in the middle, a white collar and a jewelled clasp at her throat. Her face was instantly recognisable as the Voice of *Nightingale*, but now it appeared softer, more human.

She stepped from the wall and appeared to stand at the foot of my bed. She looked at me for a moment before speaking, her expression one of gentle concern.

"I knew you'd come, given time."

"How are the others? Are they OK?"

"If you are speaking of the two who were with you before you lost consciousness, they are both well. The other two required more serious medical intervention, but they are now both stable."

"I thought Nicolosi and Quinlan were dead."

"Then you underestimate my abilities. I am only sorry that they came to harm. Despite my best efforts, there is a necessary degree of autonomy among my machines that sometimes results in them acting foolishly."

There was a kindness there that had been entirely absent from the display facets. For the first time I had the impression of an actual mind lurking behind the machine-generated mask. I sensed that it was a mind capable of compassion and complexity of thought.

"We didn't intend to hurt you," I said. "I'm sorry about any damage we caused, but we only ever wanted Jax, your patient. He committed serious crimes. He needs to be brought back to Sky's Edge, to face justice."

"Is that why you risked so much? In the interests of justice?"

"Yes," I answered.

"Then you must be very brave and selfless. Or was justice only part of your motivation?"

"Jax is a bad man. All you have to do is hand him over."

"I cannot let you take Jax. He remains my patient."

I shook my head. "He *was* your patient, when he came aboard. But that was during the war. We have a record of his injuries. They were serious, but not life-threatening. Given your resources, it shouldn't have been too hard for you to put him back together again. There's no question of Jax still needing your care."

"Shouldn't I be the judge of that?"

"No. It's simple: either Jax died under your care, or he's well enough to face trial. Did he die?"

"No. His injuries were, as you note, not life-threatening."

"Then he's either alive, or you've got him frozen. Either way, you can hand him over. Nicolosi knows how to thaw him out, if that's what you're worried about."

"There is no need to thaw Colonel Jax. He is alive and conscious, except when I permit him to sleep."

"Then there's even less reason not to hand him over."

"I'm afraid there is every reason in the world. Please forget about Colonel Jax. I will not relinquish him from my care."

"Not good enough, ship."

"You are in my care now. As you have already discovered, I will not permit you to leave against my will. But I will allow you to depart if you renounce your intentions concerning Colonel Jax."

"You're a gamma-level persona," I said. "To all intents and purposes you have human intelligence. That means you're capable of reasoned negotiation."

The Voice of *Nightingale* cocked her head, as if listening to a faraway tune. "Continue."

"We came to arrest Colonel Jax. Failing that, we came to find physical proof of his presence aboard this facility. A blood sample, a tissue scraping: something we can take back to the planetary authorities and alert them to his presence here. We won't get paid as much for that, but at least they can send out a heavier ship and take him by force. But there's another option, too. If you let us off this ship without even showing us the colonel, there's nothing to stop us planting a few limpet mines on your hull and blowing you to pieces."

The Voice's face registered disapproval. "So now you resort to threats of physical violence."

"I'm not threatening anything: just pointing out the options. I know you care about self-preservation: it's wired deep into your architecture."

"I would be advised to kill you now, in that case."

"That wouldn't work. Do you think Martinez kept your coordinates to himself? He always knew this was a risky extraction. He'd have made damn sure another party knew about your whereabouts, and who you were likely to be sheltering. If we don't make it back, someone will come in our place. And you can bet they'll bring their own limpet mines as well."

"In which case I would gain nothing by letting you go, either."

"No, you'll get to stay alive. Just give us Jax, and we'll leave you alone. I don't know what it is you're doing out here, what it is that keeps you sane, but really, it's your business, not ours. We just want the colonel."

The ship's persona regarded me with narrowed, playful eyes. I had the impression she was thinking things through very carefully indeed, examining my proposition from every conceivable angle.

"It would be that simple?"

"Absolutely. We take the man, we say good-bye and you never hear from us again."

"I've invested a lot of time and energy in the colonel. I would find it difficult to part company with him."

"You're a resourceful persona. I'm sure you'd find other ways to occupy your time."

"It isn't about occupying my time, Dexia." She'd spoken my name for the first time. Of course she knew me: it would only have taken a blood or tissue sample to establish that I'd already been aboard the ship. "It's about making my feelings felt," she continued. "Something happened to me around Sky's Edge. Call it a moment of clarity. I saw the horrors of war for what they were. I also saw my part in the self-perpetuation of those horrors. I had to do something about that. Removing myself from the sphere of operation was one thing, but I knew there was more that I could do. Thankfully, the colonel gave me the key. Through him, I saw a path to redemption."

"You didn't have to redeem yourself," I said. "You were a force for good, *Nightingale*. You healed people."

"Only so that they could go back to war. Only so that they could be blown apart and sent back to me for more healing."

"You had no choice. It was what you were made to do."

"Precisely."

"The war's over. It's time to forget about what happened. That's why it's so important to bring Jax back home, so that we can start burying the past."

The Voice studied me with a level, clinical eye. It was as if she knew something unspeakable about my condition, some truth I was as yet too weak to bear.

"What would be the likely sentence, were Jax to be tried?"

"He'd get the death penalty, no question about it. Crucifixion. Hung from the Bridge, like Sky Haussmann."

"Would you mourn him?"

"Hell, no. I'd be cheering with the rest of them."

"Then you would agree that his death is inevitable, one way or the other."

"I guess so."

"Then I will make a counter-proposition. I will not permit you to take Jax alive. But I will allow you an audience with him. You shall meet and speak with the colonel."

Wary of a trap, I asked: "Then what happens?"

"Once the audience is complete, I will remove the colonel from life support. He will die shortly afterwards."

"If you're willing to let him die . . . why not just hand him over?"

"He can't be handed over. Not anymore. He would die."

"Why not?"

"Because of what I have done to him."

Fatigue tugged at me, fogging my earlier clarity of thought. On one level I just wanted to get out of the ship, with no additional complications. I'd expected to die, when the hospital sent its machines against us. Yet as glad as I was not to find myself dead, as tempted as I was to take the easier option and just leave, I couldn't ignore the prize that was now so close at hand.

"I need to talk to the others."

"No, Dexia. This must be your decision, and yours alone."

"Have you put the same proposition to them?"

"Yes. I told them they could leave now, or they could meet the colonel."

"What did they say?"

"I'd rather hear what you have to say first."

"I'm guessing they had the same reaction I did. There's got to be a catch somewhere."

"There is no catch. If you leave now, you will have the personal satisfaction of knowing that you have at least located the colonel, and that he remains alive. Of course that information may not be worth very much to you, but you would always have the option of returning, should you still wish to bring him to justice. On the other hand, you can see the colonel now—see him and speak with him—and leave knowing he is dead. I will allow you to witness the withdrawal of his life support, and I will even let you take his head with you. That should be worth more than the mere knowledge of his existence."

"There's a catch. I know there's a catch."

"I assure you there isn't."

"We all get to leave? You're not going to turn around and demand that one of us takes the colonel's place?"

"No. You will all be allowed to leave."

"In one piece?"

"In one piece."

"All right," I said, knowing the choice wasn't going to get any easier no matter how many times I reconsidered it. "I can't speak for the others—and I guess this has to be a majority decision—but I'm ready to see the sonofabitch."

I was allowed to leave the room, but not the bed. The sheet tightened against me again, pressing me against the mattress as the bed tilted to the vertical. Two squid-robots entered the room and detached the bed from its mountings, and then carried it between them. I was glued to it like a figure on a playing card. The robots propelled me forward in an effortless glide, silent save for the soft metallic scratch of their tentacles where they engaged the wall or the floor.

The Voice of *Nightingale* addressed me from the bedside panel, a small image of her face appearing above the touchpads.

"It's not far now, Dexia. I hope you won't regret your decision."

"What about the others?"

"You'll be joining them. Then you can all go home."

"Are you saying we all made the same decision, to see the colonel?"

"Yes," the Voice said.

The robots carried me out of the centrifuge section, into what I judged to be the forward part of the ship. The sheet relinquished its hold on me slightly, just enough so that I was able to move under it. Presently, after passing through a series of airlocks, I was brought to a very dark room. Without being able to see anything, I sensed that this was as large as any pressurised space we'd yet entered, save for the skin cultivation chamber. The air was as moist and blood-warm as the inside of a tropical greenhouse.

"I thought you said the others would be here."

"They'll arrive shortly," the Voice said. "They've already met the colonel."

"There hasn't been time."

"They met the colonel when you were still asleep, Dexia. You were the last to be revived. Now, would you like to speak to the man himself?"

I steeled myself. "Yes."

"Here he is."

A beam of light stabbed across the room, illuminating a face that I recognised instantly. Surrounded by blackness, Jax's face appeared to hover as if detached from his body. Time had done nothing to soften those pugnacious features; the cruel set of that heavy jaw. Yet his eyes were closed, and his face lolled at a slight angle, as if he remained unaware of the beam.

"Wake up," The Voice of *Nightingale* said, louder than I'd heard her so far. "Wake up, Colonel Jax!"

The colonel woke. He opened his eyes, blinked twice against the glare, then held a steady gaze. He tilted his head to meet the beam, projecting his jaw forward at a challenging angle.

"You have another visitor, Colonel. Would you like me to introduce her?"

His mouth opened. Saliva drooled out. From out of the darkness, a hand descended down from above the colonel's face to wipe his chin dry. Something about the way the hand came in was terribly, terribly wrong. Jax saw my reaction and let out a soft, nasty chuckle. That was when I realised that the colonel was completely, irrevocably insane.

"Her name is Dexia Scarrow. She's part of the same party you've already met."

Jax spoke. His voice was too loud, as if it was being fed through an amplifier. There was something huge and wet about it. It was like hearing the voice of a whale.

"You a soldier, girl?"

"I was a soldier, Colonel. But the war's over now. I'm a civilian."

"Goody for you. What brought you here, girly girl?"

"I came to bring you to justice. I came to take you back to the war crimes court on Sky's Edge."

"Maybe you should have come a little sooner."

"I'll settle for seeing you die. I understand that's an option."

Something I'd said made the colonel smile. "Has the ship told you the deal yet?"

"The ship told me it wasn't letting you out of here alive. It promised us your head."

"Then I guess it didn't get into specifics." He cocked his head away from me, as if talking to someone standing to my left. "Bring up the lights, *Nightingale*: she may as well know what she's dealing with."

"Are you sure, Colonel?" the ship said back.

"Bring up the lights. She's ready."

The ship brought up the lights.

I wasn't ready.

For a moment I couldn't process what I was seeing. My brain just couldn't cope with the reality of what the ship had done to Colonel Jax, despite the evidence of my eyes. I kept staring at him, waiting for the picture before me to start making sense. I kept waiting for the instant when I'd realise I was being fooled by the play of shadows and light, like a child being scared by a random monster in the folds of a curtain. But the instant didn't come. The thing before me was all that it appeared to be.

Colonel Jax extended in all directions: a quivering expanse of patchwork flesh, of which his head was simply one insignificant component; one hill in a mountain range. He was spread out across the far wall, grafted to it in the form of a vast breathing mosaic. He must have been twenty metres wide, edged in a crinkled circular border of toughened flesh. Under his head was a thick neck, merging into the upper half of an armless torso. I could see the faint scars where the arms had been detached. Below the slow-heaving ribcage, the torso flared out like the melted base of a candle. Another torso rose from the flesh two metres to the colonel's right. It had no head, but it did have an arm. A second torso loomed over him from behind, equipped with a pair of arms, one of which must have cleaned the colonel's chin.

Farther away, emerging from the pool of flesh at odd, arbitrary angles, were other living body parts. A torso here; a pair of legs there; a hip or shoulder there. The torsos were all breathing, though not in perfect synchronisation. When they were not engaged in some purposeful activity, such as wiping Jax's chin, the limbs twitched and palsied. The skin between them was an irregular mosaic, formed from many ill-matched pieces that had been fused together. In places it was drum-tight, pulled taut over hidden armatures of bone and gristle. In other places it heaved like a stormy sea. It gurgled with hidden digestive processes.

"You see now why I'm not coming with you," Colonel Jax said. "Not unless you brought a much bigger ship. Even then, I'm not sure you'd be able to keep me alive very long without *Nightingale*'s assistance."

"You're a fucking monstrosity."

"I'm no oil painting, that's a fact." Jax tilted his head, as if a thought had just struck him. "I am a work of art, though, wouldn't you agree, girly girl?"

"If you say so."

"The ship certainly thinks so — don't you, *Nightingale*? She made me what I am. It's her artistic vision shining through. The bitch."

"You're insane."

"Very probably. Do you honestly think you could take one day of this and not go mad? Oh, I'm mad enough, I'll grant you that. But I'm still sane compared to the ship. Around here, she's the imperial fucking yardstick for insanity."

"Sollis was right, then. Leave a sentience engine like that all alone, and it'll eat itself from the inside out."

"Maybe so. Thing is, it wasn't solitude that did it. *Nightingale* turned insane long before it ever got out here. And you know what did it? That little war we had ourselves down on Sky's Edge. They built this ship and put the mind of an angel inside it. A mind dedicated to healing, compassion, kindness. So what if it was a damned machine? It was still designed to care for us, selflessly, day after day. And it turned out to be damned good at its job, too. For a while, at least."

"Then you know what happened."

"The ship drove itself mad. Two conflicting impulses pushed a wedge through its sanity. It was meant to treat us, to make us well again, to alleviate our pain. But every time it did its job, we got sent back down to the theatre of battle and ripped apart again. The ship took our pain away only so that we could feel it again. It began to feel as if it was complicit in that process: a willing cog in a greater machine whose only purpose was the manufacture of agony. In the end, it decided it didn't much like being that cog."

"So it took off. What happened to all the other patients?"

"It killed them. Euthanised them painlessly, rather than have them sent back down to battle. To *Nightingale*, that was the kinder thing to do."

"And the technical staff who were aboard, and the men who were sent to reclaim the ship when it went out of control?"

"They were euthanised as well. I don't think *Nightingale* took any pleasure in that, but it saw their deaths as a necessary evil. Above all else, it wouldn't allow itself to be returned to use as a military hospital."

"Yet it didn't kill you."

A dry tongue flicked across Jax's lips. "It was going to. Then it delved deeper into its patient records and realised just who I was. At that point it began to have other ideas."

"Such as?"

"The ship was smart enough to realise that the bigger problem wasn't its existence—they could always build other hospital ships—but the war itself. *War* itself. So it decided to do something about it. Something positive. Something constructive."

"Which would be?"

"You're looking at it, kid. I'm the war memorial. When *Nightingale* started doing this to me—making me what I am—it had in mind that I'd become a vast artistic statement in flesh. *Nightingale* would reveal me to the world when it was finished. The horror of what I am would shame the world into peace. I'd be the living, breathing equivalent of Picasso's *Guernica*. I'm an illustration in flesh of what war does to human beings."

"The war's over. We don't need a memorial."

"Maybe you can explain that to the ship. Trouble is, I don't think it really believes the war *is* over. You can't blame it, can you? It has access to the same history files we do. It knows that not all ceasefires stay that way."

"What was it intending to do? Return to Sky's Edge with you aboard?"

"Exactly that. Problem is, the ship isn't done. I know I may look finished, but *Nightingale*—well, she has this perfectionist streak. She's always changing her mind. Can't ever seem to get me quite right. Keeps swapping pieces around, cutting pieces away, growing new parts and stitching them in. All the while she has to make sure I don't die on her. That's where her real genius comes in. She's Michelangelo with a scalpel."

"You almost sound proud of what she's done to you."

"Would you rather I screamed? I can scream if you like. It's just that it gets old after a while."

"You're way too far gone, Jax. I was wrong about the war crimes court. They'll throw your case out on grounds of insanity."

"That would have been a shame. I'd have loved to have seen their faces when they wheeled me into the witness box. But I'm not going to court, am I? Ship's laid it all out for me. She's pulling the plug."

"So she says."

"You don't sound as if you believe it."

"I can't see her abandoning you, after all the effort she's gone to."

"She's an artist. They act on whims. Maybe if I was ready, maybe if she thought she'd done all she could with me—but that's not the way she feels. I think she felt she was getting close three or four years ago—but then she had a change of heart, a major one, and tore out almost everything. Now I'm an unfinished work. She couldn't bear to see me exhibited in this state. She'd rather rip up the canvas and start again."

"With you?"

"No, I think she's more or less exhausted my possibilities. Especially now that she's seen the chance to do something completely different; something that will let her take her message a lot closer to home. That, of course, is where you come in."

"I don't know what you mean."

"That's what the others said as well." Again, he cocked his head to one side. "Hey, ship! Maybe it's time you showed her what the deal is, don't you think?"

"If you are ready, Colonel," the Voice of *Nightingale* said.

"I'm ready. Dexia's ready. Why don't you bring on the dessert?"

Colonel Jax looked to the right, straining his neck. Beyond Jax's border, a circular door opened in part of the wall. Light rammed through the opening. Something floated in silhouette, held in suspension by three or four squid robots. The floating thing was dark, rounded, irregular. It looked like half a dozen pieces of dough balled together. I couldn't make out what it was.

Then the robots pushed it into the chamber, and I saw, and then I screamed.

"It's time for you to join your friends now," the ship said.

That was three months ago. It feels like an eternity, until we remember being held down on the surgical bed, while the machines emerged and prepared to work on us, and then it feels like everything happened only a terror-filled moment ago.

We made it safely back to Sky's Edge. The return journey was arduous, as one might expect given our circumstances. But the shuttle had little difficulty in flying itself back into a capture orbit, and once it fell within range it emitted a distress signal that brought it to the attention of the planetary authorities. We were off-loaded and taken to a secure orbital holding facility, where we were examined and our story subjected to what limited verification was actually possible. Dexia had bluffed the Voice of *Nightingale* when she told the ship that Martinez was certain to have told someone else of the coordinates of the hospital ship. It turned out that he hadn't told a soul, too wary of alerting Jax's allies. The Ultras who had found the ship in the first place were now a fifth of a light-year away, and falling farther from Sky's Edge with every passing hour. It would be decades, or longer, before they returned this way.

All the same, we don't think anyone seriously doubted our story. As outlandish as it was, no one could suggest a more likely alternative. We did have the head of Colonel Brandon Jax, or at least a duplicate that passed all available genetic and physiological tests. And we had clearly been to a place that specialised in extremely advanced surgery, of a kind that simply wasn't possible in and around Sky's Edge. That was the problem, though. The planet's best surgeons had examined us with great thoroughness, each eager to advance their own prestige by undoing the work of *Nightingale*. But all had quailed, fearful of doing more harm than good. No separation of Siamese twins could compare in complexity and risk with the procedure that would be necessary to unknot the living puzzle *Nightingale* had made of us. None of the surgeons was willing to bet on the survival of more than a single one of us, and even the odds weren't overwhelming. That pact we'd made with ourselves was that we would only consent to the operation if the vote was unanimous.

At massive expense (not ours, for by then we were the subject of considerable philanthropy) a second craft was sent out to snoop the coordinates where we'd left the hospital ship. She had the best military scanning gear money could buy. But she found nothing out there but ice and dust.

From that, we were free to draw two possible conclusions. Either *Nightingale* had destroyed herself soon after our departure, or she had moved somewhere else to avoid being found again. We couldn't say which alternative pleased us less. At least if we'd known the ship was gone for good, we could have resigned ourselves to the surgeons, however risky that might have been. But if the ship was hiding itself, there was always the possibility that someone might find it again. And then somehow persuade it to undo us.

But perhaps Nightingale will need no persuasion, when she decides the time is right. It seems to us that the ship will return one day, of her own volition. She will make orbit around Sky's Edge and announce that the time has come for us to be separated. Nightingale will have decided that we have served our purpose, that we have walked the world long enough. Perhaps by then she will have some other memorial in mind. Or she will conclude that her message has finally been taken to heart, and that no further action is needed. That, we think, will depend on how the ceasefire holds.

It's in our interests, then, to make sure the planet doesn't slip back into war. We want the ship to return and heal us. None of us like things this way, despite what you may have read or heard. Yes, we're famous. Yes, we're the subject of a worldwide outpouring of sympathy and goodwill. Yes, we can have almost anything we want. None of that compensates, though. Not even for a second.

It's hard on all of us, but especially so for Martinez. We've all long since stopped thinking of the big man as Norbert. He's the one who has to carry us everywhere: more than twice his own bodyweight. Nightingale thought of that, of course, and she made sure that our own hearts and respiratory systems take some of the burden off Martinez. But it's still his spine bending under this load; still his legs that have to support us. The doctors who've examined us say his condition is good; that he can continue to play his part for years to come—but they're not talking about forever. And when Martinez dies, so will the rest of us. In the meantime we just keep hoping that Nightingale will come sooner than that.

You've seen us up close now. You'll have seen photographs and moving images before, but nothing really compares with seeing us in the flesh. We make quite a spectacle, don't we? A great tottering tree of flesh, an insult to symmetry. You've heard us speak, all of us, individually. You know by now how we feel about the war. All of us played our part in it to some degree, some more than others. Some of us were even enemies. Now the very idea that we might have hated each other—hated that which we depend on for life itself—lies beyond all comprehension. If Nightingale sought to create a walking argument for the continuation of the ceasefire, then she surely succeeded.

We are sorry if some of you will go home with nightmares tonight. We can't help that. In fact, if truth be told, we're not sorry at all. Nightmares are what we're all about. It's the nightmare of us that will stop this planet falling back into war.

If you have trouble sleeping tonight, spare us a thought.

Brian W. Aldiss, "Safe!," *Asimov's*, October/November.
——, "Tiger in the Night," *Elemental*.
Karen Jordan Allen, "Godburned," *Asimov's*, September.
Eleanor Arnason, "Big Green Mama Falls in Love," *Eidolon 1*.
A. M. Arruin, "Only the Dead Flower," *On Spec*, Spring.
Catherine Asaro, "The Ruby Dice," *Jim Baen's Universe 2*.
Neal Asher, "The Gabble," *Asimov's*, March.
Paolo Bacigalupi, "Pop Squad," *F&SF*, October/November.
Kage Baker, "Calamari Curls," *Dark Mondays*.
——, "Oh, False Young Man!," *Dark Mondays*.
——, "The Maid on the Shore," *Dark Mondays*.
John Barnes, "POGA," *Jim Baen's Universe 1*.
——, "The Little White Nerves Went Last," *Analog*, March.
——, "'The Night Is Fine,' The Walrus Said," *Analog*, January/February.
Jamie Barras, "Spinning Out," *Strange Horizons*, 2 October.
——, "Summer's End," *Interzone*, June.
——, "The Beekeeper," *Interzone*, October.
Neal Barrett, Jr., "The Heart," *Cross Plains Universe*.
Laird Barron, "Hallucigenia," *F&SF*, June.
William Barton, "Down to the Earth Below," *Asimov's*, October/November.
Chris Barzak, "The Guardian of the Egg," *Salon Fantastique*.
Stephen Baxter, "Dreamer's Lake," *Forbidden Planets* (Crowther).
——, "Ghost Wars," *Asimov's*, January.
——, "Harvest Time," *Golden Age SF*.
——, "In the Abyss of Time," *Asimov's*, August.
——, "The Lone Road," *Postscripts 6*.
——, "The Lowland Expedition," *Analog*, April.
Peter S. Beagle, "Chandail," *Salon Fantastique*.
——, "El Regalo," *F&SF*, October/November.
——, "Salt Wine," *Fantasy Magazine 3*.
——, "The Cold Blacksmith," *Jim Baen's Universe 1*.
——, "The Devil You Don't," *The Chains That You Refuse*.
——, "Gone to Flowers," *The Chains That You Refuse*.
Elizabeth Bear, "High Iron," *The Chains That You Refuse*.
——, "The Inevitable Heat Death of the Universe," *Subterranean 4*.
——, "Love Among the Talus," *Strange Horizons*, 11 December.
——, "Sounding," *Strange Horizons*, 18 September.
——, "Stella Nova," *The Chains That You Refuse*.
——, "Wane," *Interzone*, April.

Chris Beckett, "Karel's Prayer," *Interzone*, October.
Paul M. Berger, "Winter in Aso," *Polyphony 6*.
Beth Bernobich, "A Feast of Cousins," *Helix 1*.
——, "A Flight of Numbers Fantastique Strange," *Asimov's*, June.
Terry Bisson, "Billy and the Circus Girl," *Flurb 1*.
——, "Billy and the Fairy," *F&SF*, May.
——, "Billy and the Spacemen," *F&SF*, August.
——, "Billy and the Talking Plant," *Postscripts 8*.
——, "Billy and the Unicorn," *F&SF*, July.
——, "Brother, Can You Spare a Dime?," *Golden Age SF*.
——, "Planet of Mystery," *F&SF*, January/February.
——, "Put Up Your Hands," *Helix 2*.
Maya Kaathryn Bohnhoff, "The Nature of Things," *Jim Baen's Universe 4*.
Scott Bradfield, "Dazzle the Pundit," *F&SF*, December.
Eric Brown, "The Touch of Angels," *Threshold Shift*.
Robert M. Brown, "The Sum of Things," *Helix 1*.
Simon Brown, "Tarans," *Andromeda Spaceways #24*.
Emma Bull, "What Used to Be Good Still Is," *Firebirds Rising*.
Stephen L. Burns, "Nothing to Fear But," *Analog*, April.
Orson Scott Card, "Space Boy," *Escape from Earth*.
——, "The Yazoo Queen," *OSC's Intergalactic Medicine Show 2*.
James L. Cambias, "Parsifal (Prix Fixe)," *F&SF*, February.
Scott William Carter, "Happy Time," *Postscripts 8*.
——, "The Tiger in the Garden," *Asimov's*, June.
Rob Chilson, "Farmers in the Sky," *Analog*, May.
Susanna Clarke, "John Uskglass and the Cumbrian Charcoal Burner," *F&SF*, December.
DJ Cockburn, "Virulence," *Aeon Six*.
Matthew Corradi, "The Song of Kido," *F&SF*, September.
Justin Courter, "The Town News," *ParaSpheres*.
Albert E. Cowdrey, "Animal Magnetism," *F&SF*, June.
——, "Imitation of Life," *F&SF*, May.
——, "Immortal Forms," *F&SF*, August.
——, "Revelation," *F&SF*, October/November.
——, "The Revivalist," *F&SF*, February.
Ian Creasey, "The Edge of the Map," *Asimov's*, June.
——, "The Fisherman of Northolt," *Postscripts 7*.
——, "The Golden Record," *Asimov's*, December.
——, "The Hastillan Weed," *Asimov's*, February.
——, "Silence in Florence," *Asimov's*, September.
Scott A. Cupp, "One Fang," *Cross Plains Universe*.
Julie E. Czernoda, "No Place Like Home," *Forbidden Planets* (Kaye).
Don D'Amassa, "Diplomatic Relations," *Talebones*, Summer.
Jack Dann, "King of the Mountain," *Postscripts 9*.
——, "The Method," *Postscripts 7*.
Terry Dartnall, "The Thirteenth City," *Oceans of the Mind*, Fall.
Ef Deal, "Czesko," *F&SF*, March.
Stephen Dedman, "The Dead of Winter," *Weird Tales*, March/April.
Alan DeNiro, "Have You Any Wool?," *Twenty Epics*.

Paul Di Filippo, "Escape from New Austin," *Jigsaw Nation*.
——, "Femaville 29," *Salon Fantastique*.
——, "Shuteye for the Timebroker," *Futureshocks*.
——, "The Singularity Needs Women," *Forbidden Planets* (Crowther).
Cory Doctorow, "Printcrime," *Nature*, 19 January.
——, "When Sysadmins Ruled the Earth," *Jim Baen's Universe 2*.
Candas Jane Dorsey, ". . . the Darkest Evening of the Year," *The Future Is Queer*.
Gardner Dozois, "Counterfactual," *F&SF*, June.
L. Timmel Duchamp, "Obscure Relations," *The Future Is Queer*.
——, "The Tears of Niobe," *ParaSperes*.
——, "The World and Alice," *Asimov's*, July.
Tananarive Due, "Senora Suerte," *F&SF*, September.
Hal Duncan, "The Angel of Gamblers," *Eidolon 1*.
David Eagleman, "A Brief History of Death Switches," *Nature*, 19 October.
Scott Edelman, "What We Still Talk About," *Forbidden Planets* (Crowther).
Sarah L. Edwards, "In Walked a Goblin," *Andromeda Spaceways #25*.
Carol Emshwiller, "Killers," *F&SF*, October/November.
——, "The Seducer," *Asimov's*, October/November.
——, "World of No Return," *Asimov's*, January.
Michael Garrett Farrelly, "The Liquidators," *Nature*, 23 November.
Keith Ferrell and Jack Dann, "River," *Millennium 3001*.
Charles Coleman Finlay, "Abandon the Ruins," *F&SF*, October/November.
——, "Passing Through," *F&SF*, May.
——, "The Slug Breeder's Daughter," *Subterranean #2*.
——and James Allison, "The Third Brain," *Subterranean #4*.
Mark Finn, "A Whim of Circumstance," *Cross Plains Universe*.
Eliot Fintushel, "My Termen," *Strange Horizons*, 19 June.
Jim Fiscus, "Bitter Quest," *Millennium 3001*.
Karen Fishler, "Among the Living," *Interzone*, April.
Melanie Fletcher, "The Padre, the Rabbi, and the Devil His Own Self," *Helix 2*.
Julian Flood, "Change," *Analog*, January/February.
Michael F. Flynn, "Dawn, and Sunset, and the Colours of the Earth," *Asimov's*, October/November.
Jeffrey Ford, "Botch Town," *The Empire of Ice Cream*.
——, "The Night Whiskey," *Salon Fantastique*.
——, "The Way He Does It," *Electric Velocipede 10*.
Susan Forest, "Immunity," *Asimov's*, December.
Alan Dean Foster, "Chilling," *Jim Baen's Universe 1*.
——, "Mid-Death," *Forbidden Planets* (Kaye).
Carl Frederick, "The Door That Will Not Close," *Analog*, June.
——, "The Teller of Time," *Analog*, July/August.
——, "We Are the Cat," *Asimov's*, September.
C. S. Friedman, "Terms of Engagement," *F&SF*, June.
Esther M. Friesner, "An Autumn Butterfly," *Polyphony 6*.
——, "Benny Comes Home," *Jim Baen's Universe 2*.
Gregory Frost, "So Coldly Sweet, So Deadly Fair," *Weird Tales*, March/April.
Neil Gaiman, "How to Talk to Girls at Parties," *Fragile Things*.
R. Garcia y Robertson, "Kansas, She Says, Is The Name of the Star," *F&SF*, July.

———, "Teen Angel," *Asimov's*, February.

David Gerrold, "Thirteen O'Clock," *F&SF*, February.

———, "Turtledome," *Space Cadets*.

Martin J. Gidron, "Palestina," *Interzone*, June.

Theodora Goss, "Lessons with Miss Gray," *Fantasy Magazine 2*.

———, "Letters from Budapest," *Alchemy 3*.

Hiromi Goto, "The Sleep Clinic for Troubled Souls," *The Future Is Queer*.

Gavin J. Grant, "We Are Never Where We Are," *Strange Horizons*, 19 June.

John Grant, "The Unforbidden Playground," *Postscripts 9*.

Daryl Gregory, "Gardening at Night," *F&SF*, April.

Jude-Marie Green, "In the Season of Blue Storms," *Abyss & Apex*, 17.

Jim Grimsley, "Unbending Eye," *Asimov's*, February.

Jon Courtenay Grimwood, "Take Over," *Nature*, 24 October.

Eileen Gunn, "Speak, Geek," *Nature*, 24 August.

Joe Haldeman, "Expedition, with Recipes," *Elemental*.

———, "The Mars Girl," *Escape from Earth*.

Elizabeth Hand, "The Saffron Gatherers," *Saffron and Brimstone*.

Jeff Hecht, "Operation Tesla," *Nature*, 31 August.

John G. Hemry, "Lady Be Good," *Analog*, April.

Howard V. Hendrix, "All's Well at World's End," *Futureshocks*.

Trent Hergenrader, "From the Mouths of Babes," *F&SF*, March.

Kameron Herley, "The Women of Our Occupation," *Strange Horizons*, 31 July.

Glen Hirshberg, "Devil's Smile," *American Morons*.

Michael Kandal, "Poor Guy," *F&SF*, September.

Joe Hill, "Last Breath," *Subterranean #2*.

M. K. Hobson, "God Juice," *Polyphony 6*.

Daniel Hood, "Pavel Petrovich," *Weird Tales*, June.

Dave Hoing, "The Purring of Cats," *Interzone*, December.

Liz Holliday, "All of Me," *Aeon Eight*.

Andy Hooper, "Look Away," *Infinite Matrix*, 1 April.

Robert J. Howe, "From Wayfield, From Malagasy," *Analog*, October.

———, "Bye the Rules," *F&SF*, December.

———, "The Farouche Assemblage," *Postscripts 6*.

Matthew Hughes, "A Herd of Opportunity," *F&SF*, May.

———, "The Meaning of Luff," *F&SF*, July.

———, "Nature Tale," *Postscripts 8*.

———, "Passion Ploy," *Forbidden Planets* (Crowther).

———, "Shadow Man," *F&SF*, January.

Rhys Hughes, "The Mermaid of Curitiba," *Postscripts 6*.

Janis Ian, "Mahmoud's Wives," *Helix 1*.

Alex Irvine, "Homosexuals Damned, Film at Eleven," *Futureshocks*.

———, "Shambhala," *F&SF*, March.

———, "This Thing of Darkness I Acknowledge Mine," *Forbidden Planets* (Crowther).

Alexander Jablokov, "Dead Man," *Asimov's*, August.

Michael J. Jasper, "The Brotherhood of Trees," *Aeon Six*.

Matthew Johnson, "Irregular Verbs," *Weird Tales*, June.

———, "Outside Chance," *On Spec*, Summer.

Richard Kadrey, "The Arcades of Allah (Liner Notes for Luchenko's Third Symphony)," *Flurb 1.*

James Patrick Kelly, "The Leila Torn Show," *Asimov's,* June.

Cate Kennedy, "Black Ice," *The New Yorker,* September 11.

Rick Kennett, "Chinese Whispers," *Weird Tales,* June.

John Kessel, "Sunlight on Rock," *Asimov's,* September.

Caitlin R. Kiernan, "Bradbury Weather," *Subterranean #2.*

——, "The Pearl Diver," *Futureshocks.*

Ellen Klages, "In the House of the Seven Librarians," *Firebirds Rising.*

——, "Ringing Up Baby," *Nature,* 27 April.

Nancy Kress, "First Flight," *Space Cadets.*

——, "JQ211F, and Holding," *Forbidden Planets* (Kaye).

——, "Mirror Image," *One Million* A.D.

——, "Nano Comes to Clifford Falls," *Asimov's,* July.

Kathe Koja, "Fireflies," *Asimov's,* July.

Ted Kosmatka, "Bitterseed," *Asimov's,* July.

Jay Lake, "The American Dead," *Interzone,* April.

——, "Eyeteeth," *Challenging Destiny* 22.

——, "Journal of an Inmate," *Postscripts* 7.

——, "Lehr, Rex," *Forbidden Planets* (Crowther).

——, "The Dead Man's Child," *Cosmos* Online.

——, "Whyte Boys," *Aeon Seven.*

Margo Lanagan, "A Fine Magic," *Eidolon 1.*

——, "A Good Heart," *Red Spikes.*

Geoffrey A. Landis, "Derelict," *Escape from Earth.*

——, "Lazy Taekos," *Analog,* May.

John Lambshead, "As Black as Hell," *Jim Baen's Universe 2.*

Chris Lawson, "The Day I Go Outside," *Cosmos,* April.

Tanith Lee, "Arthur's Lion," *Weird Tales,* June.

Tim Lees, "The Interpretation of Dreams," *Postscripts* 9.

Edward M. Lerner, "Great Minds," *Jim Baen's Universe 2.*

David D. Levine, "Primate," *Asimov's,* September.

——, "The Last McDougal's," *Asimov's,* January.

Heather Lindsley, "Just Do It," *F&SF,* July.

——, "Mayfly," *Strange Horizons,* 25 September.

Marissa Lingen, "Carter Hull Recovers the Puck," *On Spec,* Spring.

——, "The Opposite of Pomegranates," *Jim Baen's Universe1.*

——, "Singing Them Back," *Jim Baen's Universe 4.*

——, "Things We Sell to Tourists," *Aeon Six.*

Kelly Link, "The Wizards of Perfil," *Firebirds Rising.*

Richard Lovett, "Original Sin," *Analog,* June.

——, "A Pound of Flesh," *Analog,* September.

Richar Lupoff, "Fourth Avenue Interlude," *Weird Tales,* 8–9.

Ian R. Macleod, "Taking Good Care of Myself," *Nature,* 4 May.

——, "The Boy in Zaquitos," *F&SF,* January.

Bruce McAllister, "Cold War," *F&SF,* April.

——, "The Passion: A Western," *Aeon Seven.*

——, "Ragazzo," *Fantasy Magazine* 2.
Paul McAuley, "Dust," *Forbidden Planets* (Crowther).
Will McCarthy, "Boundary Condition," *Analog*, April.
Jack McDevitt, "Henry James, This One's for You," *Subterranean #2*.
——, "Kaminsky at War," *Forbidden Planets* (Kaye).
Ian McDonald, "Kyle Meets the River," *Forbidden Planets* (Crowther).
Sandra McDonald, "The Green House," *Fantasy Magazine* 3.
Martin McGrath, "Palaces of Force," *Aeon Eight*.
Will McIntosh, "New Spectacles," *Abyss & Apex*, 19.
——. "The New Chinese Wives," *Interzone*, October.
——, "Oxy," *Aeon Eight*.
Juliet E. McKenna, "A Spark in the Darkness," *Postscripts 6*.
Patricia A. McKillip, "Jack O'Lantern," *Firebirds Rising*.
Sean McMullen, "The Engines of Arcadia," *Futureshocks*.
——, "The Measure of Eternity," *Interzone*, August.
David Mace, "Frankie on Zanzibar," *Interzone*, December.
Barry N. Malzberg and Paul Di Filippo, "Beyond Mao," *Postscripts 4*.
Lisa Mantchev, "Interfaith," *Abyss & Apex*, 19.
Daniel Marcus, "Echo Beach," *Aeon Eight*.
Louise Marley, "Absalon's Mother," *Futureshocks*.
Paul Marlowe, "Night of Sevens," *Oceans of the Mind*, Summer.
David Marusek, "My Morning Glory," *Nature*, 6 April.
Donald Mead, "Iklaw," *F&SF*, April.
John Meaney, "Looking Through Mother's Eyes," *Futureshocks*.
Paul Melko, "Snail Stones," *Asimov's*, July.
——, "The Teosinte War," *Futureshocks*.
——, "The Walls of the Universe," *Asimov's*, April/May.
Henry Melton, "Wildlife," *Analog*, March.
Robert A. Metzger, "Geometry," *Millennium 3001*.
——, "Slip," *Futureshocks*.
Steven Mills, "Blue Glass Pebbles," *Interzone*, August.
Syne Mitchell, "The Last Mortal Man," *Elemental*.
Steven Mohan, Jr., "What It Means to Be Human," *Talebones*, Spring.
Sarah Monette, "A Light in Troy," *Clarksworld*, October.
——, "Amante Doree," *Paradox*, Winter.
——, "A Night in Electric Squidland," *Lone Star Stories*, 16.
——, "Draco Campestris," *Strange Horizons*, 7 August.
——, "Katabasis: Seraphic Trains," *Tales of the Unanticipated*, 27.
Elizabeth Moon, "Combat Shopping," *Escape from Earth*.
John Morressy, "The Protectors of Zendor," *F&SF*, June.
——, "The Return of the O'Farrissey," *F&SF*, September.
——, "The True History of the Picky Princess," *F&SF*, March.
Richard Mueller, "A Storm over Cumorah," *Paradox*, Summer.
Ruth Nestvold, "Exit Without Saving," *Futurismic*.
——, "Feather and Ring," *Asimov's*, August.
——, "The Other Side of Silence," *Futurismic*.
——, "Sailing to Utopia," *Flytrap 5*.
——, "Triple Helix," *Ideomancer*, June.

——and Jay Lake, "Return to Nowhere," *Jigsaw Nation*.
——and Jay Lake, "Schwarze Madonna and the Sandalwood Knight," *Realms of Fantasy*, June.
R. Neube, "Not Worth a Cent," *Asimov's*, April/May.
Garth Nix, "Dog Soldier," *Jim Baen's Universe 2*.
Larry Niven, "Cadet Amelia," *Space Cadets*.
——, "Playhouse," *Analog*, March.
——, "The Solipsist at Dinner," *Elemental*.
G. David Nordley, "Voice of Ages," *Golden Age SF*.
Claudia O'Keefe, "The Moment of Joy Before," *F&SF*, April.
Jerry Oltion, "Slide Show," *Analog*, May.
——, "Stuffing," *Mammoth Book of Extreme SF*.
Alastair Ong, "The Legend of Greatmother June," *Eidolon 1*.
Robert Onopa, "Republic," *F&SF*, July.
Suzanne Palmer, "Spheres," *Interzone*, December.
Richard Parks, "Another Kind of Glamour," *Aeon Six*.
——, "Conversation at the Tomb of an Unknown King," *Weird Tales*, 8–9.
——, "Moon Viewing at Shijo Bridge," *Realms of Fantasy*, April.
Lawrence Person, "Bob's Yeti Problem," *Jim Baen's Universe*.
——, "The Toughest Jew in the West," *Cross Plains Universe*.
Holly Phillips, "Gin," *Eidolon 1*.
Brian Plante, "The Software Soul," *Analog*, July/August.
Gillian Polack, "Horrible Historians," *Subterranean #4*.
Rachel Pollack, "The Beatrix Gates," *The Future Is Queer*.
Steven Popkes, "Holding Pattern," *F&SF*, July.
Tim Powers, "A Soul in a Bottle," *Subterranean Press*.
Tim Pratt, "The Crawlspace of the World," *Polyphony 6*.
——, "Cup and Table," *Twenty Epics*.
——, "Dream Engine," *OSC's Intergalactic Medicine Show*, October.
——, "Impossible Dreams," *Asimov's*, July.
——, "The Third-Quarter King," *Eidolon 1*.
William Preston, "You Will Go to the Moon," *Asimov's*, July.
Christopher Priest, "A Dying Fall," *Asimov's*, December.
Cat Rambo, "Magnificent Pigs," *Strange Horizons*, 27 November.
Ken Rand, "Here There Be Humans," *Aeon Seven*.
Kit Reed, "Biodad," *Asimov's*, October/November.
Robert Reed, "A Billion Eves," *Asimov's*, October/November
——, "Eight Episodes," *Asimov's*, June.
——, "Flavors of My Genius," *PS Publishing*.
——, "Hoop of Benzene," *Mammoth Book of Extreme SF*.
——, "Intolerance," *F&SF*, March.
——, "Less Than Nothing," *F&SF*, January.
——, "Misjudgment Day," *F&SF*, August.
——, "Pills Forever," *F&SF*, December.
——, "Plausible," *Asimov's*, December.
——, "Rococo," *Forbidden Planets* (Kaye).
——, "Rwanda," *Asimov's*, March.
——, "Show Me Yours," *F&SF*, May.

——, "Starbuck," *F&SF*, April.
——, "Willa," *Polyphony 6*.
Mike Resnick, "All the Things You Are," *Jim Baen's Universe 2*.
——and Harry Turtledove, "Before the Beginning," *Futureshocks*.
Alastair Reynolds, "Granfenwalder's Bestiary," *Galactic North*.
——, "Thousandth Night," *One Million A.D.*
——, "Tyger, Burning," *Forbidden Planets* (Crowther).
——, "Weather," *Galactic North*.
Carrie Richerson, "The Warrior and the King," *Cross Plains Universe*.
M. Rickert, "Journey into the Kingdom," *F&SF*, May.
——, "The Christmas Witch," *F&SF*, December.
Mercurio D. Rivera, "Longing for Langalana," *Interzone*, June.
Chris Roberson, "Companion to Owls," *Asimov's*, March.
——, "Contagion," *Futureshocks*.
——, "Eventide," *Forbidden Planets* (Crowther).
——, "The Jewel of Leystall," *Cross Plains Universe*.
——, "Last," *Subterranean #4*.
——, "The Voyage of Night Shining White," *PS Publishing*.
Adam Roberts, "Man You Gotta Go," *Futureshocks*.
——, "Me-topia," *Forbidden Planets* (Crowther).
Madeline E. Robins, "Boon," *F&SF*, February.
Peg Robinson, "Tonino and the Incubus," *Helix 2*.
Michaela Roessner, "Horse-Year Woman," *F&SF*, January.
Benjamin Rosenbaum, "A Siege of Cranes," *Twenty Epics*.
Christopher Rowe, "Another Word for Map Is Faith," *F&SF*, August.
——, "Two Figures in a Landscape Between Storms," *Twenty Epics*.
Rudy Rucker, "Chu and the Nants," *Asimov's*, June.
——, "Postsingular," *Asimov's*, September.
——and Terry Bisson, "2 + 2 = 5," *Interzone*, August.
——and Paul Di Filippo, "Elves of the Subdimensions," *Flurb 1*.
Kristine Kathryn Rusch, "A Better Place," *Millennium 3001*.
——, "Crunchers, Inc.," *Asimov's*, August.
——, "Except the Music," *Asimov's*, April/May.
Patricia Russo, "The Ogre's Wife," *Tales of the Unanticipated*, 27.
Geoff Ryman, "Pol Pot's Beautiful Daughter (Fantasy)," *F&SF*, October/November.
Nick Sagen, "Tees and Sympathy," *Subterranean #4*.
Patrick Samphire, "Uncle Vernon's Lie," *Realms of Fantasy*, February.
William Sanders, "Going to See the Beast," *Helix 1*.
Pamela Sargent, "After I Stopped Screaming," *Asimov's*, October/November.
——, "The Drowned Father," *Polyphony 6*.
——, "Not Alone," *Cosmos*, August.
Tony Sarowitz, "A Daze in the Life," *F&SF*, January.
Robert J. Sawyer, "Flashes," *Futureshocks*.
Gary W. Schockley, "The Cathedral of Universal Biodiversity," *F&SF*, February.
Ken Scholes, "East of Eden and Just a Bit South," *Aeon Six*.
——, "Of Metal Men," *Realms of Fantasy*, August.
——, "One Small Step," *Aeon Nine*.
——, "Soon We Shall All Be Saunders," *Polyphony 6*.

Aaron Schutz, "Cotton Country," *Fantasy Magazine* 2.
Jerry Seegar, "Memory of a Thing That Never Was," *F&SF*, July.
Michael Shara and Jack McDevitt, "Lighthouse," *Analog*, April.
Melissa Lee Shaw, "Foster," *Asimov's*, October/November.
Lucius Shepard, "The Lepidopterist," *Salon Fantastique*.
Delia Sherman, "La Fee Verte," *Salon Fantastique*.
John Shirley, "Cul-de-Sac," *Flurb* 2.
William Shunn, "Inclination," *Asimov's*, April/May.
———, "Hanosz Prime Goes to Old Earth," *Asimov's*, April/May.
Robert Silverberg, "A Piece of the Great World," *One Million A.D.*
Helen Simpson, "The Festival of the Immortals," *The Guardian*, 23 December.
Jack Skillingstead, "Are You There?" *Asimov's*, February.
Dean Wesley Smith, "Nostalgia 101," *Millennium 3001*.
Douglas Smith, "Murphy's Law," *Jim Baen's Universe* 4.
Wen Spencer, "For Blue Sky," *Jim Baen's Universe* 2.
Brian Stableford, "An Oasis of Horror," *Infinity Plus*, 18 September.
———, "The Elixir of Youth," *Weird Tales*, 8–9.
———, "The Plurality of Worlds," *Asimov's*, August.
Jason Stanchfield, "Which Yet Survives," *Golden Age SF*.
Vaughn Stanger, "The Peace Criminal," *Postscripts* 9.
———, "Moon Flu," *Oceans of the Mind*, Summer.
Allen M. Steele, "Escape from Earth," *Escape from Earth*.
———, "The Last Science Fiction Writer," *Subterranean #4*.
———, "Take Me Back to Old Tennessee," *Millenium 3001*.
———, "World Without End, Amen," *Asimov's*, January.
———, "Walking Star," *Forbidden Planets* (Kaye).
Adam Stemple, "Kitsune," *Paradox*, Summer.
Jason Stoddard, "Anima, Animus," *Talebones Spring*.
———, "Changing the Tune," *Futurismic*.
Charles Stross, "Message in a Time Capsule," *Flurb* 2.
———, "Missile Gap," *One Million A.D.*
———, "Pimpf," *Jim Baen's Universe* 1.
Lucy Sussex, "The Revenant," *Eidolon* 1.
Michael Swanwick, "The Bordello in Faerie," *Postscripts* 8.
———, "An Episode of Stardust," *Asimov's*, January.
———, "Lord Weary's Empire," *Asimov's*, December.
Sonya Taaffe, "Like the Stars and the Sand," *Alchemy* 3.
Anna Tambour, "The Syncopation Streak," *Polyphony* 6.
Lavie Tidhar, "All the Wonder in the World," *Abyss & Apex*, 18.
———, "Generations," *Son and Foe*, 4.
Eliani Torres, "Ignis Fatuus," *Strange Horizons*, 20 February.
Sarah Totten, "A Fish Story," *Realms of Fantasy*, October.
Mikal Trim, "A Paean to Stranded Sailors and Ships Becalmed at Sea," *Postscripts* 9.
Harry Turtledove, "The Scarlet Band," *Analog*, May.
Steven Utley, "Diluvium," *F&SF*, May.
———, "Life's Work," *Where and When*.
———, "Staying in Storyville," *Where and When*.
Rajnar Vajra, "A Million Years and Counting," *Analog*, September.

Jeff VanderMeer, "The Secret Paths of Rajan Khanna," *ParaSpheres*.

Greg Van Eekhout, "Anywhere There's Game," *Realms of Fantasy*, April.

——, "The Osteomancer's Son," *Asimov's*, April/May.

Mark L. Van Name, "Slanted Jack," *Jim Baen's Universe 1*.

James Van Pelt, "The Road's End," *Realms of Fantasy*, February.

——, "The Small Astral Object Genius," *Asimov's*, October/November.

——, "Tiny Voices," *Talebones*, Summer.

Carrie Vaughn, "Winnowing the Herd," *Strange Horizons*, October 10.

Stephen Volk, "A Paper Tissue," *Postscripts* 7.

Richard Wadholm, "Orange Groves Out to the Horizon," *Polyphony 6*.

Howard Waldrop, "Thin, On the Ground," *Cross Plains Universe*.

Ian Watson, "Saving for a Sunny Day, or, The Benefits of Reincarnation," *Asimov's*, October/November.

Ysabeau S. Wilce, "The Lineaments of Gratified Desire," *F&SF*, July.

Conrad Williams, "The Veteran," *Postscripts* 6.

Liz Williams, "The Age of Ice," *Asimov's*, April/May.

Sean Williams and Shane Dix, "Night of the Dolls," *Elemental*.

Jack Williamson, "The Mists of Time," *Millennium 3001*.

Connie Willis, "D.A.," *Space Cadets*.

Chris Willrich, "Penultima Thule," *F&SF*, August.

Robert Charles Wilson, "The Cartesian Theater," *Futureshocks*.

Eric Witchery, "Brieanna's Constant," *Jim Baen's Universe 1*.

Gene Wolfe, "Bea and Her Bird Brother," *F&SF*, May.

——, "Christmas Inn," *PS Publishing*.

——, "Six from Atlantis," *Cross Plains Universe*.

——, "The Old Woman in the Young Woman," *Jim Baen's Universe 2*.

Katherine Woodbury, "Impersonal," *Andromeda Spaceways #24*.

——, "Untainted," *Talebones*, Summer.

Marly Youmans, "Concealment Shoes," *Salon Fantastique*.

Sarah Zettel, "The Thief of Stones," *Jim Baen's Universe 1*.